P9-CQG-688

George Eliot

George Eliot

MIDDLEMARCH • SILAS MARNER • AMOS BARTON

CHANCELLOR PRESS

Middlemarch was first published in 1871-2
Silas Marner was first published in 1861
Amos Barton was first published in 1858

This collected volume first published in paperback
in 1994 by Chancellor Press an imprint of
Octopus Publishing Group Ltd

This edition published in 2001 by
Chancellor Press, an imprint of Bounty Books,
a division of Octopus Publishing Group Ltd,
2—4 Heron Quays, London E14 4JP

Reprinted 2002

Distributed in the United States by
Sterling Publishing Co., Inc.
387 Sterling Park South Avenue, New York, NY 10016-8810

Design and arrangement ' 1994 Octopus Publishing Group Ltd

ISBN 0 7537 0392 0

A CIP catalogue record for this title is available at the
British Library.

Printed by Mackays of Chatham, England

Contents

MIDDLEMARCH

↝ PRELUDE ↜

WHO THAT CARES MUCH TO KNOW the history of man, and how the mysterious mixture behaves under the varying experiments of Time, has not dwelt, at least briefly, on the life of Saint Theresa, has not smiled with some gentleness at the thought of the little girl walking forth one morning hand-in-hand with her still smaller brother, to go and seek martyrdom in the country of the Moors? Out they toddled from rugged Avila, wide-eyed and helpless-looking as two fawns, but with human hearts, already beating to a national idea; until domestic reality met them in the shape of uncles, and turned them back from their great resolve. That child-pilgrimage was a fit beginning. Theresa's passionate, ideal nature demanded an epic life: what were many-volumed romances of chivalry and the social conquests of a brilliant girl to her? Her flame quickly burned up that light fuel; and, fed from within, soared after some illimitable satisfaction, some object which would never justify weariness, which would reconcile self-despair with the rapturous consciousness of life beyond self. She found her epos in the reform of a religious order.

That Spanish woman who lived three hundred years ago was certainly not the last of her kind. Many Theresas have been born who found for themselves no epic life wherein there was a constant unfolding of far-resonant action; perhaps only a life of mistakes, the offspring of a certain spiritual grandeur ill-matched with the meanness of opportunity; perhaps a tragic failure which found no sacred poet and sank unwept into oblivion. With dim lights and tangled circumstance they tried to shape their thought and deed in noble agreement; but after all, to common eyes their struggles seemed mere inconsistency and formlessness; for these later-born Theresas were helped by no coherent social faith and order which could perform the function of knowledge for the ardently willing soul. Their ardour alternated between a vague ideal and the common yearning of womanhood; so that the one was disapproved as extravagance, and the other condemned as a lapse.

Some have felt that these blundering lives are due to the inconvenient indefiniteness with which the Supreme Power has fashioned the natures of women: if there were one level of feminine incompetence as strict as the ability to count three and no more, the social lot of women might be treated with scientific certitude. Meanwhile the indefiniteness remains, and the limits of variation are really much wider than any one would

1

imagine from the sameness of women's coiffure and the favourite love-stories in prose and verse. Here and there a cygnet is reared uneasily among the ducklings in the brown pond, and never finds the living stream in fellowship with its own oary-footed kind. Here and there is born a Saint Theresa, foundress of nothing, whose loving heart-beats and sobs after an unattained goodness tremble off and are dispersed among hindrances, instead of centring in some long-recognizable deed.

BOOK ONE
MISS BROOKE

♂ ONE ♀

Since I can do no good because a woman,
Reach constantly at something that is near it.
The Maid's Tragedy: BEAUMONT AND FLETCHER

MISS BROOKE HAD THAT KIND OF beauty which seems to be thrown into relief by poor dress. Her hand and wrist were so finely formed that she could wear sleeves not less bare of style than those in which the Blessed Virgin appeared to Italian painters; and her profile as well as her stature and bearing seemed to gain the more dignity from her plain garments, which by the side of provincial fashion gave her the impressiveness of a fine quotation from the Bible, – or from one of our elder poets, – in a paragraph of to-day's newspaper. She was usually spoken of as being remarkably clever, but with the addition that her sister Celia had more common-sense. Nevertheless, Celia wore scarcely more trimmings; and it was only to close observers that her dress differed from her sister's, and had a shade of coquetry in its arrangements; for Miss Brooke's plain dressing was due to mixed conditions, in most of which her sister shared. The pride of being ladies had something to do with it: the Brooke connections, though not exactly aristocratic, were unquestionably 'good': if you inquired backward for a generation or two, you would not find any yard-measuring or parcel-tying forefathers – anything lower than an admiral or a clergyman; and there was even an ancestor discernible as a Puritan gentleman who served under Cromwell, but afterwards conformed, and managed to come out of all political troubles as the proprietor of a respectable family estate. Young women of such birth, living in a quiet country-house, and attending a village church hardly larger than a parlour, naturally regarded frippery as the ambition of a huckster's daughter. Then there was well-bred economy, which in those days made show in dress the first item to be deducted from, when any margin was required for expenses more distinctive of rank. Such reasons would have been enough to account for plain dress, quite apart from religious feeling; but in Miss Brooke's case, religion alone would have determined it; and Celia mildly acquiesced in all her sister's sentiments, only infusing them with that common-sense which is able to accept momentous doctrines without any eccentric agitation. Dorothea knew many passages of Pascal's *Pensées* and of Jeremy Taylor by heart; and to her the destinies of mankind, seen by the light of Christianity, made the solicitudes of feminine fashion appear an

5

occupation for Bedlam. She could not reconcile the anxieties of a spiritual life involving eternal consequences, with a keen interest in guimp and artificial protrusions of drapery. Her mind was theoretic, and yearned by its nature after some lofty conception of the world which might frankly include the parish of Tipton and her own rule of conduct there; she was enamoured of intensity and greatness, and rash in embracing whatever seemed to her to have those aspects; likely to seek martyrdom, to make retractions, and then to incur martyrdom after all in a quarter where she had not sought it. Certainly such elements in the character of a marriage-able girl tended to interfere with her lot, and hinder it from being decided according to custom, by good looks, vanity, and merely canine affection. With all this, she, the elder of the sisters, was not yet twenty, and they had both been educated, since they were about twelve years old and had lost their parents, on plans at once narrow and promiscuous, first in an English family and afterwards in a Swiss family at Lausanne, their bachelor uncle and guardian trying in this way to remedy the disadvantages of their orphaned condition.

It was hardly a year since they had come to live at Tipton Grange with their uncle, a man nearly sixty, of acquiescent temper, miscellaneous opinions, and uncertain vote. He had travelled in his younger years, and was held in this part of the county to have contracted a too rambling habit of mind. Mr Brooke's conclusions were as difficult to predict as the weather: it was only safe to say that he would act with benevolent intentions, and that he would spend as little money as possible in carrying them out. For the most glutinously indefinite minds enclose some hard grains of habit; and a man has been seen lax about all his own interests except the retention of his snuff-box, concerning which he was watchful, suspicious, and greedy of clutch.

In Mr Brooke the hereditary strain of Puritan energy was clearly in abeyance; but in his niece Dorothea it glowed alike through faults and virtues, turning sometimes into impatience of her uncle's talk or his way of 'letting things be' on his estate, and making her long all the more for the time when she would be of age and have some command of money for generous schemes. She was regarded as an heiress, for not only had the sisters seven hundred a-year each from their parents, but if Dorothea married and had a son, that son would inherit Mr Brooke's estate, presumably worth about three thousand a-year – a rental which seemed wealth to provincial families, still discussing Mr Peel's late conduct on the Catholic Question, innocent of future gold-fields, and of that gorgeous plutocracy which has so nobly exalted the necessities of genteel life.

And how should Dorothea not marry? – a girl so handsome and with such prospects? Nothing could hinder it but her love of extremes, and her insistence on regulating life according to notions which might cause a wary man to hesitate before he made her an offer, or even might lead her at last to refuse all offers. A young lady of some birth and fortune, who knelt suddenly down on a brick floor by the side of a sick labourer and prayed fervidly as if she thought herself living in the time of the Apostles – who had strange whims of fasting like a Papist, and of sitting up at night to read old theological books! Such a wife might awaken you some fine morning with a new scheme for the application of her income which would interfere with political economy and the keeping of saddle-horses: a man would naturally think twice before he risked himself in such fellowship. Women were expected to have weak opinions; but the great safeguard of society and of domestic life was, that opinions were not acted on. Sane people did what their neighbours did, so that if any lunatics were at large, one might know and avoid them.

The rural opinion about the new young ladies, even among the cottagers, was generally in favour of Celia, as being so amiable and innocent-looking, while Miss Brooke's large eyes seemed, like her religion, too unusual and striking. Poor Dorothea! compared with her, the innocent-looking Celia was knowing and worldly-wise; so much subtler is a human mind than the outside tissues which make a sort of blazonry or clock-face for it.

Yet those who approached Dorothea, though prejudiced against her by this alarming hearsay, found that she had a charm unaccountably reconcilable with it. Most men thought her bewitching when she was on horseback. She loved the fresh air and the various aspects of the country, and when her eyes and cheeks glowed with mingled pleasure she looked very little like a devotee. Riding was an indulgence which she allowed herself in spite of conscientious qualms; she felt that she enjoyed it in a pagan sensuous way, and always looked forward to renouncing it.

She was open, ardent, and not in the least self-admiring; indeed, it was pretty to see how her imagination adorned her sister Celia with attractions altogether superior to her own, and if any gentleman appeared to come to the Grange from some other motive than that of seeing Mr Brooke, she concluded that he must be in love with Celia: Sir James Chettam, for example, whom she constantly considered from Celia's point of view, inwardly debating whether it would be good for Celia to accept him. That he should be regarded as a suitor to herself would have seemed to her a ridiculous irrelevance. Dorothea, with all her eagerness to know the truths of life, retained very childlike ideas about marriage. She felt sure that she would have accepted the judicious Hooker, if she had been born in time to save him from that wretched mistake he made in matrimony; or John Milton when his blindness had come on; or any of the other great men whose odd habits it would have been glorious piety to endure; but an amiable handsome baronet, who said 'Exactly' to her remarks even when she expressed uncertainty, – how could he affect her as a lover? The really delightful marriage must be that where your husband was a sort of father, and could teach you even Hebrew, if you wished it.

These peculiarities of Dorothea's character caused Mr Brooke to be all the more blamed in neighbouring families for not securing some middle-aged lady as guide and companion to his nieces. But he himself dreaded so much the sort of superior woman likely to be available for such a position, that he allowed himself to be dissuaded by Dorothea's objections, and was in this case brave enough to defy the world – that is to say, Mrs Cadwallader the Rector's wife, and the small group of gentry with whom he visited in the north-east corner of Loamshire. So Miss Brooke presided in her uncle's household, and did not at all dislike her new authority, with the homage that belonged to it.

Sir James Chettam was going to dine at the Grange to-day with another gentleman whom the girls had never seen, and about whom Dorothea felt some venerating expectation. This was the Reverend Edward Casaubon, noted in the county as a man of profound learning, understood for many years to be engaged on a great work concerning religious history; also as a man of wealth enough to give lustre to his piety, and having views of his own which were to be more clearly ascertained on the publication of his book. His very name carried an impressiveness hardly to be measured without a precise chronology of scholarship.

Early in the day Dorothea had returned from the infant school which she had set going in the village, and was taking her usual place in the pretty sitting-room which divided the bedrooms of the sisters, bent on finishing a plan for some buildings (a kind of work which she delighted in), when Celia, who had been watching her with a hesitating desire to propose something, said –

'Dorothea dear, if you don't mind – if you are not very busy – suppose we looked at mamma's jewels to-day, and divided them? It is exactly six months to-day since uncle gave them to you, and you have not looked at them yet.'

Celia's face had the shadow of a pouting expression in it, the full presence of the pout being kept back by an habitual awe of Dorothea and principle; two associated facts which might show a mysterious electricity if you touched them incautiously. To her relief, Dorothea's eyes were full of laughter as she looked up.

'What a wonderful little almanac you are, Celia! Is it six calendar or six lunar months?'

'It is the last day of September now, and it was the first of April when uncle gave them to you. You know, he said that he had forgotten them till then. I believe you have never thought of them since you locked them up in the cabinet here.'

'Well, dear, we should never wear them, you know.' Dorothea spoke in a full cordial tone, half caressing, half explanatory. She had her pencil in her hand, and was making tiny side-plans on a margin.

Celia coloured, and looked very grave. 'I think, dear, we are wanting in respect to mamma's memory, to put them by and take no notice of them. And,' she added, after hesitating a little, with a rising sob of mortification, 'necklaces are quite usual now; and Madame Poinçon, who was stricter in some things even than you are, used to wear ornaments. And Christians generally – surely there are women in heaven now who wore jewels.' Celia was conscious of some mental strength when she really applied herself to argument.

'You would like to wear them?' exclaimed Dorothea, an air of astonished discovery animating her whole person with a dramatic action which she had caught from that very Madame Poinçon who wore the ornaments. 'Of course, then, let us have them out. Why did you not tell me before? But the keys, the keys!' She pressed her hands against the sides of her head and seemed to despair of her memory.

'They are here,' said Celia, with whom this explanation had been long meditated and prearranged.

'Pray open the large drawer of the cabinet and get out the jewel-box.'

The casket was soon open before them, and the various jewels spread out, making a bright parterre on the table. It was no great collection, but a few of the ornaments were really of remarkable beauty, the finest that was obvious at first being a necklace of purple amethysts set in exquisite gold-work, and a pearl cross with five brilliants in it. Dorothea immediately took up the necklace and fastened it round her sister's neck, where it fitted almost as closely as a bracelet; but the circle suited the Henrietta-Maria style of Celia's head and neck, and she could see that it did, in the pier-glass opposite.

'There, Celia! you can wear that with your Indian muslin. But this cross you must wear with your dark dresses.'

Celia was trying not to smile with pleasure. 'O Dodo, you must keep the cross yourself.'

'No, no, dear, no,' said Dorothea, putting up her hand with careless deprecation.

'Yes, indeed you must; it would suit you – in your black dress, now,' said Celia, insistingly. 'You *might* wear that.'

'Not for the world, not for the world. A cross is the last thing I would wear as a trinket.' Dorothea shuddered slightly.

'Then you will think it wicked in me to wear it,' said Celia, uneasily.

'No, dear, no,' said Dorothea, stroking her sister's cheek. 'Souls have complexions too: what will suit one will not suit another.'

'But you might like to keep it for mamma's sake.'

'No. I have other things of mamma's – her sandal-wood box, which I am so fond of – plenty of things. In fact, they are all yours, dear. We need discuss them no longer. There – take away your property.'

Celia felt a little hurt. There was a strong assumption of superiority in this Puritanic toleration, hardly less trying to the blond flesh of an unenthusiastic sister than a Puritanic persecution.

'But how can I wear ornaments if you, who are the elder sister, will never wear them?'

'Nay, Celia, that is too much to ask, that I should wear trinkets to keep you in countenance. If I were to put on such a necklace as that, I should feel as if I had been pirouetting. The world would go round with me, and I should not know how to walk.'

Celia had unclasped the necklace and drawn it off. 'It would be a little tight for your neck; something to lie down and hang would suit you better,' she said, with some satisfaction. The complete unfitness of the necklace from all points of view for Dorothea, made Celia happier in taking it. She was opening some ring-boxes, which disclosed a fine emerald with diamonds, and just then the sun passing beyond a cloud sent a bright gleam over the table.

'How very beautiful these gems are!' said Dorothea, under a new current of feeling, as sudden as the gleam. 'It is strange how deeply colours seem to penetrate one, like scent. I suppose that is the reason why gems are used as spiritual emblems in the Revelation of St John. They look like fragments of heaven. I think that emerald is more beautiful than any of them.'

'And there is a bracelet to match it,' said Celia. 'We did not notice this at first.'

'They are lovely,' said Dorothea, slipping the ring and bracelet on her finely-turned finger and wrist, and holding them towards the window on a level with her eyes. All the while her thought was trying to justify her delight in the colours by merging them in her mystic religious joy.

'You *would* like those, Dorothea,' said Celia, rather falteringly, beginning to think with wonder that her sister showed some weakness, and also that emeralds would suit her own complexion even better than purple amethysts. 'You must keep that ring and bracelet – if nothing else. But see, these agates are very pretty – and quiet.'

'Yes! I will keep these – this ring and bracelet,' said Dorothea. Then, letting her hand fall on the table, she said in another tone – 'Yet what miserable men find such things, and work at them, and sell them!' She paused again, and Celia thought that her sister was going to renounce the ornaments, as in consistency she ought to do.

'Yes, dear, I will keep these,' said Dorothea, decidedly. 'But take all the rest away, and the casket.'

She took up her pencil without removing the jewels, and still looking at them. She thought of often having them by her, to feed her eye at these little fountains of pure colour.

'Shall you wear them in company?' said Celia, who was watching her with real curiosity as to what she would do.

Dorothea glanced quickly at her sister. Across all her imaginative adornment of those whom she loved, there darted now and then a keen discernment, which was not without a scorching quality. If Miss Brooke ever attained perfect meekness, it would not be for lack of inward fire.

'Perhaps,' she said, rather haughtily. 'I cannot tell to what level I may sink.'

Celia blushed, and was unhappy; she saw that she had offended her sister, and dared not say even anything pretty about the gift of the ornaments which she put back into the box and carried away. Dorothea too was unhappy, as she went on with her plan-drawing, questioning the purity of her own feeling and speech in the scene which had ended with that little explosion.

Celia's consciousness told her that she had not been at all in the wrong: it was quite natural and justifiable that she should have asked that question, and she repeated to herself that Dorothea was inconsistent: either she should have taken her full share of the jewels, or, after what she had said, she should have renounced them altogether.

'I am sure – at least, I trust,' thought Celia, 'that the wearing of a necklace will not interfere with my prayers. And I do not see that I should be bound by Dorothea's opinions now we are going into society, though of course she herself ought to be bound by them. But Dorothea is not always consistent.'

Thus Celia, mutely bending over her tapestry, until she heard her sister calling her.

'Here, Kitty, come and look at my plan; I shall think I am a great architect, if I have not got incompatible stairs and fireplaces.'

As Celia bent over the paper, Dorothea put her cheek against her sister's arm caressingly. Celia understood the action. Dorothea saw that she had been in the wrong, and Celia pardoned her. Since they could remember, there had been a mixture of criticism and awe in the attitude of Celia's mind towards her elder sister. The younger had always worn a yoke; but is there any yoked creature without its private opinions?

❧ TWO ❧

*'Dime: no ves aquel caballero que hácia nostros viene sobre un caballo
rucio rodado que trae puesto en la cabeza un yelmo de oro?' 'Lo que
veo y columbro,' respondió Sancho, 'no es sino un hombre sobre un
asno pardo como el mío, que trae sobre la cabeza una cosa que
relumbra.' 'Pues ése es el yelmo de Mambrino,' dijo Don Quijote.*

CERVANTES

'Seest thou not yon cavalier who cometh toward us on a
dapple-grey steed, and weareth a golden helmet?' 'What I
see,' answered Sancho, 'is nothing but a man on a grey ass like
my own, who carries something shiny on his head.' 'Just so,'
answered Don Quixote: 'and that resplendent object is the
helmet of Mambrino.'

SIR HUMPHRY DAVY?' SAID MR BROOKE, over the soup, in his easy smiling
way, taking up Sir James Chettam's remark that he was studying Davy's
Agricultural Chemistry. 'Well, now, Sir Humphry Davy: I dined with him
years ago at Cartwright's, and Wordsworth was there too – the poet
Wordsworth, you know. Now there was something singular. I was at
Cambridge when Wordsworth was there, and I never met him – and I
dined with him twenty years afterwards at Cartwright's. There's an
oddity in things, now. But Davy was there: he was a poet too. Or, as I may
say, Wordsworth was poet one, and Davy was poet two. That was true in
every sense, you know.'

Dorothea felt a little more uneasy than usual. In the beginning of dinner,
the party being small and the room still, these motes from the mass of
a magistrate's mind fell too noticeably. She wondered how a man like
Mr Casaubon would support such triviality. His manners, she thought,
were very dignified; the set of his iron-grey hair and his deep eye-sockets
made him resemble the portrait of Locke. He had the spare form and the
pale complexion which became a student; as different as possible from
the blooming Englishman of the red-whiskered type represented by Sir
James Chettam.

'I am reading the *Agricultural Chemistry,*' said this excellent baronet,
'because I am going to take one of the farms into my own hands, and see if
something cannot be done in setting a good pattern of farming among my
tenants. Do you approve of that, Miss Brooke?'

'A great mistake, Chettam,' interposed Mr Brooke, 'going into electrify-ing your land and that kind of thing, and making a parlour of your cow-house. It won't do. I went into science a great deal myself at one time; but I saw it would not do. It leads to everything; you can let nothing alone. No, no – see that your tenants don't sell their straw, and that kind of thing; and give them draining-tiles, you know. But your fancy-farming will not do – the most expensive sort of whistle you can buy; you may as well keep a pack of hounds.'

'Surely,' said Dorothea, 'it is better to spend money in finding out how men can make the most of the land which supports them all, than in keeping dogs and horses only to gallop over it. It is not a sin to make yourself poor in performing experiments for the good of all.'

She spoke with more energy than is expected of so young a lady, but Sir James had appealed to her. He was accustomed to do so, and she had often thought that she could urge him to many good actions when he was her brother-in-law.

Mr Casaubon turned his eyes very markedly on Dorothea while she was speaking, and seemed to observe her newly.

'Young ladies don't understand political economy, you know,' said Mr Brooke, smiling towards Mr Casaubon. 'I remember when we were all reading Adam Smith. *There* is a book, now. I took in all the new ideas at one time – human perfectibility, now. But some say, history moves in circles; and that may be very well argued; I have argued it myself. The fact is, human reason may carry you a little too far – over the hedge, in fact. It carried me a good way at one time; but I saw it would not do. I pulled up; I pulled up in time. But not too hard. I have always been in favour of a little theory: we must have Thought; else we shall be landed back in the dark ages. But talking of books, there is Southey's *Peninsular War*. I am reading that of a morning. You know Southey?'

'No,' said Mr Casaubon, not keeping pace with Mr Brooke's impetuous reason, and thinking of the book only. 'I have little leisure for such litera-ture just now. I have been using up my eyesight on old characters lately; the fact is, I want a reader for my evenings; but I am fastidious in voices, and I cannot endure listening to an imperfect reader. It is a misfortune, in some senses: I feed too much on the inward sources; I live too much with the dead. My mind is something like the ghost of an ancient, wandering about the world and trying mentally to construct it as it used to be, in spite of ruin and confusing changes. But I find it necessary to use the utmost caution about my eyesight.'

This was the first time that Mr Casaubon had spoken at any length. He delivered himself with precision, as if he had been called upon to make a public statement; and the balanced sing-song neatness of his speech, occasionally corresponded to by a movement of his head, was the more conspicuous from its contrast with good Mr Brooke's scrappy slovenli-ness. Dorothea said to herself that Mr Casaubon was the most interesting man she had ever seen, not excepting even Monsieur Liret, the Vaudois clergyman who had given conferences on the history of the Waldenses. To reconstruct a past world, doubtless with a view to the highest purposes of truth – what a work to be in any way present at, to assist in, though only as a lamp-holder! This elevating thought lifted her above her annoyance at being twitted with her ignorance of political economy, that never-explained science which was thrust as an extinguisher over all her lights.

'But you are fond of riding, Miss Brooke,' Sir James presently took an opportunity of saying. 'I should have thought you would enter a little into the pleasures of hunting. I wish you would let me send over a chesnut horse for you to try. It has been trained for a lady. I saw you on Saturday cantering over the hill on a nag not worthy of you. My groom shall bring Corydon for you every day, if you will only mention the time.'

'Thank you, you are very good. I mean to give up riding. I shall not ride any more,' said Dorothea, urged to this brusque resolution by a little annoyance that Sir James would be soliciting her attention when she wanted to give it all to Mr Casaubon.

'No, that is too hard,' said Sir James, in a tone of reproach that showed strong interest. 'Your sister is given to self-mortification, is she not?' he continued, turning to Celia, who sat at his right hand.

'I think she is,' said Celia, feeling afraid lest she should say something that would not please her sister, and blushing as prettily as possible above her necklace. 'She likes giving up.'

'If that were true, Celia, my giving up would be self-indulgence, not self-mortification. But there may be good reasons for choosing not to do what is very agreeable,' said Dorothea.

Mr Brooke was speaking at the same time, but it was evident that Mr Casaubon was observing Dorothea, and she was aware of it.

'Exactly,' said Sir James. 'You give up from some high, generous motive.'

'No, indeed, not exactly. I did not say that of myself,' answered Dorothea, reddening. Unlike Celia, she rarely blushed, and only from high delight or anger. At this moment she felt angry with the perverse Sir James. Why did he not pay attention to Celia, and leave her to listen to Mr Casaubon? – if that learned man would only talk, instead of allowing himself to be talked to by Mr Brooke, who was just then informing him that the Reformation either meant something or it did not, that he himself was a Protestant to the core, but that Catholicism was a fact; and as to refusing an acre of your ground for a Romanist chapel, all men needed the bridle of religion, which, properly speaking, was the dread of a Hereafter.

'I made a great study of theology at one time,' said Mr Brooke, as if to explain the insight just manifested. 'I know something of all schools. I knew Wilberforce in his best days. Do you know Wilberforce?'

Mr Casaubon said, 'No.'

'Well, Wilberforce was perhaps not enough of a thinker; but if I went

into Parliament, as I have been asked to do, I should sit on the independent bench, as Wilberforce did, and work at philanthropy.'

Mr Casaubon bowed, and observed that it was a wide field.

'Yes,' said Mr Brooke, with an easy smile, 'but I have documents. I
began a long while ago to collect documents. They want arranging, but
when a question has struck me, I have written to somebody and got an
answer. I have documents at my back. But now, how do you arrange your
documents?'

'In pigeon-holes partly,' said Mr Casaubon, with rather a startled air of
effort.

'Ah, pigeon-holes will not do. I have tried pigeon-holes, but everything
gets mixed in pigeon-holes: I never know whether a paper is in A or Z.'

'I wish you would let me sort your papers for you, uncle,' said Dorothea. 'I would letter them all, and then make a list of subjects under each
letter.'

Mr Casaubon gravely smiled approval, and said to Mr Brooke, 'You
have an excellent secretary at hand, you perceive.'

'No, no,' said Mr Brooke, shaking his head; 'I cannot let young ladies
meddle with my documents. Young ladies are too flighty.'

Dorothea felt hurt. Mr Casaubon would think that her uncle had some
special reason for delivering this opinion, whereas the remark lay in his
mind as lightly as the broken wing of an insect among all the other
fragments there, and a chance current had sent it alighting on *her*.

When the two girls were in the drawing-room alone, Celia said –

'How very ugly Mr Casaubon is!'

'Celia! He is one of the most distinguished-looking men I ever saw.
He is remarkably like the portrait of Locke. He has the same deep eye-
sockets.'

'Had Locke those two white moles with hairs on them?'

'Oh, I daresay! when people of a certain sort looked at him,' said
Dorothea, walking away a little.

'Mr Casaubon is so sallow.'

'All the better. I suppose you admire a man with the complexion of a
cochon de lait.'

'Dodo!' exclaimed Celia, looking after her in surprise. 'I never heard
you make such a comparison before.'

'Why should I make it before the occasion came? It is a good comparison: the match is perfect.'

Miss Brooke was clearly forgetting herself, and Celia thought so.

'I wonder you show temper, Dorothea.'

'It is so painful in you, Celia, that you will look at human beings as if
they were merely animals with a toilette, and never see the great soul in a
man's face.'

'Has Mr Casaubon a great soul?' Celia was not without a touch of naïve
malice.

'Yes, I believe he has,' said Dorothea, with the full voice of decision. 'Everything I see in him corresponds to his pamphlet on Biblical Cosmology.'

'He talks very little,' said Celia.

'There is no one for him to talk to.'

Celia thought privately, 'Dorothea quite despises Sir James Chettam; I believe she would not accept him.' Celia felt that this was a pity. She had never been deceived as to the object of the baronet's interest. Sometimes, indeed, she had reflected that Dodo would perhaps not make a husband happy who had not her way of looking at things; and stifled in the depths of her heart was the feeling that her sister was too religious for family comfort. Notions and scruples were like spilt needles, making one afraid of treading, or sitting down, or even eating.

When Miss Brooke was at the tea-table, Sir James came to sit down by her, not having felt her mode of answering him at all offensive. Why should he? He thought it probable that Miss Brooke liked him, and manners must be very marked indeed before they cease to be interpreted by preconceptions either confident or distrustful. She was thoroughly charming to him, but of course he theorized a little about his attachment. He was made of excellent human dough, and had the rare merit of knowing that his talents, even if let loose, would not set the smallest stream in the county on fire: hence he liked the prospect of a wife to whom he could say, 'What shall we do?' about this or that; who could help her husband out with reasons, and would also have the property qualification for doing so. As to the excessive religiousness alleged against Miss Brooke, he had a very indefinite notion of what it consisted in, and thought that it would die out with marriage. In short, he felt himself to be in love in the right place, and was ready to endure a great deal of predominance, which, after all, a man could always put down when he liked. Sir James had no idea that he should ever like to put down the predominance of this handsome girl, in whose cleverness he delighted. Why not? A man's mind – what there is of it – has always the advantage of being masculine – as the smallest birch-tree is of a higher kind than the most soaring palm – and even his ignorance is of a sounder quality. Sir James might not have originated this estimate; but a kind Providence furnishes the limpest personality with a little gum or starch in the form of tradition.

'Let me hope that you will rescind that resolution about the horse, Miss Brooke,' said the persevering admirer. 'I assure you, riding is the most healthy of exercises.'

'I am aware of it,' said Dorothea, coldly. 'I think it would do Celia good – if she would take to it.'

'But you are such a perfect horsewoman.'

'Excuse me; I have had very little practice, and I should be easily thrown.'

'Then that is a reason for more practice. Every lady ought to be a perfect horsewoman, that she may accompany her husband.'

'You see how widely we differ, Sir James. I have made up my mind that I ought not to be a perfect horsewoman, and so I should never correspond to your pattern of a lady.' Dorothea looked straight before her, and spoke with cold brusquerie, very much with the air of a handsome boy, in amusing contrast with the solicitous amiability of her admirer.

'I should like to know your reasons for this cruel resolution. It is not possible that you should think horsemanship wrong.'

'It is quite possible that I should think it wrong for me.'

'Oh, why?' said Sir James, in a tender tone of remonstrance. Mr Casaubon had come up to the table, tea-cup in hand, and was listening.

'We must not inquire too curiously into motives,' he interposed, in his measured way. 'Miss Brooke knows that they are apt to become feeble in the utterance: the aroma is mixed with the grosser air. We must keep the germinating grain away from the light.'

Dorothea coloured with pleasure, and looked up gratefully to the speaker. Here was a man who could understand the higher inward life, and with whom there could be some spiritual communion; nay, who could illuminate principle with the widest knowledge: a man whose learning almost amounted to a proof of whatever he believed!

Dorothea's inferences may seem large; but really life could never have gone on at any period but for this liberal allowance of conclusion, which has facilitated marriage under the difficulties of civilization. Has anyone ever pinched into its pilulous smallness the cobweb of pre-matrimonial acquaintanceship?

'Certainly,' said good Sir James. 'Miss Brooke shall not be urged to tell reasons she would rather be silent upon. I am sure her reasons would do her honour.'

He was not in the least jealous of the interest with which Dorothea had looked up at Mr Casaubon: it never occurred to him that a girl to whom he was meditating an offer of marriage could care for a dried bookworm towards fifty, except, indeed, in a religious sort of way, as for a clergyman of some distinction.

However, since Miss Brooke had become engaged in a conversation with Mr Casaubon about the Vaudois clergy, Sir James betook himself to Celia, and talked to her about her sister; spoke of a house in town, and asked whether Miss Brooke disliked London. Away from her sister, Celia talked quite easily, and Sir James said to himself that the second Miss Brooke was certainly very agreeable as well as pretty, though not, as some people pretended, more clever and sensible than the elder sister. He felt that he had chosen the one who was in all respects the superior; and a man naturally likes to look forward to having the best. He would be the very Mawworm of bachelors who pretended not to expect it.

❧ THREE ❧

Say, goddess, what ensued, when Raphaël,
The affable archangel . . .

                                                    Eve

The story heard attentive, and was filled
With admiration, and deep muse, to hear
Of things so high and strange.

                    Paradise Lost, BK. vii

IF IT HAD REALLY OCCURRED TO Mr Casaubon to think of Miss Brooke as a suitable wife for him, the reasons that might induce her to accept him were already planted in her mind, and by the evening of the next day the reasons had budded and bloomed. For they had had a long conversation in the morning, while Celia, who did not like the company of Mr Casaubon's moles and sallowness, had escaped to the vicarage to play with the curate's ill-shod but merry children.

Dorothea by this time had looked deep into the ungauged reservoir of Mr Casaubon's mind, seeing reflected there in vague labyrinthine extension every quality she herself brought; had opened much of her own experience to him, and had understood from him the scope of his great work, also of attractively labyrinthine extent. For he had been as instructive as Milton's 'affable archangel'; and with something of the archangelic manner he told her how he had undertaken to show (what indeed had been attempted before, but not with that thoroughness, justice of comparison, and effectiveness of arrangement at which Mr Casaubon aimed) that all the mythical systems or erratic mythical fragments in the world were corruptions of a tradition originally revealed. Having once mastered the true position and taken a firm footing there, the vast field of mythical constructions became intelligible, nay, luminous with the reflected light of correspondences. But to gather in this great harvest of truth was no light or speedy work. His notes already made a formidable range of volumes, but the crowning task would be to condense these voluminous still-accumulating results and bring them, like the earlier vintage of Hippocratic books, to fit a little shelf. In explaining this to Dorothea, Mr Casaubon expressed himself nearly as he would have done to a fellow-student, for he had not two styles of talking at command: it is true that when he used a Greek or Latin phrase he always gave the English with scrupulous care, but he would probably have done this in any case. A learned provincial clergyman is accustomed to think of his acquaintances as of 'lords, knyghtes, and other noble and worthi men, that conne Latyn but lytille'.

Dorothea was altogether captivated by the wide embrace of this conception. Here was something beyond the shallows of ladies'-school literature: here was a living Bossuet, whose work would reconcile complete knowledge with devoted piety; here was a modern Augustine who united the glories of doctor and saint.

The sanctity seemed no less clearly marked than the learning, for when Dorothea was impelled to open her mind on certain themes which she could speak of to no one whom she had before seen at Tipton, especially on the secondary importance of ecclesiastical forms and articles of belief compared with that spiritual religion, that submergence of self in communion with Divine perfection which seemed to her to be expressed in the best Christian books of widely-distant ages, she found in Mr Casaubon a listener who understood her at once, who could assure her of his own agreement with that view when duly tempered with wise conformity, and could mention historical examples before unknown to her.

'He thinks with me,' said Dorothea to herself, 'or rather, he thinks a whole world of which my thought is but a poor two-penny mirror. And his feelings too, his whole experience – what a lake compared with my little pool!'

Miss Brooke argued from words and dispositions not less unhesitatingly than other young ladies of her age. Signs are small measurable things, but interpretations are illimitable, and in girls of sweet, ardent nature, every sign is apt to conjure up wonder, hope, belief, vast as a sky, and coloured by a diffused thimbleful of matter in the shape of knowledge. They are not always too grossly deceived; for Sinbad himself may have fallen by good luck on a true description, and wrong reasoning sometimes lands poor mortals in right conclusions: starting a long way off the true point, and proceeding by loops and zig-zags, we now and then arrive just where we ought to be. Because Miss Brooke was hasty in her trust, it is not therefore clear that Mr Casaubon was unworthy of it.

He stayed a little longer than he had intended, on a slight pressure of invitation from Mr Brooke, who offered no bait except his own documents on machine-breaking and rick-burning. Mr Casaubon was called into the library to look at these in a heap, while his host picked up first one and then the other to read aloud from in a skipping and uncertain way, passing from one unfinished passage to another with a 'Yes, now, but here!' and finally pushing them all aside to open the journal of his youthful Continental travels.

'Look here – here is all about Greece, Rhamnus, the ruins of Rhamnus – you are a great Grecian, now. I don't know whether you have given much study to the topography. I spent no end of time in making out these things – Helicon, now. Here, now! – "We started the next morning for Parnassus, the double-peaked Parnassus." All this volume is about Greece, you know,' Mr Brooke wound up, rubbing his thumb transversely along the edges of the leaves as he held the book forward.

Mr Casaubon made a dignified though somewhat sad audience; bowed in the right place, and avoided looking at anything documentary as far as possible, without showing disregard or impatience; mindful that this desultoriness was associated with the institutions of the country, and that the man who took him on this severe mental scamper was not only an amiable host, but a landholder and *custos rotulorum*. Was his endurance aided also by the reflection that Mr Brooke was the uncle of Dorothea?

Certainly he seemed more and more bent on making her talk to him, on drawing her out, as Celia remarked to herself; and in looking at her, his face was often lit up by a smile like pale wintry sunshine. Before he left the next morning, while taking a pleasant walk with Miss Brooke along the gravelled terrace, he had mentioned to her that he felt the disadvantage of loneliness, the need of that cheerful companionship with which the presence of youth can lighten or vary the serious toils of maturity. And he delivered this statement with as much careful precision as if he had been a diplomatic envoy whose words would be attended with results. Indeed, Mr Casaubon was not used to expect that he should have to repeat or revise his communications of a practical or personal kind. The inclinations which he had deliberately stated on the 2d of October he would think it enough to refer to by the mention of that date; judging by the standard of his own memory, which was a volume where a *vide supra* could serve instead of repetitions, and not the ordinary long-used blotting-book which only tells of forgotten writing. But in this case Mr Casaubon's confidence was not likely to be falsified, for Dorothea heard and retained what he said with the eager interest of a fresh young nature to which every variety in experience is an epoch.

It was three o'clock in the beautiful breezy autumn day when Mr Casaubon drove off to his Rectory at Lowick, only five miles from Tipton; and Dorothea, who had on her bonnet and shawl, hurried along the shrubbery and across the park that she might wander through the bordering wood with no other visible companionship than that of Monk, the Great St Bernard dog, who always took care of the young ladies in their walks. There had risen before her the girl's vision of a possible future for herself to which she looked forward with trembling hope, and she wanted to wander on in that visionary future without interruption. She walked briskly in the brisk air, the colour rose in her cheeks, and her straw-bonnet (which our contemporaries might look at with conjectural curiosity as at an obsolete form of basket) fell a little backward. She would perhaps be hardly characterized enough if it were omitted that she wore her brown hair flatly braided and coiled behind so as to expose the outline of her head in a daring manner at a time when public feeling required the meagreness of nature to be dissimulated by tall barricades of frizzed curls and bows, never surpassed by any great race except the Feejeean. This was a trait of Miss Brooke's asceticism. But there was nothing of an ascetic's expression in her bright full eyes, as she looked before her, not consciously seeing, but absorbing into the intensity of her mood, the solemn glory of the afternoon with its long swathes of light between the far-off rows of limes, whose shadows touched each other.

All people, young or old (that is, all people in those ante-reform times), would have thought her an interesting object if they had referred the glow in her eyes and cheeks to the newly-awakened ordinary images of young love: the illusions of Chloe about Strephon have been sufficiently consecrated in poetry, as the pathetic loveliness of all spontaneous trust ought to be. Miss Pippin adoring young Pumpkin and dreaming along endless vistas of unwearying companionship, was a little drama which never tired our fathers and mothers, and had been put into all costumes. Let but Pumpkin have a figure which would sustain the disadvantages of the short-waisted swallow-tail, and everybody felt it not only natural but necessary to the perfection of womanhood, that a sweet girl should be at once convinced of his virtue, his exceptional ability, and above all, his perfect sincerity. But perhaps no persons then living – certainly none in the neighbourhood of Tipton – would have had a sympathetic understanding for the dreams of a girl whose notions about marriage took their colour entirely from an exalted enthusiasm about the ends of life, an enthusiasm which was lit chiefly by its own fire, and included neither the niceties of the *trousseau*, the pattern of plate, nor even the honours and sweet joys of the blooming matron.

It had now entered Dorothea's mind that Mr Casaubon might wish to make her his wife, and the idea that he would do so touched her with a sort of reverential gratitude. How good of him – nay, it would be almost as if a winged messenger had suddenly stood beside her path and held out his hand towards her! For a long while she had been oppressed by the indefiniteness which hung in her mind, like a thick summer haze, over all her desire to make her life greatly effective. What could she do, what ought she to do? – she, hardly more than a budding woman, but yet with an active conscience and a great mental need, not to be satisfied by a girlish instruction comparable to the nibblings and judgments of a discursive mouse. With some endowment of stupidity and conceit, she might have thought that a Christian young lady of fortune should find her ideal of life in village charities, patronage of the humbler clergy, the perusal of *Female Scripture Characters*, unfolding the private experience of Sara under the Old Dispensation, and Dorcas under the New, and the care of her soul over her embroidery in her own boudoir – with a background of prospective marriage to a man who, if less strict than herself as being involved in affairs religiously inexplicable, might be prayed for and seasonably exhorted. From such contentment poor Dorothea was shut out. The intensity of her religious disposition, the coercion it exercised over her life, was but one aspect of a nature altogether ardent, theoretic, and intellectually consequent: and with such a nature, struggling in the bands of a narrow teaching, hemmed in by a social life which seemed nothing but a labyrinth of petty courses, a walled-in maze of small paths that led no whither, the outcome was sure to strike others as at once exaggeration and inconsistency. The thing which seemed to her best, she wanted to justify by the completest knowledge; and not to live in a pretended admission of rules which were never acted on. Into this soul-hunger as yet all her youthful passion was poured; the union which attracted her was one that would deliver her from her girlish subjection to her own ignorance, and give her the freedom of voluntary submission to a guide who would take her along the grandest path.

'I should learn everything then,' she said to herself, still walking quickly along the bridle road through the wood. 'It would be my duty to study that I might help him the better in his great works. There would be nothing trivial about our lives. Everyday-things with us would mean the greatest things. It would be like marrying Pascal. I should learn to see the truth by the same light as great men have seen it by. And then I should know what to do, when I got older: I should see how it was possible to lead a grand life here – now – in England. I don't feel sure about doing good in any way now: everything seems like going on a mission to a people whose language I don't know; – unless it were building good cottages – there can be no doubt about that. Oh, I hope I should be able to get the people well housed in Lowick! I will draw plenty of plans while I have time.'

Dorothea checked herself suddenly with self-rebuke for the presumptuous way in which she was reckoning on uncertain events, but she was spared any inward effort to change the direction of her thoughts by the appearance of a cantering horseman round a turning of the road. The well-groomed chestnut horse and two beautiful setters could leave no doubt that the rider was Sir James Chettam. He discerned Dorothea, jumped off his horse at once, and, having delivered it to his groom, advanced towards her with something white on his arm, at which the two setters were barking in an excited manner.

'How delightful to meet you, Miss Brooke,' he said, raising his hat and showing his sleekly-waving blond hair. 'It has hastened the pleasure I was looking forward to.'

Miss Brooke was annoyed at the interruption. This amiable baronet, really a suitable husband for Celia, exaggerated the necessity of making himself agreeable to the elder sister. Even a prospective brother-in-law may be an oppression if he will always be presupposing too good an understanding with you, and agreeing with you even when you contradict him. The thought that he had made the mistake of paying his addresses to herself could not take shape: all her mental activity was used up in persuasions of another kind. But he was positively obtrusive at this moment, and his dimpled hands were quite disagreeable. Her roused temper made her colour deeply, as she returned his greeting with some haughtiness.

Sir James interpreted the heightened colour in the way most gratifying to himself, and thought he never saw Miss Brooke looking so handsome.

'I have brought a little petitioner,' he said, 'or rather I have brought him to see if he will be approved before his petition is offered.' He showed the white object under his arm, which was a tiny Maltese puppy, one of nature's most naïve toys.

'It is painful to me to see these creatures that are bred merely as pets,' said Dorothea, whose opinion was forming itself that very moment (as opinions will) under the heat of irritation.

'Oh, why?' said Sir James, as they walked forward.

'I believe all the petting that is given them does not make them happy. They are too helpless: their lives are too frail. A weasel or a mouse that gets its own living is more interesting. I like to think that the animals about us have souls something like our own, and either carry on their own little affairs or can be companions to us, like Monk here. Those creatures are parasitic.'

'I am so glad I know that you do not like them,' said good Sir James. 'I should never keep them for myself, but ladies usually are fond of these Maltese dogs. Here, John, take this dog, will you?'

The objectionable puppy, whose nose and eyes were equally black and expressive, was thus got rid of, since Miss Brooke decided that it had better not have been born. But she felt it necessary to explain.

'You must not judge of Celia's feeling from mine. I think she likes these small pets. She had a tiny terrier once, which she was very fond of. It made me unhappy, because I was afraid of treading on it. I am rather short-sighted.'

'You have your own opinion about everything, Miss Brooke, and it is always a good opinion.'

What answer was possible to such stupid complimenting?

'Do you know, I envy you that,' Sir James said, as they continued walking at the rather brisk pace set by Dorothea.

'I don't quite understand what you mean.'

'Your power of forming an opinion. I can form an opinion of persons. I know when I like people. But about other matters, do you know, I have often a difficulty in deciding. One hears very sensible things said on opposite sides.'

'Or that seem sensible. Perhaps we don't always discriminate between sense and nonsense.'

Dorothea felt that she was rather rude.

'Exactly,' said Sir James. 'But you seem to have the power of discrimination.'

'On the contrary, I am often unable to decide. But that is from ignorance. The right conclusion is there all the same, though I am unable to see it.'

'I think there are few who would see it more readily. Do you know, Lovegood was telling me yesterday that you had the best notion in the world of a plan for cottages – quite wonderful for a young lady, he thought. You had a real *genus*, to use his expression. He said you wanted Mr Brooke to build a new set of cottages, but he seemed to think it hardly probable that your uncle would consent. Do you know, that is one of the things I wish to do – I mean, on my own estate? I should be so glad to carry out that plan of yours, if you would let me see it. Of course, it is sinking money; that is why people object to it. Labourers can never pay rent to make it answer. But, after all, it is worth doing.'

'Worth doing! yes, indeed,' said Dorothea, energetically, forgetting her previous small vexations. 'I think we deserve to be beaten out of our beautiful houses with a scourge of small cords – all of us who let tenants live in such sties as we see round us. Life in cottages might be happier than ours, if they were real houses fit for human beings from whom we expect duties and affections.'

'Will you show me your plan?'

'Yes, certainly. I daresay it is very faulty. But I have been examining all the plans for cottages in Loudon's book, and picked out what seem the best things. Oh what a happiness it would be to set the pattern about here! I think, instead of Lazarus at the gate, we should put the pig-sty cottages outside the park gate.'

Dorothea was in the best temper now. Sir James, as brother-in-law, building model cottages on his estate, and then, perhaps, others being built at Lowick, and more and more elsewhere in imitation – it would be as if the spirit of Oberlin had passed over the parishes to make the life of poverty beautiful!

Sir James saw all the plans, and took one away to consult upon with Lovegood. He also took away a complacent sense that he was making great progress in Miss Brooke's good opinion. The Maltese puppy was not offered to Celia; an omission which Dorothea afterwards thought of with surprise; but she blamed herself for it. She had been engrossing Sir James. After all, it was a relief that there was no puppy to tread upon.

Celia was present while the plans were being examined, and observed Sir James's illusion. 'He thinks that Dodo cares about him, and she only cares about her plans. Yet I am not certain that she would refuse him if she thought he would let her manage everything and carry out all her notions. And how very uncomfortable Sir James would be! I cannot bear notions.'

It was Celia's private luxury to indulge in this dislike. She dared not confess it to her sister in any direct statement, for that would be laying herself open to a demonstration that she was somehow or other at war with all goodness. But on safe opportunities, she had an indirect mode of making her negative wisdom tell upon Dorothea, and calling her down from her rhapsodic mood by reminding her that people were staring, not listening. Celia was not impulsive: what she had to say could wait, and came from her always with the same quiet, staccato evenness. When people talked with energy and emphasis she watched their faces and features merely. She never could understand how well-bred persons consented to sing and open their mouths in the ridiculous manner requisite for that vocal exercise.

It was not many days before Mr Casaubon paid a morning visit, on which he was invited again for the following week to dine and stay the night. Thus Dorothea had three more conversations with him, and was convinced that her first impressions had been just. He was all she had at first imagined him to be: almost everything he had said seemed like a specimen from a mine, or the inscription on the door of a museum which might open on the treasures of past ages; and this trust in his mental wealth was all the deeper and more effective on her inclination because it was now obvious that his visits were made for her sake. This accomplished man condescended to think of a young girl, and take the pains to talk to her, not with absurd compliment, but with an appeal to her understanding, and sometimes with instructive correction. What delightful companionship. Mr Casaubon seemed even unconscious that trivialities existed, and never handed round that small-talk of heavy men which is as acceptable as stale bride-cake brought forth with an odour of cupboard. He talked of what he was interested in, or else he was silent and bowed with sad civility. To Dorothea this was adorable genuineness, and religious abstinence from that artificiality which uses up the soul in the efforts of pretence. For she looked as reverently at Mr Casaubon's religious elevation above herself as she did at his intellect and learning. He assented to her expressions of devout feeling, and usually with an appropriate quotation; he allowed himself to say that he had gone through some spiritual conflicts in his youth; in short, Dorothea saw that here she might reckon on understanding sympathy and guidance. On one – only one – of her favourite themes she was disappointed. Mr Casaubon apparently did not care about building cottages, and diverted the talk to the extremely narrow accommodation which was to be had in the dwellings of the ancient Egyptians, as if to check a too high standard. After he was gone, Dorothea dwelt with some agitation on this indifference of his; and her mind was much exercised with arguments drawn from the varying conditions of climate which modify human needs, and from the admitted wickedness of pagan despots. Should she not urge these arguments on Mr Casaubon when he came again? But further reflection told her that she was presumptuous in demanding his attention to such a subject; he would not disapprove of her occupying herself with it in leisure moments, as other women expected to occupy themselves with their dress and embroidery – would not forbid it when – Dorothea felt rather ashamed as she detected herself in these speculations. But her uncle had been invited to go to Lowick to stay a couple of days: was it reasonable to suppose that Mr Casaubon delighted in Mr Brooke's society for its own sake, either with or without documents?

Meanwhile that little disappointment made her delight the more in Sir James Chettam's readiness to set on foot the desired improvements. He came much oftener than Mr Casaubon, and Dorothea ceased to find him disagreeable since he showed himself so entirely in earnest; for he had already entered with much practical ability into Lovegood's estimates, and was charmingly docile. She proposed to build a couple of cottages, and transfer two families from their old cabins, which could then be pulled down, so that new ones could be built on the old sites. Sir James said, 'Exactly,' and she bore the word remarkably well.

Certainly these men who had so few spontaneous ideas might be very useful members of society under good feminine direction, if they were fortunate in choosing their sisters-in-law! It is difficult to say whether there was or was not a little wilfulness in her continuing blind to the possibility that another sort of choice was in question in relation to her. But her life was just now full of hope and action: she was not only thinking of her plans, but getting down learned books from the library and reading many things hastily (that she might be a little less ignorant in talking to Mr Casaubon), all the while being visited with conscientious questionings whether she were not exalting theses poor doings above measure and contemplating them with that self-satisfaction which was the last doom of ignorance and folly.

⊂ྀ FOUR ຊ

> 1st Gent. Our deeds are fetters that we forge ourselves.
> 2nd Gent. Ay, truly: but I think it is the world
>   That brings the iron.

'SIR JAMES SEEMS DETERMINED TO DO everything you wish,' said Celia, as they were driving home from an inspection of the new building-site.

'He is a good creature, and more sensible than any one would imagine,' said Dorothea, inconsiderately.

'You mean that he appears silly.'

'No, no,' said Dorothea, recollecting herself, and laying her hand on her sister's a moment, 'but he does not talk equally well on all subjects.'

'I should think none but disagreeable people do,' said Celia, in her usual purring way. 'They must be very dreadful to live with. Only think! at breakfast, and always.'

Dorothea laughed. 'O Kitty, you are a wonderful creature!' She pinched Celia's chin, being in the mood now to think her very winning and lovely – fit hereafter to be an eternal cherub, and if it were not doctrinally wrong to say so, hardly more in need of salvation than a squirrel. 'Of course people need not be always talking well. Only one tells the quality of their minds when they try to talk well.'

'You mean that Sir James tries and fails.'

'I was speaking generally. Why do you catechize me about Sir James? It is not the object of his life to please me.'

'Now, Dodo, can you really believe that?'

'Certainly. He thinks of me as a future sister – that is all.' Dorothea had never hinted this before, waiting, from a certain shyness on such subjects which was mutual between the sisters, until it should be introduced by some decisive event. Celia blushed, but said at once –

'Pray do not make that mistake any longer, Dodo. When Tantripp was brushing my hair the other day, she said that Sir James's man knew from Mrs Cadwallader's maid that Sir James was to marry the eldest Miss Brooke.'

'How can you let Tantripp talk such gossip to you, Celia?' said Dorothea, indignantly, not the less angry because details asleep in her memory were now awakened to confirm the unwelcome revelation. 'You must have asked her questions. It is degrading.'

'I see no harm at all in Tantripp's talking to me. It is better to hear what people say. You see what mistakes you make by taking up notions. I am quite sure that Sir James means to make you an offer; and he believes that you will accept him, especially since you have been so pleased with him about the plans. And uncle too – I know he expects it. Every one can see that Sir James is very much in love with you.'

The revulsion was so strong and painful in Dorothea's mind that the tears welled up and flowed abundantly. All her dear plans were embittered, and she thought with disgust of Sir James's conceiving that she recognized him as her lover. There was vexation too on account of Celia.

'How could he expect it?' she burst forth in her most impetuous manner. 'I have never agreed with him about anything but the cottages: I was barely polite to him before.'

'But you have been so pleased with him since then; he has begun to feel quite sure that you are fond of him.'

'Fond of him, Celia! How can you choose such odious expressions?' said Dorothea, passionately.

'Dear me, Dorothea, I suppose it would be right for you to be fond of a man whom you accepted for a husband.'

'It is offensive to me to say that Sir James could think I was fond of him. Besides, it is not the right word for the feeling I must have towards the man I would accept as a husband.'

'Well, I am sorry for Sir James. I thought it right to tell you, because you went on as you always do, never looking just where you are, and treading in the wrong place. You always see what nobody else sees; it is impossible to satisfy you; yet you never see what is quite plain. That's your way, Dodo.' Something certainly gave Celia unusual courage; and she was not sparing the sister of whom she was occasionally in awe. Who can tell what just criticisms Murr the Cat may be passing on us beings of wider speculation?

'It is very painful,' said Dorothea, feeling scourged. 'I can have no more to do with the cottages. I must be uncivil to him. I must tell him I will have nothing to do with them. It is very painful.' Her eyes filled again with tears.

'Wait a little. Think about it. You know he is going away for a day or two to see his sister. There will be nobody besides Lovegood.' Celia could not help relenting. 'Poor Dodo,' she went on, in an amiable staccato. 'It is very hard: it is your favourite *fad* to draw plans.'

'*Fad* to draw plans; Do you think I only care about my fellow-creatures' houses in that childish way? I may well make mistakes. How can one ever do anything nobly Christian, living among people with such petty thoughts?'

No more was said: Dorothea was too much jarred to recover her temper and behave so as to show that she admitted any error in herself. She was disposed rather to accuse the intolerable narrowness and the purblind conscience of the society around her: and Celia was no longer the eternal cherub, but a thorn in her spirit, a pink-and-white nullifidian, worse than any discouraging presence in the *Pilgrim's Progress*. The *fad* of drawing plans! What was life worth – what great faith was possible when the whole effect of one's actions could be withered up into such parched rubbish as that? When she got out of the carriage, her cheeks were pale and her eyelids red. She was an image of sorrow, and her uncle, who met her in the hall, would have been alarmed, if Celia had not been close to her looking so pretty and composed, that he at once concluded Dorothea's tears to have their origin in her excessive religiousness. He had returned, during their absence, from a journey to the country town, about a petition for the pardon of some criminal.

'Well, my dears,' he said, kindly, as they went up to kiss him, 'I hope nothing disagreeable has happened while I have been away.'

'No, uncle,' said Celia, 'we have been to Freshitt to look at the cottages. We thought you would have been at home by lunch.'

'I came by Lowick to lunch – you didn't know I came by Lowick. And I have brought a couple of pamphlets for you, Dorothea – in the library, you know; they lie on the table in the library.'

It seemed as if an electric stream went through Dorothea, thrilling her from despair into expectation. They were pamphlets about the early Church. The oppression of Celia, Tantripp, and Sir James was shaken off, and she walked straight to the library. Celia went upstairs. Mr Brooke was detained by a message, but when he re-entered the library, he found Dorothea seated and already deep in one of the pamphlets, which had some marginal manuscript of Mr Casaubon's, – taking it in as eagerly as she might have taken in the scent of a fresh bouquet after a dry, hot, dreary walk.

She was getting away from Tipton and Freshitt, and her own sad liability to tread in the wrong places on her way to the New Jerusalem.

Mr Brooke sat down in his arm-chair, stretched his legs towards the wood-fire, which had fallen into a wondrous mass of glowing dice between the dogs, and rubbed his hands gently, looking very mildly towards Dorothea, but with a neutral leisurely air, as if he had nothing particular to say. Dorothea closed her pamphlet, as soon as she was aware of her uncle's presence, and rose as if to go. Usually she would have been interested about her uncle's merciful errand on behalf of the criminal, but her late agitation had made her absent-minded.

'I came back by Lowick, you know,' said Mr Brooke, not as if with any intention to arrest her departure, but apparently from his usual tendency to say what he had said before. This fundamental principle of human speech was markedly exhibited in Mr Brooke. 'I lunched there and saw Casaubon's library, and that kind of thing. There's a sharp air, driving. Won't you sit down, my dear? You look cold.'

Dorothea felt quite inclined to accept the invitation. Sometimes, when her uncle's easy way of taking things did not happen to be exasperating, it was rather soothing. She threw off her mantle and bonnet, and sat down opposite to him, enjoying the glow, but lifting up her beautiful hands for a screen. They were not thin hands, or small hands; but powerful, feminine, maternal hands. She seemed to be holding them up in propitiation for her passionate desire to know and to think, which in the unfriendly mediums of Tipton and Freshitt had issued in crying and red eyelids.

She bethought herself now of the condemned criminal. 'What news have you brought about the sheep-stealer, uncle?'

'What, poor Bunch? – well, it seems we can't get him off – he is to be hanged.'

Dorothea's brow took an expression of reprobation and pity.

'Hanged, you know,' said Mr Brooke, with a quiet nod. 'Poor Romilly! he would have helped us. I knew Romilly. Casaubon didn't know Romilly. He is a little buried in books, you know, Casaubon is.'

'When a man has great studies and is writing a great work, he must of course give up seeing much of the world. How can he go about making acquaintances?'

'That's true. But a man mopes, you know. I have always been a bachelor too, but I have that sort of disposition that I never moped; it was my way to go about everywhere and take in everything. I never moped: but I can see that Casaubon does, you know. He wants a companion – a companion, you know.'

'It would be a great honour to any one to be his companion,' said Dorothea, energetically.

'You like him, eh?' said Mr Brooke, without showing any surprise, or other emotion. 'Well, now, I've known Casaubon ten years, ever since he came to Lowick. But I never got anything out of him – any ideas, you know. However, he is a tiptop man and may be a bishop – that kind of thing, you know, if Peel stays in. And he has a very high opinion of you, my dear.'

Dorothea could not speak.

'The fact is, he has a very high opinion indeed of you. And he speaks uncommonly well – does Casaubon. He has deferred to me, you not being of age. In short, I have promised to speak to you, though I told him I thought there was not much chance. I was bound to tell him that. I said, my niece is very young, and that kind of thing. But I didn't think it necessary to go into everything. However, the long and the short of it is, that he has asked my permission to make you an offer of marriage – of marriage, you know,' said Mr Brooke, with his explanatory nod. 'I thought it better to tell you, my dear.'

No one could have detected any anxiety in Mr Brooke's manner, but he did really wish to know something of his niece's mind, that, if there were any need for advice, he might give it in time. What feeling he, as a magistrate who had taken in so many ideas, could make room for, was unmixedly kind. Since Dorothea did not speak immediately, he repeated, 'I thought it better to tell you, my dear.'

'Thank you, uncle,' said Dorothea, in a clear unwavering tone. 'I am very grateful to Mr Casaubon. If he makes me an offer, I shall accept him. I admire and honour him more than any man I ever saw.'

Mr Brooke paused a little, and then said in a lingering low tone. 'Ah? . . . Well! He is a good match in some respects. But now, Chettam is a good match. And our land lies together. I shall never interfere against your wishes, my dear. People should have their own way in marriage, and that sort of thing – up to a certain point, you know. I have always said that, up to a certain point. I wish you to marry well; and I have good reason to believe that Chettam wishes to marry you. I mention it, you know.'

'It is impossible that I should ever marry Sir James Chettam,' said Dorothea. 'If he thinks of marrying me, he has made a great mistake.'

'That is it, you see. One never knows. I should have thought Chettam was just the sort of man a woman would like, now.'

'Pray do not mention him in that light again, uncle,' said Dorothea, feeling some of her late irritation revive.

Mr Brooke wondered, and felt that women were an inexhaustible subject of study, since even he at his age was not in a perfect state of scientific prediction about them! Here was a fellow like Chettam with no chance at all.

'Well, but Casaubon, now. There is no hurry – I mean for you. It's true, every year will tell upon him. He is over five-and-forty, you know. I should say a good seven-and-twenty years older than you. To be sure, – if you like learning and standing, and that sort of thing, we can't have everything. And his income is good – he has a handsome property independent of the Church – his income is good. Still he is not young, and I must not conceal from you, my dear, that I think his health is not over-strong. I know nothing else against him.'

'I should not wish to have a husband very near my own age,' said Dorothea, with grave decision. 'I should wish to have a husband who was above me in judgment and in all knowledge.'

Mr Brooke repeated his subdued, 'Ah? – I thought you had more of your own opinion than most girls. I thought you liked your own opinion – liked it, you know.'

'I cannot imagine myself living without some opinions, but I should wish to have good reasons for them, and a wise man could help me to see which opinions had the best foundation, and would help me to live according to them.'

'Very true. You couldn't put the thing better – couldn't put it better, beforehand, you know. But there are oddities in things,' continued Mr Brooke, whose conscience was really roused to do the best he could for his niece on this occasion. 'Life isn't cast in a mould – not cut out by rule and line, and that sort of thing. I never married myself, and it will be the better for you and yours. The fact is, I never loved any one well enough to put myself into a noose for them. It *is* a noose, you know. Temper, now. There is temper. And a husband likes to be master.'

'I know that I must expect trials, uncle. Marriage is a state of higher duties. I never thought of it as mere personal ease,' said poor Dorothea.

'Well, you are not fond of show, a great establishment, balls, dinners, that kind of thing. I can see that Casaubon's ways might suit you better than Chettam's. And you shall do as you like, my dear. I would not hinder Casaubon; I said so at once; for there is no knowing how anything may turn out. You have not the same tastes as every young lady; and a clergy-man and scholar – who may be a bishop – that kind of thing – may suit you better than Chettam. Chettam is a good fellow, a good sound-hearted fellow, you know; but he doesn't go much into ideas. I did, when I was his age. But Casaubon's eyes, now. I think he has hurt them a little with too much reading.'

'I should be all the happier, uncle, the more room there was for me to help him,' said Dorothea, ardently.

'You have quite made up your mind, I see. Well, my dear, the fact is, I have a letter for you in my pocket.' Mr Brooke handed the letter to Dorothea, but as she rose to go away, he added, 'There is not too much hurry, my dear. Think about it, you know.'

When Dorothea had left him, he reflected that he had certainly spoken strongly: he had put the risks of marriage before her in a striking manner.

It was his duty to do so. But as to pretending to be wise for young people, – no uncle, however much he had travelled in his youth, absorbed the new ideas, and dined with celebrities now deceased, could pretend to judge what sort of marriage would turn out well for a young girl who preferred Casaubon to Chettam. In short, woman was a problem which, since Mr Brooke's mind felt blank before it, could be hardly less complicated than the revolutions of an irregular solid.

ᗥ FIVE ᗡ

Hard students are commonly troubled with gowts, catarrhs, rheums, cachexia, bradypepsia, bad eyes, stone, and collick, crudities, oppilations, vertigo, winds, consumptions, and all such diseases as come by overmuch sitting: they are most part lean, dry, ill-coloured . . . and all through immoderate pains and extraordinary studies. If you will not believe the truth of this, look upon great Tostatus and Thomas Aquainas' works; and tell me whether those men took pains.

Burton's Anatomy of Melancholy, p. 1, s. 2.

THIS WAS MR CASAUBON'S LETTER.

My dear Miss Brooke, – I have your guardian's permission to address you on a subject than which I have none more at heart. I am not, I trust, mistaken in the recognition of some deeper correspondence than that of date in the fact that a consciousness of need in my own life had arisen contemporaneously with the possibility of my becoming acquainted with you. For in the first hour of meeting you, I had an impression of your eminent and perhaps exclusive fitness to supply that need (connected, I may say, with such activity of the affections as even the preoccupations of a work too special to be abdicated could not uninterruptedly dissimulate); and each succeeding opportunity for observation has given the impression an added depth by convincing me more emphatically of that fitness which I had preconceived, and thus evoking more decisively those affections to which I have but now referred. Our conversations have, I think, made sufficiently clear to you the tenor of my life and purposes: a tenor unsuited, I am aware, to the commoner order of minds. But I have discerned in you an elevation of thought and a capability of devotedness, which I had hitherto not conceived to be compatible either with the early bloom of youth or with those graces of sex that may be said at once to win and to confer distinction when combined, as they notably are in you, with the mental qualities above indicated. It was, I confess, beyond my hope to meet with this rare combination of elements both solid and attractive, adapted to supply aid in graver labours and to cast a charm over vacant hours; and but for the event of my introduction to you (which, let me again say, I trust not to be superficially coincident with foreshadowing needs, but providentially related thereto as stages towards the completion of a life's plan), I should presumably have gone on to the last without any attempt to lighten my solitariness by a matrimonial union.

Such, my dear Miss Brooke, is the accurate statement of my feelings; and I rely on your kind indulgence in venturing now to ask you how far your own are of a nature to confirm my happy presentiment. To be accepted by you as your husband and the earthly guardian of your welfare, I should regard as the highest of providential gifts. In return I can at least offer you an affection hitherto unwasted, and the faithful consecration of a life which, however short in the sequel, has no backward pages whereon, if you choose to turn them, you will find records such as might justly cause you either bitterness or shame. I await the expression of your sentiments with an anxiety which it would be the part of wisdom (were it possible) to divert by a more arduous labour than usual. But in this order of experience I am still young, and in looking forward to an unfavourable possibility I cannot but feel that resignation to solitude will be more difficult after the temporary illumination of hope. In any case, I shall remain, yours with sincere devotion.

Edward Casaubon

Dorothea trembled while she read this letter; then she fell on her knees, buried her face, and sobbed. She could not pray under the rush of solemn emotion in which thoughts became vague and images floated uncertainly, she could but cast herself, with a childlike sense of reclining in the lap of a divine consciousness which sustained her own. She remained in that attitude till it was time to dress for dinner.

How could it occur to her to examine the letter, to look at it critically as a profession of love? Her whole soul was possessed by the fact that a fuller life was opening before her: she was a neophyte about to enter on a higher grade of initiation. She was going to have room for the energies which stirred uneasily under the dimness and pressure of her own ignorance and the petty peremptoriness of the world's habits.

Now she would be able to devote herself to large yet definite duties; now she would be allowed to live continually in the light of a mind that she could reverence. This hope was not unmixed with the glow of proud delight – the joyous maiden surprise that she was chosen by the man whom her admiration had chosen. All Dorothea's passion was transfused through a mind struggling towards an ideal life; the radiance of her transfigured girlhood fell on the first object that came within its level. The impetus with which inclination became resolution was heightened by those little events of the day which had roused her discontent with the actual conditions of her life.

After dinner, when Celia was playing an 'air, with variations', a small kind of tinkling which symbolized the aesthetic part of the young ladies' education, Dorothea went up to her room to answer Mr Casaubon's letter. Why should she defer the answer? She wrote it over three times, not because she wished to change the wording, but because her hand was unusually uncertain, and she could not bear that Mr Casaubon should think her handwriting bad and illegible. She piqued herself on writing a hand in which each letter was distinguishable without any large range of conjecture, and she meant to make much use of this accomplishment, to save Mr Casaubon's eyes. Three times she wrote.

My dear Mr Casaubon, – I am very grateful to you for loving me, and thinking me worthy to be your wife. I can look forward to no better happiness than that which would be one with yours. If I said more, it would only be the same thing written out at greater length, for I cannot now dwell on any other thought than that I may be through life, yours devotedly,

Dorothea Brooke

Later in the evening she followed her uncle into the library to give him the letter, that he might send it in the morning. He was surprised, but his surprise only issued in a few moments' silence, during which he pushed about various objects on his writing-table, and finally stood with his back to the fire, his glasses on his nose, looking at the address of Dorothea's letter.

'Have you thought enough about this, my dear?' he said at last.

'There was no need to think long, uncle. I know of nothing to make me vacillate. If I changed my mind, it must be because of something important and entirely new to me.'

'Ah! – then you have accepted him? Then Chettam has no chance? Has Chettam offended you – offended you, you know? What is it you don't like in Chettam?'

'There is nothing that I like in him,' said Dorothea, rather impetuously.

Mr Brooke threw his head and shoulders backward as if some one had thrown a light missile at him. Dorothea immediately felt some self-rebuke, and said –

'I mean in the light of a husband. He is very kind, I think – really very good about the cottages. A well-meaning man.'

'But you must have a scholar, and that sort of thing? Well, it lies a little in our family. I had it myself – that love of knowledge, and going into everything – a little too much – it took me too far; though that sort of thing doesn't often run in the female line; or it runs underground like the rivers in Greece, you know – it comes out in the sons. Clever sons, clever mothers. I went a good deal into that, at one time. However, my dear, I have always said that people should do as they like in these things up to a certain point. I couldn't, as your guardian, have consented to a bad match. But Casaubon stands well: his position is good. I am afraid Chettam will be hurt, though, and Mrs Cadwallader will blame me.'

That evening, of course, Celia knew nothing of what had happened. She attributed Dorothea's abstracted manner, and the evidence of further crying since they had got home, to the temper she had been in about Sir James Chettam and the buildings, and was careful not to give further offence: having once said what she wanted to say, Celia had no disposition to recur to disagreeable subjects. It had been her nature when a child never to quarrel with anyone – only to observe with wonder that they quarrelled with her, and looked like turkey-cocks; whereupon she was ready to play at cat's cradle with them whenever they recovered themselves. And as to Dorothea, it had always been her way to find something wrong in her sister's words, though Celia inwardly protested that she always said just how things were, and nothing else: she never did and never could put words together out of her own head. But the best of Dodo was, that she did not keep angry for long together. Now, though they had hardly spoken to each other all the evening, yet when Celia put by her work, intending to go to bed, a proceeding in which she was always much the earlier, Dorothea, who was seated on a low stool, unable to occupy herself except in meditation, said, with the musical intonation which in moments of deep but quiet feeling made her speech like a fine bit of recitative –

'Celia, dear, come and kiss me,' holding her arms open as she spoke.

Celia knelt down to get the right level and gave her little butterfly kiss, while Dorothea encircled her with gentle arms and pressed her lips gravely on each cheek in turn.

'Don't sit up, Dodo, you are so pale tonight: go to bed soon,' said Celia, in a comfortable way, without any touch of pathos.

'No, dear, I am very, very happy,' said Dorothea, fervently.

'So much the better,' thought Celia. 'But how strangely Dodo goes from one extreme to the other.'

The next day, at luncheon, the butler, handing something to Mr Brooke, said, 'Jonas is come back, sir, and has brought this letter.'

Mr Brooke read the letter, and then, nodding toward Dorothea, said, 'Casaubon, my dear: he will be here to dinner; he didn't wait to write more – didn't wait, you know.'

It could not seem remarkable to Celia that a dinner guest should be announced to her sister beforehand, but her eyes following the same direction as her uncle's, she was struck with the peculiar effect of the announcement on Dorothea. It seemed as if something like the reflection of a white sunlit wing had passed across her features, ending in one of her rare blushes. For the first time it entered into Celia's mind that there might be something more between Mr Casaubon and her sister than his delight in bookish talk and her delight in listening. Hitherto she had classed the admiration for this 'ugly' and learned acquaintance with the admiration for Monsieur Liret at Lausanne, also ugly and learned. Dorothea had never been tired of listening to old Monsieur Liret when Celia's feet were as cold as possible, and when it had really become dreadful to see the skin of his bald head moving about. Why then should her enthusiasm not extend to Mr Casaubon simply in the same way as to Monsieur Liret? And it seemed probable that all learned men had a sort of schoolmaster's view of young people.

But now Celia was really startled at the suspicion which had darted into her mind. She was seldom taken by surprise in this way, her marvellous quickness in observing a certain order of signs generally preparing her to expect such outward events as she had an interest in. Not that she now imagined Mr Casaubon to be already an accepted lover: she had only begun to feel disgust at the possibility that anything in Dorothea's mind could tend toward such an issue. Here was something really to vex her about Dodo: it was all very well not to accept Sir James Chettam, but the idea of marrying Mr Casaubon! Celia felt a sort of shame mingled with a sense of the ludicrous. But perhaps Dodo, if she were really bordering on such an extravagance, might be turned away from it: experience had often shown that her impressibility might be calculated on. The day was damp, and they were not going to walk out, so they both went up to their sitting-room; and there Celia observed that Dorothea, instead of settling down with her usual diligent interest to some occupation, simply leaned her elbow on an open book and looked out of the window at the great cedar silvered with the damp. She herself had taken up the making of a toy for the curate's children, and was not going to enter on any subject too precipitately.

Dorothea was in fact thinking that it was desirable for Celia to know of the momentous change in Mr Casaubon's position since he had last been in the house: it did not seem fair to leave her in ignorance of what would necessarily affect her attitude towards him; but it was impossible not to shrink from telling her. Dorothea accused herself of some meanness in this timidity: it was always odious to her to have any small fears or contrivances about her actions, but at this moment she was seeking the highest aid possible that she might not dread the corrosiveness of Celia's pretty carnally minded prose. Her reverie was broken, and the difficulty of decision banished, by Celia's small and rather guttural voice speaking in its usual tone, of a remark aside or a 'by the by'.

'Is any one else coming to dine besides Mr Casaubon?'

'Not that I know of.'

'I hope there is some one else. Then I shall not hear him eat his soup so.'

'What is there remarkable about his soup-eating?'

'Really, Dodo, can't you hear how he scrapes his spoon? And he always blinks before he speaks. I don't know whether Locke blinked, but I'm sure I am sorry for those who sat opposite to him, if he did.'

'Celia,' said Dorothea, with emphatic gravity, 'pray don't make any more observations of that kind.'

'Why not? They are quite true,' returned Celia, who had her reasons for persevering, though she was beginning to be a little afraid.

'Many things are true which only the commonest minds observe.'

'Then I think the commonest minds must be rather useful. I think it is a pity Mr Casaubon's mother had not a commoner mind: she might have taught him better.' Celia was inwardly frightened, and ready to run away, now she had hurled this light javelin.

Dorothea's feelings had gathered to an avalanche, and there could be no further preparation.

'It is right to tell you, Celia, that I am engaged to marry Mr Casaubon.'

Perhaps Celia had never turned so pale before. The paper man she was making would have had his leg injured, but for her habitual care of whatever she held in her hands. She laid the fragile figure down at once, and sat perfectly still for a few moments. When she spoke there was a tear gathering.

'O Dodo, I hope you will be happy.' Her sisterly tenderness could not but surmount other feelings at this moment, and her fears were the fears of affection.

Dorothea was still hurt and agitated.

'It is quite decided, then?' said Celia, in an awed undertone. 'And uncle knows?'

'I have accepted Mr Casaubon's offer. My uncle brought me the letter that contained it; he knew about it beforehand.'

'I beg your pardon, if I have said anything to hurt you, Dodo,' said Celia, with a slight sob. She never could have thought that she should feel as she did. There was something funereal in the whole affair, and Mr Casaubon seemed to be the officiating clergyman, about whom it would be indecent to make remarks.

'Never mind, Kitty, do not grieve. We should never admire the same people. I often offend in something of the same way; I am apt to speak too strongly of those who don't please me.'

In spite of this magnanimity Dorothea was still smarting: perhaps as much from Celia's subdued astonishment as from her small criticisms. Of course all the world round Tipton would be out of sympathy with this marriage. Dorothea knew of no one who thought as she did about life and its best objects.

Nevertheless before the evening was at an end she was very happy. In an hour's *tête-à-tête* with Mr Casaubon she talked to him with more freedom than she had ever felt before, even pouring out her joy at the thought of devoting herself to him, and of learning how she might best share and further all his great ends. Mr Casaubon was touched with an unknown delight (what man would not have been?) at this childlike unrestrained ardour: he was not surprised (what lover would have been?) that he should be the object of it.

'My dear young lady – Miss Brooke – Dorothea!' he said, pressing her hand between his hands, 'this is a happiness greater than I had ever imagined to be in reserve for me. That I should ever meet with a mind and person so rich in the mingled graces which could render marriage desirable, was far indeed from my conception. You have all – nay, more than all – those qualities which I have ever regarded as the characteristic excellences of womanhood. The great charm of your sex is its capability of an ardent self-sacrificing affection, and herein we see its fitness to round and complete the existence of our own. Hitherto I have known few pleasures save of the severer kind: my satisfactions have been those of the solitary student. I have been little disposed to gather flowers that would wither in my hand, but now I shall pluck them with eagerness, to place them in your bosom.'

No speech could have been more thoroughly honest in its intention: the frigid rhetoric at the end was as sincere as the bark of a dog, or the cawing of an amorous rook. Would it not be rash to conclude that there was no passion behind those sonnets to Delia which strike us as the thin music of a mandolin?

Dorothea's faith supplied all that Mr Casaubon's words seemed to leave unsaid: what believer sees a disturbing omission or infelicity? The text, whether of prophet or of poet, expands for whatever we can put into it, and even his bad grammar is sublime.

'I am very ignorant – you will quite wonder at my ignorance,' said Dorothea. 'I have so many thoughts that may be quite mistaken; and now I shall be able to tell them all to you, and ask you about them. But,' she added, with rapid imagination of Mr Casaubon's probable feeling, 'I will not trouble you too much; only when you are inclined to listen to me. You must often be weary with the pursuit of subjects in your own track. I shall gain enough if you will take me with you there.'

'How should I be able now to persevere in any path without your companionship?' said Mr Casaubon, kissing her candid brow, and feeling that heaven had vouchsafed him a blessing in every way suited to his peculiar wants. He was being unconsciously wrought upon by the charms of a nature which was entirely without hidden calculations either for immediate effects or for remoter ends. It was this which made Dorothea so childlike, and according to some judges, so stupid, with all her reputed cleverness; as, for example, in the present case of throwing herself, meta-phorically speaking, at Mr Casaubon's feet, and kissing his unfashionable shoe-ties as if he were a Protestant Pope. She was not in the least teaching Mr Casaubon to ask if he were good enough for her, but merely asking herself anxiously how she could be good enough for Mr Casaubon. Before he left the next day it had been decided that the marriage should take place within six weeks. Why not? Mr Casaubon's house was ready. It was not a parsonage, but a considerable mansion, with much land attached to it. The parsonage was inhabited by the curate, who did all the duty except preaching the morning sermon.

⊲ SIX ⊳

My lady's tongue is like the meadow blades,
That cut you stroking them with idle hand.
Nice cutting is her function: she divides
With spiritual edge the millet-seed,
And makes intangible savings.

As mr Casaubon's carriage was passing out of the gateway, it arrested the entrance of a pony phaeton driven by a lady with a servant seated behind. It was doubtful whether the recognition had been mutual, for Mr Casaubon was looking absently before him; but the lady was quick-eyed, and threw a nod and a 'how do you do?' in the nick of time. In spite of her shabby bonnet and very old Indian shawl, it was plain that the lodge-keeper regarded her as an important personage, from the low curtsey which was dropped on the entrance of the small phaeton.

'Well, Mrs Fitchett, how are your fowls laying now?' said the high-coloured, dark-eyed lady, with the clearest chiselled utterance.

'Pretty well for laying, madam, but they've ta'en to eating their eggs: I've no peace o' mind with 'em at all.'

'O the cannibals! Better sell them cheap at once. What will you sell them a couple? One can't eat fowls of a bad character at a high price.'

'Well, madam, half-a-crown: I couldn't let 'em go, not under.'

'Half-a-crown, these times! Come now – for the Rector's chicken-broth on a Sunday. He has consumed all ours that I can spare. You are half paid with the sermon, Mrs Fitchett, remember that. Take a pair of tumbler-pigeons for them – little beauties. You must come and see them. You have no tumblers among your pigeons.'

'Well, madam, Master Fitchett shall go and see 'em after work. He's very hot on new sorts; to oblige *you*.'

'Oblige me! It will be the best bargain he ever made. A pair of church pigeons for a couple of wicked Spanish fowls that eat their own eggs! Don't you and Fitchett boast too much, that is all!'

The phaeton was driven onwards with the last words, leaving Mrs

Fitchett laughing and shaking her head slowly, with an interjectional 'Surely, surely!' – from which it might be inferred that she would have found the country-side somewhat duller if the Rector's lady had been less free-spoken and less of a skinflint. Indeed, both the farmers and labourers in the parishes of Freshitt and Tipton would have felt a sad lack of conversation but for the stories about what Mrs Cadwallader said and did: a lady of immeasurably high birth, descended, as it were, from unknown earls, dim as the crowd of heroic shades – who pleaded poverty, pared down prices, and cut jokes in the most companionable manner, though with a turn of tongue that let you know who she was. Such a lady gave a neighbourliness to both rank and religion, and mitigated the bitterness of uncommuted tithe. A much more exemplary character with an infusion of sour dignity would not have furthered their comprehension of the Thirty-nine Articles, and would have been less socially uniting.

Mr Brooke, seeing Mrs Cadwallader's merits from a different point of view, winced a little when her name was announced in the library, where he was sitting alone.

'I see you have had our Lowick Cicero here,' she said, seating herself comfortably, throwing back her wraps, and showing a thin but well-built figure. 'I suspect you and he are brewing some bad politics, else you would not be seeing so much of the lively man. I shall inform against you: remember you are both suspicious characters since you took Peel's side about the Catholic Bill. I shall tell everybody that you are going to put up for Middlemarch on the Whig side when old Pinkerton resigns, and that Casaubon is going to help you in an underhand manner: going to bribe the voters with pamphlets, and throw open the public-houses to distribute them. Come, confess!'

'Nothing of the sort,' said Mr Brooke, smiling and rubbing his eyeglasses, but really blushing a little at the impeachment. 'Casaubon and I don't talk politics much. He doesn't care much about the philanthropic side of things; punishments, and that kind of thing. He only cares about Church questions. That is not my line of action, you know.'

'Ra-a-ther too much, my friend. I have heard of your doings. Who was it that sold his bit of land to the Papists at Middlemarch? I believe you bought it on purpose. You are a perfect Guy Faux. See if you are not burnt in effigy this 5th of November coming. Humphrey would not come to quarrel with you about it, so I am come.'

'Very good. I was prepared to be persecuted for not persecuting – not persecuting, you know.'

'There you go! That is a piece of clap-trap you have got ready for the hustings. Now, *do not* let them lure you to the hustings, my dear Mr Brooke. A man always makes a fool of himself, speechifying: there's no excuse but being on the right side, so that you can ask a blessing on your humming and hawing. You will lose yourself, I forewarn you. You will make a Saturday pie of all parties' opinions, and be pelted by everybody.'

'That is what I expect, you know,' said Mr Brooke, not wishing to betray how little he enjoyed this prophetic sketch – 'what I expect as an independent man. As to the Whigs, a man who goes with the thinkers is not likely to be hooked on by any party. He may go with them up to a certain point – up to a certain point, you know. But that is what you ladies never understand.'

'Where your certain point is? No. I should like to be told how a man can have any certain point when he belongs to no party – leading a roving life, and never letting his friends know his address. "Nobody knows where Brooke will be – there's no counting on Brooke" – that is what people say of you, to be quite frank. Now, do turn respectable. How will you like going to Sessions with everybody looking shy on you, and you with a bad conscience and an empty pocket?'

'I don't pretend to argue with a lady on politics,' said Mr Brooke, with an air of smiling indifference, but feeling rather unpleasantly conscious that this attack of Mrs Cadwallader's had opened the defensive campaign to which certain rash steps had exposed him. 'Your sex are not thinkers, you know – *varium et mutabile semper* – that kind of thing. You don't know Virgil. I knew' – Mr Brooke reflected in time that he had not had the personal acquaintance of the Augustan poet – 'I was going to say, poor Stoddart, you know. That was what *he* said. You ladies are always against an independent attitude – a man's caring for nothing but truth, and that sort of thing. And there is no part of the county where opinion is narrower than it is here – I don't mean to throw stones, you know, but somebody is wanted to take the independent line; and if I don't take it, who will?'

'Who? Why, any upstart who has got neither blood nor position. People of standing should consume their independent nonsense at home, not hawk it about. And you! who are going to marry your niece, as good as your daughter, to one of our best men. Sir James would be cruelly annoyed: it will be too hard on him if you turn round now and make yourself a Whig signboard.'

Mr Brooke again winced inwardly, for Dorothea's engagement had no sooner been decided, than he had thought of Mrs Cadwallader's prospective taunts. It might have been easy for ignorant observers to say, 'Quarrel with Mrs Cadwallader'; but where is a country gentleman to go who quarrels with his oldest neighbours? Who could taste the fine flavour in the name of Brooke if it were delivered casually, like wine without a seal? Certainly a man can only be cosmopolitan up to a certain point.

'I hope Chettam and I shall always be good friends; but I am sorry to say there is no prospect of his marrying my niece,' said Mr Brooke, much relieved to see through the window that Celia was coming in.

'Why not?' said Mrs Cadwallader, with a sharp note of surprise. 'It is hardly a fortnight since you and I were talking about it.'

'My niece has chosen another suitor – has chosen him, you know. I have had nothing to do with it. I should have preferred Chettam; and I should have said Chettam was the man any girl would have chosen. But there is no accounting for these things. Your sex is capricious, you know.'

'Why, whom do you mean to say that you are going to let her marry?' Mrs Cadwallader's mind was rapidly surveying the possibilities of choice for Dorothea.

But here Celia entered, blooming from a walk in the garden, and the greeting with her delivered Mr Brooke from the necessity of answering immediately. He got up hastily, and saying, 'By the way, I must speak to Wright about the horses,' shuffled quickly out of the room.

'My dear child, what is this? – this about your sister's engagement?' said Mrs Cadwallader.

'She is engaged to marry Mr Casaubon,' said Celia, resorting, as usual, to the simplest statement of fact, and enjoying this opportunity of speaking to the Rector's wife alone.

'This is frightful. How long has it been going on?'

'I only knew of it yesterday. They are to be married in six weeks.'

'Well, my dear, I wish you joy of your brother-in-law.'

'I am so sorry for Dorothea.'

'Sorry! It is her doing, I suppose.'

'Yes: she says Mr Casaubon has a great soul.'

'With all my heart.'

'O Mrs Cadwallader, I don't think it can be nice to marry a man with a great soul.'

'Well, my dear, take warning. You know the look of one now; when the next comes and wants to marry you, don't you accept him.'

'I'm sure I never should.'

'No; one such in a family is enough. So your sister never cared about Sir James Chettam? What would you have said to *him* for a brother-in-law?'

'I should have liked that very much. I am sure he would have been a good husband. Only,' Celia added, with a slight blush (she sometimes seemed to blush as she breathed), 'I don't think he would have suited Dorothea.'

'Not high-flown enough?'

'Dodo is very strict. She thinks so much about everything, and is so particular about what one says. Sir James never seemed to please her.'

'She must have encouraged him, I am sure. That is not very creditable.'

'Please don't be angry with Dodo; she does not see things. She thought so much about the cottages, and she *was* rude to Sir James sometimes; but he is so kind, he never noticed it.'

'Well,' said Mrs Cadwallader, putting on her shawl, and rising, as if in haste, 'I must go straight to Sir James and break this to him. He will have brought his mother back by this time, and I must call. Your uncle will never tell him. We are all disappointed, my dear. Young people should think of their families in marrying. I set a bad example – married a poor clergyman, and made myself a pitiable object among the De Bracys –

obliged to get my coals by stratagem, and pray to heaven for my salad oil. However, Casaubon has money enough; I must do him that justice. As to his blood, I suppose the family quarterings are three cuttle-fish sable, and a commentator rampant. By the by, before I go, my dear, I must speak to your Mrs Carter about pastry. I want to send my young cook to learn of her. Poor people with four children, like us, you know, can't afford to keep a good cook. I have no doubt Mrs Carter will oblige me. Sir James's cook is a perfect dragon.'

In less than an hour, Mrs Cadwallader had circumvented Mrs Carter and driven to Freshitt Hall, which was not far from her own parsonage, her husband being resident in Freshitt and keeping a curate in Tipton.

Sir James Chettam had returned from the short journey which had kept him absent for a couple of days, and had changed his dress, intending to ride over to Tipton Grange. His horse was standing at the door when Mrs Cadwallader drove up, and he immediately appeared there himself, whip in hand. Lady Chettam had not yet returned, but Mrs Cadwallader's errand could not be despatched in the presence of grooms, so she asked to be taken into the conservatory close by, to look at the new plants; and on coming to a contemplative stand, she said –

'I have a great shock for you; I hope you are not so far gone in love as you pretended to be.'

It was of no use protesting against Mrs Cadwallader's way of putting things. But Sir James's countenance changed a little. He felt a vague alarm.

'I do believe Brooke is going to expose himself after all. I accused him of meaning to stand for Middlemarch on the Liberal side, and he looked silly and never denied it – talked about the independent line, and the usual nonsense.'

'Is that all?' said Sir James, much relieved.

'Why,' rejoined Mrs Cadwallader, with a sharper note, 'you don't mean to say that you would like him to turn public man in that way – making a sort of political Cheap Jack of himself?'

'He might be dissuaded, I should think. He would not like the expense.'

'That is what I told him. He is vulnerable to reason there – always a few grains of common-sense in an ounce of miserliness. Miserliness is a capital quality to run in families; it's the safe side for madness to dip on. And there must be a little crack in the Brooke family, else we should not see what we are to see.'

'What? Brooke standing for Middlemarch?'

'Worse than that. I really feel a little responsible. I always told you Miss Brooke would be such a fine match. I knew there was a great deal of nonsense in her – a flighty sort of Methodistical stuff. But these things wear out of girls. However, I am taken by surprise for once.'

'What do you mean, Mrs Cadwallader?' said Sir James. His fear lest Miss Brooke should have run away to join the Moravian Brethren, or some preposterous sect unknown to good society, was a little allayed by the knowledge that Mrs Cadwallader always made the worst of things. 'What has happened to Miss Brooke? Pray speak out.'

'Very well. She is engaged to be married.' Mrs Cadwallader paused a few moments. observing the deeply-hurt expression in her friend's face, which he was trying to conceal by a nervous smile, while he whipped his boot; but she soon added, 'Engaged to Casaubon.'

Sir James let his whip fall and stooped to pick it up. Perhaps his face had never before gathered so much concentrated disgust as when he turned to Mrs Cadawaller and repeated, 'Casaubon?'

'Even so. You know my errand now.'

'Good God! It is horrible! He is no better than a mummy!' (The point of view has to be allowed for, as that of a blooming and disappointed rival.)

'She says, he is a great soul. – A great bladder for dried peas to rattle in!' said Mrs Cadwallader.

'What business has an old bachelor like that to marry?' said Sir James. 'He has one foot in the grave.'

'He means to draw it out again, I suppose.'

'Brooke ought not to allow it: he should insist on its being put off till she is of age. She would think better of it then. What is a guardian for?'

'As if you could ever squeeze a resolution out of Brooke!'

'Cadwallader might talk to him.'

'Not he! Humphrey finds everybody charming. I never can get him to abuse Casaubon. He will even speak well of the bishop, though I tell him it is unnatural in a beneficed clergyman: what can one do with a husband who attends so little to the decencies? I hide it as well as I can by abusing everybody myself. Come, come, cheer up! you are well rid of Miss Brooke, a girl who would have been requiring you to see the stars by daylight. Between ourselves, little Celia is worth two of her, and likely after all to be the better match. For this marriage to Casaubon is as good as going to a nunnery.'

'Oh, on my own account – it is for Miss Brooke's sake I think her friends should try to use their influence.'

'Well, Humphrey doesn't know yet. But when I tell him, you may depend on it he will say, "Why not? Casaubon is a good fellow – and young – young enough." These charitable people never know vinegar from wine till they have swallowed it and got the colic. However, if I were a man I should prefer Celia, especially when Dorothea was gone. The truth is, you have been courting one and have won the other. I can see that she admires you almost as much as a man expects to be admired. If it were any one but me who said so, you might think it exaggeration. Good-bye!'

Sir James handed Mrs Cadwallader to the phaeton, and then jumped on his horse. He was not going to renounce his ride because of his friend's unpleasant news – only to ride the faster in some other direction than that of Tipton Grange.

Now, why on earth should Mrs Cadwallader have been at all busy about Miss Brooke's marriage; and why, when one match that she liked to think she had a hand in was frustrated, should she have straightway contrived the preliminaries of another? Was there any ingenious plot, any hide-and-seek course of action, which might be detected by a careful telescopic watch? Not at all: a telescope might have swept the parishes of Tipton and Freshitt, the whole area visited by Mrs Cadwallader in her phaeton, without witnessing any interview that could excite suspicion, or any scene from which she did not return with the same unperturbed keenness of eye and the same high natural colour. In fact, if that convenient vehicle had existed in the days of the Seven Sages, one of them would doubtless have remarked, that you can know little of women by following them about in their pony phaetons. Even with a microscope directed on a water-drop we find ourselves making interpretations which turn out to be rather coarse; for whereas under a weak lens you may seem to see a creature exhibiting an active voracity into which other smaller creatures actively play as if they were so many animated tax-pennies, a stronger lens reveals to you certain tiniest hairlets which make vortices for these victims while the swallower waits passively at his receipt of custom. In this way, metaphorically speaking, a strong lens applied to Mrs Cadwallader's matchmaking will show a play of minute causes producing what may be called thought and speech vortices to bring her the sort of food she needed.

Her life was rurally simple, quite free from secrets either foul, dangerous, or otherwise important, and not consciously affected by the great affairs of the world. All the more did the affairs of the great world interest her, when communicated in the letters of high-born relations: the way in which fascinating younger sons had gone to the dogs by marrying their mistresses; the fine old-blooded idiocy of young Lord Tapir, and the furious gouty humours of old Lord Megatherium; the exact crossing of genealogies which had brought a coronet into a new branch and widened the relations of scandal, – these were topics of which she retained details with the utmost accuracy, and reproduced them in an excellent pickle of epigrams, which she herself enjoyed the more because she believed as unquestioningly in birth and no-birth as she did in game and vermin. She would never have disowned any one on the ground of poverty: a De Bracy reduced to take his dinner in a basin would have seemed to her an example of pathos worth exaggerating, and I fear his aristocratic vices would not have horrified her. But her feeling towards the vulgar rich was a sort of religious hatred: they had probably made all their money out of high retail prices, and Mrs Cadwallader detested high prices for everything that was not paid in kind at the Rectory: such people were no part of God's design in making the world; and their accent was an affliction to the ears. A town where such monsters abounded was hardly more than a sort of low comedy, which could not be taken account of in a well-bred scheme of the universe. Let any lady who is inclined to be hard on Mrs

Cadwallader inquire into the comprehensiveness of her own beautiful views, and be quite sure that they afford accommodation for all the lives which have the honour to coexist with hers.

With such a mind, active as phosphorus, biting everything that came near into the form that suited it, how could Mrs Cadwallader feel that the Miss Brookes and their matrimonial prospects were alien to her? especially as it had been the habit of years for her to scold Mr Brooke with the friendliest frankness, and let him know in confidence that she thought him a poor creature. From the first arrival of the young ladies in Tipton she had prearranged Dorothea's marriage with Sir James, and if it had taken place would have been quite sure that it was her doing: that it should not take place after she had preconceived it, caused her an irritation which every thinker will sympathize with. She was the diplomatist of Tipton and Freshitt, and for anything to happen in spite of her was an offensive irregularity. As to freaks like this of Miss Brooke's, Mrs Cadwallader had no patience with them, and now saw that her opinion of this girl had been infected with some of her husband's weak charitableness: those Methodistical whims, that air of being more religious than the rector and curate together, came from a deeper and more constitutional disease than she had been willing to believe.

'However,' said Mrs Cadwallader, first to herself and afterwards to her husband, 'I throw her over: there was a chance, if she had married Sir James, of her becoming a sane, sensible woman. He would never have contradicted her, and when a woman is not contradicted, she has no motive for obstinacy in her absurdities. But now I wish her joy of her hair shirt.'

It followed that Mrs Cadwallader must decide on another match for Sir James, and having made up her mind that it was to be the younger Miss Brooke, there could not have been a more skilful move toward the success of her plan than her hint to the baronet that he had made an impression on Celia's heart. For he was not one of those gentlemen who languish after the unattainable Sappho's apple that laughs from the topmost bough – the charms which

> Smile like the knot of cowslips on the cliff,
> Not to be come at by the willing hand.

He had no sonnets to write, and it could not strike him agreeably that he was not an object of preference to the woman whom he had preferred. Already the knowledge that Dorothea had chosen Mr Casaubon had bruised his attachment and relaxed its hold. Although Sir James was a sportsman, he had some other feelings towards women than towards grouse and foxes, and did not regard his future wife in the light of prey, valuable chiefly for the excitements of the chase. Neither was he so well acquainted with the habits of primitive races as to feel that an ideal combat for her, tomahawk in hand, so to speak, was necessary to the historical continuity of the marriage-tie. On the contrary, having the amiable vanity which knits us to those who are fond of us, and disinclines us to those who are indifferent, and also a good grateful nature, the mere idea that a woman had a kindness towards him spun little threads of tenderness from out his heart towards hers.

Thus it happened, that after Sir James had ridden rather fast for half an hour in a direction away from Tipton Grange, he slackened his pace, and at last turned into a road which would lead him back by a shorter cut. Various feelings wrought in him the determination after all to go to the Grange to-day as if nothing new had happened. He could not help rejoicing that he had never made the offer and been rejected; mere friendly politeness required that he should call to see Dorothea about the cottages, and now happily Mrs Cadwallader had prepared him to offer his congratulations, if necessary, without showing too much awkwardness. He really did not like it: giving up Dorothea was very painful to him; but there was something in the resolve to make this visit forthwith and conquer all show of feeling, which was a sort of file-biting and counterirritant. And without his distinctly recognizing the impulse, there certainly was present in him the sense that Celia would be there, and that he should pay her more attention than he had done before.

We mortals, men and women, devour many a disappointment between breakfast and dinner-time; keep back the tears and look a little pale about the lips, and in answer to inquiries say, 'Oh, nothing!' Pride helps us; and pride is not a bad thing when it only urges us to hide our own hurts – not to hurt others.

ᴄᴏ SEVEN ᵥ

Piacer e popone
Vuol la sua stagione.
– Italian Proverb

MR CASAUBON, AS MIGHT BE EXPECTED, spent a great deal of his time at the Grange in these weeks, and the hindrance which courtship occasioned to the progress of his great work – the Key to all Mythologies – naturally made him look forward the more eagerly to the happy termination of courtship. But he had deliberately incurred the hindrance, having made up his mind that it was now time for him to adorn his life with the graces of female companionship, to irradiate the gloom which fatigue was apt to hang over the intervals of studious labour with the play of female fancy, and to secure in this, his culminating age, the solace of female tendance for his declining years. Hence he determined to abandon himself to the stream of feeling, and perhaps was surprised to find what an exceedingly shallow rill it was. As in droughty regions baptism by immersion could only be performed symbolically, so Mr Casaubon found that sprinkling was the utmost approach to a plunge which his stream would afford him; and he concluded that the poets had much exaggerated the force of masculine passion. Nevertheless, he observed with pleasure that Miss Brooke showed an ardent submissive affection which promised to fulfil his most agreeable previsions of marriage. It had once or twice crossed his mind that possibly there was some deficiency in Dorothea to account for the moderation of his abandonment; but he was unable to discern the deficiency, or to figure to himself a woman who would have pleased him better; so that there was clearly no reason to fall back upon but the exaggerations of human tradition.

'Could I not be preparing myself now to be more useful?' said Dorothea to him, one morning, early in the time of courtship; 'could I not learn to read Latin and Greek aloud to you, as Milton's daughters did to their father, without understanding what they read?'

'I fear that would be wearisome to you,' said Mr Casaubon, smiling; 'and, indeed, if I remember rightly, the young women you have mentioned regarded that exercise in unknown tongues as a ground for rebellion against the poet.'

'Yes; but in the first place they were very naughty girls, else they would have been proud to minister to such a father; and in the second place they might have studied privately and taught themselves to understand what they read, and then it would have been interesting. I hope you don't expect me to be naughty and stupid?'

'I expect you to be all that an exquisite young lady can be in every possible relation of life. Certainly it might be a great advantage if you were able to copy the Greek character, and to that end it were well to begin with a little reading.'

Dorothea seized this as a precious permission. She would not have asked Mr Casaubon at once to teach her the languages, dreading of all things to be tiresome instead of helpful; but it was not entirely out of devotion to her future husband that she wished to know Latin and Greek. Those provinces of masculine knowledge seemed to her a standing-ground from which all truth could be seen more truly. As it was, she constantly doubted her own conclusions, because she felt her own ignorance: how could she be confident that one-roomed cottages were not for the glory of God, when men who knew the classics appeared to conciliate indifference to the cottages with zeal for the glory? Perhaps even Hebrew might be necessary – at least the alphabet and a few roots – in order to arrive at the core of things, and judge soundly on the social duties of the

Christian. And she had not reached that point of renunciation at which she would have been satisfied with having a wise husband; she wished, poor child, to be wise herself. Miss Brooke was certainly very naïve with all her alleged cleverness. Celia, whose mind had never been thought too powerful, saw the emptiness of other people's pretensions much more readily. To have in general but little feeling, seems to be the only security against feeling too much on any particular occasion.

However, Mr Casaubon consented to listen and teach for an hour together, like a schoolmaster of little boys, or rather like a lover, to whom a mistress's elementary ignorance and difficulties have a touching fitness. Few scholars would have disliked teaching the alphabet under such circumstances. But Dorothea herself was a little shocked and discouraged at her own stupidity, and the answers she got to some timid questions about the value of the Greek accents gave her a painful suspicion that here indeed there might be secrets not capable of explanation to a woman's reason.

Mr Brooke had no doubt on that point, and expressed himself with his usual strength upon it one day that he came into the library while the reading was going forward.

'Well, but now, Casaubon, such deep studies, classics, mathematics, that kind of thing, are too taxing for a woman – too taxing, you know.'

'Dorothea is learning to read the characters simply,' said Mr Casaubon, evading the question. 'She had the very considerate thought of saving my eyes.'

'Ah, well, without understanding, you know – that may not be so bad. But there is a lightness about the feminine mind – a touch and go – music, the fine arts, that kind of thing – they should study those up to a certain point, women should; but in a light way, you know. A woman should be able to sit down and play you or sing you a good old English tune. That is what I like; though I have heard most things – been at the opera in Vienna: Gluck, Mozart, everything of that sort. But I'm a conservative in music – it's not like ideas, you know. I stick to the good old tunes.'

'Mr Casaubon is not fond of the piano, and I am very glad he is not,' said Dorothea, whose slight regard for domestic music and feminine fine art must be forgiven her, considering the small tinkling and smearing in which they chiefly consisted at that dark period. She smiled and looked up at her betrothed with grateful eyes. If he had always been asking her to play the 'Last Rose of Summer,' she would have required much resignation. 'He says there is only an old harpsichord at Lowick, and it is covered with books.'

'Ah, there you are behind Celia, my dear. Celia, now, plays very prettily, and is always ready to play. However, since Casaubon does not like it, you are all right. But it's a pity you should not have little recreations of that sort, Casaubon: the bow always strung – that kind of thing, you know – will not do.'

'I never could look on it in the light of a recreation to have my ears teased with measured noises,' said Mr Casaubon. 'A tune much iterated has the ridiculous effect of making the words in my mind perform a sort of minuet to keep time – an effect hardly tolerable, I imagine, after boyhood. As to the grander forms of music, worthy to accompany solemn celebrations, and even to serve as an educating influence according to the ancient conception, I say nothing, for with these we are not immediately concerned.'

'No; but music of that sort I should enjoy,' said Dorothea. 'When we were coming home from Lausanne my uncle took us to hear the great organ at Freiberg, and it made me sob.'

'That kind of thing is not healthy, my dear,' said Mr Brooke. 'Casaubon, she will be in your hands now: you must teach my niece to take things more quietly, eh, Dorothea?'

He ended with a smile, not wishing to hurt his niece, but really thinking that it was perhaps better for her to be early married to so sober a fellow as Casaubon, since she would not hear of Chettam.

'It is wonderful, though,' he said to himself as he shuffled out of the room – 'it is wonderful that she should have liked him. However, the match is good. I should have been travelling out of my brief to have hindered it, let Mrs Cadwallader say what she will. He is pretty certain to be a bishop, is Casaubon. That was a very seasonable pamphlet of his on the Catholic Question: – a deanery at least. They owe him a deanery.'

And here I must vindicate a claim to philosophical reflectiveness, by remarking that Mr Brooke on this occasion little thought of the Radical speech which, at a later period, he was led to make on the incomes of the bishops. What elegant historian would neglect a striking opportunity for pointing out that his heroes did not foresee the history of the world, or even their own actions? – For example, that Henry of Navarre, when a Protestant baby, little thought of being a Catholic monarch; or that Alfred the Great, when he measured his laborious nights with burning candles, had no idea of future gentlemen measuring their idle days with watches. Here is a mine of truth, which, however vigorously it may be worked, is likely to outlast our coal.

But of Mr Brooke I make a further remark perhaps less warranted by precedent – namely, that if he had foreknown his speech, it might not have made any great difference. To think with pleasure of his niece's husband having a large ecclesiastical income was one thing – to make a Liberal speech was another thing; and it is a narrow mind which cannot look at a subject from various points of view.

∝ EIGHT ∾

Oh, rescue her! I am her brother now,
And you her father. Every gentle maid
Should have a guardian in each gentleman.

IT WAS WONDERFUL TO SIR JAMES Chettam how well he continued to like
going to the Grange after he had once encountered the difficulty of seeing
Dorothea for the first time in the light of a woman who was engaged to
another man. Of course the forked lightning seemed to pass through him
when he first approached her, and he remained conscious throughout the
interview of hiding uneasiness; but, good as he was, it must be owned
that his uneasiness was less than it would have been if he had thought his
rival a brilliant and desirable match. He had no sense of being eclipsed by
Mr Casaubon; he was only shocked that Dorothea was under a melancholy illusion, and his mortification lost some of its bitterness by being
mingled with compassion.

Nevertheless, while Sir James said to himself that he had completely
resigned her, since with the perversity of a Desdemona she had not
affected a proposed match that was clearly suitable and according to
nature; he could not yet be quite passive under the idea of her engagement
to Mr Casaubon. On the day when he first saw them together in the light
of his present knowledge, it seemed to him that he had not taken the affair
seriously enough. Brooke was really culpable; he ought to have hindered
it. Who could speak to him? Something might be done perhaps even now,
at least to defer the marriage. On his way home he turned into the Rectory
and asked for Mr Cadwallader. Happily, the Rector was at home, and his
visitor was shown into the study, where all the fishing-tackle hung. But he
himself was in a little room adjoining, at work with his turning apparatus,
and he called to the baronet to join him there. The two were better friends
than any other land-holder and clergyman in the county – a significant
fact which was in agreement with the amiable expression of their faces.

Mr Cadwallader was a large man, with full lips and a sweet smile; very
plain and rough in his exterior, but with that solid imperturbable ease
and good-humour which is infectious, and like great grassy hills in the
sunshine, quiets even an irritated egoism, and makes it rather ashamed
of itself. 'Well, how are you?' he said, showing a hand not quite fit
to be grasped. 'Sorry I missed you before. Is there anything particular?
You look vexed.'

51

Sir James's brow had a little crease in it, a little depression of the eyebrow, which he seemed purposely to exaggerate as he answered.

'It is only this conduct of Brooke's. I really think somebody should speak to him.'

'What? meaning to stand?' said Mr Cadwallader, going on with the arrangement of the reels which he had just been turning. 'I hardly think he means it. But where's the harm, if he likes it? Any one who objects to Whiggery should be glad when the Whigs don't put up the strongest fellow. They won't overturn the Constitution with our friend Brooke's head for a battering ram.'

'Oh, I don't mean that,' said Sir James, who, after putting down his hat and throwing himself into a chair, had begun to nurse his leg and examine the sole of his boot with much bitterness. 'I mean this marriage. I mean his letting that blooming young girl marry Casaubon.'

'What is the matter with Casaubon? I see no harm in him – if the girl likes him.'

'She is too young to know what she likes. Her guardian ought to interfere. He ought not to allow the thing to be done in this headlong manner. I wonder a man like you, Cadwallader – a man with daughters, can look at the affair with indifference: and with such a heart as yours! Do think seriously about it.'

'I am not joking; I am as serious as possible,' said the Rector, with a provoking little inward laugh. 'You are as bad as Elinor. She has been wanting me to go and lecture Brooke; and I have reminded her that her friends had a very poor opinion of the match she made when she married me.'

'But look at Casaubon,' said Sir James, indignantly. 'He must be fifty, and I don't believe he could ever have been much more than the shadow of a man. Look at his legs!'

'Confound you handsome young fellows! you think of having it all your own way in the world. You don't understand women. They don't admire you half so much as you admire yourselves. Elinor used to tell her sisters that she married me for my ugliness – it was so various and amusing that it had quite conquered her prudence.'

'You! it was easy enough for a woman to love you. But this is no question of beauty. I don't *like* Casaubon.' This was Sir James's strongest way of implying that he thought ill of a man's character.

'Why? what do you know against him?' said the Rector, laying down his reels, and putting his thumbs into his arm-holes with an air of attention.

Sir James paused. He did not usually find it easy to give his reasons: it seemed to him strange that people should not know them without being told, since he only felt what was reasonable. At last he said –

'Now, Cadwallader, has he got any heart?'

'Well, yes. I don't mean of the melting sort, but a sound kernel, *that* you may be sure of. He is very good to his poor relations; pensions several of the women, and is educating a young fellow at a good deal of expense. Casaubon acts up to his sense of justice. His mother's sister made a bad match – a Pole, I think – lost herself – at any rate was disowned by her family. If it had not been for that, Casaubon would not have had so much money by half. I believe he went himself to find out his cousins, and see what he could do for them. Every man would not ring so well as that, if you tried his metal. *You* would, Chettam; but not every man.'

'I don't know,' said Sir James, colouring. 'I am not so sure of myself.' He paused a moment, and then added, 'That was a right thing for Casaubon to do. But a man may wish to do what is right, and yet be a sort of parchment code. A woman may not be happy with him. And I think when a girl is so young as Miss Brooke is, her friends ought to interfere a little to hinder her from doing anything foolish. You laugh, because you fancy I have some feeling on my own account. But upon my honour, it is not that. I should feel just the same if I were Miss Brooke's brother or uncle.'

'Well, but what should you do?'

'I should say that the marriage must not be decided on until she was of age. And depend upon it, in that case, it would never come off. I wish you saw it as I do – I wish you would talk to Brooke about it.'

Sir James rose as he was finishing his sentence. For he saw Mrs Cadwallader entering from the study. She held by the hand her youngest girl, about five years old, who immediately ran to papa, and was made comfortable on his knee.

'I hear what you are talking about,' said the wife. 'But you will make no impression on Humphrey. As long as the fish rise to his bait, everybody is what he ought to be. Bless you, Casaubon has got a trout stream, and does not care about fishing in it himself: could there be a better fellow?'

'Well, there is something in that,' said the Rector, with his quiet, inward laugh. 'It is a very good quality in a man to have a trout stream.'

'But seriously,' said Sir James, whose vexation had not yet spent itself, 'don't you think the Rector might do some good by speaking?'

'Oh, I told you beforehand what he would say,' answered Mrs Cadwallader, lifting up her eyebrows. 'I have done what I could: I wash my hands of the marriage.'

'In the first place,' said the Rector, looking rather grave, 'it would be nonsensical to expect that I could convince Brooke, and make him act accordingly. Brooke is a very good fellow, but pulpy; he will run into any mould, but he won't keep shape.'

'He might keep shape long enough to defer the marriage,' said Sir James.

'But, my dear Chettam, why should I use my influence to Casaubon's disadvantage, unless I were much surer than I am that I should be acting for the advantage of Miss Brooke? I know no harm of Casaubon. I don't care about his Xisuthrus and Fee-fo-fum and the rest; but then he doesn't care about my fishing-tackle. As to the line he took on the Catholic Question, that was unexpected; but he has always been civil to me, and I don't see why I should spoil his sport. For anything I can tell, Miss Brooke may be happier with him than she would be with any other man.'

'Humphrey! I have no patience with you. You know you would rather dine under the hedge than with Casaubon alone. You have nothing to say to each other.'

'What has that to do with Miss Brooke's marrying him? She does not do it for my amusement.'

'He has got no good red blood in his body,' said Sir James.

'No. Somebody put a drop under a magnifying-glass, and it was all semicolons and parentheses,' said Mrs Cadwallader.

'Why does he not bring out his book, instead of marrying?' said Sir James, with a disgust which he held warranted by the sound feeling of an English layman.

'Oh, he dreams footnotes, and they run away with all his brains. They say, when he was a little boy, he made an abstract of "Hop o' my Thumb," and he has been making abstracts ever since. Ugh! And that is the man Humphrey goes on saying that a woman may be happy with.'

'Well, he is what Miss Brooke likes,' said the Rector. 'I don't profess to understand every young lady's taste.'

'But if she were your own daughter?' said Sir James.

'That would be a different affair. She is *not* my daughter, and I don't feel called upon to interfere. Casaubon is as good as most of us. He is a scholarly clergyman, and creditable to the cloth. Some Radical fellow speechifying at Middlemarch said Casaubon was the learned straw-chopping incumbent, and Freke was the brick-and-mortar incumbent, and I was the angling incumbent. And upon my word, I don't see that one is worse or better than the other.' The Rector ended with his silent laugh. He always saw the joke of any satire against himself. His conscience was large and easy, like the rest of him: it did only what it could do without any trouble.

Clearly, there would be no interference with Miss Brooke's marriage through Mr Cadwallader; and Sir James felt with some sadness that she was to have perfect liberty of misjudgment. It was a sign of his good disposition that he did not slacken at all in his intention of carrying out Dorothea's design of the cottages. Doubtless this persistence was the best course for his own dignity: but pride only helps us to be generous; it never makes us so, any more than vanity makes us witty. She was now enough aware of Sir James's position with regard to her, to appreciate the rectitude of his perseverance in a landlord's duty, to which he had at first been urged by a lover's complaisance, and her pleasure in it was great enough to count for something even in her present happiness. Perhaps she gave to Sir James Chettam's cottages all the interest she could spare from Mr Casaubon, or rather from the symphony of hopeful dreams, admiring trust, and passionate self-devotion which that learned gentleman had set playing in her soul. Hence it happened that in the good baronet's succeeding visits, while he was beginning to pay small attentions to Celia, he found himself talking with more and more pleasure to Dorothea. She was perfectly unconstrained and without irritation towards him now, and he was gradually discovering the delight there is in frank kindness and companionship between a man and a woman who have no passion to hide or confess.

⊂ﬞ NINE ℔

1st Gent. An ancient land in ancient oracles
  Is called 'law-thirsty': all the struggle there
  Was after order and a perfect rule.
  Pray, where lie such lands now? . . .
2nd Gent. Why, where they lay of old – in human souls.

Mr CASAUBON'S BEHAVIOUR ABOUT SETTLEMENTS was highly satisfactory to Mr Brooke, and the preliminaries of marriage rolled smoothly along, shortening the weeks of courtship. The betrothed bride must see her future home, and dictate any changes that she would like to have made there. A woman dictates before marriage in order that she may have an appetite for submission afterwards. And certainly, the mistakes that we male and female mortals make when we have our own way might fairly raise some wonder that we are so fond of it.

On a grey but dry November morning Dorothea drove to Lowick in company with her uncle and Celia. Mr Casaubon's home was the manor-house. Close by, visible from some parts of the garden, was the little church, with the old parsonage opposite. In the beginning of his career, Mr Casaubon had only held the living, but the death of his brother had put him in possession of the manor also. It had a small park, with a fine old oak here and there, and an avenue of limes towards the south-west front, with a sunk fence between park and pleasure-ground, so that from the drawing-room windows the glance swept uninterruptedly along a slope of greensward till the limes ended in a level of corn and pastures, which often seemed to melt into a lake under the setting sun. This was the happy side of the house, for the south and east looked rather melancholy even under the brightest morning. The grounds here were more confined, the flower-beds showed no very careful tendance, and large clumps of trees, chiefly of sombre yews, had risen high, not ten yards from the windows. The building, of greenish stone, was in the old English style, not ugly, but small-windowed and melancholy-looking: the sort of house that must have children, many flowers, open windows, and little vistas of bright things, to make it seem a joyous home. In this latter end of autumn, with a sparse remnant of yellow leaves falling slowly athwart the dark evergreens in a stillness without sunshine, the house too had an air of autumnal decline, and Mr Casaubon, when he presented himself, had no bloom that could be thrown into relief by that background.

'Oh dear!' Celia said to herself, 'I am sure Freshitt Hall would have been pleasanter than this.' She thought of the white freestone, the pillared portico, and the terrace full of flowers, Sir James smiling above them like a prince issuing from his enchantment in a rose-bush, with a handkerchief swiftly metamorphosed from the most delicately-odorous petals – Sir James, who talked so agreeably, always about things which had common-sense in them, and not about learning! Celia had those light young feminine tastes which grave and weather-worn gentlemen sometimes prefer in a wife; but happily Mr Casaubon's bias had been different, for he would have had no chance with Celia.

Dorothea, on the contrary, found the house and grounds all that she could wish: the dark book-shelves in the long library, the carpets and curtains with colours subdued by time, the curious old maps and bird's-eye views on the walls of the corridor, with here and there an old vase below, had no oppression for her, and seemed more cheerful than the casts and pictures at the Grange, which her uncle had long ago brought home from his travels – they being probably among the ideas he had taken in at one time. To poor Dorothea these severe classical nudities and smirking Renaissance-Correggiosities were painfully inexplicable, staring into the midst of her Puritanic conceptions: she had never been taught how she could bring them into any sort of relevance with her life. But the owners of Lowick apparently had not been travellers, and Mr Casaubon's studies of the past were not carried on by means of such aids.

Dorothea walked about the house with delightful emotion. Everything seemed hallowed to her: this was to be the home of her wifehood, and she looked up with eyes full of confidence to Mr Casaubon when he drew her attention specially to some actual arrangement and asked her if she would like an alteration. All appeals to her taste she met gratefully but saw nothing to alter. His efforts at exact courtesy and formal tenderness had no defect for her. She filled up all blanks with unmanifested perfections, interpreting him as she interpreted the works of Providence, and account-ing for seeming discords by her own deafness to the higher harmonies. And there are many blanks left in the weeks of courtship, which a loving faith fills with happy assurance.

'Now, my dear Dorothea, I wish you to favour me by pointing out which room you would like to have as your boudoir,' said Mr Casaubon, showing that his views of the womanly nature were sufficiently large to include that requirement.

'It is very kind of you to think of that,' said Dorothea, 'but I assure you I would rather have all those matters decided for me. I shall be much happier to take everything as it is – just as you have been used to have it, or as you will yourself choose it to be. I have no motive for wishing anything else.'

'O Dodo,' said Celia, 'will you not have the bow-windowed room upstairs?'

Mr Casaubon led the way thither. The bow window looked down the avenue of limes; the furniture was all of a faded blue, and there were miniatures of ladies and gentlemen with powdered hair hanging in a group. A piece of tapestry over a door also showed a blue-green world with a pale stag in it. The chairs and tables were thin-legged and easy to upset. It was a room where one might fancy the ghost of a tight-laced lady revisiting the scene of her embroidery. A light book-case contained duodecimo volumes of polite literature in calf, completing the furniture.

'Yes,' said Mr Brooke, 'this would be a pretty room with some new hangings, sofas, and that sort of thing. A little bare now.'

'No, uncle,' said Dorothea, eagerly. 'Pray do not speak of altering anything. There are so many other things in the world that want altering – I like to take these things as they are. And you like them as they are, don't you?' she added, looking at Mr Casaubon. 'Perhaps this was your mother's room when she was young.'

'It was,' he said, with his slow bend of the head.

'This is your mother,' said Dorothea, who had turned to examine the group of miniatures. 'It is like the tiny one you brought me; only, I should think a better portrait. And this one opposite, who is this?'

'Her elder sister. They were, like you and your sister, the only two children of their parents, who hang above them, you see.'

'The sister is pretty,' said Celia, implying that she thought less favourably of Mr Casaubon's mother. It was a new opening to Celia's imagination, that he came of a family who had all been young in their time – the ladies wearing necklaces.

'It is a peculiar face,' said Dorothea, looking closely. 'Those deep grey eyes rather near together – and the delicate irregular nose with a sort of ripple in it – and all the powdered curls hanging backward. Altogether it seems to me peculiar rather than pretty. There is not even a family likeness between her and your mother.'

'No. And they were not alike in their lot.'

'You did not mention her to me,' said Dorothea.

'My aunt made an unfortunate marriage. I never saw her.'

Dorothea wondered a little, but felt that it would be indelicate just then to ask for any information which Mr Casaubon did not proffer, and she turned to the window to admire the view. The sun had lately pierced the grey, and the avenue of limes cast shadows.

'Shall we not walk in the garden now?' said Dorothea.

'And you would like to see the church, you know,' said Mr Brooke. 'It is a droll little church. And the village. It all lies in a nut-shell. By the way, it will suit you, Dorothea; for the cottages are like a row of alms-houses – little gardens, gillyflowers, that sort of thing.'

'Yes, please,' said Dorothea, looking at Mr Casaubon, 'I should like to see all that.' She had got nothing from him more graphic about the Lowick cottages than that they were 'not bad'.

They were soon on a gravel walk which led chiefly between grassy borders and clumps of trees, this being the nearest way to the church, Mr Casaubon said. At the little gate leading into the churchyard there was a pause while Mr Casaubon went to the parsonage close by to fetch a key. Celia, who had been hanging a little in the rear, came up presently, when she saw that Mr Casaubon was gone away, and said in her easy staccato, which always seemed to contradict the suspicion of any malicious intent –

'Do you know, Dorothea, I saw some one quite young coming up one of the walks.'

'Is that astonishing, Celia?'

'There may be a young gardener, you know – why not?' said Mr Brooke. 'I told Casaubon he should change his gardener.'

'No, not a gardener,' said Celia; 'a gentleman with a sketch-book. He had light-brown curls. I only saw his back. But he was quite young.'

'The curate's son, perhaps,' said Mr Brooke. 'Ah, there is Casaubon again, and Tucker with him. He is going to introduce Tucker. You don't know Tucker yet.'

Mr Tucker was the middle-aged curate, one of the 'inferior clergy', who are usually not wanting in sons. But after the introduction, the conversation did not lead to any question about his family, and the startling apparition of youthfulness was forgotten by every one but Celia. She inwardly declined to believe that the light-brown curls and slim figure could have any relationship to Mr Tucker, who was just as old and musty-looking as she would have expected Mr Casaubon's curate to be; doubtless an excellent man who would go to heaven (for Celia wished not to be unprincipled), but the corners of his mouth were so unpleasant. Celia thought with some dismalness of the time she should have to spend as bridesmaid at Lowick, where the curate had probably no pretty little children whom she could like, irrespective of principle.

Mr Tucker was invaluable in their walk; and perhaps Mr Casaubon had not been without foresight on this head, the curate being able to answer all Dorothea's questions about the villagers and the other parishioners. Everybody, he assured her, was well off in Lowick: not a cottager in those double cottages at a low rent but kept a pig, and the strips of garden at the back were well tended. The small boys wore excellent corduroy, the girls went out as tidy servants, or did a little straw-plaiting at home: no looms here, no Dissent; and though the public disposition was rather towards laying by money than towards spirituality, there was not much vice. The speckled fowls were so numerous that Mr Brooke observed, 'Your farmers leave some barley for the women to glean, I see. The poor folks here might have a fowl in their pot, as the good French king used to wish for all his people. The French eat a good many fowls – skinny fowls, you know.'

'I think it was a very cheap wish of his,' said Dorothea, indignantly. 'Are kings such monsters that a wish like that must be reckoned a royal virtue?'

'And if he wished them a skinny fowl,' said Celia, 'that would not be nice. But perhaps he wished them to have fat fowls.'

'Yes, but the word has dropped out of the text, or perhaps was *sub-auditum*; that is, present in the king's mind, but not uttered,' said Mr Casaubon, smiling and bending his head towards Celia, who immediately dropped backward a little, because she could not bear Mr Casaubon to blink at her.

Dorothea sank into silence on the way back to the house. She felt some disappointment, of which she was yet ashamed, that there was nothing for her to do in Lowick; and in the next few minutes her mind had glanced over the possibility, which she would have preferred, of finding that her home would be in a parish which had a larger share of the world's misery, so that she might have had more active duties in it. Then, recurring to the future actually before her, she made a picture of more complete devotion to Mr Casaubon's aims, in which she would await new duties. Many such might reveal themselves to the higher knowledge gained by her in that companionship.

Mr Tucker soon left them, having some clerical work which would not allow him to lunch at the Hall; and as they were re-entering the garden through the little gate, Mr Casaubon said –

'You seem a little sad, Dorothea. I trust you are pleased with what you have seen.'

'I am feeling something which is perhaps foolish and wrong,' answered Dorothea, with her usual openness – 'almost wishing that the people wanted more to be done for them here. I have known so few ways of making my life good for anything. Of course, my notions of usefulness must be narrow. I must learn new ways of helping people.'

'Doubtless,' said Mr Casaubon. 'Each position has its corresponding duties. Yours, I trust, as the mistress of Lowick, will not leave any yearning unfulfilled.'

'Indeed, I believe that,' said Dorothea, earnestly. 'Do not suppose that I am sad.'

'That is well. But, if you are not tired, we will take another way to the house than that by which we came.'

Dorothea was not at all tired, and a little circuit was made towards a fine yew-tree, the chief hereditary glory of the grounds on this side of the house. As they approached it, a figure, conspicuous on a dark background of evergreens, was seated on a bench, sketching the old tree. Mr Brooke, who was walking in front with Celia, turned his head, and said –

'Who is that youngster, Casaubon?'

They had come very near when Mr Casaubon answered –

'That is a young relative of mine, a second cousin: the grandson, in fact,' he added, looking at Dorothea, 'of the lady whose portrait you have been noticing, my aunt Julia.'

The younger man had laid down his sketch-book and risen. His bushy light-brown curls, as well as his youthfulness, identified him at once with Celia's apparition.

'Dorothea, let me introduce to you my cousin, Mr Ladislaw. Will, this is Miss Brooke.'

The cousin was so close now, that, when he lifted his hat, Dorothea could see a pair of grey eyes rather near together, a delicate irregular nose with a little ripple in it, and hair falling backward; but there was a mouth and chin of a more prominent, threatening aspect than belonged to the type of the grandmother's miniature. Young Ladislaw did not feel it necessary to smile, as if he were charmed with this introduction to his future second cousin and her relatives; but wore rather a pouting air of discontent.

'You are an artist, I see,' said Mr Brooke, taking up the sketch-book and turning it over in his unceremonious fashion.

'No, I only sketch a little. There is nothing fit to be seen there,' said young Ladislaw, colouring, perhaps with temper rather than modesty.

'Oh, come, this is a nice bit, now. I did a little in this way myself at one time, you know. Look here, now; this is what I call a nice thing, done with what we used to call *brio*.' Mr Brooke held out towards the two girls a large coloured sketch of stony ground and trees, with a pool.

'I am no judge of these things,' said Dorothea, not coldly, but with an eager deprecation of the appeal to her. 'You know, uncle, I never see the beauty of those pictures which you say are so much praised. They are a language I do not understand. I suppose there is some relation between pictures and nature which I am too ignorant to feel – just as you see what a Greek sentence stands for which means nothing to me.' Dorothea looked up at Mr Casaubon, who bowed his head towards her while Mr Brooke said, smiling nonchalantly –

'Bless me, now, how different people are! But you had a bad style of teaching, you know – else this is just the thing for girls – sketching, fine art and so on. But you took to drawing plans; you don't understand *morbidezza*, and that kind of thing. You will come to my house, I hope, and I will show you what I did in this way,' he continued, turning to young Ladislaw, who had to be recalled from his preoccupation in observing Dorothea. Ladislaw had made up his mind that she must be an unpleasant girl, since she was going to marry Casaubon, and what she said of her stupidity about pictures would have confirmed that opinion even if he had believed her. As it was, he took her words for a covert judgment, and was certain that she thought his sketch detestable. There was too much cleverness in her apology: she was laughing both at her uncle and himself. But what a voice! It was like the voice of a soul that had once lived in an Aeolian harp. This must be one of Nature's inconsistencies. There could be no sort of passion in a girl who would marry Casaubon. But he turned from her, and bowed his thanks for Mr Brooke's invitation.

'We will turn over my Italian engravings together,' continued that good-natured man. 'I have no end of those things, that I have laid by for years. One gets rusty in this part of the country, you know. Not you, Casaubon; you stick to your studies; but my best ideas get undermost – out of use, you know. You clever young men must guard against indolence. I was too indolent, you know: else I might have been anywhere at one time.'

'That is a seasonable admonition,' said Mr Casaubon; 'but now we will pass on to the house, lest the young ladies should be tired of standing.'

When their backs were turned, young Ladislaw sat down to go on with his sketching, and as he did so his face broke into an expression of amusement which increased as he went on drawing, till at last he threw back his head and laughed aloud. Partly it was the reception of his own artistic production that tickled him; partly the notion of his grave cousin as the lover of that girl; and partly Mr Brooke's definition of the place he might have held but for the impediment of indolence. Mr Will Ladislaw's sense of the ludicrous lit up his features very agreeably: it was the pure enjoyment of comicality, and had no mixture of sneering and self-exaltation.

'What is your nephew going to do with himself, Casaubon?' said Mr Brooke, as they went on.

'My cousin, you mean – not my nephew.'

'Yes, yes, cousin. But in the way of a career, you know.'

'The answer to that question is painfully doubtful. On leaving Rugby he declined to go to an English university, where I would gladly have placed him, and chose what I must consider the anomalous course of studying at Heidelberg. And now he wants to go abroad again, without any special object, save the vague purpose of what he calls culture, preparation for he knows not what. He declines to choose a profession.'

'He has no means but what you furnish, I suppose.'

'I have always given him and his friends reason to understand that I would furnish in moderation what was necessary for providing him with a scholarly education, and launching him respectably. I am therefore bound to fulfil the expectation so raised,' said Mr Casaubon, putting his conduct in the light of mere rectitude: a trait of delicacy which Dorothea noticed with admiration.

'He has a thirst for travelling; perhaps he may turn out a Bruce or a Mungo Park,' said Mr Brooke. 'I had a notion of that myself at one time.'

'No, he has no bent towards exploration, or the enlargement of our geognosis: that would be a special purpose which I could recognize with some approbation, though without felicitating him on a career which so often ends in premature and violent death. But so far is he from having any desire for a more accurate knowledge of the earth's surface, that he said he should prefer not to know the sources of the Nile, and that there should be some unknown regions preserved as hunting-grounds for the poetic imagination.'

'Well, there is something in that, you know,' said Mr Brooke, who had certainly an impartial mind.

'It is, I fear, nothing more than a part of his general inaccuracy and indisposition to thoroughness of all kinds, which would be a bad augury for him in any profession, civil or sacred, even were he so far submissive to ordinary rule as to choose one.'

'Perhaps he has conscientious scruples founded on his own unfitness,' said Dorothea, who was interesting herself in finding a favourable explanation. 'Because the law and medicine should be very serious professions to undertake, should they not? People's lives and fortunes depend on them.'

'Doubtless; but I fear that my young relative Will Ladislaw is chiefly determined in his aversion to these callings by a dislike to steady application, and to that kind of acquirement which is needful instrumentally, but is not charming or immediately inviting to self-indulgent taste. I have insisted to him on what Aristotle has stated with admirable brevity, that for the achievement of any work regarded as an end there must be a prior exercise of many energies or acquired facilities of a secondary order, demanding patience. I have pointed to my own manuscript volumes, which represent the toil of years preparatory to a work not yet accomplished. But in vain. To careful reasoning of this kind he replies by calling himself Pegasus, and every form of prescribed work "harness".'

Celia laughed. She was surprised to find that Mr Casaubon could say something quite amusing.

'Well, you know, he may turn out a Byron, a Chatterton, a Churchill – that sort of thing – there's no telling,' said Mr Brooke. 'Shall you let him go to Italy, or wherever else he wants to go?'

'Yes; I have agreed to furnish him with moderate supplies for a year or so; he asks no more. I shall let him be tried by the test of freedom.'

'That is very kind of you,' said Dorothea, looking up at Mr Casaubon with delight. 'It is noble. After all, people may really have in them some vocation which is not quite plain to themselves, may they not? They may seem idle and weak because they are growing. We should be very patient with each other, I think.'

'I suppose it is being engaged to be married that has made you think patience good,' said Celia, as soon as she and Dorothea were alone together, taking off their wrappings.

'You mean that I am very impatient, Celia.'

'Yes; when people don't do and say just what you like.' Celia had become less afraid of 'saying things' to Dorothea since this engagement; cleverness seemed to her more pitiable than ever.

◁ TEN ▷

He had catched a great cold, had he had no other clothes to wear than the skin of a bear not yet killed.

FULLER

YOUNG LADISLAW DID NOT PAY THAT visit to which Mr Brooke had invited him, and only six days afterwards Mr Casaubon mentioned that his young relative had started for the Continent, seeming by this cold vagueness to waive inquiry. Indeed, Will had declined to fix on any more precise destination than the entire area of Europe. Genius, he held, is necessarily intolerant of fetters: on the one hand it must have the utmost play for its spontaneity; on the other, it may confidently await those messages from the universe which summon it to its peculiar work, only placing itself in an attitude of receptivity towards all sublime chances. The attitudes of receptivity are various, and Will had sincerely tried many of them. He was not excessively fond of wine, but he had several times taken too much, simply as an experiment in that form of ecstasy; he had fasted till he was faint, and then supped on lobster; he had made himself ill with doses of opium. Nothing greatly original had resulted from these measures; and the effects of the opium had convinced him that there was an entire dissimilarity between his constitution and De Quincey's. The superadded circumstance which would evolve the genius had not yet come; the universe had not yet beckoned. Even Caesar's fortune at one time was but a grand presentiment. We know what a masquerade all development is, and what effective shapes may be disguised in helpless embryos. – In fact, the world is full of hopeful analogies and handsome dubious eggs called possibilities. Will saw clearly enough the pitiable instances of long incubation producing no chick, and but for gratitude would have laughed at Casaubon, whose plodding application, rows of note-books, and small taper of learned theory exploring the tossed ruins of the world, seemed to enforce a moral entirely encouraging to Will's generous reliance on the intentions of the universe with regard to himself. He held that reliance to be a mark of genius; and certainly it is no mark to the contrary; genius consisting neither in self-conceit nor in humility, but in a power to make or do, not anything in general, but something in particular. Let him start for the Continent, then, without our pronouncing on his future. Among all forms of mistake, prophecy is the most gratuitous.

But at present this caution against a too hasty judgment interests me more in relation to Mr Casaubon than to his young cousin. If to Dorothea Mr Casaubon had been the mere occasion which had set alight the fine inflammable material of her youthful illusions, does it follow that he was fairly represented in the minds of those less impassioned personages who have hitherto delivered their judgments concerning him? I protest against any absolute conclusion, any prejudice derived from Mrs Cadwallader's contempt for a neighbouring clergyman's alleged greatness of soul, of Sir James Chettam's poor opinion of his rival's legs, – from Mr Brooke's failure to elicit a companion's ideas, or from Celia's criticism of a middle-aged scholar's personal appearance. I am not sure that the greatest man of his age, if ever that solitary superlative existed, could escape these unfavourable reflections of himself in various small mirrors; and even Milton, looking for his portrait in a spoon, must submit to have the facial angle of a bumpkin. Moreover, if Mr Casaubon, speaking for himself, has rather chilling rhetoric, it is not therefore certain that there is no good work or fine feeling in him. Did not an immortal physicist and interpreter of hieroglyphs write detestable verses? Has the theory of the solar system been advanced by graceful manners and conversational tact? Suppose we turn from outside estimates of a man, to wonder, with keener interest, what is the report of his own consciousness about his doings or capacity: with what hindrances he is carrying on his daily labours; what fading of hopes, or what deeper fixity of self-delusion the years are marking off within him; and with what spirit he wrestles against universal pressure, which will one day be too heavy for him, and bring his heart to its final pause. Doubtless his lot is important in his own eyes; and the chief reason that we think he asks too large a place in our consideration must be our want of room for him, since we refer him to the Divine regard with perfect confidence; nay, it is even held sublime for our neighbour to expect the utmost there, however little he may have got from us. Mr Casaubon, too, was the centre of his own world; if he was liable to think that others were providentially made for him, and especially to consider them in the light of their fitness for the author of a Key to all Mythologies, this trait is not quite alien to us, and, like the other mendicant hopes of mortals, claims some of our pity.

Certainly this affair of his marriage with Miss Brooke touched him more nearly than it did any one of the persons who have hitherto shown their disapproval of it, and in the present stage of things I feel more tenderly towards his experience of success than towards the disappointment of the amiable Sir James. For in truth, as the day fixed for his marriage came nearer, Mr Casaubon did not find his spirits rising; nor did the contemplation of that matrimonial garden-scene, where, as all experience showed, the path was to be bordered with flowers, prove persistently more enchanting to him than the accustomed vaults where he walked taper in hand. He did not confess to himself, still less could he have breathed to another, his surprise that though he had won a lovely and noble-hearted girl he had not won delight, – which he had also regarded as an object to be found by search. It is true that he knew all the classical passages implying the contrary; but knowing classical passages, we find, is a mode of motion, which explains why they leave so little extra force for their personal application.

Poor Mr Casaubon had imagined that his long studious bachelorhood had stored up for him a compound interest of enjoyment, and that large drafts on his affections would not fail to be honoured; for we all of us, grave or light, get our thoughts entangled in metaphors, and act fatally on the strength of them. And now he was in danger of being saddened by the very conviction that his circumstances were unusually happy: there was nothing external by which he could account for a certain blankness of sensibilty which came over him just when his expectant gladness should have been most lively, just when he exchanged the accustomed dulness of his Lowick library for his visits to the Grange. Here was a weary experience in which he was as utterly condemned to loneliness as in the despair which sometimes threatened him while toiling in the morass of authorship without seeming nearer to the goal. And his was that worst loneliness which would shrink from sympathy. He could not but wish that Dorothea should think him not less happy than the world would expect her successful suitor to be; and in relation to his authorship he leaned on her young trust and veneration, he liked to draw forth her fresh interest in listening, as a means of encouragement to himself: in talking to her he presented all his performance and intention with the reflected confidence of the pedagogue, and rid himself for the time of that chilling ideal audience which crowded his laborious uncreative hours with the vaporous pressure of Tartarean shades.

For to Dorothea, after that toy-box history of the world adapted to young ladies which had made the chief part of her education, Mr Casaubon's talk about his great book was full of new vistas; and this sense of revelation, this surprise of a nearer introduction to Stoics and Alexandrians, as people who had ideas not totally unlike her own, kept in abeyance for the time her usual eagerness for a binding theory which could bring her own life and doctrine into strict connection with that amazing past, and give the remotest sources of knowledge some bearing on her actions. That more complete teaching would come – Mr Casaubon would tell her all that: she was looking forward to higher initiation in ideas, as she was looking forward to marriage, and blending her dim conceptions of both. It would be a great mistake to suppose that Dorothea would have cared about any share in Mr Casaubon's learning as mere accomplishment; for though opinion in the neighbourhood of Freshitt and Tipton had pronounced her clever, that epithet would not have described her to circles in whose more precise vocabulary cleverness implies mere aptitude for knowing and doing, apart from character. All her eagerness for acquirement lay within that full current of sympathetic motive in which her ideas and impulses were habitually swept along. She did not want to deck herself with knowledge – to wear it loose from the nerves and blood that fed her action; and if she had written a book she must have done it as Saint Theresa did, under the command of an authority that constrained her conscience. But something she yearned for by which her life might be filled with action at once rational and ardent; and since the time was gone by for guiding visions and spiritual directors, since prayer heightened yearning but not instruction, what lamp was there but knowledge? Surely learned men kept the only oil; and who more learned than Mr Casaubon?

Thus in these brief weeks Dorothea's joyous grateful expectation was unbroken, and however her lover might occasionally be conscious of flatness, he could never refer it to any slackening of her affectionate interest.

The season was mild enough to encourage the project of extending the wedding journey as far as Rome, and Mr Casaubon was anxious for this because he wished to inspect some manuscripts in the Vatican.

'I still regret that your sister is not to accompany us,' he said one morning, some time after it had been ascertained that Celia objected to go, and that Dorothea did not wish for her companionship. 'You will have many lonely hours, Dorothea, for I shall be constrained to make the utmost use of my time during our stay in Rome, and I should feel more at liberty if you had a companion.'

The words 'I should feel more at liberty' grated on Dorothea. For the first time in speaking to Mr Casaubon she coloured from annoyance.

'You must have misunderstood me very much,' she said, 'if you think I should not enter into the value of your time – if you think that I should not willingly give up whatever interfered with your using it to the best purpose.'

'That is very amiable in you, my dear Dorothea,' said Mr Casaubon, not in the least noticing that she was hurt; 'but if you had a lady as your companion, I could put you both under the care of a cicerone, and we could thus achieve two purposes in the same space of time.'

'I beg you will not refer to this again,' said Dorothea, rather haughtily. But immediately she feared that she was wrong, and turning toward him she laid her hand on his, adding in a different tone, 'Pray do not be anxious about me. I shall have so much to think of when I am alone. And Tantripp will be a sufficient companion, just to take care of me. I could not bear to have Celia: she would be miserable.'

It was time to dress. There was to be a dinner-party that day, the last of the parties which were held at the Grange as proper preliminaries to the wedding, and Dorothea was glad of a reason for moving away at once on the sound of the bell, as if she needed more than her usual amount of preparation. She was ashamed of being irritated from some cause she could not define even to herself; for though she had no intention to be untruthful, her reply had not touched the real hurt within her. Mr Casaubon's words had been quite reasonable, yet they had brought a vague instantaneous sense of aloofness on his part.

'Surely I am in a strangely selfish weak state of mind,' she said to herself. 'How can I have a husband who is so much above me without knowing that he needs me less than I need him?'

Having convinced herself that Mr Casaubon was altogether right, she recovered her equanimity, and was an agreeable image of serene dignity when she came into the drawing-room in her silver-grey dress – the simple lines of her dark-brown hair parted over her brow and coiled massively behind, in keeping with the entire absence from her manner and expression of all search after mere effect. Sometimes when Dorothea was in company, there seemed to be as complete an air of repose about her as if she had been a picture of Santa Barbara looking out from her tower into the clear air; but these intervals of quietude made the energy of her speech and emotion the more remarked when some outward appeal had touched her.

She was naturally the subject of many observations this evening, for the dinner-party was large and rather more miscellaneous as to the male portion than any which had been held at the Grange since Mr Brooke's nieces had resided with him, so that the talking was done in duos and trios more or less inharmonious. There was the newly-elected mayor of Middlemarch, who happened to be a manufacturer; the philanthropic banker his brother-in-law, who predominated so much in the town that some called him a Methodist, others a hypocrite, according to the resources of their vocabulary; and there were various professional men. In fact Mrs Cadwallader said that Brooke was beginning to treat the Middlemarchers, and that she preferred the farmers at the tithe-dinner, who drank her health unpretentiously, and were not ashamed of their grandfathers' furniture. For in that part of the country, before Reform had done its notable part in developing the political consciousness, there was a clearer distinction of ranks and a dimmer distinction of parties; so that Mr Brooke's miscellaneous invitations seemed to belong to that general laxity which came from his inordinate travel and habit of taking too much in the form of ideas.

Already, as Miss Brooke passed out of the dining-room, opportunity was found for some interjectional 'asides'.

'A fine woman, Miss Brooke! an uncommonly fine woman, by God!' said Mr Standish, the old lawyer, who had been so long concerned with the landed gentry that he had become landed himself, and used that oath in a deep-mouthed manner as a sort of armorial bearings, stamping the speech of a man who held a good position.

Mr Bulstrode, the banker, seemed to be addressed, but that gentleman disliked coarseness and profanity, and merely bowed. The remark was taken up by Mr Chichely, a middle-aged bachelor and coursing celebrity, who had a complexion something like an Easter egg, a few hairs carefully arranged, and a carriage implying the consciousness of a distinguished appearance.

'Yes, but not my style of woman: I like a woman who lays herself out a little more to please us. There should be a little filigree about a woman – something of the coquette. A man likes a sort of challenge. The more of a dead set she makes at you the better.'

'There's some truth in that,' said Mr Standish, disposed to be genial. 'And, by God, it's usually the way with them. I suppose it answers some wise ends: Providence made them so, eh, Bulstrode?'

'I should be disposed to refer coquetry to another source,' said Mr Bulstrode. 'I should rather refer it to the devil.'

'Ay, to be sure, there should be a little devil in a woman,' said Mr Chichely, whose study of the fair sex seemed to have been detrimental to his theology. 'And I like them blond, with a certain gait, and a swan neck. Between ourselves, the mayor's daughter is more to my taste than Miss Brooke or Miss Celia either. If I were a marrying man I should choose Miss Vincy before either of them.'

'Well, make up, make up,' said Mr Standish, jocosely; 'you see the middle-aged fellows carry the day.'

Mr Chichely shook his head with much meaning: he was not going to incur the certainty of being accepted by the woman he would choose.

The Miss Vincy who had the honour of being Mr Chichely's ideal was of course not present; for Mr Brooke, always objecting to go too far, would not have chosen that his nieces should meet the daughter of a Middlemarch manufacturer, unless it were on a public occasion. The feminine part of the company included none whom Lady Chettam or Mrs Cadwallader could object to; for Mrs Renfrew, the colonel's widow, was not only unexceptionable in point of breeding, but also interesting on the ground of her complaint, which puzzled the doctors, and seemed clearly a case wherein the fulness of professional knowledge might need the supplement of quackery. Lady Chettam, who attributed her own remarkable health to home-made bitters united with constant medical attendance, entered with much exercise of the imagination into Mrs Renfrew's account of symptoms, and into the amazing futility in her case of all strengthening medicines.

'Where can all the strength of those medicines go, my dear?' said the mild but stately dowager, turning to Mrs Cadwallader reflectively, when Mrs Renfrew's attention was called away.

'It strengthens the disease,' said the Rector's wife, much too well-born not to be an amateur in medicine. 'Everything depends on the constitution: some people make fat, some blood, and some bile – that's my view of the matter; and whatever they take is a sort of grist to the mill.'

'Then she ought to take medicines that would reduce – reduce the disease, you know, if you are right, my dear. And I think what you say is reasonable.'

'Certainly it is reasonable. You have two sorts of potatoes, fed on the same soil. One of them grows more and more watery – '

'Ah! like this poor Mrs Renfrew – that is what I think. Dropsy! There is no swelling yet – it is inward. I should say she ought to take drying medicines, shouldn't you? – or a dry hot-air bath. Many things might be tried, of a drying nature.'

'Let her try a certain person's pamphlets,' said Mrs Cadwallader in an undertone, seeing the gentlemen enter. '*He* does not want drying.'

'Who, my dear?' said Lady Chettam, a charming woman, not so quick as to nullify the pleasure of explanation.

'The bridegroom – Casaubon. He has certainly been drying up faster since the engagement: the flame of passion, I suppose.'

'I should think he is far from having a good constitution,' said Lady Chettam, with a still deeper undertone. 'And then his studies – so very dry, as you say.'

'Really, by the side of Sir James, he looks like a death's head skinned over for the occasion. Mark my words: in a year from this time that girl will hate him. She looks up to him as an oracle now, and by-and-by she will be at the other extreme, All flightiness!'

'How very shocking! I fear she is headstrong. But tell me – you know all about him – is there anything very bad? What is the truth?'

'The truth? he is as bad as the wrong physic – nasty to take, and sure to disagree.'

'There could not be anything worse than that,' said Lady Chettam, with so vivid a conception of the physic that she seemed to have learned something exact about Mr Casaubon's disadvantages. 'However, James will hear nothing about Miss Brooke. He says she is the mirror of women still.'

'That is a generous make-believe of his. Depend upon it, he likes little Celia better, and she appreciates him. I hope you like my little Celia?'

'Certainly; she is fonder of geraniums, and seems more docile, though not so fine a figure. But we were talking of physic: tell me about this new young surgeon, Mr Lydgate. I am told he is wonderfully clever: he certainly looks it – a fine brow indeed.'

'He is a gentleman. I heard him talking to Humphrey. He talks well.'

'Yes. Mr Brooke says he is one of the Lydgates of Northumberland, really well connected. One does not expect it in a practitioner of that kind. For my own part, I like a medical man more on a footing with the servants;

they are often all the cleverer. I assure you I found poor Hicks's judgment unfailing; I never knew him wrong. He was coarse and butcher-like, but he knew my constitution. It was a loss to me his going off so suddenly. Dear me, what a very animated conversation Miss Brooke seems to be having with this Mr Lydgate!'

'She is talking cottages and hospitals with him,' said Mrs Cadwallader, whose ears and power of interpretation were quick. 'I believe he is a sort of philanthropist, so Brooke is sure to take him up.'

'James,' said Lady Chettam when her son came near, 'bring Mr Lydgate and introduce him to me. I want to test him.'

The affable dowager declared herself delighted with this opportunity of making Mr Lydgate's acquaintance, having heard of his success in treating fever on a new plan.

Mr Lydgate had the medical accomplishment of looking perfectly grave whatever nonsense was talked to him, and his dark steady eyes gave him impressiveness as a listener. He was as little as possible like the lamented Hicks, especially in a certain careless refinement about his toilette and utterance. Yet Lady Chettam gathered much confidence in him. He confirmed her view of her own constitution as being peculiar, by admitting that all constitutions might be called peculiar, and he did not deny that hers might be more peculiar than others. He did not approve of a too lowering system, including reckless cupping, nor, on the other hand, of incessant port wine and bark. He said 'I think so' with an air of so much deference accompanying the insight of agreement, that she formed the most cordial opinion of his talents.

'I am quite pleased with your *protégé*,' she said to Mr Brooke before going away.

'My *protégé*? – dear me! – who is that?' said Mr Brooke.

'This young Lydgate, the new doctor. He seems to me to understand his profession admirably.'

'Oh, Lydgate! he is not my *protégé*, you know; only I knew an uncle of his who sent me a letter about him. However, I think he is likely to be first-rate – has studied in Paris, knew Broussais; has ideas, you know – wants to raise the profession.'

'Lydgate has lots of ideas, quite new, about ventilation and diet, that sort of thing,' resumed Mr Brooke, after he had handed out Lady Chettam, and had returned to be civil to a group of Middlemarchers.

'Hang it, do you think that is quite sound? – upsetting the old treatment, which has made Englishmen what they are?' said Mr Standish.

'Medical knowledge is at a low ebb among us,' said Mr Bulstrode, who spoke in a subdued tone, and had rather a sickly air. 'I, for my part, hail the advent of Mr Lydgate. I hope to find good reason for confiding the new hospital to his management.'

'That is all very fine,' replied Mr Standish, who was not fond of Mr Bulstrode; 'if you like him to try experiments on your hospital patients, and kill a few people for charity, I have no objection. But I am not going to hand money out of my purse to have experiments tried on me. I like treatment that has been tested a little.'

'Well, you know, Standish, every dose you take is an experiment – an experiment, you know,' said Mr Brooke, nodding towards the lawyer.

'Oh, if you talk in that sense!' said Mr Standish, with as much disgust at such non-legal quibbling as a man can well betray towards a valuable client.

'I should be glad of any treatment that would cure me without reducing me to a skeleton, like poor Grainger,' said Mr Vincy, the mayor, a florid man, who would have served for a study of flesh in striking contrast with the Franciscan tints of Mr Bulstrode. 'It's an uncommonly dangerous thing to be left without any padding against the shafts of disease, as somebody said, – and I think it a very good expression myself.'

Mr Lydgate, of course, was out of hearing. He had quitted the party early, and would have thought it altogether tedious but for the novelty of certain introductions, especially the introduction to Miss Brooke, whose youthful bloom, with her approaching marriage to that faded scholar, and her interest in matters socially useful, gave her the piquancy of an unusual combination.

'She is a good creature – that fine girl – but a little too earnest,' he thought. 'It is troublesome to talk to such women. They are always wanting reasons, yet they are too ignorant to understand the merits of any question, and usually fall back on their moral sense to settle things after their own taste.'

Evidently Miss Brooke was not Mr Lydgate's style of woman any more than Mr Chichely's. Considered, indeed, in relation to the latter, whose mind was matured, she was altogether a mistake, and calculated to shock his trust in final causes, including the adaptation of fine young women to purple-faced bachelors. But Lydgate was less ripe, and might possibly have experience before him which would modify his opinion as to the most excellent things in woman.

Miss Brooke, however, was not again seen by either of these gentlemen under her maiden name. Not long after that dinner-party she had become Mrs Casaubon, and was on her way to Rome.

∽ ELEVEN ∾

But deeds and language such as men do use,
And persons such as comedy would choose,
When she would show an image of the times,
And sport with human follies, not with crimes.

BEN JONSON

LYDGATE, IN FACT, WAS ALREADY CONSCIOUS of being fascinated by a woman strikingly different from Miss Brooke: he did not in the least suppose that he had lost his balance and fallen in love but he had said of that particular woman, 'She is grace itself; she is perfectly lovely and accomplished. That is what a woman ought to be: she ought to produce the effect of exquisite music.' Plain women he regarded as he did the other severe facts of life, to be faced with philosophy and investigated by science. But Rosamond Vincy seemed to have the true melodic charm; and when a man has seen the woman whom he would have chosen if he had intended to marry speedily, his remaining a bachelor will usually depend on her resolution rather than on his. Lydgate believed that he should not marry for several years: not marry until he had trodden out a good clear path for himself away from the broad road which was quite ready made. He had seen Miss Vincy above his horizon almost as long as it had taken Mr Casaubon to become engaged and married: but this learned gentleman was possessed of a fortune; he had assembled his voluminous notes, and had made that sort of reputation which precedes performance, – often the larger part of a man's fame. He took a wife, as we have seen, to adorn the remaining quadrant of his course, and be a little moon that would cause hardly a calculable perturbation. But Lydgate was young, poor, ambitious. He had his half-century before him instead of behind him, and he had come to Middlemarch bent on doing many things that were not directly fitted to make his fortune or even secure him a good income. To a man under such circumstances, taking a wife is something more than a question of adornment, however highly he may rate this; and Lydgate was disposed to give it the first place among wifely functions. To his taste, guided by a single conversation, here was the point on which Miss Brooke would be found wanting, notwithstanding her undeniable beauty. She did not look at things from the proper feminine angle. The society of such women was about as relaxing as going from your work to teach the

72

second form, instead of reclining in a paradise with sweet laughs for bird-notes, and blue eyes for a heaven.

Certainly nothing at present could seem much less important to Lydgate than the turn of Miss Brooke's mind, or to Miss Brooke than the qualities of the woman who had attracted this young surgeon. But any one watching keenly the stealthy convergence of human lots, sees a slow preparation of effects from one life on another, which tells like a calculated irony on the indifference or the frozen stare with which we look at our unintroduced neighbour. Destiny stands by sarcastic with our *dramatis personae* folded in her hand.

Old provincial society had its share of this subtle movement: had not only its striking downfalls, its brilliant young professional dandies who ended by living up an entry with a drab and six children for their establishment, but also those less marked vicissitudes which are constantly shifting the boundaries of social intercourse, and begetting new consciousness of interdependence. Some slipped a little downward, some got higher footing: people denied aspirates, gained wealth, and fastidious gentlemen stood for boroughs; some were caught in political currents, some in ecclesiastical, and perhaps found themselves surprisingly grouped in consequence; while a few personages or families that stood with rock firmness amid all this fluctuation, were slowly presenting new aspects in spite of solidity, and altering with the double change of self and beholder. Municipal town and rural parish gradually made fresh threads of connection – gradually, as the old stocking gave way to the savings-bank, and the worship of the solar guinea became extinct, while squires and baronets, and even lords who had once lived blamelessly afar from the civic mind, gathered the faultiness of closer acquaintanceship. Settlers, too, came from distant counties, some with an alarming novelty of skill, others with an offensive advantage in cunning. In fact, much the same sort of movement and mixture went on in old England as we find in older Herodotus, who also, in telling what had been, thought it well to take a woman's lot for his starting-point; though Io, as a maiden apparently beguiled by attractive merchandise, was the reverse of Miss Brooke, and in this respect perhaps bore more resemblance to Rosamond Vincy, who had excellent taste in costume, with that nymph-like figure and pure blondness which gave the largest range to choice in the flow and colour of drapery. But these things made only part of her charm. She was admitted to be the flower of Mrs Lemon's school, the chief school in the county, where the teaching included all that was demanded in the accomplished female – even to extras, such as the getting in and out of a carriage. Mrs Lemon herself had always held up Miss Vincy as an example: no pupil, she said, exceeded that young lady for mental acquisition and propriety of speech, while her musical execution was quite exceptional. We cannot help the way in which people speak of us, and probably if Mrs Lemon had undertaken to describe Juliet or Imogen, these heroines would not have seemed poetical. The first vision of Rosamond would have been enough with most judges to dispel any prejudice excited by Mrs Lemon's praise.

Lydgate could not be long in Middlemarch without having that agreeable vision, or even without making the acquaintance of the Vincy family; for though Mr Peacock whose practice he had paid something to enter on, had not been their doctor (Mrs Vincy not liking the lowering system adopted by him), he had many patients among their connections and acquaintances. For who of any consequence in Middlemarch was not connected or at least acquainted with the Vincys? They were old manufacturers, and had kept a good house for three generations, in which there had naturally been much intermarrying with neighbours more or less decidedly genteel. Mr Vincy's sister had made a wealthy match in accepting Mr Bulstrode, who, however, as a man not born in the town, and altogether of dimly known origin, was considered to have done well in uniting himself with a real Middlemarch family; on the other hand, Mr Vincy had descended a little, having taken an innkeeper's daughter. But on this side too there was a cheering sense of money; for Mrs Vincy's sister had been second wife to rich old Mr Featherstone, and had died childless years ago, so that her nephews and nieces might be supposed to touch the affections of the widower. And it happened that Mr Bulstrode and Mr Featherstone, two of Peacock's most important patients, had, from different causes, given an especially good reception to his successor, who had raised some partisanship as well as discussion. Mr Wrench, medical attendant to the Vincy family, very early had grounds for thinking lightly of Lydgate's professional discretion, and there was no report about him which was not retailed at the Vincy's, where visitors were frequent. Mr Vincy was more inclined to general good-fellowship than to taking sides, but there was no need for him to be hasty in making any new man's acquaintance. Rosamond silently wished that her father would invite Mr Lydgate. She was tired of the faces and figures she had always been used to – the various irregular profiles and gaits and turns of phrase distinguishing those Middlemarch young men whom she had known as boys. She had been at school with girls of higher position, whose brothers, she felt sure, it would have been possible for her to be more interested in, than in these inevitable Middlemarch companions. But she would not have chosen to mention her wish to her father; and he, for his part, was in no hurry on the subject. An alderman about to be mayor must by-and-by enlarge his dinner-parties, but at present there were plenty of guests at his well-spread table.

That table often remained covered with the relics of the family breakfast long after Mr Vincy had gone with his second son to the warehouse, and when Miss Morgan was already far on in morning lessons with the younger girls in the school-room. It awaited the family laggard, who found any sort of inconvenience (to others) less disagreeable than getting up when he was called. This was the case one morning of the October in which we have lately seen Mr Casaubon visiting the Grange; and though the room was a little overheated with the fire, which had sent the spaniel panting to a remote corner, Rosamond, for some reason, continued to sit at her embroidery longer than usual, now and then giving herself a little shake, and laying her work on her knee to contemplate it with an air of hesitating weariness. Her mamma, who had returned from an excursion to the kitchen, sat on the other side of the small work-table with an air of more entire placidity, until, the clock again giving notice that it was going to strike, she looked up from the lace-mending which was occupying her plump fingers and rang the bell.

'Knock at Mr Fred's door again, Pritchard, and tell him it has struck half-past ten.'

This was said without any change in the radiant good-humour of Mrs Vincy's face, in which forty-five years had delved neither angles nor parallels; and pushing back her pink cap-strings, she let her work rest on her lap, while she looked admiringly at her daughter.

'Mamma,' said Rosamond, 'when Fred comes down I wish you would not let him have red herrings. I cannot bear the smell of them all over the house at this hour of the morning.'

'Oh, my dear, you are so hard on your brothers! It is the only fault I have to find with you. You are the sweetest temper in the world, but are so tetchy with your brothers.'

'Not tetchy, mamma; you never hear me speak in an unladylike way.'

'Well, but you want to deny them things.'

'Brothers are so unpleasant.'

'Oh, my dear, you must allow for young men. Be thankful if they have good hearts. A woman must learn to put up with little things. You will be married some day.'

'Not to any one who is like Fred.'

'Don't decry your own brother, my dear. Few young men have less against them, although he couldn't take his degree – I'm sure I can't understand why, for he seems to me most clever. And you know yourself he was thought equal to the best society at college. So particular as you are, my dear, I wonder you are not glad to have such a gentlemanly young man for a brother. You are always finding fault with Bob because he is not Fred.'

'Oh no, mamma, only because he is Bob.'

'Well, my dear, you will not find any Middlemarch young man who has not something against him.'

'But' – here Rosamond's face broke into a smile which suddenly revealed two dimples. She herself thought unfavourably of these dimples and smiled little in general society. 'But I shall not marry any Middlemarch young man.'

'So it seems, my love, for you have as good as refused the pick of them; and if there's better to be had, I'm sure there's no girl better deserves it.'

'Excuse me, mamma – I wish you would not say, "the pick of them".'

'Why, what else are they?'

'I mean, mamma, it is rather a vulgar expression.'

'Very likely, my dear; I never was a good speaker. What should I say?'

'The best of them.'

'Why, that seems just as plain and common. If I had had time to think, I should have said, "the most superior young men". But with your education you must know.'

'What must Rosy know, mother?' said Mr Fred, who had slid in unobserved through the half-open door while the ladies were bending over their work, and now going up to the fire stood with his back towards it, warming the soles of his slippers.

'Whether it's right to say "superior young men",' said Mrs Vincy ringing the bell.

'Oh, there are so many superior teas and sugars now. Superior is getting to be shopkeepers' slang.'

'Are you beginning to dislike slang, then?' said Rosamond, with mild gravity.

'Only the wrong sort. All choice of words is slang. It marks a class.'

'There is correct English: that is not slang.'

'I beg your pardon: correct English is the slang of prigs who write history and essays. And the strongest slang of all is the slang of poets.'

'You will say anything, Fred, to gain your point.'

'Well, tell me whether it is slang or poetry to call an ox a *leg-plaiter*.'

'Of course you can call it poetry if you like.'

'Aha, Miss Rosy, you don't know Homer from slang. I shall invent a new game; I shall write bits of slang and poetry on slips, and give them to you to separate.'

'Dear me, how amusing it is to hear young people talk!' said Mrs Vincy, with cheerful admiration.

'Have you got nothing else for my breakfast, Pritchard?' said Fred, to the servant who brought in coffee and buttered toast; while he walked round the table surveying the ham, potted beef, and other cold remnants, with an air of silent rejection, and polite forbearance from signs of disgust.

'Should you like eggs, sir?'

'Eggs, no! Bring me a grilled bone.'

'Really, Fred,' said Rosamond, when the servant had left the room, 'if you must have hot things for breakfast, I wish you would come down earlier. You can get up at six o'clock to go out hunting; I cannot understand why you find it so difficult to get up on other mornings.'

'That is your want of understanding, Rosy. I can get up to go hunting because I like it.'

'What would you think of me if I came down two hours after every one else and ordered grilled bone?'

'I should think you were an uncommonly fast young lady,' said Fred, eating his toast with the utmost composure.

'I cannot see why brothers are to make themselves disagreeable, any more than sisters.'

'I don't make myself disagreeable; it is you who find me so. Disagreeable is a word that describes your feelings and not my actions.'

'I think it describes the smell of grilled bone.'

'Not at all. It describes a sensation in your little nose associated with certain finicking notions which are the classics of Mrs Lemon's school. Look at my mother: you don't see her objecting to everything except what she does herself. She is my notion of a pleasant woman.'

'Bless you both, my dears, and don't quarrel,' said Mrs Vincy, with motherly cordiality. 'Come, Fred, tell us all about the new doctor. How is your uncle pleased with him?'

'Pretty well, I think. He asks Lydgate all sorts of questions and then screws up his face while he hears the answers, as if they were pinching his toes. That's his way. Ah, here comes my grilled bone.'

'But how came you to stay out so late, my dear? You only said you were going to your uncle's.'

'Oh, I dined at Plymdale's. We had whist. Lydgate was there too.'

'And what do you think of him? He is very gentlemanly, I suppose. They say he is of excellent family – his relations quite county people.'

'Yes,' said Fred. 'There was a Lydgate at John's who spent no end of money. I find this man is a second cousin of his. But rich men may have very poor devils for second cousins.'

'It always makes a difference, though, to be of good family,' said Rosamond, with a tone of decision which showed that she had thought on this subject. Rosamond felt that she might have been happier if she had not been the daughter of a Middlemarch manufacturer. She disliked anything which reminded her that her mother's father had been an innkeeper. Certainly any one remembering the fact might think that Mrs Vincy had the air of a very handsome good-humoured landlady, accustomed to the most capricious orders of gentlemen.

'I thought it was odd his name was Tertius,' said the bright-faced matron, 'but of course it's a name in the family. But now, tell us exactly what sort of man he is.'

'Oh, tallish, dark, clever – talks well – rather a prig, I think.'

'I never can make out what you mean by a prig,' said Rosamond.

'A fellow who wants to show that he has opinions.'

'Why, my dear, doctors must have opinions,' said Mrs Vincy. 'What are they there for else?'

'Yes, mother, the opinions are paid for. But a prig is a fellow who is always making you a present of his opinions.'

'I suppose Mary Garth admires Mr Lydgate,' said Rosamond, not without a touch of innuendo.

'Really, I can't say,' said Fred, rather glumly, as he left the table, and taking up a novel which he had brought down with him, threw himself into an arm-chair. 'If you are jealous of her, go oftener to Stone Court yourself and eclipse her.'

'I wish you would not be so vulgar, Fred. If you have finished, pray ring the bell.'

'It is true, though – what your brother says, Rosamond,' Mrs Vincy began, when the servant had cleared the table. 'It is a thousand pities you haven't patience to go and see your uncle more, so proud of you as he is, and wanted you to live with him. There's no knowing what he might have done for you as well as for Fred. God knows, I'm fond of having you at home with me, but I can part with my children for their good. And now it stands to reason that your uncle Featherstone will do something for Mary Garth.'

'Mary Garth can bear being at Stone Court, because she likes that better than being a governess,' said Rosamond, folding up her work. 'I would rather not have anything left to me if I must earn it by enduring much of my uncle's cough and his ugly relations.'

'He can't be long for this world, my dear; I wouldn't hasten his end, but what with asthma and that inward complaint, let us hope there is something better for him in another. And I have no ill-will towards Mary Garth, but there's justice to be thought of. And Mr Featherstone's first wife brought him no money, as my sister did. Her nieces and nephews can't have so much claim as my sister's. And I must say I think Mary Garth a dreadful plain girl – more fit for a governess.'

'Every one would not agree with you there, mother,' said Fred, who seemed to be able to read and listen too.

'Well, my dear,' said Mrs Vincy, wheeling skilfully, 'if she *had* some fortune left her, – a man marries his wife's relations, and the Garths are so poor, and live in such a small way. But I shall leave you to your studies, my dear; for I must go and do some shopping.'

'Fred's studies are not very deep,' said Rosamond, rising with her mamma, 'he is only reading a novel.'

'Well, well, by-and-by he'll go to his Latin and things,' said Mrs Vincy, soothingly, stroking her son's head. 'There's a fire in the smoking-room on purpose. It's your father's wish, you know – Fred, my dear – and I always tell him you will be good, and go to college again to take your degree.'

Fred drew his mother's hand down to his lips, but said nothing.

'I suppose you are not going out riding to-day?' said Rosamond, lingering a little after her mamma was gone.

'No; why?'

'Papa says I may have the chestnut to ride now.'

'You can go with me to-morrow, if you like. Only I am going to Stone Court, remember.'

'I want the ride so much, it is indifferent to me where we go.' Rosamond really wished to go to Stone Court, of all other places.

'Oh, I say, Rosy,' said Fred, as she was passing out of the room, 'if you are going to the piano, let me come and play some airs with you.'

'Pray do not ask me this morning.'

'Why not this morning?'

'Really, Fred, I wish you would leave off playing the flute. A man looks very silly playing the flute. And you play so out of tune.'

'When next any one makes love to you, Miss Rosamond, I will tell him how obliging you are.'

'Why should you expect me to oblige you by hearing you play the flute, any more than I should expect you to oblige me by not playing it?'

'And why should you expect me to take you out riding?'

This question led to an adjustment, for Rosamond had set her mind on that particular ride.

So Fred was gratified with nearly an hour's practice of 'Ar hyd y nos', 'Ye banks and braes', and other favourite airs from his 'Instructor on the Flute'; a wheezy performance, into which he threw much ambition and an irrepressible hopefulness.

∾ TWELVE ∾

He had more tow on his distaffe
Than Gerveis knew.

CHAUCER

THE RIDE TO STONE COURT, WHICH Fred and Rosamond took the next morning, lay through a pretty bit of midland landscape, almost all meadows and pastures, with hedgerows still allowed to grow in bushy beauty and to spread out coral fruit for the birds. Little details gave each field a particular physiognomy, dear to the eyes that have looked on them from childhood: the pool in the corner where the grasses were dank and trees leaned whisperingly; the great oak shadowing a bare place in mid-pasture; the high bank where the ash-trees grew; the sudden slope of the old marl-pit making a red background for the burdock; the huddled roofs and ricks of the homestead without a traceable way of approach; the grey gate and fences against the depths of the bordering wood; and the stray hovel, its old, old thatch full of mossy hills and valleys with wondrous modulations of light and shadow such as we travel far to see in later life, and see larger, but not more beautiful. These are the things that make the gamut of joy in landscape to midland-bred souls – the things they toddled among, or perhaps learned by heart standing between their father's knees while he drove leisurely.

But the road, even the byroad, was excellent; for Lowick, as we have seen, was not a parish of muddy lanes and poor tenants: and it was into Lowick parish that Fred and Rosamond entered after a couple of miles' riding. Another mile would bring them to Stone Court, and at the end of the first half, the house was already visible, looking as if it had been arrested in its growth towards a stone mansion by an unexpected budding of farm-buildings on its left flank, which had hindered it from becoming anything more than the substantial dwelling of a gentleman farmer. It was not the less agreeable an object in the distance for the cluster of pinnacled corn-ricks which balanced the fine row of walnuts on the right.

Presently it was possible to discern something that might be a gig on the circular drive before the front door.

'Dear me,' said Rosamond, 'I hope none of my uncle's horrible relations are there.'

'They are, though. That is Mrs Waule's gig – the last yellow gig left, I should think. When I see Mrs Waule in it, I understand how yellow can have been worn for mourning. That gig seems to me more funereal than a hearse. But then Mrs Waule always has black crape on. How does she manage it, Rosy? Her friends can't always be dying.'

'I don't know at all. And she is not in the least evangelical,' said Rosamond, reflectively, as if that religious point of view would have fully accounted for perpetual crape. 'And not poor,' she added, after a moment's pause.

'No, by George! They are as rich as Jews, those Waules and Featherstones; I mean, for people like them, who don't want to spend anything. And yet they hang about my uncle like vultures, and are afraid of a farthing going away from their side of the family. But I believe he hates them all.'

The Mrs Waule who was so far from being admirable in the eyes of these distant connections, had happened to say this very morning (not at all with a defiant air, but in a low, muffled, neutral tone, as of a voice heard through cotton wool) that she did not wish 'to enjoy their good opinion'. She was seated, as she observed, on her own brother's hearth, and had been Jane Featherstone five-and-twenty years before she had been Jane Waule, which entitled her to speak when her own brother's name had been made free with by those who had no right to it.

'What are you driving at there?' said Mr Featherstone, holding his stick between his knees and settling his wig, while he gave her a momentary sharp glance, which seemed to react on him like a draught of cold air and set him coughing.

Mrs Waule had to defer her answer till he was quiet again, till Mary Garth had supplied him with fresh syrup, and he had begun to rub the gold knob of his stick, looking bitterly at the fire. It was a bright fire, but it made no difference to the chill-looking purplish tint of Mrs Waule's face, which was as neutral as her voice; having mere chinks for eyes, and lips that hardly moved in speaking.

'The doctors can't master that cough, brother. It's just like what I have; for I'm your own sister, constitution and everything. But, as I was saying, it's a pity Mrs Vincy's family can't be better conducted.'

'Tchah! you said nothing o' the sort. You said somebody had made free with my name.'

'And no more than can be proved, if what everybody says is true. My brother Solomon tells me it's the talk up and down in Middlemarch how unsteady young Vincy is, and has been for ever gambling at billiards since home he came.'

'Nonsense!' What's a game at billiards? It's a good gentlemanly game; and young Vincy is not a clodhopper. If your son John took to billiards, now, he'd make a fool of himself.'

'Your nephew John never took to billiards or any other game, brother, and is far from losing hundreds of pounds, which, if what everybody says is true, must be found somewhere else than out of Mr Vincy the father's pocket. For they say he's been losing money for years, though nobody would think so, to see him go coursing and keeping open house as they do. And I've heard say Mr Bulstrode condemns Mrs Vincy beyond anything for her flightiness, and spoiling her children so.'

'What's Bulstrode to me? I don't bank with him.'

'Well, Mrs Bulstrode is Mr Vincy's own sister, and they do say that Mr Vincy mostly trades on the Bank money; and you may see yourself, brother, when a woman past forty has pink strings always flying, and that light way of laughing at everything, it's very unbecoming. But indulging your children is one thing, and finding money to pay their debts is another. And it's openly said that young Vincy has raised money on his expectations. I don't say what expectations. Miss Garth hears me, and is welcome to tell again. I know young people hang together.'

'No, thank you, Mrs Waule,' said Mary Garth. 'I dislike hearing scandal too much to wish to repeat it.'

Mr Featherstone rubbed the knob of his stick and made a brief convulsive show of laughter, which had much the same genuineness as an old whist-player's chuckle over a bad hand. Still looking at the fire, he said –

'And who pretends to say Fred Vincy hasn't got expectations? Such a fine, spirited fellow is like enough to have 'em.'

There was a slight pause before Mrs Waule replied, and when she did so, her voice seemed to be slightly moistened with tears, though her face was still dry.

'Whether or no, brother, it is naturally painful to me and my brother Solomon to hear your name made free with, and your complaint being such as may carry you off sudden, and people who are no more

Featherstones than the Merry-Andrew at the fair, openly reckoning on your property coming to *them*. And me your own sister, and Solomon your own brother! And if that's to be it, what has it pleased the Almighty to make families for?' Here Mrs Waule's tears fell, but with moderation.

'Come, out with it, Jane!' said Mr Featherstone, looking at her. 'You mean to say, Fred Vincy has been getting somebody to advance him money on what he says he knows about my will, eh?'

'I never said so, brother' (Mrs Waule's voice had again become dry and unshaken). 'It was told me by my brother Solomon last night when he called coming from market to give me advice about the old wheat, me being a widow, and my son John only three-and-twenty, though steady beyond anything. And he had it from most undeniable authority, and not one, but many.'

'Stuff and nonsense! I don't believe a word of it. It's all a got-up story. Go to the window, Missy; I thought I heard a horse. See if the doctor's coming.'

'Not got up by me, brother, nor yet by Solomon, who, whatever else he may be – and I don't deny he has oddities – has made his will and parted his property equal between such kin as he's friends with; though, for my part, I think there are times when some should be considered more than others. But Solomon makes it no secret what he means to do.'

'The more fool he!' said Mr Featherstone, with some difficulty; breaking into a severe fit of coughing that required Mary Garth to stand near him, so that she did not find out whose horses they were which presently paused stamping on the gravel before the door.

Before Mr Featherstone's cough was quiet, Rosamond entered, bearing up her riding-habit with much grace. She bowed ceremoniously to Mrs Waule, who said stiffly, 'How do you do, miss?' smiled and nodded silently to Mary, and remained standing till the coughing should cease and allow her uncle to notice her.

'Heyday, Miss,' he said at last, 'you have a fine colour. Where's Fred?'

'Seeing about the horses. He will be in presently.'

'Sit down, sit down. Mrs Waule, you'd better go.'

Even those neighbours who had called Peter Featherstone an old fox, had never accused him of being insincerely polite, and his sister was quite used to the peculiar absence of ceremony with which he marked his sense of blood-relationship. Indeed, she herself was accustomed to think that entire freedom from the necessity of behaving agreeably was included in the Almighty's intentions about families. She rose slowly without any sign of resentment, and said in her usual muffled monotone, 'Brother, I hope the new doctor will be able to do something for you. Solomon says there's great talk of his cleverness. I'm sure it's my wish you should be spared. And there's none more ready to nurse you than your own sister and your own nieces, if you'd only say the word. There's Rebecca, and Joanna, and Elizabeth, you know.'

'Ay, ay, I remember – you'll see I've remembered 'em all – all dark and ugly. They'd need some money, eh? There never was any beauty in the women of our family; but the Featherstones have always had some money, and the Waules too. Waule had money too. A warm man was Waule. Ay, ay; money's a good egg; and if you've got money to leave behind you, lay it in a warm nest. Good-bye, Mrs Waule.'

Here Mr Featherstone pulled at both sides of his wig as if he wanted to deafen himself, and his sister went away ruminating on this oracular speech of his. Notwithstanding her jealousy of the Vincys and of Mary Garth, there remained as the nethermost sediment in her mental shallows a persuasion that her brother Peter Featherstone could never leave his chief property away from his blood-relations: – else, why had the Almighty carried off his two wives both childless, after he had gained so much by manganese and things, turning up when nobody expected it? – and why was there a Lowick parish church, and the Waules and Powder-ells all sitting in the same pew for generations, and the Featherstone pew next to them, if, the Sunday after her brother Peter's death, everybody was to know that the property was gone out of the family? The human mind has at no period accepted a moral chaos; and so preposterous a result was not strictly conceivable. But we are frightened at much that is not strictly conceivable.

When Fred came in the old man eyed him with a peculiar twinkle, which the younger had often had reason to interpret as pride in the satisfactory details of his appearance.

'You two misses go away,' said Mr Featherstone. 'I want to speak to Fred.'

'Come into my room, Rosamond, you will not mind the cold for a little while,' said Mary. The two girls had not only known each other in childhood, but had been at the same provincial school together (Mary as an articled pupil), so that they had many memories in common, and liked very well to talk in private. Indeed, this *tête-à-tête* was one of Rosamond's objects in coming to Stone Court.

Old Featherstone would not begin the dialogue till the door had been closed. He continued to look at Fred with the same twinkle and with one of his habitual grimaces, alternately screwing and widening his mouth; and when he spoke, it was in a low tone, which might be taken for that of an informer ready to be bought off, rather than for the tone of an offended senior. He was not a man to feel any strong moral indignation even on account of trespasses against himself. It was natural that others should want to get an advantage over him, but then, he was a little too cunning for them.

'So, sir, you've been paying ten per cent, for money which you've promised to pay off by mortgaging my land when I'm dead and gone, eh? You put my life at a twelvemonth, say. But I can alter my will yet.'

Fred blushed. He had not borrowed money in that way, for excellent reasons. But he was conscious of having spoken with some confidence (perhaps with more than he exactly remembered) about his prospect of getting Featherstone's land as a future means of paying present debts.

'I don't know what you refer to, sir. I have certainly never borrowed any money on such an insecurity. Please to explain.'

'No, sir, it's you must explain. I can alter my will yet, let me tell you. I'm of sound mind – can reckon compound interest in my head, and remember every fool's name as well as I could twenty years ago. What the deuce? I'm under eighty. I say, you must contradict this story.'

'I have contradicted it, sir,' Fred answered, with a touch of impatience, not remembering that his uncle did not verbally discriminate contradicting from disproving, though no one was further from confounding the two ideas than old Featherstone, who often wondered that so many fools took his own assertions for proofs. 'But I contradict it again. The story is a silly lie.'

'Nonsense! you must bring dockiments. It comes from authority.'

'Name the authority, and make him name the man of whom I borrowed the money, and then I can disprove the story.'

'It's pretty good authority, I think – a man who knows most of what goes on in Middlemarch. It's that fine, religious, charitable uncle o' yours. Come now!' Here Mr Featherstone had his peculiar inward shake which signified merriment.

'Mr Bulstrode?'

'Who else, eh?'

'Then the story has grown into this lie out of some sermonizing words he may have let fall about me. Do they pretend that he named the man who lent me the money?'

'If there is such a man, depend upon it Bulstrode knows him. But, supposing you only tried to get the money lent, and didn't get it – Bulstrode 'ud know that too. You bring me a writing from Bulstrode to say he doesn't believe you've ever promised to pay your debts out o' my land. Come now!'

Mr Featherstone's face required its whole scale of grimaces as a muscular outlet to his silent triumph in the soundness of his faculties.

Fred felt himself to be in a disgusting dilemma.

'You must be joking, sir. Mr Bulstrode, like other men, believes scores of things that are not true, and he has a prejudice against me. I could easily get him to write that he knew no facts in proof of the report you speak of, though it might lead to unpleasantness. But I could hardly ask him to write down what he believes or does not believe about me.' Fred paused an instant, and then added, in politic appeal to his uncle's vanity, 'That is hardly a thing for a gentleman to ask.'

But he was disappointed in the result.

'Ay, I know what you mean. You'd sooner offend me than Bulstrode. And what's he? – he's got no land hereabout that ever I heard tell of. A speckilating fellow! He may come down any day, when the devil leaves off backing him. And that's what his religion means: he wants God A'mighty to come in. That's nonsense! There's one thing I made out pretty clear when I used to go to church – and it's this: God A'mighty sticks to the land. He promises land, and He gives land, and He makes chaps rich with corn and cattle. But you take the other side. You like Bulstrode and speckilation better than Featherstone and land.'

'I beg your pardon, sir,' said Fred, rising, standing with his back to the fire and beating his boot with his whip. 'I like neither Bulstrode nor speculation.' He spoke rather sulkily, feeling himself stalemated.

'Well, well, you can do without *me*, that's pretty clear,' said old Featherstone, secretly disliking the possibility that Fred would show himself at all independent. 'You neither want a bit of land to make a squire of you instead of a starving parson, nor a lift of a hundred pound by the way. It's all one to me. I can make five codicils if I like, and I shall keep my bank-notes for a nest-egg. It's all one to me.'

Fred coloured again. Featherstone had rarely given him presents of money, and at this moment it seemed almost harder to part with the immediate prospect of bank-notes than with the more distant prospect of the land.

'I am not ungrateful, sir. I never meant to show disregard for any kind intentions you might have towards me. On the contrary.'

'Very good. Then prove it. You bring me a letter from Bulstrode saying he doesn't believe you've been cracking and promising to pay your debts out o' my land, and then, if there's any scrape you've got into, we'll see if I can back you a bit. Come now! That's a bargain. Here, give me your arm. I'll try and walk round the room.'

Fred, in spite of his irritation, had kindness enough in him to be a little sorry for the unloved, unvenerated old man, who with his dropsical legs looked more than usually pitiable in walking. While giving his arm, he thought that he should not himself like to be an old fellow with his constitution breaking up; and he waited good-temperedly, first before the window to hear the wonted remarks about the guinea-fowls and the weathercock, and then before the scanty book-shelves, of which the chief glories in dark calf were Josephus, Culpepper, Klopstock's *Messiah*, and several volumes of the *Gentleman's Magazine*.

'Read me the names o' the books. Come now! you're a college man.'

Fred gave him the titles.

'What did Missy want with more books? What must you be bringing her more books for?'

'They amuse her, sir. She is very fond of reading.'

'A little too fond,' said Mr Featherstone, captiously. 'She was for reading when she sat with me. But I put a stop to that. She's got the newspaper to read out loud. That's enough for one day, I should think. I can't abide to see her reading to herself. You mind and not bring her any more books, do you hear?'

'Yes, sir, I hear.' Fred had received this order before, and had secretly disobeyed it. He intended to disobey it again.

'Ring the bell,' said Mr Featherstone; 'I want Missy to come down.'

Rosamond and Mary had been talking faster than their male friends. They did not think of sitting down, but stood at the toilette-table near the window while Rosamond took off her hat, adjusted her veil, and applied little touches of her finger-tips to her hair – hair of infantile fairness, neither flaxen nor yellow. Mary Garth seemed all the plainer standing at an angle between the two nymphs – the one in the glass, and the one out of it, who looked at each other with eyes of heavenly blue, deep enough to hold the most exquisite meanings an ingenious beholder could put into them, and deep enough to hide the meanings of the owner if these should happen to be less exquisite. Only a few children in Middlemarch looked blond by the side of Rosamond, and the slim figure displayed by her riding-habit had delicate undulations. In fact, most men in Middlemarch, except her brothers, held that Miss Vincy was the best girl in the world, and some called her an angel. Mary Garth, on the contrary, had the aspect of an ordinary sinner: she was brown; her curly dark hair was rough and stubborn; her stature was low; and it would not be true to declare, in satisfactory antithesis, that she had all the virtues. Plainness has its peculiar temptations and vices quite as much as beauty; it is apt either to feign amiability, or, not feigning it, to show all the repulsiveness of discontent: at any rate, to be called an ugly thing in contrast with that lovely creature your companion, is apt to produce some effect beyond a sense of fine veracity and fitness in the phrase. At the age of two-and-twenty Mary had certainly not attained that perfect good sense and good principle which are usually recommended to the less fortunate girl, as if they were to be obtained in quantities ready mixed, with a flavour of resignation as required. Her shrewdness had a streak of satiric bitterness continually renewed and never carried utterly out of sight, except by a strong current of gratitude towards those who, instead of telling her that she ought to be contented, did something to make her so. Advancing womanhood had tempered her plainness, which was of a good human sort, such as the mothers of our race have very commonly worn in all latitudes under a more or less becoming headgear. Rembrandt would have painted her with pleasure, and would have made her broad features look out of the canvas with intelligent honesty. For honesty, truth-telling fairness, was Mary's reigning virtue: she neither tried to create illusions, nor indulged in them for her own behoof, and when she was in a good mood she had humour enough in her to laugh at herself. When she and Rosamond happened both to be reflected in the glass, she said laughingly –

'What a brown patch I am by the side of you, Rosy! You are the most unbecoming companion.'

'Oh no! No one thinks of your appearance, you are so sensible and useful, Mary. Beauty is of very little consequence in reality,' said Rosamond, turning her head towards Mary, but with eyes swerving towards the new view of her neck in the glass.

'You mean *my* beauty,' said Mary, rather sardonically.

Rosamond thought, 'Poor Mary, she takes the kindest things ill.' Aloud she said, 'What have you been doing lately?'

'I? Oh, minding the house – pouring out syrup – pretending to be amiable and contented – learning to have a bad opinion of everybody.'

'It is a wretched life for you.'

'No,' said Mary, curtly, with a little toss of her head. 'I think my life is pleasanter than your Miss Morgan's.'

'Yes; but Miss Morgan is so uninteresting, and not young.'

'She is interesting to herself, I suppose; and I am not at all sure that everything gets easier as one gets older.'

'No,' said Rosamond, reflectively; 'one wonders what such people do, without any prospect. To be sure, there is religion as a support. But,' she added, dimpling, 'it is very different with you, Mary. You may have an offer.'

'Has any one told you he means to make me one?'

'Of course not. I mean, there is a gentleman who may fall in love with you, seeing you almost every day.'

A certain change in Mary's face was chiefly determined by the resolve not to show any change.

'Does that always make people fall in love?' she answered, carelessly; 'it seems to me quite as often a reason for detesting each other.'

'Not when they are interesting and agreeable. I hear that Mr Lydgate is both.'

'Oh, Mr Lydgate!' said Mary, with an unmistakable lapse into indifference. 'You want to know something about him,' she added, not choosing to indulge Rosamond's indirectness.

'Merely, how you like him.'

'There is no question of liking at present. My liking always wants some little kindness to kindle it. I am not magnanimous enough to like people who speak to me without seeming to see me.'

'Is he so haughty?' said Rosamond, with heightened satisfaction. 'You know that he is of good family?'

'No; he did not give that as a reason.'

'Mary! you are the oddest girl. But what sort of looking man is he? Describe him to me.'

'How can one describe a man? I can give you an inventory: heavy eyebrows, dark eyes, a straight nose, thick dark hair, large solid white hands – and – let me see – oh, an exquisite cambric pocket handkerchief. But you will see him. You know this is about the time of his visits.'

Rosamond blushed a little, but said, meditatively, 'I rather like a haughty manner. I cannot endure a rattling young man.'

'I did not tell you that Mr Lydgate was haughty; but *il y en a pour tous les goûts*, as little Mamselle used to say, and if any girl can choose the particular sort of conceit she would like, I should think it is you, Rosy.'

'Haughtiness is not conceit; I call Fred conceited.'

'I wish no one said any worse of him. He should be more careful. Mrs Waule has been telling uncle that Fred is very unsteady.' Mary spoke from a girlish impulse which got the better of her judgment. There was a vague uneasiness associated with the word 'unsteady' which she hoped Rosamond might say something to dissipate. But she purposely abstained from mentioning Mrs Waule's more special insinuation.

'Oh, Fred is horrid!' said Rosamond. She would not have allowed herself so unsuitable a word to any one but Mary.

'What do you mean by horrid?'

'He is so idle, and makes papa so angry, and says he will not take orders.'

'I think Fred is quite right.'

'How can you say he is quite right, Mary? I thought you had more sense of religion.'

'He is not fit to be a clergyman.'

'But he ought to be fit.'

'Well, then, he is not what he ought to be. I know some other people who are in the same case.'

'But no one approves of them. I should not like to marry a clergyman; but there must be clergymen.'

'It does not follow that Fred must be one.'

'But when papa has been at the expense of educating him for it! And only suppose, if he should have no fortune left him?'

'I can suppose that very well,' said Mary, dryly.

'Then I wonder you can defend Fred,' said Rosamond, inclined to push this point.

'I don't defend him,' said Mary, laughing; 'I would defend any parish from having him for a clergyman.'

'But of course if he were a clergyman, he must be different.'

'Yes, he would be a great hypocrite; and he is not that yet.'

'It is of no use saying anything to you, Mary. You always take Fred's part.'

'Why should I not take his part?' said Mary, lighting up. 'He would take mine. He is the only person who takes the least trouble to oblige me.'

'You make me feel very uncomfortable, Mary,' said Rosamond, with her gravest mildness; 'I would not tell mamma for the world.'

'What would you not tell her?' said Mary, angrily.

'Pray do not go into a rage, Mary,' said Rosamond, mildly as ever.

'If your mamma is afraid that Fred will make me an offer, tell her that I would not marry him if he asked me. But he is not going to do so, that I am aware. He certainly never has asked me.'

'Mary, you are always so violent.'

'And you are always so exasperating.'

'I? What can you blame me for?'

'Oh, blameless people are always the most exasperating. There is the bell – I think we must go down.'

'I did not mean to quarrel,' said Rosamond, putting on her hat.

'Quarrel? Nonsense; we have not quarrelled. If one is not to get into a rage sometimes, what is the good of being friends?'

'Am I to repeat what you have said?'

'Just as you please. I never say what I am afraid of having repeated. But let us go down.'

Mr Lydgate was rather late this morning, but the visitors stayed long enough to see him; for Mr Featherstone asked Rosamond to sing to him, and she herself was so kind as to propose a second favourite song of his – 'Flow on, thou shining river' – after she had sung 'Home, sweet home' (which she detested). This hard-headed old Overreach approved of the sentimental song, as the suitable garnish for girls, and also as fundamentally fine, sentiment being the right thing for a song.

Mr Featherstone was still applauding the last performance, and assuring Missy that her voice was as clear as a blackbird's, when Mr Lydgate's horse passed the window.

His dull expectation of the usual disagreeable routine with an aged patient – who can hardly believe that medicine would not 'set him up' if the doctor were only clever enough – added to his general disbelief in Middlemarch charms, made a doubly effective background to this vision of Rosamond, whom old Featherstone made haste ostentatiously to introduce as his niece, though he had never thought it worth while to speak of Mary Garth in that light. Nothing escaped Lydgate in Rosamond's graceful behaviour: how delicately she waived the notice which the old man's want of taste had thrust upon her by a quiet gravity, not showing her dimples on the wrong occasion, but showing them afterwards in speaking to Mary, to whom she addressed herself with so much good-natured interest, that Lydgate, after quickly examining Mary more fully than he had done before, saw an adorable kindness in Rosamond's eyes. But Mary from some cause looked rather out of temper.

'Miss Rosy has been singing me a song – you've nothing to say against that, eh, doctor?' said Mr Featherstone. 'I like it better than your physic.'

'That has made me forget how the time was going,' said Rosamond, rising to reach her hat, which she had laid aside before singing, so that her flower-like head on its white stem was seen in perfection above her riding-habit. 'Fred, we must really go.'

'Very good,' said Fred, who had his own reasons for not being in the best spirits, and wanted to get away.

'Miss Vincy is a musician?' said Lydgate, following her with his eyes. (Every nerve and muscle in Rosamond was adjusted to the consciousness that she was being looked at. She was by nature an actress of parts that entered into her *physique*: she even acted her own character, and so well, that she did not know it to be precisely her own.)

'The best in Middlemarch, I'll be bound,' said Mr Featherstone, 'let the next be who she will. Eh, Fred? Speak up for your sister.'

'I'm afraid I'm out of court, sir. My evidence would be good for nothing.'

'Middlemarch has not a very high standard, uncle,' said Rosamond, with a pretty lightness, going towards her whip, which lay at a distance. Lydgate was quick in anticipating her. He reached the whip before she did, and turned to present it to her. She bowed and looked at him: he of course was looking at her, and their eyes met with that peculiar meeting which is never arrived at by effort, but seems like a sudden divine clearance of haze. I think Lydgate turned a little paler than usual, but Rosamond blushed deeply and felt a certain astonishment. After that, she was really anxious to go, and did not know what sort of stupidity her uncle was talking of when she went to shake hands with him.

Yet this result, which she took to be a mutual impression, called falling in love, was just what Rosamond had contemplated beforehand. Ever since that important new arrival in Middlemarch she had woven a little future, of which something like this scene was the necessary beginning. Strangers, whether wrecked and clinging to a raft, or duly escorted and accompanied by portmanteaus, have always had a circumstantial fascination for the virgin mind, against which native merit has urged itself in vain. And a stranger was absolutely necessary to Rosamond's social romance, which had always turned on a lover and bridegroom who was not a Middlemarcher, and who had no connections at all like her own: of late, indeed, the construction seemed to demand that he should somehow be related to a baronet. Now that she and the stranger had met, reality proved much more moving than anticipation, and Rosamond could not doubt that this was the great epoch of her life. She judged of her own symptoms as those of awakening love, and she held it still more natural that Mr Lydgate should have fallen in love at first sight of her. These things happened so often at balls, and why not by the morning light, when the complexion showed all the better for it? Rosamond, though no older than Mary, was rather used to being fallen in love with; but she, for her part, had remained indifferent and fastidiously critical towards both fresh sprig and faded bachelor. And here was Mr Lydgate suddenly corresponding to her ideal, being altogether foreign to Middlemarch, carrying a certain air of distinction congruous with good family, and possessing connections which offered vistas of that middle-class heaven, rank; a man of talent, also, whom it would be especially delightful to enslave: in fact, a man who had touched her nature quite newly, and brought a vivid interest into her life which was better than any fancied 'might-be' such as she was in the habit of opposing to the actual.

Thus, in riding home, both the brother and the sister were preoccupied and inclined to be silent. Rosamond, whose basis for her structure had the usual airy slightness, was of remarkably detailed and realistic imagination when the foundation had been once presupposed; and before they had ridden a mile she was far on in the costume and introductions of her wedded life, having determined on her house in Middlemarch, and foreseen the visits she would pay to her husband's high-bred relatives at a distance, whose finished manners she could appropriate as thoroughly as she had done her school accomplishments, preparing herself thus for vaguer elevations which might ultimately come. There was nothing financial, still less sordid, in her previsions: she cared about what were considered refinements, and not about the money that was to pay for them.

Fred's mind, on the other hand, was busy with an anxiety which even his ready hopefulness could not immediately quell. He saw no way of eluding Featherstone's stupid demand without incurring consequences which he liked less even than the task of fulfilling it. His father was already out of humour with him, and would be still more so if he were the occasion of any additional coolness between his own family and the Bulstrodes. Then, he himself hated having to go and speak to his uncle Bulstrode, and perhaps after drinking wine he had said many foolish things about Featherstone's property, and these had been magnified by report. Fred felt that he made a wretched figure as a fellow who bragged about expectations from a queer old miser like Featherstone, and went to beg for certificates at his bidding. But – those expectations! He really had them, and he saw no agreeable alternative if he gave them up; besides, he had lately made a debt which galled him extremely, and old Featherstone had almost bargained to pay it off. The whole affair was miserably small: his debts were small, even his expectations were not anything so very magnificent. Fred had known men to whom he would have been ashamed of confessing the smallness of his scrapes. Such ruminations naturally produced a streak of misanthropic bitterness. To be born the son of a Middlemarch manufacturer, and inevitable heir to nothing in particular, while such men as Mainwaring and Vyan – certainly life was a poor business, when a spirited young fellow, with a good appetite for the best of everything, had so poor an outlook.

It had not occurred to Fred that the introduction of Bulstrode's name in the matter was a fiction of old Featherstone's; nor could this have made any difference to his position. He saw plainly enough that the old man wanted to exercise his power by tormenting him a little, and also probably to get some satisfaction out of seeing him on unpleasant terms with Bulstrode. Fred fancied that he saw to the bottom of his uncle Featherstone's soul, though in reality half what he saw there was no more than the reflex of his own inclinations. The difficult task of knowing another soul is not for young gentlemen whose consciousness is chiefly made up of their own wishes.

Fred's main point of debate with himself was, whether he should tell his father, or try to get through the affair without his father's knowledge. It was probably Mrs Waule who had been talking about him; and if Mary Garth had repeated Mrs Waule's report to Rosamond, it would be sure to reach his father, who would as surely question him about it. He said to Rosamond, as they slackened their pace –

'Rosy, did Mary tell you that Mrs Waule had said anything about me?'

'Yes, indeed, she did.'

'What?'

'That you were very unsteady.'

'Was that all?'

'I should think that was enough, Fred.'

'You are sure she said no more?'

'Mary mentioned nothing else. But really, Fred, I think you ought to be ashamed.'

'Oh, fudge! don't lecture me. What did Mary say about it?'

'I am not obliged to tell you. You care so very much what Mary says, and you are too rude to allow me to speak.'

'Of course I care what Mary says. She is the best girl I know.'

'I should never have thought she was a girl to fall in love with.'

'How do you know what men would fall in love with? Girls never know.'

'At least, Fred, let me advise *you* not to fall in love with her, for she says she would not marry you if you asked her.'

'She might have waited till I did ask her.'

'I knew it would nettle you, Fred.'

'Not at all. She would not have said so if you had not provoked her.'

Before reaching home, Fred concluded that he would tell the whole affair as simply as possible to his father, who might perhaps take on himself the unpleasant business of speaking to Bulstrode.

BOOK TWO
OLD AND YOUNG

❦ THIRTEEN ❧

> *1st Gent.* How class your man? – as better than the most,
>   Or, seeming better, worse beneath that cloak?
>   As saint or knave, pilgrim or hypocrite?
> *2nd Gent.* Nay, tell me how you class your wealth of books,
>   The drifted relics of all time. As well
>   Sort them at once by size and livery:
>   Vellum, tall copies, and the common calf
>   Will hardly cover more diversity
>   Than all your labels cunningly devised
>   To class your unread authors.

IN CONSEQUENCE OF WHAT HE HAD heard from Fred, Mr Vincy determined to speak with Mr Bulstrode in his private room at the Bank at half-past one, when he was usually free from other callers. But a visitor had come in at one o'clock, and Mr Bulstrode had so much to say to him, that there was little chance of the interview being over in half an hour. The banker's speech was fluent, but it was also copious, and he used up an appreciable amount of time in brief meditative pauses. Do not imagine his sickly aspect to have been of the yellow, black-haired sort: he had a pale blond skin, thin grey-besprinkled brown hair, light-grey eyes, and a large forehead. Loud men called his subdued tone an undertone, and sometimes implied that it was inconsistent with openness; though there seems to be no reason why a loud man should not be given to concealment of anything except his own voice, unless it can be shown that Holy Writ has placed the seat of candour in the lungs. Mr Bulstrode had also a deferential bending attitude in listening, and an apparently fixed attentiveness in his eyes which made those persons who thought themselves worth hearing infer that he was seeking the utmost improvement from their discourse. Others, who expected to make no great figure, disliked this kind of moral lantern turned on them. If you are not proud of your cellar, there is no thrill of satisfaction in seeing your guest hold up his wine-glass to the light and look judicial. Such joys are reserved for conscious merit. Hence Mr Bulstrode's close attention was not agreeable to the publicans and sinners in Middlemarch; it was attributed by some to his being a Pharisee, and by others to his being Evangelical. Less superficial reasoners among them wished to know who his father and grandfather were, observing that five-and-twenty years ago nobody had ever heard of a

Bulstrode in Middlemarch. To his present visitor, Lydgate, the scrutinizing look was a matter of indifference: he simply formed an unfavourable opinion of the banker's constitution, and concluded that he had an eager inward life with little enjoyment of tangible things.

'I shall be exceedingly obliged if you will look in on me here occasionally, Mr Lydgate,' the banker observed, after a brief pause. 'If, as I dare to hope, I have the privilege of finding you a valuable coadjutor in the interesting matter of hospital management, there will be many questions which we shall need to discuss in private. As to the new hospital, which is nearly finished, I shall consider what you have said about the advantages of the special destination for fevers. The decision will rest with me, for though Lord Medlicote has given the land and timber for the building, he is not disposed to give his personal attention to the object.'

'There are few things better worth the pains in a provincial town like this,' said Lydgate. 'A fine fever hospital in addition to the old infirmary might be the nucleus of a medical school here, when once we get our medical reforms; and what would do more for medical education than the spread of such schools over the country? A born provincial man who has a grain of public spirit as well as a few ideas, should do what he can to resist the rush of everything that is a little better than common towards London. Any valid professional aims may often find a freer, if not a richer field, in the provinces.'

One of Lydgate's gifts was a voice habitually deep and sonorous, yet capable of becoming very low and gentle at the right moment. About his ordinary bearing there was a certain fling, a fearless expectation of success, a confidence in his own powers and integrity much fortified by contempt for petty obstacles or seductions of which he had had no experience. But this proud openness was made lovable by an expression of unaffected good-will. Mr Bulstrode perhaps liked him the better for the difference between them in pitch and manners; he certainly liked him the better, as Rosamond did, for being a stranger in Middlemarch. One can begin so many things with a new person! – even begin to be a better man.

'I shall rejoice to furnish your zeal with fuller opportunities,' Mr Bulstrode answered; 'I mean, by confiding to you the superintendence of my new hospital, should a maturer knowledge favour that issue, for I am determined that so great an object shall not be shackled by our two physicians. Indeed, I am encouraged to consider your advent to this town as a gracious indication that a more manifest blessing is now to be awarded to my efforts, which have hitherto been much withstood. With regard to the old infirmary, we have gained the initial point – I mean your election. And now I hope you will not shrink from incurring a certain amount of jealousy and dislike from your professional brethren by presenting yourself as a reformer.'

'I will not profess bravery,' said Lydgate, smiling, 'but I acknowledge a good deal of pleasure in fighting, and I should not care for my profession, if I did not believe that better methods were to be found and enforced there as well as everywhere else.'

'The standard of that profession is low in Middlemarch, my dear sir,' said the banker. 'I mean in knowledge and skill; not in social status, for our medical men are most of them connected with respectable towns-people here. My own imperfect health has induced me to give some attention to those palliative resources which the divine mercy has placed within our reach. I have consulted eminent men in the metropolis, and I am painfully aware of the backwardness under which medical treatment labours in our provincial districts.'

'Yes; – with our present medical rules and education, one must be satisfied now and then to meet with a fair practitioner. As to all the higher questions which determine the starting-point of a diagnosis – as to the philosophy of medical evidence – any glimmering of these can only come from a scientific culture of which country practitioners have usually no more notion than the man in the moon.'

Mr Bulstrode, bending and looking intently, found the form which Lydgate had given to his agreement not quite suited to his comprehension. Under such circumstances a judicious man changes the topic and enters on ground where his own gifts may be more useful.

'I am aware,' he said, 'that the peculiar bias of medical ability is towards material means. Nevertheless, Mr Lydgate, I hope we shall not vary in sentiment as to a measure in which you are not likely to be actively concerned, but in which your sympathetic concurrence may be an aid to me. You recognize, I hope, the existence of spiritual interests in your patients?'

'Certainly I do. But those words are apt to cover different meanings to different minds.'

'Precisely. And on such subjects wrong teaching is as fatal as no teaching. Now a point which I have much at heart to secure is a new regulation as to clerical attendance at the old infirmary. The building stands in Mr Farebrother's parish. You know Mr Farebrother?'

'I have seen him. He gave me his vote. I must call to thank him. He seems a very bright pleasant little fellow. And I understand he is a naturalist.'

'Mr Farebrother, my dear sir, is a man deeply painful to contemplate. I suppose there is not a clergyman in this country who has greater talents.' Mr Bulstrode paused and looked meditative.

'I have not yet been pained by finding any excessive talent in Middle-march,' said Lydgate, bluntly.

'What I desire,' Mr Bulstrode continued, looking still more serious, 'is that Mr Farebrother's attendance at the hospital should be superseded by the appointment of a chaplain – of Mr Tyke, in fact – and that no other spiritual aid should be called in.'

'As a medical man I could have no opinion on such a point unless I knew Mr Tyke, and even then I should require to know the cases in which he was applied.' Lydgate smiled, but he was bent on being circumspect.

'Of course you cannot enter fully into the merits of this measure at present. But' – here Mr Bulstrode began to speak with a more chiselled emphasis – 'the subject is likely to be referred to the medical board of the infirmary, and what I trust I may ask of you is, that in virtue of the co-operation between us which I now look forward to, you will not, so far as you are concerned, be influenced by my opponents in this matter.'

'I hope I shall have nothing to do with clerical disputes,' said Lydgate. 'The path I have chosen is to work well in my own profession.'

'My reponsibility, Mr Lydgate, is of a broader kind. With me, indeed, this question is one of sacred accountableness; whereas with my opponents, I have good reason to say that it is an occasion for gratifying a spirit of worldly opposition. But I shall not therefore drop one iota of my convictions, or cease to identify myself with that truth which an evil generation hates. I have devoted myself to this object of hospital improvement, but I will boldly confess to you, Mr Lydgate, that I should have no interest in hospitals if I believed that nothing more was concerned therein than the cure of mortal diseases. I have another ground of action, and in the face of persecution I will not conceal it.'

Mr Bulstrode's voice had become a loud and agitated whisper as he said the last words.

'There we certainly differ,' said Lydgate. But he was not sorry that the door was now opened, and Mr Vincy was announced. That florid sociable personage was become more interesting to him since he had seen Rosamond. Not that, like her, he had been weaving any future in which their lots were united; but a man naturally remembers a charming girl with pleasure, and is willing to dine where he may see her again. Before he took leave, Mr Vincy had given that invitation which he had been 'in no hurry about,' for Rosamond at breakfast had mentioned that she thought her uncle Featherstone had taken the new doctor into great favour.

Mr Bulstrode, alone with his brother-in-law, poured himself out a glass of water, and opened a sandwich-box.

'I cannot persuade you to adopt my regimen, Vincy?'

'No, no; I've no opinion of that system. Life wants padding,' said Mr Vincy, unable to omit his portable theory. 'However,' he went on, accenting the word, as if to dismiss all irrelevance, 'what I came here to talk about was a little affair of my young scapegrace, Fred's.'

'That is a subject on which you and I are likely to take quite as different views as on diet, Vincy.'

'I hope not this time.' (Mr Vincy was resolved to be good humoured.) 'The fact is, it's about a whim of old Featherstone's. Somebody has been cooking up a story out of spite, and telling it to the old man, to try to set him against Fred. He's very fond of Fred, and is likely to do something handsome for him; indeed, he has as good as told Fred that he means to leave him his land, and that makes other people jealous.'

'Vincy, I must repeat, that you will not get any concurrence from me as to the course you have pursued with your eldest son. It was entirely from worldly vanity that you destined him for the Church: with a family of three sons and four daughters, you were not warranted in devoting money to an expensive education which has succeeded in nothing but in giving him extravagant idle habits. You are now reaping the consequences.'

To point out other people's errors was a duty that Mr Bulstrode rarely shrank from, but Mr Vincy was not equally prepared to be patient. When a man has the immediate prospect of being mayor, and is ready, in the interests of commerce, to take up a firm attitude on politics generally, he has naturally a sense of his importance to the framework of things which seems to throw questions of private conduct into the background. And this particular reproof irritated him more than any other. It was eminently superfluous to him to be told that he was reaping the consequences. But he felt his neck under Bulstrode's yoke; and though he usually enjoyed kicking, he was anxious to refrain from that relief.

'As to that, Bulstrode, it's no use going back. I'm not one of your pattern men, and I don't pretend to be. I couldn't foresee everything in the trade; there wasn't a finer business in Middlemarch than ours, and the lad was clever. My poor brother was in the Church, and would have done well – had got preferment already, but that stomach fever took him off: else he might have been a dean by this time. I think I was justified in what I tried to do for Fred. If you come to religion, it seems to me a man shouldn't want to carve out his meat to an ounce beforehand: – one must trust a little to Providence and be generous. It's a good British feeling to try and raise your family a little: in my opinion, it's a father's duty to give his sons a fine chance.'

'I don't wish to act otherwise than as your best friend, Vincy, when I say that what you have been uttering just now is one mass of worldliness and inconsistent folly.'

'Very well,' said Mr Vincy, kicking in spite of resolutions, 'I never profess to be anything but worldly; and, what's more, I don't see anybody else who is not worldly. I suppose you don't conduct business on what you call unworldly principles. The only difference I see is that one worldliness is a little bit honester than another.'

'This kind of discussion is unfruitful, Vincy,' said Mr Bulstrode, who, finishing his sandwich, had thrown himself back in his chair, and shaded his eyes as if weary. 'You had some more particular business.'

'Yes, yes. The long and short of it is, somebody has told old Featherstone, giving you as the authority, that Fred has been borrowing or trying to borrow money on the prospect of his land. Of course you never said any such nonsense. But the old fellow will insist on it that Fred should bring him a denial in your handwriting; that is, just a bit of a note saying you don't believe a word of such stuff, either of his having borrowed or tried to borrow in such a fool's way. I suppose you can have no objection to do that.'

'Pardon me. I have an objection. I am by no means sure that your son, in his recklessness and ignorance – I will use no severer word – has not tried to raise money by holding out his future prospects, or even that some one may not have been foolish enough to supply him on so vague a presumption: there is plenty of such lax money-lending as of other folly in the world.'

'But Fred gives me his honour that he has never borrowed money on the pretence of any understanding about his uncle's land. He is not a liar. I don't want to make him better than he is. I have blown him up well – nobody can say I wink at what he does. But he is not a liar. And I should have thought – but I may be wrong – that there was no religion to hinder a man from believing the best of a young fellow, when you don't know worse. It seems to me it would be a poor sort of religion to put a spoke in his wheel by refusing to say you don't believe such harm of him as you've got no good reason to believe.'

'I am not at all sure that I should be befriending your son by smoothing his way to the future possession of Featherstone's property. I cannot regard wealth as a blessing to those who use it simply as a harvest for this world. You do not like to hear these things, Vincy, but on this occasion I feel called upon to tell you that I have no motive for furthering such a disposition of property as that which you refer to. I do not shrink from saying that it will not tend to your son's eternal welfare or to the glory of God. Why then should you expect me to pen this kind of affidavit, which has no object but to keep up a foolish partiality and secure a foolish bequest?'

'If you mean to hinder everybody from having money but saints and evangelists, you must give up some profitable partnerships, that's all I can say,' Mr Vincy burst out very bluntly. 'It may be for the glory of God, but it is not for the glory of the Middlemarch trade, that Plymdale's house uses those blue and green dyes it gets from the Brassing manufactory; they rot the silk, that's all I know about it. Perhaps if other people knew so much of the profit went to the glory of God, they might like it better. But I don't mind so much about that – I could get up a pretty row, if I chose.'

Mr Bulstrode paused a little before he answered. 'You pain me very much by speaking in this way, Vincy. I do not expect you to understand my grounds of action – it is not an easy thing even to thread a path for principles in the intricacies of the world – still less to make the thread clear for the careless and the scoffing. You must remember, if you please, that I stretch my tolerance towards you as my wife's brother, and that it little becomes you to complain of me as withholding material help towards the worldly position of your family. I must remind you that it is not your own prudence or judgment that has enabled you to keep your place in the trade.'

'Very likely not; but you have been no loser by my trade yet,' said Mr Vincy, thoroughly nettled (a result which was seldom much retarded by previous resolutions). 'And when you married Harriet, I don't see how you could expect that our families should not hang by the same nail. If you've changed your mind, and want my family to come down in the world, you'd better say so. I've never changed: I'm a plain Churchman now, just as I used to be before doctrines came up. I take the world as I find it, in trade and everything else. I'm contented to be no worse than my neighbours. But if you want us to come down in the world, say so. I shall know better what to do then.'

'You talk unreasonably. Shall you come down in the world for want of this letter about your son?'

'Well, whether or not, I consider it very unhandsome of you to refuse it. Such doings may be lined with religion, but outside they have a nasty, dog-in-the-manger look. You might as well slander Fred: it comes pretty near to it when you refuse to say you didn't set a slander going. It's this sort of thing – this tyrannical spirit, wanting to play bishop and banker everywhere – it's this sort of thing makes a man's name stink.'

'Vincy, if you insist on quarrelling with me, it will be exceedingly painful to Harriet as well as myself,' said Mr Bulstrode, with a trifle more eagerness and paleness than usual.

'I don't want to quarrel. It's for my interest – and perhaps for yours too – that we should be friends. I bear you no grudge; I think no worse of you than I do of other people. A man who half starves himself, and goes the length of family prayers, and so on, that you do, believes in his religion whatever it may be: you could turn over your capital just as fast with cursing and swearing: – plenty of fellows do. You like to be master, there's no denying that; you must be first chop in heaven, else you won't like it much. But you're my sister's husband, and we ought to stick together; and if I know Harriet, she'll consider it your fault if we quarrel because you strain at a gnat in this way, and refuse to do Fred a good turn. And I don't mean to say I shall bear it well. I consider it unhandsome.'

Mr Vincy rose, began to button his greatcoat, and looked steadily at his brother-in-law, meaning to imply a demand for a decisive answer.

This was not the first time that Mr Bulstrode had begun by admonishing Mr Vincy, and had ended by seeing a very unsatisfactory reflection of himself in the coarse unflattering mirror which that manufacturer's mind presented to the subtler lights and shadows of his fellow-men; and perhaps his experience ought to have warned him how the scene would end. But a full-fed fountain will be generous with its waters even in the rain, when they are worse than useless; and a fine fount of admonition is apt to be equally irrepressible.

It was not in Mr Bulstrode's nature to comply directly in consequence of uncomfortable suggestions. Before changing his course, he always needed to shape his motives and bring them into accordance with his habitual standard. He said, at last –

'I will reflect a little, Vincy. I will mention the subject to Harriet. I shall probably send you a letter.'

'Very well. As soon as you can, please. I hope it will all be settled before I see you to-morrow.'

❧ FOURTEEN ❧

Follows here the strict receipt
For that sauce to dainty meat,
Named Idleness, which many eat
By preference, and call it sweet:
First watch for morsels, like a hound,
Mix well with buffets, stir them round
With good thick oil of flatteries,
And froth with mean self-lauding lies.
Serve warm: the vessels you must choose
To keep it in are dead men's shoes.

MR BULSTRODE'S CONSULTATION OF HARRIET seemed o have had the effect desired by Mr Vincy, for early the next morning a letter came which Fred could carry to Mr Featherstone as the required testimony.

The old gentleman was staying in bed on account of the cold weather, and as Mary Garth was not to be seen in the sitting-room Fred went upstairs immediately and presented the letter to his uncle, who, propped up comfortably on a bed-rest, was not less able than usual to enjoy his consciousness of wisdom in distrusting and frustrating mankind. He put on his spectacles to read the letter, pursing up his lips and drawing down their corners.

'*Under the circumstances I will not decline to state my conviction* – tchah! what fine words the fellow puts! He's as fine as an auctioneer – *that your son Frederic has not obtained any advance of money on bequests promised by Mr Featherstone* – promised? who said I had ever promised? I promise nothing – I shall make codicils as long as I like – *and that considering the nature of such a proceeding, it is unreasonable to presume that a young man of sense and character would attempt it* – ah, but the gentleman doesn't say you *are* a young man of sense and character, mark you that, sir! – *as to my own concern with any report of such a nature, I distinctly affirm that I never made any statement to the effect that your son had borrowed money on any property that might accrue to him on Mr Featherstone's demise* – bless my heart! "property – accrue – demise!" Lawyer Standish is nothing to him. He couldn't speak finer if he wanted to borrow. Well,' Mr Featherstone here looked over his spectacles at Fred, while he handed back the letter to him with a contemptuous gesture, 'you don't suppose I believe a thing because Bulstrode writes it out fine, eh?' .

Fred coloured. 'You wished to have the letter, sir. I should think it very likely that Mr Bulstrode's denial is as good as the authority which told you what he denies.'

'Every bit. I never said I believed either one or the other. And now what d'you expect?' said Mr Featherstone, curtly, keeping on his spectacles, but withdrawing his hands under his wraps.

'I expect nothing, sir.' Fred with difficulty restrained himself from venting his irritation. 'I came to bring you the letter. If you like, I will bid you good morning.'

'Not yet, not yet. Ring the bell; I want Missy to come.'

It was a servant who came in answer to the bell.

'Tell Missy to come!' said Mr Featherstone, impatiently. 'What business had she to go away?' He spoke in the same tone when Mary came.

'Why couldn't you sit still here till I told you to go? I want my waistcoat now. I told you always to put it on the bed.'

Mary's eyes looked rather red, as if she had been crying. It was clear that Mr Featherstone was in one of his most snappish humours this morning, and though Fred had now the prospect of receiving the much-needed present of money, he would have preferred being free to turn round on the old tyrant and tell him that Mary Garth was too good to be at his beck. Though Fred had risen as she entered the room, she had barely noticed him, and looked as if her nerves were quivering with the expectation that something would be thrown at her. But she never had anything worse than words to dread. When she went to reach the waistcoat from a peg, Fred went up to her and said, 'Allow me.'

'Let it alone! You bring it, Missy, and lay it down here,' said Mr Featherstone. 'Now you go away again till I call you,' he added, when the waistcoat was laid down by him. It was usual with him to season his pleasure in showing favour to one person by being especially disagreeable to another, and Mary was always at hand to furnish the condiment. When his own relatives came she was treated better. Slowly he took out a bunch of keys from the waistcoat-pocket, and slowly he drew forth a tin box which was under the bed-clothes.

'You expect I'm going to give you a little fortune, eh?' he said, looking above his spectacles and pausing in the act of opening the lid.

'Not at all, sir. You were good enough to speak of making me a present the other day, else, of course, I should not have thought of the matter.' But Fred was of a hopeful disposition, and a vision had presented itself of a sum just large enough to deliver him from a certain anxiety. When Fred got into debt, it always seemed to him highly probable that something or other – he did not necessarily conceive what – would come to pass enabling him to pay in due time. And now that the providential occurrence was apparently close at hand, it would have been sheer absurdity to think that the supply would be short of the need: as absurd as a faith that believed in half a miracle for want of strength to believe in a whole one.

The deep-veined hands fingered many bank-notes one after the other, laying them down flat again, while Fred leaned back in his chair, scorning to look eager. He held himself to be a gentleman at heart, and did not like courting an old fellow for his money. At last, Mr Featherstone eyed him again over his spectacles and presented him with a little sheaf of notes; Fred could see distinctly that there were but five, as the less significant edges gaped towards him. But then, each might mean fifty pounds. He took them, saying –

'I am very much obliged to you, sir,' and was going to roll them up without seeming to think of their value. But this did not suit Mr Featherstone, who was eyeing him intently.

'Come, don't you think it worth your while to count 'em? You take money like a lord; I suppose you lose it like one.'

'I thought I was not to look a gift-horse in the mouth, sir. But I shall be very happy to count them.'

Fred was not so happy, however, after he had counted them. For they actually presented the absurdity of being less than his hopefulness had decided that they must be. What can the fitness of things mean, if not their fitness to a man's expectations? Failing this, absurdity and atheism gape behind him. The collapse for Fred was severe when he found that he held no more than five twenties, and his share in the higher education of this country did not seem to help him. Nevertheless he said, with rapid changes in his fair complexion –

'It is very handsome of you, sir.'

'I should think it is,' said Mr Featherstone, locking his box and replacing it, then taking off his spectacles deliberately, and at length, as if his inward meditation had more deeply convinced him, repeating, 'I should think it *is* handsome.'

'I assure you, sir, I am very grateful,' said Fred, who had had time to recover his cheerful air.

'So you ought to be. You want to cut a figure in the world, and I reckon Peter Featherstone is the only one you've got to trust to.' Here the old man's eyes gleamed with a curiously-mingled satisfaction in the consciousness that this smart young fellow relied upon him, and that the smart young fellow was rather a fool for doing so.

'Yes, indeed; I was not born to very splendid chances. Few men have been more cramped than I have been,' said Fred, with some sense of surprise at his own virtue, considering how hardly he was dealt with. 'It really seems a little too bad to have to ride a broken-winded hunter, and see men, who are not half such good judges as yourself, able to throw away any amount of money on buying bad bargains.'

'Well, you can buy yourself a fine hunter now. Eighty pounds is enough for that, I reckon – and you'll have twenty pound over to get yourself out of any little scrape,' said Mr Featherstone, chuckling slightly.

'You are very good, sir,' said Fred, with a fine sense of contrast between the words and his feeling.

'Ay, rather a better uncle than your fine uncle Bulstrode. You won't get much out of his spekilations, I think. He's got a pretty strong string round your father's leg, by what I hear, eh?'

'My father never tells me anything about his affairs, sir.'

'Well, he shows some sense there. But other people find 'em out without his telling. *He'll* never have much to leave you: he'll most-like die without a will – he's the sort of man to do it – let 'em make him mayor of Middlemarch as much as they like. But you won't get much by his dying without a will, though you *are* the eldest son.'

Fred thought that Mr Featherstone had never been so disagreeable before. True, he had never before given him quite so much money at once.

'Shall I destroy this letter of Mr Bulstrode's, sir?' said Fred, rising with the letter as if he would put it in the fire.

'Ay, ay, I don't want it. It's worth no money to me.'

Fred carried the letter to the fire, and thrust the poker through it with much zest. He longed to get out of the room, but he was a little ashamed before his inner self, as well as before his uncle, to run away immediately after pocketing the money. Presently, the farm bailiff came up to give his master a report, and Fred, to his unspeakable relief, was dismissed with the injunction to come again soon.

He had longed not only to be set free from his uncle, but also to find Mary Garth. She was now in her usual place by the fire, with sewing in her hands and a book open on the little table by her side. Her eyelids had lost some of their redness now, and she had her usual air of self-command.

'Am I wanted up-stairs?' she said, half rising as Fred entered.

'No; I am only dismissed, because Simmons is gone up.'

Mary sat down again, and resumed her work. She was certainly treating him with more indifference than usual: she did not know how affectionately indignant he had felt on her behalf up-stairs.

'May I stay here a little, Mary, or shall I bore you?'

'Pray sit down,' said Mary; 'you will not be so heavy a bore as Mr John Waule, who was here yesterday, and he sat down without asking my leave.'

'Poor fellow! I think he is in love with you.'

'I am not aware of it. And to me it is one of the most odious things in a girl's life, that there must always be some supposition of falling in love coming between her and any man who is kind to her, and to whom she is grateful. I should have thought that I, at least, might have been safe from all that. I have no ground for the nonsensical vanity of fancying everybody who comes near me is in love with me.'

Mary did not mean to betray a feeling, but in spite of herself she ended in a tremulous tone of vexation.

'Confound John Waule! I did not mean to make you angry. I didn't know you had any reason for being grateful to him. I forgot what a great service you think it if any one snuffs a candle for you.' Fred also had his pride, and was not going to show that he knew what had called forth this outburst of Mary's.

'Oh, I am not angry, except with the ways of the world. I do like to be spoken to as if I had common-sense. I really often feel as if I could understand a little more than I ever hear even from young gentlemen who have been to college.' Mary had recovered, and she spoke with a suppressed rippling undercurrent of laughter pleasant to hear.

'I don't care how merry you are at my expense this morning,' said Fred. 'I thought you looked so sad when you came up-stairs. It is a shame you should stay here to be bullied in that way.'

'Oh, I have an easy life – by comparison. I have tried being a teacher, but I am not fit for that: my mind is too fond of wandering on its own way. I think any hardship is better than pretending to do what one is paid for, and never really doing it. Everything here I can do as well as any one else could; perhaps better than some – Rosy, for example. Though she is just the sort of beautiful creature that is imprisoned with ogres in fairy tales.'

'*Rosy!*' cried Fred, in a tone of profound brotherly scepticism.

'Come, Fred!' said Mary, emphatically; 'you have no right to be so critical.'

'Do you mean anything particular – just now?'

'No, I mean something general – always.'

'Oh, that I am idle and extravagant. Well, I am not fit to be a poor man. I should not have made a bad fellow if I had been rich.'

'You would have done your duty in that state of life to which it has not pleased God to call you,' said Mary, laughing.

'Well, I couldn't do my duty as a clergyman, any more than you could do yours as a governess. You ought to have a little fellow-feeling there, Mary.'

'I never said you ought to be a clergyman. There are other sorts of work. It seems to me very miserable not to resolve on some course and act accordingly.'

'So I could, if – ' Fred broke off, and stood up, leaning against the mantelpiece.

'If you were sure you should not have a fortune?'

'I did not say that. You want to quarrel with me. It is too bad of you to be guided by what other people say about me.'

'How can I want to quarrel with you! I should be quarrelling with all my new books,' said Mary, lifting the volume on the table. 'However naughty you may be to other people, you are good to me.'

'Because I like you better than any one else. But I know you despise me.'

'Yes, I do – a little,' said Mary, nodding, with a smile.

'You would admire a stupendous fellow, who would have wise opinions about everything.'

'Yes, I should.' Mary was sewing swiftly, and seemed provokingly mistress of the situation. When a conversation has taken a wrong turn for us, we only get farther and farther into the swamp of awkwardness. This was what Fred Vincy felt.

'I suppose a women is never in love with any one she has always known – ever since she can remember; as a man often is. It is always some new fellow who strikes a girl.'

'Let me see,' said Mary, the corners of her mouth curling archly; 'I must go back on my experience. There is Juliet – she seems an example of what you say. But then Ophelia had probably known Hamlet a long while; and Brenda Troil – she had known Mordaunt Merton ever since they were children; but then he seems to have been an estimable young man; and Minna was still more deeply in love with Cleveland, who was a stranger. Waverley was new to Flora MacIvor; but then she did not fall in love with him. And there are Olivia and Sophia Primrose, and Corinne – they may be said to have fallen in love with new men. Altogether, my experience is rather mixed.'

Mary looked up with some roguishness at Fred, and that look of hers was very dear to him, though the eyes were nothing more than clear windows where observation sate laughingly. He was certainly an affectionate fellow, and as he had grown from boy to man, he had grown in love with his old playmate, notwithstanding that share in the higher education of the country which had exalted his views of rank and income.

'When a man is not loved, it is no use for him to say that he could be a better fellow – could do anything – I mean, if he were sure of being loved in return.'

'Not of the least use in the world for him to say he *could* be better. Might, could, would – they are contemptible auxiliaries.'

'I don't see how a man is to be good for much unless he has some one woman to love him dearly.'

'I think the goodness should come before he expects that.'

'You know better, Mary. Women don't love their men for their goodness.'

'Perhaps not. But if they love them, they never think them bad.'

'It is hardly fair to say I am bad.'

'I said nothing at all about you.'

'I never shall be good for anything, Mary, if you will not say that you love me – if you will not promise to marry me – I mean, when I am able to marry.'

'If I did love you, I would not marry you: I would certainly not promise ever to marry you.'

'I think that is quite wicked, Mary. If you love me, you ought to promise to marry me.'

'On the contrary, I think it would be wicked in me to marry you even if I did love you.'

'You mean, just as I am, without any means of maintaining a wife. Of course: I am but three-and-twenty.'

'In that last point you will alter. But I am not so sure of any other alteration. My father says an idle man ought not to exist, much less be married.'

'Then I am to blow my brains out?'

'No; on the whole I should think you would do better to pass your examination. I have heard Mr Farebrother say it is disgracefully easy.'

'That is all very fine. Anything is easy to him. Not that cleverness has anything to do with it. I am ten times cleverer than many men who pass.'

'Dear me!' said Mary, unable to repress her sarcasm. 'That accounts for the curates like Mr Crowse. Divide your cleverness by ten, and the quotient – dear me! – is able to take a degree. But that only shows you are ten times more idle than the others.'

'Well, if I did pass, you would not want me to go into the Church?'

'That is not the question – what I want you to do. You have a conscience of your own, I suppose. There! there is Mr Lydgate. I must go and tell my uncle.'

'Mary,' said Fred, seizing her hand as she rose; 'if you will not give me some encouragement, I shall get worse instead of better.'

'I will not give you any encouragement,' said Mary, reddening. 'Your friends would dislike it, and so would mine. My father would think it a disgrace to me if I accepted a man who got into debt, and would not work!'

Fred was stung, and released her hand. She walked to the door, but there she turned and said: 'Fred, you have always been so good, so generous to me. I am not ungrateful. But never speak to me in that way again.'

'Very well,' said Fred, sulkily, taking up his hat and whip. His complexion showed patches of pale pink and dead white. Like many a plucked idle young gentleman, he was thoroughly in love, and with a plain girl, who had no money! But having Mr Featherstone's land in the background, and a persuasion that, let Mary say what she would, she really did care for him, Fred was not utterly in despair.

When he got home, he gave four of the twenties to his mother, asking her to keep them for him. 'I don't want to spend that money, mother. I want it to pay a debt with. So keep it safe away from my fingers.'

'Bless you, my dear' said Mrs Vincy. She doted on her eldest son and her youngest girl (a child of six), whom others thought her two naughtiest children. The mother's eyes are not always deceived in their partiality: she at least can best judge who is the tender, filial-hearted child. And Fred was certainly very fond of his mother. Perhaps it was his fondness for another person also that made him particularly anxious to take some security against his own liability to spend the hundred pounds. For the creditor to whom he owed a hundred and sixty held a firmer security in the shape of a bill signed by Mary's father.

☙ FIFTEEN ❧

Black eyes you have left, you say
Blue eyes fail to draw you;
Yet you seem more rapt to-day,
Than of old we saw you.

Oh I track the fairest fair
Through new haunts of pleasure;
Footprints here and echoes there
Guide me to my treasure:

Lo! She turns – immortal youth
Wrought to mortal stature,
Fresh as starlight's aged truth –
Many-named Nature!

A GREAT HISTORIAN, AS HE INSISTED on calling himself, who had the happiness to be dead a hundred and twenty years ago, and so to take his place among the colossi whose huge legs our living pettiness is observed to walk under, glories in his copious remarks and digressions as the least imitable part of his work, and especially in those initial chapters to the successive books of his history, where he seems to bring his arm-chair to the proscenium and chat with us in all the lusty ease of his fine English. But Fielding lived when the days were longer (for time, like money, is measured by our needs), when summer afternoons were spacious, and the clock ticked slowly in the winter evenings. We belated historians must not linger after his example; and if we did so, it is probable that our chat would be thin and eager, as if delivered from a camp-stool in a parrot-house. I at least have so much to do in unravelling certain human lots, and seeing how they were woven and interwoven, that all the light I can command must be concentrated on this particular web, and not dispersed over that tempting range of relevancies called the universe.

At present I have to make the new settler Lydgate better known to any one interested in him than he could possibly be even to those who had seen the most of him since his arrival in Middlemarch. For surely all must admit that a man may be puffed and belauded, envied, ridiculed, counted upon as a tool and fallen in love with, or at least selected as a future husband, and yet remain virtually unknown – known merely as a cluster of signs for his neighbours' false suppositions. There was a general impression, however, that Lydgate was not altogether a common country doctor, and in Middlemarch at that time such an impression was significant of great things being expected from him. For everybody's family doctor was remarkably clever, and was understood to have immeasurable skill in the management and training of the most skittish or vicious diseases. The evidence of his cleverness was of the higher intuitive order, lying in his lady patients' immovable conviction, and was unassailable by any objection except that their intuitions were opposed by others equally strong; each lady who saw medical truth in Wrench and 'the strengthening treatment' regarding Toller and 'the lowering system' as medical perdition. For the heroic times of copious bleeding and blistering had not yet departed, still less the times of thorough-going theory, when disease in general was called by some bad name, and treated accordingly without shilly-shally – as if, for example, it were to be called insurrection, which must not be fired on with blank-cartridge, but have its blood drawn at once. The strengtheners and the lowerers were all 'clever' men in somebody's opinion, which is really as much as can be said for any living talents. Nobody's imagination had gone so far as to conjecture that Mr Lydgate could know as much as Dr Sprague and Dr Minchin, the two physicians, who alone could offer any hope when danger was extreme, and when the smallest hope was worth a guinea. Still, I repeat, there was a general impression that Lydgate was something rather more uncommon than any general practitioner in Middlemarch. And this was true. He was but seven-and-twenty, an age at which many men are not quite common – at which they are hopeful of achievement, resolute in avoidance, thinking that Mammon shall never put a bit in their mouths and get astride their backs, but rather that Mammon, if they have anything to do with him, shall draw their chariot.

He had been left an orphan when he was fresh from a public school. His father, a military man, had made but little provision for three children, and when the boy Tertius asked to have a medical education, it seemed easier to his guardians to grant his request by apprenticing him to a country practitioner than to make any objections on the score of family dignity. He was one of the rarer lads who early get a decided bent and make up their minds that there is something particular in life which they would like to do for its own sake, and not because their fathers did it. Most of us who turn to any subject we love remember some morning or evening hour when we got on a high stool to reach down an untried volume, or sat with parted lips listening to a new talker, or for very lack of books began to listen to the voices within, as the first traceable beginning of our love. Something of that sort happened to Lydgate. He was a quick fellow, and when hot from play, would toss himself in a corner, and in five minutes be deep in any sort of book that he could lay his hands on: if it were Rasselas or Gulliver, so much the better, but Bailey's Dictionary would do, or the Bible with the Apocrypha in it. Something he must read, when he was not riding the pony, or running and hunting, or listening to the talk of men. All this was true of him at ten years of age; he had then read through *Chrysal, or the Adventures of a Guinea,* which was neither milk for babes, nor any chalky mixture meant to pass for milk, and it had already occurred to him that books were stuff, and that life was stupid. His school studies had not much modified that opinion, for though he 'did' his classics and mathematics, he was not pre-eminent in them. It was said of him, that Lydgate could do anything he liked, but he had certainly not yet liked to do anything remarkable. He was a vigorous animal with a ready understanding, but no spark had yet kindled in him an intellectual passion; knowledge seemed to him a very superficial affair, easily mastered: judging from the conversation of his elders, he had apparently got already more than was necessary for mature life. Probably this was not an exceptional result of expensive teaching at that period of short-waisted coats, and other fashions which have not yet recurred. But, one vacation, a wet day sent him to the small home library to hunt once more for a book which might have some freshness for him: in vain! unless, indeed, he took down a dusty row of volumes with grey-paper backs and dingy labels – the volumes of an old Cyclopaedia which he had never disturbed. It would at least be a novelty to disturb them. They were on the highest shelf, and he stood on a chair to get them down. But he opened the volume which he first took from the shelf: somehow, one is apt to read in a makeshift attitude, just where it might seem inconvenient to do so. The page he opened on was under the heading of Anatomy, and the first passage that drew his eyes was on the valves of the heart. He was not much acquainted with valves of any sort, but he knew that *valvae* were folding doors, and through this crevice came a sudden light startling him with his first vivid notion of finely adjusted mechanism in the human frame. A liberal education had of course left him free to read the indecent passages in the school classics, but beyond a general sense of secrecy and obscenity in connection with his internal structure, had left his imagination quite unbiassed, so that for anything he knew his brains lay in small bags at his temples, and he had no more thought of representing to himself how his blood circulated than how paper served instead of gold. But the moment of vocation had come, and before he got down from his chair, the world was made new to him by a presentiment of endless processes filling the vast spaces planked out of his sight by that wordy ignorance which he had supposed to be knowledge. From that hour Lydgate felt the growth of an intellectual passion.

We are not afraid of telling over and over again how a man comes to fall in love with a woman and be wedded to her, or else be fatally parted from her. Is it due to excess of poetry or of stupidity that we are never weary of describing what King James called a woman's 'makdom and her fairnesse', never weary of listening to the twanging of the old Troubadour strings, and are comparatively uninterested in that other kind of 'makdom and fairnesse' which must be wooed with industrious thought and patient renunciation of small desires? In the story of this passion, too, the development varies: sometimes it is the glorious marriage, sometimes frustration and final parting. And not seldom the catastrophe is bound up with the other passion, sung by the Troubadours. For in the multitude of middle-aged men who go about their vocations in a daily course determined for them much in the same way as the tie of their cravats, there is always a good number who once meant to shape their own deeds and alter the world a little. The story of their coming to be shapen after the average and fit to be packed by the gross, is hardly ever told even in their consciousness; for perhaps their ardour in generous unpaid toil cooled as imperceptibly as the ardour of other youthful loves, till one day their earlier self walked like a ghost in its old home and made the new furniture ghastly. Nothing in the world more subtle than the process of their gradual change! In the beginning they inhaled it unknowingly; you and I may have sent some of our breath towards infecting them, when we uttered our conforming falsities or drew our silly conclusions: or perhaps it came with the vibrations from a woman's glance.

Lydgate did not mean to be one of those failures, and there was the better hope of him because his scientific interest soon took the form of a professional enthusiasm: he had a youthful belief in his bread-winning work, not to be stifled by that initiation in makeshift called his 'prentice days; and he carried to his studies in London, Edinburgh, and Paris, the conviction that the medical profession as it might be was the finest in the world; presenting the most perfect interchange between science and art; offering the most direct alliance between intellectual conquest and the social good. Lydgate's nature demanded this combination: he was an emotional creature, with a flesh-and-blood sense of fellowship which withstood all the abstractions of special study. He cared not only for 'cases', but for John and Elizabeth, especially Elizabeth.

There was another attraction in this profession: it wanted reform, and gave a man an opportunity for some indignant resolve to reject its venal decorations and other humbug, and to be the possessor of genuine though undemanded qualifications. He went to study in Paris with the determination that when he came home again he would settle in some provincial town as a general practitioner, and resist the irrational severance between medical and surgical knowledge in the interest of his own scientific pursuits, as well as of the general advance: he would keep away from the range of London intrigues, jealousies, and social truckling, and win celebrity, however slowly, as Jenner had done, by the independent value of his work. For it must be remembered that this was a dark period; and in spite of venerable colleges which used great efforts to secure purity of knowledge by making it scarce, and to exclude error by a rigid exclusiveness in relation to fees and appointments, it happened that very ignorant young gentlemen were promoted in town, and many more got a legal right to practise over large areas in the country. Also, the high standard held up to the public mind by the College of Physicians, which gave its peculiar sanction to the expensive and highly-rarified medical instruction obtained by graduates of Oxford and Cambridge, did not hinder quackery from having an excellent time of it; for since professional practice chiefly consisted in giving a great many drugs, the public inferred that it might be better off with more drugs still if they could only be got cheaply, and hence swallowed large cubic measures of physic prescribed by unscrupulous ignorance which had taken no degrees. Considering that statistics had not yet embraced a calculation as to the number of ignorant or canting doctors which absolutely must exist in the teeth of all changes, it seemed to Lydgate that a change in the units was the most direct mode of changing the numbers. He meant to be a unit who would make a certain amount of difference towards that spreading change which would one day tell appreciably upon the averages, and in the meantime have the pleasure of making an advantageous difference to the viscera of his own patients. But he did not simply aim at a more genuine kind of practice than was common. He was ambitious of a wider effect: he was fired with the possibility that he might work out the proof of an anatomical conception and make a link in the chain of discovery.

Does it seem incongruous to you that a Middlemarch surgeon should dream of himself as a discoverer? Most of us, indeed, know little of the great originators until they have been lifted up among the constellations and already rule our fates. But that Herschel, for example, who 'broke the barriers of the heavens' – did he not once play a provincial church-organ, and give music-lessons to stumbling pianists? Each of those Shining Ones had to walk on the earth among neighbours who perhaps thought much more of his gait and his garments than of anything which was to give him a title to everlasting fame: each of them had his little local personal history sprinkled with small temptations and sordid cares, which made the retarding friction of his course towards final companionship with the immortals. Lydgate was not blind to the dangers of such friction, but he had plenty of confidence in his resolution to avoid it as far as possible: being seven-and-twenty, he felt himself experienced. And he was not going to have his vanities provoked by contact with the showy worldly successes of the capital, but to live among people who could hold no rivalry with that pursuit of a great idea which was to be a twin object with the assiduous practice of his profession. There was fascination in the hope that the two purposes would illuminate each other: the careful observation and inference which was his daily work, the use of the lens to further his judgment in special cases, would further his thought as an instrument of larger inquiry. Was not this the typical pre-eminence of his profession? He would be a good Middlemarch doctor, and by that very means keep himself in the track of far-reaching investigation. On one point he may fairly claim approval at this particular stage of his career; he did not mean to imitate those philanthropic models who make a profit out of poisonous pickles to support themselves while they are exposing adulteration, or hold shares in a gambling-hell that they may have leisure to represent the cause of public morality. He intended to begin in his own case some particular reforms which were quite certainly within his reach, and much less of a problem than the demonstrating of an anatomical conception. One of these reforms was to act stoutly on the strength of a recent legal decision, and simply prescribe, without dispensing drugs or taking percentage from druggists. This was an innovation for one who had chosen to adopt the style of general practitioner in a country town, and would be felt as offensive criticism by his professional brethren. But Lydgate meant to innovate in his treatment also, and he was wise enough to see that the best security for his practising honestly according to his belief was to get rid of systematic temptations to the contrary.

Perhaps that was a more cheerful time for observers and theorizers than the present; we are apt to think it the finest era of the world when America was beginning to be discovered, when a bold sailor, even if he were wrecked, might alight on a new kingdom; and about 1829 the dark territories of Pathology were a fine America for a spirited young adventurer. Lydgate was ambitious above all to contribute towards enlarging the scientific, rational basis of his profession. The more he became interested in special questions of disease, such as the nature of fever or fevers, the more keenly he felt the need for that fundamental knowledge of structure which just at the beginning of the century had been illuminated by the brief and glorious career of Bichat, who died when he was only one-and-thirty, but, like another Alexander, left a realm large enough for many heirs. That great Frenchman first carried out the conception that living bodies, fundamentally considered, are not associations of organs which can be understood by studying them first apart, and then as it were federally; but must be regarded as consisting of certain primary webs or tissues, out of which the various organs – brain, heart, lungs, and so on – are compacted, as the various accommodations of a house are built up in various proportions of wood, iron, stone, brick, zinc, and the rest, each material having its peculiar composition and proportions. No man, one sees, can understand and estimate the entire structure or its parts – what are its frailties and what its repairs, without knowing the nature of the materials. And the conception wrought out by Bichat, with his detailed study of the different tissues, acted necessarily on medical questions as the turning of gas-light would act on a dim, oil-lit street, showing new connections and hitherto hidden facts of structure which must be taken into account in considering the symptoms of maladies and the action of medicaments. But results which depend on human conscience and intelligence work slowly, and now at the end of 1829, most medical practice was still strutting or shambling along the old paths, and there was still scientific work to be done which might have seemed to be a direct sequence of Bichat's. This great seer did not go beyond the consideration of the tissues as ultimate facts in the living organism, marking the limit of anatomical analysis; but it was open to another mind to say, have not these structures some common basis from which they have all started, as your sarsnet, gauze, net, satin and velvet from the raw cocoon? Here would be another light, as of oxy-hydrogen, showing the very grain of things, and revising all former explanations. Of this sequence to Bichat's work, already vibrating along many currents of the European mind, Lydgate was enamoured; he longed to demonstrate the more intimate relations of living structure and help to define men's thought more accurately after the true order. The work had not yet been done, but only prepared for those who knew how to use the preparation. What was the primitive tissue? In that way Lydgate put the question – not quite in the way required by the awaiting answer; but such missing of the right word befalls many seekers. And he counted on quiet intervals to be watchfully seized, for taking up the threads of investigation – on many hints to be won from diligent application, not only of the scalpel, but of the microscope, which research had begun to use again with new enthusiasm of reliance. Such was Lydgate's plan of his future: to do good small work for Middlemarch, and great work for the world.

He was certainly a happy fellow at this time: to be seven-and-twenty, without any fixed vices, with a generous resolution that his action should be beneficent, and with ideas in his brain that made life interesting quite apart from the *cultus* of horse-flesh and other mystic rites of costly observance, which the eight hundred pounds left him after buying his practice would certainly not have gone far in paying for. He was at a starting-point which makes many a man's career a fine subject for betting, if there were any gentlemen given to that amusement who could appreciate the complicated probabilities of an arduous purpose, with all the possible thwartings and furtherings of circumstance, all the niceties of inward balance, by which a man swims and makes his point or else is carried headlong. The risk would remain, even with close knowledge of Lydgate's character; for character too is a process and an unfolding. The man was still in the making, as much as the Middlemarch doctor and immortal discoverer, and there were both virtues and faults capable of shrinking or expanding. The faults will not, I hope, be a reason for the withdrawal of your interest in him. Among our valued friends is there not some one or other who is a little too self-confident and disdainful; whose distinguished mind is a little spotted with commonness; who is a little pinched here and protuberant there with native prejudices; or whose better energies are liable to lapse down the wrong channel under the influence of transient solicitations? All these things might be alleged against Lydgate, but then, they are the periphrases of a polite preacher, who talks of Adam, and would not like to mention anything painful to the pew-renters. The particular faults from which these delicate generalities are distilled have distinguishable physiognomies, diction, accent, and grimaces; filling up parts in very various dramas. Our vanities differ as our noses do: all conceit is not the same conceit, but varies in correspondence with the minutiae of mental make in which one of us differs from another. Lydgate's conceit was of the arrogant sort, never simpering, never impertinent, but massive in its claims and benevolently contemptuous. He would do a great deal for noodles, being sorry for them, and feeling quite sure that they could have no power over him: he had thought of joining the Saint Simonians when he was in Paris, in order to turn them against some of their own doctrines. All his faults were marked by kindred traits, and were those of a man who had a fine baritone, whose clothes hung well upon him, and who even in his ordinary gestures had an air of inbred distinction. Where then lay the spots of commonness? says a young lady enamoured of that careless grace. How could there be any commonness in a man so well-bred, so ambitious of social distinction, so generous and unusual in his views of social duty? As easily as there may be stupidity in a man of genius if you take him unawares on the wrong subject, or as many a man who has the best will to advance the social millennium might be ill-inspired in imagining its lighter pleasures; unable to go beyond Offenbach's music, or the brilliant punning in the last burlesque. Lydgate's spots of commonness lay in the complexion of his prejudices, which, in spite of noble intentions and sympathy, were half of them such as are found in ordinary men of the world: that distinction of mind which belonged to his intellectual ardour, did not penetrate his feeling and judgment about furniture, or women, or the desirability of its being known (without his telling) that he was better born than other country surgeons. He did not mean to think of furniture at present; but whenever he did so, it was to be feared that neither biology nor schemes of reform would lift him above the vulgarity of feeling that there would be an incompatibility in his furniture not being of the best.

As to women, he had once already been drawn headlong by impetuous folly, which he meant to be final, since marriage at some distant period would of course not be impetuous. For those who want to be acquainted with Lydgate it will be good to know what was that case of impetuous folly, for it may stand as an example of the fitful swerving of passion to which he was prone, together with the chivalrous kindness which helped to make him morally lovable. The story can be told without many words. It happened when he was studying in Paris, and just at the time when, over and above his other work, he was occupied with some galvanic experiments. One evening, tired with his experimenting, and not being able to elicit the facts he needed, he left his frogs and rabbits to some repose under their trying and mysterious dispensation of unexplained shocks, and went to finish his evening at the theatre of the Porte Saint Martin, where there was a melodrama which he had already seen several times; attracted, not by the ingenious work of the collaborating authors, but by an actress whose part it was to stab her lover, mistaking him for the evil-designing duke of the piece. Lydgate was in love with this actress, as a man is in love with a woman whom he never expects to speak to. She was a Provençale, with dark eyes, a Greek profile, and rounded majestic form, having that sort of beauty which carries a sweet matronliness even in youth, and her voice was a soft cooing. She had but lately come to Paris, and bore a virtuous reputation, her husband acting with her as the unfortunate lover. It was her acting which was 'no better than it should be', but the public was satisfied. Lydgate's only relaxation now was to go and look at this woman, just as he might have thrown himself under the breath of the sweet south on a bank of violets for a while, without prejudice to his galvanism, to which he would presently return. But this evening the old drama had a new catastrophe. At the moment when the heroine was to act the stabbing of her lover, and he was to fall gracefully, the wife veritably stabbed her husband, who fell as death willed. A wild shriek pierced the house, and the Provençale fell swooning: a shriek and a swoon were demanded by the play, but the swooning too was real this time. Lydgate leaped and climbed, he hardly knew how, on to the stage, and was active in help, making the acquaintance of his heroine by finding a contusion on her head and lifting her gently in his arms. Paris rang with the story of this death: – was it a murder? Some of the actress's warmest admirers were inclined to believe in her guilt, and liked her the better for it (such was the taste of those times); but Lydgate was not one of these. He vehemently contended for her innocence, and the remote impersonal passion for her beauty which he had felt before, had passed now into personal devotion, and tender thought of her lot. The notion of murder was absurd; no motive was discoverable, the young couple being understood to dote on each other; and it was not unprecedented that an accidental slip of the foot should have brought these grave consequences. The legal investigation ended in Madame Laure's release. Lydgate by this time had had many interviews with her, and found her more and more adorable. She talked little; but that was an additional charm. She was melancholy, and seemed grateful; her presence was enough, like that of the evening light. Lydgate was madly anxious about her affection, and jealous lest any other man than himself should win it and ask her to marry him.

But instead of re-opening her engagement at the Porte Saint Martin, where she would have been all the more popular for the fatal episode, she left Paris without warning, forsaking her little court of admirers. Perhaps no one carried inquiry far except Lydgate, who felt that all science had come to a stand-still while he imagined the unhappy Laure, stricken by ever-wandering sorrow, herself wandering, and finding no faithful comforter. Hidden actresses, however, are not so difficult to find as some other hidden facts, and it was not long before Lydgate gathered indications that Laure had taken the route to Lyons. He found her at last acting with great success at Avignon under the same name, looking more majestic than ever as a forsaken wife carrying her child in her arms. He spoke to her after the play, was received with the usual quietude which seemed to him beautiful as clear depths of water, and obtained leave to visit her the next day; when he was bent on telling her that he adored her, and on asking her to marry him. He knew that this was like the sudden impulse of a madman – incongruous even with his habitual foibles. No matter! It was the one thing which he was resolved to do. He had two selves within him apparently, and they must learn to accommodate each other and bear reciprocal impediments. Strange, that some of us, with quick alternate vision, see beyond our infatuations, and even while we rave on the heights, behold the wide plain where our persistent self pauses and awaits us.

To have approached Laure with any suit that was not reverentially tender would have been simply a contradiction of his whole feeling towards her.

'You have come all the way from Paris to find me?' she said to him the next day, sitting before him with folded arms, and looking at him with eyes that seemed to wonder as an untamed ruminating animal wonders. 'Are all Englishmen like that?'

'I came because I could not live without trying to see you. You are lonely; I love you; I want you to consent to be my wife: I will wait, but I want you to promise that you will marry me – no one else.'

Laure looked at him in silence with a melancholy radiance from under her grand eyelids, until he was full of rapturous certainty, and knelt close to her knees.

'I will tell you something,' she said, in her cooing way, keeping her arms folded. 'My foot really slipped.'

'I know, I know,' said Lydgate, deprecatingly. 'It was a fatal accident – a dreadful stroke of calamity that bound me to you the more.'

Again Laure paused a little and then said, slowly, '*I meant to do it.*'

Lydgate, strong man as he was, turned pale and trembled: moments seemed to pass before he rose and stood at a distance from her.

'There was a secret, then,' he said at last, even vehemently. 'He was brutal to you: you hated him.'

'No! he wearied me; he was too fond: he would live in Paris, and not in my country; that was not agreeable to me.'

'Great God!' said Lydgate, in a groan of horror. 'And you planned to murder him?'

'I did not plan: it came to me in the play – *I meant to do it.*'

Lydgate stood mute, and unconsciously pressed his hat on while he looked at her. He saw this woman – the first to whom he had given his young adoration – amid the throng of stupid criminals.

'You are a good young man,' she said. 'But I do not like husbands. I will never have another.'

Three days afterwards Lydgate was at his galvanism again in his Paris chambers, believing that illusions were at an end for him. He was saved from hardening effects by the abundant kindness of his heart and his belief that human life might be made better. But he had more reason than ever for trusting his judgment, now that it was so experienced; and henceforth he would take a strictly scientific view of woman, entertaining no expectations, but such as were justified beforehand.

No one in Middlemarch was likely to have such a notion of Lydgate's past as has here been faintly shadowed, and indeed the respectable townsfolk there were not more given than mortals generally to any eager attempt at exactness in the representation to themselves of what did not come under their own senses. Not only young virgins of that town, but grey-bearded men also, were often in haste to conjecture how a new acquaintance might be wrought into their purposes, contented with very vague knowledge as to the way in which life had been shaping him for that instrumentality. Middlemarch, in fact, counted on swallowing Lydgate and assimilating him very comfortably.

ᏅᏊ SIXTEEN ᏅᏊ

All that in woman is adored
In thy fair self I find –
For the whole sex can but afford
The handsome and the kind.
SIR CHARLES SEDLEY

THE QUESTION WHETHER MR TYKE should be appointed as salaried chaplain to the hospital was an exciting topic to the Middlemarchers; and Lydgate heard it discussed in a way that threw much light on the power exercised in the town by Mr Bulstrode. The banker was evidently a ruler, but there was an opposition party, and even among his supporters there were some who allowed it to be seen that their support was a compromise, and who frankly stated their impression that the general scheme of things, and especially the casualties of trade, required you to hold a candle to the devil.

Mr Bulstrode's power was not due simply to his being a country banker, who knew the financial secrets of most traders in the town and could touch the springs of their credit; it was fortified by a beneficence that was at once ready and severe – ready to confer obligations, and severe in watching the result. He had gathered, as an industrious man always at his post, a chief share in administering the town charities, and his private charities were both minute and abundant. He would take a great deal of pains about apprenticing Tegg the shoemaker's son, and he would watch over Tegg's churchgoing; he would defend Mrs Strype the washerwoman against Stubb's unjust exaction on the score of her drying-ground, and he would himself scrutinize a calumny against Mrs Strype. His private minor loans were numerous, but he would inquire strictly into the circumstances both before and after. In this way a man gathers a domain in his neighbours' hope and fear as well as gratitude; and power, when once it has got into that subtle region, propagates itself, spreading out of all proportion to its external means. It was a principle with Mr Bulstrode to gain as much power as possible, that he might use it for the glory of God. He went through a great deal of spiritual conflict and inward argument in order to adjust his motives, and make clear to himself what God's glory required. But, as we have seen, his motives were not always rightly appreciated. There were many crass minds in Middlemarch whose reflective scales could only weigh things in the lump; and they had a strong suspicion that since Mr Bulstrode could not enjoy life in their fashion, eating and drinking so little as he did, and worreting himself about everything, he must have a sort of vampire's feast in the sense of mastery.

The subject of the chaplaincy came up at Mr Vincy's table when Lydgate was dining there, and the family connection with Mr Bulstrode did not, he observed, prevent some freedom of remark even on the part of the host himself, though his reasons against the proposed arrangement turned entirely on his objection to Mr Tyke's sermons, which were all doctrine, and his preference for Mr Farebrother, whose sermons were free from that taint. Mr Vincy liked well enough the notion of the chaplain's having a salary, supposing it were given to Farebrother, who was as good a little fellow as ever breathed, and the best preacher anywhere, and companionable too.

'What line shall you take, then?' said Mr Chichely, the coroner, a great coursing comrade of Mr Vincy's.

'Oh, I'm precious glad I'm not one of the Directors now. I shall vote for referring the matter to the Directors and the Medical Board together. I shall roll some of my responsibility on your shoulders, Doctor,' said Mr Vincy, glancing first at Dr Sprague, the senior physician of the town, and then at Lydgate, who sat opposite. 'You medical gentlemen must consult which sort of black draught you will prescribe, eh, Mr Lydgate?'

'I know little of either,' said Lydgate; 'but in general, appointments are apt to be made too much a question of personal liking. The fittest man for a particular post is not always the best fellow or the most agreeable. Sometimes, if you wanted to get a reform, your only way would be to pension off the good fellows whom everybody is fond of, and put them out of the question.'

Dr Sprague, who was considered the physician of most 'weight', though Dr Minchin was usually said to have more 'penetration', divested his large heavy face of all expression, and looked at his wineglass while Lydgate was speaking. Whatever was not problematical and suspected about this young man – for example, a certain showiness as to foreign ideas, and a disposition to unsettle what had been settled and forgotten by his elders – was positively unwelcome to a physician whose standing had been fixed thirty years before by a treatise on Meningitis, of which at least one copy marked 'own' was bound in calf. For my part I have some fellow-feeling with Dr Sprague: one's self-satisfaction is an untaxed kind of property which it is very unpleasant to find depreciated.

Lydgate's remark, however, did not meet the sense of the company. Mr Vincy said, that if he could have *his* way, he would not put disagreeable fellows anywhere.

'Hang your reforms!' said Mr Chichely. 'There's no greater humbug in the world. You never hear of a reform, but it means some trick to put in new men. I hope you are not one of the *Lancet's* men, Mr Lydgate – wanting to take the coronership out of the hands of the legal profession: your words appear to point that way.'

'I disapprove of Wakley,' interposed Dr Sprague, 'no man more: he is an ill-intentioned fellow, who would sacrifice the respectability of the profession, which everybody knows depends on the London Colleges, for the sake of getting some notoriety for himself. There are men who don't mind about being kicked blue if they can only get talked about. But Wakley is right sometimes,' the Doctor added, judicially. 'I could mention one or two points in which Wakley is in the right.'

'Oh, well,' said Mr Chichely, 'I blame no man for standing up in favour of his own cloth; but, coming to argument, I should like to know how a coroner is to judge of evidence if he has not had a legal training?'

'In my opinion,' said Lydgate, 'legal training only makes a man more incompetent in questions that require knowledge of another kind. People talk about evidence as if it could really be weighed in scales by a blind Justice. No man can judge what is good evidence on any particular subject, unless he knows that subject well. A lawyer is no better than an old woman at a *post-mortem* examination. How is he to know the action of a poison? You might as well say that scanning verse will teach you to scan the potato crops.'

'You are aware, I suppose, that it is not the coroner's business to conduct the *post-mortem*, but only to take the evidence of the medical witness?' said Mr Chichely, with some scorn.

'Who is often almost as ignorant as the coroner himself,' said Lydgate. 'Questions of medical jurisprudence ought not to be left to the chance of decent knowledge in a medical witness, and the coroner ought not to be a man who will believe that strychnine will destroy the coats of the stomach if an ignorant practitioner happens to tell him so.'

Lydgate had really lost sight of the fact that Mr Chichely was his Majesty's coroner, and ended innocently with the question, 'Don't you agree with me, Dr Sprague?'

'To a certain extent – with regard to populous districts, and in the metropolis,' said the Doctor. 'But I hope it will be long before this part of the country loses the services of my friend Chichely, even though it might get the best man in our profession to succeed him. I am sure Vincy will agree with me.'

'Yes, yes, give me a coroner who is a good coursing man,' said Mr Vincy, jovially. 'And in my opinion, you're safest with a lawyer. Nobody can know everything. Most things are "visitation of God". And as to poisoning, why, what you want to know is the law. Come, shall we join the ladies?'

Lydgate's private opinion was that Mr Chichely might be the very coroner without bias as to the coats of the stomach, but he had not meant to be personal. This was one of the difficulties of moving in good Middlemarch society: it was dangerous to insist on knowledge as a qualification for any salaried office. Fred Vincy had called Lydgate a prig, and now Mr Chichely was inclined to call him prick-eared, especially when, in the drawing-room, he seemed to be making himself eminently agreeable to Rosamond, whom he had easily monopolized in a *tête-à-tête*, since Mrs Vincy herself sat at the tea-table. She resigned no domestic function to her daughter; and the matron's blooming good-natured face, with the too volatile pink strings floating from her fine throat, and her cheery manners to husband and children, were certainly among the great attractions of the Vincy house – attractions which made it all the easier to fall in love with the daughter. The tinge of unpretentious, inoffensive vulgarity in Mrs Vincy gave more effect to Rosamond's refinement, which was beyond what Lydgate had expected.

Certainly, small feet and perfectly turned shoulders aid the impression of refined manners, and the right thing said seems quite astonishingly right when it is accompanied with exquisite curves of lip and eyelid. And Rosamond could say the right thing; for she was clever with that sort of cleverness which catches every tone except the humorous. Happily she never attempted to joke, and this perhaps was the most decisive mark of her cleverness.

She and Lydgate readily got into conversation. He regretted that he had not heard her sing the other day at Stone Court. The only pleasure he allowed himself during the latter part of his stay in Paris was to go and hear music.

'You have studied music, probably?' said Rosamond.

'No, I know the notes of many birds, and I know many melodies by ear; but the music that I don't know at all, and have no notion about, delights me – affects me. How stupid the world is that it does not make more use of such a pleasure within its reach!'

'Yes, and you will find Middlemarch very tuneless. There are hardly any good musicians. I only know two gentlemen who sing at all well.'

'I suppose it is the fashion to sing comic songs in a rhythmic way, leaving you to fancy the tune – very much as if it were tapped on a drum?'

'Ah, you have heard Mr Bowyer,' said Rosamond, with one of her rare smiles. 'But we are speaking very ill of our neighbours.'

Lydgate was almost forgetting that he must carry on the conversation, in thinking how lovely this creature was, her garment seeming to be made out of the faintest blue sky, herself so immaculately blond, as if the petals of some gigantic flower had just opened and disclosed her; and yet with this infantile blondness showing so much ready, self-possessed grace. Since he had had the memory of Laure, Lydgate had lost all taste for large-eyed silence: the divine cow no longer attracted him, and Rosamond was her very opposite. But he recalled himself.

'You will let me hear some music to-night, I hope.'

'I will let you hear my attempts, if you like,' said Rosamond. 'Papa is sure to insist on my singing. But I shall tremble before you, who have heard the best singers in Paris. I have heard very little: I have only once been to London. But our organist at St Peter's is a good musician, and I go on studying with him.'

'Tell me what you saw in London.'

'Very little.' (A more naïve girl would have said, 'Oh, everything!' But Rosamond knew better.) 'A few of the ordinary sights, such as raw country girls are always taken to.'

'Do you call yourself a raw country girl?' said Lydgate, looking at her with an involuntary emphasis of admiration, which made Rosamond blush with pleasure. But she remained simply serious, turned her long neck a little, and put up her hand to touch her wondrous hair-plaits – an habitual gesture with her as pretty as any movements of a kitten's paw. Not that Rosamond was in the least like a kitten: she was a sylph caught young and educated at Mrs Lemon's.

'I assure you my mind is raw,' she said immediately; 'I pass at Middlemarch. I am not afraid of talking to our old neighbours. But I am really afraid of you.'

'An accomplished woman almost always knows more than we men, though her knowledge is of a different sort. I am sure you could teach me a thousand things – as an exquisite bird could teach a bear if there were any common language between them. Happily, there is a common language between women and men, and so the bears can get taught.'

'Ah, there is Fred beginning to strum! I must go and hinder him from jarring all your nerves,' said Rosamond, moving to the other side of the room, where Fred having opened the piano, at his father's desire, that Rosamond might give them some music, was parenthetically performing 'Cherry Ripe!' with one hand. Able men who have passed their examinations will do these things sometimes, not less than the plucked Fred.

'Fred, pray defer your practising till to-morrow; you will make Mr Lydgate ill,' said Rosamond. 'He has an ear.'

Fred laughed, and went on with his tune to the end.

Rosamond turned to Lydgate, smiling gently, and said, 'You perceive, the bears will not always be taught.'

'Now then, Rosy!' said Fred, springing from the stool and twisting it upward for her, with a hearty expectation of enjoyment. 'Some good rousing tunes first.'

Rosamond played admirably. Her master at Mrs Lemon's school (close to a county town with a memorable history that had its relics in church and castle) was one of those excellent musicians here and there to be found in our provinces, worthy to compare with many a noted Kapellmeister in a country which offers more plentiful conditions of musical celebrity. Rosamond, with the executant's instinct, had seized his manner of playing, and gave forth his large rendering of noble music with the precision of an echo. It was almost startling, heard for the first time. A hidden soul seemed to be flowing forth from Rosamond's fingers; and so indeed it was, since souls live on in perpetual echoes, and to all fine expression there goes somewhere an originating activity, if it be only that of an interpreter. Lydgate was taken possession of, and began to believe in her as something exceptional. After all, he thought, one need not be surprised to find the rare conjunctions of nature under circumstances apparently unfavourable: come where they may, they always depend on conditions that are not obvious. He sat looking at her, and did not rise to pay her any compliments, leaving that to others, now that his admiration was deepened.

Her singing was less remarkable, but also well trained, and sweet to hear as a chime perfectly in tune. It is true she sang 'Meet me by the moonlight' and 'I've been roaming'; for mortals must share the fashions of their time, and none but the ancients can be always classical. But Rosamond could also sing 'Black-eyed Susan' with effect, or Haydn's canzonets, or *Voi, che sapete*', or *'Batti, batti'* – she only wanted to know what her audience liked.

Her father looked round at the company, delighting in their admiration. Her mother sat, like a Niobe before her troubles, with her youngest little girl on her lap, softly beating the child's hand up and down in time to the music. And Fred, notwithstanding his general scepticism about Rosy, listened to her music with perfect allegiance, wishing he could do the same thing on his flute. It was the pleasantest family party that Lydgate had seen since he came to Middlemarch. The Vincys had the readiness to enjoy, the rejection of all anxiety, and the belief in life as a merry lot, which made a house exceptional in most county towns at that time, when Evangelicalism had cast a certain suspicion as of plague-infection over the few amusements which survived in the provinces. At the Vincys' there was always whist, and the card-tables stood ready now, making some of the company secretly impatient of the music. Before it ceased Mr Farebrother came in – a handsome, broad-chested but otherwise small man, about forty, whose black was very threadbare: the brilliancy was all in his quick grey eyes. He came like a pleasant change in the light, arresting little Louisa with fatherly nonsense as she was being led out of the room by Miss Morgan, greeting everybody with some special word, and seeming to condense more talk into ten minutes than had been held all through the evening. He claimed from Lydgate the fulfilment of a promise to come and see him. 'I can't let you off, you know, because I have some beetles to show you. We collectors feel an interest in every new man till he has seen all we have to show him.'

But soon he swerved to the whist-table, rubbing his hands and saying, 'Come now, let us be serious! Mr Lydgate? not play? Ah! you are too young and light for this kind of thing.'

Lydgate said to himself that the clergyman whose abilities were so painful to Mr Bulstrode appeared to have found an agreeable resort in this certainly not erudite household. He could half understand it: the good-humour, the good looks of elder and younger, and the provision for passing the time without any labour of intelligence, might make the house beguiling to people who had no particular use for their odd hours.

Everything looked blooming and joyous except Miss Morgan, who was brown, dull, and resigned, and altogether, as Mrs Vincy often said, just the sort of person for a governess. Lydgate did not mean to pay many such visits himself. They were a wretched waste of the evenings; and now, when he had talked a little more to Rosamond, he meant to excuse himself and go.

'You will not like us at Middlemarch, I feel sure,' she said, when the whist-players were settled. 'We are very stupid, and you have been used to something quite different.'

'I suppose all country towns are pretty much alike,' said Lydgate. 'But I have noticed that one always believes one's own town to be more stupid than any other. I have made up my mind to take Middlemarch as it comes, and shall be much obliged if the town will take me in the same way. I have certainly found some charms in it which are much greater than I had expected.'

'You mean the rides towards Tipton and Lowick; every one is pleased with those,' said Rosamond, with simplicity.

'No, I mean something much nearer to me.'

Rosamond rose and reached her netting, and then said, 'Do you care about dancing at all? I am not quite sure whether clever men ever dance.'

'I would dance with you, if you would allow me.'

'Oh!' said Rosamond, with a slight deprecatory laugh. 'I was only going to say that we sometimes have dancing, and I wanted to know whether you would feel insulted if you were asked to come.'

'Not on the condition I mentioned.'

After this chat Lydgate thought that he was going, but on moving towards the whist-tables, he got interested in watching Mr Farebrother's play, which was masterly, and also his face, which was a striking mixture of the shrewd and the mild. At ten o'clock supper was brought in (such were the customs of Middlemarch), and there was punch-drinking; but Mr Fare brother had only a glass of water. He was winning, but there seemed to be no reason why the renewal of rubbers should end, and Lydgate at last took his leave.

But as it was not eleven o'clock, he chose to walk in the brisk air towards the tower of St Botolph's, Mr Farebrother's church, which stood out dark, square, and massive against the starlight. It was the oldest church in Middlemarch; the living, however, was but a vicarage worth barely four hundred a-year. Lydgate had heard that, and he wondered now whether Mr Farebrother cared about the money he won at cards; thinking 'He seems a very pleasant fellow, but Bulstrode may have his good reasons.' Many things would be easier to Lydgate if it should turn out that Mr Bulstrode was generally justifiable. 'What is his religious doctrine to me, if he carries some good notions along with it? One must use such brains as are to be found.'

These were actually Lydgate's first meditations as he walked away from Mr Vincy's, and on this ground I fear that many ladies will consider him hardly worthy of their attention. He thought of Rosamond and her music only in the second place; and though, when her turn came, he dwelt on the image of her for the rest of his walk, he felt no agitation, and had no sense that any new current had set into his life. He could not marry yet; he wished not to marry for several years; and therefore he was not ready to entertain the notion of being in love with a girl whom he happened to admire. He did admire Rosamond exceedingly; but that madness which had once beset him about Laure was not, he thought, likely to recur in relation to any other woman. Certainly, if falling in love had been at all in question, it would have been quite safe with a creature like this Miss Vincy, who had just the kind of intelligence one would desire in a woman – polished, refined, docile, lending itself to finish in all the delicacies of life, and enshrined in a body which expressed this with a force of demonstration that excluded the need for other evidence. Lydgate felt sure that if ever he married, his wife would have that feminine radiance, that distinctive womanhood which must be classed with flowers and music, that sort of beauty which by its very nature was virtuous, being moulded only for pure and delicate joys.

But since he did not mean to marry for the next five years – his more pressing business was to look into Louis' new book on Fever, which he was specially interested in, because he had known Louis in Paris, and had followed many anatomical demonstrations in order to ascertain the specific differences of typhus and typhoid. He went home and read far into the smallest hour, bringing a much more testing vision of details and relations into this pathological study than he had ever thought it necessary to apply to the complexities of love and marriage, these being subjects on which he felt himself amply informed by literature, and that traditional wisdom which is handed down in the genial conversation of men. Whereas Fever had obscure conditions, and gave him that delightful labour of the imagination which is not mere arbitrariness, but the exercise of disciplined power – combining and constructing with the clearest eye for probabilities and the fullest obedience to knowledge; and then, in yet more energetic alliance with impartial Nature, standing aloof to invent tests by which to try its own work.

Many men have been praised as vividly imaginative on the strength of their profuseness in indifferent drawing or cheap narration: – reports of very poor talk going on in distant orbs; or portraits of Lucifer coming down on his bad errands as a large ugly man with bat's wings and spurts of phosphorescence; or exaggerations of wantonness that seem to reflect life in a diseased dream. But these kinds of inspiration Lydgate regarded as rather vulgar and vinous compared with the imagination that reveals subtle actions inaccessible by any sort of lens, but tracked in that outer darkness through long pathways of necessary sequence by the inward light which is the last refinement of Energy, capable of bathing even the ethereal atoms in its ideally illuminated space. He for his part had tossed away all cheap inventions where ignorance finds itself able and at ease: he was enamoured of that arduous invention which is the very eye of research, provisionally framing its object and correcting it to more and more exactness of relation; he wanted to pierce the obscurity of those minute processes which prepare human misery and joy, those invisible thoroughfares which are the first lurking-places of anguish, mania, and crime, that delicate poise and transition which determine the growth of happy or unhappy consciousness.

As he threw down his book, stretched his legs towards the embers in the grate, and clasped his hands at the back of his head, in that agreeable after-glow of excitement when thought lapses from examination of a specific object into a suffusive sense of its connections with all the rest of our existence – seems, as it were, to throw itself on its back after vigorous swimming and float with the repose of unexhausted strength – Lydgate felt a triumphant delight in his studies, and something like pity for those less lucky men who were not of his profession.

'If I had not taken that turn when I was a lad,' he thought, 'I might have got into some stupid draught-horse work or other, and lived always in blinkers. I should never have been happy in any profession that did not call forth the highest intellectual strain, and yet keep me in good warm contact with my neighbours. There is nothing like the medical profession for that: one can have the exclusive scientific life that touches the distance and befriend the old fogies in the parish too. It is rather harder for a clergyman: Farebrother seems to be an anomaly.'

This last thought brought back the Vincys and all the pictures of the evening. They floated in his mind agreeably enough, and as he took up his bed-candle his lips were curled with that incipient smile which is apt to accompany agreeable recollections. He was an ardent fellow, but at present his ardour was absorbed in love of his work and in the ambition of making his life recognized as a factor in the better life of mankind – like other heroes of science who had nothing but an obscure country practice to begin with.

Poor Lydgate! or shall I say, Poor Rosamond! Each lived in a world of which the other knew nothing. It had not occurred to Lydgate that he had been a subject of eager meditation to Rosamond, who had neither any reason for throwing her marriage into distant perspective, nor any pathological studies to divert her mind from that ruminating habit, that inward repetition of looks, words, and phrases, which makes a large part of the lives of most girls. He had not meant to look at her or speak to her with more than the inevitable amount of admiration and compliment which a man must give to a beautiful girl; indeed, it seemed to him that his enjoyment of her music had remained almost silent, for he feared falling into the rudeness of telling her his great surprise at her possession of such accomplishment. But Rosamond had registered every look and word, and estimated them as the opening incidents of a preconceived romance – incidents which gather value from the foreseen development and climax. In Rosamond's romance it was not necessary to imagine much about the inward life of the hero, or of his serious business in the world: of course, he had a profession and was clever, as well as sufficiently handsome; but the piquant fact about Lydgate was his good birth, which distinguished him from all Middlemarch admirers, and presented marriage as a prospect of rising in rank and getting a little nearer to that celestial condition on earth in which she would have nothing to do with vulgar people, and perhaps at last associate with relatives quite equal to the county people who looked down on the Middlemarchers. It was part of Rosamond's cleverness to discern very subtly the faintest aroma of rank, and once when she had seen the Miss Brookes accompanying their uncle at the county assizes, and seated among the aristocracy, she had envied them, notwithstanding their plain dress.

If you think it incredible that to imagine Lydgate as a man of family could cause thrills of satisfaction which had anything to do with the sense that she was in love with him, I will ask you to use your power of comparison a little more effectively, and consider whether red cloth and epaulets have never had an influence of that sort. Our passions do not live apart in locked chambers, but, dressed in their small wardrobe of notions, bring their provisions to a common table and mess together, feeding out of the common store according to their appetite.

Rosamond, in fact, was entirely occupied not exactly with Tertius Lydgate as he was in himself, but with his relation to her; and it was excusable in a girl who was accustomed to hear that all young men might, could, would be, or actually were in love with her, to believe at once that Lydgate could be no exception. His looks and words meant more to her than other men's, because she cared more for them: she thought of them diligently, and diligently attended to that perfection of appearance, behaviour, sentiments, and all other elegancies, which would find in Lydgate a more adequate admirer than she had yet been conscious of.

For Rosamond, though she would never do anything that was disagreeable to her, was industrious; and now more than ever she was active in sketching her landscapes and market-carts and portraits of friends, in practising her music, and in being from morning till night her own standard of a perfect lady, having always an audience in her own consciousness, with sometimes the not unwelcome addition of a more variable external audience in the numerous visitors of the house. She found time also to read the best novels, and even the second best, and she knew much poetry by heart. Her favourite poem was 'Lalla Rookh'.

'The best girl in the world! He will be a happy fellow who gets her!' was the sentiment of the elderly gentlemen who visited the Vincys; and the rejected young men thought of trying again, as is the fashion in country towns where the horizon is not thick with coming rivals. But Mrs Plymdale thought that Rosamond had been educated to a ridiculous pitch, for what was the use of accomplishments which would be all laid aside as soon as she was married? While her aunt Bulstrode, who had a sisterly faithfulness towards her brother's family, had two sincere wishes for Rosamond – that she might show a more serious turn of mind, and that she might meet with a husband whose wealth corresponded to her habits.

❧ SEVENTEEN ❧

The clerkly person smiled and said,
Promise was a pretty maid,
But being poor she died unwed.

THE REV. CAMDEN FAREBROTHER, WHOM Lydgate went to see the next evening, lived in an old parsonage, built of stone, venerable enough to match the church which it looked out upon. All the furniture too in the house was old, but with another grade of age – that of Mr Farebrother's father and grandfather. There were painted white chairs, with gilding and wreaths on them, and some lingering red silk damask with slits in it. There were engraved portraits of Lord Chancellors and other celebrated lawyers of the last century; and there were old pier-glasses to reflect them, as well as the little satin-wood tables and the sofas resembling a prolongation of uneasy chairs, all standing in relief against the dark wainscot. This was the physiognomy of the drawing-room into which Lydgate was shown; and there were three ladies to receive him, who were also old-fashioned, and of a faded but genuine respectability: Mrs Farebrother, the Vicar's white-haired mother, befrilled and kerchiefed with dainty cleanliness, upright, quick-eyed and still under seventy; Miss Noble, her sister, a tiny old lady of meeker aspect, with frills and kerchief decidedly more worn and mended; and, Miss Winifred Farebrother, the Vicar's elder sister, well-looking like himself, but nipped and subdued as single women are apt to be who spend their lives in uninterrupted subjection to their elders. Lydgate had not expected to see so quaint a group: knowing simply that Mr Farebrother was a bachelor, he had thought of being ushered into a snuggery where the chief furniture would probably be books and collections of natural objects. The Vicar himself seemed to wear rather a changed aspect, as most men do when acquaintances made elsewhere see them for the first time in their own homes; some indeed showing like an actor of genial parts disadvantageously cast for the curmudgeon in a new piece. This was not the case with Mr Farebrother: he seemed a trifle milder and more silent, the chief talker being his mother, while he only put in a good-humoured moderating remark here and there. The old lady was evidently accustomed to tell her company what they ought to think, and to regard no subject as quite safe without her steering. She was afforded leisure for this function by having all her little wants attended to by Miss Winifred. Meanwhile tiny Miss Noble carried on her

130

arm a small basket, into which she diverted a bit of sugar, which she had first dropped in her saucer as if by mistake; looking round furtively afterwards, and reverting to her tea-cup with a small innocent noise as of a tiny timid quadruped. Pray think no ill of Miss Noble. That basket held small savings from her more portable food, destined for the children of her poor friends among whom she trotted on fine mornings; fostering and petting all needy creatures being so spontaneous a delight to her, that she regarded it much as if it had been a pleasant vice that she was addicted to. Perhaps she was conscious of being tempted to steal from those who had much that she might give to those who had nothing, and carried in her conscience the guilt of that repressed desire. One must be poor to know the luxury of giving!

Mrs Farebrother welcomed the guest with a lively formality and precision. She presently informed him that they were not often in want of medical aid in that house. She had brought up her children to wear flannel and not to over-eat themselves, which last habit she considered the chief reason why people needed doctors. Lydgate pleaded for those whose fathers and mothers had over-eaten themselves, but Mrs Farebrother held that view of things dangerous: Nature was more just than that; it would be easy for any felon to say that his ancestors ought to have been hanged instead of him. If those who had bad fathers and mothers were bad themselves, they were hanged for that. There was no need to go back on what you couldn't see.

'My mother is like old George the Third,' said the Vicar, 'she objects to metaphysics.'

'I object to what is wrong, Camden. I say, keep hold of a few plain truths, and make everything square with them. When I was young, Mr Lydgate, there never was any question about right and wrong. We knew our catechism, and that was enough; we learned our creed and our duty. Every respectable Church person had the same opinions. But, now if you speak out of the Prayer-book itself, you are liable to be contradicted.'

'That makes rather a pleasant time of it for those who like to maintain their own point,' said Lydgate.

'But my mother always gives way,' said the Vicar, slyly.

'No, no, Camden, you must not lead Mr Lydgate into a mistake about *me*. I shall never show that disrespect to my parents, to give up what they taught me. Any one may see what comes of turning. If you change once, why not twenty times?'

'A man might see good arguments for changing once, and not see them for changing again,' said Lydgate, amused with the decisive old lady.

'Excuse me there. If you go upon arguments, they are never wanting, when a man has no constancy of mind. My father never changed, and he preached plain moral sermons without argument, and was a good man – few better. When you get me a good man made out of arguments, I will get you a good dinner with reading you the cookery-book. That's my opinion, and I think anybody's stomach will bear me out.'

'About the dinner certainly, mother,' said Mr Farebrother.

'It is the same thing, the dinner or the man. I am nearly seventy, Mr Lydgate, and I go upon experience. I am not likely to follow new lights, though there are plenty of them here as elsewhere. I say, they came in with the mixed stuffs that will neither wash nor wear. It was not so in my youth: a Churchman was a Churchman, and a clergyman, you might be pretty sure was a gentleman, if nothing else. But now he may be no better than a Dissenter, and want to push aside my son on pretence of doctrine. But whoever may wish to push him aside, I am proud to say, Mr Lydgate, that he will compare with any preacher in this kingdom, not to speak of this town, which is but a low standard to go by; at least, to my thinking, for I was born and bred at Exeter.'

'A mother is never partial,' said Mr Farebrother, smiling. 'What do you think Tyke's mother says about him?'

'Ah, poor creature! what indeed?' said Mrs Farebrother, her sharpness blunted for the moment by her confidence in maternal judgments. 'She says the truth to herself, depend upon it.'

'And what is the truth?' said Lydgate. 'I am curious to know.'

'Oh, nothing bad at all,' said Mr Farebrother. 'He is a zealous fellow: not very learned, and not very wise, I think – because I don't agree with him.'

'Why, Camden!' said Miss Winifred, 'Griffin and his wife told me only to-day, that Mr Tyke said they should have no more coals if they came to hear you preach.'

Mrs Farebrother laid down her knitting, which she had resumed after her small allowance of tea and toast, and looked at her son as if to say 'You hear that?' Miss Noble said, 'Oh, poor things! poor things!' in reference, probably, to the double loss of preaching and coal. But the Vicar answered quietly –

'That is because they are not my parishioners. And I don't think my sermons are worth a load of coals to them.'

'Mr Lydgate,' said Mrs Farebrother, who could not let this pass, 'you don't know my son: he always undervalues himself. I tell him he is undervaluing the God who made him, and made him a most excellent preacher.'

'That must be a hint for me to take Mr Lydgate away to my study, mother,' said the Vicar, laughing. 'I promised to show you my collection,' he added, turning to Lydgate; 'shall we go?'

All three ladies remonstrated. Mr Lydgate ought not to be hurried away without being allowed to accept another cup of tea: Miss Winifred had abundance of good tea in the pot. Why was Camden in such haste to take a visitor to his den? There was nothing but pickled vermin, and drawers full of blue-bottles and moths, with no carpet on the floor. Mr Lydgate must excuse it. A game at cribbage would be far better. In short, it was plain that a vicar might be adored by his womankind as the king of men and preachers, and yet be held by them to stand in much need of their direction. Lydgate, with the usual shallowness of a young bachelor, wondered that Mr Farebrother had not taught them better.

'My mother is not used to my having visitors who can take any interest in my hobbies,' said the Vicar, as he opened the door of his study, which was indeed as bare of luxuries for the body as the ladies had implied, unless a short porcelain pipe and a tobacco-box were to be excepted.

'Men of your profession don't generally smoke,' he said. Lygate smiled and shook his head. 'Nor of mine either, properly, I suppose. You will hear that pipe alleged against me by Bulstrode and Company. They don't know how pleased the devil would be if I gave it up.'

'I understand. You are of an excitable temper, and want a sedative. I am heavier, and should get idle with it. I should rush into idleness, and stagnate there with all my might.'

'And you mean to give it all to your work. I am some ten or twelve years older than you, and have come to a compromise. I feed a weakness or two lest they should get clamorous. See,' continued the Vicar, opening several small drawers, 'I fancy I have made an exhaustive study of the entomology of this district. I am going on both with the fauna and flora; but I have at least done my insects well. We are singularly rich in orthoptera: I don't know whether – Ah! you have got hold of that glass jar – you are looking into that instead of my drawers. You don't really care about these things?'

'Not by the side of this lovely anencephalous monster. I have never had time to give myself much to natural history. I was early bitten with an interest in structure, and it is what lies most directly in my profession. I have no hobby besides. I have the sea to swim in there.'

'Ah! you are a happy fellow,' said Mr Farebrother, turning on his heel and beginning to fill his pipe. 'You don't know what it is to want spiritual tobacco – bad emendations of old texts, or small items about a variety of *Aphis brassicae*, with the well-known signature of Philomicron, for the *Twaddler's Magazine*; or a learned treatise on the entomology of the Pentateuch, including all the insects not mentioned, but probably met with by the Israelites in their passage through the desert; with a monograph on the Ant, as treated by Solomon, showing the harmony of the Book of Proverbs with the results of modern research. You don't mind my fumigating you?'

Lydgate was more surprised at the openness of this talk than at its implied meaning – that the Vicar felt himself not altogether in the right vocation. The neat fitting-up of drawers and shelves, and the bookcase filled with expensive illustrated books on Natural History, made him think again of the winnings at cards and their destination. But he was beginning to wish that the very best construction of everything that Mr Farebrother did should be the true one. The Vicar's frankness seemed not of the repulsive sort that comes from an uneasy consciousness seeking to forestall the judgment of others, but simply the relief of a desire to do with as little pretence as possible. Apparently he was not without a sense that his freedom of speech might seem premature, for he presently said –

'I have not yet told you that I have the advantage of you, Mr Lydgate, and know you better than you know me. You remember Trawley, who shared your apartment at Paris for some time? I was a correspondent of his, and he told a good deal about you. I was not quite sure when you first came that you were the same man. I was very glad when I found that you were. Only I don't forget that you have not had the like prologue about me.'

Lydgate divined some delicacy of feeling here, but did not half understand it. 'By the way,' he said, 'what has become of Trawley? I have quite lost sight of him. He was hot on the French social systems, and talked of going to the Backwoods to found a sort of Pythagorean community. Is he gone?'

'Not at all. He is practising at a German bath, and has married a rich patient.'

'Then my notions wear the best, so far,' said Lydgate, with a short scornful laugh. 'He would have it, the medical profession was an inevitable system of humbug. I said, the fault was in the men – men who truckle to lies and folly. Instead of preaching against humbug outside the walls, it might be better to set up a disinfecting apparatus within. In short – I am reporting my own conversation – you may be sure I had all the good sense on my side.'

'Your scheme is a good deal more difficult to carry out than the Pythagorean community, though. You have not only got the old Adam in yourself against you, but you have got all those descendants of the original Adam who form the society around you. You see, I have paid twelve or thirteen years more than you for my knowledge of difficulties. But' – Mr Farebrother broke off a moment, and then added, 'you are eyeing that glass vase again. Do you want to make an exchange? You shall not have it without a fair barter.'

'I have some sea-mice – fine specimens – in spirits. And I will throw in Robert Brown's new thing – *Microscopic Observations on the Pollen of Plants* – if you don't happen to have it already.'

'Why, seeing how you long for the monster, I might ask a higher price. Suppose I ask you to look through my drawers and agree with me about all my new species?' The Vicar, while he talked in this way, alternately moved about with his pipe in his mouth, and returned to hang rather fondly over his drawers. 'That would be good discipline, you know, for a young doctor who has to please his patients in Middlemarch. You must learn to be bored, remember. However, you shall have the monster on your own terms.'

'Don't you think men overrate the necessity for humouring everybody's nonsense, till they get despised by the very fools they humour?' said

Lydgate, moving to Mr Farebrother's side, and looking rather absently at the insects ranged in fine gradation, with names subscribed in exquisite writing: 'The shortest way is to make your value felt, so that people must put up with you whether you flatter them or not.'

'With all my heart. But then you must be sure of having the value, and you must keep yourself independent. Very few men can do that. Either you slip out of service altogether, and become good for nothing, or you wear the harness and draw a good deal where your yoke-fellows pull you. But do look at these delicate orthoptera!'

Lydgate had after all to give some scrutiny to each drawer, the Vicar laughing at himself, and yet persisting in the exhibition.

'Apropos of what you said about wearing harness,' Lydgate began, after they had sat down, 'I made up my mind some time ago to do with as little of it as possible. That was why I determined not to try anything in London, for a good many years at least. I didn't like what I saw when I was studying there – so much empty bigwiggism, and obstructive trickery. In the country, people have less pretension to knowledge, and are less of companions, but for that reason they affect one's *amour-propre* less: one makes less bad blood, and can follow one's own course more quietly.'

'Yes – well – you have got a good start; you are in the right profession, the work you feel yourself most fit for. Some people miss that, and repent too late. But you must not be too sure of keeping your independence.'

'You mean of family ties?' said Lydgate, conceiving that these might press rather tightly on Mr Farebrother.

'Not altogether. Of course they make many things more difficult. But a good wife – a good unworldly woman – may really help a man, and keep him more independent. There's a parishioner of mine – a fine fellow, but who would hardly have pulled through as he has done without his wife. Do you know the Garths? I think they were not Peacock's patients.'

'No; but there is a Miss Garth at old Featherstone's, at Lowick.'

'Their daughter: an excellent girl.'

'She is very quiet – I have hardly noticed her.'

'She has taken notice of you, though, depend upon it.'

'I don't understand,' said Lydgate; he could hardly say 'Of course.'

'Oh, she gauges everybody. I prepared her for confirmation – she is a favourite of mine.'

Mr Farebrother puffed a few moments in silence, Lydgate not caring to know more about the Garths. At last the Vicar laid down his pipe, stretched out his legs, and turned his bright eyes with a smile towards Lydgate, saying –

'But we Middlemarchers are not so tame as you take us to be. We have our intrigues and our parties. I am a party man, for example, and Bulstrode is another. If you vote for me you will offend Bulstrode.'

'What is there against Bulstrode?' said Lydgate, emphatically.

'I did not say there was anything against him except that. If you vote against him you will make him your enemy.'

'I don't know that I need mind about that,' said Lydgate, rather proudly; 'but he seems to have good ideas about hospitals, and he spends large sums on useful public objects. He might help me a good deal in carrying out my ideas. As to his religious notions – why, as Voltaire said, incantations will destroy a flock of sheep if administered with a certain quantity of arsenic. I look for the man who will bring the arsenic, and don't mind about his incantations.'

'Very good. But then you must not offend your arsenic-man. You will not offend me, you know,' said Mr Farebrother, quite unaffectedly. 'I don't translate my own convenience into other people's duties. I am opposed to Bulstrode in many ways. I don't like the set he belongs to: they are a narrow ignorant set, and do more to make their neighbours uncomfortable than to make them better. Their system is a sort of worldly-spiritual cliqueism: they really look on the rest of mankind as a doomed carcase which is to nourish them for heaven. But,' he added, smilingly, 'I don't say that Bulstrode's new hospital is a bad thing; and as to his wanting to oust me from the old one – why, if he thinks me a mischievous fellow, he is only returning a compliment. And I am not a model clergyman – only a decent makeshift.'

Lydgate was not at all sure that the Vicar maligned himself. A model clergyman, like a model doctor, ought to think his own profession the finest in the world, and take all knowledge as mere nourishment to his moral pathology and therapeutics. He only said, 'What reason does Bulstrode give for superseding you?'

'That I don't teach his opinions – which he calls spiritual religion; and that I have no time to spare. Both statements are true. But then I could make time, and I should be glad of the forty pounds. That is the plain fact of the case. But let us dismiss it. I only wanted to tell you that if you vote for your arsenic-man, you are not to cut me in consequence. I can't spare you. You are a sort of circumnavigator come to settle among us, and will keep up my belief in the antipodes. Now tell me all about them in Paris.'

✑ EIGHTEEN ✐

Oh, sir, the loftiest hopes on earth
Draw lots with meaner hopes: heroic breasts,
Breathing bad air, run risk of pestilence;
Or, lacking lime-juice when they cross the Line,
May languish with the scurvy.

SOME WEEKS PASSED AFTER THIS CONVERSATION before the question of the
chaplaincy gathered any practical import for Lydgate, and without telling
himself the reason, he deferred the predetermination on which side he
should give his vote. It would really have been a matter of total indifference to him – that is to say, he would have taken the more convenient side,
and given his vote for the appointment of Tyke without any hesitation – if
he had not cared personally for Mr Farebrother.

But his liking for the Vicar of St Botolph's grew with growing acquaintanceship. That, entering into Lydgate's position as a newcomer who had
his own professional objects to secure, Mr Farebrother should have taken
pains rather to warn off than to obtain his interest, showed an unusual
delicacy and generosity which Lydgate's nature was keenly alive to. It
went along with other points of conduct in Mr Farebrother which were
exceptionally fine, and made his character resemble those southern landscapes which seem divided between natural grandeur and social slovenli-
ness. Very few men could have been as filial and chivalrous as he was to
the mother, aunt, and sister, whose dependence on him had in many ways
shaped his life rather uneasily for himself; few men who feel the pressure
of small needs are so nobly resolute not to dress up their inevitably self-
interested desires in a pretext of better motives. In these matters he was
conscious that his life would bear the closest scrutiny; and perhaps the
consciousness encouraged a little defiance towards the critical strictness of
persons whose celestial intimacies seemed not to improve their domestic
manners, and whose lofty aims were not needed to account for their
actions. Then, his preaching was ingenious and pithy, like the preaching
of the English Church in its robust age, and his sermons were delivered
without book. People outside his parish went to hear him; and, since to fill
the church was always the most difficult part of a clergyman's function,
here was another ground for a careless sense of superiority. Besides, he
was a likeable man: sweet-tempered, ready-witted, frank, without grins of
suppressed bitterness or other conversational flavours which make half

of us an affliction to our friends. Lydgate liked him heartily, and wished for his friendship.

With this feeling uppermost, he continued to waive the question of the chaplaincy, and to persuade himself that it was not only no proper business of his, but likely enough never to vex him with a demand for his vote. Lydgate, at Mr Bulstrode's request, was laying down plans for the internal arrangements of the new hospital, and the two were often in consultation. The banker was always presupposing that he could count in general on Lydgate as a coadjutor, but made no special recurrence to the coming decision between Tyke and Farebrother. When the General Board of the Infirmary had met, however, and Lydgate had notice that the question of the chaplaincy was thrown on a council of the directors and medical men, to meet on the following Friday, he had a vexed sense that he must make up his mind on this trivial Middlemarch business. He could not help hearing within him the distinct declaration that Bulstrode was prime minister, and that the Tyke affair was a question of office or no office; and he could not help an equally pronounced dislike to giving up the prospect of office. For his observation was constantly confirming Mr Farebrother's assurance that the banker would not overlook opposition. 'Confound their petty politics!' was one of his thoughts for three mornings in the meditative process of shaving, when he had begun to feel that he must really hold a court of conscience on this matter. Certainly there were valid things to be said against the election of Mr Farebrother: he had too much on his hands already, especially considering how much time he spent on non-clerical occupations. Then again it was a continually repeated shock, disturbing Lydgate's esteem, that the Vicar should obviously play for the sake of money, liking the play indeed, but evidently liking some end which it served. Mr Farebrother contended on theory for the desirability of all games, and said that Englishmen's wit was stagnant for want of them; but Lydgate felt certain that he would have played very much less but for the money. There was a billiard-room at the Green Dragon, which some anxious mothers and wives regarded as the chief temptation in Middlemarch. The Vicar was a first-rate billiard-player, and though he did not frequent the Green Dragon, there were reports that he had sometimes been there in the daytime and had won money. And as to the chaplaincy, he did not pretend that he cared for it, except for the sake of the forty pounds. Lydgate was no Puritan, but he did not care to play, and winning money at it had always seemed a meanness to him; besides, he had an ideal of life which made this subservience of conduct to the gaining of small sums thoroughly hateful to him. Hitherto in his own life his wants had been supplied without any trouble to himself, and his first impulse was always to be liberal with half-crowns as matters of no importance to a gentleman; it had never occurred to him to devise a plan for getting half-crowns. He had always known in a general way that he was not rich, but he had never felt poor, and he had no power of imagining the part which the want of money plays in determining the actions of men. Money had never been a motive to him. Hence he was not ready to frame excuses for this deliberate pursuit of small gains. It was altogether repulsive to him, and he never entered into any calculation of the ratio between the Vicar's income and his more or less necessary expenditure. It was possible that he would not have made such a calculation in his own case.

And now, when the question of voting had come, this repulsive fact told more strongly against Mr Farebrother than it had done before. One would know much better what to do if men's characters were more consistent, and especially if one's friends were invariably fit for any function they desired to undertake! Lydgate was convinced that if there had been no valid objection to Mr Farebrother, he would have voted for him whatever Bulstrode might have felt on the subject: he did not intend to be a vassal of Bulstrode's. On the other hand, there was Tyke, a man entirely given to his clerical office, who was simply curate at a chapel of ease in St Peter's parish, and had time for extra duty. Nobody had anything to say against Mr Tyke, except that they could not bear him, and suspected him of cant. Really, from his point of view, Bulstrode was thoroughly justified.

But whichever way Lydgate began to incline, there was something to make him wince; and being a proud man, he was a little exasperated at being obliged to wince. He did not like frustrating his own best purposes by getting on bad terms with Bulstrode; he did not like voting against Farebrother, and helping to deprive him of function and salary; and the question occurred whether the additional forty pounds might not leave the Vicar free from that ignoble care about winning at cards. Moreover, Lydgate did not like the consciousness that in voting for Tyke he should be voting on the side obviously convenient for himself. But would the end really be his own convenience? Other people would say so, and would allege that he was currying favour with Bulstrode for the sake of making himself important and getting on in the world. What then? He for his own part knew that if his personal prospects simply had been concerned, he would not have cared a rotten nut for the banker's friendship or enmity. What he really cared for was a medium for his work, a vehicle for his ideas; and after all, was he not bound to prefer the object of getting a good hospital, where he could demonstrate the specific distinctions of fever and test therapeutic results, before anything else connected with this chaplaincy? For the first time Lydgate was feeling the hampering thread-like pressure of small social conditions, and their frustrating complexity. At the end of his inward debate, when he set out for the hospital, his hope was really in the chance that discussion might somehow give a new aspect to the question, and make the scale dip so as to exclude the necessity for voting. I think he trusted a little also to the energy which is begotten by circumstances – some feeling rushing warmly and making resolve easy, while debate in cool blood had only made it more difficult. However it was, he did not distinctly say to himself on which side he would vote; and all the while he was inwardly resenting the subjection which had been forced upon him. It would have seemed beforehand like a ridiculous piece of bad logic that he, with his unmixed resolutions of independence and his select purpose, would find himself at the very outset in the grasp of petty alternatives, each of which was repugnant to him. In his student's chambers, he had pre-arranged his social action quite differently.

Lydgate was late in setting out, but Dr Sprague, the two other surgeons, and several of the directors had arrived early; Mr Bulstrode, treasurer and chairman, being among those who were still absent. The conversation seemed to imply that the issue was problematical, and that a majority for Tyke was not so certain as had been generally supposed. The two physicians, for a wonder, turned out to be unanimous, or rather, though of different minds, they concurred in action. Dr Sprague, the rugged and weighty, was, as every one had foreseen, an adherent of Mr Farebrother. The Doctor was more than suspected of having no religion, but somehow Middlemarch tolerated this deficiency in him as if he had been a Lord Chancellor; indeed it is probable that his professional weight was the more believed in, the world-old association of cleverness with the evil principle being still potent in the minds even of lady-patients who had the strictest ideas of frilling and sentiment. It was perhaps this negation in the Doctor which made his neighbours call him hard-headed and dry-witted; conditions of texture which were also held favourable to the storing of judgments connected with drugs. At all events, it is certain that if any medical man had come to Middlemarch with the reputation of having very definite religious views, of being given to prayer, and of otherwise showing an active piety, there would have been a general presumption against his medical skill.

On this ground it was (professionally speaking) fortunate for Dr Minchin that his religious sympathies were of a general kind, and such as gave a distant medical sanction to all serious sentiment, whether of Church or Dissent, rather than any adhesion to particular tenets. If Mr Bulstrode insisted, as he was apt to do, on the Lutheran doctrine of justification, as that by which a church must stand or fall, Dr Minchin in return was quite sure that man was not a mere machine or a fortuitous conjunction of atoms; if Mrs Wimple insisted on a particular providence in relation to her stomach complaint, Dr Minchin for his part liked to keep the mental windows open and objected to fixed limits; if the Unitarian brewer jested about the Athanasian Creed, Dr Minchin quoted Pope's *Essay on Man*. He objected to the rather free style of anecdote in which Dr Sprague indulged, preferring well-sanctioned quotations, and liking refinement of all kinds: it was generally known that he had some kinship to a bishop, and sometimes spent his holidays at the 'palace'.

Dr Minchin was soft-handed, pale-complexioned, and of rounded outline, not to be distinguished from a mild clergyman in appearance: whereas Dr Sprague was superfluously tall; his trousers got creased at the knees, and showed an excess of boot at a time when straps seemed necessary to any dignity of bearing; you heard him go in and out, and up and down, as if he had come to see after the roofing. In short, he had weight, and might be expected to grapple with a disease and throw it; while Dr Minchin might be better able to detect it lurking and to circumvent it. They enjoyed about equally the mysterious privilege of medical reputation, and concealed with much etiquette their contempt for each other's skill. Regarding themselves as Middlemarch institutions, they were ready to combine against all innovators, and against non-professionals given to interference. On this ground they were both in their hearts equally averse to Mr Bulstrode, though Dr Minchin had never been in open hostility with him, and never differed from him without elaborate explanation to Mrs Bulstrode, who had found that Dr Minchin alone understood her constitution. A layman who pried into the professional conduct of medical men, and was always obtruding his reforms, – though he was less directly embarrassing to the two physicians than to the surgeon-apothecaries who attended paupers by contract, was nevertheless offensive to the professional nostril as such; and Dr Minchin shared fully in the new pique against Bulstrode, excited by his apparent determination to patronize Lydgate. The long-established practitioners, Mr Wrench and Mr Toller, were just now standing apart and having a friendly colloquy, in which they agreed that Lydgate was a jackanapes, just made to serve Bulstrode's purpose. To non-medical friends they had already concurred in praising the other young practitioner, who had come into the town on Mr Peacock's retirement without further recommendation than his own merits and such argument for solid professional acquirement as might be gathered from his having apparently wasted no time on other branches of knowledge. It was clear that Lydgate, by not dispensing drugs, intended to cast imputations on his equals, and also to obscure the limit between his own rank as a general practitioner and that of the physicians, who, in the interest of the profession, felt bound to maintain its various grades. Especially against a man who had not been to either of the English universities and enjoyed the absence of anatomical and bedside study there, but came with a libellous pretension to experience in Edinburgh and Paris, where observation might be abundant indeed, but hardly sound.

Thus it happened that on this occasion Bulstrode became identified with Lydgate, and Lydgate with Tyke; and owing to this variety of interchangeable names for the chaplaincy question, diverse minds were enabled to form the same judgment concerning it.

Dr Sprague said at once bluntly to the group assembled when he entered, 'I go for Farebrother. A salary, with all my heart. But why take it from the Vicar? He has none too much – has to insure his life, besides keeping house, and doing a vicar's charities. Put forty pounds in his pocket and you'll do no harm. He's a good fellow, is Farebrother, with as little of the parson about him as will serve to carry orders.'

'Ho, ho! Doctor,' said old Mr Powderell, a retired ironmonger of some standing – his interjection being something between a laugh and a Parliamentary disapproval. 'We must let you have your say. But what we have to consider is not anybody's income – it's the souls of the poor sick people' – here Mr Powderell's voice and face had a sincere pathos in them. 'He is a real Gospel preacher, is Mr Tyke. I should vote against my conscience if I voted against Mr Tyke – I should indeed.'

'Mr Tyke's opponents have not asked any one to vote against his conscience, I believe,' said Mr Hackbutt, a rich tanner of fluent speech, whose glittering spectacles and erect hair were turned with some severity towards innocent Mr Powderell. 'But in my judgment it behoves us, as Directors, to consider whether we will regard it as our whole business to carry out propositions emanating from a single quarter. Will any member of the committee aver that he would have entertained the idea of displacing the gentleman who has always discharged the function of chaplain here, if it had not been suggested to him by parties whose disposition it is to regard every institution of this town as a machinery for carrying out their own views? I tax no man's motives: let them lie between himself and a higher Power: but I do say, that there are influences at work here which are incompatible with genuine independence, and that a crawling servility is usually dictated by circumstances which gentlemen so conducting themselves could not afford either morally or financially to avow. I myself am a layman, but I have given no inconsiderable attention to the divisions in the Church and . . . '

'Oh, damn the divisions!' burst in Mr Frank Hawley, lawyer and townclerk, who rarely presented himself at the board, but now looked in hurriedly, whip in hand. 'We have nothing to do with them here. Farebrother has been doing the work – what there was – without pay, and if pay is to be given, it should be given to him. I call it a confounded job to take the thing away from Farebrother.'

'I think it would be as well for gentlemen not to give their remarks a personal bearing,' said Mr Plymdale. 'I shall vote for the appointment of Mr Tyke, but I should not have known, if Mr Hackbutt hadn't hinted it, that I was a Servile Crawler.'

'I disclaim any personalities. I expressly said, if I may be allowed to repeat, or even to conclude what I was about to say – '

'Ah, here's Minchin!' said Mr Frank Hawley; at which everybody turned away from Mr Hackbutt, leaving him to feel the uselessness of superior gifts in Middlemarch. 'Come, Doctor, I must have you on the right side, eh?'

'I hope so,' said Dr Minchin, nodding and shaking hands here and there. 'At whatever cost to my feelings.'

'If there's any feeling here, it should be feeling for the man who is turned out, I think,' said Mr Frank Hawley.

'I confess I have feelings on the other side also. I have a divided esteem,' said Dr Minchin, rubbing his hands. 'I consider Mr Tyke an exemplary man – none more so – and I believe him to be proposed from unimpeachable motives. I, for my part, wish that I could give him my vote. But I am constrained to take a view of the case which gives the preponderance to Mr Farebrother's claims. He is an amiable man, an able preacher, and has been longer among us.'

Old Mr Powderell looked on, sad and silent. Mr Plymdale settled his cravat, uneasily.

'You don't set up Farebrother as a pattern of what a clergyman ought to be, I hope,' said Mr Larcher, the eminent carrier, who had just come in. 'I have no ill-will towards him, but I think we owe something to the public, not to speak of anything higher, in these appointments. In my opinion Farebrother is too lax for a clergyman. I don't wish to bring up particulars against him; but he will make a little attendance here go as far as he can.'

'And a devilish deal better than too much,' said Mr Hawley, whose bad language was notorious in that part of the county. 'Sick people can't bear so much praying and preaching. And that methodistical sort of religion is bad for the spirits – bad for the inside, eh!' he added, turning quickly round to the four medical men who were assembled.

But any answer was dispensed with by the entrance of three gentlemen, with whom there were greetings more or less cordial. These were the Reverend Edward Thesiger, Rector of St Peter's, Mr Bulstrode and our friend Mr Brooke of Tipton, who had lately allowed himself to be put on the board of directors in his turn, but had never before attended, his attendance now being due to Mr Bulstrode's exertions. Lydgate was the only person still expected

Every one now sat down, Mr Bulstrode presiding, pale and self-restrained as usual. Mr Thesiger, a moderate evangelical, wished for the appointment of his friend Mr Tyke, a zealous, able man, who, officiating at a chapel of ease, had not a cure of souls too extensive to leave him ample time for the new duty. It was desirable that chaplaincies of this kind should be entered on with a fervent intention: they were peculiar opportunities for spiritual influence; and while it was good that a salary should be allotted, there was the more need for scrupulous watching lest the office should be perverted into a mere question of salary. Mr Thesiger's manner had so much quiet propriety that objectors could only simmer in silence.

Mr Brooke believed that everybody meant well in the matter. He had not himself attended to the affairs of the Infirmary, though he had a strong interest in whatever was for the benefit of Middlemarch, and was most happy to meet the gentlemen present on any public question – 'any public question, you know,' Mr Brooke repeated, with his nod of perfect understanding. 'I am a good deal occupied as a magistrate, and in the collection of documentary evidence, but I regard my time as being at the disposal of the public – and, in short, my friends have convinced me that a chaplain with a salary – a salary, you know – is a very good thing, and I am happy to be able to come here and vote for the appointment of Mr Tyke, who, I understand, is an unexceptionable man, apostolic and eloquent and everything of that kind – and I am the last man to withhold my vote – under the circumstances, you know.'

'It seems to me that you have been crammed with one side of the question, Mr Brooke,' said Mr Frank Hawley, who was afraid of nobody, and was a Tory suspicious of electioneering intentions. 'You don't seem to know that one of the worthiest men we have has been doing duty as chaplain here for years without pay, and that Mr Tyke is proposed to supersede him.'

'Excuse me, Mr Hawley,' said Mr Bulstrode. 'Mr Brooke has been fully informed of Mr Farebrother's character and position.'

'By his enemies,' flashed out Mr Hawley.

'I trust there is no personal hostility concerned here,' said Mr Thesiger.

'I'll swear there is, though,' retorted Mr Hawley.

'Gentlemen,' said Mr Bulstrode, in a subdued tone, 'the merits of the question may be very briefly stated, and if any one present doubts that every gentleman who is about to give his vote has not been fully informed, I can now recapitulate the considerations that should weigh on either side.'

'I don't see the good of that,' said Mr Hawley. 'I suppose we all know whom we mean to vote for. Any man who wants to do justice does not wait till the last minute to hear both sides of the question. I have no time to lose, and I propose that the matter be put to the vote at once.'

A brief but still hot discussion followed before each person wrote 'Tyke' or 'Farebrother' on a piece of paper and slipped it into a glass tumbler; and in the meantime Mr Bulstrode saw Lydgate enter.

'I perceive that the votes are equally divided at present,' said Mr Bulstrode, in a clear biting voice. Then, looking up at Lydgate –

'There is a casting-vote still to be given. It is yours, Mr Lydgate: will you be good enough to write?'

'The thing is settled now,' said Mr Wrench, rising. 'We all know how Mr Lydgate will vote.'

'You seem to speak with some peculiar meaning, sir,' said Lydgate, rather defiantly, and keeping his pencil suspended.

'I merely mean that you are expected to vote with Mr Bulstrode. Do you regard that meaning as offensive?'

'It may be offensive to others. But I shall not desist from voting with him on that account.'

Lydgate immediately wrote down 'Tyke'.

So the Rev. Walter Tyke became chaplain to the Infirmary, and Lydgate continued to work with Mr Bulstrode. He was really uncertain whether Tyke were not the more suitable candidate, and yet his consciousness told him that if he had been quite free from indirect bias he should have voted for Mr Farebrother. The affair of the chaplaincy remained a sore point in his memory as a case in which this petty medium of Middlemarch had been too strong for him. How could a man be satisfied with a decision between such alternatives and under such circumstances? No more than he can be satisfied with his hat, which he has chosen from among such shapes as the resources of the age offer him, wearing it at best with a resignation which is chiefly supported by comparison.

But Mr Farebrother met him with the same friendliness as before. The character of the publican and sinner is not always practically incompatible with that of the modern Pharisee, for the majority of us scarcely see more distinctly the faultiness of our own conduct than the faultiness of our own arguments, or the dulness of our own jokes. But the Vicar of St Botolph's had certainly escaped the slightest tincture of the Pharisee, and by dint of admitting to himself that he was too much as other men were, he had become remarkably unlike them in this – that he could excuse others for thinking slightly of him, and could judge impartially of their conduct even when it told against him.

'The world has been too strong for *me*, I know,' he said one day to Lydgate. 'But then I am not a mighty man – I shall never be a man of renown. The choice of Hercules is a pretty fable; but Prodicus makes it easy work for the hero, as if the first resolves were enough. Another story says that he came to hold the distaff, and at last wore the Nessus shirt. I suppose one good resolve might keep a man right if everybody else's resolve helped him.'

The Vicar's talk was not always inspiriting: he had escaped being a Pharisee, but he had not escaped that low estimate of possibilities which we rather hastily arrive at as an inference from our own failure. Lydgate thought that there was a pitiable infirmity of will in Mr Farebrother.

◁ NINETEEN ▷

L'altra vedete ch'ha fatto alla guancia
Della sua palma, sospirando, letto.
Purgatorio, vii

WHEN GEORGE THE FOURTH WAS STILL reigning over the privacies of Windsor, when the Duke of Wellington was Prime Minister, and Mr Vincy was mayor of the old corporation in Middlemarch, Mrs Casaubon, born Dorothea Brooke, had taken her wedding journey to Rome. In those days the world in general was more ignorant of good and evil by forty years than it is at present. Travellers did not often carry full information on Christian art either in their heads or their pockets; and even the most brilliant English critic of the day mistook the flower-flushed tomb of the ascended Virgin for an ornamental vase due to the painter's fancy. Romanticism, which has helped to fill some dull blanks with love and knowledge, had not yet penetrated the times with its leaven and entered into everybody's food; it was fermenting still as a distinguishable vigorous enthusiasm in certain long-haired German artists at Rome, and the youth of other nations who worked or idled near them were sometimes caught in the spreading movement.

One fine morning a young man whose hair was not immoderately long, but abundant and curly, and who was otherwise English in his equipment, had just turned his back on the Belvedere Torso in the Vatican and was looking out on the magnificent view of the mountains from the adjoining round vestibule. He was sufficiently absorbed not to notice the approach of a dark-eyed, animated German who came up to him and placing a hand on his shoulder, said with a strong accent, 'Come here, quick! else she will have changed her pose.'

Quickness was ready at the call, and the two figures passed lightly along by the Meleager towards the hall where the reclining Ariadne, then called the Cleopatra, lies in the marble voluptuousness of her beauty, the drapery folding around her with a petal-like ease and tenderness. They were just in time to see another figure standing against a pedestal near the reclining marble: a breathing blooming girl, whose form, not shamed by the Ariadne, was clad in Quakerish grey drapery; her long cloak, fastened at the neck, was thrown backward from her arms, and one beautiful ungloved hand pillowed her cheek, pushing somewhat backward the white beaver bonnet which made a sort of halo to her face around the simply braided dark-brown hair. She was not looking at the sculpture, probably not thinking of it: her large eyes were fixed dreamily on a streak of sunlight which fell across the floor. But she became conscious of the two strangers who suddenly paused as if to contemplate the Cleopatra, and, without looking at them, immediately turned away to join a maid-servant and courier who were loitering along the hall at a little distance off.

'What do you think of that for a fine bit of antithesis?' said the German, searching in his friend's face for responding admiration, but going on volubly without waiting for any other answer. 'There lies antique beauty, not corpse-like even in death, but arrested in the complete contentment of its sensuous perfection: and here stands beauty in its breathing life, with the consciousness of Christian centuries in its bosom. But she should be dressed as a nun; I think she looks almost what you call a Quaker; I would dress her as a nun in my picture. However, she is married! I saw her wedding-ring on that wonderful left hand, otherwise I should have thought the sallow *Geistlicher* was her father. I saw him parting from her a good while ago, and just now I found her in that magnificent pose. Only think! he is perhaps rich, and would like to have her portrait taken. Ah! it is no use looking after her – there she goes! Let us follow her home!'

'No, no,' said his companion, with a little frown.

'You are singular, Ladislaw. You look struck together. Do you know her?'

'I know that she is married to my cousin,' said Will Ladislaw, sauntering down the hall with a preoccupied air, while his German friend kept at his side and watched him eagerly.

'What, the *Geistlicher*? He looks more like an uncle – a more useful sort of relation.'

'He is not my uncle. I tell you he is my second cousin,' said Ladislaw, with some irritation.

'*Schön, schön*. Don't be snappish. You are not angry with me for thinking Mrs Second-Cousin the most perfect young Madonna I ever saw?'

'Angry? nonsense. I have only seen her once before, for a couple of minutes, when my cousin introduced her to me, just before I left England. They were not married then. I didn't know they were coming to Rome.'

'But you will go to see them now – you will find out what they have for an address – since you know the name. Shall we go to the post? And you could speak about the portrait.'

'Confound you, Naumann! I don't know what I shall do. I am not so brazen as you.'

'Bah! that is because you are dilettantish and amateurish. If you were an artist, you would think of Mistress Second-Cousin as antique form animated by Christian sentiment – a sort of Christian Antigone – sensuous force controlled by spiritual passion.'

'Yes, and that your painting her was the chief outcome of her existence – the divinity passing into higher completeness and all but exhausted in the act of covering your bit of canvas. I am amateurish if you like: I do *not* think that all the universe is straining towards the obscure significance of your pictures.'

'But it is, my dear! – so far as it is straining through me, Adolf Naumann: that stands firm,' said the good-natured painter, putting a hand on Ladislaw's shoulder, and not in the least disturbed by the unaccountable touch of ill-humour in his tone. 'See now! My existence pre-supposes the existence of the whole universe – does it *not*? and my function is to paint – and as a painter I have a conception which is altogether *genialisch*, of your great-aunt or second grandmother as a subject for a picture; therefore, the universe is straining towards that picture through that particular hook or claw which is put forth in the shape of me – not true?'

'But how if another claw in the shape of me is straining to thwart it? – the case is a little less simple then.'

'Not at all: the result of the struggle is the same thing – picture or no picture – logically.' Will could not resist this imperturbable temper, and the cloud in his face broke into sunshiny laughter.

'Come now, my friend – you will help?' said Naumann, in a hopeful tone.

'No; nonsense, Naumann! English ladies are not at everybody's service as models. And you want to express too much with your painting. You would only have made a better or worse portrait with a background which every connoisseur would give a different reason for or against. And what is a portrait of a woman? Your painting and Plastik are poor stuff after all. They perturb and dull conceptions instead of raising them. Language is a finer medium.'

'Yes, for those who can't paint,' said Naumann. 'There you have perfect right. I did not recommend you to paint, my friend.'

The amiable artist carried his sting, but Ladislaw did not choose to appear stung. He went on as if he had not heard.

'Language gives a fuller image, which is all the better for being vague. After all, the true seeing is within; and painting stares at you with an insistent imperfection. I feel that especially about representations of women. As if a woman were a mere coloured superficies! You must wait for movement and tone. There is a difference in their very breathing: they change from moment to moment. – This woman whom you have just seen, for example: how would you paint her voice, pray? But her voice is much diviner than anything you have seen of her.'

'I see, I see. You are jealous. No man must presume to think that he can paint your ideal. This is serious, my friend! Your great-aunt! "*Der Neffe als Onkel*" in a tragic sense – *ungeheuer!*'

'You and I shall quarrel, Naumann, if you call that lady my aunt again.'

'How is she to be called then?'

'Mrs Casaubon.'

'Good. Suppose I get acquainted with her in spite of you, and find that she very much wishes to be painted?'

'Yes, suppose!' said Will Ladislaw, in a contemptuous undertone, intended to dismiss the subject. He was conscious of being irritated by ridiculously small causes, which were half of his own creation. Why was he making any fuss about Mrs Casaubon? And yet he felt as if something had happened to him with regard to her. There are characters which are continually creating collisions and nodes for themselves in dramas which nobody is prepared to act with them. Their susceptibilities will clash against objects that remain innocently quiet.

৫ TWENTY ৩

A child forsaken, waking suddenly,
Whose gaze afeard on all things round doth rove,
And seeth only that it cannot see
The meeting eyes of love.

TWO HOURS LATER, DOROTHEA WAS SEATED in an inner room or boudoir of a handsome apartment in the Via Sistina.

I am sorry to add that she was sobbing bitterly, with such abandonment to this relief of an oppressed heart as a woman habitually controlled by pride on her own account and thoughtfulness for others will sometimes allow herself when she feels securely alone. And Mr Casaubon was certain to remain away for some time at the Vatican.

Yet Dorothea had no distinctly shapen grievance that she could state even to herself; and in the midst of her confused thought and passion, the mental act that was struggling forth into clearness was a self-accusing cry that her feeling of desolation was the fault of her own spiritual poverty. She had married the man of her choice, and with the advantage over most girls that she had contemplated her marriage chiefly as the beginning of new duties: from the very first she had thought of Mr Casaubon as having a mind so much above her own, that he must often be claimed by studies which she could not entirely share; moreover, after the brief narrow experience of her girlhood she was beholding Rome, the city of visible history, where the past of a whole hemisphere seems moving in funeral procession with strange ancestral images and trophies gathered from afar.

But this stupendous fragmentariness heightened the dreamlike strangeness of her bridal life. Dorothea had now been five weeks in Rome, and in the kindly mornings when autumn and winter seemed to go hand in hand like a happy aged couple one of whom would presently survive in chiller loneliness, she had driven about at first with Mr Casaubon, but of late chiefly with Tantripp and their experienced courier. She had been led through the best galleries, had been taken to the chief points of view, had been shown the greatest ruins and the most glorious churches, and she had ended by oftenest choosing to drive out to the Campagna where she could feel alone with the earth and sky, away from the oppressive masquerade of ages, in which her own life too seemed to become a masque with enigmatical costumes.

To those who have looked at Rome with the quickening power of a knowledge which breathes a growing soul into all historic shapes, and traces out the suppressed transitions which unite all contrasts, Rome may still be the spiritual centre and interpreter of the world. But let them conceive one more historical contrast: the gigantic broken revelations of that Imperial and Papal city thrust abruptly on the notions of a girl who had been brought up in English and Swiss Puritanism, fed on meagre Protestant histories and on art chiefly of the hand-screen sort; a girl whose ardent nature turned all her small allowance of knowledge into principles, fusing her actions into their mould, and whose quick emotions gave the most abstract things the quality of a pleasure or a pain; a girl who had lately become a wife, and from the enthusiastic acceptance of untried duty found herself plunged in tumultuous preoccupation with her personal lot. The weight of unintelligible Rome might lie easily on bright nymphs to whom it formed a background for the brilliant picnic of Anglo-foreign society; but Dorothea had no such defence against deep impressions. Ruins and basilicas, palaces and colossi, set in the midst of a sordid present, where all that was living and warm-blooded seemed sunk in the deep degeneracy of a superstition divorced from reverence; the dimmer but yet eager Titanic life gazing and struggling on walls and ceilings; the long vistas of white forms whose marble eyes seemed to hold the monotonous light of an alien world: all this vast wreck of ambitious ideals, sensuous and spiritual, mixed confusedly with the signs of breathing forgetfulness and degradation, at first jarred her as with an electric shock, and then urged themselves on her with that ache belonging to a glut of confused ideas which check the flow of emotion. Forms both pale and glowing took possession of her young sense, and fixed themselves in her memory even when she was not thinking of them, preparing strange associations which remained through her after-years. Our moods are apt to bring with them images which succeed each other like the magic-lantern pictures of a doze; and in certain states of dull forlornness Dorothea all her life continued to see the vastness of St Peter's, the huge bronze canopy, the excited intention in the attitudes and garments of the prophets and evangelists in the mosaics above, and the red drapery which was being hung for Christmas spreading itself everywhere like a disease of the retina.

Not that this inward amazement of Dorothea's was anything very exceptional: many souls in their young nudity are tumbled out among incongruities and left to 'find their feet' among them, while their elders go about their business. Nor can I suppose that when Mrs Casaubon is discovered in a fit of weeping six weeks after her wedding, the situation will be regarded as tragic. Some discouragement, some faintness of heart at the new real future which replaces the imaginary, is not unusual, and we do not expect people to be deeply moved by what is not unusual. That element of tragedy which lies in the very fact of frequency, has not yet wrought itself into the coarse emotion of mankind; and perhaps our frames could hardly bear much of it. If we had a keen vision and feeling of all ordinary human life, it would be like hearing the grass grow and the squirrel's heart beat, and we should die of that roar which lies on the other side of silence. As it is, the quickest of us walk about well wadded with stupidity.

However, Dorothea was crying, and if she had been required to state the cause, she could only have done so in some such general words as I have already used: to have been driven to be more particular would have been like trying to give a history of the lights and shadows; for that new real future which was replacing the imaginary drew its material from the endless minutiae by which her view of Mr Casaubon and her wifely relation, now that she was married to him, was gradually changing with the secret motion of a watch-hand from what it had been in her maiden dream. It was too early yet for her fully to recognize or at least admit the change, still more for her to have readjusted that devotedness which was so necessary a part of her mental life that she was almost sure sooner or later to recover it. Permanent rebellion, the disorder of a life without some loving reverent resolve, was not possible to her; but she was now in an interval when the very force of her nature heightened its confusion. In this way, the early months of marriage often are times of critical tumult – whether that of a shrimp-pool or of deeper waters – which afterwards subsides into cheerful peace.

But was not Mr Casaubon just as learned as before? Had his forms of expression changed, or his sentiments become less laudable? O waywardness of womanhood! did his chronology fail him, or his ability to state not only a theory but the names of those who held it; or his provision for giving the heads of any subject on demand? And was not Rome the place in all the world to give free play to such accomplishments? Besides, had not Dorothea's enthusiasm especially dwelt on the prospect of relieving the weight and perhaps the sadness with which great tasks lie on him who has to achieve them? – And that such weight pressed on Mr Casaubon was only plainer than before.

All these are crushing questions; but whatever else remained the same, the light had changed, and you cannot find the pearly dawn at noonday. The fact is unalterable, that a fellow-mortal with whose nature you are acquainted solely through the brief entrances and exits of a few imaginative weeks called courtship, may, when seen in the continuity of married companionship, be disclosed as something better or worse than what you have preconceived, but will certainly not appear altogether the same. And it would be astonishing to find how soon the change is felt if we had no kindred changes to compare with it. To share lodgings with a brilliant dinner-companion, or to see your favourite politician in the Ministry, may bring about changes quite as rapid: in these cases too we begin by knowing little and believing much, and we sometimes end by inverting the quantities.

Still, such comparisons might mislead, for no man was more incapable of flashy make-believe than Mr Casaubon: he was as genuine a character as any ruminant animal, and he had not actively assisted in creating any illusions about himself. How was it that in the weeks since her marriage, Dorothea had not distinctly observed but felt with a stifling depression, that the large vistas and wide fresh air which she had dreamed of finding in her husband's mind were replaced by ante-rooms and winding passages which seemed to lead nowhither? I suppose it was that in courtship everything is regarded as provisional and preliminary, and the smallest sample of virtue or accomplishment is taken to guarantee delightful stores which the broad leisure of marriage will reveal. But the door-sill of marriage once crossed, expectation is concentrated on the present. Having once embarked on your marital voyage, it is impossible not to be aware that you make no way and that the sea is not within sight – that, in fact, you are exploring an enclosed basin.

In their conversation before marriage, Mr Casaubon had often dwelt on some explanation or questionable detail of which Dorothea did not see the bearing; but such imperfect coherence seemed due to the brokenness of their intercourse, and, supported by her faith in their future, she had listened with fervid patience to a recitation of possible arguments to be brought against Mr Casaubon's entirely new view of the Philistine god Dagon and other fish-deities, thinking that hereafter she should see this subject which touched him so nearly from the same high ground whence doubtless it had become so important to him. Again, the matter-of-course statement and tone of dismissal with which he treated what to her were the most stirring thoughts, was easily accounted for as belonging to the sense of haste and preoccupation in which she herself shared during their engagement. But now, since they had been in Rome, with all the depths of her emotion roused to tumultuous activity, and with life made a new problem by new elements, she had been becoming more and more aware, with a certain terror, that her mind was continually sliding into inward fits of anger or repulsion, or else into forlorn weariness. How far the judicious Hooker or any other hero of erudition would have been the same at Mr Casaubon's time of life, she had no means of knowing, so that he could not have the advantage of comparison; but her husband's way of commenting on the strangely impressive objects around them had begun to affect her with a sort of mental shiver: he had perhaps the best intention of acquitting himself worthily, but only of acquitting himself. What was fresh to her mind was worn out to his; and such capacity of thought and feeling as had ever been stimulated in him by the general life of mankind had long shrunk to a sort of dried preparation, a lifeless embalmment of knowledge.

When he said, 'Does this interest you, Dorothea? Shall we stay a little longer? I am ready to stay if you wish it,' – it seemed to her as if going or staying were alike dreary. Or, 'Should you like to go to the Farnesina,

Dorothea? It contains celebrated frescoes designed or painted by Raphael, which most persons think it worth while to visit.'

'But do you care about them?' was always Dorothea's question.

'They are, I believe, highly esteemed. Some of them represent the fable of Cupid and Psyche, which is probably the romantic invention of a literary period, and cannot, I think, be reckoned as a genuine mythical product. But if you like these wall-paintings we can easily drive thither; and you will then, I think, have seen the chief works of Raphael, any of which it were a pity to omit in a visit to Rome. He is the painter who has been held to combine the most complete grace of form with sublimity of expression. Such at least I have gathered to be the opinion of cognoscenti.'

This kind of answer given in a measured official tone, as of a clergyman reading according to the rubric, did not help to justify the glories of the Eternal City, or to give her the hope that if she knew more about them the world would be joyously illuminated for her. There is hardly any contact more depressing to a young ardent creature than that of a mind in which years full of knowledge seem to have issued in a blank absence of interest or sympathy.

On other subjects indeed Mr Casaubon showed a tenacity of occupation and an eagerness which are usually regarded as the effect of enthusiasm, and Dorothea was anxious to follow this spontaneous direction of his thoughts, instead of being made to feel that she dragged him away from it. But she was gradually ceasing to expect with her former delightful confidence that she should see any wide opening where she followed him. Poor Mr Casaubon himself was lost among small closets and winding stairs, and in an agitated dimness about the Cabeiri, or in an exposure of other mythologists' ill-considered parallels, easily lost sight of any purpose which had prompted him to these labours. With his taper stuck before him he forgot the absence of windows, and in bitter manuscript remarks on other men's notions about the solar deities, he had become indifferent to the sunlight.

These characteristics, fixed and unchangeable as bone in Mr Casaubon, might have remained longer unfelt by Dorothea if she had been encouraged to pour forth her girlish and womanly feeling – if he would have held her hands between his and listened with the delight of tenderness and understanding to all the little histories which made up her experience, and would have given her the same sort of intimacy in return, so that the past life of each could be included in their mutual knowledge and affection – or if she could have fed her affection with those childlike caresses which are the bent of every sweet woman, who has begun by showering kisses on the hard pate of her bald doll, creating a happy soul within that woodenness from the wealth of her own love. That was Dorothea's bent. With all her yearning to know what was afar from her and to be widely benignant, she had ardour enough for what was near, to have kissed Mr Casaubon's coat-sleeve, or to have caressed his shoe-latchet, if he would have made any other sign of acceptance than pronouncing her, with his unfailing propriety, to be of a most affectionate and truly feminine nature, indicating at the same time by politely reaching a chair for her that he regarded these manifestations as rather crude and startling. Having made his clerical toilette with due care in the morning, he was prepared only for those amenities of life which were suited to the well-adjusted stiff cravat of the period, and to a mind weighted with unpublished matter.

And by a sad contradiction Dorothea's ideas and resolves seemed like melting ice floating and lost in the warm flood of which they had been but another form. She was humiliated to find herself a mere victim of feeling, as if she could know nothing except through that medium: all her strength was scattered in fits of agitation, of struggle, of despondency, and then again in visions of more complete renunciation, transforming all hard conditions into duty. Poor Dorothea! she was certainly troublesome – to herself chiefly; but this morning for the first time she had been troublesome to Mr Casaubon.

She had begun, while they were taking coffee, with a determination to shake off what she inwardly called her selfishness, and turned a face all cheerful attention to her husband when he said, 'My dear Dorothea, we must now think of all that is yet left undone, as a preliminary to our departure. I would fain have returned home earlier that we might have been at Lowick for the Christmas; but my inquiries here have been protracted beyond their anticipated period. I trust, however, that the time here has not been passed unpleasantly to you. Among the sights of Europe, that of Rome has ever been held one of the most striking and in some respects edifying. I well remember that I considered it an epoch in my life when I visited it for the first time; after the fall of Napoleon, an event which opened the Continent to travellers. Indeed I think it is one among several cities to which an extreme hyperbole has been applied – "See Rome and die": but in your case I would propose an emendation and say, See Rome as a bride, and live thenceforth as a happy wife.'

Mr Casaubon pronounced this little speech with the most conscientious intention, blinking a little and swaying his head up and down, and concluding with a smile. He had not found marriage a rapturous state, but he had no idea of being anything else than an irreproachable husband, who would make a charming young woman as happy as she deserved to be.

'I hope you are thoroughly satisfied with our stay – I mean, with the result so far as your studies are concerned,' said Dorothea, trying to keep her mind fixed on what most affected her husband.

'Yes,' said Mr Casaubon, with that peculiar pitch of voice which makes the word half a negative. 'I have been led farther than I had foreseen, and various subjects for annotation have presented themselves which, though I have no direct need of them, I could not pretermit. The task, notwithstanding the assistance of my amanuensis, has been a somewhat laborious one, but your society has happily prevented me from that too continuous prosecution of thought beyond the hours of study which has been the snare of my solitary life.'

'I am very glad that my presence has made any difference to you,' said Dorothea, who had a vivid memory of evenings in which she had supposed that Mr Casaubon's mind had gone too deep during the day to be able to get to the surface again. I fear there was a little temper in her reply. 'I hope when we get to Lowick, I shall be more useful to you, and be able to enter a little more into what interests you.'

'Doubtless, my dear,' said Mr Casaubon, with a slight bow. 'The notes I have here made will want sifting, and you can, if you please, extract them under my direction.'

'And all your notes,' said Dorothea, whose heart had already burned within her on this subject so that now she could not help speaking with her tongue. 'All those rows of volumes – will you not now do what you used to speak of? – will you not make up your mind what part of them you will use, and begin to write the book which will make your vast knowledge useful to the world? I will write to your dictation, or I will copy and extract what you tell me: I can be of no other use.' Dorothea, in a most unaccountable, darkly-feminine manner, ended with a slight sob and eyes full of tears.

The excessive feeling manifested would alone have been highly disturbing to Mr Casaubon, but there were other reasons why Dorothea's words were among the most cutting and irritating to him that she could have been impelled to use. She was as blind to his inward troubles as he to hers; she had not yet learned those hidden conflicts in her husband which claim our pity. She had not yet listened patiently to his heart-beats, but only felt that her own was beating violently. In Mr Casaubon's ear, Dorothea's voice gave loud emphatic iteration to those muffled suggestions of consciousness which it was possible to explain as mere fancy, the illusion of exaggerated sensitiveness: always when such suggestions are unmistakably repeated from without, they are resisted as cruel and unjust. We are angered even by the full acceptance of our humiliating confessions – how much more by hearing in hard distinct syllables from the lips of a near observer, those confused murmurs which we try to call morbid, and strive against as if they were the oncoming of numbness! And this cruel outward accuser was there in the shape of a wife – nay, of a young bride, who, instead of observing his abundant pen scratches and amplitude of paper with the uncritical awe of an elegant-minded canary-bird, seemed to present herself as a spy watching everything with a malign power of inference. Here, towards this particular point of the compass, Mr Casaubon had a sensitiveness to match Dorothea's, and an equal quickness to imagine more than the fact. He had formerly observed with approbation her capacity for worshipping the right object; he now foresaw with sudden terror that this capacity might be replaced by presumption, this worship by the most exasperating of all criticism, – that which sees vaguely a great many fine ends and has not the least notion what it costs to reach them.

For the first time since Dorothea had known him, Mr Casaubon's face had a quick angry flush upon it.

'My love,' he said, with irritation reined in by propriety, 'you may rely upon me for knowing the times and the seasons, adapted to the different stages of a work which is not to be measured by the facile conjectures of ignorant onlookers. It had been easy for me to gain a temporary effect by a mirage of baseless opinion; but it is ever the trial of the scrupulous explorer to be saluted with the impatient scorn of chatterers who attempt only the smallest achievements, being indeed equipped for no other. And it were well if all such could be admonished to discriminate judgments of which the true subject-matter lies entirely beyond their reach, from those of which the elements may be compassed by a narrow and superficial survey.'

This speech was delivered with an energy and readiness quite unusual with Mr Casaubon. It was not indeed entirely an improvisation, but had taken shape in inward colloquy, and rushed out like the round grains from a fruit when sudden heat cracks. Dorothea was not only his wife: she was a personification of that shallow world which surrounds the ill-appreciated or desponding author.

Dorothea was indignant in her turn. Had she not been repressing everything in her except the desire to enter into some fellowship with her husband's chief interests?

'My judgment *was* a very superficial one – such as I am capable of forming,' she answered, with a prompt resentment, that needed no rehearsal. 'You showed me the rows of notebooks – you have often spoken of them – you have often said that they wanted digesting. But I never heard you speak of the writing that is to be published. Those were very simple facts, and my judgment went no farther. I only begged you to let me be of some good to you.'

Dorothea rose to leave the table and Mr Casaubon made no reply, taking up a letter which lay beside him as if to reperuse it. Both were shocked at their mutual situation – that each should have betrayed anger towards the other. If they had been at home, settled at Lowick in ordinary life among their neighbours, the clash would have been less embarrassing: but on a wedding journey, the express object of which is to isolate two people on the ground that they are all the world to each other, the sense of disagreement is, to say the least, confounding and stultifying. To have changed your longitude extensively, and placed yourselves in a moral solitude in order to have small explosions, to find conversation difficult and to hand a glass of water without looking, can hardly be regarded as satisfactory fulfilment even to the toughest minds. To Dorothea's inexperienced sensitiveness, it seemed like a catastrophe, changing all prospects; and to Mr

Casaubon it was a new pain, he never having been on a wedding journey before, or found himself in that close union which was more of a subjection than he had been able to imagine, since this charming young bride not only obliged him to much consideration on her behalf (which he had sedulously given), but turned out to be capable of agitating him cruelly just where he most needed soothing. Instead of getting a soft fence against the cold, shadowy, unapplausive audience of his life, had he only given it a more substantial presence?

Neither of them felt it possible to speak again at present. To have reversed a previous arrangement and declined to go out would have been a show of persistent anger which Dorothea's conscience shrank from, seeing that she already began to feel herself guilty. However just her indignation might be, her ideal was not to claim justice, but to give tenderness. So when the carriage came to the door, she drove with Mr Casaubon to the Vatican, walked with him through the stony avenue of inscriptions, and when she parted with him at the entrance to the Library, went on through the Museum out of mere listlessness as to what was around her. She had not spirit to turn round and say that she would drive anywhere. It was when Mr Casaubon was quitting her that Naumann had first seen her, and he had entered the long gallery of sculpture at the same time with her; but here Naumann had to await Ladislaw, with whom he was to settle a bet of champagne about an enigmatical mediaeval-looking figure there. After they had examined the figure, and had walked on finishing their dispute, they had parted, Ladislaw lingering behind while Naumann had gone into the Hall of Statues, where he again saw Dorothea, and saw her in that brooding abstraction which made her pose remarkable. She did not really see the streak of sunlight on the floor more than she saw the statues: she was inwardly seeing the light of years to come in her own home and over the English fields and elms and hedge-bordered highroads: and feeling that the way in which they might be filled with joyful devotedness was not so clear to her as it had been. But in Dorothea's mind there was a current into which all thought and feeling were apt sooner or later to flow – the reaching forward of the whole consciousness towards the fullest truth, the least partial good. There was clearly something better than anger and despondency.

♋ TWENTY-ONE ♌

Hire facounde eke full womanly and plain,
No contrefeted termes had she
To semen wise.

CHAUCER

IT WAS IN THAT WAY DOROTHEA CAME to be sobbing as soon as she was securely alone. But she was presently roused by a knock at the door, which made her hastily dry her eyes before saying, 'Come in.' Tantripp had brought a card, and said that there was a gentleman waiting in the lobby. The courier had told him that only Mrs Casaubon was at home, but he said he was a relation of Mr Casaubon's: would she see him?

'Yes,' said Dorothea, without pause; 'show him into the salon.' Her chief impressions about young Ladislaw were that when she had seen him at Lowick she had been made aware of Mr Casaubon's generosity towards him, and also that she had been interested in his own hesitation about his career. She was alive to anything that gave her an opportunity for active sympathy, and at this moment it seemed as if the visit had come to shake her out of her self-absorbed discontent – to remind her of her husband's goodness, and make her feel that she had now the right to be his helpmate in all kind deeds. She waited a minute or two, but when she passed into the next room there were just signs enough that she had been crying to make her open face look more youthful and appealing than usual. She met Ladislaw with that exquisite smile of goodwill which is unmixed with vanity, and held out her hand to him. He was the elder by several years, but at that moment he looked much the younger, for his transparent complexion flushed suddenly, and he spoke with a shyness extremely unlike the ready indifference of his manner with his male companion, while Dorothea became all the calmer with a wondering desire to put him at ease.

'I was not aware that you and Mr Casaubon were in Rome, until this morning, when I saw you in the Vatican Museum,' he said. 'I knew you at once – but – I mean, that I concluded Mr Casaubon's address would be found at the Poste Restante, and I was anxious to pay my respects to him and you as early as possible.'

'Pray sit down. He is not here now, but he will be glad to hear of you, I am sure,' said Dorothea, seating herself unthinkingly between the fire and the light of the tall window, and pointing to a chair opposite, with the quietude of a benignant matron. The signs of girlish sorrow in her face were only the more striking. 'Mr Casaubon is much engaged; but you will leave your address – will you not? – and he will write to you.'

'You are very good,' said Ladislaw, beginning to lose his diffidence in the interest with which he was observing the signs of weeping which had altered her face. 'My address is on my card. But if you will allow me I will call again to-morrow at an hour when Mr Casaubon is likely to be at home.'

'He goes to read in the Library of the Vatican every day, and you can hardly see him except by an appointment. Especially now. We are about to leave Rome, and he is very busy. He is usually away almost from breakfast till dinner. But I am sure he will wish you to dine with us.'

Will Ladislaw was struck mute for a few moments. He had never been fond of Mr Casaubon, and if it had not been for the sense of obligation, would have laughed at him as a Bat of erudition. But the idea of this dried-up pedant, this elaborator of small explanations about as important as the surplus stock of false antiquities kept in a vendor's back chamber, having first got this adorable young creature to marry him, and then passing his honeymoon away from her, groping after his mouldy futilities (Will was given to hyperbole) – this sudden picture stirred him with a sort of comic disgust: he was divided between the impulse to laugh aloud and the equally unseasonable impulse to burst into scornful invective. For an instant he felt that the struggle was causing a queer contortion of his mobile features, but with a good effort he resolved it into nothing more offensive than a merry smile.

Dorothea wondered; but the smile was irresistible, and shone back from her face too. Will Ladislaw's smile was delightful, unless you were angry with him beforehand: it was a gush of inward light illuminating the transparent skin as well as the eyes, and playing about every curve and line as if some Ariel were touching them with a new charm, and banishing for ever the traces of moodiness. The reflection of that smile could not but have a little merriment in it too, even under dark eyelashes still moist, as Dorothea said inquiringly, 'Something amuses you?'

'Yes,' said Will, quick in finding resources. 'I am thinking of the sort of figure I cut the first time I saw you, when you annihilated my poor sketch with your criticism.'

'My criticism?' said Dorothea, wondering still more. 'Surely not. I always feel particularly ignorant about painting.'

'I suspected you of knowing so much, that you knew how to say just what was most cutting. You said – I daresay you don't remember it as I do – that the relation of my sketch to nature was quite hidden from you. At least, you implied that.' Will could laugh now as well as smile.

'That was really my ignorance,' said Dorothea, admiring Will's good humour. 'I must have said so only because I never could see any beauty in the pictures which my uncle told me all judges thought very fine. And I have gone about with just the same ignorance in Rome. There are comparatively few paintings that I can really enjoy. At first when I enter a room where the walls are covered with frescoes, or with rare pictures, I feel a kind of awe – like a child present at great ceremonies where there are grand robes and processions; I feel myself in the presence of some higher life than my own. But when I begin to examine the pictures one by one, the life goes out of them, or else is something violent and strange to me. It must be my own dulness. I am seeing so much all at once, and not understanding half of it. That always makes one feel stupid. It is painful to be told that anything is very fine and not be able to feel that it is fine – something like being blind, while people talk of the sky.'

'Oh, there is a great deal in the feeling for art which must be acquired,' said Will. (It was impossible now to doubt the directness of Dorothea's confession.) 'Art is an old language with a great many artificial affected styles, and sometimes the chief pleasure one gets out of knowing them is the mere sense of knowing. I enjoy the art of all sorts here immensely; but I suppose if I could pick my enjoyment to pieces I should find it made up of many different threads. There is something in daubing a little one's self, and having an idea of the process.'

'You mean perhaps to be a painter?' said Dorothea, with a new direction of interest. 'You mean to make painting your profession. Mr Casaubon will like to hear that you have chosen a profession.'

'No, oh no,' said Will, with some coldness. 'I have quite made up my mind against it. It is too one-sided a life. I have been seeing a great deal of the German artists here: I travelled from Frankfort with one of them. Some are fine, even brilliant fellows – but I should not like to get into their way of looking at the world entirely from the studio point of view.'

'That I can understand,' said Dorothea, cordially. 'And in Rome it seems as if there were so many things which are more wanted in the world than pictures. But if you have a genius for painting, would it not be right to take that as a guide? Perhaps you might do better things than these – or different, so that there might not be so many pictures almost all alike in the same place.'

There was no mistaking this simplicity, and Will was won by it into frankness. 'A man must have a very rare genius to make changes of that sort. I am afraid mine would not carry me even to the pitch of doing well what has been done already, at least not so well as to make it worth while. And I should never succeed in anything by dint of drudgery. If things don't come easily to me I never get them.'

'I have heard Mr Casaubon say that he regrets your want of patience,' said Dorothea, gently. She was rather shocked at this mode of taking all life as a holiday.

'Yes, I know Mr Casaubon's opinion. He and I differ.'

The slight streak of contempt in his hasty reply offended Dorothea. She was all the more susceptible about Mr Casaubon because of her morning's trouble.

'Certainly you differ,' she said, rather proudly. 'I did not think of comparing you: such power of persevering devoted labour as Mr Casaubon's is not common.'

Will saw that she was offended, but this only gave an additional impulse to the new irritation of his latent dislike towards Mr Casaubon. It was too intolerable that Dorothea should be worshipping this husband: such weakness in a woman is pleasant to no man but the husband in question. Mortals are easily tempted to pinch the life out of their neighbour's buzzing glory, and think that such killing is no murder.

'No, indeed,' he answered, promptly. 'And therefore it is a pity that it should be thrown away, as so much English scholarship is, for want of knowing what is being done by the rest of the world. If Mr Casaubon read German he would save himself a great deal of trouble.'

'I do not understand you,' said Dorothea, startled and anxious.

'I merely mean,' said Will, in an offhand way, 'that the Germans have taken the lead in historical inquiries, and they laugh at results which are got by groping about in the woods with a pocket-compass while they have made good roads. When I was with Mr Casaubon I saw that he deafened himself in that direction: it was almost against his will that he read a Latin treatise written by a German. I was very sorry.'

Will only thought of giving a good pinch that would annihilate that vaunted laboriousness, and was unable to imagine the mode in which Dorothea would be wounded. Young Mr Ladislaw was not at all deep himself in German writers; but very little achievement is required in order to pity another man's shortcomings.

Poor Dorothea felt a pang at the thought that the labour of her husband's life might be void, which left her no energy to spare for the question whether this young relative who was so much obliged to him ought not to have repressed his observation. She did not even speak, but sat looking at her hands, absorbed in the piteousness of that thought.

Will, however, having given that annihilating pinch, was rather ashamed, imagining from Dorothea's silence that he had offended her still more; and having also a conscience about plucking the tail-feathers from a benefactor.

'I regretted it especially,' he resumed, taking the usual course from detraction to insincere eulogy, 'because of my gratitude and respect towards my cousin. It would not signify so much in a man whose talents and character were less distinguished.'

Dorothea raised her eyes, brighter than usual with excited feeling, and said, in her saddest recitative, 'How I wish I had learned German when I was at Lausanne! There were plenty of German teachers. But now I can be of no use.'

There was a new light, but still a mysterious light, for Will in Dorothea's last words. The question how she had come to accept Mr Casaubon – which he had dismissed when he first saw her by saying that she must be disagreeable in spite of appearances – was not now to be answered on any such short and easy method. Whatever else she might be, she was not disagreeable. She was not coldly clever and indirectly satirical, but adorably simple and full of feeling. She was an angel beguiled. It would be a unique delight to wait and watch for the melodious fragments in which her heart and soul came forth so directly and ingenuously. The Aeolian harp again came into his mind.

She must have made some original romance for herself in this marriage. And if Mr Casaubon had been a dragon who had carried her off to his lair with his talons simply and without legal forms, it would have been an unavoidable feat of heroism to release her and fall at her feet. But he was something more unmanageable than a dragon: he was a benefactor with collective society at his back, and he was at that moment entering the room in all the unimpeachable correctness of his demeanour, while Dorothea was looking animated with a newly aroused alarm and regret, and Will was looking animated with his admiring speculation about her feelings.

Mr Casaubon felt a surprise which was quite unmixed with pleasure, but he did not swerve from his usual politeness of greeting, when Will rose and explained his presence. Mr Casaubon was less happy than usual, and this perhaps made him look all the dimmer and more faded; else, the effect might easily have been produced by the contrast of his young cousin's appearance. The first impression on seeing Will was one of sunny brightness, which added to the uncertainty of his changing expression. Surely, his very features changed their form; his jaw looked sometimes large and sometimes small; and the little ripple in his nose was a preparation for metamorphosis. When he turned his head quickly his hair seemed to shake out light, and some persons thought they saw decided genius in this coruscation. Mr Casaubon, on the contrary, stood rayless.

As Dorothea's eyes were turned anxiously on her husband she was perhaps not insensible to the contrast, but it was only mingled with other causes in making her more conscious of that new alarm on his behalf which was the first stirring of a pitying tenderness fed by the realities of his lot and not by her own dreams. Yet it was a source of greater freedom to her that Will was there; his young equality was agreeable, and also perhaps his openness to conviction. She felt an immense need of some one to speak to, and she had never before seen any one who seemed so quick and pliable, so likely to understand everything.

Mr Casaubon gravely hoped that Will was passing his time profitably as well as pleasantly in Rome – had thought his intention was to remain in South Germany – but begged him to come and dine to-morrow, when he would converse more at large: at present he was somewhat weary. Ladislaw understood, and accepting the invitation immediately took his leave.

Dorothea's eyes followed her husband anxiously, while he sank down wearily at the end of a sofa, and resting his elbow supported his head and looked on the floor. A little flushed, and with bright eyes, she seated herself beside him, and said,

'Forgive me for speaking so hastily to you this morning. I was wrong. I fear I hurt you and made the day more burdensome.'

'I am glad that you feel that, my dear,' said Mr Casaubon. He spoke quietly and bowed his head a little, but there was still an uneasy feeling in his eyes as he looked at her.

'But you do forgive me?' said Dorothea, with a quick sob. In her need for some manifestation of feeling she was ready to exaggerate her own fault. Would not love see returning penitence afar off, and fall on its neck and kiss it?

'My dear Dorothea – "who with repentance is not satisfied, is not of heaven nor earth". – You do not think me worthy to be banished by that severe sentence,' said Mr Casaubon, exerting himself to make a strong statement, and also to smile faintly.

Dorothea was silent, but a tear which had come up with the sob would insist on falling.

'You are excited, my dear. And I also am feeling some unpleasant consequences of too much mental disturbance,' said Mr Casaubon. In fact, he had it in his thought to tell her that she ought not to have received young Ladislaw in his absence; but he abstained, partly from the sense that it would be ungracious to bring a new complaint in the moment of her penitent acknowledgment, partly because he wanted to avoid further agitation of himself by speech, and partly because he was too proud to betray that jealousy of disposition which was not so exhausted on his scholarly compeers that there was none to spare in other directions. There is a sort of jealousy which needs very little fire; it is hardly a passion, but a blight bred in the cloudy, damp despondency of uneasy egoism.

'I think it is time for us to dress,' he added, looking at his watch. They both rose, and there was never any further allusion between them to what had passed on this day.

But Dorothea remembered it to the last with the vividness with which we all remember epochs in our experience when some dear expectation dies, or some new motive is born. To-day she had begun to see that she had been under a wild illusion in expecting a response to her feeling from Mr Casaubon, and she had felt the waking of a presentiment that there might be a sad consciousness in his life which made as great a need on his side as on her own.

We are all of us born in moral stupidity, taking the world as an udder to feed our supreme selves: Dorothea had early begun to emerge from that stupidity, but yet it had been easier to her to imagine how she would devote herself to Mr Casaubon, and become wise and strong in his strength and wisdom, than to conceive with that distinctness which is no longer reflection but feeling – an idea wrought back to the directness of sense, like the solidity of objects – that he had an equivalent centre of self, whence the lights and shadows must always fall with a certain difference.

◁ TWENTY-TWO ▷

Nous causâmes longtemps; elle était simple et bonne.
Ne sachant pas le mal, elle faisait le bien;
Des richesses du ceour elle me fit l'aumône,
Et tout en écoutant comme le ceour se donne,
Sans oser y penser, je lui donnai le mien;
Elle emporta ma vie, et n'en sut jamais rien.
ALFRED DE MUSSET

WILL LADISLAW WAS DELIGHTFULLY AGREEABLE at dinner the next day, and gave no opportunity for Mr Casaubon to show disapprobation. On the contrary it seemed to Dorothea that Will had a happier way of drawing her husband into conversation and of deferentially listening to him than she had ever observed in any one before. To be sure, the listeners about Tipton were not highly gifted! Will talked a good deal himself, but what he said was thrown in with such rapidity, and with such an unimportant air of saying something by the way, that it seemed a gay little chime after the great bell. If Will was not always perfect, this was certainly one of his good days. He described touches of incident among the poor people in Rome, only to be seen by one who could move about freely; he found himself in agreement with Mr Casaubon as to the unsound opinions of Middleton concerning the relations of Judaism and Catholicism; and passed easily to a half-enthusiastic half-playful picture of the enjoyment he got out of the very miscellaneousness of Rome, which made the mind flexible with constant comparison, and saved you from seeing the world's ages as a set of box-like partitions without vital connection. Mr Casaubon's studies, Will observed, had always been of too broad a kind for that, and he had perhaps never felt any such sudden effect, but for himself he confessed that Rome had given him quite a new sense of history as a whole; the fragments stimulated his imagination and made him constructive. Then occasionally, but not too often, he appealed to Dorothea, and discussed what she said, as if her sentiment were an item to be considered in the final judgment even of the Madonna di Foligno or the Laocoon. A sense of contributing to form the world's opinion makes conversation particularly cheerful; and Mr Casaubon too was not without his pride in his young wife, who spoke better than most women, as indeed he had perceived in choosing her.

Since things were going on so pleasantly, Mr Casaubon's statement that his labours in the Library would be suspended for a couple of days, and that after a brief renewal he should have no further reason for staying in Rome, encouraged Will to urge that Mrs Casaubon should not go away without seeing a studio or two. Would not Mr Casaubon take her? That sort of thing ought not to be missed; it was quite special: it was a form of life that grew like a small fresh vegetation with its population of insects on huge fossils. Will would be happy to conduct them – not to anything wearisome, only to a few examples.

Mr Casaubon, seeing Dorothea look earnestly towards him, could not but ask her if she would be interested in such visits: he was now at her service during the whole day; and it was agreed that Will should come on the morrow and drive with them.

Will could not omit Thorwaldsen, a living celebrity about whom even Mr Casaubon inquired, but before the day was far advanced he led the way to the studio of his friend Adolf Naumann, whom he mentioned as one of the chief renovators of Christian art, one of those who had not only revived but expanded that grand conception of supreme events as mysteries at which the successive ages were spectators, and in relation to which the great souls of all periods became as it were contemporaries. Will added that he had made himself Naumann's pupil for the nonce.

'I have been making some oil-sketches under him,' said Will. 'I hate copying. I must put something of my own in. Naumann has been painting the Saints drawing the Car of the Church, and I have been making a sketch of Marlowe's Tamburlaine Driving the Conquered Kings in his Chariot. I am not so ecclesiastical as Naumann, and I sometimes twit him with his excess of meaning. But this time I mean to outdo him in breadth of intention. I take Tamburlaine in his chariot for the tremendous course of the world's physical history lashing on the harnessed dynasties. In my opinion, that is a good mythical interpretation.' Will here looked at Mr Casaubon, who received this off-hand treatment of symbolism very uneasily, and bowed with a neutral air.

'The sketch must be very grand, if it conveys so much,' said Dorothea. 'I should need some explanation even of the meaning you give. Do you intend Tamburlaine to represent earthquakes and volcanoes?'

'O yes,' said Will, laughing, 'and migrations of races and clearings of forests – and America and the steam-engine. Everything you can imagine!'

'What a difficult kind of shorthand!' said Dorothea, smiling towards her husband. 'It would require all your knowledge to be able to read it.'

Mr Casaubon blinked furtively at Will. He had a suspicion that he was being laughed at. But it was not possible to include Dorothea in the suspicion.

They found Naumann painting industriously, but no model was present; his pictures were advantageously arranged, and his own plain vivacious person set off by a dove-coloured blouse and a maroon velvet cap, so that everything was as fortunate as if he had expected the beautiful young English lady exactly at that time.

The painter in his confident English gave little dissertations on his finished and unfinished subjects, seeming to observe Mr Casaubon as much as he did Dorothea. Will burst in here and there with ardent words of praise, marking out particular merits in his friend's work; and Dorothea felt that she was getting quite new notions as to the significance of Madonnas seated under inexplicable canopied thrones with the simple country as a background, and of saints with architectural models in their hands, or knives accidentally wedged in their skulls. Some things which had seemed monstrous to her were gathering intelligibility and even a natural meaning; but all this was apparently a branch of knowledge in which Mr Casaubon had not interested himself.

'I think I would rather feel that painting is beautiful than have to read it as an enigma; but I should learn to understand these pictures sooner than yours with the very wide meaning,' said Dorothea, speaking to Will.

'Don't speak of my painting before Naumann,' said Will. 'He will tell you, it is all *pfuscherei*⁶, which is his most opprobrious word!'

'Is that true?' said Dorothea, turning her sincere eyes on Naumann, who made a slight grimace and said,

'Oh, he does not mean it seriously with painting. His walk must be *belles-lettres*. That is wi-ide.'

Naumann's pronunciation of the vowel seemed to stretch the word satirically. Will did not half like it, but managed to laugh; and Mr Casaubon, while he felt some disgust at the artist's German accent, began to entertain a little respect for his judicious severity.

The respect was not diminished when Naumann, after drawing Will aside for a moment and looking, first at a large canvas, then at Mr Casaubon, came forward again and said,

'My friend Ladislaw thinks you will pardon me, sir, if I say that a sketch of your head would be invaluable to me for the St Thomas Aquinas in my picture there. It is too much to ask; but I so seldom see just what I want – the idealistic in the real.'

'You astonish me greatly, sir,' said Mr Casaubon, his looks improved with a glow of delight; 'but if my poor physiognomy, which I have been accustomed to regard as of the commonest order, can be of any use to you in furnishing some traits for the angelical doctor, I shall feel honoured. That is to say, if the operation will not be a lengthy one; and if Mrs Casaubon will not object to the delay.'

As for Dorothea, nothing could have pleased her more, unless it had been a miraculous voice pronouncing Mr Casaubon the wisest and worthiest among the sons of men. In that case her tottering faith would have become firm again.

Naumann's apparatus was at hand in wonderful completeness, and the sketch went on at once as well as the conversation. Dorothea sat down and subsided into calm silence, feeling happier than she had done for a long while before. Every one about her seemed good, and she said to herself that Rome, if she had only been less ignorant, would have been full of beauty; its sadness would have been winged with hope. No nature could be less suspicious than hers; when she was a child she believed in the gratitude of wasps and the honourable susceptibility of sparrows, and was proportionately indignant when their baseness was made manifest.

The adroit artist was asking Mr Casaubon questions about English politics, which brought long answers, and Will meanwhile had perched himself on some steps in the background overlooking all.

Presently Naumann said – 'Now if I could lay this by for half an hour and take it up again – come and look, Ladislaw – I think it is perfect so far.'

Will vented those adjuring interjections which imply that admiration is too strong for syntax; and Naumann said in a tone of piteous regret –

'Ah – now – if I could but have had more – but you have other engagements – I could not ask it – or even to come again to-morrow.'

'O let us stay!' said Dorothea. 'We have nothing to do to-day except to go about, have we?' she added, looking entreatingly at Mr Casaubon. 'It would be a pity not to make the head as good as possible.'

'I am at your service, sir, in the matter,' said Mr Casaubon, with polite condescension. 'Having given up the interior of my head to idleness, it is as well that the exterior should work in this way.'

'You are unspeakably good – now I am happy!' said Naumann, and then went on in German to Will, pointing here and there to the sketch as if he were considering that. Putting it aside for a moment, he looked round vaguely, as if seeking some occupation for his visitors, and afterwards turning to Mr Casaubon said,

'Perhaps the beautiful bride, the gracious lady, would not be unwilling to let me fill up the time by trying to make a slight sketch of her – not, of course, as you see, for that picture – only as a single study.'

Mr Casaubon, bowing, doubted not that Mrs Casaubon would oblige him, and Dorothea said, at once, 'Where shall I put myself?'

Naumann was all apologies in asking her to stand, and allow him to adjust her attitude to which she submitted without any of the affected airs and laughs frequently thought necessary on such occasions, when the painter said, 'It is as Santa Clara that I want you to stand – leaning so, with your cheek against your hand – so – looking at that stool, please, so!'

Will was divided between the inclination to fall at the Saint's feet and kiss her robe, and the temptation to knock Naumann down while he was adjusting her arm. All this was impudence and desecration, and he repented that he had brought her.

The artist was diligent, and Will recovering himself moved about and occupied Mr Casaubon as ingeniously as he could; but he did not in the end prevent the time from seeming long to that gentleman, as was clear from his expressing a fear that Mrs Casaubon would be tired. Naumann took the hint and said –

'Now, sir, if you can oblige me again, I will release the lady-wife.'

So Mr Casaubon's patience held out further, and when after all it turned out that the head of Saint Thomas Aquinas would be more perfect if another sitting could be had, it was granted for the morrow. On the morrow Santa Clara too was retouched more than once. The result of all was so far from displeasing to Mr Casaubon that he arranged for the purchase of the picture in which Saint Thomas Aquinas sat among the doctors of the Church in a disputation too abstract to be represented, but listened to with more or less attention by an audience above. The Santa Clara, which was spoken of in the second place, Naumann declared himself to be dissatisfied with – he could not, in conscience, engage to make a worthy picture of it; so about the Santa Clara the arrangement was conditional.

I will not dwell on Naumann's jokes at the expense of Mr Casaubon that evening, or on his dithyrambs about Dorothea's charm, in all which Will joined, but with a difference. No sooner did Naumann mention any detail of Dorothea's beauty, than Will got exasperated at his presumption: there was grossness in his choice of the most ordinary words, and what business had he to talk of her lips? She was not a woman to be spoken of as other women were. Will could not say just what he thought, but he became irritable. And yet, when after some resistance he had consented to take the Casaubons to his friend's studio, he had been allured by the gratification of his pride in being the person who could grant Naumann such an opportunity of studying her loveliness – or rather her divineness, for the ordinary phrases which might apply to mere bodily prettiness were not applicable to her. (Certainly all Tipton and its neighbourhood, as well as Dorothea herself, would have been surprised at her beauty being made so much of. In that part of the world Miss Brooke had been only a 'fine young woman'.)

'Oblige me by letting the subject drop, Naumann. Mrs Casaubon is not to be talked of as if she were a model,' said Will. Naumann stared at him.

'*Schön*! I will talk of my Aquinas. The head is not a bad type, after all. I daresay the great scholastic himself would have been flattered to have his portrait asked for. Nothing like these starchy doctors for vanity! It was as I thought: he cared much less for her portrait than his own.'

'He's a cursed white-blooded pedantic coxcomb,' said Will, with gnashing impetuosity. His obligations to Mr Casaubon were not known to his hearer, but Will himself was thinking of them, and wishing that he could discharge them all by a cheque.

Naumann gave a shrug and said, 'It is good they go away soon, my dear. They are spoiling your fine temper.'

All Will's hope and contrivance were now concentrated on seeing Dorothea when she was alone. He only wanted her to take more emphatic notice of him; he only wanted to be something more special in her remembrance than he could yet believe himself likely to be. He was rather impatient under that open ardent goodwill, which he saw was her usual state of feeling. The remote worship of a woman throned out of their reach plays a great part in men's lives, but in most cases the worshipper longs for some queenly recognition, some approving sign by which his soul's sovereign may cheer him without descending from her high place. That was precisely what Will wanted. But there were plenty of contradictions in his imaginative demands. It was beautiful to see how Dorothea's eyes turned with wifely anxiety and beseeching to Mr Casaubon: she would have lost some of her halo if she had been without that duteous preoccupation: and yet at the next moment the husband's sandy absorption of such nectar was too intolerable; and Will's longing to say damaging things about him was perhaps not the less tormenting because he felt the strongest reasons for restraining it.

Will had not been invited to dine the next day. Hence he persuaded himself that he was bound to call, and that the only eligible time was the middle of the day, when Mr Casaubon would not be at home.

Dorothea, who had not been made aware that her former reception of Will had displeased her husband, had no hesitation about seeing him, especially as he might be come to pay a farewell visit. When he entered she was looking at some cameos which she had been buying for Celia. She greeted Will as if his visit were quite a matter of course, and said at once, having a cameo bracelet in her hand,

'I am so glad you are come. Perhaps you understand all about cameos, and can tell me if these are really good. I wished to have you with us in choosing them, but Mr Casaubon objected; he thought there was not time. He will finish his work to-morrow, and we shall go away in three days. I have been uneasy about these cameos. Pray sit down and look at them.'

'I am not particularly knowing, but there can be no great mistake about these little Homeric bits: they are exquisitely neat. And the colour is fine: it will just suit you.'

'O, they are for my sister, who has quite a different complexion. You saw her with me at Lowick: she is light-haired and very pretty – at least I think so. We were never so long away from each other in our lives before. She is a great pet, and never was naughty in her life. I found out before I came away that she wanted me to buy her some cameos, and I should be sorry for them not to be good – after their kind.' Dorothea added the last words with a smile.

'You seem not to care about cameos,' said Will, seating himself at some distance from her, and observing her while she closed the cases.

'No, frankly, I don't think them a great object in life,' said Dorothea.

'I fear you are a heretic about art generally. How is that? I should have expected you to be very sensitive to the beautiful everywhere.'

'I suppose I am dull about many things,' said Dorothea, simply. 'I should like to make life beautiful – I mean everybody's life. And then all this immense expense of art, that seems somehow to lie outside life and make it no better for the world, pains one. It spoils my enjoyment of anything when I am made to think that most people are shut out from it.'

'I call that the fanaticism of sympathy,' said Will, impetuously. 'You might say the same of landscape, of poetry, of all refinement. If you carried it out you ought to be miserable in your own goodness, and turn evil that you might have no advantage over others. The best piety is to enjoy – when you can. You are doing the most then to save the earth's character as an agreeable planet. And enjoyment radiates. It is of no use to try and take care of all the world; that is being taken care of when you feel delight – in art or in anything else. Would you turn all the youth of the world into a tragic chorus, wailing and moralizing over misery? I suspect that you have some false belief in the virtues of misery, and want to make your life a martyrdom.' Will had gone further than he intended, and checked himself. But Dorothea's thought was not taking just the same direction as his own, and she answered without any special emotion –

'Indeed you mistake me. I am not a sad, melancholy creature. I am never unhappy long together. I am angry and naughty – not like Celia: I have a great outburst, and then all seems glorious again. I cannot help believing in glorious things in a blind sort of way. I should be quite willing to enjoy the art here, but there is so much that I don't know the reason of – so much that seems to me a consecration of ugliness rather than beauty. The painting and sculpture may be wonderful, but the feeling is often low and brutal, and sometimes even ridiculous. Here and there I see what takes me at once as noble – something that I might compare with the Alban Mountains or the sunset from the Pincian Hill: but that makes it the greater pity that there is so little of the best kind among all that mass of things over which men have toiled so.'

'Of course there is always a great deal of poor work: the rarer things want that soil to grow in.'

'O dear,' said Dorothea, taking up that thought into the chief current of anxiety, 'I see it must be very difficult to do anything good. I have often felt since I have been in Rome that most of our lives would look much uglier and more bungling than the pictures, if they could be put on the wall.'

Dorothea parted her lips again as if she were going to say more, but changed her mind and paused.

'You are too young – it is an anachronism for you to have such thoughts,' said Will energetically, with a quick shake of the head, habitual to him. 'You talk as if you had never known any youth. It is monstrous – as if you had had a vision of Hades in your childhood, like the boy in the legend. You have been brought up in some of those horrible notions that choose the sweetest women to devour – like Minotaurs. And now you will go and be shut up in that stone prison at Lowick: you will be buried alive. It makes me savage to think of it! I would rather never have seen you than think of you with such a prospect.'

Will again feared that he had gone too far; but the meaning we attach to words depends on our feeling, and his tone of angry regret had so much kindness in it for Dorothea's heart, which had always been giving out ardour and had never been fed with much from the living beings around her, that she felt a new sense of gratitude and answered with a gentle smile.

'It is very good of you to be anxious about me. It is because you did not like Lowick yourself: you had set your heart on another kind of life. But Lowick is my chosen home.'

The last sentence was spoken with an almost solemn cadence, and Will did not know what to say, since it would not be useful for him to embrace her slippers, and tell her that he would die for her: it was clear that she required nothing of the sort; and they were both silent for a moment or two, when Dorothea began again with an air of saying at last what had been in her mind beforehand.

'I wanted to ask you again about something you said the other day. Perhaps it was half of it your lively way of speaking: I notice that you like to put things strongly; I myself often exaggerate when I speak hastily.'

'What was it?' said Will, observing that she spoke with a timidity quite new in her. 'I have a hyperbolical tongue: it catches fire as it goes. I daresay I shall have to retract.'

'I mean what you said about the necessity of knowing German – I mean, for the subjects that Mr Casaubon is engaged in. I have been thinking about it; and it seems to me that with Mr Casaubon's learning he must have before him the same materials as German scholars – has he not?' Dorothea's timidity was due to an indistinct consciousness that she was in the strange situation of consulting a third person about the adequacy of Mr Casaubon's learning.

'Not exactly the same materials,' said Will, thinking that he would be duly reserved. 'He is not an Orientalist, you know. He does not profess to have more than second-hand knowledge there.'

'But there are very valuable books about antiquities which were written a long while ago by scholars who knew nothing about these modern things; and they are still used. Why should Mr Casaubon's not be valuable, like theirs?' said Dorothea, with more remonstrant energy. She was impelled to have the argument aloud, which she had been having in her own mind.

'That depends on the line of study taken,' said Will, also getting a tone of rejoinder. 'The subject Mr Casaubon has chosen is as changing as chemistry: new discoveries are constantly making new points of view. Who wants a system on the basis of the four elements, or a book to refute Paracelsus? Do you not see that it is no use now to be crawling a little way after men of the last century – men like Bryant – and correcting their mistakes? – living in a lumber-room and furbishing up broken-legged theories about Chus and Mizraim?'

'How can you bear to speak so lightly?' said Dorothea, with a look between sorrow and anger. 'If it were as you say, what could be sadder than so much ardent labour all in vain? I wonder it does not affect you more painfully, if you really think that a man like Mr Casaubon, of so much goodness, power, and learning, should in any way fail in what has been the labour of his best years.' She was beginning to be shocked that she had got to such a point of supposition, and indignant with Will for having led her to it.

'You questioned me about the matter of fact, not of feeling,' said Will. 'But if you wish to punish me for the fact, I submit. I am not in a position to express my feeling toward Mr Casaubon: it would be at best a pensioner's eulogy.'

'Pray excuse me,' said Dorothea, colouring deeply. 'I am aware, as you say, that I am in fault, in having introduced the subject. Indeed, I am wrong altogether. Failure after long perseverance is much grander than never to have a striving good enough to be called a failure.'

'I quite agree with you,' said Will, determined to change the situation – 'so much so that I have made up my mind not to run that risk of never attaining a failure. Mr Casaubon's generosity has perhaps been dangerous to me, and I mean to renounce the liberty it has given me. I mean to go back to England shortly and work my own way – depend on nobody else than myself.'

'That is fine – I respect that feeling,' said Dorothea, with returning kindness. 'But Mr Casaubon, I am sure, has never thought of anything in the matter except what was most for your welfare.'

'She has obstinacy and pride enough to serve instead of love, now she has married him,' said Will to himself. Aloud he said, rising,

'I shall not see you again.'

'O stay till Mr Casaubon comes,' said Dorothea, earnestly. 'I am so glad we met in Rome. I wanted to know you.'

'And I have made you angry,' said Will. 'I have made you think ill of me.'

'Oh no! My sister tells me I am always angry with people who do not say just what I like. But I hope I am not given to think ill of them.

In the end I am usually obliged to think ill of myself, for being so impatient.'

'Still, you don't like me; I have made myself an unpleasant thought to you.'

'Not at all,' said Dorothea, with the most open kindness. 'I like you very much.'

Will was not quite contented, thinking that he would apparently have been of more importance if he had been disliked. He said nothing, but looked dull, not to say sulky.

'And I am quite interested to see what you will do,' Dorothea went on cheerfully. 'I believe devoutly in a natural difference of vocation. If it were not for that belief, I suppose I should be very narrow – there are so many things, besides painting, that I am quite ignorant of. You would hardly believe how little I have taken in of music and literature, which you know so much of. I wonder what your vocation will turn out to be: perhaps you will be a poet?'

'That depends. To be a poet is to have a soul so quick to discern, that no shade of quality escapes it, and so quick to feel, that discernment is but a hand playing with finely ordered variety on the chords of emotion – a soul in which knowledge passes instantaneously into feeling, and feeling flashes back as a new organ of knowledge. One may have that condition by fits only.'

'But you leave out the poems,' said Dorothea. 'I think they are wanted to complete the poet. I understand what you mean about knowledge passing into feeling, for that seems to be just what I experience. But I am sure I could never produce a poem.'

'You *are* a poem – and that is to be the best part of a poet – what makes up the poet's consciousness in his best moods,' said Will, showing such originality as we all share with the morning and the spring-time and other endless renewals.

'I am very glad to hear it,' said Dorothea, laughing out her words in a birdlike modulation, and looking at Will with playful gratitude in her eyes. 'What very kind things you say to me!'

'I wish I could ever do anything that would be what you call kind – that I could ever be of the slightest service to you. I fear I shall never have the opportunity.' Will spoke with fervour.

'Oh yes!' said Dorothea, cordially. 'It will come; and I shall remember how well you wish me. I quite hoped that we should be friends when I first saw you – because of your relationship to Mr Casaubon.' There was a certain liquid brightness in her eyes, and Will was conscious that his own were obeying a law of nature and filling too. The allusion to Mr Casaubon would have spoiled all if anything at that moment could have spoiled the subduing power, the sweet dignity, of her noble unsuspicious in-experience.

'And there is one thing even now that you can do,' said Dorothea, rising and walking a little way under the strength of a recurring impulse. 'Promise me that you will not again, to any one, speak of that subject – I mean, about Mr Casaubon's writings – I mean in that kind of way. It was I who led to it. It was my fault. But promise me.' She had returned from her brief pacing and stood opposite Will, looking gravely at him.

'Certainly, I will promise you,' said Will, reddening however. If he never said a cutting word about Mr Casaubon again and left off receiving favours from him, it would clearly be permissible to hate him the more. The poet must know how to hate, says Goethe; and Will was at least ready with that accomplishment. He said that he must go now without waiting for Mr Casaubon, whom he would come to take leave of at the last moment. Dorothea gave him her hand, and they exchanged a simple 'Good-bye.'

But going out of the *porte cochère* he met Mr Casaubon, and that gentleman, expressing the best wishes for his cousin, politely waived the pleasure of any further leave-taking on the morrow, which would be sufficiently crowded with the preparations for departure.

'I have something to tell you about our cousin, Mr Ladislaw, which I think will heighten your opinion of him,' said Dorothea to her husband in the course of the evening. She had mentioned immediately on his entering that Will had just gone away, and would come again, but Mr Casaubon had said, 'I met him outside, and we made our final adieux, I believe,' saying this with the air and tone by which we imply that any subject, whether private or public, does not interest us enough to wish for a further remark upon it. So Dorothea had waited.

'What is that, my love?' said Mr Casaubon (he always said 'my love', when his manner was the coldest).

'He has made up his mind to leave off wandering at once, and to give up his dependence on your generosity. He means soon to go back to England, and work his own way. I thought you would consider that a good sign,' said Dorothea, with an appealing look into her husband's neutral face.

'Did he mention the precise order of occupation to which he would addict himself?'

'No. But he said that he felt the danger which lay for him in your generosity. Of course he will write to you about it. Do you not think better of him for his resolve?'

'I shall await his communication on the subject,' said Mr Casaubon.

'I told him I was sure that the thing you considered in all you did for him was his own welfare. I remembered your goodness in what you said about him when I first saw him at Lowick,' said Dorothea, putting her hand on her husband's.

'I had a duty towards him,' said Mr Casaubon, laying his other hand on Dorothea's in conscientious acceptance of her caress, but with a glance which he could not hinder from being uneasy. 'The young man, I confess, is not otherwise an object of interest to me, nor need we, I think, discuss his future course, which it is not ours to determine beyond the limits which I have sufficiently indicated.'

Dorothea did not mention Will again.

BOOK THREE
WAITING FOR DEATH

ꙮ TWENTY-THREE ꙮ

'Your horses of the Sun,' he said,
'And first-rate whip Apollo!
Whate'er they be, I'll eat my head,
But I will beat them hollow.'

FRED VINCY, WE HAVE SEEN, HAD A DEBT on his mind, and though no such immaterial burthen could depress that buoyant-hearted young gentleman for many hours together, there were circumstances connected with this debt which made the thought of it unusually importunate. The creditor was Mr Bambridge, a horse-dealer of the neighbourhood, whose company was much sought in Middlemarch by young men understood to be 'addicted to pleasure'. During the vacations Fred had naturally required more amusements than he had ready money for, and Mr Bambridge had been accommodating enough not only to trust him for the hire of horses and the accidental expense of ruining a fine hunter, but also to make a small advance by which he might be able to meet some losses at billiards. The total debt was a hundred and sixty pounds. Bambridge was in no alarm about his money, being sure that young Vincy had backers; but he had required something to show for it, and Fred had at first given a bill with his own signature. Three months later he had renewed this bill with the signature of Caleb Garth. On both occasions Fred had felt confident that he should meet the bill himself, having ample funds at disposal in his own hopefulness. You will hardly demand that his confidence should have a basis in external facts; such confidence, we know, is something less coarse and materialistic: it is a comfortable disposition leading us to expect that the wisdom of providence or the folly of our friends, the mysteries of luck or the still greater mystery of our high individual value in the universe, will bring about agreeable issues, such as are consistent with our good taste in costume, and our general preference for the best style of thing. Fred felt sure that he should have a present from his uncle, that he should have a run of luck, that by dint of 'swapping' he should gradually metamorphose a horse worth forty pounds into a horse that would fetch a hundred at any moment – 'judgment' being always equivalent to an unspecified sum in hard cash. And in any case, even supposing negations which only a morbid distrust could imagine, Fred had always (at that time) his father's pocket as a last resource, so that his assets of hopefulness had a sort of gorgeous superfluity about them. Of what might be the capacity of his father's pocket. Fred had only a vague notion: was not trade elastic? And would not the deficiencies of one year be made up for by the surplus of another? The Vincys lived in an easy profuse way, not with any new ostentation, but according to the family habits and traditions, so that the children had no standard of economy, and the elder ones retained some of their infantine notion that their father might pay for anything if he would. Mr Vincy himself had expensive Middlemarch habits – spent money on coursing, on his cellar, and on dinner-giving, while mamma had those running accounts with tradespeople, which give a cheerful sense of getting everything one wants without any question of payment. But it was in the nature of fathers, Fred knew, to bully one about expenses: there was always a little storm over his extravagance if he had to disclose a debt, and Fred disliked bad weather within doors. He was too filial to be disrespectful to his father, and he bore the thunder with the certainty that it was transient; but in the meantime it was disagreeable to see his mother cry, and also to be obliged to look sulky instead of having fun; for Fred was so good-tempered that if he looked glum under scolding, it was chiefly for propriety's sake. The easier course, plainly, was to renew the bill with a friend's signature. Why not? With the superfluous securities of hope at his command, there was no reason why he should not have increased other people's liabilities to any extent, but for the fact that men whose names were good for anything were usually pessimists, indisposed to believe that the universal order of things would necessarily be agreeable to an agreeable young gentleman.

With a favour to ask we review our list of friends, do justice to their more amiable qualities, forgive their little offences, and concerning each in turn, try to arrive at the conclusion that he will be eager to oblige us, our own eagerness to be obliged being as communicable as other warmth. Still there is always a certain number who are dismissed as but moderately eager until the others have refused; and it happened that Fred checked off all his friends but one, on the ground that applying to them would be disagreeable; being implicitly convinced that he at least (whatever might be maintained about mankind generally) had a right to be free from anything disagreeable. That he should ever fall into a thoroughly unpleasant position – wear trousers shrunk with washing, eat cold mutton, have to walk for want of a horse, or to 'duck under' in any sort of way – was an absurdity irreconcilable with those cheerful intuitions implanted in him by nature. And Fred winced under the idea of being looked down upon as wanting funds for small debts. Thus it came to pass that the friend whom he chose to apply to was at once the poorest and the kindest – namely, Caleb Garth.

The Garths were very fond of Fred, as he was of them; for when he and Rosamond were little ones, and the Garths were better off, the slight connection between the two families through Mr Featherstone's double marriage (the first to Mr Garth's sister, and the second to Mrs Vincy's) had led to an acquaintance which was carried on between the children rather than the parents: the children drank tea together out of their toy tea-cups, and spent whole days together in play. Mary was a little hoyden, and Fred at six years old thought her the nicest girl in the world, making her his wife with a brass ring which he had cut from an umbrella. Through all the stages of his education he had kept his affection for the Garths, and his habit of going to their house as a second home, though any intercourse between them and the elders of his family had long ceased. Even when Caleb Garth was prosperous, the Vincys were on condescending terms with him and his wife, for there were nice distinctions of rank in Middlemarch; and though old manufacturers could not any more than dukes be connected with none but equals, they were conscious of an inherent social superiority which was defined with great nicety in practice, though hardly expressible theoretically. Since then Mr Garth had failed in the building business, which he had unfortunately added to his other avocations of surveyor, valuer, and agent, had conducted that business for a time entirely for the benefit of his assignees, and had been living narrowly, exerting himself to the utmost that he might after all pay twenty shillings in the pound. He had now achieved this, and from all who did not think it a bad precedent, his honourable exertions had won him due esteem; but in no part of the world is genteel visiting founded on esteem, in the absence of suitable furniture and complete dinner-service. Mrs Vincy had never been at her ease with Mrs Garth, and frequently spoke of her as a woman who had had to work for her bread – meaning that Mrs Garth had been a teacher before her marriage; in which case an intimacy with Lindley Murray and Mangnall's *Questions* was something like a draper's discrimination of calico trademarks, or a courier's acquaintance with foreign countries: no woman who was better off needed that sort of thing. And since Mary had been keeping Mr Featherstone's house, Mrs Vincy's want of liking for the Garths had been converted into something more positive, by alarm lest Fred should engage himself to this plain girl, whose parents 'lived in such a small way'. Fred, being aware of this, never spoke at home of his visits to Mrs Garth, which had of late become more frequent, the increasing ardour of his affection for Mary inclining him the more towards those who belonged to her.

Mr Garth had a small office in the town, and to this Fred went with his request. He obtained it without much difficulty, for a large amount of painful experience had not sufficed to make Caleb Garth cautious about his own affairs, or distrustful of his fellow-men when they had not proved themselves untrustworthy; and he had the highest opinion of Fred, was 'sure the lad would turn out well – an open affectionate fellow, with a good bottom to his character – you might trust him for anything'. Such was Caleb's psychological argument. He was one of those rare men who are rigid to themselves and indulgent to others. He had a certain shame about his neighbours' errors, and never spoke of them willingly; hence he was not likely to divert his mind from the best mode of hardening timber and other ingenious devices in order to preconceive those errors. If he had to blame any one, it was necessary for him to move all the papers within his reach, or describe various diagrams with his stick, or make calculations with the odd money in his pocket, before he could begin; and he would rather do other men's work than find fault with their doing. I fear he was a bad disciplinarian.

When Fred stated the circumstances of his debt, his wish to meet it without troubling his father, and the certainty that the money would be forthcoming so as to cause no one any inconvenience, Caleb pushed his spectacles upward, listened, looked into his favourite's clear young eyes, and believed him, not distinguishing confidence about the future from veracity about the past; but he felt that it was an occasion for a friendly hint as to conduct, and that before giving his signature he must give a rather strong admonition. Accordingly, he took the paper and lowered his spectacles, measured the space at his command, reached his pen and examined it, dipped it in the ink and examined it again, then pushed the paper a little way from him, lifted up his spectacles again, showed a deepened depression in the outer angle of his bushy eyebrows, which gave his face a peculiar mildness (pardon these details for once – you would have learned to love them if you had known Caleb Garth), and said in a comfortable tone –

'It was a misfortune, eh, that breaking the horse's knees? And then, these exchanges, they don't answer when you have 'cute jockies to deal with. You'll be wiser another time, my boy.'

Whereupon Caleb drew down his spectacles, and proceeded to write his signature with the care which he always gave to that performance; for whatever he did in the way of business he did well. He contemplated the large well-proportioned letters and final flourish, with his head a trifle on one side for an instant, then handed it to Fred, said 'Good-bye,' and returned forthwith to his absorption in a plan for Sir James Chettam's new farm-buildings.

Either because his interest in this work thrust the incident of the signature from his memory, or for some reason of which Caleb was more conscious, Mrs Garth remained ignorant of the affair.

Since it occurred, a change had come over Fred's sky, which altered his view of the distance, and was the reason why his uncle Featherstone's present of money was of importance enough to make his colour come and go, first with a too definite expectation, and afterwards with a proportionate disappointment. His failure in passing his examination had made his accumulation of college debts the more unpardonable by his father, and there had been an unprecedented storm at home. Mr Vincy had sworn that if he had anything more of that sort to put up with, Fred should turn out and get his living how he could; and he had never yet quite recovered his good-humoured tone to his son, who had especially enraged him by saying at this stage of things that he did not want to be a clergyman, and would rather not 'go on with that'. Fred was conscious that he would have been yet more severely dealt with if his family as well as himself had not secretly regarded him as Mr Featherstone's heir; that old gentleman's pride in him, and apparent fondness for him, serving in the stead of more exemplary conduct – just as when a youthful nobleman steals jewellery we call the act kleptomania, speak of it with a philosophical smile, and never think of his being sent to the house of correction as if he were a ragged boy who had stolen turnips. In fact, tacit expectations of what would be done for him by Uncle Featherstone determined the angle at which most people viewed Fred Vincy in Middlemarch; and in his own consciousness, what Uncle Featherstone would do for him in an emergency or what he would do simply as an incorporated luck, formed always an immeasurable depth of aërial perspective. But that present of bank-notes, once made, was measurable, and being applied to the amount of the debt, showed a deficit which had still to be filled up either by Fred's 'judgment' or by luck in some other shape. For that little episode of the alleged borrowing, in which he had made his father the agent in getting the Bulstrode certificate, was a new reason against going to his father for money towards meeting his actual debt. Fred was keen enough to foresee that anger would confuse distinctions, and that his denial of having borrowed expressly on the strength of his uncle's will would be taken as a falsehood. He had gone to his father and told him one vexatious affair, and he had left another untold: in such cases the complete revelation always produces the impression of a previous duplicity. Now Fred piqued himself on keeping clear of lies, and even fibs; he often shrugged his shoulders and made a significant grimace at what he called Rosamond's fibs (it is only brothers who can associate such ideas with a lovely girl); and rather than incur the accusation of falsehood he would even incur some trouble and self-restraint. It was under strong inward pressure of this kind that Fred had taken the wise step of depositing the eighty pounds with his mother. It was a pity that he had not at once given them to Mr Garth; but he meant to make the sum complete with another sixty, and with a view to this, he had kept twenty pounds in his own pocket as a sort of seed-corn, which, planted by judgment, and watered by luck, might yield more than threefold – a very poor rate of multiplication when the field is a young gentleman's infinite soul, with all the numerals at command.

Fred was not a gambler: he had not that specific disease in which the suspension of the whole nervous energy on a chance or risk becomes as necessary as the dram to the drunkard; he had only the tendency to that diffusive form of gambling which has no alcoholic intensity, but is carried on with the healthiest chyle-fed blood, keeping up a joyous imaginative activity which fashions events according to desire, and having no fears about its own weather, only sees the advantage there must be to others in going aboard with it. Hopefulness has a pleasure in making a throw of any kind, because the prospect of success is certain; and only a more generous pleasure in offering as many as possible a share in the stake. Fred liked play, especially billiards, as he liked hunting or riding a steeplechase; and he only liked it the better because he wanted money and hoped to win. But the twenty pounds' worth of seed-corn had been planted in vain in the seductive green plot – all of it at least which had not been dispersed by the roadside – and Fred found himself close upon the term of payment with no money at command beyond the eighty pounds which he had deposited with his mother. The broken-winded horse which he rode represented a present which had been made to him a long while ago by his uncle Featherstone: his father always allowed him to keep a horse, Mr Vincy's own habits making him regard this as a reasonable demand even for a son who was rather exasperating. This horse, then, was Fred's property, and in his anxiety to meet the imminent bill he determined to sacrifice a possession without which life would certainly be worth little. He made the resolution with a sense of heroism – heroism forced on him by the dread of breaking his word to Mr Garth, by his love for Mary and awe of her opinion. He would start for Houndsley horsefair which was to be held the next morning, and – simply sell his horse, bringing back the money by coach? – Well, the horse would hardly fetch more than thirty pounds, and there was no knowing what might happen: it would be folly to balk himself of luck beforehand. It was a hundred to one that some good chance would fall in his way: the longer he thought of it, the less possible it seemed that he should not have a good chance, and the less reasonable that he should not equip himself with the powder and shot for bringing it down. He would ride to Houndsley with Bambridge and with Horrock 'the vet', and without asking them anything expressly, he should virtually get the benefit of their opinion. Before he set out, Fred got the eighty pounds from his mother.

Most of those who saw Fred riding out of Middlemarch in company with Bambridge and Horrock, on his way of course to Houndsley horsefair, thought that young Vincy was pleasure-seeking as usual; and but for an unwonted consciousness of grave matters on hand, he himself would have had a sense of dissipation, and of doing what might be expected of a gay young fellow. Considering that Fred was not at all coarse, that he rather looked down on the manners and speech of young men who had not been to the university, and that he had written stanzas as pastoral and unvoluptuous as his flute-playing, his attraction towards Bambridge and Horrock was an interesting fact which even the love of horse-flesh would not wholly account for without that mysterious influence of Naming which determinates so much of mortal choice. Under any other name than 'pleasure' the society of Messieurs Bambridge and Horrock must certainly have been regarded as monotonous; and to arrive with them at Houndsley on a drizzling afternoon, to get down at the Red Lion in a street shaded with coal-dust, and dine in a room furnished with a dirt-enamelled map of the county, a bad portrait of an anonymous horse in a stable, His Majesty George the Fourth with legs and cravat, and various leaden spittoons, might have seemed a hard business, but for the sustaining power of nomenclature which determined that the pursuit of these things was 'gay'.

In Mr Horrock there was certainly an apparent unfathomableness which offered play to the imagination. Costume, at a glance, gave him a thrilling association with horses (enough to specify the hat-brim, which took the slightest upward angle just to escape the suspicion of bending downwards), and nature had given him a face which by dint of Mongolian eyes, and a nose, mouth, and chin, seeming to follow his hat-brim in a moderate inclination upwards, gave the effect of a subdued unchangeable sceptical smile, of all expressions the most tyrannous over a susceptible mind, and, when accompanied by adequate silence, likely to create the reputation of an invincible understanding, an infinite fund of humour – too dry to flow, and probably in a state of immovable crust, – and a critical judgment which, if you could ever be fortunate enough to know it, would be *the* thing and no other. It is a physiognomy seen in all vocations, but perhaps it has never been more powerful over the youth of England than in a judge of horses.

Mr Horrock, at a question from Fred about his horse's fetlock, turned sideways in his saddle, and watched the horse's action for the space of three minutes, then turned forward, twitched his own bridle, and remained silent with a profile neither more nor less sceptical than it had been.

The part thus played in dialogue by Mr Horrock was terribly effective. A mixture of passions was excited in Fred – a mad desire to thrash Horrock's opinion into utterance, restrained by anxiety to retain the advantage of his friendship. There was always the chance that Horrock might say something quite invaluable at the right moment.

Mr Bambridge had more open manners, and appeared to give forth his ideas without economy. He was loud, robust, and was sometimes spoken of as being 'given to indulgence' – chiefly in swearing, drinking, and beating his wife. Some people who had lost by him called him a vicious man; but he regarded horse-dealing as the finest of the arts, and might have argued plausibly that it had nothing to do with morality. He was undeniably a prosperous man, bore his drinking better than others bore their moderation, and, on the whole, flourished like the green bay tree. But his range of conversation was limited, and like the fine old tune, 'Drops of brandy', gave you after a while a sense of returning upon itself in a way that might make weak heads dizzy. But a slight infusion of Mr Bambridge was felt to give tone and character to several circles in Middlemarch; and he was a distinguished figure in the bar and billiard-room at the Green Dragon. He knew some anecdotes about the heroes of the turf, and various clever tricks of Marquesses and Viscounts which seemed to prove that blood asserted its pre-eminence even among black-legs, but the minute retentiveness of his memory was chiefly shown about the horses he had himself bought and sold; the number of miles they would trot you in no time without turning a hair being, after the lapse of years, still a subject of passionate asseveration, in which he would assist the imagination of his hearers by solemnly swearing that they never saw anything like it. In short, Mr Bambridge was a man of pleasure and a gay companion.

Fred was subtle, and did not tell his friends that he was going to Houndsley bent on selling his horse: he wished to get indirectly at their genuine opinion of its value, not being aware that a genuine opinion was the last thing likely to be extracted from such eminent critics. It was not Mr Bambridge's weakness to be a gratuitous flatterer. He had never before been so much struck with the fact that this unfortunate bay was a roarer to a degree which required the roundest word for perdition to give you any idea of it.

'You made a bad hand at swapping when you went to anybody but me, Vincy! Why, you never threw your leg across a finer horse than that chestnut, and you gave him for this brute. If you set him cantering, he goes on like twenty sawyers. I never heard but one worse roarer in my life, and that was a roan: it belonged to Pegwell, the corn-factor; he used to drive him in his gig seven years ago, and he wanted me to take him, but I said, "Thank you, Peg, I don't deal in wind-instruments." That was what I said. It went the round of the country, that joke did. But, what the hell! the horse was a penny trumpet to that roarer of yours.'

'Why, you said just now his was worse than mine,' said Fred, more irritable than usual.

'I said a lie, then,' said Mr Bambridge, emphatically. 'There wasn't a penny to choose between 'em.'

Fred spurred his horse, and they trotted on a little way. When they slackened again, Mr Bambridge said –

'Not but what the roan was a better trotter than yours.'

'I'm quite satisfied with his paces, I know,' said Fred, who required all the consciousness of being in gay company to support him; 'I say, his trot is an uncommonly clean one, eh, Horrock?'

Mr Horrock looked before him with as complete a neutrality as if he had been a portrait by a great master.

Fred gave up the fallacious hope of getting a genuine opinion; but on reflection he saw that Bambridge's depreciation and Horrock's silence were both virtually encouraging, and indicated that they thought better of the horse than they chose to say.

That very evening, indeed, before the fair had set in, Fred thought he saw a favourable opening for disposing advantageously of his horse, but an opening which made him congratulate himself on his foresight in bringing with him his eighty pounds. A young farmer, acquainted with Mr Bambridge, came into the Red Lion, and entered into conversation about parting with a hunter, which he introduced at once as Diamond, implying that it was a public character. For himself he only wanted a useful hack, which would draw upon occasion; being about to marry and to give up hunting. The hunter was in a friend's stable at some little distance; there was still time for gentlemen to see it before dark. The friend's stable had to be reached through a back street where you might as easily have been poisoned without expense of drugs as in any grim street of that unsanitary period. Fred was not fortified against disgust by brandy, as his companions were, but the hope of having at last seen the horse that would enable him to make money was exhilarating enough to lead him over the same ground again the first thing in the morning. He felt sure that if he did not come to a bargain with the farmer, Bambridge would; for the stress of circumstances, Fred felt, was sharpening his acuteness and endowing him with all the constructive power of suspicion. Bambridge had run down Diamond in a way that he never would have done (the horse being a friend's) if he had not thought of buying it; every one who looked at the animal – even Horrock – was evidently impressed with its merit. To get all the advantage of being with men of this sort, you must know how to draw your inferences, and not be a spoon who takes things literally. The colour of the horse was a dappled grey, and Fred happened to know that Lord Medlicote's man was on the look-out for just such a horse. After all his running down, Bambridge let it out in the course of the evening, when the farmer was absent, that he had seen worse horses go for eighty pounds. Of course he contradicted himself twenty times over, but when you know what is likely to be true you can test a man's admissions. And Fred could not but reckon his own judgment of a horse was worth something. The farmer had paused over Fred's respectable though broken-winded steed long enough to show that he thought it worth consideration, and it seemed probable that he would take it, with five-and-twenty pounds in addition, as the equivalent of Diamond. In that case Fred, when he had parted with his new horse for at least eighty pounds, would be fifty-five pounds in pocket by the transaction, and would have a hundred and thirty-five pounds towards meeting the bill; so that the deficit temporarily thrown on Mr Garth would at the utmost be twenty-five pounds. By the time he was hurrying on his clothes in the morning, he saw so clearly the importance of not losing this rare chance, that if Bambridge and Horrock had both dissuaded him, he would not have been deluded into a direct interpretation of their purpose: he would have been aware that those deep hands held something else than a young fellow's interest. With regard to horses, distrust was your only clue. But scepticism, as we know, can never be thoroughly applied, else life would come to a standstill: something we must believe in and do, and whatever that something may be called, it is virtually our own judgment, even when it seems like the most slavish reliance on another. Fred believed in the excellence of his bargain, and even before the fair had well set in, had got possession of the dappled grey, at the price of his old horse and thirty pounds in addition – only five pounds more than he had expected to give.

But he felt a little worried and wearied, perhaps with mental debate, and without waiting for the further gaieties of the horse-fair, he set out alone on his fourteen miles' journey, meaning to take it very quietly and keep his horse fresh.

◁ TWENTY-FOUR ▷

The offender's sorrow brings but small relief
To him who wears the strong offence's cross.
SHAKESPEARE: *Sonnets*

I AM SORRY TO SAY THAT ONLY THE third day after the propitious events at Houndsley Fred Vincy had fallen into worse spirits than he had known in his life before. Not that he had been disappointed as to the possible market for his horse, but that before the bargain could be concluded with Lord Medlicote's man, this Diamond, in which hope to the amount of eighty pounds had been invested, had without the slightest warning exhibited in the stable a most vicious energy in kicking, had just missed killing the groom, and had ended in laming himself severely by catching his leg in a rope that overhung the stable-board. There was no more redress for this than for the discovery of bad temper after marriage – which of course old companions were aware of before the ceremony. For some reason or other, Fred had none of his usual elasticity under this stroke of ill-fortune: he was simply aware that he had only fifty pounds, that there was no chance of his getting any more at present, and that the bill for a hundred and sixty would be presented in five days. Even if he had applied to his father on the plea that Mr Garth should be saved from loss, Fred felt smartingly that his father would angrily refuse to rescue Mr Garth from the consequence of what he would call encouraging extravagance and deceit. He was so utterly downcast that he could frame no other project than to go straight to Mr Garth and tell him the sad truth, carrying with him the fifty pounds, and getting that sum at least safely out of his own hands. His father, being at the warehouse, did not yet know of the accident: when he did, he would storm about the vicious brute being brought into his stable; and before meeting that lesser annoyance

Fred wanted to get away with all his courage to face the greater. He took his father's nag, for he had made up his mind that when he had told Mr Garth, he would ride to Stone Court and confess all to Mary. In fact, it is probable that but for Mary's existence and Fred's love for her, his conscience would have been much less active both in previously urging the debt on his thought and in impelling him not to spare himself after his usual fashion by deferring an unpleasant task, but to act as directly and simply as he could. Even much stronger mortals than Fred Vincy hold half their rectitude in the mind of the being they love best. 'The theatre of all my actions is fallen,' said an antique personage when his chief friend was dead; and they are fortunate who get a theatre where the audience demands their best. Certainly it would have made a considerable difference to Fred at that time if Mary Garth had had no decided notions as to what was admirable in character.

Mr Garth was not at the office, and Fred rode on to his house, which was a little way outside the town – a homely place with an orchard in front of it, a rambling, old-fashioned, half-timbered building, which before the town had spread had been a farmhouse, but was now surrounded with the private gardens of the townsmen. We get the fonder of our houses if they have a physiognomy of their own, as our friends have. The Garth family, which was rather a large one, for Mary had four brothers and one sister, were very fond of their old house, from which all the best furniture had long been sold. Fred liked it too, knowing it by heart even to the attic which smelt deliciously of apples and quinces, and until to-day he had never come to it without pleasant expectations; but his heart beat uneasily now with the sense that he should probably have to make his confession before Mrs Garth, of whom he was rather more in awe than of her husband. Not that she was inclined to sarcasm and to impulsive sallies, as Mary was. In her present matronly age at least, Mrs Garth never committed herself by over-hasty speech; having, as she said, borne the yoke in her youth, and learned self-control. She had that rare sense which discerns what is unalterable, and submits to it without murmuring. Adoring her husband's virtues, she had very early made up her mind to his incapacity of minding his own interests, and had met the consequences cheerfully. She had been magnanimous enough to renounce all pride in teapots or children's frilling, and had never poured any pathetic confidences into the ears of her feminine neighbours concerning Mr Garth's want of prudence and the sums he might have had if he had been like other men. Hence these fair neighbours thought her either proud or eccentric, and sometimes spoke of her to their husbands as 'your fine Mrs Garth'. She was not without her criticism of them in return, being more accurately instructed than most matrons in Middlemarch, and – where is the blameless woman? – apt to be a little severe towards her own sex, which in her opinion was framed to be entirely subordinate. On the other hand, she was disproportionately indulgent towards the failings of men, and was often heard to say that these were natural. Also, it must be admitted that Mrs Garth was a trifle too emphatic in her resistance to what she held to be follies: the passage from governess into housewife had wrought itself a little too strongly into her consciousness, and she rarely forgot that while her grammar and accent were above the town standard, she wore a plain cap, cooked the family dinner, and darned all the stockings. She had sometimes taken pupils in a peripatetic fashion, making them follow her about in the kitchen with their book or slate. She thought it good for them to see that she could make an excellent lather while she corrected their blunders 'without looking', that a woman with her sleeves tucked up above her elbows might know all about the Subjunctive Mood or the Torrid Zone – that, in short, she might possess 'education' and other good things ending in 'tion', and worthy to be pronounced emphatically, without being a useless doll. When she made remarks to this edifying effect, she had a firm little frown on her brow, which yet did not hinder her face from looking benevolent, and her words which came forth like a procession were uttered in a fervid agreeable contralto. Certainly, the exemplary Mrs Garth had her droll aspects, but her character sustained her oddities, as a very fine wine sustains a flavour of skin.

Towards Fred Vincy she had a motherly feeling, and had always been disposed to excuse his errors, though she would probably not have excused Mary for engaging herself to him, her daughter being included in that more rigorous judgment which she applied to her own sex. But this very fact of her exceptional indulgence towards him made it the harder to Fred that he must now inevitably sink in her opinion. And the circumstances of his visit turned out to be still more unpleasant than he had expected; for Caleb Garth had gone out early to look at some repairs not far off. Mrs Garth at certain hours was always in the kitchen, and this morning she was carrying on several occupations at once there – making her pies at the well-scoured deal table on one side of that airy room, observing Sally's movements at the oven and dough-tub through an open door, and giving lessons to her youngest boy and girl, who were standing opposite to her at the table with their books and slates before them. A tub and a clothes-horse at the other end of the kitchen indicated an intermittent wash of small things also going on.

Mrs Garth, with her sleeves turned above her elbows, deftly handling her pastry – applying her rolling-pin and giving ornamental pinches, while she expounded with grammatical fervour what were the right views about the concord of verbs and pronouns with 'nouns of multitude or signifying many', was a sight agreeably amusing. She was of the same curly-haired, square-faced type as Mary, but handsomer, with more delicacy of feature, a pale skin, a solid matronly figure, and a remarkable firmness of glance. In her snowy-frilled cap she reminded one of that delightful Frenchwoman whom we have all seen marketing, basket on arm. Looking at the mother, you might hope that the daughter would become like her, which is a prospective advantage equal to a dowry – the mother too often standing behind the daughter like a malignant prophecy – 'Such as I am, she will shortly be.'

'Now let us go through that once more,' said Mrs Garth, pinching an apple-puff which seemed to distract Ben, an energetic young male with a heavy brow, from due attention to the lesson. ' "Not without regard to the import of the word as conveying unity or plurality of idea" – tell me again what that means, Ben.'

(Mrs Garth, like more celebrated educators, had her favourite ancient paths, and in a general wreck of society would have tried to hold her 'Lindley Murray' above the waves.)

'Oh – it means – you must think what you mean,' said Ben, rather peevishly. 'I hate grammar. What's the use of it?'

'To teach you to speak and write correctly, so that you can be understood,' said Mrs Garth, with severe precision. 'Should you like to speak as old Job does?'

'Yes,' said Ben, stoutly; 'it's funnier. He says, "Yo goo" – that's just as good as "You go".'

'But he says, "A ship's in the garden", instead of "a sheep" said Letty, with an air of superiority. 'You might think he meant a ship off the sea.'

'No, you mightn't, if you weren't silly,' said Ben. 'How could a ship off the sea come there?'

'These things belong only to pronunciation, which is the least part of grammar,' said Mrs Garth. 'That apple peel is to be eaten by the pigs, Ben; if you eat it, I must give them your piece of pastry. Job has only to speak about very plain things. How do you think you would write or speak about anything more difficult, if you knew no more of grammar than he does? You would use wrong words, and put words in the wrong places, and instead of making people understand you, they would turn away from you as a tiresome person. What would you do then?'

'I shouldn't care, I should leave off,' said Ben, with a sense that this was an agreeable issue where grammar was concerned.

'I see you are getting tired and stupid, Ben,' said Mrs Garth, accustomed to these obstructive arguments from her male offspring. Having finished her pies, she moved towards the clothes-horse, and said, 'Come here and tell me the story I told you on Wednesday, about Cincinnatus.'

'I know! he was a farmer,' said Ben.

'Now, Ben, he was a Roman – let *me* tell,' said Letty, using her elbow contentiously.

'You silly thing, he was a Roman farmer, and he was ploughing.'

'Yes, but before that – that didn't come first – people wanted him,' said Letty.

'Well, but you must say what sort of a man he was first,' insisted Ben. 'He was a wise man, like my father, and that made the people want his

advice. And he was a brave man, and could fight. And so could my father
– couldn't he, mother?'

'Now, Ben, let me tell the story straight on, as mother told it us,' said
Letty, frowning. 'Please, mother, tell Ben not to speak.'

'Letty, I am ashamed of you,' said her mother, wringing out the caps
from the tub. 'When your brother began, you ought to have waited to see
if he could not tell the story. How rude you look, pushing and frowning,
as if you wanted to conquer with your elbows! Cincinnatus, I am sure,
would have been sorry to see his daughter behave so.' (Mrs Garth delivered this awful sentence with much majesty of enunciation, and Letty
felt that between repressed volubility and general disesteem, that of the
Romans inclusive, life was already a painful affair.) 'Now, Ben.'

'Well – oh – well – why, there was a great deal of fighting, and they were
all blockheads, and – I can't tell it just how you told it – but they wanted a
man to be captain and king and everything – '

'Dictator, now,' said Letty, with injured looks, and not without a wish to
make her mother repent.

'Very well, dictator!' said Ben, contemptuously. 'But that isn't a good
word: he didn't tell them to write on slates.'

'Come, come, Ben, you are not so ignorant as that,' said Mrs Garth,
carefully serious. 'Hark, there is a knock at the door! Run, Letty, and
open it.'

The knock was Fred's; and when Letty said that her father was not in
yet, but that her mother was in the kitchen, Fred had no alternative. He
could not depart from his usual practice of going to see Mrs Garth in the
kitchen if she happened to be at work there. He put his arm round Letty's
neck silently, and led her into the kitchen without his usual jokes and
caresses.

Mrs Garth was surprised to see Fred at this hour, but surprise was not a
feeling that she was given to express, and she only said, quietly continuing her work –

'You, Fred, so early in the day? You look quite pale. Has anything
happened?'

'I want to speak to Mr Garth,' said Fred, not yet ready to say more –
'and to you also,' he added, after a little pause, for he had no doubt that
Mrs Garth knew everything about the bill, and he must in the end speak
of it before her, if not to her solely.

'Caleb will be in again in a few minutes,' said Mrs Garth, who imagined
some trouble between Fred and his father. 'He is sure not to be long,
because he has some work at his desk that must be done this morning. Do
you mind staying with me, while I finish my matters here?'

'But we needn't go on about Cincinnatus, need we?' said Ben, who had
taken Fred's whip out of his hand, and was trying its efficiency on the cat.

'No, go out now. But put that whip down. How very mean of you to
whip poor old Tortoise! Pray take the whip from him, Fred.'

'Come, old boy, give it me,' said Fred, putting out his hand.

'Will you let me ride on your horse to-day?' said Ben, rendering up the whip, with an air of not being obliged to do it.

'Not to-day – another time. I am not riding my own horse.'

'Shall you see Mary to-day?'

'Yes, I think so,' said Fred, with an unpleasant twinge.

'Tell her to come home soon, and play at forfeits, and make fun.'

'Enough, enough, Ben! run away,' said Mrs Garth, seeing that Fred was teased.

'Are Letty and Ben your only pupils now, Mrs Garth?' said Fred, when the children were gone and it was needful to say something that would pass the time. He was not yet sure whether he should wait for Mr Garth, or use any good opportunity in conversation to confess to Mrs Garth herself, give her the money and ride away.

'One – only one. Fanny Hackbutt comes at half-past eleven. I am not getting a great income now,' said Mrs Garth, smiling. 'I am at a low ebb with pupils. But I have saved my little purse for Alfred's premium: I have ninety-two pounds. He can go to Mr Hanmer's now; he is just at the right age.'

This did not lead well towards the news that Mr Garth was on the brink of losing ninety-two pounds and more. Fred was silent. 'Young gentlemen who go to college are rather more costly than that,' Mrs Garth innocently continued, pulling out the edging on a cap-border. 'And Caleb thinks that Alfred will turn out a distinguished engineer: he wants to give the boy a good chance. There he is! I hear him coming in. We will go to him in the parlour, shall we?'

When they entered the parlour Caleb had thrown down his hat and was seated at his desk.

'What, Fred, my boy?' he said in a tone of mild surprise, holding his pen still undipped. 'You are here betimes.' But missing the usual expression of cheerful greeting in Fred's face, he immediately added, 'Is there anything up at home? – anything the matter?'

'Yes, Mr Garth, I am come to tell something that I am afraid will give you a bad opinion of me. I am come to tell you and Mrs Garth that I can't keep my word. I can't find the money to meet the bill after all. I have been unfortunate; I have only got these fifty pounds towards the hundred and sixty.'

While Fred was speaking, he had taken out the notes and laid them on the desk before Mr Garth. He had burst forth at once with the plain fact, feeling boyishly miserable and without verbal resources. Mrs Garth was mutely astonished, and looked at her husband for an explanation. Caleb blushed, and after a little pause said –

'Oh, I didn't tell you, Susan: I put my name to a bill for Fred; it was for a hundred and sixty pounds. He made sure he could meet it himself.'

There was an evident change in Mrs Garth's face, but it was like a change below the surface of water which remains smooth. She fixed her eyes on Fred, saying –

'I suppose you have asked your father for the rest of the money and he has refused you.'

'No,' said Fred, biting his lip, and speaking with more difficulty; 'but I know it will be of no use to ask him; and unless it were of use, I should not like to mention Mr Garth's name in the matter.'

'It has come at an unfortunate time,' said Caleb, in his hesitating way, looking down at the notes and nervously fingering the paper, 'Christmas upon us – I'm rather hard up just now. You see, I have to cut out everything like a tailor with short measure. What can we do, Susan? I shall want every farthing we have in the bank. It's a hundred and ten pounds, the deuce take it!'

'I must give you the ninety-two pounds that I have put by for Alfred's premium,' said Mrs Garth, gravely and decisively, though a nice ear might have discerned a slight tremor in some of the words. 'And I have no doubt that Mary has twenty pounds saved from her salary by this time. She will advance it.'

Mrs Garth had not again looked at Fred, and was not in the least calculating what words she should use to cut him the most effectively. Like the eccentric woman she was, she was at present absorbed in considering what was to be done, and did not fancy that the end could be better achieved by bitter remarks or explosions. But she had made Fred feel for the first time something like the tooth of remorse. Curiously enough, his pain in the affair beforehand had consisted almost entirely in the sense that he must seem dishonourable, and sink in the opinion of the Garths: he had not occupied himself with the inconvenience and possible injury that his breach might occasion them, for this exercise of the imagination on other people's needs is not common with hopeful young gentlemen. Indeed we are most of us brought up in the notion that the highest motive for not doing a wrong is something irrespective of the beings who would suffer the wrong. But at this moment he suddenly saw himself as a pitiful rascal who was robbing two women of their savings.

'I shall certainly pay it all, Mrs Garth – ultimately,' he stammered out.

'Yes, ultimately,' said Mrs Garth, who having a special dislike to fine words on ugly occasions, could not now repress an epigram. 'But boys cannot well be apprenticed ultimately: they should be apprenticed at fifteen.' She had never been so little inclined to make excuses for Fred.

'I was the most in the wrong, Susan,' said Caleb. 'Fred made sure of finding the money. But I'd no business to be fingering bills. I suppose you have looked all round and tried all honest means?' he added fixing his merciful grey eyes on Fred. Caleb was too delicate to specify Mr Featherstone.

'Yes, I have tried everything – I really have. I should have had a hundred and thirty pounds ready but for a misfortune with a horse which

I was about to sell. My uncle had given me eighty pounds, and I paid away thirty with my old horse in order to get another which I was going to sell for eighty or more – I meant to go without a horse – but now it has turned out vicious and lamed itself. I wish I and the horses too had been at the devil, before I had brought this on you. There's no one else I care so much for: you and Mrs Garth have always been so kind to me. However, it's no use saying that. You will always think me a rascal now.'

Fred turned round and hurried out of the room, conscious that he was getting rather womanish, and feeling confusedly that his being sorry was not of much use to the Garths. They could see him mount, and quickly pass through the gate.

'I am disappointed in Fred Vincy,' said Mrs Garth. 'I would not have believed beforehand that he would have drawn you into his debts. I knew he was extravagant, but I did not think that he would be so mean as to hang his risks on his oldest friend, who could the least afford to lose.'

'I was a fool, Susan.'

'That you were,' said the wife, nodding and smiling. 'But I should not have gone to publish it in the market place. Why should you keep such things from me? It is just so with your buttons; you let them burst off without telling me, and go out with your wristband hanging. If I had only known I might have been ready with some better plan.'

'You are sadly cut up, I know, Susan,' said Caleb, looking feelingly at her. 'I can't abide your losing the money you've scraped together for Alfred.'

'It is very well that I *had* scraped it together; and it is you who will have to suffer, for you must teach the boy yourself. You must give up your bad habits. Some men take to drinking, and you have taken to working without pay. You must indulge yourself a little less in that. And you must ride over to Mary, and ask the child what money she has.'

Caleb had pushed his chair back, and was leaning forward, shaking his head slowly, and fitting his finger-tips together with much nicety.

'Poor Mary!' he said. 'Susan,' he went on in a lowered tone, 'I'm afraid she may be fond of Fred.'

'Oh no! She always laughs at him; and he is not likely to think of her in any other than a brotherly way.'

Caleb made no rejoinder, but presently lowered his spectacles, drew up his chair to the desk, and said, 'Deuce take the bill – I wish it was at Hanover! These things are a sad interruption to business!'

The first part of this speech comprised his whole store of maledictory expression, and was uttered with a slight snarl easy to imagine. But it would be difficult to convey to those who never heard him utter the word 'business', the peculiar tone of fervid veneration, of religious regard, in which he wrapped it, as a consecrated symbol is wrapped in its gold-fringed linen.

Caleb Garth often shook his head in meditation on the value, the indispensable might of that myriad-headed, myriad-handed labour by which the social body is fed, clothed, and housed. It had laid hold of his imagination in boyhood. The echoes of the great hammer where roof or keel were a-making, the signal-shouts of the workmen, the roar of the furnace, the thunder and plash of the engine, were a sublime music to him; the felling and lading of timber, and the huge trunk vibrating star-like in the distance along the highway, the crane at work on the wharf, the piled-up produce in warehouses, the precision and variety of muscular effort wherever exact work had to be turned out, – all these sights of his youth had acted on him as poetry without the aid of the poets, had made a philosophy for him without the aid of philosophers, a religion without the aid of theology. His early ambition had been to have as effective a share as possible in this sublime labour, which was peculiarly dignified by him with the name of 'business'; and though he had only been a short time under a surveyor, and had been chiefly his own teacher, he knew more of land, building, and mining than most of the special men in the county.

His classification of human employments was rather crude, and, like the categories of more celebrated men, would not be acceptable in these advanced times. He divided them into 'business, politics, preaching, learning, and amusement'. He had nothing to say against the last four; but he regarded them as a reverential pagan regarded other gods than his own. In the same way, he thought very well of all ranks, but he would not himself have liked to be of any rank in which he had not such close contact with 'business' as to get often honourably decorated with marks of dust and mortar, the damp of the engine, or the sweet soil of the woods and fields. Though he had never regarded himself as other than an orthodox Christian, and would argue on prevenient grace if the subject were proposed to him, I think his virtual divinities were good practical schemes, accurate work, and the faithful completion of undertakings: his prince of darkness was a slack workman. But there was no spirit of denial in Caleb, and the world seemed so wondrous to him that he was ready to accept any number of systems, like any number of firmaments, if they did not obviously interfere with the best land-drainage, solid building, correct measuring, and judicious boring (for coal). In fact, he had a reverential soul with a strong practical intelligence. But he could not manage finance: he knew values well, but he had no keenness of imagination for monetary results in the shape of profit and loss: and having ascertained this to his cost, he determined to give up all forms of his beloved 'business' which required that talent. He gave himself up entirely to the many kinds of work which he could do without handling capital, and was one of those precious men within his own district whom everybody would choose to work for them, because he did his work well, charged very little, and often declined to charge at all. It is no wonder, then, that the Garths were poor, and 'lived in a small way'. However, they did not mind it.

❦ TWENTY-FIVE ❧

Love seeketh not itself to please,
Nor for itself hath any care,
But for another gives its ease,
And builds a heaven in hell's despair.
. . . .
Love seeketh only self to please,
To bind another to its delight,
Joys in another's loss of ease,
And builds a hell in heaven's despite.
Songs of Experience: W. BLAKE

FRED VINCY WANTED TO ARRIVE AT Stone Court when Mary could not expect him, and when his uncle was not down-stairs: in that case she might be sitting alone in the wainscoted parlour. He left his horse in the yard to avoid making a noise on the gravel in front, and entered the parlour without other notice than the noise on the door-handle. Mary was in her usual corner, laughing over Mrs Piozzi's recollections of Johnson, and looked up with the fun still in her face. It gradually faded as she saw Fred approach her without speaking, and stand before her with his elbow on the mantelpiece, looking ill. She too was silent, only raising her eyes to him inquiringly.

'Mary,' he began, 'I am a good-for-nothing blackguard.'

'I should think one of those epithets would do at a time,' said Mary, trying to smile, but feeling alarmed.

'I know you will never think well of me any more. You will think me a liar. You will think me dishonest. You will think I didn't care for you, or your father and mother. You always do make the worst of me, I know.'

'I cannot deny that I shall think all that of you, Fred, if you give me good reasons. But please to tell me at once what you have done. I would rather know the painful truth than imagine it.'

'I owed money – a hundred and sixty pounds. I asked your father to put his name to a bill. I thought it would not signify to him. I made sure of paying the money myself, and I have tried as hard as I could. And now, I have been so unlucky – a horse has turned out badly – I can only pay fifty pounds. And I can't ask my father for the money: he would not give me a farthing. And my uncle gave me a hundred a little while ago. So what can I do? And now your father has no ready money to spare, and your mother will have to pay away her ninety-two pounds that she has saved, and she says your savings must go too. You see what a – '

'Oh, poor mother, poor father!' said Mary, her eyes filling with tears, and a little sob rising which she tried to repress. She looked straight before her and took no notice of Fred, all the consequences at home becoming present to her. He too remained silent for some moments, feeling more miserable than ever.

'I wouldn't have hurt you so for the world, Mary,' he said at last. 'You can never forgive me.'

'What does it matter whether I forgive you?' said Mary passionately. 'Would that make it any better for my mother to lose the money she has been earning by lessons for four years, that she might send Alfred to Mr Hanmer's? Should you think all that pleasant enough if I forgave you?'

'Say what you like, Mary. I deserve it all.'

'I don't want to say anything,' said Mary, more quietly; 'my anger is of no use.' She dried her eyes, threw aside her book, rose and fetched her sewing.

Fred followed her with his eyes, hoping that they would meet hers, and in that way find access for his imploring penitence. But no! Mary could easily avoid looking upward.

'I do care about your mother's money going,' he said, when she was seated again and sewing quickly. 'I wanted to ask you, Mary – don't you think that Mr Featherstone – if you were to tell him – tell him, I mean, about apprenticing Alfred – would advance the money?'

'My family is not fond of begging, Fred. We would rather work for our money. Besides, you say that Mr Featherstone has lately given you a hundred pounds. He rarely makes presents; he has never made presents to us. I am sure my father will not ask him for anything; and even if I chose to beg of him, it would be of no use.'

'I am so miserable, Mary – if you knew how miserable I am, you would be sorry for me.'

'There are other things to be more sorry for than that. But selfish people always think their own discomfort of more importance than anything else in the world: I see enough of that every day.'

'It is hardly fair to call me selfish. If you knew what things other young men do, you would think me a good way off the worst.'

'I know that people who spend a great deal of money on themselves without knowing how they shall pay, must be selfish. They are always thinking of what they can get for themselves, and not of what other people may lose.'

'Any man may be unfortunate, Mary, and find himself unable to pay when he meant it. There is not a better man in the world than your father, and yet he got into trouble.'

'How dare you make any comparison between my father and you, Fred?' said Mary, in a deep tone of indignation. 'He never got into trouble by thinking of his own idle pleasures, but because he was always thinking of the work he was doing for other people. And he has fared hard, and worked hard to make good everybody's loss.'

'And you think that I shall never try to make good anything, Mary. It is not generous to believe the worst of a man. When you have got any power over him, I think you might try and use it to make him better; but that is what you never do. However, I'm going,' Fred ended, languidly. 'I shall never speak to you about anything again. I'm very sorry for all the trouble I've caused – that's all.'

Mary had dropped her work out of her hand and looked up. There is often something maternal even in a girlish love, and Mary's hard experience had wrought her nature to an impressibility very different from that hard slight thing which we call girlishness. At Fred's last words she felt an instantaneous pang, something like what a mother feels at the imagined sobs or cries of her naughty truant child, which may lose itself and get harm. And when, looking up, her eyes met his dull despairing glance, her pity for him surmounted her anger and all her other anxieties.

'Oh, Fred, how ill you look! Sit down a moment. Don't go yet. Let me tell uncle that you are here. He has been wondering that he has not seen you for a whole week.' Mary spoke hurriedly, saying the words that came first without knowing very well what they were, but saying them in a half-soothing, half-beseeching tone, and rising as if to go away to Mr Featherstone. Of course Fred felt as if the clouds had parted and a gleam had come: he moved and stood in her way.

'Say one word, Mary, and I will do anything. Say you will not think the worst of me – will not give me up altogether.'

'As if it were any pleasure to me to think ill of you,' said Mary, in a mournful tone. 'As if it were not very painful to me to see you an idle frivolous creature. How can you bear to be so contemptible, when others are working and striving, and there are so many things to be done – how can you bear to be fit for nothing in the world that is useful? And with so much good in your disposition, Fred, – you might be worth a great deal.'

'I will try to be anything you like, Mary, if you will say that you love me.'

'I should be ashamed to say that I loved a man who must always be hanging on others, and reckoning on what they would do for him. What will you be when you are forty? Like Mr Bowyer, I suppose – just as idle, living in Mrs Beck's front parlour – fat and shabby, hoping somebody will invite you to dinner – spending your morning in learning a comic song – oh no! learning a tune on the flute.'

Mary's lips had begun to curl with a smile as soon as she had asked that question about Fred's future (young souls are mobile), and before she ended, her face had its full illumination of fun. To him it was like the cessation of an ache that Mary could laugh at him, and with a passive sort of smile he tried to reach her hand; but she slipped away quickly towards the door and said, 'I shall tell uncle. You *must* see him for a moment or two.'

Fred secretly felt that his future was guaranteed against the fulfilment of Mary's sarcastic prophecies, apart from that 'anything' which he was ready to do if she would define it. He never dared in Mary's presence to approach the subject of his expectations from Mr Featherstone, and she always ignored them, as if everything depended on himself. But if ever he actually came into the property, she must recognize the change in his position. All this passed through his mind somewhat languidly, before he went up to see his uncle. He stayed but a little while, excusing himself on the ground that he had a cold; and Mary did not reappear before he left the house. But as he rode home, he began to be more conscious of being ill, than of being melancholy.

When Caleb Garth arrived at Stone Court soon after dusk, Mary was not surprised, although he seldom had leisure for paying her a visit, and was not at all fond of having to talk with Mr Featherstone. The old man, on the other hand, felt himself ill at ease with a brother-in-law whom he could not annoy, who did not mind about being considered poor, had nothing to ask of him, and understood all kinds of farming and mining business better than he did. But Mary had felt sure that her parents would want to see her, and if her father had not come, she would have obtained leave to go home for an hour or two the next day. After discussing prices during tea with Mr Featherstone, Caleb rose to bid him good-bye, and said, 'I want to speak to you, Mary.'

She took a candle into another large parlour, where there was no fire, and setting down the feeble light on the dark mahogany table, turned round to her father, and putting her arms round his neck kissed him with childish kisses which he delighted in, – the expression of his large brows softening as the expression of a great beautiful dog softens when it is caressed. Mary was his favourite child, and whatever Susan might say, and right as she was on all other subjects, Caleb thought it natural that Fred or any one else should think Mary more lovable than other girls.

'I've got something to tell you, my dear,' said Caleb in his hesitating way. 'No very good news; but then it might be worse.'

'About money, father? I think I know what it is.'

'Ay? how can that be? You see, I've been a bit of a fool again, and put my name to a bill, and now it comes to paying; and your mother has got to part with her savings, that's the worst of it, and even they won't quite make things even. We wanted a hundred and ten pounds: your mother has ninety-two, and I have none to spare in the bank; and she thinks that you will have some savings.'

'Oh yes; I have more than four-and-twenty pounds. I thought you would come, father, so I put it in my bag. See! beautiful white notes and gold.'

Mary took out the folded money from her reticule and put it into her father's hand.

'Well, but how – we only want eighteen – here, put the rest back, child, – but how did you know about it?' said Caleb, who, in his unconquerable indifference to money, was beginning to be chiefly concerned about the relation the affair might have to Mary's affections.

'Fred told me this morning.'

'Ah! Did he come on purpose?'

'Yes, I think so. He was a good deal distressed.'

'I'm afraid Fred is not to be trusted, Mary,' said the father, with hesitating tenderness. 'He means better than he acts, perhaps. But I should think it a pity for anybody's happiness to be wrapped up in him, and so would your mother.'

'And so should I, father,' said Mary, not looking up, but putting the back of her father's hand against her cheek.

'I don't want to pry, my dear. But I was afraid there might be something between you and Fred, and I wanted to caution you. You see, Mary' – here Caleb's voice became more tender; he had been pushing his hat about on the table and looking at it, but finally he turned his eyes on his daughter – 'a woman, let her be as good as she may, has got to put up with the life her husband makes for her. Your mother has had to put up with a good deal because of me.'

Mary turned the back of her father's hand to her lips and smiled at him.

'Well, well, nobody's perfect, but' – here Mr Garth shook his head to help out the inadequacy of words – 'what I am thinking of is – what it must be for a wife when she's never sure of her husband, when he hasn't got a principle in him to make him more afraid of doing the wrong thing by others than of getting his own toes pinched. That's the long and the short of it, Mary. Young folks may get fond of each other before they know what life is, and they may think it all holiday if they can only get together; but it soon turns into working day, my dear. However, you have more sense than most, and you haven't been kept in cotton-wool: there may be no occasion for me to say this, but a father trembles for his daughter, and you are all by yourself here.'

'Don't fear for me, father,' said Mary, gravely meeting her father's eyes; 'Fred has always been very good to me; he is kind-hearted and affectionate, and not false, I think, with all his self-indulgence. But I will never engage myself to one who has no manly independence, and who goes on loitering away his time on the chance that others will provide for him. You and my mother have taught me too much pride for that.'

'That's right – that's right. Then I am easy,' said Mr Garth, taking up his hat. 'But it's hard to run away with your earnings, child.'

'Father!' said Mary, in her deepest tone of remonstrance. 'Take pocketfuls of love besides to them all at home,' was her last word before he closed the outer door on himself.

'I suppose your father wanted your earnings,' said old Mr Featherstone, with his usual power of unpleasant surmise, when Mary returned to him. 'He makes but a tight fit, I reckon. You're of age now; you ought to be saving for yourself.'

'I consider my father and mother the best part of myself, sir,' said Mary, coldly.

Mr Featherstone grunted: he could not deny that an ordinary sort of girl like her might be expected to be useful, so he thought of another rejoinder, disagreeable enough to be always apropos. 'If Fred Vincy comes to-morrow, now, don't you keep him chattering: let him come up to me.'

◁ TWENTY-SIX ▷

He beats me and I rail at him: O worthy satisfaction! would it were otherwise – that I could beat him while he railed at me.
Troilus and Cressida

BUT FRED DID NOT GO TO STONE COURT the next day, for reasons that were quite peremptory. From those visits to unsanitary Houndsley streets in search of Diamond, he had brought back not only a bad bargain in horse-flesh, but the further misfortune of some ailment which for a day or two had seemed mere depression and headache, but which got so much worse when he returned from his visit to Stone Court that, going into the dining-room, he threw himself on the sofa, and in answer to his mother's anxious question, said, 'I feel very ill: I think you must send for Wrench.'

Wrench came but did not apprehend anything serious, spoke of a 'slight derangement', and did not speak of coming again on the morrow. He had a due value for the Vincys' house, but the wariest men are apt to be a little dulled by routine, and on worried mornings will sometimes go through their business with the zest of the daily bell-ringer. Mr Wrench was a small, neat, bilious man, with a well-dressed wig: he had a laborious practice, an irascible temper, a lymphatic wife, and seven children; and he was already rather late before setting out on a four-miles' drive to meet Dr Minchin on the other side of Tipton, the decease of Hicks, a rural prac-titioner, having increased Middlemarch practice in that direction. Great statesmen err, and why not small medical men? Mr Wrench did not neg-lect sending the usual white parcels, which this time had black and drastic contents. Their effect was not alleviating to poor Fred, who, however, unwilling as he said to believe that he was 'in for an illness', rose at his usual hour the next morning and went downstairs meaning to breakfast, but succeeded in nothing but in sitting and shivering by the fire. Mr Wrench was again sent for, but was gone on his rounds, and Mrs Vincy, seeing her darling's changed looks and general misery, began to cry and said she would send for Dr Sprague.

'Oh nonsense, mother! It's nothing,' said Fred, putting out his hot dry hand to her, 'I shall soon be all right. I must have taken cold in that nasty damp ride.'

'Mamma!' said Rosamond, who was seated near the window (the dining-room windows looked on that highly respectable street called Lowick Gate), 'there is Mr Lydgate, stopping to speak to some one. If I were you I would call him in. He has cured Ellen Bulstrode. They say he cures every one.'

Mrs Vincy sprang to the window and opened it in an instant, thinking only of Fred and not of medical etiquette. Lydgate was only two yards off on the other side of some iron palisading, and turned round at the sudden sound of the sash, before she called to him. In two minutes he was in the room, and Rosamond went out, after waiting just long enough to show a pretty anxiety conflicting with her sense of what was becoming.

Lydgate had to hear a narrative in which Mrs Vincy's mind insisted with remarkable instinct on every point of minor importance, especially on what Mr Wrench had said and had not said about coming again. That there might be an awkward affair with Wrench, Lydgate saw at once; but the case was serious enough to make him dismiss that consideration: he was convinced that Fred was in the pink-skinned stage of typhoid fever, and that he had taken just the wrong medicines. He must go to bed immediately, must have a regular nurse, and various appliances and precautions must be used, about which Lydgate was particular. Poor Mrs Vincy's terror at these indications of danger found vent in such words as came most easily. She thought it 'very ill usage on the part of Mr Wrench, who had attended their house so many years in preference to Mr Peacock, though Mr Peacock was equally a friend. Why Mr Wrench should neglect her children more than others, she could not for the life of her understand. He had not neglected Mrs Larcher's when they had the measles, nor indeed would Mrs Vincy have wished that he should. And if anything should happen . . .'

Here poor Mrs Vincy's spirit quite broke down, and her Niobe-throat and good-humoured face were sadly convulsed. This was in the hall out of Fred's hearing, but Rosamond had opened the drawing-room door, and now came forward anxiously. Lydgate apologized for Mr Wrench, said that the symptoms yesterday might have been disguising, and that this form of fever was very equivocal in its beginnings: he would go immediately to the druggists and have a prescription made up in order to lose no time, but he would write to Mr Wrench and tell him what had been done.

'But you must come again – you must go on attending Fred. I can't have my boy left to anybody who may come or not. I bear nobody ill-will, thank God, and Mr Wrench saved me in the pleurisy, but he'd better have let me die – if – if – '

'I will meet Mr Wrench here, then, shall I?' said Lydgate, really believing that Wrench was not well prepared to deal wisely with a case of this kind.

'Pray make that arrangement, Mr Lydgate,' said Rosamond, coming to her mother's aid, and supporting her arm to lead her away.

When Mr Vincy came home he was very angry with Wrench, and did not care if he never came into his house again. Lydgate should go on now, whether Wrench liked it or not. It was no joke to have fever in the house. Everybody must be sent to now, not to come to dinner on Thursday. And Pritchard needn't get up any wine: brandy was the best thing against infection. 'I shall drink brandy,' added Mr Vincy emphatically – as much as to say, this was not an occasion for firing with blank-cartridges. 'He's an uncommonly unfortunate lad, is Fred. He'd need have some luck by-and-by to make up for all this – else I don't know who'd have an eldest son.'

'Don't say so, Vincy,' said the mother, with a quivering lip, 'if you don't want him to be taken from me.'

'It will worret you to death, Lucy; *that* I can see,' said Mr Vincy, more mildly. 'However, Wrench shall know what I think of the matter.' (What Mr Vincy thought confusedly was, that the fever might somehow have been hindered if Wrench had shown the proper solicitude about his – the Mayor's – family.) 'I'm the last man to give in to the cry about new doctors or new parsons, either – whether they're Bulstrode's men or not. But Wrench shall know what I think, take it as he will.'

Wrench did not take it at all well. Lydgate was as polite as he could be in his offhand way, but politeness in a man who has placed you at a disadvantage is only an additional exasperation, especially if he happens to have been an object of dislike beforehand. Country practitioners used to be an irritable species, susceptible on the point of honour; and Mr Wrench was one of the most irritable among them. He did not refuse to meet Lydgate in the evening, but his temper was somewhat tried on the occasion. He had to hear Mrs Vincy say –

'Oh, Mr Wrench, what have I ever done that you should use me so? – To go away, and never to come again! And my boy might have been stretched a corpse!'

Mr Vincy, who had been keeping up a sharp fire on the enemy Infection, and was a good deal heated in consequence, started up when he heard Wrench come in, and went into the hall to let him know what he thought.

'I'll tell you what, Wrench, this is beyond a joke,' said the Mayor, who of late had had to rebuke offenders with an official air, and now broadened himself by putting his thumbs in his armholes. – 'To let fever get unawares into a house like this. There are some things that ought be be actionable, and are not so – that's my opinion.'

But irrational reproaches were easier to bear than the sense of being instructed, or rather the sense that a younger man, like Lydgate, inwardly considered him in need of instruction, for 'in point of fact', Mr Wrench afterwards said, Lydgate paraded flighty, foreign notions, which would not wear. He swallowed his ire for the moment, but he afterwards wrote to decline further attendance in the case. The house might be a good one, but Mr Wrench was not going to truckle to anybody on a professional matter. He reflected, with much probability on his side, that Lydgate would by-and-by be caught tripping too, and that his ungentlemanly attempts to discredit the sale of drugs by his professional brethren would by-and-by recoil on himself. He threw out biting remarks on Lydgate's tricks, worthy only of a quack, to get himself a factitious reputation with credulous people. That cant about cures was never got up by sound practitioners.

This was a point on which Lydgate smarted as much as Wrench could desire. To be puffed by ignorance was not only humiliating, but perilous, and not more enviable than the reputation of the weather-prophet. He was impatient of the foolish expectations amidst which all work must be carried on, and likely enough to damage himself as much as Mr Wrench could wish, by an unprofessional openness.

However, Lydgate was installed as medical attendant on the Vincys, and the event was a subject of general conversation in Middlemarch. Some said, that the Vincys had behaved scandalously, that Mr Vincy had threatened Wrench, and that Mrs Vincy had accused him of poisoning her son. Others were of opinion that Mr Lydgate's passing by was providential, that he was wonderfully clever in fevers, and that Bulstrode was in the right to bring him forward. Many people believed that Lydgate's coming to the town at all was really due to Bulstrode; and Mrs Taft, who was always counting stitches and gathered her information in misleading fragments caught between the rows of her knitting, had got it into her head that Mr Lydgate was a natural son of Bulstrode's, a fact which seemed to justify her suspicions of evangelical laymen.

She one day communicated this piece of knowledge to Mrs Farebrother, who did not fail to tell her son of it, observing –

'I should not be surprised at anything in Bulstrode, but I should be sorry to think it of Mr Lydgate.'

'Why, mother,' said Mr Farebrother, after an explosive laugh, 'you know very well that Lydgate is of a good family in the North. He never heard of Bulstrode before he came here.'

'That is satisfactory so far as Mr Lydgate is concerned, Camden,' said the old lady, with an air of precision. 'But as to Bulstrode – the report may be true of some other son.'

⚘ TWENTY-SEVEN ⚘

Let the high Muse chant loves Olympian:
We are but mortals, and must sing of man.

AN EMINENT PHILOSOPHER AMONG MY friends, who can dignify even your ugly furniture by lifting it into the serene light of science, has shown me this pregnant little fact. Your pier-glass or extensive surface of polished steel made to be rubbed by a housemaid, will be minutely and multitudinously scratched in all directions; but place now against it a lighted candle as a centre of illumination, and lo! the scratches will seem to arrange themselves in a fine series of concentric circles round that little sun. It is demonstrable that the scratches are going everywhere impartially, and it is only your candle which produces the flattering illusion of a concentric arrangement, its light falling with an exclusive optical selection. These things are a parable. The scratches are events, and the candle is the egoism of any person now absent – of Miss Vincy, for example. Rosamond had a Providence of her own who had kindly made her more charming than other girls, and who seemed to have arranged Fred's illness and Mr Wrench's mistake in order to bring her and Lydgate within effective proximity. It would have been to contravene these arrangements if Rosamond had consented to go away to Stone Court or elsewhere, as her parents wished her to do, especially since Mr Lydgate thought the precaution needless. Therefore, while Miss Morgan and the children were sent away to a farmhouse the morning after Fred's illness had declared itself, Rosamond refused to leave papa and mamma.

Poor mamma indeed was an object to touch any creature born of woman; and Mr Vincy, who doated on his wife, was more alarmed on her account than on Fred's. But for his insistence she would have taken no rest: her brightness was all bedimmed; unconscious of her costume which had always been so fresh and gay, she was like a sick bird with languid eye and plumage ruffled, her senses dulled to the sights and sounds that used most to interest her. Fred's delirium, in which he seemed to be wandering out of her reach, tore her heart. After her first outburst against Mr Wrench she went about very quietly: her one low cry was to Lydgate. She would follow him out of the room and put her hand on his arm moaning out, 'Save my boy.' Once she pleaded, 'He has always been good to me, Mr Lydgate: he never had a hard word for his mother,' – as if poor Fred's suffering were an accusation against him. All the deepest fibres of the mother's memory were stirred, and the young man whose voice took a gentler tone when he spoke to her, was one with the babe whom she had loved, with a love new to her, before he was born. 'I have good hope, Mrs Vincy,' Lydgate would say. 'Come down with me and let us talk about the food.' In that way he led her to the parlour where Rosamond was, and made a change for her, surprising her into taking some tea or broth which had been prepared for her. There was a constant understanding between him and Rosamond on these matters. He almost always saw her before going to the sick-room, and she appealed to him as to what she could do for mamma. Her presence of mind and adroitness in carrying out his hints were admirable, and it is not wonderful that the idea of seeing Rosamond began to mingle itself with his interest in the case. Especially when the critical stage was passed, and he began to feel confident of Fred's recovery. In the more doubtful time, he had advised calling in Dr Sprague (who, if he could, would rather have remained neutral on Wrench's account); but after two consultations, the conduct of the case was left to Lydgate, and there was every reason to make him assiduous. Morning and evening he was at Mr Vincy's, and gradually the visits became cheerful as Fred became simply feeble, and lay not only in need of the utmost petting but conscious of it, so that Mrs Vincy felt as if after all the illness had made a festival for her tenderness.

Both father and mother held it an added reason for good spirits, when old Mr Featherstone sent messages by Lydgate, saying that Fred must make haste and get well, as he, Peter Featherstone, could not do without him, and missed his visits sadly. The old man himself was getting bed-ridden. Mrs Vincy told these messages to Fred when he could listen, and he turned towards her his delicate, pinched face, from which all the thick blond hair had been cut away, and in which the eyes seemed to have got larger, yearning for some word about Mary – wondering what she felt about his illness. No word passed his lips; but 'to hear with eyes belongs to love's rare wit', and the mother in the fulness of her heart not only divined Fred's longing, but felt ready for any sacrifice in order to satisfy him.

'If I can only see my boy strong again,' she said, in her loving folly; 'and who knows? – perhaps master of Stone Court! and he can marry anybody he likes then.'

'Not if they won't have me, mother,' said Fred. The illness had made him childish, and tears came as he spoke.

'Oh, take a bit of jelly, my dear,' said Mrs Vincy, secretly incredulous of any such refusal.

She never left Fred's side when her husband was not in the house, and thus Rosamond was in the unusual position of being much alone. Lydgate, naturally, never thought of staying long with her, yet it seemed that the brief impersonal conversations they had together were creating that peculiar intimacy which consists in shyness. They were obliged to look at each other in speaking, and somehow the looking could not be carried through as the matter of course which it really was. Lydgate began to feel this sort of consciousness unpleasant, and one day looked down, or anywhere, like an ill-worked puppet. But this turned out badly: the next day, Rosamond looked down, and the consequence was that when their eyes met again, both were more conscious than before. There was no help for this in science, and as Lydgate did not want to flirt, there seemed to be no help for it in folly. It was therefore a relief when neighbours no longer considered the house in quarantine, and when the chances of seeing Rosamond alone were very much reduced.

But that intimacy of mutual embarrassment, in which each feels that the other is feeling something, having once existed, its effect is not to be done away with. Talk about the weather and other well-bred topics is apt to seem a hollow device, and behaviour can hardly become easy unless it frankly recognizes a mutual fascination – which of course need not mean anything deep or serious. This was the way in which Rosamond and Lydgate slid gracefully into ease, and made their intercourse lively again. Visitors came and went as usual, there was once more music in the drawing-room, and all the extra hospitality of Mr Vincy's mayoralty returned. Lydgate, whenever he could, took his seat by Rosamond's side, and lingered to hear her music, calling himself her captive – meaning, all the while, not to be her captive. The preposterousness of the notion that he could at once set up a satisfactory establishment as a married man was a sufficient guarantee against danger. This play at being a little in love was agreeable, and did not interfere with graver pursuits. Flirtation, after all, was not necessarily a singeing process. Rosamond, for her part, had never enjoyed the days so much in her life before: she was sure of being admired by some one worth captivating, and she did not distinguish flirtation from love, either in herself or in another. She seemed to be sailing with a fair wind just whither she would go, and her thoughts were much occupied with a handsome house in Lowick Gate which she hoped would by-and-by be vacant. She was quite determined, when she was married, to rid herself adroitly of all the visitors who were not agreeable to her at her father's; and she imagined the drawing-room in her favourite house with various styles of furniture.

Certainly her thoughts were much occupied with Lydgate himself; he seemed to her almost perfect: if he had known his notes so that his enchantment under her music had been less like an emotional elephant's, and if he had been able to discriminate better the refinements of her taste in dress, she could hardly have mentioned a deficiency in him. How different he was from young Plymdale or Mr Caius Larcher! Those young men had not a notion of French, and could speak on no subject with striking knowledge, except perhaps the dyeing and carrying trades, which of course they were ashamed to mention; they were Middlemarch gentry, elated with their silver-headed whips and satin stocks, but embarrassed in their manners, and timidly jocose: even Fred was above them, having at least the accent and manner of a university man. Whereas Lydgate was always listened to, bore himself with the careless politeness of conscious superiority, and seemed to have the right clothes on by a certain natural affinity, without ever having to think about them. Rosamond was proud when he entered the room, and when he approached her with a distinguishing smile, she had a delicious sense that she was the object of enviable homage. If Lydgate had been aware of all the pride he excited in that delicate bosom, he might have been just as well pleased as any other man, even the most densely ignorant of humoral pathology or fibrous tissue: he held it one of the prettiest attitudes of the feminine mind to adore a man's pre-eminence without too precise a knowledge of what it consisted in.

But Rosamond was not one of those helpless girls who betray themselves unawares, and whose behaviour is awkwardly driven by their impulses, instead of being steered by wary grace and propriety. Do you imagine that her rapid forecast and rumination concerning house-furniture and society were ever discernible in her conversation, even with her mamma? On the contrary, she would have expressed the prettiest surprise and disapprobation if she had heard that another young lady had been detected in that immodest prematureness – indeed, would probably have disbelieved in its possibility. For Rosamond never showed any unbecoming knowledge, and was always that combination of correct sentiments, music, dancing, drawing, elegant note-writing, private album for extracted verse, and perfect blond loveliness, which made the irresistible woman for the doomed man of that date. Think no unfair evil of her, pray: she had no wicked plots, nothing sordid or mercenary; in fact, she never thought of money except as something necessary which other people would always provide. She was not in the habit of devising falsehoods, and if her statements were no direct clue to fact, why, they were not intended in that light – they were among her elegant accomplishments, intended to please. Nature had inspired many arts in finishing Mrs Lemon's favourite pupil, who by general consent (Fred's excepted) was a rare compound of beauty, cleverness, and amiability.

Lydgate found it more and more agreeable to be with her, and there was no constraint now, there was a delightful interchange of influence in their eyes, and what they said had that superfluity of meaning for them, which is observable with some sense of flatness by a third person; still they had no interviews or asides from which a third person need have been excluded. In fact, they flirted; and Lydgate was secure in the belief that they did nothing else. If a man could not love and be wise, surely he could flirt and be wise at the same time? Really, the men in Middlemarch, except Mr Farebrother, were great bores, and Lydgate did not care about commercial politics or cards: what was he to do for relaxation? He was often invited to the Bulstrodes'; but the girls there were hardly out of the schoolroom; and Mrs Bulstrode's naïve way of conciliating piety and worldliness, the nothingness of this life and the desirability of cut glass, the consciousness at once of filthy rags and the best damask, was not a sufficient relief from the weight of her husband's invariable seriousness. The Vincys' house, with all its faults, was the pleasanter by contrast; besides, it nourished Rosamond – sweet to look at as a half-opened blush-rose, and adorned with accomplishments for the refined amusement of man.

But he made some enemies, other than medical, by his success with Miss Vincy. One evening he came into the drawing-room rather late, when several other visitors were there. The card-table had drawn off the elders, and Mr Ned Plymdale (one of the good matches in Middlemarch, though not one of its leading minds) was in *tête-à-tête* with Rosamond. He had brought the last *Keepsake*, the gorgeous watered-silk publication which marked modern progress at that time; and he considered himself very fortunate that he could be the first to look over it with her, dwelling on the ladies and gentlemen with shiny copper-plate cheeks and copper-plate smiles, and pointing to comic verses as capital and sentimental stories as interesting. Rosamond was gracious, and Mr Ned was satisfied that he had the very best thing in art and literature as a medium for 'paying addresses' – the very thing to please a nice girl. He had also reasons, deep rather than ostensible, for being satisfied with his own appearance. To superficial observers his chin had too vanishing an aspect, looking as if it were being gradually reabsorbed. And it did indeed cause him some difficulty about the fit of his satin stocks, for which chins were at that time useful.

'I think the Honourable Mrs S. is something like you,' said Mr Ned. He kept the book open at the bewitching portrait, and looked at it rather languishingly.

'Her back is very large; she seems to have sat for that,' said Rosamond, not meaning any satire, but thinking how red young Plymdale's hands were, and wondering why Lydgate did not come. She went on with her tatting all the while.

'I did not say she was as beautiful as you are,' said Mr Ned, venturing to look from the portrait to its rival.

'I suspect you of being an adroit flatterer,' said Rosamond, feeling sure that she should have to reject this young gentleman a second time.

But now Lydgate came in; the book was closed before he reached Rosamond's corner, and as he took his seat with easy confidence on the other side of her, young Plymdale's jaw fell like a barometer towards the cheerless side of change. Rosamond enjoyed not only Lydgate's presence but its effect: she liked to excite jealousy.

'What a late comer you are!' she said, as they shook hands. 'Mamma had given you up a little while ago. How do you find Fred?'

'As usual; going on well, but slowly. I want him to go away – to Stone Court, for example. But your mamma seems to have some objection.'

'Poor fellow!' said Rosamond, prettily. 'You will see Fred so changed,' she added, turning to the other suitor; 'we have looked to Mr Lydgate as our guardian angel during his illness.'

Mr Ned smiled nervously, while Lydgate, drawing the *Keepsake* towards him and opening it, gave a short scornful laugh and tossed up his chin, as if in wonderment at human folly.

'What are you laughing at so profanely?' said Rosamond, with bland neutrality.

'I wonder which would turn out to be the silliest – the engravings or the writing here,' said Lydgate, in his most convinced tone, while he turned over the pages quickly, seeming to see all through the book in no time, and showing his large white hands to much advantage, as Rosamond thought. 'Do look at this bridegroom coming out of church: did you ever see such a "sugared invention" – as the Elizabethans used to say? Did any haberdasher ever look so smirking? Yet I will answer for it the story makes him one of the first gentlemen in the land.'

'You are so severe, I am frightened at you,' said Rosamond, keeping her amusement duly moderate. Poor young Plymdale had lingered with admiration over this very engraving, and his spirit was stirred.

'There are a great many celebrated people writing in the *Keepsake*, at all events,' he said, in a tone at once piqued and timid. 'This is the first time I have heard it called silly.'

'I think I shall turn round on you and accuse you of being a Goth,' said Rosamond, looking at Lydgate with a smile. 'I suspect you know nothing about Lady Blessington and L. E. L.' Rosamond herself was not without relish for these writers, but she did not readily commit herself by admiration, and was alive to the slightest hint that anything was not, according to Lydgate, in the very highest taste.

'But Sir Walter Scott – I suppose Mr Lydgate knows him,' said young Plymdale, a little cheered by this advantage.

'Oh, I read no literature now,' said Lydgate, shutting the book, and pushing it away. 'I read so much when I was a lad, that I suppose it will last me all my life. I used to know Scott's poems by heart.'

'I should like to know when you left off,' said Rosamond, 'because then I might be sure that I knew something which you did not know.'

'Mr Lydgate would say that was not worth knowing,' said Mr Ned, purposely caustic.

'On the contrary,' said Lydgate, showing no smart, but smiling with exasperating confidence at Rosamond. 'It would be worth knowing by the fact that Miss Vincy could tell it me.'

Young Plymdale soon went to look at the whist-playing, thinking that Lydgate was one of the most conceited, unpleasant fellows it had ever been his ill-fortune to meet.

'How rash you are!' said Rosamond, inwardly delighted. 'Do you see that you have given offence?'

'What – is it Mr Plymdale's book? I am sorry. I didn't think about it.'

'I shall begin to admit what you said of yourself when you first came here – that you are a bear, and want teaching by the birds.'

'Well, there is a bird who can teach me what she will. Don't I listen to her willingly?'

To Rosamond it seemed as if she and Lydgate were as good as engaged. That they were some time to be engaged had long been an idea in her mind; and ideas, we know, tend to a more solid kind of existence, the necessary materials being at hand. It is true, Lydgate had the counter idea of remaining unengaged; but this was a mere negative, a shadow cast by other resolves which themselves were capable of shrinking. Circumstances was almost sure to be on the side of Rosamond's idea, which had a shaping activity and looked through watchful blue eyes, whereas Lydgate's lay blind and unconcerned as a jelly-fish which gets melted without knowing it.

That evening when he went home, he looked at his phials to see how a process of maceration was going on, with undisturbed interest; and he wrote out his daily notes with as much precision as usual. The reveries from which it was difficult for him to detach himself were ideal constructions of something else than Rosamond's virtues, and the primitive tissue was still his fair unknown. Moreover, he was beginning to feel some zest for the growing though half-suppressed feud between him and the other medical men, which was likely to become more manifest, now that Bulstrode's method of managing the new hospital was about to be declared; and there were various inspiriting signs that his non-acceptance by some of Peacock's patients might be counter-balanced by the impression he had produced in other quarters. Only a few days later, when he had happened to overtake Rosamond on the Lowick road and had got down from his horse to walk by her side until he had quite protected her from a passing drove, he had been stopped by a servant on horseback with a message calling him in to a house of some importance where Peacock had never attended; and it was the second instance of this kind. The servant was Sir James Chettam's, and the house was Lowick Manor.

ᥴ TWENTY-EIGHT ᥳ

1st Gent. All times are good to seek your wedded home
   Bringing a mutual delight.
2nd Gent.   Why, true.
   The calendar hath not an evil day
   For souls made one by love, and even death
   Were sweetness, if it came like rolling waves
   While they two clasped each other, and foresaw
   No life apart.

MR AND MRS CASAUBON, RETURNING FROM their wedding journey, arrived at Lowick Manor in the middle of January. A light snow was falling as they descended at the door, and in the morning, when Dorothea passed from her dressing-room into the blue-green boudoir that we know of, she saw the long avenue of limes lifting their trunks from a white earth, and spreading white branches against the dun and motionless sky. The distant flat shrank in uniform whiteness and low-hanging uniformity of cloud. The very furniture in the room seemed to have shrunk since she saw it before: the stag in the tapestry looked more like a ghost in his ghostly blue-green world; the volumes of polite literature in the bookcase looked more like immovable imitations of books. The bright fire of dry oak-boughs burning on the dogs seemed an incongruous renewal of life and glow – like the figure of Dorothea herself as she entered carrying the red-leather cases containing the cameos for Celia.

She was glowing from her morning toilette as only healthful youth can glow; there was gem-like brightness on her coiled hair and in her hazel eyes; there was warm red life in her lips; her throat had a breathing whiteness above the differing white of the fur which itself seemed to wind about her neck and cling down her blue-grey pelisse with a tenderness gathered from her own, a sentient commingled innocence which kept its loveliness against the crystalline purity of the out-door snow. As she laid the cameo-cases on the table in the bow-window, she unconsciously kept her hands on them, immediately absorbed in looking out on the still, white enclosure which made her visible world.

Mr Casaubon, who had risen early complaining of palpitation, was in the library giving audience to his curate Mr Tucker. By-and-by Celia would come in her quality of bridesmaid as well as sister, and through the next weeks there would be wedding visits received and given; all in continuance of that transitional life understood to correspond with the excitement of bridal felicity, and keeping up the sense of busy ineffectiveness, as of a dream which the dreamer begins to suspect. The duties of her married life, contemplated as so great beforehand, seemed to be shrinking with the furniture and the white vapour-walled landscape. The clear heights where she expected to walk in full communion had become difficult to see even in her imagination; the delicious repose of the soul on a complete superior had been shaken into uneasy effort and alarmed with dim presentiment. When would the days begin of that active wifely devotion which was to strengthen her husband's life and exalt her own? Never perhaps, as she had preconceived them; but somehow – still somehow. In this solemnly pledged union of her life, duty would present itself in some new form of inspiration and give a new meaning to wifely love.

Meanwhile there was the snow and the low arch of dun vapour – there was the stifling oppression of that gentlewoman's world, where everything was done for her and none asked for her aid – where the sense of connection with a manifold pregnant existence had to be kept up painfully as an inward vision, instead of coming from without in claims that would have shaped her energies. – 'What shall I do?' 'Whatever you please, my dear': that had been her brief history since she had left off learning morning lessons and practising silly rhythms on the hated piano. Marriage, which was to bring guidance into worthy and imperative occupation, had not yet freed her from the gentlewoman's oppressive liberty: it had not even filled her leisure with the ruminant joy of unchecked tenderness. Her blooming full-pulsed youth stood there in a moral imprisonment which made itself one with the chill, colourless, narrowed landscape, with the shrunken furniture, the never-read books, and the ghostly stag in a pale fantastic world that seemed to be vanishing from the daylight.

In the first minutes when Dorothea looked out she felt nothing but the dreary oppression; then came a keen remembrance, and turning away from the window she walked round the room. The ideas and hopes which were living in her mind when she first saw this room nearly three months before were present now only as memories: she judged them as we judge transient and departed things. All existence seemed to beat with a lower pulse than her own, and her religious faith was a solitary cry, the struggle out of a nightmare in which every object was withering and shrinking away from her. Each remembered thing in the room was disenchanted, was deadened as an unlit transparency, till her wandering gaze came to the group of miniatures, and there at last she saw something which had gathered new breath and meaning: it was the miniature of Mr Casaubon's aunt Julia, who had made the unfortunate marriage – of Will Ladislaw's grandmother. Dorothea could fancy that it was alive now – the delicate woman's face which yet had a head-strong look, a peculiarity difficult to interpret. Was it only her friends who thought her marriage unfortunate?

or did she herself find it out to be a mistake, and taste the salt bitterness of her tears in the merciful silence of the night? What breadths of experience Dorothea seemed to have passed over since she first looked at this miniature! She felt a new companionship with it, as if it had an ear for her and could see how she was looking at it. Here was a woman who had known some difficulty about marriage. Nay, the colours deepened, the lips and chin seemed to get larger, the hair and eyes seemed to be sending out light, the face was masculine and beamed on her with that full gaze which tells her on whom it falls that she is too interesting for the slightest movement of her eyelid to pass unnoticed and uninterpreted. The vivid presentation came like a pleasant glow to Dorothea: she felt herself smiling, and turning from the miniature sat down and looked up as if she were again talking to a figure in front of her. But the smile disappeared as she went on meditating, and at last she said aloud –

'Oh, it was cruel to speak so! How sad how dreadful!'

She rose quickly and went out of the room, hurrying along the corridor, with the irresistible impulse to go and see her husband and inquire if she could do anything for him. Perhaps Mr Tucker was gone and Mr Casaubon was alone in the library. She felt as if all her morning's gloom would vanish if she could see her husband glad because of her presence.

But when she reached the head of the dark oak staircase, there was Celia coming up, and below there was Mr Brooke, exchanging welcomes and congratulations with Mr Casaubon.

'Dodo!' said Celia, in her quiet staccato; then kissed her sister, whose arms encircled her, and said no more. I think they both cried a little in a furtive manner, while Dorothea ran down-stairs to greet her uncle.

'I need not ask how you are, my dear,' said Mr Brooke, after kissing her forehead. 'Rome has agreed with you, I see – happiness, frescoes, the antique – that sort of thing. Well, it's very pleasant to have you back again, and you understand all about art now, eh? But Casaubon is a little pale, I tell him – a little pale, you know. Studying hard in his holidays is carrying it rather too far. I overdid it at one time' – Mr Brooke still held Dorothea's hand, but had turned his face to Mr Casaubon – 'about topography, ruins, temples – I thought I had a clue, but I saw it would carry me too far, and nothing might have come of it. You may go any length in that sort of thing, and nothing may come of it, you know.'

Dorothea's eyes also were turned up to her husband's face with some anxiety at the idea that those who saw him afresh after absence might be aware of signs which she had not noticed.

'Nothing to alarm you, my dear,' said Mr Brooke, observing her expression. 'A little English beef and mutton will soon make a difference. It was all very well to look pale, sitting for the portrait of Aquinas, you know – we got your letter just in time. But Aquinas, now – he was a little too subtle, wasn't he? Does anybody read Aquinas?'

'He is not indeed an author adapted to superficial minds,' said Mr Casaubon, meeting these timely questions with dignified patience.

'You would like coffee in your own room, uncle?' said Dorothea, coming to the rescue.

'Yes; and you must go to Celia: she has great news to tell you, you know. I leave it all to her.'

The blue-green boudoir looked much more cheerful when Celia was seated there in a pelisse exactly like her sister's, surveying the cameos with a placid satisfaction, while the conversation passed on to other topics.

'Do you think it nice to go to Rome on a wedding journey?' said Celia, with her ready delicate blush which Dorothea was used to on the smallest occasion.

'It would not suit all – not you, dear, for example,' said Dorothea, quietly. No one would ever know what she thought of a wedding journey to Rome.

'Mrs Cadwallader says it is nonsense, people going a long journey when they are married. She says they get tired to death of each other, and can't quarrel comfortably, as they would at home. And Lady Chettam says she went to Bath.' Celia's colour changed again and again – seemed

> To come and go with tidings from the heart,
> As it a running messenger had been.

It must mean more than Celia's blushing usually did.

'Celia! has something happened?' said Dorothea, in a tone full of sisterly feeling. 'Have you really any great news to tell me?'

'It was because you went away, Dodo. Then there was nobody but me for Sir James to talk to,' said Celia, with a certain roguishness in her eyes.

'I understand. It is as I used to hope and believe,' said Dorothea, taking her sister's face between her hands, and looking at her half anxiously. Celia's marriage seemed more serious than it used to do.

'It was only three days ago,' said Celia. 'And Lady Chettam is very kind.'

'And you are very happy?'

'Yes. We are not going to be married yet. Because everything is to be got ready. And I don't want to be married so very soon, because I think it is nice to be engaged. And we shall be married all our lives after.'

'I do believe you could not marry better, Kitty. Sir James is a good, honourable man,' said Dorothea, warmly.

'He has gone on with the cottages, Dodo. He will tell you about them when he comes. Shall you be glad to see him?'

'Of course I shall. How can you ask me?'

'Only I was afraid you would be getting so learned,' said Celia,

regarding Mr Casaubon's learning as a kind of damp which might in due
time saturate a neighbouring body.

◁ TWENTY-NINE ▷

I found that no genius in another could please me. My
unfortunate paradoxes had entirely dried up that source of
comfort.

GOLDSMITH

ONE MORNING, SOME WEEKS AFTER HER arrival at Lowick, Dorothea – but
why always Dorothea? Was her point of view the only possible one with
regard to this marriage? I protest against all our interest, all our effort at
understanding being given to the young skins that look blooming in spite
of trouble; for these too will get faded, and will know the older and more
eating griefs which we are helping to neglect. In spite of the blinking eyes
and white moles objectionable to Celia, and the want of muscular curve
which was morally painful to Sir James, Mr Casaubon had an intense
consciousness within him, and was spiritually a-hungered like the rest of
us. He had done nothing exceptional in marrying – nothing but what
society sanctions, and considers an occasion for wreaths and bouquets. It
had occurred to him that he must not any longer defer his intention of
matrimony, and he had reflected that in taking a wife, a man of good
position should expect and carefully choose a blooming young lady – the
younger the better, because more educable and submissive – of a rank
equal to his own, of religious principles, virtuous disposition, and good
understanding. On such a young lady he would make handsome settlements, and he would neglect no arrangement for her happiness: in return,
he should receive family pleasures and leave behind him that copy of
himself which seemed so urgently required of a man – to the sonneteers
of the sixteenth century. Times had altered since then, and no sonneteer
had insisted on Mr Casaubon's leaving a copy of himself; moreover,
he had not yet succeeded in issuing copies of his mythological key; but he
had always intended to acquit himself by marriage, and the sense that
he was fast leaving the years behind him, that the world was getting
dimmer and that he felt lonely, was a reason to him for losing no more
time in overtaking domestic delights before they too were left behind by
the years.

And when he had seen Dorothea he believed that he had found even
more than he demanded: she might really be such a helpmate to him as

would enable him to dispense with a hired secretary, an aid which Mr Casaubon had never yet employed and had a suspicious dread of. (Mr Casaubon was nervously conscious that he was expected to manifest a powerful mind.) Providence, in its kindness, had supplied him with the wife he needed. A wife, a modest young lady, with the purely appreciative, unambitious abilities of her sex, is sure to think her husband's mind powerful. Whether Providence had taken equal care of Miss Brooke in presenting her with Mr Casaubon was an idea which could hardly occur to him. Society never made the preposterous demand that a man should think as much about his own qualifications for making a charming girl happy as he thinks of hers for making himself happy. As if a man could choose not only his wife but his wife's husband! Or as if he were bound to provide charms for his posterity in his own person! – When Dorothea accepted him with effusion, that was only natural; and Mr Casaubon believed that his happiness was going to begin.

He had not had much foretaste of happiness in his previous life. To know intense joy without a strong bodily frame, one must have an enthusiastic soul. Mr Casaubon had never had a strong bodily frame, and his soul was sensitive without being enthusiastic: it was too languid to thrill out of self-consciousness into passionate delight; it went on fluttering in the swampy ground where it was hatched, thinking of its wings and never flying. His experience was of that pitiable kind which shrinks from pity, and fears most of all that it should be known: it was that proud narrow sensitiveness which has not mass enough to spare for transformation into sympathy, and quivers thread-like in small currents of self-preoccupation or at best of an egoistic scrupulosity. And Mr Casaubon had many scruples: he was capable of a severe self-restraint; he was resolute in being a man of honour according to the code; he would be unimpeachable by any recognized opinion. In conduct these ends had been attained; but the difficulty of making his Key to all Mythologies unimpeachable weighed like lead upon his mind; and the pamphlets – or 'Parerga' as he called them – by which he tested his public and deposited small monumental records of his march, were far from having been seen in all their significance. He suspected the Archdeacon of not having read them; he was in painful doubt as to what was really thought of them by the leading minds of Brasenose, and bitterly convinced that his old acquaintance Carp had been the writer of that depreciatory recension which was kept locked in a small drawer of Mr Casaubon's desk, and also in a dark closet of his verbal memory. These were heavy impressions to struggle against, and brought that melancholy embitterment which is the consequence of all excessive claim: even his religious faith wavered with his wavering trust in his own authorship, and the consolations of the Christian hope in immortality seemed to lean on the immortality of the still unwritten Key to all Mythologies. For my part I am very sorry for him. It is an uneasy lot at best, to be what we call highly taught and yet not to enjoy: to be present at this great spectacle of life and never to be liberated from a small hungry shivering self – never to be fully possessed by the glory we behold, never to have our consciousness rapturously transformed into the vividness of a thought, the ardour of a passion, the energy of an action, but always to be scholarly and uninspired, ambitious and timid, scrupulous and dim-sighted. Becoming a dean or even a bishop would make little difference, I fear, to Mr Casaubon's uneasiness. Doubtless some ancient Greek has observed that behind the big mask and the speaking-trumpet, there must always be our poor little eyes peeping as usual and our timorous lips more or less under anxious control.

To this mental estate mapped out a quarter of a century before, to sensibilities thus fenced in, Mr Casaubon had thought of annexing happiness with a lovely young bride; but even before marriage, as we have seen, he found himself under a new depression in the consciousness that the new bliss was not blissful to him. Inclination yearned back to its old, easier custom. And the deeper he went in domesticity the more did the sense of acquitting himself and acting with propriety predominate over any other satisfaction. Marriage, like religion and erudition, nay, like authorship itself, was fated to become an outward requirement, and Edward Casaubon was bent on fulfilling unimpeachably all requirements. Even drawing Dorothea into use in his study, according to his own intention before marriage, was an effort which he was always tempted to defer, and but for her pleading insistence it might never have begun. But she had succeeded in making it a matter of course that she should take her place at an early hour in the library and have work either of reading aloud or copying assigned her. The work had been easier to define because Mr Casaubon had adopted an immediate intention: there was to be a new Parergon, a small monograph on some lately-traced indications concerning the Egyptian mysteries whereby certain assertions of Warburton's could be corrected. References were extensive even here, but not altogether shoreless; and sentences were actually to be written in the shape wherein they would be scanned by Brasenose and a less formidable posterity. These minor monumental productions were always exciting to Mr Casaubon: digestion was made difficult by the interference of citations, or by the rivalry of dialectical phrases ringing against each other in his brain. And from the first there was to be a Latin dedication about which everything was uncertain except that it was not to be addressed to Carp: it was a poisonous regret to Mr Casaubon that he had once addressed a dedication to Carp in which he had numbered that member of the animal kingdom among the *viros nullo aevo perituros*, a mistake which would infallibly lay the dedicator open to ridicule in the next age, and might even be chuckled over by Pike and Tench in the present.

Thus Mr Casaubon was in one of his busiest epochs, and as I began to say a little while ago, Dorothea joined him early in the library where he had breakfasted alone. Celia at this time was on a second visit to Lowick, probably the last before her marriage, and was in the drawing-room expecting Sir James.

Dorothea had learned to read the signs of her husband's mood, and she saw that the morning had become more foggy there during the last hour. She was going silently to her desk when he said, in that distant tone which implied that he was discharging a disagreeable duty –

'Dorothea, here is a letter for you, which was enclosed in one addressed to me.'

It was a letter of two pages, and she immediately looked at the signature.

'Mr Ladislaw! What can he have to say to me?' she exclaimed, in a tone of pleased surprise. 'But,' she added, looking at Mr Casaubon, 'I can imagine what he has written to you about.'

'You can, if you please, read the letter,' said Mr Casaubon, severely pointing to it with his pen, and not looking at her. 'But I may as well say beforehand, that I must decline the proposal it contains to pay a visit here. I trust I may be excused for desiring an interval of complete freedom from such distractions as have been hitherto inevitable, and especially from guests whose desultory vivacity makes their presence a fatigue.'

There had been no clashing of temper between Dorothea and her husband since that little explosion in Rome, which had left such strong traces in her mind that it had been easier ever since to quell emotion than to incur the consequence of venting it. But this ill-tempered anticipation that she could desire visits which might be disagreeable to her husband, this gratuitous defence of himself against selfish complaint on her part, was too sharp a sting to be meditated on until after it had been resented. Dorothea had thought that she could have been patient with John Milton, but she had never imagined him behaving in this way; and for a moment Mr Casaubon seemed to be stupidly undiscerning and odiously unjust. Pity, that 'newborn babe' which was by-and-by to rule many a storm within her, did not 'stride the blast' on this occasion. With her first words, uttered in a tone that shook him, she startled Mr Casaubon into looking at her, and meeting the flash of her eyes.

'Why do you attribute to me a wish for anything that would annoy you? You speak to me as if I were something you had to contend against. Wait at least till I appear to consult my own pleasure apart from yours.'

'Dorothea, you are hasty,' answered Mr Casaubon, nervously.

Decidedly, this woman was too young to be on the formidable level of wifehood – unless she had been pale and featureless and taken everything for granted.

'I think it was you who were first hasty in your false suppositions about my feeling,' said Dorothea, in the same tone. The fire was not dissipated yet, and she thought it was ignoble in her husband not to apologize to her.

'We will, if you please, say no more on this subject, Dorothea. I have neither leisure nor energy for this kind of debate.'

Here Mr Casaubon dipped his pen and made as if he would return to his writing, though his hand trembled so much that the words seemed to be written in an unknown character. There are answers which, in turning away wrath, only send it to the other end of the room, and to have a discussion coolly waived when you feel that justice is all on your own side is even more exasperating in marriage than in philosophy.

Dorothea left Ladislaw's two letters unread on her husband's writing-table and went to her own place, the scorn and indignation within her rejecting the reading of these letters, just as we hurl away any trash towards which we seem to have been suspected of mean cupidity. She did not in the least divine the subtle sources of her husband's bad temper about these letters; she only knew that they had caused him to offend her. She began to work at once, and her hand did not tremble; on the contrary, in writing out the quotations which had been given to her the day before, she felt that she was forming her letters beautifully, and it seemed to her that she saw the construction of the Latin she was copying, and which she was beginning to understand, more clearly than usual. In her indignation there was a sense of superiority, but it went out for the present in firmness of stroke, and did not compress itself into an inward articulate voice pronouncing the once 'affable archangel' a poor creature.

There had been this apparent quiet for half an hour, and Dorothea had not looked away from her own table, when she heard the loud bang of a book on the floor, and turning quickly saw Mr Casaubon on the library-steps clinging forward as if he were in some bodily distress. She started up and bounded towards him in an instant: he was evidently in great straits for breath. Jumping on a stool she got close to his elbow and said with her whole soul melted into tender alarm –

'Can you lean on me, dear?'

He was still for two or three minutes, which seemed endless to her, unable to speak or move, gasping for breath. When at last he descended the three steps and fell backwards in the large chair which Dorothea had drawn close to the foot of the ladder, he no longer gasped but seemed helpless and about to faint. Dorothea rang the bell violently, and presently Mr Casaubon was helped to the couch: he did not faint, and was gradually reviving, when Sir James Chettam came in, having been met in the hall with the news that Mr Casaubon had 'had a fit in the library'.

'Good God! this is just what might have been expected,' was his immediate thought. If his prophetic soul had been urged to particularize, it seemed to him that 'fits' would have been the definite expression alighted upon. He asked his informant, the butler, whether the doctor had been sent for. The butler never knew his master want the doctor before; but would it not be right to send for a physician?

When Sir James entered the library, however, Mr Casaubon could make some signs of his usual politeness, and Dorothea, who in the reaction from her first terror had been kneeling and sobbing by his side, now rose and herself proposed that some one should ride off for a medical man.

'I recommend you to send for Lydgate,' said Sir James. 'My mother has called him in, and she has found him uncommonly clever. She has had a poor opinion of the physicians since my father's death.'

Dorothea appealed to her husband, and he made a silent sign of approval. So Mr Lydgate was sent for and he came wonderfully soon, for the messenger, who was Sir James Chettam's man and knew Mr Lydgate, met him leading his horse along the Lowick road and giving his arm to Miss Vincy.

Celia, in the drawing-room, had known nothing of the trouble till Sir James told her of it. After Dorothea's account, he no longer considered the illness a fit, but still something 'of that nature'.

'Poor dear Dodo – how dreadful!' said Celia, feeling as much grieved as her own perfect happiness would allow. Her little hands were clasped, and enclosed by Sir James's as a bud is enfolded by a liberal calyx. 'It is very shocking that Mr Casaubon should be ill; but I never did like him. And I think he is not half fond enough of Dorothea; and he ought to be, for I am sure no one else would have had him – do you think they would?'

'I always thought it a horrible sacrifice of your sister,' said Sir James.

'Yes. But poor Dodo never did do what other people do, and I think she never will.'

'She is a noble creature,' said the loyal-hearted Sir James. He had just had a fresh impression of this kind, as he had seen Dorothea stretching her tender arm under her husband's neck and looking at him with unspeakable sorrow. He did not know how much penitence there was in the sorrow.

'Yes,' said Celia, thinking it was very well for Sir James to say so, but he would not have been comfortable with Dodo. 'Shall I go to her? Could I help her, do you think?'

'I think it would be well for you just to go and see her before Lydgate comes,' said Sir James, magnanimously. 'Only don't stay long.'

While Celia was gone, he walked up and down remembering what he had originally felt about Dorothea's engagement, and feeling a revival of his disgust at Mr Brooke's indifference. If Cadwallader – if every one else had regarded the affair as he, Sir James, had done, the marriage might have been hindered. It was wicked to let a young girl blindly decide her fate in that way, without any effort to save her. Sir James had long ceased to have any regrets on his own account: his heart was satisfied with his engagement to Celia. But he had a chivalrous nature (was not the disinterested service of woman among the ideal glories of old chivalry?): his disregarded love had not turned to bitterness; its death had made sweet odours – floating memories that clung with a consecrating effect to Dorothea. He could remain her brotherly friend, interpreting her actions with generous trustfulness.

✑ THIRTY ✑

Qui veut délasser hors de propos, lasse.

PASCAL

MR CASAUBON HAD NO SECOND ATTACK of equal severity with the first, and in a few days began to recover his usual condition. But Lydgate seemed to think the case worth a great deal of attention. He not only used his stethoscope (which had not become a matter of course in practice at that time), but sat quietly by his patient and watched him. To Mr Casaubon's questions about himself, he replied that the source of the illness was the common error of intellectual men – a too eager and monotonous application: the remedy was, to be satisfied with moderate work, and to seek variety of relaxation. Mr Brooke, who sat by on one occasion, suggested that Mr Casaubon should go fishing, as Cadwallader did, and have a turning-room, make toys, table-legs, and that kind of thing.

'In short you recommend me to anticipate the arrival of my second childhood,' said poor Mr Casaubon, with some bitterness. 'These things,' he added, looking at Lydgate, 'would be to me such relaxation as tow-picking is to prisoners in a house of correction.'

'I confess,' said Lydgate, smiling, 'amusement is rather an unsatisfactory prescription. It is something like telling people to keep up their spirits. Perhaps I had better say, that you must submit to be mildly bored rather than to go on working.'

'Yes, yes,' said Mr Brooke. 'Get Dorothea to play back-gammon with you in the evenings. And shuttlecock, now – I don't know a finer game than shuttlecock for the daytime. I remember it all the fashion. To be sure, your eyes might not stand that, Casaubon. But you must unbend, you know. Why, you might take to some light study: conchology, now: I always think that must be a light study. Or get Dorothea to read you light things, Smollett – *Roderick Random, Humphry Clinker*: they are a little broad, but she may read anything now she's married, you know. I remember they made me laugh uncommonly – there's a droll bit about a postilion's breeches. We have no such humour now. I have gone through all these things, but they might be rather new to you.'

'As new as eating thistles,' would have been an answer to represent Mr Casaubon's feelings. But he only bowed resignedly, with due respect to his wife's uncle, and observed that doubtless the works he mentioned had 'served as a resource to a certain order of mind'.

'You see,' said the able magistrate to Lydgate, when they were outside the door, 'Casaubon has been a little narrow: it leaves him rather at a loss when you forbid him his particular work, which I believe is something very deep indeed – in the line of research, you know. I would never give way to that; I was always versatile. But a clergyman is tied a little tight. If they would make him a bishop, now! – he did a very good pamphlet for Peel. He would have more movement then, more show; he might get a little flesh. But I recommend you to talk to Mrs Casaubon. She is clever enough for anything, is my niece. Tell her, her husband wants liveliness, diversion: put her on amusing tactics.'

Without Mr Brooke's advice, Lydgate had determined on speaking to Dorothea. She had not been present while her uncle was throwing out his pleasant suggestions as to the mode in which life at Lowick might be enlivened, but she was usually by her husband's side, and the unaffected signs of intense anxiety in her face and voice about whatever touched his mind or health, made a drama which Lydgate was inclined to watch. He said to himself that he was only doing right in telling her the truth about her husband's probable future, but he certainly thought also that it would be interesting to talk confidentially with her. A medical man likes to make psychological observations, and sometimes in the pursuit of such studies is too easily tempted into momentous prophecy which life and death easily set at nought. Lydgate had often been satirical on this gratuitous prediction, and he meant now to be guarded.

He asked for Mrs Casaubon, but being told that she was out walking, he was going away, when Dorothea and Celia appeared, both glowing from their struggle with the March wind. When Lydgate begged to speak with her alone, Dorothea opened the library door which happened to be the nearest, thinking of nothing at the moment but what he might have to say about Mr Casaubon. It was the first time she had entered this room since her husband had been taken ill, and the servant had chosen not to open the shutters. But there was light enough to read by from the narrow upper panes of the windows.

'You will not mind this sombre light,' said Dorothea, standing in the middle of the room. 'Since you forbade books, the library has been out of the question. But Mr Casaubon will soon be here again, I hope. Is he not making progress?'

'Yes, much more rapid progress than I at first expected. Indeed, he is already nearly in his usual state of health.'

'You do not fear that the illness will return?' said Dorothea, whose quick ear had detected some significance in Lydgate's tone.

'Such cases are peculiarly difficult to pronounce upon,' said Lydgate. 'The only point on which I can be confident is that it will be desirable to be very watchful on Mr Casaubon's account lest he should in any way strain his nervous power.'

'I beseech you to speak quite plainly,' said Dorothea, in an imploring tone. 'I cannot bear to think that there might be something which I did not know, and which, if I had known it, would have made me act differently.' The words came out like a cry: it was evident that they were the voice of some mental experience which lay not very far off.

'Sit down,' she added, placing herself on the nearest chair, and throwing off her bonnet and gloves, with an instinctive discarding of formality where a great question of destiny was concerned.

'What you say now justifies my own view,' said Lydgate. 'I think it is one's function as a medical man to hinder regrets of that sort as far as possible. But I beg you to observe that Mr Casaubon's case is precisely of the kind in which the issue is most difficult to pronounce upon. He may possibly live for fifteen years or more, without much worse health than he has had hitherto.'

Dorothea had turned very pale, and when Lydgate paused she said in a low voice, 'You mean if we are very careful.'

'Yes – careful against mental agitation of all kinds, and against excessive application.'

'He would be miserable, if he had to give up his work,' said Dorothea, with a quick prevision of that wretchedness.

'I am aware of that. The only course is to try by all means, direct and indirect, to moderate and vary his occupations. With a happy concurrence of circumstances, there is, as I said, no immediate danger from that affection of the heart which I believe to have been the cause of his late attack. On the other hand, it is possible that the disease may develop itself more rapidly: it is one of those cases in which death is sometimes sudden. Nothing should be neglected which might be affected by such an issue.'

There was silence for a few moments, while Dorothea sat as if she had been turned to marble, though the life within her was so intense that her mind had never before swept in brief time over an equal range of scenes and motives.

'Help me, pray,' she said, at last, in the same low voice as before. 'Tell me what I can do.'

'What do you think of foreign travel? You have been lately in Rome, I think.'

The memories which made this resource utterly hopeless were a new current that shook Dorothea out of her pallid immobility.

'Oh, that would not do – that would be worse than anything,' she said with a more childlike despondency, while the tears rolled down. 'Nothing will be of any use that he does not enjoy.'

'I wish that I could have spared you this pain,' said Lydgate, deeply touched, yet wondering about her marriage. Women just like Dorothea had not entered into his traditions.

'It was right of you to tell me. I thank you for telling me the truth.'

'I wish you to understand that I shall not say anything to enlighten Mr Casaubon himself. I think it desirable for him to know nothing more than that he must not overwork himself, and must observe certain rules. Anxiety of any kind would be precisely the most unfavourable condition for him.'

Lydgate rose, and Dorothea mechanically rose at the same time, unclasping her cloak and throwing it off as if it stifled her. He was bowing and quitting her, when an impulse which if she had been alone would have turned into a prayer, made her say with a sob in her voice –

'Oh, you are a wise man, are you not? You know all about life and death. Advise me. Think what I can do. He has been labouring all his life and looking forward. He minds about nothing else. And I mind about nothing else – '

For years after Lydgate remembered the impression produced in him by this involuntary appeal – this cry from soul to soul, without other consciousness than their moving with kindred natures in the same embroiled medium, the same troublous fitfully-illuminated life. But what could he say now except that he should see Mr Casaubon again to-morrow?

When he was gone, Dorothea's tears gushed forth, and relieved her stifling oppression. Then she dried her eyes, reminded that her distress must not be betrayed to her husband; and looked round the room thinking that she must order the servant to attend to it as usual, since Mr Casaubon might now at any moment wish to enter. On his writing-table there were letters which had lain untouched since the morning when he was taken ill, and among them, as Dorothea well remembered, there were young Ladislaw's letters, the one addressed to her still unopened. The associations of these letters had been made the more painful by that sudden attack of illness which she felt that the agitation caused by her anger might have helped to bring on: it would be time enough to read them when they were again thrust upon her, and she had had no inclination to fetch them from the library. But now it occurred to her that they should be put out of her husband's sight: whatever might have been the sources of his annoyance about them, he must, if possible, not be annoyed again; and she ran her eyes first over the letter addressed to him to assure herself whether or not it would be necessary to write in order to hinder the offensive visit.

Will wrote from Rome, and began by saying that his obligations to Mr Casaubon were too deep for all thanks not to seem impertinent. It was plain that if he were not grateful, he must be the poorest-spirited rascal who had ever found a generous friend. To expand in wordy thanks would be like saying, 'I am honest'. But Will had come to perceive that his defects – defects which Mr Casaubon had himself often pointed to – needed for their correction that more strenuous position which his relative's generosity had hitherto prevented from being inevitable. He trusted that he should make the best return, if return were possible, by showing the effectiveness of the education for which he was indebted, and by ceasing in future to need any diversion towards himself of funds on which others might have a better claim. He was coming to England to try his fortune, as many other young men were obliged to do whose only capital was in their brains. His friend Naumann had desired him to take charge of the 'Dispute' – the picture painted for Mr Casaubon, with whose permission, and Mrs Casaubon's, Will would convey it to Lowick in person. A letter addressed to the Poste Restante in Paris within the fortnight would hinder him, if necessary, from arriving at an inconvenient moment. He enclosed a letter to Mrs Casaubon in which he continued a discussion about art, begun with her in Rome.

Opening her own letter Dorothea saw that it was a lively continuance of his remonstrance with her fanatical sympathy and her want of sturdy neutral delight in things as they were – an outpouring of his young vivacity which it was impossible to read just now. She had immediately to consider what was to be done about the other letter: there was still time perhaps to prevent Will from coming to Lowick. Dorothea ended by giving the letter to her uncle, who was still in the house, and begging him to let Will know that Mr Casaubon had been ill, and that his health would not allow the reception of any visitors.

No one more ready than Mr Brooke to write a letter: his only difficulty was to write a short one, and his ideas in this case expanded over the three large pages and the inward foldings. He had simply said to Dorothea –

'To be sure, I will write, my dear. He's a very clever young fellow – this young Ladislaw – I daresay will be a rising young man. It's a good letter – marks his sense of things, you know. However, I will tell him about Casaubon.'

But the end of Mr Brooke's pen was a thinking organ, evolving sentences, especially of a benevolent kind, before the rest of his mind could well overtake them. It expressed regrets and proposed remedies, which, when Mr Brooke read them, seemed felicitously worded – surprisingly the right thing, and determined a sequel which he had never before thought of. In this case, his pen found it such a pity that young Ladislaw should not have come into the neighbourhood just at that time, in order that Mr Brooke might make his acquaintance more fully, and that they might go over the long-neglected Italian drawings together – it also felt such an interest in a young man who was starting in life with a stock of ideas – that by the end of the second page it had persuaded Mr Brooke to invite young Ladislaw, since he could not be received at Lowick, to come to Tipton Grange. Why not? They could find a great many things to do together, and this was a period of peculiar growth – the political horizon was expanding, and – in short, Mr Brooke's pen went off into a little speech which it had lately reported for that imperfectly-edited organ the *Middlemarch Pioneer*. While Mr Brooke was sealing this letter, he felt elated with an influx of dim projects: – a young man capable of putting ideas into form, the *Pioneer* purchased to clear the pathway for a new candidate, documents utilized – who knew what might come of it all? Since Celia was going to marry immediately, it would be very pleasant to have a young fellow at table with him, at least for a time.

But he went away without telling Dorothea what he had put into the letter, for she was engaged with her husband, and – in fact, these things were of no importance to her.

◁ THIRTY-ONE ▷

How will you know the pitch of that great bell
Too large for you to stir? Let but a flute
Play 'neath the fine-mixed metal: listen close
Till the right note flows forth, a silvery rill:
Then shall the huge bell tremble – then the mass
With myriad waves concurrent shall respond
In low soft unison.

LYDGATE THAT EVENING SPOKE TO MISS VINCY of Mrs Casaubon, and laid some emphasis on the strong feeling she appeared to have for that formal studious man thirty years older than herself.

'Of course she is devoted to her husband,' said Rosamond, implying a notion of necessary sequence which the scientific man regarded as the prettiest possible for a woman; but she was thinking at the same time that it was not so very melancholy to be mistress of Lowick Manor with a husband likely to die soon. 'Do you think her very handsome?'

'She certainly is handsome, but I have not thought about it,' said Lydgate.

'I suppose it would be unprofessional,' said Rosamond, dimpling. 'But how your practice is spreading! You were called in before to the Chettams, I think; and now, the Casaubons.'

'Yes,' said Lydgate, in a tone of compulsory admission. 'But I don't really like attending such people so well as the poor. The cases are more monotonous, and one has to go through more fuss and listen more deferentially to nonsense.'

'Not more than in Middlemarch,' said Rosamond. 'And at least you go through wide corridors and have the scent of rose-leaves everywhere.'

'That is true, Mademoiselle de Montmorenci,' said Lydgate, just bending his head to the table and lifting with his fourth finger her delicate handkerchief which lay at the mouth of her reticule, as if to enjoy its scent, while he looked at her with a smile.

But this agreeable holiday freedom with which Lydgate hovered about the flower of Middlemarch, could not continue indefinitely. It was not more possible to find social isolation in that town than elsewhere, and two people persistently flirting could by no means escape from 'the various entanglements, weights, blows, clashings, motions, by which things severally go on'. Whatever Miss Vincy did must be remarked, and she was perhaps the more conspicuous to admirers and critics because just now Mrs Vincy, after some struggle, had gone with Fred to stay a little while at Stone Court, there being no other way of at once gratifying old Featherstone and keeping watch against Mary Garth, who appeared a less tolerable daughter-in-law in proportion as Fred's illness disappeared.

Aunt Bulstrode, for example, came a little oftener into Lowick Gate to see Rosamond, now she was alone. For Mrs Bulstrode had a true sisterly feeling for her brother; always thinking that he might have married better, but wishing well to the children. Now Mrs Bulstrode had a long-standing intimacy with Mrs Plymdale. They had nearly the same preferences in silks, patterns for underclothing, china-ware, and clergymen; they confided their little troubles of health and household management to each other, and various little points of superiority on Mrs Bulstrode's side, namely, more decided seriousness, more admiration for mind, and a house outside the town, sometimes served to give colour to their conversation without dividing them: well-meaning women both, knowing very little of their own motives.

Mrs Bulstrode, paying a morning visit to Mrs Plymdale, happened to say that she could not stay longer, because she was going to see poor Rosamond.

'Why do you say "poor Rosamond"?' said Mrs Plymdale, a round-eyed sharp little woman, like a tamed falcon.

'She is so pretty, and has been brought up in such thoughtlessness. The mother, you know, had always that levity about her which makes me anxious for the children.'

'Well, Harriet, if I am to speak my mind,' said Mrs Plymdale, with emphasis, 'I must say, anybody would suppose you and Mr Bulstrode would be delighted with what has happened, for you have done everything to put Mr Lydgate forward.'

'Selina, what do you mean?' said Mrs Bulstrode in genuine surprise.

'Not but what I am truly thankful for Ned's sake,' said Mrs Plymdale. 'He could certainly better afford to keep such a wife than some people can; but I should wish him to look elsewhere. Still a mother has anxieties, and some young men would take to a bad life in consequence. Besides, if I was obliged to speak, I should say I was not fond of strangers coming into a town.'

'I don't know, Selina,' said Mrs Bulstrode, with a little emphasis in her turn. 'Mr Bulstrode was a stranger here at one time. Abraham and Moses were strangers in the land, and we are told to entertain strangers.

And especially,' she added, after a slight pause, 'when they are unexceptionable.'

'I was not speaking in a religious sense, Harriet. I spoke as a mother.'

'Selina, I am sure you have never heard me say anything against a niece
of mine marrying your son.'

'Oh, it is pride in Miss Vincy – I am sure it is nothing else,' said Mrs
Plymdale, who had never before given all her confidence to 'Harriet' on
this subject. 'No young man in Middlemarch was good enough for her: I
have heard her mother say as much. That is not a Christian spirit, I think.
But now, from all I hear, she has found a man as proud as herself.'

'You don't mean that there is anything between Rosamond and Mr
Lydgate?' said Mrs Bulstrode, rather mortified at finding out her own
ignorance.

'Is it possible you don't know, Harriet?'

'Oh, I go about so little; and I am not fond of gossip; I really never hear
any. You see so many people that I don't see. Your circle is rather different
from ours.'

'Well, but your own niece and Mr Bulstrode's great favourite – and
yours too, I am sure, Harriet! I thought, at one time, you meant him for
Kate, when she is a little older.'

'I don't believe there can be anything serious at present,' said Mrs
Bulstrode. 'My brother would certainly have told me.'

'Well, people have different ways, but I understand that nobody can see
Miss Vincy and Mr Lydgate together without taking them to be engaged.
However, it is not my business. Shall I put up the pattern of mittens?'

After this Mrs Bulstrode drove to her niece with a mind newly weighted. She was herself handsomely dressed, but she noticed with a little
more regret than usual that Rosamond, who was just come in and met her
in walking-dress, was almost as expensively equipped. Mrs Bulstrode was
a feminine, smaller edition of her brother, and had none of her husband's
low-toned pallor. She had a good honest glance and used no circum-
locution.

'You are alone, I see, my dear,' she said, as they entered the drawing-
room together, looking round gravely. Rosamond felt sure that her aunt
had something particular to say, and they sat down near each other.
Nevertheless, the quilling inside Rosamond's bonnet was so charming
that it was impossible not to desire the same kind of thing for Kate, and
Mrs Bulstrode's eyes, which were rather fine, rolled round that ample
quilled circuit, while she spoke.

'I have just heard something about you that has surprised me very
much, Rosamond.'

'What is that, aunt?' Rosamond's eyes also were roaming over her
aunt's large embroidered collar.

'I can hardly believe it – that you should be engaged without my knowing it – without your father's telling me.' Here Mrs Bulstrode's eyes finally rested on Rosamond's, who blushed deeply, and said –

'I am not engaged, aunt.'

'How is it that every one says so, then – that it is the town's talk?'

'The town's talk is of very little consequence, I think,' said Rosamond, inwardly gratified.

'Oh, my dear, be more thoughtful; don't despise your neighbours so. Remember you are turned twenty-two now, and you will have no fortune: your father, I am sure, will not be able to spare you anything. Mr Lydgate is very intellectual and clever; I know there is an attraction in that. I like talking to such men myself; and your uncle finds him very useful. But the profession is a poor one here. To be sure, this life is not everything; but it is seldom a medical man has true religious views – there is too much pride of intellect. And you are not fit to marry a poor man.'

'Mr Lydgate is not a poor man, aunt. He has very high connections.'

'He told me himself he was poor.'

'That is because he is used to people who have a high style of living.'

'My dear Rosamond, *you* must not think of living in high style.'

Rosamond looked down and played with her reticule. She was not a fiery young lady and had no sharp answers, but she meant to live as she pleased.

'Then it is really true?' said Mrs Bulstrode, looking very earnestly at her niece. 'You are thinking of Mr Lydgate: there is some understanding between you, though your father doesn't know. Be open, my dear Rosamond: Mr Lydgate has really made you an offer?'

Poor Rosamond's feelings were very unpleasant. She had been quite easy as to Lydgate's feeling and intention, but now when her aunt put this question she did not like being unable to say Yes. Her pride was hurt, but her habitual control of manner helped her.

'Pray excuse me, aunt. I would rather not speak on the subject.'

'You would not give your heart to a man without a decided prospect, I trust, my dear. And think of the two excellent offers I know of that you have refused! – and one still within your reach, if you will not throw it away. I knew a very great beauty who married badly at last, by doing so. Mr Ned Plymdale is a nice young man – some might think good-looking; and an only son; and a large business of that kind is better than a profession. Not that marrying is everything. I would have you seek first the kingdom of God. But a girl should keep her heart within her own power.'

'I should never give it to Mr Ned Plymdale, if it were. I have already refused him. If I loved, I should love at once and without change,' said Rosamond, with a great sense of being a romantic heroine, and playing the part prettily.

'I see how it is, my dear,' said Mrs Bulstrode, in a melancholy voice, rising to go. 'You have allowed your affections to be engaged without return.'

'No, indeed, aunt,' said Rosamond, with emphasis.

'Then you are quite confident that Mr Lydgate has a serious attachment to you?'

Rosamond's cheeks by this time were persistently burning, and she felt much mortification. She chose to be silent, and her aunt went away all the more convinced.

Mr Bulstrode in things worldly and indifferent was disposed to do what his wife bade him, and she now, without telling her reasons, desired him on the next opportunity to find out in conversation with Mr Lydgate whether he had any intention of marrying soon. The result was a decided negative. Mr Bulstrode, on being cross-questioned, showed that Lydgate had spoken as no man would who had any attachment that could issue in matrimony. Mrs Bulstrode now felt that she had a serious duty before her, and she soon managed to arrange a *tête-à-tête* with Lydgate, in which she passed from inquiries about Fred Vincy's health, and expressions of her sincere anxiety for her brother's large family, to general remarks on the dangers which lay before young people with regard to their settlement in life. Young men were often wild and disappointing, making little return for the money spent on them, and a girl was exposed to many circumstances which might interfere with her prospects.

'Especially when she has great attractions, and her parents see much company,' said Mrs Bulstrode. 'Gentlemen pay her attention, and engross her all to themselves, for the mere pleasure of the moment, and that drives off others. I think it is a heavy responsibility, Mr Lydgate, to interfere with the prospects of any girl.' Here Mrs Bulstrode fixed her eyes on him, with an unmistakable purpose of warning, if not of rebuke.

'Clearly,' said Lydgate, looking at her – perhaps even staring a little in return. 'On the other hand, a man must be a great coxcomb to go about with a notion that he must not pay attention to a young lady lest she should fall in love with him, or lest others should think she must.'

'Oh, Mr Lydgate, you know well what your advantages are. You know that our young men here cannot cope with you. Where you frequent a house it may militate very much against a girl's making a desirable settlement in life, and prevent her from accepting offers even if they are made.'

Lydgate was less flattered by his advantage over the Middlemarch Orlandos than he was annoyed by the perception of Mrs Bulstrode's meaning. She felt that she had spoken as impressively as it was necessary to do, and that in using the superior word 'militate' she had thrown a noble drapery over a mass of particulars which were still evident enough.

Lydgate was fuming a little, pushed his hair back with one hand, felt curiously in his waistcoat-pocket with the other, and then stooped to beckon the tiny black spaniel, which had the insight to decline his hollow caresses. It would not have been decent to go away, because he had been dining with other guests, and had just taken tea. But Mrs Bulstrode, having no doubt that she had been understood, turned the conversation.

Solomon's Proverbs, I think, have omitted to say, that as the sore palate findeth grit, so an uneasy consciousness heareth innuendoes. The next day Mr Farebrother, parting from Lydgate in the street, supposed that they should meet at Vincy's in the evening. Lydgate answered curtly, no – he had work to do – he must give up going out in the evening.

'What, you are going to get lashed to the mast, eh, and are stopping your ears?' said the Vicar. 'Well, if you don't mean to be won by the sirens, you are right to take precautions in time.'

A few days before, Lydgate would have taken no notice of these words as anything more than the Vicar's usual way of putting things. They seemed now to convey an innuendo which confirmed the impression that he had been making a fool of himself and behaving so as to be misunderstood: not, he believed, by Rosamond herself; she, he felt sure, took everything as lightly as he intended it. She had an exquisite tact and insight in relation to all points of manners; but the people she lived among were blunderers and busybodies. However, the mistake should go no farther. He resolved – and kept his resolution – that he would not go to Mr Vincy's except on business.

Rosamond became very unhappy. The uneasiness first stirred by her aunt's questions grew and grew till at the end of ten days that she had not seen Lydgate, it grew into terror at the blank that might possibly come – into foreboding of that ready, fatal sponge which so cheaply wipes out the hopes of mortals. The world would have a new dreariness for her, as a wilderness that a magician's spells had turned for a little while into a garden. She felt that she was beginning to know the pang of disappointed love, and that no other man could be the occasion of such delightful aerial building as she had been enjoying for the last six months. Poor Rosamond lost her appetite and felt as forlorn as Ariadne – as a charming stage Ariadne left behind with all her boxes full of costumes and no hope of a coach.

There are many wonderful mixtures in the world which are all alike called love, and claim the privileges of a sublime rage which is an apology for everything (in literature and the drama). Happily Rosamond did not think of committing any desperate act: she plaited her fair hair as beautifully as usual, and kept herself proudly calm. Her most cheerful supposition was that her aunt Bulstrode had interfered in some way to hinder Lydgate's visits: everything was better than a spontaneous indifference in him. Any one who imagines ten days too short a time – not for falling into leanness, lightness, or other measurable effects of passion, but – for the whole spiritual circuit of alarmed conjecture and disappointment, is ignorant of what can go on in the elegant leisure of a young lady's mind.

On the eleventh day, however, Lydgate when leaving Stone Court was requested by Mrs Vincy to let her husband know that there was a marked change in Mr Featherstone's health, and that she wished him to come to Stone Court on that day. Now Lydgate might have called at the warehouse, or might have written a message on a leaf of his pocket-book and left it at the door. Yet these simple devices apparently did not occur to him, from which we may conclude that he had no strong objection to calling at the house at an hour when Mr Vincy was not at home, and leaving the message with Miss Vincy. A man may, from various motives, decline to give his company, but perhaps not even a sage would be gratified that nobody missed him. It would be a graceful, easy way of piecing on the new habits to the old, to have a few playful words with Rosamond about his resistance to dissipation, and his firm resolve to take long fasts even from sweet sounds. It must be confessed, also, that momentary speculations as to all the possible grounds for Mrs Bulstrode's hints had managed to get woven like slight clinging hairs into the more substantial web of his thoughts.

Miss Vincy was alone, and blushed so deeply when Lydgate came in that he felt a corresponding embarrassment, and instead of any playfulness, he began at once to speak of his reason for calling, and to beg her, almost formally, to deliver the message to her father. Rosamond, who at the first moment felt as if her happiness were returning, was keenly hurt by Lydgate's manner; her blush had departed, and she assented coldly, without adding an unnecessary word, some trivial chain-work which she had in her hands enabling her to avoid looking at Lydgate higher than his chin. In all failures, the beginning is certainly the half of the whole. After sitting two long moments while he moved his whip and could say nothing, Lydgate rose to go, and Rosamond, made nervous by her struggle between mortification and the wish not to betray it, dropped her chain as if startled, and rose too, mechanically. Lydgate instantaneously stooped to pick up the chain. When he rose he was very near to a lovely little face set on a fair long neck which he had been used to see turning about under the most perfect management of self-contented grace. But as he raised his eyes now he saw a certain helpless quivering which touched him quite newly, and made him look at Rosamond with a questioning flash. At this moment she was as natural as she had ever been when she was five years old: she felt that her tears had risen, and it was no use to try to do anything else than let them stay like water on a blue flower or let them fall over her cheeks, even as they would.

That moment of naturalness was the crystallizing feather-touch: it shook flirtation into love. Remember that the ambitious man who was looking at those Forget-me-nots under the water was very warm-hearted and rash. He did not know where the chain went; an idea had thrilled through the recesses within him which had a miraculous effect in raising the power of passionate love lying buried there in no sealed sepulchre, but under the lightest, easily pierced mould. His words were quite abrupt and awkward; but the tone made them sound like an ardent, appealing avowal.

'What is the matter? you are distressed. Tell me – pray.'

Rosamond had never been spoken to in such tones before. I am not sure that she knew what the words were; but she looked at Lydgate and the tears fell over her cheeks. There could have been no more complete answer than that silence, and Lydgate, forgetting everything else, completely mastered by the outrush of tenderness at the sudden belief that this sweet young creature depended on him for her joy, actually put his arms round her, folding her gently and protectingly – he was used to being gentle with the weak and suffering – and kissed each of the two large tears. This was a strange way of arriving at an understanding, but it was a short way. Rosamond was not angry, but she moved backward a little in timid happiness, and Lydgate could now sit near her and speak less incompletely. Rosamond had to make her little confession, and he poured out words of gratitude and tenderness with impulsive lavishment. In half an hour he left the house an engaged man, whose soul was not his own, but the woman's to whom he had bound himself.

He came again in the evening to speak with Mr Vincy, who, just returned from Stone Court, was feeling sure that it would not be long before he heard of Mr Featherstone's demise. The felicitous word 'demise', which had seasonably occurred to him, had raised his spirits even above their usual evening pitch. The right word is always a power, and communicates its definiteness to our action. Considered as a demise, old Featherstone's death assumed a merely legal aspect, so that Mr Vincy could tap his snuff-box over it and be jovial, without even an intermittent affectation of solemnity; and Mr Vincy hated both solemnity and affectation. Who was ever awe-struck about a testator, or sang a hymn on the title to real property? Mr Vincy was inclined to take a jovial view of all things that evening: he even observed to Lydgate that Fred had got the family constitution after all, and would soon be as fine a fellow as ever again; and when his approbation of Rosamond's engagement was asked for, he gave it with astonishing facility, passing at once to general remarks on the desirableness of matrimony for young men and maidens, and apparently deducing from the whole the appropriateness of a little more punch.

↺ THIRTY-TWO ↻

They'll take suggestion as a cat laps milk.
Tempest: SHAKESPEARE

THE TRIUMPHANT CONFIDENCE OF THE MAYOR founded on Mr Featherstone's insistent demand that Fred and his mother should not leave him, was a feeble emotion compared with all that was agitating the breasts of the old man's blood-relations, who naturally manifested more their sense of the family tie and were more visibly numerous now that he had become bedridden. Naturally: for when 'poor Peter' had occupied his arm-chair in the wainscoated parlour, no assiduous beetles for whom the cook prepares boiling water could have been less welcome on a hearth which they had reasons for preferring, than those persons whose Featherstone blood was ill-nourished, not from penuriousness on their part, but from poverty. Brother Solomon and Sister Jane were rich, and the family candour and total abstinence from false politeness with which they were always received seemed to them no argument that their brother in the solemn act of making his will would overlook the superior claims of wealth. Themselves at least he had never been unnatural enough to banish from his house, and it seemed hardly eccentric that he should have kept away Brother Jonah, Sister Martha, and the rest, who had no shadow of such claims. They knew Peter's maxim, that money was a good egg, and should be laid in a warm nest.

But Brother Jonah, Sister Martha, and all the needy exiles, held a different point of view. Probabilities are as various as the faces to be seen at will in fretwork or paperhangings: every form is there, from Jupiter to Judy, if you only look with creative inclination. To the poorer and least favoured it seemed likely that since Peter had done nothing for them in his life, he would remember them at the last. Jonah argued that men like to make a surprise of their wills, while Martha said that nobody need be surprised if he left the best part of his money to those who least expected it. Also it was not to be thought but that an own brother 'lying there' with dropsy in his legs must come to feel that blood was thicker than water, and if he didn't alter his will, he might have money by him. At any rate some blood-relations should be on the premises and on the watch against those who were hardly relations at all. Such things had been known as forged wills and disputed wills, which seemed to have the golden-hazy advantage of somehow enabling non-legatees to live out of them. Again, those

who were no blood-relations might be caught making away with things –
and poor Peter 'lying there' helpless! Somebody should be on the watch.
But in this conclusion they were at one with Solomon and Jane; also some
nephews, nieces, and cousins, arguing with still greater subtilty as to what
might be done by a man able to 'will away' his property and give himself
large treats of oddity, felt in a handsome sort of way that there was a
family interest to be attended to, and thought of Stone Court as a place
which it would be nothing but right for them to visit. Sister Martha,
otherwise Mrs Cranch, living with some wheeziness in the Chalky Flats,
could not undertake the journey; but her son, as being poor Peter's own
nephew, could represent her advantageously, and watch lest his uncle
Jonah should make an unfair use of the improbable things which seemed
likely to happen. In fact there was a general sense running in the Featherstone blood that everybody must watch everybody else, and that it would
be well for everybody else to reflect that the Almighty was watching him.

Thus Stone Court continually saw one or other blood-relation alighting
or departing, and Mary Garth had the unpleasant task of carrying their
messages to Mr Featherstone, who would see none of them, and sent her
down with the still more unpleasant task of telling them so. As manager
of the household she felt bound to ask them in good provincial fashion to
stay and eat; but she chose to consult Mrs Vincy on the point of extra
downstairs consumption now that Mr Featherstone was laid up.

'Oh, my dear, you must do things handsomely where there's last illness
and a property. God knows, I don't grudge them every ham in the house –
only, save the best for the funeral. Have some stuffed veal always, and a
fine cheese in cut. You must expect to keep open house in these last
illnesses,' said liberal Mrs Vincy, once more of cheerful note and bright
plumage.

But some of the visitors alighted and did not depart after the handsome
treating to veal and ham. Brother Jonah, for example (there are such
unpleasant people in most families; perhaps even in the highest aristocracy there are Brobdingnag specimens, gigantically in debt and bloated at
greater expense) – Brother Jonah, I say, having come down in the world,
was mainly supported by a calling which he was modest enough not to
boast of, though it was much better than swindling either on exchange or
turf, but which did not require his presence at Brassing so long as he had a
good corner to sit in and a supply of food. He chose the kitchen-corner,
partly because he liked it best, and partly because he did not want to sit
with Solomon, concerning whom he had a strong brotherly opinion.
Seated in a famous arm-chair and in his best suit, constantly within sight
of good cheer, he had a comfortable consciousness of being on the premises, mingled with fleeting suggestions of Sunday and the bar at the Green
Man; and he informed Mary Garth that he should not go out of reach of
his brother Peter while that poor fellow was above ground. The troublesome ones in a family are usually either the wits or the idiots. Jonah was

the wit among the Featherstones, and joked with the maid-servants when they came about the hearth, but seemed to consider Miss Garth a suspicious character, and followed her with cold eyes.

Mary would have borne this one pair of eyes with comparative ease, but unfortunately there was young Cranch, who, having come all the way from the Chalky Flats to represent his mother and watch his uncle Jonah, also felt it his duty to stay and to sit chiefly in the kitchen to give his uncle company. Young Cranch was not exactly the balancing point between the wit and the idiot, – verging slightly towards the latter type, and squinting so as to leave everything in doubt about his sentiments except that they were not of a forcible character. When Mary Garth entered the kitchen and Mr Jonah Featherstone began to follow her with his cold detective eyes, young Cranch turning his head in the same direction seemed to insist on it that she should remark how he was squinting, as if he did it with design, like the gypsies when Borrow read the New Testament to them. This was rather too much for poor Mary; sometimes it made her bilious, sometimes it upset her gravity. One day that she had an opportunity she could not resist describing the kitchen scene to Fred, who would not be hindered from immediately going to see it, affecting simply to pass through. But no sooner did he face the four eyes than he had to rush through the nearest door, which happened to lead to the dairy, and there under the high roof and among the pans he gave way to laughter which made a hollow resonance perfectly audible in the kitchen. He fled by another doorway, but Mr Jonah, who had not before seen Fred's white complexion, long legs, and pinched delicacy of face, prepared many sarcasms in which these points of appearance were wittily combined with the lowest moral attributes.

'Why, Tom, you don't wear such gentlemanly trousers – you haven't got half such fine long legs,' said Jonah to his nephew, winking at the same time, to imply that there was something more in these statements than their undeniableness. Tom looked at his legs, but left it uncertain whether he preferred his moral advantages to a more vicious length of limb and reprehensible gentility of trouser.

In the large wainscoated parlour too there were constantly pairs of eyes on the watch, and own relatives eager to be 'sitters-up'. Many came, lunched, and departed, but Brother Solomon and the lady who had been Jane Featherstone for twenty-five years before she was Mrs Waule found it good to be there every day for hours, without other calculable occupation than that of observing the cunning Mary Garth (who was so deep that she could be found out in nothing) and giving occasional dry wrinkly indications of crying – as if capable of torrents in a wetter season – at the thought that they were not allowed to go into Mr Featherstone's room. For the old man's dislike of his own family seemed to get stronger as he got less able to amuse himself by saying biting things to them. Too languid to sting, he had the more venom refluent in his blood.

Not fully believing the message sent through Mary Garth, they had presented themselves together within the door of the bedroom, both in black – Mrs Waule having a white handkerchief partially unfolded in her hand – and both with faces in a sort of half-mourning purple; while Mrs Vincy with her pink cheeks and pink ribbons flying was actually administering a cordial to their own brother, and the light-complexioned Fred, his short hair curling as might be expected in a gambler's, was lolling at his ease in a large chair.

Old Featherstone no sooner caught sight of these funereal figures appearing in spite of his orders than rage came to strengthen him more successfully than the cordial. He was propped up on a bedrest, and always had his gold-headed stick lying by him. He seized it now and swept it backwards and forwards in as large an area as he could, apparently to ban these ugly spectres, crying in a hoarse sort of screech –

'Back, back, Mrs Waule! Back, Solomon!'

'Oh, Brother Peter,' Mrs Waule began – but Solomon put his hand before her repressingly. He was a large-cheeked man, nearly seventy, with small furtive eyes, and was not only of much blander temper but thought himself much deeper than his brother Peter; indeed not likely to be deceived in any of his fellow-men, inasmuch as they could not well be more greedy and deceitful than he suspected them of being. Even the invisible powers, he thought, were likely to be soothed by a bland parenthesis here and there – coming from a man of property, who might have been as impious as others.

'Brother Peter,' he said, in a wheedling yet gravely official tone, 'it's nothing but right I should speak to you about the Three Crofts and the Manganese. The Almighty knows what I've got on my mind ...'

'Then He knows more than I want to know,' said Peter, laying down his stick with a show of truce which had a threat in it too, for he reversed the stick so as to make the gold handle a club in case of closer fighting, and looked hard at Solomon's bald head.

'There's things you might repent of, Brother, for want of speaking to me,' said Solomon, not advancing, however. 'I could sit up with you to-night, and Jane with me, willingly, and you might take your own time to speak, or let me speak.'

'Yes, I shall take my own time – you needn't offer me yours,' said Peter.

'But you can't take your own time to die in, Brother,' began Mrs Waule, with her usual woolly tone. 'And when you lie speechless you may be tired of having strangers about you, and you may think of me and my children – ' but here her voice broke under the touching thought which she was attributing to her speechless brother; the mention of ourselves being naturally affecting.

'No, I shan't,' said old Featherstone, contradictiously. 'I shan't think of any of you. I've made my will, I tell you, I've made my will.' Here he turned his head towards Mrs Vincy, and swallowed some more of his cordial.

'Some people would be ashamed to fill up a place belonging by rights to others,' said Mrs Waule, turning her narrow eyes in the same direction.

'Oh, Sister,' said Solomon, with ironical softness, 'you and me are not fine, and handsome, and clever enough: we must be humble and let smart people push themselves before us.'

Fred's spirit could not bear this: rising and looking at Mr Featherstone, he said, 'Shall my mother and I leave the room, sir, that you may be alone with your friends?'

'Sit down, I tell you,' said old Featherstone, snappishly. 'Stop where you are. Good-bye, Solomon,' he added, trying to wield his stick again, but failing now that he had reversed the handle. 'Good-bye, Mrs Waule. Don't you come again.'

'I shall be down-stairs, Brother, whether or no,' said Solomon. 'I shall do *my* duty, and it remains to be seen what the Almighty will allow.'

'Yes, in property going out of families,' said Mrs Waule, in continuation, – 'and where there's steady young men to carry on. But I pity them who are not such, and I pity their mothers. Good-bye, Brother Peter.'

'Remember, I'm the eldest after you, Brother, and prospered from the first, just as you did, and have got land already by the name of Featherstone,' said Solomon, relying much on that reflection, as one which might be suggested in the watches of the night. 'But I bid you good-bye for the present.'

Their exit was hastened by their seeing old Mr Featherstone pull his wig on each side and shut his eyes with his mouth-widening grimace, as if he were determined to be deaf and blind.

None the less they came to Stone Court daily and sat below at the post of duty, sometimes carrying on a slow dialogue in an undertone in which the observation and response were so far apart, that any one hearing them might have imagined himself listening to speaking automata, in some doubt whether the ingenious mechanism would really work, or wind itself up for a long time in order to stick and be silent. Solomon and Jane would have been sorry to be quick: what that led to might be seen on the other side of the wall in the person of Brother Jonah.

But their watch in the wainscoted parlour was sometimes varied by the presence of other guests from far or near. Now that Peter Featherstone was up-stairs, his property could be discussed with all that local enlightenment to be found on the spot: some rural and Middlemarch neighbours expressed much agreement with the family and sympathy with their interest against the Vincys, and feminine visitors were even moved to tears, in conversation with Mrs Waule, when they recalled the fact that they themselves had been disappointed in times past by codicils and marriages for spite on the part of ungrateful elderly gentlemen, who, it might have supposed, had been spared for something better. Such conversation paused suddenly, like an organ when the bellows are let drop, if Mary Garth came into the room; and all eyes were turned on her as a possible legatee, or one who might get access to iron chests.

But the younger men who were relatives or connections of the family, were disposed to admire her in this problematic light, as a girl who showed much conduct, and who among all the chances that were flying might turn out to be at least a moderate prize. Hence she had her share of compliments and polite attentions.

Especially from Mr Borthrop Trumbull, a distinguished bachelor and auctioneer of those parts, much concerned in the sale of land and cattle: a public character, indeed, whose name was seen on widely distributed placards, and who might reasonably be sorry for those who did not know of him. He was second cousin to Peter Featherstone, and had been treated by him with more amenity than any other relative, being useful in matters of business; and in that programme of his funeral which the old man had himself dictated, he had been named as a Bearer. There was no odious cupidity in Mr Borthrop Trumbull – nothing more than a sincere sense of his own merit, which, he was aware, in case of rivalry might tell against competitors; so that if Peter Featherstone, who so far as he, Trumbull, was concerned, had behaved like as good a soul as ever breathed, should have done anything handsome by him, all he could say was, that he had never fished and fawned, but had advised him to the best of his experience, which now extended over twenty years from the time of his apprenticeship at fifteen, and was likely to yield a knowledge of no surreptitious kind. His admiration was far from being confined to himself, but was accustomed professionally as well as privately to delight in estimating things at a high rate. He was an amateur of superior phrases, and never used poor language without immediately correcting himself – which was fortunate, as he was rather loud, and given to predominate, standing or walking about frequently, pulling down his waistcoat with the air of a man who is very much of his own opinion, trimming himself rapidly with his forefinger, and marking each new series in these movements by a busy play with his large seals. There was occasionally a little fierceness in his demeanour, but it was directed chiefly against false opinion, of which there is so much to correct in the world that a man of some reading and experience necessarily has his patience tried. He felt that the Featherstone family generally was of limited understanding, but being a man of the world and a public character, took everything as a matter of course, and even went to converse with Mr Jonah and young Cranch in the kitchen, not doubting that he had impressed the latter greatly by his leading questions concerning the Chalky Flats. If anybody had observed that Mr Borthrop Trumbull, being an auctioneer, was bound to know the nature of everything, he would have smiled and trimmed himself silently with the sense that he came pretty near that. On the whole, in an auctioneering way, he was an honourable man, not ashamed of his business, and feeling that 'the celebrated Peel, now Sir Robert', if introduced to him, would not fail to recognize his importance.

'I don't mind if I have a slice of that ham, and a glass of that ale, Miss Garth, if you will allow me,' he said, coming into the parlour at half past eleven, after having had the exceptional privilege of seeing old Featherstone, and standing with his back to the fire between Mrs Waule and Solomon. 'It's not necessary for you to go out; – let me ring the bell.'

'Thank you,' said Mary, 'I have an errand.'

'Well, Mr Trumbull, you're highly favoured,' said Mrs Waule.

'What, seeing the old man?' said the auctioneer, playing with his seals dispassionately. 'Ah, you see he has relied on me considerably.' Here he pressed his lips together, and frowned meditatively.

'Might anybody ask what their brother has been saying?' said Solomon, in a soft tone of humility, in which he had a sense of luxurious cunning, he being a rich man and not in need of it.

'Oh yes, anybody may ask,' said Mr Trumbull, with loud and good-humoured though cutting sarcasm. 'Anybody may interrogate. Any one may give their remarks an interrogative turn,' he continued, his sonorousness rising with his style. 'This is constantly done by good speakers, even when they anticipate no answer. It is what we call a figure of speech – speech at a high figure, as one may say.' The eloquent auctioneer smiled at his own ingenuity.

'I shouldn't be sorry to hear he'd remembered *you*, Mr Trumbull,' said Solomon. 'I never was against the deserving. It's the undeserving I'm against.'

'Ah, there it is, you see, there it is,' said Mr Trumbull, significantly. 'It can't be denied that undeserving people have been legatees, and even residuary legatees. It is so, with testamentary dispositions.' Again he pursed up his lips and frowned a little.

'Do you mean to say for certain, Mr Trumbull, that my brother has left his land away from our family?' said Mrs Waule, on whom, as an unhopeful woman, those long words had a depressing effect.

'A man might as well turn his land into charity land at once as leave it to some people,' observed Solomon, his sister's question having drawn no answer.

'What, Blue-Coat land?' said Mrs Waule, again. 'Oh, Mr Trumbull, you never can mean to say that. It would be flying in the face of the Almighty that's prospered him.'

While Mrs Waule was speaking, Mr Borthrop Trumbull walked away from the fireplace towards the window, patrolling with his forefinger round the inside of his stock, then along his whiskers and the curves of his hair. He now walked to Miss Garth's work-table, opened a book which lay there, and read the title aloud with pompous emphasis as if he were offering it for sale:

'*Anne of Geierstein* (pronounced Jeersteen) or the Maiden of the Mist, by the Author of *Waverley.*' Then turning the page, he began sonorously – 'The course of four centuries has well-nigh elapsed since the series of events which are related in the following chapters took place on the Continent.' He pronounced the last truly admirable word with the accent on the last syllable, not as unaware of vulgar usage, but feeling that this novel delivery enhanced the sonorous beauty which his reading had given to the whole.

And now the servant came in with the tray, so that the moments for answering Mrs Waule's question had gone by safely, while she and Solomon, watching Mr Trumbull's movements, were thinking that high learning interfered sadly with serious affairs. Mr Borthrop Trumbull really knew nothing about old Featherstone's will; but he could hardly have been brought to declare any ignorance unless he had been arrested for misprision of treason.

'I shall take a mere mouthful of ham and a glass of ale,' he said, reassuringly. 'As a man with public business, I take a snack when I can. I will back this ham,' he added, after swallowing some morsels with alarming haste, 'against any ham in the three kingdoms. In my opinion it is better than the hams at Freshitt Hall – and I think I am a tolerable judge.'

'Some don't like so much sugar in their hams,' said Mrs Waule. 'But my poor brother would always have sugar.'

'If any person demands better, he is at liberty to do so; but, God bless me, what an aroma! I should be glad to buy-in that quality, I know. There is some gratification to a gentleman' – here Mr Trumbull's voice conveyed an emotional remonstrance – 'in having this kind of ham set on his table.'

He pushed aside his plate, poured out his glass of ale and drew his chair a little forward, profiting by the occasion to look at the inner side of his legs, which he stroked approvingly – Mr Trumbull having all those less frivolous airs and gestures which distinguish the predominant races of the north.

'You have an interesting work there, I see, Miss Garth,' he observed, when Mary re-entered. 'It is by the author of *Waverley*: that is Sir Walter Scott. I have bought one of his works myself – a very nice thing, a very superior publication, entitled *Ivanhoe.* You will not get any writer to beat him in a hurry, I think – he will not, in my opinion, be speedily surpassed. I have just been reading a portion at the commencement of *Anne of Jeersteen.* It commences well.' (Things never began with Mr Borthrop Trumbull: they always commenced, both in private life and on his handbills.) 'You are a reader, I see. Do you subscribe to our Middlemarch library?'

'No,' said Mary. 'Mr Fred Vincy brought this book.'

'I am a great bookman myself,' returned Mr Trumbull. 'I have no less than two hundred volumes in calf, and I flatter myself they are well selected. Also pictures by Murillo, Rubens, Teniers, Titian, Vandyck, and others. I shall be happy to lend you any work you like to mention, Miss Garth.'

'I am much obliged,' said Mary, hastening away again, 'but I have little time for reading.'

'I should say my brother has done something for *her* in his will,' said Mr Solomon, in a very low undertone, when she had shut the door behind her, pointing with his head towards the absent Mary.

'His first wife was a poor match for him, though,' said Mrs Waule. 'She brought him nothing: and this young woman is only her niece. And very proud. And my brother has always paid her wage.'

'A sensible girl though, in my opinion,' said Mr Trumbull, finishing his ale and starting up with an emphatic adjustment of his waistcoat. 'I have observed her when she has been mixing medicine in drops. She minds what she is doing, sir. That is a great point in a woman, and a great point for our friend upstairs, poor dear old soul. A man whose life is of any value should think of his wife as a nurse: that is what I should do, if I married; and I believe I have lived single long enough not to make a mistake in that line. Some men must marry to elevate themselves a little, but when I am in need of that, I hope some one will tell me so – I hope some individual will apprise me of the fact. I wish you good-morning, Mrs Waule. Good-morning, Mr Solomon. I trust we shall meet under less melancholy auspices.'

When Mr Trumbull had departed with a fine bow, Solomon, leaning forward, observed to his sister, 'You may depend, Jane, my brother has left that girl a lumping sum.'

'Anybody would think so, from the way Mr Trumbull talks,' said Jane. Then, after a pause, 'He talks as if my daughters wasn't to be trusted to give drops.'

'Auctioneers talk wild,' said Solomon. 'Not but what Trumbull has made money.'

∽ THIRTY-THREE ∾

Close up his eyes and draw the curtain close;
And let us all to meditation.

2 Henry VI

THAT NIGHT AFTER TWELVE O'CLOCK Mary Garth relieved the watch in Mr Featherstone's room, and sat there alone through the small hours. She often chose this task, in which she found some pleasure, notwithstanding the old man's testiness whenever he demanded her attentions. There were intervals in which she could sit perfectly still, enjoying the outer stillness and the subdued light. The red fire with its gently audible movement seemed like a solemn existence calmly independent of the petty passions, the imbecile desires, the straining after worthless uncertainties, which were daily moving her contempt. Mary was fond of her own thoughts, and could amuse herself well sitting in twilight with her hands in her lap; for, having early had strong reason to believe that things were not likely to be arranged for her peculiar satisfaction, she wasted no time in astonishment and annoyance at that fact. And she had already come to take life very much as a comedy in which she had a proud, nay, a generous resolution not to act the mean or treacherous part. Mary might have become cynical if she had not had parents whom she honoured, and a well of affectionate gratitude within her, which was all the fuller because she had learned to make no unreasonable claims.

She sat to-night revolving, as she was wont, the scenes of the day, her lips often curling with amusement at the oddities to which her fancy added fresh drollery: people were so ridiculous with their illusions, carrying their fools' caps unawares, thinking their own lies opaque while everybody else's were transparent, making themselves exceptions to everything, as if when all the world looked yellow under a lamp they alone were rosy. Yet there were some illusions under Mary's eyes which were not quite comic to her. She was secretly convinced, though she had no other grounds than her close observation of old Featherstone's nature, that in spite of his fondness for having the Vincys about him, they were as likely to be disappointed as any of the relations whom he kept at a distance. She had a good deal of disdain for Mrs Vincy's evident alarm lest she and Fred should be alone together, but it did not hinder her from thinking anxiously of the way in which Fred would be affected, if it should turn out that his uncle had left him as poor as ever. She could make a butt of Fred when he was present, but she did not enjoy his follies when he was absent.

Yet she liked her thoughts: a vigorous young mind not overbalanced by passion, finds a good in making acquaintance with life, and watches its own powers with interest. Mary had plenty of merriment within.

Her thought was not veined by any solemnity or pathos about the old man on the bed: such sentiments are easier to affect than to feel about an aged creature whose life is not visibly anything but a remnant of vices. She had always seen the most disagreeable side of Mr Featherstone: he was not proud of her, and she was only useful to him. To be anxious about a soul that is always snapping at you must be left to the saints of the earth; and Mary was not one of them. She had never returned him a harsh word, and had waited on him faithfully: that was her utmost. Old Featherstone himself was not in the least anxious about his soul, and had declined to see Mr Tucker on the subject.

To-night he had not once snapped, and for the first hour or two he lay remarkably still, until at last Mary heard him rattling his bunch of keys against the tin box which he always kept in the bed beside him. About three o'clock he said, with remarkable distinctness, 'Missy, come here!'

Mary obeyed and found that he had already drawn the tin box from under the clothes, though he usually asked to have this done for him; and he had selected the key. He now unlocked the box, and, drawing from it another key, looked straight at her with eyes that seemed to have recovered all their sharpness and said, 'How many of 'em are in the house?'

'You mean of your own relations, sir,' said Mary, well used to the old man's way of speech. He nodded slightly and she went on.

'Mr Jonah Featherstone and young Cranch are sleeping here.'

'Oh ay, they stick, do they? and the rest – they come every day, I'll warrant – Solomon and Jane, and all the young uns? They come peeping, and counting and casting up?'

'Not all of them every day. Mr Solomon and Mrs Waule are here every day, and the others come often.'

The old man listened with a grimace while she spoke, and then said, relaxing his face, 'The more fools they. You hearken, Missy. It's three o'clock in the morning, and I've got all my faculties as well as ever I had in my life. I know all my property, and where the money's put out, and everything. And I've made everything ready to change my mind, and do as I like at the last. Do you hear, Missy? I've got my faculties.'

'Well, sir?' said Mary, quietly.

He now lowered his tone with an air of deeper cunning. 'I've made two wills, and I'm going to burn one. Now you do as I tell you. This is the key of my iron chest, in the closet there. You push well at the side of the brass plate at the top, till it goes like a bolt: then you can put the key in the front lock and turn it. See and do that; and take out the topmost paper – Last Will and Testament – big printed.'

'No, sir,' said Mary, in a firm voice, 'I cannot do that.'

'Not do it? I tell you, you must,' said the old man, his voice beginning to shake under the shock of this resistance.

'I cannot touch your iron chest or your will. I must refuse to do anything that might lay me open to suspicion.'

I tell you, I'm in my right mind. Shan't I do as I like at the last? I made two wills on purpose. Take the key, I say.'

'No, sir, I will not,' said Mary, more resolutely still. Her repulsion was getting stronger.

'I tell you, there's no time to lose.'

'I cannot help that, sir. I will not let the close of your life soil the beginning of mine. I will not touch your iron chest or your will.' She moved to a little distance from the bedside.

The old man paused with a blank stare for a little while, holding the one key erect on the ring; then with an agitated jerk he began to work with his bony left hand at emptying the tin box before him.

'Missy,' he began to say, hurriedly, 'look here! take the money – the notes and gold – look here – take it – you shall have it all – do as I tell you.'

He made an effort to stretch out the key towards her as far as possible, and Mary again retreated.

'I will not touch your key or your money, sir. Pray don't ask me to do it again. If you do, I must go and call your brother.'

He let his hand fall, and for the first time in her life Mary saw old Peter Featherstone begin to cry childishly. She said, in as gentle a tone as she could command, 'Pray put up your money, sir'; and then went away to her seat by the fire, hoping this would help to convince him that it was useless to say more. Presently he rallied and said eagerly –

'Look here, then. Call the young chap. Call Fred Vincy.'

Mary's heart began to beat more quickly. Various ideas rushed through her mind as to what the burning of a second will might imply. She had to make a difficult decision in a hurry.

'I will call him, if you will let me call Mr Jonah and others with him.'

'Nobody else, I say. The young chap. I shall do as I like.'

'Wait till broad daylight, sir, when every one is stirring. Or let me call Simmons now, to go and fetch the lawyer. He can be here in less than two hours.'

'Lawyer? What do I want with the lawyer? Nobody shall know – I say, nobody shall know. I shall do as I like.'

'Let me call some one else, sir,' said Mary, persuasively. She did not like her position – alone with the old man, who seemed to show a strange flaring of nervous energy which enabled him to speak again and again without falling into his usual cough; yet she desired not to push unnecessarily the contradiction which agitated him. 'Let me, pray, call some one else.'

'You let me alone, I say. Look here, Missy. Take the money. You'll never have the chance again. It's pretty nigh two hundred – there's more in the box, and nobody knows how much there was. Take it and do as I tell you.'

Mary, standing by the fire, saw its red light falling on the old man, propped up on his pillows and bed-rest, with his bony hand holding out the key, and the money lying on the quilt before him. She never forgot that vision of a man wanting to do as he liked at the last. But the way in which he had put the offer of the money urged her to speak with harder resolution than ever.

'It is of no use, sir. I will not do it. Put up your money. I will not touch your money. I will do anything else I can to comfort you; but I will not touch your keys or your money.'

'Anything else – anything else!' said old Featherstone, with hoarse rage, which, as if in a nightmare, tried to be loud, and yet was only just audible. 'I want nothing else. You come here – you come here.'

Mary approached him cautiously, knowing him too well. She saw him dropping his keys and trying to grasp his stick, while he looked at her like an aged hyena, the muscles of his face getting distorted with the effort of his hand. She paused at a safe distance.

'Let me give you some cordial,' she said, quietly, 'and try to compose yourself. You will perhaps go to sleep. And to-morrow by daylight you can do as you like.'

He lifted the stick, in spite of her being beyond his reach, and threw it with a hard effort which was but impotence. It fell, slipping over the foot of the bed. Mary let it lie, and retreated to her chair by the fire. By-and-by she would go to him with the cordial. Fatigue would make him passive. It was getting towards the chillest moment of the morning, the fire had got low, and she could see through the chink between the moreen window-curtains the light whitened by the blind. Having put some wood on the fire and thrown a shawl over her, she sat down, hoping that Mr Feather-stone might now fall asleep. If she went near him the irritation might be kept up. He had said nothing after throwing the stick, but she had seen him taking his keys again and laying his right hand on the money. He did not put it up, however, and she thought that he was dropping off to sleep.

But Mary herself began to be more agitated by the remembrance of what she had gone through, than she had been by the reality – questioning those acts of hers which had come imperatively and excluded all question in the critical moment.

Presently the dry wood sent out a flame which illuminated every crev-ice, and Mary saw that the old man was lying quietly with his head turned a little on one side. She went towards him with inaudible steps, and thought that his face looked strangely motionless; but the next moment the movement of the flame communicating itself to all objects made her uncertain. The violent beating of her heart rendered her perceptions so doubtful that even when she touched him and listened for his breathing, she could not trust her conclusions. She went to the window and gently propped aside the curtain and blind, so that the still light of the sky fell on the bed.

The next moment she ran to the bell and rang it energetically. In a very little while there was no longer any doubt that Peter Featherstone was dead, with his right hand clasping the keys, and his left hand lying on the heap of notes and gold.

BOOK FOUR

THREE LOVE
PROBLEMS

ℭ THIRTY-FOUR ℮

1st Gent. Such men as this are feathers, chips, and straws,
  Carry no weight, no force.
2nd Gent.   But levity
  Is casual too, and makes the sum of weight,
  For power finds its place in lack of power;
  Advance is cession, and the driven ship
  May run aground because the helmsman's thought
  Lacked force to balance opposites.

IT WAS ON A MORNING OF MAY THAT Peter Featherstone was buried. In the prosaic neighbourhood of Middlemarch, May was not always warm and sunny, and on this particular morning a chill wind was blowing the blossoms from the surrounding gardens on to the green mounds of Lowick churchyard. Swiftly moving clouds only now and then allowed a gleam to light up any object, whether ugly or beautiful, that happened to stand within its golden shower. In the churchyard the objects were remarkably various, for there was a little country crowd waiting to see the funeral. The news had spread that it was to be a 'big burying'; the old gentleman had left written directions about everything, and meant to have a funeral 'beyond his betters'. This was true; for old Featherstone had not been a Harpagon whose passions had all been devoured by the ever-lean and ever-hungry passion of saving, and who would drive a bargain with his undertaker beforehand. He loved money, but he also loved to spend it in gratifying his peculiar tastes, and perhaps he loved it best of all as a means of making others feel his power more or less uncomfortably. If any one will here contend that there must have been traits of goodness in old Featherstone, I will not presume to deny this; but I must observe that goodness is of a modest nature, easily discouraged, and when much elbowed in early life by unabashed vices, is apt to retire into extreme privacy, so that it is more easily believed in by those who construct a selfish old gentleman theoretically, than by those who form the narrower judgments based on his personal acquaintance. In any case, he had been bent on having a handsome funeral, and on having persons 'bid' to it who would rather have stayed at home. He had even desired that female relatives should follow him to the grave, and poor sister Martha had taken a difficult journey for this purpose from the Chalky Flats. She and Jane would have been altogether cheered (in a tearful manner) by this sign that a brother who disliked seeing them while he was living had been prospectively fond of their presence when he should have become a testator, if the sign had not been made equivocal by being extended to Mrs Vincy, whose expense in handsome crape seemed to imply the most presumptuous hopes, aggravated by a bloom of complexion which told pretty plainly that she was not a blood-relation, but of that generally objectionable class called wife's kin.

We are all of us imaginative in some form or other, for images are the brood of desire; and poor old Featherstone, who laughed much at the way in which others cajoled themselves, did not escape the fellowship of illusion. In writing the programme for his burial he certainly did not make clear to himself that his pleasure in the little drama of which it formed a part was confined to anticipation. In chuckling over the vexations he could inflict by the rigid clutch of his dead hand, he inevitably mingled his consciousness with that livid stagnant presence, and so far as he was preoccupied with a future life, it was with one of gratification inside his coffin. Thus old Featherstone was imaginative, after his fashion.

However, the three mourning-coaches were filled according to the written orders of the deceased. There were pall-bearers on horse-back, with the richest scarves and hatbands, and even the under-bearers had trappings of woe which were of a good well-priced quality. The black procession, when dismounted, looked the larger for the smallness of the churchyard; the heavy human faces and the black draperies shivering in the wind seemed to tell of a world strangely incongruous with the lightly-dropping blossoms and the gleams of sunshine on the daisies. The clergyman who met the procession was Mr Cadwallader – also according to the request of Peter Featherstone, prompted as usual by peculiar reasons. Having a contempt for curates, whom he always called understrappers, he was resolved to be buried by a beneficed clergyman. Mr Casaubon was out of the question, not merely because he declined duty of this sort, but because Featherstone had an especial dislike to him as the rector of his own parish, who had a lien on the land in the shape of tithe, also as the deliverer of morning sermons, which the old man, being in his pew and not at all sleepy, had been obliged to sit through with an inward snarl. He had an objection to a parson stuck up above his head preaching to him. But his relations with Mr Cadwallader had been of a different kind: the trout-stream which ran through Mr Casaubon's land took its course through Featherstone's also, so that Mr Cadwallader was a parson who had had to ask a favour instead of preaching. Moreover, he was one of the high gentry living four miles away from Lowick, and was thus exalted to an equal sky with the sheriff of the county and other dignities vaguely regarded as necessary to the system of things. There would be a satisfaction in being buried by Mr Cadwallader, whose very name offered a fine opportunity for pronouncing wrongly if you liked.

This distinction conferred on the Rector of Tipton and Freshitt was the reason why Mrs Cadwallader made one of the group that watched old Featherstone's funeral from an upper window of the manor. She was not fond of visiting that house, but she liked, as she said, to see collections of strange animals such as there would be at this funeral; and she had persuaded Sir James and the young Lady Chettam to drive the Rector and herself to Lowick in order that the visit might be altogether pleasant.

'I will go anywhere with you, Mrs Cadwallader,' Celia had said; 'but I don't like funerals.'

'Oh, my dear, when you have a clergyman in your family you must accommodate your tastes: I did that very early. When I married Humphrey I made up my mind to like sermons, and I set out by liking the end very much. That soon spread to the middle and the beginning, because I couldn't have the end without them.'

'No, to be sure not,' said the Dowager Lady Chettam, with stately emphasis.

The upper window from which the funeral could be well seen was in the room occupied by Mr Casaubon when he had been forbidden to work; but he had resumed nearly his habitual style of life now in spite of warnings and prescriptions, and after politely welcoming Mrs Cadwallader had slipped again into the library to chew a cud of erudite mistake about Cush and Mizraim.

But for her visitors Dorothea too might have been shut up in the library, and would not have witnessed this scene of old Featherstone's funeral, which, aloof as it seemed to be from the tenor of her life, always afterwards came back to her at the touch of certain sensitive points in memory, just as the vision of St Peter's at Rome was inwoven with moods of despondency. Scenes which make vital changes in our neighbours' lot are but the background of our own, yet, like a particular aspect of the fields and trees, they become associated for us with the epochs of our own history, and make a part of that unity which lies in the selection of our keenest consciousness.

The dream-like association of something alien and ill-understood with the deepest secrets of her experience seemed to mirror that sense of loneliness which was due to the very ardour of Dorothea's nature. The country gentry of old time lived in a rarefied social air: dotted apart on their stations up the mountain they looked down with imperfect discrimination on the belts of thicker life below. And Dorothea was not at ease in the perspective and chilliness of that height.

'I shall not look any more,' said Celia, after the train had entered the church, placing herself behind her husband's elbow so that she could slyly touch his coat with her cheek. 'I daresay Dodo likes it: she is fond of melancholy things and ugly people.'

'I am fond of knowing something about the people I live among,' said Dorothea, who had been watching everything with the interest of a monk on his holiday tour. 'It seems to me we know nothing of our neighbours, unless they are cottagers. One is constantly wondering what sort of lives other people lead, and how they take things. I am quite obliged to Mrs Cadwallader for coming and calling me out of the library.'

'Quite right to feel obliged to me,' said Mrs Cadwallader. 'Your rich Lowick farmers are as curious as any buffaloes or bisons, and I daresay you don't half see them at church. They are quite different from your uncle's tenants or Sir James's – monsters – farmers without landlords – one can't tell how to class them.'

'Most of these followers are not Lowick people,' said Sir James; 'I suppose they are legatees from a distance, or from Middlemarch. Lovegood tells me the old fellow has left a good deal of money as well as land.'

'Think of that now! when so many younger sons can't dine at their own expense,' said Mrs Cadwallader. 'Ah,' turning round at the sound of the opening door, 'here is Mr Brooke. I felt that we were incomplete before, and here is the explanation. You are come to see this odd funeral, of course?'

'No, I came to look after Casaubon – to see how he goes on, you know. And to bring a little news – a little news, my dear,' said Mr Brooke, nodding at Dorothea as she came towards him. 'I looked into the library, and I saw Casaubon over his books. I told him it wouldn't do: I said, "This will never do, you know: think of your wife, Casaubon." And he promised me to come up. I didn't tell him my news: I said, he must come up.'

'Ah, now they are coming out of church,' Mrs Cadwallader exclaimed. 'Dear me, what a wonderfully mixed set! Mr Lydgate as doctor, I suppose. But that is really a good-looking woman, and the fair young man must be her son. Who are they, Sir James, do you know?'

'I see Vincy, the mayor of Middlemarch; they are probably his wife and son,' said Sir James, looking interrogatively at Mr Brooke, who nodded and said –

'Yes, a very decent family – a very good fellow is Vincy; a credit to the manufacturing interest. You have seen him at my house, you know.'

'Ah, yes: one of your secret committee,' said Mrs Cadwallader, provokingly.

'A coursing fellow, though,' said Sir James, with a fox-hunter's disgust.

'And one of those who suck the life out of the wretched handloom weavers in Tipton and Freshitt. That is how his family look so fair and sleek,' said Mrs Cadwallader. 'Those dark, purple-faced people are an excellent foil. Dear me, they are like a set of jugs! Do look at Humphrey: one might fancy him an ugly archangel towering above them in his white surplice.'

'It's a solemn thing, though, a funeral,' said Mr Brooke, 'if you take it in that light, you know.'

'But I am not taking it in that light. I can't wear my solemnity too often, else it will go to rags. It was time the old man died, and none of these people are sorry.'

'How piteous!' said Dorothea. 'This funeral seems to me the most dismal thing I ever saw. It is a blot on the morning. I cannot bear to think that any one should die and leave no love behind.'

She was going to say more, but she saw her husband enter and seat himself a little in the background. The difference his presence made to her was not always a happy one: she felt that he often inwardly objected to her speech.

'Positively,' exclaimed Mrs Cadwallader, 'there is a new face come out from behind that broad man queerer than any of them: a little round head with bulging eyes – a sort of frog-face – do look. He must be of another blood, I think.'

'Let me see!' said Celia, with awakened curiosity, standing behind Mrs Cadwallader and leaning forward over her head. 'Oh, what an odd face!' Then with a quick change to another sort of surprised expression, she added, 'Why, Dodo, you never told me that Mr Ladislaw was come again!'

Dorothea felt a shock of alarm: every one noticed her sudden paleness as she looked up immediately at her uncle, while Mr Casaubon looked at her.

'He came with me, you know; he is my guest – puts up with me at the Grange,' said Mr Brooke, in his easiest tone, nodding at Dorothea, as if the announcement were just what she might have expected. 'And we have brought the picture at the top of the carriage. I knew you would be pleased with the surprise, Casaubon. There you are to the very life – as Aquinas, you know. Quite the right sort of thing. And you will hear young Ladislaw talk about it. He talks uncommonly well – points out this, that, and the other – knows art and everything of that kind – companionable, you know – is up with you in any track – what I've been wanting a long while.'

Mr Casaubon bowed with cold politeness, mastering his irritation, but only so far as to be silent. He remembered Will's letter quite as well as Dorothea did; he had noticed that it was not among the letters which had been reserved for him on his recovery, and secretly concluding that Dorothea had sent word to Will not to come to Lowick, he had shrunk with proud sensitiveness from ever recurring to the subject. He now inferred that she had asked her uncle to invite Will to the Grange; and she felt it impossible at that moment to enter into any explanation.

Mrs Cadwallader's eyes diverted from the churchyard, saw a good deal of dumb show which was not so intelligible to her as she could have desired, and could not repress the question, 'Who is Mr Ladislaw?'

'A young relative of Mr Casaubon's,' said Sir James, promptly. His good-nature often made him quick and clear-seeing in personal matters, and he had divined from Dorothea's glance at her husband that there was some alarm in her mind.

'A very nice young fellow – Casaubon has done everything for him,' explained Mr Brooke. 'He repays your expense in him, Casaubon,' he went on, nodding encouragingly. 'I hope he will stay with me a long while and we shall make something of my documents. I have plenty of ideas and facts, you know, and I can see he is just the man to put them into shape – remembers what the right quotations are, *omne tulit punctum*, and that sort of thing – gives subjects a kind of turn. I invited him some time ago when you were ill, Casaubon: Dorothea said you couldn't have anybody in the house, you know, and she asked me to write.'

Poor Dorothea felt that every word of her uncle's was about as pleasant as a grain of sand in the eye of Mr Casaubon. It would be altogether unfitting now to explain that she had not wished her uncle to invite Will Ladislaw. She could not in the least make clear to herself the reasons for her husband's dislike to his presence – a dislike painfully impressed on her by the scene in the library; but she felt the unbecomingness of saying anything that might convey a notion of it to others. Mr Casaubon, indeed, had not thoroughly represented those mixed reasons to himself; irritated feeling with him, as with all of us, seeking rather for justification than for self-knowledge. But he wished to repress outward signs, and only Dorothea could discern the changes in her husband's face before he observed with more of dignified bending and sing-song than usual –

'You are exceedingly hospitable, my dear sir; and I owe you acknowledgments for exercising your hospitality towards a relative of mine.'

The funeral was ended now, and the churchyard was being cleared.

'Now you can see him, Mrs Cadwallader,' said Celia. 'He is just like a miniature of Mr Casaubon's aunt that hangs in Dorothea's boudoir – quite nice-looking.'

'A very pretty sprig,' said Mrs Cadwallader, dryly. 'What is your nephew to be, Mr Casaubon?'

'Pardon me, he is not my nephew. He is my cousin.'

'Well, you know,' interposed Mr Brooke, 'he is trying his wings. He is just the sort of young fellow to rise. I should be glad to give him an opportunity. He would make a good secretary, now, like Hobbes, Milton, Swift – that sort of man.'

'I understand,' said Mrs Cadwallader. 'One who can write speeches.'

'I'll fetch him in now, eh, Casaubon?' said Mr Brooke. 'He wouldn't come in till I had announced him, you know. And we'll go down and look at the picture. There you are to the life: a deep subtle sort of thinker with his forefinger on the page, while Saint Bonaventure or somebody else, rather fat and florid, is looking up at the Trinity. Everything is symbolical, you know – the higher style of art: I like that up to a certain point, but not too far – it's rather straining to keep up with, you know. But you are at home in that, Casaubon. And your painter's flesh is good – solidity, transparency, everything of that sort. I went into that a great deal at one time. However, I'll go and fetch Ladislaw.'

❈ THIRTY-FIVE ❧

Non, je ne comprends pas de plus charmant plaisir
Que de voir d'héritiers une troupe affligée,
Le maintien interdit, et la mine allongée,
Lire un long testament où pales, étonnés,
On leur laisse un bonsoir avec un pied de nez.
Pour voir au natural leur tristesse profonde,
Je reviendrais, je crois, exprès de l'autre monde.
REGNARD: *Le Légataire Universel*

WHEN THE ANIMALS ENTERED THE ARK in pairs, one may imagine that allied species made much private remark on each other, and were tempted to think that so many forms feeding on the same store of fodder were eminently superfluous, as tending to diminish the rations. (I fear the part played by the vultures on that occasion would be too painful for art to represent, those birds being disadvantageously naked about the gullet, and apparently without rites and ceremonies.)

The same sort of temptation befell the Christian Carnivora who formed Peter Featherstone's funeral procession; most of them having minds bent on a limited store which each would have liked to get the most of. The long-recognized blood-relations and connections by marriage made already a goodly number, which, multiplied by possibilities, presented a fine range for jealous conjecture and pathetic hopefulness. Jealousy of the Vincys had created a fellowship in hostility among all persons of the Featherstone blood, so that in the absence of any decided indication that one of themselves was to have more than the rest, the dread lest that long-legged Fred Vincy should have the land was necessarily dominant, though it left abundant feeling and leisure for vaguer jealousies, such as were entertained towards Mary Garth. Solomon found time to reflect that Jonah was undeserving, and Jonah to abuse Solomon as greedy; Jane, the elder sister, held that Martha's children ought not to expect so much as the young Waules; and Martha, more lax on the subject of primogeniture, was sorry to think that Jane was so 'having'. These nearest of kin were naturally impressed with the unreasonableness of expectations in cousins and second cousins, and used their arithmetic in reckoning the large sums that small legacies might mount to, if there were too many of them. Two cousins were present to hear the will, and a second cousin besides Mr Trumbull. This second cousin was a Middlemarch mercer of polite manners and superfluous aspirates. The two cousins were elderly men from Brassing, one of them conscious of claims on the score of inconvenient expense sustained by him in presents of oysters and other eatables to his rich cousin Peter; the other entirely saturnine, leaning his hands and chin on a stick, and conscious of claims based on no narrow performance but on merit generally: both blameless citizens of Brassing, who wished that Jonah Featherstone did not live there. The wit of a family is usually best received among strangers.

'Why, Trumbull himself is pretty sure of five hundred – *that* you may depend, – I shouldn't wonder if my brother promised him,' said Solomon, musing aloud with his sisters, the evening before the funeral.

'Dear, dear!' said poor Sister Martha, whose imagination of hundreds had been habitually narrowed to the amount of her unpaid rent.

But in the morning all the ordinary currents of conjecture were disturbed by the presence of a strange mourner who had plashed among them as if from the moon. This was the stranger described by Mrs Cadwallader as frog-face: a man perhaps about two or three and thirty, whose prominent eyes, thin-lipped, downward-curved mouth, and hair sleekly brushed away from a forehead that sank suddenly above the ridge of the eyebrows, certainly gave his face a batrachian unchangeableness of expression. Here, clearly, was a new legatee; else why was he bidden as a mourner? Here were new possibilities, raising a new uncertainty, which almost checked remark in the mourning coaches. We are all humiliated by the sudden discovery of a fact which has existed very comfortably and perhaps been staring at us in private while we have been making up our world entirely without it. No one had seen this questionable stranger before except Mary Garth, and she knew nothing more of him than that he had twice been to Stone Court when Mr Featherstone was down-stairs, and had sat alone with him for several hours. She had found an opportunity of mentioning this to her father, and perhaps Caleb's were the only eyes, except the lawyer's, which examined the stranger with more of inquiry than of disgust or suspicion. Caleb Garth, having little expectation and less cupidity, was interested in the verification of his own guesses, and the calmness with which he half-smilingly rubbed his chin and shot intelligent glances much as if he were valuing a tree, made a fine contrast with the alarm or scorn visible in other faces when the unknown mourner, whose name was understood to be Rigg, entered the wainscoted parlour and took his seat near the door to make part of the audience when the will should be read. Just then Mr Solomon and Mr Jonah were gone up-stairs with the lawyer to search for the will; and Mrs Waule, seeing two vacant seats between herself and Mr Borthrop Trumbull, had the spirit to move next to that great authority, who was handling his watch-seals and trimming his outlines with a determination not to show anything so compromising to a man of ability as wonder or surprise.

'I suppose you know everything about what my poor brother's done,

Mr Trumbull,' said Mrs Waule, in the lowest of her woolly tones, while she turned her crape-shadowed bonnet towards Mr Trumbull's ear.

'My good lady, whatever was told me was told in confidence,' said the auctioneer, putting his hand up to screen that secret.

'Them who've made sure of their good-luck may be disappointed yet,' Mrs Waule continued, finding some relief in this communication.

'Hopes are often delusive,' said Mr Trumbull, still in confidence.

'Ah!' said Mrs Waule, looking across at the Vincys, and then moving back to the side of her sister Martha.

'It's wonderful how close poor Peter was,' she said, in the same undertones. 'We none of us know what he might have had on his mind: I only hope and trust he wasn't a worse liver than we think of, Martha.'

Poor Mrs Cranch was bulky, and, breathing asthmatically, had the additional motive for making her remarks unexceptionable and giving them a general bearing, that even her whispers were loud and liable to sudden bursts like those of a deranged barrel-organ.

'I never *was* covetous, Jane,' she replied; 'but I have six children and have buried three, and I didn't marry into money. The eldest, that sits there, is but nineteen – so I leave you to guess. And stock always short, and land most awkward. But if ever I've begged and prayed, it's been to God above; though where there's one brother a bachelor and the other childless after twice marrying – anybody might think!'

Meanwhile, Mr Vincy had glanced at the passive face of Mr Rigg, and had taken out his snuff-box and tapped it, but had put it back again unopened as an indulgence which, however clarifying to the judgment, was unsuited to the occasion. 'I shouldn't wonder if Featherstone had better feelings than any of us gave him credit for,' he observed, in the ear of his wife. 'This funeral shows a thought about everybody: it looks well when a man wants to be followed by his friends, and if they are humble, not to be ashamed of them. I should be all the better pleased if he'd left lots of small legacies. They may be uncommonly useful to fellows in a small way.'

'Everything is as handsome as could be, crape and silk and everything,' said Mrs Vincy, contentedly.

But I am sorry to say that Fred was under some difficulty in repressing a laugh, which would have been more unsuitable than his father's snuff-box. Fred had overheard Mr Jonah suggesting something about a 'love-child', and with this thought in his mind, the stranger's face, which happened to be opposite him, affected him too ludicrously. Mary Garth, discerning his distress in the twitchings of his mouth, and his recourse to a cough, came cleverly to his rescue by asking him to change seats with her, so that he got into a shadowy corner. Fred was feeling as good-naturedly as possible towards everybody, including Rigg; and having some relenting towards all these people who were less lucky than he was aware of being himself, he would not for the world have behaved amiss; still, it was particularly easy to laugh.

But the entrance of the lawyer and the two brothers drew every one's attention.

The lawyer was Mr Standish, and he had come to Stone Court this morning believing that he knew thoroughly well who would be pleased and who disappointed before the day was over. The will he expected to read was the last of three which he had drawn up for Mr Featherstone. Mr Standish was not a man who varied his manners: he behaved with the same deep-voiced, offhand-civility to everybody, as if he saw no difference in them, and talked chiefly of the hay crop, which would be 'very fine, by God!', of the last bulletins concerning the King, and of the Duke of Clarence, who was a sailor every inch of him, and just the man to rule over an island like Britain.

Old Featherstone had often reflected as he sat looking at the fire that Standish would be surprised some day: it is true that if he had done as he liked at the last, and burnt the will drawn up by another lawyer, he would not have secured that minor end; still he had had his pleasure in ruminating on it. And certainly Mr Standish was surprised, but not at all sorry; on the contrary, he rather enjoyed the zest of a little curiosity in his own mind, which the discovery of a second will added to the prospective amazement on the part of the Featherstone family.

As to the sentiments of Solomon and Jonah, they were held in utter suspense: it seemed to them that the old will would have a certain validity, and that there might be such an interlacement of poor Peter's former and latter intentions as to create endless 'lawing' before anybody came by their own – an inconvenience which would have at least the advantage of going all round. Hence the brothers showed a thoroughly neutral gravity as they re-entered with Mr Standish; but Solomon took out his white handkerchief again with a sense that in any case there would be affecting passages, and crying at funerals, however dry, was customarily served up in lawn.

Perhaps the person who felt the most throbbing excitement at this moment was Mary Garth, in the consciousness that it was she who had virtually determined the production of this second will, which might have momentous effects on the lot of some persons present. No soul except herself knew what had passed on that final night.

'The will I hold in my hand,' said Mr Standish, who, seated at the table in the middle of the room, took his time about everything, including the coughs with which he showed a disposition to clear his voice, 'was drawn up by myself and executed by our deceased friend on the 9th of August 1825. But I find that there is a subsequent instrument hitherto unknown to me, bearing date the 20th of July 1826, hardly a year later than the previous one. And there is farther, I see' – Mr Standish was cautiously travelling over the document with his spectacles – 'a codicil to this latter will, bearing date March the 1st, 1828.'

'Dear, dear!' said Sister Martha, not meaning to be audible, but driven to some articulation under this pressure of dates.

'I shall begin by reading the earlier will,' continued Mr Standish, 'since such, as appears by his not having destroyed the document, was the intention of deceased.'

The preamble was felt to be rather long, and several besides Solomon shook their heads pathetically, looking on the ground: all eyes avoided meeting other eyes, and were chiefly fixed either on the spots in the table-cloth or on Mr Standish's bald head; excepting Mary Garth's. When all the rest were trying to look nowhere in particular, it was safe for her to look at them. And at the sound of the first 'give and bequeath' she could see all complexions changing subtly, as if some faint vibration were passing through them, save that of Mr Rigg. He sat in unaltered calm, and, in fact, the company, preoccupied with more important problems, and with the complication of listening to bequests which might or might not be revoked, had ceased to think of him. Fred blushed, and Mr Vincy found it impossible to do without his snuff-box in his hand, though he kept it closed.

The small bequests came first, and even the recollection that there was another will and that poor Peter might have thought better of it, could not quell the rising disgust and indignation. One likes to be done well by in every tense, past, present, and future. And here was Peter capable five years ago of leaving only two hundred apiece to his own brothers and sisters, and only a two hundred apiece to his own nephews and nieces: the Garths were not mentioned, but Mrs Vincy and Rosamond were each to have a hundred. Mr Trumbull was to have the gold-headed cane and fifty pounds; the other second cousins and the cousins present were each to have the like handsome sum, which, as the saturnine cousin observed, was a sort of legacy that left a man nowhere; and there was much more of such offensive dribbling in favour of persons not present – problematical, and, it was to be feared, low connections. Altogether, reckoning hastily, here were about three thousand disposed of. Where then had Peter meant the rest of the money to go – and where the land? and what was revoked and what not revoked – and was the revocation for better or for worse? All emotion must be conditional, and might turn out to be the wrong thing. The men were strong enough to bear up and keep quiet under this confused suspense: some letting their lower lip fall, others pursing it up, according to the habit of their muscles. But Jane and Martha sank under the rush of questions, and began to cry; poor Mrs Cranch being half moved with the consolation of getting any hundreds at all without working for them, and half aware that her share was scanty; whereas Mrs Waule's mind was entirely flooded with the sense of being an own sister and getting little, while somebody else was to have much. The general expectation now was that the 'much' would fall to Fred Vincy, but the Vincys themselves were surprised when ten thousand pounds in specified investments were declared to be bequeathed to him: – was the land coming too? Fred bit his lips: it was difficult to help smiling, and Mrs Vincy felt herself the happiest of women – possible revocation shrinking out of sight in this dazzling vision.

There was still a residue of personal property as well as the land, but the whole was left to one person, and that person was – O possibilities! O expectations founded on the favour of 'close' old gentlemen! O endless vocatives that would still leave expression slipping helpless from the measurement of mortal folly! – that residuary legatee was Joshua Rigg, who was also sole executor, and who was to take thenceforth the name of Featherstone.

There was a rustling which seemed like a shudder running round the room. Every one stared afresh at Mr Rigg, who apparently experienced no surprise.

'A most singular testamentary disposition!' exclaimed Mr Trumbull, preferring for once that he should be considered ignorant in the past. 'But there is a second will – there is a further document. We have not yet heard the final wishes of the deceased.'

Mary Garth was feeling that what they had yet to hear were not the final wishes. The second will revoked everything except the legacies to the low persons before mentioned (some alterations in these being the occasion of the codicil), and the bequest of all the land lying in Lowick parish, with all the stock and household furniture, to Joshua Rigg. The residue of the property was to be devoted to the erection and endowment of almshouses for old men, to be called Featherstone's Almshouses, and to be built on a piece of land near Middlemarch already bought for the purpose by the testator, he wishing – so the document declared – to please God Almighty. Nobody present had a farthing; but Mr Trumbull had the gold-headed cane. It took some time for the company to recover the power of expression. Mary dared not look at Fred.

Mr Vincy was the first to speak – after using his snuff-box energetically – and he spoke with loud indignation. 'The most unaccountable will I ever heard! I should say he was not in his right mind when he made it. I should say this last will was void,' added Mr Vincy, feeling that this expression put the thing in the true light. 'Eh, Standish?'

'Our deceased friend always knew what he was about, I think,' said Mr Standish. 'Everything is quite regular. Here is a letter from Clemmens of Brassing tied with the will. He drew it up. A very respectable solicitor.'

'I never noticed any alienation of mind – any aberration of intellect in the late Mr Featherstone,' said Borthrop Trumbull, 'but I call this will eccentric. I was always willingly of service to the old soul; and he intimated pretty plainly a sense of obligation which would show itself in his will. The gold-headed cane is farcical considered as an acknowledgment to me; but happily I am above mercenary considerations.'

'There's nothing very surprising in the matter that I can see,' said Caleb Garth. 'Anybody might have had more reason for wondering if the will had been what you might expect from an open-minded straightforward man. For my part, I wish there was no such thing as a will.'

'That's a strange sentiment to come from a Christian man, by God!' said the lawyer. 'I should like to know how you will back that up, Garth!'

'Oh,' said Caleb, leaning forward, adjusting his fingertips with nicety and looking meditatively on the ground. It always seemed to him that words were the hardest part of 'business'.

But here Mr Jonah Featherstone made himself heard. 'Well, he always was a fine hypocrite, was my brother Peter. But this will cuts out everything. If I'd known, a waggon and six horses shouldn't have drawn me from Brassing. I'll put a white hat and drab coat on to-morrow.'

'Dear, dear,' wept Mrs Cranch, 'and we've been at the expense of travelling, and that poor lad sitting idle here so long! It's the first time I ever heard my brother Peter was so wishful to please God Almighty; but if I was to be struck helpless I must say it's hard – I can think no other.'

'It'll do him no good where he's gone, that's my belief,' said Solomon, with a bitterness which was remarkably genuine, though his tone could not help being sly. 'Peter was a bad liver, and almshouses won't cover it, when he's had the impudence to show it at the last.'

'And all the while had got his own lawful family – brothers and sisters and nephews and nieces – and has sat in church with 'em whenever he thought well to come,' said Mrs Waule. 'And might have left his property so respectable, to them that's never been used to extravagance or unsteadiness in no manner of way – and not so poor but what they could have saved every penny and made more of it. And me – the trouble I've been at, times and times, to come here and be sisterly – and him with things on his mind all the while that might make anybody's flesh creep. But if the Almighty's allowed it, He means to punish him for it. Brother Solomon, I shall be going, if you'll drive me.'

'I've no desire to put my foot on the premises again,' said Solomon. 'I've got land of my own and property of my own to will away.'

'It's a poor tale how luck goes in the world,' said Jonah. 'It never answers to have a bit of spirit in you. You'd better be a dog in the manger. But those above ground might learn a lesson. One fool's will is enough in a family.'

'There's more ways than one of being a fool,' said Solomon. 'I shan't leave my money to be poured down the sink, and I shan't leave it to fondlings from Africay. I like Featherstones that were brewed such, and not turned Featherstones with sticking the name on 'em.'

Solomon addressed these remarks in a loud aside to Mrs Waule as he rose to accompany her. Brother Jonah felt himself capable of much more stinging wit than this, but he reflected that there was no use in offending the new proprietor of Stone Court, until you were certain that he was quite without intentions of hospitality towards witty men whose name he was about to bear.

Mr Joshua Rigg, in fact, appeared to trouble himself little about any innuendoes, but showed a notable change of manner, walking coolly up to Mr Standish and putting business questions with much coolness. He had a high chirping voice and a vile accent. Fred, whom he no longer moved to laughter, thought him the lowest monster he had ever seen. But Fred was feeling rather sick. The Middlemarch mercer waited for an opportunity of engaging Mr Rigg in conversation: there was no knowing how many pairs of legs the new proprietor might require hose for, and profits were more to be relied on than legacies. Also, the mercer, as a second cousin, was dispassionate enough to feel curiosity.

Mr Vincy, after his one outburst, had remained proudly silent, though too much preoccupied with unpleasant feelings to think of moving, till he observed that his wife had gone to Fred's side and was crying silently while she held her darling's hand. He rose immediately, and turning his back on the company while he said to her in an undertone, – 'Don't give way, Lucy; don't make a fool of yourself, my dear, before these people,' he added in his usual loud voice – 'Go and order the phaeton, Fred; I have no time to waste.'

Mary Garth had before this been getting ready to go home with her father. She met Fred in the hall, and now for the first time had the courage to look at him. He had that withered sort of paleness which will sometimes come on young faces, and his hand was very cold when she shook it. Mary too was agitated: she was conscious that fatally, without will of her own, she had perhaps made a great difference to Fred's lot.

'Good-bye,' she said, with affectionate sadness. 'Be brave, Fred. I do believe you are better without the money. What was the good of it to Mr Featherstone?'

'That's all very fine,' said Fred, pettishly. 'What is a fellow to do? I *must* go into the Church now.' (He knew that this would vex Mary: very well; then she must tell him what else he could do.) 'And I thought I should be able to pay your father at once and make everything right. And you have not even a hundred pounds left you. What shall you do now, Mary?'

'Take another situation, of course, as soon as I can get one. My father has enough to do to keep the rest, without me. Good-bye.'

In a very short time Stone Court was cleared of well-brewed Featherstones and other long-accustomed visitors. Another stranger had been brought to settle in the neighbourhood of Middlemarch, but in the case of Mr Rigg Featherstone there was more discontent with immediate visible consequence than speculation as to the effect which his presence might have in the future. No soul was prophetic enough to have any foreboding as to what might appear on the trail of Joshua Rigg.

And here I am naturally led to reflect on the means of elevating a low subject. Historical parallels are remarkably efficient in this way. The chief objection to them is, that the diligent narrator may lack space, or (what is often the same thing) may not be able to think of them with any degree of particularity, though he may have a philosophical confidence that if known they would be illustrative. It seems an easier and shorter way to dignity, to observe that – since there never was a true story which could not be told in parables where you might put a monkey for a margrave, and *vice versa* – whatever has been or is to be narrated by me about low people, may be ennobled by being considered a parable; so that if any bad habits and ugly consequences are brought into view, the reader may have the relief of regarding them as not more than figuratively ungenteel, and may feel himself virtually in company with persons of some style. Thus while I tell the truth about loobies, my reader's imagination need not be entirely excluded from an occupation with lords; and the petty sums which any bankrupt of high standing would be sorry to retire upon, may be lifted to the level of high commercial transactions by the inexpensive addition of proportional ciphers.

As to any provincial history in which the agents are all of high moral rank, that must be of a date long posterior to the first Reform Bill, and Peter Featherstone, you perceive, was dead and buried some months before Lord Grey came into office.

❧ THIRTY-SIX ❧

'Tis strange to see the humours of these men,
These great aspiring spirits, that should be wise:
. . . .
For being the nature of great spirits to love
To be where they may be most eminent;
They, rating of themselves so farre above
Us in conceit, with whom they do frequent,
Imagine how we wonder and esteeme
All that they do or say; which makes them strive
To make our admiration more extreme,
Which they suppose they cannot, 'less they give
Notice of their extreme and highest thoughts.
                    DANIEL: *Tragedy of Philotas*

MR VINCY WENT HOME FROM THE reading of the will with his point of view considerably changed in relation to many subjects. He was an open-minded man, but given to indirect modes of expressing himself: when he was disappointed in a market for his silk braids, he swore at the groom; when his brother-in-law Bulstrode had vexed him, he made cutting remarks on Methodism; and it was now apparent that he regarded Fred's idleness with a sudden increase of severity, by his throwing an embroidered cap out of the smoking-room on to the hall-floor.

'Well, sir,' he observed, when that young gentleman was moving off to bed, 'I hope you've made up your mind now to go up next term and pass your examination. I've taken my resolution, so I advise you to lose no time in taking yours.'

Fred made no answer: he was too utterly depressed. Twenty-four hours ago he had thought that instead of needing to know what he should do, he should by this time know that he needed to do nothing: that he should hunt in pink, have a first-rate hunter, ride to cover on a fine hack, and be generally respected for doing so; moreover, that he should be able at once to pay Mr Garth, and that Mary could not longer have any reason for not marrying him. And all this was to have come without study or other inconvenience, purely by the favour of Providence in the shape of an old gentleman's caprice. But now, at the end of twenty-four hours, all those firm expectations were upset. It was 'rather hard lines' that while he was

266

smarting under this disappointment he should be treated as if he could have helped it. But he went away silently and his mother pleaded for him.

'Don't be hard on the poor boy, Vincy. He'll turn out well yet, though that wicked man has deceived him. I feel as sure as I sit here, Fred will turn out well – else why was he brought back from the brink of the grave? And I call it a robbery: it was like giving him the land, to promise it; and what is promising, if making everybody believe is not promising? And you see he did leave him ten thousand pounds, and then took it away again.'

'Took it away again!' said Mr Vincy, pettishly. 'I tell you the lad's an unlucky lad, Lucy. And you've always spoiled him.'

'Well, Vincy, he was my first, and you made a fine fuss with him when he came. You were as proud as proud,' said Mrs Vincy, easily recovering her cheerful smile.

'Who knows what babies will turn to? I was fool enough, I daresay,' said the husband – more mildly, however.

'But who has handsomer, better children than ours? Fred is far beyond other people's sons: you may hear it in his speech, that he has kept college company. And Rosamond – where is there a girl like her? She might stand beside any lady in the land, and only look the better for it. You see – Mr Lydgate has kept the highest company and been everywhere, and he fell in love with her at once. Not but what I could have wished Rosamond had not engaged herself. She might have met somebody on a visit who would have been a far better match; I mean at her schoolfellow Miss Willoughby's. There are relations in that family quite as high as Mr Lydgate's.'

'Damn relations!' said Mr Vincy; 'I've had enough of them. I don't want a son-in-law who has got nothing but his relations to recommend him.'

'Why, my dear,' said Mrs Vincy, 'you seemed as pleased as could be about it. It's true, I wasn't at home; but Rosamond told me you hadn't a word to say against the engagement. And she has begun to buy in the best linen and cambric for her underclothing.'

'Not by my will,' said Mr Vincy. 'I shall have enough to do this year, with an idle scamp of a son, without paying for wedding-clothes. The times are as tight as can be; everybody is being ruined; and I don't believe Lydgate has got a farthing. I shan't give my consent to their marrying. Let 'em wait, as their elders have done before 'em.'

'Rosamond will take it hard, Vincy, and you know you never could bear to cross her.'

'Yes, I could. The sooner the engagement's off, the better. I don't believe he'll ever make an income, the way he goes on. He makes enemies; that's all I hear of his making.'

'But he stands very high with Mr Bulstrode, my dear. The marriage would please *him*, I should think.'

'Please the deuce!' said Mr Vincy. 'Bulstrode won't pay for their keep. And if Lydgate thinks I'm going to give money for them to set up housekeeping, he's mistaken, that's all. I expect I shall have to put down my horses soon. You'd better tell Rosy what I say.'

This was a not infrequent procedure with Mr Vincy – to be rash in jovial assent, and on becoming subsequently conscious that he had been rash, to employ others in making the offensive retractation. However, Mrs Vincy, who never willingly opposed her husband, lost no time the next morning in letting Rosamond know what he had said. Rosamond, examining some muslin-work, listened in silence, and at the end gave a certain turn of her graceful neck, of which only long experience could teach you that it meant perfect obstinacy.

'What do you say, my dear?' said her mother, with affectionate deference.

'Papa does not mean anything of the kind,' said Rosamond, quite calmly. 'He has always said that he wished me to marry the man I loved. And I shall marry Mr Lydgate. It is seven weeks now since papa gave his consent. And I hope we shall have Mrs Bretton's house.'

'Well, my dear, I shall leave you to manage your papa. You always do manage everybody. But if we ever do go and get damask, Sadler's is the place – far better than Hopkins's. Mrs Bretton's is very large though: I should love you to have such a house; but it will take a great deal of furniture – carpeting and everything, besides plate and glass. Do you think Mr Lydgate expects it?'

'You cannot imagine that I should ask him, mamma. Of course he understands his own affairs.'

'But he may have been looking for money, my dear, and we all thought of your having a pretty legacy as well as Fred; – and now everything is so dreadful – there's no pleasure in thinking of anything, with that poor boy disappointed as he is.'

'That has nothing to do with my marriage, mamma. Fred must leave off being idle. I am going up-stairs to take this work to Miss Morgan: she does the open-hemming very well. Mary Garth might do some work for me now, I should think. Her sewing is exquisite; it is the nicest thing I know about Mary. I should so like to have all my cambric frilling double-hemmed. And it takes a long time.'

Mrs Vincy's belief that Rosamond could manage her papa was well founded. Apart from his dinners and his coursing, Mr Vincy, blustering as he was, had as little of his own way as if he had been a prime minister: the force of circumstances was easily too much for him, as it is for most pleasure-loving florid men; and the circumstance called Rosamond was particularly forcible by means of that mild persistence which, as we know, enables a white soft living substance to make its way in spite of opposing rock. Papa was not a rock: he had no other fixity than that fixity of alternating impulses sometimes called habit, and this was altogether unfavourable to his taking the only decisive line of conduct in relation to his daughter's engagement – namely, to inquire thoroughly into Lydgate's circumstances, declare his own inability to furnish money, and forbid alike either a speedy marriage or an engagement which must be too lengthy. That seems very simple and easy in the statement; but a disagreeable resolve formed in the chill hours of the morning had as many conditions against it as the early frost, and rarely persisted under the warming influences of the day. The indirect though emphatic expression of opinion to which Mr Vincy was prone suffered much restraint in this case: Lydgate was a proud man towards whom innuendoes were obviously unsafe, and throwing his hat on the floor was out of the question. Mr Vincy was a little in awe of him, a little vain that he wanted to marry Rosamond, a little indisposed to raise a question of money in which his own position was not advantageous, a little afraid of being worsted in dialogue with a man better educated and more highly bred than himself, and a little afraid of doing what his daughter would not like. The part Mr Vincy preferred playing was that of the generous host whom nobody criticizes. In the earlier half of the day there was business to hinder any formal communication of an adverse resolve; in the later there was dinner, wine, whist, and general satisfaction. And in the meanwhile the hours were each leaving their little deposit and gradually forming the final reason for inaction, namely, that action was too late.

The accepted lover spent most of his evenings in Lowick Gate, and a love-making not at all dependent on money-advances from fathers-in-law, or prospective income from a profession, went on flourishingly under Mr Vincy's own eyes. Young love-making – that gossamer web! Even the points it clings to – the things whence its subtle interlacings are swung – are scarcely perceptible; momentary touches of finger-tips, meetings of rays from blue and dark orbs, unfinished phrases, lightest changes of cheek and lip, faintest tremors. The web itself is made of spontaneous beliefs and indefinable joys, yearnings of one life towards another, visions of completeness, indefinite trust. And Lydgate fell to spinning that web from his inward self with wonderful rapidity, in spite of experience supposed to be finished off with the drama of Laure – in spite too of medicine and biology; for the inspection of macerated muscle or of eyes presented in a dish (like Santa Lucia's), and other incidents of scientific inquiry, are observed to be less incompatible with poetic love than a native dulness or a lively addiction to the lowest prose. As for Rosamond, she was in the water-lily's expanding wonderment at its own fuller life, and she too was spinning industriously at the mutual web. All this went on in the corner of the drawing-room where the piano stood, and subtle as it was, the light made it a sort of rainbow visible to many observers besides Mr Farebrother. The certainty that Miss Vincy and Mr Lydgate were engaged became general in Middlemarch without the aid of formal announcement.

Aunt Bulstrode was again stirred to anxiety; but this time she addressed herself to her brother, going to the warehouse expressly to avoid Mrs Vincy's volatility. His replies were not satisfactory.

'Walter, you never mean to tell me that you have allowed all this to go on without inquiry into Mr Lydgate's prospects?' said Mrs Bulstrode, opening her eyes with wider gravity at her brother, who was in his peevish warehouse humour. 'Think of this girl brought up in luxury – in too worldly a way, I am sorry to say – what will she do on a small income?'

'Oh, confound it, Harriet! what can I do when men come into the town without any asking of mine? Did you shut your house up against Lydgate? Bulstrode has pushed him forward more than anybody. I never made any fuss about the young fellow. You should go and talk to your husband about it, not me.'

'Well, really, Walter, how can Mr Bulstrode be to blame? I am sure he did not wish for the engagement.'

'Oh, if Bulstrode had not taken him by the hand, I should never have invited him.'

'But you called him in to attend on Fred, and I am sure that was a mercy,' said Mrs Bulstrode, losing her clue in the intricacies of the subject.

'I don't know about mercy,' said Mr Vincy, testily. 'I know I am worried more than I like with my family. I was a good brother to you, Harriet, before you married Bulstrode, and I must say he doesn't always show that friendly spirit towards your family that might have been expected of him.' Mr Vincy was very little like a Jesuit, but no accomplished Jesuit could have turned a question more adroitly. Harriet had to defend her husband instead of blaming her brother, and the conversation ended at a point as far from the beginning as some recent sparring between the brothers-in-law at a vestry meeting.

Mrs Bulstrode did not repeat her brother's complaints to her husband, but in the evening she spoke to him of Lydgate and Rosamond. He did not share her warm interest, however; and only spoke with resignation of the risks attendant on the beginning of medical practice and the desirability of prudence.

'I am sure we are bound to pray for that thoughtless girl – brought up as she has been,' said Mrs Bulstrode, wishing to rouse her husband's feelings.

'Truly, my dear,' said Mr Bulstrode, assentingly. 'Those who are not of this world can do little else to arrest the errors of the obstinately worldly. That is what we must accustom ourselves to recognize with regard to your brother's family. I could have wished that Mr Lydgate had not entered into such a union; but my relations with him are limited to that use of his gifts for God's purposes which is taught us by the divine government under each dispensation.'

Mrs Bulstrode said no more, attributing some dissatisfaction which she felt to her own want of spirituality. She believed that her husband was one of those men whose memoirs should be written when they died.

As to Lydgate himself, having been accepted, he was prepared to accept all the consequences which he believed himself to foresee with perfect clearness. Of course he must be married in a year – perhaps even in half a year. This was not what he had intended; but other schemes would not be hindered: they would simply adjust themselves anew. Marriage, of course, must be prepared for in the usual way. A house must be taken instead of the rooms he at present occupied; and Lydgate, having heard Rosamond speak with admiration of old Mrs Bretton's house (situated in Lowick Gate), took notice when it fell vacant after the old lady's death, and immediately entered into treaty for it.

He did this in an episodic way, very much as he gave orders to his tailor for every requisite of perfect dress, without any notion of being extravagant. On the contrary, he would have despised any ostentation of expense; his profession had familiarized him with all grades of poverty, and he cared much for those who suffered hardships. He would have behaved perfectly at a table where the sauce was served in a jug with the handle off, and he would have remembered nothing about a grand dinner except that a man was there who talked well. But it had never occurred to him that he should live in any other than what he would have called an ordinary way, with green glasses for hock, and excellent waiting at table. In warming himself at French social theories he had brought away no smell of scorching. We may handle even extreme opinions with impunity while our furniture, our dinner-giving, and preference for armorial bearings in our own case, link us indissolubly with the established order. And Lydgate's tendency was not towards extreme opinions: he would have liked no barefooted doctrines, being particular about his boots: he was no radical in relation to anything but medical reform and the prosecution of discovery. In the rest of practical life he walked by hereditary habit; half from that personal pride and unreflecting egoism which I have already called commonness, and half from that naïveté which belonged to pre-occupation with favourite ideas.

Any inward debate Lydgate had as to the consequence of this engagement which had stolen upon him, turned on the paucity of time rather than of money. Certainly, being in love and being expected continually by some one who always turned out to be prettier than memory could represent her to be, did interfere with the diligent use of spare hours which might serve some 'plodding fellow of a German' to make the great, imminent discovery. This was really an argument for not deferring the marriage too long, as he implied to Mr Farebrother, one day that the Vicar came to his room with some pond-products which he wanted to examine under a better microscope than his own, and, finding Lydgate's tableful of apparatus and specimens in confusion, said sarcastically,

'Eros has degenerated; he began by introducing order and harmony, and now he brings back chaos.'

'Yes, at some stages,' said Lydgate, lifting his brows and smiling, while he began to arrange his microscope. 'But a better order will begin after.'

'Soon?' said the Vicar.

'I hope so, really. This unsettled state of affairs uses up the time, and when one has notions in science, every moment is an opportunity. I feel sure that marriage must be the best thing for a man who wants to work steadily. He has everything at home then – no teasing with personal speculations. He can get calmness and freedom.'

'You are an enviable dog,' said the Vicar, 'to have such a prospect – Rosamond, calmness and freedom, all to your share. Here am I with nothing but my pipe and pond animalcules. Now, are you ready?'

Lydgate did not mention to the Vicar another reason he had for wishing to shorten the period of courtship. It was rather irritating to him, even with the wine of love in his veins, to be obliged to mingle so often with the family part at the Vincys', and to enter so much into Middlemarch gossip, protracted good cheer, whist-playing, and general futility. He had to be deferential when Mr Vincy decided questions with trenchant ignorance, especially as to those liquors which were the best inward pickle, preserving you from the effects of bad air. Mrs Vincy's openness and simplicity were quite unstreaked with suspicion as to the subtle offence she might give to the taste of her intended son-in-law; and altogether Lydgate had to confess to himself that he was descending a little in relation to Rosamond's family. But that exquisite creature herself suffered in the same sort of way: – it was at least one delightful thought that in marrying her, he could give her a much-needed transplantation.

'Dear!' he said to her one evening, in his gentlest tone, as he sat down by her and looked closely at her face –

But I must first say that he had found her alone in the drawing-room where the great old-fashioned window, almost as large as the side of the room, was opened to the summer scents of the garden at the back of the house. Her father and mother were gone to a party, and the rest were all out with the butterflies.

'Dear! your eyelids are red.'

'Are they?' said Rosamond. 'I wonder why.' It was not in her nature to pour forth wishes or grievances. They only came forth gracefully on solicitation.

'As if you could hide it from me!' said Lydgate, laying his hand tenderly on both of hers. 'Don't I see a tiny drop on one of the lashes? Things trouble you, and you don't tell me. That is unloving.'

'Why should I tell you what you cannot alter? They are everyday things: – perhaps they have been a little worse lately.'

'Family annoyances. Don't fear speaking. I guess them.'

'Papa has been more irritable lately. Fred makes him angry, and this morning there was a fresh quarrel because Fred threatens to throw his whole education away, and do something quite beneath him. And besides – '

Rosamond hesitated, and her cheeks were gathering a slight flush. Lydgate had never seen her in trouble since the morning of their engagement, and he had never felt so passionately towards her as at this moment. He kissed the hesitating lips gently, as if to encourage them.

'I feel that papa is not quite pleased about our engagement,' Rosamond continued, almost in a whisper; 'and he said last night that he should certainly speak to you and say it must be given up.'

'Will you give it up?' said Lydgate, with quick energy – almost angrily.

'I never give up anything that I choose to do,' said Rosamond, recovering her calmness at the touching of this cord.

'God bless you!' said Lydgate, kissing her again. This constancy of purpose in the right place was adorable. He went on:–

'It is too late now for your father to say that our engagement must be given up. You are of age, and I claim you as mine. If anything is done to make you unhappy, – that is a reason for hastening our marriage.'

An unmistakable delight shone forth from the blue eyes that met his, and the radiance seemed to light up all his future with mild sunshine. Ideal happiness (of the kind known in the Arabian Nights, in which you are invited to step from the labour and discord of the street into a paradise where everything is given to you and nothing claimed) seemed to be an affair of a few weeks' waiting, more or less.

'Why should we defer it?' he said, with ardent insistence. 'I have taken the house now: everything else can soon be got ready – can it not? You will not mind about new clothes. Those can be bought afterwards.'

'What original notions you clever men have!' said Rosamond, dimpling with more thorough laughter than usual at this humorous incongruity. 'This is the first time I ever heard of wedding-clothes being bought after marriage.'

'But you don't mean to say you would insist on my waiting months for the sake of clothes?' said Lydgate, half thinking that Rosamond was tormenting him prettily, and half fearing that she really shrank from speedy marriage. 'Remember, we are looking forward to a better sort of happiness than this – being continually together, independent of others, and ordering our lives as we will. Come, dear, tell me how soon you can be altogether mine.'

There was a serious pleading in Lydgate's tone, as if he felt that she would be injuring him by any fantastic delays. Rosamond became serious too, and slightly meditative; in fact, she was going through many intricacies of lace-edging and hosiery and petticoat-tucking, in order to give an answer that would at least be approximate.

'Six weeks would be ample – say so, Rosamond,' insisted Lydgate, releasing her hands to put his arm gently round her.

One little hand immediately went to pat her hair, while she gave her neck a meditative turn, and then said seriously –

'There would be the house-linen and the furniture to be prepared. Still mamma could see to those while we were away.'

'Yes, to be sure. We must be away a week or so.'

'Oh, more than that!' said Rosamond, earnestly. She was thinking of her evening dresses for the visit to Sir Godwin Lydgate's, which she had long been secretly hoping for as a delightful employment of at least one quarter of the honeymoon, even if she deferred her introduction to the uncle who was a doctor of divinity (also a pleasing though sober kind of rank, when sustained by blood). She looked at her lover with some wondering remonstrance as she spoke, and he readily understood that she might wish to lengthen the sweet time of double solitude.

'Whatever you wish, my darling, when the day is fixed. But let us take a decided course, and put an end to any discomfort you may be suffering. Six weeks! – I am sure they would be ample.'

'I could certainly hasten the work,' said Rosamond. 'Will you, then, mention it to papa? – I think it would be better to write to him.' She blushed and looked at him as the garden flowers look at us when we walk forth happily among them in the transcendent evening light: is there not a soul beyond utterance, half-nymph, half-child, in those delicate petals which glow and breathe about the centres of deep colour?

He touched her ear and a little bit of neck under it with his lips, and they sat quite still for many minutes which flowed by them like a small gurgling brook with the kisses of the sun upon it. Rosamond thought that no one could be more in love than she was; and Lydgate thought that after all his wild mistakes and absurd credulity, he had found perfect womanhood – felt as if already breathed upon by exquisite wedded affection such as would be bestowed by an accomplished creature who venerated his high musings and momentous labours and would never interfere with them; who would create order in the home and accounts with still magic, yet keep her fingers ready to touch the lute and transform life into romance at any moment; who was instructed to the true womanly limit and not a hair's-breadth beyond – docile, therefore, and ready to carry out behests which came from beyond that limit. It was plainer now than ever that his notion of remaining much longer a bachelor had been a mistake: marriage would not be an obstruction but a furtherance. And happening the next day to accompany a patient to Brassing, he saw a dinner-service there which struck him as so exactly the right thing that he bought it at once. It saved time to do these things just when you thought of them, and Lydgate hated ugly crockery. The dinner-service in question was expensive, but that might be in the nature of dinner-services. Furnishing was necessarily expensive; but then it had to be done only once.

'It must be lovely,' said Mrs Vincy, when Lydgate mentioned his purchase with some descriptive touches. 'Just what Rosy ought to have. I trust in heaven it won't be broken!'

'One must hire servants who will not break things,' said Lydgate. (Certainly, this was reasoning with an imperfect vision of sequences. But at that period there was no sort of reasoning which was not more or less sanctioned by men of science.)

Of course it was unnecessary to defer the mention of anything to mamma, who did not readily take views that were not cheerful, and being a happy wife herself, had hardly any feeling but pride in her daughter's marriage. But Rosamond had good reasons for suggesting to Lydgate that papa should be appealed to in writing. She prepared for the arrival of the letter by walking with her papa to the warehouse the next morning, and telling him on the way that Mr Lydgate wished to be married soon.

'Nonsense, my dear,' said Mr Vincy. 'What has he got to marry on? You'd much better give up the engagement. I've told you so pretty plainly before this. What have you had such an education for, if you are to go and marry a poor man? It's a cruel thing for a father to see.'

'Mr Lydgate is not poor, papa. He bought Mr Peacock's practice, which, they say, is worth eight or nine hundred a-year.'

'Stuff and nonsense! What's buying a practice? He might as well buy next year's swallows. It'll all slip through his fingers.'

'On the contrary, papa, he will increase the practice. See how he has been called in by the Chettams and Casaubons.'

'I hope he knows I shan't give anything – with this disappointment about Fred, and Parliament going to be dissolved, and machine-breaking everywhere, and an election coming on – '

'Dear papa! what can that have to do with my marriage?'

'A pretty deal to do with it! We may all be ruined for what I know – the country's in that state! Some say it's the end of the world, and be hanged if I don't think it looks like it. Anyhow, it's not a time for me to be drawing money out of my business, and I should wish Lydgate to know that.'

'I am sure he expects nothing, papa. And he has such very high connections: he is sure to rise in one way or another. He is engaged in making scientific discoveries.'

Mr Vincy was silent.

'I cannot give up my only prospect of happiness, papa. Mr Lydgate is a gentleman. I could never love any one who was not a perfect gentleman. You would not like me to go into a consumption, as Arabella Hawley did. And you know that I never change my mind.'

Again papa was silent.

'Promise me, papa, that you will consent to what we wish. We shall never give each other up; and you know that you have always objected to long courtships and late marriages.'

There was a little more urgency of this kind, till Mr Vincy said, 'Well, well, child, he must write to me first before I can answer him,' – and Rosamond was certain that she had gained her point.

Mr Vincy's answer consisted chiefly in a demand that Lydgate should insure his life – a demand immediately conceded. This was a delightfully reassuring idea supposing that Lydgate died, but in the meantime not a self-supporting idea. However, it seemed to make everything comfortable about Rosamond's marriage; and the necessary purchases went on with

much spirit. Not without prudential considerations, however. A bride
(who is going to visit at a baronet's) must have a few first-rate pocket
handkerchiefs; but beyond the absolutely necessary half-dozen, Rosamond contented herself without the very highest style of embroidery and
Valenciennes. Lydgate also, finding that his sum of eight hundred pounds
had been considerably reduced since he had come to Middlemarch,
restrained his inclination for some plate of an old pattern which was
shown to him when he went into Kibble's establishment at Brassing to
buy forks and spoons. He was too proud to act as if he presupposed that
Mr Vincy would advance money to provide furniture; and though, since it
would not be necessary to pay for everything at once, some bills would be
left standing over, he did not waste time in conjecturing how much his
father-in-law would give in the form of dowry, to make payment easy. He
was not going to do anything extravagant, but the requisite things must
be bought, and it would be bad economy to buy them of a poor quality.
All these matters were by the by. Lydgate foresaw that science and his
profession were the objects he should alone pursue enthusiastically; but
he could not imagine himself pursuing them in such a home as Wrench
had – the doors all open, the oil-cloth worn, the children in soiled pinafores, and lunch lingering in the form of bones, black-handled knives, and
willow-pattern. But Wrench had a wretched lymphatic wife who made a
mummy of herself indoors in a large shawl; and he must have altogether
begun with an ill-chosen domestic apparatus.

Rosamond, however, was on her side much occupied with conjectures,
though her quick imitative perception warned her against betraying them
too crudely.

'I shall like so much to know your family,' she said one day, when the
wedding-journey was being discussed. 'We might perhaps take a direction that would allow us to see them as we returned. Which of your uncles
do you like best?'

'Oh, – my uncle Godwin, I think. He is a good-natured old fellow.'

'You were constantly at his house at Quallingham, when you were a
boy, were you not? I should so like to see the old spot and everything you
were used to. Does he know you are going to be married?'

'No,' said Lydgate, carelessly, turning in his chair and rubbing his
hair up.

'Do send him word of it, you naughty undutiful nephew. He will perhaps ask you to take me to Quallingham; and then you could show me
about the grounds, and I could imagine you there when you were a boy.
Remember, you see me in my home, just as it has been since I was a child.
It is not fair that I should be so ignorant of yours. But perhaps you would
be a little ashamed of me. I forgot that.'

Lydgate smiled at her tenderly, and really accepted the suggestion
that the proud pleasure of showing so charming a bride was worth some

trouble. And now he came to think of it, he would like to see the old spots with Rosamond.

'I will write to him, then. But my cousins are bores.'

It seemed magnificent to Rosamond to be able to speak so slightingly of a baronet's family, and she felt much contentment in the prospect of being able to estimate them contemptuously on her own account.

But mamma was near spoiling all, a day or two later, by saying,

'I hope your uncle Sir Godwin will not look down on Rosy, Mr Lydgate. I should think he would do something handsome. A thousand or two can be nothing to a baronet.'

'Mamma!' said Rosamond, blushing deeply; and Lydgate pitied her so much that he remained silent and went to the other end of the room to examine a print curiously, as if he had been absent-minded. Mamma had a little filial lecture afterwards, and was docile as usual. But Rosamond reflected that if any of those high-bred cousins who were bores, should be induced to visit Middlemarch, they would see many things in her own family which might shock them. Hence it seemed desirable that Lydgate should by-and-by get some first-rate position elsewhere than in Middlemarch; and this could hardly be difficult in the case of a man who had a titled uncle and could make discoveries. Lydgate, you perceive, had talked fervidly to Rosamond of his hopes as to the highest uses of his life, and had found it delightful to be listened to by a creature who would bring him the sweet furtherance of satisfying affection – beauty – repose – such help as our thoughts get from the summer sky and the flower-fringed meadows.

Lydgate relied much on the psychological difference between what for the sake of variety I will call goose and gander: especially on the innate submissiveness of the goose as beautifully corresponding to the strength of the gander.

♋ THIRTY-SEVEN ♋

Thrice happy she that is so well assured
Unto herself, and settled so in heart,
That neither will for better be allured
Ne fears to worse with any chance to start,
But like a steddy ship doth strongly part
The raging waves, and keeps her course aright:
Ne aught for tempest doth from it depart,
Ne aught for fairer weather's false delight.
Such self-assurance need not fear the spight
Of grudging foes; ne favour seek of friends;
But in the stay of her own stedfast might
Neither to one herself nor other bends.
　　Most happy she that most assured doth rest,
　　But he most happy who such one loves best.
                                    SPENSER

THE DOUBT HINTED BY MR VINCY WHETHER it were only the general election or the end of the world that was coming on, now that George the Fourth was dead, Parliament dissolved, Wellington and Peel generally depreciated and the new King apologetic, was a feeble type of the uncertainties in provincial opinion at that time. With the glow-worm lights of country places, how could men see which were their own thoughts in the confusion of a Tory Ministry passing Liberal measures, of Tory nobles and electors being anxious to return Liberals rather than friends of the recreant Ministers, and of outcries for remedies which seemed to have a mysteriously remote bearing on private interest and were made suspicious by the advocacy of disagreeable neighbours? Buyers of the Middlemarch newspapers found themselves in an anomalous position: during the agitation on the Catholic Question many had given up the *Pioneer* – which had a motto from Charles James Fox and was in the van of progress – because it had taken Peel's side about the Papists, and had thus blotted its Liberalism with a toleration of Jesuitry and Baal; but they were ill-satisfied with the *Trumpet*, which – since its blasts against Rome, and in the general flaccidity of the public mind (nobody knowing who would support whom) – had become feeble in its blowing.

It was a time, according to a noticeable article in the *Pioneer*, when the crying needs of the country might well counteract a reluctance to public action on the part of men whose minds had from long experience acquired breadth as well as concentration, decision of judgment as well as tolerance, dispassionateness as well as energy – in fact, all those qualities which in the melancholy experience of mankind have been the least disposed to share lodgings.

Mr Hackbutt, whose fluent speech was at that time floating more widely than usual, and leaving much uncertainty as to its ultimate channel, was heard to say in Mr Hawley's office that the article in question 'emanated' from Brooke of Tipton, and that Brooke had secretly bought the *Pioneer* some months ago.

'That means mischief, eh?' said Mr Hawley. 'He's got the freak of being a popular man now, after dangling about like a stray tortoise. So much the worse for him. I've had my eye on him for some time. He shall be prettily pumped upon. He's a damned bad landlord. What business has an old county man to come currying favour with a low set of dark-blue freemen? As to his paper, I only hope he may do the writing himself. It would be worth our paying for.'

'I understand he has got a very brilliant young fellow to edit it, who can write the highest style of leading article, quite equal to anything in the London papers. And he means to take very high ground on Reform.'

'Let Brooke reform his rent-roll. He's a cursed old screw, and the buildings all over his estate are going to rack. I suppose this young fellow is some loose fish from London.'

'His name is Ladislaw. He is said to be of foreign extraction.'

'I know the sort,' said Mr Hawley; 'some emissary. He'll begin with flourishing about the Rights of Man and end with murdering a wench. That's the style.'

'You must concede that there are abuses, Hawley,' said Mr Hackbutt, foreseeing some political disagreement with his family lawyer. 'I myself should never favour immoderate views – in fact I take my stand with Huskisson – but I cannot blind myself to the consideration that the non-representation of large towns – '

'Large towns be damned!' said Mr Hawley, impatient of exposition. 'I know a little too much about Middlemarch elections. Let 'em quash every pocket borough to-morrow, and bring in every mushroom town in the kingdom – they'll only increase the expense of getting into Parliament. I go upon facts.'

Mr Hawley's disgust at the notion of the *Pioneer* being edited by an emissary, and of Brooke becoming actively political – as if a tortoise of desultory pursuits should protrude its small head ambitiously and become rampant – was hardly equal to the annoyance felt by some members of Mr Brooke's own family. The result had oozed forth gradually, like the discovery that your neighbour has set up an unpleasant kind of manufacture which will be permanently under your nostrils without legal remedy. The *Pioneer* had been secretly bought even before Will Ladislaw's arrival, the expected opportunity having offered itself in the readiness of the proprietor to part with valuable property which did not pay; and in the interval since Mr Brooke had written his invitation, those germinal ideas of making his mind tell upon the world at large which had been present in him from his younger years, but had hitherto lain in some obstruction, had been sprouting under cover.

The development was much furthered by a delight in his guest which proved greater even than he had anticipated. For it seemed Will was not only at home in all those artistic and literary subjects which Mr Brooke had gone into at one time, but that he was strikingly ready at seizing the points of the political situation, and dealing with them in that large spirit which, aided by adequate memory, lends itself to quotation and general effectiveness of treatment.

'He seems to me a kind of Shelley, you know,' Mr Brooke took an opportunity of saying, for the gratification of Mr Casaubon. 'I don't mean as to anything objectionable – laxities or atheism, or anything of that kind, you know – Ladislaw's sentiments in every way I am sure are good – indeed, we were talking a great deal together last night. But he has the same sort of enthusiasm for liberty, freedom, emancipation – a fine thing under guidance – under guidance, you know. I think I shall be able to put him on the right tack; and I am the more pleased because he is a relation of yours, Casaubon.'

If the right tack implied anything more precise than the rest of Mr Brooke's speech, Mr Casaubon silently hoped that it referred to some occupation at a great distance from Lowick. He had disliked Will while he helped him, but he had begun to dislike him still more now that Will had declined his help. That is the way with us when we have any uneasy jealousy in our disposition: if our talents are chiefly of the burrowing kind, our honey-sipping cousin (whom we have grave reasons for objecting to) is likely to have a secret contempt for us, and any one who admires him passes an oblique criticism on ourselves. Having the scruples of rectitude in our souls, we are above the meanness of injuring him – rather we meet all his claims on us by active benefits; and the drawing of cheques for him, being a superiority which he must recognize, gives our bitterness a milder infusion. Now Mr Casaubon had been deprived of that superiority (as anything more than a remembrance) in a sudden, capricious manner. His antipathy to Will did not spring from the common jealousy of a winter-worn husband: it was something deeper, bred by his lifelong claims and discontents; but Dorothea, now that she was present – Dorothea, as a young wife who herself had shown an offensive capability of criticism, necessarily gave concentration to the uneasiness which had before been vague.

Will Ladislaw on his side felt that his dislike was flourishing at the expense of his gratitude; and spent much inward discourse in justifying the dislike. Casaubon hated him – he knew that very well; on his first entrance he could discern a bitterness in the mouth and a venom in the glance which would almost justify declaring war in spite òf past benefits. He was much obliged to Casaubon in the past, but really the act of marrying this wife was a set-off against the obligation. It was a question whether gratitude which refers to what is done for one's self ought not to give way to indignation at what is done against another. And Casaubon had done a wrong to Dorothea in marrying her. A man was bound to know himself better than that, and if he chose to grow grey crunching bones in a cavern, he had no business to be luring a girl into his companionship. 'It is the most horrible of virgin sacrifices,' said Will; and he painted to himself what were Dorothea's inward sorrows as if he had been writing a choric wail. But he would never lose sight of her: he would watch over her – if he gave up everything else in life he would watch over her, and she should know that she had one slave in the world. Will had – to use Sir Thomas Browne's phrase – a 'passionate prodigality' of statement both to himself and others. The simple truth was that nothing then invited him so strongly as the presence of Dorothea.

Invitations of the formal kind had been wanting, however, for Will had never been asked to go to Lowick. Mr Brooke, indeed, confident of doing everything agreeable which Casaubon, poor fellow, was too much absorbed to think of, had arranged to bring Ladislaw to Lowick several times (not neglecting meanwhile to introduce him elsewhere on every opportunity as 'a young relative of Casaubon's'). And though Will had not seen Dorothea alone, their interviews had been enough to restore her former sense of young companionship with one who was cleverer than herself, yet seemed ready to be swayed by her. Poor Dorothea before her marriage had never found much room in other minds for what she cared most to say; and she had not, as we know, enjoyed her husband's superior instruction so much as she had expected. If she spoke with any keenness of interest to Mr Casaubon, he heard her with an air of patience as if she had given a quotation from the Delectus familiar to him from his tender years, and sometimes mentioned curtly what ancient sects or personages had held similar ideas, as if there were too much of that sort in stock already; at other times he would inform her that she was mistaken, and reassert what her remark had questioned.

But Will Ladislaw always seemed to see more in what she said than she herself saw. Dorothea had little vanity, but she had the ardent woman's need to rule beneficently by making the joy of another soul. Hence the mere chance of seeing Will occasionally was like a lunette opened in the wall of her prison, giving her a glimpse of the sunny air; and this pleasure began to nullify her original alarm at what her husband might think about the introduction of Will as her uncle's guest. On this subject Mr Casaubon had remained dumb.

But Will wanted to talk with Dorothea alone, and was impatient of slow circumstances. However slight the terrestrial intercourse between Dante and Beatrice or Petrarch and Laura, time changes the proportion of things, and in later days it is preferable to have fewer sonnets and more conversation. Necessity excused stratagem, but stratagem was limited by the dread of offending Dorothea. He found out at last that he wanted to take a particular sketch at Lowick; and one morning when Mr Brooke had to drive along the Lowick road on his way to the county town, Will asked to be set down with his sketch-book and camp-stool at Lowick, and without announcing himself at the Manor settled himself to sketch in a position where he must see Dorothea if she came out to walk – and he knew that she usually walked an hour in the morning.

But the stratagem was defeated by the weather. Clouds gathered with treacherous quickness, the rain came down, and Will was obliged to take shelter in the house. He intended, on the strength of relationship, to go into the drawing-room and wait there without being announced; and seeing his old acquaintance the bütler in the hall, he said, 'Don't mention that I am here, Pratt; I will wait till luncheon; I know Mr Casaubon does not like to be disturbed when he is in the library.'

'Master is out, sir; there's only Mrs Casaubon in the library. I'd better tell her you're here sir,' said Pratt, a red-cheeked man given to lively converse with Tantripp, and often agreeing with her that it must be dull for Madam.

'Oh, very well; this confounded rain has hindered me from sketching,' said Will, feeling so happy that he affected indifference with delightful ease.

In another minute he was in the library, and Dorothea was meeting him with her sweet unconstrained smile.

'Mr Casaubon has gone to the Archdeacon's,' she said, at once. 'I don't know whether he will be at home again long before dinner. He was uncertain how long he should be. Did you want to say anything particular to him?'

'No; I came to sketch, but the rain drove me in. Else I would not have disturbed you yet. I supposed that Mr Casaubon was here and I know he dislikes interruption at this hour.'

'I am indebted to the rain, then. I am so glad to see you.' Dorothea uttered these common words with the simple sincerity of an unhappy child, visited at school.

'I really came for the chance of seeing you alone,' said Will, mysteriously forced to be just as simple as she was. He could not stay to ask himself, why not? 'I wanted to talk about things, as we did in Rome. It always makes a difference when other people are present.'

'Yes,' said Dorothea, in her clear full tone of assent. 'Sit down.' She seated herself on a dark ottoman with the brown books behind her, looking in her plain dress of some thin woollen-white material, without a single ornament on her besides her wedding-ring, as if she were under a vow to be different from all other women; and Will sat down opposite her at two yards' distance, the light falling on his bright curls and delicate but rather petulant profile, with its defiant curves of lip and chin. Each looked at the other as if they had been two flowers which had opened then and there. Dorothea for the moment forgot her husband's mysterious irritation against Will: it seemed fresh water at her thirsty lips to speak without fear to the one person whom she had found receptive; for in looking backward through sadness she exaggerated a past solace.

'I have often thought that I should like to talk to you again,' she said, immediately. 'It seems strange to me how many things I said to you.'

'I remember them all,' said Will, with the unspeakable content in his soul of feeling that he was in the presence of a creature worthy to be perfectly loved. I think his own feelings at that moment were perfect, for we mortals have our divine moments, when love is satisfied in the completeness of the beloved object.

'I have tried to learn a great deal since we were in Rome,' said Dorothea. 'I can read Latin a little, and I am beginning to understand just a little Greek. I can help Mr Casaubon better now. I can find out references for him and save his eyes in many ways. But it is very difficult to be learned; it seems as if people were worn out on the way to great thoughts, and can never enjoy them because they are too tired.'

'If a man has a capacity for great thoughts, he is likely to overtake them before he is decrepit,' said Will, with irrepressible quickness. But through certain sensibilities Dorothea was as quick as he, and seeing her face change, he added, immediately, 'But it is quite true that the best minds have been sometimes overstrained in working out their ideas.'

'You correct me,' said Dorothea. 'I expressed myself ill. I should have said that those who have great thoughts get too much worn in working them out. I used to feel about that, even when I was a little girl; and it always seemed to me that the use I should like to make of my life would be to help some one who did great works, so that his burthen might be lighter.'

Dorothea was led on to this bit of autobiography without any sense of making a revelation. But she had never before said anything to Will which threw so strong a light on her marriage. He did not shrug his shoulders; and for want of that muscular outlet he thought the more irritably of beautiful lips kissing holy skulls and other emptinesses ecclesiastically enshrined. Also he had to take care that his speech should not betray that thought.

'But you may easily carry the help too far,' he said, 'and get over-wrought yourself. You are not too much shut up? You already look paler. It would be better for Mr Casaubon to have a secretary; he could easily get a man who would do half his work for him. It would save him more effectually, and you need only help him in lighter ways.'

'How can you think of that?' said Dorothea, in a tone of earnest remonstrance. 'I should have no happiness if I did not help him in his work.

What could I do? There is no good to be done in Lowick. The only thing I desire is to help him more. And he objects to a secretary: please not to mention that again.'

'Certainly not, now I know your feeling. But I have heard both Mr Brooke and Sir James Chettam express the same wish.'

'Yes,' said Dorothea, 'but they don't understand – they want me to be a great deal on horseback, and have the garden altered and new conservatories, to fill up my days. I thought you could understand that one's mind has other wants,' she added, rather impatiently – 'besides, Mr Casaubon cannot bear to hear of a secretary.'

'My mistake is excusable,' said Will. 'In old days I used to hear Mr Casaubon speak as if he looked forward to having a secretary. Indeed he held out the prospect of that office to me. But I turned out to be – not good enough for it.'

Dorothea was trying to extract out of this an excuse for her husband's evident repulsion, as she said, with a playful smile, 'You were not a steady worker enough.'

'No,' said Will, shaking his head backward somewhat after the manner of a spirited horse. And then, the old irritable demon prompting him to give another good pinch at the moth-wings of poor Mr Casaubon's glory, he went on, 'And I have seen since that Mr Casaubon does not like any one to overlook his work and know thoroughly what he is doing. He is too doubtful – too uncertain of himself. I may not be good for much, but he dislikes me because I disagree with him.'

Will was not without his intentions to be always generous, but our tongues are little triggers which have usually been pulled before general intentions can be brought to bear. And it was too intolerable that Casaubon's dislike of him should not be fairly accounted for to Dorothea. Yet when he had spoken he was rather uneasy as to the effect on her.

But Dorothea was strangely quiet – not immediately indignant as she had been on a like occasion in Rome. And the cause lay deep. She was no longer struggling against the perception of facts, but adjusting herself to their clearest perception; and now when she looked steadily at her husband's failure, still more at his possible consciousness of failure, she seemed to be looking along the one track where duty became tenderness. Will's want of reticence might have been met with more severity, if he had not already been recommended to her mercy by her husband's dislike, which must seem hard to her till she saw better reason for it.

She did not answer at once, but after looking down ruminatingly she said, with some earnestness, 'Mr Casaubon must have overcome his dislike of you so far as his actions were concerned: and that is admirable.'

'Yes; he has shown a sense of justice in family matters. It was an abominable thing that my grandmother should have been disinherited because she made what they called a *mésalliance*, though there was nothing to be said against her husband except that he was a Polish refugee who gave lessons for his bread.'

'I wish I knew all about her!' said Dorothea. 'I wonder how she bore the change from wealth to poverty: I wonder whether she was happy with her husband! Do you know much about them?'

'No: only that my grandfather was a patriot – a bright fellow – could speak many languages – musical – got his bread by teaching all sorts of things. They both died rather early. And I never knew much of my father, beyond what my mother told me; but he inherited the musical talents. I remember his slow walk and his long thin hands; and one day remains with me when he was lying ill, and I was very hungry, and had only a little bit of bread.'

'Ah, what a different life from mine!' said Dorothea, with keen interest, clasping her hands on her lap. 'I have always had too much of everything. But tell me how it was – Mr Casaubon could not have known about you then.'

'No; but my father had made himself known to Mr Casaubon, and that was my last hungry day. My father died soon after, and my mother and I were well taken care of. Mr Casaubon always expressly recognized it as his duty to take care of us because of the harsh injustice which had been shown to his mother's sister. But now I am telling you what is not new to you.'

In his inmost soul Will was conscious of wishing to tell Dorothea what was rather new even in his own construction of things – namely, that Mr Casaubon had never done more than pay a debt towards him. Will was much too good a fellow to be easy under the sense of being ungrateful. And when gratitude has become a matter of reasoning there are many ways of escaping from its bonds.

'No,' answered Dorothea; 'Mr Casaubon has always avoided dwelling on his honourable actions.' She did not feel that her husband's conduct was depreciated; but this notion of what justice had required in his relations with Will Ladislaw took strong hold on her mind. After a moment's pause, she added, 'He had never told me that he supported your mother. Is she still living?'

'No; she died by an accident – a fall – four years ago. It is curious that my mother, too, ran away from her family, but not for the sake of a husband. She never would tell me anything about her family, except that she forsook them to get her own living – went on the stage, in fact. She was a dark-eyed creature, with crisp ringlets, and never seemed to be getting old. You see I come of rebellious blood on both sides,' Will ended, smiling brightly at Dorothea, while she was still looking with serious intentness before her, like a child seeing a drama for the first time.

But her face, too, broke into a smile as she said, 'That is your apology, I suppose, for having yourself been rather rebellious; I mean, to Mr Casaubon's wishes. You must remember that you have not done what he thought best for you. And if he dislikes you – you were speaking of dislike a little while ago – but I should rather say, if he has shown any painful feelings towards you, you must consider how sensitive he has become from the wearing effect of study. Perhaps,' she continued, getting into a pleading tone, 'my uncle has not told you how serious Mr Casaubon's illness was. It would be petty of us who are well and can bear things, to think much of small offences from those who carry a weight of trial.'

'You teach me better,' said Will. 'I will never grumble on that subject again.' There was a gentleness in his tone which came from the unutter-able contentment of perceiving – what Dorothea was hardly conscious of – that she was travelling into the remoteness of pure pity and loyalty towards her husband. Will was ready to adore her pity and loyalty, if she would associate himself with her in manifesting them 'I have really sometimes been a perverse fellow,' he went on, 'but I will never again, if I can help it, do or say what you would disapprove.'

'That is very good of you,' said Dorothea, with another open smile. 'I shall have a little kingdom then, where I shall give laws. But you will soon go away, out of my rule, I imagine. You will soon be tired of staying at the Grange.'

'That is a point I wanted to mention to you – one of the reasons why I wished to speak to you alone. Mr Brooke proposes that I should stay in this neighbourhood. He has bought one of the Middlemarch newspapers, and he wishes me to conduct that, and also to help him in other ways.'

'Would not that be a sacrifice of higher prospects for you?' said Dorothea.

'Perhaps; but I have always been blamed for thinking of prospects, and not settling to anything. And here is something offered to me. If you would not like me to accept it, I will give it up. Otherwise I would rather stay in this part of the country than go away. I belong to nobody anywhere else.'

'I should like you to stay very much,' said Dorothea, at once, as simply and readily as she had spoken at Rome. There was not the shadow of a reason in her mind at the moment why she should not say so.

'Then I will stay,' said Ladislaw, shaking his head backward, rising and going towards the window, as if to see whether the rain had ceased.

But the next moment, Dorothea, according to a habit which was getting continually stronger, began to reflect that her husband felt differently from herself, and she coloured deeply under the double embarrassment of having expressed what might be in opposition to her husband's feeling, and of having to suggest this opposition to Will. His face was not turned towards her, and this made it easier to say –

'But my opinion is of little consequence on such a subject. I think you should be guided by Mr Casaubon. I spoke without thinking of anything else than my own feeling, which has nothing to do with the real question.

But it now occurs to me – perhaps Mr Casaubon might see that the proposal was not wise. Can you not wait now and mention it to him?'

'I can't wait to-day,' said Will, inwardly scared by the possibility that Mr Casaubon would enter. 'The rain is quite over now. I told Mr Brooke not to call for me: I would rather walk the five miles. I shall strike across Halsell Common, and see the gleams on the wet grass. I like that.'

He approached her to shake hands quite hurriedly, longing but not daring to say, 'Don't mention the subject to Mr Casaubon.' No, he dared not, could not say it. To ask her to be less simple and direct would be like breathing on the crystal that you want to see the light through. And there was always the other great dread – of himself becoming dimmed and for ever ray-shorn in her eyes.

'I wish you could have stayed,' said Dorothea, with a touch of mournfulness, as she rose and put out her hand. She also had her thought which she did not like to express: – Will certainly ought to lose no time in consulting Mr Casaubon's wishes, but for her to urge this might seem an undue dictation.

So they only said 'Good-bye', and Will quitted the house, striking across the fields so as not to run any risk of encountering Mr Casaubon's carriage, which, however, did not appear at the gate until four o'clock. That was an unpropitious hour for coming home: it was too early to gain the moral support under *ennui* of dressing his person for dinner, and too late to undress his mind of the day's frivolous ceremony and affairs, so as to be prepared for a good plunge into the serious business of study. On such occasions he usually threw himself into an easy-chair in the library, and allowed Dorothea to read the London papers to him, closing his eyes the while. To-day, however, he declined that relief, observing that he had already had too many public details urged upon him; but he spoke more cheerfully than usual, when Dorothea asked about his fatigue, and added with that air of formal effort which never forsook him even when he spoke without his waistcoat and cravat –

'I have had the gratification of meeting my former acquaintance, Dr Spanning, to-day, and of being praised by one who is himself a worthy recipient of praise. He spoke very handsomely of my late tractate on the Egyptian Mysteries, – using, in fact, terms which it would not become me to repeat.' In uttering the last clause, Mr Casaubon leaned over the elbow of his chair, and swayed his head up and down, apparently as a muscular outlet instead of that recapitulation which would not have been becoming.

'I am very glad you have had that pleasure,' said Dorothea, delighted to see her husband less weary than usual at this hour. 'Before you came I had been regretting that you happened to be out to-day.'

'Why so, my dear?' said Mr Casaubon, throwing himself backward again.

'Because Mr Ladislaw has been here; and he has mentioned a proposal of my uncle's which I should like to know your opinion of.' Her husband she felt was really concerned in this question. Even with her ignorance of the world she had a vague impression that the position offered to Will was out of keeping with his family connections, and certainly Mr Casaubon had a claim to be consulted. He did not speak, but merely bowed.

'Dear uncle, you know, has many projects. It appears that he has bought one of the Middlemarch newspapers, and he has asked Mr Ladislaw to stay in this neighbourhood and conduct the paper for him, besides helping him in other ways.'

Dorothea looked at her husband while she spoke, but he had at first blinked and finally closed his eyes, as if to save them; while his lips became more tense. 'What is your opinion?' she added, rather timidly, after a slight pause.

'Did Mr Ladislaw come on purpose to ask my opinion?' said Mr Casaubon, opening his eyes narrowly with a knife-edge look at Dorothea. She was really uncomfortable on the point he inquired about, but she only became a little more serious, and her eyes did not swerve.

'No,' she answered, immediately, 'he did not say that he came to ask your opinion. But when he mentioned the proposal, he of course expected me to tell you of it.'

Mr Casaubon was silent.

'I feared that you might feel some objection. But certainly a young man with so much talent might be very useful to my uncle – might help him to do good in a better way. And Mr Ladislaw wishes to have some fixed occupation. He has been blamed, he says, for not seeking something of that kind, and he would like to stay in this neighbourhood because no one cares for him elsewhere.'

Dorothea felt that this was a consideration to soften her husband. However, he did not speak, and she presently recurred to Dr Spanning and the Archdeacon's breakfast. But there was no longer sunshine on these subjects.

The next morning, without Dorothea's knowledge, Mr Casaubon dispatched the following letter, beginning 'Dear Mr Ladislaw' (he had always before addressed him as 'Will'): –

Mrs Casaubon informs me that a proposal has been made to you, and (according to an inference by no means stretched) has on your part been in some degree entertained, which involves your residence in this neighbourhood in a capacity which I am justified in saying touches my own position in such a way as renders it not only natural and warrantable in me when that effect is viewed under the influence of legitimate feeling, but incumbent on me when the same effect is considered in the light of my responsibilities, to state at once that your acceptance of the proposal above indicated would be highly offensive to me. That I have some claim to the exercise of a veto here, would not, I believe, be denied by any reasonable person cognizant of the relations between us: relations which, though thrown into the past by your recent procedure, are not thereby annulled in their character of determining antecedents. I will not here make reflections on any person's judgment. It is enough for me to point out to yourself that there are certain social fitnesses and proprieties which should hinder a somewhat near relative of mine from becoming in anywise conspicuous in this vicinity in a status not only much beneath my own, but associated at best with the sciolism of literary or political adventurers. At any rate, the contrary issue must exclude you from further reception at my house. – Yours faithfully,

Edward Casaubon

Meanwhile Dorothea's mind was innocently at work towards the further embitterment of her husband; dwelling, with a sympathy that grew to agitation, on what Will had told her about his parents and grandparents. Any private hours in her day were usually spent in her blue-green boudoir, and she had come to be very fond of its pallid quaintness. Nothing had been outwardly altered there; but while the summer had gradually advanced over the western fields beyond the avenue of elms, the bare room had gathered within it those memories of an inward life which fill the air as with a cloud of good or bad angels, the invisible yet active forms of our spiritual triumphs or our spiritual falls. She had been so used to struggle for and to find resolve in looking along the avenue towards the arch of western light that the vision itself had gained a communicating power. Even the pale stag seemed to have reminding glances and to mean mutely, 'Yes, we know.' And the group of delicately-touched miniatures had made an audience as of beings no longer disturbed about their own earthly lot, but still humanly interested. Especially the mysterious 'Aunt Julia' about whom Dorothea had never found it easy to question her husband.

And now, since her conversation with Will, many fresh images had gathered round that Aunt Julia who was Will's grandmother: the presence of that delicate miniature, so like a living face that she knew, helping to concentrate her feelings. What a wrong, to cut off the girl from the family protection and inheritance only because she had chosen a man who was poor! Dorothea, early troubling her elders with questions about the facts around her, had wrought herself into some independent clearness as to the historical, political reasons why eldest sons had superior rights, and why land should be entailed: those reasons, impressing her with a certain awe, might be weightier than she knew, but here was a question of ties which left them uninfringed. Here was a daughter whose child – even according to the ordinary aping of aristocratic institutions by people who are no more aristocratic than retired grocers, and who have no more land to 'keep together' than a lawn and a paddock – would have a prior claim. Was inheritance a question of liking or of responsibility? All the energy of

Dorothea's nature went on the side of responsibility – the fulfilment of claims founded on our own deeds, such as marriage and parentage.

It was true, she said to herself, that Mr Casaubon had a debt to the Ladislaws – that he had to pay back what the Ladislaws had been wronged of. And now she began to think of her husband's will which had been made at the time of their marriage, leaving the bulk of his property to her, with proviso in case of her having children. That ought to be altered; and no time ought to be lost. This very question which had just arisen about Will Ladislaw's occupation, was the occasion for placing things on a new, right footing. Her husband, she felt sure, according to all his previous conduct, would be ready to take the just view, if she proposed it – she, in whose interest an unfair concentration of the property had been urged. His sense of right had surmounted and would continue to surmount anything that might be called antipathy. She suspected that her uncle's scheme was disapproved by Mr Casaubon, and this made it seem all the more opportune that a fresh understanding should be begun, so that instead of Will's starting penniless and accepting the first function that offered itself, he should find himself in possession of a rightful income which should be paid by her husband during his life, and, by an immediate alteration of the will, should be secured at his death. The vision of all this as what ought to be done seemed to Dorothea like a sudden letting in of daylight, waking her from her previous stupidity and incurious self-absorbed ignorance about her husband's relation to others. Will Ladislaw had refused Mr Casaubon's future aid on a ground that no longer appeared right to her; and Mr Casaubon had never himself seen fully what was the claim upon him. 'But he will!' said Dorothea. 'The great strength of his character lies here. And what are we doing with our money? We make no use of half of our income. My own money buys me nothing but an uneasy conscience.'

There was a peculiar fascination for Dorothea in this division of property intended for herself, and always regarded by her as excessive. She was blind, you see, to many things obvious to others – likely to tread in the wrong places, as Celia had warned her; yet her blindness to whatever did not lie in her own pure purpose carried her safely by the side of precipices where vision would have been perilous with fear.

The thoughts which had gathered vividness in the solitude of her boudoir occupied her incessantly through the day on which Mr Casaubon had sent his letter to Will. Everything seemed hindrance to her till she could find an opportunity of opening her heart to her husband. To his preoccupied mind all subjects were to be approached gently, and she had never since his illness lost from her consciousness the dread of agitating him. But when young ardour is set brooding over the conception of a prompt deed, the deed itself seems to start forth with independent life, mastering ideal obstacles. The day passed in a sombre fashion, not unusual, though Mr Casaubon was perhaps unusually silent; but there were hours of the night which might be counted on as opportunities of conversation; for Dorothea, when aware of her husband's sleeplessness, had established the habit of rising, lighting a candle, and reading him to sleep again. And this night she was from the beginning sleepless, excited by resolves. He slept as usual for a few hours, but she had risen softly and had sat in the darkness for nearly an hour before he said –

'Dorothea, since you are up, will you light a candle?'

'Do you feel ill, dear?' was her first question, as she obeyed him.

'No, not at all; but I shall be obliged, since you are up, if you will read me a few pages of Lowth.'

'May I talk to you a little, instead?' said Dorothea.

'Certainly.'

'I have been thinking about money all day – that I have always had too much, and especially the prospect of too much.'

'These, my dear Dorothea, are providential arrangements.'

'But if one has too much in consequence of others being wronged, it seems to me that the divine voice which tells us to set that wrong right must be obeyed.'

'What, my love, is the bearing of your remark?'

'That you have been too liberal in arrangements for me – I mean, with regard to property; and that makes me unhappy.'

'How so? I have none but comparatively distant connections.'

'I have been led to think about your aunt Julia, and how she was left in poverty only because she married a poor man, an act which was not disgraceful, since he was not unworthy. It was on that ground, I know, that you educated Mr Ladislaw and provided for his mother.'

Dorothea waited a few moments for some answer that would help her onward. None came, and her next words seemed the more forcible to her, falling clear upon the dark silence.

'But surely we should regard his claim as a much greater one, even to the half of that property which I know that you have destined for me. And I think he ought at once to be provided for on that understanding. It is not right that he should be in the dependence of poverty while we are rich. And if there is any objection to the proposal he mentioned, the giving him his true place and his true share would set aside any motive for his accepting it.'

'Mr Ladislaw has probably been speaking to you on this subject?' said Mr Casaubon, with a certain biting quickness not habitual to him.

'Indeed, no!' said Dorothea, earnestly. 'How can you imagine it, since he has so lately declined everything from you? I fear you think too hardly of him, dear. He only told me a little about his parents and grand-parents, and almost all in answer to my questions. You are so good, so just – you have done everything you thought to be right. But it seems to me clear that more than that is right; and I must speak about it, since I am the person who would get what is called benefit by that "more" not being done.'

There was a perceptible pause before Mr Casaubon replied, not quickly as before, but with a still more biting emphasis.

'Dorothea, my love, this is not the first occasion, but it were well that it should be the last, on which you have assumed a judgment on subjects beyond your scope. Into the question how far conduct, especially in the matter of alliances, constitutes a forfeiture of family claims, I do not now enter. Suffice it, that you are not here qualified to discriminate. What I now wish you to understand is, that I accept no revision, still less dictation within that range of affairs which I have deliberated upon as distinctly and properly mine. It is not for you to interfere between me and Mr Ladislaw, and still less to encourage communications from him to you which constitute a criticism on my procedure.'

Poor Dorothea, shrouded in the darkness, was in a tumult of conflicting emotions. Alarm at the possible effect on himself of her husband's strongly-manifested anger, would have checked any expression of her own resentment, even if she had been quite free from doubt and compunction under the consciousness that there might be some justice in his last insinuation. Hearing him breathe quickly after he had spoken, she sat listening, frightened, wretched – with a dumb inward cry for help to bear this nightmare of a life in which every energy was arrested by dread. But nothing else happened, except that they both remained a long while sleepless, without speaking again.

The next day, Mr Casaubon received the following answer from Will Ladislaw: –

Dear Mr Casaubon, – I have given all due consideration to your letter of yesterday, but I am unable to take precisely your view of our mutual position. With the fullest acknowledgment of your generous conduct to me in the past, I must still maintain that an obligation of this kind cannot fairly fetter me as you appear to expect that it should. Granted that a benefactor's wishes may constitute a claim; there must always be a reservation as to the quality of those wishes. They may possibly clash with more imperative considerations. Or a benefactor's veto might impose such a negation on a man's life that the consequent blank might be more cruel than the benefaction was generous. I am merely using strong illustrations. In the present case I am unable to take your view of the bearing which my acceptance of occupation – not enriching certainly, but not dishonourable – will have on your own position, which seems to me too substantial to be affected in that shadowy manner. And though I do not believe that any change in our relations will occur (certainly none has yet occurred) which can nullify the obligations imposed on me by the past, pardon me for not seeing that those obligations should restrain me from using the ordinary freedom of living where I choose, and maintaining myself by any lawful occupation I may choose. Regretting that there exists this difference between us as to a relation in which the conferring of benefits has been entirely on your side – I remain, yours with persistent obligation,

Will Ladislaw

Poor Mr Casaubon felt (and must not we, being impartial, feel with him a little?) that no man had juster cause for disgust and suspicion than he. Young Ladislaw, he was sure, meant to defy and annoy him, meant to win Dorothea's confidence and sow her mind with disrespect, and perhaps aversion, towards her husband. Some motive beneath the surface had been needed to account for Will's sudden change of course in rejecting Mr Casaubon's aid and quitting his travels; and this defiant determination to fix himself in the neighbourhood by taking up something so much at variance with his former choice as Mr Brooke's Middlemarch projects, revealed clearly enough that the undeclared motive had relation to Dorothea. Not for one moment did Mr Casaubon suspect Dorothea of any doubleness: he had no suspicions of her, but he had (what was little less uncomfortable) the positive knowledge that her tendency to form opinions about her husband's conduct was accompanied with a disposition to regard Will Ladislaw favourably and be influenced by what he said. His own proud reticence had prevented him from ever being undeceived in the supposition that Dorothea had originally asked her uncle to invite Will to his house.

And now, on receiving Will's letter, Mr Casaubon had to consider his duty. It would never have been easy to call his action anything else than duty; but in this case, contending motives thrust him back into negations.

Should he apply directly to Mr Brooke, and demand of that troublesome gentleman to revoke his proposal? Or should he consult Sir James Chettam, and get him to concur in remonstrance against a step which touched the whole family? In either case Mr Casaubon was aware that failure was just as probable as success. It was impossible for him to mention Dorothea's name in the matter, and without some alarming urgency Mr Brooke was as likely as not, after meeting all representations with apparent assent, to wind up by saying, 'Never fear, Casaubon! Depend upon it, young Ladislaw will do you credit. Depend upon it, I have put my finger on the right thing.' And Mr Casaubon shrank nervously from communicating on the subject with Sir James Chettam, between whom and himself there had never been cordiality, and who would immediately think of Dorothea without any mention of her.

Poor Mr Casaubon was distrustful of everybody's feeling towards him, especially as a husband. To let any one suppose that he was jealous would be to admit their (suspected) view of his disadvantages: to let them know that he did not find marriage particularly blissful would imply his conversion to their (probably) earlier disapproval. It would be as bad as letting Carp, and Brasenose generally, know how backward he was in organizing the matter for his 'Key to all Mythologies.' All through his life Mr Casaubon had been trying not to admit even to himself the inward sores of self-doubt and jealousy. And on the most delicate of all personal subjects, the habit of proud suspicious reticence told doubly.

Thus Mr Casaubon remained proudly, bitterly silent. But he had forbidden Will to come to Lowick Manor, and he was mentally preparing other means of frustration.

◁ THIRTY-EIGHT �763

C'est beaucoup que le jugement des hommes sur les actions
humaines; tôt ou tard il devient efficace.

GUIZOT

SIR JAMES CHETTAM COULD NOT LOOK with any satisfaction on Mr Brooke's new courses; but it was easier to object than to hinder. Sir James accounted for his having come in alone one day to lunch with the Cadwalladers by saying –

'I can't talk to you as I want, before Celia: it might hurt her. Indeed, it would not be right.'

'I know what you mean – the *Pioneer* at the Grange!' darted in Mrs Cadwallader, almost before the word was off her friend's tongue. 'It is frightful – this taking to buying whistles and blowing them in everybody's hearing. Lying in bed all day and playing at dominoes, like poor Lord Plessy, would be more private and bearable.'

'I see they are beginning to attack our friend Brooke in the *Trumpet*,' said the Rector, lounging back and smiling easily, as he would have done if he had been attacked himself. 'There are tremendous sarcasms against a Landlord not a hundred miles from Middlemarch, who receives his own rents, and makes no returns.'

'I do wish Brooke would leave that off,' said Sir James, with his little frown of annoyance.

'Is he really going to be put in nomination, though?' said Mr Cadwallader. 'I saw Farebrother yesterday – he's Whiggish himself, hoists Brougham and Useful Knowledge, that's the worst I know of him; – and he says that Brooke is getting up a pretty strong party. Bulstrode, the banker, is his foremost man. But he thinks Brooke would come off badly at a nomination.'

'Exactly,' said Sir James, with earnestness. 'I have been inquiring into the thing, for I've never known anything about Middlemarch politics before – the county being my business. What Brooke trusts to, is that they are going to turn out Oliver because he is a Peelite. But Hawley tells me that if they send up a Whig at all it is sure to be Bagster, one of those candidates who come from heaven knows where, but dead against Ministers, and an experienced Parliamentary man. Hawley's rather rough: he forgot that he was speaking to me. He said if Brooke wanted a pelting, he could get it cheaper than by going to the hustings.'

'I warned you all of it,' said Mrs Cadwallader, waving her hands outward. 'I said to Humphrey long ago, Mr Brooke is going to make a splash in the mud. And now he has done it.'

'Well, he might have taken it into his head to marry,' said the Rector. 'That would have been a graver mess than a little flirtation with politics.'

'He may do that afterwards,' said Mrs Cadwallader – 'when he has come out on the other side of the mud with an ague.'

'What I care for most is his own dignity,' said Sir James. 'Of course I care the more because of the family. But he's getting on in life now, and I don't like to think of his exposing himself. They will be raking up everything against him.'

'I suppose it's no use trying any persuasion,' said the Rector. 'There's such an odd mixture of obstinacy and changeableness in Brooke. Have you tried him on the subject?'

'Well, no,' said Sir James; 'I feel a delicacy in appearing to dictate. But I have been talking to this young Ladislaw that Brooke is making a factotum of. Ladislaw seems clever enough for anything. I thought it as well to hear what he had to say; and he is against Brooke's standing this time. I think he'll turn him round: I think the nomination may be staved off.'

'I know,' said Mrs Cadwallader, nodding. 'The independent member hasn't got his speeches well enough by heart.'

'But this Ladislaw – there again is a vexatious business,' said Sir James. 'We have had him two or three times to dine at the Hall (you have met him, by the by) as Brooke's guest and a relation of Casaubon's, thinking he was only on a flying visit. And now I find he's in everybody's mouth in Middlemarch as the editor of the *Pioneer*. There are stories going about him as a quill-driving alien, a foreign emissary, and what not.'

'Casaubon won't like that,' said the Rector.

'There *is* some foreign blood in Ladislaw,' returned Sir James. 'I hope he won't go into extreme opinions and carry Brooke on.'

'Oh, he's a dangerous young sprig, that Mr Ladislaw,' said Mrs Cadwallader, 'with his opera songs and his ready tongue. A sort of Byronic hero – an amorous conspirator, it strikes me. And Thomas Aquinas is not fond of him. I could see that, the day the picture was brought.'

'I don't like to begin on the subject with Casaubon,' said Sir James. 'He has more right to interfere than I. But it's a disagreeable affair all round.

What a character for anybody with decent connections to show himself in! – one of those newspaper fellows! You have only to look at Keck, who manages the *Trumpet*. I saw him the other day with Hawley. His writing is sound enough, I believe, but he's such a low fellow, that I wished he had been on the wrong side.'

'What can you expect with these peddling Middlemarch papers?' said the Rector. 'I don't suppose you could get a high style of man anywhere to be writing up interests he doesn't really care about, and for pay that hardly keeps him in at elbows.'

'Exactly: that makes it so annoying that Brooke should have put a man who has a sort of connection with the family in a position of that kind. For my part, I think Ladislaw is rather a fool for accepting.'

'It is Aquinas's fault,' said Mrs Cadwallader. 'Why didn't he use his interest to get Ladislaw made an *attaché* or sent to India? That is how families get rid of troublesome sprigs.'

'There is no knowing to what lengths the mischief may go,' said Sir James, anxiously. 'But if Casaubon says nothing, what can I do?'

'Oh, my dear Sir James,' said the Rector, 'don't let us make too much of all this. It is likely enough to end in mere smoke. After a month or two Brooke and this Master Ladislaw will get tired of each other; Ladislaw will take wing; Brooke will sell the *Pioneer*, and everything will settle down again as usual.'

'There is one good chance – that he will not like to feel his money oozing away,' said Mrs Cadwallader. 'If I knew the items of election expenses I could scare him. It's no use plying him with wide words like Expenditure: I wouldn't talk of phlebotomy, I would empty a pot of leeches upon him. What we good stingy people don't like, is having our sixpences sucked away from us.'

'And he will not like having things raked up against him,' said Sir James. 'There is the management of his estate. They have begun upon that already. And it really is painful for me to see. It is a nuisance under one's very nose. I do think one is bound to do the best for one's land and tenants, especially in these hard times.'

'Perhaps the *Trumpet* may rouse him to make a change, and some good may come of it all,' said the Rector. 'I know I should be glad. I should hear less grumbling when my tithe is paid. I don't know what I should do if there were not a modus in Tipton.'

'I want him to have a proper man to look after things – I want him to take on Garth again,' said Sir James. 'He got rid of Garth twelve years ago, and everything has been going wrong since. I think of getting Garth to manage for me – he has made such a capital plan for my buildings; and Lovegood is hardly up to the mark. But Garth would not undertake the Tipton estate again unless Brooke left it entirely to him.'

'In the right of it too,' said the Rector. 'Garth is an independent fellow: an original, simple-minded fellow. One day, when he was doing some valuation for me, he told me point-blank that clergymen seldom understood anything about business, and did mischief when they meddled; but he said it as quietly and respectfully as if he had been talking to me about sailors. He would make a different parish of Tipton, if Brooke would let him manage. I wish, by the help of the *Trumpet*, you could bring that round.'

'If Dorothea had kept near her uncle, there would have been some chance,' said Sir James. 'She might have got some power over him in time, and she was always uneasy about the estate. She had wonderfully good notions about such things. But now Casaubon takes her up entirely. Celia complains a good deal. We can hardly get her to dine with us since he had that fit.' Sir James ended with a look of pitying disgust, and Mrs Cadwallader shrugged her shoulders as much as to say that *she* was not likely to see anything new in that direction.

'Poor Casaubon!' the Rector said. 'That was a nasty attack. I thought he looked shattered the other day at the Archdeacon's.'

'In point of fact,' resumed Sir James, not choosing to dwell on 'fits', 'Brooke doesn't mean badly by his tenants or any one else, but he has got that way of paring and clipping at expenses.'

'Come, that's a blessing,' said Mrs Cadwallader. 'That helps him to find himself in the morning. He may not know his own opinions, but he does know his own pocket.'

'I don't believe a man is in pocket by stinginess on his land,' said Sir James.

'Oh, stinginess may be abused like other virtues: it will not do to keep one's own pigs lean,' said Mrs Cadwallader, who had risen to look out of the window. 'But talk of an independent politician and he will appear.'

'What, Brooke?' said her husband.

'Yes. Now, you ply him with the *Trumpet*, Humphrey; and I will put the leeches on him. What will you do, Sir James?'

'The fact is, I don't like to begin about it with Brooke, in our mutual position; the whole thing is so unpleasant. I do wish people would behave like gentlemen,' said the good baronet, feeling that this was a simple and comprehensive programme for social well-being.

'Here you all are, eh?' said Mr Brooke, shuffling round and shaking hands. 'I was going up to the Hall by-and-by, Chettam. But it's pleasant to find everybody, you know. Well, what do you think of things? – going on a little fast! It was true enough, what Lafitte said – "Since yesterday, a century has passed away": – they're in the next century, you know, on the other side of the water. Going on faster than we are.'

'Why, yes,' said the Rector, taking up the newspaper. 'Here is the *Trumpet* accusing you of lagging behind – did you see?'

'Eh? no,' said Mr Brooke, dropping his gloves into his hat and hastily adjusting his eye-glass. But Mr Cadwallader kept the paper in his hand, saying, with a smile in his eyes –

'Look here! all this is about a landlord not a hundred miles from Middlemarch, who receives his own rents. They say he is the most retrogressive man in the county. I think you must have taught them that word in the *Pioneer*.

'Oh, that is Keck – an illiterate fellow, you know. Retrogressive, now! Come, that's capital. He thinks it means destructive: they want to make me out a destructive, you know,' said Mr Brooke, with that cheerfulness which is usually sustained by an adversary's ignorance.

'I think he knows the meaning of the word. Here is a sharp stroke or two.

If we had to describe a man who is retrogressive in the most evil sense of the word – we should say, he is one who would dub himself a reformer of our constitution, while every interest for which he is immediately responsible is going to decay: a philanthropist who cannot bear one rogue to be hanged, but does not mind five honest tenants being half-starved: a man who shrieks at corruption, and keeps his farms at rack-rent: who roars himself red at rotten boroughs, and does not mind if every field on his farms has a rotten gate: a man very open-hearted to Leeds and Manchester, no doubt; he would give any number of representatives who will pay for their seats out of their own pockets: what he objects to giving, is a little return on rent-days to help a tenant to buy stock, or an outlay on repairs to keep the weather out at a tenant's barn-door or make his house look a little less like an Irish cottier's. But we all know the wag's definition of a philanthropist: a man whose charity increases directly as the square of the distance.

And so on. All the rest is to show what sort of legislator a philanthropist is likely to make,' ended the Rector, throwing down the paper, and clasping his hands at the back of his head, while he looked at Mr Brooke with an air of amused neutrality.

'Come, that's rather good you know,' said Mr Brooke, taking up the paper and trying to bear the attack as easily as his neighbour did, but colouring and smiling rather nervously; 'that about roaring himself red at rotten boroughs – I never made a speech about rotten boroughs in my life. And as to roaring myself red and that kind of thing – these men never understand what is good satire. Satire, you know, should be true up to a certain point. I recollect they said that in *The Edinburgh* somewhere – it must be true up to a certain point.'

'Well, that is really a hit about the gates,' said Sir James, anxious to tread carefully. 'Dagley complained to me the other day that he hadn't got a decent gate on his farm. Garth has invented a new pattern of gate – I wish you would try it. One ought to use some of one's timber in that way.'

'You go in for fancy farming, you know, Chettam,' said Mr Brooke, appearing to glance over the columns of the *Trumpet*. 'That's your hobby, and you don't mind the expense.'

'I thought the most expensive hobby in the world was standing for Parliament,' said Mrs Cadwallader. 'They said the last unsuccessful candidate at Middlemarch – Giles, wasn't his name? – spent ten thousand pounds and failed because he did not bribe enough. What a bitter reflection for a man!'

'Somebody was saying,' said the Rector, laughingly, 'that East Retford was nothing to Middlemarch, for bribery.'

'Nothing of the kind,' said Mr Brooke. 'The Tories bribe, you know: Hawley and his set bribe with treating, hot codlings, and that sort of thing; and they bring the voters drunk to the poll. But they are not going to have it their own way in future – not in future, you know. Middlemarch is a little backward, I admit – the freemen are a little backward. But we shall educate them – we shall bring them on, you know. The best people there are on our side.'

'Hawley says you have men on your side who will do you harm,' remarked Sir James. 'He says Bulstrode the banker will do you harm.'

'And that if you got pelted,' interposed Mrs Cadwallader, 'half the rotten eggs would mean hatred of your committee-man. Good heavens! Think what it must be to be pelted for wrong opinions. And I seem to remember a story of a man they pretended to chair and let him fall into a dust-heap on purpose!'

'Pelting is nothing to their finding holes in one's coat,' said the Rector. 'I confess that's what I should be afraid of, if we parsons had to stand at the hustings for preferment. I should be afraid of their reckoning up all my fishing days. Upon my word, I think the truth is the hardest missile one can be pelted with.'

'The fact is,' said Sir James, 'if a man goes into public life he must be prepared for the consequences. He must make himself proof against calumny.'

'My dear Chettam, that is all very fine, you know,' said Mr Brooke. 'But how will you make yourself proof against calumny? You should read history – look at ostracism, persecution, martyrdom, and that kind of thing. They always happen to the best men, you know. But what is that in Horace? – *fiat justitia, ruat* . . . something or other.'

'Exactly,' said Sir James, with a little more heat than usual. 'What I mean by being proof against calumny is being able to point to the fact as a contradiction.'

'And it is not martyrdom to pay bills that one has run into one's self,' said Mrs Cadwallader.

But it was Sir James's evident annoyance that most stirred Mr Brooke. 'Well, you know, Chettam,' he said, rising, taking up his hat and leaning on his stick, 'you and I have a different system. You are all for outlay with your farms. I don't want to make out that my system is good under all circumstances – under all circumstances, you know.'

'There ought to be a new valuation made from time to time,' said Sir James. 'Returns are very well occasionally, but I like a fair valuation. What do you say, Cadwallader?'

'I agree with you. If I were Brooke, I would choke the *Trumpet* at once by getting Garth to make a new valuation of the farms, and giving him *carte blanche* about gates and repairs: that's my view of the political situation,' said the Rector, broadening himself by sticking his thumbs in his arm-holes, and laughing towards Mr Brooke.

'That's a showy sort of thing to do, you know,' said Mr Brooke. 'But I should like you to tell me of another landlord who has distressed his tenants for arrears as little as I have. I let the old tenants stay on. I'm uncommonly easy, let me tell you – uncommonly easy. I have my own ideas, and I take my stand on them, you know. A man who does that is always charged with eccentricity, inconsistency, and that kind of thing. When I change my line of action, I shall follow my own ideas.'

After that, Mr Brooke remembered that there was a packet which he had omitted to send off from the Grange, and he bade everybody hurriedly good-bye.

'I didn't want to take a liberty with Brooke,' said Sir James; 'I see he is nettled. But as to what he says about old tenants, in point of fact no new tenant would take the farms on the present terms.'

'I have a notion that he will be brought round in time,' said the Rector. 'But you were pulling one way, Elinor, and we were pulling another. You wanted to frighten him away from expense, and we want to frighten him into it. Better let him try to be popular and see that his character as a landlord stands in his way. I don't think it signifies two straws about the *Pioneer*, or Ladislaw, or Brooke's speechifying to the Middlemarchers. But it does signify about the parishioners in Tipton being comfortable.'

'Excuse me, it is you two who are on the wrong tack,' said Mrs Cadwallader. 'You should have proved to him that he loses money by bad management, and then we all should have pulled together. If you put him a-horseback on politics, I warn you of the consequences. It was all very well to ride on sticks at home and call them ideas.'

⌬ THIRTY-NINE ⌬

If, as I have, you also doe,
　　Vertue attired in woman see,
And dare love that, and say so too,
　　And forget the He and She;

And if this love, though placed so,
　　From prophane men you hide,
Which will no faith on this bestow,
　　Or, if they doe, deride:

Then you have done a braver thing
　　Than all the Worthies did,
And a braver thence will spring,
　　Which is, to keep that hid.

DR DONNE

SIR JAMES CHETTAM'S MIND WAS NOT fruitful in devices, but his growing anxiety to 'act on Brooke', once brought close to his constant belief in Dorothea's capacity for influence, became formative and issued in a little plan; namely, to plead Celia's indisposition as a reason for fetching Dorothea by herself to the Hall, and to leave her at the Grange with the carriage on the way, after making her fully aware of the situation concerning the management of the estate.

In this way it happened that one day near four o'clock, when Mr Brooke and Ladislaw were seated in the library, the door opened and Mrs Casaubon was announced.

Will, the moment before, had been low in the depths of boredom, and, obliged to help Mr Brooke in arranging 'documents' about hanging sheep-stealers, was exemplifying the power our minds have of riding several horses at once by inwardly arranging measures towards getting a lodging for himself in Middlemarch and cutting short his constant residence at the Grange; while there flitted through all these steadier images a tickling vision of a sheep-stealing epic written with Homeric particularity. When Mrs Casaubon was announced he started up as from an electric shock, and felt a tingling at his finger-ends. Any one observing him would have seen a change in his complexion, in the adjustment of his facial muscles, in the vividness of his glance, which might have made them imagine that

301

every molecule in his body had passed the message of a magic touch. And so it had. For effective magic is transcendent nature; and who shall measure the subtlety of those touches which convey the quality of soul as well as body, and make a man's passion for one woman differ from his passion for another as joy in the morning light over valley and river and white mountain-top differs from joy among Chinese lanterns and glass panels? Will, too, was made of very impressible stuff. The bow of a violin drawn near him cleverly, would at one stroke change the aspect of the world for him, and his point of view shifted as easily as his mood. Dorothea's entrance was the freshness of morning.

'Well, my dear, this is pleasant, now,' said Mr Brooke, meeting and kissing her. 'You have left Casaubon with his books, I suppose. That's right. We must not have you getting too learned for a woman, you know.'

'There is no fear of that, uncle,' said Dorothea, turning to Will and shaking hands with open cheerfulness, while she made no other form of greeting, but went on answering her uncle. 'I am very slow. When I want to be busy with books, I am often playing truant among my thoughts. I find it is not so easy to be learned as to plan cottages.'

She seated herself beside her uncle opposite to Will, and was evidently preoccupied with something that made her almost unmindful of him. He was ridiculously disappointed, as if he had imagined that her coming had anything to do with him.

'Why, yes, my dear, it was quite your hobby to draw plans. But it was good to break that off a little. Hobbies are apt to run away with us, you know; it doesn't do to be run away with. We must keep the reins. I have never let myself be run away with; I always pulled up. That is what I tell Ladislaw. He and I are alike, you know: he likes to go into everything. We are working at capital punishment. We shall do a great deal together, Ladislaw and I.'

'Yes,' said Dorothea, with characteristic directness, 'Sir James has been telling me that he is in hope of seeing a great change made soon in your management of the estate – that you are thinking of having the farms valued, and repairs made, and the cottages improved, so that Tipton may look quite another place. Oh, how happy!' – she went on, clasping her hands, with a return to that more childlike impetuous manner which had been subdued since her marriage. 'If I were at home still, I should take to riding again, that I might go about with you and see all that! And you are going to engage Mr Garth, who praised my cottages, Sir James says.'

'Chettam is a little hasty, my dear,' said Mr Brooke, colouring slightly. 'A little hasty, you know. I never said I should do anything of the kind. I never said I should *not* do it, you know.'

'He only feels confident that you will do it,' said Dorothea, in a voice as clear and unhesitating as that of a young chorister chanting a *credo*, 'because you mean to enter Parliament as a member who cares for the improvement of the people, and one of the first things to be made better is the state of the land and the labourers. Think of Kit Downes, uncle, who lives with his wife and seven children in a house with one sitting-room and one bed-room hardly larger than this table! – and those poor Dagleys, in their tumble-down farmhouse, where they live in the back kitchen and leave the other rooms to the rats! That is one reason why I did not like the pictures here, dear uncle – which you think me stupid about. I used to come from the village with all that dirt and coarse ugliness like a pain within me, and the simpering pictures in the drawing-room seemed to me like a wicked attempt to find delight in what is false, while we don't mind how hard the truth is for the neighbours outside our walls. I think we have no right to come forward and urge wider changes for good, until we have tried to alter the evils which lie under our own hands.'

Dorothea had gathered emotion as she went on, and had forgotten everything except the relief of pouring forth her feelings, unchecked: an experience once habitual with her, but hardly ever present since her marriage, which had been a perpetual struggle of energy with fear. For the moment, Will's admiration was accompanied with a chilling sense of remoteness. A man is seldom ashamed of feeling that he cannot love a woman so well when he sees a certain greatness in her: nature having intended greatness for men. But nature has sometimes made sad over-sights in carrying out her intentions; as in the case of good Mr Brooke, whose masculine consciousness was at this moment in rather a stammering condition under the eloquence of his niece. He could not immediately find any other mode of expressing himself than that of rising, fixing his eye-glass, and fingering the papers before him. At last he said –

'There is something in what you say, my dear, something in what you say – but not everything – eh, Ladislaw. You and I don't like our pictures and statues being found fault with. Young ladies are a little ardent, you know – a little one-sided, my dear. Fine art, poetry, that kind of thing, elevates a nation – *emollit mores* – you understand a little Latin now. But – eh, what?'

These interrogatives were addressed to the footman who had come in to say that the keeper had found one of Dagley's boys with a leveret in his hand, just killed.

'I'll come, I'll come. I shall let him off easily, you know,' said Mr Brooke aside to Dorothea, shuffling away very cheerfully.

'I hope you feel how right this change is that I – that Sir James wishes for,' said Dorothea to Will, as soon as her uncle was gone.

'I do, now I have heard you speak about it. I shall not forget what you have said. But can you think of something else at this moment? I may not have another opportunity of speaking to you about what has occurred,' said Will, rising with a movement of impatience, and holding the back of his chair with both hands.

'Pray tell me what it is,' said Dorothea, anxiously, also rising and going to the open window, where Monk was looking in, panting and wagging his tail. She leaned her back against the window-frame, and laid her hand on the dog's head; for though, as we know, she was not fond of pets that must be held in the hands or trodden on, she was always attentive to the feelings of dogs, and very polite if she had to decline their advances.

Will followed her only with his eyes and said, 'I presume you know that Mr Casaubon has forbidden me to go to his house.'

'No, I did not,' said Dorothea, after a moment's pause. She was evidently much moved. 'I am very, very sorry,' she added, mournfully. She was thinking of what Will had no knowledge of – the conversation between her and her husband in the darkness; and she was anew smitten with hopelessness that she could influence Mr Casaubon's action. But the marked expression of her sorrow convinced Will that it was not all given to him personally, and that Dorothea had not been visited by the idea that Mr Casaubon's dislike and jealousy of him turned upon herself. He felt an odd mixture of delight and vexation: of delight that he could dwell and be cherished in her thought as in a pure home, without suspicion and without stint – of vexation because he was of too little account with her, was not formidable enough, was treated with an unhesitating benevolence which did not flatter him. But his dread of any change in Dorothea was stronger than his discontent, and he began to speak again in a tone of mere explanation.

'Mr Casaubon's reason is, his displeasure at my taking a position here which he considers unsuited to my rank as his cousin. I have told him that I cannot give way on this point. It is a little too hard on me to expect that my course in life is to be hampered by prejudices which I think ridiculous. Obligation may be stretched till it is no better than a brand of slavery stamped on us when we were too young to know its meaning. I would not have accepted the position if I had not meant to make it useful and honourable. I am not bound to regard family dignity in any other light.'

Dorothea felt wretched. She thought her husband altogether in the wrong, on more grounds than Will had mentioned.

'It is better for us not to speak on the subject,' she said, with a tremulousness not common in her voice, 'since you and Mr Casaubon disagree. You intend to remain?' She was looking out on the lawn, with melancholy meditation.

'Yes; but I shall hardly ever see you now,' said Will, in a tone of almost boyish complaint.

'No,' said Dorothea, turning her eyes full upon him, 'hardly ever. But I shall hear of you. I shall know what you are doing for my uncle.'

'I shall know hardly anything about you,' said Will. 'No one will tell me anything.'

'Oh, my life is very simple,' said Dorothea, her lips curling with an exquisite smile, which irradiated her melancholy. 'I am always at Lowick.'

'That is a dreadful imprisonment,' said Will, impetuously.

'No, don't think that,' said Dorothea. 'I have no longings.'

He did not speak, but she replied to some change in his expression. 'I mean, for myself. Except that I should like not to have so much more than my share without doing anything for others. But I have a belief of my own, and it comforts me.'

'What is that?' said Will, rather jealous of the belief.

'That by desiring what is perfectly good, even when we don't quite know what it is and cannot do what we would, we are part of the divine power against evil – widening the skirts of light and making the struggle with darkness narrower.'

'That is a beautiful mysticism – it is a – '

'Please not to call it by any name,' said Dorothea, putting out her hands entreatingly. 'You will say it is Persian, or something else geographical. It is my life. I have found it out, and cannot part with it. I have always been finding out my religion since I was a little girl. I used to pray so much – now I hardly ever pray. I try not to have desires merely for myself, because they may not be good for others, and I have too much already. I only told you, that you might know quite well how my days go at Lowick.'

'God bless you for telling me!' said Will, ardently, and rather wondering at himself. They were looking at each other like two fond children who were talking confidentially of birds.

'What is *your* religion?' said Dorothea. 'I mean – not what you know about religion, but the belief that helps you most?'

'To love what is good and beautiful when I see it,' said Will. 'But I am a rebel: I don't feel bound, as you do, to submit to what I don't like.'

'But if you like what is good, that comes to the same thing,' said Dorothea, smiling.

'Now you are subtle,' said Will.

'Yes; Mr Casaubon often says I am too subtle. I don't feel as if I were subtle,' said Dorothea, playfully. 'But how long my uncle is! I must go and look for him. I must really go on to the Hall. Celia is expecting me.'

Will offered to tell Mr Brooke, who presently came and said that he would step into the carriage and go with Dorothea as far as Dagley's, to speak about the small delinquent who had been caught with the leveret. Dorothea renewed the subject of the estate as they drove along, but Mr Brooke, not being taken unawares, got the talk under his own control.

'Chettam, now,' he replied; 'he finds fault with me, my dear; but I should not preserve my game if it were not for Chettam, and he can't say that *that* expense is for the sake of the tenants, you know. It's a little against my feeling: – poaching, now, if you come to look into it – I have often thought of getting up the subject. Not long ago, Flavell, the Methodist preacher, was brought up for knocking down a hare that came across his path when he and his wife were walking out together. He was pretty quick, and knocked it on the neck.'

'That was very brutal, I think,' said Dorothea.

'Well, now, it seemed rather black to me, I confess, in a Methodist preacher, you know. And Johnson said, "You may judge what a hypocrite he is." And upon my word, I thought Flavell looked very little like "the highest style of man" – as somebody calls the Christian – Young, the poet Young, I think – you know Young? Well, now, Flavell in his shabby black gaiters, pleading that he thought the Lord had sent him and his wife a good dinner, and he had a right to knock it down, though not a mighty hunter before the Lord, as Nimrod was – I assure you it was rather comic: Fielding would have made something of it – or Scott, now – Scott might have worked it up. But really, when I came to think of it, I couldn't help liking that the fellow should have a bit of hare to say grace over. It's all a matter of prejudice – prejudice with the law on its side, you know – about the stick and the gaiters, and so on. However, it doesn't do to reason about things; and law is law. But I got Johnson to be quiet, and I hushed the matter up. I doubt whether Chettam would not have been more severe, and yet he comes down on me as if I were the hardest man in the county. But we are here at Dagley's.'

Mr Brooke got down at the farmyard-gate, and Dorothea drove on. It is wonderful how much uglier things will look when we only suspect that we are blamed for them. Even our own persons in the glass are apt to change their aspect for us after we have heard some frank remark on their less admirable points; and on the other hand it is astonishing how pleasantly conscience takes our encroachments on those who never complain or have nobody to complain for them. Dagley's homestead never looked before so dismal to Mr Brooke as it did to-day, with his mind thus sore about the fault-finding of the *Trumpet*, echoed by Sir James.

It is true that an observer, under that softening influence of the fine arts which makes other people's hardships picturesque, might have been delighted with this homestead called Freeman's End: the old house had dormer-windows in the dark-red roof, two of the chimneys were choked with ivy, the large porch was blocked up with bundles of sticks, and half the windows were closed with grey worm-eaten shutters about which the jasmine-boughs grew in wild luxuriance; the mouldering garden wall with hollyhocks peeping over it was a perfect study of highly-mingled subdued colour, and there was an aged goat (kept doubtless on interesting superstitious grounds) lying against the open back-kitchen door. The mossy thatch of the cowshed, the broken grey barn-doors, the pauper labourers in ragged breeches who had nearly finished unloading a waggon of corn into the barn ready for early thrashing; the scanty dairy of cows being tethered for milking and leaving one half of the shed in brown emptiness; the very pigs and white ducks seeming to wander about the uneven neglected yard as if in low spirits from feeding on a too meagre quality of rinsings – all these objects under the quiet light of a sky marbled with high clouds would have made a sort of picture which we have all paused over as a 'charming bit', touching other sensibilities than those which are stirred by the depression of the agricultural interest, with the sad lack of farming capital, as seen constantly in the newspapers of that time. But these troublesome associations were just now strongly present to Mr Brooke, and spoiled the scene for him. Mr Dagley himself made a figure in the landscape, carrying a pitchfork and wearing his milking-hat – a very old beaver flattened in front. His coat and breeches were the best he had, and he would not have been wearing them on this week-day occasion if he had not been to market and returned later than usual, having given himself the rare treat of dining at the public table of the Blue Bull. How he came to fall into this extravagance would perhaps be matter of wonderment to himself on the morrow; but before dinner something in the state of the country, a slight pause in the harvest before the Far Dips were cut, the stories about the new King and the numerous handbills on the walls, had seemed to warrant a little recklessness. It was a maxim about Middlemarch, and regarded as self-evident, that good meat should have good drink, which last Dagley interpreted as plenty of table ale well followed up by rum-and-water. These liquors have so far truth in them that they were not false enough to make poor Dagley seem merry: they only made his discontent less tongue-tied than usual. He had also taken too much in the shape of muddy political talk, a stimulant dangerously disturbing to his farming conservatism, which consisted in holding that whatever is, is bad, and any change is likely to be worse. He was flushed, and his eyes had a decidedly quarrelsome stare as he stood still grasping his pitchfork, while the landlord approached with his easy shuffling walk, one hand in his trouser-pocket and the other swinging round a thin walking-stick.

'Dagley, my good fellow,' began Mr Brooke, conscious that he was going to be very friendly about the boy.

'Oh, ay, I'm a good feller, am I? Thank ye, sir, thank ye,' said Dagley, with a loud snarling irony which made Fag the sheepdog stir from his seat and prick his ears; but seeing Monk enter the yard after some outside loitering, Fag seated himself again in an attitude of observation. 'I'm glad to hear I'm a good feller.'

Mr Brooke reflected that it was market-day, and that his worthy tenant had probably been dining, but saw no reason why he should not go on, since he could take the precaution of repeating what he had to say to Mrs Dagley.

'Your little lad Jacob has been caught killing a leveret, Dagley: I have told Johnson to lock him up in the empty stable an hour or two, just to frighten him, you know. But he will be brought home by-and-by, before night: and you'll just look after him, will you, and give him a reprimand, you know?'

'No, I woon't: I'll be dee'd if I'll leather my boy to please you or anybody else, not if you was twenty landlords istid o' one, and that a bad un.'

Dagley's words were loud enough to summon his wife to the back-kitchen door – the only entrance ever used, and one always open except in bad weather – and Mr Brooke, saying soothingly, 'Well, well, I'll speak to your wife – I didn't mean beating, you know,' turned to walk to the house. But Dagley, only the more inclined to 'have his say' with a gentleman who walked away from him, followed at once, with Fag slouching at his heels and sullenly evading some small and probably charitable advances on the part of Monk.

'How do you do, Mrs Dagley?' said Mr Brooke, making some haste. 'I came to tell you about your boy: I don't want you to give him the stick, you know.' He was careful to speak quite plainly this time.

Overworked Mrs Dagley – a thin, worn woman, from whose life pleasure had so entirely vanished that she had not even any Sunday clothes which could give her satisfaction in preparing for church – had already had a misunderstanding with her husband since he had come home, and was in low spirits, expecting the worst. But her husband was beforehand in answering.

'No, nor he woon't hev the stick, whether you want it or no,' pursued Dagley, throwing out his voice, as if he wanted it to hit hard. 'You've got no call to come an' talk about sticks o' these primises, as you woon't give a stick tow'rt mending. Go to Middlemarch to ax for *your* charrickter.'

'You'd far better hold your tongue, Dagley,' said the wife, 'and not kick your own trough over. When a man as is father of a family has been an' spent money at market and made himself the worse for liquor, he's done enough mischief for one day. But I should like to know what my boy's done, sir.'

'Niver do you mind what he's done,' said Dagley, more fiercely, 'it's my business to speak, an' not yourn. An' I wull speak, too. I'll hev my say – supper or no. An' what I say is, as I've lived upo' your ground from my father and grandfather afore me, an' hev dropped our money into't, an' me an' my children might lie an' rot on the ground for top-dressin' as we can't find the money to buy, if the King wasn't to put a stop.'

'My good fellow, you're drunk, you know,' said Mr Brooke, confidentially, but not judiciously. 'Another day, another day,' he added, turning as if to go.

But Dagley immediately fronted him, and Fag at his heels growled low, as his master's voice grew louder and more insulting, while Monk also drew close in silent dignified watch. The labourers on the waggon were pausing to listen, and it seemed wiser to be quite passive than to attempt a ridiculous flight pursued by a bawling man.

'I'm no more drunk nor you are, nor so much,' said Dagley. 'I can carry my liquor, an' I know what I mean. An' I meean as the King 'ull put a stop to't, for them say it as knows it, as there's to be a Rinform, and them landlords as never done the right thing by their tenants 'ull be treated i' that way as they'll hev to scuttle off. An' there's them i' Middlemarch knows what the Rinform is – an' as knows who'll hev to scuttle. Says they, "I know who *your* landlord is." An' says I, "I hope you're the better for knowin' him, I arn't." Says they, "He's a close-fisted un." "Ay, ay," says I. "He's a man for the Rinform," says they. That's what they says. An' I made out what the Rinform were – an' it were to send you an' your likes a scuttlin'; an' wi' pretty strong-smellin' things too. An' you may do as you like now, for I'm none afeard on you. An' you'd better let my boy aloan, an' look to yoursen, afore the Rinform has got upo' your back. That's what I'n got to say,' concluded Mr Dagley, striking his fork into the ground with a firmness which proved inconvenient as he tried to draw it up again.

At this last action Monk began to bark loudly, and it was a moment for Mr Brooke to escape. He walked out of the yard as quickly as he could, in some amazement at the novelty of his situation. He had never been insulted on his own land before, and had been inclined to regard himself as a general favourite (we are all apt to do so, when we think of our own amiability more than of what other people are likely to want of us). When he had quarrelled with Caleb Garth twelve years before he had thought that the tenants would be pleased at the landlord's taking everything into his own hands.

Some who follow the narrative of his experience may wonder at the midnight darkness of Mr Dagley; but nothing was easier in those times than for an hereditary farmer of his grade to be ignorant, in spite somehow of having a rector in the twin parish who was a gentleman to the backbone, a curate nearer at hand who preached more learnedly than the rector, a landlord who had gone into everything, especially fine art and social improvement, and all the lights of Middlemarch only three miles off. As to the facility with which mortals escape knowledge, try an average acquaintance in the intellectual blaze of London, and consider what that eligible person for a dinner-party would have been if he had learned scant skill in 'summing' from the parish-clerk of Tipton, and read a chapter in the Bible with immense difficulty, because such names as Isaiah or Apollos remained unmanageable after twice spelling. Poor Dagley read a few verses sometimes on a Sunday evening, and the world was at least not darker to him than it had been before. Some things he knew thoroughly, namely, the slovenly habits of farming, and the awkwardness of weather, stock, and crops, at Freeman's End – so called apparently by way of sarcasm, to imply that a man was free to quit it if he chose, but that there was no earthly 'beyond' open to him.

⊘ FORTY ⊘

Wise in his daily work was he:
   To fruits of diligence,
And not to faiths or polity,
   He plied his utmost sense.
These perfect in their little parts,
   Whose work is all their prize –
Without them how could laws, or arts,
   Or towered cities rise?

In watching effects, if only of an electric battery, it is often necessary
to change our place and examine a particular mixture or group at some
distance from the point where the movement we are interested in was set
up. The group I am moving towards is at Caleb Garth's breakfast-table in
the large parlour where the maps and desk were: father, mother, and five
of the children. Mary was just now at home waiting for a situation, while
Christy, the boy next to her, was getting cheap learning and cheap fare in
Scotland, having to his father's disappointment taken to books instead of
that sacred calling 'business'.

The letters had come – nine costly letters, for which the postman had
been paid three and twopence, and Mr Garth was forgetting his tea and
toast while he read his letters and laid them open one above the other,
sometimes swaying his head slowly, sometimes screwing up his mouth in
inward debate, but not forgetting to cut off a large red seal unbroken,
which Letty snatched up like an eager terrier.

The talk among the rest went on unrestrainedly, for nothing disturbed
Caleb's absorption except shaking the table when he was writing.

Two letters of the nine had been for Mary. After reading them, she had
passed them to her mother, and sat playing with her teaspoon absently,
till with a sudden recollection she returned to her sewing, which she had
kept on her lap during breakfast.

'Oh, don't sew, Mary!' said Ben, pulling her arm down. 'Make me a
peacock with this bread-crumb.' He had been kneading a small mass for
the purpose.

'No, no, Mischief!' said Mary, good-humouredly, while she pricked his
hand lightly with her needle. 'Try and mould it yourself: you have seen
me do it often enough. I must get this sewing done. It is for Rosamond

Vincy: she is to be married next week, and she can't be married without this handkerchief.' Mary ended merrily, amused with the last notion.

'Why can't she, Mary?' said Letty, seriously interested in this mystery, and pushing her head so close to her sister that Mary now turned the threatening needle towards Letty's nose.

'Because this is one of a dozen, and without it there would only be eleven,' said Mary, with a grave air of explanation, so that Letty sank back with a sense of knowledge.

'Have you made up your mind, my dear?' said Mrs Garth, laying the letters down.

'I shall go to the school at York,' said Mary. 'I am less unfit to teach in a school than in a family. I like to teach classes best. And, you see, I must teach: there is nothing else to be done.'

'Teaching seems to me the most delightful work in the world,' said Mrs Garth, with a touch of rebuke in her tone. 'I could understand your objection to it if you had not knowledge enough, Mary, or if you disliked children.'

'I suppose we never quite understand why another dislikes what we like, mother,' said Mary, rather curtly. 'I am not fond of a school-room: I like the outside world better. It is a very inconvenient fault of mine.'

'It must be very stupid to be always in a girls' school,' said Alfred, 'Such a set of nincompoops, like Mrs Ballard's pupils walking two and two.'

'And they have no games worth playing at,' said Jim. 'They can neither throw nor leap. I don't wonder at Mary's not liking it.'

'What is that Mary doesn't like, eh?' said the father, looking over his spectacles and pausing before he opened his next letter.

'Being among a lot of nincompoop girls,' said Alfred.

'Is it the situation you had heard of, Mary?' said Caleb, gently, looking at his daughter.

'Yes, father: the school at York. I have determined to take it. It is quite the best. Thirty-five pounds a-year, and extra pay for teaching the smallest strummers at the piano.'

'Poor child! I wish she could stay at home with us, Susan,' said Caleb, looking plaintively at his wife.

'Mary would not be happy without doing her duty,' said Mrs Garth, magisterially, conscious of having done her own.

'It wouldn't make me happy to do such a nasty duty as that,' said Alfred – at which Mary and her father laughed silently, but Mrs Garth said, gravely –

'Do find a fitter word than nasty, my dear Alfred, for everything that you think disagreeable. And suppose that Mary could help you to go to Mr Hanmer's with the money she gets?'

'That seems to me a great shame. But she's an old brick,' said Alfred, rising from his chair, and pulling Mary's head backward to kiss her.

Mary coloured and laughed, but could not conceal that the tears were coming. Caleb, looking on over his spectacles, with the angles of his eyebrows falling, had an expression of mingled delight and sorrow as he returned to the opening of his letter; and even Mrs Garth, her lips curling with a calm contentment, allowed that inappropriate language to pass without correction, although Ben immediately took it up, and sang, 'She's an old brick, old brick, old brick!' to a cantering measure, which he beat out with his fist on Mary's arm.

But Mrs Garth's eyes were now drawn towards her husband, who was already deep in the letter he was reading. His face had an expression of grave surprise, which alarmed her a little, but he did not like to be questioned while he was reading, and she remained anxiously watching till she saw him suddenly shaken by a little joyous laugh as he turned back to the beginning of the letter, and looking at her above his spectacles, said, in a low tone, 'What do you think, Susan?'

She went and stood behind him, putting her hand on his shoulder, while they read the letter together. It was from Sir James Chettam, offering to Mr Garth the management of the family estates at Freshitt and else-where, and adding that Sir James had been requested by Mr Brooke of Tipton to ascertain whether Mr Garth would be disposed at the same time to resume the agency of the Tipton property. The Baronet added in very obliging words that he himself was particularly desirous of seeing the Freshitt and Tipton estates under the same management, and he hoped to be able to show that the double agency might be held on terms agreeable to Mr Garth, whom he would be glad to see at the Hall at twelve o'clock on the following day.

'He writes handsomely, doesn't he, Susan?' said Caleb, turning his eyes upward to his wife, who raised her hand from his shoulder to his ear, while she rested her chin on his head. 'Brooke didn't like to ask me himself, I can see,' he continued, laughing silently.

'Here is an honour to your father, children,' said Mrs Garth, looking round at the five pair of eyes, all fixed on the parents. 'He is asked to take a post again by those who dismissed him long ago. That shows that he did his work well, so that they feel the want of him.'

'Like Cincinnatus – hooray!' said Ben, riding on his chair, with a pleasant confidence that discipline was relaxed.

'Will they come to fetch him, mother?' said Letty, thinking of the Mayor and Corporation in their robes.

Mrs Garth patted Letty's head and smiled, but seeing that her husband was gathering up his letters and likely soon to be out of reach in that sanctuary 'business', she pressed his shoulder and said emphatically.

'Now, mind you ask fair pay, Caleb.'

'Oh, yes,' said Caleb, in a deep voice of assent, as if it would be unreasonable to suppose anything else of him. 'It'll come to between four and five hundred, the two together.' Then with a little start of remembrance he said, 'Mary, write and give up that school. Stay and help your mother. I'm as pleased as Punch, now I've thought of that.'

No manner could have been less like that of Punch triumphant than Caleb's, but his talents did not lie in finding phrases, though he was very particular about his letter-writing, and regarded his wife as a treasury of correct language.

There was almost an uproar among the children now, and Mary held up the cambric embroidery towards her mother entreatingly, that it might be put out of reach while the boys dragged her into a dance. Mrs Garth, in placid joy, began to put the cups and plates together, while Caleb pushing his chair from the table, as if he were going to move to the desk, still sat holding his letters in his hand and looking on the ground meditatively, stretching out the fingers of his left hand, according to a mute language of his own. At last he said –

'It's a thousand pities Christy didn't take to business, Susan. I shall want help by-and-by. And Alfred must go off to the engineering – I've made up my mind to that.' He fell into meditation and finger rhetoric again for a little while, and then continued: – 'I shall make Brooke have new agreements with the tenants, and I shall draw up a rotation of crops. And I'll lay a wager we can get fine bricks out of the clay at Bott's corner. I must look into that: it would cheapen the repairs. It's a fine bit of work, Susan! A man without a family would be glad to do it for nothing.'

'Mind you don't, though,' said his wife, lifting up her finger.

'No, no; but it's a fine thing to come to a man when he's seen into the nature of business; to have a chance of getting a bit of the country into good fettle, as they say, and putting men into the right way with their farming, and getting a bit of good contriving and solid building done – that those who are living and those who come after will be the better for. I'd sooner have it than a fortune. I hold it the most honourable work that is.' Here Caleb laid down his letters, thrust his fingers between the buttons of his waistcoat, and sat upright, but presently proceeded with some awe in his voice and moving his head slowly aside – 'It's a great gift of God, Susan.'

'That it is, Caleb,' said his wife, with answering fervour. 'And it will be a blessing to your children to have had a father who did such work: a father whose good work remains though his name may be forgotten.' She could not say any more to him then about the pay.

In the evening, when Caleb, rather tired with his day's work, was seated in silence with his pocket-book open on his knee, while Mrs Garth and Mary were at their sewing, and Letty in a corner was whispering a dialogue with her doll, Mr Farebrother came up the orchard walk, dividing the bright August lights and shadows with the tufted grass and the apple-tree boughs. We know that he was fond of his parishioners the Garths, and had thought Mary worth mentioning to Lydgate. He used to the full the clergyman's privilege of disregarding the Middlemarch discrimination of ranks, and always told his mother that Mrs Garth was more of a lady than any matron in the town. Still, you see, he spent his evenings at the Vincys', where the matron, though less of a lady, presided over a well-lit drawing-room and whist. In those days human intercourse was not determined solely by respect. But the Vicar did heartily respect the Garths, and a visit from him was no surprise to that family. Nevertheless he accounted for it even while he was shaking hands, by saying, 'I come as an envoy, Mrs Garth: I have something to say to you and Garth on behalf of Fred Vincy. The fact is, poor fellow,' he continued, as he seated himself and looked round with his bright glance at the three who were listening to him, 'he has taken me into his confidence.'

Mary's heart beat rather quickly: she wondered how far Fred's confidence had gone.

'We haven't seen the lad for months,' said Caleb. 'I couldn't think what was become of him.'

'He has been away on a visit,' said the Vicar, 'because home was a little too hot for him, and Lydgate told his mother that the poor fellow must not begin to study yet. But yesterday he came and poured himself out to me. I am very glad he did, because I have seen him grow up from a youngster of fourteen, and I am so much at home in the house that the children are like nephews and nieces to me. But it is a difficult case to advise upon. However, he has asked me to come and tell you that he is going away, and that he is so miserable about his debt to you, and his inability to pay, that he can't bear to come himself even to bid you good-bye.'

'Tell him it doesn't signify a farthing,' said Caleb, waving his hand. 'We've had the pinch and have got over it. And now I'm going to be as rich as a Jew.'

'Which means,' said Mrs Garth, smiling at the Vicar, 'that we are going to have enough to bring up the boys well and to keep Mary at home.'

'What is the treasure-trove?' said Mr Farebrother.

'I'm going to be agent for two estates, Freshitt and Tipton; and perhaps for a pretty little bit of land in Lowick besides: it's all the same family connection, and employment spreads like water if it's once set going. It makes me very happy, Mr Farebrother' – here Caleb threw back his head a little, and spread his arms on the elbows of his chair – 'that I've got an opportunity again with the letting of the land, and carrying out a notion or two with improvements. It's a most uncommonly cramping thing, as I've often told Susan, to sit on horseback and look over the hedges at the wrong thing, and not be able to put your hand to it to make it right. What people do who go into politics I can't think: it drives me almost mad to see mismanagement over only a few hundred acres.'

It was seldom that Caleb volunteered so long a speech, but his happiness had the effect of mountain air: his eyes were bright, and the words came without effort.

'I congratulate you heartily, Garth,' said the Vicar. 'This is the best sort of news I could have had to carry to Fred Vincy, for he dwelt a good deal on the injury he had done you in causing you to part with money – robbing you of it, he said – which you wanted for other purposes. I wish Fred was not such an idle dog; he has some very good points, and his father is a little hard upon him.'

'Where is he going?' said Mrs Garth, rather coldly.

'He means to try again for his degree, and he is going up to study before term. I have advised him to do that. I don't urge him to enter the Church – on the contrary. But if he will go and work so as to pass, that will be some guarantee that he has energy and a will; and he is quite at sea; he doesn't know what else to do. So far he will please his father, and I have promised in the meantime to try and reconcile Vincy to his son's adopting some other line of life. Fred says frankly he is not fit for a clergyman, and I would do anything I could to hinder a man from the fatal step of choosing the wrong profession. He quoted to me what you said, Miss Garth – do you remember it?' (Mr Farebrother used to say 'Mary' instead of 'Miss Garth', but it was part of his delicacy to treat her with the more deference because, according to Mrs Vincy's phrase, she worked for her bread.)

Mary felt uncomfortable, but, determined to take the matter lightly, answered at once, 'I have said so many impertinent things to Fred – we are such old playfellows.'

'You said, according to him, that he would be one of those ridiculous clergymen who help to make the whole clergy ridiculous. Really, that was so cutting that I felt a little cut myself.'

Caleb laughed. 'She gets her tongue from you, Susan,' he said, with some enjoyment.

'Not its flippancy, father,' said Mary, quickly, fearing that her mother would be displeased. 'It is rather too bad of Fred to repeat my flippant speeches to Mr Farebrother.'

'It was certainly a hasty speech, my dear,' said Mrs Garth, with whom speaking evil of dignities was a high misdemeanour. 'We should not value our Vicar the less because there was a ridiculous curate in the next parish.'

'There's something in what she says, though,' said Caleb, not disposed to have Mary's sharpness undervalued. 'A bad workman of any sort makes his fellows mistrusted. Things hang together,' he added, looking on the floor and moving his feet uneasily with a sense that words were scantier than thoughts.

'Clearly,' said the Vicar, amused. 'By being contemptible we set men's minds to the tune of contempt. I certainly agree with Miss Garth's view of the matter, whether I am condemned by it or not. But as to Fred Vincy, it is only fair he should be excused a little: old Featherstone's delusive behaviour did help to spoil him. There was something quite diabolical in not leaving him a farthing after all. But Fred has the good taste not to dwell on that. And what he cares most about is having offended you, Mrs Garth; he supposes you will never think well of him again.'

'I have been disappointed in Fred,' said Mrs Garth, with decision. 'But I shall be ready to think well of him again when he gives me good reason to do so.'

At this point Mary went out of the room, taking Letty with her.

'Oh, we must forgive young people when they're sorry,' said Caleb, watching Mary close the door. 'And as you say, Mr Farebrother, there was the very devil in that old man. Now Mary's gone out, I must tell you a thing – it's only known to Susan and me, and you'll not tell it again. The old scoundrel wanted Mary to burn one of the wills the very night he died, when she was sitting up with him by herself, and he offered her a sum of money that he had in the box by him if she would do it. But Mary, you understand, could do no such thing – would not be handling his iron chest, and so on. Now, you see, the will he wanted burnt was this last, so that if Mary had done what he wanted, Fred Vincy would have had ten thousand pounds. The old man did turn to him at the last. That touches poor Mary close; she couldn't help it – she was in the right to do what she did, but she feels, as she says, much as if she had knocked down somebody's property and broken it against her will, when she was rightfully defending herself. I feel with her, somehow, and if I could make any amends to the poor lad, instead of bearing him a grudge for the harm he did us, I should be glad to do it. Now, what is your opinion, sir? Susan doesn't agree with me. She says – tell what you say, Susan.'

'Mary could not have acted otherwise, even if she had known what would be the effect on Fred,' said Mrs Garth, pausing from her work, and looking at Mr Farebrother. 'And she was quite ignorant of it. It seems to me, a loss which falls on another because we have done right is not to lie upon our conscience.'

The Vicar did not answer immediately, and Caleb said, 'It's the feeling. The child feels in that way, and I feel with her. You don't mean your horse to tread on a dog when you're backing out of the way; but it goes through you, when it's done.'

'I am sure Mrs Garth would agree with you there,' said Mr Farebrother, who for some reason seemed more inclined to ruminate than to speak. 'One could hardly say that the feeling you mention about Fred is wrong – or rather, mistaken – though no man ought to make a claim on such feeling.'

'Well, well,' said Caleb; 'it's a secret. You will not tell Fred.'

'Certainly not. But I shall carry the other good news – that you can afford the loss he caused you.'

Mr Farebrother left the house soon after, and seeing Mary in the orchard with Letty, went to say good-bye to her. They made a pretty picture in the western light which brought out the brightness of the apples on the old scant-leaved boughs – Mary in her lavender gingham and black ribbons holding a basket, while Letty in her well-worn nankin picked up the fallen apples. If you want to know more particularly how Mary looked, ten to one you will see a face like hers in the crowded street tomorrow, if you are there on the watch: she will not be among those daughters of Zion who are haughty, and walk with stretched-out necks and wanton eyes, mincing as they go: let all those pass, and fix your eyes on some small plump brownish person of firm but quiet carriage, who looks about her, but does not suppose that anybody is looking at her. If she has a broad face and square brow, well-marked eyebrows and curly dark hair, a certain expression of amusement in her glance which her mouth keeps the secret of, and for the rest features entirely insignificant – take that ordinary but not disagreeable person for a portrait of Mary Garth. If you made her smile she would show you perfect little teeth; if you made her angry, she would not raise her voice, but would probably say one of the bitterest things you have ever tasted the flavour of; if you did her a kindness, she would never forget it. Mary admired the keen-faced handsome little Vicar in his well-brushed threadbare clothes more than any man she had had the opportunity of knowing. She had never heard him say a foolish thing, though she knew that he did unwise ones; and perhaps foolish sayings were more objectionable to her than any of Mr Farebrother's unwise doings. At least, it was remarkable that the actual imperfections of the Vicar's clerical character never seemed to call forth the same scorn and dislike which she showed beforehand for the predicted imperfections of the clerical character sustained by Fred Vincy. These irregularities of judgment, I imagine, are found even in riper minds than Mary Garth's: our impartiality is kept for abstract merit and demerit, which none of us ever saw. Will any one guess towards which of these widely different men Mary had the peculiar woman's tenderness? – the one she was most inclined to be severe on, or the contrary?

'Have you any message for your old playfellow, Miss Garth?' said the Vicar, as he took a fragrant apple from the basket which she held towards him, and put it in his pocket. 'Something to soften down that harsh judgment? I am going straight to see him.'

'No,' said Mary, shaking her head, and smiling. 'If I were to say that he would not be ridiculous as a clergyman, I must say that he would be something worse than ridiculous. But I am very glad to hear that he is going away to work.'

'On the other hand, I am very glad to hear that you are not going away to work. My mother, I am sure, will be all the happier if you will come to see her at the vicarage: you know she is fond of having young people to talk to, and she has a great deal to tell about old times. You will really be doing a kindness.'

'I should like it very much, if I may,' said Mary. 'Everything seems too happy for me all at once. I thought it would always be part of my life to long for home, and losing that grievance makes me feel rather empty: I suppose it served instead of sense to fill up my mind?'

'May I go with you, Mary?' whispered Letty – a most inconvenient child, who listened to everything. But she was made exultant by having her chin pinched and her cheek kissed by Mr Farebrother – an incident which she narrated to her mother and father.

As the Vicar walked to Lowick, any one watching him closely might have seen him twice shrug his shoulders. I think that the rare Englishmen who have this gesture are never of the heavy type – for fear of any lumbering instance to the contrary, I will say, hardly ever; they have usually a fine temperament and much tolerance towards the smaller errors of men (themselves inclusive). The Vicar was holding an inward dialogue in which he told himself that there was probably something more between Fred and Mary Garth than the regard of old playfellows, and replied with a question whether that bit of womanhood were not a great deal too choice for that crude young gentleman. The rejoinder to this was the first shrug. Then he laughed at himself for being likely to have felt jealous, as if he had been a man able to marry, which, added he, it is as clear as any balance-sheet that I am not. Whereupon followed the second shrug.

What could two men, so different from each other, see in this 'brown patch', as Mary called herself? It was certainly not her plainness that attracted them (and let all plain young ladies be warned against the dangerous encouragement given them by Society to confide in their want of beauty). A human being in this aged nation of ours is a very wonderful whole, the slow creation of long interchanging influences; and charm is a result of two such wholes, the one loving and the one loved.

When Mr and Mrs Garth were sitting alone, Caleb said, 'Susan, guess what I'm thinking of.'

'The rotation of crops,' said Mrs Garth, smiling at him, above her knitting, 'or else the backdoors of the Tipton cottages.'

'No,' said Caleb, gravely; 'I am thinking that I could do a great turn for Fred Vincy. Christy's gone, Alfred will be gone soon, and it will be five years before Jim is ready to take to business. I shall want help, and Fred might come in and learn the nature of things and act under me, and it might be the making of him into a useful man, if he gives up being a parson. What do you think?'

'I think, there is hardly anything honest that his family would object to more,' said Mrs Garth, decidedly.

'What care I about their objecting?' said Caleb, with a sturdiness which he was apt to show when he had an opinion. 'The lad is of age and must get his bread. He has sense enough and quickness enough; he likes being on the land, and it's my belief that he could learn business well if he gave his mind to it.'

'But would he? His father and mother wanted him to be a fine gentleman, and I think he has the same sort of feeling himself. They all think us beneath them. And if the proposal came from you, I am sure Mrs Vincy would say that we wanted Fred for Mary.'

'Life is a poor tale, if it is to be settled by nonsense of that sort,' said Caleb, with disgust.

'Yes, but there is a certain pride which is proper, Caleb.'

'I call it improper pride to let fools' notions hinder you from doing a good action. There's no sort of work,' said Caleb, with fervour, putting out his hand and moving it up and down to mark his emphasis, 'that could ever be done well, if you minded what fools say. You must have it inside you that your plan is right, and that plan you must follow.'

'I will not oppose any plan you have set your mind on, Caleb,' said Mrs Garth, who was a firm woman, but knew that there were some points on which her mild husband was yet firmer. 'Still, it seems to be fixed that Fred is to go back to college: will it not be better to wait and see what he will choose to do after that? It is not easy to keep people against their will. And you are not yet quite sure enough of your own position, or what you will want.'

'Well, it may be better to wait a bit. But as to my getting plenty of work for two, I'm pretty sure of that. I've always had my hands full with scattered things, and there's always something fresh turning up. Why, only yesterday – bless me, I don't think I told you! – it was rather odd that two men should have been at me on different sides to do the same bit of valuing. And who do you think they were?' said Caleb, taking a pinch of snuff and holding it up between his fingers, as if it were a part of his exposition. He was fond of a pinch when it occurred to him, but he usually forgot that this indulgence was at his command.

His wife held down her knitting and looked attentive.

'Why, that Rigg, or Rigg Featherstone, was one. But Bulstrode was before him, so I'm going to do it for Bulstrode. Whether it's mortgage or purchase they're going for, I can't tell yet.'

'Can that man be going to sell the land just left him – which he has taken the name for?' said Mrs Garth.

'Deuce knows,' said Caleb, who never referred the knowledge of discreditable doings to any higher power than the deuce. 'But Bulstrode has long been wanting to get a handsome bit of land under his fingers – that I know. And it's a difficult matter to get, in this part of the country.'

Caleb scattered his snuff carefully instead of taking it, and then added, 'The ins and outs of things are curious. Here is the land they've been all along expecting for Fred, which it seems the old man never meant to leave him a foot of, but left it to this side-slip of a son that he kept in the dark, and thought of his sticking there and vexing everybody as well as he could have vexed 'em himself if he could have kept alive. I say, it would be curious if it got into Bulstrode's hands after all. The old man hated him, and never would bank with him.'

'What reason could the miserable creature have for hating a man whom he had nothing to do with?' said Mrs Garth.

'Pooh! where's the use of asking for such fellows' reasons? The soul of man,' said Caleb, with the deep tone and grave shake of the head which always came when he used this phrase – 'the soul of man, when it gets fairly rotten, will bear you all sorts of poisonous toad-stools, and no eye can see whence came the seed thereof.'

It was one of Caleb's quaintnesses, that in his difficulty of finding speech for his thought, he caught, as it were, snatches of diction which he associated with various points of view or states of mind; and whenever he had a feeling of awe, he was haunted by a sense of Biblical phraseology, though he could hardly have given a strict quotation.

◁ FORTY-ONE ▷

By swaggering could I never thrive,
For the rain it raineth every day.
Twelfth Night

THE TRANSACTIONS REFERRED TO BY CALEB Garth, as having gone forward between Mr Bulstrode and Mr Joshua Rigg Featherstone concerning the land attached to Stone Court, had occasioned the interchange of a letter or two between these personages.

Who shall tell what may be the effect of writing? If it happens to have been cut in stone, though it lie face downmost for ages on a forsaken beach, or 'rest quietly under the drums and tramplings of many conquests', it may end by letting us into the secret of usurpations and other scandals gossiped about long empires ago: – this world being apparently a huge whispering-gallery. Such conditions are often minutely represented in our petty lifetime. As the stone which has been kicked by generations of clowns may come by curious little links of effect under the eyes of a scholar, through whose labours it may at last fix the date of invasions and unlock religions, so a bit of ink and paper which has long been an innocent wrapping or stop-gap may at last be laid open under the one pair of eyes which have knowledge enough to turn it into the opening of a catastrophe. To Uriel watching the progress of planetary history from the Sun, the one result would be just as much of a coincidence as the other.

Having made this rather lofty comparison I am less uneasy in calling attention to the existence of low people by whose interference, however little we may like it, the course of the world is very much determined. It would be well, certainly, if we could help to reduce their number, and something might perhaps be done by not lightly giving occasion to their existence. Socially speaking, Joshua Rigg would have been generally pronounced a superfluity. But those who like Peter Featherstone never had a copy of themselves demanded, are the very last to wait for such a request either in prose or verse. The copy in this case bore more of outside resemblance to the mother, in whose sex frog-features, accompanied with fresh-coloured cheeks and a well-rounded figure, are compatible with much charm for a certain order of admirers. The result is sometimes a frog-faced male, desirable, surely, to no order of intelligent beings. Especially when he is suddenly brought into evidence to frustrate other people's expectations – the very lowest aspect in which a social super-fluity can present himself.

But Mr Rigg Featherstone's low characteristics were all of the sober, water-drinking kind. From the earliest to the latest hour of the day he was always as sleek, neat, and cool as the frog he resembled, and old Peter had secretly chuckled over an offshoot almost more calculating, and far more imperturbable, than himself. I will add that his finger-nails were scrupu-lously attended to, and that he meant to marry a well-educated young lady (as yet unspecified) whose person was good, and whose connections, in a solid middle-class way, were undeniable. Thus his nails and modesty were comparable to those of most gentlemen; though his ambition had been educated only by the opportunities of a clerk and accountant in the smaller commercial houses of a seaport. He thought the rural Feather-stones very simple absurd people, and they in their turn regarded his 'bringing up' in a seaport town as an exaggeration of the monstrosity that their brother Peter, and still more Peter's property, should have had such belongings.

The garden and gravel approach, as seen from the two windows of the wainscoted parlour at Stone Court, were never in better trim than now, when Mr Rigg Featherstone stood, with his hands behind him, looking out on these grounds as their master. But it seemed doubtful whether he looked out for the sake of contemplation or of turning his back to a person who stood in the middle of the room, with his legs considerably apart and his hands in his trouser-pockets: a person in all respects a contrast to the sleek and cool Rigg. He was a man obviously on the way towards sixty, very florid and hairy, with much grey in his bushy whiskers and thick curly hair, a stoutish body which showed to disadvantage the somewhat worn joinings of his clothes, and the air of a swaggerer, who would aim at being noticeable even at a show of fireworks, regarding his own remarks on any other person's performance as likely to be more interesting than the performance itself.

His name was John Raffles, and he sometimes wrote jocosely W.A.G. after his signature, observing when he did so, that he was once taught by Leonard Lamb, of Finsbury, who wrote B.A. after his name, and that he, Raffles, originated the witticism of calling that celebrated principal Ba-Lamb. Such were the appearance and mental flavour of Mr Raffles, both of which seemed to have a stale odour of traveller's rooms in the commercial hotels of that period.

'Come, now, Josh,' he was saying, in a full rumbling tone, 'look at it in this light: here is your poor mother going into the vale of years, and you could afford something handsome now to make her comfortable.'

'Not while you live. Nothing would make her comfortable while you live,' returned Rigg, in his cool high voice. 'What I give her, you'll take.'

'You bear me a grudge, Josh, that I know. But come, now – as between man and man – without humbug – a little capital might enable me to make a first-rate thing of the shop. The tobacco trade is growing. I should cut my own nose off in not doing the best I could at it. I should stick to it like a flea to a fleece for my own sake. I should always be on the spot. And nothing would make your poor mother so happy. I've pretty well done with my wild oats – turned fifty-five. I want to settle down in my chimney-corner. And if I once buckled to the tobacco trade, I could bring an amount of brains and experience to bear on it that would not be found elsewhere in a hurry. I don't want to be bothering you one time after another, but to get things once for all into the right channel. Consider that, Josh – as between man and man – and with your poor mother to be made easy for her life. I was always fond of the old woman, *by* Jove.'

'Have you done?' said Mr Rigg, quietly, without looking away from the window.

'Yes, *I've* done,' said Raffles, taking hold of his hat, which stood before him on the table, and giving it a sort of oratorical push.

'Then just listen to me. The more you say anything, the less I shall believe it. The more you want me to do a thing, the more reason I shall have for never doing it. Do you think I mean to forget your kicking me when I was a lad, and eating all the best victual away from me and my mother? Do you think I forget your always coming home to sell and pocket everything and going off again leaving us in the lurch? I should be glad to see you whipped at the cart-tail. My mother was a fool to you: she'd no right to give me a father-in-law, and she's been punished for it. She shall have her weekly allowance paid and no more: and that shall be stopped if you dare to come on to these premises again, or to come into this country after me again. The next time you show yourself inside the gates here, you shall be driven off with the dogs and the waggoner's whip.'

As Rigg pronounced the last words he turned round and looked at Raffles with his prominent frozen eyes. The contrast was as striking as it could have been eighteen years before, when Rigg was a most unengaging kickable boy, and Raffles was the rather thickset Adonis of bar-rooms and back-parlours. But the advantage now was on the side of Rigg, and auditors of this conversation might probably have expected that Raffles would retire with the air of a defeated dog. Not at all. He made a grimace which was habitual with him whenever he was 'out' in a game; then subsided into a laugh, and drew a brandy-flask from his pocket.

'Come, Josh,' he said, in a cajoling tone, 'give us a spoonful of brandy, and a sovereign to pay the way back, and I'll go. Honour bright! I'll go like a bullet, *by* Jove!'

'Mind,' said Rigg, drawing out a bunch of keys, 'if I ever see you again, I shan't speak to you. I don't own you any more than if I saw a crow; and if you want to own me you'll get nothing by it but a character for being what you are – a spiteful, brassy, bullying rogue.'

'That's a pity, now, Josh,' said Raffles, affecting to scratch his head and wrinkle his brows upwards as if he were nonplussed.

'I'm very fond of you; by Jove, I am! There's nothing I like better than plaguing you – you're so like your mother; and I must do without it. But the brandy and the sovereign's a bargain.'

He jerked forward the flask and Rigg went to a fine old oaken bureau with his keys. But Raffles had reminded himself by his movement with the flask that it had become dangerously loose from its leather covering, and catching sight of a folded paper which had fallen within the fender, he took it up and shoved it under the leather so as to make the glass firm.

By that time Rigg came forward with a brandy-bottle, filled the flask, and handed Raffles a sovereign, neither looking at him nor speaking to him. After locking up the bureau again, he walked to the window and gazed out as impassibly as he had done at the beginning of the interview, while Raffles took a small allowance from the flask, screwed it up, and deposited it in his side-pocket, with provoking slowness, making a grimace at his stepson's back.

'Farewell, Josh – and if for ever!' said Raffles, turning back his head as he opened the door.

Rigg saw him leave the grounds and enter the lane. The grey day had turned to a light drizzling rain, which freshened the hedgerows and the grassy borders of the byroads, and hastened the labourers who were loading the last shocks of corn. Raffles, walking with the uneasy gait of a town loiterer obliged to do a bit of country journeying on foot, looked as incongruous amid this moist rural quiet and industry as if he had been a baboon escaped from a menagerie. But there were none to stare at him except the long-weaned calves, and none to show dislike of his appearance except the little water-rats which rustled away at his approach.

He was fortunate enough when he got on to the highroad to be overtaken by the stage-coach, which carried him to Brassing; and there he took the new-made railway, observing to his fellow-passengers that he considered it pretty well seasoned now it had done for Huskisson. Mr Raffles on most occasions kept up the sense of having been educated at an academy, and being able, when he chose, to pass well everywhere; indeed, there was not one of his fellow-men whom he did not feel himself in a position to ridicule and torment, confident of the entertainment which he thus gave to all the rest of the company.

He played this part now with as much spirit as if his journey had been entirely successful, resorting at frequent intervals to his flask. The paper with which he had wedged it was a letter signed *Nicholas Bulstrode*, but Raffles was not likely to disturb it from its present useful position.

♋ FORTY-TWO ♋

How much, methinks, I could despise this man,
Were I not bound in charity against it!
SHAKESPEARE: *Henry VIII*

ONE OF THE PROFESSIONAL CALLS MADE by Lydgate soon after his return from his wedding-journey was to Lowick Manor, in consequence of a letter which had requested him to fix a time for his visit.

Mr Casaubon had never put any question concerning the nature of his illness to Lydgate, nor had he even to Dorothea betrayed any anxiety as to how far it might be likely to cut short his labours or his life. On this point, as on all others, he shrank from pity; and if the suspicion of being pitied for anything in his lot surmised or known in spite of himself was embittering, the idea of calling forth a show of compassion by frankly admitting an alarm or a sorrow was necessarily intolerable to him. Every proud mind knows something of this experience, and perhaps it is only to be overcome by a sense of fellowship deep enough to make all efforts at isolation seem mean and petty instead of exalting.

But Mr Casaubon was now brooding over something through which the question of his health and life haunted his silence with a more harassing importunity even than through the autumnal unripeness of his authorship. It is true that this last might be called his central ambition; but there are some kinds of authorship in which by far the largest result is the uneasy susceptibility accumulated in the consciousness of the author – one knows of the river by a few streaks amid a long-gathered deposit of uncomfortable mud. That was the way with Mr Casaubon's hard intellectual labours. Their most characteristic result was not the 'Key to all Mythologies', but a morbid consciousness that others did not give him the place which he had not demonstrably merited – a perpetual suspicious conjecture that the views entertained of him were not to his advantage – a melancholy absence of passion in his efforts at achievement, and a passionate resistance to the confession that he had achieved nothing.

Thus his intellectual ambition which seemed to others to have absorbed and dried him, was really no security against wounds, least of all against those which came from Dorothea. And he had begun now to frame possibilities for the future which were somehow more embittering to him than anything his mind had dwelt on before.

Against certain facts he was helpless: against Will Ladislaw's existence, his defiant stay in the neighbourhood of Lowick, and his flippant state of mind with regard to the possessor of authentic, well-stamped erudition: against Dorothea's nature, always taking on some new shape of ardent activity, and even in submission and silence covering fervid reasons which it was an irritation to think of: against certain notions and likings which had taken possession of her mind in relation to subjects that he could not possibly discuss with her. There was no denying that Dorothea was as virtuous and lovely a young lady as he could have obtained for a wife; but a young lady turned out to be something more troublesome than he had conceived. She nursed him, she read to him, she anticipated his wants, and was solicitous about his feelings; but there had entered into the husband's mind the certainty that she judged him, and that her wifely devotedness was like a penitential expiation of unbelieving thoughts – was accompanied with a power of comparison by which himself and his doings were seen too luminously as a part of things in general. His discontent passed vapour-like through all her gentle loving manifestations, and clung to that inappreciative world which she had only brought nearer to him.

Poor Mr Casaubon! This suffering was the harder to bear because it seemed like a betrayal: the young creature who had worshipped him with perfect trust had quickly turned into the critical wife; and early instances of criticism and resentment had made an impression which no tenderness and submission afterwards could remove. To his suspicious interpretation Dorothea's silence now was a suppressed rebellion; a remark from her which he had not in any way anticipated was an assertion of conscious superiority; her gentle answers had an irritating cautiousness in them; and when she acquiesced it was a self-approved effort of forbearance. The tenacity with which he strove to hide this inward drama made it the more vivid for him; as we hear with the more keenness what we wish others not to hear.

Instead of wondering at this result of misery in Mr Casaubon, I think it quite ordinary. Will not a tiny speck very close to our vision blot out the glory of the world, and leave only a margin by which we see the blot? I know no speck so troublesome as self. And who, if Mr Casaubon had chosen to expound his discontents – his suspicions that he was not any longer adored without criticism – could have denied that they were founded on good reasons? On the contrary, there was a strong reason to be added, which he had not himself taken explicitly into account – namely, that he was not unmixedly adorable. He suspected this, however, as he suspected other things, without confessing it, and like the rest of us, felt how soothing it would have been to have a companion who would never find it out.

This sore susceptibility in relation to Dorothea was thoroughly prepared before Will Ladislaw had returned to Lowick, and what had occurred since then had brought Mr Casaubon's power of suspicious construction into exasperated activity. To all the facts which he knew, he added imaginary facts both present and future which became more real to him than those, because they called up a stronger dislike, a more predominating bitterness. Suspicion and jealousy of Will Ladislaw's intentions, suspicion and jealousy of Dorothea's impressions, were constantly at their weaving work. It would be quite unjust to him to suppose that he could have entered into any coarse misinterpretation of Dorothea: his own habits of mind and conduct, quite as much as the open elevation of her nature, saved him from any such mistake. What he was jealous of was her opinion, the sway that might be given to her ardent mind in its judgments, and the future possibilities to which these might lead her. As to Will, though until his last defiant letter he had nothing definite which he would choose formally to allege against him, he felt himself warranted in believing that he was capable of any design which could fascinate a rebellious temper and an undisciplined impulsiveness. He was quite sure that Dorothea was the cause of Will's return from Rome, and his determination to settle in the neighbourhood; and he was penetrating enough to imagine that Dorothea had innocently encouraged this course. It was as clear as possible that she was ready to be attached to Will and to be pliant to his suggestions: they had never had a tête-à-tête without her bringing away from it some new troublesome impression, and the last interview that Mr Casaubon was aware of (Dorothea, on returning from Freshitt Hall, had for the first time been silent about having seen Will) had led to a scene which roused an angrier feeling against them both than he had ever known before. Dorothea's outpouring of her notions about money, in the darkness of the night, had done nothing but bring a mixture of more odious foreboding into her husband's mind.

And there was the shock lately given to his health always sadly present with him. He was certainly much revived; he had recovered all his usual power of work: the illness might have been mere fatigue, and there might still be twenty years of achievement before him, which would justify the thirty years of preparation. That prospect was made the sweeter by a flavour of vengeance against the hasty sneers of Carp & Company; for even when Mr Casaubon was carrying his taper among the tombs of the past, those modern figures came athwart the dim light, and interrupted his diligent exploration. To convince Carp of his mistake, so that he would have to eat his own words with a good deal of indigestion, would be an agreeable accident of triumphant authorship, which the prospect of living to future ages on earth and to all eternity in heaven could not exclude from contemplation. Since, thus, the prevision of his own unending bliss could not nullify the bitter savours of irritated jealousy and vindictiveness, it is the less surprising that the probability of a transient earthly bliss for other persons, when he himself should have entered into glory, had not a potently sweetening effect. If the truth should be that some undermining disease was at work within him, there might be large opportunity for some people to be the happier when he was gone; and if one of those people should be Will Ladislaw, Mr Casaubon objected so strongly that it seemed as if the annoyance would make part of his disembodied existence.

This is a very bare and therefore a very incomplete way of putting the case. The human soul moves in many channels, and Mr Casaubon, we know, had a sense of rectitude and an honourable pride in satisfying the requirements of honour, which compelled him to find other reasons for his conduct than those of jealousy and vindictiveness. The way in which Mr Casaubon put the case was this:–

'In marrying Dorothea Brooke I had to care for her wellbeing in case of my death. But wellbeing is not to be secured by ample, independent possession of property; on the contrary, occasions might arise in which such possession might expose her to the more danger. She is ready prey to any man who knows how to play adroitly either on her affectionate ardour or her Quixotic enthusiasm; and a man stands by with that very intention in his mind – a man with no other principle than transient caprice, and who has a personal animosity towards me – I am sure of it – an animosity which is fed by the consciousness of his ingratitude, and which he has constantly vented in ridicule of which I am as well assured as if I had heard it. Even if I live I shall not be without uneasiness as to what he may attempt through indirect influence. This man has gained Dorothea's ear: he has fascinated her attention; he has evidently tried to impress her mind with the notion that he has claims beyond anything I have done for him. If I die – and he is waiting here on the watch for that – he will persuade her to marry him. That would be calamity for her and success for him. *She* would not think it calamity: he would make her believe anything; she has a tendency to immoderate attachment which she inwardly reproaches me for not responding to, and already her mind is occupied with his fortunes. He thinks of an easy conquest and of entering into my nest. That I will hinder! Such a marriage would be fatal to Dorothea. Has he ever persisted in anything except from contradiction? In knowledge, he has always tried to be showy at small cost. In religion he could be, as long as it suited him, the facile echo of Dorothea's vagaries. When was sciolism ever dissociated from laxity? I utterly distrust his morals, and it is my duty to hinder to the utmost the fulfilment of his designs.'

The arrangements made by Mr Casaubon on his marriage left strong measures open to him, but in ruminating on them his mind inevitably dwelt so much on the probabilities of his own life that the longing to get the nearest possible calculation had at last overcome his proud reticence, and had determined him to ask Lydgate's opinion as to the nature of his illness.

He had mentioned to Dorothea that Lydgate was coming by appointment at half-past three, and in answer to her anxious question, whether he had felt ill, replied, – 'No, I merely wish to have his opinion concerning some habitual symptoms. You need not see him, my dear. I shall give orders that he may be sent to me in the Yew-Tree Walk, where I shall be taking my usual exercise.'

When Lydgate entered the Yew-Tree Walk he saw Mr Casaubon slowly receding with his hands behind him according to his habit, and his head bent forward. It was a lovely afternoon; the leaves from the lofty limes were falling silently across the sombre evergreens, while the lights and shadows slept side by side: there was no sound but the cawing of the rooks, which to the accustomed ear is a lullaby, or that last solemn lullaby, a dirge. Lydgate, conscious of an energetic frame in its prime, felt some compassion when the figure which he was likely soon to overtake turned round, and in advancing towards him showed more markedly than ever the signs of premature age – the student's bent shoulders, the emaciated limbs, and the melancholy lines of the mouth. 'Poor fellow,' he thought, 'some men with his years are like lions; one can tell nothing of their age except that they are full grown.'

'Mr Lydgate,' said Mr Casaubon, with his invariably polite air, 'I am exceedingly obliged to you for your punctuality. We will, if you please, carry on our conversation in walking to and fro.'

'I hope your wish to see me is not due to the return of unpleasant symptoms,' said Lydgate, filling up a pause.

'Not immediately – no. In order to account for that wish I must mention – what it were otherwise needless to refer to – that my life, on all collateral accounts insignificant, derives a possible importance from the incompleteness of labours which have extended through all its best years. In short, I have long had on hand a work which I would fain leave behind me in such a state, at least, that it might be committed to the press by – others. Were I assured that this is the utmost I can reasonably expect, that assurance would be a useful circumscription of my attempts, and a guide in both the positive and negative determination of my course.'

Here Mr Casaubon paused, removed one hand from his back and thrust it between the buttons of his single-breasted coat. To a mind largely instructed in the human destiny hardly anything could be more interesting than the inward conflict implied in his formal measured address, delivered with the usual sing-song and motion of the head. Nay, are there many situations more sublimely tragic than the struggle of the soul with the demand to renounce a work which has been all the significance of its life – a significance which is to vanish as the waters which come and go where no man has need of them? But there was nothing to strike others as sublime about Mr Casaubon, and Lydgate, who had some contempt at hand for futile scholarship, felt a little amusement mingling with his pity. He was at present too ill acquainted with disaster to enter into the pathos of a lot where everything is below the level of tragedy except the passionate egoism of the sufferer.

'You refer to the possible hindrances from want of health?' he said, wishing to help forward Mr Casaubon's purpose, which seemed to be clogged by some hesitation.

'I do. You have not implied to me that the symptoms which – I am bound to testify – you watched with scrupulous care, were those of a fatal disease. But were it so, Mr Lydgate, I should desire to know the truth without reservation, and I appeal to you for an exact statement of your conclusions: I request it as a friendly service. If you can tell me that my life is not threatened by anything else than ordinary casualties, I shall rejoice, on grounds which I have already indicated. If not, knowledge of the truth is even more important to me.'

'Then I can no longer hesitate as to my course,' said Lydgate; 'but the first thing I must impress on you is that my conclusions are doubly uncertain – uncertain not only because of my fallibility, but because diseases of the heart are eminently difficult to found predictions on. In any case, one can hardly increase appreciably the tremendous uncertainty of life.'

Mr Casaubon winced perceptibly, but bowed.

'I believe that you are suffering from what is called fatty degeneration of the heart, a disease which was first divined and explored by Laennec, the man who gave us the stethoscope, not so very many years ago. A good deal of experience – a more lengthened observation – is wanted on the subject. But after what you have said, it is my duty to tell you that death from this disease is often sudden. At the same time, no such result can be predicted. Your condition may be consistent with a tolerably comfortable life for another fifteen years, or even more. I could add no information to this, beyond anatomical or medical details, which would leave expectation at precisely the same point.'

Lydgate's instinct was fine enough to tell him that plain speech, quite free from ostentatious caution, would be felt by Mr Casaubon as a tribute of respect.

'I thank you, Mr Lydgate,' said Mr Casaubon, after a moment's pause. 'One thing more I have still to ask: did you communicate what you have now told me to Mrs Casaubon?'

'Partly – I mean, as to the possible issues.' Lydgate was going to explain why he had told Dorothea, but Mr Casaubon, with an unmistakable desire to end the conversation, waved his hand slightly, and said again, 'I thank you,' proceeding to remark on the rare beauty of the day.

Lydgate, certain that his patient wished to be alone, soon left him; and the black figure with hands behind and head bent forward continued to pace the walk where the dark yew-trees gave him a mute companionship in melancholy, and the little shadows of bird or leaf that fleeted across the isles of sunlight, stole along in silence as in the presence of a sorrow. Here was a man who now for the first time found himself looking into the eyes of death – who was passing through one of those rare moments of experience when we feel the truth of a commonplace, which is as different from what we call knowing it, as the vision of waters upon the earth is different from the delirious vision of the water which cannot be had to cool the burning tongue. When the commonplace 'We must all die' transforms itself suddenly into the acute consciousness 'I must die – and soon', then death grapples us, and his fingers are cruel; afterwards, he may come to fold us in his arms as our mother did, and our last moment of dim earthly discerning may be like the first. To Mr Casaubon now, it was as if he suddenly found himself on the dark river-brink and heard the plash of the oncoming oar, not discerning the forms, but expecting the summons. In such an hour the mind does not change its lifelong bias, but carries it onwards in imagination to the other side of death, gazing backward – perhaps with the divine calm of beneficence, perhaps with the petty anxieties of self-assertion. What was Mr Casaubon's bias his acts will give us a clue to. He held himself to be, with some private scholarly reservations, a believing Christian, as to estimates of the present and hopes of the future. But what we strive to gratify, though we may call it a distant hope, is an immediate desire; the future estate for which men drudge up city alleys exists already in their imagination and love. And Mr Casaubon's immediate desire was not for divine communion and light divested of earthly conditions; his passionate longings, poor man, clung low and mist-like in very shady places.

Dorothea had been aware when Lydgate had ridden away, and she had stepped into the garden, with the impulse to go at once to her husband. But she hesitated, fearing to offend him by obtruding herself; for her ardour, continually repulsed, served, with her intense memory, to heighten her dread, as thwarted energy subsides into a shudder; and she wandered slowly round the nearer clumps of trees until she saw him advancing. Then she went towards him, and might have represented a heaven-sent angel coming with a promise that the short hours remaining should yet be filled with that faithful love which clings the closer to a comprehended grief. His glance in reply to hers was so chill that she felt her timidity increased; yet she turned and passed her hand through his arm.

Mr Casaubon kept his hands behind him and allowed her pliant arm to cling with difficulty against his rigid arm.

There was something horrible to Dorothea in the sensation which this unresponsive hardness inflicted on her. That is a strong word, but not too strong: it is in these acts called trivialities that the seeds of joy are for ever wasted, until men and women look round with haggard faces at the devastation their own waste has made, and say, the earth bears no harvest of sweetness – calling their denial knowledge. You may ask why, in the name of manliness, Mr Casaubon should have behaved in that way. Consider that his was a mind which shrank from pity: have you ever watched in such a mind the effect of a suspicion that what is pressing it as a grief may be really a source of contentment, either actual or future, to the being who already offends by pitying? Besides, he knew little of Dorothea's sensations, and had not reflected that on such an occasion as the present they were comparable in strength to his own sensibilities about Carp's criticisms.

Dorothea did not withdraw her arm, but she could not venture to speak. Mr Casaubon did not say, 'I wish to be alone', but he directed his steps in silence towards the house, and as they entered by the glass door on this eastern side, Dorothea withdrew her arm and lingered on the matting, that she might leave her husband quite free. He entered the library and shut himself in, alone with his sorrow.

She went up to her boudoir. The open bow-window let in the serene glory of the afternoon lying in the avenue, where the lime-trees cast long shadows. But Dorothea knew nothing of the scene. She threw herself on a chair, not heeding that she was in the dazling sun-rays: if there were discomfort in that, how could she tell that it was not part of her inward misery?

She was in the reaction of a rebellious anger stronger than any she had felt since her marriage. Instead of tears there came words:—

'What have I done – what am I – that he should treat me so? He never knows what is in my mind – he never cares. What is the use of anything I do? He wishes he had never married me.'

She began to hear herself, and was checked into stillness. Like one who has lost his way and is weary, she sat and saw as in one glance all the paths of her young hope which she should never find again. And just as clearly in the miserable light she saw her own and her husband's solitude – how they walked apart so that she was obliged to survey him. If he had drawn her towards him, she would never have surveyed him – never have said, 'Is he worth living for?' but would have felt him simply a part of her own life. Now she said bitterly, 'It is his fault, not mine.' In the jar of her whole being, Pity was overthrown. Was it her fault that she had believed in him – had believed in his worthiness? – And what, exactly, was he? – She was able enough to estimate him – she who waited on his glances with trembling, and shut her best soul in prison, paying it only hidden visits, that she might be petty enough to please him. In such a crisis as this, some women begin to hate.

The sun was low when Dorothea was thinking that she would not go down again, but would send a message to her husband saying that she was not well and preferred remaining up-stairs. She had never deliberately allowed her resentment to govern her in this way before, but she believed now that she could not see him again without telling him the truth about her feeling, and she must wait till she could do it without interruption. He might wonder and be hurt at her message. It was good that he should wonder and be hurt. Her anger said, as anger is apt to say, that God was with her – that all heaven, though it were crowded with spirits watching them, must be on her side. She had determined to ring her bell, when there came a rap at the door.

Mr Casaubon had sent to say that he would have his dinner in the library. He wished to be quite alone this evening, being much occupied.

'I shall not dine, then, Tantripp.'

'Oh, madam, let me bring you a little something?'

'No; I am not well. Get everything ready in my dressing-room, but pray do not disturb me again.'

Dorothea sat almost motionless in her meditative struggle, while the evening slowly deepened into night. But the struggle changed continually, as that of a man who begins with a movement towards striking and ends with conquering his desire to strike. The energy that would animate a crime is not more than is wanted to inspire a resolved submission, when the noble habit of the soul reasserts itself. That thought with which Dorothea had gone out to meet her husband – her conviction that he had been asking about the possible arrest of all his work, and that the answer must have wrung his heart, could not be long without rising beside the image of him, like a shadowy monitor looking at her anger with sad remonstrance. It cost her a litany of pictured sorrows and of silent cries that she might be the mercy for those sorrows – but the resolved submission did come; and when the house was still, and she knew that it was near the time when Mr Casaubon habitually went to rest, she opened her door gently and stood outside in the darkness waiting for his coming up-stairs with a light in his hand. If he did not come soon she thought that she would go down and even risk incurring another pang. She would never again expect anything else. But she did hear the library door open, and slowly the light advanced up the staircase without noise from the foot-steps on the carpet. When her husband stood opposite to her, she saw that his face was more haggard. He started slightly on seeing her, and she looked up at him beseechingly, without speaking.

'Dorothea!' he said, with a gentle surprise in his tone. 'Were you waiting for me?'

'Yes, I did not like to disturb you.'

'Come, my dear, come. You are young, and need not to extend your life by watching.'

When the kind quiet melancholy of that speech fell on Dorothea's ears, she felt something like the thankfulness that might well up in us if we had narrowly escaped hurting a lamed creature. She put her hand into her husband's, and they went along the broad corridor together.

BOOK FIVE

THE DEAD HAND

✑ FORTY-THREE ✑

This figure hath high price: 'twas wrought with love
Ages ago in finest ivory;
Nought modish in it, pure and noble lines
Of generous womanhood that fits all time.
That too is costly ware; majolica
Of deft design, to please a lordly eye:
The smile, you see, is perfect – wonderful
As mere Faience! a table ornament
To suit the richest mounting.

DOROTHEA SELDOM LEFT HOME WITHOUT her husband, but she did occasionally drive into Middlemarch alone, on little errands of shopping or charity such as occur to every lady of any wealth when she lives within three miles of a town. Two days after that scene in the Yew-Tree Walk, she determined to use such an opportunity in order if possible to see Lydgate and learn from him whether her husband had really felt any depressing change of symptoms which he was concealing from her, and whether he had insisted on knowing the utmost about himself. She felt almost guilty in asking for knowledge about him from another, but the dread of being without it – the dread of that ignorance which would make her unjust or hard – overcame every scruple. That there had been some crisis in her husband's mind she was certain: he had the very next day begun a new method of arranging his notes, and had associated her quite newly in carrying out his plan. Poor Dorothea needed to lay up stores of patience.

It was about four o'clock when she drove to Lydgate's house in Lowick Gate, wishing, in her immediate doubt of finding him at home, that she had written beforehand. And he was not at home.

'Is Mrs Lydgate at home?' said Dorothea, who had never, that she knew of, seen Rosamond, but now remembered the fact of the marriage. Yes, Mrs Lydgate was at home.

'I will go in and speak to her, if she will allow me. Will you ask her if she can see me – see Mrs Casaubon, for a few minutes?'

When the servant had gone to deliver that message, Dorothea could hear sounds of music through an open window – a few notes from a man's voice and then a piano bursting into roulades. But the roulades broke off suddenly, and then the servant came back saying that Mrs Lydgate would be happy to see Mrs Casaubon.

When the drawing-room door opened and Dorothea entered, there was a sort of contrast not infrequent in country life when the habits of the different ranks were less blent than now. Let those who know, tell us exactly what stuff it was that Dorothea wore in those days of mild autumn – that thin white woollen stuff soft to the touch and soft to the eye. It always seemed to have been lately washed, and to smell of the sweet hedges – was always in the shape of a pelisse with sleeves hanging all out of the fashion. Yet if she had entered before a still audience as Imogen or Cato's daughter, the dress might have seemed right enough: the grace and dignity were in her limbs and neck; and about her simply parted hair and candid eyes the large round poke which was then in the fate of women, seemed no more odd as a head-dress than the gold trencher we call a halo. By the present audience of two persons, no dramatic heroine could have been expected with more interest than Mrs Casaubon. To Rosamond she was one of those county divinities not mixing with Middlemarch mortality, whose slightest marks of manner or appearance were worthy of her study; moreover, Rosamond was not without satisfaction that Mrs Casaubon should have an opportunity of studying *her*. What is the use of being exquisite if you are not seen by the best judges? and since Rosamond had received the highest compliments at Sir Godwin Lydgate's, she felt quite confident of the impression she must make on people of good birth. Dorothea put out her hand with her usual simple kindness, and looked admiringly at Lydgate's lovely bride – aware that there was a gentleman standing at a distance, but seeing him merely as a coated figure at a wide angle. The gentleman was too much occupied with the presence of the one woman to reflect on the contrast between the two – a contrast that would certainly have been striking to a calm observer. They were both tall, and their eyes were on a level; but imagine Rosamond's infantine blondness and wondrous crown of hair-plaits, with her pale-blue dress of a fit and fashion so perfect that no dressmaker could look at it without emotion, a large embroidered collar which it was to be hoped all beholders would know the price of, her small hands duly set off with rings, and that controlled self-consciousness of manner which is the expensive substitute for simplicity.

'Thank you very much for allowing me to interrupt you,' said Dorothea, immediately. 'I am anxious to see Mr Lydgate, if possible, before I go home, and I hoped that you might possibly tell me where I could find him, or even allow me to wait for him, if you expect him soon.'

'He is at the New Hospital,' said Rosamond; 'I am not sure how soon he will come home. But I can send for him.'

'Will you let me go and fetch him?' said Will Ladislaw, coming forward. He had already taken up his hat before Dorothea entered. She coloured with surprise, but put out her hand with a smile of unmistakable pleasure, saying –

'I did not know it was you: I had no thought of seeing you here.'

'May I go to the Hospital and tell Mr Lydgate that you wish to see him?' said Will.

'It would be quicker to send the carriage for him,' said Dorothea, 'if you will be kind enough to give the message to the coachman.'

Will was moving to the door when Dorothea, whose mind had flashed in an instant over many connected memories, turned quickly and said, 'I will go myself, thank you. I wish to lose no time before getting home again. I will drive to the Hospital and see Mr Lydgate there. Pray excuse me, Mrs Lydgate. I am very much obliged to you.'

Her mind was evidently arrested by some sudden thought, and she left the room hardly conscious of what was immediately around her – hardly conscious that Will opened the door for her and offered her his arm to lead her to the carriage. She took the arm but said nothing. Will was feeling rather vexed and miserable, and found nothing to say on his side. He handed her into the carriage in silence, they said good-bye, and Dorothea drove away.

In the five minutes' drive to the Hospital she had time for some reflections that were quite new to her. Her decision to go, and her preoccupation in leaving the room, had come from the sudden sense that there would be a sort of deception in her voluntarily allowing any further intercourse between herself and Will which she was unable to mention to her husband, and already her errand in seeking Lydgate was a matter of concealment. That was all that had been explicitly in her mind; but she had been urged also by a vague discomfort. Now that she was alone in her drive, she heard the notes of the man's voice and the accompanying piano, which she had not noted much at the time, returning on her inward sense; and she found herself thinking with some wonder that Will Ladislaw was passing his time with Mrs Lydgate in her husband's absence. And then she could not help remembering that he had passed some time with her under like circumstances, so why should there be any unfitness in the fact? But Will was Mr Casaubon's relative, and one towards whom she was bound to show kindness. Still there had been signs which perhaps she ought to have understood as implying that Mr Casaubon did not like his cousin's visits during his own absence. 'Perhaps I have been mistaken in many things,' said poor Dorothea to herself, while the tears came rolling and she had to dry them quickly. She felt confusedly unhappy, and the image of Will which had been so clear to her before was mysteriously spoiled. But the carriage stopped at the gate of the Hospital. She was soon walking round the grass plots with Lydgate, and her feelings recovered the strong bent which had made her seek for this interview.

Will Ladislaw, meanwhile, was mortified, and knew the reason of it clearly enough. His chances of meeting Dorothea were rare; and here for the first time there had come a chance which had set him at a disadvantage. It was not only, as it had been hitherto, that she was not supremely occupied with him, but that she had seen him under circumstances in which he might appear not to be supremely occupied with her. He felt thrust to a new distance from her, amongst the circles of Middlemarchers who made no part of her life. But that was not his fault: of course, since he had taken his lodgings in the town, he had been making as many acquaintances as he could, his position requiring that he should know everybody and everything. Lydgate was really better worth knowing than any one else in the neighbourhood, and he happened to have a wife who was musical and altogether worth calling upon. Here was the whole history of the situation in which Diana had descended too unexpectedly on her worshipper. It was mortifying. Will was conscious that he should not have been at Middlemarch but for Dorothea; and yet his position there was threatening to divide him from her with those barriers of habitual sentiment which are more fatal to the persistence of mutual interest than all the distance between Rome and Britain. Prejudices about rank and status were easy enough to defy in the form of a tyrannical letter from Mr Casaubon; but prejudices, like odorous bodies, have a double existence both solid and subtle – solid as the pyramids, subtle as the twentieth echo of an echo, or as the memory of hyacinths which once scented the darkness. And Will was of a temperament to feel keenly the presence of subtleties: a man of clumsier perceptions would not have felt, as he did, that for the first time some sense of unfitness in perfect freedom with him had sprung up in Dorothea's mind, and that their silence, as he conducted her to the carriage, had had a chill in it. Perhaps Casaubon, in his hatred and jealousy, had been insisting to Dorothea that Will had slid below her socially. Confound Casaubon!

Will re-entered the drawing-room, took up his hat, and looking irritated as he advanced towards Mrs Lydgate, who had seated herself at her work-table, said –

'It is always fatal to have music or poetry interrupted. May I come another day and just finish about the rendering of "Lungi dal caro bene"?'

'I shall be happy to be taught,' said Rosamond. 'But I am sure you admit that the interruption was a very beautiful one. I quite envy your acquaintance with Mrs Casaubon. Is she very clever? She looks as if she were.'

'Really, I never thought about it,' said Will, sulkily.

'That is just the answer Tertius gave me, when I first asked him if she were handsome. What is it that you gentlemen are thinking of when you are with Mrs Casaubon?'

'Herself,' said Will, not indisposed to provoke the charming Mrs Lydgate. 'When one sees a perfect woman, one never thinks of her attributes – one is conscious of her presence.'

'I shall be jealous when Tertius goes to Lowick,' said Rosamond, dimpling, and speaking with aëry lightness. 'He will come back and think nothing of me.'

'That does not seem to have been the effect on Lydgate hitherto. Mrs Casaubon is too unlike other women for them to be compared with her.'

'You are a devout worshipper, I perceive. You often see her, I suppose.'

'No,' said Will, almost pettishly. 'Worship is usually a matter of theory rather than of practice. But I am practising it to excess just at this moment – I must really tear myself away.'

'Pray come again some evening: Mr Lydgate will like to hear the music, and I cannot enjoy it so well without him.'

When her husband was at home again, Rosamond said, standing in front of him and holding his coat-collar with both her hands, 'Mr Ladislaw was here singing with me when Mrs Casaubon came in. He seemed vexed. Do you think he disliked her seeing him at our house? Surely your position is more than equal to his – whatever may be his relation to the Casaubons.'

'No, no; it must be something else if he were really vexed. Ladislaw is a sort of gypsy; he thinks nothing of leather and prunella.'

'Music apart, he is not always very agreeable. Do you like him?'

'Yes: I think he is a good fellow: rather miscellaneous and *bric-à-brac*, but likable.'

'Do you know, I think he adores Mrs Casaubon.'

'Poor devil!' said Lydgate, smiling and pinching his wife's ears.

Rosamond felt herself beginning to know a great deal of the world, especially in discovering – what when she was in her unmarried girlhood had been inconceivable to her except as a dim tragedy in bygone costumes – that women, even after marriage, might make conquests and enslave men. At that time young ladies in the country, even when educated at Mrs Lemon's, read little French literature later than Racine, and public prints had not cast their present magnificent illumination over the scandals of life. Still, vanity, with a woman's whole mind and day to work in, can construct abundantly on slight hints, especially on such a hint as the possibility of indefinite conquests. How delightful to make captives from the throne of marriage with a husband as crown-prince by your side – himself in fact a subject – while the captives look up for ever hopeless, losing their rest probably, and if their appetite too, so much the better! But Rosamond's romance turned at present chiefly on her crown-prince, and it was enough to enjoy his assured subjection. When he said, 'Poor devil!' she asked, with playful curiosity –

'Why so?'

'Why, what can a man do when he takes to adoring one of you mermaids? He only neglects his work and runs up bills.'

'I am sure you do not neglect your work. You are always at the Hospital, or seeing poor patients, or thinking about some doctor's quarrel; and then at home you always want to pore over your microscope and phials. Confess you like those things better than me.'

'Haven't you ambition enough to wish that your husband should be something better than a Middlemarch doctor?' said Lydgate, letting his hands fall on to his wife's shoulders, and looking at her with affectionate gravity. 'I shall make you learn my favourite bit from an old poet –

> Why should our pride make such a stir to be
> And be forgot? What good is like to this,
> To do worthy the writing, and to write
> Worthy the reading and the world's delight?

What I want, Rosy, is to do worthy the writing, – and to write out myself what I have done. A man must work, to do that, my pet.'

'Of course, I wish you to make discoveries: no one could more wish you to attain a high position in some better place than Middlemarch. You cannot say that I have ever tried to hinder you from working. But we cannot live like hermits. You are not discontented with me, Tertius?'

'No, dear, no. I am too entirely contented.'

'But what did Mrs Casaubon want to say to you?'

'Merely to ask about her husband's health. But I think she is going to be splendid to our New Hospital: I think she will give us two hundred a-year.'

◁ FORTY-FOUR ▷

> I would not creep along the coast, but steer
> Out in mid-sea, by guidance of the stars.

WHEN DOROTHEA, WALKING ROUND THE laurel-planted plots of the New Hospital with Lydgate, had learned from him that there were no signs of change in Mr Casaubon's bodily condition beyond the mental sign of anxiety to know the truth about his illness, she was silent for a few moments, wondering whether she had said or done anything to rouse this new anxiety. Lydgate, not willing to let slip an opportunity of furthering a favourite purpose, ventured to say –

'I don't know whether your or Mr Casaubon's attention has been drawn to the needs of our New Hospital. Circumstances have made it seem rather egotistic in me to urge the subject; but that is not my fault; it is because there is a fight being made against it by the other medical men. I think you are generally interested in such things, for I remember that when I first had the pleasure of seeing you at Tipton Grange before your marriage you were asking me some questions about the way in which the health of the poor was affected by their miserable housing.'

'Yes, indeed,' said Dorothea, brightening. 'I shall be quite grateful to you if you will tell me how I can help to make things a little better. Everything of that sort has slipped away from me since I have been married. I mean,' she said, after a moment's hesitation, 'that the people in our village are tolerably comfortable, and my mind has been too much taken up for me to inquire further. But here – in such a place as Middlemarch – there must be a great deal to be done.'

'There is everything to be done,' said Lydgate, with abrupt energy. 'And this Hospital is a capital piece of work, due entirely to Mr Bulstrode's exertions, and in a great degree to his money. But one man can't do everything in a scheme of this sort. Of course he looked forward to help. And now there's a mean, petty feud set up against the thing in the town, by certain persons who want to make it a failure.'

'What can be their reasons?' said Dorothea, with naïve surprise.

'Chiefly Mr Bulstrode's unpopularity, to begin with. Half the town would almost take trouble for the sake of thwarting him. In this stupid world most people never consider that a thing is good to be done unless it is done by their own set. I had no connection with Bulstrode before I came here. I look at him quite impartially, and I see that he has some notions – that he has set things on foot – which I can turn to good public purpose. If a fair number of the better educated men went to work with the belief that their observations might contribute to the reform of medical doctrine and practice, we should soon see a change for the better. That's my point of view. I hold that by refusing to work with Mr Bulstrode I should be turning my back on an opportunity of making my profession more generally serviceable.'

'I quite agree with you,' said Dorothea, at once fascinated by the situation sketched in Lydgate's words. 'But what is there against Mr Bulstrode? I know that my uncle is friendly with him.'

'People don't like his religious tone,' said Lydgate, breaking off there.

'That is all the stronger reason for despising such an opposition,' said Dorothea, looking at the affairs of Middlemarch by the light of the great persecutions.

'To put the matter quite fairly, they have other objections to him: – he is masterful and rather unsociable, and he is concerned with trade, which has complaints of its own that I know nothing about. But what has that to do with the question whether it would not be a fine thing to establish here a more valuable hospital than any they have in the county? The immediate motive to the opposition, however, is the fact that Bulstrode has put the medical direction into my hands. Of course I am glad of that. It gives me an opportunity of doing some good work, – and I am aware that I have to justify his choice of me. But the consequence is, that the whole profession in Middlemarch have set themselves tooth and nail against the Hospital, and not only refuse to co-operate themselves, but try to blacken the whole affair and hinder subscriptions.'

'How very petty!' exclaimed Dorothea, indignantly.

'I suppose one must expect to fight one's way: there is hardly anything to be done without it. And the ignorance of people about here is stupendous. I don't lay claim to anything else than having used some opportunities which have not come within everybody's reach; but there is no stifling the offence of being young, and a newcomer, and happening to know something more than the old inhabitants. Still, if I believe that I can set going a better method of treatment – if I believe that I can pursue certain observations and inquiries which may be a lasting benefit to medical practice, I should be a base truckler if I allowed any consideration of personal comfort to hinder me. And the course is all the clearer from there being no salary in question to put my persistence in an equivocal light.'

'I am glad you have told me this, Mr Lydgate,' said Dorothea, cordially. 'I feel sure I can help a little. I have some money, and don't know what to do with it – that is often an uncomfortable thought to me. I am sure I can spare two hundred a-year for a grand purpose like this. How happy you must be, to know things that you feel sure will do great good! I wish I could awake with that knowledge every morning. There seems to be so much trouble taken that one can hardly see the good of!'

There was a melancholy cadence in Dorothea's voice as she spoke these last words. But she presently added, more cheerfully, 'Pray come to Lowick and tell us more of this. I will mention the subject to Mr Casaubon. I must hasten home now.'

She did mention it that evening, and said that she should like to subscribe two hundred a-year – she had seven hundred a-year as the equivalent of her own fortune, settled on her at her marriage. Mr Casaubon made no objection beyond a passing remark that the sum might be disproportionate in relation to other good objects, but when Dorothea in her ignorance resisted that suggestion, he acquiesced. He did not care himself about spending money, and was not reluctant to give it. If he ever felt keenly any question of money it was through the medium of another passion than the love of material property.

Dorothea told him that she had seen Lydgate, and recited the gist of her conversation with him about the Hospital. Mr Casaubon did not question her further, but he felt sure that she had wished to know what had passed between Lydgate and himself. 'She knows that I know,' said the ever-restless voice within; but that increase of tacit knowledge only thrust further off any confidence between them. He distrusted her affection; and what loneliness is more lonely than distrust?

⚘ FOURTY-FIVE ⚘

It is the humour of many heads to extol the days of their
forefathers, and declaim against the wickedness of times
present. Which notwithstanding they cannot handsomely do,
without the borrowed help and satire of times past;
condemning the vices of their own times, by the expressions of
vices in times which they commend, which cannot but argue
the community of vice in both. Horace, therefore, Juvenal, and
Persius, were no prophets, although their lines did seem to
indigitate and point at our times.
            SIR THOMAS BROWNE: *Pseudodoxia Epidemica*

THAT OPPOSITION TO THE NEW FEVER hospital which Lydgate had sketched
to Dorothea was, like other oppositions, to be viewed in many different
lights. He regarded it as a mixture of jealousy and dunder-headed prejudice. Mr Bulstrode saw in it not only medical jealousy but a determination
to thwart himself, prompted mainly by a hatred of that vital religion of
which he had striven to be an effectual lay representative – a hatred which
certainly found pretexts apart from religion such as were only too easy to
find in the entanglements of human action. These might be called the
ministerial views. But oppositions have the illimitable range of objections
at command, which need never stop short at the boundary of knowledge,
but can draw for ever on the vasts of ignorance. What the opposition in
Middlemarch said about the New Hospital and its administration had
certainly a great deal of echo in it, for heaven has taken care that everybody shall not be an originator; but there were differences which represented every social shade between the polished moderation of Dr Minchin
and the trenchant assertion of Mrs Dollop, the landlady of the Tankard in
Slaughter Lane.

Mrs Dollop became more and more convinced by her own asseveration,
that Doctor Lydgate meant to let the people die in the Hospital, if not to
poison them, for the sake of cutting them up without saying by your leave
or with your leave; for it was a known 'fac' that he had wanted to cut up
Mrs Goby, as respectable a woman as any in Parley Street, who had money
in trust before her marriage – a poor tale for a doctor, who if he was good
for anything should know what was the matter with you before you died,
and not want to pry into your inside after you were gone. If that was not
reason, Mrs Dollop wished to know what was; but there was a prevalent

343

feeling in her audience that her opinion was a bulwark, and that if it were overthrown there would be no limits to the cutting-up of bodies, as had been well seen in Burke and Hare with their pitch-plaisters – such a hanging business as that was not wanted in Middlemarch!

And let it not be supposed that opinion at the Tankard in Slaughter Lane was unimportant to the medical profession: that old authentic public-house – the original Tankard known by the name of Dollop's – was the resort of a great Benefit Club, which had some months before put to the vote whether its long-standing medical man, 'Doctor Gambit', should not be cashiered in favour of 'this Doctor Lydgate', who was capable of performing the most astonishing cures, and rescuing people altogether given up by other practitioners. But the balance had been turned against Lydgate by two members, who for some private reasons held that this power of resuscitating persons as good as dead was an equivocal recommendation, and might interfere with providential favours. In the course of the year, however, there had been a change in the public sentiment, of which the unanimity at Dollop's was an index.

A good deal more than a year ago, before anything was known of Lydgate's skill, the judgments on it had naturally been divided, depending on a sense of likelihood, situated perhaps in the pit of the stomach or in the pineal gland, and differing in its verdicts, but not the less valuable as a guide in the total deficit of evidence. Patients who had chronic diseases or whose lives had long been worn threadbare, like old Featherstone's, had been at once inclined to try him; also, many who did not like paying their doctor's bills, thought agreeably of opening an account with a new doctor and sending for him without stint if the children's temper wanted a dose, occasions when the old practitioners were often crusty; and all persons thus inclined to employ Lydgate held it likely that he was clever. Some considered that he might do more than others 'where there was liver'; – at least there would be no harm in getting a few bottles of 'stuff' from him, since if these proved useless it would still be possible to return to the Purifying Pills, which kept you alive, if they did not remove the yellowness. But these were people of minor importance. Good Middlemarch families were of course not going to change their doctor without reason shown; and everybody who had employed Mr Peacock did not feel obliged to accept a new man merely in the character of his successor, objecting that he was 'not likely to be equal to Peacock'.

But Lydgate had not been long in the town before there were particulars enough reported of him to breed much more specific expectations and to intensify differences into partisanship; some of the particulars being of that impressive order of which the significance is entirely hidden, like a statistical amount without a standard of comparison, but with a note of exclamation at the end. The cubic feet of oxygen yearly swallowed by a full-grown man – what a shudder they might have created in some Middlemarch circles! 'Oxygen! nobody knows what that may be – is it any wonder the cholera has got to Dantzic? And yet there are people who say quarantine is no good!'

One of the facts quickly rumoured was that Lydgate did not dispense drugs. This was offensive both to the physicians whose exclusive distinction seemed infringed on, and to the surgeon-apothecaries with whom he ranged himself; and only a little while before, they might have counted on having the law on their side against a man who without calling himself a London-made M.D. dared to ask for pay except as a charge on drugs. But Lydgate had not been experienced enough to foresee that his new course would be even more offensive to the laity; and to Mr Mawmsey, an important grocer in the Top Market, who, though not one of his patients, questioned him in an affable manner on the subject, he was injudicious enough to give a hasty popular explanation of his reasons, pointing out to Mr Mawmsey that it must lower the character of practitioners, and be a constant injury to the public, if their only mode of getting paid for their work was by their making out long bills for draughts, boluses, and mixtures.

'It is in that way that hard-working medical men may come to be almost as mischievous as quacks,' said Lydgate, rather thoughtlessly. 'To get their own bread they must overdose the king's lieges; and that's a bad sort of treason, Mr Mawmsey – undermines the constitution in a fatal way.'

Mr Mawmsey was not only an overseer (it was about a question of outdoor pay that he was having an interview with Lydgate), he was also asthmatic and had an increasing family: thus, from a medical point of view, as well as from his own, he was an important man; indeed, an exceptional grocer, whose hair was arranged in a flame-like pyramid, and whose retail deference was of the cordial, encouraging kind – jocosely complimentary, and with a certain considerate abstinence from letting out the full force of his mind. It was Mr Mawmsey's friendly jocoseness in questioning him which had set the tone of Lydgate's reply. But let the wise be warned against too great readiness at explanation: it multiplies the sources of mistake, lengthening the sum for reckoners sure to go wrong.

Lydgate smiled as he ended his speech, putting his foot into the stirrup, and Mr Mawmsey laughed more than he would have done if he had known who the king's lieges were, giving his 'Good morning, sir, good morning, sir' with the air of one who saw everything clearly enough. But in truth his views were perturbed. For years he had been paying bills with strictly-made items, so that for every half-crown and eighteenpence he was certain something measurable had been delivered. He had done this with satisfaction, including it among his responsibilities as a husband and father, and regarding a longer bill than usual as a dignity worth mentioning. Moreover, in addition to the massive benefit of the drugs to 'self and family', he had enjoyed the pleasure of forming an acute judgment as to their immediate effects, so as to give an intelligent statement for the guidance of Mr Gambit – a practitioner just a little lower in status than

Wrench or Toller, and especially esteemed as an accoucheur, of whose ability Mr Mawmsey had the poorest opinion on all other points, but in doctoring, he was wont to say in an undertone, he placed Gambit above any of them.

Here were deeper reasons than the superficial talk of a new man, which appeared still flimsier in the drawing-room over the shop, when they were recited to Mrs Mawmsey, a woman accustomed to be made much of as a fertile mother, – generally under attendance more or less frequent from Mr Gambit, and occasionally having attacks which required Dr Minchin.

'Does this Mr Lydgate mean to say there is no use in taking medicine?' said Mrs Mawmsey, who was slightly given to drawling. 'I should like him to tell me how I could bear up at Fair time, if I didn't take strengthening medicine for a month beforehand. Think of what I have to provide for calling customers, my dear!' – here Mrs Mawmsey turned to an intimate female friend who sat by – 'a large veal pie – a stuffed fillet – a round of beef – ham, tongue, *et* cetera, *et* cetera! But what keeps me up best is the pink mixture, not the brown. I wonder, Mr Mawmsey, with *your* experience, you could have patience to listen. *I* should have told him at once that I knew a little better than that.'

'No, no, no,' said Mr Mawmsey; 'I was not going to tell him my opinion. Hear everything and judge for yourself is my motto. But he didn't know who he was talking to. I was not to be turned on *his* finger. People often pretend to tell me things, when they might as well say, "Mawmsey, you're a fool." But I smile at it: I humour everybody's weak place. If physic had done harm to self and family, I should have found it out by this time.'

The next day Mr Gambit was told that Lydgate went about saying physic was of no use.

'Indeed!' said he, lifting his eyebrows with cautious surprise. (He was a stout husky man with a large ring on his fourth finger.) 'How will he cure his patients then?'

'That is what *I* say,' returned Mrs Mawmsey, who habitually gave weight to her speech by loading her pronouns. 'Does *he* suppose that people will pay him only to come and sit with them and go away again?'

Mrs Mawmsey had had a great deal of sitting from Mr Gambit, including very full accounts of his own habits of body and other affairs; but of course he knew there was no innuendo in her remark, since his spare time and personal narrative had never been charged for. So he replied, humorously –

'Well, Lydgate is a good-looking young fellow, you know.'

'Not one that *I* would employ,' said Mrs Mawmsey. '*Others* may do as they please.'

Hence Mr Gambit could go away from the chief grocer's without fear of rivalry, but not without a sense that Lydgate was one of those hypocrites who try to discredit others by advertising their own honesty, and that it might be worth some people's while to show him up. Mr Gambit, however, had a satisfactory practice, much pervaded by the smells of retail trading which suggested the reduction of cash payments to a balance. And he did not think it worth his while to show Lydgate up until he knew how. He had not indeed great resources of education, and had had to work his own way against a good deal of professional contempt; but he made none the worse accoucheur for calling the breathing apparatus 'longs'.

Other medical men felt themselves more capable. Mr Toller shared the highest practice in the town and belonged to an old Middlemarch family: there were Tollers in the law and everything else above the line of retail trade. Unlike our irascible friend Wrench, he had the easiest way in the world of taking things which might be supposed to annoy him, being a well-bred, quietly facetious man, who kept a good house, was very fond of a little sporting when he could get it, very friendly with Mr Hawley, and hostile to Mr Bulstrode. It may seem odd that with such pleasant habits he should have been given to the heroic treatment, bleeding and blistering and starving his patients, with a dispassionate disregard to his personal example; but the incongruity favoured the opinion of his ability among his patients, who commonly observed that Mr Toller had lazy manners, but his treatment was as active as you could desire: – no man, said they, carried more seriousness into his profession: he was a little slow in coming, but when he came he *did* something. He was a great favourite in his own circle, and whatever he implied to any one's disadvantage told doubly from his careless ironical tone.

He naturally got tired of smiling and saying, 'Ah!' when he was told that Mr Peacock's successor did not mean to dispense medicines; and Mr Hackbutt one day mentioning it over the wine at a dinner-party, Mr Toller said, laughingly, 'Dibbitts will get rid of his stale drugs, then. I'm fond of little Dibbitts – I'm glad he's in luck.'

'I see your meaning. Toller,' said Mr Hackbutt, 'and I am entirely of your opinion. I shall take an opportunity of expressing myself to that effect. A medical man should be responsible for the quality of the drugs consumed by his patients. That is the *rationale* of the system of charging which has hitherto obtained; and nothing is more offensive than this ostentation of reform, where there is no real amelioration.'

'Ostentation, Hackbutt?' said Mr Toller, ironically. 'I don't see that. A man can't very well be ostentatious of what nobody believes in. There's no reform in the matter: the question is, whether the profit on the drugs is paid to the medical man by the druggist or by the patient, and whether there shall be extra pay under the name of attendance.'

'Ah, to be sure; one of your damned new versions of old humbug,' said Mr Hawley, passing the decanter to Mr Wrench.

Mr Wrench, generally abstemious, often drank wine rather freely at a party, getting the more irritable in consequence.

'As to humbug, Hawley,' he said, 'that's a word easy to fling about. But what I contend against is the way medical men are fouling their own nest, and setting up a cry about the country as if a general practitioner who dispenses drugs couldn't be a gentleman. I throw back the imputation with scorn. I say, the most ungentlemanly trick a man can be guilty of is to come among the members of his profession with innovations which are a libel on their time-honoured procedure. That is my opinion, and I am ready to maintain it against any one who contradicts me.' Mr Wrench's voice had become exceedingly sharp.

'I can't oblige you there, Wrench,' said Mr Hawley, thrusting his hands into his trouser-pockets.

'My dear fellow,' said Mr Toller, striking in pacifically, and looking at Mr Wrench, 'the physicians have their toes trodden on more than we have. If you come to dignity it is a question for Minchin and Sprague.'

'Does medical jurisprudence provide nothing against these infringements?' said Mr Hackbutt, with a disinterested desire to offer his lights. 'How does the law stand, eh, Hawley?'

'Nothing to be done there,' said Mr Hawley. 'I looked into it for Sprague. You'd only break your nose against a damned judge's decision.'

'Pooh! no need of law,' said Mr Toller. 'So far as practice is concerned the attempt is an absurdity. No patient will like it – certainly not Peacock's, who have been used to depletion. Pass the wine.'

Mr Toller's prediction was partly verified. If Mr and Mrs Mawmsey, who had no idea of employing Lydgate, were made uneasy by his supposed declaration against drugs, it was inevitable that those who called him in should watch a little anxiously to see whether he did 'use all the means he might use' in the case. Even good Mr Powderell, who in his constant charity of interpretation was inclined to esteem Lydgate the more for what seemed a conscientious pursuit of a better plan, had his mind disturbed with doubts during his wife's attack of erysipelas, and could not abstain from mentioning to Lydgate that Mr Peacock on a similar occasion had administered a series of boluses which were not otherwise definable than by their remarkable effect in bringing Mrs Powderell round before Michaelmas from an illness which had begun in a remarkably hot August. At last, indeed, in the conflict between his desire not to hurt Lydgate and his anxiety that no 'means' should be lacking, he induced his wife privately to take Widgeon's Purifying Pills, an esteemed Middlemarch medicine, which arrested every disease at the fountain by setting to work at once upon the blood. This co-operative measure was not to be mentioned to Lydgate, and Mr Powderell himself had no certain reliance on it, only hoping that it might be attended with a blessing.

But in this doubtful stage of Lydgate's introduction he was helped by what we mortals rashly call good fortune. I suppose no doctor ever came newly to a place without making cures that surprised somebody – cures which may be called fortune's testimonials, and deserve as much credit as the written or printed kind. Various patients got well while Lydgate was attending them, some even of dangerous illnesses; and it was remarked that the new doctor with his new ways had at least the merit of bringing people back from the brink of death. The trash talked on such occasions was the more vexatious to Lydgate, because it gave precisely the sort of prestige which an incompetent and unscrupulous man would desire, and was sure to be imputed to him by the simmering dislike of the other medical men as an encouragement on his own part of ignorant puffing. But even his proud outspokenness was checked by the discernment that it was as useless to fight against the interpretations of ignorance as to whip the fog; and 'good fortune' insisted on using those interpretations.

Mrs Larcher having just become charitably concerned about alarming symptoms in her charwoman, when Dr Minchin called, asked him to see her then and there, and to give her a certificate for the Infirmary; where-upon after examination he wrote a statement of the case as one of tumour, and recommended the bearer Nancy Nash as an out-patient. Nancy, call-ing at home on her way to the Infirmary, allowed the staymaker and his wife, in whose attic she lodged, to read Dr Minchin's paper, and by this means became a subject of compassionate conversation in the neigh-bouring shops of Churchyard Lane as being afflicted with a tumour at first declared to be as large and hard as a duck's egg, but later in the day to be about the size of 'your fist'. Most hearers agreed that it would have to be cut out, but one had known of oil and another of 'squitchineal' as adequate to soften and reduce any lump in the body when taken enough of into the inside – the oil by gradually 'soopling', the squitchineal by eating away.

Meanwhile when Nancy presented herself at the Infirmary it happened to be one of Lydgate's days there. After questioning and examining her, Lydgate said to the house-surgeon in an undertone, 'It's not tumour: it's cramp.' He ordered her a blister and some steel mixture, and told her to go home and rest, giving her at the same time a note to Mrs Larcher, who, she said, was her best employer, to testify that she was in need of good food.

But by-and-by Nancy, in her attic, became portentously worse, the sup-posed tumour having indeed given way to the blister, but only wandered to another region with angrier pain. The staymaker's wife went to fetch Lydgate, and he continued for a fortnight to attend Nancy in her own home, until under his treatment she got quite well and went to work again. But the case continued to be described as one of tumour in Church-yard Lane and other streets – nay, by Mrs Larcher also; for when Lydgate's remarkable cure was mentioned to Dr Minchin, he naturally did not like to say, 'The case was not one of tumour, and I was mistaken in describing it as such,' but answered, 'Indeed! ah! I saw it was a surgical case, not of a fatal kind.' He had been inwardly annoyed, however, when he had asked at the Infirmary about the woman he had recommended two days before, to hear from the house-surgeon, a youngster who was not sorry to vex Minchin with impunity, exactly what had occurred: he privately pronounced that it was indecent in a general practitioner to contradict a physician's diagnosis in that open manner, and afterwards agreed with Wrench that Lydgate was disagreeably inattentive to etiquette. Lydgate did not make the affair a ground for valuing himself or (very particularly) despising Minchin, such rectification of misjudgments often happening among men of equal qualifications. But report took up this amazing case of tumour, not clearly distinguished from cancer, and considered the more awful for being of the wandering sort; till much prejudice against Lydgate's method as to drugs was overcome by the proof of his marvellous skill in the speedy restoration of Nancy Nash after she had been rolling and rolling in agonies from the presence of a tumour both hard and obstinate, but nevertheless compelled to yield.

How could Lydgate help himself? It is offensive to tell a lady when she is expressing her amazement at your skill, that she is altogether mistaken and rather foolish in her amazement. And to have entered into the nature of diseases would only have added to his breaches of medical propriety. Thus he had to wince under a promise of success given by that ignorant praise which misses every valid quality.

In the case of a more conspicuous patient, Mr Borthrop Trumbull, Lydgate was conscious of having shown himself something better than an everyday doctor, though here too it was an equivocal advantage that he won. The eloquent auctioneer was seized with pneumonia, and having been a patient of Mr Peacock's, sent for Lydgate, whom he had expressed his intention to patronize. Mr Trumbull was a robust man, a good subject for trying the expectant theory upon – watching the course of an interesting disease when left as much as possible to itself, so that the stages might be noted for future guidance; and from the air with which he described his sensations Lydgate surmised that he would like to be taken into his medical man's confidence, and be represented as a partner in his own cure. The auctioneer heard, without much surprise, that his was a constitution which (always with due watching) might be left to itself, so as to offer a beautiful example of a disease with all its phases seen in clear delineation, and that he probably had the rare strength of mind voluntarily to become the test of a rational procedure, and thus make the disorder of his pulmonary functions a general benefit to society.

Mr Trumbull acquiesced at once, and entered strongly into the view that an illness of his was no ordinary occasion for medical science.

'Never fear, sir; you are not speaking to one who is altogether ignorant of the *vis medicatrix*,' said he, with his usual superiority of expression, made rather pathetic by difficulty of breathing. And he went without shrinking through his abstinence from drugs, much sustained by application of the thermometer which implied the importance of his temperature, by the sense that he furnished objects for the microscope, and by learning many new words which seemed suited to the dignity of his secretions. For Lydgate was acute enough to indulge him with a little technical talk.

It may be imagined that Mr Trumbull rose from his couch with a disposition to speak of an illness in which he had manifested the strength of his mind as well as constitution; and he was not backward in awarding credit to the medical man who had discerned the quality of patient he had to deal with. The auctioneer was not an ungenerous man, and liked to give others their due, feeling that he could afford it. He had caught the words 'expectant method', and rang chimes on this and other learned phrases to accompany the assurance that Lydgate 'knew a thing or two more than the rest of the doctors – was far better versed in the secrets of his profession than the majority of his compeers'.

This had happened before the affair of Fred Vincy's illness had given to Mr Wrench's enmity towards Lydgate more definite personal ground. The newcomer already threatened to be a nuisance in the shape of rivalry, and was certainly a nuisance in the shape of practical criticism or reflections on his hard-driven elders, who had had something else to do than to busy themselves with untried notions. His practice had spread in one or two quarters, and from the first the report of his high family had led to his being pretty generally invited, so that the other medical men had to meet him at dinner in the best houses; and having to meet a man whom you dislike is not observed always to end in mutual attachment. There was hardly ever so much unanimity among them as in the opinion that Lydgate was an arrogant young fellow, and yet ready for the sake of ultimately predominating to show a crawling subservience to Bulstrode. That Mr Farebrother, whose name was a chief flag of the anti-Bulstrode party, always defended Lydgate and made a friend of him, was referred to Farebrother's unaccountable way of fighting on both sides.

Here was plenty of preparation for the outburst of professional disgust at the announcement of the laws Mr Bulstrode was laying down for the direction of the New Hospital, which were the more exasperating because there was no present possibility of interfering with his will and pleasure, everybody except Lord Medlicote having refused help towards the building, on the ground that they preferred giving to the Old Infirmary. Mr Bulstrode met all the expenses, and had ceased to be sorry that he was purchasing the right to carry out his notions of improvement without hindrance from prejudiced coadjutors; but he had had to spend large sums and the building had lingered. Caleb Garth had undertaken it, had failed during its progress, and before the interior fittings were begun had retired from the management of the business; and when referring to the Hospital he often said that however Bulstrode might ring if you tried him, he liked good solid carpentry and masonry, and had a notion both of drains and chimneys. In fact, the Hospital had become an object of intense interest to Bulstrode, and he would willingly have continued to spare a large yearly sum that he might rule it dictatorially without any Board; but he had another favourite object which also required money for its accomplishment: he wished to buy some land in the neighbourhood of Middlemarch, and therefore he wished to get considerable contributions towards maintaining the Hospital. Meanwhile he framed his plan of management. The Hospital was to be reserved for fever in all its forms; Lydgate was to be chief medical superintendent, that he might have free authority to pursue all comparative investigations which his studies, particularly in Paris, had shown him the importance of, the other medical visitors having a consultative influence, but no power to contravene Lydgate's ultimate decisions; and the general management was to be lodged exclusively in the hands of five directors associated with Mr Bulstrode, who were to have votes in the ratio of their contributions, the Board itself filling up any vacancy in its numbers, and no mob of small contributors being admitted to a share of government.

There was an immediate refusal on the part of every medical man in the town to become a visitor at the Fever Hospital.

'Very well,' said Lydgate to Mr Bulstrode, 'we have a capital house-surgeon and dispenser, a clear-headed, neat-handed fellow; we'll get Webb from Crabsley, as good a country practitioner as any of them, to come over twice a-week, and in case of any exceptional operation, Protheroe will come from Brassing. I must work the harder, that's all, and I have given up my post at the Infirmary. The plan will flourish in spite of them, and then they'll be glad to come in. Things can't last as they are: there must be all sorts of reform soon, and then these fellows may be glad to come and study here.' Lydgate was in high spirits.

'I shall not flinch, you may depend upon it, Mr Lydgate,' said Mr Bulstrode. 'While I see you carrying out high intentions with vigour, you shall have my unfailing support. And I have humble confidence that the blessing which has hitherto attended my efforts against the spirit of evil in this town will not be withdrawn. Suitable directors to assist me I have no doubt of securing. Mr Brooke of Tipton has already given me his concurrence, and a pledge to contribute yearly: he has not specified the sum – probably not a great one. But he will be a useful member of the Board.'

A useful member was perhaps to be defined as one who would originate nothing, and always vote with Mr Bulstrode.

The medical aversion to Lydgate was hardly disguised now. Neither Dr Sprague nor Dr Minchin said that he disliked Lydgate's knowledge, or his disposition to improve treatment: what they disliked was his arrogance, which nobody felt to be altogether deniable. They implied that he was insolent, pretentious, and given to that reckless innovation for the sake of noise and show which was the essence of the charlatan.

The word charlatan once thrown on the air could not be let drop. In those days the world was agitated about the wondrous doings of Mr

St John Long, 'noblemen and gentlemen' attesting his extraction of a fluid like mercury from the temples of a patient.

Mr Toller remarked one day, smilingly, to Mrs Taft, that 'Bulstrode had found a man to suit him in Lydgate; a charlatan in religion is sure to like other sorts of charlatans.'

'Yes, indeed, I can imagine,' said Mrs Taft, keeping the number of thirty stitches carefully in her mind all the while; 'there are so many of that sort. I remember Mr Cheshire, with his irons, trying to make people straight when the Almighty had made them crooked.'

'No, no,' said Mr Toller, 'Cheshire was all right – all fair and above board. But there's St John Long – that's the kind of fellow we call a charlatan, advertising cures in ways nobody knows anything about; a fellow who wants to make a noise by pretending to go deeper than other people. The other day he was pretending to tap a man's brain and get quicksilver out of it.'

'Good gracious! what dreadful trifling with people's constitutions!' said Mrs Taft.

After this it came to be held in various quarters that Lydgate played even with respectable constitutions for his own purposes, and how much more likely that in his flighty experimenting he should make sixes and sevens of hospital patients. Especially it was to be expected, as the land-lady of the Tankard had said, that he would recklessly cut up their dead bodies. For Lydgate having attended Mrs Goby, who died apparently of a heart-disease not very clearly expressed in the symptoms, too daringly asked leave of her relatives to open the body, and thus gave an offence quickly spreading beyond Parley Street, where that lady had long resided on an income such as made this association of her body with the victims of Burke and Hare a flagrant insult to her memory.

Affairs were in this stage when Lydgate opened the subject of the Hospital to Dorothea. We see that he was bearing enmity and silly miscon-ception with much spirit, aware that they were partly created by his good share of success.

'They will not drive me away,' he said, talking confidentially in Mr Farebrother's study. 'I have got a good opportunity here, for the ends I most care about; and I am pretty sure to get income enough for our wants. By-and-by I shall go on as quietly as possible: I have no seductions now away from home and work. And I am more and more convinced that it will be possible to demonstrate the homogeneous origin of all the tissues. Raspail and others are on the same track, and I have been losing time.'

'I have no power of prophecy there,' said Mr Farebrother, who had been puffing at his pipe thoughtfully while Lydgate talked; 'but as to the hostility in the town, you'll weather it if you are prudent.'

'How am I to be prudent?' said Lydgate, 'I just do what comes before me to do. I can't help people's ignorance and spite, any more than Vesalius could. It isn't possible to square one's conduct to silly conclusions which nobody can foresee.'

'Quite true; I didn't mean that. I meant only two things. One is, keep yourself as separable from Bulstrode as you can: of course, you can go on doing good work of your own by his help; but don't get tied. Perhaps it seems like personal feeling in me to say so – and there's a good deal of that, I own – but personal feeling is not always in the wrong if you boil it down to the impressions which make it simply an opinion.'

'Bulstrode is nothing to me,' said Lydgate, carelessly, 'except on public grounds. As to getting very closely united to him, I am not fond enough of him for that. But what was the other thing you meant?' said Lydgate, who was nursing his leg as comfortably as possible, and feeling in no great need of advice.

'Why, this. Take care – *experto crede* – take care not to get hampered about money matters. I know, by a word you let fall one day, that you don't like my playing at cards so much for money. You are right enough there. But try and keep clear of wanting small sums that you haven't got. I am perhaps talking rather superfluously; but a man likes to assume superiority over himself, by holding up his bad example and sermonizing on it.'

Lydgate took Mr Farebrother's hints very cordially, though he would hardly have borne them from another man. He could not help remembering that he had lately made some debts, but these had seemed inevitable, and he had no intention now to do more than keep house in a simple way. The furniture for which he owed would not want renewing; nor even the stock of wine for a long while.

Many thoughts cheered him at that time – and justly. A man conscious of enthusiasm for worthy aims is sustained under petty hostilities by the memory of great workers who had to fight their way not without wounds, and who hover in his mind as patron saints, invisibly helping. At home, that same evening when he had been chatting with Mr Farebrother, he had his long legs stretched on the sofa, his head thrown back, and his hands clasped behind it according to his favourite ruminating attitude, while Rosamond sat at the piano, and played one tune after another, of which her husband only knew (like the emotional elephant he was!) that they fell in with his mood as if they had been melodious sea-breezes.

There was something very fine in Lydgate's look just then, and any one might have been encouraged to bet on his achievement. In his dark eyes and on his mouth and brow there was that placidity which comes from the fulness of contemplative thought – the mind not searching, but beholding, and the glance seeming to be filled with what is behind it.

Presently Rosamond left the piano and seated herself on a chair close to the sofa and opposite her husband's face.

'Is that enough music for you, my lord?' she said, folding her hands before her and putting on a little air of meekness.

'Yes, dear, if you are tired,' said Lydgate, gently, turning his eyes and resting them on her, but not otherwise moving. Rosamond's presence at that moment was perhaps no more than a spoonful brought to the lake, and her woman's instinct in this matter was not dull.

'What is absorbing you?' she said, leaning forward and bringing her face nearer to his.

He moved his hands and placed them gently behind her shoulders.

'I am thinking of a great fellow, who was about as old as I am three hundred years ago, and had already begun a new era in anatomy.'

'I can't guess,' said Rosamond, shaking her head. 'We used to play at guessing historical characters at Mrs Lemon's, but not anatomists.'

'I'll tell you. His name was Vesalius. And the only way he could get to know anatomy as he did, was by going to snatch bodies at night, from graveyards and places of execution.'

'Oh!' said Rosamond, with a look of disgust on her pretty face, 'I am very glad you are not Vesalius. I should have thought he might find some less horrible way than that.'

'No, he couldn't,' said Lydgate, going on too earnestly to take much notice of her answer. 'He could only get a complete skeleton by snatching the whitened bones of a criminal from the gallows, and burying them, and fetching them away by bits secretly, in the dead of night.'

'I hope he is not one of your great heroes,' said Rosamond, half-playfully, half-anxiously, 'else I shall have you getting up in the night to go to St Peter's churchyard. You know how angry you told me the people were about Mrs Goby. You have enemies enough already.'

'So had Vesalius, Rosy. No wonder the medical fogies in Middlemarch are jealous, when some of the greatest doctors living were fierce upon Vesalius because they had believed in Galen, and he showed that Galen was wrong. They called him a liar and a poisonous monster. But the facts of the human frame were on his side; and so he got the better of them.'

'And what happened to him afterwards?' said Rosamond, with some interest.

'Oh, he had a good deal of fighting to the last. And they did exasperate him enough at one time to make him burn a good deal of his work. Then he got shipwrecked just as he was coming from Jerusalem to take a great chair at Padua. He died rather miserably.'

There was a moment's pause before Rosamond said, 'Do you know, Tertius, I often wish you had not been a medical man.'

'Nay, Rosy, don't say that,' said Lydgate, drawing her closer to him. 'That is like saying you wish you had married another man.'

'Not at all; you are clever enough for anything: you might easily have been something else. And your cousins at Quallingham all think that you have sunk below them in your choice of a profession.'

'The cousins at Quallingham may go to the devil!' said Lydgate with scorn. 'It was like their impudence if they said anything of the sort to you.'

'Still,' said Rosamond, 'I do *not* think it is a nice profession, dear.' We know that she had much quiet perseverance in her opinion.

'It is the grandest profession in the world, Rosamond,' said Lydgate, gravely. 'And to say that you love me without loving the medical man in me, is the same sort of thing as to say that you like eating a peach but don't like its flavour. Don't say that again, dear, it pains me.'

'Very well, Doctor Grave-face,' said Rosy, dimpling, 'I will declare in future that I dote on skeletons, and body-snatchers, and bits of things in phials, and quarrels with everybody, that end in your dying miserably.'

'No, no, not so bad as that,' said Lydgate, giving up remonstrance and petting her resignedly.

᦯ FORTY-SIX ᴆ

Pues no podemos haber aquello que queremos, queramos aquello que podremos.

Since we cannot get what we like, let us like what we can get.

Spanish Proverb

WHILE LYDGATE, SAFELY MARRIED AND with the Hospital under his command, felt himself struggling for Medical Reform against Middlemarch, Middlemarch was becoming more and more conscious of the national struggle for another kind of Reform.

By the time that Lord John Russell's measure was being debated in the House of Commons, there was a new political animation in Middlemarch, and a new definition of parties which might show a decided change of balance if a new election came. And there were some who already predicted this event, declaring that a Reform Bill would never be carried by the actual Parliament. This was what Will Ladislaw dwelt on to Mr Brooke as a reason for congratulation that he had not yet tried his strength at the hustings.

'Things will grow and ripen as if it were a comet year,' said Will. 'The public temper will soon get to a cometary heat, now the question of Reform has set in. There is likely to be another election before long, and by that time Middlemarch will have got more ideas into its head. What we have to work at now is the *Pioneer* and political meetings.'

'Quite right, Ladislaw; we shall make a new thing of opinion here,' said Mr Brooke. 'Only I want to keep myself independent about Reform, you know: I don't want to go too far. I want to take up Wilberforce's and

Romilly's line, you know, and work at Negro Emancipation, Criminal Law – that kind of thing. But of course I should support Grey.'

'If you go in for the principle of Reform, you must be prepared to take what the situation offers,' said Will. 'If everybody pulled for his own bit against everybody else, the whole question would go to tatters.'

'Yes, yes, I agree with you – I quite take that point of view. I should put it in that light. I should support Grey, you know. But I don't want to change the balance of the constitution, and I don't think Grey would.'

'But that is what the country wants,' said Will. 'Else there would be no meaning in political unions or any other movement that knows what it's about. It wants to have a House of Commons which is not weighted with nominees of the landed class, but with representatives of the other interests. And as to contending for a reform short of that, it is like asking for a bit of an avalanche which has already begun to thunder.'

'That is fine, Ladislaw: that is the way to put it. Write that down, now. We must begin to get documents about the feeling of the country, as well as the machine-breaking and general distress.'

'As to documents,' said Will, 'a two-inch card will hold plenty. A few rows of figures are enough to deduce misery from, and a few more will show the rate at which the political determination of the people is growing.'

'Good: draw that out a little more at length, Ladislaw. That is an idea, now: write it out in the *Pioneer*. Put the figures and deduce the misery, you know; and put the other figures and deduce – and so on. You have a way of putting things. Burke, now: – when I think of Burke, I can't help wishing somebody had a pocket-borough to give you, Ladislaw. You'd never get elected, you know. And we shall always want talent in the House: reform as we will, we shall always want talent. That avalanche and the thunder, now, was really a little like Burke. I want that sort of thing – not ideas, you know, but a way of putting them.'

'Pocket-boroughs would be a fine thing,' said Ladislaw, 'if they were always in the right pocket, and there were always a Burke at hand.'

Will was not displeased with that complimentary comparison, even from Mr Brooke; for it is a little too trying to human flesh to be conscious of expressing one's self better than others and never to have it noticed, and in the general dearth of admiration for the right thing, even a chance bray of applause falling exactly in time is rather fortifying. Will felt that his literary refinements were usually beyond the limits of Middlemarch perception; nevertheless, he was beginning thoroughly to like the work of which when he began he had said to himself rather languidly, 'Why not?' – and he studied the political situation with as ardent an interest as he had ever given to poetic metres or medievalism. It is undeniable that but for the desire to be where Dorothea was, and perhaps the want of knowing what else to do, Will would not at this time have been meditating on the needs of the English people or criticizing English statesmanship: he would probably have been rambling in Italy sketching plans for several dramas, trying prose and finding it too jejune, trying verse and finding it too artificial, beginning to copy 'bits' from old pictures, leaving off because they were 'no good', and observing that, after all, self-culture was the principal point; while in politics he would have been sympathizing warmly with liberty and progress in general. Our sense of duty must often wait for some work which shall take the place of dilettantism and make us feel that the quality of our action is not a matter of indifference.

Ladislaw had now accepted his bit of work, though it was not that indeterminate loftiest thing which he had once dreamed of as alone worthy of continuous effort. His nature warmed easily in the presence of subjects which were visibly mixed with life and action, and the easily-stirred rebellion in him helped the glow of public spirit. In spite of Mr Casaubon and the banishment from Lowick, he was rather happy; getting a great deal of fresh knowledge in a vivid way and for practical purposes, and making the *Pioneer* celebrated as far as Brassing (never mind the smallness of the area; the writing was not worse than much that reaches the four corners of the earth).

Mr Brooke was occasionally irritating; but Will's impatience was relieved by the division of his time between visits to the Grange and retreats to his Middlemarch lodgings, which gave variety to his life.

'Shift the pegs a little,' he said to himself, 'and Mr Brooke might be in the Cabinet, while I was Under-Secretary. That is the common order of things: the little waves make the large ones and are of the same pattern. I am better here than in the sort of life Mr Casaubon would have trained me for, where the doing would be all laid down by a precedent too rigid for me to react upon. I don't care for prestige or high pay.'

As Lydgate had said of him, he was a sort of gypsy, rather enjoying the sense of belonging to no class; he had a feeling of romance in his position, and a pleasant consciousness of creating a little surprise wherever he went. That sort of enjoyment had been disturbed when he had felt some new distance between himself and Dorothea in their accidental meeting at Lydgate's, and his irritation had gone out towards Mr Casaubon, who had declared beforehand that Will would lose caste. 'I never had any caste,' he would have said, if that prophecy had been uttered to him, and the quick blood would have come and gone like breath in his transparent skin. But it is one thing to like defiance, and another thing to like its consequences.

Meanwhile, the town opinion about the new editor of the *Pioneer* was tending to confirm Mr Casaubon's view. Will's relationship in that distinguished quarter did not, like Lydgate's high connections, serve as an advantageous introduction: if it was rumoured that young Ladislaw was Mr Casaubon's nephew or cousin, it was also rumoured that 'Mr Casaubon would have nothing to do with him'.

'Brooke has taken him up,' said Mr Hawley, 'because that is what no man in his senses could have expected. Casaubon has devilish good reasons, you may be sure, for turning the cold shoulder on a young fellow whose bringing-up he paid for. Just like Brooke – one of those fellows who would praise a cat to sell a horse.'

And some oddities of Will's, more or less poetical, appeared to support Mr Keck, the editor of the *Trumpet*, in asserting that Ladislaw if the truth were known, was not only a Polish emissary but crack-brained, which accounted for the preternatural quickness and glibness of his speech when he got on to a platform – as he did whenever he had an opportunity, speaking with a facility which cast reflections on solid Englishmen generally. It was disgusting to Keck to see a strip of a fellow, with light curls round his head, get up and speechify by the hour against institutions 'which had existed when he was in his cradle'. And in a leading article of the *Trumpet*, Keck characterized Ladislaw's speech at a Reform meeting as 'the violence of an energumen – a miserable effort to shroud in the brilliancy of fireworks the daring of irresponsible statements and the poverty of a knowledge which was of the cheapest and most recent description.'

'That was a rattling article yesterday, Keck,' said Dr Sprague, with sarcastic intentions. 'But what is an energumen?'

'Oh, a term that came up in the French Revolution,' said Keck.

This dangerous aspect of Ladislaw was strangely contrasted with other habits which became matter of remark. He had a fondness, half artistic, half affectionate, for little children – the smaller they were on tolerably active legs, and the funnier their clothing, the better Will liked to surprise and please them. We know that in Rome he was given to ramble about among the poor people, and the taste did not quit him in Middlemarch.

He had somehow picked up a troop of droll children, little hatless boys with their galligaskins much worn and scant shirting to hang out, little girls who tossed their hair out of their eyes to look at him, and guardian brothers at the mature age of seven. This troop he had led out on gypsy excursions to Halsell Wood at nutting-time, and since the cold weather had set in he had taken them on a clear day to gather sticks for a bonfire in the hollow of a hillside, where he drew out a small feast of gingerbread for them, and improvised a Punch-and-Judy drama with some private home-made puppets. Here was one oddity. Another was, that in houses where he got friendly, he was given to stretch himself at full length on the rug while he talked, and was apt to be discovered in this attitude by occasional callers for whom such an irregularity was likely to confirm the notions of his dangerously mixed blood and general laxity.

But Will's articles and speeches naturally recommended him in families which the new strictness of party division had marked off on the side of Reform. He was invited to Mr Bulstrode's; but here he could not lie down on the rug, and Mrs Bulstrode felt that his mode of talking abut Catholic countries, as if there were any truce with Antichrist, illustrated the usual tendency to unsoundness in intellectual men.

At Mr Farebrother's, however, whom the irony of events had brought on the same side with Bulstrode in the national movement, Will became a favourite with the ladies; especially with little Miss Noble, whom it was one of his oddities to escort when he met her in the street with her little basket, giving her his arm in the eyes of the town, and insisting on going with her to pay some call where she distributed her small filchings from her own share of sweet things.

But the house where he visited oftenest and lay most on the rug was Lydgate's. The two men were not at all alike, but they agreed none the worse. Lydgate was abrupt but not irritable, taking little notice of megrims in healthy people; and Ladislaw did not usually throw away his susceptibilities on those who took no notice of them. With Rosamond, on the other hand, he pouted and was wayward – nay, often uncomplimentary, much to her inward surprise; nevertheless he was gradually becoming necessary to her entertainment by his companionship in her music, his varied talk, and his freedom from the grave preoccupation which, with all her husband's tenderness and indulgence, often made his manners unsatisfactory to her, and confirmed her dislike of the medical profession.

Lydgate, inclined to be sarcastic on the superstitious faith of the people in the efficacy of 'the bill', while nobody cared about the low state of pathology, sometimes assailed Will with troublesome questions. One evening in March, Rosamond in her cherry-coloured dress with swansdown trimming about the throat sat at the tea-table; Lydgate, lately come in tired from his outdoor work, was seated sideways on an easy-chair by the fire with one leg over the elbow, his brow looking a little troubled as his eyes rambled over the columns of the *Pioneer*, while Rosamond, having noticed that he was perturbed, avoided looking at him, and inwardly thanked heaven that she herself had not a moody disposition. Will Ladislaw was stretched on the rug contemplating the curtain-pole abstractedly, and humming very low the notes of 'When first I saw thy face'; while the house spaniel, also stretched out with small choice of room, looked from between his paws at the usurper of the rug with silent but strong objection.

Rosamond bringing Lydgate his cup of tea, he threw down the paper, and said to Will, who had started up and gone to the table –

'It's no use your puffing Brooke as a reforming landlord, Ladislaw: they only pick the more holes in his coat in the *Trumpet*.'

'No matter; those who read the *Pioneer* don't read the *Trumpet*,' said Will, swallowing his tea and walking about. 'Do you suppose the public reads with a view to its own conversion? We should have a witches' brewing with a vengeance then – "Mingle, mingle, mingle, mingle. You that mingle may" – and nobody would know which side he was going to take.'

'Farebrother says, he doesn't believe Brooke would get elected if the opportunity came: the very men who profess to be for him would bring another member out of the bag at the right moment.'

'There's no harm in trying. It's good to have resident members.'

'Why?' said Lydgate, who was much given to use that inconvenient word in a curt tone.

'They represent the local stupidity better,' said Will, laughing, and shaking his curls; 'and they are kept on their best behaviour in the neighbourhood. Brooke is not a bad fellow, but he has done some good things on his estate that he never would have done but for this Parliamentary bite.'

'He's not fitted to be a public man,' said Lydgate, with contemptuous decision. 'He would disappoint everybody who counted on him: I can see that at the Hospital. Only, there Bulstrode holds the reins and drives him.'

'That depends on how you fix your standard of public men,' said Will. 'He's good enough for the occasion: when the people have made up their mind as they are making it up now, they don't want a man – they only want a vote.'

'That is the way with you political writers, Ladislaw – crying up a measure as if it were a universal cure, and crying up men who are a part of the very disease that wants curing.'

'Why not? Men may help to cure themselves off the face of the land without knowing it,' said Will, who could find reasons impromptu, when he had not thought of a question beforehand.

'That is no excuse for encouraging the superstitious exaggeration of hopes about this particular measure, helping the cry to swallow it whole and to send up voting popinjays who are good for nothing but to carry it. You go against rottenness, and there is nothing more thoroughly rotten than making people believe that society can be cured by a political hocus-pocus.'

'That's very fine, my dear fellow. But your cure must begin somewhere, and put it that a thousand things which debase a population can never be reformed without this particular reform to begin with. Look what Stanley said the other day – that the House had been tinkering long enough at small questions of bribery, inquiring whether this or that voter has had a guinea when everybody knows that the seats have been sold wholesale. Wait for wisdom and conscience in public agents – fiddlestick! The only conscience we can trust to is the massive sense of wrong in a class, and the best wisdom that will work is the wisdom of balancing claims. That's my text – which side is injured? I support the man who supports their claims; not the virtuous upholder of the wrong.'

'That general talk about a particular case is mere question-begging, Ladislaw. When I say, I go in for the dose that cures, it doesn't follow that I go in for opium in a given case of gout.'

'I am not begging the question we are upon – whether we are to try for nothing till we find immaculate men to work with. Should you go on that plan? If there were one man who would carry you a medical reform and another who would oppose it, should you inquire which had the better motives or even the better brains?'

'Oh, of course,' said Lydgate, seeing himself checkmated by a move which he had often used himself, 'if one did not work with such men as are at hand, things must come to a dead-lock. Suppose the worst opinion in the town about Bulstrode were a true one, that would not make it less true that he has the sense and the resolution to do what I think ought to be done in the matters I know and care most about; but that is the only ground on which I go with him,' Lydgate added rather proudly, bearing in mind Mr Farebrother's remarks. 'He is nothing to me otherwise; I would not cry him up on any personal ground – I would keep clear of that.'

'Do you mean that I cry up Brooke on any personal ground?' said Will Ladislaw, nettled, and turning sharp round. For the first time he felt offended with Lydgate; not the less so, perhaps, because he would have declined any close inquiry into the growth of his relation to Mr Brooke.

'Not at all,' said Lydgate, 'I was simply explaining my own action. I meant that a man may work for a special end with others whose motives and general course are equivocal, if he is quite sure of his personal independence, and that he is not working for his private interest – either place or money.'

'Then, why don't you extend your liberality to others?' said Will, still nettled. 'My personal independence is as important to me as yours is to you. You have no more reason to imagine that I have personal expectations from Brooke, than I have to imagine that you have personal expectations from Bulstrode. Motives are points of honour, I suppose – nobody can prove them. But as to money and place in the world,' Will ended, tossing back his head, 'I think it is pretty clear that I am not determined by considerations of that sort.'

'You quite mistake me, Ladislaw,' said Lydgate, surprised. He had been preoccupied with his own vindication, and had been blind to what Ladislaw might infer on his own account. 'I beg your pardon for unintentionally annoying you. In fact, I should rather attribute to you a romantic disregard of your own worldly interests. On the political question, I referred simply to intellectual bias.'

'How very unpleasant you both are this evening!' said Rosamond. 'I cannot conceive why money should have been referred to. Politics and medicine are sufficiently disagreeable to quarrel upon. You can both of you go on quarrelling with all the world and with each other on those two topics.'

Rosamond looked mildly neutral as she said this, rising to ring the bell, and then crossing to her work-table.

'Poor Rosy!' said Lydgate, putting out his hand to her as she was passing him. 'Disputation is not amusing to cherubs. Have some music. Ask Ladislaw to sing with you.'

When Will was gone Rosamond said to her husband, 'What put you out of temper this evening, Tertius?'

'Me? It was Ladislaw who was out of temper. He is like a bit of tinder.'

'But I mean, before that. Something had vexed you before you came in, you looked cross. And that made you begin to dispute with Mr Ladislaw. You hurt me very much when you look so, Tertius.'

'Do I? Then I am a brute,' said Lydgate, caressing her penitently.

'What vexed you?'

'Oh, outdoor things – business.'

It was really a letter insisting on the payment of a bill for furniture. But Rosamond was expecting to have a baby, and Lydgate wished to save her from any perturbation.

◁ FORTY-SEVEN ▷

Was never true love loved in vain,
For truest love is highest gain.
No art can make it: it must spring
Where elements are fostering.
 So in heaven's spot and hour
 Springs the little native flower,
 Downward root and upward eye,
 Shapen by the earth and sky.

IT HAPPENED TO BE ON A SATURDAY EVENING that Will Ladislaw had that little discussion with Lydgate. Its effect when he went to his own rooms was to make him sit up half the night, thinking over again, under a new irritation, all that he had before thought of his having settled in Middlemarch and harnessed himself with Mr Brooke. Hesitations before he had taken the step had since turned into susceptibility to every hint that he would have been wiser not to take it; and hence came his heat towards Lydgate – a heat which still kept him restless. Was he not making a fool of himself? – and at a time when he was more than ever conscious of being something better than a fool? And for what end?

Well, for no definite end. True, he had dreamy visions of possibilities: there is no human being who having both passions and thoughts does not think in consequence of his passions – does not find images rising in his mind which soothe the passion with hope or sting it with dread. But this, which happens to us all, happens to some with a wide difference; and Will was not one of those whose wit 'keeps the roadway': he had his bypaths

where there were little joys of his own choosing, such as gentlemen cantering on the highroad might have thought rather idiotic. The way in which
he made a sort of happiness for himself out of his feeling for Dorothea
was an example of this. It may seem strange, but it is the fact, that the
ordinary vulgar vision of which Mr Casaubon suspected him – namely,
that Dorothea might become a widow, and that the interest he had established in her mind might turn into acceptance of him as a husband – had
no tempting, arresting power over him; he did not live in the scenery of
such an event, and follow it out, as we all do with that imagined 'otherwise' which is our practical heaven. It was not only that he was unwilling
to entertain thoughts which could be accused of baseness, and was
already uneasy in the sense that he had to justify himself from the charge
of ingratitude – the latent consciousness of many other barriers between
himself and Dorothea besides the existence of her husband, had helped to
turn away his imagination from speculating on what might befall Mr
Casaubon. And there were yet other reasons. Will, we know, could not
bear the thought of any flaw appearing in his crystal: he was at once
exasperated and delighted by the calm freedom with which Dorothea
looked at him and spoke to him, and there was something so exquisite in
thinking of her just as she was, that he could not long for a change which
must somehow change her. Do we not shun the street version of a fine
melody? – or shrink from the news that the rarity – some bit of chiselling
or engraving perhaps – which we have dwelt on even with exultation in
the trouble it has cost us to snatch glimpses of it, is really not an
uncommon thing, and may be obtained as an everyday possession? Our
good depends on the quality and breadth of our emotion; and to Will, a
creature who cared little for what are called the solid things of life and
greatly for its subtler influences, to have within him such a feeling as he
had towards Dorothea, was like the inheritance of a fortune. What others
might have called the futility of his passion, made an additional delight
for his imagination: he was conscious of a generous movement, and of
verifying in his own experience that higher love-poetry which had charmed his fancy. Dorothea, he said to himself, was for ever enthroned in his
soul: no other woman could sit higher than her footstool; and if he could
have written out in immortal syllables the effect she wrought within him,
he might have boasted after the example of old Drayton, that –

> Queens hereafter might be glad to live
> Upon the alms of her superfluous praise.

But this result was questionable. And what else could he do for Dorothea?
What was his devotion worth to her? It was impossible to tell. He would
not go out of her reach. He saw no creature among her friends to whom he
could believe that she spoke with the same simple confidence as to him.

She had once said that she would like him to stay; and stay he would, whatever fire-breathing dragons might hiss around her.

This had always been the conclusion of Will's hesitations. But he was not without contradictoriness and rebellion even towards his own resolve. He had often got irritated, as he was on this particular night, by some outside demonstration that his public exertions with Mr Brooke as a chief could not seem as heroic as he would like them to be, and this was always associated with the other ground of irritation – that notwithstanding his sacrifice of dignity for Dorothea's sake, he could hardly ever see her. Whereupon, not being able to contradict these unpleasant facts, he contradicted his own strongest bias and said, 'I am a fool.'

Nevertheless, since the inward debate necessarily turned on Dorothea, he ended, as he had done before, only by getting a livelier sense of what her presence would be to him; and suddenly reflecting that the morrow would be Sunday, he determined to go to Lowick Church and see her. He slept upon that idea, but when he was dressing in the rational morning light, Objection said –

'That will be a virtual defiance of Mr Casaubon's prohibition to visit Lowick, and Dorothea will be displeased.'

'Nonsense!' argued Inclination, 'it would be too monstrous for him to hinder me from going out to a pretty country church on a spring morning. And Dorothea will be glad.'

'It will be clear to Mr Casaubon that you have come either to annoy him or to see Dorothea.'

'It is not true that I go to annoy him, and why should I not go to see Dorothea? Is he to have everything to himself and be always comfortable? Let him smart a little, as other people are obliged to do. I have always liked the quaintness of the church and congregation; besides, I know the Tuckers: I shall go into their pew.'

Having silenced Objection by force of unreason, Will walked to Lowick as if he had been on the way to Paradise, crossing Halsell Common and skirting the woods, where the sunlight fell broadly under the budding boughs, bringing out the beauties of moss and lichen, and fresh green growths piercing the brown. Everything seemed to know that it was Sunday, and to approve of his going to Lowick Church. Will easily felt happy when nothing crossed his humour, and by this time the thought of vexing Mr Casaubon had become rather amusing to him, making his face break into its merry smile, pleasant to see as the breaking of sunshine on the water – though the occasion was not exemplary. But most of us are apt to settle within ourselves that the man who blocks our way is odious, and not to mind causing him a little of the disgust which his personality excites in ourselves. Will went along with a small book under his arm and a hand in each side-pocket, never reading, but chanting a little, as he made scenes of what would happen in church and coming out. He was experimenting in tunes to suit some words of his own, sometimes trying a

ready-made melody, sometimes improvising. The words were not exactly
a hymn, but they certainly fitted his Sunday experience: –

> O me, O me, what frugal cheer
> My love doth feed upon!
> A touch, a ray, that is not here,
> A shadow that is gone:
>
> A dream of breath that might be near,
> An inly-echoed tone,
> The thought that one may think me dear,
> The place where one was known,
>
> The tremor of a banished fear,
> An ill that was not done –
> O me, O me, what frugal cheer
> My love doth feed upon!

Sometimes, when he took off his hat, shaking his head backward, and
showing his delicate throat as he sang, he looked like an incarnation of the
spring whose spirit filled the air – a bright creature, abundant in uncertain
promises.

The bells were still ringing when he got to Lowick, and he went into the
curate's pew before any one else arrived there. But he was still left alone
in it when the congregation had assembled. The curate's pew was
opposite the rector's at the entrance of the small chancel, and Will had
time to fear that Dorothea might not come while he looked round at the
group of rural faces which made the congregation from year to year
within the white-washed walls and dark old pews, hardly with more
change than we see in the boughs of a tree which breaks here and there
with age, but yet has young shoots. Mr Rigg's frog-face was something
alien and unaccountable, but notwithstanding this shock to the order of
things, there were still the Waules and the rural stock of the Powderells in
their pews side by side: Brother Samuel's cheek had the same purple
round as ever, and the three generations of decent cottagers came as of old
with a sense of duty to their betters generally – the smaller children
regarding Mr Casaubon, who wore the black gown and mounted to the
highest box, as probably the chief of all betters, and the one most awful if
offended. Even in 1831 Lowick was at peace, not more agitated by Reform
than by the solemn tenor of the Sunday sermon. The congregation had
been used to seeing Will at church in former days, and no one took much
note of him except the quire, who expected him to make a figure in the
singing.

Dorothea did at last appear in this quaint background, walking up the
short aisle in her white beaver bonnet and grey cloak – the same she had

worn in the Vatican. Her face being, from her entrance, towards the chancel, even her short-sighted eyes soon discerned Will, but there was no outward show of her feeling except a slight paleness and a grave bow as she passed him. To his own surprise Will felt suddenly uncomfortable, and dared not look at her after they had bowed to each other. Two minutes later, when Mr Casaubon came out of the vestry, and, entering the pew, seated himself in face of Dorothea, Will felt his paralysis more complete. He could look nowhere except at the quire in the little gallery over the vestry-door: Dorothea was perhaps pained, and he had made a wretched blunder. It was no longer amusing to vex Mr Casaubon, who had the advantage probably of watching him and seeing that he dared not turn his head. Why had he not imagined this beforehand? – but he could not expect that he should sit in that square pew alone, unrelieved by any Tuckers, who had apparently departed from Lowick altogether, for a new clergyman was in the desk. Still he called himself stupid now for not foreseeing that it would be impossible for him to look towards Dorothea – nay, that she might feel his coming an impertinence. There was no delivering himself from his cage, however; and Will found his places and looked at his book as if he had been a schoolmistress, feeling that the morning service had never been so immeasurably long before, that he was utterly ridiculous, out of temper, and miserable. This was what a man got by worshipping the sight of a woman! The clerk observed with surprise that Mr Ladislaw did not join in the tune of Hanover, and reflected that he might have a cold.

Mr Casaubon did not preach that morning, and there was no change in Will's situation until the blessing had been pronounced and every one rose. It was the fashion at Lowick for 'the betters' to go out first. With a sudden determination to break the spell that was upon him, Will looked straight at Mr Casaubon. But that gentleman's eyes were on the button of the pew-door, which he opened, allowing Dorothea to pass, and following her immediately without raising his eyelids. Will's glance had caught Dorothea's as she turned out of the pew, and again she bowed, but this time with a look of agitation, as if she were repressing tears. Will walked out after them, but they went on towards the little gate leading out of the churchyard into the shrubbery, never looking round.

It was impossible for him to follow them, and he could only walk back sadly at mid-day along the same road which he had trodden hopefully in the morning. The lights were all changed for him both without and within.

❧ FORTY-EIGHT ❧

Surely the golden hours are turning grey
And dance no more, and vainly strive to run:
I see their white locks streaming in the wind –
Each face is haggard as it looks at me,
Slow turning in the constant clasping round
Storm-driven.

DOROTHEA'S DISTRESS WHEN SHE WAS leaving the church came chiefly from the perception that Mr Casaubon was determined not to speak to his cousin, and that Will's presence at church had served to mark more strongly the alienation between them. Will's coming seemed to her quite excusable, nay, she thought it an amiable movement in him towards a reconciliation which she herself had been constantly wishing for. He had probably imagined, as she had, that if Mr Casaubon and he could meet easily, they would shake hands and friendly intercourse might return. But now Dorothea felt quite robbed of that hope. Will was banished further than ever, for Mr Casaubon must have been newly embittered by this thrusting upon him of a presence which he refused to recognize.

He had not been very well that morning, suffering from some difficulty in breathing, and had not preached in consequence; she was not surprised, therefore, that he was nearly silent at luncheon, still less that he made no allusion to Will Ladislaw. For her own part she felt that she could never again introduce that subject. They usually spent apart the hours between luncheon and dinner on a Sunday; Mr Casaubon in the library dozing chiefly, and Dorothea in her boudoir, where she was wont to occupy herself with some of her favourite books. There was a little heap of them on the table in the bow-window – of various sorts, from Herodotus, which she was learning to read with Mr Casaubon, to her old companion Pascal, and Keble's *Christian Year*. But to-day she opened one after another, and could read none of them. Everything seemed dreary: the portents before the birth of Cyrus – Jewish antiquities – oh dear! – devout epigrams – the sacred chime of favourite hymns – all alike were as flat as tunes beaten on wood: even the spring flowers and the grass had a dull shiver in them under the afternoon clouds that hid the sun fitfully: even the sustaining thoughts which had become habits seemed to have in them the weariness of long future days in which she would still live with them for her sole companions. It was another or rather a fuller sort of companionship that poor Dorothea was hungering for, and the hunger had grown from the perpetual effort demanded by her married life. She was always trying to be what her husband wished, and never able to repose on his delight in what she was. The thing that she liked, that she spontaneously cared to have, seemed to be always excluded from her life; for if it was only granted and not shared by her husband it might as well have been denied. About Will Ladislaw there had been a difference between them from the first, and it had ended, since Mr Casaubon had so severely repulsed Dorothea's strong feeling about his claims on the family property, by her being convinced that she was in the right and her husband in the wrong, but that she was helpless. This afternoon the helplessness was more wretchedly benumbing than ever: she longed for objects who could be dear to her, and to whom she could be dear. She longed for work which would be directly beneficent like the sunshine and the rain, and now it appeared that she was to live more and more in a virtual tomb, where there was the apparatus of a ghastly labour producing what would never see the light. To-day she had stood at the door of the tomb and seen Will Ladislaw receding into the distant world of warm activity and fellowship – turning his face towards her as he went.

Books were of no use. Thinking was of no use. It was Sunday, and she could not have the carriage to go to Celia, who had lately had a baby. There was no refuge now from spiritual emptiness and discontent, and Dorothea had to bear her bad mood, as she would have borne a headache.

After dinner, at the hour when she usually began to read aloud, Mr Casaubon proposed that they should go into the library, where, he said, he had ordered a fire and lights. He seemed to have revived and to be thinking intently.

In the library Dorothea observed that he had newly arranged a row of his note-books on a table, and now he took up and put into her hand a well-known volume, which was a table of contents to all the others.

'You will oblige me, my dear,' he said, seating himself, 'if instead of other reading this evening, you will go through this aloud, pencil in hand, and at each point where I say 'mark', will make a cross with your pencil. This is the first step in a sifting process which I have long had in view, and as we go on I shall be able to indicate to you certain principles of selection whereby you will, I trust, have an intelligent participation in my purpose.'

This proposal was only one more sign added to many since his memorable interview with Lydgate, that Mr Casaubon's original reluctance to let Dorothea work with him had given place to the contrary disposition, namely, to demand much interest and labour from her.

After she had read and marked for two hours, he said, 'We will take the volume up-stairs – and the pencil, if you please – and in case of reading in the night, we can pursue this task. It is not wearisome to you, I trust, Dorothea?'

'I prefer always reading what you like best to hear,' said Dorothea, who told the simple truth; for what she dreaded was to exert herself in reading or anything else which left him as joyless as ever.

It was a proof of the force with which certain characteristics in Dorothea impressed those around her, that her husband, with all his jealousy and suspicion, had gathered implicit trust in the integrity of her promises, and her power of devoting herself to her idea of the right and best. Of late he had begun to feel that these qualities were a peculiar possession for himself, and he wanted to engross them.

The reading in the night did come. Dorothea in her young weariness had slept soon and fast: she was awakened by a sense of light, which seemed to her at first like a sudden vision of sunset after she had climbed a steep hill: she opened her eyes and saw her husband wrapped in his warm gown seating himself in the arm-chair near the fire-place where the embers were still glowing. He had lit two candles, expecting that Dorothea would awake, but not liking to rouse her by more direct means.

'Are you ill, Edward?' she said, rising immediately.

'I felt some uneasiness in a reclining posture. I will sit here for a time.' She threw wood on the fire, wrapped herself up, and said, 'You would like me to read to you?'

'You would oblige me greatly by doing so, Dorothea,' said Mr Casaubon, with a shade more meekness than usual in his polite manner. 'I am wakeful: my mind is remarkably lucid.'

'I fear that the excitement may be too great for you,' said Dorothea, remembering Lydgate's cautions.

'No, I am not conscious of undue excitement. Thought is easy.' Dorothea dared not insist, and she read for an hour or more on the same plan as she had done in the evening, but getting over the pages with more quickness. Mr Casaubon's mind was more alert, and he seemed to anticipate what was coming after a very slight verbal indication, saying, 'That will do – mark that' or 'Pass on to the next head – I omit the second excursus on Crete.' Dorothea was amazed to think of the bird-like speed with which his mind was surveying the ground where it had been creeping for years. At last he said –

'Close the book now, my dear. We will resume our work to-morrow. I have deferred it too long, and would gladly see it completed. But you observe that the principle on which my selection is made, is to give adequate, and not disproportionate illustration to each of the theses enumerated in my introduction, as at present sketched. You have perceived that distinctly, Dorothea?'

'Yes,' said Dorothea, rather tremulously. She felt sick at heart.

'And now I think that I can take some repose,' said Mr Casaubon. He lay down again and begged her to put out the lights. When she had lain down too, and there was a darkness only broken by a dull glow on the hearth, he said –

'Before I sleep, I have a request to make, Dorothea.'

'What is it?' said Dorothea, with a dread in her mind.

'It is that you will let me know, deliberately, whether, in case of my death, you will carry out my wishes: whether you will avoid doing what I should deprecate, and apply yourself to do what I should desire.'

Dorothea was not taken by surprise: many incidents had been leading her to the conjecture of some intention on her husband's part which might make a new yoke for her. She did not answer immediately.

'You refuse?' said Mr Casaubon, with more edge in his tone.

'No, I do not yet refuse,' said Dorothea, in a clear voice, the need of freedom asserting itself within her; 'but it is too solemn – I think it is not right – to make a promise when I am ignorant what it will bind me to. Whatever affection prompted I would do without promising.'

'But you would use your own judgment: I ask you to obey mine; you refuse.'

'No, dear, no!' said Dorothea, beseechingly, crushed by opposing fears. 'But may I wait and reflect a little while? I desire with my whole soul to do what will comfort you; but I cannot give any pledge suddenly – still less a pledge to do I know not what.'

'You cannot then confide in the nature of my wishes?'

'Grant me till to-morrow,' said Dorothea beseechingly.

'Till to-morrow then,' said Mr Casaubon.

Soon she could hear that he was sleeping, but there was no more sleep for her. While she constrained herself to lie still lest she should disturb him, her mind was carrying on a conflict in which imagination ranged its forces first on one side and then on the other. She had no presentiment that the power which her husband wished to establish over her future action had relation to anything else than his work. But it was clear enough to her that he would expect her to devote herself to sifting those mixed heaps of material, which were to be the doubtful illustration of principles still more doubtful. The poor child had become altogether unbelieving as to the trustworthiness of that Key which had made the ambition and the labour of her husband's life. It was not wonderful that, in spite of her small instruction, her judgment in this matter was truer than his: for she looked with unbiassed comparison and healthy sense at probabilities on which he had risked all his egoism. And now she pictured to herself the days, and months, and years which she must spend in sorting what might be called shattered mummies, and fragments of a tradition which was itself a mosaic wrought from crushed ruins – sorting them as food for a theory which was already withered in the birth like an elfin child. Doubtless a vigorous error vigorously pursued has kept the embryos of truth a-breathing: the quest of gold being at the same time a questioning of substances, the body of chemistry is prepared for its soul, and Lavoisier is born. But Mr Casaubon's theory of the elements which made the seed of all tradition was not likely to bruise itself unawares against discoveries: it floated among flexible conjectures no more solid than those etymologies which seemed strong because of likeness in sound, until it was shown that likeness in sound made them impossible: it was a method of interpretation which was not tested by the necessity of forming anything which had sharper collisions than an elaborate notion of Gog and Magog: it was as free from interruption as a plan for threading the stars together. And Dorothea had so often had to check her weariness and impatience over this questionable riddle-guessing, as it revealed itself to her instead of the fellowship in high knowledge which was to make life worthier! She could understand well enough now why her husband had come to cling to her, as possibly the only hope left that his labours would ever take a shape in which they could be given to the world. At first it had seemed that he wished to keep even her aloof from any close knowledge of what he was doing; but gradually the terrible stringency of human need – the prospect of a too speedy death –

And here Dorothea's pity turned from her own future to her husband's past – nay, to his present hard struggle with a lot which had grown out of that past: the lonely labour, the ambition breathing hardly under the pressure of self-distrust; the goal receding, and the heavier limbs; and now at last the sword visibly trembling above him! And had she not wished to marry him that she might help him in his life's labour? – But she had thought the work was to be something greater, which she could serve in devoutly for its own sake. Was it right, even to soothe his grief – would it be possible, even if she promised – to work as in a treadmill fruitlessly?

And yet, could she deny him? Could she say, 'I refuse to content this pining hunger?' It would be refusing to do for him dead, what she was almost sure to do for him living. If he lived, as Lydgate had said he might, for fifteen years or more, her life would certainly be spent in helping him and obeying him.

Still, there was a deep difference between that devotion to the living, and that indefinite promise of devotion to the dead. While he lived, he could claim nothing that she would not still be free to remonstrate against, and even to refuse. But – the thought passed through her mind more than once, though she could not believe in it – might he not mean to demand something more from her than she had been able to imagine, since he wanted her pledge to carry out his wishes without telling her exactly what they were? No; his heart was bound up in his work only: that was the end for which his failing life was to be eked out by hers.

And now, if she were to say, 'No! if you die, I will put no finger to your work' – it seemed as if she would be crushing that bruised heart.

For four hours Dorothea lay in this conflict, till she felt ill and bewildered, unable to resolve, praying mutely. Helpless as a child which has sobbed and sought too long, she fell into a late morning sleep, and when she waked Mr Casaubon was already up. Tantripp told her that he had read prayers, breakfasted, and was in the library.

'I never saw you look so pale, madam,' said Tantripp, a solid-figured woman who had been with the sisters at Lausanne.

'Was I ever high-coloured, Tantripp?' said Dorothea, smiling faintly.

'Well, not to say high-coloured, but with a bloom like a Chiny rose. But always smelling those leather books, what can be expected? Do rest a little this morning, madam. Let me say you are ill and not able to go into that close library.'

'Oh no, no! let me make haste,' said Dorothea. 'Mr Casaubon wants me particularly.'

When she went down she felt sure that she should promise to fulfil his wishes; but that would be later in the day – not yet.

As Dorothea entered the library, Mr Casaubon turned round from the table where he had been placing some books, and said –

'I was waiting for your appearance, my dear. I had hoped to set to work at once this morning, but I find myself under some indisposition, probably from too much excitement yesterday. I am going now to take a turn in the shrubbery, since the air is milder.'

'I am glad to hear that,' said Dorothea. 'Your mind, I feared, was too active last night.'

'I would fain have it set at rest on the point I last spoke of, Dorothea. You can now, I hope, give me an answer.'

'May I come out to you in the garden presently?' said Dorothea, winning a little breathing space in that way.

'I shall be in the Yew-Tree Walk for the next half-hour,' said Mr Casaubon, and then he left her.

Dorothea, feeling very weary, rang and asked Tantripp to bring her some wraps. She had been sitting still for a few minutes, but not in any renewal of the former conflict: she simply felt that she was going to say 'Yes' to her own doom: she was too weak, too full of dread at the thought of inflicting a keen-edged blow on her husband, to do anything but submit completely. She sat still and let Tantripp put on her bonnet and shawl, a passivity which was unusual with her, for she liked to wait on herself.

'God bless you, madam!' said Tantripp, with an irrepressible movement of love towards the beautiful, gentle creature for whom she felt unable to do anything more, now that she had finished tying the bonnet.

This was too much for Dorothea's highly-strung feeling, and she burst into tears, sobbing against Tantripp's arm. But soon she checked herself, dried her eyes, and went out at the glass door into the shrubbery.

'I wish every book in that library was built into a caticom for your master,' said Tantripp to Pratt, the butler, finding him in the breakfast-room. She had been at Rome, and visited the antiquities, as we know; and she always declined to call Mr Casaubon anything but 'your master', when speaking to the other servants.

Pratt laughed. He liked his master very well, but he liked Tantripp better.

When Dorothea was out on the gravel walks, she lingered among the nearer clumps of trees, hesitating, as she had done once before, though from a different cause. Then she had feared lest her effort at fellowship should be unwelcome; now she dreaded going to the spot where she foresaw that she must bind herself to a fellowship from which she shrank. Neither law nor the world's opinion compelled her to this – only her husband's nature and her own compassion, only the ideal and not the real yoke of marriage. She saw clearly enough the whole situation, yet she was fettered: she could not smite the stricken soul that entreated hers. If that were weakness, Dorothea was weak. But the half-hour was passing, and she must not delay longer. When she entered the Yew-Tree Walk she could not see her husband; but the walk had bends, and she went, expecting to catch sight of his figure wrapped in a blue cloak, which, with a warm velvet cap, was his outer garment on chill days for the garden. It occurred to her that he might be resting in the summer-house, towards which the path diverged a little. Turning the angle, she could see him seated on the bench, close to a stone table. His arms were resting on the table, and his brow was bowed down on them, the blue cloak being dragged forward and screening his face on each side.

'He exhausted himself last night,' Dorothea said to herself, thinking at first that he was asleep, and that the summer-house was too damp a place to rest in. But then she remembered that of late she had seen him take that attitude when she was reading to him, as if he found it easier than any other; and that he would sometimes speak, as well as listen, with his face down in that way. She went into the summer-house and said, 'I am come, Edward; I am ready.'

He took no notice, and she thought that he must be fast asleep. She laid her hand on his shoulder, and repeated, 'I am ready!' Still he was motionless; and with a sudden confused fear, she leaned down to him, took off his velvet cap, and leaned her cheek close to his head, crying in a distressed tone,

'Wake, dear, wake! Listen to me. I am come to answer.'

But Dorothea never gave her answer.

Later in the day, Lydgate was seated by her bedside, and she was talking deliriously, thinking aloud, and recalling what had gone through her mind the night before. She knew him, and called him by his name, but appeared to think it right that she should explain everything to him; and again, and again, begged him to explain everything to her husband.

'Tell him I shall go to him soon: I am ready to promise. Only, thinking about it was so dreadful – it has made me ill. Not very ill. I shall soon be better. Go and tell him.'

But the silence in her husband's ear was never more to be broken.

≪ FORTY-NINE ≫

A task too strong for wizard spells
This squire had brought about;
'Tis easy dropping stones in wells,
But who shall get them out?

'I WISH TO GOD WE COULD HINDER Dorothea from knowing this,' said Sir James Chettam, with the little frown on his brow, and an expression of intense disgust about his mouth.

He was standing on the hearth-rug in the library at Lowick Grange, and speaking to Mr Brooke. It was the day after Mr Casaubon had been buried, and Dorothea was not yet able to leave her room.

'That would be difficult, you know, Chettam, as she is an executrix, and she likes to go into these things – property, land, that kind of thing. She has her notions, you know,' said Mr Brooke, sticking his eye-glasses on nervously, and exploring the edges of a folded paper which he held in his hand; 'and she would like to act – depend upon it, as an executrix Dorothea would want to act. And she was twenty-one last December, you know. I can hinder nothing.'

Sir James looked at the carpet for a minute in silence, and then lifting his eyes suddenly fixed them on Mr Brooke, saying, 'I will tell you what we can do. Until Dorothea is well, all business must be kept from her, and as soon as she is able to be moved she must come to us. Being with Celia and the baby will be the best thing in the world for her, and will pass away the time. And meanwhile you must get rid of Ladislaw: you must send him out of the country.' Here Sir James's look of disgust returned in all its intensity.

Mr Brooke put his hands behind him, walked to the window and straightened his back with a little shake before he replied:

'That is easily said, Chettam, easily said, you know.'

'My dear sir,' persisted Sir James, restraining his indignation within respectful forms, 'it was you who brought him here, and you who keep him here – I mean by the occupation you give him.'

'Yes, but I can't dismiss him in an instant without assigning reasons, my dear Chettam. Ladislaw has been invaluable, most satisfactory. I consider that I have done this part of the country a service by bringing him – by bringing him, you know.' Mr Brooke ended with a nod, turning round to give it.

'It's a pity this part of the country didn't do without him, that's all I have to say about it. At any rate, as Dorothea's brother-in-law, I feel warranted in objecting strongly to his being kept here by any action on the part of her friends. You admit, I hope, that I have a right to speak about what concerns the dignity of my wife's sister?'

Sir James was getting warm.

'Of course, my dear Chettam, of course. But you and I have different ideas – different – '

'Not about this action of Casaubon's, I should hope,' interrupted Sir James. 'I say that he has most unfairly compromised Dorothea. I say that there never was a meaner, more ungentlemanly action than this – a codicil of this sort to a will which he made at the time of his marriage with the knowledge and reliance of her family – a positive insult to Dorothea!'

'Well, you know, Casaubon was a little twisted about Ladislaw. Ladislaw has told me the reason – dislike of the bent he took, you know – Ladislaw didn't think much of Casaubon's notions, Thoth and Dagon – that sort of thing: and I fancy that Casaubon didn't like the independent position Ladislaw had taken up. I saw the letters between them, you know. Poor Casaubon was a little buried in books – he didn't know the world.'

'It's all very well for Ladislaw to put that colour on it,' said Sir James. 'But I believe Casaubon was only jealous of him on Dorothea's account, and the world will suppose that she gave him some reason; and that is what makes it so abominable – coupling her name with this young fellow's.'

'My dear Chettam, it won't lead to anything, you know,' said Mr Brooke, seating himself and sticking on his eye-glass again. 'It's all of a piece with Casaubon's oddity. This paper, now, "Synoptical Tabulation" and so on, "for the use of Mrs Casaubon", it was locked up in the desk with the will. I suppose he meant Dorothea to publish his researches, eh? and she'll do it, you know; she has gone into his studies uncommonly.'

'My dear sir,' said Sir James, impatiently, 'that is neither here nor there. The question is, whether you don't see with me the propriety of sending young Ladislaw away?'

'Well, no, not the urgency of the thing. By-and-by, perhaps, it may come round. As to gossip, you know, sending him away won't hinder gossip. People say what they like to say, not what they have chapter and verse for,' said Mr Brooke, becoming acute about the truths that lay on the side of his own wishes. 'I might get rid of Ladislaw up to a certain point – take away the *Pioneer* from him, and that sort of thing; but I couldn't send him out of the country if he didn't choose to go – didn't choose, you know.'

Mr Brooke, persisting as quietly as if he were only discussing the nature of last year's weather, and nodding at the end with his usual amenity, was an exasperating form of obstinacy.

'Good God!' said Sir James, with as much passion as he ever showed, 'let us get him a post; let us spend money on him. If he could go in the suite of some Colonial Governor! Grampus might take him – and I could write to Fulke about it.'

'But Ladislaw won't be shipped off like a head of cattle, my dear fellow; Ladislaw has his ideas. It's my opinion that if he were to part from me tomorrow, you'd only hear the more of him in the country. With his talent for speaking and drawing up documents, there are few men who could come up to him as an agitator – an agitator, you know.'

'Agitator!' said Sir James, with bitter emphasis, feeling that the syllables of this word properly repeated were a sufficient exposure of its hatefulness.

'But be reasonable, Chettam. Dorothea, now. As you say, she had better go to Celia as soon as possible. She can stay under your roof, and in the meantime things may come round quietly. Don't let us be firing off our guns in a hurry, you know. Standish will keep our counsel, and the news will be old before it's known. Twenty things may happen to carry off Ladislaw – without my doing anything, you know.'

'Then I am to conclude that you decline to do anything?'

'Decline, Chettam? – no – I don't say decline. But I really don't see what I could do. Ladislaw is a gentleman.'

'I am glad to hear it!' said Sir James, his irritation making him forget himself a little. 'I am sure Casaubon was not.'

'Well, it would have been worse if he had made the codicil to hinder her from marrying again at all, you know.'

'I don't know that,' said Sir James. 'It would have been less indelicate.'

'One of poor Casaubon's freaks! That attack upset his brain a little. It all goes for nothing. She doesn't *want* to marry Ladislaw.'

'But this codicil is framed so as to make everybody believe that she did. I don't believe anything of the sort about Dorothea,' said Sir James – then frowningly, 'but I suspect Ladislaw. I tell you frankly, I suspect Ladislaw.'

'I couldn't take any immediate action on that ground, Chettam. In fact, if it were possible to pack him off – send him to Norfolk Island – that sort of thing – it would look all the worse for Dorothea to those who knew about it. It would seem as if we distrusted her – distrusted her, you know.'

That Mr Brooke had hit on an undeniable argument, did not tend to soothe Sir James. He put out his hand to reach his hat, implying that he did not mean to contend further, and said, still with some heat –

'Well, I can only say that I think Dorothea was sacrificed once, because her friends were too careless. I shall do what I can, as her brother, to protect her now.'

'You can't do better than get her to Freshitt as soon as possible, Chettam. I approve that plan altogether,' said Mr Brooke, well pleased that he had won the argument. It would have been highly inconvenient to him to part with Ladislaw at that time, when a dissolution might happen any day, and electors were to be convinced of the course by which the interests of

the country would be best served. Mr Brooke sincerely believed that this
end could be secured by his own return to Parliament: he offered the
forces of his mind honestly to the nation.

⚬ FIFTY ⚬

'This Loller here wol prechen us somewhat.'
'Nay by my father's soule! that schal he nat,'
Sayde the Schipman, 'here schal he not preche,
He schal no gospel glosen here ne teche.
We leven all in the gret God,' quod he.
He wolden sowen some diffcultee.

Canterbury Tales

DOROTHEA HAD BEEN SAFE AT FRESHITT Hall nearly a week before she had
asked any dangerous questions. Every morning now she sat with Celia in
the prettiest of up-stairs sitting-rooms, opening into a small conservatory – Celia all in white and lavender like a bunch of mixed violets,
watching the remarkable acts of the baby, which were so dubious to her
inexperienced mind that all conversation was interrupted by appeals for
their interpretation made to the oracular nurse. Dorothea sat by in her
widow's dress, with an expression which rather provoked Celia, as being
much too sad; for not only was baby quite well, but really when a husband
had been so dull and troublesome while he lived, and besides that had –
well, well! Sir James, of course, had told Celia everything, with a strong
representation how important it was that Dorothea should not know it
sooner than was inevitable.

But Mr Brooke had been right in predicting that Dorothea would not
long remain passive where action had been assigned to her; she knew the
purport of her husband's will made at the time of their marriage, and her
mind, as soon as she was clearly conscious of her position, was silently
occupied with what she ought to do as the owner of Lowick Manor with
the patronage of the living attached to it.

One morning when her uncle paid his usual visit, though with an
unusual alacrity in his manner which he accounted for by saying that it
was now pretty certain Parliament would be dissolved forthwith, Dorothea said –

'Uncle, it is right now that I should consider who is to have the living at
Lowick. After Mr Tucker had been provided for, I never heard my husband say that he had any clergyman in his mind as a successor to himself.

I think I ought to have the keys now and go to Lowick to examine all my husband's papers. There may be something that would throw light on his wishes.'

'No hurry, my dear,' said Mr Brooke, quietly. 'By-and-by, you know, you can go, if you like. But I cast my eyes over things in the desks and drawers – there was nothing – nothing but deep subjects, you know – besides the will. Everything can be done by-and-by. As to the living, I have had an application for interest already – I should say rather good. Mr Tyke has been strongly recommended to me – I had something to do with getting him an appointment before. An apostolic man, I believe – the sort of thing that would suit you, my dear.'

'I should like to have fuller knowledge about him, uncle, and judge for myself, if Mr Casaubon has not left any expression of his wishes. He has perhaps made some addition to his will – there may be some instructions for me,' said Dorothea, who had all the while had this conjecture in her mind with relation to her husband's work.

'Nothing about the rectory, my dear – nothing,' said Mr Brooke, rising to go away, and putting out his hand to his nieces: 'nor about his researches, you know. Nothing in the will.'

Dorothea's lip quivered.

'Come, you must not think of these things yet, my dear. By-and-by, you know.'

'I am quite well now, uncle: I wish to exert myself.'

'Well, well, we shall see. But I must run away now – I have no end of work now – it's a crisis – a political crisis, you know. And here is Celia and her little man – you are an aunt, you know, now, and I am a sort of grandfather,' said Mr Brooke, with placid hurry, anxious to get away and tell Chettam that it would not be his (Mr Brooke's) fault if Dorothea insisted on looking into everything.

Dorothea sank back in her chair when her uncle had left the room, and cast her eyes down meditatively on her crossed hands.

'Look, Dodo! look at him! Did you ever see anything like that?' said Celia in her comfortable staccato.

'What, Kitty?' said Dorothea, lifting her eyes rather absently.

'What? why, his upper lip; see how he is drawing it down, as if he meant to make a face. Isn't it wonderful! He may have his little thoughts. I wish nurse were here. Do look at him.'

A large tear, which had been for some time gathering, rolled down Dorothea's cheek as she looked up and tried to smile.

'Don't be sad, Dodo; kiss baby. What are you brooding over so? I am sure you did everything, and a great deal too much. You should be happy now.'

'I wonder if Sir James would drive me to Lowick. I want to look over everything – to see if there were any words written for me.'

'You are not to go till Mr Lydgate says you may go. And he has not said so yet (here you are, nurse; take baby and walk up and down the gallery). Besides, you have got a wrong notion in your head as usual, Dodo – I can see that: it vexes me.'

'Where am I wrong, Kitty?' said Dorothea, quite meekly. She was almost ready now to think Celia wiser than herself, and was really wondering with some fear what her wrong notion was. Celia felt her advantage, and was determined to use it. None of them knew Dodo as well as she did, or knew how to manage her. Since Celia's baby was born, she had had a new sense of her mental solidity and calm wisdom. It seemed clear that where there was a baby, things were right enough, and that error, in general, was a mere lack of that central poising force.

'I can see what you are thinking of as well as can be, Dodo,' said Celia. 'You are wanting to find out if there is anything uncomfortable for you to do now, only because Mr Casaubon wished it. As if you had not been uncomfortable enough before. And he doesn't deserve it, and you will find that out. He has behaved very badly. James is as angry with him as can be. And I had better tell you, to prepare you.'

'Celia,' said Dorothea, entreatingly, 'you distress me. Tell me at once what you mean.' It glanced through her mind that Mr Casaubon had left the property away from her – which would not be so very distressing.

'Why, he has made a codicil to his will, to say the property was all to go away from you if you married – I mean – '

'That is of no consequence,' said Dorothea, breaking in impetuously.

'But if you married Mr Ladislaw, not anybody else,' Celia went on with persevering quietude. 'Of course that is of no consequence in one way – you never *would* marry Mr Ladislaw; but that only makes it worse of Mr Casaubon.'

The blood rushed to Dorothea's face and neck painfully. But Celia was administering what she thought a sobering dose of fact. It was taking up notions that had done Dodo's health so much harm. So she went on in her neutral tone, as if she had been remarking on baby's robes.

'James says so. He says it is abominable, and not like a gentleman. And there never *was* a better judge than James. It is as if Mr Casaubon wanted to make people believe that you would wish to marry Mr Ladislaw – which is ridiculous. Only James says it was to hinder Mr Ladislaw from wanting to marry you for your money – just as if he ever would think of making you an offer. Mrs Cadwallader said you might as well marry an Italian with white mice! But I must just go and look at baby,' Celia added, without the least change of tone, throwing a light shawl over her, and tripping away.

Dorothea by this time had turned cold again, and now threw herself back helplessly in her chair. She might have compared her experience at that moment to the vague, alarmed consciousness that her life was taking on a new form, that she was undergoing a metamorphosis in which memory would not adjust itself to the stirring of new organs. Everything was changing its aspect: her husband's conduct, her own duteous feeling towards him, every struggle between them – and yet more, her whole relation to Will Ladislaw. Her world was in a state of convulsive change; the only thing she could say distinctly to herself was, that she must wait and think anew. One change terrified her as if it had been a sin; it was a violent shock of repulsion from her departed husband, who had had hidden thoughts, perhaps perverting everything she said and did. Then again she was conscious of another change which also made her tremulous; it was a sudden strange yearning of heart towards Will Ladislaw. It had never before entered her mind that he could, under any circumstances, be her lover: conceive the effect of the sudden revelation that another had thought of him in that light – that perhaps he himself had been conscious of such a possibility, – and this with the hurrying, crowding vision of unfitting conditions, and questions not soon to be solved.

It seemed a long while – she did not know how long – before she heard Celia saying, 'That will do, nurse; he will be quiet on my lap now. You can go to lunch, and let Garratt stay in the next room.' 'What I think, Dodo,' Celia went on, observing nothing more than that Dorothea was leaning back in her chair, and likely to be passive, 'is that Mr Casaubon was spiteful. I never did like him, and James never did. I think the corners of his mouth were dreadfully spiteful. And now he has behaved in this way, I am sure religion does not require you to make yourself uncomfortable about him. If he has been taken away, that is a mercy, and you ought to be grateful. *We* should not grieve, should we, baby?' said Celia confidentially to that unconscious centre and poise of the world, who had the most remarkable fists all complete even to the nails, and hair enough, really, when you took his cap off, to make – you didn't know what: – in short, he was Bouddha in a Western form.

At this crisis Lydgate was announced, and one of the first things he said was, 'I fear you are not so well as you were, Mrs Casaubon; have you been agitated? allow me to feel your pulse.' Dorothea's hand was of a marble coldness.

'She wants to go to Lowick, to look over papers,' said Celia. 'She ought not, ought she?'

Lydgate did not speak for a few moments. Then he said, looking at Dorothea, 'I hardly know. In my opinion Mrs Casaubon should do what would give her the most repose of mind. That repose will not always come from being forbidden to act.'

'Thank you,' said Dorothea, exerting herself, 'I am sure that is wise. There are so many things which I ought to attend to. Why should I sit here idle?' Then, with an effort to recall subjects not connected with her agitation, she added, abruptly, 'You know every one in Middlemarch, I think, Mr Lydgate. I shall ask you to tell me a great deal. I have serious things to do now. I have a living to give away. You know Mr Tyke and all the – ' But Dorothea's effort was too much for her; she broke off and burst into sobs.

Lydgate made her drink a dose of sal-volatile.

'Let Mrs Casaubon do as she likes,' he said to Sir James, whom he asked to see before quitting the house. 'She wants perfect freedom, I think, more than any other prescription.'

His attendance on Dorothea while her brain was excited, had enabled him to form some true conclusions concerning the trials of her life. He felt sure that she had been suffering from the strain and conflict of self-repression; and that she was likely now to feel herself only in another sort of pinfold than that from which she had been released.

Lydgate's advice was all the easier for Sir James to follow when he found that Celia had already told Dorothea the unpleasant fact about the will. There was no help for it now – no reason for any further delay in the execution of necessary business. And the next day Sir James complied at once with her request that he would drive her to Lowick.

'I have no wish to stay there at present,' said Dorothea; 'I could hardly bear it. I am much happier at Freshitt with Celia. I shall be able to think better about what should be done at Lowick by looking at it from a distance. And I should like to be at the Grange a little while with my uncle, and go about in all the old walks and among the people in the village.'

'Not yet, I think. Your uncle is having political company, and you are better out of the way of such doings,' said Sir James, who at that moment thought of the Grange chiefly as a haunt of young Ladislaw's. But no word passed between him and Dorothea about the objectionable part of the will; indeed, both of them felt that the mention of it between them would be impossible. Sir James was shy, even with men, about disagreeable subjects; and the one thing that Dorothea would have chosen to say, if she had spoken on the matter at all, was forbidden to her at present because it seemed to be a further exposure of her husband's injustice. Yet she did wish that Sir James could know what had passed between her and her husband about Will Ladislaw's moral claim on the property: it would then, she thought, be apparent to him as it was to her, that her husband's strange indelicate proviso had been chiefly urged by his bitter resistance to that idea of claim, and not merely by personal feelings more difficult to talk about. Also, it must be admitted, Dorothea wished that this could be known for Will's sake, since her friends seemed to think of him as simply an object of Mr Casaubon's charity. Why should he be compared with an Italian carrying white mice? That word quoted from Mrs Cadwallader seemed like a mocking travesty wrought in the dark by an impish finger.

At Lowick Dorothea searched desk and drawer – searched all her husband's places of deposit for private writing, but found no paper addressed especially to her, except that 'Synoptical Tabulation' which was probably only the beginning of many intended directions for her guidance. In carrying out this bequest of labour to Dorothea, as in all else, Mr Casaubon had been slow and hesitating, oppressed in the plan of transmitting his work, as he had been in executing it, by the sense of moving heavily in a dim and clogging medium: distrust of Dorothea's competence to arrange what he had prepared was subdued only by distrust of any other redactor. But he had come at last to create a trust for himself out of Dorothea's nature: she could do what she resolved to do: and he willingly imagined her toiling under the fetters of a promise to erect a tomb with his name upon it. (Not that Mr Casaubon called the future volumes a tomb; he called them the Key to all Mythologies.) But the months gained on him and left his plans belated: he had only had time to ask for that promise by which he sought to keep his cold grasp on Dorothea's life.

The grasp had slipped away. Bound by a pledge given from the depths of her pity, she would have been capable of undertaking a toil which her judgment whispered was vain for all uses except that consecration of faithfulness which is a supreme use. But now her judgment, instead of being controlled by duteous devotion, was made active by the embittering discovery that in her past union there had lurked the hidden alienation of secrecy and suspicion. The living, suffering man was no longer before her to awaken her pity: there remained only the retrospect of painful subjection to a husband whose thoughts had been lower than she had believed, whose exorbitant claims for himself had even blinded his scrupulous care for his own character, and made him defeat his own pride by shocking men of ordinary honour. As for the property which was the sign of that broken tie, she would have been glad to be free from it and have nothing more than her original fortune which had been settled on her, if there had not been duties attached to ownership, which she ought not to flinch from. About this property many troublous questions insisted on rising: had she not been right in thinking that the half of it ought to go to Will Ladislaw – but was it not impossible now for her to do that act of justice? Mr Casaubon had taken a cruelly effective means of hindering her: even with indignation against him in her heart, any act that seemed a triumphant eluding of his purpose revolted her.

After collecting papers of business which she wished to examine she locked up again the desks and drawers – all empty of personal words for her – empty of any sign that in her husband's lonely brooding his heart had gone out to her in excuse or explanation; and she went back to Freshitt with the sense that around his last hard demand and his last injurious assertion of his power, the silence was unbroken.

Dorothea tried now to turn her thoughts towards immediate duties, and one of these was of a kind which others were determined to remind her of. Lydgate's ear had caught eagerly her mention of the living, and as soon as he could, he reopened the subject, seeing here a possibility of making amends for the casting-vote he had once given with an ill-satisfied conscience.

'Instead of telling you anything about Mr Tyke,' he said, 'I should like to speak of another man – Mr Farebrother, the Vicar of St Botolph's. His living is a poor one, and gives him a stinted provision for himself and his family. His mother, aunt, and sister all live with him, and depend upon him. I believe he has never married because of them. I never heard such good preaching as his – such plain, easy eloquence. He would have done to preach at St Paul's Cross after old Latimer. His talk is just as good about all subjects: original, simple, clear. I think him a remarkable fellow; he ought to have done more than he has done.'

'Why has he not done more?' said Dorothea, interested now in all who had slipped below their own intention.

'That's a hard question,' said Lydgate. 'I find myself that it's uncommonly difficult to make the right thing work: there are so many strings pulling at once. Farebrother often hints that he has got into the wrong profession; he wants a wider range than that of a poor clergyman, and I suppose he has no interest to help him on. He is very fond of Natural History and various scientific matters, and he is hampered in reconciling these tastes with his position. He has no money to spare – hardly enough to use; and that has led him into card-playing – Middlemarch is a great place for whist. He does play for money, and wins a good deal. Of course that takes him into company a little beneath him, and makes him slack about some things; and yet, with all that, looking at him as a whole, I think he is one of the most blameless men I ever knew. He has neither venom nor doubleness in him, and those often go with a more correct outside.'

'I wonder whether he suffers in his conscience because of that habit,' said Dorothea; 'I wonder whether he wishes he could leave it off.'

'I have no doubt he would leave it off, if he were transplanted into plenty: he would be glad of the time for other things.'

'My uncle says that Mr Tyke is spoken of as an apostolic man,' said Dorothea, meditatively. She was wishing it were possible to restore the times of primitive zeal, and yet thinking of Mr Farebrother with a strong desire to rescue him from his chance-gotten money.

'I don't pretend to say that Farebrother is apostolic,' said Lydgate. 'His position is not quite like that of the Apostles: he is only a parson among parishioners whose lives he has to try and make better. Practically I find that what is called being apostolic now, is an impatience of everything in which the parson doesn't cut the principal figure. I see something of that in Mr Tyke at the Hospital: a good deal of his doctrine is a sort of pinching hard to make people uncomfortably aware of him. Besides, an apostolic man at Lowick! – he ought to think, as St Francis did, that it is needful to preach to the birds.'

'True,' said Dorothea. 'It is hard to imagine what sort of notions our farmers and labourers get from their teaching. I have been looking into a volume of sermons by Mr Tyke: such sermons would be of no use at

Lowick – I mean, about imputed righteousness and the prophecies in the Apocalypse. I have always been thinking of the different ways in which Christianity is taught, and whenever I find one way that makes it a wider blessing than any other, I cling to that as the truest – I mean that which takes in the most good of all kinds, and brings in the most people as sharers in it. It is surely better to pardon too much, than to condemn too much. But I should like to see Mr Farebrother and hear him preach.'

'Do,' said Lydgate; 'I trust to the effect of that. He is very much beloved, but he has his enemies too: there are always people who can't forgive an able man for differing from them. And that money-winning business is really a blot. You don't, of course, see many Middlemarch people: but Mr Ladislaw, who is constantly seeing Mr Brooke, is a great friend of Mr Farebrother's old ladies, and would be glad to sing the Vicar's praises. One of the old ladies – Miss Noble, the aunt – is a wonderfully quaint picture of self-forgetful goodness, and Ladislaw gallants her about sometimes. I met them one day in a back street: you know Ladislaw's look – a sort of Daphnis in coat and waistcoat; and this little old maid reaching up to his arm – they looked like a couple dropped out of a romantic comedy. But the best evidence about Farebrother is to see him and hear him.'

Happily Dorothea was in her private sitting-room when this conversation occurred, and there was no one present to make Lydgate's innocent introduction of Ladislaw painful to her. As was usual with him in matters of personal gossip, Lydgate had quite forgotten Rosamond's remark that she thought Will adored Mrs Casaubon. At that moment he was only caring for what would recommend the Farebrother family; and he had purposely given emphasis to the worst that could be said about the Vicar, in order to forestall objections. In the weeks since Mr Casaubon's death he had hardly seen Ladislaw, and he had heard no rumour to warn him that Mr Brooke's confidential secretary was a dangerous subject with Mrs Casaubon. When he was gone, his picture of Ladislaw lingered in her mind and disputed the ground with that question of the Lowick living. What was Will Ladislaw thinking about her? Would he hear of that fact which made her cheeks burn as they never used to do? And how would he feel when he heard it? – But she could see as well as possible how he smiled down at the little old maid. An Italian with white mice! – on the contrary, he was a creature who entered into every one's feelings, and could take the pressure of their thought instead of urging his own with iron resistance.

❧ FIFTY-ONE ❧

Party is Nature too, and you shall see
By force of Logic how they both agree:
The Many in the One, the One in Many;
All is not Some, nor Some the same as Any:
Genus holds species, both are great or small;
One genus highest, one not high at all;
Each species has its differentia too,
This is not That, and He was never You,
Though this and that are AYES, and you and he
Are like as one to one, or three to three.

No GOSSIP ABOUT MR CASAUBON'S WILL had yet reached Ladislaw: the air seemed to be filled with the dissolution of Parliament and the coming election, as the old wakes and fairs were filled with the rival clatter of itinerant shows; and more private noises were taken little notice of. The famous 'dry election' was at hand, in which the depths of public feeling might be measured by the low flood-mark of drink. Will Ladislaw was one of the busiest at this time; and though Dorothea's widowhood was continually in his thought, he was so far from wishing to be spoken to on the subject, that when Lydgate sought him out to tell him what had passed about the Lowick living, he answered rather waspishly –

'Why should you bring me into the matter? I never see Mrs Casaubon, and am not likely to see her, since she is at Freshitt. I never go there. It is Tory ground, where I and the *Pioneer* are no more welcome than a poacher and his gun.'

The fact was that Will had been made the more susceptible by observing that Mr Brooke, instead of wishing him, as before, to come to the Grange oftener than was quite agreeable to himself, seemed now to contrive that he should go there as little as possible. This was a shuffling concession of Mr Brooke's to Sir James Chettam's indignant remonstrance; and Will, awake to the slightest hint in this direction, concluded that he was to be kept away from the Grange on Dorothea's account. Her friends, then, regarded him with some suspicion? Their fears were quite superfluous: they were very much mistaken if they imagined that he would put himself forward as a needy adventurer trying to win the favour of a rich woman.

Until now Will had never fully seen the chasm between himself and Dorothea – until now that he was come to the brink of it, and saw her on the other side. He began, not without some inward rage, to think of going away from the neighbourhood: it would be impossible for him to show any further interest in Dorothea without subjecting himself to disagreeable imputations – perhaps even in her mind, which others might try to poison.

'We are for ever divided,' said Will. 'I might as well be at Rome; she would be no farther from me.' But what we call our despair is often only the painful eagerness of unfed hope. There were plenty of reasons why he should not go – public reasons why he should not quit his post at this crisis, leaving Mr Brooke in the lurch when he needed 'coaching' for the election, and when there was so much canvassing, direct and indirect, to be carried on. Will could not like to leave his own chessmen in the heat of a game; and any candidate on the right side, even if his brain and marrow had been as soft as was consistent with a gentlemanly bearing, might help to turn a majority. To coach Mr Brooke and keep him steadily to the idea that he must pledge himself to vote for the actual Reform Bill, instead of insisting on his independence and power of pulling up in time, was not an easy task. Mr Farebrother's prophecy of a fourth candidate 'in the bag' had not yet been fulfilled, neither the Parliamentary Candidate Society nor any other power on the watch to secure a reforming majority seeing a worthy nodus for interference while there was a second reforming candidate like Mr Brooke, who might be returned at his own expense; and the fight lay entirely between Pinkerton the old Tory member, Bagster, the new Whig member returned at the last election, and Brooke the future independent member, who was to fetter himself for this occasion only. Mr Hawley and his party would bend all their forces to the return of Pinkerton, and Mr Brooke's success must depend either on plumpers which would leave Bagster in the rear, or on the new minting of Tory votes into reforming votes. The latter means, of course, would be preferable.

This prospect of converting votes was a dangerous distraction to Mr Brooke: his impression that waverers were likely to be allured by wavering statements, and also the liability of his mind to stick afresh at opposing arguments as they turned up in his memory, gave Will Ladislaw much trouble.

'You know there are tactics in these things,' said Mr Brooke; 'meeting people half-way – tempering your ideas – saying, "Well now, there's something in that", and so on. I agree with you that this is a peculiar occasion – the country with a will of its own – political unions – that sort of thing – but we sometimes cut with rather too sharp a knife, Ladislaw. These ten-pound householders, now: why ten? Draw the line somewhere – yes: but why just at ten? That's a difficult question, now, if you go into it.'

'Of course it is,' said Will, impatiently. 'But if you are to wait till we get a logical Bill, you must put yourself forward as a revolutionist, and then Middlemarch would not elect you, I fancy. As for trimming, this is not a time for trimming.'

Mr Brooke always ended by agreeing with Ladislaw, who still appeared to him a sort of Burke with a leaven of Shelley; but after an interval the wisdom of his own methods reasserted itself, and he was again drawn into using them with much hopefulness. At this stage of affairs he was in excellent spirits, which even supported him under large advances of money; for his powers of convincing and persuading had not yet been tested by anything more difficult than a chairman's speech, introducing other orators, or a dialogue with a Middlemarch voter, from which he came away with a sense that he was a tactician by nature, and that it was a pity he had not gone earlier into this kind of thing. He was a little conscious of defeat, however, with Mr Mawmsey, a chief representative in Middlemarch of that great social power, the retail trader, and naturally one of the most doubtful voters in the borough – willing for his own part to supply an equal quality of teas and sugars to reformer and anti-reformer, as well as to agree impartially with both, and feeling like the burgesses of old that this necessity of electing members was a great burthen to a town; for even if there were no danger in holding out hopes to all parties beforehand, there would be the painful necessity at last of disappointing respectable people whose names were on his books. He was accustomed to receive large orders from Mr Brooke of Tipton; but then, there were many of Pinkerton's committee whose opinions had a great weight of grocery on their side. Mr Mawmsey thinking that Mr Brooke, as not too 'clever in his intellects', was the more likely to forgive a grocer who gave a hostile vote under pressure, had become confidential in his back parlour.

'As to Reform, sir, put it in a family light,' he said, rattling the small silver in his pocket, and smiling affably. 'Will it support Mrs Mawmsey, and enable her to bring up six children when I am no more? I put the question *fictiously,* knowing what must be the answer. Very well, sir. I ask you what, as a husband and a father, I am to do when gentlemen come to me and say, "Do as you like, Mawmsey; but if you vote against us, I shall get my groceries elsewhere; when I sugar my liquor I like to feel that I am benefiting the country by maintaining tradesmen of the right colour." Those very words have been spoken to me, sir, in the very chair where you are now sitting. I don't mean by your honourable self, Mr Brooke.'

'No, no, no – that's narrow, you know. Until my butler complains to me of your goods, Mr Mawmsey,' said Mr Brooke, soothingly, 'until I hear that you send bad sugars, spices – that sort of thing – I shall never order him to go elsewhere.'

'Sir, I am your humble servant, and greatly obliged,' said Mr Mawmsey, feeling that politics were clearing up a little. 'There would be some pleasure in voting for a gentleman who speaks in that honourable manner.'

'Well, you know, Mr Mawmsey, you would find it the right thing to put yourself on our side. This Reform will touch everybody by-and-by – a thoroughly popular measure – a sort of A, B, C, you know, that must come first before the rest can follow. I quite agree with you that you've got to look at the thing in a family light: but public spirit, now. We're all one family, you know – it's all one cupboard. Such a thing as a vote, now: why, it may help to make men's fortunes at the Cape – there's no knowing what may be the effect of a vote,' Mr Brooke ended, with a sense of being a little out at sea, though finding it still enjoyable. But Mr Mawmsey answered in a tone of decisive check.

'I beg your pardon, sir, but I can't afford that. When I give a vote I must know what I'm doing; I must look to what will be the effects on my till and ledger, speaking respectfully. Prices, I'll admit, are what nobody can know the merits of; and the sudden falls after you've bought in currants, which are a goods that will not keep – I've never myself seen into the ins and outs there; which is a rebuke to human pride. But as to one family, there's debtor and creditor, I hope; they're not going to reform that away; else I should vote for things staying as they are. Few men have less need to cry for change than I have, personally speaking – that is, for self and family. I am not one of those who have nothing to lose; I mean as to respectability both in parish and private business, and noways in respect of your honourable self and custom, which you was good enough to say you would not withdraw from me, vote or no vote, while the article sent in was satisfactory.'

After this conversation Mr Mawmsey went up and boasted to his wife that he had been rather too many for Brooke of Tipton, and that he didn't mind so much now about going to the poll.

Mr Brooke on this occasion abstained from boasting of his tactics to Ladislaw, who for his part was glad enough to persuade himself that he had no concern with any canvassing except the purely argumentative sort, and that he worked no meaner engine than knowledge. Mr Brooke, necessarily, had his agents, who understood the nature of the Middlemarch voter and the means of enlisting his ignorance on the side of the Bill – which were remarkably similar to the means of enlisting it on the side against the Bill. Will stopped his ears. Occasionally Parliament, like the rest of our lives, even to our eating and apparel, could hardly go on if our imaginations were too active about processes. There were plenty of dirty-handed men in the world to do dirty business; and Will protested to himself that his share in bringing Mr Brooke through would be quite innocent.

But whether he should succeed in that mode of contributing to the majority on the right side was very doubtful to him. He had written out various speeches and memoranda for speeches, but he had begun to perceive that Mr Brooke's mind, if it had the burthen of remembering any train of thought, would let it drop, run away in search of it, and not easily come back again. To collect documents is one mode of serving your country, and to remember the contents of a document is another. No! the only way in which Mr Brooke could be coerced into thinking of the right arguments at the right time was to be well plied with them till they took up all the room in his brain. But here there was the difficulty of finding room, so many things having been taken in beforehand. Mr Brooke himself observed that his ideas stood rather in his way when he was speaking.

However, Ladislaw's coaching was forthwith to be put to the test, for before the day of nomination Mr Brooke was to explain himself to the worthy electors of Middlemarch from the balcony of the White Hart, which looked out advantageously at an angle of the market-place, commanding a large area in front and two converging streets. It was a fine May morning and everything seemed hopeful: there was some prospect of an understanding between Bagster's committee and Brooke's, to which Mr Bulstrode, Mr Standish as a Liberal lawyer, and such manufacturers as Mr Plymdale and Mr Vincy, gave a solidity which almost counterbalanced Mr Hawley and his associates who sat for Pinkerton at the Green Dragon. Mr Brooke, conscious of having weakened the blasts of the *Trumpet* against him, by his reforms as a landlord in the last half year, and hearing himself cheered a little as he drove into the town, felt his heart tolerably light under his buff-coloured waistcoat. But with regard to critical occasions, it often happens that all moments seem comfortably remote until the last.

'This looks well, eh?' said Mr Brooke as the crowd gathered. 'I shall have a good audience, at any rate. I like this, now – this kind of public made up of one's own neighbours, you know.'

The weavers and tanners of Middlemarch, unlike Mr Mawmsey, had never thought of Mr Brooke as a neighbour, and were not more attached to him than if he had been sent in a box from London. But they listened without much disturbance to the speakers who introduced the candidate, though one of them – a political personage from Brassing, who came to tell Middlemarch its duty – spoke so fully, that it was alarming to think what the candidate could find to say after him. Meanwhile the crowd became denser, and as the political personage neared the end of his speech, Mr Brooke felt a remarkable change in his sensations while he still handled his eye-glass, trifled with documents before him, and exchanged remarks with his committee, as a man to whom the moment of summons was indifferent.

'I'll take another glass of sherry, Ladislaw,' he said, with an easy air, to Will, who was close behind him, and presently handed him the supposed fortifier. It was ill-chosen; for Mr Brooke was an abstemious man, and to drink a second glass of sherry quickly at no great interval from the first was a surprise to his system which tended to scatter his energies instead of collecting them. Pray pity him: so many English gentlemen make themselves miserable by speechifying on entirely private grounds! whereas Mr Brooke wished to serve his country by standing for Parliament – which, indeed, may also be done on private grounds, but being once undertaken does absolutely demand some speechifying.

It was not about the beginning of his speech that Mr Brooke was at all anxious; this, he felt sure, would be all right; he should have it quite pat, cut out as neatly as a set of couplets from Pope. Embarking would be easy, but the vision of open sea that might come after was alarming. 'And questions, now,' hinted the demon just waking up in his stomach, 'somebody may put questions about the schedules – Ladislaw,' he continued, aloud, 'just hand me the memorandum of the schedules.'

When Mr Brooke presented himself on the balcony, the cheers were quite loud enough to counterbalance the yells, groans, brayings, and other expressions of adverse theory, which were so moderate that Mr Standish (decidedly an old bird) observed in the ear next to him, 'This looks dangerous, by God! Hawley has got some deeper plan than this.' Still, the cheers were exhilarating, and no candidate could look more amiable than Mr Brooke, with the memorandum in his breast-pocket, his left hand on the rail of the balcony, and his right trifling with his eye-glass. The striking points in his appearance were his buff waistcoat, short-clipped blond hair, and neutral physiognomy. He began with some confidence.

'Gentlemen – Electors of Middlemarch!'

This was so much the right thing that a little pause after it seemed natural.

'I'm uncommonly glad to be here – I was never so proud and happy in my life – never so happy, you know.'

This was a bold figure of speech, but not exactly the right thing; for, unhappily, the pat opening had slipped away – even couplets from Pope may be but 'fallings from us, vanishings', when fear clutches us, and a glass of sherry is hurrying like smoke among our ideas. Ladislaw, who stood at the window behind the speaker, thought, 'It's all up now. The only chance is that, since the best thing won't always do, floundering may answer for once.' Mr Brooke, meanwhile, having lost other clues, fell back on himself and his qualifications – always an appropriate graceful subject for a candidate.

'I am a close neighbour of yours, my good friends – you've known me on the bench a good while – I've always gone a good deal into public questions – machinery, now, and machine-breaking – you're many of you concerned with machinery, and I've been going into that lately. It won't do, you know, breaking machines: everything must go on – trade, manufactures, commerce, interchange of staples – that kind of thing – since Adam Smith, that must go on. We must look all over the globe: – "Observation with extensive view", must look everywhere "from China to Peru", as somebody says – Johnson, I think, *The Rambler*, you know. That is what I have done up to a certain point – not as far as Peru; but I've not always stayed at home – I saw it wouldn't do. I've been in the Levant, where some of your Middlemarch goods go – and then, again, in the Baltic. The Baltic, now.'

Plying among his recollections in this way, Mr Brooke might have got along, easily to himself, and would have come back from the remotest seas without trouble; but a diabolical procedure had been set up by the enemy. At one and the same moment there had risen above the shoulders of the crowd, nearly opposite Mr Brooke, and within ten yards of him, the effigy of himself; buff-coloured waistcoat, eye-glass, and neutral physiognomy, painted on rag; and there had arisen apparently in the air, like the note of the cuckoo, a parrot-like, Punch-voiced echo of his words. Everybody looked up at the open windows in the houses at the opposite angles of the converging streets; but they were either blank, or filled by laughing listeners. The most innocent echo has an impish mockery in it when it follows a gravely persistent speaker, and this echo was not at all innocent; if it did not follow with the precision of a natural echo, it had a wicked choice of the words it overtook. By the time it said, 'The Baltic, now', the laugh which had been running through the audience became a general shout, and but for the sobering effects of party and that great public cause which the entanglement of things had identified with 'Brooke of Tipton', the laugh might have caught his committee. Mr Bulstrode asked, reprehensively, what the new police was doing; but a voice could not well be collared, and an attack on the effigy of the candidate would have been too equivocal, since Hawley probably meant it to be pelted.

Mr Brooke himself was not in a position to be quickly conscious of anything except a general slipping away of ideas within himself: he had even a little singing in the ears, and he was the only person who had not yet taken distinct account of the echo or discerned the image of himself. Few things hold the perceptions more thoroughly captive than anxiety about what we have got to say. Mr Brooke heard the laughter; but he had expected some Tory efforts at disturbance, and he was at this moment additionally excited by the tickling, stinging sense that his lost exordium was coming back to fetch him from the Baltic.

'That reminds me,' he went on, thrusting a hand into his side-pocket, with an easy air, 'if I wanted a precedent, you know – but we never want a precedent for the right thing – but there is Chatham, now; I can't say I should have supported Chatham, or Pitt, the younger Pitt – he was not a man of ideas, and we want ideas, you know.'

'Blast your ideas! we want the Bill,' said a loud rough voice from the crowd below.

Immediately the invisible Punch, who had hitherto followed Mr Brooke, repeated, 'Blast your ideas! we want the Bill.' The laugh was louder than ever, and for the first time Mr Brooke, being himself silent, heard distinctly the mocking echo. But it seemed to ridicule his interrupter, and in that light was encouraging; so he replied with amenity –

'There is something in what you say, my good friend, and what do we meet for but to speak our minds – freedom of opinion, freedom of the press, liberty – that kind of thing? The Bill, now – you shall have the Bill' – here Mr Brooke paused a moment to fix on his eye-glass and take the paper from his breast-pocket, with a sense of being practical and coming to particulars. The invisible Punch followed:–

'You shall have the Bill, Mr Brooke, per electioneering contest, and a seat outside Parliament as delivered, five thousand pounds, seven shillings, and fourpence.'

Mr Brooke, amid the roars of laughter, turned red, let his eye-glass fall, and looking about him confusedly, saw the image of himself, which had come nearer. The next moment he saw it dolorously bespattered with eggs. His spirit rose a little, and his voice too.

'Buffoonery, tricks, ridicule the test of truth – all that is very well' – here an unpleasant egg broke on Mr Brooke's shoulder, as the echo said, 'All that is very well'; then came a hail of eggs, chiefly aimed at the image, but occasionally hitting the original, as if by chance. There was a stream of new men pushing among the crowd; whistles, yells, bellowings, and fifes made all the greater hubbub because there was shouting and struggling to put them down. No voice would have had wing enough to rise above the uproar, and Mr Brooke, disagreeably anointed, stood his ground no longer. The frustration would have been less exasperating if it had been less gamesome and boyish: a serious assault of which the newspaper reporter 'can aver that it endangered the learned gentleman's ribs', or can respectfully bear witness to 'the soles of that gentleman's boots having been visible above the railing,' has perhaps more consolations attached to it.

Mr Brooke re-entered the committee-room, saying, as carelessly as he could, 'This is a little too bad, you know. I should have got the ear of the people by-and-by – but they didn't give me time. I should have gone into the Bill by-and-by, you know,' he added, glancing at Ladislaw. 'However, things will come all right at the nomination.'

But it was not resolved unanimously that things would come right; on the contrary, the committee looked rather grim, and the political personage from Brassing was writing busily, as if he were brewing new devices.

'It was Bowyer who did it,' said Mr Standish, evasively. 'I know it as well as if he had been advertised. He's uncommonly good at ventriloquism, and he did it uncommonly well, by God! Hawley has been having him to dinner lately: there's a fund of talent in Bowyer.'

'Well, you know, you never mentioned him to me, Standish, else I would have invited him to dine,' said poor Mr Brooke, who had gone through a great deal of inviting for the good of his country.

'There's not a more paltry fellow in Middlemarch than Bowyer,' said Ladislaw, indignantly, 'but it seems as if the paltry fellows were always to turn the scale.'

Will was thoroughly out of temper with himself as well as with his 'principal', and he went to shut himself in his rooms with a half-formed resolve to throw up the *Pioneer* and Mr Brooke together. Why should he stay? If the impassable gulf between himself and Dorothea were ever to be filled up, it must rather be by his going away and getting into a thoroughly different position than by staying here and slipping into deserved contempt as an understrapper of Brooke's. Then came the young dream of wonders that he might do – in five years, for example: political writing, political speaking, would get a higher value now public life was going to be wider and more national, and they might give him such distinction that he would not seem to be asking Dorothea to step down to him. Five years: – if he could only be sure that she cared for him more than for others; if he could only make her aware that he stood aloof until he could tell his love without lowering himself – then he could go away easily, and begin a career which at five-and-twenty seemed probable enough in the inward order of things, where talent brings fame, and fame everything else which is delightful. He could speak and he could write; he could master any subject if he chose, and he meant always to take the side of reason and justice, on which he would carry all his ardour. Why should he not one day be lifted above the shoulders of the crowd, and feel that he had won that eminence well? Without doubt he would leave Middlemarch, go to town, and make himself fit for celebrity by 'eating his dinners'.

But not immediately: not until some kind of sign had passed between him and Dorothea. He could not be satisfied until she knew why, even if he were the man she would choose to marry, he would not marry her. Hence he must keep his post and bear with Mr Brooke a little longer.

But he soon had reason to suspect that Mr Brooke had anticipated him in the wish to break up their connection. Deputations without and voices within had concurred in inducing that philanthropist to take a stronger measure than usual for the good of mankind; namely, to withdraw in favour of another candidate, to whom he left the advantages of his canvassing machinery. He himself called this a strong measure, but observed that his health was less capable of sustaining excitement than he had imagined.

'I have felt uneasy about the chest – it won't do to carry that too far,' he said to Ladislaw in explaining the affair. 'I must pull up. Poor Casaubon was a warning, you know. I've made some heavy advances, but I've dug a channel. It's rather coarse work – this electioneering, eh, Ladislaw? I daresay you are tired of it. However, we have dug a channel with the *Pioneer* – put things in a track, and so on. A more ordinary man than you might carry it on now – more ordinary, you know.'

'Do you wish me to give it up?' said Will, the quick colour coming in his face, as he rose from the writing-table, and took a turn of three steps with his hands in his pockets. 'I am ready to do so whenever you wish it.'

'As to wishing, my dear Ladislaw, I have the highest opinion of your powers, you know. But about the *Pioneer*, I have been consulting a little with some of the men on our side, and they are inclined to take it into their hands – indemnify me to a certain extent – carry it on, in fact. And under the circumstances, you might like to give up – might find a better field. These people might not take that high view of you which I have always taken, as an *alter ego*, a right hand – though I always looked forward to your doing something else. I think of having a run into France. But I'll write you any letters, you know – to Althorpe and people of that kind. I've met Althorpe.'

'I am exceedingly obliged to you,' said Ladislaw proudly. 'Since you are going to part with the *Pioneer*, I need not trouble you about the steps I shall take. I may choose to continue here for the present.'

After Mr Brooke had left him Will said to himself, 'The rest of the family have been urging him to get rid of me, and he doesn't care now about my going. I shall stay as long as I like. I shall go of my own movement, and not because they are afraid of me.'

◁ FIFTY-TWO ▷

His heart
The lowliest duties on itself did lay.
WORDSWORTH

ON THAT JUNE EVENING WHEN MR Farebrother knew that he was to have the Lowick living, there was joy in the old-fashioned parlour, and even the portraits of the great lawyers seemed to look on with satisfaction. His mother left her tea and toast untouched, but sat with her usual pretty primness, only showing her emotion by that flush in the cheeks and brightness in the eyes which give an old woman a touching momentary identity with her far-off youthful self, and saying decisively –

'The greatest comfort, Camden, is that you have deserved it.'

'When a man gets a good berth, mother, half the deserving must come after,' said the son, brimful of pleasure, and not trying to conceal it. The gladness in his face was of that active kind which seems to have energy enough not only to flash outwardly, but to light up busy vision within: one seemed to see thoughts, as well as delight, in his glances.

'Now, aunt,' he went on, rubbing his hands and looking at Miss Noble, who was making tender little beaver-like noises, 'there shall be sugar-candy always on the table for you to steal and give to the children, and you shall have a great many new stockings to make presents of, and you shall darn your own more than ever!'

Miss Noble nodded at her nephew with a subdued half-frightened laugh, conscious of having already dropped an additional lump of sugar into her basket on the strength of the new preferment.

'As for you, Winny' – the Vicar went on – 'I shall make no difficulty about your marrying any Lowick bachelor – Mr Solomon Featherstone, for example, as soon as I find you are in love with him.'

Miss Winifred, who had been looking at her brother all the while and crying heartily, which was her way of rejoicing, smiled through her tears and said, 'You must set me the example, Cam: *you* must marry now.'

'With all my heart. But who is in love with me? I am a seedy old fellow,' said the Vicar, rising, pushing his chair away and looking down at himself. 'What do you say, mother?'

'You are a handsome man, Camden: though not so fine a figure of a man as your father,' said the old lady.

'I wish you would marry Miss Garth, brother,' said Miss Winifred. 'She would make us so lively at Lowick.'

'Very fine! You talk as if young women were tied up to be chosen, like poultry at market; as if I had only to ask and everybody would have me,' said the Vicar, not caring to specify.

'We don't want everybody,' said Miss Winifred. 'But *you* would like Miss Garth, mother, shouldn't you?'

'My son's choice shall be mine,' said Mrs Farebrother, with majestic discretion; 'and a wife would be most welcome, Camden. You will want your whist at home when we go to Lowick, and Henrietta Noble never was a whist-player.' (Mrs Farebrother always called her tiny old sister by that magnificent name.)

'I shall do without whist now, mother.'

'Why so, Camden? In my time whist was thought an undeniable amusement for a good churchman,' said Mrs Farebrother, innocent of the meaning that whist had for her son, and speaking rather sharply, as at some dangerous countenancing of new doctrine.

'I shall be too busy for whist; I shall have two parishes,' said the Vicar, preferring not to discuss the virtues of that game.

He had already said to Dorothea, 'I don't feel bound to give up St Botolph's. It is protest enough against the pluralism they want to reform if I give somebody else most of the money. The stronger thing is not to give up power, but to use it well.'

'I have thought of that,' said Dorothea. 'So far as self is concerned. I think it would be easier to give up power and money than to keep them. It seems very unfitting that I should have this patronage, yet I felt that I ought not to let it be used by some one else insead of me.'

'It is I who am bound to act so that you will not regret your power,' said Mr Farebrother.

His was one of the natures in which conscience gets the more active when the yoke of life ceases to gall them. He made no display of humility on the subject, but in his heart he felt rather ashamed that his conduct had shown laches which others who did not get benefices were free from.

'I used often to wish I had been something else than a clergyman,' he said to Lydgate, 'but perhaps it will be better to try and make as good a clergyman out of myself as I can. That is the well-beneficed point of view, you perceive, from which difficulties are much simplified,' he ended, smiling.

The Vicar did feel then as if his share of duties would be easy. But Duty has a trick of behaving unexpectedly – something like a heavy friend whom we have amiably asked to visit us, and who breaks his leg within our gates.

Hardly a week later, Duty presented itself in his study under the disguise of Fred Vincy, now returned from Omnibus College with his bachelor's degree.

'I am ashamed to trouble you, Mr Farebrother,' said Fred, whose fair open face was propitiating, 'but you are the only friend I can consult. I told you everything once before, and you were so good that I can't help coming to you again.'

'Sit down, Fred, I'm ready to hear and do anything I can,' said the Vicar, who was busy packing some small objects for removal, and went on with his work.

'I wanted to tell you – ' Fred hesitated an instant and then went on plungingly, 'I might go into the Church now; and really, look where I may, I can't see anything else to do. I don't like it, but I know it's uncommonly hard on my father to say so, after he has spent a good deal of money in educating me for it.' Fred paused again an instant, and then repeated, 'and I can't see anything else to do.'

'I did talk to your father about it, Fred, but I made little way with him. He said it was too late. But you have got over one bridge now: what are your other difficulties?'

'Merely that I don't like it. I don't like divinity, and preaching, and feeling obliged to look serious. I like riding across country, and doing as other men do. I don't mean that I want to be a bad fellow in any way; but I've no taste for the sort of thing people expect of a clergyman. And yet what else am I to do? My father can't spare me any capital, else I might go into farming. And he has no room for me in his trade. And of course I can't begin to study for law or physic now, when my father wants me to earn something. It's all very well to say I'm wrong to go into the Church; but those who say so might as well tell me to go into the backwoods.'

Fred's voice had taken a tone of grumbling remonstrance, and Mr Farebrother might have been inclined to smile if his mind had not been too busy in imagining more than Fred told him.

'Have you any difficulties about doctrines – about the Articles?' he said, trying hard to think of the question simply for Fred's sake.

'No, I suppose the Articles are right. I am not prepared with any arguments to disprove them, and much better, cleverer fellows than I am go in for them entirely. I think it would be rather ridiculous in me to urge scruples of that sort, as if I were a judge,' said Fred, quite simply.

'I suppose, then, it has occurred to you that you might be a fair parish priest without being much of a divine?'

'Of course, if I am obliged to be a clergyman, I shall try and do my duty, though I mayn't like it. Do you think anybody ought to blame me?'

'For going into the Church under the circumstances? That depends on your conscience, Fred – how far you have counted the cost, and seen what your position will require of you. I can only tell you about myself, that I have always been too lax, and have been uneasy in consequence.'

'But there is another hindrance,' said Fred, colouring. 'I did not tell you before, though perhaps I may have said things that made you guess it. There is somebody I am very fond of: I have loved her ever since we were children.'

'Miss Garth, I suppose?' said the Vicar, examining some labels very closely.

'Yes. I shouldn't mind anything if she would have me. And I know I could be a good fellow then.'

'And you think she returns the feeling?'

'She never will say so; and a good while ago she made me promise not to speak to her about it again. And she has set her mind especially against my being a clergyman; I know that. But I can't give her up. I do think she cares about me. I saw Mrs Garth last night and she said that Mary was staying at Lowick Rectory with Miss Farebrother.'

'Yes, she is very kindly helping my sister. Do you wish to go there?'

'No, I want to ask a great favour of you. I am ashamed to bother you in this way; but Mary might listen to what you said, if you mentioned the subject to her – I mean about my going into the Church.'

'That is rather a delicate task, my dear Fred. I shall have to presuppose your attachment to her; and to enter on the subject as you wish me to do, will be asking her to tell me whether she returns it.'

'That is what I want her to tell you,' said Fred, bluntly. 'I don't know what to do, unless I can get at her feeling.'

'You mean that you would be guided by that as to your going into the Church?'

'If Mary said she would never have me I might as well go wrong in one way as another.'

'That is nonsense, Fred: Men outlive their love, but they don't outlive the consequences of their recklessness.'

'Not my sort of love: I have never been without loving Mary. If I had to give her up, it would be like beginning to live on wooden legs.'

'Will she not be hurt at my intrusion?'

'No, I feel sure she will not. She respects you more than any one, and she would not put you off with fun as she does me. Of course I could not have told any one else, or asked any one else to speak to her, but you. There is no one else who could be such a friend to both of us.' Fred paused a moment, and then said, rather complainingly, 'And she ought to acknowledge that I have worked in order to pass. She ought to believe that I would exert myself for her sake.'

There was a moment's silence before Mr Farebrother laid down his work, and putting out his hand to Fred said –

'Very well, my boy. I will do what you wish.'

That very day Mr Farebrother went to Lowick parsonage on the nag which he had just set up. 'Decidedly I am an old stalk,' he thought, 'the young growths are pushing me aside.'

He found Mary in the garden gathering roses and sprinkling the petals on a sheet. The sun was low, and tall trees sent their shadows across the grassy walks where Mary was moving without bonnet or parasol. She did not observe Mr Farebrother's approach along the grass, and had just stooped down to lecture a small black-and-tan terrier, which would persist in walking on the sheet and smelling at the rose-leaves as Mary sprinkled them. She took his forepaws in one hand, and lifted up the forefinger of the other, while the dog wrinkled his brows and looked embarrassed. 'Fly, Fly, I am ashamed of you,' Mary was saying in a grave contralto. 'This is not becoming in a sensible dog; anybody would think you were a silly young gentleman.'

'You are unmerciful to young gentlemen, Miss Garth,' said the Vicar, within two yards of her.

Mary started up and blushed. 'It always answers to reason with Fly,' she said, laughingly.

'But not with young gentlemen?'

'Oh, with some, I suppose; since some of them turn into excellent men.'

'I am glad of that admission, because I want at this very moment to interest you in a young gentleman.'

'Not a silly one, I hope,' said Mary, beginning to pluck the roses again, and feeling her heart beat uncomfortably.

'No; though perhaps wisdom is not his strong point, but rather affection and sincerity. However, wisdom lies more in those two qualities than people are apt to imagine. I hope you know by those marks what young gentleman I mean.'

'Yes, I think I do,' said Mary, bravely, her face getting more serious, and her hands cold; 'it must be Fred Vincy.'

'He has asked me to consult you about his going into the Church. I hope you will not think that I consented to take a liberty in promising to do so.'

'On the contrary, Mr Farebrother,' said Mary, giving up the roses, and folding her arms, but unable to look up, 'whenever you have anything to say to me I feel honoured.'

'But before I enter on that question, let me just touch a point on which your father took me into confidence; by the way, it was that very evening on which I once before fulfilled a mission from Fred, just after he had gone to college. Mr Garth told me what happened on the night of Featherstone's death – how you refused to burn the will; and he said that you had some heart-prickings on that subject, because you had been the innocent means of hindering Fred from getting his ten thousand pounds. I have kept that in mind, and I have heard something that may relieve you on that score – may show you that no sin-offering is demanded from you there.'

Mr Farebrother paused a moment and looked at Mary. He meant to give Fred his full advantage, but it would be well, he thought, to clear her mind of any superstitions, such as women sometimes follow when they do a man the wrong of marrying him as an act of atonement. Mary's cheeks had begun to burn a little, and she was mute.

'I mean, that your action made no real difference to Fred's lot. I find that the first will would not have been legally good after the burning of the last; it would not have stood if it had been disputed, and you may be sure it would have been disputed. So, on that score, you may feel your mind free.'

'Thank you, Mr Farebrother,' said Mary, earnestly. 'I am grateful to you for remembering my feelings.'

'Well, now I may go on. Fred, you know, has taken his degree. He has worked his way so far, and now the question is, what is he to do? That question is so difficult that he is inclined to follow his father's wishes and enter the Church, though you know better than I do that he was quite set against that formerly. I have questioned him on the subject and I confess I see no insuperable objection to his being a clergyman, as things go. He says that he could turn his mind to doing his best in that vocation, on one condition. If that condition were fulfilled I would do my utmost in helping Fred on. After a time – not, of course, at first – he might be with me as my curate, and he would have so much to do that his stipend would be nearly what I used to get as vicar. But I repeat that there is a condition without which all this cannot come to pass. He has opened his heart to me, Miss Garth, and asked me to plead for him. The condition lies entirely in your feeling.'

Mary looked so much moved, that he said after a moment, 'Let us walk a little'; and when they were walking he added, 'To speak quite plainly, Fred will not take any course which would lessen the chance that you would consent to be his wife; but with that prospect, he will try his best at anything you approve.'

'I cannot possibly say that I will ever be his wife, Mr Farebrother: but I certainly never will be his wife if he becomes a clergyman. What you say is most generous and kind; I don't mean for a moment to correct your judgment. It is only that I have my girlish, mocking way of looking at things,' said Mary, with a returning sparkle of playfulness in her answer which only made its modesty more charming.

'He wishes me to report exactly what you think,' said Mr Farebrother.

'I could not love a man who is ridiculous,' said Mary, not choosing to go deeper. 'Fred has sense and knowledge enough to make him respectable, if he likes, in some good worldly business, but I can never imagine him preaching and exhorting and pronouncing blessings, and praying by the sick, without feeling as if I were looking at a caricature. His being a clergyman would be only for gentility's sake, and I think there is nothing more contemptible than such imbecile gentility. I used to think that of Mr Crowse, with his empty face and neat umbrella, and mincing little speeches. What right have such men to represent Christianity – as if it were an institution for getting up idiots genteelly – as if – ' Mary checked herself. She had been carried along as if she had been speaking to Fred instead of Mr Farebrother.

'Young women are severe; they don't feel the stress of action as men do, though perhaps I ought to make you an exception there. But you don't put Fred Vincy on so low a level as that?'

'No, indeed; he has plenty of sense, but I think he would not show it as a clergyman. He would be a piece of professional affectation.'

'Then the answer is quite decided. As a clergyman he could have no hope?'

Mary shook her head.

'But if he braved all the difficulties of getting his bread in some other way – will you give him the support of hope? May he count on winning you?'

'I think Fred ought not to need telling again what I have already said to him,' Mary answered, with a slight resentment in her manner. 'I mean that he ought not to put such questions until he has done something worthy, instead of saying that he could do it.'

Mr Farebrother was silent for a minute or more, and then, as they turned and paused under the shadow of a maple at the end of a grassy walk, said, 'I understand that you resist any attempt to fetter you, but either your feeling for Fred Vincy excludes your entertaining another attachment, or it does not: either he may count on your remaining single until he shall have earned your hand, or he may in any case be disappointed. Pardon me, Mary – you know I used to catechize you under that name – but when the state of a woman's affections touches the happiness of another life – of more lives than one – I think it would be the nobler course for her to be perfectly direct and open.'

Mary in her turn was silent, wondering not at Mr Farebrother's manner but at his tone, which had a grave restrained emotion in it. When the strange idea flashed across her that his words had reference to himself, she was incredulous and ashamed of entertaining it. She had never thought that any man could love her except Fred, who had espoused her with the umbrella ring, when she wore socks and little strapped shoes; still less that she could be of any importance to Mr Farebrother, the cleverest man in her narrow circle. She had only time to feel that all this was hazy and perhaps illusory; but one thing was clear and determined – her answer.

'Since you think it my duty, Mr Farebrother, I will tell you that I have too strong a feeling for Fred to give him up for any one else. I should never be quite happy if I thought he was unhappy for the loss of me. It has taken such deep root in me – my gratitude to him for always loving me best, and minding so much if I hurt myself, from the time when we were very little. I cannot imagine any new feeling coming to make that weaker. I should like better than anything to see him worthy of every one's respect. But please tell him I will not promise to marry him till then; I should shame and grieve my father and mother. He is free to choose some one else.'

'Then I have fulfilled my commission thoroughly,' said Mr Farebrother, putting out his hand to Mary, 'and I shall ride back to Middlemarch forthwith. With this prospect before him, we shall get Fred into the right niche somehow, and I hope I shall live to join your hands. God bless you!'

'Oh, please stay, and let me give you some tea,' said Mary. Her eyes filled with tears, for something indefinable, something like the resolute suppression of a pain in Mr Farebrother's manner, made her feel suddenly miserable, as she had once felt when she saw her father's hands trembling in a moment of trouble.

'No, my dear, no. I must get back.'

In three minutes the Vicar was on horseback again, having gone magnanimously through a duty much harder than the renunciation of whist, or even than the writing of penitential meditations.

⌀ FIFTY-THREE ଚ

It is but a shallow haste which concludeth insincerity from
what outsiders call inconsistency – putting a dead
mechanism of 'ifs' and 'therefores' for the living myriad of
hidden suckers whereby the belief and the conduct are
wrought into mutual sustainment.

MR BULSTRODE, WHEN HE WAS HOPING to acquire a new interest in Lowick,
had naturally had an especial wish that the new clergyman should be one
whom he thoroughly approved; and he believed it to be a chastisement
and admonition directed to his own shortcomings and those of the nation
at large, that just about the time when he came in possession of the deeds
which made him the proprietor of Stone Court, Mr Farebrother 'read
himself' into the quaint little church and preached his first sermon to the
congregation of farmers, labourers, and village artisans. It was not that Mr
Bulstrode intended to frequent Lowick Church or to reside at Stone Court
for a good while to come: he had bought the excellent farm and fine
homestead simply as a retreat which he might gradually enlarge as to the
land and beautify as to the dwelling, until it should be conducive to
the divine glory that he should enter on it as a residence, partially withdrawing from his present exertions in the administration of business, and
throwing more conspicuously on the side of Gospel truth the weight of
local landed proprietorship, which Providence might increase by unforeseen occasions of purchase. A strong leading in this direction seemed to
have been given in the surprising facility of getting Stone Court, when
every one had expected that Mr Rigg Featherstone would have clung to it
as the Garden of Eden. That was what poor old Peter himself had
expected; having often, in imagination, looked up through the sods above
him, and, unobstructed by perspective, seen his frog-faced legatee enjoying the fine old place to the perpetual surprise and disappointment of
other survivors.

But how little we know what would make paradise for our neighbours!
We judge from our own desires, and our neighbours themselves are not
always open enough even to throw out a hint of theirs. The cool and
judicious Joshua Rigg had not allowed his parent to perceive that Stone
Court was anything less than the chief good in his estimation, and he had
certainly wished to call it his own. But as Warren Hastings looked at gold
and thought of buying Daylesford, so Joshua Rigg looked at Stone Court

and thought of buying gold. He had a very distinct and intense vision of his chief good, the vigorous greed which he had inherited having taken a special form by dint of circumstance: and his chief good was to be a money-changer. From his earliest employment as an errand-boy in a seaport, he had looked though the windows of the money-changers as other boys look through the windows of the pastry-cooks; the fascination had wrought itself gradually into a deep special passion; he meant, when he had property, to do many things, one of them being to marry a genteel young person; but these were all accidents and joys that imagination could dispense with. The one joy after which his soul thirsted was to have a money-changer's shop on a much-frequented quay, to have locks all round him of which he held the keys, and to look sublimely cool as he handled the breeding coins of all nations, while helpless Cupidity looked at him enviously from the other side of an iron lattice. The strength of that passion had been a power enabling him to master all the knowledge necessary to gratify it. And when others were thinking that he had settled at Stone Court for life, Joshua himself was thinking that the moment now was not far off when he should settle on the North Quay with the best appointments in safes and locks.

Enough. We are concerned with looking at Joshua Rigg's sale of his land from Mr Bulstrode's point of view, and he interpreted it as a cheering dispensation conveying perhaps a sanction to a purpose which he had for some time entertained without external encouragement; he interpreted it thus, but not too confidently, offering up his thanksgiving in guarded phraseology. His doubts did not arise from the possible relations of the event to Joshua Rigg's destiny, which belonged to the unmapped regions not taken under the providential government, except perhaps in an imperfect colonial way; but they arose from reflecting that this dispensation too might be a chastisement for himself, as Mr Farebrother's induction to the living clearly was.

This was not what Mr Bulstrode said to any man for the sake of deceiving him: it was what he said to himself – it was as genuinely his mode of explaining events as any theory of yours may be, if you happen to disagree with him. For the egoism which enters into our theories does not affect their sincerity; rather, the more our egoism is satisfied, the more robust is our belief.

However, whether for sanction or for chastisement, Mr Bulstrode, hardly fifteen months after the death of Peter Featherstone, had become the proprietor of Stone Court, and what Peter would say 'if he were worthy to know', had become an inexhaustible and consolatory subject of conversation to his disappointed relatives. The tables were now turned on that dear brother departed, and to contemplate the frustration of his cunning by the superior cunning of things in general was a cud of delight to Solomon. Mrs Waule had a melancholy triumph in the proof that it did not answer to make false Featherstones and cut off the genuine; and Sister

Martha receiving the news in the Chalky Flats said, 'Dear, dear! then the Almighty could have been none so pleased with the alms-houses after all.'

Affectionate Mrs Bulstrode was particularly glad of the advantage which her husband's health was likely to get from the purchase of Stone Court. Few days passed without his riding thither and looking over some part of the farm with the bailiff, and the evenings were delicious in that quiet spot, when the new hayricks lately set up were sending forth odours to mingle with the breath of the rich old garden. One evening, while the sun was still above the horizon and burning in golden lamps among the great walnut boughs, Mr Bulstrode was pausing on horseback outside the front gate waiting for Caleb Garth, who had met him by appointment to give an opinion on a question of stable drainage, and was now advising the bailiff in the rick-yard.

Mr Bulstrode was conscious of being in a good spiritual frame and more than usually serene, under the influence of his innocent recreation. He was doctrinally convinced that there was a total absence of merit in himself; but that doctrinal conviction may be held without pain when the sense of demerit does not take a distinct shape in memory and revive the tingling of shame or the pang of remorse. Nay, it may be held with intense satisfaction when the depth of our sinning is but a measure for the depth of forgiveness, and clenching proof that we are peculiar instruments of the divine intention. The memory has as many moods as the temper, and shifts its scenery like a diorama. At this moment Mr Bulstrode felt as if the sunshine were all one with that of far-off evenings when he was a very young man and used to go out preaching beyond Highbury. And he would willingly have had that service of exhortation in prospect now. The texts were there still, and so was his own facility in expounding them. His brief reverie was interrupted by the return of Caleb Garth, who also was on horseback, and was just shaking his bridle before starting, when he exclaimed –

'Bless my heart! what's this fellow in black coming along the lane? He's like one of those men one sees about after the races.' Mr Bulstrode turned his horse and looked along the lane, but made no reply. The comer was our slight acquaintance Mr Raffles, whose appearance presented no other change than such as was due to a suit of black and a crape hat-band. He was within three yards of the horsemen now, and they could see the flash of recognition in his face as he whirled his stick upward, looking all the while at Mr Bulstrode, and at last exclaiming: –

'By Jove, Nick, it's you! I couldn't be mistaken, though the five-and-twenty years have played old Bogey with us both! How are you, eh? you didn't expect to see *me* here. Come, shake us by the hand.'

To say that Mr Raffles's manner was rather excited would be only one mode of saying that it was evening. Caleb Garth could see that there was a moment of struggle and hesitation in Mr Bulstrode, but it ended in his putting out his hand coldly to Raffles and saying –

'I did not indeed expect to see you in this remote country place.'

'Well, it belongs to a stepson of mine,' said Raffles, adjusting himself in a swaggering attitude. 'I came to see him here before. I'm not so surprised at seeing you, old fellow, because I picked up a letter – what you may call a providential thing. It's uncommonly fortunate I met you, though; for I don't care about seeing my stepson: he's not affectionate, and his poor mother's gone now. To tell the truth, I came out of love to you, Nick: I came to get your address, for – look here!' Raffles drew a crumpled paper from his pocket.

Almost any other man than Caleb Garth might have been tempted to linger on the spot for the sake of hearing all he could about a man whose acquaintance with Bulstrode seemed to imply passages in the banker's life so unlike anything that was known of him in Middlemarch that they must have the nature of a secret to pique curiosity. But Caleb was peculiar: certain human tendencies which are commonly strong were almost absent from his mind; and one of these was curiosity about personal affairs. Especially if there was anything discreditable to be found out concerning another man, Caleb preferred not to know it: and if he had to tell anybody under him that his evil doings were discovered, he was more embarrassed than the culprit. He now spurred his horse, and saying, 'I wish you good evening, Mr Bulstrode; I must be getting home,' set off at a trot.

'You didn't put your full address to this letter,' Raffles continued. 'That was not like the first-rate man of business you used to be. "The Shrubs", – they may be anywhere: you live near at hand, eh? – have cut the London concern altogether – perhaps turned country squire – have a rural mansion to invite me to. Lord, how many years it is ago! The old lady must have been dead a pretty long while – gone to glory without the pain of knowing how poor her daughter was, eh? But, by Jove! you're very pale and pasty, Nick. Come, if you're going home, I'll walk by your side.'

Mr Bulstrode's usual paleness had in fact taken an almost deathly hue. Five minutes before, the expanse of his life had been submerged in its evening sunshine which shone backward to its remembered morning: sin seemed to be a question of doctrine and inward penitence, humiliation an exercise of the closet, the bearing of his deeds a matter of private vision adjusted solely by spiritual relations and conceptions of the divine purposes. And now, as if by some hideous magic, this loud red figure had risen before him in unmanageable solidity – an incorporate past which had not entered into his imagination of chastisements. But Mr Bulstrode's thought was busy, and he was not a man to act or speak rashly.

'I was going home,' he said, 'but I can defer my ride a little. And you can, if you please, rest here.'

'Thank you,' said Raffles, making a grimace. 'I don't care now about seeing my stepson. I'd rather go home with you.'

'Your stepson, if Mr Rigg Featherstone was he, is here no longer. I am master here now.'

Raffles opened wide eyes, and gave a long whistle of surprise, before he said, 'Well, then, I've no objection. I've had enough walking from the coach-road. I never was much of a walker, or rider either. What I like is a smart vehicle and a spirited cob. I was always a little heavy in the saddle. What a pleasant surprise it must be to you to see me, old fellow!' he continued, as they turned towards the house. 'You don't say so; but you never took your luck heartily – you were always thinking of improving the occasion – you'd such a gift for improving your luck.'

Mr Raffles seemed greatly to enjoy his own wit, and swung his leg in a swaggering manner which was rather too much for his companion's judicious patience.

'If I remember rightly,' Mr Bulstrode observed, with chill anger, 'our acquaintance many years ago had not the sort of intimacy which you are now assuming, Mr Raffles. Any services you desire of me will be the more readily rendered if you will avoid a tone of familiarity which did not lie in our former intercourse, and can hardly be warranted by more than twenty years of separation.'

'You don't like being called Nick? Why, I always called you Nick in my heart, and though lost to sight, to memory dear. By Jove! my feelings have ripened for you like fine old cognac. I hope you've got some in the house now. Josh filled my flask well the last time.'

Mr Bulstrode had not yet fully learned that even the desire for cognac was not stronger in Raffles than the desire to torment, and that a hint of annoyance always served him as a fresh cue. But it was at least clear that further objection was useless, and Mr Bulstrode, in giving orders to the housekeeper for the accommodation of the guest, had a resolute air of quietude.

There was the comfort of thinking that this housekeeper had been in the service of Rigg also, and might accept the idea that Mr Bulstrode entertained Raffles merely as a friend of her former master. When there was food and drink spread before his visitor in the wainscoted parlour, and no witness in the room, Mr Bulstrode said –

'Your habits and mine are so different, Mr Raffles, that we can hardly enjoy each other's society. The wisest plan for both of us will therefore be to part as soon as possible. Since you say that you wished to meet me, you probably considered that you had some business to transact with me. But under the circumstances I will invite you to remain here for the night, and I will myself ride over here early to-morrow morning – before breakfast, in fact, when I can receive any communication you have to make to me.'

'With all my heart,' said Raffles, 'this is a comfortable place – a little dull for a continuance; but I can put up with it for a night, with this good liquor and the prospect of seeing you again in the morning. You're a much better host than my stepson was; but Josh owed me a bit of a grudge for marrying his mother; and between you and me there was never anything but kindness.'

Mr Bulstrode, hoping that the peculiar mixture of joviality and sneering in Raffles's manner was a good deal the effect of drink, had determined to wait till he was quite sober before he spent more words upon him. But he rode home with a terribly lucid vision of the difficulty there would be in arranging any result that could be permanently counted on with this man. It was inevitable that he should wish to get rid of John Raffles, though his reappearance could not be regarded as lying outside the divine plan. The spirit of evil might have sent him to threaten Mr Bulstrode's subversion as an instrument of good; but the threat must have been permitted, and was a chastisement of a new kind. It was an hour of anguish for him very different from the hours in which his struggle had been securely private, and which had ended with a sense that his secret misdeeds were pardoned and his services accepted. Those misdeeds, even when committed – had they not been half sanctified by the singleness of his desire to devote himself and all he possessed to the furtherance of the divine scheme? And was he after all to become a mere stone of stumbling and a rock of offence? For who would understand the work within him? Who would not, when there was the pretext of casting disgrace upon him, confound his whole life and the truths he had espoused in one heap of obloquy?

In his closest meditations the life-long habit of Mr Bulstrode's mind clad his most egoistic terrors in doctrinal references to superhuman ends. But even while we are talking and meditating about the earth's orbit and the solar system, what we feel and adjust our movements to is the stable earth and the changing day. And now within all the automatic succession of theoretic phrases – distinct and inmost as the shiver and the ache of oncoming fever when we are discussing abstract pain – was the forecast of disgrace in the presence of his neighbours and of his own wife. For the pain, as well as the public estimate of disgrace, depends on the amount of previous profession. To men who only aim at escaping felony, nothing short of the prisoner's dock is disgrace. But Mr Bulstrode had aimed at being an eminent Christian.

It was not more than half-past seven in the morning when he again reached Stone Court. The fine old place never looked more like a delightful home than at that moment; the great white lilies were in flower, the nasturtiums, their pretty leaves all silvered with dew, were running away over the low stone wall; the very noises all around had a heart of peace within them. But everything was spoiled for the owner as he walked on the gravel in front and awaited the descent of Mr Raffles, with whom he was condemned to breakfast.

It was not long before they were seated together in the wainscoted parlour over their tea and toast, which was as much as Raffles cared to take at that early hour. The difference between his morning and evening self was not so great as his companion had imagined that it might be; the delight in tormenting was perhaps even the stronger because his spirits were rather less highly pitched. Certainly his manners seemed more disagreeable by the morning light.

'As I have little time to spare, Mr Raffles,' said the banker, who could hardly do more than sip his tea and break his toast without eating it, 'I shall be obliged if you will mention at once the ground on which you wished to meet with me. I presume that you have a home elsewhere and will be glad to return to it.'

'Why, if a man has got any heart, doesn't he want to see an old friend, Nick? – I must call you Nick – we always did call you young Nick when we knew you meant to marry the old widow. Some said you had a handsome family likeness to old Nick, but that was your mother's fault, calling you Nicholas. Aren't you glad to see me again? I expected an invite to stay with you at some pretty place. My own establishment is broken up now my wife's dead. I've no particular attachment to any spot; I would as soon settle hereabout as anywhere.'

'May I ask why you returned from America? I considered that the strong wish you expressed to go there, when an adequate sum was furnished, was tantamount to an engagement that you would remain there for life.'

'Never knew that a wish to go to a place was the same thing as a wish to stay. But I did stay a matter of ten years; it didn't suit me to stay any longer. And I'm not going again, Nick.' Here Mr Raffles winked slowly as he looked at Mr Bulstrode.

'Do you wish to be settled in any business? What is your calling now?'

'Thank you, my calling is to enjoy myself as much as I can. I don't care about working any more. If I did anything it would be a little travelling in the tobacco line – or something of that sort, which takes a man into agreeable company. But not without an independence to fall back upon. That's what I want: I'm not so strong as I was, Nick, though I've got more colour than you. I want an independence.'

'That could be supplied to you, if you would engage to keep at a distance,' said Mr Bulstrode, perhaps with a little too much eagerness in his undertone.

'That must be as it suits my convenience,' said Raffles, coolly. 'I see no reason why I shouldn't make a few acquaintances hereabout. I'm not ashamed of myself as company for anybody. I dropped my portmanteau at the turnpike when I got down – change of linen – genuine – honour bright! – more than fronts and wristbands; and with this suit of mourning, straps and everything, I should do you credit among the nobs here.' Mr Raffles had pushed away his chair and looked down at himself, particularly at his straps. His chief intention was to annoy Bulstrode, but he really thought that his appearance now would produce a good effect, and that he was not only handsome and witty, but clad in a mourning style which implied solid connections.

'If you intend to rely on me in any way, Mr Raffles,' said Bulstrode, after a moment's pause, 'you will expect to meet my wishes.'

'Ah, to be sure,' said Raffles, with a mocking cordiality. 'Didn't I always do it? Lord, you made a pretty thing out of me, and I got but little. I've often thought since, I might have done better by telling the old woman that I'd found her daughter and her grandchild: it would have suited my feelings better; I've got a soft place in my heart. But you've buried the old lady by this time, I suppose – it's all one to her now. And you've got your fortune out of that profitable business which had such a blessing on it. You've taken to being a nob, buying land, being a country bashaw. Still in the Dissenting line, eh? Still godly? Or taken to the Church as more genteel?'

This time Mr Raffles's slow wink and slight protrusion of his tongue was worse than a nightmare, because it held the certitude that it was not a nightmare, but a waking misery. Mr Bulstrode felt a shuddering nausea, and did not speak, but was considering diligently whether he should not leave Raffles to do as he would, and simply defy him as a slanderer. The man would soon show himself disreputable enough to make people disbelieve him. 'But not when he tells any ugly-looking truth about *you*,' said discerning consciousness. And again: it seemed no wrong to keep Raffles at a distance, but Mr Bulstrode shrank from the direct falsehood of denying true statements. It was one thing to look back on forgiven sins, nay, to explain questionable conformity to lax customs, and another to enter deliberately on the necessity of falsehood.

But since Bulstrode did not speak, Raffles ran on, by way of using time to the utmost.

'I've not had such fine luck as you, by Jove! Things went confoundedly with me in New York; those Yankees are cool hands, and a man of gentlemanly feelings has no chance with them. I married when I came back – a nice woman in the tobacco trade – very fond of me – but the trade was restricted, as we say. She had been settled there a good many years by a friend; but there was a son too much in the case. Josh and I never hit it off. However, I made the most of the position, and I've always taken my glass in good company. It's been all on the square with me; I'm as open as the day. You won't take it ill of me that I didn't look you up before; I've got a complaint that makes me a little dilatory. I thought you were trading and praying away in London still, and didn't find you there. But you see I was sent to you, Nick – perhaps for a blessing to both of us.'

Mr Raffles ended with a jocose snuffle: no man felt his intellect more superior to religious cant. And if the cunning which calculates on the meanest feelings in men could be called intellect, he had his share, for under the blurting rallying tone with which he spoke to Bulstrode, there was an evident selection of statements, as if they had been so many moves at chess. Mean-while Bulstrode had determined on his move, and he said, with gathered resolution—

'You will do well to reflect, Mr Raffles, that it is possible for a man to overreach himself in the effort to secure undue advantage. Although I am not in any way bound to you, I am willing to supply you with a regular annuity – in quarterly payments – so long as you fulfil a promise to remain at a distance from this neighbourhood. It is in your power to choose. If you insist on remaining here, even for a short time, you will get nothing from me. I shall decline to know you.'

'Ha ha!' said Raffles, with an affected explosion, 'that reminds me of a droll dog of a thief who declined to know the constable.'

'Your allusions are lost on me, sir,' said Bulstrode, with white heat; 'the law has no hold on me either through your agency or any other.'

'You can't understand a joke, my good fellow. I only meant that I should never decline to know you. But let us be serious. Your quarterly payment won't quite suit me. I like my freedom.'

Here Raffles rose and stalked once or twice up and down the room, swinging his leg, and assuming an air of masterly meditation. At last he stopped opposite Bulstrode, and said, 'I'll tell you what! Give us a couple of hundreds – come, that's modest – and I'll go away – honour bright! – pick up my portmanteau and go away. But I shall not give up my liberty for a dirty annuity. I shall come and go where I like. Perhaps it may suit me to stay away, and correspond with a friend; perhaps not. Have you the money with you?'

'No, I have one hundred,' said Bulstrode, feeling the immediate riddance too great a relief to be rejected on the ground of future uncertainties. 'I will forward you the other if you will mention an address.'

'No, I'll wait here till you bring it,' said Raffles. 'I'll take a stroll, and have a snack, and you'll be back by that time.'

Mr Bulstrode's sickly body, shattered by the agitations he had gone through since the last evening, made him feel abjectly in the power of this loud invulnerable man. At that moment he snatched at a temporary repose to be won on any terms. He was rising to do what Raffles suggested, when the latter said, lifting up his finger as if with a sudden recollection –

'I did have another look after Sarah again, though I didn't tell you; I'd a tender conscience about that pretty young woman. I didn't find her, but I found out her husband's name, and I made a note of it. But hang it, I lost my pocket-book. However, if I heard it, I should know it again. I've got my faculties as if I was in my prime, but names wear out, by Jove! Sometimes I'm no better than a confounded tax-paper before the names are filled in. However, if I hear of her and her family, you shall know, Nick. You'd like to do something for her, now she's your step-daughter.'

'Doubtless,' said Mr Bulstrode, with the usual steady look of his light-grey eyes; 'though that might reduce my power of assisting you.'

As he walked out of the room, Raffles winked slowly at his back, and then turned towards the window to watch the banker riding away –

virtually at his command. His lips first curled with a smile and then opened with a short triumphant laugh.

'But what the deuce *was* the name?' he presently said, half aloud, scratching his head, and wrinkling his brows horizontally. He had not really cared or thought about this point of forgetfulness until it occurred to him in his invention of annoyances for Bulstrode.

'It began with L; it was almost all l's, I fancy,' he went on, with a sense that he was getting hold of the slippery name. But the hold was too slight, and he soon got tired of this mental chase; for few men were more impatient of private occupation or more in need of making themselves continually heard than Mr Raffles. He preferred using his time in pleasant conversation with the bailiff and the housekeeper, from whom he gathered as much as he wanted to know about Mr Bulstrode's position in Middlemarch.

After all, however, there was a dull space of time which needed relieving with bread and cheese and ale, and when he was seated alone with these resources in the wainscoted parlour, he suddenly slapped his knee, and exclaimed, 'Ladislaw!' That action of memory which he had tried to set going, and had abandoned in despair, had suddenly completed itself without conscious effort – a common experience, agreeable as a completed sneeze, even if the name remembered is of no value. Raffles immediately took out his pocket-book and wrote down the name, not because he expected to use it, but merely for the sake of not being at a loss if he ever did happen to want it. He was not going to tell Bulstrode: there was no actual good in telling, and to a mind like that of Mr Raffles there is always probable good in a secret.

He was satisfied with his present success, and by three o'clock that day he had taken up his portmanteau at the turnpike and mounted the coach, relieving Mr Bulstrode's eyes of an ugly black spot on the landscape at Stone Court, but not relieving him of the dread that the black spot might reappear and become inseparable even from the vision of his hearth.

BOOK SIX

THE WIDOW AND
THE WIFE

ᴏᒓ FIFTY-FOUR ᕤ

Negli occhi porta la mia donna Amore;
Per che si fa gentil ciò ch'ella mira:
Ov' ella passa, ogni uom ver lei si gira,
E cui saluta fa tremar lo core.
Sicchè, bassando il viso, tutto smore,
E d' ogni suo difetto allor sospira:
Fuggon dinanzi a lei Superbia ed Ira:
Aiutatemi, donne, a farle onore.
Ogni dolcezza, ogni pensiero umile
Nasce nel core a chi parlar la sente;
Ond' è beato chi prima la vide.
Quel ch'ella par quand' un poco sorride,
Non si può dicer, nè tener a mente,
Si è nuovo miracolo gentile.

DANTE: *La Vita Nuova*

BY THAT DELIGHTFUL MORNING WHEN the hayricks at Stone Court were scenting the air quite impartially, as if Mr Raffles had been a guest worthy of finest incense, Dorothea had again taken up her abode at Lowick Manor. After three months Freshitt had become rather oppressive: to sit like a model for St Catherine looking rapturously at Celia's baby would not do for many hours in the day, and to remain in that momentous babe's presence with persistent disregard was a course that could not have been tolerated in a childless sister. Dorothea would have been capable of carrying baby joyfully for a mile if there had been need, and of loving it the more tenderly for that labour; but to an aunt who does not recognize her infant nephew as Bouddha, and has nothing to do for him but to admire, his behaviour is apt to appear monotonous, and the interest of watching him exhaustible.

This possibility was quite hidden from Celia, who felt that Dorothea's childless widowhood fell in quite prettily with the birth of little Arthur (baby was named after Mr Brooke).

'Dodo is just the creature not to mind about having anything of her own – children or anything!' said Celia to her husband. 'And if she had had a baby, it never could have been such a dear as Arthur. Could it, James?'

'Not if it had been like Casaubon,' said Sir James, conscious of some indirectness in his answer, and of holding a strictly private opinion as to the perfections of his first-born.

'No! just imagine? Really it was a mercy,' said Celia; 'and I think it is very nice for Dodo to be a widow. She can be just as fond of our baby as if it were her own, and she can have as many notions of her own as she likes.'

'It is a pity she was not a queen,' said the devout Sir James.

'But what should we have been then? We must have been something else,' said Celia, objecting to so laborious a flight of imagination. 'I like her better as she is.'

Hence, when she found that Dorothea was making arrangements for her final departure to Lowick, Celia raised her eyebrows with disappointment, and in her quiet unemphatic way shot a needle-arrow of sarcasm.

'What will you do at Lowick, Dodo? You say yourself there is nothing to be done there: everybody is so clean and well off, it makes you quite melancholy. And here you have been so happy going all about Tipton with Mr Garth into the worst backyards. And now uncle is abroad, you and Mr Garth can have it all your own way; and I am sure James does everything you tell him.'

'I shall often come here, and I shall see how baby grows all the better,' said Dorothea.

'But you will never see him washed,' said Celia: 'and that is quite the best part of the day.' She was almost pouting: it did seem to her very hard in Dodo to go away from the baby when she might stay.

'Dear Kitty, I will come and stay all night on purpose,' said Dorothea: 'but I want to be alone now, and in my own home. I wish to know the Farebrothers better, and to talk to Mr Farebrother about what there is to be done in Middlemarch.'

Dorothea's native strength of will was no longer all converted into resolute submission. She had a great yearning to be at Lowick, and was simply determined to go, not feeling bound to tell all her reasons. But every one around her disapproved. Sir James was much pained, and offered that they should all migrate to Cheltenham for a few months with the sacred ark, otherwise called a cradle: at that period a man could hardly know what to propose if Cheltenham were rejected.

The Dowager Lady Chettam, just returned from a visit to her daughter in town, wished, at least, that Mrs Vigo should be written to, and invited to accept the office of companion to Mrs Casaubon: it was not credible that Dorothea as a young widow would think of living alone in the house at Lowick. Mrs Vigo had been reader and secretary to royal personages, and in point of knowledge and sentiments even Dorothea could have nothing to object to her.

Mrs Cadwallader said, privately, 'You will certainly go mad in that house alone, my dear. You will see visions. We have all got to exert ourselves a little to keep sane, and call things by the same names as other people call them by. To be sure, for younger sons and women who have no money, it is a sort of provision to go mad: they are taken care of then. But you must not run into that. I daresay you are a little bored here with our good dowager; but think what a bore you might become yourself to your fellow-creatures if you were always playing tragedy queen and taking things sublimely. Sitting alone in that library at Lowick you may fancy yourself ruling the weather; you must get a few people round you who wouldn't believe you if you told them. That is a good lowering medicine.'

'I never called everything by the same name that all the people about me did,' said Dorothea, stoutly.

'But I suppose you have found out your mistake, my dear,' said Mrs Cadwallader, 'and that is a proof of sanity.'

Dorothea was aware of the sting, but it did not hurt her. 'No,' she said, 'I still think that the greater part of the world is mistaken about many things. Surely one may be sane and yet think so, since the greater part of the world has often had to come round from its opinion.'

Mrs Cadwallader said no more on that point to Dorothea, but to her husband she remarked, 'It will be well for her to marry again as soon as it is proper, if one could get her among the right people. Of course the Chettams would not wish it. But I see clearly a husband is the best thing to keep her in order. If we were not so poor I would invite Lord Triton. He will be marquis some day, and there is no denying that she would make a good marchioness: she looks handsomer than ever in her mourning.'

'My dear Elinor, do let the poor woman alone. Such contrivances are of no use,' said the easy Rector.

'No use? How are matches made, except by bringing men and women together? And it is a shame that her uncle should have run away and shut up the Grange just now. There ought to be plenty of eligible matches invited to Freshitt and the Grange. Lord Triton is precisely the man: full of plans for making the people happy in a soft-headed sort of way. That would just suit Mrs Casaubon.'

'Let Mrs Casaubon choose for herself, Elinor.'

'That is the nonsense you wise men talk! How can she choose if she has no variety to choose from? A woman's choice usually means taking the only man she can get. Mark my words, Humphrey. If her friends don't exert themselves, there will be a worse business than the Casaubon business yet.'

'For heaven's sake don't touch on that topic, Elinor! It is a very sore point with Sir James. He would be deeply offended if you entered on it to him unnecessarily.'

'I have never entered on it,' said Mrs Cadwallader, opening her hands. 'Celia told me all about the will at the beginning, without any asking of mine.'

'Yes, yes; but they want the thing hushed up, and I understand that the young fellow is going out of the neighbourhood.'

Mrs Cadwallader said nothing, but gave her husband three significant nods, with a very sarcastic expression in her dark eyes.

Dorothea quietly persisted in spite of remonstrance and persuasion. So by the end of June the shutters were all opened at Lowick Manor, and the morning gazed calmly into the library, shining on the rows of note-books as it shines on the weary waste planted with huge stones, the mute memorial of a forgotten faith; and the evening laden with roses entered silently into the blue-green boudoir where Dorothea chose oftenest to sit. At first she walked into every room, questioning the eighteen months of her married life, and carrying on her thoughts as if they were a speech to be heard by her husband. Then, she lingered in the library and could not be at rest till she had carefully ranged all the note-books as she imagined that he would wish to see them, in orderly sequence. The pity which had been the restraining compelling motive in her life with him still clung about his image, even while she remonstrated with him in indignant thought and told him that he was unjust. One little act of hers may perhaps be smiled at as superstitious. The 'Synoptical Tabulation for the use of Mrs Casaubon', she carefully enclosed and sealed, writing within the envelope,

I could not use it. Do you not see now that I could not submit my soul to yours, by working hopelessly at what I have no belief in? – Dorothea.

Then she deposited the paper in her own desk.

That silent colloquy was perhaps only the more earnest because underneath and through it all there was always the deep longing which had really determined her to come to Lowick. The longing was to see Will Ladislaw. She did not know any good that could come of their meeting: she was helpless; her hands had been tied from making up to him for any unfairness in his lot. But her soul thirsted to see him. How could it be otherwise? If a princess in the days of enchantment had seen a four-footed creature from among those which live in herds come to her once and again with a human gaze which rested upon her with choice and beseeching, what would she think of in her journeying, what would she look for when the herds passed her? Surely for the gaze which had found her, and which she would know again. Life would be no better than candle-light tinsel and daylight rubbish if our spirits were not touched by what has been, to issues of longing and constancy. It was true that Dorothea wanted to know the Farebrothers better, and especially to talk to the new rector, but also true that remembering what Lydgate had told her about Will Ladislaw and little Miss Noble, she counted on Will's coming to Lowick to see the Farebrother family. The very first Sunday, *before* she entered the church, she saw him as she had seen him the last time she was there, alone in the clergyman's pew; but *when* she entered his figure was gone.

In the week-days when she went to see the ladies at the Rectory, she listened in vain for some word that they might let fall about Will; but it seemed to her that Mrs Farebrother talked of every one else in the neighbourhood and out of it.

'Probably some of Mr Farebrother's Middlemarch hearers may follow him to Lowick sometimes. Do you not think so?' said Dorothea, rather despising herself for having a secret motive in asking the question.

'If they are wise they will, Mrs Casaubon,' said the old lady. 'I see that you set a right value on my son's preaching. His grandfather on my side was an excellent clergyman, but his father was in the law: – most exemplary and honest nevertheless, which is a reason for our never being rich. They say Fortune is a woman and capricious. But sometimes she is a good woman and gives to those who merit, which has been the case with you, Mrs Casaubon, who have given a living to my son.'

Mrs Farebrother recurred to her knitting with a dignified satisfaction in her neat little effort at oratory, but this was not what Dorothea wanted to hear. Poor thing! she did not even know whether Will Ladislaw was still at Middlemarch, and there was no one whom she dared to ask, unless it were Lydgate. But just now she could not see Lydgate without sending for him or going to seek him. Perhaps Will Ladislaw, having heard of that strange ban against him left by Mr Casaubon, had felt it better that he and she should not meet again, and perhaps she was wrong to wish for a meeting that others might find many good reasons against. Still 'I do wish it' came at the end of those wise reflections as naturally as a sob after holding the breath. And the meeting did happen, but in a formal way quite unexpected by her.

One morning, about eleven, Dorothea was seated in her boudoir with a map of the land attached to the manor and other papers before her, which were to help her in making an exact statement for herself of her income and affairs. She had not yet applied herself to her work, but was seated with her hands folded on her lap, looking out along the avenue of limes to the distant fields. Every leaf was at rest in the sunshine, the familiar scene was changeless, and seemed to represent the prospect of her life, full of motiveless ease – motiveless, if her own energy could not seek out reasons for ardent action. The widow's cap of those times made an oval frame for the face, and had a crown standing up; the dress was an experiment in the utmost laying on of crape; but this heavy solemnity of clothing made her face look all the younger, with its recovered bloom, and the sweet, inquiring candour of her eyes.

Her reverie was broken by Tantripp, who came to say that Mr Ladislaw was below, and begged permission to see Madam if it were not too early.

'I will see him,' said Dorothea, rising immediately. 'Let him be shown into the drawing-room.'

The drawing-room was the most neutral room in the house to her – the one least associated with the trials of her married life: the damask matched the wood-work, which was all white and gold; there were two tall mirrors and tables with nothing on them – in brief, it was a room where you had no reason for sitting in one place rather than in another. It was below the boudoir, and had also a bow-window looking out on the avenue. But when Pratt showed Will Ladislaw into it the window was open; and a winged visitor, buzzing in and out now and then without minding the furniture, made the room look less formal and uninhabited.

'Glad to see you here again, sir,' said Pratt, lingering to adjust a blind.

'I am only come to say good-bye, Pratt,' said Will, who wished even the butler to know that he was too proud to hang about Mrs Casaubon now she was a rich widow.

'Very sorry to hear it, sir,' said Pratt, retiring. Of course, as a servant who was to be told nothing, he knew the fact of which Ladislaw was still ignorant, and had drawn his inferences; indeed, had not differed from his betrothed Tantripp when she said, 'Your master was as jealous as a fiend – and no reason. Madam would look higher than Mr Ladislaw, else I don't know her. Mrs Cadwallader's maid says there's a lord coming who is to marry her when the mourning's over.'

There were not many moments for Will to walk about with his hat in his hand before Dorothea entered. The meeting was very different from that first meeting in Rome when Will had been embarrassed and Dorothea calm. This time he felt miserable but determined, while she was in a state of agitation which could not be hidden. Just outside the door she had felt that this longed-for meeting was after all too difficult, and when she saw Will advancing towards her, the deep blush which was rare in her came with painful suddenness. Neither of them knew how it was, but neither of them spoke. She gave her hand for a moment, and then they went to sit down near the window, she on one settee and he on another opposite. Will was peculiarly uneasy: it seemed to him not like Dorothea that the mere fact of her being a widow should cause such a change in her manner of receiving him; and he knew of no other condition which could have affected their previous relation to each other – except that, as his imagination at once told him, her friends might have been poisoning her mind with their suspicions of him.

'I hope I have not presumed too much in calling,' said Will; 'I could not bear to leave the neighbourhood and begin a new life without seeing you to say good-bye.'

'Presumed? Surely not. I should have thought it unkind if you had not wished to see me,' said Dorothea, her habit of speaking with perfect genuineness asserting itself through all her uncertainty and agitation. 'Are you going away immediately?'

'Very soon, I think. I intend to go to town and eat my dinners as a barrister, since, they say, that is the preparation for all public business. There will be a great deal of political work to be done by-and-by, and I mean to try and do some of it. Other men have managed to win an honourable position for themselves without family or money.'

'And that will make it all the more honourable,' said Dorothea, ardently. 'Besides, you have so many talents. I have heard from my uncle how well you speak in public, so that every one is sorry when you leave off, and how clearly you can explain things. And you care that justice should be done to every one. I am so glad. When we were in Rome, I thought you only cared for poetry and art, and the things that adorn life for us who are well off. But now I know you think about the rest of the world.'

While she was speaking Dorothea had lost her personal embarrassment and had become like her former self. She looked at Will with a direct glance, full of delighted confidence.

'You approve of my going away for years, then, and never coming here again till I have made myself of some mark in the world?' said Will, trying hard to reconcile the utmost pride with the utmost effort to get an expression of strong feeling from Dorothea.

She was not aware how long it was before she answered. She had turned her head and was looking out of the window on the rose-bushes, which seemed to have in them the summers of all the years when Will would be away. This was not judicious behaviour. But Dorothea never thought of studying her manners: she thought only of bowing to a sad necessity which divided her from Will. Those first words of his about his intentions had seemed to make everything clear to her: he knew, she supposed, all about Mr Casaubon's final conduct in relation to him, and it had come to him with the same sort of shock as to herself. He had never felt more than friendship for her – had never had anything in his mind to justify what she felt to be her husband's outrage on the feelings of both: and that friendship he still felt. Something which may be called an inward silent sob had gone on in Dorothea before she said with a pure voice, just trembling in the last words as if only from its liquid flexibility –

'Yes, it must be right for you to do as you say. I shall be very happy when I hear that you have made your value felt. But you must have patience. It will perhaps be a long while.'

Will never quite knew how it was that he saved himself from falling down at her feet, when the 'long while' came forth with its gentle tremor. He used to say that the horrible hue and surface of her crape dress was most likely the sufficient controlling force. He sat still, however, and only said –

'I shall never hear from you. And you will forget all about me.'

'No,' said Dorothea, 'I shall never forget you. I have never forgotten any one whom I once knew. My life has never been crowded, and seems not likely to be so. And I have a great deal of space for memory at Lowick, haven't I?' She smiled.

'Good God!' Will burst out passionately, rising with his hat still in his hand, and walking to a marble table, where he suddenly turned and leaned his back against it. The blood had mounted to his face and neck, and he looked almost angry. It had seemed to him as if they were like two creatures slowly turning to marble in each other's presence, while their hearts were conscious and their eyes were yearning. But there was no help for it. It should never be true of him that in this meeting to which he had come with bitter resolution he had ended by a confession which might be interpreted into asking for her fortune. Moreover, it was actually true that he was fearful of the effect which such confessions might have on Dorothea herself.

She looked at him from that distance in some trouble, imagining that there might have been an offence in her words. But all the while there was a current of thought in her about his probable want of money, and the impossibility of her helping him. If her uncle had been at home, something might have been done through him! It was this preoccupation with the hardship of Will's wanting money, while she had what ought to have been his share, which led her to say, seeing that he remained silent and looked away from her –

'I wonder whether you would like to have that miniature which hangs up-stairs – I mean that beautiful miniature of your grandmother. I think it is not right for me to keep it, if you would wish to have it. It is wonderfully like you.'

'You are very good,' said Will, irritably. 'No; I don't mind about it. It is not very consoling to have one's own likeness. It would be more consoling if others wanted to have it.'

'I thought you would like to cherish her memory – I thought – ' Dorothea broke off in an instant, her imagination suddenly warning her away from Aunt Julia's history – 'you would surely like to have the miniature as a family memorial.'

'Why should I have that, when I have nothing else! A man with only a portmanteau for his stowage must keep his memorials in his head.'

Will spoke at random: he was merely venting his petulance; it was a little too exasperating to have his grandmother's portrait offered him at that moment. But to Dorothea's feeling his words had a peculiar sting. She rose and said with a touch of indignation as well as hauteur –

'You are much the happier of us two, Mr Ladislaw, to have nothing.'

Will was startled. Whatever the words might be, the tone seemed like a dismissal; and quitting his leaning posture, he walked a little way towards her. Their eyes met, but with a strange questioning gravity. Something was keeping their minds aloof, and each was left to conjecture what was in the other. Will had really never thought of himself as having a claim of inheritance on the property which was held by Dorothea, and would have required a narrative to make him understand her present feeling.

'I never felt it a misfortune to have nothing till now,' he said. 'But poverty may be as bad as leprosy, if it divides us from what we most care for.'

The words cut Dorothea to the heart, and made her relent. She answered in a tone of sad fellowship.

'Sorrow comes in so many ways. Two years ago I had no notion of that – I mean of the unexpected way in which trouble comes, and ties our hands, and makes us silent when we long to speak. I used to despise women a little for not shaping their lives more, and doing better things. I was very fond of doing as I liked, but I have almost given it up,' she ended, smiling playfully.

'I have not given up doing as I like, but I can very seldom do it,' said Will. He was standing two yards from her with his mind full of contradictory desires and resolves – desiring some unmistakable proof that she loved him, and yet dreading the position into which such a proof might bring him. 'The thing one most longs for may be surrounded with conditions that would be intolerable.'

At this moment Pratt entered and said, 'Sir James Chettam is in the library, madam.'

Ask Sir James to come in here,' said Dorothea, immediately. It was as if the same electric shock had passed through her and Will. Each of them felt proudly resistant, and neither looked at the other, while they awaited Sir James's entrance.

After shaking hands with Dorothea, he bowed as slightly as possible to Ladislaw, who repaid the slightness exactly, and then going towards Dorothea, said –

'I must say good-bye, Mrs Casaubon; and probably for a long while.'

Dorothea put out her hand and said her good-bye cordially. The sense that Sir James was depreciating Will, and behaving rudely to him, roused her resolution and dignity: there was no touch of confusion in her manner. And when Will had left the room, she looked with such calm self-possession at Sir James, saying, 'How is Celia?' that he was obliged to behave as if nothing had annoyed him. And what would be the use of behaving otherwise! Indeed, Sir James shrank with so much dislike from the association even in thought of Dorothea with Ladislaw as her possible lover, that he would himself have wished to avoid an outward show of displeasure which would have recognized the disagreeable possibility. If any one had asked him why he shrank in that way, I am not sure that he would at first have said anything fuller or more precise than '*that* Ladislaw!' – though on reflection he might have urged that Mr Casaubon's codicil, barring Dorothea's marriage with Will, except under a penalty, was enough to cast unfitness over any relation at all between them. His aversion was all the stronger because he felt himself unable to interfere.

But Sir James was a power in a way unguessed by himself. Entering at that moment, he was an incorporation of the strongest reasons through which Will's pride became a repellent force, keeping him asunder from Dorothea.

❦ FIFTY-FIVE ❧

Hath she her faults? I would you had them too.
They are the fruity must of soundest wine
Or say, they are regenerating fire
Such as hath turned the dense black element
Into a crystal pathway for the sun.

IF YOUTH IS THE SEASON OF HOPE, it is often so only in the sense that our elders are hopeful about us; for no age is so apt as youth to think its emotions, partings, and resolves are the last of their kind. Each crisis seems final, simply because it is new. We are told that the oldest inhabitants in Peru do not cease to be agitated by the earthquakes, but they probably see beyond each shock, and reflect that there are plenty more to come.

To Dorothea, still in that time of youth when the eyes with their long full lashes look out after their rain of tears unsoiled and unwearied as a freshly-opened passion-flower, that morning's parting with Will Ladislaw seemed to be the close of their personal relations. He was going away into the distance of unknown years, and if ever he came back he would be another man. The actual state of his mind – his proud resolve to give the lie beforehand to any suspicion that he would play the needy adventurer seeking a rich woman – lay quite out of her imagination, and she had interpreted all his behaviour easily enough by her supposition that Mr Casaubon's codicil seemed to him, as it did to her, a gross and cruel interdict on any active friendship between them. Their young delight in speaking to each other, and saying what no one else would care to hear, was for ever ended, and become a treasure of the past. For this very reason she dwelt on it without inward check. That unique happiness too was dead, and in its shadowed silent chamber she might vent the passionate grief which she herself wondered at. For the first time she took down the miniature from the wall and kept it before her, liking to blend the woman who had been too hardly judged with the grandson whom her own heart and judgment defended. Can any one who has rejoiced in woman's tenderness think it a reproach to her that she took the little oval picture in her palm and made a bed for it there, and leaned her cheek upon it, as if that would soothe the creature who had suffered unjust condemnation? She did not know then that it was Love who had come to her briefly as in a dream before awaking, with the hues of morning on his wings – that it

424

was Love to whom she was sobbing her farewell as his image was banished by the blameless rigour of irresistible day. She only felt that there was something irrevocably amiss and lost in her lot, and her thoughts about the future were the more readily shapen into resolve. Ardent souls, ready to construct their coming lives, are apt to commit themselves to the fulfilment of their own visions.

One day that she went to Freshitt to fulfil her promise of staying all night and seeing baby washed, Mrs Cadwallader came to dine, the Rector being gone on a fishing excursion. It was a warm evening, and even in the delightful drawing-room, where the fine old turf sloped from the open window towards a lilied pool and well-planted mounds, the heat was enough to make Celia in her white muslin and light curls reflect with pity on what Dodo must feel in her black dress and close cap. But this was not until some episodes with baby were over, and had left her mind at leisure. She had seated herself and taken up a fan for some time before she said, in her quiet guttural –

'Dear Dodo, do throw off that cap. I am sure your dress must make you feel ill.'

'I am so used to the cap – it has become a sort of shell,' said Dorothea, smiling. 'I feel rather bare and exposed when it is off.'

'I *must* see you without it; it makes us all warm,' said Celia, throwing down her fan, and going to Dorothea. It was a pretty picture to see this little lady in white muslin unfastening the widow's cap from her more majestic sister, and tossing it on to a chair. Just as the coils and braids of dark-brown hair had been set free, Sir James entered the room. He looked at the released head, and said, 'Ah!' in a tone of satisfaction.

'It was I who did it, James,' said Celia. 'Dodo need not make such a slavery of her mourning; she need not wear that cap any more among her friends.'

'My dear Celia,' said Lady Chettam, 'a widow must wear her mourning at least a year.'

'Not if she marries again before the end of it,' said Mrs Cadwallader, who had some pleasure in startling her good friend the Dowager. Sir James was annoyed, and leaned forward to play with Celia's Maltese dog.

'That is very rare, I hope,' said Lady Chettam, in a tone intended to guard against such events. 'No friend of ours ever committed herself in that way except Mrs Beevor, and it was very painful to Lord Grinsell when she did so. Her first husband was objectionable, which made it the greater wonder. And severely she was punished for it. They said Captain Beevor dragged her about by the hair, and held up loaded pistols at her.'

'Oh, if she took the wrong man!' said Mrs Cadwallader, who was in a decidedly wicked mood. 'Marriage is always bad then, first or second. Priority is a poor recommendation in a husband if he has got no other. I would rather have a good second husband than an indifferent first.'

'My dear, your clever tongue runs away with you,' said Lady Chettam.

'I am sure you would be the last woman to marry again prematurely, if our dear Rector were taken away.'

'Oh, I make no vows; it might be a necessary economy. It is lawful to marry again, I suppose; else we might as well be Hindoos instead of Christians. Of course if a woman accepts the wrong man, she must take the consequences, and one who does it twice over deserves her fate. But if she can marry blood, beauty, and bravery – the sooner the better.'

'I think the subject of our conversation is very ill-chosen,' said Sir James, with a look of disgust. 'Suppose we change it.'

'Not on my account, Sir James,' said Dorothea, determined not to lose the opportunity of freeing herself from certain oblique references to excellent matches. 'If you are speaking on my behalf, I can assure you that no question can be more indifferent and impersonal to me than second marriage. It is no more to me than if you talked of women going fox-hunting: whether it is admirable in them or not, I shall not follow them. Pray let Mrs Cadwallader amuse herself on that subject as much as on any other.'

'My dear Mrs Casaubon,' said Lady Chettam, in her stateliest way, 'you do not, I hope, think there was any allusion to you in my mentioning Mrs Beevor. It was only an instance that occurred to me. She was step-daughter to Lord Grinsell: he married Mrs Teveroy for his second wife. There could be no possible allusion to you.'

'Oh no,' said Celia. 'Nobody chose the subject; it all came out of Dodo's cap. Mrs Cadwallader only said what was quite true. A woman could not be married in a widow's cap, James.'

'Hush, my dear!' said Mrs Cadwallader. 'I will not offend again. I will not even refer to Dido or Zenobia. Only what are we to talk about? I, for my part, object to the discussion of Human Nature, because that is the nature of rectors' wives.'

Later in the evening, after Mrs Cadwallader was gone, Celia said privately to Dorothea, 'Really, Dodo, taking your cap off made you like yourself again in more ways than one. You spoke up just as you used to do, when anything was said to displease you. But I could hardly make out whether it was James that you thought wrong, or Mrs Cadwallader.'

'Neither,' said Dorothea. 'James spoke out of delicacy to me, but he was mistaken in supposing that I minded what Mrs Cadwallader said. I should only mind if there were a law obliging me to take any piece of blood and beauty that she or anybody else recommended.'

'But you know, Dodo, if you ever did marry, it would be all the better to have blood and beauty,' said Celia, reflecting that Mr Casaubon had not been richly endowed with those gifts, and that it would be well to caution Dorothea in time.

'Don't be anxious, Kitty; I have quite other thoughts about my life. I shall never marry again,' said Dorothea, touching her sister's chin, and looking at her with indulgent affection. Celia was nursing her baby, and Dorothea had come to say good-night to her.

'Really – quite?' said Celia. 'Not anybody at all – if he were very wonderful indeed?'

Dorothea shook her head slowly. 'Not anybody at all. I have delightful plans. I should like to take a great deal of land, and drain it, and make a little colony, where everybody should work, and all the work should be done well. I should know every one of the people and be their friend. I am going to have great consultations with Mr Garth: he can tell me almost everything I want to know.'

'Then you *will* be happy, if you have a plan, Dodo,' said Celia. 'Perhaps little Arthur will like plans when he grows up, and then he can help you.'

Sir James was informed that same night that Dorothea was really quite set against marrying anybody at all, and was going to take to 'all sorts of plans', just like what she used to have. Sir James made no remark. To his secret feeling, there was something repulsive in a woman's second marriage, and no match would prevent him from feeling it a sort of desecration for Dorothea. He was aware that the world would regard such a sentiment as preposterous, especially in relation to a woman of one-and-twenty; the practice of 'the world' being to treat of a young widow's second marriage as certain and probably near, and to smile with meaning if the widow acts accordingly. But if Dorothea did choose to espouse her solitude, he felt that the resolution would well become her.

❧ FIFTY-SIX ❧

How happy is he born and taught,
That serveth not another's will?
Whose armour is his honest thought,
And simple truth his only skill?
. . . .
This man is freed from servile bands
Of hope to rise, or fear to fall:
Lord of himself, though not of lands,
And having nothing, yet hath all.

SIR HENRY WOTTON

DOROTHEA'S CONFIDENCE IN CALEB Garth's knowledge, which had begun on her hearing that he approved of her cottages, had grown fast during her stay at Freshitt, Sir James having induced her to take rides over the two estates in company with himself and Caleb, who quite returned her admiration, and told his wife that Mrs Casaubon had a head for business most uncommon in a woman. It must be remembered that by 'business' Caleb never meant money transactions, but the skilful application of labour.

'Most uncommon!' repeated Caleb. 'She said a thing I often used to think myself when I was a lad: – "Mr Garth, I should like to feel, if I lived to be old, that I had improved a great piece of land and built a great many good cottages, because the work is of a healthy kind while it is being done, and after it is done, men are the better for it." Those were the very words: she sees into things in that way.'

'But womanly, I hope,' said Mrs Garth, half suspecting that Mrs Casaubon might not hold the true principle of subordination.

'Oh, you can't think!' said Caleb, shaking his head. 'You would like to hear her speak, Susan. She speaks in such plain words, and a voice like music. Bless me! it reminds me of bits in the *Messiah* – "and straightway there appeared a multitude of the heavenly host, praising God and saying"; it has a tone with it that satisfies your ear.'

Caleb was very fond of music, and when he could afford it went to hear an oratorio that came within his reach, returning from it with a profound reverence for this mighty structure of tones, which made him sit meditatively, looking on the floor and throwing much unutterable language into his outstretched hands.

With this good understanding between them, it was natural that Dorothea asked Mr Garth to undertake any business connected with the three farms and the numerous tenements attached to Lowick Manor; indeed, his expectation of getting work for two was being fast fulfilled. As he said, 'Business breeds.' And one form of business which was beginning to breed just then was the construction of railways. A projected line was to run through Lowick parish where the cattle had hitherto grazed in a peace unbroken by astonishment; and thus it happened that the infant struggles of the railway system entered into the affairs of Caleb Garth, and determined the course of this history with regard to two persons who were dear to him.

The submarine railway may have its difficulties; but the bed of the sea is not divided among various landed proprietors with claims for damages not only measurable but sentimental. In the hundred to which Middlemarch belonged railways were as exciting a topic as the Reform Bill or the imminent horrors of Cholera, and those who held the most decided views on the subject were women and landholders. Women both old and young regarded travelling by steam as presumptuous and dangerous, and argued against it by saying that nothing should induce them to get into a railway carriage; while proprietors, differing from each other in their arguments as much as Mr Solomon Featherstone differed from Lord Medlicote, were yet unanimous in the opinion that in selling land, whether to the Enemy of mankind or to a company obliged to purchase, these pernicious agencies must be made to pay a very high price to landowners for permission to injure mankind.

But the slower wits, such as Mr Solomon and Mrs Waule, who both occupied land of their own, took a long time to arrive at this conclusion, their minds halting at the vivid conception of what it would be to cut the Big Pasture in two, and turn it into three-cornered bits, which would be 'nohow'; while accommodation-bridges and high payments were remote and incredible.

'The cows will all cast their calves, Brother,' said Mrs Waule, in a tone of deep melancholy, 'if the railway comes across the Near Close; and I shouldn't wonder at the mare too, if she was in foal. It's a poor tale if a widow's property is to be spaded away, and the law say nothing to it. What's to hinder 'em from cutting right and left if they begin? It's well known, I can't fight.'

'The best way would be to say nothing, and set somebody on to send 'em away with a flea in their ear, when they came spying and measuring,' said Solomon. 'Folks did that about Brassing, by what I can understand. It's all a pretence, if the truth was known, about their being forced to take one way. Let 'em go cutting in another parish. And I don't believe in any pay to make amends for bringing a lot of ruffians to trample your crops. Where's a company's pocket?'

'Brother Peter, God forgive him, got money out of a company,' said Mrs

Waule. 'But that was for the manganese. That wasn't for railways to blow you to pieces right and left.'

'Well, there's this to be said, Jane,' Mr Solomon concluded, lowering his voice in a cautious manner – 'the more spokes we put in their wheel, the more they'll pay us to let 'em go on, if they must come whether or not.'

This reasoning of Mr Solomon's was perhaps less thorough than he imagined, his cunning bearing about the same relation to the course of railways as the cunning of a diplomatist bears to the general chill or catarrh of the solar system. But he set about acting on his views in a thoroughly diplomatic manner, by stimulating suspicion. His side of Lowick was the most remote from the village, and the houses of the labouring people were either lone cottages or were collected in a hamlet called Frick, where a water-mill and some stone-pits made a little centre of slow, heavy-shouldered industry.

In the absence of any precise idea as to what railways were, public opinion in Frick was against them; for the human mind in that grassy corner had not the proverbial tendency to admire the unknown, holding rather that it was likely to be against the poor man, and that suspicion was the only wise attitude with regard to it. Even the rumour of Reform had not yet excited any millennial expectations in Frick, there being no definite promise in it, as of gratuitous grains to fatten Hiram Ford's pig, or of a publican at the 'Weights and Scales' who would brew beer for nothing, or of an offer on the part of the three neighbouring farmers to raise wages during winter. And without distinct good of this kind in its promises, Reform seemed on a footing with the bragging of pedlars, which was a hint for distrust to every knowing person. The men of Frick were not ill-fed, and were less given to fanaticism than to a strong muscular suspicion; less inclined to believe that they were peculiarly cared for by heaven, than to regard heaven itself as rather disposed to take them in – a disposition observable in the weather.

Thus the mind of Frick was exactly of the sort for Mr Solomon Featherstone to work upon, he having more plenteous ideas of the same order, with a suspicion of heaven and earth which was better fed and more entirely at leisure. Solomon was overseer of the roads at that time, and on his slow-paced cob often took his rounds by Frick to look at the workmen getting the stones there, pausing with a mysterious deliberation, which might have misled you into supposing that he had some other reason for staying than the mere want of impulse to move. After looking for a long while at any work that was going on, he would raise his eyes a little and look at the horizon; finally he would shake his bridle, touch his horse with the whip, and get it to move slowly onward. The hour-hand of a clock was quick by comparison with Mr Solomon, who had an agreeable sense that he could afford to be slow. He was in the habit of pausing for a cautious, vaguely-designing chat with every hedger or ditcher on his way, and was especially willing to listen even to news which he had heard before, feeling himself at an advantage over all narrators in partially disbelieving them. One day, however, he got into a dialogue with Hiram Ford, a waggoner, in which he himself contributed information. He wished to know whether Hiram had seen fellows with staves and instruments spying about: they called themselves railroad people, but there was no telling what they were, or what they meant to do. The least they pretended was that they were going to cut Lowick Parish into sixes and sevens.

'Why, there'll be no stirrin' from one pla-ace to another,' said Hiram, thinking of his waggon and horses.

'Not a bit,' said Mr Solomon. 'And cutting up fine land such as this parish! Let 'em go into Tipton, say I. But there's no knowing what there is at the bottom of it. Traffick is what they put for'ard; but it's to do harm to the land and the poor man in the long-run.'

'Why, they're Lunnon chaps, I reckon,' said Hiram, who had a dim notion of London as a centre of hostility to the country.

'Ay, to be sure. And in some parts against Brassing, by what I've heard say, the folks fell on 'em when they were spying and broke their peep-holes as they carry, and drove 'em away, so as they knew better than come again.'

'It war good foon, I'd be bound,' said Hiram, whose fun was much restricted by circumstances.

'Well, I wouldn't meddle with 'em myself,' said Solomon. 'But some say this country's seen its best days, and the sign is, as it's being overrun with these fellows trampling right and left, and wanting to cut it up into railways; and all for the big traffic to swallow up the little, so as there shan't be a team left on the land, nor a whip to crack.'

'I'll crack *my* whip about their ear'n, afore they bring it to that, though,' said Hiram, while Mr Solomon, shaking his bridle, moved onward.

Nettle-seed needs no digging. The ruin of this country-side by railroads was discussed, not only at the 'Weights and Scales', but in the hay-field, where the muster of working hands gave opportunities for talk such as were rarely had through the rural year.

One morning, not long after that interview between Mr Farebrother and Mary Garth, in which she confessed to him her feeling for Fred Vincy, it happened that her father had some business which took him to Yoddrell's farm in the direction of Frick: it was to measure and value an outlying piece of land belonging to Lowick Manor, which Caleb expected to dispose of advantageously for Dorothea (it must be confessed that his bias was towards getting the best possible terms from railroad companies). He put up his gig at Yoddrell's, and in walking with his assistant and measuring-chain to the scene of his work, he encountered the party of the company's agents, who were adjusting their spirit-level. After a little chat he left them, observing that by-and-by they would reach him again where he was going to measure. It was one of those grey mornings after light rains, which become delicious about twelve o'clock, when the clouds part a little, and the scent of the earth is sweet along the lanes and by the hedgerows.

The scent would have been sweeter to Fred Vincy, who was coming along the lanes on horseback, if his mind had not been worried by unsuccessful efforts to imagine what he was to do, with his father on one side expecting him straightway to enter the Church, with Mary on the other threatening to forsake him if he did enter it, and with the working-day world showing no eager need whatever of a young gentleman without capital and generally unskilled. It was the harder to Fred's disposition because his father, satisfied that he was no longer rebellious, was in good humour with him, and had sent him on this pleasant ride to see after some greyhounds. Even when he had fixed on what he should do, there would be the task of telling his father. But it must be admitted that the fixing, which had to come first, was the more difficult task: – what secular avocation on earth was there for a young man (whose friends could not get him an 'appointment') which was at once gentlemanly, lucrative, and to be followed without special knowledge? Riding along the lanes by Frick in this mood, and slackening his pace while he reflected whether he should venture to go round by Lowick Parsonage to call on Mary, he could see over the hedges from one field to another. Suddenly a noise roused his attention, and on the far side of a field on his left hand he could see six or seven men in smock-frocks with hay-forks in their hands making an offensive approach towards the four railway agents who were facing them, while Caleb Garth and his assistant were hastening across the field to join the threatened group. Fred, delayed a few moments by having to find the gate, could not gallop up to the spot before the party in smock-frocks, whose work of turning the hay had not been too pressing after swallowing their mid-day beer, were driving the men in coats before them with their hay-forks; while Caleb Garth's assistant, a lad of seventeen, who had snatched up the spirit-level at Caleb's order, had been knocked down and seemed to be lying helpless. The coated men had the advantage as runners, and Fred covered their retreat by getting in front of the smock-frocks and charging them suddenly enough to throw their chase into confusion. 'What do you confounded fools mean?' shouted Fred, pursuing the divided group in a zig-zag, and cutting right and left with his whip. 'I'll swear to every one of you before the magistrate. You've knocked the lad down and killed him, for what I know. You'll every one of you be hanged at the next assizes, if you don't mind,' said Fred, who afterwards laughed heartily as he remembered his own phrases.

The labourers had been driven through the gateway into their hay-field, and Fred had checked his horse, when Hiram Ford, observing himself at a safe challenging distance, turned back and shouted a defiance which he did not know to be Homeric.

'Yo're a coward, yo are. Yo git off your horse, young measter, and I'll have a round wi' ye, I wull. Yo daredn't come on wi'out your hoss an' whip. I'd soon knock the breath out on ye, I would.'

'Wait a minute, and I'll come back presently, and have a round with you all in turn, if you like,' said Fred, who felt confidence in his power of boxing with his dearly-beloved brethren. But just now he wanted to hasten back to Caleb and the prostrate youth.

The lad's ankle was strained, and he was in much pain from it, but he was no further hurt, and Fred placed him on the horse that he might ride to Yoddrell's and be taken care of there.

'Let them put the horse in the stable, and tell the surveyors they can come back for their traps,' said Fred. 'The ground is clear now.'

'No, no,' said Caleb, 'here's a breakage. They'll have to give up for to-day, and it will be as well. Here, take the things before you on the horse, Tom. They'll see you coming, and they'll turn back.'

'I'm glad I happened to be here at the right moment, Mr Garth,' said Fred, as Tom rode away. 'No knowing what might have happened if the cavalry had not come up in time.'

'Ay, ay, it was lucky,' said Caleb, speaking rather absently, and looking towards the spot where he had been at work at the moment of interruption. 'But – deuce take it – this is what comes of men being fools – I'm hindered of my day's work. I can't get along without somebody to help me with the measuring chain. However!' He was beginning to move towards the spot with a look of vexation, as if he had forgotten Fred's presence, but suddenly he turned round and said quickly, 'What have you got to do to-day, young fellow?'

'Nothing, Mr Garth. I'll help you with pleasure – can I?' said Fred, with a sense that he should be courting Mary when he was helping her father.

'Well, you mustn't mind stooping and getting hot.'

'I don't mind anything. Only I want to go first and have a round with that hulky fellow who turned to challenge me. It would be a good lesson for him. I shall not be five minutes.'

'Nonsense!' said Caleb, with his most peremptory intonation. 'I shall go and speak to the men myself. It's all ignorance. Somebody has been telling them lies. The poor fools don't know any better.'

'I shall go with you, then,' said Fred.

'No, no; stay where you are. I don't want your young blood. I can take care of myself.'

Caleb was a powerful man and knew little of any fear except the fear of hurting others and the fear of having to speechify. But he felt it his duty at this moment to try and give a little harangue. There was a striking mixture in him – which came from his having always been a hard-working man himself – of rigorous notions about workmen and practical indulgence towards them. To do a good day's work and to do it well, he held to be part of their welfare, as it was the chief part of his own happiness; but he had a strong sense of fellowship with them. When he advanced towards the labourers they had not gone to work again, but were standing in that form of rural grouping which consists in each turning a shoulder towards the other, at a distance of two or three yards. They looked rather sulkily at Caleb, who walked quickly with one hand in his pocket and the other thrust between the buttons of his waistcoat, and had his everyday mild air when he paused among them.

'Why, my lads, how's this?' he began, taking as usual to brief phrases, which seemed pregnant to himself, because he had many thoughts lying under them, like the abundant roots of a plant that just manages to peep above the water. 'How came you to make such a mistake as this! Somebody has been telling you lies. You thought those men up there wanted to do mischief.'

'Aw!' was the answer, dropped at intervals by each according to his degree of unreadiness.

'Nonsense! No such thing! They're looking out to see which way the railroad is to take. Now, my lads, you can't hinder the railroad: it will be made whether you like it or not. And if you go fighting against it, you'll get yourselves into trouble. The law gives those men leave to come here on the land. The owner has nothing to say against it, and if you meddle with them you'll have to do with the constable and Justice Blakesley, and with the handcuffs and Middlemarch jail. And you might be in for it now, if anybody informed against you.'

Caleb paused here, and perhaps the greatest orator could not have chosen either his pause or his images better for the occasion.

'But come, you didn't mean any harm. Somebody told you the railroad was a bad thing. That was a lie. It may do a bit of harm here and there, to this and to that; and so does the sun in heaven. But the railway's a good thing.'

'Aw! good for the big folks to make money out on,' said old Timothy Cooper, who had stayed behind turning his hay while the others had been gone on their spree; – 'I'n seen lots o' things turn up sin' I war a young un – the war an' the peace, and the canells, an' the oald King George, an' the Regen', an' the new King George, an' the new un as has got a new ne-ame – an' it's been all aloike to the poor mon. What's the canells been t' him? They'n brought him neyther me-at nor be-acon, nor wage to lay by, if he didn't save it wi' clemmin' his own inside. Times ha' got wusser for him sin' I war a young un. An' so it'll be wi' the railroads. They'll on'y leave the poor mon furder behind. But them are fools as meddle, and so I told the chaps here. This is the big folks's world, this is. But yo're for the big folks, Muster Garth, yo are.'

Timothy was a wiry old labourer, of a type lingering in those times – who had his savings in a stocking-foot, lived in a lone cottage, and was not to be wrought on by any oratory, having as little of the feudal spirit, and believing as little, as if he had not been totally unacquainted with the Age of Reason and the Rights of Man. Caleb was in a difficulty known to any person attempting in dark times and unassisted by miracle to reason with rustics who are in possession of an undeniable truth which they know through a hard process of feeling, and can let it fall like a giant's club on your neatly-carved argument for a social benefit which they do *not* feel. Caleb had no cant at command, even if he could have chosen to use it; and he had been accustomed to meet all such difficulties in no other way than by doing his 'business' faithfully. He answered –

'If you don't think well of me, Tim, never mind; that's neither here nor there now. Things may be bad for the poor man – bad they are; but I want the lads here not to do what will make things worse for themselves. The cattle may have a heavy load, but it won't help 'em to throw it over into the roadside pit, when it's partly their own fodder.'

'We war on'y for a bit o' foon,' said Hiram, who was beginning to see consequences. 'That war all we war arter.'

'Well, promise me not to meddle again, and I'll see that nobody informs against you.'

'I'n ne'er meddled, an' I'n no call to promise,' said Timothy.

'No, but the rest. Come, I'm as hard at work as any of you to-day, and I cąn't spare much time. Say you'll be quiet without the constable.'

'Aw, we wooant meddle – they may do as they loike for oos' – were the forms in which Caleb got his pledges; and then he hastened back to Fred, who had followed him, and watched him in the gateway.

They went to work, and Fred helped vigorously. His spirits had risen, and he heartily enjoyed a good slip in the moist earth under the hedgerow, which soiled his perfect summer trousers. Was it his successful onset which had elated him, or the satisfaction of helping Mary's father? Something more. The accidents of the morning had helped his frustrated imagination to shape an employment for himself which had several attractions. I am not sure that certain fibres in Mr Garth's mind had not resumed their old vibration towards the very end which now revealed itself to Fred. For the effective accident is but the touch of fire where there is oil and tow; and it always appeared to Fred that the railway brought the needed touch. But they went on in silence except when their business demanded speech. At last, when they had finished and were walking away, Mr Garth said –

'A young fellow needn't be a B.A. to do this sort of work, eh, Fred?'

'I wish I had taken to it before I had thought of being a B.A.,' said Fred. He paused a moment, and then added, more hesitatingly, 'Do you think I am too old to learn your business, Mr Garth?'

'My business is of many sorts, my boy,' said Mr Garth, smiling. 'A good deal of what I know can only come from experience: you can't learn it off as you learn things out of a book. But you are young enough to lay a foundation yet.' Caleb pronounced the last sentence emphatically, but paused in some uncertainty. He had been under the impression lately that Fred had made up his mind to enter the Church.

'You do think I could do some good at it, if I were to try?' said Fred, more eagerly.

'That depends,' said Caleb, turning his head on one side and lowering his voice, with the air of a man who felt himself to be saying something deeply religious. 'You must be sure of two things: you must love your work, and not be always looking over the edge of it, wanting your play to begin. And the other is, you must not be ashamed of your work, and think it would be more honourable to you to be doing something else. You must have a pride in your own work and in learning to do it well, and not be always saying, "There's this and there's that – if I had this or that to do, I might make something of it." No matter what a man is – I wouldn't give twopence for him' – here Caleb's mouth looked bitter, and he snapped his fingers – 'whether he was the prime minister or the rick-thatcher, if he didn't do well what he undertook to do.'

'I can never feel that I should do that in being a clergyman,' said Fred, meaning to take a step in argument.

'Then let it alone, my boy,' said Caleb, abruptly, 'else you'll never be easy. Or, if you *are* easy, you'll be a poor stick.'

'That is very nearly what Mary thinks about it,' said Fred, colouring. 'I think you must know what I feel for Mary, Mr Garth: I hope it does not displease you that I have always loved her better than any one else, and that I shall never love any one as I love her.'

The expression of Caleb's face was visibly softening while Fred spoke. But he swung his head with a solemn slowness, and said –

'That makes things more serious, Fred, if you want to take Mary's happiness into your keeping.'

'I know that, Mr Garth,' said Fred, eagerly, 'and I would do anything for *her*. She says she will never have me if I go into the Church; and I shall be the most miserable devil in the world if I lose all hope of Mary. Really, if I could get some other profession, business – anything that I am at all fit for, I would work hard, I would deserve your good opinion. I should like to have to do with outdoor things. I know a good deal about land and cattle already. I used to believe, you know – though you will think me rather foolish for it – that I should have land of my own. I am sure knowledge of that sort would come easily to me, especially if I could be under you in any way.'

'Softly, my boy,' said Caleb, having the image of 'Susan' before his eyes. 'What have you said to your father about all this?'

'Nothing, yet; but I must tell him. I am only waiting to know what I can do instead of entering the Church. I am very sorry to disappoint him, but a man ought to be allowed to judge for himself when he is four-and-twenty. How could I know when I was fifteen, what it would be right for me to do now? My education was a mistake.'

'But hearken to this, Fred,' said Caleb. 'Are you sure Mary is fond of you, or would ever have you?'

'I asked Mr Farebrother to talk to her, because she had forbidden me – I didn't know what else to do,' said Fred, apologetically. 'And he says that I have every reason to hope, if I can put myself in an honourable position – I mean, out of the Church. I daresay you think it unwarrantable in me, Mr Garth, to be troubling you and obtruding my own wishes about Mary, before I have done anything at all for myself. Of course I have not the least claim – indeed, I have already a debt to you which will never be discharged, even when I have been able to pay it in the shape of money.'

'Yes, my boy, you have a claim,' said Caleb, with much feeling in his voice. 'The young ones have always a claim on the old to help them forward. I was young myself once and had to do without much help; but help would have been welcome to me, if it had been only for the fellow-feeling's sake. But I must consider. Come to me to-morrow at the office, at nine o'clock. At the office, mind.'

Mr Garth would take no important step without consulting Susan, but it must be confessed that before he reached home he had taken his resolution. With regard to a large number of matters about which other men are decided or obstinate, he was the most easily manageable man in the world. He never knew what meat he would choose, and if Susan had said that they ought to live in a four-roomed cottage, in order to save, he would have said, 'Let us go', without inquiring into details. But where Caleb's feeling and judgment strongly pronounced, he was a ruler; and in spite of his mildness and timidity in reproving, every one about him knew that on the exceptional occasions when he chose, he was absolute. He never, indeed, chose to be absolute except on some one else's behalf. On ninety-nine points Mrs Garth decided, but on the hundredth she was often aware that she would have to perform the singularly difficult task of carrying out her own principle, and to make herself subordinate.

'It is come round as I thought, Susan,' said Caleb, when they were seated alone in the evening. He had already narrated the adventure which had brought about Fred's sharing in his work, but had kept back the further result. 'The children *are* fond of each other – I mean, Fred and Mary.'

Mrs Garth laid her work on her knee, and fixed her penetrating eyes anxiously on her husband.

'After we'd done our work, Fred poured it all out to me. He can't bear to be a clergyman, and Mary says she won't have him if he is one; and the lad would like to be under me and give his mind to business. And I've determined to take him and make a man of him.'

'Caleb!' said Mrs Garth, in a deep contralto, expressive of resigned astonishment.

'It's a fine thing to do,' said Mr Garth, settling himself firmly against the back of his chair, and grasping the elbows. 'I shall have trouble with him, but I think I shall carry it through. The lad loves Mary, and a true love for a good woman is a great thing, Susan. It shapes many a rough fellow.'

'Has Mary spoken to you on the subject?' said Mrs Garth, secretly a little hurt that she had to be informed on it herself.

'Not a word. I asked her about Fred once; I gave her a bit of a warning. But she assured me she would never marry an idle, self-indulgent man – nothing since. But it seems Fred set on Mr Farebrother to talk to her, because she had forbidden him to speak himself, and Mr Farebrother has found out that she is fond of Fred, but says he must not be a clergyman. Fred's heart is fixed on Mary, that I can see: it gives me a good opinion of the lad – and we always liked him, Susan.'

'It is a pity for Mary, I think,' said Mrs Garth.

'Why – a pity?'

'Because, Caleb, she might have had a man who is worth twenty Fred Vincys.'

'Ah?' said Caleb, with surprise.

'I firmly believe that Mr Farebrother is attached to her, and meant to make her an offer; but of course now that Fred has used him as an envoy, there is an end to that better prospect.' There was a severe precision in Mrs Garth's utterance. She was vexed and disappointed, but she was bent on abstaining from useless words.

Caleb was silent for a few moments under a conflict of feelings. He looked at the floor and moved his head and hands in accompaniment to some inward argumentation. At last he said –

'That would have made me very proud and happy, Susan, and I should have been glad for your sake. I've always felt that your belongings have never been on a level with you. But you took me, though I was a plain man.'

'I took the best and cleverest man I had ever known,' said Mrs Garth, convinced that *she* would never have loved any one who came short of that mark.

'Well, perhaps others thought you might have done better. But it would have been worse for me. And that is what touches me close about Fred. The lad is good at bottom, and clever enough to do, if he's put in the right way; and he loves and honours my daughter beyond anything, and she has given him a sort of promise according to what he turns out. I say, that young man's soul is in my hand; and I'll do the best I can for him, so help me God! It's my duty, Susan.'

Mrs Garth was not given to tears, but there was a large one rolling down her face before her husband had finished. It came from the pressure of various feelings, in which there was much affection and some vexation. She wiped it away quickly, saying –

'Few men besides you would think it a duty to add to their anxieties in that way, Caleb.'

'That signifies nothing – what other men would think. I've got a clear feeling inside me, and that I shall follow; and I hope your heart will go with me, Susan, in making everything as light as can be to Mary, poor child.'

Caleb, leaning back in his chair, looked with anxious appeal towards his wife. She rose and kissed him, saying, 'God bless you, Caleb! Our children have a good father.'

But she went out and had a hearty cry to make up for the suppression of her words. She felt sure that her husband's conduct would be misunderstood, and about Fred she was rational and unhopeful. Which would turn out to have the more foresight in it – her rationality or Caleb's ardent generosity?

When Fred went to the office the next morning, there was a test to be gone through which he was not prepared for.

'Now, Fred,' said Caleb, 'you will have some desk-work. I have always done a good deal of writing myself, but I can't do without help, and as I want you to understand the accounts and get the values into your head, I mean to do without another clerk. So you must buckle to. How are you at writing and arithmetic?'

Fred felt an awkward movement of the heart: he had not thought of desk-work; but he was in a resolute mood, and not going to shrink. 'I'm not afraid of arithmetic, Mr Garth: it always came easily to me. I think you know my writing.'

'Let us see,' said Caleb, taking up a pen, examining it carefully and handing it, well dipped, to Fred with a sheet of ruled paper. 'Copy me a line or two of that valuation, with the figures at the end.'

At that time the opinion existed that it was beneath a gentleman to write legibly, or with a hand in the least suitable to a clerk. Fred wrote the lines demanded in a hand as gentlemanly as that of any viscount or bishop of the day: the vowels were all alike and the consonants only distinguishable as turning up or down, the strokes had a blotted solidity and the letters disdained to keep the line – in short, it was a manuscript of that venerable kind easy to interpret when you know beforehand what the writer means.

As Caleb looked on, his visage showed a growing depression, but when Fred handed him the paper he gave something like a snarl, and rapped the paper passionately with the back of his hand. Bad work like this dispelled all Caleb's mildness.

'The deuce!' he exclaimed, snarlingly. 'To think that this is a country where a man's education may cost hundreds and hundreds, and it turns you out this!' Then in a more pathetic tone, pushing up his spectacles and looking at the unfortunate scribe, 'The Lord have mercy on us, Fred, I can't put up with this!'

'What can I do, Mr Garth?' said Fred, whose spirits had sunk very low, not only at the estimate of his handwriting, but at the vision of himself as liable to be ranked with office-clerks.

'Do? Why, you must learn to form your letters and keep the line. What's the use of writing at all if nobody can understand it?' asked Caleb, ener-getically, quite preoccupied with the bad quality of the work. 'Is there so little business in the world that you must be sending puzzles over the country? But that's the way people are brought up. I should lose no end of time with the letters some people send me, if Susan did not make them out for me. It's disgusting.' Here Caleb tossed the paper from him.

Any stranger peeping into the office at that moment might have wondered what was the drama between the indignant man of business, and the fine-looking young fellow whose blond complexion was getting rather patchy as he bit his lip with mortification. Fred was struggling with many thoughts. Mr Garth had been so kind and encouraging at the beginning of their interview, that gratitude and hopefulness had been at a high pitch, and the downfall was proportionate. He had not thought of desk-work – in fact, like the majority of young gentlemen, he wanted an occupation which should be free from disagreeables. I cannot tell what might have been the consequences if he had not distinctly promised himself that he would go to Lowick to see Mary and tell her that he was engaged to work under her father. He did not like to disappoint himself there.

'I am very sorry,' were all the words that he could muster. But Mr Garth was already relenting.

'We must make the best of it, Fred,' he began, with a return to his usual quiet tone. 'Every man can learn to write. I taught myself. Go at it with a will, and sit up at night if the day-time isn't enough. We'll be patient, my boy. Callum shall go on with the books for a bit, while you are learning. But now I must be off,' said Caleb, rising. 'You must let your father know our agreement. You'll save me Callum's salary, you know, when you can write; and I can afford to give you eighty pounds for the first year, and more after.'

When Fred made the necessary disclosure to his parents, the relative effect on the two was a surprise which entered very deeply into his memory. He went straight from Mr Garth's office to the warehouse, rightly feeling that the most respectful way in which he could behave to his father, was to make the painful communication as gravely and for-mally as possible. Moreover, the decision would be more certainly under-stood to be final, if the interview took place in his father's gravest hours, which were always those spent in his private room at the warehouse.

Fred entered on the subject directly, and declared briefly what he had done and was resolved to do, expressing at the end his regret that he should be the cause of disappointment to his father, and taking the blame on his own deficiencies. The regret was genuine, and inspired Fred with strong, simple words.

Mr Vincy listened in profound surprise without uttering even an excla-mation, a silence which in his impatient temperament was a sign of unusual emotion. He had not been in good spirits about trade that morning, and the slight bitterness in his lips grew intense as he listened. When Fred had ended, there was a pause of nearly a minute, during which Mr Vincy replaced a book in his desk and turned the key emphatically. Then he looked at his son steadily, and said –

'So you've made up your mind at last, sir?'

'Yes, father.'

'Very well; stick to it. I've no more to say. You've thrown away your education, and gone down a step in life, when I had given you the means of rising, that's all.'

'I am very sorry that we differ, father. I think I can be quite as much of a gentleman at the work I have undertaken, as if I had been a curate. But I am grateful to you for wishing to do the best for me.'

'Very well; I have no more to say. I wash my hands of you. I only hope, when you have a son of your own he will make a better return for the pains you spend on him.'

This was very cutting to Fred. His father was using that unfair advantage possessed by us all when we are in a pathetic situation and see our own past as if it were simply part of the pathos. In reality, Mr Vincy's wishes about his son had had a great deal of pride, inconsiderateness, and egoistic folly in them. But still the disappointed father held a strong lever; and Fred felt as if he were being banished with a malediction.

'I hope you will not object to my remaining at home, sir?' he said, after rising to go; 'I shall have a sufficient salary to pay for my board, as of course I should wish to do.'

'Board, be hanged!' said Mr Vincy, recovering himself in his disgust at the notion that Fred's keep would be missed at his table. 'Of course your mother will want you to stay. But I shall keep no horse for you, you understand; and you will pay your own tailor. You will do with a suit or two less, I fancy, when you have to pay for 'em.'

Fred lingered; there was still something to be said. At last it came.

'I hope you will shake hands with me, father, and forgive me the vexation I have caused you.'

Mr Vincy from his chair threw a quick glance upward at his son, who had advanced near to him, and then gave his hand, saying hurriedly, 'Yes, yes, let us say no more.'

Fred went through much more narrative and explanation with his mother, but she was inconsolable, having before her eyes what perhaps her husband had never thought of, the certainty that Fred would marry Mary Garth, that her life would henceforth be spoiled by a perpetual infusion of Garths and their ways, and that her darling boy, with his beautiful face and stylish air 'beyond anybody else's son in Middlemarch', would be sure to get like that family in plainness of appearance and carelessness about his clothes. To her it seemed that there was a Garth conspiracy to get possession of the desirable Fred, but she dared not enlarge on this opinion, because a slight hint of it had made him 'fly out' at her as he had never done before. Her temper was too sweet for her to show any anger; but she felt that her happiness had received a bruise, and for several days merely to look at Fred made her cry a little as if he were the subject of some baleful prophecy. Perhaps she was the slower to recover her usual cheerfulness because Fred had warned her that she must not reopen the sore question with his father, who had accepted his decision and forgiven him. If her husband had been vehement against Fred, she would have been urged into defence of her darling. It was the end of the fourth day when Mr Vincy said to her –

'Come, Lucy, my dear, don't be so down-hearted. You have always spoiled the boy, and you must go on spoiling him.'

'Nothing ever did cut me so before, Vincy,' said the wife, her fair throat and chin beginning to tremble again, 'only his illness.'

'Pooh, pooh, never mind! We must expect to have trouble with our children. Don't make it worse by letting me see you out of spirits.'

'Well, I won't,' said Mrs Vincy, roused by this appeal and adjusting herself with a little shake as of a bird which lays down its ruffled plumage.

'It won't do to begin making a fuss about one,' said Mr Vincy, wishing to combine a little grumbling with domestic cheerfulness. 'There's Rosamond as well as Fred.'

'Yes, poor thing. I'm sure I felt for her being disappointed of her baby; but she got over it nicely.'

'Baby, pooh! I can see Lydgate is making a mess of his practice, and getting into debt too, by what I hear. I shall have Rosamond coming to me with a pretty tale one of these days. But they'll get no money from me, I know. Let *his* family help him. I never did like that marriage. But it's no use talking. Ring the bell for lemons, and don't look dull any more, Lucy. I'll drive you and Louisa to Riverston to-morrow.'

✑ FIFTY-SEVEN ✐

They numbered scarce eight summers when a name
  Rose on their souls and stirred such motions there
As thrill the buds and shape their hidden frame
  At penetration of the quickening air:
His name who told of loyal Evan Dhu,
  Of quaint Bradwardine, and Vich Ian Vor,
Making the little world their childhood knew
  Large with a land of mountain, lake, and scaur,
And larger yet with wonder, love, belief
  Toward Walter Scott, who living far away
Sent them this wealth of joy and noble grief.
  The book and they must part, but day by day,
    In lines that thwart like portly spiders ran,
    They wrote the tale, from Tully Veolan.

THE EVENING THAT FRED VINCY WALKED to Lowick Parsonage (he had begun to see that this was a world in which even a spirited young man must sometimes walk for want of a horse to carry him) he set out at five o'clock and called on Mrs Garth by the way, wishing to assure himself that she accepted their new relations willingly.

He found the family group, dogs and cats included, under the great apple-tree in the orchard. It was a festival with Mrs Garth, for her eldest son, Christy, her peculiar joy and pride, had come home for a short holiday – Christy, who held it the most desirable thing in the world to be a tutor, to study all literatures and be a regenerate Porson, and who was an incorporate criticism on poor Fred, a sort of object-lesson given to him by the educational mother. Christy himself, a square-browed, broad-shouldered masculine edition of his mother not much higher than Fred's shoulder – which made it the harder that he should be held superior – was always as simple as possible, and thought no more of Fred's disinclination to scholarship than of a giraffe's' wishing that he himself were more of the same height. He was lying on the ground now by his mother's chair, with his straw-hat laid flat over his eyes, while Jim on the other side was reading aloud from that beloved writer who has made a chief part in the happiness of many young lives. The volume was *Ivanhoe*, and Jim was in the great archery scene at the tournament, but suffered much interruption from Ben, who had fetched his own old bow and arrows, and was making

443

himself dreadfully disagreeable, Letty thought, by begging all present to observe his random shots, which no one wished to do except Brownie, the active-minded but probably shallow mongrel, while the grizzled New-foundland lying in the sun looked on with the dull-eyed neutrality of extreme old age. Letty herself, showing as to her mouth and pinafore some slight signs that she had been assisting at the gathering of the cherries which stood in a coral-heap on the tea-table, was now seated on the grass, listening open-eyed to the reading.

But the centre of interest was changed for all by the arrival of Fred Vincy. When, seating himself on a garden-stool, he said that he was on his way to Lowick Parsonage, Ben, who had thrown down his bow, and snatched up a reluctant half-grown kitten instead, strode across Fred's outstretched leg and said, 'Take me!'

'Oh, and me too,' said Letty.

'You can't keep up with Fred and me,' said Ben.

'Yes, I can. Mother, please say that I am to go,' urged Letty, whose life was much checkered by resistance to her depreciation as a girl.

'I shall stay with Christy,' observed Jim; as much as to say that he had the advantage of these simpletons; whereupon Letty put her hand up to her head and looked with jealous indecision from the one to the other.

'Let us all go and see Mary,' said Christy, opening his arms.

'No, my dear child, we must not go in a swarm to the parsonage. And that old Glasgow suit of yours would never do. Besides, your father will come home. We must let Fred go alone. He can tell Mary that you are here, and she will come back to-morrow.'

Christy glanced at his own threadbare knees, and then Fred's beautiful white trousers. Certainly Fred's tailoring suggested the advantage of an English university, and he had a graceful way even of looking warm and of pushing his hair back with his handkerchief.

'Children, run away,' said Mrs Garth; 'it is too warm to hang about your friends. Take your brother and show him the rabbits.'

The eldest understood, and led off the children immediately. Fred felt that Mrs Garth wished to give him an opportunity of saying anything that he had to say, but he could only begin by observing –

'How glad you must be to have Christy here!'

'Yes; he has come sooner than I expected. He got down from the coach at nine o'clock, just after his father went out. I am longing for Caleb to come and hear what wonderful progress Christy is making. He has paid his expenses for the last year by giving lessons, carrying on hard study at the same time. He hopes soon to get a private tutorship and go abroad.'

'He is a great fellow,' said Fred, to whom these cheerful truths had a medicinal taste, 'and no trouble to anybody.' After a slight pause, he added, 'But I fear you will think that I am going to be a great deal of trouble to Mr Garth.'

'Caleb likes taking trouble: he is one of those men who always do more than any one would have thought of asking them to do,' answered Mrs Garth. She was knitting, and could either look at Fred or not, as she chose – always an advantage when one is bent on loading speech with salutary meaning; and though Mrs Garth intended to be duly reserved, she did wish to say something that Fred might be the better for.

'I know you think me very undeserving, Mrs Garth, and with good reason,' said Fred, his spirit rising a little at the perception of something like a disposition to lecture him. 'I happen to have behaved just the worst to the people I can't help wishing for the most from. But while two men like Mr Garth and Mr Farebrother have not given me up, I don't see why I should give myself up.' Fred thought it might be well to suggest these masculine examples to Mrs Garth.

'Assuredly,' said she, with gathering emphasis. 'A young man for whom two such elders had devoted themselves would indeed be culpable if he threw himself away and made their sacrifices vain.'

Fred wondered a little at this strong language, but only said, 'I hope it will not be so with me, Mrs Garth, since I have some encouragement to believe that I may win Mary. Mr Garth has told you about that? You were not surprised, I daresay?' Fred ended, innocently referring only to his own love as probably evident enough.

'Not surprised that Mary has given you encouragement?' returned Mrs Garth, who thought it would be well for Fred to be more alive to the fact that Mary's friends could not possibly have wished this beforehand, whatever the Vincys might suppose. 'Yes, I confess I *was* surprised.'

'She never did give me any – not the least in the world, when I talked to her myself,' said Fred, eager to vindicate Mary. 'But when I asked Mr Farebrother to speak for me, she allowed him to tell me there was a hope.'

The power of admonition which had begun to stir in Mrs Garth had not yet discharged itself. It was a little too provoking even for *her* self-control that this blooming youngster should flourish on the disappointments of sadder and wiser people – making a meal of a nightingale and never knowing it – and that all the while his family should suppose that hers was in eager need of this sprig; and her vexation had fermented the more actively because of its total repression towards her husband. Exemplary wives will sometimes find scape-goats in this way. She now said with energetic decision. 'You made a great mistake, Fred, in asking Mr Farebrother to speak for you.'

'Did I?' said Fred, reddening instantaneously. He was alarmed, but at a loss to know what Mrs Garth meant, and added, in an apologetic tone, 'Mr Farebrother has always been such a friend of ours; and Mary, I knew, would listen to him gravely; and he took it on himself quite readily.'

'Yes, young people are usually blind to everything but their own wishes, and seldom imagine how much those wishes cost others,' said Mrs Garth. She did not mean to go beyond this salutary general doctrine, and threw her indignation into a needless unwinding of her worsted, knitting her brow at it with a grand air.

'I cannot conceive how it could be any pain to Mr Farebrother,' said Fred, who nevertheless felt that surprising conceptions were beginning to form themselves.

'Precisely; you cannot conceive,' said Mrs Garth, cutting her words as neatly as possible.

For a moment Fred looked at the horizon with a dismayed anxiety, and then turning with a quick movement said almost sharply –

'Do you mean to say, Mrs Garth, that Mr Farebrother is in love with Mary?'

'And if it were so, Fred, I think you are the last person who ought to be surprised,' returned Mrs Garth, laying her knitting down beside her and folding her arms. It was an unwonted sign of emotion in her that she should put her work out of her hands. In fact her feelings were divided between the satisfaction of giving Fred his discipline and the sense of having gone a little too far. Fred took his hat and stick and rose quickly.

'Then you think I am standing in his way, and in Mary's too?' he said, in a tone which seemed to demand an answer.

Mrs Garth could not speak immediately. She had brought herself into the unpleasant position of being called on to say what she really felt, yet what she knew there were strong reasons for concealing. And to her the consciousness of having exceeded in words was peculiarly mortifying. Besides, Fred had given out unexpected electricity, and he now added, 'Mr Garth seemed pleased that Mary should be attached to me. He could not have known anything of this.'

Mrs Garth felt a severe twinge at this mention of her husband, the fear that Caleb might think her in the wrong not being easily endurable. She answered, wanting to check unintended consequences –

'I spoke from inference only. I am not aware that Mary knows anything of the matter.'

But she hesitated to beg that he would keep entire silence on a subject which she had herself unnecessarily mentioned, not being used to stoop in that way; and while she was hesitating there was already a rush of unintended consequences under the apple-tree where the tea-things stood. Ben, bouncing across the grass with Brownie at his heels, and seeing the kitten dragging the knitting by a lengthening line of wool, shouted and clapped his hands; Brownie barked, the kitten, desperate, jumped on the tea-table and upset the milk, then jumped down again and swept half the cherries with it; and Ben, snatching up the half-knitted sock-top, fitted it over the kitten's head as a new source of madness, while Letty arriving cried out to her mother against this cruelty – it was a history as full of sensation as 'This is the house that Jack built.' Mrs Garth was obliged to interfere, the other young ones came up and the *tête-à-tête* with Fred was ended. He got away as soon as he could, and Mrs Garth could only imply some retraction of her severity by saying 'God bless you' when she shook hands with him.

She was unpleasantly conscious that she had been on the verge of speaking as 'one of the foolish women speaketh' – telling first and entreating silence after. But she had not entreated silence, and to prevent Caleb's blame she determined to blame herself and confess all to him that very night. It was curious what an awful tribunal the mild Caleb's was to her, whenever he set it up. But she meant to point out to him that the revelation might do Fred Vincy a great deal of good.

No doubt it was having a strong effect on him as he walked to Lowick. Fred's light hopeful nature had perhaps never had so much of a bruise as from this suggestion that if he had been out of the way Mary might have made a thoroughly good match. Also he was piqued that he had been what he called such a stupid lout as to ask that intervention from Mr Farebrother. But it was not in a lover's nature – it was not in Fred's – that the new anxiety raised about Mary's feeling should not surmount every other. Notwithstanding his trust in Mr Farebrother's generosity, notwithstanding what Mary had said to him, Fred could not help feeling he had a rival: it was a new consciousness, and he objected to it extremely, not being in the least ready to give up Mary for her good, being ready rather to fight for her with any man whatsoever. But the fighting with Mr Farebrother must be of a metaphorical kind, which was much more difficult to Fred than the muscular. Certainly this experience was a discipline for Fred hardly less sharp than his disappointment about his uncle's will. The iron had not entered his soul, but he had begun to imagine what the sharp edge would be. It did not once occur to Fred that Mrs Garth might be mistaken about Mr Farebrother, but he suspected that she might be wrong about Mary. Mary had been staying at the parsonage lately, and her mother might know very little of what had been passing in her mind.

He did not feel easier when he found her looking cheerful with the three ladies in the drawing-room. They were in animated discussion on some subject which was dropped when he entered, and Mary was copying the labels from a heap of shallow cabinet drawers, in a minute handwriting which she was skilled in. Mr Farebrother was somewhere in the village, and the three ladies knew nothing of Fred's peculiar relation to Mary: it was impossible for either of them to propose that they should walk round the garden, and Fred predicted to himself that he should have to go away without saying a word to her in private. He told her first of Christy's arrival and then of his own engagement with her father; and he was comforted by seeing that this latter news touched her keenly. She said hurriedly, 'I am so glad,' and then bent over her writing to hinder any one from noticing her face. But here was a subject which Mrs Farebrother could not let pass.

'You don't mean, my dear Miss Garth, that you are glad of a young man giving up the Church for which he was educated: you only mean that things being so, you are glad that he should be under an excellent man like your father.'

'No, really, Mrs Farebrother, I am glad of both, I fear,' said Mary, cleverly getting rid of one rebellious tear. 'I have a dreadfully secular mind. I never liked any clergyman except the Vicar of Wakefield and Mr Farebrother.'

'Now why, my dear?' said Mrs Farebrother, pausing on her large wooden knitting-needles and looking at Mary. 'You have always a good reason for your opinions, but this astonishes me. Of course I put out of the question those who preach new doctrine. But why should you dislike clergymen?'

'Oh dear,' said Mary, her face breaking into merriment as she seemed to consider a moment. 'I don't like their neckcloths.'

'Why, you don't like Camden's, then,' said Miss Winifred, in some anxiety.

'Yes, I do,' said Mary. 'I don't like the other clergymen's neckcloths, because it is they who wear them.'

'How very puzzling!' said Miss Noble, feeling that her own intellect was probably deficient.

'My dear, you are joking. You would have better reasons than these for slighting so respectable a class of men,' said Mrs Farebrother, majestically.

'Miss Garth has such severe notions of what people should be that it is difficult to satisfy her,' said Fred.

'Well, I am glad at least that she makes an exception in favour of my son,' said the old lady.

Mary was wondering at Fred's piqued tone, when Mr Farebrother came in and had to hear the news about the engagement under Mr Garth. At the end he said with quiet satisfaction, '*That* is right;' and then bent to look at Mary's labels and praise her handwriting. Fred felt horribly jealous – was glad, of course, that Mr Farebrother was so estimable, but wished that he had been ugly and fat as men at forty sometimes are. It was clear what the end would be, since Mary openly placed Farebrother above everybody, and these women were all evidently encouraging the affair. He was feeling sure that he should have no chance of speaking to Mary, when Mr Farebrother said –

'Fred, help me to carry these drawers back into my study – you have never seen my fine new study. Pray come too, Miss Garth. I want you to see a stupendous spider I found this morning.'

Mary at once saw the Vicar's intention. He had never since the memorable evening deviated from his old pastoral kindness towards her, and her momentary wonder and doubt had quite gone to sleep. Mary was accustomed to think rather rigorously of what was probable, and if a belief flattered her vanity she felt warned to dismiss it as ridiculous, having early had much exercise in such dismissals. It was as she had foreseen: when Fred had been asked to admire the fittings of the study, and she had been asked to admire the spider, Mr Farebrother said –

'Wait here a minute or two. I am going to look out an engraving which Fred is tall enough to hang for me. I shall be back in a few minutes.' And then he went out. Nevertheless, the first word Fred said to Mary was –

'It is of no use, whatever I do, Mary. You are sure to marry Farebrother at last.' There was some rage in his tone.

'What do you mean, Fred?' Mary exclaimed indignantly, blushing deeply, and surprised out of all her readiness in reply.

'It is impossible that you should not see it all clearly enough – you who see everything.'

'I only see that you are behaving very ill, Fred, in speaking so of Mr Farebrother after he has pleaded your cause in every way. How can you have taken up such an idea?'

Fred was rather deep, in spite of his irritation. If Mary had really been unsuspicious, there was no good in telling her what Mrs Garth had said.

'It follows as a matter of course,' he replied. 'When you are continually seeing a man who beats me in everything, and whom you set up above everybody, I can have no fair chance.'

'You are very ungrateful, Fred,' said Mary. 'I wish I had never told Mr Farebrother that I cared for you in the least.'

'No, I am not ungrateful; I should be the happiest fellow in the world if it were not for this. I told your father everything, and he was very kind; he treated me as if I were his son. I could go at the work with a will, writing and everything, if it were not for this.'

'For this? for what?' said Mary, imagining now that something specific must have been said or done.

'This dreadful certainty that I shall be bowled out by Farebrother.' Mary was appeased by her inclination to laugh.

'Fred,' she said, peeping round to catch his eyes, which were sulkily turned away from her, 'you are too delightfully ridiculous. If you were not such a charming simpleton, what a temptation this would be to play the wicked coquette, and let you suppose that somebody besides you made love to me.'

'Do you really like me best, Mary?' said Fred, turning eyes full of affection on her, and trying to take her hand.

'I don't like you at all at this moment,' said Mary, retreating, and putting her hands behind her. 'I only said that no mortal ever made love to me besides you. And that is no argument that a very wise man ever will,' she ended, merrily.

'I wish you would tell me that you could not possibly ever think of him,' said Fred.

'Never dare to mention this any more to me, Fred,' said Mary, getting serious again. 'I don't know whether it is more stupid or ungenerous in you not to see that Mr Farebrother has left us together on purpose that we might speak freely. I am disappointed that you should be so blind to his delicate feeling.'

There was no time to say any more before Mr Farebrother came back with the engraving; and Fred had to return to the drawing-room still with a jealous dread in his heart, but yet with comforting arguments from Mary's words and manner. The result of the conversation was on the whole more painful to Mary: inevitably her attention had taken a new attitude, and she saw the possibility of new interpretations. She was in a position in which she seemed to herself to be slighting Mr Farebrother, and this, in relation to a man who is much honoured, is always dangerous to the firmness of a grateful woman. To have a reason for going home the next day was a relief, for Mary earnestly desired to be always clear that she loved Fred best. When a tender affection has been storing itself in us through many of our years, the idea that we could accept any exchange for it seems to be a cheapening of our lives. And we can set a watch over our affections and our constancy as we can over other treasures.

'Fred has lost all his other expectations; he must keep this,' Mary said to herself, with a smile curling her lips. It was impossible to help fleeting visions of another kind – new dignities and an acknowledged value of which she had often felt the absence. But these things with Fred outside them, Fred forsaken and looking sad for the want of her, could never tempt her deliberate thought.

ଔ FIFTY-EIGHT ଚ

For there can live no hatred in thine eye,
Therefore in that I cannot know thy change:
In many's looks the false heart's history
Is writ in moods and frowns and wrinkles strange;
But Heaven in thy creation did decree
That in thy face sweet love should ever dwell;
Whate'er thy thoughts or thy heart's workings be,
Thy looks should nothing thence but sweetness tell.
SHAKESPEARE: *Sonnets*

AT THE TIME WHEN MR VINCY UTTERED that presentiment about Rosamond, she herself had never had the idea that she should be driven to make the sort of appeal which he foresaw. She had not yet had any anxiety about ways and means, although her domestic life had been expensive as well as eventful. Her baby had been born prematurely, and all the embroidered robes and caps had to be laid by in darkness. This misfortune was attributed entirely to her having persisted in going out on horseback one day when her husband had desired her not to do so; but it must not be supposed that she had shown temper on the occasion, or rudely told him that she would do as she liked.

What led her particularly to desire horse-exercise was a visit from Captain Lydgate, the baronet's third son, who, I am sorry to say, was detested by our Tertius of that name as a vapid fop 'parting his hair from brow to nape in a despicable fashion' (not followed by Tertius himself), and showing an ignorant security that he knew the proper thing to say on every topic. Lydgate inwardly cursed his own folly that he had drawn down this visit by consenting to go to his uncle's on the wedding-tour, and he made himself rather disagreeable to Rosamond by saying so in private. For to Rosamond this visit was a source of unprecedented but gracefully concealed exultation. She was so intensely conscious of having a cousin who was a baronet's son staying in the house, that she imagined the knowledge of what was implied by his presence to be diffused through all other minds; and when she introduced Captain Lydgate to her guests, she had a placid sense that his rank penetrated them as if it had been an odour. The satisfaction was enough for the time to melt away some disappointment in the conditions of marriage with a medical man even of good birth: it seemed now that her marriage was visibly as well as ideally floating her above the Middlemarch level, and the future looked bright with letters and visits to and from Quallingham, and vague advancement in consequence for Tertius. Especially as, probably at the Captain's suggestion, his married sister, Mrs Mengan, had come with her maid, and stayed two nights on her way from town. Hence it was clearly worth while for Rosamond to take pains with her music and the careful selection of her lace.

As to Captain Lydgate himself, his low brow, his aquiline nose bent on one side, and his rather heavy utterance, might have been disadvantageous in any young gentleman who had not a military bearing and moustache to give him what is doted on by some flower-like blond heads as 'style'. He had, moreover, that sort of high-breeding which consists in being free from the petty solicitudes of middle-class gentility, and he was a great critic of feminine charms. Rosamond delighted in his admiration now even more than she had done at Quallingham, and he found it easy to spend several hours of the day in flirting with her. The visit altogether was one of the pleasantest larks he had ever had, not the less so perhaps because he suspected that his queer cousin Tertius wished him away: though Lydgate, who would rather (hyperbolically speaking) have died than have failed in polite hospitality, suppressed his dislike, and only pretended generally not to hear what the gallant officer said, consigning the task of answering him to Rosamond. For he was not at all a jealous husband, and preferred leaving a feather-headed young gentleman alone with his wife to bearing him company.

'I wish you would talk more to the Captain at dinner, Tertius,' said Rosamond, one evening when the important guest was gone to Loamford to see some brother officers stationed there. 'You really look so absent sometimes – you seem to be seeing through his head into something behind it, instead of looking at him.'

'My dear Rosy, you don't expect me to talk much to such a conceited ass as that, I hope,' said Lydgate, brusquely. 'If he got his head broken, I might look at it with interest, not before.'

'I cannot conceive why you should speak of your cousin so contemptuously,' said Rosamond, her fingers moving at her work while she spoke with a mild gravity which had a touch of disdain in it.

'Ask Ladislaw if he doesn't think your Captain the greatest bore he ever met with. Ladislaw has almost forsaken the house since he came.'

Rosamond thought she knew perfectly well why Mr Ladislaw disliked the Captain: he was jealous, and she liked his being jealous.

'It is impossible to say what will suit eccentric persons,' she answered, 'but in my opinion Captain Lydgate is a thorough gentleman, and I think you ought not, out of respect to Sir Godwin, to treat him with neglect.'

'No, dear; but we have had dinners for him. And he comes in and goes out as he likes. He doesn't want me.'

'Still, when he is in the room, you might show him more attention. He may not be a phoenix of cleverness in your sense; his profession is different; but it would be all the better for you to talk a little on his subjects. I think his conversation is quite agreeable. And he is anything but an unprincipled man.'

'The fact is, you would wish me to be a little more like him, Rosy,' said Lydgate, in a sort of resigned murmur, with a smile which was not exactly tender, and certainly not merry. Rosamond was silent and did not smile again; but the lovely curves of her face looked good-tempered enough without smiling.

Those words of Lydgate's were like a sad milestone marking how far he had travelled from his old dreamland, in which Rosamond Vincy appeared to be that perfect piece of womanhood who would reverence her husband's mind after the fashion of an accomplished mermaid, using her comb and looking-glass and singing her song for the relaxation of his adored wisdom alone. He had begun to distinguish between that imagined adoration and the attraction towards a man's talent because it gives him prestige, and is like an order in his button-hole or an Honourable before his name.

It might have been supposed that Rosamond had travelled too, since she had found the pointless conversation of Mr Ned Plymdale perfectly wearisome; but to most mortals there is a stupidity which is unendurable and a stupidity which is altogether acceptable – else, indeed, what would become of social bonds? Captain Lydgate's stupidity was delicately scented, carried itself with 'style', talked with a good accent and was closely related to Sir Godwin. Rosamond found it quite agreeable and caught many of its phrases.

Therefore, since Rosamond, as we know, was fond of horseback, there were plenty of reasons why she should be tempted to resume her riding when Captain Lydgate, who had ordered his man with two horses to follow him and put up at the Green Dragon, begged her to go out on the grey which he warranted to be gentle and trained to carry a lady – indeed he had bought it for his sister, and was taking it to Quallingham. Rosamond went out the first time without telling her husband, and came back before his return; but the ride had been so thorough a success, and she declared herself so much the better in consequence, that he was informed of it with full reliance on his consent that she should go riding again.

On the contrary Lydgate was more than hurt – he was utterly confounded that she had risked herself on a strange horse without referring the matter to his wish. After the first almost thundering exclamations of astonishment, which sufficiently warned Rosamond of what was coming, he was silent for some moments.

'However, you have come back safely,' he said, at last, in a decisive tone. 'You will not go again, Rosy; that is understood. If it were the quietest, most familiar horse in the world, there would always be the chance of accident. And you know very well that I wished you to give up riding the roan on that account.'

'But there is the chance of accident indoors, Tertius.'

'My darling, don't talk nonsense,' said Lydgate, in an imploring tone; 'surely I am the person to judge for you. I think it is enough that I say you are not to go again.'

Rosamond was arranging her hair before dinner, and the reflection of her head in the glass showed no change in its loveliness except a little turning aside of the long neck. Lydgate had been moving about with his hands in his pockets, and now paused near her, as if he awaited some assurance.

'I wish you would fasten up my plaits, dear,' said Rosamond, letting her arms fall with a little sigh, so as to make a husband ashamed of standing there like a brute. Lydgate had often fastened the plaits before, being among the deftest of men with his large finely-formed fingers. He swept up the soft festoons of plaits and fastened in the tall comb (to such uses do men come!); and what could he do then but kiss the exquisite nape which was shown in all its delicate curves? But when we do what we have done before, it is often with a difference. Lydgate was still angry, and had not forgotten his point.

'I shall tell the Captain that he ought to have known better than offer you his horse,' he said, as he moved away.

'I beg you will not do anything of the kind, Tertius,' said Rosamond, looking at him with something more marked than usual in her speech. 'It will be treating me as if I were a child. Promise that you will leave the subject to me.'

There did seem to be some truth in her objection. Lydgate said, 'Very well,' with a surly obedience, and thus the discussion ended with his promising Rosamond, and not with her promising him.

In fact, she had been determined not to promise. Rosamond had that victorious obstinacy which never wastes its energy in impetuous resistance. What she liked to do was to her the right thing and all her cleverness was directed to getting the means of doing it. She meant to go out riding again on the grey, and she did go on the next opportunity of her husband's absence, not intending that he should know until it was late enough not to signify to her. The temptation was certainly great: she was very fond of the exercise, and the gratification of riding on a fine horse, with Captain Lydgate, Sir Godwin's son, on another fine horse by her side, and of being met in this position by any one but her husband, was something as good as her dreams before marriage: moreover, she was riveting the connection with the family at Quallingham, which must be a wise thing to do.

But the gentle grey, unprepared for the crash of a tree that was being felled on the edge of Halsell Wood, took fright, and caused a worse fright to Rosamond, leading finally to the loss of her baby. Lydgate could not show his anger towards her, but he was rather bearish to the Captain, whose visit naturally soon came to an end.

In all future conversations on the subject, Rosamond was mildly certain that the ride had made no difference, and that if she had stayed at home the same symptoms would have come on and would have ended in the same way, because she had felt something like them before.

Lydgate could only say, 'Poor, poor darling!' but he secretly wondered over the terrible tenacity of this mild creature. There was gathering within him an amazed sense of his powerlessness over Rosamond. His superior knowledge and mental force, instead of being, as he had imagined, a shrine to consult on all occasions, was simply set aside on every practical question. He had regarded Rosamond's cleverness as precisely of the receptive kind which became a woman. He was now beginning to find out what that cleverness was – what was the shape into which it had run as into a close network aloof and independent. No one quicker than Rosamond to see causes and effects which lay within the track of her own tastes and interests: she had seen clearly Lydgate's pre-eminence in Middlemarch society, and could go on imaginatively tracing still more agreeable social effects when his talent should have advanced him; but for her, his professional and scientific ambition had no other relation to these desirable effects than if they had been the fortunate discovery of an ill-smelling oil. And that oil apart, with which she had nothing to do, of course she believed in her own opinion more than she did in his. Lydgate was astounded to find in numberless trifling matters, as well as in this last serious case of the riding, that affection did not make her compliant. He had no doubt that the affection was there, and had no presentiment that he had done anything to repel it. For his own part he said to himself that he loved her as tenderly as ever, and could make up his mind to her negations; but – well! Lydgate was much worried, and conscious of new elements in his life as noxious to him as an inlet of mud to a creature that has been used to breathe and bathe and dart after its illuminated prey in the clearest of waters.

Rosamond was soon looking lovelier than ever at her work-table, enjoying drives in her father's phaeton and thinking it likely that she might be invited to Quallingham. She knew that she was a much more exquisite ornament to the drawing-room there than any daughter of the family, and in reflecting that the gentlemen were aware of that, did not perhaps sufficiently consider whether the ladies would be eager to see themselves surpassed.

Lydgate, relieved from anxiety about her, relapsed into what she inwardly called his moodiness – a name which to her covered his thoughtful preoccupation with other subjects than herself, as well as that uneasy look of the brow and distaste for all ordinary things as if they were mixed with bitter herbs, which really made a sort of weather-glass to his vexation and foreboding. These latter states of mind had one cause amongst others, which he had generously but mistakenly avoided mentioning to Rosamond, lest it should affect her health and spirits. Between him and her indeed there was that total missing of each other's mental track, which is too evidently possible even between persons who are continually thinking of each other. To Lydgate it seemed that he had been spending month after month in sacrificing more than half of his best intent and best power to his tenderness for Rosamond; bearing her little claims and interruptions without impatience, and above all, bearing without betrayal of bitterness to look through less and less of interfering illusion at the blank unreflecting surface her mind presented to his ardour for the more impersonal ends of his profession and his scientific study, an ardour which he had fancied that the ideal wife must somehow worship as sublime, though not in the least knowing why. But his endurance was mingled with a self-discontent which, if we know how to be candid, we shall confess to make more than half our bitterness under grievances, wife or husband included. It always remains true that if we had been greater, circumstance would have been less strong against us. Lydgate was aware that his concessions to Rosamond were often little more than the lapse of slackening resolution, the creeping paralysis apt to seize an enthusiasm which is out of adjustment to a constant portion of our lives. And on Lydgate's enthusiasm there was constantly pressing not a simple weight of sorrow, but the biting presence of a petty degrading care, such as casts the blight of irony over all higher effort.

This was the care which he had hitherto abstained from mentioning to Rosamond; and he believed, with some wonder, that it had never entered her mind, though certainly no difficulty could be less mysterious. It was an inference with a conspicuous handle to it, and had been easily drawn by indifferent observers, that Lydgate was in debt; and he could not succeed in keeping out of his mind for long together that he was every day getting deeper into that swamp, which tempts men towards it with such a pretty covering of flowers and verdure. It is wonderful how soon a man gets up to his chin there – in a condition in which, in spite of himself, he is forced to think chiefly of release, though he had a scheme of the universe in his soul.

Eighteen months ago Lydgate was poor, but had never known the eager want of small sums, and felt rather a burning contempt for any who descended a step in order to gain them. He was now experiencing something worse than a simple deficit; he was assailed by the vulgar hateful trials of a man who has bought and used a great many things which might have been done without, and which he is unable to pay for, though the demand for payment has become pressing.

How this came about may be easily seen without much arithmetic or knowledge of prices. When a man in setting up a house and preparing for marriage finds that his furniture and other initial expenses come to between four and five hundred pounds more than he has capital to pay for; when at the end of a year it appears that his household expenses, horses and et ceteras, amount to nearly a thousand, while the proceeds of the practice reckoned from the old books to be worth eight hundred per annum have sunk like a summer pond and make hardly five hundred chiefly in unpaid entries, the plain inference is that, whether he minds it or not, he is in debt. Those were less expensive times than our own, and provincial life was comparatively modest; but the ease with which a medical man who had lately bought a practice, who thought that he was obliged to keep two horses, whose table was supplied without stint, and who paid an insurance on his life and a high rent for house and garden, might find his expenses doubling his receipts, can be conceived by any one who does not think these details beneath his consideration. Rosamond, accustomed from her childhood to an extravagant household, thought that good housekeeping consisted simply in ordering the best of everything – nothing else 'answered'; and Lydgate supposed that 'if things were done at all, they must be done properly' – he did not see how they were to live otherwise. If each head of household expenditure had been mentioned to him beforehand, he would have probably observed that 'it could hardly come to much', and if any one had suggested a saving on a particular article – for example, the substitution of cheap fish for dear – it would have appeared to him simply a penny-wise, mean notion.

Rosamond, even without such an occasion as Captain Lydgate's visit, was fond of giving invitations, and Lydgate, though he often thought the guests tiresome, did not interfere. The sociability seemed a necessary part of professional prudence, and the entertainment must be suitable. It is true Lydgate was constantly visiting the homes of the poor and adjusting his prescriptions of diet to their small means; but, dear me! has it not by this time ceased to be remarkable – is it not rather what we expect in men, that they should have numerous strands of experience lying side by side and never compare them with each other? Expenditure – like ugliness and errors – becomes a totally new thing when we attach our own personality to it, and measure it by that wide difference which is manifest (in our own sensations) between ourselves and others. Lydgate believed himself to be careless about his dress, and he despised a man who calculated the effects of his costume; it seemed to him only a matter of course that he had abundance of fresh garments – such things were naturally ordered in sheaves. It must be remembered that he had never hitherto felt the check of importunate debt, and he walked by habit, not by self-criticism. But the check had come.

Its novelty made it the more irritating. He was amazed, disgusted that conditions so foreign to all his purposes, so hatefully disconnected with the objects he cared to occupy himself with, should have lain in ambush and clutched him when he was unaware. And there was not only the actual debt; there was the certainty that in his present position he must go on deepening it. Two furnishing tradesmen at Brassing, whose bills had been incurred before his marriage, and whom uncalculated current expenses had ever since prevented him from paying, had repeatedly sent him unpleasant letters which had forced themselves on his attention. This could hardly have been more galling to any disposition than to Lydgate's, with his intense pride – his dislike of asking a favour or being under an obligation to any one. He had scorned even to form conjectures about Mr Vincy's intentions on money matters, and nothing but extremity could have induced him to apply to his father-in-law, even if he had not been made aware in various indirect ways since his marriage that Mr Vincy's own affairs were not flourishing, and that the expectation of help from him would be resented. Some men easily trust in the readiness of friends; it had never in the former part of his life occurred to Lydgate that he should need to do so: he had never thought what borrowing would be to him; but now that the idea had entered his mind, he felt that he would rather incur any other hardship. In the meantime he had no money or prospects of money; and his practice was not getting more lucrative.

No wonder that Lydgate had been unable to suppress all signs of inward trouble during the last few months, and now that Rosamond was regaining brilliant health, he meditated taking her entirely into confidence on his difficulties. New conversance with tradesmen's bills had forced his reasoning into a new channel of comparison: he had begun to consider from a new point of view what was necessary and unnecessary in goods ordered, and to see that there must be some change of habits. How could such a change be made without Rosamond's concurrence? The immediate occasion of opening the disagreeable fact on her was forced upon him.

Having no money, and having privately sought advice as to what security could possibly be given by a man in his position, Lydgate had offered the one good security in his power to the less peremptory creditor, who was a silversmith and jeweller, and who consented to take on himself the upholsterer's credit also, accepting interest for a given term. The security necessary was a bill of sale on the furniture of his house, which might make a creditor easy for a reasonable time about a debt amounting to less than four hundred pounds; and the silversmith, Mr Dover, was willing to reduce it by taking back a portion of the plate and any other article which was as good as new. 'Any other article' was a phrase delicately implying jewellery, and more particularly some purple amethysts costing thirty pounds, which Lydgate had bought as a bridal present.

Opinions may be divided as to his wisdom in making this present: some may think that it was a graceful attention to be expected from a man like Lydgate, and that the fault of any troublesome consequences lay in the pinched narrowness of provincial life at that time, which offered no conveniences for professional people whose fortune was not proportioned to their tastes; also, in Lydgate's ridiculous fastidiousness about asking his friends for money.

However, it had seemed a question of no moment to him on that fine morning when he went to give a final order for plate: in the presence of other jewels enormously expensive, and as an addition to orders of which the amount had not been exactly calculated, thirty pounds for ornaments so exquisitely suited to Rosamond's neck and arms could hardly appear excessive when there was no ready cash for it to exceed. But at this crisis Lydgate's imagination could not help dwelling on the possibility of letting the amethysts take their place again among Mr Dover's stock, though he shrank from the idea of proposing this to Rosamond. Having been roused to discern consequences which he had never been in the habit of tracing, he was preparing to act on this discernment with some of the rigour (by no means all) that he would have applied in pursuing experiment. He was nerving himself to this rigour as he rode from Brassing, and meditated on the representations he must make to Rosamond.

It was evening when he got home. He was intensely miserable, this strong man of nine-and-twenty and of many gifts. He was not saying angrily within himself that he had made a profound mistake; but the mistake was at work in him like a recognized chronic disease, mingling its uneasy importunities with every prospect, and enfeebling every thought. As he went along the passage to the drawing-room, he heard the piano and singing. Of course, Ladislaw was there. It was some weeks since Will had parted from Dorothea, yet he was still at the old post in Middlemarch.

Lydgate had no objection in general to Ladislaw's coming, but just now he was annoyed that he could not find his hearth free. When he opened the door the two singers went on towards the keynote, raising their eyes and looking at him indeed, but not regarding his entrance as an interruption. To a man galled with his harness as poor Lydgate was, it is not soothing to see two people warbling at him, as he comes in with the sense that the painful day has still pains in store. His face, already paler than usual, took on a scowl as he walked across the room and flung himself into a chair.

The singers, feeling themselves excused by the fact that they had had only three bars to sing, now turned round.

'How are you, Lydgate?' said Will, coming forward to shake hands.

Lydgate took his hand, but did not think it necessary to speak.

'Have you dined, Tertius? I expected you much earlier,' said Rosamond, who had already seen that her husband was in a 'horrible humour'. She seated herself in her usual place as she spoke.

'I have dined. I should like some tea, please,' said Lydgate, curtly, still scowling and looking markedly at his legs stretched out before him.

Will was too quick to need more. 'I shall be off,' he said reaching his hat.

'Tea is coming,' said Rosamond; 'pray don't go.'

'Yes, Lydgate is bored,' said Will, who had more comprehension of Lydgate than Rosamond had, and was not offended by his manner, easily imagining outdoor causes of annoyance.

'There is the more need for you to stay,' said Rosamond, playfully, and in her lightest accent; 'he will not speak to me all the evening.'

'Yes, Rosamond, I shall,' said Lydgate, in his strong baritone. 'I have some serious business to speak to you about.'

No introduction of the business could have been less like that which Lydgate had intended; but her indifferent manner had been too provoking.

'There! you see,' said Will. 'I'm going to the meeting about the Mechanics' Institute. Good-bye;' and he went quickly out of the room.

Rosamond did not look at her husband, but presently rose and took her place before the tea-tray. She was thinking that she had never seen him so disagreeable. Lydgate turned his dark eyes on her and watched her as she delicately handled the tea-service with her taper fingers, and looked at the objects immediately before her with no curve in her face disturbed, and yet with an ineffable protest in her air against all people with unpleasant manners. For the moment he lost the sense of his wound in a sudden speculation about this new form of feminine impassibility revealing itself in the sylph-like frame which he had once interpreted as the sign of a ready intelligent sensitiveness. His mind glancing back to Laure while he looked at Rosamond, he said inwardly, 'Would *she* kill me because I wearied her?' and then, 'It is the way with all women.' But this power of generalizing which gives men so much the superiority in mistake over the dumb animals, was immediately thwarted by Lydgate's memory of wondering impressions from the behaviour of another woman – from Dorothea's looks and tones of emotion about her husband when Lydgate began to attend him – from her passionate cry to be taught what would best comfort that man for whose sake it seemed as if she must quell every impulse in her except the yearnings of faithfulness and compassion. These revived impressions succeeded each other quickly and dreamily in Lydgate's mind while the tea was being brewed. He had shut his eyes in the last instant of reverie while he heard Dorothea saying, 'Advise me – think what I can do – he has been all his life labouring and looking forward. He minds about nothing else – and I mind about nothing else.'

That voice of deep-souled womanhood had remained within him as the enkindling conceptions of dead and sceptred genius had remained within him (is there not a genius for feeling nobly which also reigns over human spirits and their conclusions?): the tones were a music from which he was falling away – he had really fallen into a momentary doze, when Rosamond said in her silvery neutral way, 'Here is your tea, Tertius,' setting it on the small table by his side, and then moved back to her place without looking at him. Lydgate was too hasty in attributing insensibility to her; after her own fashion, she was sensitive enough, and took lasting impressions. Her impression now was one of offence and repulsion. But then, Rosamond had no scowls and had never raised her voice: she was quite sure that no one could justly find fault with her.

Perhaps Lydgate and she had never felt so far off each other before; but there were strong reasons for not deferring his revelation, even if he had not already begun it by that abrupt announcement; indeed some of the angry desire to rouse her into more sensibility on his account which had prompted him to speak prematurely, still mingled with his pain in the prospect of her pain. But he waited till the tray was gone, the candles were lit, and the evening quiet might be counted on: the interval had left time for repelled tenderness to return into the old course. He spoke kindly.

'Dear Rosy, lay down your work and come and sit by me,' he said, gently, pushing away the table, and stretching out his arm to draw a chair near his own.

Rosamond obeyed. As she came towards him in her drapery of transparent faintly-tinted muslin, her slim yet round figure never looked more graceful; as she sat down by him and laid one hand on the elbow of his chair, at last looking at him and meeting his eyes, her delicate neck and cheek and purely-cut lips never had more of that untarnished beauty which touches us in spring-time and infancy and all sweet freshness. It touched Lydgate now, and mingled the early moments of his love for her with all the other memories which were stirred in this crisis of deep trouble. He laid his ample hand softly on hers, saying –

'Dear!' with the lingering utterance which affection gives to the word. Rosamond too was still under the power of that same past, and her husband was still in part the Lydgate whose approval had stirred delight.

She put his hair lightly away from his forehead, then laid her other hand on his, and was conscious of forgiving him.

'I am obliged to tell you what will hurt you, Rosy. But there are things which husband and wife must think of together. I daresay it has occurred to you already that I am short of money.'

Lydgate paused; but Rosamond turned her neck and looked at a vase on the mantelpiece.

'I was not able to pay for all the things we had to get before we were married, and there have been expenses since which I have been obliged to meet. The consequence is, there is a large debt at Brassing – three hundred and eighty pounds – which has been pressing on me a good while, and in fact we are getting deeper every day, for people don't pay me the faster because others want the money. I took pains to keep it from you while you were not well; but now we must think together about it, and you must help me.'

'What can I do, Tertius?' said Rosamond, turning her eyes on him again. That little speech of four words, like so many others in all languages, is capable by varied vocal inflexions of expressing all states of mind from helpless dimness to exhaustive argumentative perception, from the completest self-devoting fellowship to the most neutral aloofness. Rosamond's thin utterance threw into the words: 'What can I do!' as much neutrality as they could hold. They fell like a mortal chill on Lydgate's roused tenderness. He did not storm in indignation – he felt too sad a sinking of the heart. And when he spoke again it was more in the tone of a man who forces himself to fulfil a task.

'It is necessary for you to know, because I have to give security for a time, and a man must come to make an inventory of the furniture.'

Rosamond coloured deeply. 'Have you not asked papa for money?' she said, as soon as she could speak.

'No.'

'Then I must ask him!' she said, releasing her hands from Lydgate's and rising to stand at two yards distance from him.

'No, Rosy,' said Lydgate, decisively. 'It is too late to do that. The inventory will be begun to-morrow. Remember it is a mere security: it will make no difference: it is a temporary affair. I insist upon it that your father shall not know, unless I choose to tell him,' added Lydgate, with a more peremptory emphasis.

This certainly was unkind, but Rosamond had thrown him back on evil expectation as to what she would do in the way of quiet steady disobedience. The unkindness seemed unpardonable to her: she was not given to weeping and disliked it, but now her chin and lips began to tremble and the tears welled up. Perhaps it was not possible for Lydgate, under the double stress of outward material difficulty and of his own proud resistance to humiliating consequences, to imagine fully what this sudden trial was to a young creature who had known nothing but indulgence, and whose dreams had all been of new indulgence, more exactly to her taste. But he did wish to spare her as much as he could, and her tears cut him to the heart. He could not speak again immediately; but Rosamond did not go on sobbing: she tried to conquer her agitation and wiped away her tears, continuing to look before her at the mantelpiece.

'Try not to grieve, darling,' said Lydgate, turning his eyes up towards her. That she had chosen to move away from him in this moment of her trouble made everything harder to say, but he must absolutely go on. 'We must brace ourselves to do what is necessary. It is I who have been in fault: I ought to have seen that I could not afford to live in this way. But many things have told against me in my practice, and it really just now has ebbed to a low point. I may recover it, but in the meantime we must pull up – we must change our way of living. We shall weather it. When I have given this security I shall have time to look about me; and you are so clever that if you turn your mind to managing you will school me into carefulness. I have been a thoughtless rascal about squaring prices – but come, dear, sit down and forgive me.'

Lydgate was bowing his neck under the yoke like a creature who had talons, but who had Reason too, which often reduces us to meekness. When he had spoken the last words in an imploring tone, Rosamond returned to the chair by his side. His self-blame gave her some hope that he would attend to her opinion, and she said –

'Why can you not put off having the inventory made? You can send the men away to-morrow when they come.'

'I shall not send them away,' said Lydgate, the peremptoriness rising again. Was it of any use to explain?

'If we left Middlemarch, there would of course be a sale, and that would do as well.'

'But we are not going to leave Middlemarch.'

'I am sure, Tertius, it would be much better to do so. Why can we not go to London? Or near Durham, where your family is known?'

'We can go nowhere without money, Rosamond.'

'Your friends would not wish you to be without money. And surely these odious tradesmen might be made to understand that, and to wait, if you would make proper representations to them.'

'This is idle, Rosamond,' said Lydgate angrily. 'You must learn to take my judgment on questions you don't understand. I have made necessary arrangements, and they must be carried out. As to friends, I have no expectations whatever from them, and shall not ask them for anything.'

Rosamond sat perfectly still. The thought in her mind was that if she had known how Lydgate would behave, she would never have married him.

'We have no time to waste now on unnecessary words, dear,' said Lydgate, trying to be gentle again. 'There are some details that I want to consider with you. Dover says he will take a good deal of the plate back again, and any of the jewellery we like. He really behaves·very well.'

'Are we to go without spoons and forks then?' said Rosamond, whose very lips seemed to get thinner with the thinness of her utterance. She was determined to make no further resistance or suggestions.

'Oh no, dear!' said Lydgate. 'But look here,' he continued, drawing a paper from his pocket and opening it; 'here is Dover's account. See, I have marked a number of articles, which if we returned them would reduce the amount by thirty pounds and more. I have not marked any of the jewellery.' Lydgate had really felt this point of the jewellery very bitter to himself; but he had overcome the feeling by severe argument. He could not propose to Rosamond that she return any particular present of his, but he had told himself that he was bound to put Dover's offer before her, and her inward prompting might make the affair easy.

'It is useless for me to look, Tertius,' said Rosamond, calmly; 'you will return what you please.' She would not turn her eyes on the paper, and Lydgate, flushing up to the roots of his hair, drew it back and let it fall on his knee. Meanwhile Rosamond quietly went out of the room, leaving Lydgate helpless and wondering. Was she not coming back? It seemed that she had no more identified herself with him than if they had been creatures of different species and opposing interests. He tossed his head and thrust his hands deep into his pockets with a sort of vengeance. There was still science – there were still good objects to work for. He must give a tug still – all the stronger because other satisfactions were going.

But the door opened and Rosamond re-entered. She carried the leather box containing the amethysts, and a tiny ornamental basket which contained other boxes, and laying them on the chair where she had been sitting, she said, with perfect propriety in her air –

'This is all the jewellery you ever gave me. You can return what you like of it, and of the plate also. You will not, of course, expect me to stay at home to-morrow. I shall go to papa's.'

To many women the look Lydgate cast at her would have been more terrible than one of anger: it had in it a despairing acceptance of the distance she was placing between them.

'And when shall you come back again?' he said, with a bitter edge on his accent.

''Oh, in the evening. Of course I shall not mention the subject to mamma.' Rosamond was convinced that no woman could behave more irreproachably than she was behaving; and she went to sit down at her work-table. Lydgate sat meditating a minute or two, and the result was that he said, with some of the old emotion in his tone –

'Now we have been united, Rosy, you should not leave me to myself in the first trouble that has come.'

'Certainly not,' said Rosamond; 'I shall do everything it becomes me to do.'

'It is not right that the thing should be left to servants, or that I should have to speak to them about it. And I shall be obliged to go out – I don't know how early. I understand your shrinking from the humiliation of these money affairs. But, my dear Rosamond, as a question of pride, which I feel just as much as you can, it is surely better to manage the thing ourselves, and let the servants see as little of it as possible; and since you are my wife, there is no hindering your share in my disgraces – if there were disgraces.'

Rosamond did not answer immediately, but at last she said, 'Very well, I will stay at home.'

'I shall not touch these jewels Rosy. Take them away again. But I will write out a list of plate that we may return, and that can be packed up and sent at once.'

'The servants will know *that*,' said Rosamond, with the slightest touch of sarcasm.

'Well, we must meet some disagreeables as necessities. Where is the ink, I wonder?' said Lydgate, rising, and throwing the account on the larger table where he meant to write.

Rosamond went to reach the inkstand, and after setting it on the table was going to turn away, when Lydgate, who was standing close by, put his arm round her and drew her towards him, saying,

'Come, darling, let us make the best of things. It will only be for a time, I hope, that we shall have to be stingy and particular. Kiss me.'

His native warm-heartedness took a great deal of quenching, and it is a part of manliness for a husband to feel keenly the fact that an inexperienced girl has got into trouble by marrying him. She received his kiss and returned it faintly, and in this way an appearance of accord was recovered for the time. But Lydgate could not help looking forward with dread to the inevitable future discussions about expenditure and the necessity for a complete change in their way of living.

⊘ FIFTY-NINE ⊘

They said of old the Soul had human shape;
But smaller, subtler than the fleshly self,
So wandered forth for airing when it pleased.
And see! beside her cherub-face there floats
A pale-lipped form aerial whispering
Its promptings in that little shell her ear.

NEWS IS OFTEN DISPERSED AS THOUGHTLESSLY and effectively as that pollen which the bees carry off (having no idea how powdery they are) when they are buzzing in search of their particular nectar. This fine comparison has reference to Fred Vincy, who on that evening at Lowick Parsonage heard a lively discussion among the ladies on the news which their old servant had got from Tantripp concerning Mr Casaubon's strange mention of Mr Ladislaw in a codicil to his will made not long before his death. Miss Winifred was astounded to find that her brother had known the fact before, and observed that Camden was the most wonderful man for knowing things and not telling them; whereupon Mary Garth said that the codicil had perhaps got mixed up with the habits of spiders, which Miss Winifred never would listen to. Mrs Farebrother considered that the news had something to do with their having only once seen Mr Ladislaw at Lowick, and Miss Noble made many small compassionate mewings.

Fred knew little and cared less about Ladislaw and the Casaubons, and his mind never recurred to that discussion till one day calling on Rosamond at his mother's request to deliver a message as he passed, he happened to see Ladislaw going away. Fred and Rosamond had little to say to each other now that marriage had removed her from collision with the unpleasantness of brothers. and especially now that he had taken what she held the stupid and even reprehensible step of giving up the Church to take to such a business as Mr Garth's. Hence Fred talked by preference of what he considered indifferent news, and 'à propos of that young Ladislaw' mentioned what he had heard at Lowick Parsonage.

Now Lydgate, like Mr Farebrother, knew a great deal more than he told, and when he had once been set thinking about the relation between Will and Dorothea his conjectures had gone beyond the fact. He imagined that there was a passionate attachment on both sides, and this struck him as much too serious to gossip about. He remembered Will's irritability when he had mentioned Mrs Casaubon, and was the more circumspect.

On the whole his surmises, in addition to what he knew of the fact, increased his friendliness and tolerance towards Ladislaw, and made him understand the vacillation which kept him at Middlemarch after he had said that he should go away. It was significant of the separateness between Lydgate's mind and Rosamond's that he had no impulse to speak to her on the subject; indeed, he did not quite trust her reticence towards Will. And he was right there; though he had no vision of the way in which her mind would act in urging her to speak.

When she had repeated Fred's news to Lydgate, he said, 'Take care you don't drop the faintest hint to Ladislaw, Rosy. He is likely to fly out as if you insulted him. Of course it is a painful affair.'

Rosamond turned her neck and patted her hair, looking the image of placid indifference. But the next time Will came when Lydgate was away, she spoke archly about his not going to London as he had threatened.

'I know all about it. I have a confidential little bird,' said she, showing very pretty airs of her head over the bit of work held high between her active fingers. 'There is a powerful magnet in this neighbourhood.'

'To be sure there is. Nobody knows that better than you,' said Will, with light gallantry, but inwardly prepared to be angry.

'It is really the most charming romance: Mr Casaubon jealous, and foreseeing that there was no one else whom Mrs Casaubon would like so much to marry, and no one who would so much like to marry her as a certain gentleman and then laying a plan to spoil all by making her forfeit her property if she did marry that gentleman – and then – and then – and then – oh, I have no doubt the end will be thoroughly romantic.'

'Great God! what do you mean?' said Will, flushing over face and ears, his features seeming to change as if he had had a violent shake. 'Don't joke; tell me what you mean.'

'You don't really know?' said Rosamond, no longer playful, and desiring nothing better than to tell in order that she might evoke effects.

'No!' he returned, impatiently.

'Don't know that Mr Casaubon has left it in his will that if Mrs Casaubon marries you she is to forfeit all her property?'

'How do you know that it is true?' said Will, eagerly.

'My brother Fred heard it from the Farebrothers.'

Will started up from his chair and reached his hat.

'I daresay she likes you better than the property,' said Rosamond, looking at him from a distance.

'Pray don't say any more about it,' said Will, in a hoarse undertone extremely unlike his usual light voice. 'It is a foul insult to her and to me.' Then he sat down absently, looking before him, but seeing nothing.

'Now you are angry with *me*,' said Rosamond. 'It is too bad to bear *me* malice. You ought to be obliged to me for telling you.'

'So I am,' said Will, abruptly, speaking with that kind of double soul which belongs to dreamers who answer questions.

'I expect to hear of the marriage,' said Rosamond, playfully.

'Never! You will never hear of the marriage!'

With those words uttered impetuously, Will rose, put out his hand to Rosamond, still with the air of a somnambulist, and went away.

When he was gone, Rosamond left her chair and walked to the other end of the room, leaning when she got there against a *chiffonnière*, and looking out of the window wearily. She was oppressed by ennui, and by that dissatisfaction which in women's minds is continually turning into a trivial jealousy, referring to no real claims, springing from no deeper passion than the vague exactingness of egoism, and yet capable of impelling action as well as speech. 'There really is nothing to care for much,' said poor Rosamond inwardly, thinking of the family at Quallingham, who did not write to her; and that perhaps Tertius when he came home would tease her about expenses. She had already secretly disobeyed him by asking her father to help them, and he had ended decisively by saying, 'I am more likely to want help myself.'

ᴄᴊ SIXTY ᴆ

Good phrases are surely, and ever were, very commendable.
JUSTICE SHALLOW

A FEW DAYS AFTERWARDS – IT WAS already the end of August – there was an occasion which caused some excitement in Middlemarch: the public, if it chose, was to have the advantage of buying, under the distinguished auspices of Mr Borthrop Trumbull, the furniture, books, and pictures, which anybody might see by the handbills to be the best in every kind, belonging to Edwin Larcher, Esq. This was not one of the sales indicating the depression of trade; on the contrary, it was due to Mr Larcher's great success in the carrying business, which warranted his purchase of a mansion near Riverston already furnished in high style by an illustrious Spa physician – furnished indeed with such large framefuls of expensive flesh-painting in the dining-room, that Mrs Larcher was nervous until reassured by finding the subjects to be Scriptural. Hence the fine opportunity to purchasers which was well pointed out in the handbills of Mr Borthrop Trumbull, whose acquaintance with the history of art enabled him to state that the hall furniture, to be sold without reserve, comprised a piece of carving by a contemporary of Gibbons.

At Middlemarch in those times a large sale was regarded as a kind of festival. There was a table spread with the best cold eatables, as at a superior funeral; and facilities were offered for that generous drinking of cheerful glasses which might lead to generous and cheerful bidding for undesirable articles. Mr Larcher's sale was the more attractive in the fine weather because the house stood just at the end of the town, with a garden and stables attached, in that pleasant issue from Middlemarch called the London Road, which was also the road to the New Hospital and to Mr Bulstrode's retired residence, known as The Shrubs. In short, the auction was as good as a fair, and drew all classes with leisure at command: to some, who risked making bids in order simply to raise prices, it was almost equal to betting at the races. The second day, when the best furniture was to be sold, 'everybody' was there; even Mr Thesiger, the rector of St Peter's, had looked in for a short time, wishing to buy the carved table, and had rubbed elbows with Mr Bambridge and Mr Horrock. There was a wreath of Middlemarch ladies accommodated with seats round the large table in the dining-room, where Mr Borthrop Trumbull was mounted with desk and hammer; but the rows chiefly of masculine faces behind were often varied by incomings and outgoings both from the door and the large bow-window opening on to the lawn.

'Everybody' that day did not include Mr Bulstrode, whose health could not well endure crowds and draughts. But Mrs Bulstrode had particularly wished to have a certain picture – a *Supper at Emmaus*, attributed in the catalogue to Guido, and at the last moment before the day of the sale Mr Bulstrode had called at the office of the *Pioneer*, of which he was now one of the proprietors, to beg of Mr Ladislaw as a great favour that he would obligingly use his remarkable knowledge of pictures on behalf of Mrs Bulstrode, and judge of the value of this particular painting – 'if,' added the scrupulously polite banker, 'attendance at the sale would not interfere with the arrangements for your departure, which I know is imminent.'

This proviso might have sounded rather satirically in Will's ear if he had been in a mood to care about such satire. It referred to an understanding entered into many weeks before with the proprietors of the paper, that he should be at liberty any day he pleased to hand over the management to the sub-editor whom he had been training; since he wished finally to quit Middlemarch. But indefinite visions of ambition are weak against the ease of doing what is habitual or beguilingly agreeable; and we all know the difficulty of carrying out a resolve when we secretly long that it may turn out to be unnecessary. In such states of mind the most incredulous person has a private leaning towards miracle: impossible to conceive how our wish could be fulfilled, still – very wonderful things have happened! Will did not confess this weakness to himself, but he lingered. What was the use of going to London at that time of the year? The Rugby men who would remember him were not there; and so far as political writing was concerned, he would rather for a few weeks go on with the *Pioneer*. At the present moment, however, when Mr Bulstrode was speaking to him, he had both a strengthened resolve to go and an equally strong resolve not to go till he had once more seen Dorothea. Hence he replied that he had reasons for deferring his departure a little, and would be happy to go to the sale.

Will was in a defiant mood, his consciousness being deeply stung with the thought that the people who looked at him probably knew a fact tantamount to an accusation against him as a fellow with low designs which were to be frustrated by a disposal of property. Like most people who assert their freedom with regard to conventional distinction, he was prepared to be sudden and quick at quarrel with any one who might hint that he had personal reasons for that assertion – that there was anything in his blood, his bearing, or his character to which he gave the mask of an opinion. When he was under an irritating impression of this kind he would go about for days with a defiant look, the colour changing in his transparent skin as if he were on the *qui vive*, watching for something which he had to dart upon.

This expression was peculiarly noticeable in him at the sale, and those who had only seen him in his moods of gentle oddity or of bright enjoyment would have been struck with a contrast. He was not sorry to have this occasion for appearing in public before the Middlemarch tribes of Toller, Hackbutt, and the rest, who looked down on him as an adventurer, and were in a state of brutal ignorance about Dante – who sneered at his Polish blood, and were themselves of a breed very much in need of crossing. He stood in a conspicuous place not far from the auctioneer, with a forefinger in each side-pocket and his head thrown backward, not caring to speak to anybody, though he had been cordially welcomed as a connoissure by Mr Trumbull, who was enjoying the utmost activity of his great faculties.

And surely among all men whose vocation requires them to exhibit their powers of speech, the happiest is a prosperous provincial auctioneer keenly alive to his own jokes and sensible of his encyclopaedic knowledge. Some saturnine, sour-blooded persons might object to be constantly insisting on the merits of all articles from bootjacks to 'Berghems'; but Mr Borthrop Trumbull had a kindly liquid in his veins; he was an admirer by nature, and would have liked to have the universe under his hammer, feeling that it would go at a higher figure for his recommendation.

Meanwhile Mrs Larcher's drawing-room furniture was enough for him. When Will Ladislaw had come in, a second fender, said to have been forgotten in its right place, suddenly claimed the auctioneer's enthusiasm, which he distributed on the equitable principle of praising those things most which were most in need of praise. The fender was of polished steel, with much lancet-shaped open-work and a sharp edge.

'Now, ladies,' said he, 'I shall appeal to you. Here is a fender, which at any other sale would hardly be offered without reserve, being, as I may say, for quality of steel and quaintness of design, a kind of thing' – here Mr Trumbull dropped his voice and became slightly nasal, trimming his outlines with his left finger – 'that might not fall in with ordinary tastes. Allow me to tell you that by-and-by this style of workmanship will be the only one in vogue – half-a-crown, you said? thank you – going at half-a-crown, this characteristic fender; and I have particular information that the antique style is very much sought after in high quarters. Three shillings – three-and-sixpence – hold it well up, Joseph. Look, ladies, at the chastity of the design – I have no doubt myself that it was turned out in the last century! Four shillings, Mr Mawmsey? – four shillings.'

'It's not a thing I would put in *my* drawing-room,' said Mrs Mawmsey, audibly, for the warning of the rash husband. 'I wonder *at* Mrs Larcher. Every blessed child's head that fell against it would be cut in two. The edge is like a knife.'

'Quite true,' rejoined Mr Trumbull, quickly, 'and most uncommonly useful to have a fender at hand that will cut, if you have a leather shoetie or a bit of string that wants cutting and no knife at hand: many a man has been left hanging because there was no knife to cut him down. Gentlemen, here's a fender that if you had the misfortune to hang yourselves would cut you down in no time – with astonishing celerity – four-and-sixpence – five – five-and-sixpence – an appropriate thing for a spare bedroom where there was a four-poster and a guest a little out of his mind – six shillings – thank you, Mr Clintup – going at six shillings – going – gone!' The auctioneer's glance, which had been searching round him with a preternatural susceptibility to all signs of bidding, here dropped on the paper before him, and his voice too dropped into a tone of indifferent despatch as he said, 'Mr Clintup. Be handy, Joseph.'

'It was worth six shillings to have a fender you could always tell that joke on,' said Mr Clintup, laughing low and apologetically to his next neighbour. He was a diffident though distinguished nurseryman, and feared that the audience might regard his bid as a foolish one.

Meanwhile Joseph had brought a trayful of small articles. 'Now, ladies,' said Mr Trumbull, taking up one of the articles, 'this tray contains a very recherchy lot – a collection of trifles for the drawing-room table – and trifles make the sum of human things – nothing more important than trifles – (yes, Mr Ladislaw, yes, by-and-by) – but pass the tray round, Joseph – these bijoux must be examined, ladies. This I have in my hand is an ingenious contrivance – a sort of practical rebus I may call it: here, you see, it looks like an elegant heart-shaped box, portable – for the pocket; there, again, it becomes like a splendid double flower – an ornament for the table; and now' – Mr Trumbull allowed the flower to fall alarmingly into strings of heart-shaped leaves – 'a book of riddles! No less than five hundred printed in a beautiful red. Gentlemen, if I had less of a conscience, I should not wish you to bid high for this lot – I have a longing for it myself. What can promote innocent mirth, and I may say virtue, more than a good riddle? – it hinders profane language, and attaches a man to the society of refined females. This ingenious article itself, without the elegant domino-box, card-basket, &c., ought alone to give a high price to the lot. Carried in the pocket it might make an individual welcome in any society. Four shillings, sir? – four shillings for this remarkable collection of riddles with the et ceteras. Here is a sample: "How must you spell honey to make it catch lady-birds? Answer – money." You hear? – lady-birds – honey – money. This is an amusement to sharpen the intellect: it has a sting – it has what we call satire, and wit without indecency. Four-and-sixpence – five shillings.'

The bidding ran on with warming rivalry, Mr Bowyer was a bidder, and this was too exasperating. Bowyer couldn't afford it, and only wanted to hinder every other man from making a figure. The current carried even Mr Horrock with it, but this committal of himself to an opinion fell from him with so little sacrifice of his neutral expression, that the bid might not have been detected as his but for the friendly oaths of Mr Bambridge, who wanted to know what Horrock would do with the blasted stuff only fit for haberdashers given over to that state of perdition which the horse-dealer so cordially recognized in the majority of earthly existences. The lot was finally knocked down at a guinea to Mr Spilkins, a young Slender of the neighbourhood, who was reckless with his pocket-money and felt his want of memory for riddles.

'Come, Trumbull, this is too bad – you've been putting some old maid's rubbish into the sale,' murmured Mr Toller, getting close to the auctioneer. 'I want to see how the prints go, and I must be off soon.'

'Immediately, Mr Toller. It was only an act of benevolence which your noble heart would approve. Joseph! quick with the prints – Lot 235. Now, gentlemen, you who are connoissures, you are going to have a treat. Here is an engraving of the Duke of Wellington surrounded by his staff on the Field of Waterloo: and notwithstanding recent events which have, as it were, enveloped our great Hero in a cloud, I will be bold to say – for a man in my line must not be blown about by political winds – that a finer subject – of the modern order, belonging to our own time and epoch – the understanding of man could hardly conceive: angels might, perhaps, but not men, sirs, not men.'

'Who painted it?' said Mr Powderell, much impressed.

'It is a proof before the letter, Mr Powderell – the painter is not known,' answered Trumbull, with a certain gaspingness in his last words, after which he pursed up his lips and stared round him.

'I'll bid a pound!' said Mr Powderell, in a tone of resolved emotion, as of a man ready to put himself in the breach. Whether from awe or pity, nobody raised the price on him.

Next came two Dutch prints which Mr Toller had been eager for, and after he had secured them he went away. Other prints, and afterwards some paintings, were sold to leading Middlemarchers who had come with a special desire for them, and there was a more active movement of the audience in and out; some who had bought what they wanted, going away, others coming in either quite newly or from a temporary visit to the refreshments which were spread under the marquee on the lawn. It was this marquee that Mr Bambridge was bent on buying, and he appeared to like looking inside it frequently, as a foretaste of its possession. On the last occasion of his return from it he was observed to bring with him a new companion, a stranger to Mr Trumbull and every one else, whose appearance, however, led to the supposition that he might be a relative of the horse-dealer's – also 'given to indulgence'. His large whiskers, imposing swagger, and swing of the leg, made him a striking figure; but his suit of black, rather shabby at the edges, caused the prejudicial inference that he was not able to afford himself as much indulgence as he liked.

'Who is it you've picked up, Bam?' said Mr Horrock, aside.

'Ask him yourself,' returned Mr Bambridge. 'He said he'd just turned in from the road.'

Mr Horrock eyed the stranger, who was leaning back against his stick with one hand, using his toothpick with the other, and looking about him with a certain restlessness apparently under the silence imposed on him by circumstances.

At length the *Supper at Emmaus* was brought forward, to Will's immense relief, for he was getting so tired of the proceedings that he had drawn back a little and leaned his shoulder against the wall just behind the auctioneer. He now came forward again, and his eye caught the conspicuous stranger, who, rather to his surprise, was staring at him markedly. But Will was immediately appealed to by Mr Trumbull.

'Yes, Mr Ladislaw, yes; this interests you as a connoi*ssure*, I think. It is some pleasure,' the auctioneer went on with a rising fervour, 'to have a picture like this to show to a company of ladies and gentlemen – a picture worth any sum to an individual whose means were on a level with his judgment. It is a painting of the Italian school – by the celebrated *Guydo*, the greatest painter in the world, the chief of the Old Masters, as they are called – I take it, because they were up to a thing or two beyond most of us – in possession of secrets now lost to the bulk of mankind. Let me tell you, gentlemen, I have seen a great many pictures by the Old Masters, and they are not all up to this mark – some of them are darker than you might like, and not family subjects. But here is a *Guydo* – the frame alone is worth pounds – which any lady might be proud to hang up – a suitable thing for what we call a refectory in a charitable institution, if any gentleman of the Corporation wished to show his munifi*cence*. Turn it a little, sir? yes. Joseph, turn it a little to Mr Ladislaw – Mr Ladislaw, having been abroad, understands the merit of these things, you observe.'

All eyes were for a moment turned towards Will, who said, coolly, 'Five pounds.' The auctioneer burst out in deep remonstrance –

'Ah! Mr Ladislaw! the frame alone is worth that. Ladies and gentlemen, for the credit of the town! Suppose it should be discovered hereafter that a gem of art has been amongst us in this town, and nobody in Middlemarch

awake to it. Five guineas – five seven-six – five ten. Still, ladies, still! It is a
gem, and "Full many a gem", as the poet says, has been allowed to go at
a nominal price because the public knew no better, because it was offered
in circles where there was – I was going to say a low feeling, but no! – Six
pounds – six guineas – a *Guydo* of the first order going at six guineas – it is
an insult to religion, ladies; it touches us all as Christians, gentlemen, that
a subject like this should go at such a low figure – six pounds ten –
seven – .'

The bidding was brisk, and Will continued to share in it, remembering
that Mrs Bulstrode had a strong wish for the picture, and thinking that he
might stretch the price to twelve pounds. But it was knocked down to him
at ten guineas, whereupon he pushed his way towards the bow-window
and went out. He chose to go under the marquee to get a glass of water,
being hot and thirsty: it was empty of other visitors, and he asked the
woman in attendance to fetch him some fresh water; but before she was
well gone he was annoyed to see entering the florid stranger who had
stared at him. It struck Will at this moment that the man might be one of
those political parasitic insects of the bloated kind who had once or twice
claimed acquaintance with him as having heard him speak on the Reform
question, and who might think of getting a shilling by news. In this light
his person, already rather heating to behold on a summer's day appeared
the more disagreeable, and Will, half-seated on the elbow of a garden-
chair, turned his eyes carefully away from the corner. But this signified
little to our acquaintance Mr Raffles, who never hesitated to thrust himself
on unwilling observation, if it suited his purpose to do so. He moved a
step or two till he was in front of Will, and said with full-mouthed haste,
'Excuse me, Mr Ladislaw – was your mother's name Sarah Dunkirk?'

Will, starting to his feet, moved backward a step, frowning and saying
with some fierceness, 'Yes, sir, it was. And what is that to you?'

It was in Will's nature that the first spark it threw out was a direct
answer of the question and a challenge of the consequences. To have said,
'What is that to you?' in the first instance, would have seemed like shuffling – as if he minded who knew anything about his origin!

Raffles on his side had not the same eagerness for a collision which was
implied in Ladislaw's threatening air. The slim young fellow with his
girl's complexion looked like a tiger-cat ready to spring on him. Under
such circumstances Mr Raffles's pleasure in annoying his company was
kept in abeyance.

'No offence, my good sir, no offence; I only remember your mother –
knew her when she was a girl. But it is your father that you feature, sir. I
had the pleasure of seeing your father too. Parents alive, Mr Ladislaw?'

'No!' thundered Will, in the same attitude as before.

'Should be glad to do you a service, Mr Ladislaw – by Jove, I should!
Hope to meet again.'

Hereupon Raffles, who had lifted his hat with the last words, turned himself round with a swing of his leg and walked away. Will looked after him a moment, and could see that he did not re-enter the auction room, but appeared to be walking towards the road. For an instant he thought that he had been foolish not to let the man go on talking; – but no! on the whole he preferred doing without knowledge from that source.

Later in the evening, however, Raffles overtook him in the street, and appearing either to have forgotten the roughness of his former reception or to intend avenging it by a forgiving familiarity, greeted him jovially and walked by his side, remarking at first on the pleasantness of the town and neighbourhood. Will at first suspected that the man had been drinking and was considering how to shake him off when Raffles said –

'I've been abroad myself, Mr Ladislaw – I've seen the world – used to parley-vous a little. It was at Boulogne I saw your father – a most uncommon likeness you are of him, by Jove! mouth – nose – eyes – hair turned off your brow just like this – a little in the foreign style. John Bull doesn't do much of that. But your father was very ill when I saw him. Lord, lord! hands you might see through. You were a small youngster, then. Did he get well?'

'No,' said Will, curtly.

'Ah! Well! I've often wondered what became of your mother. She ran away from her friends when she was a young lass – a proud-spirited lass, and pretty, by Jove! *I* knew the reason why she ran away,' said Raffles, winking slowly as he looked sideways at Will.

'You know nothing dishonourable of her, sir,' said Will, turning on him rather savagely. But Mr Raffles just now was not sensitive to shades of manner.

'Not a bit!' said he, tossing his head decisively. 'She was a little too honourable to like her friends – that was it!' Here Raffles again winked slowly. 'Lord bless you, I knew all about 'em – a little in what you may call the respectable thieving line – the high style of receiving-house – none of your holes and corners – first-rate. Slap-up shop, high profits and no mistake. But Lord! Sarah would have known nothing about it – a dashing young lady she was – fine boarding-school – fit for a lord's wife – only Archie Duncan threw it at her out of spite, because she would have nothing to do with him. And so she ran away from the whole concern. I travelled for 'em, sir, in a gentlemanly way – at a high salary. They didn't mind her running away at first – godly folk, sir, very godly – and she was for the stage. The son was alive then, and the daughter was at a discount. Hallo! here we are at the Blue Bull. What do you say, Mr Ladislaw? shall we turn in and have a glass?'

'No, I must say good evening,' said Will; dashing up a passage which led to Lowick Gate, and almost running to get out of Raffles's reach.

He walked a long while on the Lowick Road away from the town, glad of the starlit darkness when it came. He felt as if he had had dirt cast on him amidst shouts of scorn. There was this to confirm the fellow's statement – that his mother never would tell him the reason why she had run away from her family.

Well! what was he, Will Ladislaw, the worse, supposing the truth about that family to be the ugliest? His mother had braved hardship in order to separate herself from it. But if Dorothea's friends had known this story – if the Chettams had known it – they would have had a fine colour to give their suspicions, a welcome ground for thinking him unfit to come near her. However, let them suspect what they pleased, they would find themselves in the wrong. They would find out that the blood in his veins was as free from the taint of meanness as theirs.

CR SIXTY-ONE ℅

*'Inconsistencies,' answered Imlac, 'cannot both be right,
but imputed to man they may both be true.'*

RASSELAS

THE SAME NIGHT, WHEN MR BULSTRODE returned from a journey to Brassing on business, his good wife met him in the entrance-hall and drew him into his private sitting-room.

'Nicholas,' she said, fixing her honest eyes upon him anxiously, 'there has been such a disagreeable man here asking for you – it has made me quite uncomfortable.'

'What kind of man, my dear?' said Mr Bulstrode, dreadfully certain of the answer.

'A red-faced man with large whiskers, and most impudent in his manner. He declared he was an old friend of yours, and said you would be sorry not to see him. He wanted to wait for you here, but I told him he could see you at the Bank to-morrow. Most impudent he was! – stared at me, and said his friend Nick had luck in wives. I don't believe he would have gone away if Blucher had not happened to break his chain and come running round on the gravel – for I was in the garden; so I said, "You'd better go away – the dog is very fierce, and I can't hold him." Do you really know anything of such a man?'

'I believe I know who he is, my dear,' said Bulstrode, in his usual subdued voice, 'an unfortunate, dissolute wretch, whom I helped too much in days gone by. However, I presume you will not be troubled by him again. He will probably come to the Bank – to beg, doubtless.'

No more was said on the subject until the next day, when Mr Bulstrode had returned from the town and was dressing for dinner. His wife, not sure that he was come home, looked into his dressing-room and saw him with his coat and cravat off, leaning one arm on a chest of drawers and staring absently at the ground. He started nervously and looked up as she entered.

'You look very ill, Nicholas. Is there anything the matter?'

'I have a good deal of pain in my head,' said Mr Bulstrode, who was so frequently ailing that his wife was always ready to believe in this cause of depression.

'Sit down and let me sponge it with vinegar.'

Physically Mr Bulstrode did not want the vinegar, but morally the affectionate attention soothed him. Though always polite, it was his habit to receive such services with marital coolness, as his wife's duty. But to-day, while she was bending over him, he said, 'You are very good, Harriet,' in a tone which had something new in it to her ear; she did not know exactly what the novelty was, but her woman's solicitude shaped itself into a darting thought that he might be going to have an illness.

'Has anything worried you?' she said. 'Did that man come to you at the Bank?'

'Yes; it was as I had supposed. He is a man who at one time might have done better. But he has sunk into a drunken debauched creature.'

'Is he quite gone away?' said Mrs Bulstrode, anxiously; but for certain reasons she refrained from adding, 'it was very disagreeable to hear him calling himself a friend of yours.' At that moment she would not have liked to say anything which implied her habitual consciousness that her husband's earlier connections were not quite on a level with her own. Not that she knew much about them. That her husband had at first been employed in a bank, that he had afterwards entered into what he called city business and gained a fortune before he was three-and-thirty, that he had married a widow who was much older than himself – a Dissenter, and in other ways probably of that disadvantageous quality usually perceptible in a first wife if inquired into with the dispassionate judgment of a second – was almost as much as she had cared to learn beyond the glimpses which Mr Bulstrode's narrative occasionally gave of his early bent towards religion, his inclination to be a preacher, and his association with missionary and philanthropic efforts. She believed in him as an excellent man whose piety carried a peculiar eminence in belonging to a layman, whose influence had turned her own mind towards seriousness, and whose share of perishable good had been the means of raising her own position. But she also liked to think that it was well in every sense for Mr Bulstrode to have won the hand of Harriet Vincy; whose family was undeniable in a Middlemarch light – a better light surely than any thrown in London thoroughfares or dissenting chapel-yards. The unreformed provincial mind distrusted London; and while true religion was everywhere saving, honest Mrs Bulstrode was convinced that to be saved in the Church was more respectable. She so much wished to ignore towards others that her husband had ever been a London Dissenter, that she liked to keep it out of sight even in talking to him. He was quite aware of this; indeed in some respects he was rather afraid of this ingenuous wife, whose imitative piety and native worldliness were equally sincere, who had nothing to be ashamed of, and whom he had married out of a thorough inclination still subsisting. But his fears were such as belong to a man who cares to maintain his recognized supremacy: the loss of high consideration from his wife as from every one else who did not clearly hate him out of enmity to the truth, would be as the beginning of death to him. When she said –

'Is he quite gone away?'

'Oh, I trust so,' he answered, with an effort to throw as much sober unconcern into his tone as possible.

But in truth Mr Bulstrode was very far from a state of quiet trust. In the interview at the Bank, Raffles had made it evident that his eagerness to torment was almost as strong in him as any other greed. He had frankly said that he had turned out of the way to come to Middlemarch, just to look about him and see whether the neighbourhood would suit him to live in. He had certainly had a few debts to pay more than he expected, but the two hundred pounds were not gone yet: a cool five-and-twenty would suffice him to go away with for the present. What he had wanted chiefly was to see his friend Nick and family, and know all about the prosperity of a man to whom he was so much attached. By-and-by he might come back for a longer stay. This time Raffles declined to be 'seen off the premises', as he expressed it – declined to quit Middlemarch under Bulstrode's eyes. He meant to go by coach the next day – if he chose.

Bulstrode felt himself helpless. Neither threats nor coaxing could avail: he could not count on any persistent fear nor on any promise. On the contrary, he felt a cold certainty at his heart that Raffles – unless providence sent death to hinder him – would come back to Middlemarch before long. And that certainty was a terror.

It was not that he was in danger of legal punishment or of beggary: he was in danger only of seeing disclosed to the judgment of his neighbours and the mournful perception of his wife certain facts of his past life which would render him an object of scorn and an opprobrium of the religion with which he had diligently associated himself. The terror of being judged sharpens the memory: it sends an inevitable glare over that long-unvisited past which has been habitually recalled only in general phrases. Even without memory, the life is bound into one by a zone of dependence in growth and decay: but intense memory forces a man to own his blame-worthy past. With memory set smarting like a reopened wound, a man's past is not simply a dead history, an outworn preparation of the present: it is not a repented error shaken loose from the life: it is a still quivering part of himself, bringing shudders and bitter flavours and the tinglings of a merited shame.

Into this second life Bulstrode's past had now risen, only the pleasures of it seeming to have lost their quality. Night and day, without interruption save of brief sleep which only wove retrospect and fear into a fantastic present, he felt the scenes of his earlier life coming between him and everything else, as obstinately as when we look through the window from a lighted room, the objects we turn our backs on are still before us, instead of the grass and the trees. The successive events inward and outward were there in one view: though each might be dwelt on in turn, the rest still kept their hold in the consciousness.

Once more he saw himself the young banker's clerk, with an agreeable person, as clever in figures as he was fluent in speech and fond of theological definition: an eminent though young member of a Calvinistic dissenting church at Highbury, having had striking experience in conviction of sin and sense of pardon. Again he heard himself called for as Brother Bulstrode in prayer meetings, speaking on religious platforms, preaching in private houses. Again he felt himself thinking of the ministry as possibly his vocation, and inclined towards missionary labour. That was the happiest time of his life: that was the spot he would have chosen now to awake in and find the rest a dream. The people among whom Brother Bulstrode was distinguished were very few, but they were very near to him, and stirred his satisfaction the more; his power stretched through a narrow space, but he felt its effect the more intensely. He believed without effort in the peculiar work of grace within him, and in the signs that God intended him for special instrumentality.

Then came the moment of transition; it was with the sense of promotion he had when he, an orphan educated at a commercial charity-school, was invited to a fine villa belonging to Mr Dunkirk, the richest man in the congregation. Soon he became an intimate there, honoured for his piety by the wife, marked out for his ability by the husband, whose wealth was due to a flourishing city and west-end trade. That was the setting-in of a new current for his ambition, directing his prospects of 'instrumentality' towards the uniting of distinguished religious gifts with successful business.

By-and-by came a decided external leading: a confidential subordinate partner died, and nobody seemed to the principal so well fitted to fill the severely-felt vacancy as his young friend Bulstrode, if he would become confidential accountant. The offer was accepted. The business was a pawnbroker's, of the most magnificent sort both in extent and profits; and on a short acquaintance with it Bulstrode became aware that one source of magnificent profit was the easy reception of any goods offered without strict inquiry as to where they came from. But there was a branch house at the west end, and no pettiness or dinginess to give suggestions of shame.

He remembered his first moments of shrinking. They were private, and were filled with arguments; some of these taking the form of prayer. The business was established and had old roots; is it not one thing to set up a new gin-palace and another to accept an investment in an old one? The profits made out of lost souls – where can the line be drawn at which they begin in human transactions? Was it not even God's way of saving His chosen? 'Thou knowest,' – the young Bulstrode had said then, as the older Bulstrode was saying now – 'Thou knowest how loose my soul sits from these things – how I view them all as implements for tilling Thy garden rescued here and there from the wilderness.'

Metaphors and precedents were not wanting; peculiar spiritual experiences were not wanting which at last made the retention of his position seem a service demanded of him: the vista of a fortune had already opened itself, and Bulstrode's shrinking remained private. Mr Dunkirk had never expected that there would be any shrinking at all: he had never conceived that trade had anything to do with the scheme of salvation. And it was true that Bulstrode found himself carrying on two distinct lives; his religious activity could not be incompatible with his business as soon as he had argued himself into not feeling it incompatible.

Mentally surrounded with that past again, Bulstrode had the same pleas – indeed, the years had been perpetually spinning them into intricate thickness, like masses of spider-web, padding the moral sensibility; nay, as age made egoism more eager but less enjoying, his soul had become more saturated with the belief that he did everything for God's sake, being indifferent to it for his own. And yet – if he could be back in that far-off spot with his youthful poverty – why, then he would choose to be a missionary.

But the train of causes in which he had locked himself went on. There was trouble in the fine villa at Highbury. Years before, the only daughter had run away, defied her parents, and gone on the stage; and now the only boy died, and after a short time Mr Dunkirk died also. The wife, a simple pious woman, left with all the wealth in and out of the magnificent trade, of which she never knew the precise nature, had come to believe in Bulstrode, and innocently adore him as women often adore their priest or 'man-made' minister. It was natural that after a time marriage should have been thought of between them. But Mrs Dunkirk had qualms and yearnings about her daughter, who had long been regarded as lost both to God and her parents. It was known that the daughter had married, but she was utterly gone out of sight. The mother, having lost her boy, imagined a grandson, and wished in a double sense to reclaim her daughter. If she were found, there would be a channel for property – perhaps a wide one, in the provision for several grandchildren. Efforts to find her must be made before Mrs Dunkirk would marry again. Bulstrode concurred; but after advertisement as well as other modes of inquiry had been tried, the mother believed that her daughter was not to be found, and consented to marry without reservation of property.

The daughter had been found; but only one man besides Bulstrode knew it, and he was paid for keeping silence and carrying himself away.

That was the bare fact which Bulstrode was now forced to see in the rigid outline with which acts present themselves to onlookers. But for himself at that distant time, and even now in burning memory, the fact was broken into little sequences, each justified as it came by reasonings which seemed to prove it righteous. Bulstrode's course up to that time had, he thought, been sanctioned by remarkable providences, appearing to point the way for him to be the agent in making the best use of a large property and withdrawing it from perversion. Death and other striking dispositions, such as feminine trustfulness, had come, and Bulstrode would have adopted Cromwell's words – 'Do you call these bare events? The Lord pity you!' The events were comparatively small, but the essential condition was there – namely, that they were in favour of his own ends. It was easy for him to settle what was due from him to others by inquiring what were God's intentions with regard to himself. Could it be for God's service that this fortune should in any considerable proportion go to a young woman and her husband who were given up to the lightest pursuits, and might scatter it abroad in triviality – people who seemed to lie outside the path of remarkable providences? Bulstrode had never said to himself beforehand, 'The daughter shall not be found' – nevertheless when the moment came he kept her existence hidden; and when other moments followed, he soothed the mother with consolation in the probability that the unhappy young woman might be no more.

There were hours in which Bulstrode felt that his action was unrighteous; but how could he go back? He had mental exercises, called himself nought, laid hold on redemption, and went on in his course of instrumentality. And after five years Death again came to widen his path, by taking away his wife. He did gradually withdraw his capital, but he did not make the sacrifices requisite to put an end to the business, which was carried on for thirteen years afterwards before it finally collapsed. Meanwhile Nicholas Bulstrode had used his hundred thousand discreetly, and was becoming provincially, solidly important – a banker, a Churchman, a public benefactor; also a sleeping partner in trading concerns, in which his ability was directed to economy in the raw material, as in the case of the dyes which rotted Mr Vincy's silk. And now, when this respectability had lasted undisturbed for nearly thirty years – when all that preceded it had long lain benumbed in the consciousness – that past had risen and immersed his thoughts as if with the terrible irruption of a new sense overburthening the feeble being.

Meanwhile, in his conversation with Raffles, he had learned something momentous, something which entered actively into the struggle of his longings and terrors. There, he thought, lay an opening towards spiritual, perhaps towards material rescue.

The spiritual kind of rescue was a genuine need with him. There may be coarse hypocrites, who consciously affect beliefs and emotions for the sake of gulling the world, but Bulstrode was not one of them. He was simply a man whose desires had been stronger than his theoretic beliefs, and who had gradually explained the gratification of his desires into satisfactory agreement with those beliefs. If this be hypocrisy, it is a process which shows itself occasionally in us all, to whatever confession we belong, and whether we believe in the future perfection of our race or in the nearest date fixed for the end of the world; whether we regard the earth as a putrefying nidus for a saved remnant, including ourselves, or have a passionate belief in the solidarity of mankind.

The service he could do to the cause of religion had been through life the ground he alleged to himself for his choice of action: it had been the motive which he had poured out in his prayers. Who would use money and position better than he meant to use them? Who could surpass him in self-abhorrence and exaltation of God's cause? And to Mr Bulstrode God's cause was something distinct from his own rectitude of conduct: it enforced a discrimination of God's enemies, who were to be used merely as instruments, and whom it would be well if possible to keep out of money and consequent influence. Also, profitable investments in trades where the power of the prince of this world showed its most active devices, became sanctified by a right application of the profits in the hands of God's servant.

This implicit reasoning is essentially no more peculiar to evangelical belief than the use of wide phrases for narrow motives is peculiar to Englishmen. There is no general doctrine which is not capable of eating out our morality if unchecked by the deep-seated habit of direct fellow-feeling with individual fellow-men.

But a man who believes in something else than his own greed, has necessarily a conscience or standard to which he more or less adapts himself. Bulstrode's standard had been his serviceableness to God's cause: 'I am sinful and nought – a vessel to be consecrated by use – but use me!' – had been the mould into which he had constrained his immense need of being something important and predominating. And now had come a moment in which that mould seemed in danger of being broken and utterly cast away.

What if the acts he had reconciled himself to, because they made him a stronger instrument of the divine glory, were to become the pretext of the scoffer, and a darkening of that glory? If this were to be the ruling of Providence, he was cast out from the temple as one who had brought unclean offerings.

He had long poured out utterances of repentance. But to-day a repentance had come which was of a bitterer flavour, and a threatening Providence urged him to a kind of propitiation which was not simply a doctrinal transaction. The divine tribunal had changed its aspect for him; self-prostration was no longer enough, and he must bring restitution in his hand. It was really before his God that Bulstrode was about to attempt such restitution as seemed possible: a great dread had seized his susceptible frame, and the scorching approach of shame wrought in him a new spiritual need. Night and day, while the resurgent threatening past was making a conscience within him, he was thinking by what means he could recover peace and trust – by what sacrifice he could stay the rod. His belief in these moments of dread was, that if he spontaneously did something right, God would save him from the consequences of wrong-doing. For religion can only change when the emotions which fill it are changed; and the religion of personal fear remains nearly at the level of the savage.

He had seen Raffles actually going away on the Brassing coach, and this was a temporary relief; it removed the pressure of an immediate dread, but did not put an end to the spiritual conflict and the need to win protection. At last he came to a difficult resolve, and wrote a letter to Will Ladislaw, begging him to be at The Shrubs that evening for a private interview at nine o'clock. Will had felt no particular surprise at the request, and connected it with some new notions about the *Pioneer*; but when he was shown into Mr Bulstrode's private room, he was struck with the painfully worn look on the banker's face, and was going to say, 'Are you ill?' when, checking himself in that abruptness, he only inquired after Mrs Bulstrode, and her satisfaction with the picture bought for her.

'Thank you, she is quite satisfied; she has gone out with her daughters this evening. I begged you to come, Mr Ladislaw, because I have a com-munication of a very private – indeed, I will say, of a sacredly confidential nature, which I desire to make to you. Nothing, I daresay, has been farther from your thoughts than that there had been important ties in the past which could connect your history with mine.'

Will felt something like an electric shock. He was already in a state of keen sensitiveness and hardly allayed agitation on the subject of ties in the past, and his presentiments were not agreeable. It seemed like the fluctuations of a dream – as if the action begun by that loud bloated stranger were being carried on by this pale-eyed sickly-looking piece of respectability, whose subdued tone and glib formality of speech were at this moment almost as repulsive to him as their remembered contrast. He answered, with a marked change of colour –

'No, indeed, nothing.'

'You see before you, Mr Ladislaw, a man who is deeply stricken. But for the urgency of conscience and the knowledge that I am before the bar of One who seeth not as man seeth, I should be under no compulsion to make the disclosure which has been my object in asking you to come here to-night. So far as human laws go, you have no claim on me whatever.'

Will was even more uncomfortable than wondering. Mr Bulstrode had paused, leaning his head on his hand, and looking at the floor. But he now fixed his examining glance on Will and said –

'I am told that your mother's name was Sarah Dunkirk, and that she ran away from her friends to go on the stage. Also, that your father was at one time much emaciated by illness. May I ask if you can confirm these statements?'

'Yes, they are all true,' said Will, struck with the order in which an inquiry had come, that might have been expected to be preliminary to the banker's hints. But Mr Bulstrode had tonight followed the order of his emotions; he entertained no doubt that the opportunity for restitution had come, and he had an overpowering impulse towards the penitential expression by which he was deprecating chastisement.

'Do you know any particulars of your mother's family?' he continued.

'No; she never liked to speak of them. She was a very generous, honourable woman,' said Will, almost angrily.

'I do not wish to allege anything against her. Did she never mention her mother to you at all?'

'I have heard her say that she thought her mother did not know the reason of her running away. She said "poor mother" in a pitying tone.'

'That mother became my wife,' said Bulstrode, and then paused a moment before he added, 'you have a claim on me, Mr Ladislaw: as I said before, not a legal claim, but one which my conscience recognizes. I was enriched by that marriage – a result which would probably not have taken place – certainly not to the same extent – if your grandmother could have discovered her daughter. That daughter, I gather, is no longer living!'

'No,' said Will, feeling suspicion and repugnance rising so strongly within him, that without quite knowing what he did, he took his hat from the floor and stood up. The impulse within him was to reject the disclosed connection.

'Pray be seated, Mr Ladislaw,' said Bulstrode, anxiously. 'Doubtless you are startled by the suddenness of this discovery. But I entreat your patience with one who is already bowed down by inward trial.'

Will reseated himself, feeling some pity which was half contempt for this voluntary self-abasement of an elderly man.

'It is my wish, Mr Ladislaw, to make amends for the deprivation which befell your mother. I know that you are without fortune, and I wish to supply you adequately from a store which would have probably already been yours had your grandmother been certain of your mother's existence and been able to find her.'

Mr Bulstrode paused. He felt that he was performing a striking piece of scrupulosity in the judgment of his auditor, and a penitential act in the eyes of God. He had no clue to the state of Will Ladislaw's mind, smarting as it was from the clear hint of Raffles, and with its natural quickness in construction stimulated by the expectation of discoveries which he would have been glad to conjure back into darkness. Will made no answer for several moments, till Mr Bulstrode, who at the end of his speech had cast his eyes on the floor, now raised them with an examining glance, which Will met fully, saying –

'I suppose you did know of my mother's existence, and knew where she might have been found.'

Bulstrode shrank – there was a visible quivering in his face and hands. He was totally unprepared to have his advances met in this way, or to find himself urged into more revelation than he had beforehand set down as needful. But at that moment he dared not tell a lie, and he felt suddenly uncertain of his ground which he had trodden with some confidence before.

'I will not deny that you conjecture rightly,' he answered, with a faltering in his tone. 'And I wish to make atonement to you as the one still remaining who has suffered a loss through me. You enter, I trust, into my purpose, Mr Ladislaw, which has a reference to higher than merely human claims, and as I have already said, is entirely independent of any legal compulsion. I am ready to narrow my own resources and the prospects of my family by binding myself to allow you five hundred pounds yearly during my life, and to leave you a proportional capital at my death – nay, to do still more, if more should be definitely necessary to any laudable project on your part.' Mr Bulstrode had gone on to particulars in the expectation that these would work strongly on Ladislaw, and merge other feelings in grateful acceptance.

But Will was looking as stubborn as possible, with his lip pouting and his fingers in his side-pockets. He was not in the least touched, and said firmly –

'Before I make any reply to your proposition, Mr Bulstrode, I must beg you to answer a question or two. Were you connected with the business by which that fortune you speak of was originally made?'

Mr Bulstrode's thought was, 'Raffles has told him.' How could he refuse to answer when he had volunteered what drew forth the question? He answered, 'Yes.'

'And was that business – or was it not – a thoroughly dishonourable one – nay, one that, if its nature had been made public, might have ranked those concerned in it with thieves and convicts?'

Will's tone had a cutting bitterness: he was moved to put his question as nakedly as he could.

Bulstrode reddened with irrepressible anger. He had been prepared for a scene of self-abasement, but his intense pride and his habit of supremacy overpowered penitence, and even dread, when this young man, whom he had meant to benefit, turned on him with the air of a judge.

'The business was established before I became acquainted with it, sir; nor is it for you to institute an inquiry of that kind,' he answered, not raising his voice, but speaking with quick defiantness.

'Yes, it is,' said Will, starting up again with his hat in his hand. 'It is eminently mine to ask such questions, when I have to decide whether I will have transactions with you and accept your money. My unblemished honour is important to me. It is important to me to have no stain on my birth and connections. And now I find there is a stain which I can't help. My mother felt it, and tried to keep as clear of it as she could, and so will I. You shall keep your ill-gotten money. If I had any fortune of my own, I would willingly pay it to any one who could disprove what you have told me. What I have to thank you for is that you kept the money till now, when I can refuse it. It ought to lie with a man's self that he is a gentleman. Good-night, sir.'

Bulstrode was going to speak, but Will with determined quickness was out of the room in an instant, and in another the hall-door had closed behind him. He was too strongly possessed with passionate rebellion against this inherited blot which had been thrust on his knowledge to reflect at present whether he had not been too hard on Bulstrode – too arrogantly merciless towards a man of sixty, who was making efforts at retrieval when time had rendered them in vain.

No third person listening could have thoroughly understood the impetuosity of Will's repulse or the bitterness of his words. No one but himself then knew how everything connected with the sentiment of his own dignity had an immediate bearing for him on his relation to Dorothea and to Mr Casaubon's treatment of him. And in the rush of impulses by which he flung back that offer of Bulstrode's, there was mingled the sense that it would have been impossible for him ever to tell Dorothea that he had accepted it.

As for Bulstrode – when Will was gone he suffered a violent reaction, and wept like a woman. It was the first time he had encountered an open expression of scorn from any man higher than Raffles; and with that scorn hurrying like venom through his system, there was no sensibility left to consolations. But the relief of weeping had to be checked. His wife and daughters soon came home from hearing the address of an Oriental missionary, and were full of regret that papa had not heard, in the first instance, the interesting things which they tried to repeat to him.

Perhaps, through all other hidden thoughts, the one that breathed most comfort, was that Will Ladislaw at least was not likely to publish what had taken place that evening.

♂ SIXTY-TWO ♀

He was a squyer of lowe degre,
That loved the king's daughter of Hungrie.
Old Romance

WILL LADISLAW'S MIND WAS NOW WHOLLY bent on seeing Dorothea again,
and forthwith quitting Middlemarch. The morning after his agitating
scene with Bulstrode he wrote a brief letter to her, saying that various
causes had detained him in the neighbourhood longer than he had
expected, and asking her permission to call again at Lowick at some hour
which she would mention on the earliest possible day, he being anxious to
depart, but unwilling to do so until she had granted him an interview. He
left the letter at the office, ordering the messenger to carry it to Lowick
Manor, and wait for an answer.

Ladislaw felt the awkwardness of asking for more last words. His
former farewell had been made in the hearing of Sir James Chettam, and
had been announced as final even to the butler. It is certainly trying to a
man's dignity to reappear when he is not expected to do so: a first farewell
has pathos in it, but to come back for a second lends an opening to
comedy, and it was possible even that there might be bitter sneers afloat
about Will's motives for lingering. Still it was on the whole more satisfactory to his feeling to take the directest means of seeing Dorothea, than to
use any device which might give an air of chance to a meeting of which he
wished her to understand that it was what he earnestly sought. When
he had parted from her before, he had been in ignorance of facts which
gave a new aspect to the relation between them, and made a more
absolute severance than he had then believed in. He knew nothing of
Dorothea's private fortune, and being little used to reflect on such matters,
took it for granted that according to Mr Casaubon's arrangement marriage
to him, Will Ladislaw, would mean that she consented to be penniless.
That was not what he could wish for even in his secret heart, or even if she
had been ready to meet such hard contrast for his sake. And then, too,
there was the fresh smart of that disclosure about his mother's family,
which if known would be an added reason why Dorothea's friends should
look down upon him as utterly below her. The secret hope that after some
years he might come back with the sense that he had at least a personal
value equal to her wealth, seemed now the dreamy continuation of a

dream. This change would surely justify him in asking Dorothea to receive him once more.

But Dorothea on that morning was not at home to receive Will's note. In consequence of a letter from her uncle announcing his intention to be at home in a week, she had driven first to Freshitt to carry the news, meaning to go on to the Grange to deliver some orders with which her uncle had intrusted her – thinking, as he said, 'a little mental occupation of this sort good for a widow'.

If Will Ladislaw could have overheard some of the talk at Freshitt that morning, he would have felt all his suppositions confirmed as to the readiness of certain people to sneer at his lingering in the neighbourhood. Sir James, indeed, though much relieved concerning Dorothea, had been on the watch to learn Ladislaw's movements, and had an instructed informant in Mr Standish, who was necessarily in his confidence on this matter. That Ladislaw had stayed in Middlemarch nearly two months after he had declared that he was going immediately, was a fact to embitter Sir James's suspicions, or at least to justify his aversion to a 'young fellow' whom he represented to himself as slight, volatile, and likely to show such recklessness as naturally went along with a position unriveted by family ties or a strict profession. But he had just heard something from Standish which, while it justified these surmises about Will, offered a means of nullifying all danger with regard to Dorothea.

Unwonted circumstances may make us all rather unlike ourselves: there are conditions under which the most majestic person is obliged to sneeze, and our emotions are liable to be acted on in the same incongruous manner. Good Sir James was this morning so far unlike himself that he was irritably anxious to say something to Dorothea on a subject which he usually avoided as if it had been a matter of shame to them both. He could not use Celia as a medium, because he did not choose that she should know the kind of gossip he had in his mind; and before Dorothea happened to arrive he had been trying to imagine how, with his shyness and unready tongue, he could ever manage to introduce his communication. Her unexpected presence brought him to utter hopelessness in his own power of saying anything unpleasant; but desperation suggested a resource; he sent the groom on an unsaddled horse across the park with a pencilled note to Mrs Cadwallader, who already knew the gossip, and would think it no compromise of herself to repeat it as often as required.

Dorothea was detained on the good pretext that Mr Garth, whom she wanted to see, was expected at the Hall within the hour, and she was still talking to Caleb on the gravel when Sir James, on the watch for the rector's wife, saw her coming and met her with the needful hints.

'Enough! I understand,' said Mrs Cadwallader. 'You shall be innocent. I am such a blackamoor that I cannot smirch myself.'

'I don't mean that it's of any consequence,' said Sir James, disliking that Mrs Cadwallader should understand too much. 'Only it is desirable that Dorothea should know there are reasons why she should not receive him again; and I really can't say so to her. It will come lightly from you.'

It came very lightly indeed. When Dorothea quitted Caleb and turned to meet them, it appeared that Mrs Cadwallader had stepped across the park by the merest chance in the world, just to chat with Celia in a matronly way about the baby. And so Mr Brooke was coming back? Delightful – coming back, it was to be hoped, quite cured of Parliamentary fever and pioneering. *Apropos* of the *Pioneer* – somebody had prophesied that it would soon be like a dying dolphin, and turn all colours for want of knowing how to help itself, because Mr Brooke's *protégé*, the brilliant young Ladislaw, was gone or going. Had Sir James heard that?

The three were walking along the gravel slowly, and Sir James, turning aside to whip a shrub, said he had heard something of that sort.

'All false!' said Mrs Cadwallader. 'He is not gone, or going, apparently; the *Pioneer* keeps its colour, and Mr Orlando Ladislaw is making a sad dark-blue scandal by warbling continually with your Mr Lydgate's wife, who they tell me is as pretty as pretty can be. It seems nobody ever goes into the house without finding this young gentleman lying on the rug or warbling at the piano. But the people in manufacturing towns are always disreputable.'

'You began by saying that one report was false, Mrs Cadwallader, and I believe this is false too,' said Dorothea, with indignant energy; 'at least, I feel sure it is a misrepresentation. I will not hear any evil spoken of Mr Ladislaw: he has already suffered too much injustice.'

Dorothea when thoroughly moved cared little what any one thought of her feelings: and even if she had been able to reflect, she would have held it petty to keep silence at injurious words about Will from fear of being herself misunderstood. Her face was flushed and her lip trembled.

Sir James, glancing at her, repented of his stratagem; but Mrs Cadwallader, equal to all occasions, spread the palms of her hands outward and said, 'Heaven grant it, my dear! – I mean that all bad tales about anybody may be false. But it is a pity that young Lydgate should have married one of these Middlemarch girls. Considering he's a son of somebody, he might have got a woman with good blood in her veins, and not too young, who would have put up with his profession. There's Clara Harfager, for instance, whose friends don't know what to do with her and she has a portion. Then we might have had her among us. However! – it's no use being wise for other people. Where is Celia? Pray let us go in.'

'I am going on immediately to Tipton,' said Dorothea rather haughtily. 'Good-bye.'

Sir James could say nothing as he accompanied her to the carriage. He was altogether discontented with the result of a contrivance which had cost him some secret humiliation beforehand.

Dorothea drove along between the berried hedge-rows and the shorn corn-fields, not seeing or hearing anything around. The tears came and rolled down her cheeks, but she did not know it. The world, it seemed, was turning ugly and hateful, and there was no place for her trustfulness. 'It is not true – it is not true!' was the voice within her that she listened to; but all the while a remembrance to which there had always clung a vague uneasiness would thrust itself on her attention – the remembrance of that day when she had found Will Ladislaw with Mrs Lydgate, and had heard his voice accompanied by the piano.

'He said he would never do anything that I disapproved – I wish I could have told him that I disapproved of that,' said poor Dorothea, inwardly, feeling a strange alternation between anger with Will and the passionate defence of him. 'They all try to blacken him before me; but I will care for no pain, if he is not to blame. I always believed he was good.' – These were her last thoughts before she felt that the carriage was passing under the archway of the lodge-gate at the Grange, when she hurriedly pressed her handkerchief to her face and began to think of her errands. The coachman begged leave to take out the horses for half an hour as there was something wrong with a shoe; and Dorothea, having the sense that she was going to rest, took off her gloves and bonnet, while she was leaning against a statue in the entrance-hall, and talking to the house-keeper. At last she said –

'I must stay here a little, Mrs Kell. I will go into the library and write you some memoranda from my uncle's letter, if you will open the shutters for me.'

'The shutters are open, madam,' said Mrs Kell, following Dorothea, who had walked along as she spoke. 'Mr Ladislaw is there, looking for something.'

(Will had come to fetch a portfolio of his own sketches which he had missed in the act of packing his movables, and did not choose to leave behind.)

Dorothea's heart seemed to turn over as if it had had a blow, but she was not perceptibly checked: in truth, the sense that Will was there was for the moment all-satisfying to her, like the sight of something precious that one has lost. When she reached the door she said to Mrs Kell –

'Go in first, and tell him that I am here.'

Will had found his portfolio, and had laid it on the table at the far end of the room, to turn over the sketches and please himself by looking at the memorable piece of art which had a relation to nature too mysterious for Dorothea. He was smiling at it still, and shaking the sketches into order with the thought that he might find a letter from her awaiting him at Middlemarch, when Mrs Kell close to his elbow said –

'Mrs Casaubon is coming in, sir.'

Will turned round quickly, and the next moment Dorothea was entering. As Mrs Kell closed the door behind her they met: each was looking at the other, and consciousness was overflowed by something that suppressed utterance. It was not confusion that kept them silent, for they both felt that parting was near, and there is no shamefacedness in a sad parting.

She moved automatically towards her uncle's chair against the writing-table, and Will, after drawing it out a little for her, went a few paces off and stood opposite her.

'Pray sit down,' said Dorothea, crossing her hands on her lap; 'I am very glad you were here.' Will thought that her face looked just as it did when she first shook hands with him in Rome; for her widow's cap, fixed in her bonnet, had gone off with it, and he could see that she had lately been shedding tears. But the mixture of anger in her agitation had vanished at the sight of him; she had been used, when they were face to face, always to feel confidence and the happy freedom which comes with mutual understanding, and how could other people's words hinder that effect on a sudden? Let the music which can take possession of our frame and fill the air with joy for us, sound once more – what does it signify that we heard it found fault with in its absence?

'I have sent a letter to Lowick Manor to-day, asking leave to see you,' said Will, seating himself opposite to her. 'I am going away immediately, and I could not go without speaking to you again.'

'I thought we had parted when you came to Lowick many weeks ago – you thought you were going then,' said Dorothea, her voice trembling a little.

'Yes; but I was in ignorance then of things which I know now – things which have altered my feelings about the future. When I saw you before, I was dreaming that I might come back some day. I don't think I ever shall – now.' Will paused here.

'You wished me to know the reasons?' said Dorothea, timidly.

'Yes,' said Will, impetuously, shaking his head backward, and looking away from her with irritation in his face. 'Of course I must wish it. I have been grossly insulted in your eyes and in the eyes of others. There has been a mean implication against my character. I wish you to know that under no circumstances would I have lowered myself by – under no circumstances would I have given men the chance of saying that I sought money under the pretext of seeking – something else. There was no need of other safeguard against me – the safeguard of wealth was enough.'

Will rose from his chair with the last word and went – he hardly knew where; but it was to the projecting window nearest him, which had been open as now about the same season a year ago, when he and Dorothea had stood within it and talked together. Her whole heart was going out at this moment in sympathy with Will's indignation: she only wanted to convince him that she had never done him injustice, and he seemed to have turned away from her as if she too had been part of the unfriendly world.

'It would be very unkind of you to suppose that I ever attributed any meanness to you,' she began. Then in her ardent way, wanting to plead with him, she moved from her chair and went in front of him to her old place in the window, saying, 'Do you suppose that I ever disbelieved in you?'

When Will saw her there, he gave a start and moved backward out of the window, without meeting her glance. Dorothea was hurt by this movement following up the previous anger of his tone. She was ready to say that it was as hard on her as on him, and that she was helpless; but those strange particulars of their relation which neither of them could explicitly mention kept her always in dread of saying too much. At this moment she had no belief that Will would in any case have wanted to marry her, and she feared using words which might imply such a belief. She only said earnestly, recurring to his last word –

'I am sure no safeguard was ever needed against you.'

Will did not answer. In the stormy fluctuation of his feelings these words of hers seemed to him cruelly neutral, and he looked pale and miserable after his angry outburst. He went to the table and fastened up his portfolio, while Dorothea looked at him from the distance. They were wasting these last moments together in wretched silence. What could he say, since what had got obstinately uppermost in his mind was the passionate love for her which he forbade himself to utter? What could she say, since she might offer him no help – since she was forced to keep the money that ought to have been his? – since to-day he seemed not to respond as he used to do to her thorough trust and liking?

But Will at last turned away from his portfolio and approached the window again.

'I must go,' he said, with that peculiar look of the eyes which sometimes accompanies bitter feeling, as if they had been tired and burned with gazing too close at a light.

'What shall you do in life?' said Dorothea, timidly. 'Have your intentions remained just the same as when we said good-bye before?'

'Yes,' said Will, in a tone that seemed to waive the subject as uninteresting. 'I shall work away at the first thing that offers. I suppose one gets a habit of doing without happiness or hope.'

'Oh, what sad words!' said Dorothea, with a dangerous tendency to sob. Then trying to smile, she added, 'We used to agree that we were alike in speaking too strongly.'

'I have not spoken too strongly now,' said Will, leaning back against the angle of the wall. 'There are certain things which a man can only go through once in his life; and he must know some time or other that the best is over with him. This experience has happened to me while I am very young – that is all. What I care more for than I can ever care for anything else is absolutely forbidden to me – I don't mean merely by being out of my reach, but forbidden me, even if it were within my reach, by my own pride and honour – by everything I respect myself for. Of course I shall go on living as a man might do who had seen heaven in a trance.'

Will paused, imagining that it would be impossible for Dorothea to misunderstand this; indeed he felt that he was contradicting himself and offending against his self-approval in speaking to her so plainly; but still – it could not be fairly called wooing a woman to tell her that he would never woo her. It must be admitted to be a ghostly kind of wooing.

But Dorothea's mind was rapidly going over the past with quite another vision than his. The thought that she herself might be what Will most cared for did throb through her an instant, but then came doubt: the memory of the little they had lived through together turned pale and shrank before the memory which suggested how much fuller might have been the intercourse between Will and some one else with whom he had had constant companionship. Everything he had said might refer to that other relation, and whatever had passed between him and herself was thoroughly explained by what she had always regarded as their simple friendship and the cruel obstruction thrust upon it by her husband's injurious act. Dorothea stood silent, with her eyes cast down dreamily, while images crowded upon her which left the sickening certainty that Will was referring to Mrs Lydgate. But why sickening? He wanted her to know that here too his conduct should be above suspicion.

Will was not surprised at her silence. His mind also was tumultuously busy while he watched her, and he was feeling rather wildly that something must happen to hinder their parting – some miracle, clearly nothing in their own deliberate speech. Yet, after all, had she any love for him? – he could not pretend to himself that he would rather believe her to be without that pain. He could not deny that a secret longing for the assurance that she loved him was at the root of all his words.

Neither of them knew how long they stood in that way. Dorothea was raising her eyes, and was about to speak, when the door opened and her footman came to say –

'The horses are ready, madam, whenever you like to start.'

'Presently,' said Dorothea. Then turning to Will, she said, 'I have some memoranda to write for the housekeeper.'

'I must go,' said Will, when the door had closed again – advancing towards her. 'The day after to-morrow I shall leave Middlemarch.'

'You have acted in every way rightly,' said Dorothea, in a low tone, feeling a pressure at her heart which made it difficult to speak.

She put out her hand, and Will took it for an instant without speaking, for her words had seemed to him cruelly cold and unlike herself. Their eyes met, but there was discontent in his, and in hers there was only sadness. He turned away and took his portfolio under his arm.

'I have never done you injustice. Please remember me,' said Dorothea, repressing a rising sob.

'Why should you say that?' said Will, with irritation. 'As if I were not in danger of forgetting everything else.'

He had really a movement of anger against her at that moment, and it impelled him to go away without pause. It was all one flash to Dorothea – his last words – his distant bow to her as he reached the door – the sense that he was no longer there. She sank into the chair, and for a few moments sat there like a statue, while images and emotions were hurrying upon her. Joy came first, in spite of the threatening train behind it – joy in the impression that it was really herself whom Will loved and was renouncing, that there was really no other love less permissible, more blameworthy, which honour was hurrying him away from. They were parted all the same, but – Dorothea drew a deep breath and felt her strength return – she could think of him unrestrainedly. At that moment the parting was easy to bear: the first sense of loving and being loved excluded sorrow. It was as if some hard icy pressure had melted, and her consciousness had room to expand; her past was come back to her with larger interpretation. The joy was not the less – perhaps it was the more complete just then – because of the irrevocable parting; for there was no reproach, no contemptuous wonder to imagine in any eye or from any lips. He had acted so as to defy reproach, and make wonder respectful.

Any one watching her might have seen that there was a fortifying thought within her. Just as when inventive power is working with glad ease some small claim on the attention is fully met as if it were only a cranny opened to the sunlight, it was easy now for Dorothea to write her memoranda. She spoke her last words to the housekeeper in cheerful tones, and when she seated herself in the carriage her eyes were bright and her cheeks blooming under the dismal bonnet. She threw back the heavy 'weepers', and looked before her, wondering which road Will had taken. It was in her nature to be proud that he was blameless, and through all her feelings there ran this vein – 'I was right to defend him.'

The coachman was used to drive his greys at a good pace, Mr Casaubon being unenjoying and impatient in everything away from his desk, and wanting to get to the end of all journeys; and Dorothea was now bowled along quickly. Driving was pleasant, for rain in the night had laid the dust, and the blue sky looked far off, away from the region of the great clouds that sailed in masses. The earth looked like a happy place under the vast heavens, and Dorothea was wishing that she might overtake Will and see him once more.

After a turn of the road, there he was with the portfolio under his arm; but the next moment she was passing him while he raised his hat, and she felt a pang at being seated there in a sort of exaltation, leaving him behind. She could not look back at him. It was as if a crowd of indifferent objects had thrust them asunder, and forced them along different paths, taking them farther and farther away from each other, and making it useless to look back. She could no more make any sign that would seem to say,

'Need we part?' than she could stop the carriage to wait for him. Nay, what a world of reasons crowded upon her against any movement of her thought towards a future that might reverse the decision of this day!

'I only wish I had known before – I wish he knew – then we could be quite happy in thinking of each other, though we are for ever parted. And if I could but have given him the money, and made things easier for him!' – were the longings that came back the most persistently. And yet, so heavily did the world weigh on her in spite of her independent energy, that with this idea of Will as in need of such help and at a disadvantage with the world, there came always the vision of that unfittingness of any closer relation between them which lay in the opinion of every one connected with her. She felt to the full all the imperativeness of the motives which urged Will's conduct. How could he dream of her defying the barrier that her husband had placed between them? – how could she ever say to herself that she would defy it?

Will's certainty, as the carriage grew smaller in the distance, had much more bitterness in it. Very slight matters were enough to gall him in his sensitive mood, and the sight of Dorothea driving past him while he felt himself plodding along as a poor devil seeking a position in a world which in his present temper offered him little that he coveted, made his conduct seem a mere matter of necessity, and took away the sustainment of resolve. After all, he had no assurance that she loved him: could any man pretend that he was simply glad in such a case to have the suffering all on his own side?

That evening Will spent with the Lydgates; the next evening he was gone.

BOOK SEVEN
TWO TEMPTATIONS

∾ SIXTY-THREE ∾

These little things are great to little man.
GOLDSMITH

'HAVE YOU SEEN MUCH OF YOUR SCIENTIFIC phoenix, Lydgate, lately?'
said Mr Toller at one of his Christmas dinner-parties, speaking to Mr
Farebrother on his right hand.

'Not much I am sorry to say,' answered the Vicar, accustomed to parry
Mr Toller's banter about his belief in the new medical light. 'I am out of
the way, and he is too busy.'

'Is he? I am glad to hear it,' said Dr Minchin, with mingled suavity and
surprise.

'He gives a great deal of time to the New Hospital,' said Mr Farebrother,
who had his reasons for continuing the subject: 'I hear of that from my
neighbour, Mrs Casaubon, who goes there often. She says Lydgate is
indefatigable, and is making a fine thing of Bulstrode's institution. He
is preparing a new ward in case of the cholera coming to us.'

'And preparing theories of treatment to try on the patients, I suppose,'
said Mr Toller.

'Come, Toller, be candid,' said Mr Farebrother. 'You are too clever not to
see the good of a bold fresh mind in medicine, as well as in everything
else; and as to cholera, I fancy, none of you are very sure what you ought
to do. If a man goes a little too far along a new road, it is usually himself
that he harms more than any one else.'

'I am sure you and Wrench ought to be obliged to him,' said Dr Minchin, looking towards Toller, 'for he has sent you the cream of Peacock's
patients.'

'Lydgate has been living at a great rate for a young beginner,' said
Mr Harry Toller, the brewer. 'I suppose his relations in the North back
him up.'

'I hope so,' said Mr Chichely, 'else he ought not to have married that
nice girl we were all so fond of. Hang it, one has a grudge against a man
who carries off the prettiest girl in the town.'

'Ay, by God! and the best too,' said Mr Standish.

'My friend Vincy didn't half like the marriage, I know that,' said Mr
Chichely. 'He wouldn't do much. How the relations on the other side may
have come down I can't say.' There was an emphatic kind of reticence in
Mr Chichely's manner of speaking.

'Oh, I shouldn't think Lydgate ever looked to practice for a living,' said Mr Toller, with a slight touch of sarcasm; and there the subject was dropped.

This was not the first time that Mr Farebrother had heard hints of Lydgate's expenses being obviously too great to be met by his practice, but he thought it not unlikely that there were resources of expectations which excused the large outlay at the time of Lydgate's marriage, and which might hinder any bad consequences from the disappointment in his practice. One evening, when he took the pains to go to Middlemarch on purpose to have a chat with Lydgate as of old, he noticed in him an air of excited effort quite unlike his usual easy way of keeping silence or breaking it with abrupt energy whenever he had anything to say. Lydgate talked persistently when they were in his work-room, putting arguments for and against the probability of certain biological views; but he had none of those definite things to say or to show which give the way-marks of a patient uninterrupted pursuit, such as he used himself to insist on, saying that 'there must be a systole and diastole in all inquiry,' and that 'a man's mind must be continually expanding and shrinking between the whole human horizon and the horizon of an object-glass.' That evening he seemed to be talking widely for the sake of resisting any personal bearing; and before long they went into the drawing-room, where Lydgate, having asked Rosamond to give them music, sank back in his chair in silence, but with a strange light in his eyes. 'He may have been taking an opiate,' was a thought that crossed Mr Farebrother's mind – 'tic-douloureux perhaps – or medical worries.'

It did not occur to him that Lydgate's marriage was not delightful: he believed, as the rest did, that Rosamond was an amiable, docile creature, though he had always thought her rather uninteresting – a little too much the pattern-card of the finishing-school; and his mother could not forgive Rosamond because she never seemed to see that Henrietta Noble was in the room. 'However, Lydgate fell in love with her,' said the Vicar to himself, 'and she must be to his taste.'

Mr Farebrother was aware that Lydgate was a proud man, but having very little corresponding fibre in himself, and perhaps too little care about personal dignity, except the dignity of not being mean or foolish, he could hardly allow enough for the way in which Lydgate shrank, as from a burn, from the utterance of any word about his private affairs. And soon after that conversation at Mr Toller's, the Vicar learned something which made him watch the more eagerly for an opportunity of indirectly letting Lydgate know that if he wanted to open himself about any difficulty there was a friendly ear ready.

The opportunity came at Mr Vincy's, where, on New Year's Day, there was a party, to which Mr Farebrother was irresistibly invited, on the plea that he must not forsake his old friends on the first new year of his being a greater man, and Rector as well as Vicar. And this party was thoroughly friendly: all the ladies of the Farebrother family were present; the Vincy children all dined at the table, and Fred had persuaded his mother that if she did not invite Mary Garth, the Farebrothers would regard it as a slight to themselves, Mary being their particular friend. Mary came and Fred was in high spirits, though his enjoyment was of a checkered kind – triumph that his mother should see Mary's importance with the chief personages in the party being much streaked with jealousy when Mr Farebrother sat down by her. Fred used to be much more easy about his own accomplishments in the days when he had not begun to dread being 'bowled out by Farebrother', and this terror was still before him. Mrs Vincy, in her fullest matronly bloom, looked at Mary's little figure, rough wavy hair, and visage quite without lilies and roses, and wondered; trying unsuccessfully to fancy herself caring about Mary's appearance in wedding clothes, or feeling complacency in grandchildren who would 'feature' the Garths. However, the party was a merry one, and Mary was particularly bright; being glad, for Fred's sake, that his friends were getting kinder to her, and being also quite willing that they should see how much she was valued by others whom they must admit to be the judges.

Mr Farebrother noticed that Lydgate seemed bored, and that Mr Vincy spoke as little as possible to his son-in-law. Rosamond was perfectly graceful and calm, and only a subtle observation such as the Vicar had not been roused to bestow on her would have perceived the total absence of that interest in her husband's presence which a loving wife is sure to betray, even if etiquette keeps her aloof from him. When Lydgate was taking part in the conversation, she never looked towards him any more than if she had been a sculptured Psyche modelled to look another way: and when, after being called out for an hour or two, he re-entered the room, she seemed unconscious of the fact, which eighteen months before would have had the effect of a numeral before cyphers. In reality, however, she was intensely aware of Lydgate's voice and movements; and her pretty good-tempered air of unconsciousness was a studied negation by which she satisfied her inward opposition to him without compromise of propriety. When the ladies were in the drawing-room after Lydgate had been called away from the dessert, Mrs Farebrother, when Rosamond happened to be near her, said – 'You have to give up a great deal of your husband's society, Mrs Lydgate.'

'Yes, the life of a medical man is very arduous; especially when he is so devoted to his profession as Mr Lydgate is,' said Rosamond, who was standing, and moved easily away at the end of this correct little speech.

'It is dreadfully dull for her when there is no company,' said Mrs Vincy, who was seated at the old lady's side. 'I am sure I thought so when Rosamond was ill, and I was staying with her. You know, Mrs Farebrother, ours is a cheerful house. I am of a cheerful disposition myself, and Mr Vincy always likes something to be going on. That is what Rosamond has been used to. Very different from a husband out at odd hours, and never knowing when he will come home, and of a close, proud disposition, *I* think' – indiscreet Mrs Vincy did lower her tone slightly with this parenthesis. 'But Rosamond always had an angel of a temper; her brothers used very often not to please her, but she was never the girl to show temper; from a baby she was always as good as good, and with a complexion beyond anything. But my children are all good-tempered, thank God.'

This was easily credible to any one looking at Mrs Vincy as she threw back her broad cap-strings, and smiled towards her three little girls, aged from seven to eleven. But in that smiling glance she was obliged to include Mary Garth, whom the three girls had got into a corner to make her tell them stories. Mary was just finishing the delicious tale of Rumpelstiltskin, which she had well by heart, because Letty was never tired of communicating it to her ignorant elders from a favourite red volume. Louisa, Mrs Vincy's darling, now ran to her with wide-eyed serious excitement, crying, 'O mamma, mamma, the little man stamped so hard on the floor he couldn't get his leg out again!'

'Bless you, my cherub!' said mamma; 'you shall tell me all about it tomorrow. Go and listen!' and then, as her eyes followed Louisa back towards the attractive corner, she thought that if Fred wished her to invite Mary again she would make no objection, the children being so pleased with her.

But presently the corner became still more animated, for Mr Farebrother came in, and seating himself behind Louisa, took her on his lap: whereupon the girls insisted that he must hear Rumpelstiltskin, and Mary must tell it over again. He insisted too, and Mary, without fuss, began in her neat fashion, with precisely the same words as before. Fred, who had also seated himself near, would have felt unmixed triumph in Mary's effectiveness if Mr Farebrother had not been looking at her with evident admiration, while he dramatized an intense interest in the tale to please the children.

'You will never care any more about my one-eyed giant, Loo,' said Fred at the end.

'Yes, I shall. Tell about him now,' said Louisa.

'Oh, I daresay; I am quite cut out. Ask Mr Farebrother.'

'Yes,' added Mary; 'ask Mr Farebrother to tell you about the ants whose beautiful house was knocked down by a giant named Tom, and he thought they didn't mind because he couldn't hear them cry, or see them use their pocket-handkerchiefs.'

'Please,' said Louisa, looking up at the Vicar.

'No, no, I am a grave old parson. If I try to draw a story out of my bag a sermon comes instead. Shall I preach you a sermon?' said he, putting on his short-sighted glasses, and pursing up his lips.

'Yes,' said Louisa, falteringly.

'Let me see, then. Against cakes: how cakes are bad things, especially if they are sweet and have plums in them.'

Louisa took the affair rather seriously, and got down from the Vicar's knee to go to Fred.

'Ah, I see it will not do to preach on New Year's Day,' said Mr Farebrother, rising and walking away. He had discovered of late that Fred had become jealous of him, and also that he himself was not losing his preference for Mary above all other women.

'A delightful young person is Miss Garth,' said Mrs Farebrother, who had been watching her son's movements.

'Yes,' said Mrs Vincy, obliged to reply, as the old lady turned to her expectantly. 'It is a pity she is not better-looking.'

'I cannot say that,' said Mrs Farebrother, decisively. 'I like her countenance. We must not always ask for beauty, when a good God has seen fit to make an excellent young woman without it. I put good manners first, and Miss Garth will know how to conduct herself in any station.'

The old lady was a little sharp in her tone, having a prospective reference to Mary's becoming her daughter-in-law; for there was this inconvenience in Mary's position with regard to Fred, that it was not suitable to be made public, and hence the three ladies at Lowick Parsonage were still hoping that Camden would choose Miss Garth.

New visitors entered, and the drawing-room was given up to music and games, while whist-tables were prepared in the quiet room on the other side of the hall. Mr Farebrother played a rubber to satisfy his mother, who regarded her occasional whist as a protest against scandal and novelty of opinion, in which light even a revoke had its dignity. But at the end he got Mr Chichely to take his place, and left the room. As he crossed the hall, Lydgate had just come in and was taking off his greatcoat.

'You are the man I was going to look for,' said the Vicar; and instead of entering the drawing-room, they walked along the hall and stood against the fireplace, where the frosty air helped to make a glowing bank. 'You see, I can leave the whist-table easily enough,' he went on, smiling at Lydgate, 'now I don't play for money. I owe that to you, Mrs Casaubon says.'

'How?' said Lydgate, coldly.

'Ah, you didn't mean me to know it; I call that ungenerous reticence. You should let a man have the pleasure of feeling that you have done him a good turn. I don't enter into some people's dislike of being under an obligation; upon my word, I prefer being under an obligation to everybody for behaving well to me.'

'I can't tell what you mean,' said Lydgate, 'unless it is that I once spoke of you to Mrs Casaubon. But I did not think that she would break her promise not to mention that I had done so,' said Lydgate, leaning his back against the corner of the mantelpiece, and showing no radiance in his face.

'It was Brooke who let it out, only the other day. He paid me the compliment of saying that he was very glad I had the living, though you had come across his tactics, and had praised me up as a Ken and a

Tillotson, and that sort of thing, till Mrs Casaubon would hear of no one else.'

'Oh, Brooke is such a leaky-minded fool,' said Lydgate contemptuously.

'Well, I was glad of the leakiness then. I don't see why you shouldn't like me to know that you have wished to do me a service, my dear fellow. And you certainly have done me one. It's rather a strong check to one's self-complacency to find how much of one's right doing depends on not being in want of money. A man will not be tempted to say the Lord's Prayer backward to please the devil, if he doesn't want the devil's services. I have no need to hang on the smiles of chance now.'

'I don't see that there's any money-getting without chance,' said Lydgate; 'if a man gets it in a profession, it's pretty sure to come by chance.'

Mr Farebrother thought he could account for this speech, in striking contrast with Lydgate's former way of talking, as the perversity which will often spring from the moodiness of a man ill at ease in his affairs. He answered in a tone of good-humoured admission –

'Ah, there's enormous patience wanted with the way of the world. But it is easier for a man to wait patiently when he has friends who love him, and ask for nothing better than to help him through, so far as it lies in their power.'

'Oh yes,' said Lydgate, in a careless tone, changing his attitude and looking at his watch. 'People make much more of their difficulties than they need to do.'

He knew as distinctly as possible that this was an offer of help to himself from Mr Farebrother, and he could not bear it. So strangely determined are we mortals, that, after having been long gratified with the sense that he had privately done the Vicar a service, the suggestion that the Vicar discerned his need of a service in return made him shrink into unconquerable reticence. Besides, behind all making of such offers what else must come? – that he should 'mention his case', imply that he wanted specific things. At that moment, suicide seemed easier.

Mr Farebrother was too keen a man not to know the meaning of that reply, and there was a certain massiveness in Lydgate's manner and tone, corresponding with his physique, which if he repelled your advances in the first instance seemed to put persuasive devices out of question.

'What time are you?' said the Vicar, devouring his wounded feeling.

'After eleven,' said Lydgate. And they went into the drawing-room.

◅ SIXTY-FOUR ▻

1st Gent. Where lies the power, there let the blame lie too.
2nd Gent. Nay, power is relative; you cannot fright
 The coming pest with border fortresses,
 Or catch your carp with subtle argument.
 All force is twain in one: cause is not cause
 Unless effect be there; and action's self
 Must needs contain a passive. So command
 Exists but with obedience.

EVEN IF LYDGATE HAD BEEN INCLINED to be quite open about his affairs, he knew that it would hardly have been in Mr Farebrother's power to give him the help he immediately wanted. With the year's bills coming in from his tradesmen, with Dover's threatening hold on his furniture, and with nothing to depend on but slow dribbling payments from patients who must not be offended – for the handsome fees he had had from Freshitt Hall and Lowick Manor had been easily absorbed – nothing less than a thousand pounds would have freed him from actual embarrassment, and left a residue which, according to the favourite phrase of hopefulness in such circumstances, would have given him 'time to look about him'.

Naturally the merry Christmas bringing the happy New Year, when fellow-citizens expect to be paid for the trouble and goods they have smilingly bestowed on their neighbours, had so tightened the pressure of sordid cares on Lydgate's mind that it was hardly possible for him to think unbrokenly of any other subject, even the most habitual and soliciting. He was not an ill-tempered man; his intellectual activity, the ardent kindness of his heart, as well as his strong frame, would always, under tolerably easy conditions, have kept him above the petty uncontrolled susceptibilities which make bad temper. But he was now a prey to that worst irritation which arises not simply from annoyance, but from the second consciousness underlying those annoyances, of wasted energy and a degrading preoccupation, which was the reverse of all his former purposes. '*This* is what I am thinking of; and *that* is what I might have been thinking of', was the bitter incessant murmur within him, making every difficulty a double goad to impatience.

Some gentlemen have made an amazing figure in literature by general discontent with the universe as a trap of dulness into which their great souls have fallen by mistake; but the sense of a stupendous self and an insignificant world may have its consolations. Lydgate's discontent was much harder to bear; it was the sense that there was a grand existence in thought and effective action lying around him, while his self was being narrowed into the miserable isolation of egoistic fears, and vulgar anxieties for events that might allay such fears. His troubles will perhaps appear miserably sordid, and beneath the attention of lofty persons who can know nothing of debt except on a magnificent scale. Doubtless they were sordid; and for the majority, who are not lofty, there is no escape from sordidness but by being free from money-craving, with all its base hopes and temptations, its watching for death, its hinted requests, its horse-dealer's desire to make bad work pass for good, its seeking for function which ought to be another's, its compulsion often to long for Luck in the shape of a wide calamity.

It was because Lydgate writhed under the idea of getting his neck beneath this vile yoke that he had fallen into a bitter moody state which was continually widening Rosamond's alienation from him. After the first disclosure about the bill of sale, he had made many efforts to draw her into sympathy with him about possible measures for narrowing their expenses, and with the threatening approach of Christmas his propositions grew more and more definite. 'We can do with only one servant, and live on very little,' he said, 'and I shall manage with one horse.' For Lydgate, as we have seen, had begun to reason, with a more distinct vision, about the expenses of living, and any shape of pride he had given to appearances of that sort was meagre compared with the pride which made him revolt from exposure as a debtor, or from asking men to help him with their money.

'Of course you can dismiss the other two servants, if you like,' said Rosamond; 'but I should have thought it would be very injurious to your position for us to live in a poor way. You must expect your practice to be lowered.'

'My dear Rosamond, it is not a question of choice. We have begun too expensively. Peacock, you know, lived in a much smaller house than this. It is my fault: I ought to have known better, and I deserve a thrashing – if there were anybody who had a right to give it me – for bringing you into the necessity of living in a poorer way than you have been used to. But we married because we loved each other, I suppose. And that may help us to pull along till things get better. Come dear, put down that work and come to me.'

He was really in chill gloom about her at that moment, but he dreaded a future without affection, and was determined to resist the oncoming of division between them. Rosamond obeyed him, and he took her on his knee, but in her secret soul she was utterly aloof from him. The poor thing saw only that the world was not ordered to her liking, and Lydgate was part of that world. But he held her waist with one hand and laid the other gently on both of hers; for this rather abrupt man had much tenderness in his manners towards women, seeming to have always present in his imagination the weakness of their frames and the delicate poise of their health both in body and mind. And he began again to speak persuasively.

'I find, now I look into things a little, Rosy, that it is wonderful what an amount of money slips away in our housekeeping. I suppose the servants are careless, and we have had a great many people coming. But there must be many in our rank who manage with much less: they must do with commoner things, I suppose, and look after the scraps. It seems, money goes but a little way in these matters, for Wrench has everything as plain as possible, and he has a very large practice.'

'Oh, if you think of living as the Wrenches do!' said Rosamond, with a little turn of her neck. 'But I have heard you express your disgust at that way of living.'

'Yes, they have very bad taste in everything – they make economy look ugly. We needn't do that. I only meant that they avoid expenses, although Wrench has a capital practice.'

'Why should not you have a good practice, Tertius? Mr Peacock had. You should be more careful not to offend people, and you should send out medicines as the others do. I am sure you began well, and you got several good houses. It cannot answer to be eccentric; you should think what will be generally liked,' said Rosamond, in a decided little tone of admonition.

Lydgate's anger rose; he was prepared to be indulgent towards feminine weakness, but not towards feminine dictation. The shallowness of a waternixie's soul may have a charm until she becomes didactic. But he controlled himself, and only said, with a touch of despotic firmness –

'What I am to do in my practice, Rosy, it is for me to judge. That is not the question between us. It is enough for you to know that our income is likely to be a very narrow one – hardly four hundred, perhaps less, for a long time to come, and we must try to rearrange our lives in accordance with that fact.'

Rosamond was silent for a moment or two, looking before her, and then said, 'My uncle Bulstrode ought to allow you a salary for the time you give to the Hospital: it is not right that you should work for nothing.'

'It was understood from the beginning that my services would be gratuitous. That, again, need not enter into our discussion. I have pointed out what is the only probability,' said Lydgate, impatiently. Then checking himself, he went on more quietly –

'I think I see one resource which would free us from a good deal of the present difficulty. I hear that young Ned Plymdale is going to be married to Miss Sophy Toller. They are rich, and it is not often that a good house is vacant in Middlemarch. I feel sure that they would be glad to take this house from us with most of our furniture, and they would be willing to pay handsomely for the lease. I can employ Trumbull to speak to Plymdale about it.'

Rosamond left her husband's knee and walked slowly to the other end of the room; when she turned round and walked towards him it was evident that the tears had come, and that she was biting her underlip and clasping her hands to keep herself from crying. Lydgate was wretched – shaken with anger and yet feeling that it would be unmanly to vent the anger just now.

'I am very sorry, Rosamond; I know this is painful.'

'I thought, at least, when I had borne to send the plate back and have that man taking an inventory of the furniture – I should have thought *that* would suffice.'

'I explained it to you at the time, dear. That was only a security and behind that security there is a debt. And that debt must be paid within the next few months, else we shall have our furniture sold. If young Plymdale will take our house and most of our furniture, we shall be able to pay that debt, and some others too, and we shall be quit of a place too expensive for us. We might take a smaller house: Trumbull, I know, has a very decent one to let at thirty pounds a year, and this is ninety.' Lydgate uttered this speech in the curt hammering way with which we usually try to nail down a vague mind to imperative facts. Tears rolled silently down Rosamond's cheeks; she just pressed her handkerchief against them, and stood looking at the large vase on the mantelpiece. It was a moment of more intense bitterness than she had ever felt before. At last, she said, without hurry and with careful emphasis –

'I could never have believed that you would like to act in that way.'

'Like it?' burst out Lydgate, rising from his chair, thrusting his hands in his pockets and stalking away from the hearth; 'it's not a question of liking. Of course, I don't like it; it's the only thing I can do.' He wheeled round there, and turned towards her.

'I should have thought there were many other means than that,' said Rosamond. 'Let us have a sale and leave Middlemarch altogether.'

'To do what? What is the use of my leaving my work in Middlemarch to go where I have none? We should be just as penniless elsewhere as we are here,' said Lydgate still more angrily.

'If we are to be in that position it will be entirely your own doing, Tertius,' said Rosamond, turning round to speak with the fullest conviction. 'You will not behave as you ought to do to your own family. You offended Captain Lydgate. Sir Godwin was very kind to me when we were at Quallingham, and I am sure if you showed proper regard to him and told him your affairs, he would do anything for you. But rather than that, you like giving up our house and furniture to Mr Ned Plymdale.'

There was something like fierceness in Lydgate's eyes, as he answered with new violence, 'Well then, if you will have it so, I do like it. I admit that I like it better than making a fool of myself by going to beg where it's of no use. Understand then, that it is what I *like* to do.'

There was a tone in the last sentence which was equivalent to the clutch of his strong hand on Rosamond's delicate arm. But for all that, his will was not a whit stronger than hers. She immediately walked out of the room in silence, but with an intense determination to hinder what Lydgate liked to do.

He went out of the house, but as his blood cooled he felt that the chief result of the discussion was a deposit of dread within him at the idea of opening with his wife in future subjects which might again urge him to violent speech. It was as if a fracture in delicate crystal had begun, and he was afraid of any movement that might make it fatal. His marriage would be a mere piece of bitter irony if they could not go on loving each other. He had long ago made up his mind to what he thought was her negative character – her want of sensibility, which showed itself in disregard both of his specific wishes and of his general aims. The first great disappointment had been borne: the tender devotedness and docile adoration of the ideal wife must be renounced, and life must be taken up on a lower stage of expectation, as it is by men who have lost their limbs. But the real wife had not only her claims, she had still a hold on his heart, and it was his intense desire that the hold should remain strong. In marriage, the certainty, 'She will never love me much', is easier to bear than the fear, 'I shall love her no more.' Hence, after that outburst, his inward effort was entirely to excuse her, and to blame the hard circumstances which were partly his fault. He tried that evening, by petting her, to heal the wound he had made in the morning, and it was not in Rosamond's nature to be repellent or sulky; indeed, she welcomed the signs that her husband loved her and was under control. But this was something quite distinct from loving *him*.

Lydgate would not have chosen soon to recur to the plan of parting with the house: he was resolved to carry it out, and say as little more about it as possible. But Rosamond herself touched on it at breakfast by saying, mildly –

'Have you spoken to Trumbull yet?'

'No,' said Lydgate, 'but I shall call on him as I go by this morning. No time must be lost.' He took Rosamond's question as a sign that she withdrew her inward opposition, and kissed her head caressingly when he got up to go away.

As soon as it was late enough to make a call, Rosamond went to Mrs Plymdale, Mr Ned's mother, and entered with pretty congratulations into the subject of the coming marriage. Mrs Plymdale's maternal view was, that Rosamond might possibly now have retrospective glimpses of her own folly; and feeling the advantages to be at present all on the side of her son, was too kind a woman not to behave graciously.

'Yes, Ned is most happy, I must say. And Sophy Toller is all I could desire in a daughter-in-law. Of course her father is able to do something handsome for her – that is only what would be expected with a brewery like his. And the connection is everything we should desire. But that is not what I look at. She is a very nice girl – no airs, no pretensions, though on a level with the first. I don't mean with the titled aristocracy. I see very little good in people aiming out of their own sphere. I mean that Sophy is equal to the best in the town, and she is contented with that.'

'I have always thought her very agreeable,' said Rosamond.

'I look upon it as a reward for Ned, who never held his head too high, that he should have got into the very best connection,' continued Mrs Plymdale, her native sharpness softened by a fervid sense that she was taking a correct view. 'And such particular people as the Tollers are, they might have objected because some of our friends are not theirs. It is well known that your aunt Bulstrode and I have been intimate from our youth, and Mr Plymdale has always been on Mr Bulstrode's side. And I myself prefer serious opinions. But the Tollers have welcomed Ned all the same.'

'I am sure he is very deserving, well-principled young man,' said Rosamond, with a neat air of patronage, in return for Mrs Plymdale's wholesome corrections.

'Oh, he has not the style of a captain in the army, or that sort of carriage as if everybody was beneath him, or that showy kind of talking, and singing, and intellectual talent. But I am thankful he has not. It is a poor preparation both for here and Hereafter.'

'Oh dear, yes; appearances have very little to do with happiness,' said Rosamond. 'I think there is every prospect of their being a happy couple. What house will they take?'

'Oh, as for that, they must put up with what they can get. They have been looking at the house in St Peter's Place, next to Mr Hackbutt's; it belongs to him, and he is putting it nicely in repair. I suppose they are not likely to hear of a better. Indeed, I think Ned will decide the matter to-day.'

'I should think it is a nice house; I like St Peter's Place.'

'Well, it is near the Church, and a genteel situation. But the windows are narrow, and it is all ups and downs. You don't happen to know of any other that would be at liberty?' said Mrs Plymdale, fixing her round black eyes on Rosamond with the animation of a sudden thought in them.

'Oh no; I hear so little of those things.'

Rosamond had not foreseen that question and answer in setting out to pay her visit; she had simply meant to gather any information which would help her to avert the parting with her own house under circumstances thoroughly disagreeable to her. As to the untruth in her reply, she no more reflected on it than she did on the untruth there was in her saying that appearances had very little to do with happiness. Her object, she was convinced, was thoroughly justifiable: it was Lydgate whose intention was inexcusable: and there was a plan in her mind which, when she had carried it out fully, would prove how very false a step it would have been for him to have descended from his position.

She returned home by Mr Borthrop Trumbull's office, meaning to call there, It was the first time in her life that Rosamond had thought of doing anything in the form of business, but she felt equal to the occasion. That she should be obliged to do what she intensely disliked, was an idea which turned her quiet tenacity into active invention. Here was a case in which it could not be enough simply to disobey and be serenely, placidly obstinate: she must act according to her judgment, and she said to herself that her judgment was right – 'indeed, if it had not been, she would not have wished to act on it.'

Mr Trumbull was in the back-room of his office, and received Rosamond with his finest manners, not only because he had much sensibility to her charms, but because the good-natured fibre in him was stirred by his certainty that Lydgate was in difficulties, and that this uncommonly pretty woman – this young lady with the highest personal attractions – was likely to feel the pinch of trouble – to find herself involved in circumstances beyond her control. He begged her to do him the honour to take a seat, and stood before her trimming and comporting himself with an eager solicitude, which was chiefly benevolent. Rosamond's first question was, whether her husband had called on Mr Trumbull that morning, to speak about disposing of their house.

'Yes, ma'am, yes, he did; he did so,' said the good auctioneer, trying to throw something soothing into his iteration. 'I was about to fulfil his order if possible, this afternoon. He wished me not to procrastinate.'

'I called to tell you not to go any further, Mr Trumbull; and I beg of you not to mention what has been said on the subject. Will you oblige me?'

'Certainly I will, Mrs Lydgate, certainly. Confidence is sacred with me on business or any other topic. I am then to consider the commission withdrawn?' said Mr Trumbull, adjusting the long ends of his blue cravat with both hands, and looking at Rosamond deferentially.

'Yes, if you please. I find that Mr Ned Plymdale has taken a house – the one in St Peter's Place next to Mr Hackbutt's. Mr Lydgate would be annoyed that his orders should be fulfilled uselessly. And besides that, there are other circumstances which render the proposal unnecessary.'

'Very good, Mrs Lydgate, very good. I am at your commands, whenever you require any service of me,' said Mr Trumbull, who felt pleasure in conjecturing that some new resources had been opened. 'Rely on me, I beg. The affair shall go no further.'

That evening Lydgate was a little comforted by observing that Rosamond was more lively than she had usually been of late, and even seemed interested in doing what would please him without being asked. He thought, 'If she will be happy and I can rub through, what does it all signify? It is only a narrow swamp that we have to pass in a long journey. If I can get my mind clear again, I shall do.'

He was so much cheered that he began to search for an account of experiments which he had long ago meant to look up, and had neglected out of that creeping self-despair which comes in the train of petty anxieties. He felt again some of the old delightful absorption in a far-reaching inquiry, while Rosamond played the quiet music which was as helpful to his meditation as the plash of an oar on the evening lake. It was rather late; he had pushed away all the books, and was looking at the fire with his hands clasped behind his head in forgetfulness of everything except the construction of a new controlling experiment, when Rosamond, who had left the piano and was leaning back in her chair watching him, said –

'Mr Ned Plymdale has taken a house already.'

Lydgate, startled and jarred, looked up in silence for a moment, like a man who has been disturbed in his sleep. Then flushing with an unpleasant consciousness, he asked –

'How do you know?'

'I called at Mrs Plymdale's this morning, and she told me that he had taken the house in St Peter's Place next to Mr Hackbutt's.'

Lydgate was silent. He drew his hands from behind his head and pressed them against the hair which was hanging, as it was apt to do, in a mass on his forehead, while he rested his elbow on his knees. He was feeling bitter disappointment, as if he had opened a door out of a suffocating place and had found it walled up; but he also felt sure that Rosamond was pleased with the cause of his disappointment. He preferred not looking at her and not speaking, until he had got over the first spasm of vexation. After all, he said in his bitterness, what can a woman care about so much as house and furniture? a husband without them is an absurdity. When he looked up and pushed his hair aside, his dark eyes had a miserable blank non-expectance of sympathy in them, but he only said coolly –

'Perhaps some one else may turn up. I told Trumbull to be on the look-out if he failed with Plymdale.'

Rosamond made no remark. She trusted to the chance that nothing more would pass between her husband and the auctioneer until some issue should have justified her interference; at any rate, she had hindered the event which she immediately dreaded. After a pause, she said –

'How much money is it that those disagreeable people want?'

'What disagreeable people?'

'Those who took the list – and the others. I mean, how much money would satisfy them so that you need not be troubled any more?'

Lydgate surveyed her for a moment, as if he were looking for symptoms, and then said, 'Oh, if I could have got six hundred from Plymdale for furniture and as premium, I might have managed. I could have paid off Dover, and given enough on account to the others to make them wait patiently, if we contracted our expenses.'

'But I mean how much should you want if we stayed in this house?'

'More than I am likely to get anywhere,' said Lydgate, with rather a grating sarcasm in his tone. It angered him to perceive that Rosamond's mind was wandering over impracticable wishes instead of facing possible efforts.

'Why should you not mention the sum?' said Rosamond, with a mild indication that she did not like his manners.

'Well,' said Lydgate, in a guessing tone, 'it would take at least a thousand to set me at ease. But,' he added incisively, 'I have to consider what I shall do without it, not with it.'

Rosamond said no more.

But the next day she carried out her plan of writing to Sir Godwin Lydgate. Since the Captain's visit, she had received a letter from him, and also one from Mrs Mengan, his married sister, condoling with her on the loss of her baby, and expressing vaguely the hope that they should see her again at Quallingham. Lydgate had told her that this politeness meant nothing: but she was secretly convinced that any backwardness in Lydgate's family towards him was due to his cold and contemptuous behaviour, and she answered the letters in her most charming manner, feeling some confidence that a specific invitation would follow. But there had been total silence. The Captain evidently was not a great penman, and Rosamond reflected that the sisters might have been abroad. However, the season was come for thinking of friends at home, and at any rate Sir Godwin, who had chucked her under the chin, and pronounced her to be like the celebrated beauty, Mrs Croly, who had made a conquest of him in 1790, would be touched by any appeal from her, and would find it pleasant for her sake to behave as he ought to do towards his nephew. Rosamond was naïvely convinced of what an old gentleman ought to do to prevent her from suffering annoyance. And she wrote what she considered the most judicious letter possible – one which would strike Sir Godwin as a proof of her excellent sense – pointing out how desirable it was that Tertius should quit such a place as Middlemarch for one more fitted to his talents, how the unpleasant character of the inhabitants had hindered his professional success, and how in consequence he was in money difficulties, from which it would require a thousand pounds thoroughly to extricate him. She did not say that Tertius was unaware of her intention to write; for she had the idea that his supposed sanction of her letter would be in accordance with what she did say of his great regard for his uncle Godwin as the relative who had always been his best friend. Such was the force of poor Rosamond's tactics now she applied them to affairs.

This had happened before the party on New Year's Day, and no answer had yet come from Sir Godwin. But on the morning of that day Lydgate had to learn that Rosamond had revoked his order to Borthrop Trumbull. Feeling it necessary that she should be gradually accustomed to the idea of their quitting the house in Lowick Gate, he overcame his reluctance to speak to her again on the subject, and when they were breakfasting, said –

'I shall try to see Trumbull this morning, and tell him to advertise the house in the *Pioneer* and the *Trumpet*. If the thing were advertised, some one might be inclined to take it who would not otherwise have thought of a change. In these country places many people go on in their old houses when their families are too large for them, for want of knowing where they can find another. And Trumbull seems to have got no bite at all.'

Rosamond knew that the inevitable moment was come. 'I ordered Trumbull not to inquire further,' she said, with a careful calmness which was evidently defensive.

Lydgate stared at her in mute amazement. Only half an hour before he had been fastening up her plaits for her, and talking the 'little language' of affection, which Rosamond, though not returning it, accepted, as if she had been a serene and lovely image, now and then miraculously dimpling towards her votary. With such fibres still astir in him, the shock he received could not at once be distinctly anger; it was confused pain. He laid down the knife and fork with which he was carving, and throwing himself back in his chair, said at last, with a cool irony in his tone –

'May I ask when and why you did so?'

'When I knew that the Plymdales had taken a house, I called to tell him not to mention ours to them; and at the same time I told him not to let the affair go on any further. I knew that it would be very injurious to you if it were known that you wished to part with your house and furniture, and I had a very strong objection to it. I think that was reason enough.'

'It was of no consequence then that I had told you imperative reasons of another kind; of no consequence that I had come to a different conclusion, and given an order accordingly?' said Lydgate, bitingly, the thunder and lightning gathering about his brow and eyes.

The effect of any one's anger on Rosamond had always been to make her shrink in cold dislike, and to become all the more calmly correct, in the conviction that she was not the person to misbehave, whatever others might do. She replied –

'I think I had a perfect right to speak on a subject which concerns me at least as much as you.'

'Clearly – you had a right to speak, but only to me. You had no right to contradict my orders secretly, and treat me as if I were a fool,' said Lydgate, in the same tone as before. Then with some added scorn. 'Is it possible to make you understand what the consequences will be? Is it of any use for me to tell you again why we *must* try to part with the house?'

'It is not necessary for you to tell me again,' said Rosamond, in a voice that fell and trickled like cold water-drops. 'I remembered what you said. You spoke just as violently as you do now. But that does not alter my opinion that you ought to try every other means rather than take a step which is so painful to me. And as to advertising the house, I think it would be perfectly degrading to you.'

'And suppose I disregard your opinion as you disregard mine?'

'You can do do so, of course. But I think you ought to have told me before we were married that you would place me in the worst position, rather than give up your own will.'

Lydgate did not speak, but tossed his head on one side, and twitched the corners of his mouth in despair. Rosamond, seeing that he was not looking at her, rose and set his cup of coffee before him; but he took no notice of it, and went on with an inward drama and argument, occasionally moving in his seat, resting one arm on the table, and rubbing his hand against his hair. There was a conflux of emotions and thoughts in him that would not let him either give thorough way to his anger or persevere with simple rigidity of resolve. Rosamond took advantage of his silence.

'When we were married every one felt that your position was very high. I could not have imagined then that you would want to sell our furniture, and take a house in Bride Street, where the rooms are like cages. If we are to live in that way let us at least leave Middlemarch.'

'These would be very strong considerations,' said Lydgate, half ironically – still there was a withered paleness about his lips as he looked at his coffee, and did not drink – 'these would be very strong considerations if I did not happen to be in debt.'

'Many persons must have been in debt in the same way, but if they are respectable, people trust them. I am sure I have heard papa say that the Torbits were in debt, and they went on very well. It cannot be good to act rashly,' said Rosamond, with serene wisdom.

Lydgate sat paralysed by opposing impulses: since no reasoning he could apply to Rosamond seemed likely to conquer her assent, he wanted to smash and grind some object on which he could at least produce an impression, or else to tell her brutally that he was master, and she must obey. But he not only dreaded the effect of such extremities on their mutual life – he had a growing dread of Rosamond's quiet elusive obstinacy, which would not allow any assertion of power to be final; and again, she had touched him in a spot of keenest feeling by implying that she had been deluded with a false vision of happiness in marrying him. As to saying that he was master, it was not the fact. The very resolution to which he had wrought himself by dint of logic and honourable pride was beginning to relax under her torpedo contact. He swallowed half his cup of coffee, and then rose to go.

'I may at least request that you will not go to Trumbull at present – until it has been seen that there are no other means,' said Rosamond. Although she was not subject to much fear, she felt it safer not to betray that she had written to Sir Godwin. 'Promise me that you will not go to him for a few weeks, or without telling me.'

Lydgate gave a short laugh. 'I think it is I who should exact a promise that you will do nothing without telling me,' he said, turning his eyes sharply upon her, and then moving to the door.

'You remember that we are going to dine at papa's,' said Rosamond, wishing that he should turn and make a more thorough concession to her. But he only said, 'Oh yes,' impatiently, and went away. She held it to be very odious in him that he did not think the painful propositions he had

had to make to her were enough, without showing so unpleasant a temper. And when she put the moderate request that he would defer going to Trumbull again, it was cruel in him not to assure her of what he meant to do. She was convinced of her having acted in every way for the best; and each grating or angry speech of Lydgate's served only as an addition to the register of offences in her mind. Poor Rosamond for months had begun to associate her husband with feelings of disappointment, and the terribly inflexible relation of marriage had lost its charm of encouraging delightful dreams. It had freed her from the disagreeables of her father's house, but it had not given her everything that she had wished and hoped. The Lydgate with whom she had been in love had been a group of airy conditions for her, most of which had disappeared, while their place had been taken by everyday details which must be lived through slowly from hour to hour, not floated through with a rapid selection of favourable aspects. The habits of Lydgate's profession, his home preoccupation with scientific subjects, which seemed to her almost like a morbid vampire's taste, his peculiar views of things which had never entered into the dialogue of courtship – all these continually-alienating influences, even without the fact of his having placed himself at a disadvantage in the town, and without that first shock of revelation about Dover's debt, would have made his presence dull to her. There was another presence which ever since the early days of her marriage, until four months ago, had been an agreeable excitement, but that was gone: Rosamond would not confess to herself how much the consequent blank had to do with her utter ennui; and it seemed to her (perhaps she was right) that an invitation to Quallingham, and an opening for Lydgate to settle elsewhere than in Middlemarch – in London, or somewhere likely to be free from unpleasantness – would satisfy her quite well, and make her indifferent to the absence of Will Ladislaw, towards whom she felt some resentment for his exaltation of Mrs Casaubon.

That was the state of things with Lydgate and Rosamond on the New Year's Day when they dined at her father's, she looking mildly neutral towards him in remembrance of his ill-tempered behaviour at breakfast, and he carrying a much deeper effect from the inward conflict in which that morning scene was only one of many epochs. His flushed effort while talking to Mr Farebrother – his effort after the cynical pretence that all ways of getting money are essentially the same, and that chance has an empire which reduces choice to a fool's illusion – was but the symptom of a wavering resolve, a benumbed response to the old stimuli of enthusiasm.

What was he to do? He saw even more keenly than Rosamond did the dreariness of taking her into the small house in Bride Street, where she would have scanty furniture around her and discontent within: a life of privation and life with Rosamond were two images which had become more and more irreconcilable ever since the threat of privation had disclosed itself. But even if his resolves had forced the two images into combination, the useful preliminaries to that hard change were not visibly within reach. And though he had not given the promise which his wife had asked for, he did not go again to Trumbull. He even began to think of taking a rapid journey to the North and seeing Sir Godwin. He had once believed that nothing would urge him into making an application for money to his uncle, but he had not then known the full pressure of alternatives yet more disagreeable. He could not depend on the effect of a letter; it was only in an interview, however disagreeable this might be to himself, that he could give a thorough explanation and could test the effectiveness of kinship. No sooner had Lydgate begun to represent this step to himself as the easiest than there was a reaction of anger that he – he who had long ago determined to live aloof from such abject calculations, such self-interested anxiety about the inclinations and the pockets of men with whom he had been proud to have no aims in common – should have fallen not simply to their level, but to the level of soliciting them.

⊂ SIXTY-FIVE ⊃

One of us two must bowen douteless,
And, sith a man is more reasonable
Than woman is, ye [men] moste be suffrable.
                CHAUCER: *Canterbury Tales*

THE BIAS OF HUMAN NATURE TO BE slow in correspondence triumphs even over the present quickening in the general pace of things: what wonder then that in 1832 old Sir Godwin Lydgate was slow to write a letter which was of consequence to others rather than to himself? Nearly three weeks of the new year were gone, and Rosamond, awaiting an answer to her winning appeal, was every day disappointed. Lydgate, in total ignorance of her expectations, was seeing the bills come in, and feeling that Dover's use of his advantage over other creditors was imminent. He had never mentioned to Rosamond his brooding purpose of going to Quallingham: he did not want to admit what would appear to her a concession to her wishes after indignant refusal, until the last moment; but he was really expecting to set off soon. A slice of the railway would enable him to manage the whole journey and back in four days.

But one morning after Lydgate had gone out, a letter came addressed to him, which Rosamond saw clearly to be from Sir Godwin. She was full of hope. Perhaps there might be a particular note to her enclosed; but Lydgate was naturally addressed on the question of money or other aid, and the fact that he was written to, nay, the very delay in writing at all, seemed to certify that the answer was thoroughly compliant. She was too much excited by these thoughts to do anything but light stitching in a warm corner of the dining-room, with the outside of this momentous letter lying on the table before her. About twelve she heard her husband's step in the passage, and tripping to open the door, she said in her lightest tones, 'Tertius, come in here – here is a letter for you.'

'Ah?' he said, not taking off his hat, but just turning her round within his arm to walk towards the spot where the letter lay. 'My uncle Godwin!' he exclaimed, while Rosamond reseated herself, and watched him as he opened the letter. She had expected him to be surprised.

While Lydgate's eyes glanced rapidly over the brief letter, she saw his face, usually of a pale brown, taking on a dry whiteness; with nostrils and lips quivering he tossed down the letter before her and said violently –

'It will be impossible to endure life with you, if you will be always acting secretly – acting in opposition to me and hiding your actions.'

He checked his speech and turned his back on her – then wheeled round and walked about, sat down, and got up again restlessly, grasping hard objects deep down in his pockets. He was afraid of saying something irremediably cruel.

Rosamond too had changed colour as she read. The letter ran this way –

Dear Tertius, – Don't set your wife to write to me when you have anything to ask. It is a roundabout wheedling sort of thing which I should not have credited you with. I never choose to write to a woman on matters of business. As to my supplying you with a thousand pounds, or only half that sum, I can do nothing of the sort. My own family drains me to the last penny. With two younger sons and three daughters, I am not likely to have cash to spare. You seem to have got through your own money pretty quickly, and to have made a mess where you are; the sooner you go somewhere else the better. But I have nothing to do with men of your profession, and can't help you there. I did the best I could for you as guardian, and let you have your own way in taking to medicine. You might have gone into the army or the Church. Your money would have held out for that, and there would have been a surer ladder before you. Your uncle Charles has had a grudge against you for not going into his profession, but not I. I have always wished you well, but you must consider yourself on your own legs entirely now. – Your affectionate uncle,

Godwin Lydgate

When Rosamond had finished reading the letter she sat quite still, with her hands folded before her, restraining any show of her keen disappointment, and intrenching herself in quiet passivity under her husband's wrath. Lydgate paused in his movements, looked at her again, and said, with biting severity –

'Will this be enough to convince you of the harm you may do by secret meddling? Have you sense enough to recognize now your incompetence to judge and act for me – to interfere with your ignorance in affairs which it belongs to me to decide on?'

The words were hard; but this was not the first time that Lydgate had been frustrated by her. She did not look at him, and made no reply.

'I had nearly resolved on going to Quallingham. It would have cost me pain enough to do it, yet it might have been of some use. But it has been of no use for me to think of anything. You have always been counteracting me secretly. You delude me with a false assent, and then I am at the mercy of your devices. If you mean to resist every wish I express, say so and defy me. I shall at least know what I am doing then.'

It is a terrible moment in young lives when the closeness of love's bond has turned to this power of galling. In spite of Rosamond's self-control a tear fell silently and rolled over her lips. She still said nothing; but under that quietude was hidden an intense effect: she was in such entire disgust with her husband that she wished that she had never seen him. Sir Godwin's rudeness towards her and utter want of feeling ranged him with Dover and all other creditors – disagreeable people who only thought of themselves, and did not mind how annoying they were to her. Even her father was unkind, and might have done more for them. In fact there was but one person in Rosamond's world whom she did not regard as blameworthy, and that was the graceful creature with blond plaits and with little hands crossed before her, who had never expressed herself unbecomingly, and had always acted for the best – the best naturally being what she best liked.

Lydgate pausing and looking at her again began to feel that half-maddening sense of helplessness which comes over passionate people when their passion is met by an innocent-looking silence whose meek victimized air seems to put them in the wrong, and at last infects even the justest indignation with a doubt of its justice. He needed to recover the full sense that he was in the right by moderating his words.

'Can you not see, Rosamond,' he began again, trying to be simply grave and not bitter, 'that nothing can be so fatal as a want of openness and confidence between us? It has happened again and again that I have expressed a decided wish, and you have seemed to assent, yet after that you have secretly disobeyed my wish. In that way I can never know what I have to trust to. There would be some hope for us if you would admit this. Am I such an unreasonable, furious brute? Why should you not be open with me?'

Still silence.

517

'Will you only say that you have been mistaken, and that I may depend on your not acting secretly in future?' said Lydgate, urgently, but with something of request in his tone which Rosamond was quick to perceive. She spoke with coolness.

'I cannot possibly make admissions or promises in answer to such words as you have used towards me. I have not been accustomed to language of that kind. You have spoken of my "secret meddling", and my "interfering ignorance", and my "false assent". I have never expressed myself in that way to you, and I think that you ought to apologize. You spoke of its being impossible to live with me. Certainly you have not made my life pleasant to me of late. I think it was to be expected that I should try to avert some of the hardships which our marriage has brought on me.' Another tear fell as Rosamond ceased speaking, and she pressed it away as quietly as the first.

Lydgate flung himself into a chair, feeling checkmated. What place was there in her mind for a remonstrance to lodge in? He laid down his hat, flung an arm over the back of his chair, and looked down for some moments without speaking. Rosamond had the double purchase over him of insensibility to the point of justice in his reproach, and of sensibility to the undeniable hardships now present in her married life. Although her duplicity in the affair of the house had exceeded what he knew, and had really hindered the Plymdales from knowing of it, she had no consciousness that her action could rightly be called false. We are not obliged to identify our own acts according to a strict classification, any more than the materials of our grocery and clothes. Rosamond felt that she was aggrieved, and that this was what Lydgate had to recognize.

As for him, the need of accommodating himself to her nature, which was inflexible in proportion to its negations, held him as with pincers. He had begun to have an alarmed foresight of her irrevocable loss of love for him, and the consequent dreariness of their life. The ready fulness of his emotions made this dread alternate quickly with the first violent movements of his anger. It would assuredly have been a vain boast in him to say that he was her master.

'You have not made my life pleasant to me of late' – 'the hardships which our marriage has brought on me' – these words were stinging his imagination as a pain makes an exaggerated dream. If he were not only to sink from his highest resolve, but to sink into the hideous fettering of domestic hate?

'Rosamond,' he said, turning his eyes on her with a melancholy look, 'you should allow for a man's words when he is disappointed and provoked. You and I cannot have opposite interests. I cannot part my happiness from yours. If I am angry with you, it is that you seem not to see how any concealment divides us. How could I wish to make anything hard to you either by my words or conduct? When I hurt you, I hurt part of my own life. I should never be angry with you if you would be quite open with me.'

'I have only wished to prevent you from hurrying us into wretchedness without any necessity,' said Rosamond, the tears coming again from a softened feeling now that her husband had softened. 'It is so very hard to be disgraced here among all the people we know, and to live in such a miserable way. I wish I had died with the baby.'

She spoke and wept with that gentleness which makes such words and tears omnipotent over a loving-hearted man. Lydgate drew his chair near to hers and pressed her delicate head against his cheek with his powerful tender hand. He only caressed her; he did not say anything; for what was there to say? He could not promise to shield her from the dreaded wretchedness, for he could see no sure means of doing so. When he left her to go out again, he told himself that it was ten times harder for her than for him: he had a life away from home, and constant appeals to his activity on behalf of others. He wished to excuse everything in her if he could – but it was inevitable that in that excusing mood he should think of her as if she were an animal of another and feebler species. Nevertheless she had mastered him.

◁ SIXTY-SIX ▷

'Tis one thing to be tempted, Escalus,
Another thing to fall.
Measure for Measure

LYDGATE CERTAINLY HAD GOOD REASON TO reflect on the service his practice did him in counteracting his personal cares. He had no longer free energy enough for spontaneous research and speculative thinking, but by the bedside of patients the direct external calls on his judgment and sympathies brought the added impulse needed to draw him out of himself. It was not simply that beneficent harness of routine which enables silly men to live respectably and unhappy men to live calmly – it was a perpetual claim on the immediate fresh application of thought, and on the consideration of another's need and trial. Many of us looking back through life would say that the kindest man we have ever known has been a medical man, or perhaps that surgeon whose fine tact, directed by deeply-informed perception, has come to us in our need with a more sublime beneficence than that of miracle-workers. Some of that twice-blessed mercy was always with Lydgate in his work at the Hospital or in private houses, serving better than any opiate to quiet and sustain him under anxieties and his sense of mental degeneracy.

Mr Farebrother's suspicion as to the opiate was true, however. Under the first galling pressure of foreseen difficulties, and the first perception that his marriage, if it were not to be a yoked loneliness, must be a state of effort to go on loving without too much care about being loved, he had once or twice tried a dose of opium. But he had no hereditary constitutional craving after such transient escapes from the hauntings of misery. He was strong, could drink a great deal of wine, but did not care about it; and when the men round him were drinking spirits, he took sugar and water, having a contemptuous pity even for the earliest stages of excitement from drink. It was the same with gambling. He had looked on at a great deal of gambling in Paris, watching it as if it had been a disease. He was no more tempted by such winning than he was by drink. He had said to himself that the only winning he cared for must be attained by a conscious process of high, difficult combination tending towards a beneficent result. The power he longed for could not be represented by agitated fingers, clutching a heap of coin, or by the half-barbarous, half-idiotic triumph in the eyes of a man who sweeps within his arms the ventures of twenty chapfallen companions.

But just as he had tried opium, so his thought now began to turn upon gambling – not with appetite for its excitement, but with a sort of wistful inward gaze after that easy way of getting money, which implied no asking and brought no responsibility. If he had been in London or Paris at that time, it is probable that such thoughts, seconded by opportunity, would have taken him into a gambling-house, no longer to watch the gamblers, but to watch them in kindred eagerness. Repugnance would have been surmounted by the immense need to win, if chance would be kind enough to let him. An incident which happened not very long after that airy notion of getting aid from his uncle had been excluded, was a strong sign of the effect that might have followed any extant opportunity of gambling.

The billiard-room at the Green Dragon was the constant resort of a certain set, most of whom, like our acquaintance Mr Bambridge, were regarded as men of pleasure. It was here that poor Fred Vincy had made part of his memorable debt, having lost money in betting, and had been obliged to borrow of that gay companion. It was generally known in Middlemarch that a good deal of money was lost and won in this way; and the consequent repute of the Green Dragon as a place of dissipation naturally heightened in some quarters the temptation to go there. Probably its regular visitants, like the initiates of free-masonry, wished that there were something a little more tremendous to keep to themselves concerning it; but they were not a closed community, and many decent seniors as well as juniors occasionally turned into the billiard-room to see what was going on. Lydgate, who had the muscular aptitude for billiards, and was fond of the game, had once or twice in the early days after his arrival in Middlemarch taken his turn with the cue at the Green Dragon; but afterwards he had no leisure for the game, and no inclination for the socialities there. One evening, however, he had occasion to seek Mr Bambridge at that resort. The horse-dealer had been engaged to get him a customer for his remaining good horse, for which Lydgate had determined to substitute a cheap hack, hoping by this reduction of style to get perhaps twenty pounds; and he cared now for every small sum, as a help towards feeding the patience of his tradesmen. To run up to the billiard-room, as he was passing, would save time.

Mr Bambridge was not yet come, but he would be sure to arrive by-and-by, said his friend Mr Horrock; and Lydgate stayed, playing a game for the sake of passing the time. That evening he had the peculiar light in the eyes and the unusual vivacity which had been once noticed in him by Mr Farebrother. The exceptional fact of his presence was much noticed in the room, where there was a good deal of Middlemarch company; and several lookers-on, as well as some of the players, were betting with animation. Lydgate was playing well, and felt confident; the bets were dropping round him, and with a swift glancing thought of the probable gain which might double the sum he was saving from his horse, he began to bet on his own play, and won again and again. Mr Bambridge had come in, but Lydgate did not notice him. He was not only excited with his play, but visions were gleaming on him of going the next day to Brassing, where there was gambling on a grander scale to be had, and where, by one powerful snatch at the devil's bait, he might carry it off without the hook, and buy his rescue from his daily solicitings.

He was still winning when two new visitors entered. One of them was a young Hawley, just come from his law studies in town, and the other was Fred Vincy, who had spent several evenings of late at this old haunt of his. Young Hawley, an accomplished billiard-player, brought a cool fresh hand to the cue. But Fred Vincy, startled at seeing Lydgate, and astonished to see him betting with an excited air, stood aside, and kept out of the circle round the table.

Fred had been rewarding resolution by a little laxity of late. He had been working heartily for six months at all outdoor occupations under Mr Garth, and by dint of severe practice had nearly mastered the defects of his handwriting, this practice being, perhaps, a little the less severe that it was often carried on in the evening at Mr Garth's under the eyes of Mary. But the last fortnight Mary had been staying at Lowick Parsonage with the ladies there, during Mr Farebrother's residence in Middlemarch, where he was carrying out some parochial plans; and Fred, not seeing anything more agreeable to do, had turned into the Green Dragon, partly to play at billiards, partly to taste the old flavour of discourse about horses, sport, and things in general, considered from a point of view which was not strenuously correct. He had not been out hunting once this season, had

had no horse of his own to ride, and had gone from place to place chiefly with Mr Garth in his gig, or on the sober cob which Mr Garth could lend him. It was a little too bad, Fred began to think, that he should be kept in the traces with more severity than if he had been a clergyman. 'I will tell you what, Mistress Mary – it will be rather harder work to learn surveying and drawing plans than it would have been to write sermons,' he had said, wishing her to appreciate what he went through for her sake; 'and as to Hercules and Theseus, they were nothing to me. They had sport, and never learned to write a book-keeping hand.' And now, Mary being out of the way for a little while, Fred, like any other strong dog who cannot slip his collar, had pulled up the staple of his chain and made a small escape, not of course meaning to go fast or far. There could be no reason why he should not play at billiards, but he was determined not to bet. As to money just now, Fred had in his mind the heroic project of saving almost all of the eighty pounds that Mr Garth offered him, and returning it, which he could easily do by giving up all futile money-spending, since he had a superfluous stock of clothes, and no expense in his board. In that way he could, in one year, go a good way towards repaying the ninety pounds of which he had deprived Mrs Garth, unhappily at a time when she needed that sum more than she did now. Nevertheless, it must be acknowledged that on this evening, which was the fifth of his recent visits to the billiard-room, Fred had not in his pocket, but in his mind, the ten pounds which he meant to reserve for himself from his half-year's salary (having before him the pleasure of carrying thirty to Mrs Garth when Mary was likely to be come home again) – he had those ten pounds in his mind as a fund from which he might risk something, if there were a chance of a good bet. Why? Well, when sovereigns were flying about, why shouldn't he catch a few? He would never go far along that road again; but a man likes to assure himself, and men of pleasure generally, what he could do in the way of mischief if he chose, and that if he abstains from making himself ill, or beggaring himself, or talking with the utmost looseness which the narrow limits of human capacity will allow, it is not because he is a spooney. Fred did not enter into formal reasons, which are a very artificial, inexact way of representing the tingling returns of old habit, and the caprices of young blood: but there was lurking in him a prophetic sense that evening, that when he began to play he should also begin to bet – that he should enjoy some punch-drinking, and in general prepare himself for feeling 'rather seedy' in the morning. It is in such indefinable movements that action often begins.

But the last thing likely to have entered Fred's expectation was that he should see his brother-in-law Lydgate – of whom he had never quite dropped the old opinion that he was a prig, and tremendously conscious of his superiority – looking excited and betting, just as he himself might have done. Fred felt a shock greater than he could quite account for by the vague knowledge that Lydgate was in debt, and that his father had refused to help him; and his own inclination to enter into the play was suddenly checked. It was a strange reversal of attitudes: Fred's blond face and blue eyes, usually bright and careless, ready to give attention to anything that held out a promise of amusement, looking involuntarily grave and almost embarrassed as if by the sight of something unfitting: while Lydgate, who had habitually an air of self-possessed strength, and a certain meditativeness that seemed to lie behind his most observant attention, was acting, watching, speaking with that excited narrow consciousness which reminds one of an animal with fierce eyes and retractile claws.

Lydgate, by betting on his own strokes, had won sixteen pounds; but young Hawley's arrival had changed the poise of things. He made first-rate strokes himself, and began to bet against Lydgate's strokes, the strain of whose nerves was thus changed from simple confidence in his own movements to defying another person's doubt in them. The defiance was more exciting than the confidence, but it was less sure. He continued to bet on his own play, but began often to fail. Still he went on, for his mind was as utterly narrowed into that precipitous crevice of play as if he had been the most ignorant lounger there. Fred observed that Lydgate was losing fast, and found himself in the new situation of puzzling his brains to think of some device by which, without being offensive, he could withdraw Lydgate's attention, and perhaps suggest to him a reason for quitting the room. He saw that others were observing Lydgate's strange unlikeness to himself, and it occurred to him that merely to touch his elbow and call him aside for a moment might rouse him from his absorption. He could think of nothing cleverer than the daring improbability of saying that he wanted to see Rosy, and wished to know if she were at home this evening; and he was going desperately to carry out this weak device, when a waiter came up to him with a message, saying that Mr Farebrother was below, and begged to speak with him.

Fred was surprised, not quite comfortably, but sending word that he would be down immediately, he went with a new impulse up to Lydgate, said, 'Can I speak to you a moment?' and drew him aside.

'Farebrother has just sent up a message to say he wants to speak to me. He is below. I thought you might like to know he was there, if you had anything to say to him.'

Fred had simply snatched up this pretext for speaking, because he could not say, 'You are losing confoundedly, and are making everybody stare at you; you had better come away.' But inspiration could hardly have served him better. Lydgate had not before seen that Fred was present, and his sudden appearance with an announcement of Mr Farebrother had the effect of a sharp concussion.

'No, no,' said Lydgate; 'I have nothing particular to say to him. But – the game is up – I must be going – I came in just to see Bambridge.'

'Bambridge is over there, but he is making a row – I don't think he's ready for business. Come down with me to Farebrother. I expect he is going to blow me up, and you will shield,' said Fred, with some adroitness.

Lydgate felt shame, but could not bear to act as if he felt it, by refusing to see Mr Farebrother; and he went down. They merely shook hands, however, and spoke of the frost; and when all three had turned into the street, the Vicar seemed quite willing to say good-bye to Lydgate. His present purpose was clearly to talk with Fred alone, and he said, kindly, 'I disturbed you, young gentleman, because I have some pressing business with you. Walk with me to St Botolph's, will you?'

It was a fine night, the sky was thick with stars, and Mr Farebrother proposed that they should make a circuit to the old church by the London road. The next thing he said was –

'I thought Lydgate never went to the Green Dragon?'

'So did I,' said Fred. 'But he said that he went to see Bambridge.'

'He was not playing then?'

Fred had not meant to tell this, but he was obliged now to say, 'Yes, he was. But I suppose it was an accidental thing. I have never seen him there before.'

'You have been going often yourself, then, lately?'

'Oh, about five or six times.'

'I think you had some good reason for giving up the habit of going there?'

'Yes. You know all about it,' said Fred, not liking to be catechized in this way. 'I made a clean breast to you.'

'I suppose that gives me a warrant to speak about the matter now. It is understood between us – is it not? – that we are on a footing of open friendship: I have listened to you, and you will be willing to listen to me. I may take my turn in talking a little about myself?'

'I am under the deepest obligation to you, Mr Farebrother,' said Fred, in a state of uncomfortable surmise.

'I will not affect to deny that you are under some obligation to me. But I am going to confess to you, Fred, that I have been tempted to reserve all that by keeping silence with you just now. When somebody said to me, "Young Vincy has taken to being at the billiard-table every night again – he won't bear the curb long"; I was tempted to do the opposite of what I am doing – to hold my tongue and wait while you went down the ladder again, – betting first and then – '

'I have not made any bets,' said Fred hastily.

'Glad to hear it. But I say, my prompting was to look on and see you take the wrong turning, wear out Garth's patience, and lose the best opportunity of your life – the opportunity which you made some rather difficult effort to secure. You can guess the feeling which raised that temptation in me – I am sure you know it. I am sure you know that the satisfaction of your affections stands in the way of mine.'

There was a pause. Mr Farebrother seemed to wait for a recognition of the fact; and the emotion perceptible in the tones of his fine voice gave solemnity to his words. But no feeling could quell Fred's alarm.

'I could not be expected to give her up,' he said, after a moment's hesitation: it was not a case for any pretence of generosity.

'Clearly not, when her affection met yours. But relations of this sort, even when they are of long standing, are always liable to change. I can easily conceive that you might act in a way to loosen the tie she feels towards you – it must be remembered that she is only conditionally bound to you – and that in that case, another man, who may flatter himself that he has a hold on her regard, might succeed in winning that firm place in her love as well as respect which you had let slip. I can easily conceive such a result,' repeated Mr Farebrother, emphatically. 'There is a companionship of ready sympathy, which might get the advantage even over the longest associations.'

It seemed to Fred that if Mr Farebrother had had a beak and talons instead of his very capable tongue, his mode of attack could hardly be more cruel. He had a horrible conviction that behind all this hypothetic statement there was knowledge of some actual change in Mary's feeling.

'Of course I know it might easily be all up with me,' he said, in a troubled voice. 'If she is beginning to compare – ' He broke off, not liking to betray all he felt, and then said, by the help of a little bitterness, 'But I thought you were friendly to me.'

'So I am; that is why we are here. But I have had a strong disposition to be otherwise. I have said to myself, "If there is a likelihood of that youngster doing himself harm, why should you interfere? Aren't you worth as much as he is, and don't your sixteen years over and above his, in which you have gone rather hungry, give you more right to satisfaction than he has? If there's a chance of his going to the dogs, let him – perhaps you could nohow hinder it – and do you take the benefit." '

There was a pause, in which Fred was seized by a most uncomfortable chill. What was coming next? He dreaded to hear that something had been said to Mary – he felt as if he were listening to a threat rather than a warning. When the Vicar began again there was a change in his tone like the encouraging transition to a major key.

'But I had once meant better than that, and I am come back to my old intention. I thought that I could hardly *secure myself* in it better, Fred, than by telling you just what had been going on in me. And now, do you understand me? I want you to make the happiness of her life and your own, and if there is any chance that a word of warning from me may turn aside any risk to the contrary – well, I have uttered it.'

There was a drop in the Vicar's voice when he spoke the last words. He paused – they were standing on a patch of green where the road diverged towards St Botolph's, and he put out his hand, as if to imply that the conversation was closed. Fred was moved quite newly. Some one highly susceptible to the contemplation of a fine act has said, that it produces a sort of regenerating shudder through the frame, and makes one feel ready to begin a new life. A good degree of that effect was just then present in Fred Vincy.

'I will try to be worthy,' he said, breaking off before he could say 'of you as well as of her'. And meanwhile Mr Farebrother had gathered the impulse to say something more.

'You must not imagine that I believe there is at present any decline in her preference of you, Fred. Set your heart at rest, that if you keep right, other things will keep right.'

'I shall never forget what you have done,' Fred answered. 'I can't say anything that seems worth saying – only I will try that your goodness shall not be thrown away.'

'That's enough. Good-bye, and God bless you.'

In that way they parted. But both of them walked about a long while before they went out of the starlight. Much of Fred's rumination might be summed up in the words, 'It certainly would have been a fine thing for her to marry Farebrother – but if she loves me best and I am a good husband?'

Perhaps Mr Farebrother's might be concentrated into a single shrug and one little speech. 'To think of the part one little woman can play in the life of a man, so that to renounce her may be a very good imitation of heroism, and to win her may be a discipline!'

ৎ SIXTY-SEVEN ৩

Now is there civil war within the soul;
Resolve is thrust from off the sacred throne
By clamorous Needs, and Pride the grand-vizier
Makes humble compact, plays the supple part
Of envoy and deft-tongued apologist
For hungry rebels.

HAPPILY LYDGATE HAD ENDED BY LOSING in the billiard-room, and brought away no encouragement to make a raid on luck. On the contrary, he felt unmixed disgust with himself the next day when he had to pay four or five pounds over and above his gains, and he carried about with him a most unpleasant vision of the figure he had made, not only rubbing elbows with the men at the Green Dragon but behaving just as they did. A philosopher fallen to betting is hardly distinguishable from a Philistine under the same circumstances: the difference will chiefly be found in his subsequent reflections, and Lydgate chewed a very disagreeable cud in that way. His reason told him how the affair might have been magnified into ruin by a slight change of scenery – if it had been a gambling-house that he had turned into, where chance could be clutched with both hands instead of being picked up with thumb and forefinger. Nevertheless, though reason strangled the desire to gamble, there remained the feeling that, with an assurance of luck to the needful amount, he would have liked to gamble, rather than take the alternative which was beginning to urge itself as inevitable.

That alternative was to apply to Mr Bulstrode. Lydgate had so many times boasted both to himself and others that he was totally independent of Bulstrode, to whose plans he had lent himself solely because they enabled him to carry out his own ideas of professional work and public benefit – he had so constantly in their personal intercourse had his pride sustained by the sense that he was making a good social use of this predominating banker, whose opinions he thought contemptible and whose motives often seemed to him an absurd mixture of contradictory impressions – that he had been creating for himself strong ideal obstacles to the proffering of any considerable request to him on his own account.

Still, early in March his affairs were at that pass in which men begin to say that their oaths were delivered in ignorance, and to perceive that the act which they had called impossible to them is becoming manifestly possible. With Dover's ugly security soon to be put in force, with the proceeds of his practice immediately absorbed in paying back-debts, and with the chance, if the worst were known, of daily supplies being refused on credit, above all with the vision of Rosamond's hopeless discontent continually haunting him, Lydgate had begun to see that he should inevitably bend himself to ask help from somebody or other. At first he had considered whether he should write to Mr Vincy; but on questioning Rosamond he found that, as he had suspected, she had already applied twice to her father, the last time being since the disappointment from Sir Godwin; and papa had said that Lydgate must look for himself. 'Papa said he had come, with one bad year after another, to trade more and more on borrowed capital, and had had to give up many indulgences: he could not spare a single hundred from the charges of his family. He said, let Lydgate ask Bulstrode: they have always been hand in glove.'

Indeed, Lydgate himself had come to the conclusion that if he must end by asking for a free loan, his relations with Bulstrode, more at least than with any other man, might take the shape of a claim which was not purely personal. Bulstrode had indirectly helped to cause the failure of his practice, and had also been highly gratified by getting a medical partner in his plans: – but who among us ever reduced himself to the sort of dependence in which Lydgate now stood, without trying to believe that he had claims which diminished the humiliation of asking? It was true that of late there had seemed to be a new languor of interest in Bulstrode about the Hospital; but his health had got worse, and showed signs of a deep-seated nervous affection. In other respects he did not appear to be changed: he had always been highly polite, but Lydgate had observed in him from the first a marked coldness about his marriage and other private circumstances, a coldness which he had hitherto preferred to any warmth of familiarity between them. He deferred the intention from day to day, his habit of acting on his conclusions being made infirm by his repugnance to every possible conclusion and its subsequent act. He saw Mr Bulstrode often, but he did not try to use any occasion for his private purpose. At one moment he thought, 'I will write a letter: I prefer that to any circuitous talk'; at another he thought, 'No; if I were talking to him, I could make a retreat before any signs of disinclination'.

Still the days passed and no letter was written, no special interview sought. In his shrinking from the humiliation of a dependent attitude towards Bulstrode, he began to familiarize his imagination with another step even more unlike his remembered self. He began spontaneously to consider whether it would be possible to carry out that puerile notion of Rosamond's, which had often made him angry, namely, that they should quit Middlemarch without seeing anything beyond that preface. The question came – 'Would any man buy the practice of me even now, for as little as it is worth? Then the sale might happen as a necessary preparation for going away.'

But against his taking this step, which he still felt to be a contemptible relinquishment of present work, a guilty turning aside from what was a real and might be a widening channel for worthy activity, to start again without any justified destination, there was this obstacle, that the purchaser, if procurable at all, might not be quickly forthcoming. And afterwards? Rosamond in a poor lodging, though in the largest city or most distant town, would not find the life that could save her from gloom, and save him from the reproach of having plunged her into it. For when a man is at the foot of the hill in his fortunes, he may stay a long while there in spite of professional accomplishment. In the British climate there is no incompatibility between scientific insight and furnished lodgings: the incompatibility is chiefly between scientific ambition and a wife who objects to that kind of residence.

But in the midst of his hesitation, opportunity came to decide him. A note from Mr Bulstrode requested Lydgate to call on him at the Bank. A hypochondriacal tendency had shown itself in the banker's constitution of late; and a lack of sleep, which was really only a slight exaggeration of an habitual dyspeptic symptom, had been dwelt on by him as a sign of threatening insanity. He wanted to consult Lydgate without delay on that particular morning, although he had nothing to tell beyond what he had told before. He listened eagerly to what Lydgate had to say in dissipation of his fears, though this too was only repetition; and this moment, in which Bulstrode was receiving a medical opinion with a sense of comfort, seemed to make the communication of a personal need to him easier than it had been in Lydgate's contemplation beforehand. He had been insisting that it would be well for Mr Bulstrode to relax his attention to business.

'One sees how any mental strain, however slight, may affect a delicate frame,' said Lydgate at that stage of the consultation when the remarks tend to pass from the personal to the general, 'by the deep stamp which anxiety will make for a time even on the young and vigorous. I am naturally very strong; yet I have been thoroughly shaken lately by an accumulation of trouble.'

'I presume that a constitution in the susceptible state in which mine at present is, would be especially liable to fall a victim to cholera, if it visited our district. And since its appearance near London, we may well besiege the Mercy-seat for our protection,' said Mr Bulstrode, not intending to evade Lydgate's allusion, but really preoccupied with alarms about himself.

'You have at all events taken your share in using good practical precautions for the town, and that is the best mode of asking for protection,' said Lydgate, with a strong distaste for the broken metaphor and bad logic of the banker's religion, somewhat increased by the apparent deafness of his sympathy. But his mind had taken up its long-prepared movement towards getting help, and was not yet arrested. He added, 'The town has done well in the way of cleansing, and finding appliances; and I think that if the cholera should come, even our enemies will admit that the arrangements in the Hospital are a public good.'

'Truly,' said Mr Bulstrode, with some coldness. 'With regard to what you say, Mr Lydgate, about the relaxation of my mental labour, I have for some time been entertaining a purpose to that effect – a purpose of a very decided character. I contemplate at least a temporary withdrawal from the management of much business, whether benevolent or commercial. Also I think of changing my residence for a time: probably I shall close or let The Shrubs, and take some place near the coast – under advice, of course, as to salubrity. That would be a measure which you would recommend?'

'Oh yes,' said Lydgate, falling backward in his chair, with ill-repressed impatience under the banker's pale earnest eyes and intense preoccupation with himself.

'I have for some time felt that I should open this subject with you in relation to our Hospital,' continued Bulstrode. 'Under the circumstances I have indicated, of course, I must cease to have any personal share in the management, and it is contrary to my views of responsibility to continue a large application of means to an institution which I cannot watch over and to some extent regulate. I shall therefore, in case of my ultimate decision to leave Middlemarch, consider that I withdraw other support to the New Hospital than that which will subsist in the fact that I chiefly supplied the expenses of building it, and have contributed further large sums to its successful working.'

Lydgate's thought, when Bulstrode paused according to his wont, was, 'He has perhaps been losing a good deal of money.' This was the most plausible explanation of a speech which had caused rather a startling change in his expectations. He said in reply –

'The loss to the Hospital can hardly be made up, I fear.'

'Hardly,' returned Bulstrode, in the same deliberate, silvery tone; 'except by some changes of plan. The only person who may be certainly counted on as willing to increase her contributions is Mrs Casaubon. I have had an interview with her on the subject, and I have pointed out to her, as I am about to do to you, that it will be desirable to win a more general support to the New Hospital by a change of system.'

Another pause, but Lydgate did not speak.

'The change I mean is an amalgamation with the Infirmary, so that the New Hospital shall be regarded as a special addition to the elder institution, having the same directing board. It will be necessary, also, that the medical management of the two shall be combined. In this way any difficulty as to the adequate maintenance of our new establishment will be removed; the benevolent interests of the town will cease to be divided.'

Mr Bulstrode had lowered his eyes from Lydgate's face to the buttons of his coat as he again paused.

'No doubt that is a good device as to ways and means,' said Lydgate, with an edge of irony in his tone. 'But I can't be expected to rejoice in it at once, since one of the first results will be that the other medical men will upset or interrupt my methods, if it were only because they are mine.'

'I myself, as you know, Mr Lydgate, highly value the opportunity of new and independent procedure which you have diligently employed: the original plan, I confess, was one which I had much at heart, under submission to the Divine Will. But since providential indications demand a renunciation from me, I renounce.'

Bulstrode showed a rather exasperating ability in this conversation. The broken metaphor and bad logic of motive which had stirred his hearer's contempt were quite consistent with a mode of putting the facts which made it difficult for Lydgate to vent his own indignation and disappointment. After some rapid reflection, he only asked,

'What did Mrs Casaubon say?'

'That was the further statement which I wished to make to you,' said Bulstrode, who had thoroughly prepared his ministerial explanation. 'She is, you are aware, a woman of most munificent disposition, and happily in possession – not I presume of great wealth, but of funds which she can well spare. She has informed me that though she had destined the chief part of those funds to another purpose, she is willing to consider whether she cannot fully take my place in relation to the Hospital. But she wishes for ample time to mature her thoughts on the subject, and I have told her that there is no need for haste – that, in fact, my own plans are not yet absolute.'

Lydgate was ready to say, 'If Mrs Casaubon would take your place, there would be gain, instead of loss.' But there was still a weight on his mind which arrested this cheerful candour. He replied, 'I suppose, then, that I may enter into the subject with Mrs Casaubon.'

'Precisely; that is what she expressly desires. Her decision, she says, will much depend on what you can tell her. But not at present: she is, I believe, just setting out on a journey. I have her letter here,' said Mr Bulstrode, drawing it out, and reading from it. ' "I am immediately otherwise engaged," she says. "I am going into Yorkshire with Sir James and Lady Chettam; and the conclusions I come to about some land which I am to see there may affect my power of contributing to the Hospital." Thus Mr Lydgate, there is no haste necessary in this matter; but I wished to apprise you beforehand of what may possibly occur.'

Mr Bulstrode returned the letter to his side-pocket, and changed his attitude as if his business were closed. Lydgate, whose renewed hope about the Hospital only made him more conscious of the facts which poisoned his hope, felt that his effort after help, if made at all, must be made now and vigorously.

'I am much obliged to you for giving me full notice,' he said, with a firm intention in his tone, yet with an interruptedness in his delivery which showed that he spoke unwillingly. 'The highest object to me is my profession, and I had identified the Hospital with the best use I can at present make of my profession. But the best use is not always the same with monetary success. Everything which has made the Hospital unpopular has helped with other causes – I think they are all connected with my professional zeal – to make me unpopular as a practitioner. I get chiefly patients who can't pay me. I should like them best, if I had nobody to pay on my own side.' Lydgate waited a little, but Bulstrode only bowed, looking at him fixedly, and he went on with the same interrupted enunciation – as if he were biting an objectionable leek.

'I have slipped into money difficulties which I can see no way out of, unless some one who trusts me and my future will advance me a sum without other security. I had very little fortune left when I came here. I have no prospects of money from my own family. My expenses, in consequence of my marriage, have been very much greater than I had expected. The result at this moment is that it would take a thousand pounds to clear me. I mean, to free me from the risk of having all my goods sold in security of my largest debt – as well as to pay other debts – and leave anything to keep us a little beforehand with our small income. I find that it is out of the question that my wife's father should make such an advance. That is why I mention my position to – to the only other man who may be held to have some personal connection with my prosperity or ruin.'

Lydgate hated to hear himself. But he had spoken now, and had spoken with unmistakable directness. Mr Bulstrode replied without haste, but also without hesitation.

'I am grieved, though, I confess, not surprised by this information, Mr Lydgate. For my own part, I regretted your alliance with my brother-in-law's family, which has always been of prodigal habits, and which has already been much indebted to me for sustainment in its present position. My advice to you, Mr Lydgate, would be, that instead of involving yourself in further obligations, and continuing a doubtful struggle, you should simply become a bankrupt.'

'That would not improve my prospect,' said Lydgate, rising, and speaking bitterly, 'even if it were a more agreeable thing in itself.'

'It is always a trial,' said Mr Bulstrode; 'but trial, my dear sir, is our portion here, and is a needed corrective. I recommend you to weigh the advice I have given.'

'Thank you,' said Lydgate, not quite knowing what he said. 'I have occupied you too long. Good-day.'

✑ SIXTY-EIGHT ✐

What suit of grace hath Virtue to put on
If Vice shall wear as good, and do as well?
If Wrong, if Craft, if Indiscretion
Act as fair parts with ends as laudable?
Which all this mighty volume of events
The world, the universal map of deeds,
Strongly controls, and proves from all descents,
That the directest course still best succeeds.
For should not grave and learn'd Experience
That looks with the eyes of all the world beside,
And with all ages holds intelligence,
Go safer than Deceit without a guide!
DANIEL: Musophilus

THAT CHANGE OF PLAN AND SHIFTING of interest which Bulstrode stated or betrayed in his conversation with Lydgate, had been determined in him by some severe experience which he had gone through since the epoch of Mr Larcher's sale, when Raffles had recognized Will Ladislaw, and when the banker had in vain attempted an act of restitution which might move Divine Providence to arrest painful consequences.

His certainty that Raffles, unless he were dead, would return to Middlemarch before long, had been justified. On Christmas Eve he had reappeared at The Shrubs. Bulstrode was at home to receive him, and hinder his communication with the rest of the family, but he could not altogether hinder the circumstances of the visit from compromising himself and alarming his wife. Raffles proved more unmanageable than he had shown himself to be in his former appearances, his chronic state of mental restlessness, the growing effect of habitual intemperance, quickly shaking off every impression from what was said to him. He insisted on staying in the house, and Bulstrode, weighing two sets of evils, felt that this was at least not a worse alternative than his going into the town. He kept him in his own room for the evening and saw him to bed, Raffles all the while amusing himself with the annoyance he was causing this decent and highly prosperous fellow-sinner, an amusement which he facetiously expressed as sympathy with his friend's pleasure in entertaining a man who had been serviceable to him, and who had not had all his earnings. There was a cunning calculation under this noisy joking – a cool resolve to

533

extract something the handsomer from Bulstrode as payment for release from this new application of torture. But his cunning had a little overcast its mark.

Bulstrode was indeed more tortured than the coarse fibre of Raffles could enable him to imagine. He had told his wife that he was simply taking care of this wretched creature, the victim of vice, who might otherwise injure himself; he implied, without the direct form of falsehood, that there was a family tie which bound him to this care, and that there were signs of mental alienation in Raffles which urged caution. He would himself drive the unfortunate being away the next morning. In these hints he felt that he was supplying Mrs Bulstrode with precautionary information for his daughters and servants, and accounting for his allowing no one but himself to enter the room even with food and drink. But he sat in an agony of fear lest Raffles should be overheard in his loud and plain references to past facts – lest Mrs Bulstrode should be even tempted to listen at the door. How could he hinder her, how betray his terror by opening the door to detect her? She was a woman of honest direct habits, and little likely to take so low a course in order to arrive at painful knowledge; but fear was stronger than the calculation of probabilities.

In this way Raffles had pushed the torture too far, and produced an effect which had not been in his plan. By showing himself hopelessly unmanageable he had made Bulstrode feel that a strong defiance was the only resource left. After taking Raffles to bed that night the banker ordered his closed carriage to be ready at half-past seven the next morning. At six o'clock he had already been long dressed, and had spent some of his wretchedness in prayer, pleading his motives for averting the worst evil if in anything he had used falsity and spoken what was not true before God. For Bulstrode shrank from a direct lie with an intensity disproportionate to the number of his more indirect misdeeds. But many of these misdeeds were like the subtle muscular movements which are not taken account of in the consciousness, though they bring about the end that we fix our mind on and desire. And it is only what we are vividly conscious of that we can vividly imagine to be seen by Omniscience.

Bulstrode carried his candle to the bedside of Raffles, who was apparently in a painful dream. He stood silent, hoping that the presence of the light would serve to waken the sleeper gradually and gently, for he feared some noise as the consequence of a too sudden awakening. He had watched for a couple of minutes or more the shudderings and pantings which seemed likely to end in waking, when Raffles, with a long half-stifled moan, started up and stared round him in terror, trembling and gasping. But he made no further noise, and Bulstrode, setting down the candle, awaited his recovery.

It was a quarter of an hour later before Bulstrode, with a cold peremptoriness of manner which he had not before shown, said, 'I came to call you thus early, Mr Raffles, because I have ordered the carriage to be ready at half-past seven, and intend myself to conduct you as far as Ilsely, where you can either take the railway or await a coach.'

Raffles was about to speak, but Bulstrode anticipated him imperiously, with the words, 'Be silent, sir, and hear what I have to say. I shall supply you with money now, and I will furnish you with a reasonable sum from time to time, on your application to me by letter; but if you choose to present yourself here again, if you return to Middlemarch, if you use your tongue in a manner injurious to me, you will have to live on such fruits as your malice can bring you, without help from me. Nobody will pay you well for blasting my name: I know the worst you can do against me, and I shall brave it if you dare to thrust yourself upon me again. Get up, sir, and do as I order you, without noise, or I will send for a policeman to take you off my premises, and you may carry your stories into every pot-house in the town, but you shall have no sixpence from me to pay your expenses there.'

Bulstrode had rarely in his life spoken with such nervous energy: he had been deliberating on this speech and its probable effects through a large part of the night; and though he did not trust to its ultimately saving him from any return of Raffles, he had concluded that it was the best throw he could make. It succeeded in enforcing submission from the jaded man this morning: his empoisoned system at this moment quailed before Bulstrode's cold, resolute bearing, and he was taken off quietly in the carriage before the family breakfast-time. The servants imagined him to be a poor relation and were not surprised that a strict man like their master, who held his head high in the world, should be ashamed of such a cousin and want to get rid of him. The banker's drive of ten miles with his hated companion was a dreary beginning of the Christmas day; but at the end of the drive, Raffles had recovered his spirits, and parted in a contentment for which there was the good reason that the banker had given him a hundred pounds. Various motives urged Bulstrode to this open-handedness, but he did not himself inquire closely into all of them. As he had stood watching Raffles in his uneasy sleep, it had certainly entered his mind that the man had been much shattered since the first gift of two hundred pounds.

He had taken care to repeat the incisive statement of his resolve not to be played on any more; and had tried to penetrate Raffles with the fact that he had shown the risks of bribing him to be quite equal to the risks of defying him. But when, freed from his repulsive presence, Bulstrode returned to his quiet home, he brought with him no confidence that he had secured more than a respite. It was as if he had had a loathsome dream, and could not shake off its images with their hateful kindred of sensations – as if on all the pleasant surroundings of his life a dangerous reptile had left his slimy traces.

Who can know how much of his most inward life is made up of the thoughts he believes other men to have about him, until that fabric of opinion is threatened with ruin?

Bulstrode was only the more conscious that there was a deposit of uneasy presentiment in his wife's mind, because she carefully avoided any allusion to it. He had been used every day to taste the flavour of supremacy and the tribute of complete deference; and the certainty that he was watched or measured with a hidden suspicion of his having some discreditable secret, made his voice totter when he was speaking to edification. Foreseeing, to men of Bulstrode's anxious temperament, is often worse than seeing; and his imagination continually heightened the anguish of an imminent disgrace. Yes, imminent; for if his defiance of Raffles did not keep the man away – and though he prayed for this result he hardly hoped for it – the disgrace was certain. In vain he said to himself that, if permitted, it would be a divine visitation, a chastisement, a preparation; he recoiled from the imagined burning; and he judged that it must be more for the Divine glory that he should escape dishonour. That recoil had at last urged him to make preparations for quitting Middle-march. If evil truth must be reported of him, he would then be at a less scorching distance from the contempt of his old neighbours; and in a new scene, where his life would not have gathered the same wide sensibility, the tormentor, if he pursued him, would be less formidable. To leave the place finally would, he knew, be extremely painful to his wife, and on other grounds he would have preferred to stay where he had struck root. Hence he made his preparations at first in a conditional way, wishing to leave on all sides an opening for his return after a brief absence, if any favourable intervention of Providence should dissipate his fears. He was preparing to transfer his management of the Bank, and to give up any active control of other commercial affairs in the neighbourhood, on the ground of his failing health, but without excluding his future resumption of such work. The measure would cause him some added expense and some diminution of income beyond what he had already undergone from the general depression of trade; and the Hospital presented itself as a principal object of outlay on which he could fairly economize.

This was the experience which had determined his conversation with Lydgate. But at this time his arrangements had most of them gone no farther than a stage at which he could recall them if they proved to be unnecessary. He continually deferred the final steps; in the midst of his fears, like many a man who is in danger of shipwreck or of being dashed from his carriage by runaway horses, he had a clinging impression that something would happen to hinder the worst, and that to spoil his life by a later transplantation might be over-hasty – especially since it was diffi-cult to account satisfactorily to his wife for the project of their indefinite exile from the only place where she would like to live.

Among the affairs Bulstrode had to care for, was the management of the farm at Stone Court in case of his absence; and on this as well as on all other matters connected with any houses and land he possessed in or about Middlemarch, he had consulted Caleb Garth. Like every one else who had business of that sort, he wanted to get the agent who was more anxious for his employer's interests than his own. With regard to Stone Court, since Bulstrode wished to retain his hold on the stock, and to have an arrangement by which he himself could, if he chose, resume his favourite recreation of superintendence, Caleb had advised him not to trust a mere bailiff, but to let the land, stock, and implements yearly, and take a proportionate share of the proceeds.

'May I trust to you to find me a tenant on these terms, Mr Garth?' said Bulstrode. 'And will you mention to me the yearly sum which would repay you for managing these affairs which we have discussed together?'

'I'll think about it,' said Caleb, in his blunt way. 'I'll see how I can make it out.'

If it had not been that he had to consider Fred Vincy's future, Mr Garth would not probably have been glad of any addition to his work, of which his wife was always fearing an excess for him as he grew older. But on quitting Bulstrode after that conversation, a very alluring idea occurred to him about this said letting of Stone Court. What if Bulstrode would agree to his placing Fred Vincy there on the understanding that he, Caleb Garth, should be responsible for the management? It would be an excellent schooling for Fred; he might make a modest income there, and still have time left to get knowledge by helping in other business. He mentioned his notion to Mrs Garth with such evident delight that she could not bear to chill his pleasure by expressing her constant fear of his undertaking too much.

'The lad would be as happy as two,' he said, throwing himself back in his chair, and looking radiant, 'if I could tell him it was all settled. Think, Susan! His mind had been running on that place for years before old Featherstone died. And it would be as pretty a turn of things as could be that he should hold the place in a good industrious way after all – by his taking to business. For it's likely enough Bulstrode might let him go on, and gradually buy the stock. He hasn't made up his mind, I can see, whether or not he shall settle somewhere else as a lasting thing. I never was better pleased with a notion in my life. And then the children might be married by-and-by, Susan.'

'You will not give any hint of the plan to Fred, until you are sure that Bulstrode would agree to the plan?' said Mrs Garth, in a tone of gentle caution. 'And as to marriage, Caleb, we old people need not help to hasten it.'

'Oh, I don't know,' said Caleb, swinging his head aside. 'Marriage is a taming thing. Fred would want less of my bit and bridle. However, I shall say nothing till I know the ground I'm treading on. I shall speak to Bulstrode again.'

He took his earliest opportunity of doing so. Bulstrode had anything but a warm interest in his nephew Fred Vincy, but he had a strong wish to secure Mr Garth's services on many scattered points of business at which he was sure to be a considerable loser, if they were under less conscientious management. On that ground he made no objection to Mr Garth's proposal; and there was also another reason why he was not sorry to give a consent which was to benefit one of the Vincy family. It was that Mrs Bulstrode, having heard of Lydgate's debts, had been anxious to know whether her husband could not do something for poor Rosamond, and had been much troubled on learning from him that Lydgate's affairs were not easily remediable, and that the wisest plan was to let them 'take their course'. Mrs Bulstrode had then said for the first time, 'I think you are always a little hard towards my family, Nicholas. And I am sure I have no reason to deny any of my relatives. Too worldly they may be, but no one ever had to say that they were not respectable.'

'My dear Harriet,' said Mr Bulstrode, wincing under his wife's eyes, which were filling with tears, 'I have supplied your brother with a great deal of capital. I cannot be expected to take care of his married children.'

That seemed to be true, and Mrs Bulstrode's remonstrance subsided into pity for poor Rosamond, whose extravagant education she had always foreseen the fruits of.

But remembering that dialogue, Mr Bulstrode felt that when he had to talk to his wife fully about his plan of quitting Middlemarch, he should be glad to tell her that he had made an arrangement which might be for the good of her nephew Fred. At present he had merely mentioned to her that he thought of shutting up The Shrubs for a few months, and taking a house on the Southern Coast.

Hence Mr Garth got the assurance he desired, namely, that in case of Bulstrode's departure from Middlemarch for an indefinite time, Fred Vincy should be allowed to have the tenancy of Stone Court on the terms proposed.

Caleb was so elated with his hope of this 'neat turn' being given to things, that if his self-control had not been braced by a little affectionate wifely scolding, he would have betrayed everything to Mary, wanting 'to give the child comfort'. However, he restrained himself, and kept in strict privacy from Fred certain visits which he was making to Stone Court, in order to look more thoroughly into the state of the land and stock, and take a preliminary estimate. He was certainly more eager in these visits than the probable speed of events required him to be; but he was stimulated by a fatherly delight in occupying his mind with this bit of probable happiness which he held in store like a hidden birthday gift for Fred and Mary.

'But suppose the whole scheme should turn out to be a castle in the air?' said Mrs Garth.

'Well, well,' replied Caleb; 'the castle will tumble about nobody's head.'

≪ SIXTY-NINE ≫

If thou hast heard a word, let it die with thee.
Ecclesiasticus

Mr Bulstrode was still seated in his manager's room at the Bank, about three o'clock of the same day on which he had received Lydgate there, when the clerk entered to say that his horse was waiting, and also that Mr Garth was outside and begged to speak with him.

'By all means,' said Bulstrode; and Caleb entered. 'Pray sit down, Mr Garth,' continued the banker, in his suavest tone. 'I am glad that you arrived just in time to find me here. I know you count your minutes.'

'Oh,' said Caleb, gently, with a slow swing of his head on one side, as he seated himself and laid his hat on the floor. He looked at the ground, leaning forward and letting his long fingers droop between his legs, while each finger moved in succession, as if it were sharing some thought which filled his large quiet brow.

Mr Bulstrode, like every one else who knew Caleb, was used to his slowness in beginning to speak on any topic which he felt to be important, and rather expected that he was about to recur to the buying of some houses in Blindman's Court, for the sake of pulling them down, as a sacrifice of property which would be well repaid by the influx of air and light on that spot. It was by propositions of this kind that Caleb was sometimes troublesome to his employers; but he had usually found Bulstrode ready to meet him in projects of improvement, and they had got on well together. When he spoke again, however, it was to say, in rather a subdued voice –

'I have just come away from Stone Court, Mr Bulstrode.'

'You found nothing wrong there, I hope,' said the banker; 'I was there myself yesterday. Abel has done well with the lambs this year.'

'Why, yes,' said Caleb, looking up gravely, 'there *is* something wrong – a stranger, who is very ill, I think. He wants a doctor, and I came to tell you of that. His name is Raffles.'

He saw the shock of his words passing through Bulstrode's frame. On this subject the banker had thought that his fears were too constantly on the watch to be taken by surprise; but he had been mistaken.

'Poor wretch!' he said in a compassionate tone, though his lips trembled a little. 'Do you know how he came there?'

'I took him myself,' said Caleb, quietly – 'took him up in my gig. He had got down from the coach, and was walking a little beyond the turning from the toll-house, and I overtook him. He remembered seeing me with you once before, at Stone Court, and he asked me to take him on. I saw he was ill: it seemed to me the right thing to do, to carry him under shelter. And now I think you should lose no time in getting advice for him.' Caleb took up his hat from the floor as he ended, and rose slowly from his seat.

'Certainly,' said Bulstrode, whose mind was very active at this moment. 'Perhaps you will yourself oblige me, Mr Garth, by calling at Mr Lydgate's as you pass – or stay! he may at this hour probably be at the Hospital. I will first send my man on the horse there with a note this instant, and then I will myself ride to Stone Court.'

Bulstrode quickly wrote a note, and went out himself to give the commission to his man. When he returned, Caleb was standing as before with one hand on the back of the chair, holding his hat with the other. In Bulstrode's mind the dominant thought was, 'Perhaps Raffles only spoke to Garth of his illness. Garth may wonder, as he must have done before, at this disreputable fellow's claiming intimacy with me; but he will know nothing. And he is friendly to me – I can be of use to him.'

He longed for some information of this hopeful conjecture, but to have asked any question as to what Raffles had said or done would have been to betray fear.

'I am exceedingly obliged to you, Mr Garth,' he said, in his usual tone of politeness. 'My servant will be back in a few minutes, and I shall then go myself to see what can be done for this unfortunate man. Perhaps you had some other business with me? If so, pray be seated.'

'Thank you,' said Caleb, making a slight gesture with his right hand to waive the invitation. 'I wish to say, Mr Bulstrode, that I must request you to put your business into some other hands than mine. I am obliged to you for your handsome way of meeting me – about the letting of Stone Court, and all other business. But I must give it up.'

A sharp certainty entered like a stab into Bulstrode's soul.

'This is sudden, Mr Garth,' was all he could say at first.

'It is,' said Caleb; 'but it is quite fixed. I must give it up.'

He spoke with a firmness which was very gentle, and yet he could see that Bulstrode seemed to cower under that gentleness, his face looking dried and his eyes swerving away from the glance which rested on him. Caleb felt a deep pity for him, but he could have used no pretexts to account for his resolve, even if they would have been of any use.

'You have been led to this, I apprehend, by some slanders concerning me uttered by that unhappy creature,' said Bulstrode, anxious now to know the utmost.

'That is true. I can't deny that I act upon what I heard from him.'

'You are a conscientious man, Mr Garth – a man, I trust, who feels himself accountable to God. You would not wish to injure me by being too ready to believe a slander,' said Bulstrode, casting about for pleas that might be adapted to his hearer's mind. 'That is a poor reason for giving up a connection which I think I may say will be mutually beneficial.'

'I would injure no man if I could help it,' said Caleb; 'even if I thought God winked at it. I hope I should have a feeling for my fellow-creature. But, sir – I am obliged to believe that this Raffles has told me the truth. And I can't be happy in working with you, or profiting by you. It hurts my mind. I must beg you to seek another agent.'

'Very well, Mr Garth. But I must at least claim to know the worst that he has told you. I must know what is the foul speech that I am liable to be the victim of,' said Bulstrode, a certain amount of anger beginning to mingle with his humiliation before this quiet man who renounced his benefits.

'That's needless,' said Caleb, waving his hand, bowing his head slightly, and not swerving from the tone which had in it the merciful intention to spare this pitiable man. 'What he has said to me will never pass from my lips, unless something now unknown forces it from me. If you led a harmful life for gain, and kept others out of their rights by deceit, to get the more for yourself, I daresay you repent – you would like to go back, and can't: that must be a bitter thing' – Caleb paused a moment and shook his head – 'it is not for me to make your life harder to you.'

'But you do – you do make it harder to me,' said Bulstrode, constrained into a genuine, pleading cry. 'You make it harder to me by turning your back on me.'

'That I'm forced to do,' said Caleb, still more gently, lifting up his hand. 'I am sorry. I don't judge you and say, he is wicked, and I am righteous. God forbid. I don't know everything. A man may do wrong, and his will may rise clear out of it, though he can't get his life clear. That's a bad punishment. If it is so with you, – well, I'm very sorry for you. But I have that feeling inside me, that I can't go on working with you. That's all, Mr Bulstrode. Everything else is buried, so far as my will goes. And I wish you good-day.'

'One moment, Mr Garth!' said Bulstrode, hurriedly. 'I may trust then to your solemn assurance that you will not repeat either to man or woman what – even if it had any degree of truth in it – is yet a malicious representation?'

Caleb's wrath was stirred, and he said, indignantly –

'Why should I have said it if I didn't mean it? I am in no fear of you. Such tales as that will never tempt my tongue.'

'Excuse me – I am agitated – I am the victim of this abandoned man.'

'Stop a bit! you have got to consider whether you didn't help to make him worse, when you profited by his vices.'

'You are wronging me by too readily believing him,' said Bulstrode, oppressed, as by a nightmare, with the inability to deny flatly what Raffles might have said; and yet feeling it an escape that Caleb had not so stated it to him as to ask for that flat denial.

'No,' said Caleb, lifting his hand deprecatingly; 'I am ready to believe better, when better is proved. I rob you of no good chance. As to speaking, I hold it a crime to expose a man's sin unless I'm clear it must be done to save the innocent. That is my way of thinking, Mr Bulstrode, and what I say, I've no need to swear. I wish you good-day.'

Some hours later, when he was at home, Caleb said to his wife, incidentally, that he had had some little differences with Bulstrode, and that in consequence, he had given up all notion of taking Stone Court, and had indeed resigned doing further business for him.

'He was disposed to interfere too much, was he?' said Mrs Garth, imagining that her husband had been touched on his sensitive point, and not been allowed to do what he thought right as to materials and modes of work.

'Oh,' said Caleb, bowing his head and waving his hand gravely. And Mrs Garth knew that this was a sign of his not intending to speak further on the subject.

As for Bulstrode, he had almost immediately mounted his horse and set off for Stone Court, being anxious to arrive there before Lydgate.

His mind was crowded with images and conjectures, which were a language to his hopes and fears, just as we hear tones from the vibrations which shake our whole system. The deep humiliation with which he had winced under Caleb Garth's knowledge of his past and rejection of his patronage, alternated with and almost gave way to the sense of safety in the fact that Garth, and no other, had been the man to whom Raffles had spoken. It seemed to him a sort of earnest that Providence intended his rescue from worse consequences; the way being thus left open for the hope of secrecy. That Raffles should be afflicted with illness, that he should have been led to Stone Court rather than elsewhere – Bulstrode's heart fluttered at the vision of probabilities which these events conjured up. If it should turn out that he was freed from all danger of disgrace – if he could breathe in perfect liberty – his life should be more consecrated than it had ever been before. He mentally lifted up this vow as if it would urge the result he longed for – he tried to believe in the potency of that prayerful resolution – its potency to determine death. He knew that he ought to say, 'Thy will be done', and he said it often. But the intense desire remained that the will of God might be the death of that hated man.

Yet when he arrived at Stone Court he could not see the change in Raffles without a shock. But for his pallor and feebleness, Bulstrode would have called the change in him entirely mental. Instead of his loud tormenting mood, he showed an intense, vague terror, and seemed to deprecate Bulstrode's anger, because the money was all gone – he had been robbed – it had half of it been taken from him. He had only come here because he was ill and somebody was hunting him – somebody was after him: he had told nobody anything, he had kept his mouth shut. Bulstrode, not knowing the significance of these symptoms, interpreted this new nervous susceptibility into a means of alarming Raffles into true confessions, and taxed him with falsehood in saying that he had not told anything, since he had just told the man who took him up in his gig and brought him to Stone Court. Raffles denied this with solemn adjurations; the fact being that the links of consciousness were interrupted in him, and that his minute terror-stricken narrative to Caleb Garth had been delivered under a set of visionary impulses which had dropped back into darkness.

Bulstrode's heart sank again at this sign that he could get no grasp over the wretched man's mind, and that no word of Raffles could be trusted as to the fact which he most wanted to know, namely, whether or not he had really kept silence to every one in the neighbourhood except Caleb Garth. The housekeeper had told him without the least constraint of manner that since Mr Garth left, Raffles had asked her for beer, and after that had not spoken, seeming very ill. On that side it might be concluded that there had been no betrayal. Mrs Abel thought, like the servants at The Shrubs, that the strange man belonged to the unpleasant 'kin' who are among the troubles of the rich; she had at first referred the kinship to Mr Rigg, and where there was property left, the buzzing presence of such large bluebottles seemed natural enough. How he could be 'kin' to Bulstrode as well was not so clear, but Mrs Abel agreed with her husband that there was 'no knowing', a proposition which had a great deal of mental food for her, so that she shook her head over it without further speculation.

In less than an hour Lydgate arrived. Bulstrode met him outside the wainscoted parlour, where Raffles was, and said –

'I have called you in, Mr Lydgate, to an unfortunate man who was once in my employment many years ago. Afterwards he went to America, and returned I fear to an idle dissolute life. Being destitute, he has a claim on me. He was slightly connected with Rigg, the former owner of this place, and in consequence found his way here. I believe he is seriously ill: apparently his mind is affected, I feel bound to do the utmost for him.'

Lydgate, who had the remembrance of his last conversation with Bulstrode strongly upon him, was not disposed to say an unnecessary word to him, and bowed slightly in answer to this account; but just before entering the room he turned automatically and said, 'What is his name?' – to know names being as much a part of the medical man's accomplishment as of the practical politician's.

'Raffles, John Raffles,' said Bulstrode, who hoped that whatever became of Raffles, Lydgate would never know any more of him.

When he had thoroughly examined and considered the patient, Lydgate ordered that he should go to bed, and be kept there in as complete quiet as possible, and then went with Bulstrode into another room.

'It is a serious case, I apprehend,' said the banker, before Lydgate began to speak.

'No – and yes,' said Lydgate, half dubiously. 'It is difficult to decide as to the possible effect of long-standing complications; but the man had a robust constitution to begin with. I should not expect this attack to be fatal, though of course the system is in a ticklish state. He should be well watched and attended to.'

'I will remain here myself,' said Bulstrode. 'Mrs Abel and her husband are inexperienced. I can easily remain here for the night, if you will oblige me by taking a note for Mrs Bulstrode.'

'I should think that is hardly necessary,' said Lydgate. 'He seems tame and terrified enough. He might become more unmanageable. But there is a man here – is there not?'

'I have more than once stayed here a few nights for the sake of seclusion,' said Bulstrode, indifferently; 'I am quite disposed to do so now. Mrs Abel and her husband can relieve or aid me, if necessary.'

'Very well. Then I need give my directions only to you,' said Lydgate, not feeling surprised at a little peculiarity in Bulstrode.

'You think, then, that the case is hopeful?' said Bulstrode, when Lydgate had ended giving his orders.

'Unless there turn out to be further complications, such as I have not at present detected – yes,' said Lydgate. 'He may pass on to a worse stage; but I should not wonder if he got better in a few days, by adhering to the treatment I have prescribed. There must be firmness. Remember, if he calls for liquors of any sort, not to give them to him. In my opinion, men in his condition are oftener killed by treatment than by the disease. Still, new symptoms may arise. I shall come again to-morrow morning.'

After waiting for the note to be carried to Mrs Bulstrode, Lydgate rode away, forming no conjectures, in the first instance, about the history of Raffles, but rehearsing the whole argument which had lately been much stirred by the publication of Dr Ware's abundant experience in America, as to the right way of treating cases of alcoholic poisoning such as this. Lydgate, when abroad, had already been interested in this question: he was strongly convinced against the prevalent practice of allowing alcohol and persistently administering large doses of opium; and he had repeatedly acted on this conviction with a favourable result.

'The man is in a diseased state,' he thought, 'but there's a good deal of wear in him still. I suppose he is an object of charity to Bulstrode. It is curious what patches of hardness and tenderness lie side by side in men's dispositions. Bulstrode seems the most unsympathetic fellow I ever saw about some people, and yet he has taken no end of trouble, and spent a great deal of money, on benevolent objects. I suppose he has some test by which he finds out whom Heaven cares for – he has made up his mind that it doesn't care for me.'

This streak of bitterness came from a plenteous source, and kept widening in the current of his thought as he neared Lowick Gate. He had not been there since his first interview with Bulstrode in the morning, having been found at the Hospital by the banker's messenger; and for the first time he was returning to his home without the vision of any expedient in the background which left him a hope of raising money enough to deliver him from the coming destitution of everything which made his married life tolerable – everything which saved him and Rosamond from that bare isolation in which they would be forced to recognize how little of a comfort they could be to each other. It was more bearable to do without tenderness for himself than to see that his own tenderness could make no amends for the lack of other things to her. The sufferings of his own pride from humiliations past and to come were keen enough, yet they were hardly distinguishable to himself from that more acute pain which dominated them – the pain of foreseeing that Rosamond would come to regard him chiefly as the cause of disappointment and unhappiness to her. He had never liked the makeshifts of poverty, and they had never before entered into his prospects for himself; but he was beginning now to imagine how two creatures who loved each other, and had a stock of thoughts in common, might laugh over their shabby furniture, and their calculations how far they could afford butter and eggs. But the glimpse of that poetry seemed as far off from him as the carelessness of the golden age; in poor Rosamond's mind there was not room enough for luxuries to look small in. He got down from his horse in a very sad mood, and went into the house, not expecting to be cheered except by his dinner, and reflecting that before the evening closed it would be wise to tell Rosamond of his application to Bulstrode and his failure. It would be well not to lose time in preparing her for the worst.

But his dinner waited long for him before he was able to eat it. For on entering he found that Dover's agent had already put a man in the house, and when he asked where Mrs Lydgate was, he was told that she was in her bedroom. He went up and found her stretched on the bed pale and silent, without an answer even in her face to any word or look of his. He sat down by the bed and leaning over her said with almost a cry of prayer –

'Forgive me for this misery, my poor Rosamond! Let us only love one another.'

She looked at him silently, still with the blank despair on her face; but the tears began to fill her blue eyes, and her lip trembled. The strong man had had too much to bear that day. He let his head fall beside hers and sobbed.

He did not hinder her from going to her father early in the morning – it seemed now that he ought not to hinder her from doing as she pleased. In half an hour she came back, and said that papa and mamma wished her to go and stay with them while things were in this miserable state. Papa said he could do nothing about the debt – if he paid this, there would be half-a-dozen more. She had better come back home again till Lydgate had got a comfortable home for her. 'Do you object, Tertius?'

'Do as you like,' said Lydgate. 'But things are not coming to a crisis immediately. There is no hurry.'

'I should not go till to-morrow,' said Rosamond; 'I shall want to pack my clothes.'

'Oh, I would wait a little longer than to-morrow – there is no knowing what may happen,' said Lydgate, with bitter irony. 'I may get my neck broken, and that may make things easier to you.'

It was Lydgate's misfortune and Rosamond's too, that his tenderness towards her, which was both an emotional prompting and a well-considered resolve, was inevitably interrupted by these outbursts of indignation either ironical or remonstrant. She thought them totally unwarranted, and the repulsion which this exceptional severity excited in her was in danger of making the more persistent tenderness unacceptable.

'I see you do not wish me to go,' she said, with chill mildness; 'why can you not say so, without that kind of violence? I shall stay until you request me to do otherwise.'

Lydgate said no more, but went out on his rounds. He felt bruised and shattered, and there was a dark line under his eyes which Rosamond had not seen before. She could not bear to look at him. Tertius had a way of taking things which made them a great deal worse for her.

‹? SEVENTY ››

Our deeds still travel with us from afar,
And what we have been makes us what we are.

BULSTRODE'S FIRST OBJECT AFTER LYDGATE had left Stone Court was to examine Raffles's pockets, which he imagined were sure to carry signs in the shape of hotel-bills of the places he had stopped in, if he had not told the truth in saying that he had come straight from Liverpool because he was ill and had no money. There were various bills crammed into his pocket-book, but none of a later date than Christmas at any other place, except one, which bore date that morning. This was crumpled up with a handbill about a horse-fair in one of his tail-pockets and represented the cost of three days' stay at an inn at Bilkley, where the fair was held – a town at least forty miles from Middlemarch. The bill was heavy, and since Raffles had no luggage with him, it seemed probable that he had left his portmanteau behind in payment, in order to save money for his travelling fare; for his purse was empty, and he had only a couple of sixpences and some loose pence in his pockets.

Bulstrode gathered a sense of safety from these indications that Raffles had really kept at a distance from Middlemarch since his memorable visit at Christmas. At a distance and among people who were strangers to Bulstrode, what satisfaction could there be to Raffles's tormenting, self-magnifying vein in telling old scandalous stories about a· Middlemarch banker? And what harm if he did talk? The chief point now was to keep watch over him as long as there was any danger of that intelligible raving, that unaccountable impulse to tell, which seemed to have acted towards Caleb Garth; and Bulstrode felt much anxiety lest some such impulse should come over him at the sight of Lydgate. He sat up alone with him through the night, only ordering the housekeeper to lie down in her clothes, so as to be ready when he called her, alleging his own indisposition to sleep, and his anxiety to carry out the doctor's orders. He did carry them out faithfully, although Raffles was incessantly asking for brandy, and declaring that he was sinking away – that the earth was sinking away from under him. He was restless and sleepless, but still quailing and manageable. On the offer of the food ordered by Lydgate, which he refused, and the denial of other things which he demanded, he seemed to concentrate all his terror on Bulstrode, imploringly deprecating his anger, his revenge on him by starvation, and declaring with strong oaths that he had never told any mortal a word against him. Even this Bulstrode felt that he would not have liked Lydgate to hear; but a more alarming sign of fitful alternation in his delirium was, that in the morning twilight Raffles suddenly seemed to imagine a doctor present, addressing him and declaring that Bulstrode wanted to starve him to death out of revenge for telling, when he never had told.

Bulstrode's native imperiousness and strength of determination served him well. This delicate-looking man, himself nervously perturbed, found the needed stimulus in his strenuous circumstances, and through that difficult night and morning, while he had the air of an animated corpse returned to movement without warmth, holding the mastery by its chill impassibility, his mind was intensely at work thinking of what he had to guard against and what would win him security. Whatever prayers he might lift up, whatever statements he might inwardly make of this man's wretched spiritual condition, and the duty he himself was under to submit to the punishment divinely appointed for him rather than to wish for evil to another – through all this effort to condense words into a solid mental state, there pierced and spread with irresistible vividness the images of the events he desired. And in the train of those images came their apology. He could not but see the death of Raffles, and see in it his own deliverance. What was the removal of this wretched creature? He was impenitent – but were not public criminals impenitent? – yet the law decided on their fate. Should Providence in this case award death, there was no sin in contemplating death as the desirable issue – if he kept his hands from hastening it – if he scrupulously did what was prescribed. Even here there might be a mistake; human prescriptions were fallible things: Lydgate had said that treatment had hastened death, – why not his own method of treatment? But of course intention was everything in the question of right and wrong.

And Bulstrode set himself to keep his intention separate from his desire. He inwardly declared that he intended to obey orders. Why should he have got into any argument about the validity of these orders? It was only the common trick of desire – which avails itself of any irrelevant scepticism, finding larger room for itself in all uncertainty about effects, in every obscurity that looks like the absence of law. Still, he did obey the orders.

His anxieties continually glanced towards Lydgate, and his remembrance of what had taken place between them the morning before was accompanied with sensibilities which had not been roused at all during the actual scene. He had then cared but little about Lydgate's painful impressions with regard to the suggested change in the Hospital, or about the disposition towards himself which what he held to be his justifiable refusal of a rather exorbitant request might call forth. He recurred to the scene now with a perception that he had probably made Lydgate his enemy, and with an awakened desire to propitiate him, or rather to create in him a strong sense of personal obligation. He regretted that he had not at once made even an unreasonable money-sacrifice. For in case of unpleasant suspicions or even knowledge gathered from the raving of Raffles, Bulstrode would have felt that he had a defence in Lydgate's mind by having conferred a momentous benefit on him. But the regret had perhaps come too late.

Strange, piteous conflict in the soul of this unhappy man, who had longed for years to be better than he was – who had taken his selfish passions into discipline and clad them in severe robes, so that he had walked with them as a devout quire, till now that a terror had risen among them, and they could chant no longer, but threw out their common cries for safety.

It was nearly the middle of the day before Lydgate arrived: he had meant to come earlier, but had been detained, he said; and his shattered looks were noticed by Bulstrode. But he immediately threw himself into the consideration of the patient, and inquired strictly into all that had occurred. Raffles was worse, would take hardly any food, was persistently wakeful and restlessly raving; but still not violent. Contrary to Bulstrode's alarmed expectation, he took little notice of Lydgate's presence, and continued to talk or murmur incoherently.

'What do you think of him?' said Bulstrode, in private.

'The symptoms are worse.'

'You are less hopeful?'

'No; I still think he may come round. Are you going to stay here yourself?' said Lydgate, looking at Bulstrode with an abrupt question, which made him uneasy, though in reality it was not due to any suspicious conjecture.

'Yes, I think so,' said Bulstrode, governing himself and speaking with deliberation. 'Mrs Bulstrode is advised of the reasons which detain me. Mrs Abel and her husband are not experienced enough to be left quite alone, and this kind of responsibility is scarcely included in their service of me. You have some fresh instructions, I presume.'

The chief new instruction that Lydgate had to give was on the administration of extremely moderate doses of opium, in case of the sleeplessness continuing after several hours. He had taken the precaution of bringing opium in his pocket, and he gave minute directions to Bulstrode as to the doses, and the point at which they should cease. He insisted on the risk of not ceasing; and repeated his order that no alcohol should be given.

'From what I see of the case,' he ended, 'narcotism is the only thing I should be much afraid of. He may wear through even without much food. There's a good deal of strength in him.'

'You look ill yourself, Mr Lydgate – a most unusual, I may say unprecedented thing in my knowledge of you,' said Bulstrode, showing a solicitude as unlike his indifference the day before, as his present recklessness about his own fatigue was unlike his habitual self-cherishing anxiety. 'I fear you are harassed.'

'Yes, I am,' said Lydgate, brusquely, holding his hat, and ready to go.

'Something new, I fear,' said Bulstrode, inquiringly. 'Pray be seated.'

'No, thank you,' said Lydgate, with some *hauteur*. 'I mentioned to you yesterday what was the state of my affairs. There is nothing to add, except that the execution has since then been actually put into my house. One can tell a good deal of trouble in a short sentence. I will say good-morning.'

'Stay, Mr Lydgate, stay,' said Bulstrode; 'I have been reconsidering this subject. I was yesterday taken by surprise and saw it superficially. Mrs Bulstrode is anxious for her niece, and I myself should grieve at a calamitous change in your position. Claims on me are numerous, but on reconsideration, I esteem it right that I should incur a small sacrifice rather than leave you unaided. You said, I think, that a thousand pounds would suffice entirely to free you from your burthens, and enable you to recover a firm stand?'

'Yes,' said Lydgate, a great leap of joy within him surmounting every other feeling; 'that would pay all my debts, and leave me a little on hand. I could set about economizing in our way of living. And by-and-by my practice might look up.'

'If you will wait a moment, Mr Lydgate, I will draw a cheque to that amount. I am aware that help, to be effectual in these cases, should be thorough.'

While Bulstrode wrote, Lydgate turned to the window thinking of his home – thinking of his life with its good start saved from frustration, its good purposes still unbroken.

'You can give me a note of hand for this, Mr Lydgate,' said the banker, advancing towards him with the cheque. 'And by-and-by, I hope, you may be in circumstances gradually to repay me. Meanwhile, I have great pleasure in thinking that you will be released from further difficulty.'

'I am deeply obliged to you,' said Lydgate. 'You have restored to me the prospect of working with some happiness and some chance of good.'

It appeared to him a very natural movement in Bulstrode that he should have reconsidered his refusal: it corresponded with the more munificent side of his character. But as he put his hack into a canter, that he might get the sooner home, and tell the good news to Rosamond, and get cash at the bank to pay over to Dover's agent, there crossed his mind, with an unpleasant impression, as from a dark-winged flight of evil augury across his vision, the thought of that contrast in himself which a few months had brought – that he should be overjoyed at being under a strong personal obligation – that he should be overjoyed at getting money for himself from Bulstrode.

The banker felt that he had done something to nullify one cause of uneasiness, and yet he was scarcely the easier. He did not measure the quantity of diseased motive which had made him wish for Lydgate's goodwill, but the quantity was none the less actively there, like an irritating agent in his blood. A man vows, and yet will not cast away the means of breaking his vow. Is it that he distinctly means to break it? Not at all; but the desires which tend to break it are at work in him dimly, and make their way into his imagination, and relax his muscles in the very moments when he is telling himself over again the reasons for his vow. Raffles, recovering quickly, returning to the free use of his odious powers – how could Bulstrode wish for that? Raffles dead was the image that brought release, and indirectly he prayed for that way of release, beseeching that, if it were possible, the rest of his days here below might be freed from the threat of an ignominy which would break him utterly as an instrument of God's service. Lydgate's opinion was not on the side of promise that this prayer would be fulfilled; and as the day advanced, Bulstrode felt himself getting irritated at the persistent life in this man, whom he would fain have seen sinking in to the silence of death: imperious will stirred murderous impulses towards this brute life, over which will, by itself, had no power. He said inwardly that he was getting too much worn; he would not sit up with the patient to-night, but leave him to Mrs Abel, who, if necessary, could call her husband.

At six o'clock, Raffles, having had only fitful perturbed snatches of sleep, from which he waked with fresh restlessness and perpetual cries that he was sinking away, Bulstrode began to administer the opium according to Lydgate's directions. At the end of half an hour or more he called Mrs Abel and told her that he found himself unfit for further watching. He must now consign the patient to her care; and he proceeded to repeat to her Lydgate's directions as to the quantity of each dose. Mrs Abel had not before known anything of Lydgate's prescriptions; she had simply prepared and brought whatever Bulstrode ordered, and had done what he pointed out to her. She began now to ask what else she should do besides administering the opium.

'Nothing at present, except the offer of the soup or the soda-water: you can come to me for further directions. Unless there is any important change, I shall not come into the room again to-night. You will ask your husband for help, if necessary. I must go to bed early.'

'You've much need, sir, I'm sure,' said Mrs Abel, 'and to take something more strengthening than what you've done.'

Bulstrode went away now without anxiety as to what Raffles might say in his raving, which had taken on a muttering incoherence not likely to create any dangerous belief. At any rate he must risk this. He went down into the wainscoated parlour first, and began to consider whether he would not have his horse saddled and go home by the moonlight, and give up caring for earthly consequences. Then, he wished that he had begged Lydgate to come again that evening. Perhaps he might deliver a different opinion, and think that Raffles was getting into a less hopeful state. Should he send for Lydgate? If Raffles were really getting worse, and slowly dying, Bulstrode felt that he could go to bed and sleep in gratitude to Providence. But was he worse? Lydgate might come and simply say that he was going on as he expected, and predict that he would by-and-by fall into a good sleep, and get well. What was the use of sending for him? Bulstrode shrank from that result. No ideas or opinions could hinder him from seeing the one probability to be, that Raffles recovered would be just the same man as before, with his strength as a tormentor renewed, obliging him to drag away his wife to spend her years apart from her friends and native place, carrying an alienating suspicion against him in her heart.

He had sat an hour and a half in this conflict by the firelight only, when a sudden thought made him rise and light the bed-candle, which he had brought down with him. The thought was, that he had not told Mrs Abel when the doses of opium must cease.

He took hold of the candlestick, but stood motionless for a long while. She might already have given him more than Lydgate had prescribed. But it was excusable in him, that he should forget part of an order, in his present wearied condition. He walked up-stairs, candle in hand, not knowing whether he should straightway enter his own room and go to bed, or turn to the patient's room and rectify his omission. He paused in the passage, with his face turned towards Raffles's room, and he could hear him moaning and murmuring. He was not asleep, then. Who could know that Lydgate's prescription would not be better disobeyed than followed, since there was still no sleep?

He turned into his own room. Before he had quite undressed, Mrs Abel rapped at the door; he opened it an inch, so that he could hear her speak low.

'If you please, sir, should I have no brandy nor nothing to give the poor creetur? He feels sinking away, and nothing else will he swaller – and but little strength in it, if he did – only the opium. And he says more and more he's sinking down through the earth.'

To her surprise, Mr Bulstrode did not answer. A struggle was going on within him.

'I think he must die for want o' support, if he goes on in that way. When I nursed my poor master, Mr Robisson, I had to give him port-wine and brandy constant, and a big glass at a time,' added Mrs Abel with a touch of remonstrance in her tone.

But again Mr Bulstrode did not answer immediately, and she continued, 'It's not a time to spare when people are at death's door, nor would you wish it, sir, I'm sure. Else I should give him our own bottle o' rum as we keep by us. But a sitter-up so as you've been, and doing everything as laid in your power – '

Here a key was thrust through the inch of doorway, and Mr Bulstrode said huskily, 'That is the key of the wine-cooler. You will find plenty of brandy there.'

Early in the morning – about six – Mr Bulstrode rose and spent some time in prayer. Does any one suppose that private prayer is necessarily candid – necessarily goes to the roots of action! Private prayer is inaudible speech, and speech is representative: who can represent himself just as he is, even in his own reflections? Bulstrode had not yet unravelled in his thought the confused promptings of the last four-and-twenty hours.

He listened in the passage, and could hear hard stertorous breathing. Then he walked out in the garden, and looked at the early rime on the grass and fresh spring leaves. When he re-entered the house, he felt startled at the sight of Mrs Abel.

'How is your patient – asleep, I think?' he said, with an attempt at cheerfulness in his tone.

'He's gone very deep, sir,' said Mrs Abel. 'He went off gradual between three and four o'clock. Would you please to go and look at him? I thought it no harm to leave him. My man's gone afield, and the little girl's seeing to the kettles.'

Bulstrode went up. At a glance he knew that Raffles was not in the sleep which brings revival, but in the sleep which streams deeper and deeper into the gulf of death.

He looked round the room and saw a bottle with some brandy in it, and the almost empty opium phial. He put the phial out of sight, and carried the brandy-bottle down-stairs with him, locking it again in the wine-cooler.

While breakfasting he considered whether he should ride to Middlemarch at once, or wait for Lydgate's arrival. He decided to wait, and told Mrs Abel that she might go about her work – he could watch in the bed-chamber.

As he sat there and beheld the enemy of his peace going irrevocably into silence, he felt more at rest than he had done for many months. His conscience was soothed by the enfolding wing of secrecy, which seemed just then like an angel sent down for his relief. He drew out his pocket-book to review various memoranda there as to the arrangements he had projected and partly carried out in the prospect of quitting Middlemarch, and considered how far he would let them stand or recall them, now that his absence would be brief. Some economies which he felt desirable might still find a suitable occasion in his temporary withdrawal from manage-ment, and he hoped still that Mrs Casaubon would take a large share in the expenses of the Hospital. In that way the moments passed, until a change in the stertorous breathing was marked enough to draw his atten-tion wholly to the bed, and forced him to think of the departing life, which had once been subservient to his own – which he had once been glad to find base enough for him to act as he would. It was his gladness then which impelled him now to be glad that the life was at an end.

And who could say that the death of Raffles had been hastened? Who knew what would have saved him?

Lydgate arrived at half-past ten, in time to witness the final pause of the breath. When he entered the room Bulstrode observed a sudden expression in his face, which was not so much surprise as a recognition that he had not judged correctly. He stood by the bed in silence for some time, with his eyes turned on the dying man, but with that subdued activity of expression which showed that he was carrying on an inward debate.

'When did this change begin?' said he, looking at Bulstrode.

'I did not watch by him last night,' said Bulstrode. 'I was over-worn, and left him under Mrs Abel's care. She said that he sank into sleep between three and four o'clock. When I came in before eight he was nearly in this condition.'

Lydgate did not ask another question, but watched in silence until he said, 'It's all over.'

This morning Lydgate was in a state of recovered hope and freedom. He had set out on his work with all his old animation, and felt strong enough to bear all the deficiencies of his married life. And he was con-scious that Bulstrode had been a benefactor to him. But he was uneasy about this case. He had not expected it to terminate as it had done. Yet he hardly knew how to put a question on the subject to Bulstrode without appearing to insult him; and if he examined the housekeeper – why, the man was dead. There seemed to be no use in implying that somebody's ignorance or imprudence had killed him. And after all, he himself might be wrong.

He and Bulstrode rode back to Middlemarch together, talking of many things – chiefly cholera and the chances of the Reform Bill in the House of Lords, and the firm resolve of the Political Unions. Nothing was said about Raffles, except that Bulstrode mentioned the necessity of having a grave for him in Lowick churchyard and observed that, so far as he knew, the poor man had no connections, except Rigg, whom he had stated to be unfriendly towards him.

On returning home Lydgate had a visit from Mr Farebrother. The Vicar had not been in town the day before, but the news that there was an execution in Lydgate's house had got to Lowick by the evening, having been carried by Mr Spicer, shoemaker and parish-clerk, who had it from his brother, the respectable bell-hanger in Lowick Gate. Since that evening when Lydgate had come down from the billiard-room with Fred Vincy, Mr Farebrother's thoughts about him had been rather gloomy. Playing at the Green Dragon once or oftener might have been a trifle in another man; but in Lydgate it was one of several signs that he was getting unlike his former self. He was beginning to do things for which he had formerly even an excessive scorn. Whatever certain dissatisfactions in marriage, which some silly tinklings of gossip had given him hints of, might have to do with this change, Mr Farebrother felt that it was chiefly connected with the debts which were being more and more distinctly reported, and he began to fear that any notion of Lydgate's having resources or friends in the background must be quite illusory. The rebuff he had met with in his first attempt to win Lydgate's confidence, disinclined him to a second; but this news of the execution being actually in the house, determined the Vicar to overcome his reluctance.

Lydgate had just dismissed a poor patient, in whom he was much interested, and he came forward to put out his hand with an open cheerfulness which surprised Mr Farebrother. Could this too be a proud rejection of sympathy and help? Never mind; the sympathy and help should be offered.

'How are you, Lydgate? I came to see you because I had heard something which made me anxious about you,' said the Vicar, in the tone of a good brother, only that there was no reproach in it. They were both seated by this time, and Lydgate answered immediately –

'I think I know what you mean. You had heard that there was an execution in the house?'

'Yes; is it true?'

'It was true,' said Lydgate, with an air of freedom, as if he did not mind talking about the affair now. 'But the danger is over; the debt is paid. I am out of my difficulties now: I shall be freed from debts, and able, I hope, to start afresh on a better plan.'

'I am very thankful to hear it,' said the Vicar, falling back in his chair, and speaking with that low-toned quickness which often follows the removal of a load. 'I like that better than all the news in the *Times*. I confess I came to you with a heavy heart.'

'Thank you for coming,' said Lydgate, cordially. 'I can enjoy the kindness all the more because I am happier. I have certainly been a good deal crushed. I'm afraid I shall find the bruises still painful by-and-by,' he added, smiling rather sadly; 'but just now I can only feel that the torture-screw is off.'

Mr Farebrother was silent for a moment, and then said earnestly, 'My dear fellow, let me ask you one question. Forgive me if I take a liberty.'

'I don't believe you will ask anything that ought to offend me.'

'Then – this is necessary to set my heart quite at rest – you have not – have you? – in order to pay your debts, incurred another debt which may harass you worse hereafter?'

'No,' said Lydgate, colouring slightly. 'There is no reason why I should not tell you – since the fact is so – that the person to whom I am indebted is Bulstrode. He has made me a very handsome advance – a thousand pounds – and he can afford to wait for repayment.'

'Well, that is generous,' said Mr Farebrother, compelling himself to approve of the man whom he disliked. His delicate feeling shrank from dwelling even in his thought on the fact that he had always urged Lydgate to avoid any personal entanglement with Bulstrode. He added immediately, 'And Bulstrode must naturally feel an interest in your welfare, after you have worked with him in a way which has probably reduced your income instead of adding to it. I am glad to think that he has acted accordingly.'

Lydgate felt uncomfortable under these kindly suppositions. They made more distinct within him the uneasy consciousness which had shown its first dim stirrings only a few hours before, that Bulstrode's motives for his sudden beneficence following close upon the chillest indifference might be merely selfish. He let the kindly suppositions pass. He could not tell the history of the loan, but it was more vividly present with him than ever, as well as the fact which the Vicar delicately ignored – that this relation of personal indebtedness to Bulstrode was what he had once been most resolved to avoid.

He began, instead of answering, to speak of his projected economies, and of his having come to look at his life from a different point of view.

'I shall set up a surgery,' he said. 'I really think I made a mistaken effort in that respect. And if Rosamond will not mind, I shall take an apprentice. I don't like these things, but if one carries them out faithfully they are not really lowering. I have had a severe galling to begin with: that will make the small rubs seem easy.'

Poor Lydgate! the 'if Rosamond will not mind', which had fallen from him involuntarily as part of his thought, was a significant mark of the yoke he bore. But Mr Farebrother, whose hopes entered strongly into the same current with Lydgate's, and who knew nothing about him that could now raise a melancholy presentiment, left him with affectionate congratulation.

❧ SEVENTY-ONE ❧

Clown . . . 'Twas in the Bunch of Grapes, where, indeed, you have
a delight to sit, have you not?
Froth. I have so; because it is an open room, and good for winter.
Clo. Why, very well then: I hope here be truths.

Measure for Measure

FIVE DAYS AFTER THE DEATH OF Raffles, Mr Bambridge was standing at his leisure under the large archway leading into the yard of the Green Dragon. He was not fond of solitary contemplation, but he had only just come out of the house, and any human figure standing at ease under the archway in the early afternoon was as certain to attract companionship as a pigeon which has found something worth pecking at. In this case there was no material object to feed upon, but the eye of reason saw a probability of mental sustenance in the shape of gossip. Mr Hopkins, the meek-mannered draper opposite, was the first to act on this inward vision, being the more ambitious of a little masculine talk because his customers were chiefly women. Mr Bambridge was rather curt to the draper, feeling that Hopkins was of course glad to talk to *him*, but that he was not going to waste much of his talk on Hopkins. Soon, however, there was a small cluster of more important listeners, who were either deposited from the passers-by, or had sauntered to the spot expressly to see if there were anything going on at the Green Dragon; and Mr Bambridge was finding it worth his while to say many impressive things about the fine studs he had been seeing and the purchases he had made on a journey in the north from which he had just returned. Gentlemen present were assured that when they could show him anything to cut out a blood mare, a bay, rising four, which was to be seen at Doncaster if they chose to go and look at it, Mr Bambridge would gratify them by being shot 'from here to Hereford'. Also, a pair of blacks which he was going to put into the break recalled vividly to his mind a pair which he had sold to Faulkner in '19, for a hundred guineas, and which Faulkner had sold for a hundred and sixty two months later – any agent who could disprove this statement being offered the privilege of calling Mr Bambridge by a very ugly name until the exercise made his throat dry.

When the discourse was at this point of animation, came up Mr Frank Hawley. He was not a man to compromise his dignity by lounging at the Green Dragon, but happening to pass along the High Street and seeing

556

Bambridge on the other side, he took some of his long strides to ask the horse-dealer whether he had found the first-rate gig-horse which he had engaged to look for. Mr Hawley was requested to wait until he had seen a grey selected at Bilkley: if that did not meet his wishes to a hair, Bambridge did not know a horse when he saw it, which seemed to be the highest conceivable unlikelihood. Mr Hawley, standing with his back to the street, was fixing a time for looking at the grey and seeing it tried, when a horseman passed slowly by.

'Bulstrode!' said two or three voices at once in a low tone, one of them, which was the draper's, respectfully fixing the 'Mr'; but nobody having more intention in this interjectional naming than if they had said 'the Riverston coach' when that vehicle appeared in the distance. Mr Hawley gave a careless glance round at Bulstrode's back, but as Bambridge's eyes followed it he made a sarcastic grimace.

'By jingo! that reminds me,' he began, lowering his voice a little, 'I picked up something else at Bilkley besides your gig-horse, Mr Hawley. I picked up a fine story about Bulstrode. Do you know how he came by his fortune? Any gentleman wanting a bit of curious information, I can give it him free of expense. If everybody got their deserts, Bulstrode might have had to say his prayers at Botany Bay.'

'What do you mean?' said Mr Hawley, thrusting his hands into his pockets, and pushing a little forward under the archway. If Bulstrode should turn out to be a rascal, Frank Hawley had a prophetic soul.

'I had it from a party who was an old chum of Bulstrode's. I'll tell you where I first picked him up,' said Bambridge, with a sudden gesture of his forefinger. 'He was at Larcher's sale, but I knew nothing of him then – he slipped through my fingers – was after Bulstrode, no doubt. He tells me he can tap Bulstrode to any amount, knows all his secrets. However, he blabbed to me at Bilkley: he takes a stiff glass. Damme if I think he meant to turn king's evidence; but he's that sort of bragging fellow, the bragging runs over hedge and ditch with him, till he'd brag of a spavin as if it 'ud fetch money. A man should know when to pull up.' Mr Bambridge made this remark with an air of disgust, satisfied that his own bragging showed a fine sense of the marketable.

'What's the man's name? Where can he be found?' said Mr Hawley.

'As to where he is to be found, I left him to it at the Saracen's Head; but his name is Raffles.'

'Raffles!' exclaimed Mr Hopkins. 'I furnished his funeral yesterday. He was buried at Lowick. Mr Bulstrode followed him. A very decent funeral.'

There was a strong sensation among the listeners. Mr Bambridge gave an ejaculation in which 'brimstone' was the mildest word, and Mr Hawley, knitting his brows and bending his head forward, exclaimed, 'What? – where did the man die?'

'At Stone Court,' said the draper. 'The housekeeper said he was a relation of the master's. He came there ill on Friday.'

'Why, it was on Wednesday I took a glass with him,' interposed Bambridge.

'Did any doctor attend him?' said Mr Hawley.

'Yes, Mr Lydgate. Mr Bulstrode sat up with him one night. He died the third morning.'

'Go on, Bambridge,' said Mr Hawley, insistently. 'What did this fellow say about Bulstrode?'

The group had already become larger, the town-clerk's presence being a guarantee that something worth listening to was going on there; and Mr Bambridge delivered his narrative in the hearing of seven. It was mainly what we know, including the fact about Will Ladislaw, with some local colour and circumstance added: it was what Bulstrode had dreaded the betrayal of – and hoped to have buried for ever with the corpse of Raffles – it was that haunting ghost of his earlier life which as he rode past the archway of the Green Dragon he was trusting that Providence had delivered him from. Yes, Providence. He had not confessed to himself yet that he had done anything in the way of contrivance to this end; he had accepted what seemed to have been offered. It was impossible to prove that he had done anything which hastened the departure of that man's soul.

But this gossip about Bulstrode spread through Middlemarch like the smell of fire. Mr Frank Hawley followed up his information by sending a clerk whom he could trust to Stone Court on a pretext of inquiring about hay, but really to gather all that could be learned about Raffles and his illness from Mrs Abel. In this way it came to his knowledge that Mr Garth had carried the man to Stone Court in his gig; and Mr Hawley in consequence took an opportunity of seeing Caleb, calling at his office to ask whether he had time to undertake an arbitration if it were required, and then asking him incidentally about Raffles. Caleb was betrayed into no word injurious to Bulstrode beyond the fact which he was forced to admit, that he had given up acting for him within the last week. Mr Hawley drew his inferences, and feeling convinced that Raffles had told his story to Garth, and that Garth had given up Bulstrode's affairs in consequence, said so a few hours later to Mr Toller. The statement was passed on until it had quite lost the stamp of an inference, and was taken as information coming straight from Garth, so that even a diligent historian might have concluded Caleb to be the chief publisher of Bulstrode's misdemeanours.

Mr Hawley was not slow to perceive that there was no handle for the law either in the revelations made by Raffles or in the circumstances of his death. He had himself ridden to Lowick village that he might look at the register and talk over the whole matter with Mr Farebrother, who was not more surprised than the lawyer that an ugly secret should have come to light about Bulstrode, though he had always had justice enough in him to hinder his antipathy from turning into conclusions. But while they were talking another combination was silently going forward in Mr Farebrother's mind, which foreshadowed what was soon to be loudly spoken of in Middlemarch as a necessary 'putting of two and two together'. With the reasons which kept Bulstrode in dread of Raffles there flashed the thought that the dread might have something to do with his munificence towards his medical man; and though he resisted the suggestion that it had been consciously accepted in any way as a bribe, he had a foreboding that this complication of things might be of malignant effect on Lydgate's reputation. He perceived that Mr Hawley knew nothing at present of the sudden relief from debt, and he himself was careful to glide away from all approaches towards the subject.

'Well,' he said, with a deep breath, wanting to wind up the illimitable discussion of what might have been, though nothing could be legally proven, 'it is a strange story. So our mercurial Ladislaw has a queer genealogy! A high-spirited young lady and a musical Polish patriot made a likely enough stock for him to spring from, but I should never have suspected a grafting of the Jew pawnbroker. However, there's no knowing what a mixture will turn out beforehand. Some sorts of dirt serve to clarify.'

'It's just what I should have expected,' said Mr Hawley, mounting his horse. 'Any cursed alien blood, Jew, Corsican, or Gypsy.'

'I know he's one of your black sheep, Hawley. But he is really a disinterested unworldly fellow,' said Mr Farebrother, smiling.

'Ay, ay, that is your Whiggish twist,' said Mr Hawley, who had been in the habit of saying apologetically that Farebrother was such a damned pleasant good-hearted fellow you would mistake him for a Tory.

Mr Hawley rode home without thinking of Lydgate's attendance on Raffles in any other light than as a piece of evidence on the side of Bulstrode. But the news that Lydgate had all at once become able not only to get rid of the execution in his house but to pay all his debts in Middlemarch was spreading fast, gathering round it conjectures and comments which gave it new body and impetus, and soon filling the ears of other persons besides Mr Hawley, who were not slow to see a significant relation between this sudden command of money and Bulstrode's desire to stifle the scandal of Raffles. That the money came from Bulstrode would infallibly have been guessed even if there had been no direct evidence of it; for it had beforehand entered into the gossip about Lydgate's affairs, that neither his father-in-law nor his own family would do anything for him, and direct evidence was furnished not only by a clerk at the Bank, but by innocent Mrs Bulstrode herself, who mentioned the loan to Mrs Plymdale, who mentioned it to her daughter-in-law of the house of Toller, who mentioned it generally. The business was felt to be so public and important that it required dinners to feed it, and many invitations were just then issued and accepted on the strength of this scandal concerning Bulstrode and Lydgate; wives, widows, and single ladies took their work and went out to tea oftener than usual; and all public conviviality, from the Green Dragon to Dollop's, gathered a zest which could not be won from the question whether the Lords would throw out the Reform Bill.

For hardly anybody doubted that some scandalous reason or other was at the bottom of Bulstrode's liberality to Lydgate. Mr Hawley, indeed, in the first instance, invited a select party, including the two physicians, with Mr Toller and Mr Wrench, expressly to hold a close discussion as to the probabilities of Raffles's illness, reciting to them all the particulars which had been gathered from Mrs Abel in connection with Lydgate's certificate, that the death was due to *delirium tremens*; and the medical gentlemen, who all stood undisturbedly on the old paths in relation to this disease, declared that they could see nothing in these particulars which could be transformed into a positive ground of suspicion. But the moral grounds of suspicion remained; the strong motives Bulstrode clearly had for wishing to be rid of Raffles, and the fact that at this critical moment he had given Lydgate the help which he must for some time have known the need for; the disposition, moreover, to believe that Bulstrode would be unscrupulous, and the absence of any indisposition to believe that Lydgate might be as easily bribed as other haughty-minded men when they have found themselves in want of money. Even if the money had been given merely to make him hold his tongue about the scandal of Bulstrode's earlier life, the fact threw an odious light on Lydgate, who had long been sneered at as making himself subservient to the banker for the sake of working himself into predominance, and discrediting the older members of his profession. Hence, in spite of the negative as to any direct sign of guilt, in relation to the death at Stone Court, Mr Hawley's select party broke up with the sense that the affair had 'an ugly look'.

But this vague conviction of indeterminable guilt, which was enough to keep up much head-shaking and biting innuendo even among substantial professional seniors, had for the general mind all the superior power of mystery over fact. Everybody liked better to conjecture how the thing was, than simply to know it; for conjecture soon became more confident than knowledge, and had a more liberal allowance for the incompatible. Even the more definite scandal concerning Bulstrode's earlier life was, for some minds, melted into the mass of mystery, as so much lively metal to be poured out in dialogue, and to take such fantastic shapes as heaven pleased.

This was the tone of thought chiefly sanctioned by Mrs Dollop, the spirited landlady of the Tankard in Slaughter Lane, who had often to resist the shallow pragmatism of customers disposed to think that their reports from the outer world were of equal force with what had 'come up' in her mind. How it had been brought to her she didn't know, but it was there before her as if it had been scored with the chalk on the chimneyboard – 'as Bulstrode should say, his inside was *that black* as if the hairs of his head knowed the thoughts of his heart, he'd tear 'em up by the roots.'

'That's odd,' said Mr Limp, a meditative shoemaker, with weak eyes and a piping voice. 'Why, I read in the *Trumpet* that was what the Duke of Wellington said when he turned his coat and went over to the Romans.'

'Very like,' said Mrs Dollop. 'If one raskill said it, it's more reason why another should. But hypo*crite* as he's been, and holding things with that high hand, as there was no parson i' the country good enough for him, he was forced to take Old Harry into his counsel, and Old Harry's been too many for him.'

'Ay, ay, he's a 'complice you can't send out o' the country,' said Mr Crabbe the glazier, who gathered much news and groped among it dimly. 'But by what I can make out, there's them says Bulstrode was for running away, for fear o' being found out, before now.'

'He'll be drove away, whether or no,' said Mr Dill, the barber, who had just dropped in. 'I shaved Fletcher, Hawley's clerk, this morning – he's got a bad finger – and he says they're all of one mind to get rid of Bulstrode. Mr Thesiger is turned against him, and wants him out o' the parish. And there's gentlemen in this town says they'd as soon dine with a fellow from the hulks. "And a deal sooner I would," says Fletcher; "for what's more against one's stomach than a man coming and making himself bad company with his religion, and giving out as the Ten Commandments are not enough for him, and all the while he's worse than half the men at the tread-mill?" Fletcher said so himself.'

'It'll be a bad thing for the town though, if Bulstrode's money goes out of it,' said Mr Limp, quaveringly.

'Ah, there's better folk spend their money worse,' said a firm-voiced dyer, whose crimson hands looked out of keeping with his good-natured face.

'But he won't keep his money, by what I can make out,' said the glazier. 'Don't they say as there's somebody can strip it off him? By what I can understan', they could take every penny off him, if they went to lawing.'

'No such thing!' said the barber, who felt himself a little above his company at Dollop's, but liked it none the worse. 'Fletcher says it's no such thing. He says they might prove over and over again whose child this young Ladislaw was, and they'd do no more than if they proved I came out of the Fens – he couldn't touch a penny.'

'Look you there now!' said Mrs Dollop, indignantly. 'I thank the Lord he took my children to Himself, if that's all the law can do for the motherless. Then by that, it's o' no use who your father and mother is. But as to listening to what one lawyer says without asking another – I wonder at a man o' your cleverness, Mr Dill. It's well known there's always two sides, if no more; else who'd go to law, I should like to know? It's a poor tale, with all the law as there is up and down, if it's no use proving whose child you are. Fletcher may say that if he likes, but I say, don't Fletcher *me!*'

Mr Dill affected to laugh in a complimentary way at Mrs Dollop, as a woman who was more than a match for the lawyers; being disposed to submit to much twitting from a landlady who had a long score against him.

'If they come to lawing, and it's all true as folks say, there's more to be looked to nor money,' said the glazier. 'There's this poor creetur as is dead and gone: by what I can make out, he'd seen the day when he was a deal finer gentleman nor Bulstrode.'

'Finer gentleman! I'll warrant him,' said Mrs Dollop, 'and a far personabler man, by what I can hear. As I said when Mr Baldwin, the tax gatherer, comes in, a-standing where you sit, and says, "Bulstrode got all his money as he brought into this town by thieving and swindling," – I said, "You don't make me no wiser, Mr Baldwin: it's set my blood a-creeping to look at him ever sin' here he came into Slaughter Lane a-wanting to buy the house over my head: folks don't look the colour o' the dough-tub and stare at you as if they wanted to see into your backbone for nothingk." That was what I said, and Mr Baldwin can bear me witness.'

'And in the rights of it too,' said Mr Crabbe. 'For by what I can make out, this Raffles, as they call him, was a lusty, fresh-coloured man as you'd wish to see, and the best o' company – though dead he lies in Lowick churchyard sure enough; and by what I can understan', there's them knows more than they *should* know about how he got there.'

'I'll believe you!' said Mrs Dollop, with a touch of scorn at Mr Crabbe's apparent dimness. 'When a man's been 'ticed to a lone house, and there's them can pay for hospitals and nurses for half the countryside choose to be sitters-up night and day, and nobody to come near but a doctor as is known to stick at nothingk, and as poor as he can hang together, and after that so flushed o' money as he can pay off Mr Byles the butcher as his bill has been running on for the best o' joints since last Michaelmas was a twelvemonth – I don't want anybody to come and tell me as there's been more going on nor the Prayer-book's got a service for – I don't want to stand winking and blinking and thinking.'

Mrs Dollop looked round with the air of a landlady accustomed to dominate her company. There was a chorus of adhesion from the more courageous; but Mr Limp, after taking a draught, placed his flat hands together and pressed them hard between his knees, looking down at them with blear-eyed contemplation, as if the scorching power of Mrs Dollop's speech had quite dried up and nullified his wits until they could be brought round again by further moisture.

'Why shouldn't they dig the man up and have the Crowner?' said the dyer. 'It's been done many and many's the time. If there's been foul play they might find it out.'

'Not they, Mr Jonas!' said Mrs Dollop, emphatically. 'I know what doctors are. They're a deal too cunning to be found out. And this Doctor Lydgate that's been for cutting up everybody before the breath was well out o' their body – it's plain enough what use he wanted to make o' looking into respectable people's insides. He knows drugs, you may be sure, as you can neither smell nor see, neither before they're swallowed nor after. Why, I've seen drops myself ordered by Doctor Gambit, as is our club doctor and a good chariker, and has brought more live children into the world nor ever another i' Middlemarch – I say I've seen drops myself as made no difference whether they was in the glass or out, and yet have griped you the next day. So I'll leave your own sense to judge. Don't tell me! All I say is, it's a mercy they didn't take this Doctor Lydgate on to our club. There's many a mother's child might ha' rued it.'

The heads of this discussion at 'Dollop's' had been the common theme among all classes in the town, had been carried to Lowick Parsonage on one side and to Tipton Grange on the other, had come fully to the ears of the Vincy family, and had been discussed with sad reference to 'poor Harriet' by all Mrs Bulstrode's friends, before Lydgate knew distinctly why people were looking strangely at him, and before Bulstrode himself suspected the betrayal of his secrets. He had not been accustomed to very cordial relations with his neighbours, and hence he could not miss the signs of cordiality; moreover, he had been taking journeys on business of various kinds, having now made up his mind that he need not quit Middlemarch, and feeling able consequently to determine on matters which he had before left in suspense.

'We will make a journey to Cheltenham in the course of a month or two,' he had said to his wife. 'There are great spiritual advantages to be had in that town along with the air and the waters, and six weeks there will be eminently refreshing to us.'

He really believed in the spiritual advantages, and meant that his life henceforth should be the more devoted because of those later sins which he represented to himself as hypothetic, praying hypothetically for their pardon: – 'if I have herein trangressed.'

As to the Hospital, he avoided saying anything further to Lydgate, fearing to manifest a too sudden change of plans immediately on the death of Raffles. In his secret soul he believed that Lydgate suspected his orders to have been intentionally disobeyed, and suspecting this he must also suspect a motive. But nothing had been betrayed to him as to the history of Raffles, and Bulstrode was anxious not to do anything which would give emphasis to his undefined suspicions. As to any certainty that a particular method of treatment would either save or kill, Lydgate himself was constantly arguing against such dogmatism; he had no right to speak, and he had every motive for being silent. Hence Bulstrode felt himself providentially secured. The only incident he had strongly winced under had been an occasional encounter with Caleb Garth, who, however, had raised his hat with mild gravity.

Meanwhile, on the part of the principal townsmen a strong determination was growing against him.

A meeting was to be held in the Town Hall on a sanitary question which had risen into pressing importance by the occurrence of a cholera case in the town. Since the Act of Parliament, which had been hurriedly passed, authorizing assessments for sanitary measures, there had been a Board for the superintendence of such measures appointed in Middlemarch, and much cleansing and preparation had been concurred in by Whigs and Tories. The question now was, whether a piece of ground outside the town should be secured as a burial-ground by means of assessment or by private subscription. The meeting was to be open, and almost everybody of importance in the town was expected to be there.

Mr Bulstrode was a member of the Board, and just before twelve o'clock he started from the Bank with the intention of urging the plan of private subscription. Under the hesitation of his projects, he had for some time kept himself in the background, and he felt that he should this morning resume his old position as a man of action and influence in the public affairs of the town where he expected to end his days. Among the various persons going in the same direction, he saw Lydgate; they joined, talked over the object of the meeting, and entered it together.

It seemed that everybody of mark had been earlier than they. But there were still spaces left near the head of the large central table, and they made their way thither. Mr Farebrother sat opposite, not far from Mr Hawley; all the medical men were there; Mr Thesiger was in the chair, and Mr Brooke of Tipton was on his right hand.

Lydgate noticed a peculiar interchange of glances when he and Bulstrode took their seats.

After the business had been fully opened by the chairman, who pointed out the advantages of purchasing by subscription a piece of ground large enough to be ultimately used as a general cemetery, Mr Bulstrode, whose rather high-pitched but subdued and fluent voice the town was used to at meetings of this sort, rose and asked leave to deliver his opinion. Lydgate could see again the peculiar interchange of glances before Mr Hawley started up, and said in his firm resonant voice, 'Mr Chairman, I request that before any one delivers his opinion on this point I may be permitted to speak on a question of public feeling, which not only by myself, but by many gentlemen present, is regarded as preliminary.'

Mr Hawley's mode of speech, even when public decorums repressed his 'awful language', was formidable in its curtness and self-possession. Mr Thesiger sanctioned the request, Mr Bulstrode sat down, and Mr Hawley continued.

'In what I have to say, Mr Chairman, I am not speaking simply on my own behalf: I am speaking with the concurrence and at the express request of no fewer than eight of my fellow-townsmen, who are immediately around us. It is our united sentiment that Mr Bulstrode should be called upon – and I do now call upon him – to resign public positions which he holds not simply as a tax-payer, but as a gentleman among gentlemen. There are practices and there are acts which, owing to circumstances, the law cannot visit, though they may be worse than many things which are legally punishable. Honest men and gentlemen, if they don't want the company of people who perpetrate such acts, have got to defend themselves as they best can, and that is what I and the friends whom I may call my clients in this affair are determined to do. I don't say that Mr Bulstrode has been guilty of shameful acts, but I call upon him either publicly to deny and confute the scandalous statements made against him by a man now dead, and who died in his house – the statement that he was for many years engaged in nefarious practices, and that he won his fortune by dishonest procedures – or else to withdraw from positions which could only have been allowed him as a gentleman among gentlemen.'

All eyes in the room were turned on Mr Bulstrode, who, since the first mention of his name, had been going through a crisis of feeling almost too violent for his delicate frame to support. Lydgate, who himself was undergoing a shock as from the terrible practical interpretation of some faint augury, felt, nevertheless, that his own movement of resentful hatred was checked by that instinct of the Healer which thinks first of bringing rescue or relief to the sufferer, when he looked at the shrunken misery of Bulstrode's livid face.

The quick vision that his life was after all a failure, that he was a dishonoured man, and must quail before the glance of those towards whom he had habitually assumed the attitude of a reprover – that God had disowned him before men and left him unscreened to the triumphant scorn of those who were glad to have their hatred justified – the sense of utter futility in that equivocation with his conscience in dealing with the life of his accomplice, an equivocation which now turned venomously upon him with the full-grown fang of a discovered lie: – all this rushed through him like the agony of terror which fails to kill, and leaves the ears still open to the returning wave of execration. The sudden sense of exposure after the re-established sense of safety came – not to the coarse organization of a criminal but – to the susceptible nerve of a man whose intensest being lay in such mastery and predominance as the conditions of his life had shaped for him.

But in that intense being lay the strength of reaction. Through all his bodily infirmity there ran a tenacious nerve of ambitious self-preserving will, which had continually leaped out like a flame, scattering all doctrinal fears, and which, even while he sat an object of compassion for the merciful, was beginning to stir and glow under his ashy paleness. Before the last words were out of Mr Hawley's mouth, Bulstrode felt that he should answer, and that his answer would be a retort. He dared not get up and say, 'I am not guilty, the whole story is false' – even if he had dared this, it would have seemed to him, under his present keen sense of betrayal, as vain as to pull, for covering to his nakedness, a frail rag which would rend at every little strain.

For a few moments there was total silence, while every man in the room was looking at Bulstrode. He sat perfectly still, leaning hard against the back of his chair; he could not venture to rise, and when he began to speak he pressed his hands upon the seat on each side of him. But his voice was perfectly audible, though hoarser than usual, and his words were distinctly pronounced, though he paused between each sentence as if short of breath. He said, turning first towards Mr Thesiger, and then looking at Mr Hawley –

'I protest before you, sir, as a Christian minister, against the sanction of proceedings towards me which are dictated by virulent hatred. Those who are hostile to me are glad to believe any libel uttered by a loose tongue against me. And their consciences become strict against me. Say that the evil-speaking of which I am to be made the victim accuses me of malpractices – ' here Bulstrode's voice rose and took on a more biting accent, till it seemed a low cry – 'who shall be my accuser? Not men whose own lives are unchristian, nay, scandalous – not men who themselves use low instruments to carry out their ends – whose profession is a tissue of chicanery – who have been spending their income on their own sensual enjoyments, while I have been devoting mine to advance the best objects with regard to this life and the next.'

After the word chicanery there was a growing noise, half of murmurs and half of hisses, while four persons started up at once – Mr Hawley, Mr Toller, Mr Chichely, and Mr Hackbutt; but Mr Hawley's outburst was instantaneous, and left the others behind in silence.

'If you mean me, sir, I call upon you and every one else to the inspection of my professional life. As to Christian or unchristian, I repudiate your canting palavering Christianity; and as to the way in which I spend my income, it is not my principle to maintain thieves and cheat offspring of their due inheritance in order to support religion and set myself up as a saintly Kill-joy. I affect no niceness of conscience – I have not found any nice standards necessary yet to measure your actions by, sir. And I again call upon you to enter into satisfactory explanations concerning the scandals against you, or else to withdraw from posts in which we at any rate decline you as a colleague. I say, sir, we decline to co-operate with a man whose character is not cleared from infamous lights cast upon it, not only by reports but by recent actions.'

'Allow me, Mr Hawley,' said the chairman; and Mr Hawley, still fuming, bowed half impatiently, and sat down with his hands thrust deep in his pockets.

'Mr Bulstrode, it is not desirable, I think, to prolong the present discussion,' said Mr Thesiger, turning to the pallid trembling man; 'I must so far concur with what has fallen from Mr Hawley in expression of a general feeling, as to think it due to your Christian profession that you should clear yourself, if possible, from unhappy aspersions. I for my part should be willing to give you full opportunity and hearing. But I must say that your present attitude is painfully inconsistent with those principles which you have sought to identify yourself with, and for the honour of which I am bound to care. I recommend you at present as your clergyman, and one who hopes for your reinstatement in respect, to quit the room, and avoid further hindrance to business.'

Bulstrode, after a moment's hesitation, took his hat from the floor and slowly rose, but he grasped the corner of the chair so totteringly that Lydgate felt sure there was not strength enough in him to walk away without support. What could he do? He could not see a man sink close to him for want of help. He rose and gave his arm to Bulstrode, and in that way led him out of the room; yet this act, which might have been one of gentle duty and pure compassion, was at this moment unspeakably bitter to him. It seemed as if he were putting his sign-manual to that association of himself with Bulstrode, of which he now saw the full meaning as it must have presented itself to other minds. He now felt the conviction that this man who was leaning tremblingly on his arm, had given him the thousand pounds as a bribe, and that somehow the treatment of Raffles had been tampered with from an evil motive. The inferences were closely linked enough: the town knew of the loan, believed it to be a bribe, and believed that he took it as a bribe.

Poor Lydgate, his mind struggling under the terrible clutch of this revelation, was all the while morally forced to take Mr Bulstrode to the Bank, send a man off for his carriage, and wait to accompany him home.

Meanwhile the business of the meeting was despatched, and fringed off into eager discussion among various groups concerning this affair of Bulstrode – and Lydgate.

Mr Brooke, who had before heard only imperfect hints of it, and was very uneasy that he had 'gone a little too far' in countenancing Bulstrode, now got himself fully informed, and felt some benevolent sadness in talking to Mr Farebrother about the ugly light in which Lydgate had come to be regarded. Mr Farebrother was going to walk back to Lowick.

'Step into my carriage,' said Mr Brooke. 'I am going round to see Mrs Casaubon. She was to come back from Yorkshire last night. She will like to see me, you know.'

So they drove along, Mr Brooke chatting with good-natured hope that there had not really been anything black in Lydgate's behaviour – a young fellow whom he had seen to be quite above the common mark, when he brought a letter from his uncle, Sir Godwin. Mr Farebrother said little: he was deeply mournful: with a keen perception of human weakness, he could not be confident that under the pressure of humiliating needs Lydgate had not fallen below himself.

When the carriage drove up to the gate of the manor, Dorothea was out on the gravel, and came to greet them.

'Well, my dear,' said Mr Brooke, 'we have just come from a meeting – a sanitary meeting, you know.'

'Was Mr Lydgate there?' said Dorothea, who looked full of health and animation, and stood with her head bare under the gleaming April lights. 'I want to see him and have a great consultation with him about the Hospital. I have engaged with Mr Bulstrode to do so.'

'Oh, my dear,' said Mr Brooke, 'we have been hearing bad news – bad news, you know.'

They walked through the garden towards the churchyard gate, Mr Farebrother wanting to go on to the parsonage; and Dorothea heard the whole sad story.

She listened with deep interest, and begged to hear twice over the facts and impressions concerning Lydgate. After a short silence, pausing at the churchyard gate, and addressing Mr Farebrother, she said energetically –

'You don't believe that Mr Lydgate is guilty of anything base? I will not believe it. Let us find out the truth and clear him!'

BOOK EIGHT
SUNSET AND SUNRISE

⃕ SEVENTY-TWO ⃔

Full souls are double mirrors, making still
An endless vista of fair things before,
Repeating things behind.

DOROTHEA'S IMPETUOUS GENEROSITY, WHICH would have leaped at once
to the vindication of Lydgate from the suspicion of having accepted
money as a bribe, underwent a melancholy check when she came to
consider all the circumstances of the case by the light of Mr Farebrother's
experience.

'It is a delicate matter to touch,' he said. 'How can we begin to inquire
into it? It must be either publicly by setting the magistrate and coroner to
work, or privately by questioning Lydgate. As to the first proceeding there
is no solid ground to go upon, else Hawley would have adopted it; and as
to opening the subject with Lydgate, I confess I should shrink from it. He
would probably take it as a deadly insult. I have more than once experienced the difficulty of speaking to him on personal matters. And – one
should know the truth about his conduct beforehand, to feel very confident of a good result.'

'I feel convinced that his conduct has not been guilty: I believe that
people are almost always better than their neighbours think they are,' said
Dorothea. Some of her intensest experience in the last two years had set
her mind strongly in opposition to any unfavourable construction of
others; and for the first time she felt rather discontented with Mr Farebrother. She disliked this cautious weighing of consequences, instead of
an ardent faith in efforts of justice and mercy, which would conquer by
their emotional force. Two days afterwards, he was dining at the Manor
with her uncle and the Chettams, and when the dessert was standing
uneaten, the servants were out of the room, and Mr Brooke was nodding
in a nap, she returned to the subject with renewed vivacity.

'Mr Lydgate would understand that if his friends hear a calumny about
him their first wish must be to justify. What do we live for, if it is not to
make life less difficult to each other? I cannot be indifferent to the troubles
of a man who advised me in *my* trouble, and attended me in my illness.'

Dorothea's tone and manner were not more energetic than they had
been when she was at the head of her uncle's table nearly three years
before, and her experience since had given her more right to express a
decided opinion. But Sir James Chettam was no longer the diffident and

acquiescent suitor: he was the anxious brother-in-law, with a devout admiration for his sister, but with a constant alarm lest she should fall under some new illusion almost as bad as marrying Casaubon. He smiled much less; when he said 'Exactly' it was more often an introduction to a dissentient opinion than in those submissive bachelor days; and Dorothea found to her surprise that she had to resolve not to be afraid of him – all the more because he was really her best friend. He disagreed with her now.

'But, Dorothea,' he said, remonstrantly, 'you can't undertake to manage a man's life for him in that way. Lydgate must know – at least he will soon come to know how he stands. If he can clear himself, he will. He must act for himself.'

'I think his friends must wait till they find an opportunity,' added Mr Farebrother. 'It is possible – I have often felt so much weakness in myself that I can conceive even a man of honourable disposition, such as I have always believed Lydgate to be, succumbing to such a temptation as that of accepting money which was offered more or less indirectly as a bribe to insure his silence about scandalous facts long gone by. I say, I can conceive this, if he were under the pressure of hard circumstances – if he had been harassed as I feel sure Lydgate has been. I would not believe anything worse of him except under stringent proof. But there is the terrible Nemesis following on some errors, that it is always possible for those who like it to interpret them into a crime: there is no proof in favour of the man outside his own consciousness and assertion.'

'Oh, how cruel!' said Dorothea, clasping her hands. 'And would you not like to be the one person who believed in that man's innocence, if the rest of the world belied him? Besides, there is a man's character beforehand to speak for him.'

'But, my dear Mrs Casaubon,' said Mr Farebrother, smiling gently at her ardour, 'character is not cut in marble – it is not something solid and unalterable. It is something living and changing, and may become diseased as our bodies do.'

'Then it may be rescued and healed,' said Dorothea. 'I should not be afraid of asking Mr Lydgate to tell me the truth, that I might help him. Why should I be afraid? Now that I am not to have the land, James, I might do as Mr Bulstrode proposed, and take his place in providing for the hospital; and I have to consult Mr Lydgate, to know thoroughly what are the prospects of doing good by keeping up the present plans. There is the best opportunity in the world for me to ask for his confidence; and he would be able to tell me things which might make all the circumstances clear. Then we would all stand by him and bring him out of his trouble. People glorify all sorts of bravery except the bravery they might show on behalf of their nearest neighbours.' Dorothea's eyes had a moist brightness in them, and the changed tones of her voice roused her uncle, who began to listen.

'It is true that a woman may venture on some efforts of sympathy which would hardly succeed if we men undertook them,' said Mr Farebrother, almost converted by Dorothea's ardour.

'Surely, a woman is bound to be cautious and listen to those who know the world better than she does,' said Sir James, with his little frown. 'Whatever you do in the end, Dorothea, you should really keep back at present, and not volunteer any meddling with this Bulstrode business. We don't know yet what may turn up. You must agree with me?' he ended, looking at Mr Farebrother.

'I do think it would be better to wait,' said the latter.

'Yes, yes, my dear,' said Mr Brooke, not quite knowing at what point the discussion had arrived, but coming up to it with a contribution which was generally appropriate. 'It is easy to go too far, you know. You must not let your ideas run away with you. And as to being in a hurry to put money into schemes – it won't do, you know. Garth has drawn me in uncommonly with repairs, draining, that sort of thing: I'm uncommonly out of pocket with one thing or another. I must pull up. As for you, Chettam, you are spending a fortune on those oak fences round your demesne.'

Dorothea, submitting uneasily to this discouragement, went with Celia into the library, which was her usual drawing-room.

'Now, Dodo, do listen to what James says,' said Celia, 'else you will be getting into a scrape. You always did, and you always will, when you set about doing as you please. And I think it is a mercy now after all that you have got James to think for you. He lets you have your plans, only he hinders you from being taken in. And that is the good of having a brother instead of a husband. A husband would not let you have your plans.'

'As if I wanted a husband!' said Dorothea. 'I only want not to have my feelings checked at every turn.' Mrs Casaubon was still undisciplined enough to burst into angry tears.

'Now, really, Dodo,' said Celia, with rather a deeper guttural than usual, 'you *are* contradictory: first one thing and then another. You used to submit to Mr Casaubon quite shamefully: I think you would have given up ever coming to see me if he had asked you.'

'Of course I submitted to him, because it was my duty; it was my feeling for him,' said Dorothea, looking through the prism of her tears.

'Then why can't you think it your duty to submit a little to what James wishes?' said Celia, with a sense of stringency in her argument. 'Because he only wishes what is for your own good. And, of course men know best about everything, except what women know better.'

Dorothea laughed and forgot her tears.

'Well, I mean about babies and those things,' explained Celia. 'I should not give up to James when I knew he was wrong, as you used to do to Mr Casaubon.'

◌ SEVENTY-THREE ◌

Pity the laden one; this wandering woe
May visit you and me.

WHEN LYDGATE HAD ALLAYED MRS BULSTRODE'S anxiety by telling her
that her husband had been seized with faintness at the meeting, but that
he trusted to see him better and would call again the next day, unless she
sent for him earlier, he went directly home, got on his horse, and rode
three miles out of the town for the sake of being out of reach.

He felt himself becoming violent and unreasonable as if raging under
the pain of stings: he was ready to curse the day on which he had come to
Middlemarch. Everything that had happened to him there seemed a mere
preparation for this hateful fatality, which had come as a blight on his
honourable ambition, and must make even people who had only vulgar
standards regard his reputation as irrevocably damaged. In such moments
a man can hardly escape being unloving. Lydgate thought of himself as
the sufferer, and of others as the agents who had injured his lot. He had
meant everything to turn out differently; and others had thrust themselves into his life and thwarted his purposes. His marriage seemed an
unmitigated calamity; and he was afraid of going to Rosamond before he
had vented himself in this solitary rage, lest the mere sight of her should
exasperate him and make him behave unwarrantably. There are episodes
in most men's lives in which their highest qualities can only cast a deter-
ring shadow over the objects that fill their inward vision: Lydgate's
tender-heartedness was present just then only as a dread lest he should
offend against it, not as an emotion that swayed him to tenderness. For he
was very miserable. Only those who know the supremacy of the intellectual life – the life which has a seed of ennobling thought and purpose
within it – can understand the grief of one who falls from that serene
activity into the absorbing soul-wasting struggle with worldly
annoyances.

How was he to live on without vindicating himself among people
who suspected him of baseness? How could he go silently away from
Middlemarch as if he were retreating before a just condemnation? And yet
how was he to set about vindicating himself?

For that scene at the meeting, which he had just witnessed, although it
had told him no particulars, had been enough to make his own situation
thoroughly clear to him. Bulstrode had been in dread of scandalous

disclosures on the part of Raffles. Lydgate could now construct all the probabilities of the case. 'He was afraid of some betrayal in my hearing: all he wanted was to bind me to him by a strong obligation: that was why he passed on a sudden from hardness to liberality. And he may have tampered with the patient – he may have disobeyed my orders. I fear he did. But whether he did or not, the world believes that he somehow or other poisoned the man and that I winked at the crime, if I didn't help in it. And yet – and yet he may not be guilty of the last offence; and it is just possible that the change towards me may have been a genuine relenting – the effect of second thoughts such as he alleged. What we call the "just possible" is sometimes true and the thing we find it easier to believe is grossly false. In his last dealings with this man Bulstrode may have kept his hands pure, in spite of my suspicion to the contrary.'

There was a benumbing cruelty in his position. Even if he renounced every other consideration than that of justifying himself – if he met shrugs, cold glances, and avoidance as an accusation, and made a public statement of all the facts as he knew them, who would be convinced? It would be playing the part of a fool to offer his own testimony on behalf of himself, and say, 'I did not take the money as a bribe.' The circumstances would always be stronger than his assertion. And besides, to come forward and tell everything about himself must include declarations about Bulstrode which would darken the suspicions of others against him. He must tell that he had not known of Raffles's existence when he first mentioned his pressing need of money to Bulstrode, and that he took the money innocently as a result of that communication, not knowing that a new motive for the loan might have arisen on his being called in to this man. And after all, the suspicion of Bulstrode's motives might be unjust.

But then came the question whether he should have acted in precisely the same way if he had not taken the money? Certainly, if Raffles had continued alive and susceptible of further treatment when he arrived, and he had then imagined any disobedience to his orders on the part of Bulstrode, he would have made a strict inquiry, and if his conjecture had been verified he would have thrown up the case, in spite of his recent heavy obligation. But if he had not received any money – if Bulstrode had never revoked his cold recommendation of bankruptcy – would he, Lydgate, have abstained from all inquiry even on finding the man dead? – would the shrinking from an insult to Bulstrode – would the dubiousness of all medical treatment and the argument that his own treatment would pass for the wrong with most members of his profession – have had just the same force or significance with him?

That was the uneasy corner of Lydgate's consciousness while he was reviewing the facts and resisting all reproach. If he had been independent, this matter of a patient's treatment and the distinct rule that he must do or see done that which he believed best for the life committed to him, would have been the point on which he would have been the sturdiest. As it was, he had rested in the consideration that disobedience to his orders, however it might have arisen, could not be considered a crime, that in the dominant opinion obedience to his orders was just as likely to be fatal, and that the affair was simply one of etiquette. Whereas, again and again, in his time of freedom, he had denounced the perversion of pathological doubt into moral doubt and had said – 'the purest experiment in treatment may still be conscientious: my business is to take care of life, and to do the best I can think of for it. Science is properly more scrupulous than dogma. Dogma gives a charter to mistake, but the very breath of science is a contest with mistake, and must keep the conscience alive.' Alas! the scientific conscience had got into the debasing company of money obligation and selfish respects.

'Is there a medical man of them all in Middlemarch who would question himself as I do?' said poor Lydgate, with a renewed outburst of rebellion against the oppression of his lot. 'And yet they will all feel warranted in making a wide space between me and them, as if I were a leper! My practice and my reputation are utterly damned – I can see that. Even if I could be cleared by valid evidence, it would make little difference to the blessed world here. I have been set down as tainted and should be cheapened to them all the same.'

Already there had been abundant signs which had hitherto puzzled him, that just when he had been paying off his debts and getting cheerfully on his feet, the townsmen were avoiding him or looking strangely at him, and in two instances it came to his knowledge that patients of his had called in another practitioner. The reasons were too plain now. The general black-balling had begun.

No wonder that in Lydgate's energetic nature the sense of a hopeless misconstruction easily turned into a dogged resistance. The scowl which occasionally showed itself on his square brow was not a meaningless accident. Already when he was re-entering the town after that ride taken in the first hours of stinging pain, he was setting his mind on remaining in Middlemarch in spite of the worst that could be done against him. He would not retreat before calumny, as if he submitted to it. He would face it to the utmost, and no act of his should show that he was afraid. It belonged to the generosity as well as defiant force of his nature that he resolved not to shrink from showing to the full his sense of obligation to Bulstrode. It was true that the association with this man had been fatal to him – true that if he had the thousand pounds still in his hands with all his debts unpaid he would have returned the money to Bulstrode, and taken beggary rather than the rescue which had been sullied with the suspicion of a bribe (for, remember, he was one of the proudest among the sons of men) – nevertheless, he would not turn away from this crushed fellow-mortal whose aid he had used, and make a pitful effort to get acquittal for himself by howling against another. 'I shall do as I think right, and explain to nobody. They will try to starve me out, but – ' he was going on with an obstinate resolve, but he was getting near home, and the thought of Rosamond urged itself again into that chief place from which it had been thrust by the agonized struggles of wounded honour and pride.

How would Rosamond take it all? Here was another weight of chain to drag, and poor Lydgate was in a bad mood for bearing her dumb mastery. He had no impulse to tell her the trouble which must soon be common to them both. He preferred waiting for the incidental disclosure which events must soon bring about.

◁ SEVENTY-FOUR ▷

Mercifully grant that we may grow aged together.
BOOK OF TOBIT: *Marriage Prayer*

IN MIDDLEMARCH A WIFE COULD NOT long remain ignorant that the town held a bad opinion of her husband. No feminine intimate might carry her friendship so far as to make a plain statement to the wife of the unpleasant fact known or believed about her husband: but when a woman with her thoughts much at leisure got them suddenly employed on something grievously disadvantageous to her neighbours, various moral impulses were called into play which tended to stimulate utterance. Candour was one. To be candid, in Middlemarch phraseology, meant, to use an early opportunity of letting your friends know that you did not take a cheerful view of their capacity, their conduct, or their position; and a robust candour never waited to be asked for its opinion. Then, again, there was the love of truth – a wide phrase, but meaning in this relation, a lively objection to seeing a wife look happier than her husband's character warranted, or manifest too much satisfaction in her lot: the poor thing should have some hint given her that if she knew the truth she would have less complacency in her bonnet, and in light dishes for a supper-party. Stronger than all, there was the regard for a friend's moral improvement, sometimes called her soul, which was likely to be benefited by remarks tending to gloom, uttered with the accompaniment of pensive staring at the furniture and a manner implying that the speaker would not tell what was on her mind, from regard to the feelings of her hearer. On the whole, one might say that an ardent charity was at work setting the virtuous mind to make a neighbour unhappy for her good.

There were hardly any wives in Middlemarch whose matrimonial misfortunes would in different ways be likely to call forth more of this moral activity than Rosamond and her aunt Bulstrode. Mrs Bulstrode was not an object of dislike, and had never consciously injured any human being. Men had always thought her a handsome comfortable woman, and had reckoned it among the signs of Bulstrode's hypocrisy that he had chosen a red-blooded Vincy, insteady of a ghastly and melancholy person suited to his low esteem for earthly pleasure. When the scandal about her husband was disclosed they remarked of her – 'Ah, poor woman! She's as honest as the day – *she* never suspected anything wrong in him, you may depend on it.' Women, who were intimate with her, talked together much of 'poor Harriet', imagined what her feelings must be when she came to know everything, and conjectured how much she had already come to know. There was no spiteful disposition towards her; rather, there was a busy benevolence anxious to ascertain what it would be well for her to feel and do under the circumstances, which of course kept the imagination occupied with her character and history from the time when she was Harriet Vincy till now. With the review of Mrs Bulstrode and her position it was inevitable to associate Rosamond, whose prospects were under the same blight with her aunt's. Rosamond was more severely criticized and less pitied, though she too, as one of the good old Vincy family who had always been known in Middlemarch, was regarded as a victim to marriage with an interloper. The Vincys had their weaknesses, but then they lay on the surface: there was never anything bad to be 'found out' concerning them. Mrs Bulstrode was vindicated from any resemblance to her husband. Harriet's faults were her own.

'She has always been showy,' said Mrs Hackbutt, making tea for a small party, 'though she has got into the way of putting her religion forward, to conform to her husband: she has tried to hold her head up above Middlemarch by making it known that she invites clergymen and heaven-knows-who from Riverston and those places.'

'We can hardly blame her for that,' said Mrs Sprague; 'because few of the best people in the town cared to associate with Bulstrode, and she must have somebody to sit down at her table.'

'Mr Thesiger has always countenanced him,' said Mrs Hackbutt. 'I think he must be sorry now.'

'But he was never fond of him in his heart – that every one knows,' said Mrs Toller. 'Mr Thesiger never goes into extremes. He keeps to the truth in what is evangelical. It is only clergymen like Mr Tyke, who want to use Dissenting hymn-books and that low kind of religion who ever found Bulstrode to their taste.'

'I understand Mr Tyke is in great distress about him,' said Mrs Hackbutt. 'And well he may be: they say the Bulstrodes have half kept the Tyke family.'

'And of course it is a discredit to his doctrines,' said Mrs Sprague, who was elderly and old-fashioned in her opinions. 'People will not make a boast of being methodistical in Middlemarch for a good while to come.'

'I think we must not set down people's bad actions to their religion,' said falcon-faced Mrs Plymdale, who had been listening hitherto.

'Oh, my dear, we are forgetting,' said Mrs Sprague. 'We ought not to be talking of this before you.'

'I am sure I have no reason to be partial,' said Mrs Plymdale, colouring. 'It's true Mr Plymdale has always been on good terms with Mr Bulstrode, and Harriet Vincy was my friend long before she married him. But I have always kept my own opinions and told her where she was wrong, poor thing. Still, in point of religion, I must say, Mr Bulstrode might have done what he has, and worse, and yet have been a man of no religion. I don't say that there has not been a little too much of that – I like moderation myself. But truth is truth. The men tried at the assizes are not all over-religious, I suppose.'

'Well,' said Mrs Hackbutt, wheeling adroitly, 'all I can say is, that I think she ought to separate from him.'

'I can't say that,' said Mrs Sprague. 'She took him for better or worse, you know.'

'But "worse" can never mean finding out that your husband is fit for Newgate,' said Mrs Hackbutt. 'Fancy living with such a man! I should expect to be poisoned.'

'Yes, I think myself it is an encouragement to crime if such men are to be taken care of and waited on by good wives,' said Mrs Tom Toller.

'And a good wife poor Harriet has been,' said Mrs Plymdale. 'She thinks her husband the first of men. It's true he has never denied her anything.'

'Well, we shall see what she will do,' said Mrs Hackbutt. 'I suppose she knows nothing yet, poor creature. I do hope and trust I shall not see her, for I should be frightened to death lest I should say anything about her husband. Do you think any hint has reached her?'

'I should hardly think so,' said Mrs Tom Toller. 'We hear that *he* is ill, and has never stirred out of the house since the meeting on Thursday; but she was with her girls at church yesterday, and they had new Tuscan bonnets. Her own had a feather in it. I have never seen that her religion made any difference in her dress.'

'She wears very neat patterns always,' said Mrs Plymdale, a little stung. 'And that feather I know she got dyed a pale lavender on purpose to be consistent. I must say it of Harriet that she wishes to do right.'

'As to her knowing what has happened, it can't be kept from her long,' said Mrs Hackbutt. 'The Vincys know, for Mr Vincy was at the meeting. It will be a great blow to him. There is his daughter as well as his sister.'

'Yes, indeed,' said Mrs Sprague. 'Nobody supposes that Mr Lydgate can go on holding up his head in Middlemarch, things look so black about the thousand pounds he took just at that man's death. It really makes one shudder.'

'Pride must have a fall,' said Mrs Hackbutt.

'I am not so sorry for Rosamond Vincy that was as I am for her aunt,' said Mrs Plymdale. 'She needed a lesson.'

'I suppose the Bulstrodes will go and live abroad somewhere,' said Mrs Sprague. 'That is what is generally done when there is anything disgraceful in a family.'

'And a most dreadful blow it will be to Harriet,' said Mrs Plymdale. 'If ever a woman was crushed, she will be. I pity her from my heart. And with all her faults, few women are better. From a girl she had the neatest ways, and was always good-hearted, and as open as the day. You might look into her drawers when you would – always the same. And so she has brought up Kate and Ellen. You may think how hard it will be for her to go among foreigners.'

'The doctor says that is what he should recommend the Lydgates to do,' said Mrs Sprague. 'He says Lydgate ought to have kept among the French.'

'That would suit *her* well enough, I daresay,' said Mrs Plymdale; 'there is that kind of lightness about her. But she got that from her mother; she never got it from her aunt Bulstrode, who always gave her good advice, and to my knowledge would rather have had her marry elsewhere.'

Mrs Plymdale was in a situation which caused her some complication of feeling. There had been not only her intimacy with Mrs Bulstrode, but also a profitable business relation of the great Plymdale dyeing house with Mr Bulstrode, which on the one hand would have inclined her to desire that the mildest view of his character should be the true one, but on the other, made her the more afraid of seeming to palliate his culpability. Again, the late alliance of her family with the Tollers had brought her in connection with the best circle, which gratified her in every direction except in the inclination to those serious views which she believed to be the best in another sense. The sharp little woman's conscience was somewhat troubled in the adjustment of these opposing 'bests' and of her griefs and satisfactions under late events, which were likely to humble those who needed humbling, but also to fall heavily on her old friend whose faults she would have preferred seeing on a background of prosperity.

Poor Mrs Bulstrode, meanwhile, had been no further shaken by the oncoming tread of calamity than in the busier stirring of that secret uneasiness which had always been present in her since the last visit of Raffles to The Shrubs. That the hateful man had come ill to Stone Court, and that her husband had chosen to remain there and watch over him, she allowed to be explained by the fact that Raffles had been employed and aided in earlier days, and that this made a tie of benevolence towards him in his degraded helplessness; and she had been since then innocently cheered by her husband's more hopeful speech about his own health and ability to continue his attention to business. The calm was disturbed when Lydgate had brought him home ill from the meeting, and in spite of comforting assurances during the next few days, she cried in private from the conviction that her husband was not suffering from bodily illness merely, but from something that afflicted his mind. He would not allow her to read to him, and scarcely to sit with him, alleging nervous susceptibility to sounds and movements; yet she suspected that in shutting himself up in his private room he wanted to be busy with his papers. Something, she felt sure, had happened. Perhaps it was some great loss of money; and she was kept in the dark. Not daring to question her husband, she said to Lydgate, on the fifth day after the meeting, when she had not left home except to go to church –

'Mr Lydgate, pray be open with me: I like to know the truth. Has anything happened to Mr Bulstrode?'

'Some little nervous shock,' said Lydgate, evasively. He felt that it was not for him to make the painful revelation.

'But what brought it on?' said Mrs Bulstrode, looking directly at him with her large dark eyes.

'There is often something poisonous in the air of public rooms,' said Lydgate. 'Strong men can stand it, but it tells on people in proportion to the delicacy of their systems. It is often impossible to account for the precise moment of an attack – or rather, to say why the strength gives way at a particular moment.'

Mrs Bulstrode was not satisfied with his answer. There remained in her the belief that some calamity had befallen her husband, of which she was to be kept in ignorance; and it was in her nature strongly to object to such concealment. She begged leave for her daughters to sit with their father, and drove into the town to pay some visits, conjecturing that if anything were known to have gone wrong in Mr Bulstrode's affairs, she should see or hear some sign of it.

She called on Mrs Thesiger, who was not at home, and then drove to Mrs Hackbutt's on the other side of the churchyard. Mrs Hackbutt saw her coming from an up-stairs window, and remembering her former alarm lest she should meet Mrs Bulstrode, felt almost bound in consistency to send word that she was not at home; but against that, there was a sudden strong desire within her for the excitement of an interview in which she was quite determined not to make the slightest allusion to what was in her mind.

Hence Mrs Bulstrode was shown into the drawing-room, and Mrs Hackbutt went to her, with more tightness of lip and rubbing of her hands than was usually observable in her, these being precautions adopted against freedom of speech. She was resolved not to ask how Mr Bulstrode was.

'I have not been anywhere except to church for nearly a week,' said Mrs Bulstrode, after a few introductory remarks. 'But Mr Bulstrode was taken so ill at the meeting on Thursday that I have not liked to leave the house.'

Mrs Hackbutt rubbed the back of one hand with the palm of the other held against her chest, and let her eyes ramble over the pattern on the rug.

'Was Mr Hackbutt at the meeting?' persevered Mrs Bulstrode.

'Yes, he was,' said Mrs Hackbutt, with the same attitude. 'The land is to be bought by subscription, I believe.'

'Let us hope that there will be no more cases of cholera to be buried in it,' said Mrs Bulstrode. 'It is an awful visitation. But I always think Middlemarch a very healthy spot. I suppose it is being used to it from a child; but I never saw the town I should like to live at better, and especially our end.'

'I am sure I should be glad that you always should live at Middlemarch, Mrs Bulstrode,' said Mrs Hackbutt, with a slight sigh. 'Still, we must learn to resign ourselves, wherever our lot may be cast. Though I am sure there will always be people in this town who will wish you well.'

Mrs Hackbutt longed to say, 'if you take my advice you will part from your husband', but it seemed clear to her that the poor woman knew nothing of the thunder ready to bolt on her head, and she herself could do no more than prepare her a little. Mrs Bulstrode felt suddenly rather chill and trembling: there was evidently something unusual behind this speech of Mrs Hackbutt's; but though she had set out with the desire to be fully informed, she found herself unable now to pursue her brave purpose, and turning the conversation by an inquiry about the young Hackbutts, she soon took her leave saying that she was going to see Mrs Plymdale. On her way thither she tried to imagine that there might have been some unusually warm sparring at the meeting between Mr Bulstrode and some of his frequent opponents – perhaps Mr Hackbutt might have been one of them. That would account for everything.

But when she was in conversation with Mrs Plymdale that comforting explanation seemed no longer tenable. 'Selina' received her with a pathetic affectionateness and a disposition to give edifying answers on the commonest topics, which could hardly have reference to an ordinary quarrel of which the most important consequence was a perturbation of Mr Bulstrode's health. Beforehand Mrs Bulstrode had thought that she would sooner question Mrs Plymdale than any one else; but she found to her surprise that an old friend is not always the person whom it is easiest to make a confidant of: there was the barrier of remembered communication under other circumstances – there was the dislike of being pitied and informed by one who had been long wont to allow her the superiority. For certain words of mysterious appropriateness that Mrs Plymdale let fall about her resolution never to turn her back on her friends, convinced Mrs Bulstrode that what had happened must be some kind of misfortune, and instead of being able to say with her native directness, 'What is it that you have in your mind?' she found herself anxious to get away before she had heard anything more explicit. She began to have an agitating certainty that the misfortune was something more than the mere loss of money, being keenly sensitive to the fact that Selina now, just as Mrs Hackbutt had done before, avoided noticing what she said about her husband, as they would have avoided noticing a personal blemish.

She said good-bye with nervous haste, and told the coachman to drive to Mr Vincy's warehouse. In that short drive her dread gathered so much force from the sense of darkness, that when she entered the private counting-house where her brother sat at his desk, her knees trembled and her usually florid face was deathly pale. Something of the same effect was produced in him by the sight of her: he rose from his seat to meet her, took her by the hand, and said, with his impulsive rashness –

'God help you, Harriet! you know all.'

That moment was perhaps worse than any which came after. It contained that concentrated experience which in great crises of emotion reveals the bias of a nature, and is prophetic of the ultimate act which will end an intermediate struggle. Without that memory of Raffles she might still have thought only of monetary ruin, but now along with her brother's look and words there darted into her mind the idea of some guilt in her husband – then, under the working of terror came the image of her husband exposed to disgrace – and then, after an instant of scorching shame in which she felt only the eyes of the world, with one leap of her heart she was at his side in mournful but unreproaching fellowship with shame and isolation. All this went on within her in a mere flash of time – while she sank into the chair, and raised her eyes to her brother, who stood over her. 'I know nothing, Walter. What is it?' she said, faintly.

He told her everything, very inartificially, in slow fragments, making her aware that the scandal went much beyond proof, especially as to the end of Raffles.

'People will talk,' he said. 'Even if a man has been acquitted by a jury, they'll talk, and nod and wink – and as far as the world goes, a man might often as well be guilty as not. It's a breakdown blow, and it damages Lydgate as much as Bulstrode. I don't pretend to say what is the truth. I only wish we had never heard the name of either Bulstrode or Lydgate. You'd better have been a Vincy all your life, and so had Rosamond.'

Mrs Bulstrode made no reply.

'But you must bear up as well as you can, Harriet. People don't blame *you*. And I'll stand by you whatever you make up your mind to do,' said the brother, with rough but well-meaning affectionateness.

'Give me your arm to the carriage, Walter,' said Mrs Bulstrode. 'I feel very weak.'

And when she got home she was obliged to say to her daughter, 'I am not well, my dear; I must go and lie down. Attend to your papa. Leave me in quiet. I shall take no dinner.'

She locked herself in her room. She needed time to get used to her maimed consciousness, her poor lopped life, before she could walk steadily to the place allotted her. A new searching light had fallen on her husband's character, and she could not judge him leniently: the twenty years in which she had believed in him and venerated him by virtue of his concealments came back with particulars that made them seem an odious deceit. He had married her with that bad past life hidden behind him and she had no faith left to protest his innocence of the worst that was imputed to him. Her honest ostentatious nature made the sharing of a merited dishonour as bitter as it could be to any mortal.

But this imperfectly-taught woman, whose phrases and habits were an odd patchwork, had a loyal spirit within her. The man whose prosperity she had shared through nearly half a life, and who had unvaryingly cherished her – now that punishment had befallen him it was not possible to her in any sense to forsake him. There is a forsaking which still sits at the same board and lies on the same couch with the forsaken soul, withering it the more by unloving proximity. She knew, when she locked her door, that she should unlock it ready to go down to her unhappy husband and espouse his sorrow, and say of his guilt, I will mourn and not reproach. But she needed time to gather up her strength; she needed to sob out her farewell to all the gladness and pride of her life. When she had resolved to go down, she prepared herself by some little acts which might seem mere folly to a hard onlooker; they were her way of expressing to all spectators visible or invisible that she had begun a new life in which she embraced humiliation. She took off all her ornaments and put on a plain black gown, and instead of wearing her much-adorned cap and large bows of hair, she brushed her hair down and put on a plain bonnet-cap, which made her look suddenly like an early Methodist.

Bulstrode, who knew that his wife had been out and had come in saying that she was not well, had spent the time in an agitation equal to hers. He had looked forward to her learning the truth from others, and had acquiesced in that probability, as something easier to him than any confession. But now that he imagined the moment of her knowledge come, he awaited the result in anguish. His daughters had been obliged to consent to leave him, and though he had allowed some food to be brought to him, he had not touched it. He felt himself perishing slowly in unpitied misery. Perhaps he should never see his wife's face with affection in it again. And if he turned to God there seemed to be no answer but the pressure of retribution.

It was eight o'clock in the evening before the door opened and his wife entered. He dared not look up at her. He sat with his eyes bent down, and as she went towards him she thought he looked smaller – he seemed so withered and shrunken. A movement of new compassion and old tenderness went through her like a great wave, and putting one hand on his which rested on the arm of the chair, and the other on his shoulder, she said, solemnly but kindly –

'Look up, Nicholas.'

He raised his eyes with a little start and looked at her half amazed for a moment: her pale face, her changed, mourning dress, the trembling about her mouth, all said, 'I know'; and her hands and eyes rested gently on him. He burst out crying and they cried together, she sitting at his side. They could not yet speak to each other of the shame which she was bearing with him, or of the acts which had brought it down on them. His confession was silent, and her promise of faithfulness was silent. Open-minded as she was, she nevertheless shrank from the words which would have expressed their mutual consciousness as she would have shrunk from flakes of fire. She could not say, 'How much is only slander and false suspicion?' and he did not say, 'I am innocent.'

◁ SEVENTY-FIVE ▷

Le sentiment de la fausseté des plaisirs présents, et l'ignorance de la vanité des plaisirs absents, causent l'inconstance.

PASCAL

ROSAMOND HAD A GLEAM OF RETURNING cheerfulness when the house was freed from the threatening figure, and when all the disagreeable creditors were paid. But she was not joyous: her married life had fulfilled none of her hopes, and had been quite spoiled for her imagination. In this brief interval of calm, Lydgate, remembering that he had often been stormy in his hours of perturbation, and mindful of the pain Rosamond had had to bear, was carefully gentle towards her; but he, too, had lost some of his old spirit, and he still felt it necessary to refer to an economical change in their way of living as a matter of course, trying to reconcile her to it gradually, and repressing his anger when she answered by wishing that he would go to live in London. When she did not make this answer, she listened languidly, and wondered what she had that was worth living for. The hard and contemptuous words which had fallen from her husband in his anger had deeply offended that vanity which he had at first called into active enjoyment; and what she regarded as his perverse way of looking at things, kept up a secret repulsion, which made her receive all his tenderness as a poor substitute for the happiness he had failed to give her. They were at a disadvantage with their neighbours, and there was no longer any outlook towards Quallingham – there was no outlook any-where except in an occasional letter from Will Ladislaw. She had felt stung and disappointed by Will's resolution to quit Middlemarch, for in spite of what she knew and guessed about his admiration for Dorothea, she secretly cherished the belief that he had, or would necessarily come to have, much more admiration for herself; Rosamond being one of those women who live much in the idea that each man they meet would have preferred them if the preference had not been hopeless. Mrs Casaubon was all very well; but Will's interest in her dated before he knew Mrs Lydgate. Rosamond took his way of talking to herself, which was a mixture of playful fault-finding and hyperbolical gallantry, as the disguise of a deeper feeling; and in his presence she felt that agreeable titillation of vanity and sense of romantic drama which Lydgate's presence had no longer the magic to create. She even fancied – what will not men and women fancy in these matters? – that Will exaggerated his admiration for Mrs Casaubon in order to pique herself. In this way poor Rosamond's brain had been busy before Will's departure. He would have made, she thought, a much more suitable husband for her than she had found in Lydgate. No notion could have been falser than this, for Rosamond's discontent in her marriage was due to the conditions of marriage itself, to its demand for self-suppression and tolerance, and not to the nature of her husband; but the easy conception of an unreal Better had a sentimental charm which diverted her ennui. She constructed a little romance which was to vary the flatness of her life: Will Ladislaw was always to be a bachelor and live near her, always to be at her command, and have an understood though never fully expressed passion for her, which would be sending out lambent flames every now and then in interesting scenes. His departure had been a proportionate disappointment, and had sadly increased her weariness of Middlemarch; but at first she had the alternative dream of pleasure in store from her intercourse with the family at Quallingham. Since then the troubles of her married life had deepened, and the absence of other relief encouraged her regretful rumination over that thin romance which she had once fed on. Men and women make sad mistakes about their own symptoms, taking their vague uneasy longings, sometimes for genius, sometimes for religion, and oftener still for a mighty love. Will Ladislaw had written chatty letters, half to her, and half to Lydgate, and she had replied: their separation, she felt, was not likely to be final, and the change she now most longed for was that Lydgate should go to live in London; everything would be agreeable in London; and she had set to work with quiet determination to win this result, when there came a sudden, delightful promise which inspirited her.

It came shortly before the memorable meeting at the town-hall, and was nothing less than a letter from Will Ladislaw to Lydgate, which turned chiefly on his new interest in plans of colonization, but mentioned incidentally, that he might find it necessary to pay a visit to Middlemarch within the next few weeks – a very pleasant necessity, he said, almost as good as holidays to a schoolboy. He hoped there was his old place on the rug, and a great deal of music in store for him. But he was quite uncertain as to the time. While Lydgate was reading the letter to Rosamond, her face looked like a reviving flower – it grew prettier and more blooming. There was nothing unendurable now: the debts were paid, Mr Ladislaw was coming, and Lydgate would be persuaded to leave Middlemarch and settle in London, which was 'so different from a provincial town'.

That was a bright bit of morning. But soon the sky became black over poor Rosamond. The presence of a new gloom in her husband, about which he was entirely reserved towards her – for he dreaded to expose his lacerated feeling to her neutrality and misconception – soon received a painfully strange explanation, alien to all her previous notions of what could affect her happiness. In the new gaiety of her spirits, thinking that Lydgate had merely a worse fit of moodiness than usual, causing him to leave her remarks unanswered, and evidently to keep out of her way as much as possible, she chose, a few days after the meeting, and without speaking to him on the subject, to send out notes of invitation for a small evening party, feeling convinced that this was a judicious step, since people seemed to have been keeping aloof from them, and wanted restoring to the old habit of intercourse. When the invitations had been accepted, she would tell Lydgate, and give him a wise admonition as to how a medical man should behave to his neighbours; for Rosamond had the gravest little airs possible about other people's duties. But all the invitations were declined, and the last answer came into Lydgate's hands.

'This is Chichely's scratch. What is he writing to you about?' said Lydgate, wonderingly, as he handed the note to her. She was obliged to let him see it, and, looking at her severely, he said –

'Why on earth have you been sending out invitations without telling me, Rosamond? I beg, I insist that you will not invite any one to this house. I suppose you have been inviting others, and they have refused too.'

She said nothing.

'Do you hear me?' thundered Lydgate.

'Yes, certainly I hear you,' said Rosamond, turning her head aside with the movement of a graceful long-necked bird.

Lydgate tossed his head without any grace and walked out of the room, feeling himself dangerous. Rosamond's thought was, that he was getting more and more unbearable – not that there was any new special reason for this peremptoriness. His indisposition to tell her anything in which he was sure beforehand that she would not be interested was growing into an unreflecting habit, and she was in ignorance of everything connected with the thousand pounds, except that the loan had come from her uncle Bulstrode. Lydgate's odious humours and their neighbours' apparent avoidance of them had an unaccountable date for her in their relief from money difficulties. If the invitations had been accepted she would have gone to invite her mamma and the rest, whom she had seen nothing of for several days; and she now put on her bonnet to go and inquire what had become of them all, suddenly feeling as if there were a conspiracy to leave her in isolation with a husband disposed to offend everybody. It was after the dinner hour, and she found her father and mother seated together alone in the drawing-room. They greeted her with sad looks, saying, 'Well, my dear!' and no more. She had never seen her father look so downcast; and seating herself near him she said –

'Is there anything the matter, papa?'

He did not answer, but Mrs Vincy, said, 'Oh, my dear, have you heard nothing? It won't be long before it reaches you.'

'Is it anything about Tertius?' said Rosamond, turning pale. The idea of trouble immediately connected itself with what had been unaccountable to her in him.

'Oh my dear, yes. To think of your marrying into this trouble. Debt was bad enough, but this will be worse.'

'Stay, stay, Lucy,' said Mr Vincy. 'Have you heard nothing about your uncle Bulstrode, Rosamond?'

'No, papa,' said the poor thing, feeling as if trouble were not anything she had before experienced, but some invisible power with an iron grasp that made her soul faint within her.

Her father told her everything, saying at the end, 'It's better for you to know, my dear. I think Lydgate must leave the town. Things have gone against him. I daresay he couldn't help it. I don't accuse him of any harm,' said Mr Vincy. He had always before been disposed to find the utmost fault with Lydgate.

The shock to Rosamond was terrible. It seemed to her that no lot could be so cruelly hard as hers – to have married a man who had become the centre of infamous suspicions. In many cases it is inevitable that the shame is felt to be the worst part of crime; and it would have required a great deal of disentangling reflection, such as had never entered into Rosamond's life, for her in these moments to feel that her trouble was less than if her husband had been certainly known to have done something criminal. All the shame seemed to be there. And she had innocently married this man with the belief that he and his family were a glory to her! She showed her usual reticence to her parents, and only said, that if Lydgate had done as she wished he would have left Middlemarch long ago.

'She bears it beyond anything,' said her mother when she was gone.

'Ah, thank God!' said Mr Vincy, who was much broken down.

But Rosamond went home with a sense of justified repugnance towards her husband. What had he really done – how had he really acted? She did not know. Why had he not told her everything? He did not speak to her on the subject, and of course she could not speak to him. It came into her mind once that she would ask her father to let her go home again; but dwelling on that prospect made it seem utter dreariness to her: a married woman gone back to live with her parents – life seemed to have no meaning for her in such a position: she could not contemplate herself in it.

The next two days Lydgate observed a change in her, and believed that she had heard the bad news. Would she speak to him about it, or would she go on for ever in the silence which seemed to imply that she believed him guilty? We must remember that he was in a morbid state of mind, in which almost all contact was pain. Certainly Rosamond in this case had equal reason to complain of reserve and want of confidence on his part; but in the bitterness of his soul he excused himself; – was he not justified in shrinking from the task of telling her, since now she knew the truth she had no impulse to speak to him? But a deeper-lying consciousness that he was in fault made him restless, and the silence between them became intolerable to him; it was as if they were both adrift on one piece of wreck and looked away from each other.

He thought, 'I am a fool. Haven't I given up expecting anything? I have married care, not help.' And that evening he said –

'Rosamond, have you heard anything that distresses you?'

'Yes,' she answered, laying down her work, which she had been carrying on with a languid semi-consciousness, most unlike her usual self.

'What have you heard?'

'Everything, I suppose. Papa told me.'

'That people think me disgraced?'

'Yes,' said Rosamond, faintly, beginning to sew again automatically.

There was silence. Lydgate thought, 'If she has any trust in me – any notion of what I am, she ought to speak now and say that she does not believe I have deserved disgrace.'

But Rosamond on her side went on moving her fingers languidly. Whatever was to be said on the subject she expected to come from Tertius. What did she know? And if he were innocent of any wrong, why did he not do something to clear himself?

This silence of hers brought a new rush of gall to that bitter mood in which Lydgate had been saying to himself that nobody believed in him – even Farebrother had not come forward. He had begun to question her with the intent that their conversation should disperse the chill fog which had gathered between them, but he felt his resolution checked by despairing resentment. Even this trouble, like the rest, she seemed to regard as if it were hers alone. He was always to her a being apart, doing what she objected to. He started from his chair with an angry impulse, and thrusting his hands in his pockets, walked up and down the room. There was an underlying consciousness all the while that he should have to master this anger, and tell her everything, and convince her of the facts. For he had almost learned the lesson that he must bend himself to her nature, and that because she came short in her sympathy, he must give the more. Soon he recurred to his intention of opening himself: the occasion must not be lost. If he could bring her to feel with some solemnity that here was a slander which must be met and not run away from, and that the whole trouble had come out of his desperate want of money, it would be a moment for urging powerfully on her that they should be one in the resolve to do with as little money as possible, so that they might weather the bad time and keep themselves independent. He would mention the definite measures which he desired to take, and win her to a willing spirit. He was bound to try this – and what else was there for him to do?

He did not know how long he had been walking uneasily backwards and forwards, but Rosamond felt that it was long, and wished that he would sit down. She too had begun to think this an opportunity for urging on Tertius what he ought to do. Whatever might be the truth about all this misery, there was one dread which asserted itself.

Lydgate at last seated himself, not in his usual chair, but in one nearer to Rosamond, leaning aside in it towards her, and looking at her gravely before he reopened the sad subject. He had conquered himself so far, and was about to speak with a sense of solemnity, as on an occasion which was not to be repeated. He had even opened his lips, when Rosamond, letting her hands fall, looked at him and said –

'Surely, Tertius – '

'Well?'

'Surely now at last you have given up the idea of staying in Middlemarch. I cannot go on living here. Let us go to London. Papa, and every one else, says you had better go. Whatever misery I have to put up with, it will be easier away from here.'

Lydgate felt miserably jarred. Instead of that critical outpouring for which he had prepared himself with effort, here was the old round to be gone through again. He could not bear it. With a quick change of countenance he rose and went out of the room.

Perhaps if he had been strong enough to persist in his determination to be the more because she was less, that evening might have had a better issue. If his energy could have borne down that check, he might still have wrought on Rosamond's vision and will. We cannot be sure that any natures, however inflexible or peculiar, will resist this effect from a more massive being than their own. They may be taken by storm and for the moment converted, becoming part of the soul which enwraps them in the ardour of its movement. But poor Lydgate had a throbbing pain within him, and his energy had fallen short of its task.

The beginning of mutual understanding and resolve seemed as far off as ever; nay, it seemed blocked out by the sense of unsuccessful effort. They lived on from day to day with their thoughts still apart, Lydgate going about what work he had in a mood of despair, and Rosamond feeling, with some justification, that he was behaving cruelly. It was of no use to say anything to Tertius; but when Will Ladislaw came, she was determined to tell him everything. In spite of her general reticence, she needed some one who would recognize her wrongs.

❧ SEVENTY-SIX ❧

To mercy, pity, peace, and love
All pray in their distress,
And to these virtues of delight,
Return their thankfulness.

For Mercy has a human heart,
Pity a human face;
And Love, the human form divine;
And Peace, the human dress.
WILLIAM BLAKE: *Songs of Innocence*

SOME DAYS LATER, LYDGATE WAS RIDING to Lowick Manor, in consequence of a summons from Dorothea. The summons had not been unexpected, since it had followed a letter from Mr Bulstrode, in which he stated that he had resumed his arrangements for quitting Middlemarch, and must remind Lydgate of his previous communications about the Hospital, to the purport of which he still adhered. It had been his duty, before taking further steps, to reopen the subject with Mrs Casaubon, who now wished, as before, to discuss the question with Lydgate. 'Your views may possibly have undergone some change,' wrote Mr Bulstrode; 'but, in that case also, it is desirable that you should lay them before her.'

Dorothea awaited his arrival with eager interest. Though, in deference to her masculine advisers, she had refrained from what Sir James had called 'interfering in this Bulstrode business', the hardship of Lydgate's position was continually in her mind, and when Bulstrode applied to her again about the Hospital, she felt that the opportunity was come to her which she had been hindered from hastening. In her luxurious home, wandering under the boughs of her own great trees, her thought was going out over the lot of others, and her emotions were imprisoned. The idea of some active good within her reach, 'haunted her . . . like a passion', and another's need having once come to her as a distinct image, preoccupied her desire with the yearning to give relief, and made her own ease tasteless. She was full of confident hope about this interview with Lydgate, never heeding what was said of his personal reserve; never heeding that she was a very young woman. Nothing could have seemed more irrelevant to Dorothea than insistence on her youth and sex when she was moved to show her human fellowship.

As she sat waiting in the library, she could do nothing but live through again all the past scenes which had brought Lydgate into her memories. They all owed their significance to her marriage and its troubles – but no; there were two occasions in which the image of Lydgate had come painfully in connection with his wife and some one else. The pain had been allayed for Dorothea, but it had left in her an awakening conjecture as to what Lydgate's marriage might be to him, a susceptibility to the slightest hint about Mrs Lydgate. These thoughts were like a drama to her, and made her eyes bright, and gave an attitude of suspense to her whole frame, though she was only looking out from the brown library on to the turf and the bright green buds which stood in relief against the dark evergreens.

When Lydgate came in, she was almost shocked at the change in his face, which was strikingly perceptible to her who had not seen him for two months. It was not the change of emaciation, but that effect which even young faces will very soon show from the persistent presence of resentment and despondency. Her cordial look, when she put out her hand to him, softened his expression, but only with melancholy.

'I have wished very much to see you for a long while, Mr Lydgate,' said Dorothea when they were seated opposite each other; 'but I put off asking you to come until Mr Bulstrode applied to me again about the Hospital. I know that the advantage of keeping the management of it separate from that of the Infirmary depends on you, or, at least, on the good which you are encouraged to hope for from having it under your control. And I am sure you will not refuse to tell me exactly what you think.'

'You want to decide whether you should give a generous support to the Hospital,' said Lydgate. 'I cannot conscientiously advise you to do it in dependence on any activity of mine. I may be obliged to leave the town.'

He spoke curtly, feeling the ache of despair as to his being able to carry out any purpose that Rosamond had set her mind against.

'Not because there is no one to believe in you?' said Dorothea, pouring out her words in clearness from a full heart. 'I know the unhappy mistakes about you. I knew them from the first moment to be mistakes. You have never done anything vile. You would not do anything dishonourable.'

It was the first assurance of belief in him that had fallen on Lydgate's ears. He drew a deep breath, and said 'Thank you.' He could say no more: it was something very new and strange in his life that these few words of trust from a woman should be so much to him.

'I beseech you to tell me how everything was,' said Dorothea, fearlessly. 'I am sure that the truth would clear you.'

Lydgate started up from his chair and went towards the window, forgetting where he was. He had so often gone over in his mind the possibility of explaining everything without aggravating appearances that would tell, perhaps, unfairly, against Bulstrode, and had so often decided against it – he had so often said to himself that his assertions would not change people's impressions – that Dorothea's words sounded like a temptation to do something which in his soberness he had pronounced to be unreasonable.

'Tell me, pray,' said Dorothea, with simple earnestness; 'then we can consult together. It is wicked to let people think evil of any one falsely, when it can be hindered.'

Lydgate turned, remembering where he was, and saw Dorothea's face looking up at him with a sweet trustful gravity. The presence of a noble nature, generous in its wishes, ardent in its charity, changes the lights for us: we begin to see things again in their larger, quieter masses, and to believe that we too can be seen and judged in the wholeness of our character. That influence was beginning to act on Lydgate, who had for many days been seeing all life as one who is dragged and struggling amid the throng. He sat down again, and felt that he was recovering his old self in the consciousness that he was with one who believed in it.

'I don't want,' he said, 'to bear hard on Bulstrode, who has lent me money of which I was in need – though I would rather have gone without it now. He is hunted down and miserable, and has only a poor thread of life in him. But I should like to tell you everything. It will be a comfort to me to speak where belief has gone beforehand, and where I shall not seem to be offering assertions of my own honesty. You will feel what is fair to another, as you feel what is fair to me.'

'Do trust me,' said Dorothea; 'I will not repeat anything without your leave. But at the very least, I could say that you have made all the circumstances clear to me, and that I know you are not in any way guilty. Mr Farebrother would believe me, and my uncle, and Sir James Chettam. Nay, there are persons in Middlemarch to whom I could go; although they don't know much of me, they would believe me. They would know that I could have no other motive than truth and justice. I would take any pains to clear you. I have very little to do. There is nothing better that I can do in the world.'

Dorothea's voice, as she made this childlike picture of what she would do, might have been almost taken as a proof that she could do it effectively. The searching tenderness of her woman's tones seemed made for a defence against ready accusers. Lydgate did not stay to think that she was Quixotic; he gave himself up, for the first time in his life, to the exquisite sense of leaning entirely on a generous sympathy, without any check of proud reserve. And he told her everything, from the time when, under the pressure of his difficulties, he unwillingly made his first application to Bulstrode; gradually, in the relief of speaking, getting into a more thorough utterance of what had gone on in his mind – entering fully into the fact that his treatment of the patient was opposed to the dominant practice, into his doubts at the last, his ideal of medical duty, and his uneasy consciousness that the acceptance of the money had made some difference in his private inclination and professional behaviour, though not in his fulfilment of any publicly recognized obligation.

'It has come to my knowledge since,' he added, 'that Hawley sent some one to examine the housekeeper at Stone Court, and she said that she gave the patient all the opium in the phial I left, as well as a good deal of brandy. But that would not have been opposed to ordinary prescriptions, even of first-rate men. The suspicions against me had no hold there: they are grounded on the knowledge that I took money, that Bulstrode had strong motives for wishing the man to die, and that he gave me the money as a bribe to concur in some malpractices or other against the patient – that in any case I accepted a bribe to hold my tongue. They are just the suspicions that cling the most obstinately, because they lie in people's inclination and can never be disproved. How my orders came to be disobeyed is a question to which I don't know the answer. It is still possible that Bulstrode was innocent of any criminal intention – even possible that he had nothing to do with the disobedience, and merely abstained from mentioning it. But all that has nothing to do with the public belief. It is one of those cases on which a man is condemned on the ground of his character – it is believed that he has committed a crime in some undefined way, because he had the motive for doing it; and Bulstrode's character has enveloped me, because I took his money. I am simply blighted – like a damaged ear of corn – the business is done and can't be undone.'

'Oh, it is hard!' said Dorothea. 'I understand the difficulty there is in your vindicating yourself. And that all this should have come to you who had meant to lead a higher life than the common, and to find out better ways – I cannot bear to rest in this as unchangeable. I know you meant that. I remember what you said to me when you first spoke to me about the Hospital. There is no sorrow I have thought more about than that – to love what is great, and try to reach it, and yet to fail.'

'Yes,' said Lydgate, feeling that here he had found room for the full meaning of his grief. 'I had some ambition. I meant everything to be different with me. I thought I had more strength and mastery. But the most terrible obstacles are such as nobody can see except oneself.'

'Suppose,' said Dorothea, meditatively. 'Suppose we kept on the Hospital according to the present plan, and you stayed here though only with the friendship and support of a few, the evil feeling towards you would gradually die out; there would come opportunities in which people would be forced to acknowledge that they had been unjust to you, because they would see that your purposes were pure. You may still win a great fame like the Louis and Laennec I have heard you speak of, and we shall all be proud of you,' she ended, with a smile.

'That might do if I had my old trust in myself,' said Lydgate, mournfully. 'Nothing galls me more than the notion of turning round and running away before this slander, leaving it unchecked behind me. Still, I can't ask any one to put a great deal of money into a plan which depends on me.'

'It would be quite worth my while,' said Dorothea, simply. 'Only think. I am very uncomfortable with my money, because they tell me I have too little for any great scheme of the sort I like best, and yet I have too much. I don't know what to do. I have seven hundred a-year of my own fortune, and nineteen hundred a-year that Mr Casaubon left me, and between three and four thousand of ready money in the bank. I wished to raise money and pay it off gradually out of my income which I don't want, to buy land with and found a village which should be a school of industry; but Sir James and my uncle have convinced me that the risk would be too great. So you see that what I should most rejoice at would be to have something good to do with my money: I should like it to make other people's lives better to them. It makes me very uneasy – coming all to me who don't want it.'

A smile broke through the gloom of Lydgate's face. The childlike grave-eyed earnestness with which Dorothea said all this was irresistible – blent into an adorable whole with her ready understanding of high experience. (Of lower experience such as plays a great part in the world, poor Mrs Casaubon had a very blurred shortsighted knowledge, little helped by her imagination.) But she took the smile as encouragement of her plan.

'I think you see now that you spoke too scrupulously,' she said, in a tone of persuasion. 'The Hospital would be one good; and making your life quite whole and well again would be another.'

Lydgate's smile had died away. 'You have the goodness as well as the money to do all that; if it could be done,' he said. 'But – '

He hesitated a little while, looking vaguely towards the window; and she sat in silent expectation. At last he turned towards her and said impetuously –

'Why should I not tell you? – you know what sort of bond marriage is. You will understand everything.'

Dorothea felt her heart beginning to beat faster. Had he that sorrow too? But she feared to say any word, and he went on immediately.

'It is impossible for me now to do anything – to take any step without considering my wife's happiness. The thing that I might like to do if I were alone, is become impossible to me. I can't see her miserable. She married me without knowing what she was going into, and it might have been better for her if she had not married me.'

'I know, I know – you could not give her pain, if you were not obliged to do it,' said Dorothea, with keen memory of her own life.

'And she has set her mind against staying. She wishes to go. The troubles she has had here have wearied her,' said Lydgate, breaking off again, lest he should say too much.

'But when she saw the good that might come of staying – ' said

Dorothea, remonstrantly, looking at Lydgate as if he had forgotten the reasons which had just been considered. He did not speak immediately.

'She would not see it,' he said at last, curtly, feeling at first that this statement must do without explanation. 'And, indeed, I have lost all spirit about carrying on my life here.' He paused a moment and then, following the impulse to let Dorothea see deeper into the difficulty of his life, he said, 'The fact is, this trouble has come upon her confusedly. We have not been able to speak to each other about it. I am not sure what is in her mind about it: she may fear that I have really done something base. It is my fault; I ought to be more open. But I have been suffering cruelly.'

'May I go and see her?' said Dorothea, eagerly. 'Would she accept my sympathy? I would tell her that you have not been blamable before any one's judgment but your own. I would tell her that you shall be cleared in every fair mind. I would cheer her heart. Will you ask her if I may go to see her? I did see her once.'

'I am sure you may,' said Lydgate, seizing the proposition with some hope. 'She would feel honoured – cheered, I think, by the proof that you at least have some respect for me. I will not speak to her about your coming – that she may not connect it with my wishes at all. I know very well that I ought not to have left anything to be told her by others, but – '

He broke off, and there was a moment's silence. Dorothea refrained from saying what was in her mind – how well she knew that there might be invisible barriers to speech between husband and wife. This was a point on which even sympathy might make a wound. She returned to the more outward aspect of Lydgate's position, saying cheerfully –

'And if Mrs Lydgate knew that there were friends who would believe in you and support you, she might then be glad that you should stay in your place and recover your hopes – and do what you meant to do. Perhaps then you would see that it was right to agree with what I proposed about your continuing at the Hospital. Surely you would, if you still have faith in it as a means of making your knowledge useful?'

Lydgate did not answer, and she saw that he was debating with himself.

'You need not decide immediately,' she said, gently. 'A few days hence it will be early enough for me to send my answer to Mr Bulstrode.'

Lydgate still waited, but at last turned to speak in his most decisive tones.

'No; I prefer that there should be no interval left for wavering. I am no longer sure enough of myself – I mean of what it would be possible for me to do under the changed circumstances of my life. It would be dishonour-able to let others engage themselves to anything serious in dependence on me. I might be obliged to go away after all; I see little chance of anything else. The whole thing is too problematic; I cannot consent to be the cause of your goodness being wasted. No – let the New Hospital be joined with the Old Infirmary, and everything go on as it might have done if I had never come. I have kept a valuable register since I have been there; I shall send it to a man who will make use of it,' he ended bitterly. 'I can think of nothing for a long while but getting an income.'

'It hurts me very much to hear you speak so hopelessly,' said Dorothea. 'It would be a happiness to your friends, who believe in your future, in your power to do great things, if you would let them save you from that. Think how much money I have; it would be like taking a burthen from me if you took some of it every year till you got free from this fettering want of income. Why should not people do these things? It is so difficult to make shares at all even. This is one way.'

'God bless you, Mrs Casaubon!' said Lydgate, rising as if with the same impulse that made his words energetic, and resting his arm on the back of the great leather chair he had been sitting in. 'It is good that you should have such feelings. But I am not the man who ought to allow himself to benefit by them. I have not given guarantees enough. I must not at least sink into the degradation of being pensioned for work that I never achieved. It is very clear to me that I must not count on anything else than getting away from Middlemarch as soon as I can manage it. I should not be able for a long while, at the very best, to get an income here, and – it is easier to make the necessary changes in a new place. I must do as other men do, and think what will please the world and bring in money; look for a little opening in the London crowd, and push myself; set up in a watering-place, or go to some southern town where there are plenty of idle English, and get myself puffed, – that is the sort of shell I must creep into and try to keep my soul alive in.'

'Now that is not brave,' said Dorothea, – 'to give up the fight.'

'No, it is not brave,' said Lydgate, 'but if a man is afraid of creeping paralysis?' Then, in another tone, 'Yet you have made a great difference in my courage by believing in me. Everything seems more bearable since I have talked to you; and if you can clear me in a few other minds, especially in Farebrother's, I shall be deeply grateful. The point I wish you not to mention is the fact of disobedience to my orders. That would soon get distorted. After all, there is no evidence for me but people's opinion of me beforehand. You can only repeat my own report of myself.'

'Mr Farebrother will believe – others will believe,' said Dorothea. 'I can say of you what will make it stupidity to suppose that you would be bribed to do a wickedness.'

'I don't know,' said Lydgate, with something like a groan in his voice. 'I have not taken a bribe yet. But there is a pale shade of bribery which is sometimes called prosperity. You will do me another great kindness, then, and come to see my wife?'

'Yes, I will. I remember how pretty she is,' said Dorothea, into whose mind every impression about Rosamond had cut deep. 'I hope she will like me.'

As Lydgate rode away, he thought, 'This young creature has a heart large enough for the Virgin Mary. She evidently thinks nothing of her own future, and would pledge away half her income at once, as if she wanted nothing for herself but a chair to sit in from which she can look down with those clear eyes at the poor mortals who pray to her. She seems to have what I never saw in any woman before – a fountain of friendship towards men – a man can make a friend of her. Casaubon must have raised some heroic hallucination in her. I wonder if she could have any other sort of passion for a man? Ladislaw? – there was certainly an unusual feeling between them. And Casaubon must have had a notion of it. Well – her love might help a man more than her money.'

Dorothea on her side had immediately formed a plan of relieving Lydgate from his obligation to Bulstrode, which she felt sure was a part, though small, of the galling pressure he had to bear. She sat down at once under the inspiration of their interview, and wrote a brief note, in which she pleaded that she had more claim than Mr Bulstrode had to the satisfaction of providing the money which had been serviceable to Lydgate – that it would be unkind in Lydgate not to grant her the position of being his helper in this small matter, the favour being entirely to her who had so little that was plainly marked out for her to do with her superfluous money. He might call her a creditor or by any other name if it did but imply that he granted her request. She enclosed a cheque for a thousand pounds, and determined to take the letter with her the next day when she went to see Rosamond.

ᐊ SEVENTY-SEVEN ᐅ

And thus thy fall hath left a kind of blot,
To mark the full-fraught man and best indued
With some suspicion.

Henry V

THE NEXT DAY LYDGATE HAD TO GO TO Brassing, and told Rosamond that he should be away until the evening. Of late she had never gone beyond her own house and garden, except to church, and once to see her papa, to whom she said, 'If Tertius goes away, you will help us to move, will you not, papa? I suppose we shall have very little money. I am sure I hope some one will help us.' And Mr Vincy had said, 'Yes, child, I don't mind a hundred or two. I can see the end of that.' With these exceptions she had sat at home in languid melancholy and suspense, fixing her mind on Will Ladislaw's coming as the one point of hope and interest, and associating this with some new urgency on Lydgate to make immediate arrangements for leaving Middlemarch and going to London, till she felt assured that the coming would be a potent cause of the going, without at all seeing how. This way of establishing sequences is too common to be fairly regarded as a peculiar folly in Rosamond. And it is precisely this sort of sequence which causes the greatest shock when it is sundered: for to see how an effect may be produced is often to see possible missings and checks; but to see nothing except the desirable cause, and close upon it the desirable effect, rids us of doubt and makes our minds strongly intuitive. That was the process going on in poor Rosamond, while she arranged all objects around her with the same nicety as ever, only with more slowness – or sat down to the piano, meaning to play, and then desisting, yet lingering on the music stool with her white fingers suspended on the wooden front, and looking before her in dreamy ennui. Her melancholy had become so marked that Lydgate felt a strange timidity before it, as a perpetual silent reproach, and the strong man, mastered by his keen sensibilities towards this fair fragile creature whose life he seemed somehow to have bruised, shrank from her look, and sometimes started at her approach, fear of her and fear for her rushing in only the more forcibly after it had been momentarily expelled by exasperation.

But this morning Rosamond descended from her room up-stairs – where she sometimes sat the whole day when Lydgate was out – equipped for a walk in the town. She had a letter to post – a letter addressed to Mr Ladislaw and written with charming discretion, but intended to hasten his arrival by a hint of trouble. The servant-maid, their sole house-servant now, noticed her coming down-stairs in her walking dress, and thought 'there never did anybody look so pretty in a bonnet, poor thing'.

Meanwhile Dorothea's mind was filled with her project of going to Rosamond, and with the many thoughts, both of the past and the probable future, which gathered round the idea of that visit. Until yesterday when Lydgate had opened to her a glimpse of some trouble in his married life, the image of Mrs Lydgate had always been associated for her with that of Will Ladislaw. Even in her most uneasy moments – even when she had been agitated by Mrs Cadwallader's painfully graphic report of gossip – her effort, nay, her strongest impulsive prompting, had been towards the vindication of Will from any sullying surmises; and when, in her meeting with him afterwards, she had at first interpreted his words as a probable allusion to a feeling towards Mrs Lydgate which he was determined to cut himself off from indulging, she had had a quick, sad, excusing vision of the charm there might be in his constant opportunities of companionship with that fair creature, who most likely shared his other tastes as she evidently did his delight in music. But there had followed his parting words – the few passionate words in which he had implied that she herself was the object of whom his love held him in dread, that it was his love for her only which he was resolved not to declare but to carry away into banishment. From the time of that parting, Dorothea, believing in

Will's love for her, believing with a proud delight in his delicate sense of honour and his determination that no one should impeach him justly, felt her heart quite at rest as to the regard he might have for Mrs Lydgate. She was sure that the regard was blameless.

There are natures in which, if they love us, we are conscious of having a sort of baptism and consecration: they bind us over to rectitude and purity by their pure belief about us; and our sins become that worst kind of sacrilege which tears down the invisible altar of trust. 'If you are not good, none is good' – those little words may give a terrific meaning to responsibility, may hold a vitriolic intensity for remorse.

Dorothea's nature was of that kind: her own passionate faults lay along the easily-counted open channels of her ardent character; and while she was full of pity for the visible mistakes of others, she had not yet any material within her experience for subtle constructions and suspicions of hidden wrong. But that simplicity of hers, holding up an ideal for others in her believing conception of them, was one of the great powers of her womanhood. And it had from the first acted strongly on Will Ladislaw. He felt, when he parted from her, that the brief words by which he had tried to convey to her his feeling about herself and the division which her fortune made between them, would only profit by their brevity when Dorothea had to interpret them: he felt that in her mind he had found his highest estimate.

And he was right there. In the months since their parting Dorothea had felt a delicious sad repose in their relation to each other, as one which was inwardly whole and without blemish. She had an active force of antagonism within her, when the antagonism turned on the defence either of plans or persons that she believed in; and the wrongs which she felt that Will had received from her husband, and the external conditions which to others were grounds for slighting him, only gave the more tenacity to her affection and admiring judgment. And now with the disclosures about Bulstrode had come another fact affecting Will's social position, which roused afresh Dorothea's inward resistance to what was said about him in that part of her world which lay within park palings.

'Young Ladislaw the grandson of a thieving Jew pawnbroker' was a phrase which had entered emphatically into the dialogues about the Bulstrode business, at Lowick, Tipton and Freshitt, and was a worse kind of placard on poor Will's back than the 'Italian with white mice'. Upright Sir James Chettam was convinced that his own satisfaction was righteous when he thought with some complacency that here was an added league to that mountainous distance between Ladislaw and Dorothea, which enabled him to dismiss any anxiety in that direction as too absurd. And perhaps there had been some pleasure in pointing Mr Brooke's attention to this ugly bit of Ladislaw's genealogy, as a fresh candle for him to see his own folly by. Dorothea had observed the animus with which Will's part in the painful story had been recalled more than once; but she had uttered no word, being checked now, as she had not been formerly in speaking of Will, by the consciousness of a deeper relation between them which must always remain in consecrated secrecy. But her silence shrouded her resistant emotion into a more thorough glow; and this misfortune in Will's lot which, it seemed, others were wishing to fling at his back as an opprobrium, only gave something more of enthusiasm to her clinging thought.

She entertained no visions of their ever coming into nearer union, and yet she had taken no posture of renunciation. She had accepted her whole relation to Will very simply as part of her marriage sorrows, and would have thought it very sinful in her to keep up an inward wail because she was not completely happy, being rather disposed to dwell on the superfluities of her lot. She could bear that the chief pleasures of her tenderness should lie in memory, and the idea of marriage came to her solely as a repulsive proposition from some suitor of whom she at present knew nothing, but whose merits, as seen by her friends, would be a source of torment to her: – 'somebody who will manage your property for you, my dear,' was Mr Brooke's attractive suggestion of suitable characteristics. 'I should like to manage it myself, if I knew what to do with it,' said Dorothea. No – she adhered to her declaration that she would never be married again, and in the long valley of her life, which looked so flat and empty of way-marks, guidance would come as she walked along the road, and saw her fellow-passengers by the way.

This habitual state of feeling about Will Ladislaw had been strong in all her waking hours since she had proposed to pay a visit to Mrs Lydgate, making a sort of background against which she saw Rosamond's figure presented to her without hindrances to her interest and compassion. There was evidently some mental separation, some barrier to complete confidence which had arisen between this wife and the husband who had yet made her happiness a law to him. That was a trouble which no third person must directly touch. But Dorothea thought with deep pity of the loneliness which must have come upon Rosamond from the suspicions cast on her husband: and there would surely be help in the manifestation of respect for Lydgate and sympathy with her.

'I shall talk to her about her husband,' thought Dorothea, as she was being driven towards the town. The clear spring morning, the scent of the moist earth, the fresh leaves just showing their creased-up wealth of greenery from out their half-opened sheaths, seemed part of the cheerfulness she was feeling from a long conversation with Mr Farebrother, who had joyfully accepted the justifying explanation of Lydgate's conduct. 'I shall take Mrs Lydgate good news, and perhaps she will like to talk to me and make a friend of me.'

Dorothea had another errand in Lowick Gate: it was about a new fine-toned bell for the school-house, and as she had to get out of her carriage very near to Lydgate's, she walked thither across the street, having told the coachman to wait for some packages. The street door was open, and the servant was taking the opportunity of looking out at the carriage which was pausing within sight when it became apparent to her that the lady who 'belonged to it' was coming towards her.

'Is Mrs Lydgate at home?' said Dorothea.

'I'm not sure, my lady; I'll see, if you'll please walk in,' said Martha, a little confused on the score of her kitchen apron, but collected enough to be sure that 'mum' was not the right title for this queenly young widow with a carriage and pair. 'Will you please to walk in, and I'll go and see.'

'Say that I am Mrs Casaubon,' said Dorothea, as Martha moved forward intending to show her into the drawing-room and then to go up-stairs to see if Rosamond had returned from her walk.

They crossed the broader part of the entrance hall, and turned up the passage which led to the garden. The drawing-room door was unlatched, and Martha, pushing it without looking into the room, waited for Mrs Casaubon to enter and then turned away, the door having swung open and swung back again without noise.

Dorothea had less of outward vision than usual this morning, being filled with images of things as they had been and were going to be. She found herself on the other side of the door without seeing anything remarkable, but immediately she heard a voice speaking in low tones which startled her as with a sense of dreaming in daylight, and advancing unconsciously a step or two beyond the projecting slab of a bookcase, she saw, in the terrible illumination of a certainty which filled up all outlines, something which made her pause motionless, without self-possession enough to speak.

Seated with his back towards her on a sofa which stood against the wall on a line with the door by which she had entered she saw Will Ladislaw: close by him and turned towards him with a flushed tearfulness which gave a new brilliancy to her face sat Rosamond, her bonnet hanging back, while Will leaning towards her clasped both her upraised hands in his and spoke with low-toned fervour.

Rosamond in her agitated absorption had not noticed the silently advancing figure; but when Dorothea, after the first immeasurable instant of this vision, moved confusedly backward and found herself impeded by some piece of furniture, Rosamond was suddenly aware of her presence, and with a spasmodic movement snatched away her hands and rose, looking at Dorothea who was necessarily arrested. Will Ladislaw, starting up, looked round also, and meeting Dorothea's eyes with a new lightning in them, seemed changing to marble. But she immediately turned them away from him to Rosamond and said in a firm voice—

'Excuse me, Mrs Lydgate, the servant did not know that you were here. I called to deliver an important letter for Mr Lydgate, which I wished to put into your own hands.'

She laid down the letter on the small table which had checked her retreat, and then including Rosamond and Will in one distant glance and bow, she went quickly out of the room, meeting in the passage the surprised Martha, who said she was sorry the mistress was not at home, and then showed the strange lady out with an inward reflection that grand people were probably more impatient than others.

Dorothea walked across the street with her most elastic step and was quickly in her carriage again.

'Drive on to Freshitt Hall,' she said to the coachman, and any one looking at her might have thought that though she was paler than usual she was never animated by a more self-possessed energy. And that was really her experience. It was as if she had drunk a great draught of scorn that stimulated her beyond the susceptibility to other feelings. She had seen something so far below her belief, that her emotions rushed back from it and made an excited throng without an object. She needed something active to turn her excitement out upon. She felt power to walk and work for a day, without meat or drink. And she would carry out the purpose with which she had started in the morning, of going to Freshitt and Tipton to tell Sir James and her uncle all that she wished them to know about Lydgate, whose married loneliness under his trial now presented itself to her with new significance, and made her more ardent in readiness to be his champion. She had never felt anything like this triumphant power of indignation in the struggle of her married life, in which there had always been a quickly subduing pang; and she took it as a sign of new strength.

'Dodo, how very bright your eyes are!' said Celia, when Sir James was gone out of the room. 'And you don't see anything you look at. Arthur or anything. You are going to do something uncomfortable, I know. Is it all about Mr Lydgate, or has something else happened?' Celia had been used to watch her sister with expectation.

'Yes, dear, a great many things have happened,' said Dodo, in her full tones.

'I wonder what,' said Celia, folding her arms cozily and leaning forward upon them.

'Oh, all the troubles of all people on the face of the earth,' said Dorothea, lifting her arms to the back of her head.

'Dear me, Dodo, are you going to have a scheme for them?' said Celia, a little uneasy at this Hamlet-like raving.

But Sir James came in again, ready to accompany Dorothea to the Grange, and she finished her expedition well, not swerving in her resolution until she descended at her own door.

❧ SEVENTY-EIGHT ❧

Would it were yesterday and I i' the grave,
With her sweet faith above for monument.

ROSAMOND AND WILL STOOD MOTIONLESS – they did not know how long –
he looking towards the spot where Dorothea had stood, and she looking
towards him with doubt. It seemed an endless time to Rosamond, in
whose inmost soul there was hardly so much annoyance as gratification
from what had just happened. Shallow natures dream of an easy sway
over the emotions of others, trusting implicitly in their own petty magic to
turn the deepest streams, and confident, by pretty gestures and remarks,
of making the thing that is not as though it were. She knew that Will had
received a severe blow, but she had been little used to imagining other
people's states of mind except as a material cut into shape by her own
wishes; and she believed in her own power to soothe or subdue. Even
Tertius, that most perverse of men, was always subdued in the long-run:
events had been obstinate, but still Rosamond would have said now, as
she did before her marriage, that she never gave up what she had set her
mind on.

She put out her arm and laid the tips of her fingers on Will's coat-sleeve.

'Don't touch me!' he said, with an utterance like the cut of a lash,
darting from her, and changing from pink to white and back again, as if
his whole frame were tingling with the pain of the sting. He wheeled
round to the other side of the room and stood opposite to her, with the
tips of his fingers in his pockets and his head thrown back, looking fiercely
not at Rosamond but at a point a few inches away from her.

She was keenly offended, but the signs she made of this were such as
only Lydgate was used to interpret. She became suddenly quiet and
seated herself, untying her hanging bonnet and laying it down with her
shawl. Her little hands which she folded before her were very cold.

It would have been safer for Will in the first instance to have taken up
his hat and gone away; but he had felt no impulse to do this; on the
contrary, he had a horrible inclination to stay and shatter Rosamond with
his anger. It seemed as impossible to bear the fatality she had drawn down
on him without venting his fury as it would be to a panther to bear the
javelin-wound without springing and biting. And yet – how could he tell
a woman that he was ready to curse her? He was fuming under a repress-
ive law which he was forced to acknowledge: he was dangerously poised,

and Rosamond's voice now brought the decisive vibration. In flute-like tones of sarcasm she said,

'You can easily go after Mrs Casaubon and explain your preference.'

'Go after her!' he burst out, with a sharp edge in his voice. 'Do you think she would turn to look at me, or value any word I ever uttered to her again at more than a dirty feather? – Explain! How can a man explain at the expense of a woman!'

'You can tell her what you please,' said Rosamond, with more tremor.

'Do you suppose she would like me better for sacrificing you? She is not a woman to be flattered because I made myself despicable – to believe that I must be true to her because I was a dastard to you.'

He began to move about with the restlessness of a wild animal that sees prey but cannot reach it. Presently he burst out again –

'I had no hope before – not much – of anything better to come. But I had one certainty – that she believed in me. Whatever people had said or done about me, she believed in me. That's gone! She'll never again think me anything but a paltry pretence – too nice to take heaven except upon flattering conditions, and yet selling myself for any devil's change by the sly. She'll think of me as an incarnate insult to her, from the first moment we . . .'

Will stopped as if he had found himself grasping something that must not be thrown and shattered. He found another vent for his rage by snatching up Rosamond's words again, as if they were reptiles to be throttled and flung off.

'Explain! Tell a man to explain how he dropped into hell! Explain my preference! I never had a *preference* for her, any more than I have a prefer-ence for breathing. No other woman exists by the side of her. I would rather touch her hand if it were dead, than I would touch any other woman's living.'

Rosamond, while these poisoned weapons were being hurled at her, was almost losing the sense of her identity, and seemed to be waking into some new terrible existence. She had no sense of chill resolute repulsion, of reticent self-justification such as she had known under Lydgate's most stormy displeasure; all her sensibility was turned into a bewildering nov-elty of pain; she felt a new terrified recoil under a lash never experienced before. What another nature felt in opposition to her own was being burnt and bitten into her consciousness. When Will had ceased to speak she had become an image of sickened misery: her lips were pale, and her eyes had a tearless dismay in them. If it had been Tertius who stood opposite to her, that look of misery would have been a pang to him, and he would have sunk by her side to comfort her, with that strong-armed comfort which she had often held very cheap.

Let it be forgiven to Will that he had no such movement of pity. He had felt no bond beforehand to this woman who had spoiled the ideal treasure of his life, and he held himself blameless. He knew that he was cruel, but he had no relenting in him yet.

After he had done speaking, he still moved about, half in absence of mind, and Rosamond sat perfectly still. At length Will, seeming to bethink himself, took up his hat, yet stood some moments irresolute. He had spoken to her in a way that made a phrase of common politeness difficult to utter; and yet, now that he had come to the point of going away from her without further speech, he shrank from it as a brutality; he felt checked and stultified in his anger. He walked towards the mantelpiece and leaned his arm on it, and waited in silence for – he hardly knew what. The vindictive fire was still burning in him, and he could utter no word of retraction; but it was nevertheless in his mind that having come back to this hearth where he had enjoyed a caressing friendship he had found calamity seated there – he had had suddenly revealed to him a trouble that lay outside the home as well as within it. And what seemed a foreboding was pressing upon him as with slow pincers: – that his life might come to be enslaved by this helpless woman who had thrown herself upon him in the dreary sadness of her heart. But he was in gloomy rebellion against the fact that his quick apprehensiveness foreshadowed to him, and when his eyes fell on Rosamond's blighted face it seemed to him that he was the more pitiable of the two: for pain must enter into its glorified life of memory before it can turn into compassion.

And so they remained for many minutes, opposite each other, far apart, in silence: Will's face still possessed by a mute rage, and Rosamond's by a mute misery. The poor thing had no force to fling out any passion in return; the terrible collapse of the illusion towards which all her hope had been strained was a stroke which had too thoroughly shaken her: her little world was in ruins, and she felt herself tottering in the midst as a lonely bewildered consciousness.

Will wished that she would speak and bring some mitigating shadow across his own cruel speech, which seemed to stand staring at them both in mockery of any attempt at revived fellowship. But she said nothing, and at last with a desperate effort over himself, he asked, 'Shall I come in and see Lydgate this evening?'

'If you like,' Rosamond answered, just audibly.

And then Will went out of the house, Martha never knowing that he had been in.

After he was gone, Rosamond tried to get up from her seat, but fell back fainting. When she came to herself again, she felt too ill to make the exertion of rising to ring the bell, and she remained helpless until the girl, surprised at her long absence, thought for the first time of looking for her in all the down-stairs rooms. Rosamond said that she had felt suddenly sick and faint, and wanted to be helped up-stairs. When there she threw herself on the bed with her clothes on, and lay in apparent torpor, as she had done once before on a memorable day of grief.

Lydgate came home earlier than he had expected, about half-past five, and found her there. The perception that she was ill threw every other thought into the background. When he felt her pulse, her eyes rested on him with more persistence than they had done for a long while, as if she felt some content that he was there. He perceived the difference in a moment, and seating himself by her put his arm gently under her, and bending over her said, 'My poor Rosamond! has something agitated you?' Clinging to him she fell into hysterical sobbings and cries, and for the next hour he did nothing but soothe and tend her. He imagined that Dorothea had been to see her, and that all this effect on her nervous system, which evidently involved some new turning towards himself, was due to the excitement of the new impressions which that visit had raised.

◁ SEVENTY-NINE ▷

Now, I saw in my dream, that just as they had ended their talk,
they drew nigh to a very miry slough, that was in the midst of
the plain; and they, being heedless, did both fall suddenly into
the bog. The name of the slough was Despond.

BUNYAN

WHEN ROSAMOND WAS QUIET, AND LYDGATE had left her, hoping that she might soon sleep under the effect of an anodyne, he went into the drawing-room to fetch a book which he had left there, meaning to spend the evening in his work-room, and he saw on the table Dorothea's letter addressed to him. He had not ventured to ask Rosamond if Mrs Casaubon had called, but the reading of this letter assured him of the fact, for Dorothea mentioned that it was to be carried by herself.

When Will Ladislaw came in a little later, Lydgate met him with a surprise which made it clear that he had not been told of the earlier visit, and Will could not say, 'Did not Mrs Lydgate tell you that I came this morning?'

'Poor Rosamond is ill,' Lydgate added immediately on his greeting.

'Not seriously, I hope,' said Will.

'No – only a slight nervous shock – the effect of some agitation. She has been overwrought lately. The truth is, Ladislaw, I am an unlucky devil. We have gone through several rounds of purgatory since you left, and I have lately got on to a worse ledge of it than ever. I suppose you are only just come down – you look rather battered – you have not been long enough in the town to hear anything?'

'I travelled all night and got to the White Hart at eight o'clock this morning. I have been shutting myself up and resting,' said Will, feeling himself a sneak, but seeing no alternative to this evasion.

And then he heard Lydgate's account of the troubles which Rosamond had already depicted to him in her way. She had not mentioned the fact of Will's name being connected with the public story – this detail not immediately affecting her – and he now heard it for the first time.

'I thought it better to tell you that your name is mixed up with the disclosures,' said Lydgate, who could understand better than most men how Ladislaw might be stung by the revelation. 'You will be sure to hear it as soon as you turn out into the town. I suppose it is true that Raffles spoke to you.'

'Yes,' said Will, sardonically. 'I shall be fortunate if gossip does not make me the most disreputable person in the whole affair. I should think the latest version must be, that I plotted with Raffles to murder Bulstrode, and ran away from Middlemarch for the purpose.'

He was thinking, 'Here is a new ring in the sound of my name to recommend it in her hearing; however – what does it signify now?'

But he said nothing of Bulstrode's offer to him. Will was very open and careless about his personal affairs, but it was among the more exquisite touches in nature's modelling of him that he had a delicate generosity which warned him into reticence here. He shrank from saying that he had rejected Bulstrode's money, in the moment when he was learning that it was Lydgate's misfortune to have accepted it.

Lydgate too was reticent in the midst of his confidence. He made no allusion to Rosamond's feeling under their trouble, and of Dorothea he only said, 'Mrs Casaubon has been the one person to come forward and say that she had no belief in any of the suspicions against me.' Observing a change in Will's face, he avoided any further mention of her, feeling himself too ignorant of their relation to each other not to fear that his words might have some hidden painful bearing on it. And it occurred to him that Dorothea was the real cause of the present visit to Middlemarch.

The two men were pitying each other, but it was only Will who guessed the extent of his companion's trouble. When Lydgate spoke with desperate resignation of going to settle in London, and said with a faint smile, 'We shall have you again, old fellow', Will felt inexpressibly mournful, and said nothing. Rosamond had that morning entreated him to urge this step on Lydgate; and it seemed to him as if he were beholding in a magic panorama a future where he himself was sliding into that pleasureless yielding to the small solicitations of circumstance, which is a commoner history of perdition than any single momentous bargain.

We are on a perilous margin when we begin to look passively at our future selves, and see our own figures led with dull consent into insipid misdoing and shabby achievement. Poor Lydgate was inwardly groaning on that margin, and Will was arriving at it. It seemed to him this evening as if the cruelty of his outburst to Rosamond had made an obligation for him, and he dreaded the obligation: he dreaded Lydgate's unsuspecting goodwill: he dreaded his own distaste for his spoiled life, which would leave him in motiveless levity.

ᔕ EIGHTY ᔕ

Stern lawgiver! yet thou dost wear
The Godhead's most benignant grace;
Nor know we anything so fair
As is the smile upon thy face;
Flowers laugh before thee on their beds,
And fragrance in thy footing treads;
Thou dost preserve the Stars from wrong:
And the most ancient Heavens, through thee, are fresh and strong.
WORDSWORTH: *Ode to Duty*

WHEN DOROTHEA HAD SEEN MR FAREBROTHER in the morning, she had promised to go and dine at the parsonage on her return from Freshitt. There was a frequent interchange of visits between her and the Farebrother family, which enabled her to say that she was not at all lonely at the Manor, and to resist for the present the severe prescription of a lady companion. When she reached home and remembered her engagement, she was glad of it; and finding that she had still an hour before she could dress for dinner, she walked straight to the schoolhouse and entered into a conversation with the master and mistress about the new bell, giving eager attention to their small details and repetitions, and getting up a dramatic sense that her life was very busy. She paused on her way back to talk to old Master Bunney who was putting in some garden-seeds, and discoursed wisely with that rural sage about the crops that would make the most return on a perch of ground, and the result of sixty years' experience as to soils – namely, that if your soil was pretty mellow it would do, but if there came wet, wet, wet to make it all of a mummy, why then –

Finding that the social spirit had beguiled her into being rather late, she dressed hastily and went over to the parsonage rather earlier than was necessary. That house was never dull, Mr Farebrother, like another White of Selborne, having continually something new to tell of his inarticulate guests and *protégés*, whom he was teaching the boys not to torment; and he had just set up a pair of beautiful goats to be pets of the village in general, and to walk at large as sacred animals. The evening went by cheerfully till after tea, Dorothea talking more than usual and dilating with Mr Farebrother on the possible histories of creatures that converse compendiously with their antennae, and for aught we know may hold reformed parliaments; when suddenly some inarticulate little sounds were heard which called everybody's attention.

'Henrietta Noble,' said Mrs Farebrother, seeing her small sister moving about the furniture-legs distressfully, 'what is the matter?'

'I have lost my tortoise-shell lozenge-box. I fear the kitten has rolled it away,' said the tiny old lady, involuntarily continuing her beaver-like notes.

'Is it a great treasure, aunt?' said Mr Farebrother, putting up his glasses and looking at the carpet.

'Mr Ladislaw gave it me,' said Miss Noble. 'A German box – very pretty; but if it falls it always spins away as far as it can.'

'Oh, if it is Ladislaw's present,' said Mr Farebrother, in a deep tone of comprehension, getting up and hunting. The box was found at last under a chiffonier, and Miss Noble grasped it with delight, saying, 'It was under a fender the last time.'

'That is an affair of the heart with my aunt,' said Mr Farebrother, smiling at Dorothea, as he reseated himself.

'If Henrietta Noble forms an attachment to any one, Mrs Casaubon,' said his mother, emphatically, – 'she is like a dog – she would take their shoes for a pillow and sleep the better.'

'Mr Ladislaw's shoes, I would,' said Henrietta Noble.

Dorothea made an attempt at smiling in return. She was surprised and annoyed to find that her heart was palpitating violently, and that it was quite useless to try after a recovery of her former animation. Alarmed at herself – fearing some further betrayal of a change so marked in its occasion, she rose and said in a low voice with undisguised anxiety, 'I must go; I have overtired myself.'

Mr Farebrother, quick in perception, rose and said, 'It is true; you must have half-exhausted yourself in talking about Lydgate. That sort of work tells upon one after the excitement is over.'

He gave her his arm back to the Manor, but Dorothea did not attempt to speak, even when he said good-night.

The limit of resistance was reached, and she had sunk back helpless within the clutch of inescapable anguish. Dismissing Tantripp with a few faint words, she locked her door, and turning away from it towards the vacant room she pressed her hands hard on the top of her head, and moaned out –

'Oh, I did love him!'

Then came the hour in which the waves of suffering shook her too thoroughly to leave any power of thought. She could only cry in loud whispers, between her sobs, after her lost belief which she had planted and kept alive from a very little seed since the days in Rome – after her lost joy of clinging with silent love and faith to one who, misprized by others, was worthy in her thought – after her lost woman's pride of reigning in his memory – after her sweet dim perspective of hope, that along some pathway they should meet with unchanged recognition and take up the backward years as a yesterday.

In that hour she repeated what the merciful eyes of solitude have looked on for ages in the spiritual struggles of man – she besought hardness and coldness and aching weariness to bring her relief from the mysterious incorporeal might of her anguish: she lay on the bare floor and let the night grow cold around her; while her grand woman's frame was shaken by sobs as if she had been a despairing child.

There were two images – two living forms that tore her heart in two, as if it had been the heart of a mother who seems to see her child divided by the sword, and presses one bleeding half to her breast while her gaze goes forth in agony towards the half which is carried away by the lying woman that has never known the mother's pang.

Here, with the nearness of an answering smile, here within the vibrating bond of mutual speech, was the bright creature whom she had trusted – who had come to her like the spirit of morning visiting the dim vault where she sat as the bride of a worn-out life; and now, with a full consciousness which had never awakened before, she stretched out her arms towards him and cried with bitter cries that their nearness was a parting vision: she discovered her passion to herself in the unshrinking utterance of despair.

And there, aloof, yet persistently with her, moving wherever she moved, was the Will Ladislaw who was a changed belief exhausted of hope, a detected illusion – no, a living man towards whom there could not yet struggle any wail of regretful pity, from the midst of scorn and indignation and jealous offended pride. The fire of Dorothea's anger was not easily spent, and it flamed out in fitful returns of spurning reproach. Why had he come obtruding his life into hers, hers that might have been whole enough without him? Why had he brought his cheap regard and his lip-born words to her who had nothing paltry to give in exchange? He knew that he was deluding her – wished, in the very moment of farewell, to make her believe that he gave her the whole price of her heart, and knew that he had spent it half before. Why had he not stayed among the crowd of whom she asked nothing – but only prayed that they might be less contemptible?

But she lost energy at last even for her loud-whispered cries and moans: she subsided into helpless sobs, and on the cold floor she sobbed herself to sleep,

In the chill hours of the morning twilight, when all was dim around her, she awoke – not with any amazed wondering where she was or what had happened, but with the clearest consciousness that she was looking into the eyes of sorrow. She rose, and wrapped warm things around her, and seated herself in a great chair where she had often watched before. She was vigorous enough to have borne that hard night without feeling ill in body, beyond some aching and fatigue; but she had waked to a new condition: she felt as if her soul had been liberated from its terrible conflict; she was no longer wrestling with her grief, but could sit down with it as a lasting companion and make it a sharer in her thoughts. For now the thoughts came thickly. It was not in Dorothea's nature, for longer than the duration of a paroxysm, to sit in the narrow cell of her calamity, in the besotted misery of a consciousness that only sees another's lot as an accident of its own.

She began now to live through that yesterday morning deliberately again, forcing herself to dwell on every detail and its possible meaning. Was she alone in that scene? Was it her event only? She forced herself to think of it as bound up with another woman's life – a woman towards whom she had set out with a longing to carry some clearness and comfort into her beclouded youth. In her first outleap of jealous indignation and disgust, when quitting the hateful room, she had flung away all the mercy with which she had undertaken that visit. She had enveloped both Will and Rosamond in her burning scorn, and it seemed to her as if Rosamond were burned out of her sight for ever. But that base prompting which makes a woman more cruel to a rival than to a faithless lover, could have no strength of recurrence in Dorothea when the dominant spirit of justice within her had once overcome the tumult and had once shown her the truer measure of things. All the active thought with which she had before been representing to herself the trials of Lydgate's lot, and this young marriage union which, like her own, seemed to have its hidden as well as evident troubles – all this vivid sympathetic experience returned to her now as a power: it asserted itself as acquired knowledge asserts itself and will not let us see as we saw in the day of our ignorance. She said to her own irremediable grief, that it should make her more helpful, instead of driving her back from effort.

And what sort of crisis might not this be in three lives whose contact with hers laid an obligation on her as if they had been suppliants bearing the sacred branch? The objects of her rescue were not to be sought out by her fancy: they were chosen for her. She yearned towards the perfect Right, that it might make a throne within her, and rule her errant will. 'What should I do – how should I act now, this very day if I could clutch my own pain, and compel it to silence, and think of those three!'

It had taken long for her to come to that question, and there was light piercing into the room. She opened her curtains, and looked out towards the bit of road that lay in view, with fields beyond, outside the entrance-gates. On the road there was a man with a bundle on his back and a woman carrying her baby; in the field she could see figures moving – perhaps the shepherd with his dog. Far off in the bending sky was the pearly light; and she felt the largeness of the world and the manifold wakings of men to labour and endurance. She was a part of that involuntary, palpitating life, and could neither look out on it from her luxurious shelter as a mere spectator, nor hide her eyes in selfish complaining.

What she would resolve to do that day did not yet seem quite clear, but something that she could achieve stirred her as with an approaching murmur which would soon gather distinctness. She took off the clothes which seemed to have some of the weariness of a hard watching in them, and began to make her toilet. Presently she rang for Tantripp, who came in her dressing-gown.

'Why, madam, you've never been in bed this blessed night,' burst out Tantripp, looking first at the bed and then at Dorothea's face, which in spite of bathing had the pale cheeks and pink eyelids of a *mater dolorosa*. 'You'll kill yourself, you *will*. Anybody might think now you had a right to give yourself a little comfort.'

'Don't be alarmed, Tantripp,' said Dorothea, smiling. 'I have slept; I am not ill. I shall be glad of a cup of coffee as soon as possible. And I want you to bring me my new dress; and most likely I shall want my new bonnet to-day.'

'They've lain there a month and more ready for you, madam, and most thankful I shall be to see you with a couple o' pounds' worth less of crape,' said Tantripp, stooping to light the fire. 'There's a reason in mourning, as I've always said; and three folds at the bottom of your skirt and a plain quilling in your bonnet – and if ever anybody looked like an angel, it's you in a net quilling – is what's consistent for a second year. At least, that's *my* thinking,' ended Tantripp, looking anxiously at the fire; 'and if anybody was to marry me flattering himself I should wear those hijeous weepers two years for him, he'd be deceived by his own vanity, that's all.'

'The fire will do, my good Tan,' said Dorothea, speaking as she used to do in the old Lausanne days, only with a very low voice; 'get me the coffee.'

She folded herself in the large chair, and leaned her head against it in fatigued quiescence, while Tantripp went away wondering at this strange contrariness in her young mistress – that just the morning when she had more of a widow's face than ever, she should have asked for her lighter mourning which she had waived before. Tantripp would never have found the clue to this mystery. Dorothea wished to acknowledge that she had not the less an active life before her because she had buried a private joy; and the tradition that fresh garments belonged to all initiation, haunting her mind, made her grasp after even that slight outward help towards calm resolve. For the resolve was not easy.

Nevertheless at eleven o'clock she was walking towards Middlemarch, having made up her mind that she would make as quietly and unnoticeably as possible her second attempt to see and save Rosamond.

EIGHTY-ONE

Du Erde warst auch diese Nacht beständig,
Und athmest neu erquickt zu meinen Füssen,
Beginnest schon mit Lust mich zu umgeben,
Du regst und rührst ein kräftiges Beschliessen
Zum höchsten Dasein immerfort zu streben.
Faust: 2r Theil

WHEN DOROTHEA WAS AGAIN AT LYDGATE's door speaking to Martha, he was in the room close by with the door ajar, preparing to go out. He heard her voice, and immediately came to her.

'Do you think that Mrs Lydgate can receive me this morning?' she said, having reflected that it would be better to leave out all allusion to her previous visit.

'I have no doubt she will,' said Lydgate, suppressing his thought about Dorothea's looks, which were as much changed as Rosamond's, 'if you will be kind enough to come in and let me tell her that you are here. She has not been very well since you were here yesterday, but she is better this morning, and I think it is very likely that she will be cheered by seeing you again.'

It was plain that Lydgate, as Dorothea had expected, knew nothing about the circumstances of her yesterday's visit; nay, he appeared to imagine that she had carried it out according to her intention. She had prepared a little note asking Rosamond to see her, which she would have given to the servant if he had not been in the way, but now she was in much anxiety as to the result of his announcement.

After leading her into the drawing-room, he paused to take a letter from his pocket and put it into her hands, saying, 'I wrote this last night, and was going to carry it to Lowick in my ride. When one is grateful for something too good for common thanks, writing is less unsatisfactory than speech – one does not at least *hear* how inadequate the words are.'

Dorothea's face brightened. 'It is I who have most to thank for, since you have let me take that place. You *have* consented?' she said, suddenly doubting.

'Yes, the cheque is going to Bulstrode to-day.'

He said no more, but went up-stairs to Rosamond, who had but lately finished dressing herself, and sat languidly wondering what she should do next, her habitual industry in small things, even in the days of her sadness, prompting her to begin some kind of occupation, which she dragged through slowly or paused in from lack of interest. She looked ill, but had recovered her usual quietude of manner, and Lydgate had feared to disturb her by any questions. He had told her of Dorothea's letter containing the cheque, and afterwards he had said, 'Ladislaw is come, Rosy; he sat with me last night; I daresay he will be here again to-day. I thought he looked rather battered and depressed.' And Rosamond had made no reply.

Now, when he came up, he said to her very gently, 'Rosy, dear, Mrs Casaubon is come to see you again; you would like to see her, would you not?' That she coloured and gave rather a startled movement did not surprise him after the agitation produced by the interview yesterday – a beneficent agitation, he thought, since it seemed to have made her turn to him again.

Rosamond dared not say no. She dared not with a tone of her voice touch the facts of yesterday. Why had Mrs Casaubon come again? The answer was a blank which Rosamond could only fill up with dread, for Will Ladislaw's lacerating words had made every thought of Dorothea a fresh smart to her. Nevertheless, in her new humiliating uncertainty she dared do nothing but comply. She did not say yes, but she rose and let Lydgate put a light shawl over her shoulders, while he said, 'I am going out immediately.' Then something crossed her mind which prompted her to say, 'Pray tell Martha not to bring any one else into the drawing-room.' And Lydgate assented, thinking that he fully understood this wish. He led her down to the drawing-room door, and then turned away, observing to himself that he was rather a blundering husband to be dependent for his wife's trust in him on the influence of another woman.

Rosamond, wrapping her soft shawl around her as she walked towards Dorothea, was inwardly wrapping her soul in cold reserve. Had Mrs Casaubon come to say anything to her about Will? If so, it was a liberty that Rosamond resented; and she prepared herself to meet every word with polite impassibility. Will had bruised her pride too sorely for her to feel any compunction towards him and Dorothea: her own injury seemed much the greater. Dorothea was not only the 'preferred' woman, but had also a formidable advantage in being Lydgate's benefactor; and to poor Rosamond's pained confused vision it seemed that this Mrs Casaubon – this woman who predominated in all things concerning her – must have come now with the sense of having the advantage, and with animosity prompting her to use it. Indeed, not Rosamond only, but any one else, knowing the outer facts of the case, and not the simple inspiration on which Dorothea acted, might well have wondered why she came.

Looking like the lovely ghost of herself, her graceful slimness wrapped in her soft white shawl, the rounded infantine mouth and cheek inevitably suggesting mildness and innocence, Rosamond paused at three yards' distance from her visitor and bowed. But Dorothea, who had taken off her gloves, from an impulse which she could never resist when she wanted a sense of freedom, came forward, and with her face full of a sad yet sweet openness, put out her hand. Rosamond could not avoid meeting her glance, could not avoid putting her small hand into Dorothea's which clasped it with gentle motherliness; and immediately a doubt of her own prepossessions began to stir within her. Rosamond's eye was quick for faces; she saw that Mrs Casaubon's face looked pale and changed since yesterday, yet gentle, and like the firm softness of her hand. But Dorothea had counted a little too much on her own strength: the clearness and intensity of her mental action this morning were the continuance of a nervous exaltation which made her frame as dangerously responsive as a bit of finest Venetian crystal; and in looking at Rosamond, she suddenly found her heart swelling, and was unable to speak – all her effort was required to keep back tears. She succeeded in that, and the emotion only passed over her face like the spirit of a sob; but it added to Rosamond's impression that Mrs Casaubon's state of mind must be something quite different from what she had imagined.

So they sat down without a word of preface on the two chairs that happened to be nearest, and happened also to be close together; though Rosamond's notion when she first bowed was that she should stay a long way off from Mrs Casaubon. But she ceased thinking how anything would turn out – merely wondering what would come. And Dorothea began to speak quite simply, gathering firmness as she went on.

'I had an errand yesterday which I did not finish; that is why I am here again so soon. You will not think me too troublesome, when I tell you that I came to talk to you about the injustice that has been shown towards Mr Lydgate. It will cheer you – will it not? – to know a great deal about him, that he may not like to speak about himself just because it is in his own vindication and to his own honour. You will like to know that your husband has warm friends, who have not left off believing in his high character? You will let me speak of this without thinking that I take a liberty?'

The cordial, pleading tones which seemed to flow with generous heedlessness above all the facts which had filled Rosamond's mind as grounds of obstruction and hatred between her and this woman, came as soothingly as a warm stream over her shrinking fears. Of course Mrs Casaubon had the facts in her mind, but she was not going to speak of anything connected with them. That relief was too great for Rosamond to feel much else at the moment. She answered prettily, in the new ease of her soul –

'I know you have been very good. I shall like to hear anything you will say to me about Tertius.'

'The day before yesterday,' said Dorothea, 'when I had asked him to come to Lowick to give me his opinion on the affairs of the Hospital, he told me everything about his conduct and feelings in this sad event which has made ignorant people cast suspicions on him. The reason he told me was because I was very bold and asked him. I believed that he had never acted dishonourably, and I begged him to tell me the history. He confessed to me that he had never told it before, not even to you, because he had a great dislike to say, "I was not wrong", as if that were proof, when there are guilty people who will say so. The truth is, he knew nothing of this man Raffles, or that there were any bad secrets about him; and he thought that Mr Bulstrode offered him the money because he repented, out of kindness, of having refused it before. All his anxiety about his patient was to treat him rightly, and he was a little uncomfortable that the case did not end as he had expected; but he thought then and still thinks that there may have been no wrong in it on any one's part. And I have told Mr Farebrother, and Mr Brooke, and Sir James Chettam: they all believe in your husband. That will cheer you, will it not? That will give you courage?'

Dorothea's face had become animated, and as it beamed on Rosamond very close to her, she felt something like bashful timidity before a superior, in the presence of this self-forgetful ardour. She said, with blushing embarrassment, 'Thank you: you are very kind.'

'And he felt that he had been so wrong not to pour out everything about this to you. But you will forgive him. It was because he feels so much more about your happiness than anything else – he feels his life bound into one with yours, and it hurts him more than anything, that his misfortunes must hurt you. He could speak to me because I am an indifferent person. And then I asked him if I might come to see you; because I felt so much for his trouble and yours. That is why I came yesterday, and why I am come to-day. Trouble is so hard to bear, is it not? – How can we live and think that any one has trouble – piercing trouble – and we could help them, and never try?'

Dorothea, completely swayed by the feeling that she was uttering, forgot everything but that she was speaking from out the heart of her own trial to Rosamond's. The emotion had wrought itself more and more into her utterance, till the tones might have gone to one's very marrow, like a low cry from some suffering creature in the darkness. And she had unconsciously laid her hand again on the little hand that she had pressed before.

Rosamond, with an overmastering pang, as if a wound within her had been probed, burst into hysterical crying as she had done the day before when she clung to her husband. Poor Dorothea was feeling a great wave of her own sorrow returning over her – her thought being drawn to the possible share that Will Ladislaw might have in Rosamond's mental tumult. She was beginning to fear that she should not be able to suppress herself enough to the end of this meeting, and while her hand was still resting on Rosamond's lap, though the hand underneath it was withdrawn, she was struggling against her own rising sobs. She tried to master herself with the thought that this might be a turning-point in three lives –

not in her own; no, there the irrevocable had happened, but – in those three lives which were touching hers with the solemn neighbourhood of danger and distress. The fragile creature who was crying close to her – there might still be time to rescue her from the misery of false incompatible bonds; and this moment was unlike any other: she and Rosamond could never be together again with the same thrilling consciousness of yesterday within them both. She felt the relation between them to be peculiar enough to give her a peculiar influence, though she had no conception that the way in which her own feelings were involved was fully known to Mrs Lydgate.

It was a newer crisis in Rosamond's experience than even Dorothea could imagine: she was under the first great shock that had shattered her dream-world in which she had been easily confident of herself and critical of others; and this strange unexpected manifestation of feeling in a woman whom she had approached with a shrinking aversion and dread, as one who must necessarily have a jealous hatred towards her, made her soul totter all the more with a sense that she had been walking in an unknown world which had just broken in upon her.

When Rosamond's convulsed throat was subsiding into calm, and she withdrew the handkerchief with which she had been hiding her face, her eyes met Dorothea's as helplessly as if they had been blue flowers. What was the use of thinking about behaviour after this crying? And Dorothea looked almost as childish, with the neglected trace of a silent tear. Pride was broken down between these two.

'We were talking about your husband,' Dorothea said, with some timidity. 'I thought his looks were sadly changed with suffering the other day. I had not seen him for many weeks before. He said he had been feeling very lonely in his trial; but I think he would have borne it all better if he had been able to be quite open with you.'

'Tertius is so angry and impatient if I say anything,' said Rosamond, imagining that he had been complaining of her to Dorothea. 'He ought not to wonder that I object to speak to him on painful subjects.'

'It was himself he blamed for not speaking,' said Dorothea. 'What he said of you was, that he could not be happy in doing anything which made you unhappy – that his marriage was of course a bond which must affect his choice about everything; and for that reason he refused my proposal that he should keep his position at the Hospital, because that would bind him to stay in Middlemarch, and he would not undertake to do anything which would be painful to you. He could say that to me, because he knows that I had much trial in my marriage, from my husband's illness, which hindered his plans and saddened him; and he knows that I have felt how hard it is to walk always in fear of hurting another who is tied to us.'

Dorothea waited a little; she had discerned a faint pleasure stealing over Rosamond's face. But there was no answer, and she went on, with a

gathering tremor, 'Marriage is so unlike everything else. There is something even awful in the nearness it brings. Even if we loved some one else
better than – than those we were married to, it would be no use' –
poor Dorothea, in her palpitating anxiety, could only seize her language
brokenly – 'I mean, marriage drinks up all our power of giving or getting
any blessedness in that sort of love. I know it may be very dear – but it
murders our marriage – and then the marriage stays with us like a murder
– and everything else is gone. And then our husband – if he loved and
trusted us, and we have not helped him, but made a curse in his life . . .'

Her voice had sunk very low: there was a dread upon her of presuming
too far, and of speaking as if she herself were perfection addressing error.
She was too much preoccupied with her own anxiety, to be aware that
Rosamond was trembling too; and filled with the need to express pitying
fellowship rather than rebuke, she put her hands on Rosamond's, and
said with more agitated rapidity, – 'I know, I know that the feeling may be
very dear – it has taken hold of us unawares – it is so hard, it may seem
like death to part with it – and we are weak – I am weak – '

The waves of her own sorrow, from out of which she was struggling to
save another, rushed over Dorothea with conquering force. She stopped in
speechless agitation, not crying, but feeling as if she were being inwardly
grappled. Her face had become of a deathlier paleness, her lips trembled,
and she pressed her hands helplessly on the hands that lay under them.

Rosamond, taken hold of by an emotion stronger than her own –
hurried along in a new movement which gave all things some new, awful,
undefined aspect – could find no words, but involuntarily she put her lips
to Dorothea's forehead which was very near her, and then for a minute
the two women clasped each other as if they had been in a shipwreck.

'You are thinking what is not true,' said Rosamond, in an eager half-
whisper, while she was still feeling Dorothea's arms round her – urged by
a mysterious necessity to free herself from something that oppressed her
as if it were blood-guiltiness.

They moved apart, looking at each other.

'When you came in yesterday – it was not as you thought,' said Rosamond in the same tone.

There was a movement of surprised attention in Dorothea. She expected
a vindication of Rosamond herself.

'He was telling me how he loved another woman, that I might know he
could never love me,' said Rosamond, getting more and more hurried as
she went on. 'And now I think he hates me because – because you mistook
him yesterday. He says it is through me that you will think ill of him –
think that he is a false person. But it shall not be through me. He has never
had any love for me – I know he has not – he has always thought slightly
of me. He said yesterday that no other woman existed for him besides
you. The blame of what happened is entirely mine. He said he could never

explain to you – because of me. He said you could never think well of him again. But now I have told you, and he cannot reproach me any more.'

Rosamond had delivered her soul under impulses which she had not known before. She had begun her confession under the subduing influence of Dorothea's emotion; and as she went on she had gathered the sense that she was repelling Will's reproaches, which were still like a knife-wound within her.

The revulsion of feeling in Dorothea was too strong to be called joy. It was a tumult in which the terrible strain of the night and morning made a resistant pain: – she could only perceive that this would be joy when she had recovered her power of feeling it. Her immediate consciousness was one of immense sympathy without check; she cared for Rosamond without struggle now, and responded earnestly to her last words:

'No, he cannot reproach you any more.'

With her usual tendency to over-estimate the good in others, she felt a great outgoing of her heart towards Rosamond for the generous effort which had redeemed her from suffering, not counting that the effort was a reflex of her own energy.

After they had been silent a little, she said –

'You are not sorry that I came this morning?'

'No, you have been very good to me,' said Rosamond. 'I did not think that you would be so good. I was very unhappy. I am not happy now. Everything is so sad.'

'But better days will come. Your husband will be rightly valued. And he depends on you for comfort. He loves you best. The worst loss would be to lose that – and you have not lost it,' said Dorothea.

She tried to thrust away the too overpowering thought of her own relief, lest she should fail to win some sign that Rosamond's affection was yearning back towards her husband.

'Tertius did not find fault with me, then?' said Rosamond, understanding now that Lydgate might have said anything to Mrs Casaubon, and that she certainly was different from other women. Perhaps there was a faint taste of jealousy in the question. A smile began to play over Dorothea's face as she said –

'No, indeed! How could you imagine it?' But here the door opened, and Lydgate entered.

'I am come back in my quality of doctor,' he said. 'After I went away, I was haunted by two pale faces: Mrs Casaubon looked as much in need of care as you, Rosy. And I thought that I had not done my duty in leaving you together; so when I had been to Coleman's I came home again. I noticed that you were walking, Mrs Casaubon, and the sky has changed – I think we may have rain. May I send some one to order your carriage to come for you?'

'Oh no! I am strong: I need the walk,' said Dorothea, rising with animation in her face. 'Mrs Lydgate and I have chatted a great deal, and it is time for me to go. I have always been accused of being immoderate and saying too much.'

She put out her hand to Rosamond, and they said an earnest, quiet good-bye without kiss or other show of effusion: there had been between them too much serious emotion for them to use the signs of it superficially.

As Lydgate took her to the door she said nothing of Rosamond, but told him of Mr Farebrother and the other friends who had listened with belief to his story.

When he came back to Rosamond, she had already thrown herself on the sofa, in resigned fatigue.

'Well, Rosy,' he said, standing over her, and touching her hair, 'what do you think of Mrs Casaubon now you have seen so much of her?'

'I think she must be better than any one,' said Rosamond, 'and she is very beautiful. If you go to talk to her so often, you will be more discontented with me than ever!'

Lydgate laughed at the 'so often'. 'But has she made you any less discontented with me?'

'I think she has,' said Rosamond, looking up in his face. 'How heavy your eyes are, Tertius – and do push your hair back.' He lifted up his large white hand to obey her, and felt thankful for this little mark of interest in him. Poor Rosamond's vagrant fancy had come back terribly scourged – meek enough to nestle under the old despised shelter. And the shelter was still there: Lydgate had accepted his narrowed lot with sad resignation. He had chosen this fragile creature, and had taken the burthen of her life upon his arms. He must walk as he could, carrying that burthen pitifully.

◁ EIGHTY-TWO ▷

My grief lies onward and my joy behind.
SHAKESPEARE: *Sonnets*

EXILES NOTORIOUSLY FEED MUCH ON HOPES, and are unlikely to stay in banishment unless they are obliged. When Will Ladislaw exiled himself from Middlemarch he had placed no stronger obstacle to his return than his own resolve, which was by no means an iron barrier, but simply a state of mind liable to melt into a minuet with other states of mind, and to find itself bowing, smiling, and giving place with polite facility. As the months went on, it had seemed more and more difficult to him to say why he should not run down to Middlemarch – merely for the sake of hearing something about Dorothea; and if on such a flying visit he should chance by some strange coincidence to meet with her, there was no reason for him to be ashamed of having taken an innocent journey which he had beforehand supposed that he should not take. Since he was hopelessly divided from her, he might surely venture into her neighbourhood; and as to the suspicious friends who kept a dragon watch over her – their opinions seemed less and less important with time and change of air.

And there had come a reason quite irrespective of Dorothea, which seemed to make a journey to Middlemarch a sort of philanthropic duty. Will had given a disinterested attention to an intended settlement on a new plan in the Far West, and the need for funds in order to carry out a good design had set him on debating with himself whether it would not be a laudable use to make of his claim on Bulstrode, to urge the application of that money which had been offered to himself as a means of carrying out a scheme likely to be largely beneficial. The question seemed a very dubious one to Will, and his repugnance to again entering into any relation with the banker might have made him dismiss it quickly, if there had not arisen in his imagination the probability that his judgment might be more safely determined by a visit to Middlemarch.

That was the object which Will stated to himself as a reason for coming down. He had meant to confide in Lydgate, and discuss the money question with him, and he had meant to amuse himself for the few evenings of his stay by having a great deal of music and badinage with fair Rosamond, without neglecting his friends at Lowick Parsonage: – if the Parsonage was close to the Manor, that was no fault of his. He had neglected the Farebrothers before his departure, from a proud resistance to the possible accusation of indirectly seeking interviews with Dorothea; but hunger tames us, and Will had become very hungry for the vision of a certain form and the sound of a certain voice. Nothing had done instead – not the opera, or the converse of zealous politicians, or the flattering reception (in dim corners) of his new hand in leading articles.

Thus he had come down, foreseeing with confidence how almost everything would be in his familiar little world; fearing, indeed, that there would be no surprises in his visit. But he had found that humdrum world in a terribly dynamic condition, in which even badinage and lyrism had turned explosive; and the first day of this visit had become the most fatal epoch of his life. The next morning he felt so harassed with the nightmare of consequences – he dreaded so much the immediate issues before him – that seeing while he breakfasted the arrival of the Riverston coach, he went out hurriedly and took his place on it, that he might be relieved, at least for a day, from the necessity of doing or saying anything in Middlemarch. Will Ladislaw was in one of those tangled crises which are commoner in experience than one might imagine, from the shallow absoluteness of men's judgments. He had found Lydgate, for whom he had the sincerest respect, under circumstances which claimed his thorough and frankly-declared sympathy; and the reason why, in spite of that claim, it would have been better for Will to have avoided all further intimacy, or even contact, with Lydgate, was precisely of the kind to make such a course appear impossible. To a creature of Will's susceptible temperament – without any neutral region of indifference in his nature, ready to turn everything that befell him into the collisions of a passionate drama – the revelation that Rosamond had made her happiness in any way dependent on him was a difficulty which his outburst of rage towards her had immeasurably increased for him. He hated his own cruelty, and yet he dreaded to show the fulness of his relenting: he must go to her again; the friendship could not be put to a sudden end; and her unhappiness was a power which he dreaded. And all the while there was no more foretaste of enjoyment in the life before him than if his limbs had been lopped off and he was making his fresh start on crutches. In the night he had debated whether he should not get on the coach, not for Riverston, but for London, leaving a note to Lydgate which would give a makeshift reason for his retreat. But there were strong cords pulling him back from that abrupt departure: the blight on his happiness in thinking of Dorothea, the crushing of that chief hope which had remained in spite of the acknowledged necessity for renunciation, was too fresh a misery for him to resign himself to it, and go straightway into a distance which was also despair.

Thus he did nothing more decided than take the Riverston coach. He came back again by it while it was still daylight, having made up his mind that he must go to Lydgate's that evening. The Rubicon, we know, was a very insignificant stream to look at; its significance lay entirely in certain invisible conditions. Will felt as if he were forced to cross his small boundary ditch, and what he saw beyond it was not empire but discontented subjection.

But it is given to us sometimes even in our everyday life to witness the saving influence of a noble nature, the divine efficacy of rescue that may lie in a self-subduing act of fellowship. If Dorothea, after her night's anguish, had not taken that walk to Rosamond – why, she perhaps would have been a woman who gained a higher character for discretion, but it would certainly not have been as well for those three who were on one hearth in Lydgate's house at half-past seven that evening.

Rosamond had been prepared for Will's visit, and she received him with a languid coldness which Lydgate accounted for by her nervous exhaustion, of which he could not suppose that it had any relation to Will. And when she sat in silence bending over a bit of work, he innocently apologized for her in an indirect way by begging her to lean backward and rest. Will was miserable in the necessity for playing the part of a friend who was making his first appearance and greeting to Rosamond, while his thoughts were busy about her feeling since that scene of yesterday, which seemed still inexorably to enclose them both, like the painful vision of a double madness. It happened that nothing called Lydgate out of the room; but when Rosamond poured out the tea, and Will came near to fetch it, she placed a tiny bit of folded paper in his saucer. He saw it and secured it quickly, but as he went back to his inn he had no eagerness to unfold the paper. What Rosamond had written to him would probably deepen the painful impressions of the evening. Still, he opened and read it by his bed-candle. There were only these few words in her neatly-flowing hand: –

> I have told Mrs Casaubon. She is not under any mistake about you. I told her because she came to see me and was very kind. You will have nothing to reproach me with now. I shall not have made any difference to you.

The effect of these words was not quite all gladness. As Will dwelt on them with excited imagination, he felt his cheeks and ears burning at the thought of what had occurred between Dorothea and Rosamond – at the uncertainty how far Dorothea might still feel her dignity wounded in having an explanation of his conduct offered to her. There might still remain in her mind a changed association with him which made an irremediable difference – a lasting flaw. With active fancy he wrought himself into a state of doubt little more easy than that of the man who has escaped from wreck by night and stands on unknown ground in the darkness. Until that wretched yesterday – except the moment of vexation long ago in the very same room and in the very same presence – all their vision, all their thought of each other, had been as in a world apart, where the sunshine fell on tall white lilies, where no evil lurked, and no other soul entered. But now – would Dorothea meet him in that world again?

⊲ EIGHTY-THREE ⊳

And now good-morrow to our waking souls
Which watch not one another out of fear;
For love all love of other sights controls,
And makes one little room, an everywhere.
                    DR DONNE

ON THE SECOND MORNING AFTER DOROTHEA'S visit to Rosamond, she had had two nights of sound sleep, and had not only lost all trace of fatigue, but felt as if she had a great deal of superfluous strength – that is to say, more strength than she could manage to concentrate on any occupation.

The day before, she had taken long walks outside the grounds, and had paid two visits to the Parsonage; but she never in her life told any one the reason why she spent her time in that fruitless manner, and this morning she was rather angry with herself for her childish restlessness. To-day was to be spent quite differently. What was there to be done in the village? Oh dear! nothing. Everybody was well and had flannel; nobody's pig had died; and it was Saturday morning, when there was a general scrubbing of floors and doorstones, and when it was useless to go into the school. But there were various subjects that Dorothea was trying to get clear upon, and she resolved to throw herself energetically into the gravest of all. She sat down in the library before her particular little heap of books on political economy and kindred matters, out of which she was trying to get light as to the best way of spending money so as not to injure one's neighbours, or – what comes to the same thing – so as to do them the most good. Here was a weighty subject which, if she could but lay hold of it, would certainly keep her mind steady. Unhappily her mind slipped off it for a whole hour; and at the end she found herself reading sentences twice over with an intense consciousness of many things, but not of any one thing contained in the text. This was hopeless. Should she order the carriage and drive to Tipton? No; for some reason or other she preferred staying at Lowick. But her vagrant mind must be reduced to order: there was an art in self-discipline; and she walked round and round the brown library considering by what sort of manoeuvre she could arrest her wandering thoughts. Perhaps a mere task was the best means – something to which she must go doggedly. Was there not the geography of Asia Minor, in which her slackness had often been rebuked by Mr Casaubon? She went to the cabinet of maps and unrolled one: this morning she might make herself finally sure that Paphlagonia was not on the Levantine coast, and fix her total darkness about the Chalybes firmly on the shores of the Euxine. A map was a fine thing to study when you were disposed to think of something else, being made up of names that would turn into a chime if you went back upon them. Dorothea set earnestly to work, bending close to her map, and uttering the names in an audible, subdued tone, which often got into a chime. She looked amusingly girlish after all her deep experience – nodding her head and marking the names off on her fingers, with a little pursing of her lip, and now and then breaking off to put her hands on each side of her face and say, 'Oh dear! oh dear!'

There was no reason why this should end any more than a merry-go-round; but it was at last interrupted by the opening of the door and the announcement of Miss Noble.

The little old lady, whose bonnet hardly reached Dorothea's shoulder, was warmly welcomed, but while her hand was being pressed she made many of her beaver-like noises, as if she had something difficult to say.

'Do sit down,' said Dorothea, rolling a chair forward. 'Am I wanted for anything? I shall be so glad if I can do anything.'

'I will not stay,' said Miss Noble, putting her hand into her small basket, and holding some article inside it nervously; 'I have left a friend in the churchyard.' She lapsed into her inarticulate sounds, and unconsciously drew forth the article which she was fingering. It was the tortoise-shell lozenge-box, and Dorothea felt the colour mounting to her cheeks.

'Mr Ladislaw,' continued the timid little woman. 'He fears he has offended you, and has begged me to ask if you will see him for a few minutes.'

Dorothea did not answer on the instant: it was crossing her mind that she could not receive him in this library, where her husband's prohibition seemed to dwell. She looked towards the window. Could she go out and meet him in the grounds? The sky was heavy, and the trees had begun to shiver as at a coming storm. Besides, she shrank from going out to him.

'Do see him, Mrs Casaubon,' said Miss Noble, pathetically; 'else I must go back and say No, and that will hurt him.'

'Yes, I will see him,' said Dorothea. 'Pray tell him to come.'

What else was there to be done? There was nothing that she longed for at the moment except to see Will: the possibility of seeing him had thrust itself insistently between her and every other object; and yet she had a throbbing excitement like an alarm upon her – a sense that she was doing something daringly defiant for his sake.

When the little lady had trotted away on her mission, Dorothea stood in the middle of the library with her hands falling clasped before her, making no attempt to compose herself in an attitude of dignified unconsciousness. What she was least conscious of just then was her own body: she was thinking of what was likely to be in Will's mind, and of the hard feelings that others had had about him. How could any duty bind her to hardness? Resistance to unjust dispraise had mingled with her feeling for him from the very first, and now in the rebound of her heart after her anguish the resistance was stronger than ever. 'If I love him too much it is because he has been used so ill': there was a voice within her saying this to some imagined audience in the library, when the door was opened, and she saw Will before her.

She did not move, and he came towards her with more doubt and timidity in his face than she had ever seen before. He was in a state of uncertainty which made him afraid lest some look or word of his should condemn him to a new distance from her; and Dorothea was afraid of her own emotion. She looked as if there were a spell upon her, keeping her motionless and hindering her from unclasping her hands, while some intense, grave yearning was imprisoned within her eyes. Seeing that she did not put out her hand as usual, Will paused a yard from her and said with embarrassment, 'I am so grateful to you for seeing me.'

'I wanted to see you,' said Dorothea, having no other words at command. It did not occur to her to sit down, and Will did not give a cheerful interpretation to this queenly way of receiving him; but he went on to say what he had made up his mind to say.

'I fear you think me foolish and perhaps wrong for coming back so soon. I have been punished for my impatience. You know – every one knows now – a painful story about my parentage. I knew of it before I went away, and I always meant to tell you of it if – if we ever met again.'

There was a slight movement in Dorothea, and she unclasped her hands, but immediately folded them over each other.

'But the affair is matter of gossip now,' Will continued. 'I wished you to know that something connected with it – something which happened before I went away – helped to bring me down here again. At least I thought it excused my coming. It was the idea of getting Bulstrode to apply some money to a public purpose – some money which he had thought of giving me. Perhaps it is rather to Bulstrode's credit that he privately offered me compensation for an old injury: he offered to give me a good income to make amends; but I suppose you know the disagreeable story?'

Will looked doubtfully at Dorothea, but his manner was gathering some of the defiant courage with which he always thought of this fact in his destiny. He added, 'You know that it must be altogether painful to me.'

'Yes – yes – I know,' said Dorothea, hastily.

'I did not choose to accept an income from such a source. I was sure that you would not think well of me if I did so,' said Will. Why should he mind saying anything of that sort to her now? She knew that he had avowed his love for her. 'I felt that' – he broke off, nevertheless.

'You acted as I should have expected you to act,' said Dorothea, her face brightening and her head becoming a little more erect on its beautiful stem.

'I did not believe that you would let any circumstance of my birth create a prejudice in you against me, though it was sure to do so in others,' said Will, shaking his head backward in his old way, and looking with a grave appeal into her eyes.

'If it were a new hardship it would be a new reason for me to cling to you,' said Dorothea, fervidly. 'Nothing could have changed me but – ' her heart was swelling, and it was difficult to go on; she made a great effort over herself to say in a low tremulous voice, 'but thinking that you were different – not so good as I had believed you to be.'

'You are sure to believe me better than I am in everything but one,' said Will, giving way to his own feeling in the evidence of hers. 'I mean, in my truth to you. When I thought you doubted of that, I didn't care about anything that was left. I thought it was all over with me, and there was nothing to try for – only things to endure.'

'I don't doubt you any longer,' said Dorothea, putting out her hand; a vague fear for him impelling her unutterable affection.

He took her hand and raised it to his lips with something like a sob. But he stood with his hat and gloves in the other hand, and might have done for the portrait of a Royalist. Still it was difficult to loose the hand, and Dorothea, withdrawing it in a confusion that distressed her, looked and moved away.

'See how dark the clouds have become, and how the trees are tossed,' she said, walking towards the window, yet speaking and moving with only a dim sense of what she was doing.

Will followed her at a little distance, and leaned against the tall back of a leather chair, on which he ventured now to lay his hat and gloves, and free himself from the intolerable durance of formality to which he had been for the first time condemned in Dorothea's presence. It must be confessed that he felt very happy at that moment leaning on the chair. He was not much afraid of anything that she might feel now.

They stood silent, not looking at each other, but looking at the evergreens which were being tossed, and were showing the pale underside of their leaves against the blackening sky. Will never enjoyed the prospect of a storm so much: it delivered him from the necessity of going away. Leaves and little branches were hurled about, and the thunder was getting nearer. The light was more and more sombre, but there came a flash of lightning which made them start and look at each other, and then smile. Dorothea began to say what she had been thinking of.

'That was a wrong thing for you to say, that you would have had nothing to try for. If we had lost our own chief good, other people's good would remain, and that is worth trying for. Some can be happy. I seemed to see that more clearly than ever, when I was the most wretched. I can hardly think how I could have borne the trouble, if that feeling had not come to me to make strength.'

'You have never felt the sort of misery I felt,' said Will; 'the misery of knowing that you must despise me.'

'But I have felt worse – it was worse to think ill – ' Dorothea had begun impetuously, but broke off.

Will coloured. He had the sense that whatever she said was uttered in the vision of a fatality that kept them apart. He was silent a moment, and then said passionately –

'We may at least have the comfort of speaking to each other without disguise. Since I must go away – since we must always be divided – you may think of me as one on the brink of the grave.'

While he was speaking there came a vivid flash of lightning which lit each of them up for the other – and the light seemed to be the terror of a hopeless love. Dorothea darted instantaneously from the window; Will followed her, seizing her hand with a spasmodic movement; and so they stood, with their hands clasped, like two children, looking out on the storm, while the thunder gave a tremendous crack and roll above them, and the rain began to pour down. Then they turned their faces towards each other, with the memory of his last words in them, and they did not loose each other's hands.

'There is no hope for me,' said Will. 'Even if you loved me as well as I love you – even if I were everything to you – I shall most likely always be very poor: on a sober calculation, one can count on nothing but a creeping lot. It is impossible for us ever to belong to each other. It is perhaps base of me to have asked for a word from you. I meant to go away into silence, but I have not been able to do what I meant.'

'Don't be sorry,' said Dorothea, in her clear tender tones. 'I would rather share all the trouble of our parting.'

Her lips trembled, and so did his. It was never known which lips were the first to move towards the other lips; but they kissed tremblingly, and then they moved apart.

The rain was dashing against the window-panes as if an angry spirit were within it, and behind it was the great swoop of the wind; it was one of those moments in which both the busy and the idle pause with a certain awe.

Dorothea sat down on the seat nearest to her, a long low ottoman in the middle of the room, and with her hands folded over each other on her lap, looked at the drear outer world. Will stood still an instant looking at her, then seated himself beside her, and laid his hand on hers, which turned itself upward to be clasped. They sat in that way without looking at each other, until the rain abated and began to fall in stillness. Each had been full of thoughts which neither of them could begin to utter.

But when the rain was quiet, Dorothea turned to look at Will. With passionate exclamation, as if some torture-screw were threatening him, he started up and said, 'It is impossible!'

He went and leaned on the back of the chair again, and seemed to be battling with his own anger, while she looked towards him sadly.

'It is as fatal as a murder or any other horror that divides people,' he burst out again; 'it is more intolerable – to have our life maimed by petty accidents.'

'No – don't say that – your life need not be maimed,' said Dorothea, gently.

'Yes, it must,' said Will, angrily. 'It is cruel of you to speak in that way – as if there were any comfort. You may see beyond the misery of it, but I don't. It is unkind – it is throwing back my love for you as if it were a trifle, to speak in that way in the face of the fact. We shall never be married.'

'Some time – we might,' said Dorothea, in a trembling voice.

'When?' said Will, bitterly. 'What is the use of counting on any success of mine? It is a mere toss up whether I shall ever do more than keep myself decently, unless I choose to sell myself as a mere pen and a mouthpiece. I can see that clearly enough. I could not offer myself to any woman, even if she had no luxuries to renounce.'

There was silence. Dorothea's heart was full of something that she wanted to say, and yet the words were too difficult. She was wholly possessed by them: at that moment debate was mute within her. And it was very hard that she could not say what she wanted to say. Will was looking out of the window angrily. If he would have looked at her and not gone away from her side, she thought everything would have been easier. At last he turned, still resting against the chair, and stretching his hand automatically towards his hat, said with a sort of exasperation, 'Good-bye.'

'Oh, I cannot bear it – my heart will break,' said Dorothea, starting from her seat, the flood of her young passion bearing down all the obstructions which had kept her silent – the great tears rising and falling in an instant: 'I don't mind about poverty – I hate my wealth.'

In an instant Will was close to her and had his arms round her, but she drew her head back and held his away gently that she might go on speaking, her large tear-filled eyes looking at his very simply, while she said in a sobbing childlike way, 'We could live quite well on my own fortune – it is too much – seven hundred-a-year – I want so little – no new clothes – and I will learn what everything costs.'

ᖇ EIGHTY-FOUR ᖇ

Though it be songe of old and yonge,
That I sholde be to blame,
Theyrs be the charge, that spoke so large
In hurtynge of my name.
The Not-Browne Mayde

IT WAS JUST AFTER THE LORDS HAD thrown out the Reform Bill: that explains how Mr Cadwallader came to be walking on the slope of the lawn near the great conservatory at Freshitt Hall, holding the *Times* in his hands behind him, while he talked with a trout-fisher's dispassionateness about the prospects of the country to Sir James Chettam. Mrs Cadwallader, the Dowager Lady Chettam, and Celia were sometimes seated on garden-chairs, sometimes walking to meet little Arthur, who was being drawn in his chariot, and, as became the infantine Bouddha, was sheltered by his sacred umbrella with handsome silken fringe.

The ladies also talked politics, though more fitfully. Mrs Cadwallader was strong on the intended creation of peers: she had it for certain from her cousin that Truberry had gone over to the other side entirely at the instigation of his wife, who had scented peerages in the air from the very first introduction of the Reform question, and would sign her soul away to take precedence of her younger sister, who had married a baronet. Lady Chettam thought that such conduct was very reprehensible, and remembered that Mrs Truberry's mother was a Miss Walsingham of Melspring. Celia confessed it was nicer to be 'Lady' than 'Mrs', and that Dodo never minded about precedence if she could have her own way. Mrs Cadwallader held that it was a poor satisfaction to take precedence when everybody about you knew that you had not a drop of good blood in your veins; and Celia again, stopping to look at Arthur, said, 'It would be nice, though, if he were a Viscount – and his lordship's little tooth coming through! He might have been, if James had been an Earl.'

'My dear Celia,' said the Dowager, 'James's title is worth far more than any new earldom. I never wished his father to be anything else than Sir James.'

'Oh, I only meant about Arthur's little tooth,' said Celia, comfortably. 'But see, here is my uncle coming.'

She tripped off to meet her uncle, while Sir James and Mr Cadwallader came forward to make one group with the ladies. Celia had slipped her arm through her uncle's, and he patted her hand with a rather melancholy 'Well, my dear!' As they approached, it was evident that Mr Brooke was looking dejected, but this was fully accounted for by the state of politics; and as he was shaking hands all round without more greeting than a 'Well, you're all here, you know,' the Rector said, laughingly –

'Don't take the throwing out of the Bill so much to heart, Brooke; you've got all the riff-raff of the country on your side.'

'The Bill, eh? ah!' said Mr Brooke, with a mild distractedness of manner. 'Thrown out, you know, eh? The Lords are going too far, though. They'll have to pull up. Sad news, you know. I mean, here at home – sad news. But you must not blame me, Chettam.'

'What is the matter?' said Sir James. 'Not another gamekeeper shot, I hope? It's what I should expect, when a fellow like Trapping Bass is let off so easily.'

'Gamekeeper? No. Let us go in; I can tell you all in the house, you know,' said Mr Brooke, nodding at the Cadwalladers, to show that he included them in his confidence. 'As to poachers like Trapping Bass, you know, Chettam,' he continued, as they were entering, 'when you are a magistrate, you'll not find it so easy to commit. Severity is all very well, but it's a great deal easier when you've got somebody to do it for you. You have a soft place in your heart yourself, you know – you're not a Draco, a Jeffreys, that sort of thing.'

Mr Brooke was evidently in a state of nervous perturbation. When he had something painful to tell, it was usually his way to introduce it among a number of disjointed particulars, as if it were a medicine that would get a milder flavour by mixing. He continued his chat with Sir James about the poachers until they were all seated, and Mrs Cadwallader, impatient of this drivelling, said –

'I'm dying to know the sad news. The gamekeeper is not shot; that is settled. What is it, then?'

'Well, it's a very trying thing, you know,' said Mr Brooke. 'I'm glad you and the Rector are here; it's a family matter – but you will help us all to bear it, Cadwallader. I've got to break it to you, my dear.' Here Mr Brooke looked at Celia – 'You've no notion what it is, you know. And, Chettam, it will annoy you uncommonly – but you see you have not been able to hinder it, any more than I have. There's something singular in things: they came round, you know.'

'It must be about Dodo,' said Celia, who had been used to think of her sister as the dangerous part of the family machinery. She had seated herself on a low stool against her husband's knee.

'For God's sake let us hear what it is!' said Sir James.

'Well, you know, Chettam, I couldn't help Casaubon's will: it was a sort of will to make things worse.'

'Exactly,' said Sir James, hastily. 'But *what* is worse?'

'Dorothea is going to be married again, you know,' said Mr Brooke, nodding towards Celia, who immediately looked up at her husband with a frightened glance, and put her hand on his knee.

Sir James was almost white with anger, but he did not speak.

'Merciful heaven!' said Mrs Cadwallader. 'Not to young Ladislaw?'

Mr Brooke nodded, saying, 'Yes; to Ladislaw,' and then fell into a prudential silence.

'You see, Humphrey!' said Mrs Cadwallader, waving her arm towards her husband. 'Another time you will admit that I have some foresight; or rather you will contradict me and be just as blind as ever. *You* supposed that the young gentleman was gone out of the country.'

'So he might be, and yet come back,' said the Rector, quietly.

'When did you learn this?' said Sir James, not liking to hear any one else speak, though finding it difficult to speak himself.

'Yesterday,' said Mr Brooke, meekly, 'I went to Lowick. Dorothea sent for me, you know. It had come about quite suddenly – neither of them had any idea two days ago – not any idea, you know. There's something singular in things. But Dorothea is quite determined – it is no use opposing. I put it strongly to her. I did my duty, Chettam. But she can act as she likes, you know.'

'It would have been better if I had called him out and shot him a year ago,' said Sir James, not from bloody-mindedness, but because he needed something strong to say.

'Really, James, that would have been very disagreeable,' said Celia.

'Be reasonable, Chettam. Look at the affair more quietly,' said Mr Cadwallader, sorry to see his good-natured friend so overmastered by anger.

'That is not so very easy for a man of any dignity – with any sense of right – when the affair happens to be in his own family,' said Sir James, still in his white indignation. 'It is perfectly scandalous. If Ladislaw had had a spark of honour he would have gone out of the country at once, and never shown his face in it again. However, I am not surprised. The day after Casaubon's funeral I said what ought to be done. But I was not listened to.'

'You wanted what was impossible, you know, Chettam,' said Mr Brooke. 'You wanted him shipped off. I told you Ladislaw was not to be done as we liked with: he had his ideas. He was a remarkable fellow – I always said he was a remarkable fellow.'

'Yes,' said Sir James, unable to repress a retort, 'it is rather a pity you formed that high opinion of him. We are indebted to that for him being lodged in this neighbourhood. We are indebted to that for seeing a woman like Dorothea degrading herself by marrying him.' Sir James made little stoppages between his clauses, the words not coming easily. 'A man so marked out by her husband's will, that delicacy ought to have forbidden her from seeing him again – who takes her out of her proper rank – into poverty – has the meanness to accept such a sacrifice – has always had an objectionable position – a bad origin – and, I *believe*, is a man of little principle and light character. That is my opinion,' Sir James ended emphatically, turning aside and crossing his leg.

'I pointed everything out to her,' said Mr Brooke, apologetically – 'I mean the poverty, and abandoning her position. I said, "My dear, you don't know what it is to live on seven hundred a-year, and have no carriage, and that kind of thing, and go amongst people who don't know who you are." I put it strongly to her. But I advise you to talk to Dorothea herself. The fact is, she has a dislike to Casaubon's property. You will hear what she says, you know.'

'No – excuse me – I shall not,' said Sir James, with more coolness. 'I cannot bear to see her again; it is too painful. It hurts me too much that a woman like Dorothea should have done what is wrong.'

'Be just, Chettam,' said the easy, large-lipped Rector, who objected to all this unnecessary discomfort. 'Mrs Casaubon may be acting imprudently: she is giving up a fortune for the sake of a man, and we men have so poor an opinion of each other that we can hardly call a woman wise who does that. But I think you should not condemn it as a wrong action, in the strict sense of the word.'

'Yes, I do,' answered Sir James. 'I think that Dorothea commits a wrong action in marrying Ladislaw.'

'My dear fellow, we are rather apt to consider an act wrong because it is unpleasant to us,' said the Rector, quietly. Like many men who take life easily, he had the knack of saying a home truth occasionally to those who felt themselves virtuously out of temper. Sir James took out his handkerchief and began to bite the corner.

'It is very dreadful of Dodo, though,' said Celia, wishing to justify her husband. 'She said she *never would* marry again – not anybody at all.'

'I heard her say the same thing myself,' said Lady Chettam, majestically, as if this were royal evidence.

'Oh, there is usually a silent exception in such cases,' said Mrs Cadwallader. 'The only wonder to me is, that any of you are surprised. You did nothing to hinder it. If you would have had Lord Triton down here to woo her with his philanthropy, he might have carried her off before the year was over. There was no safety in anything else. Mr Casaubon had prepared all this as beautifully as possible. He made himself disagreeable – or it pleased God to make him so – and then he dared her to contradict him. It's the way to make any trumpery tempting, to ticket it at a high price in that way.'

'I don't know what you mean by wrong, Cadwallader,' said Sir James, still feeling a little stung, and turning round in his chair towards the Rector. 'He's not a man we can take into the family. At least, I must speak for myself,' he continued, carefully keeping his eyes off Mr Brooke. 'I suppose others will find his society too pleasant to care about the propriety of the thing.'

'Well, you know, Chettam,' said Mr Brooke, good-humouredly, nursing his leg, 'I can't turn my back on Dorothea. I must be a father to her up to a certain point. I said, "My dear, I won't refuse to give you away." I had spoken strongly before. But I can cut off the entail, you know. It will cost money and be troublesome; but I can do it, you know.'

Mr Brooke nodded at Sir James, and felt that he was both showing his own force of resolution and propitiating what was just in the Baronet's vexation. He had hit on a more ingenious mode of parrying than he was aware of. He had touched a motive of which Sir James was ashamed. The mass of his feeling about Dorothea's marriage to Ladislaw was due partly to excusable prejudice, or even justifiable opinion, partly to a jealous repugnance hardly less in Ladislaw's case than in Casaubon's. He was convinced that the marriage was a fatal one for Dorothea. But amid that mass ran a vein of which he was too good and honourable a man to like the avowal even to himself: it was undeniable that the union of the two estates – Tipton and Freshitt – lying charmingly within a ring-fence, was a prospect that flattered him for his son and heir. Hence when Mr Brooke noddingly appealed to that motive, Sir James felt a sudden embarrassment; there was a stoppage in his throat; he even blushed. He had found more words than usual in the first jet of his anger, but Mr Brooke's propitiation was more clogging to his tongue than Mr Cadwallader's caustic hint.

But Celia was glad to have room for speech after her uncle's suggestion of the marriage ceremony, and she said, though with as little eagerness of manner as if the question had turned on an invitation to dinner, 'Do you mean that Dodo is going to be married directly, uncle?'

'In three weeks, you know,' said Mr Brooke, helplessly. 'I can do nothing to hinder it, Cadwallader,' he added, turning for a little countenance towards the Rector, who said –

'I should not make any fuss about it. If she likes to be poor, that is her affair. Nobody would have said anything if she had married the young fellow because he was rich. Plenty of beneficed clergy are poorer than they will be. Here is Elinor,' continued the provoking husband; 'she vexed her friends by marrying me: I had hardly a thousand a-year – I was a lout – nobody could see anything in me – my shoes were not the right cut – all the men wondered how a woman could like me. Upon my word, I must take Ladislaw's part until I hear more harm of him.'

'Humphrey, that is all sophistry, and you know it,' said his wife. 'Everything is all one – that is the beginning and end with you. As if you had not been a Cadwallader! Does any one suppose that I would have taken such a monster as you by any other name?'

'And a clergyman too,' observed Lady Chettam with approbation. 'Elinor cannot be said to have descended below her rank. It is difficult to say what Mr Ladislaw is, eh, James?'

Sir James gave a small grunt, which was less respectful than his usual mode of answering his mother. Celia looked up at him like a thoughtful kitten.

'It must be admitted that his blood is a frightful mixture!' said Mrs Cadwallader. 'The Casaubon cuttle-fish fluid to begin with, and then a rebellious Polish fiddler or dancing-master, was it? – and then an old clo – '

'Nonsense, Elinor,' said the Rector, rising. 'It is time for us to go.'

'After all, he is a pretty sprig,' said Mrs Cadwallader, rising too, and wishing to make amends. 'He is like the fine old Crichley portraits before the idiots came in.'

'I'll go with you,' said Mr Brooke, starting up with alacrity. 'You must all come and dine with me to-morrow, you know – eh, Celia, my dear?'

'You will, James – won't you?' said Celia, taking her husband's hand.

'Oh, of course, if you like,' said Sir James, pulling down his waistcoat, but unable yet to adjust his face good-humouredly. 'That is to say, if it is not to meet anybody else.'

'No, no, no,' said Mr Brooke, understanding the condition. 'Dorothea would not come, you know, unless you had been to see her.'

When Sir James and Celia were alone, she said, 'Do you mind about my having the carriage to go to Lowick, James?'

'What, now, directly?' he answered, with some surprise.

'Yes, it is very important,' said Celia.

'Remember, Celia, I cannot see her,' said Sir James.

'Not if she gave up marrying?'

'What is the use of saying that? – however, I'm going to the stables. I'll tell Briggs to bring the carriage round.'

Celia thought it was of great use, if not to say that, at least to take a journey to Lowick in order to influence Dorothea's mind. All through their girlhood she had felt that she could act on her sister by a word judiciously placed – by opening a little window for the daylight of her own understanding to enter among the strange coloured lamps by which Dodo habitually saw. And Celia the matron naturally felt more able to advise her childless sister. How could ány one understand Dodo so well as Celia did, or love her so tenderly?

Dorothea, busy in her boudoir, felt a glow of pleasure at the sight of her sister so soon after the revelation of her intended marriage. She had prefigured to herself, even with exaggeration, the disgust of her friends, and she had even feared that Celia might be kept aloof from her.

'O Kitty, I am delighted to see you!' said Dorothea, putting her hands on Celia's shoulder, and beaming on her. 'I almost thought you would not come to me.'

'I have not brought Arthur, because I was in a hurry,' said Celia, and they sat down on two small chairs opposite each other, with their knees touching.

'You know, Dodo, it is very bad,' said Celia, in her placid guttural, looking as prettily free from humours as possible. 'You have disappointed us all so. And I can't think that it ever *will* be – you never can go and live in that way. And then there are all your plans! You never can have thought of that. James would have taken any trouble for you, and you might have gone on all your life doing what you liked.'

'On the contrary, dear,' said Dorothea, 'I never could do anything that I liked. I have never carried out any plan yet.'

'Because you always wanted things that wouldn't do. But other plans would have come. And how *can* you marry Mr Ladislaw, that we none of us ever thought you *could* marry? It shocks James so dreadfully. And then it is all so different from what you have always been. You would have Mr Casaubon because he had such a great soul, and was so old and dismal and learned; and now, to think of marrying Mr Ladislaw, who has got no estate or anything. I suppose it is because you must be making yourself uncomfortable in some way or other.'

Dorothea laughed.

'Well, it is very serious, Dodo,' said Celia, becoming more impressive. 'How will you live? and you will go away among queer people. And I shall never see you – and you won't mind about little Arthur – and I thought you always would – '

Celia's rare tears had got into her eyes, and the corners of her mouth were agitated.

'Dear Celia,' said Dorothea, with tender gravity, 'if you don't ever see me, it will not be my fault.'

'Yes, it will,' said Celia, with the same touching distortion of her small features. 'How can I come to you or have you with me when James can't bear it? – that is because he thinks it is not right – he thinks you are so wrong, Dodo. But you always were wrong; only I can't help loving you. And nobody can think where you will live: where can you go?'

'I am going to London,' said Dorothea.

'How can you always live in a street? And you will be so poor. I could give you half my things, only how can I, when I never see you?'

'Bless you, Kitty,' said Dorothea, with gentle warmth. 'Take comfort: perhaps James will forgive me some time.'

'But it would be much better if you would not be married,' said Celia, drying her eyes, and returning to her argument; 'then there would be nothing uncomfortable. And you would not do what nobody thought you could do. James always said you ought to be a queen; but this is not at all being like a queen. You know what mistakes you have always been making, Dodo, and this is another. Nobody thinks Mr Ladislaw a proper husband for you. And you *said* you would never be married again.'

'It is quite true that I might be a wiser person, Celia,' said Dorothea, 'and that I might have done something better, if I had been better. But this is what I am going to do. I have promised to marry Mr Ladislaw; and I am going to marry him.'

The tone in which Dorothea said this was a note that Celia had long learned to recognize. She was silent, a few moments, and then said, as if she had dismissed all contest, 'Is he very fond of you, Dodo?'

'I hope so. I am very fond of him.'

'That is nice,' said Celia, comfortably. 'Only I would rather you had such a sort of husband as James is, with a place very near, that I could drive to.'

Dorothea smiled, and Celia looked rather meditative. Presently she said, 'I cannot think how it all came about.' Celia thought it would be pleasant to hear the story.

'I daresay not,' said Dorothea, pinching her sister's chin. 'If you knew how it came about, it would not seem wonderful to you.'

'Can't you tell me?' said Celia, settling her arms cozily.

'No, dear, you would have to feel with me, else you would never know.'

⊲ EIGHTY-FIVE ⊳

Then went the jury out, whose names were Mr Blindman, Mr
No-good, Mr Malice, Mr Love-lust, Mr Live-loose, Mr Heady,
Mr Highmind, Mr Enmity, Mr Liar, Mr Cruelty, Mr Hate-light,
Mr Implacable, who every one gave in his private verdict
against him among themselves, and afterwards unanimously
concluded to bring him in guilty before the judge. And first
among themselves, Mr Blindman, the foreman, said, I see
clearly that this man is a heretic. Then said Mr No-good,
Away with such a fellow from the earth! Ay, said Mr Malice,
for I hate the very look of him. Then said Mr Love-lust, I
could never endure him. Nor I, said Mr Live-loose; for he
would be always condemning my way. Hang him, hang him,
said Mr Heady. A sorry scrub, said Mr Highmind. My heart
riseth against him, said Mr Enmity. He is a rogue, said Mr
Liar. Hanging is too good for him, said Mr Cruelty. Let us
despatch him out of the way, said Mr Hate-light. Then said
Mr Implacable, Might I have all the world given me, I could
not be reconciled to him; therefore let us forthwith bring him
in guilty of death.

Pilgrim's Progress

WHEN IMMORTAL BUNYAN MAKES HIS PICTURE of the persecuting passions
bringing in their verdict of guilty, who pities Faithful? That is a rare and
blessed lot which some greatest men have not attained, to know ourselves
guiltless before a condemning crowd – to be sure that what we are
denounced for is solely the good in us. The pitiable lot is that of the man
who could not call himself a martyr even though he were to persuade
himself that the men who stoned him were but ugly passions incarnate –
who knows that he is stoned, not for professing the Right, but for not
being the man he professed to be.

This was the consciousness that Bulstrode was withering under while
he made his preparations for departing from Middlemarch, and going to
end his stricken life in that sad refuge, the indifference of new faces. The
duteous merciful constancy of his wife had delivered him from one dread,
but it could not hinder her presence from being still a tribunal before
which he shrank from confession and desired advocacy. His equivocations
with himself about the death of Raffles had sustained the conception of an

Omniscience whom he prayed to, yet he had a terror upon him which would not let him expose them to judgment by a full confession to his wife: the acts which he had washed and diluted with inward argument and motive, and for which it seemed comparatively easy to win invisible pardon – what name would she call them by? That she should ever silently call his acts Murder was what he could not bear. He felt shrouded by her doubt: he got strength to face her from the sense that she could not yet feel warranted in pronouncing that worst condemnation on him. Some time, perhaps – when he was dying – he would tell her all: in the deep shadow of that time, when she held his hand in the gathering darkness, she might listen without recoiling from his touch. Perhaps: but concealment had been the habit of his life, and the impulse to confession had no power against the dread of a deeper humiliation.

He was full of timid care for his wife, not only because he deprecated any harshness of judgment from her, but because he felt a deep distress at the sight of her suffering. She had sent her daughters away to board at a school on the coast, that his crisis might be hidden from them as far as possible. Set free by their absence from the intolerable necessity of accounting for her grief or of beholding their frightened wonder, she could live unconstrainedly with the sorrow that was every day streaking her hair with whiteness and making her eyelids languid.

'Tell me anything that you would like to have me do, Harriet,' Bulstrode had said to her; 'I mean with regard to arrangements of property. It is my intention not to sell the land I possess in this neighbourhood, but to leave it to you as a safe provision. If you have any wish on such subjects, do not conceal it from me.'

A few days afterwards, when she had returned from a visit to her brother's, she began to speak to her husband on a subject which had for some time been in her mind.

'I *should* like to do something for my brother's family, Nicholas; and I think we are bound to make some amends to Rosamond and her husband. Walter says Mr Lydgate must leave the town, and his practice is almost good for nothing, and they have very little left to settle anywhere with. I would rather do without something for ourselves, to make some amends to my poor brother's family.'

Mrs Bulstrode did not wish to go nearer to the facts than in the phrase 'make some amends'; knowing that her husband must understand her. He had a particular reason, which she was not aware of, for wincing under her suggestion. He hesitated before he said –

'It is not possible to carry out your wish in the way you propose, my dear. Mr Lydgate has virtually rejected any further service from me. He has returned the thousand pounds which I lent him. Mrs Casaubon advanced him the sum for that purpose. Here is his letter.'

The letter seemed to cut Mrs Bulstrode severely. The mention of Mrs Casaubon's loan seemed a reflection of that public feeling which held it a

matter of course that every one would avoid a connection with her husband. She was silent for some time; and the tears fell one after the other,
her chin trembling as she wiped them away. Bulstrode, sitting opposite
her, ached at the sight of that grief-worn face, which two months before
had been bright and blooming. It had aged to keep sad company with
his own withered features. Urged into some effort at comforting her, he
said –

'There is another means, Harriet, by which I might do a service to your
brother's family, if you like to act in it. And it would, I think, be beneficial
to you: it would be an advantageous way of managing the land which I
mean to be yours.'

She looked attentive.

'Garth once thought of undertaking the management of Stone Court in
order to place your nephew Fred there. The stock was to remain as it is,
and they were to pay a certain share of the profits instead of an ordinary
rent. That would be a desirable beginning for the young man, in conjunction with his employment under Garth. Would it be a satisfaction to you?'

'Yes, it would,' said Mrs Bulstrode, with some return of energy. 'Poor
Walter is so cast down: I would try anything in my power to do him some
good before I go away. We have always been brother and sister.'

'You must make the proposal to Garth yourself, Harriet,' said Mr Bulstrode, not liking what he had to say, but desiring the end he had in view,
for other reasons besides the consolation of his wife. 'You must state to
him that the land is virtually yours, and that he need have no transactions
with me. Communications can be made through Standish. I mention this,
because Garth gave up being my agent. I can put into your hands a paper
which he himself drew up, stating conditions; and you can propose his
renewed acceptance of them. I think it is not unlikely that he will accept
when you propose the thing for the sake of your nephew.'

⊘ EIGHTY-SIX ⊘

Le coeur se sature d'amour comme d'un sel divin qui le conserve; de
là l'incorruptible adhérence de ceux qui se sont aimés dès l'aube
de la vie, et la fraîcheur des vieilles amours prolongés. Il existe un
embaumement d'amour. C'est de Daphnis et Chlöe que sont faits
Philémon et Baucis. Cette vieillesse-là, ressemblance du soir avec
l'aurore.

VICTOR HUGO: *L'Homme qui rit*

MRS GARTH, HEARING CALEB ENTER THE passage about tea-time, opened the parlour-door and said, 'There you are, Caleb. Have you had your dinner?' (Mr Garth's meals were much subordinated to 'business'.)

'Oh yes, a good dinner – cold mutton and I don't know what. Where is Mary?'

'In the garden with Letty, I think.'

'Fred is not come yet?'

'No. Are you going out again without taking tea, Caleb?' said Mrs Garth, seeing that her absent-minded husband was putting on again the hat which he had just taken off.

'No, no; I'm only going to Mary a minute.'

Mary was in a grassy corner of the garden, where there was a swing loftily hung between two pear-trees. She had a pink kerchief tied over her head, making a little poke to shade her eyes from the level sunbeams, while she was giving a glorious swing to Letty, who laughed and screamed wildly.

Seeing her father, Mary left the swing and went to meet him, pushing back the pink kerchief and smiling afar off at him with the involuntary smile of loving pleasure.

'I came to look for you, Mary,' said Mr Garth. 'Let us walk about a bit.'

Mary knew quite well that her father had something particular to say: his eyebrows made their pathetic angle, and there was a tender gravity in his voice: these things had been signs to her when she was Letty's age. She put her arm within his, and they turned by the row of nut-trees.

'It will be a sad while before you can be married, Mary,' said her father, not looking at her, but at the end of the stick which he held in his other hand.

'Not a sad while, father – I mean to be merry,' said Mary, laughingly. 'I have been single and merry for four-and-twenty years and more: I

641

suppose it will not be quite as long again as that.' Then, after a little pause, she said, more gravely, bending her face before her father's, 'If you are contented with Fred?'

Caleb screwed up his mouth and turned his head aside wisely.

'Now, father, you did praise him last Wednesday. You said he had an uncommon notion of stock, and a good eye for things.'

'Did I?' said Caleb, rather slyly.

'Yes, I put it all down, and the date, *anno Domini*, and everything,' said Mary. 'You like things to be neatly booked. And then his behaviour to you, father, is really good; he has a deep respect for you; and it is impossible to have a better temper than Fred has.'

'Ay, ay; you want to coax me into thinking him a fine match.'

'No, indeed, father. I don't love him because he is a fine match.'

'What for, then?'

'Oh, dear, because I have always loved him. I should never like scolding any one else so well; and that is a point to be thought of in a husband.'

'Your mind is quite settled, then, Mary?' said Caleb, returning to his first tone. 'There's no other wish come into it since things have been going on as they have been of late?' (Caleb meant a great deal in that vague phrase;) 'because, better late than never. A woman must not force her heart – she'll do a man no good by that.'

'My feelings have not changed, father,' said Mary, calmly. 'I shall be constant to Fred as long as he is constant to me. I don't think either of us could spare the other, or like any one else better, however much we might admire them. It would make too great a difference to us – like seeing all the old places altered, and changing the name for everything. We must wait for each other a long while; but Fred knows that.'

Instead of speaking immediately, Caleb stood still and screwed his stick on the grassy walk. Then he said, with emotion in his voice, 'Well, I've got a bit of news. What do you think of Fred going to live at Stone Court, and managing the land there?'

'How can that ever be, father?' said Mary, wonderingly.

'He would manage it for his aunt Bulstrode. The poor woman has been to me begging and praying. She wants to do the lad good, and it might be a fine thing for him. With saving, he might gradually buy the stock, and he has a turn for farming.'

'Oh Fred would be so happy! It is too good to believe.'

'Ah, but mind you,' said Caleb, turning his head warningly, 'I must take it on *my* shoulders, and be responsible, and see after everything; and that will grieve your mother a bit, though she mayn't say so. Fred had need be careful.'

'Perhaps it is too much, father,' said Mary, checked in her joy. 'There would be no happiness in bringing you any fresh trouble.'

'Nay, nay; work is my delight, child, when it doesn't vex your mother. And then, if you and Fred get married,' here Caleb's voice shook just perceptibly, 'he'll be steady and saving; and you've got your mother's cleverness, and mine too, in a woman's sort of way; and you'll keep him in order. He'll be coming by-and-by, so I wanted to tell you first, because I think you'd like to tell *him* by yourselves. After that, I could talk it well over with him, and we could go into business and the nature of things.'

'Oh, you dear good father!' cried Mary, putting her hands round her father's neck, while he bent his head placidly, willing to be caressed. 'I wonder if any other girl thinks her father the best man in the world!'

'Nonsense, child; you'll think your husband better.'

'Impossible,' said Mary, relapsing into her usual tone; 'husbands are an inferior class of men, who require keeping in order.'

When they were entering the house with Letty, who had run to join them, Mary saw Fred at the orchard-gate, and went to meet him.

'What fine clothes you wear, you extravagant youth!' said Mary, as Fred stood still and raised his hat to her with playful formality. 'You are not learning economy.'

'Now that is too bad, Mary,' said Fred. 'Just look at the edges of these coat-cuffs! It is only by dint of good brushing that I look respectable. I am saving up three suits – one for a wedding-suit.'

'How very droll you will look! – like a gentleman in an old fashion-book.'

'Oh no, they will keep two years.'

'Two years! be reasonable, Fred,' said Mary, turning to walk. 'Don't encourage flattering expectations.'

'Why not? One lives on them better than on unflattering ones. If we can't be married in two years, the truth will be quite bad enough when it comes.'

'I have heard a story of a young gentleman who once encouraged flattering expectations, and they did him harm.'

'Mary, if you've got something discouraging to tell me, I shall bolt; I shall go into the house to Mr Garth. I am out of spirits. My father is so cut up – home is not like itself. I can't bear any more bad news.'

'Should you call it bad news to be told that you were to live at Stone Court, and manage the farm, and be remarkably prudent, and save money every year till all the stock and furniture were your own, and you were a distinguished agricultural character, as Mr Borthrop Trumbull says – rather stout, I fear, and with the Greek and Latin sadly weather-worn?'

'You don't mean anything except nonsense, Mary?' said Fred, colouring slightly nevertheless.

'That is what my father has just told me of as what may happen, and he never talks nonsense,' said Mary, looking up at Fred now, while he grasped her hand as they walked, till it rather hurt her; but she would not complain.

'Oh, I could be a tremendously good fellow then, Mary, and we could be married directly.'

'Not so fast, sir; how do you know that I would not rather defer our marriage for some years? That would leave you time to misbehave, and then if I liked some one else better, I should have an excuse for jilting you.'

'Pray don't joke, Mary,' said Fred, with strong feeling. 'Tell me seriously that all this is true, and that you are happy because of it – because you love me best.'

'It is all true, Fred, and I am happy because of it – because I love you best,' said Mary, in a tone of obedient recitation.

They lingered on the door-step under the steep-roofed porch, and Fred almost in a whisper said, –

'When we were first engaged, with the umbrella-ring, Mary, you used to – '

The spirit of joy began to laugh more decidedly in Mary's eyes, but the fatal Ben came running to the door with Brownie yapping behind him, and, bouncing against them, said –

'Fred and Mary! are you ever coming in? – or may I eat your cake?'

❧ FINALE ❧

EVERY LIMIT IS A BEGINNING AS WELL AS an ending. Who can quit young lives after being long in company with them, and not desire to know what befell them in their after-years? For the fragment of a life, however typical, is not the sample of an even web: promises may not be kept, and an ardent outset may be followed by declension; latent powers may find their long-waited opportunity; a past error may urge a grand retrieval.

Marriage, which has been the bourne of so many narratives, is still a great beginning, as it was to Adam and Eve, who kept their honeymoon in Eden, but had their first little one among the thorns and thistles of the wilderness. It is still the beginning of the home epic – the gradual conquest or irremediable loss of that complete union which makes the advancing years a climax, and age the harvest of sweet memories in common.

Some set out, like Crusaders of old, with a glorious equipment of hope and enthusiasm, and get broken by the way, wanting patience with each other and the world.

All who have cared for Fred Vincy and Mary Garth will like to know that these two made no such failure, but achieved a solid mutual happiness. Fred surprised his neighbours in various ways. He became rather distinguished in his side of the county as a theoretic and practical farmer, and produced a work on the *Cultivation of Green Crops and the Economy of Cattle-Feeding* which won him high congratulations at agricultural meetings. In Middlemarch admiration was more reserved: most persons there were inclined to believe that the merit of Fred's authorship was due to his wife, since they had never expected Fred Vincy to write on turnips and mangel-wurzel.

But when Mary wrote a little book for her boys, called *Stories of Great Men, taken from Plutarch,* and had it printed and published by Gripp & Co., Middlemarch, every one in the town was willing to give the credit of this work to Fred, observing that he had been to the University, 'where the ancients were studied', and might have been a clergyman if he had chosen.

In this way it was made clear that Middlemarch had never been deceived, and that there was no need to praise anybody for writing a book, since it was always done by somebody else.

Moreover, Fred remained unswervingly steady. Some years after his marriage he told Mary that his happiness was half owing to Farebrother, who gave him a strong pull-up at the right moment. I cannot say that he was never again misled by his hopefulness: the yield of crops or the profits of a cattle sale usually fell below his estimate; and he was always prone to believe that he could make money by the purchase of a horse which turned out badly – though this, Mary observed, was of course the fault of the horse, not of Fred's judgment. He kept his love of horsemanship, but he rarely allowed himself a day's hunting; and when he did so, it was remarkable that he submitted to be laughed at for cowardliness at the fences, seeming to see Mary and the boys sitting on the five-barred gate, or showing their curly heads between hedge and ditch.

There were three boys: Mary was not discontented that she brought forth men-children only; and when Fred wished to have a girl like her, she said, laughingly, 'That would be too great a trial to your mother.' Mrs Vincy in her declining years, and in the diminished lustre of her house-keeping, was much comforted by her perception that two at least of Fred's boys were real Vincys, and did not 'feature the Garths'. But Mary secretly rejoiced that the youngest of the three was very much what her father must have been when he wore a round jacket, and showed a marvellous nicety of aim in playing at marbles, or in throwing stones to bring down the mellow pears.

Ben and Letty Garth, who were uncle and aunt before they were well in their teens, disputed much as to whether nephews or nieces were more desirable; Ben contending that it was clear girls were good for less than boys, else they would not be always in petticoats, which showed how little they were meant for; whereupon Letty, who argued much from books, got angry in replying that God made coats of skins for both Adam and Eve alike – also it occurred to her that in the East the men too wore petticoats. But this latter argument, obscuring the majesty of the former, was one too many, for Ben answered contemptuously, 'The more spooneys they!' and immediately appealed to his mother whether boys were not better than girls. Mrs Garth pronounced that both were alike naughty, but that boys were undoubtedly stronger, could run faster, and throw with more precision to a greater distance. With this oracular sentence Ben was well satisfied, not minding the naughtiness; but Letty took it ill, her feeling of superiority being stronger than her muscles.

Fred never became rich – his hopefulness had not led him to expect that; but he gradually saved enough to become owner of the stock and furniture at Stone Court, and the work which Mr Garth put into his hands carried him in plenty through those 'bad times' which are always present with farmers. Mary, in her matronly days, became as solid in figure as her mother; but, unlike her, gave the boys little formal teaching, so that Mrs Garth was alarmed lest they should never be well grounded in grammar and geography. Nevertheless, they were found quite forward enough when they went to school; perhaps, because they had liked nothing so well as being with their mother. When Fred was riding home on winter evenings he had a pleasant vision beforehand of the bright hearth in the wainscoated parlour, and was sorry for other men who could not have Mary for their wife; especially for Mr Farebrother. 'He was ten times worthier of you than I was,' Fred could now say to her, magnanimously. 'To be sure he was,' Mary answered; 'and for that reason he could do better without me. But you – I shudder to think what you would have been – a curate in debt for horsehire and cambric pocket-handkerchiefs!'

On inquiry it might possibly be found that Fred and Mary still inhabit Stone Court – that the creeping plants still cast the foam of their blossoms over the fine stone-walls into the field where the walnut-trees stand in stately row – and that on sunny days the two lovers who were first engaged with the umbrella-ring may be seen in white-haired placidity at the open window from which Mary Garth, in the days of old Peter Featherstone, had often been ordered to look out for Mr Lydgate.

Lydgate's hair never became white. He died when he was only fifty, leaving his wife and children provided for by a heavy insurance on his life. He had gained an excellent practice, alternating, according to the season, between London and a Continental bathing-place; having written a treatise on Gout, a disease which has a good deal of wealth on its side. His skill was relied on by many paying patients, but he always regarded himself as a failure: he had not done what he once meant to do. His acquaintances thought him enviable to have so charming a wife, and nothing happened to shake their opinion. Rosamond never committed a second compromising indiscretion. She simply continued to be mild in her temper, inflexible in her judgment, disposed to admonish her husband, and able to frustrate him by stratagem. As the years went on he opposed her less and less, whence Rosamond concluded that he had learned the value of her opinion; on the other hand, she had a more thorough conviction of his talents now that he gained a good income, and instead of the threatened cage in Bride Street provided one all flowers and gilding, fit for the bird of paradise that she resembled. In brief, Lydgate was what is called a successful man. But he died prematurely of diphtheria, and Rosamond afterwards married an elderly and wealthy physician, who took kindly to her four children. She made a very pretty show with her daughters, driving out in her carriage, and often spoke of her happiness as 'a reward' – she did not say for what, but probably she meant that it was a reward for her patience with Tertius, whose temper never became faultless, and to the last occasionally let slip a bitter speech which was more memorable than the signs he made of his repentance. He once called her his basil plant; and when she asked for an explanation, said that basil was a plant which had flourished wonderfully on a murdered man's brains. Rosamond had a placid but strong answer to such speeches. Why then had he chosen her? It was a pity he had not had Mrs Ladislaw, whom he was always praising and placing above her. And thus the conversation ended with the advantage on Rosamond's side. But it would be unjust not to tell, that she never uttered a word in depreciation of Dorothea, keeping in religious remembrance the generosity which had come to her aid in the sharpest crisis of her life.

Dorothea herself had no dreams of being praised above other women, feeling that there was always something better which she might have done, if she had only been better and known better. Still, she never repented that she had given up position and fortune to marry Will Ladislaw, and he would have held it the greatest shame as well as sorrow to him if she had repented. They were bound to each other by a love stronger than any impulses which could have marred it. No life would have been possible to Dorothea which was not filled with emotion, and she had now a life filled also with a beneficent activity which she had not the doubtful pains of discovering and marking out for herself. Will became an ardent public man, working well in those times when reforms were begun with a young hopefulness of immediate good which has been much checked in our days, and getting at last returned to Parliament by a constituency who paid his expenses. Dorothea could have liked nothing better, since wrongs existed, than that her husband should be in the thick of a struggle against them, and that she should give him wifely help. Many who knew her, thought it a pity that so substantive and rare a creature should have been absorbed into the life of another, and be only known in a certain circle as a wife and mother. But no one stated exactly what else that was in her power she ought rather to have done – not even Sir James Chettam, who went no further than the negative prescription that she ought not to have married Will Ladislaw.

But this opinion of his did not cause a lasting alienation; and the way in which the family was made whole again was characteristic of all concerned. Mr Brooke could not resist the pleasure of corresponding with Will and Dorothea; and one morning when his pen had been remarkably fluent on the prospects of Municipal Reform, it ran off into an invitation to the Grange, which, once written, could not be done away with at less cost than the sacrifice (hardly to be conceived) of the whole valuable letter. During the months of this correspondence Mr Brooke had continually, in his talk with Sir James Chettam, been presupposing or hinting that the intention of cutting off the entail was still maintained; and the day on which his pen gave the daring invitation, he went to Freshitt expressly to intimate that he had a stronger sense than ever of the reasons for taking that energetic step as a precaution against any mixture of low blood in the heir of the Brookes.

But that morning something exciting had happened at the Hall. A letter had come to Celia which made her cry silently as she read it; and when Sir James, unused to see her in tears, asked anxiously what was the matter, she burst out in a wail such as he had never heard from her before.

'Dorothea has a little boy. And you will not let me go and see her. And I am sure she wants to see me. And she will not know what to do with the baby – she will do wrong things with it. And they thought she would die. It is very dreadful! Suppose it had been me and little Arthur, and Dodo had been hindered from coming to see me! I wish you would be less unkind, James!'

'Good heavens, Celia!' said Sir James, much wrought upon, 'what do you wish? I will do anything you like. I will take you to town to-morrow if you wish it.' And Celia did wish it.

It was after this that Mr Brooke came, and meeting the Baronet in the grounds, began to chat with him in ignorance of the news, which Sir James for some reason did not care to tell him immediately. But when the entail was touched on in the usual way, he said, 'My dear sir, it is not for me to dictate to you, but for my part I would let that alone. I would let things remain as they are.'

Mr Brooke felt so much surprise that he did not at once find out how much he was relieved by the sense that he was not expected to do anything in particular.

Such being the bent of Celia's heart, it was inevitable that Sir James should consent to a reconciliation with Dorothea and her husband. Where women love each other, men learn to smother their mutual dislike. Sir James never liked Ladislaw, and Will always preferred to have Sir James's company mixed with another kind: they were on a footing of reciprocal tolerance which was made quite easy only when Dorothea and Celia were present.

It became an understood thing that Mr and Mrs Ladislaw should pay at least two visits during the year to the Grange, and there came gradually a small row of cousins at Freshitt who enjoyed playing with the two cousins visiting Tipton as much as if the blood of these cousins had been less dubiously mixed.

Mr Brooke lived to a good old age, and his estate was inherited by Dorothea's son, who might have represented Middlemarch, but declined, thinking that his opinions had less chance of being stifled if he remained out of doors.

Sir James never ceased to regard Dorothea's second marriage as a mistake; and indeed this remained the tradition concerning it in Middlemarch, where she was spoken of to a younger generation as a fine girl who married a sickly clergyman, old enough to be her father, and in little more than a year after his death gave up her estate to marry his cousin – young enough to have been his son, with no property, and not well-born. Those who had not seen anything of Dorothea usually observed that she could not have been 'a nice woman', else she would not have married either the one or the other.

Certainly those determining acts of her life were not ideally beautiful. They were the mixed result of a young and noble impulse struggling amidst the conditions of an imperfect social state, in which great feelings will often take the aspect of error, and great faith the aspect of illusion. For there is no creature whose inward being is so strong that it is not greatly determined by what lies outside it. A new Theresa will hardly have the opportunity of reforming a conventual life, any more than a new Antigone will spend her heroic piety in daring all for the sake of a brother's burial· the medium in which their ardent deeds took shape is for ever gone. But we insignificant people with our daily words and acts are preparing the lives of many Dorotheas, some of which may present a far sadder sacrifice than that of the Dorothea whose story we know.

Her finely-touched spirit had still its fine issues, though they were not widely visible. Her full nature, like that river of which Cyrus broke the strength, spent itself in channels which had no great name on the earth. But the effect of her being on those around her was incalculably diffusive: for the growing good of the world is partly dependent on unhistoric acts; and that things are not so ill with you and me as they might have been, is half owing to the number who lived faithfully a hidden life, and rest in unvisited tombs.

SILAS MARNER

PART ONE

৩ ONE ৩

In the days when the spinning-wheels hummed busily in the farm-houses – and even great ladies, clothed in silk and thread lace, had their toy spinning-wheels of polished oak – there might be seen in districts far away among the lanes, or deep in the bosom of the hills, certain pallid undersized men, who, by the side of the brawny country-folk, looked like the remnants of a disinherited race. The shepherd's dog barked fiercely when one of these alien-looking men appeared on the upland, dark against the early winter sunset; for what dog likes a figure bent under a heavy bag? – and these pale men rarely stirred abroad without that mysterious burden. The shepherd himself, though he had good reason to believe that the bag held nothing but flaxen thread, or else the long rolls of strong linen spun from that thread, was not quite sure that this trade of weaving, indispensable though it was, could be carried on entirely without the help of the Evil One. In that far-off time superstition clung easily round every person or thing that was at all unwonted, or even intermittent and occasional merely, like the visits of the pedlar or the knife-grinder. No one knew where wandering men had their homes or their origin; and how was a man to be explained unless you at least knew somebody who knew his father and mother? To the peasants of old times, the world outside their own direct experience was a region of vagueness and mystery: to their untravelled thought a state of wandering was a conception as dim as the winter life of the swallows that came back with the spring; and even a settler, if he came from distant parts, hardly ever ceased to be viewed with a remnant of distrust, which would have prevented any surprise if a long course of inoffensive conduct on his part had ended in the commission of a crime; especially if he had any reputation for knowledge, or showed any skill in handicraft. All cleverness, whether in the rapid use of that difficult instrument the tongue, or in some other art unfamiliar to villagers, was in itself suspicious: honest folk, born and bred in a visible manner, were mostly not over-wise or clever – at least, not beyond such a matter as knowing the signs of the weather; and the process by which rapidity and dexterity of any kind were acquired was so wholly hidden, that they partook of the nature of conjuring. In this way it came to pass that those scattered linen-weavers – emigrants from the town into the country – were to the last regarded as aliens by their rustic neighbours, and usually contracted the eccentric habits which belong to a state of loneliness.

In the early years of this century, such a linen-weaver, named Silas Marner, worked at his vocation in a stone cottage that stood among the nutty hedgerows near the village of Raveloe, and not far from the edge of a deserted stone-pit. The questionable sound of Silas's loom, so unlike the natural cheerful trotting of the winnowing-machine, or the simpler rhythm of the flail, had a half-fearful fascination for the Raveloe boys, who would often leave off their nutting or birds'-nesting to peep in at the window of the stone cottage, counterbalancing a certain awe at the mysterious action of the loom, by a pleasant sense of scornful superiority, drawn from the mockery of its alternating noises, along with the bent, tread-mill attitude of the weaver. But sometimes it happened that Marner, pausing to adjust an irregularity in his thread, became aware of the small scoundrels, and, though chary of his time, he liked their intrusion so ill that he would descend from his loom, and, opening the door, would fix on them a gaze that was always enough to make them take to their legs in terror. For how was it possible to believe that those large brown protuberant eyes in Silas Marner's pale face really saw nothing very distinctly that was not close to them, and not rather that their dreadful stare could dart cramp, or rickets, or a wry mouth at any boy who happened to be in the rear? They had, perhaps, heard their fathers and mothers hint that Silas Marner could cure folks' rheumatism if he had a mind, and add, still more darkly, that if you could only speak the devil fair enough, he might save you the cost of the doctor. Such strange lingering echoes of the old demon-worship might perhaps even now be caught by the diligent listener among the grey-haired peasantry; for the rude mind with difficulty associates the ideas of power and benignity. A shadowy conception of power that by much persuasion can be induced to refrain from inflicting harm, is the shape most easily taken by the sense of the Invisible in the minds of men who have always been pressed close by primitive wants, and to whom a life of hard toil has never been illuminated by any enthusiastic religious faith. To them pain and mishap present a far wider range of possibilities than gladness and enjoyment: their imagination is almost barren of the images that feed desire and hope, but is all overgrown by recollections that are a perpetual pasture to fear. 'Is there anything you can fancy that you would like to eat?' I once said to an old labouring man, who was in his last illness, and who had refused all the food his wife had offered him. 'No,' he answered, 'I've never been used to nothing but common victual, and I can't eat that.' Experience had bred no fancies in him that could raise the phantasm of appetite.

And Raveloe was a village where many of the old echoes lingered, undrowned by new voices. Not that it was one of those barren parishes lying on the outskirts of civilization – inhabited by meagre sheep and thinly-scattered shepherds: on the contrary, it lay in the rich central plain of what we are pleased to call Merry England, and held farms which, speaking from a spiritual point of view, paid highly-desirable tithes. But it was nestled in a snug well-wooded hollow, quite an hour's journey on horseback from any turnpike, where it was never reached by the vibrations of the coach-horn, or of public opinion. It was an important-looking village, with a fine old church and large churchyard in the heart of it, and two or three large brick-and-stone homesteads, with well-walled orchards and ornamental weathercocks, standing close upon the road, and lifting more imposing fronts than the rectory, which peeped from among the trees on the other side of the churchyard: – a village which showed at once the summits of its social life, and told the practised eye that there was no great park and manor-house in the vicinity, but that there were several chiefs in Raveloe who could farm badly quite at their ease, drawing enough money from their bad farming, in those war times, to live in a rollicking fashion, and keep a jolly Christmas, Whitsun, and Easter tide.

It was fifteen years since Silas Marner had first come to Raveloe; he was then simply a pallid young man, with prominent, short-sighted brown eyes, whose appearance would have had nothing strange for people of average culture and experience, but for the villagers near whom he had come to settle it had mysterious peculiarities which corresponded with the exceptional nature of his occupation, and his advent from an unknown region called 'North'ard'. So had his way of life: – he invited no comer to step across his door-sill, and he never strolled into the village to drink a pint at the Rainbow, or to gossip at the wheelwright's: he sought no man or woman, save for the purposes of his calling, or in order to supply himself with necessaries; and it was soon clear to the Raveloe lasses that he would never urge one of them to accept him against her will – quite as if he had heard them declare that they would never marry a dead man come to life again. This view of Marner's personality was not without another ground than his pale face and unexampled eyes; for Jem Rodney, the mole-catcher, averred that one evening as he was returning homeward he saw Silas Marner leaning against a stile with a heavy bag on his back, instead of resting the bag on the stile as a man in his senses would have done; and that, on coming up to him, he saw that Marner's eyes were set like a dead man's, and he spoke to him, and shook him, and his limbs were stiff, and his hands clutched the bag as if they'd been made of iron; but just as he had made up his mind that the weaver was dead, he came all right again, like, as you might say, in the winking of an eye, and said 'Good-night', and walked off. All this Jem swore he had seen, more by token that it was the very day he had been mole-catching on Squire Cass's land, down by the old saw-pit. Some said Marner must have been in a 'fit', a word which seemed to explain things otherwise incredible; but the argumentative Mr Macey, clerk of the parish, shook his head, and asked if anybody was ever known to go off in a fit and not fall down. A fit was a stroke, wasn't it? and it was in the nature of a stroke to partly take away the use of a man's limbs and throw him on the parish, if he'd got no children to look to. No, no; it was no stroke that would let a man stand on his legs, like a horse between the shafts, and then walk off as soon as you can say 'Gee!' But there might be such a thing as a man's soul being loose from his body, and going out and in, like a bird out of its nest and back; and that was how folks got over-wise, for they went to school in this shell-less state to those who could teach them more than their neighbours could learn with their five senses and the parson. And where did Master Marner get his knowledge of herbs from – and charms too, if he liked to give them away? Jem Rodney's story was no more than what might have been expected by anybody who had seen how Marner had cured Sally Oates, and made her sleep like a baby, when her heart had been beating enough to burst her body, for two months and more, while she had been under the doctor's care. He might cure more folks if he would; but he was worth speaking fair, if it was only to keep him from doing you a mischief.

It was partly to this vague fear that Marner was indebted for protecting him from the persecution that his singularities might have drawn upon him, but still more to the fact that, the old linen-weaver in the neighbouring parish of Tarley being dead, his handicraft made him a highly welcome settler to the richer housewives of the district, and even to the more provident cottagers, who had their little stock of yarn at the year's end. Their sense of his usefulness would have counteracted any repugnance or suspicion which was not confirmed by a deficiency in the quality or the tale of the cloth he wove for them. And the years had rolled on without producing any change in the impressions of the neighbours concerning Marner, except the change from novelty to habit. At the end of fifteen years the Raveloe men said just the same things about Silas Marner as at the beginning: they did not say them quite so often, but they believed them much more strongly when they did say them. There was only one important addition which the years had brought: it was, that Master Marner had laid by a fine sight of money somewhere, and that he could buy up 'bigger men' than himself.

But while opinion concerning him had remained nearly stationary, and his daily habits had presented scarcely any visible change, Marner's inward life had been a history and a metamorphosis, as that of every fervid nature must be when it has fled, or been condemned to solitude. His life, before he came to Raveloe, had been filled with the movement, the mental activity, and the close fellowship, which, in that day as in this, marked the life of an artisan early incorporated in a narrow religious sect, where the poorest layman has the chance of distinguishing himself by gifts of speech, and has, at the very least, the weight of a silent voter in the government of his community. Marner was highly thought of in that little hidden world, known to itself as the church assembling in Lantern Yard; he was believed to be a young man of exemplary life and ardent faith; and a peculiar interest had been centred in him ever since he had fallen, at a prayer-meeting, into a mysterious rigidity and suspension of consciousness, which, lasting for an hour or more, had been mistaken for death. To have sought a medical explanation for this phenomenon would have been held by Silas himself, as well as by his minister and fellow-members, a wilful self-exclusion from the spiritual significance that might lie therein. Silas was evidently a brother selected for a peculiar discipline, and though the effort to interpret this discipline was discouraged by the absence, on his part, of any spiritual vision during his outward trance, yet it was believed by himself and others that its effect was seen in an accession of light and fervour. A less truthful man than he might have been tempted into the subsequent creation of a vision in the form of resurgent memory; a less sane man might have believed in such a creation; but Silas was both sane and honest, though, as with many honest and fervent men, culture had not defined any channels for his sense of mystery, and so it spread itself over the proper pathway of inquiry and knowledge. He had inherited from his mother some acquaintance with medicinal herbs and their preparation – a little store of wisdom which she had imparted to him as a solemn bequest – but of late years he had had doubts about the lawfulness of applying this knowledge, believing that herbs could have no efficacy without prayer, and that prayer might suffice without herbs; so that his inherited delight to wander through the fields in search of foxglove and dandelion and coltsfoot, began to wear to him the character of a temptation.

Among the members of his church there was one young man, a little older than himself, with whom he had long lived in such close friendship that it was the custom of their Lantern Yard brethren to call them David and Jonathan. The real name of the friend was William Dane, and he too was regarded as a shining instance of youthful piety, though somewhat given to over-severity towards weaker brethren, and to be so dazzled by his own light as to hold himself wiser than his teachers. But whatever blemishes others might discern in William, to his friend's mind he was faultless; for Marner had one of those impressible self-doubting natures which, at an inexperienced age, admire imperativeness and lean on contradiction. The expression of trusting simplicity in Marner's face, heightened by that absence of special observation, that defenceless, deer-like gaze which belongs to large prominent eyes, was strongly contrasted by the self-complacent suppression of inward triumph that lurked in the narrow slanting eyes and compressed lips of William Dane. One of the most frequent topics of conversation between the two friends was Assurance of salvation: Silas confessed that he could never arrive at anything higher than hope mingled with fear, and listened with longing wonder when William declared that he had possessed unshaken assurance ever since, in the period of his conversion, he had dreamed that he saw the words 'calling and election sure' standing by themselves on a white page in the open Bible. Such colloquies have occupied many a pair of pale-faced weavers, whose unnurtured souls have been like young winged things, fluttering forsaken in the twilight.

It had seemed to the unsuspecting Silas that the friendship had suffered no chill even from his formation of another attachment of a closer kind. For some months he had been engaged to a young servant-woman, waiting only for a little increase to their mutual savings in order to their marriage; and it was a great delight to him that Sarah did not object to William's occasional presence in their Sunday interviews. It was at this point in their history that Silas's cataleptic fit occurred during the prayer-meeting; and amidst the various queries and expressions of interest addressed to him by his fellow-members, William's suggestion alone jarred with the general sympathy towards a brother thus singled out for special dealings. He observed that, to him, this trance looked more like a visitation of Satan than a proof of divine favour, and exhorted his friend to see that he hid no accursed thing within his soul. Silas, feeling bound to accept rebuke and admonition as a brotherly office, felt no resentment, but only pain, at his friend's doubts concerning him; and to this was soon added some anxiety at the perception that Sarah's manner towards him began to exhibit a strange fluctuation between an effort at an increased manifestation of regard and involuntary signs of shrinking and dislike. He asked her if she wished to break off their engagement; but she denied this: their engagement was known to the church, and had been recognized in the prayer-meetings; it could not be broken off without strict investigation, and Sarah could render no reason that would be sanctioned by the feeling of the community. At this time the senior deacon was taken dangerously ill, and, being a childless widower, he was tended night and day by some of the younger brethren or sisters. Silas frequently took his turn in the night-watching with William, the one relieving the other at two in the morning. The old man, contrary to expectation, seemed to be on the way to recovery, when one night Silas, sitting up by his bedside, observed that his usual audible breathing had ceased. The candle was burning low, and he had to lift it to see the patient's face distinctly. Examination convinced him that the deacon was dead – had been dead for some time, for the limbs were rigid. Silas asked himself if he had been asleep, and looked at the clock: it was already four in the morning. How was it that William had not come? In much anxiety he went to seek for help, and soon there were several friends assembled in the house, the minister among them, while Silas went away to his work, wishing he could have met William to know the reason of his non-appearance. But at six o'clock, as he was thinking of going to seek his friend, William came, and with him the minister. They came to summon him to Lantern Yard, to meet the church members there; and to his inquiry concerning the cause of the summons the only reply was, 'You will hear.' Nothing further was said until Silas was seated in the vestry, in front of the minister, with the eyes of those who to him represented God's people fixed solemnly upon him. Then the minister, taking out a pocket-knife, showed it to Silas, and asked him if he knew where he had left that knife? Silas said, he did not know that he had left it anywhere out of his own pocket – but he was trembling at this strange interrogation. He was then exhorted not to hide his sin, but to confess and repent. The knife had been found in the bureau by the departed deacon's bedside – found in the place where the little bag of church money had lain, which the minister himself had seen the day before. Some hand had removed that bag; and whose hand could it be, if not that of the man to whom the knife belonged? For some time Silas was mute with astonishment: then he said, 'God will clear me: I know nothing about the knife being there, or the money being gone. Search me and my dwelling; you will find nothing but three pound five of my own savings, which William Dane knows I have had these six months.' At this William groaned, but the minister said, 'The proof is heavy against you, brother Marner. The money was taken in the night last past, and no man was with our departed brother but you, for William Dane declares to us that he was hindered by sudden sickness from going to take his place as usual, and you yourself said that he had not come; and, moreover, you neglected the dead body.'

'I must have slept,' said Silas. Then, after a pause, he added, 'Or I must have had another visitation like that which you have all seen me under, so that the thief must have come and gone while I was not in the body, but out of the body. But, I say again, search me and my dwelling, for I have been nowhere else.'

The search was made, and it ended – in William Dane's finding the well-known bag, empty, tucked behind the chest of drawers in Silas's chamber! On this William exhorted his friend to confess, and not to hide his sin any longer. Silas turned a look of keen reproach on him, and said, 'William, for nine years that we have gone in and out together, have you ever known me tell a lie? But God will clear me.'

'Brother,' said William, 'how do I know what you may have done in the secret chambers of your heart, to give Satan an advantage over you?'

Silas was still looking at his friend. Suddenly a deep flush came over his face, and he was about to speak impetuously, when he seemed checked again by some inward shock, that sent the flush back and made him tremble. But at last he spoke feebly, looking at William.

'I remember now – the knife wasn't in my pocket.'

William said, 'I know nothing of what you mean.' The other persons present, however, began to inquire where Silas meant to say that the knife was, but he would give no further explanation: he only said, 'I am sore stricken; I can say nothing. God will clear me.'

On their return to the vestry there was further deliberation. Any resort to legal measures for ascertaining the culprit was contrary to the principles of the church in Lantern Yard, according to which prosecution was forbidden to Christians, even had the case held less scandal to the community. But the members were bound to take other measures for finding out the truth, and they resolved on praying and drawing lots. This resolution can be a ground of surprise only to those who are unacquainted with that obscure religious life which has gone on in the alleys of our towns. Silas knelt with his brethren, relying on his own innocence being certified by immediate divine interference, but feeling that there was sorrow and mourning behind for him even then – that his trust in man had been cruelly bruised. *The lots declared that Silas Marner was guilty.* He was solemnly suspended from church-membership, and called upon to render up the stolen money: only on confession, as the sign of repentance, could he be received once more within the fold of the church. Marner listened in silence. At last, when every one rose to depart, he went towards William Dane and said, in a voice shaken by agitation –

'The last time I remember using my knife, was when I took it out to cut a strap for you. I don't remember putting it in my pocket again. *You* stole the money, and you have woven a plot to lay the sin at my door. But you may prosper, for all that: there is no just God that governs the earth righteously, but a God of lies, that bears witness against the innocent.'

There was a general shudder at this blasphemy.

William said meekly, 'I leave our brethren to judge whether this is the voice of Satan or not. I can do nothing but pray for you, Silas.'

Poor Marner went out with that despair in his soul – that shaken trust in God and man, which is little short of madness to a loving nature. In the bitterness of his wounded spirit, he said to himself, '*She* will cast me off too.' And he reflected that, if she did not believe the testimony against him, her whole faith must be upset as his was. To people accustomed to reason about the forms in which their religious feeling has incorporated itself, it is difficult to enter into that simple, untaught state of mind in which the form and the feeling have never been severed by an act of reflection. We are apt to think it inevitable that a man in Marner's position should have begun to question the validity of an appeal to the divine judgment by drawing lots; but to him this would have been an effort of independent thought such as he had never known; and he must have made the effort at a moment when all his energies were turned into the anguish of disappointed faith. If there is an angel who records the sorrows of men as well as their sins, he knows how many and deep are the sorrows that spring from false ideas for which no man is culpable.

Marner went home, and for a whole day sat alone, stunned by despair, without any impulse to go to Sarah and attempt to win her belief in his innocence. The second day he took refuge from benumbing unbelief, by getting into his loom and working away as usual; and before many hours were past, the minister and one of the deacons came to him with the message from Sarah, that she held her engagement to him at an end. Silas received the message mutely, and then turned away from the messengers to work at his loom again. In little more than a month from that time,

Sarah was married to William Dane; and not long afterwards it was known to the brethren in Lantern Yard that Silas Marner had departed from the town.

⊲ TWO ⊳

EVEN PEOPLE WHOSE LIVES HAVE BEEN made various by learning, sometimes find it hard to keep a fast hold on their habitual views of life, on their faith in the Invisible, nay, on the sense that their past joys and sorrows are a real experience, when they are suddenly transported to a new land, where the beings around them know nothing of their history, and share none of their ideas – where their mother earth shows another lap, and human life has other forms than those on which their souls have been nourished. Minds that have been unhinged from their old faith and love, have perhaps sought this Lethean influence of exile, in which the past becomes dreamy because its symbols have all vanished, and the present too is dreamy because it is linked with no memories. But even *their* experience may hardly enable them thoroughly to imagine what was the effect on a simple weaver like Silas Marner, when he left his own country and people and came to settle in Raveloe. Nothing could be more unlike his native town, set within sight of the widespread hillsides, than this low, wooded region, where he felt hidden even from the heavens by the screening trees and hedgerows. There was nothing here, when he rose in the deep morning quiet and looked out on the dewy brambles and rank tufted grass, that seemed to have any relation with that life centring in Lantern Yard, which had once been to him the altar-place of high dispensations. The white-washed walls; the little pews where well-known figures entered with a subdued rustling, and where first one well-known voice and then another, pitched in a peculiar key of petition, uttered phrases at once occult and familiar, like the amulet worn on the heart; the pulpit where the minister delivered unquestioned doctrine, and swayed to and fro, and handled the book in a long-accustomed manner; the very pauses between the couplets of the hymn, as it was given out, and the recurrent swell of voices in song: these things had been the channel of divine influences to Marner – they were the fostering home of his religious emotions – they were Christianity and God's kingdom upon earth. A weaver who finds hard words in his hymn-book knows nothing of abstractions; as the little child knows nothing of parental love, but only knows one face and one lap towards which it stretches its arms for refuge and nurture.

And what could be more unlike that Lantern Yard world than the world in Raveloe? – orchards looking lazy with neglected plenty; the large church in the wide churchyard, which men gazed at lounging at their own doors in service-time; the purple-faced farmers jogging along the lanes or turning in at the Rainbow; homesteads, where men supped heavily and slept in the light of the evening hearth, and where women seemed to be laying up a stock of linen for the life to come. There were no lips in Raveloe from which a word could fall that would stir Silas Marner's benumbed faith to a sense of pain. In the early ages of the world, we know, it was believed that each territory was inhabited and ruled by its own divinities, so that a man could cross the bordering heights and be out of the reach of his native gods, whose presence was confined to the streams and the groves and the hills among which he had lived from his birth. And poor Silas was vaguely conscious of something not unlike the feeling of primitive men, when they fled thus, in fear or in sullenness, from the face of an unpropitious deity. It seemed to him that the Power he had vainly trusted in among the streets and at the prayer-meetings, was very far away from this land in which he had taken refuge, where men lived in careless abundance, knowing and needing nothing of that trust, which, for him, had been turned to bitterness. The little light he possessed spread its beams so narrowly, that frustrated belief was a curtain broad enough to create for him the blackness of night.

His first movement after the shock had been to work in his loom; and he went on with this unremittingly, never asking himself why, now he was come to Raveloe, he worked far on into the night to finish the tale of Mrs Osgood's tablelinen sooner than she expected – without contemplating beforehand the money she would put into his hand for the work. He seemed to weave, like the spider, from pure impulse, without reflection. Every man's work, pursued steadily, tends in this way to become an end in itself, and so to bridge over the loveless chasms of his life. Silas's hand satisfied itself with throwing the shuttle, and his eye with seeing the little squares in the cloth complete themselves under his effort. Then there were the calls of hunger; and Silas, in his solitude, had to provide his own breakfast, dinner, and supper, to fetch his own water from the well, and put his own kettle on the fire; and all these immediate promptings helped, along with the weaving, to reduce his life to the unquestioning activity of a spinning insect. He hated the thought of the past; there was nothing that called out his love and fellowship toward the strangers he had come amongst; and the future was all dark, for there was no Unseen Love that cared for him. Thought was arrested by utter bewilderment, now its old narrow pathway was closed, and affection seemed to have died under the bruise that had fallen on its keenest nerves.

But at last Mrs Osgood's table-linen was finished, and Silas was paid in gold. His earnings in his native town, where he worked for a wholesale dealer, had been after a lower rate; he had been paid weekly, and of his weekly earnings a large proportion had gone to objects of piety and charity. Now, for the first time in his life, he had five bright guineas put into his hand; no man expected a share of them, and he loved no man that he should offer him a share. But what were the guineas to him who saw no vista beyond countless days of weaving? It was needless for him to ask that, for it was pleasant to him to feel them in his palm, and look at their bright faces, which were all his own: it was another element of life, like the weaving and the satisfaction of hunger, subsisting quite aloof from the life of belief and love from which he had been cut off. The weaver's hand had known the touch of hard-won money even before the palm had grown to its full breadth; for twenty years, mysterious money had stood to him as the symbol of earthly good, and the immediate object of toil. He had seemed to love it little in the years when every penny had its purpose for him; for he loved the *purpose* then. But now, when all purpose was gone, that habit of looking towards the money and grasping it with a sense of fulfilled effort made a loam that was deep enough for the seeds of desire; and as Silas walked homeward across the fields in the twilight, he drew out the money and thought it was brighter in the gathering gloom.

About this time an incident happened which seemed to open a possibility of some fellowship with his neighbours. One day, taking a pair of shoes to be mended, he saw the cobbler's wife seated by the fire, suffering from the terrible symptoms of heart-disease and dropsy, which he had witnessed as the precursors of his mother's death. He felt a rush of pity at the mingled sight and remembrance, and, recalling the relief his mother had found from a simple preparation of foxglove, he promised Sally Oates to bring her something that would ease her, since the doctor did her no good. In this office of charity, Silas felt, for the first time since he had come to Raveloe, a sense of unity between his past and present life, which might have been the beginning of his rescue from the insect-like existence into which his nature had shrunk. But Sally Oates's disease had raised her into a personage of much interest and importance among the neighbours, and the fact of her having found relief from drinking Silas Marner's 'stuff' became a matter of general discourse. When Doctor Kimble gave physic, it was natural that it should have an effect; but when a weaver, who came from nobody knew where, worked wonders with a bottle of brown waters, the occult character of the process was evident. Such a sort of thing had not been known since the Wise Woman at Tarley died; and she had charms as well as 'stuff': everybody went to her when their children had fits. Silas Marner must be a person of the same sort, for how did he know what would bring back Sally Oates's breath, if he didn't know a fine sight more than that? The Wise Woman had words that she muttered to herself, so that you couldn't hear what they were, and if she tied a bit of red thread round the child's toe the while, it would keep off the water in the head. There were women in Raveloe, at that present time, who had worn one of the Wise Woman's little bags round their necks, and, in consequence, had never had an idiot child, as Ann Coulter had. Silas Marner could very likely do as much, and more; and now it was all clear how he should have come from unknown parts, and be so 'comical-looking'. But Sally Oates must mind and not tell the doctor, for he would be sure to set his face against Marner: he was always angry about the Wise Woman, and used to threaten those who went to her that they should have none of his help any more.

Silas now found himself and his cottage suddenly beset by mothers who wanted him to charm away the whooping-cough, or bring back the milk, and by men who wanted stuff against the rheumatics or the knots in the hands; and, to secure themselves against a refusal, the applicants brought silver in their palms. Silas might have driven a profitable trade in charms as well as in his small list of drugs; but money on this condition was no temptation to him: he had never known an impulse towards falsity, and he drove one after another away with growing irritation, for the news of him as a wise man had spread even to Tarley, and it was long before people ceased to take long walks for the sake of asking his aid. But the hope in his wisdom was at length changed into dread, for no one believed him when he said he knew no charms and could work no cures, and every man and woman who had an accident or a new attack after applying to him, set the misfortune down to Master Marner's ill-will and irritated glances. Thus it came to pass that his movement of pity towards Sally Oates, which had given him a transient sense of brotherhood, heightened the repulsion between him and his neighbours, and made his isolation more complete.

Gradually the guineas, the crowns, and the half-crowns, grew to a heap, and Marner drew less and less for his own wants, trying to solve the problem of keeping himself strong enough to work sixteen hours a-day on as small an outlay as possible. Have not men, shut up in solitary imprisonment, found an interest in marking the moments by straight strokes of a certain length on the wall, until the growth of the sum of straight strokes, arranged in triangles, has become a mastering purpose? Do we not wile away moments of inanity or fatigued waiting by repeating some trivial movement or sound, until the repetition has bred a want, which is incipient habit? That will help us to understand how the love of accumulating money grows an absorbing passion in men whose imaginations, even in the very beginning of their hoard, showed them no purpose beyond it. Marner wanted the heaps of ten to grow into a square, and then into a larger square; and every added guinea, while it was itself a satisfaction, bred a new desire. In this strange world, made a hopeless riddle to him, he might, if he had had a less intense nature, have sat weaving, weaving – looking towards the end of his pattern, or towards the end of his web, till he forgot the riddle, and everything else but his immediate sensations; but the money had come to mark off his weaving into periods, and the money not only grew, but it remained with him. He began to think it was conscious of him, as his loom was, and he would on no account have exchanged those coins, which had become his familiars, for other coins with unknown faces. He handled them, he counted them, till their form and colour were like the satisfaction of a thirst to him; but it was only in the night, when his work was done, that he drew them out to enjoy their companionship. He had taken up some bricks in his floor underneath his loom, and here he had made a hole in which he set the iron pot that contained his guineas and silver coins, covering the bricks with sand whenever he replaced them. Not that the idea of being robbed presented itself often or strongly to his mind: hoarding was common in country districts in those days; there were old labourers in the parish of Raveloe who were known to have their savings by them, probably inside their flock-beds; but their rustic neighbours, though not all of them as honest as their ancestors in the days of King Alfred, had not imaginations bold enough to lay a plan of burglary. How could they have spent the money in their own village without betraying themselves? They would be obliged to 'run away' – a course as dark and dubious as a balloon journey.

So, year after year, Silas Marner had lived in this solitude, his guineas rising in the iron pot, and his life narrowing and hardening itself more and more into a mere pulsation of desire and satisfaction that had no relation to any other being. His life had reduced itself to the functions of weaving and hoarding, without any contemplation of an end towards which the functions tended. The same sort of process has perhaps been undergone by wiser men, when they have been cut off from faith and love – only, instead of a loom and a heap of guineas, they have had some erudite research, some ingenious project, or some well-knit theory. Strangely Marner's face and figure shrank and bent themselves into a constant mechanical relation to the objects of his life, so that he produced the same sort of impression as a handle or a crooked tube, which has no meaning standing apart. The prominent eyes that used to look trusting and dreamy, now looked as if they had been made to see only one kind of thing that was very small, like tiny grain, for which they hunted everywhere: and he was so withered and yellow, that, though he was not yet forty, the children always called him 'Old Master Marner'.

Yet even in this stage of withering a little incident happened, which showed that the sap of affection was not all gone. It was one of his daily tasks to fetch his water from a well a couple of fields off, and for this purpose, ever since he came to Raveloe, he had had a brown earthenware pot, which he held as his most precious utensil among the very few conveniences he had granted himself. It had been his companion for twelve years, always standing on the same spot, always lending its handle to him in the early morning, so that its form had an expression for him of willing helpfulness, and the impress of its handle on his palm gave a satisfaction mingled with that of having the fresh clear water. One day as he was returning from the well, he stumbled against the step of the stile, and his brown pot, falling with force against the stones that overarched the ditch below him, was broken in three pieces. Silas picked up the pieces and carried them home with grief in his heart. The brown pot could never be of use to him any more, but he stuck the bits together and propped the ruin in its old place for a memorial.

This is the history of Silas Marner until the fifteenth year after he came to Raveloe. The livelong day he sat in his loom, his ear filled with its monotony, his eyes bent close down on the slow growth of sameness in the brownish web, his muscles moving with such even repetition that their pause seemed almost as much a constraint as the holding of his breath. But at night came his revelry: at night he closed his shutters, and made fast his doors, and drew forth his gold. Long ago the heap of coins had become too large for the iron pot to hold them, and he had made for them two thick leather bags, which wasted no room in their resting place, but lent themselves flexibly to every corner. How the guineas shone as they came pouring out of the dark leather mouths! The silver bore no large proportion in amount to the gold, because the long pieces of linen which formed his chief work were always partly paid for in gold, and out of the silver he supplied his own bodily wants, choosing always the shillings and sixpences to spend in this way. He loved the guineas best, but he would not change the silver – the crowns and half-crowns that were his own earnings, begotten by his labour; he loved them all. He spread them out in heaps and bathed his hands in them; then he counted them and set them up in regular piles, and felt their rounded outline between his thumb and fingers, and thought fondly of the guineas that were only half-earned by the work in his loom, as if they had been unborn children – thought of the guineas that were coming slowly through the coming years, through all his life, which spread far away before him, the end quite hidden by countless days of weaving. No wonder his thoughts were still with his loom and his money when he made his journeys through the fields and the lanes to fetch and carry home his work, so that his steps never wandered to the hedge-banks and the lane-side in search of the once familiar herbs; these too belonged to the past, from which his life had shrunk away, like a rivulet that has sunk far down from the grassy fringe of its old breadth into a little shivering thread, that cuts a groove for itself in the barren sand.

But about the Christmas of that fifteenth year, a second great change came over Marner's life, and his history became blent in a singular manner with the life of his neighbours.

∞ THREE ∾

THE GREATEST MAN IN RAVELOE WAS Squire Cass, who lived in the large red house with the handsome flight of stone steps in front and the high stables behind it, nearly opposite the church. He was only one among several landed parishioners, but he alone was honoured with the title of Squire; for though Mr Osgood's family was also understood to be of timeless origin – the Raveloe imagination having never ventured back to that fearful blank when there were no Osgoods – still, he merely owned the farm he occupied; whereas Squire Cass had a tenant or two, who complained of the game to him quite as if he had been a lord.

It was still that glorious war-time which was felt to be a peculiar favour of Providence towards the landed interest, and the fall of prices had not yet come to carry the race of small squires and yeomen down that road to ruin for which extravagant habits and bad husbandry were plentifully anointing their wheels. I am speaking now in relation to Raveloe and the parishes that resembled it; for our old-fashioned country life had many different aspects, as all life must have when it is spread over a various surface, and breathed on variously by multitudinous currents from the winds of heaven to the thoughts of men, which are for ever moving and crossing each other with incalculable results. Raveloe lay low among the bushy trees and the rutted lanes, aloof from the currents of industrial energy and Puritan earnestness: the rich ate and drank freely, accepting gout and apoplexy as things that ran mysteriously in respectable families, and the poor thought that the rich were entirely in the right of it to lead a jolly life; besides, their feasting caused a multiplication of orts, which were the heirlooms of the poor. Betty Jay scented the boiling of Squire Cass's hams, but her longing was arrested by the unctuous liquor in which they were boiled; and when the seasons brought round the great merry-makings, they were regarded on all hands as a fine thing for the poor. For the Raveloe feasts were like the rounds of beef and the barrels of ale – they were on a large scale, and lasted a good while, especially in the winter-time. After ladies had packed up their best gowns and top-knots in bandboxes, and had incurred the risk of fording streams on pillions with the precious burden in rainy or snowy weather, when there was no knowing how high the water would rise, it was not to be supposed that they looked forward to a brief pleasure. On this ground it was always contrived in the dark seasons, when there was little work to be done, and the hours were long, that several neighbours should keep open house in succession. So soon as Squire Cass's standing dishes diminished in plenty and freshness, his guests had nothing to do but to walk a little higher up the village to Mr Osgood's, at the Orchards, and they found hams and chines uncut, pork-pies with the scent of the fire in them, spun butter in all its freshness – everything, in fact, that appetites at leisure could desire, in perhaps greater perfection, though not in greater abundance, than at Squire Cass's.

For the Squire's wife had died long ago, and the Red House was without that presence of the wife and mother which is the fountain of wholesome love and fear in parlour and kitchen; and this helped to account not only for there being more profusion than finished excellence in the holiday provisions, but also for the frequency with which the proud Squire condescended to preside in the parlour of the Rainbow rather than under the shadow of his own dark wainscot; perhaps, also, for the fact that his sons had turned out rather ill. Raveloe was not a place where moral censure was severe, but it was thought a weakness in the Squire that he had kept all his sons at home in idleness; and though some licence was to be allowed to young men whose fathers could afford it, people shook their heads at the courses of the second son, Dunstan, commonly called Dunsey Cass, whose taste for swopping and betting might turn out to be a sowing of something worse than wild oats. To be sure, the neighbours said, it was no matter what became of Dunsey – a spiteful jeering fellow, who seemed to enjoy his drink the more when other people went dry – always provided that his doings did not bring trouble on a family like Squire Cass's, with a monument in the church and tankards older than King George. But it would be a thousand pities if Mr Godfrey, the eldest, a fine open-faced good-natured young man who was to come into the land some day, should take to going along the same road with his brother, as he had seemed to do of late. If he went on in that way, he would lose Miss Nancy Lammeter; for it was well known that she had looked very shyly on him ever since last Whitsuntide twelvemonth, when there was so much talk about his being away from home days and days together. There was something wrong, more than common – that was quite clear; for Mr Godfrey didn't look half so fresh-coloured and open as he used to do. At one time everybody was saying, What a handsome couple he and Miss Nancy Lammeter would make! and if she could come to be mistress at the Red House, there would be a fine change, for the Lammeters had been brought up in that way, that they never suffered a pinch of salt to be wasted, and yet everybody in their household had of the best, according to his place. Such a daughter-in-law would be a saving to the old Squire, if she never brought a penny to her fortune; for it was to be feared that, notwithstanding his incomings, there were more holes in his pocket than the one where he put his own hand in. But if Mr Godfrey didn't turn over a new leaf, he might say 'Good-bye' to Miss Nancy Lammeter.

It was the once hopeful Godfrey who was standing, with his hands in his side-pockets and his back to the fire, in the dark wainscoted parlour, one late November afternoon in that fifteenth year of Silas Marner's life at Raveloe. The fading grey light fell dimly on the walls decorated with guns, whips, and foxes' brushes, on coats and hats flung on the chairs, on tankards sending forth a scent of flat ale, and on a half-choked fire, with pipes propped up in the chimney-corners: signs of a domestic life destitute of any hallowing charm, with which the look of gloomy vexation on Godfrey's blond face was in sad accordance. He seemed to be waiting and listening for some one's approach, and presently the sound of a heavy step, with an accompanying whistle, was heard across the large empty entrance-hall.

The door opened, and a thick-set, heavy-looking young man entered, with the flushed face and the gratuitously elated bearing which mark the first stage of intoxication. It was Dunsey, and at the sight of him Godfrey's face parted with some of its gloom to take on the more active expression of hatred. The handsome brown spaniel that lay on the hearth retreated under the chair in the chimney-corner.

'Well, Master Godfrey, what do you want with me?' said Dunsey, in a mocking tone. 'You're my elders and betters, you know; I was obliged to come when you sent for me.'

'Why, this is what I want – and just shake yourself sober and listen, will you?' said Godfrey, savagely. He had himself been drinking more than was good for him, trying to turn his gloom into uncalculating anger. 'I want to tell you, I must hand over that rent of Fowler's to the Squire, or else tell him I gave it you; for he's threatening to distrain for it, and it'll all be out soon, whether I tell him or not. He said, just now, before he went out, he should send word to Cox to distrain, if Fowler didn't come and pay up his arrears this week. The Squire's short o' cash, and in no humour to stand any nonsense; and you know what he threatened, if ever he found you making away with his money again. So, see and get the money, and pretty quickly, will you?'

'Oh!' said Dunsey, sneeringly, coming nearer to his brother and looking in his face. 'Suppose, now, you get the money yourself, and save me the trouble, eh? Since you was so kind as to hand it over to me, you'll not refuse me the kindness to pay it back for me: it was your brotherly love made you do it, you know.'

Godfrey bit his lips and clenched his fist. 'Don't come near me with that look, else I'll knock you down.'

'O no, you won't,' said Dunsey, turning away on his heel, however. 'Because I'm such a good-natured brother, you know. I might get you turned out of house and home, and cut off with a shilling any day. I might tell the Squire how his handsome son was married to that nice young woman, Molly Farren, and was very unhappy because he couldn't live with his drunken wife, and I should slip into your place as comfortable as could be. But you see, I don't do it – I'm so easy and good-natured. You'll take any trouble for me. You'll get the hundred pounds for me – I know you will.'

'How can I get the money?' said Godfrey, quivering. 'I haven't a shilling to bless myself with. And it's a lie that you'd slip into my place: you'd get yourself turned out too, that's all. For if you begin telling tales, I'll follow. Bob's my father's favourite – you know that very well. He'd only think himself well rid of you.'

'Never mind,' said Dunsey, nodding his head sideways as he looked out of the window. 'It'ud be very pleasant to me to go in your company – you're such a handsome brother, and we've always been so fond of quarrelling with one another, I shouldn't know what to do without you. But you'd like better for us both to stay at home together; I know you would. So you'll manage to get that little sum o'money, and I'll bid you good-bye, though I'm sorry to part.'

Dunstan was moving off, but Godfrey rushed after him and seized him by the arm, saying, with an oath,

'I tell you, I have no money: I can get no money.'

'Borrow of old Kimble.'

'I tell you, he won't lend me any more, and I shan't ask him.'

'Well, then, sell Wildfire.'

'Yes, that's easy talking. I must have the money directly.'

'Well, you've only got to ride him to the hunt to-morrow. There'll be Bryce and Keating there, for sure. You'll get more bids than one.'

'I daresay, and get back home at eight o'clock, splashed up to the chin. I'm going to Mrs Osgood's birthday dance.'

'Oho!' said Dunsey, turning his head on one side, and trying to speak in a small mincing treble. 'And there's sweet Miss Nancy coming; and we shall dance with her, and promise never to be naughty again, and be taken into favour, and – '

'Hold your tongue about Miss Nancy, you fool,' said Godfrey, turning red, 'else I'll throttle you.'

'What for?' said Dunsey, still in an artificial tone, but taking a whip from the table and beating the butt-end of it on his palm. 'You've a very good chance. I'd advise you to creep up her sleeve again: it 'ud be saving time, if Molly should happen to take a drop too much laudanum some day, and make a widower of you. Miss Nancy wouldn't mind being a second, if she didn't know it. And you've got a good-natured brother, who'll keep your secret well, because you'll be so very obliging to him.'

'I'll tell you what it is,' said Godfrey, quivering, and pale again. 'My patience is pretty near at an end. If you'd a little more sharpness in you, you might know that you may urge a man a bit too far, and make one leap as easy as another. I don't know but what it is so now: I may as well tell the Squire everything myself – I should get you off my back, if I got nothing else. And, after all, he'll know some time. She's been threatening to come herself and tell him. So, don't flatter yourself that your secrecy's worth any price you choose to ask. You drain me of money till I have got nothing to pacify *her* with, and she'll do as she threatens some day. It's all one. I'll tell my father everything myself, and you may go to the devil.'

Dunsey perceived that he had overshot his mark, and that there was a point at which even the hesitating Godfrey might be driven into decision. But he said, with an air of unconcern,

'As you please; but I'll have a draught of ale first.' And ringing the bell, he threw himself across two chairs, and began to rap the window-seat with the handle of his whip.

Godfrey stood, still with his back to the fire, uneasily moving his fingers among the contents of his side-pockets, and looking at the floor. That big muscular frame of his held plenty of animal courage, but helped him to no decision when the dangers to be braved were such as could neither be knocked down nor throttled. His natural irresolution and moral coward-ice were exaggerated by a position in which dreaded consequences seemed to press equally on all sides, and his irritation had no sooner provoked him to defy Dunstan and anticipate all possible betrayals, than the miseries he must bring on himself by such a step seemed more unen-durable to him than the present evil. The results of confession were not contingent, they were certain; whereas betrayal was not certain. From the near vision of that certainty he fell back on suspense and vacillation with a sense of repose. The disinherited son of a small squire, equally disinclined to dig and to beg, was almost as helpless as an uprooted tree, which, by the favour of earth and sky, has grown to a handsome bulk on the spot where it first shot upward. Perhaps it would have been possible to think of digging with some cheerfulness if Nancy Lammeter were to be won on those terms; but, since he must irrevocably lose *her* as well as the inheritance, and must break every tie but the one that degraded him and left him without motive for trying to recover his better self, he could imagine no future for himself on the other side of confession but that of "listing for a soldier' – the most desperate step, short of suicide, in the eyes of respectable families. No! he would rather trust to casualties than to his own resolve – rather go on sitting at the feast and sipping the wine he loved, though with the sword hanging over him and terror in his heart, than rush away into the cold darkness where there was no pleasure left. The utmost concession to Dunstan about the horse began to seem easy, compared with the fulfilment of his own threat. But his pride would not let him recommence the conversation otherwise than by continuing the quarrel. Dunstan was waiting for this, and took his ale in shorter draughts than usual.

'It's just like you,' Godfrey burst out, in a bitter tone, 'to talk about my selling Wildfire in that cool way – the last thing I've got to call my own, and the best bit of horse-flesh I ever had in my life. And if you'd got a spark of pride in you, you'd be ashamed to see the stables emptied, and everybody sneering about it. But it's my belief you'd sell yourself, if it was only for the pleasure of making somebody feel he'd got a bad bargain.'

'Ay, ay,' said Dunstan, very placably, 'you do me justice, I see. You know I'm a jewel for 'ticing people into bargains. For which reason I advise you to let *me* sell Wildfire. I'd ride him to the hunt tomorrow for you, with pleasure. I shouldn't look so handsome as you in the saddle, but it's the horse they'll bid for, and not the rider.'

'Yes, I daresay – trust my horse to you!'

'As you please,' said Dunstan, rapping the window-seat again with an air of great unconcern. 'It's *you* have got to pay Fowler's money; it's none of my business. You received the money from him when you went to Bramcote, and *you* told the Squire it wasn't paid. I'd nothing to do with that; you chose to be so obliging as give it me, that was all. If you don't want to pay the money, let it alone; it's all one to me. But I was willing to accommodate you by undertaking to sell the horse, seeing it's not convenient to you to go so far tomorrow.'

Godfrey was silent for some moments. He would have liked to spring on Dunstan, wrench the whip from his hand, and flog him to within an inch of his life; and no bodily fear could have deterred him; but he was mastered by another sort of fear, which was fed by feelings stronger even than his resentment. When he spoke again, it was in a half-conciliatory tone.

'Well, you mean no nonsense about the horse, eh? You'll sell him all fair, and hand over the money? If you don't, you know, everything 'ull go to smash, for I've got nothing else to trust to. And you'll have less pleasure in pulling the house over my head, when your own skull's broken too.'

'Ay, ay,' said Dunstan, rising, 'all right. I thought you'd come round. I'm the fellow to bring old Bryce up to the scratch. I'll get you a hundred and twenty for him, if I get you a penny.'

'But it'll perhaps rain cats and dogs tomorrow, as it did yesterday, and then you can't go,' said Godfrey, hardly knowing whether he wished for that obstacle or not.

'Not *it*,' said Dunstan. 'I'm always lucky in my weather. It might rain if you wanted to go yourself. You never hold trumps, you know – I always do. You've got the beauty, you see, and I've got the luck, so you must keep me by you for your crooked sixpence; you'll *ne*-ver get along without me.'

'Confound you, hold your tongue!' said Godfrey, impetuously. 'And take care to keep sober tomorrow, else you'll get pitched on your head coming home, and Wildfire might be the worse for it.'

'Make your tender heart easy,' said Dunstan, opening the door. 'You never knew me see double when I'd got a bargain to make; it 'ud spoil the fun. Besides, whenever I fall, I'm warranted to fall on my legs.'

With that, Dunstan slammed the door behind him, and left Godfrey to that bitter rumination on his personal circumstances which was now unbroken from day to day save by the excitement of sporting, drinking, card-playing, or the rarer and less oblivious pleasure of seeing Miss Nancy Lammeter. The subtle and varied pains springing from the higher sensibility that accompanies higher culture, are perhaps less pitiable than that dreary absence of impersonal enjoyment and consolation which leaves ruder minds to the perpetual urgent companionship of their own griefs and discontents. The lives of those rural fore-fathers, whom we are apt to think very prosaic figures – men whose only work was to ride round their land, getting heavier and heavier in their saddles, and who passed the rest of their days in the half-listless gratification of senses dulled by monotony – had a certain pathos in them nevertheless. Calamities came to *them* too, and their early errors carried hard consequences: perhaps the love of some sweet maiden, the image of purity, order, and calm, had opened their eyes to the vision of a life in which the days would not seem too long, even without rioting; but the maiden was lost, and the vision passed away, and then what was left to them, especially when they had become too heavy for the hunt, or for carrying a gun over the furrows, but to drink and get merry, or to drink and get angry, so that they might be independent of variety, and say over again with eager emphasis the things they had said already any time that twelvemonth? Assuredly, among these flushed and dull-eyed men there were some whom – thanks to their native human-kindness – even riot could never drive into brutality; men who, when their cheeks were fresh, had felt the keen point of sorrow or remorse, had been pierced by the reeds they leaned on, or had lightly put their limbs in fetters from which no struggle could loose them; and under these sad circumstances, common to us all, their thoughts could find no resting-place outside the ever-trodden round of their own petty history.

That, at least, was the condition of Godfrey Cass in this six-and-twentieth year of his life. A movement of compunction, helped by those small indefinable influences which every personal relation exerts on a pliant nature, had urged him into a secret marriage, which was a blight on his life. It was an ugly story of low passion, delusion, and waking from delusion, which needs not to be dragged from the privacy of Godfrey's bitter memory. He had long known that the delusion was partly due to a trap laid for him by Dunstan, who saw in his brother's degrading marriage the means of gratifying at once his jealous hate and his cupidity. And if Godfrey could have felt himself simply a victim, the iron bit that destiny had put into his mouth would have chafed him less intolerably. If the curses he muttered half aloud when he was alone had had no other object than Dunstan's diabolical cunning, he might have shrunk less from the consequences of avowal. But he had something else to curse – his own vicious folly, which now seemed as mad and unaccountable to him as almost all our follies and vices do when their promptings have long passed away. For four years he had thought of Nancy Lammeter, and wooed her with tacit patient worship, as the woman who made him think of the future with joy: she would be his wife, and would make home lovely to him, as his father's home had never been; and it would be easy, when she was always near, to shake off those foolish habits that were no pleasures, but only a feverish way of annulling vacancy. Godfrey's was an essentially domestic nature, bred up in a home where the hearth had no smiles, and where the daily habits were not chastised by the presence of household order. His easy disposition made him fall in unresistingly with the family courses, but the need of some tender permanent affection, the longing for some influence that would make the good he preferred easy to pursue, caused the neatness, purity, and liberal orderliness of the Lammeter household, sunned by the smile of Nancy, to seem like those fresh bright hours of the morning when temptations go to sleep and leave the ear open to the voice of the good angel, inviting to industry, sobriety, and peace. And yet the hope of this paradise had not been enough to save him from a course which shut him out of it for ever. Instead of keeping fast hold of the strong silken rope by which Nancy would have drawn him safe to the green banks where it was easy to step firmly, he had let himself be dragged back into mud and slime, in which it was useless to struggle. He had made ties for himself which robbed him of all wholesome motives and were a constant exasperation.

Still, there was one position worse than the present: it was the position he would be in when the ugly secret was disclosed; and the desire that continually triumphed over every other was that of warding off the evil day, when he would have to bear the consequences of his father's violent resentment for the wound inflicted on his family pride – would have, perhaps, to turn his back on that hereditary ease and dignity which, after all, was a sort of reason for living, and would carry with him the certainty that he was banished for ever from the sight and esteem of Nancy Lammeter. The longer the interval, the more chance there was of deliverance from some, at least, of the hateful consequences to which he had sold himself; the more opportunities remained for him to snatch the strange gratification of seeing Nancy, and gathering some faint indications of her lingering regard. Towards this gratification he was impelled, fitfully, every now and then, after having passed weeks in which he had avoided her as the far-off bright-winged prize that only made him spring forward and find his chain all the more galling. One of those fits of yearning was on him now, and it would have been strong enough to have persuaded him to trust Wildfire to Dunstan rather than disappoint the yearning, even if he had not had another reason for his disinclination towards the morrow's hunt. That other reason was the fact that the morning's meet was near Batherley, the market-town where the unhappy woman lived, whose image became more odious to him every day; and to his thought the whole vicinage was haunted by her. The yoke a man creates for himself by wrong-doing will breed hate in the kindliest nature; and the good-humoured, affectionate-hearted Godfrey Cass was fast becoming a bitter man, visited by cruel wishes, that seemed to enter, and depart, and enter again, like demons who had found in him a ready-garnished home.

What was he to do this evening to pass the time? He might as well go to the Rainbow, and hear the talk about the cock-fighting: everybody was there, and what else was there to be done? Though, for his own part, he did not care a button for cock-fighting. Snuff, the brown spaniel, who had placed herself in front of him, and had been watching him for some time, now jumped up in impatience for the expected caress. But Godfrey thrust her away without looking at her, and left the room, followed humbly by the unresenting Snuff – perhaps because she saw no other career open to her.

ᘓ FOUR ᘔ

DUNSTAN CASS, SETTING OFF IN THE raw morning, at the judiciously quiet pace of a man who is obliged to ride to cover on his hunter, had to take his way along the lane which, at its farther extremity, passed by the piece of unenclosed ground called the Stone-pit, where stood the cottage, once a stone-cutter's shed, now for fifteen years inhabited by Silas Marner. The spot looked very dreary at this season, with the moist trodden clay about it, and the red, muddy water high up in the deserted quarry. That was Dunstan's first thought as he approached it; the second was, that the old fool of a weaver, whose loom he heard rattling already, had a great deal of money hidden somewhere. How was it that he, Dunstan Cass, who had often heard talk of Marner's miserliness, had never thought of suggesting to Godfrey that he should frighten or persuade the old fellow into lending the money on the excellent security of the young Squire's prospects? The resource occurred to him now as so easy and agreeable, especially as Marner's hoard was likely to be large enough to leave Godfrey a handsome surplus beyond his immediate needs, and enable him to accommodate his faithful brother, that he had almost turned the horse's head towards home again. Godfrey would be ready enough to accept the suggestion: he would snatch eagerly at a plan that might save him from parting with Wildfire. But when Dunstan's meditation reached this point, the inclination to go on grew strong and prevailed. He didn't want to give Godfrey that pleasure: he preferred that Master Godfrey should be vexed. Moreover, Dunstan enjoyed the self-important consciousness of having a horse to sell, and the opportunity of driving a bargain, swaggering, and possibly taking somebody in. He might have all the satisfaction attendant on selling his brother's horse, and not the less have the further satisfaction of setting Godfrey to borrow Marner's money. So he rode on to cover.

Bryce and Keating were there, as Dunstan was quite sure they would be – he was such a lucky fellow.

'Hey-day,' said Bryce, who had long had his eye on Wildfire, 'you're on your brother's horse today: how's that?'

'O, I've swopped with him,' said Dunstan, whose delight in lying, grandly independent of utility, was not to be diminished by the likelihood that his hearer would not believe him – 'Wildfire's mine now.'

'What! has he swopped with you for that big-boned hack of yours?' said Bryce, quite aware that he should get another lie in answer.

'O, there was a little account between us,' said Dunsey, carelessly, 'and Wildfire made it even. I accommodated him by taking the horse, though it was against my will, for I'd got an itch for a mare o' Jortin's – as rare a bit o' blood as ever you threw your leg across. But I shall keep Wildfire, now I've got him, though I'd a bid of a hundred and fifty for him the other day, from a man over at Flitton – he's buying for Lord Cromleck – a fellow with a cast in his eye, and a green waistcoat. But I mean to stick to Wildfire: I shan't get a better at a fence in a hurry. The mare's got more blood, but she's a bit too weak in the hind-quarters.'

Bryce of course divined that Dunstan wanted to sell the horse, and Dunstan knew that he divined it (horse-dealing is only one of many human transactions carried on in this ingenious manner); and they both considered that the bargain was in its first stage, when Bryce replied ironically –

'I wonder at that now; I wonder you mean to keep him; for I never heard of a man who didn't want to sell his horse getting a bid of half as much again as the horse was worth. You'll be lucky if you get a hundred.'

Keating rode up now, and the transaction became more complicated. It ended in the purchase of the horse by Bryce for a hundred and twenty, to be paid on the delivery of Wildfire, safe and sound, at the Batherley stables. It did occur to Dunsey that it might be wise for him to give up the day's hunting, proceed at once to Batherley, and, having waited for Bryce's return, hire a horse to carry him home with the money in his pocket. But the inclination for a run, encouraged by confidence in his luck, and by a draught of brandy from his pocket-pistol at the conclusion of the bargain, was not easy to overcome, especially with a horse under him that would take the fences to the admiration of the field. Dunstan, however, took one fence too many, and got his horse pierced with a hedge-stake. His own ill-favoured person, which was quite unmarketable, escaped without injury, but poor Wildfire, unconscious of his price, turned on his flank, and painfully panted his last. It happened that Dunstan, a short time before, having had to get down to arrange his stirrup had muttered a good many curses at this interruption, which had thrown him in the rear of the hunt near the moment of glory, and under this exasperation had taken the fences more blindly. He would soon have been up with the hounds again, when the fatal accident happened; and hence he was between eager riders in advance, not troubling themselves about what happened behind them, and far-off stragglers, who were as likely as not to pass quite aloof from the line of road in which Wildfire had fallen. Dunstan, whose nature it was to care more for immediate annoyances than for remote consequences, no sooner recovered his legs, and saw that it was all over with Wildfire, than he felt a satisfaction at the absence of witnesses to a position which no swaggering could make enviable. Reinforcing himself, after his shake, with a little brandy and much swearing, he walked as fast as he could to a coppice on his right hand, through which it occurred to him that he could make his way to Batherley without danger of encountering any member of the hunt. His first intention was to hire a horse there and ride home forthwith, for to walk many miles without a gun in his hand and along an ordinary road, was as much out of the question to him as to other spirited young men of his kind. He did not much mind about taking the bad news to Godfrey, for he had to offer him at the same time the resource of Marner's money; and if Godfrey kicked, as he always did, at the notion of making a fresh debt from which he himself got the smallest share of advantage, why, he wouldn't kick long: Dunstan felt sure he could worry Godfrey into anything. The idea of Marner's money kept growing in vividness, now the want of it had become immediate; the prospect of having to make his appearance with the muddy boots of a pedestrian at Batherley, and to encounter the grinning queries of stable men, stood unpleasantly in the way of his impatience to be back at Raveloe and carry out his felicitous plan; and a casual visitation of his waistcoat-pocket, as he was ruminating, awakened his memory to the fact that the two or three small coins his fore-finger encountered there, were of too pale a colour to cover that small debt, without payment of which the stable-keeper had declared he would never do any more business with Dunsey Cass. After all, according to the direction in which the run had brought him, he was not so very much farther from home than he was from Batherley; but Dunsey, not being remarkable for clearness of head, was only led to this conclusion by the gradual perception that there were other reasons for choosing the unprecedented course of walking home. It was now nearly four o'clock, and a mist was gathering: the sooner he got into the road the better. He remembered having crossed the road and seen the finger-post only a little while before Wildfire broke down; so, buttoning his coat, twisting the lash of his hunting-whip compactly round the handle, and rapping the tops of his boots with a self-possessed air, as if to assure himself that he was not at all taken by surprise, he set off with the sense that he was undertaking a remarkable feat of bodily exertion, which somehow and at some time he should be able to dress up and magnify to the admiration of a select circle at the Rainbow. When a young gentleman like Dunsey is reduced to so exceptional a mode of locomotion as walking, a whip in his hand is a desirable corrective to a too bewildering dreamy sense of unwontedness in his position; and Dunstan, as he went along through the gathering mist, was always rapping his whip somewhere. It was Godfrey's whip, which he had chosen to take without leave because it had a gold handle; of course no one could see, when Dunstan held it, that the name *Godfrey Cass* was cut in deep letters on that gold handle – they could only see that it was a very handsome whip. Dunsey was not without fear that he might meet some acquaintance in whose eyes he would cut a pitiable figure, for mist is no screen when people get close to each other; but when he at last found himself in the well-known Raveloe lanes without having met a soul, he silently remarked that that was part of his usual good-luck. But now the mist, helped by the evening darkness, was more of a screen than he desired, for it hid the ruts into which his feet were liable to slip – hid everything, so that he had to guide his steps by dragging his whip along the low bushes in advance of the hedgerow. He must soon, he thought, be getting near the opening at the Stone-pits: he should find it out by the break in the hedgerow. He found it out, however, by another circumstance which he had not expected – namely, by certain gleams of light, which he presently guessed to proceed from Silas Marner's cottage. That cottage and the money hidden within it had been in his mind continually during his walk, and he had been imagining ways of cajoling and tempting the weaver to part with the immediate possession of his money for the sake of receiving interest. Dunstan felt as if there must be a little frightening added to the cajolery, for his own arithmetical convictions were not clear enough to afford him any forcible demonstration as to the advantages of interest; and as for security, he regarded it vaguely as a means of cheating a man by making him believe that he would be paid. Altogether, the operation on the miser's mind was a task that Godfrey would be sure to hand over to his more daring and cunning brother: Dunstan had made up his mind to that; and by the time he saw the light gleaming through the chinks of Marner's shutters, the idea of a dialogue with the weaver had become so familiar to him, that it occurred to him as quite a natural thing to make the acquaintance forthwith. There might be several conveniences attending this course: the weaver had possibly got a lantern, and Dunstan was tired of feeling his way. He was still nearly three-quarters of a mile from home, and the lane was becoming unpleasantly slippery, for the mist was passing into rain. He turned up the bank, not without some fear lest he might miss the right way, since he was not certain whether the light were in front or on the side of the cottage. But he felt the ground before him cautiously with his whip-handle, and at last arrived safely at the door. He knocked loudly, rather enjoying the idea that the old fellow would be frightened at the sudden noise. He heard no movement in reply: all was silence in the cottage. Was the weaver gone to bed, then? If so, why had he left a light? That was a strange forgetfulness in a miser. Dunstan knocked still more loudly, and, without pausing for a reply, pushed his fingers through the latch-hole, intending to shake the door and pull the latchstring up and down, not doubting that the door was fastened. But, to his surprise, at this double motion the door opened, and he found himself in front of a bright fire which lit up every corner of the cottage – the bed, the loom, the three chairs, and the table – and showed him that Marner was not there.

Nothing at that moment could be much more inviting to Dunsey than the bright fire on the brick hearth: he walked in and seated himself by it at once. There was something in front of the fire, too, that would have been inviting to a hungry man, if it had been in a different stage of cooking. It was a small bit of pork suspended from the kettle-hanger by a string passed through a large door-key, in a way known to primitive house-keepers unpossessed of jacks. But the pork had been hung at the farthest, extremity of the hanger, apparently to prevent the roasting from proceed-ing too rapidly during the owner's absence. The old staring simpleton had hot meat for his supper, then? thought Dunstan. People had always said he lived on mouldy bread, on purpose to check his appetite. But where could he be at this time, and on such an evening, leaving his supper in this stage of preparation, and his door unfastened? Dunstan's own recent difficulty in making his way suggested to him that the weaver had perhaps gone outside his cottage to fetch in fuel, or for some such brief purpose, and had slipped into the Stone-pit. That was an interesting idea to Dunstan, carrying consequences of entire novelty. If the weaver was dead, who had a right to his money? Who would know where his money was hidden? *Who would know that anybody had come to take it away?* He went no farther into the subtleties of evidence: the pressing question, 'Where *is* the money?' now took such entire possession of him as to make him quite forget that the weaver's death was not a certainty. A dull mind, once arriving at an inference that flatters a desire, is rarely able to retain the impression that the notion from which the inference started was purely problematic. And Dunstan's mind was as dull as the mind of a possible felon usually is. There were only three hiding-places where he had ever heard of cottagers' hoards being found: the thatch, the bed, and a hole in the floor. Marner's cottage had no thatch; and Dunstan's first act, after a train of thought made rapid by the stimulus of cupidity, was to go up to the bed; but while he did so, his eyes travelled eagerly over the floor, where the bricks, distinct in the fire-light, were discernible under the sprinkling of sand. But not everywhere; for there was one spot, and one only, which was quite covered with sand, and sand showing the marks of fingers, which had apparently been careful to spread it over a given space. It was near the treddles of the loom. In an instant Dunstan darted to that spot, swept away the sand with his whip, and, inserting the thin end of the hook between the bricks, found that they were loose. In haste he lifted up two bricks, and saw what he had no doubt was the object of his search;

for what could there be but money in those two leathern bags? And, from their weight, they must be filled with guineas. Dunstan felt round the hole, to be certain that it held no more; then hastily replaced the bricks, and spread the sand over them. Hardly more than five minutes had passed since he entered the cottage, but it seemed to Dunstan like a long while; and though he was without any distinct recognition of the possibility that Marner might be alive, and might re-enter the cottage at any moment, he felt an undefinable dread laying hold on him, as he rose to his feet with the bags in his hand. He would hasten out into the darkness, and then consider what he should do with the bags. He closed the door behind him immediately, that he might shut in the stream of light: a few steps would be enough to carry him beyond betrayal by the gleams from the shutter-chinks and the latch-hole. The rain and darkness had got thicker, and he was glad of it; though it was awkward walking with both hands filled, so that it was as much as he could do to grasp his whip along with one of the bags. But when he had gone a yard or two, he might take his time. So he stepped forward into the darkness.

∝ FIVE ∾

WHEN DUNSTAN CASS TURNED HIS BACK on the cottage, Silas Marner was not more than a hundred yards away from it, plodding along from the village with a sack thrown round his shoulders as an over-coat, and with a horn lantern in his hand. His legs were weary, but his mind was at ease, free from the presentiment of change. The sense of security more frequently springs from habit than from conviction, and for this reason it often subsists after such a change in the conditions as might have been expected to suggest alarm. The lapse of time during which a given event has not happened, is, in this logic of habit, constantly alleged as a reason why the event should never happen, even when the lapse of time is precisely the added condition which makes the event imminent. A man will tell you that he has worked in a mine for forty years unhurt by an accident as a reason why he should apprehend no danger, though the roof is beginning to sink; and it is often observable, that the older a man gets, the more difficult it is to him to retain a believing conception of his own death. This influence of habit was necessarily strong in a man whose life was so monotonous as Marner's – who saw no new people and heard of no new events to keep alive in him the idea of the unexpected and the changeful; and it explains, simply enough, why his mind could be at ease, though he had left his house and his treasure more defenceless than usual.

Silas was thinking with double complacency of his supper: first, because it would be hot and savoury; and secondly, because it would cost him nothing. For the little bit of pork was a present from that excellent housewife, Miss Priscilla Lammeter, to whom he had this day carried home a handsome piece of linen; and it was only on occasion of a present like this, that Silas indulged himself with roast-meat. Supper was his favourite meal, because it came at his time of revelry, when his heart warmed over his gold; whenever he had roast-meat, he always chose to have it for supper. But this evening, he had no sooner ingeniously knotted his string fast round his bit of pork, twisted the string according to rule over his door-key, passed it through the handle, and made it fast on the hanger than he remembered that a piece of very fine twine was indispensable to his 'setting up' a new piece of work in his loom early in the morning. It had slipped his memory, because, in coming from Mr Lammeter's, he had not had to pass through the village; but to lose time by going on errands in the morning was out of the question. It was a nasty fog to turn out into, but there were things Silas loved better than his own comfort; so, drawing his pork to the extremity of the hanger, and arming himself with his lantern and his old sack, he set out on what, in ordinary weather, would have been a twenty minutes' errand. He could not have locked his door without undoing his well-knotted string and retarding his supper; it was not worth his while to make that sacrifice. What thief would find his way to the Stone-pits on such a night as this? and why should he come on this particular night, when he had never come through all the fifteen years before? These questions were not distinctly present in Silas's mind; they merely serve to represent the vaguely-felt foundation of his freedom from anxiety.

He reached his door in much satisfaction that his errand was done: he opened it, and to his short-sighted eyes everything remained as he had left it, except that the fire sent out a welcome increase of heat. He trod about the floor while putting by his lantern and throwing aside his hat and sack, so as to merge the marks of Dunstan's feet on the sand in the marks of his own nailed boots. Then he moved his pork nearer to the fire, and sat down to the agreeable business of tending the meat and warming himself at the same time.

Any one who had looked at him as the red light shone upon his pale face, strange straining eyes, and meagre form, would perhaps have understood the mixture of contemptuous pity, dread, and suspicion with which he was regarded by his neighbours in Raveloe. Yet few men could be more harmless than poor Marner. In his truthful simple soul, not even the growing greed and worship of gold could beget any vice directly injurious to others. The light of his faith quite put out, and his affections made desolate, he had clung with all the force of his nature to his work and his money; and like all objects to which a man devotes himself, they had fashioned him into correspondence with themselves. His loom, as he wrought in it without ceasing, had in its turn wrought on him, and confirmed more and more the monotonous craving for its monotonous response. His gold, as he hung over it and saw it grow, gathered his power of loving together into a hard isolation like its own.

As soon as he was warm he began to think it would be a long while to wait till after supper before he drew out his guineas, and it would be pleasant to see them on the table before him as he ate his unwonted feast. For joy is the best of wine, and Silas's guineas were a golden wine of that sort.

He rose and placed his candle unsuspectingly on the floor near his loom, swept away the sand without noticing any change, and removed the bricks. The sight of the empty hole made his heart leap violently, but the belief that his gold was gone could not come at once – only terror, and the eager effort to put an end to the terror. He passed his trembling hand all about the hole, trying to think it possible that his eyes had deceived him; then he held the candle in the hole and examined it curiously, trembling more and more. At last he shook so violently that he let fall the candle, and lifted his hands to his head, trying to steady himself, that he might think. Had he put his gold somewhere else, by a sudden resolution last night, and then forgotten it? A man falling into dark waters seeks a momentary footing even on sliding stones; and Silas, by acting as if he believed in false hopes, warded off the moment of despair. He searched in every corner, he turned his bed over, and shook it, and kneaded it; he looked in his brick oven where he laid his sticks. When there was no other place to be searched, he kneeled down again and felt once more all round the hole. There was no untried refuge left for a moment's shelter from the terrible truth.

Yes, there was a sort of refuge which always comes with the prostration of thought under an overpowering passion: it was that expectation of impossibilities, that belief in contradictory images, which is still distinct from madness, because it is capable of being dissipated by the external fact. Silas got up from his knees trembling, and looked round at the table: didn't the gold lie there after all? The table was bare. Then he turned and looked behind him – looked all round his dwelling, seeming to strain his brown eyes after some possible appearance of the bags where he had already sought them in vain. He could see every object in his cottage – and his gold was not there.

Again he put his trembling hands to his head, and gave a wild ringing scream, the cry of desolation. For a few moments after, he stood motionless; but the cry had relieved him from the first maddening pressure of the truth. He turned, and tottered towards his loom, and got into the seat where he worked, instinctively seeking this as the strongest assurance of reality.

And now that all the false hopes had vanished, and the first shock of certainty was past, the idea of a thief began to present itself, and he entertained it eagerly, because a thief might be caught and made to restore the gold. The thought brought some new strength with it, and he started from his loom to the door. As he opened it the rain beat in upon him, for it was falling more and more heavily. There were no footsteps to be tracked on such a night – footsteps? When had the thief come? During Silas's absence in the daytime the door had been locked, and there had been no marks of any inroad on his return by daylight. And in the evening, too, he said to himself, everything was the same as when he had left it. The sand and bricks looked as if they had not been moved. *Was* it a thief who had taken the bags? or was it a cruel power that no hands could reach, which had delighted in making him a second time desolate? He shrank from this vaguer dread, and fixed his mind with struggling effort on the robber with hands, who could be reached by hands. His thoughts glanced at all the neighbours who had made any remarks, or asked any questions which he might now regard as a ground of suspicion. There was Jem Rodney, a known poacher, and otherwise disreputable: he had often met Marner in his journeys across the fields, and had said something jestingly about the weaver's money; nay, he had once irritated Marner, by lingering at the fire when he called to light his pipe, instead of going about his business. Jem Rodney was the man – there was ease in the thought. Jem could be found and made to restore the money: Marner did not want to punish him, but only to get back his gold which had gone from him, and left his soul like a forlorn traveller on an unknown desert. The robber must be laid hold of. Marner's ideas of legal authority were confused, but he felt that he must go and proclaim his loss; and the great people in the village – the clergyman, the constable, and Squire Cass – would make Jem Rodney, or somebody else, deliver up the stolen money. He rushed out in the rain, under the stimulus of this hope, forgetting to cover his head, not caring to fasten his door; for he felt as if he had nothing left to lose. He ran swiftly, till want of breath compelled him to slacken his pace as he was entering the village at the turning close to the Rainbow.

The Rainbow, in Marner's view, was a place of luxurious resort for rich and stout husbands, whose wives had superfluous stores of linen; it was the place where he was likely to find the powers and dignities of Raveloe, and where he could most speedily make his loss public. He lifted the latch, and turned into the bright bar or kitchen on the right hand, where the less lofty customers of the house were in the habit of assembling, the parlour on the left being reserved for the more select society in which Squire Cass frequently enjoyed the double pleasure of conviviality and condescension. But the parlour was dark to-night, the chief personages who ornamented its circle being all at Mrs Osgood's birthday dance, as Godfrey Cass was. And in consequence of this, the party on the high-screened seats in the kitchen was more numerous than usual; several personages, who would otherwise have been admitted into the parlour and enlarged the opportunity of hectoring and condescension for their betters, being content this evening to vary their enjoyment by taking their spirits-and-water where they could themselves hector and condescend in company that called for beer.

◁ SIX ▷

THE CONVERSATION, WHICH WAS AT A high pitch of animation when Silas approached the door of the Rainbow, had, as usual, been slow and intermittent when the company first assembled. The pipes began to be puffed in a silence which had an air of severity; the more important customers, who drank spirits and sat nearest the fire, staring at each other as if a bet were depending on the first man who winked; while the beer-drinkers, chiefly men in fustian jackets and smock-frocks, kept their eyelids down and rubbed their hands across their mouths, as if their draughts of beer were a funereal duty attended with embarrassing sadness. At last, Mr Snell, the landlord, a man of a neutral disposition, accustomed to stand aloof from human differences as those of beings who were all alike in need of liquor, broke silence, by saying in a doubtful tone to his cousin the butcher –

'Some folks 'ud say that was a fine beast you druv in yesterday, Bob?'

The butcher, a jolly, smiling, red-haired man, was not disposed to answer rashly. He gave a few puffs before he spat and replied, 'And they wouldn't be fur wrong, John.'

After this feeble delusive thaw, the silence set in as severely as before.

'Was it a red Durham?' said the farrier, taking up the thread of discourse after the lapse of a few minutes.

The farrier looked at the landlord, and the landlord looked at the butcher, as the person who must take the responsibility of answering.

'Red it was,' said the butcher, in his good-humoured husky treble – 'and a Durham it was.'

'Then you needn't tell *me* who you bought it of,' said the farrier, looking round with some triumph; 'I know who it is has got the red Durhams o' this country-side. And she'd a white star on her brow, I'll bet a penny?' The farrier leaned forward with his hands on his knees as he put this question, and his eyes twinkled knowingly.

'Well; yes – she might,' said the butcher, slowly, considering that he was giving a decided affirmative. 'I don't say contrairy.'

'I knew that very well,' said the farrier, throwing himself backward again, and speaking defiantly; 'if *I* don't know Mr Lammeter's cows, I should like to know who does – that's all. And as for the cow you've bought, bargain or no bargain, I've been at the drenching of her – contradick me who will.'

The farrier looked fierce, and the mild butcher's conversational spirit was roused a little.

'I'm not for contradicking no man,' he said; 'I'm for peace and quietness. Some are for cutting long ribs – I'm for cutting 'em short myself; but I don't quarrel with 'em. All I say is, it's a lovely carkiss – and anybody as was reasonable, it 'ud bring tears into their eyes to look at it.'

'Well, it's the cow as I drenched, whatever it is,' pursued the farrier, angrily; 'and it was Mr Lammeter's cow, else you told a lie when you said it was a red Durham.'

'I tell no lies,' said the butcher, with the same mild huskiness as before, 'and I contradick none – not if a man was to swear himself black: he's no meat o' mine, nor none o' my bargains. All I say is, it's a lovely carkiss. And what I say I'll stick to; but I'll quarrel wi' no man.'

'No,' said the farrier, with bitter sarcasm, looking at the company generally; 'and p'rhaps you aren't pig-headed; and p'rhaps you didn't say the cow was a red Durham; and p'rhaps you didn't say she'd got a star on her brow – stick to that, now you're at it.'

'Come, come,' said the landlord; 'let the cow alone. The truth lies atween you: you're both right and both wrong, as I allays say. And as for the cow's being Mr Lammeter's, I say nothing to that; but this I say, as the Rainbow's the Rainbow. And for the matter o' that, if the talk is to be o' the Lammeters, *you* know the most upo' that head, eh, Mr Macey? You remember when first Mr Lammeter's father come into these parts, and took the Warrens?'

Mr Macey, tailor and parish-clerk, the latter of which functions rheumatism had of late obliged him to share with a small-featured young man who sat opposite him, held his white head on one side, and twirled his thumbs with an air of complacency, slightly seasoned with criticism. He smiled pityingly, in answer to the landlord's appeal, and said –

'Ay, ay; I know, I know; but I let other folks talk. I've laid by now, and gev up to the young uns. Ask them as have been to school at Tarley: they've learnt pernouncing; that's come up since my day.'

'If you're pointing at me, Mr Macey,' said the deputy-clerk, with an air of anxious propriety, 'I'm nowise a man to speak out of my place. As the psalm says –

"I know what's right, nor only so,
But also practise what I know." '

'Well, then, I wish you'd keep hold o' the tune, when it's set for you; if you're for prac*tis*ing, I wish you'd prac*tise* that,' said a large jocose-looking man, an excellent wheel-wright in his week-day capacity, but on Sundays leader of the choir. He winked, as he spoke, at two of the company, who were known officially as the 'bassoon' and the 'key-bugle,' in the confidence that he was expressing the sense of the musical profession in Raveloe.

Mr Tookey, the deputy-clerk, who shared the unpopularity common to deputies, turned very red, but replied, with careful moderation – 'Mr Winthrop, if you'll bring me any proof as I'm in the wrong, I'm not the man to say I won't alter. But there's people set up their own ears for a standard, and expect the whole choir to follow 'em. There may be two opinions, I hope.'

'Ay, ay,' said Mr Macey, who felt very well satisfied with this attack on youthful presumption; 'you're right there, Tookey: there's allays two 'pinions; there's the 'pinion a man has of himsen, and there's the 'pinion other folks have on him. There'd be two 'pinions about a cracked bell, if the bell could hear itself.'

'Well, Mr Macey,' said poor Tookey, serious amidst the general laughter, 'I undertook to partially fill up the office of parish-clerk by Mr Crackenthorp's desire, whenever your infirmities should make you unfitting; and it's one of the rights thereof to sing in the choir – else why have you done the same yourself?'

'Ah! but the old gentleman and you are two folks,' said Ben Winthrop. 'The old gentleman's got a gift. Why, the Squire used to invite him to take a glass, only to hear him sing the "Red Rovier;" didn't he, Mr Macey? It's a nat'ral gift. There's my little lad Aaron, he's got a gift – he can sing a tune off straight, like a throstle. But as for you, Master Tookey, you'd better stick to your "Amens:" your voice is well enough when you keep it up in your nose. It's your inside as isn't right made for music: it's no better nor a hollow stalk.'

This kind of unflinching frankness was the most piquant form of joke to the company at the Rainbow, and Ben Winthrop's insult was felt by everybody to have capped Mr Macey's epigram.

'I see what it is plain enough,' said Mr Tookey, unable to keep cool any longer. 'There's a consperacy to turn me out o' the choir, as I shouldn't share the Christmas money – that's where it is. But I shall speak to Mr Crackenthorp; I'll not be put upon by no man.'

'Nay, nay, Tookey,' said Ben Winthrop. 'We'll pay you your share to keep out of it – that's what we'll do. There's things folks 'ud pay to be rid on, besides varmin.'

'Come, come,' said the landlord, who felt that paying people for their absence was a principle dangerous to society; 'a joke's a joke. We're all good friends here, I hope. We must give and take. You're both right and you're both wrong, as I say. I agree wi' Mr Macey here, as there's two opinions; and if mine was asked, I should say they're both right. Tookey's right and Winthrop's right, and they've only got to split the difference and make themselves even.'

The farrier was puffing his pipe rather fiercely, in some contempt at this trivial discussion. He had no ear for music himself, and never went to church, as being of the medical profession, and likely to be in requisition for delicate cows. But the butcher, having music in his soul, had listened with a divided desire for Tookey's defeat, and for the preservation of the peace.

'To be sure,' he said, following up the landlord's conciliatory view, 'we're fond of our old clerk; it's nat'ral, and him used to be such a singer, and got a brother as is known for the first fiddler in this country-side. Eh, it's a pity but what Solomon lived in our village, and could give us a tune when we liked; eh, Mr Macey? I'd keep him in liver and lights for nothing – that I would.'

'Ay, ay,' said Mr Macey, in the height of complacency; 'our family's been known for musicianers as far back as anybody can tell. But them things are dying out, as I tell Solomon every time he comes round; there's no voices like what there used to be, and there's nobody remembers what we remember, if it isn't the old crows.'

'Ay, you remember when first Mr Lammeter's father come into these parts, don't you, Mr Macey?' said the landlord.

'I should think I did.' said the old man, who had now gone through that complimentary process necessary to bring him up to the point of narration; 'and a fine old gentlemen he was – as fine, and finer nor the Mr Lammeter as now is. He came from a bit north'ard, so far as I could ever make out. But there's nobody rightly knows about those parts: only it couldn't be far north'ard, nor much different from this country, for he brought a fine breed o'sheep with him, so there must be pastures there, and everything reasonable. We heared tell as he'd sold his own land to come and take the Warrens, and that seemed odd for a man as had land of his own, to come and rent a farm in a strange place. But they said it was along of his wife's dying; though there's reasons in things as nobody knows on – that's pretty much what I've made out; yet some folks are so wise, they'll find you fifty reasons straight off, and all the while the real reason's winking at 'em in the corner, and they never see't. Howsomever, it was soon seen as we'd got a new parish'ner as know'd the rights and customs o' things, and kep a good house, and was well looked on by everybody. And the young man – that's the Mr Lammeter as now is, for he'd niver a sister – soon begun to court Miss Osgood, that's the sister o' the Mr Osgood as now is, and a fine handsome lass she was – eh, you can't think – they pretend this young lass is like her, but that's the way wi' people as don't know what come before 'em. I should know, for I helped the old rector, Mr Drumlow as was, I helped him marry 'em.'

Here Mr Macey paused; he always gave his narrative in instalments, expecting to be questioned according to precedent.

'Ay, and a partic'lar thing happened, didn't it, Mr Macey, so as you were likely to remember that marriage?' said the landlord, in a congratulatory tone.

'I should think there did – a *very* parti'clar thing,' said Mr Macey, nodding sideways. 'For Mr Drumlow – poor old gentlemen, I was fond on him, though he'd got a bit confused in head, what wi' age and wi' taking a drop o' summat warm when the service come of a cold morning. And young Mr Lammeter, he'd have no way but he must be married in Jani-wary, which, to be sure, 's a unreasonable time to be married in, for it isn't like a christening or a burying, as you can't help; and so Mr Drumlow – poor old gentleman, I was fond on him – but when he come to put the questions, he put 'em by the rule o' contrairy, like, and he says, "Wilt thou have this man to thy wedded wife?" says he, and then he says. "Wilt thou have this woman to thy wedded husband?" says he. But the parti-c'larest thing of all is, as nobody took any notice on it but me, and they answered straight off "yes", like as if it had been me saying "Amen" i' the right place, without listening to what went before.'

'But *you* knew what was going on well enough, didn't you, Mr Macey? You were live enough, eh?' said the butcher.

'Lor bless you!' said Mr Macey, pausing, and smiling in pity at the importance of his hearer's imagination – 'why, I was all of a tremble: it was as if I'd been a coat pulled by the two tails, like; for I couldn't stop the parson, I couldn't take upon me to do that; and yet I said to myself, I says, "Suppose they shouldn't be fast married, 'cause the words are contrairy?" and my head went working like a mill, for I was allays uncommon for turning things over and seeing all round 'em; and I says to myself, "Is't the meanin' or the words as makes folks fast i' wedlock?" For the parson meant right, and the bride and bridegroom meant right. But then, when I come to think on it, meanin' goes but a little way i' most things, for you may mean to stick things together and your glue may be bad, and then where are you? And so I says to mysen, "It isn't the meanin', it's the glue." And I was worreted as if I'd got three bells to pull at once, when we went into the vestry, and they begun to sign their names. But where's the use o' talking? – you can't think what goes on in a 'cute man's inside.'

'But you held in for all that, didn't you, Mr Macey?' said the landlord.

'Ay, I held in tight till I was by mysen wi' Mr Drumlow, and then I out wi' everything, but respectful, as I allays did. And he made light on it, and he says, "Pooh, pooh, Macey, make yourself easy," he says; "it's neither the meaning nor the words – it's the reg*ester* does it – that's the glue." So you see he settled it easy; for parsons and doctors know everything by heart, like, so as they aren't worreted wi' thinking what's the rights and wrongs o' things, as I'n been many and many's the time. And sure enough the wedding turned out all right, on'y poor Mrs Lammeter – that's Miss Osgood as was – died afore the lasses was growed up; but for prosperity and everything respectable, there's no family more looked on.'

Every one of Mr Macey's audience had heard this story many times, but it was listened to as if it had been a favourite tune, and at certain points the puffing of the pipes was momentarily suspended, that the listeners might give their whole minds to the expected words. But there was more to come; and Mr Snell, the landlord, duly put the leading question.

'Why, old Mr Lammeter had a pretty fortin, didn't they say, when he come into these parts?'

'Well, yes,' said Mr Macey; 'but I daresay it's as much as this Mr Lammeter's done to keep it whole. For there was allays a talk as nobody could get rich on the Warrens: though he holds it cheap, for it's what they call Charity Land.'

'Ay, and there's few folks know so well as you how it come to be Charity Land, eh, Mr Macey?' said the butcher.

'How should they?' said the old clerk, with some contempt. 'Why, my grandfather made the grooms' livery for that Mr Cliff as came and built the big stables at the Warrens. Why, they're stables four times as big as Squire Cass's, for he thought o' nothing but hosses and hunting, Cliff didn't – a Lunnon tailor, some folks said, as had gone mad wi' cheating. For he couldn't ride; lor bless you! they said he'd got no more grip o' the hoss than if his legs had been cross-sticks: my grandfather heared old Squire Cass say so many and many a time. But ride he would as if Old Harry had been a-driving him; and he'd a son, a lad o' sixteen; and nothing would his father have him do, but he must ride and ride – though the lad was frighted, they said. And it was a common saying as the father wanted to ride the tailor out o' the lad, and make a gentleman on him – not but what I'm a tailor myself, but in respect as God made me such, I'm proud on it, for "Macey, tailor," 's been wrote up over our door since afore the Queen's heads went out on the shillings. But Cliff, he was ashamed o' being called a tailor, and he was sore vexed as his riding was laughed at, and nobody o' the gentlefolks hereabout could abide him. Howsomever, the poor lad got sickly and died, and the father didn't live long after him, for he got queerer nor ever, and they said he used to go out i' the dead o' the night, wi' a lantern in his hand, to the stables, and set a lot o' lights burning, for he got as he couldn't sleep; and there he'd stand, cracking his whip and looking at his hosses; and they said it was a mercy as the stables didn't get burnt down wi' the poor dumb creaturs in 'em. But at last he died raving, and they found as he'd left all his property, Warrens and all, to a Lunnon Charity, and that's how the Warrens come to be Charity Land; though, as for the stables, Mr Lammeter never uses 'em – they're out o' all charicter – lor bless you! if you was to set the doors a-banging in 'em, it 'ud sound like thunder half o'er the parish.'

'Ay, but there's more going on in the stables than what folks see by daylight, eh, Mr Macey?' said the landlord.

'Ay, ay; go that way of a dark night, that's all,' said Mr Macey, winking mysteriously, 'and then make believe, if you like, as you didn't see lights i' the stables, nor hear the stamping o' the hosses, nor the cracking o' the whips, and howling, too, if it's tow'rt daybreak. "Cliff's Holiday" has been the name of it ever sin' I were a boy; that's to say, some said as it was the holiday Old Harry gev him from roasting, like. That's what my father told me, and he was a reasonable man, though there's folks nowadays know what happened afore they were born better nor they know their own business.'

'What do you say to that, eh, Dowlas?' said the landlord, turning to the farrier, who was swelling with impatience for his cue. 'There's a nut for *you* to crack.'

Mr Dowlas was the negative spirit in the company, and was proud of his position.

'Say? I say what a man *should* say as doesn't shut his eyes to look at a finger-post. I say, as I'm ready to wager any man ten pound, if he'll stand out wi' me and dry night in the pasture before the Warren stables, as we shall neither see lights nor hear noises, if it isn't the blowing of our own noses. That's what I say, and I've said it many a time; but there's nobody 'ull ventur a ten-pun' note on their ghos'es as they make so sure of.'

'Why, Dowlas, that's easy betting, that is,' said Ben Winthrop. 'You might as well bet a man as he wouldn't catch the rheumatise if he stood up to 's neck in the pool of a frosty night. It 'ua be fine fun for a man to win his bet as he'd catch the rheumatise. Folks as believe in Cliff's Holiday aren't agoing to ventur near it for a matter o' ten pound.'

'If Master Dowlas wants to know the truth on it,' said Mr Macey, with a sarcastic smile, tapping his thumbs together, 'he's no call to lay any bet – let him go and stan' by himself – there's nobody 'ull hinder him; and then he can let the parish'ners know if they're wrong.'

'Thank you! I'm obliged to you,' said the farrier, with a snort of scorn. 'If folks are fools, it's no business o' mine. *I* don't want to make out the truth about ghos'es: I know it a'ready. But I'm not against a bet – everything fair and open. Let any man bet me ten pound as I shall see Cliff's Holiday, and I'll go and stand by myself. I want no company. I'd as lief do it as I'd fill this pipe.'

'Ah, but who's to watch you, Dowlas, and see you do it? That's no fair bet,' said the butcher.

'No fair bet?' replied Mr Dowlas, angrily. 'I should like to hear any man stand up and say I want to bet unfair. Come now, Master Lundy, I should like to hear you say it.'

'Very like you would,' said the butcher. 'But it's no business o' mine. You're none o' my bargains, and I aren't agoing to try and 'bate your price. If anybody 'll bid for you at your own vallying, let him. I'm for peace and quietness, I am.'

'Yes, that's what every yapping cur is, when you hold a stick up at him,' said the farrier. 'But I'm afraid o' neither man nor ghost, and I'm ready to lay a fair bet. *I* aren't a turntail cur.'

'Ay, but there's this in it, Dowlas,' said the landlord, speaking in a tone of much candour and tolerance. 'There's folks, i' my opinion, they can't see ghos'es, not if they stood as plain as a pike-staff before 'em. And there's reason i' that. For there's my wife, now, can't smell, not if she'd the strongest o' cheese under her nose. I never see'd a ghost myself; but then I says to myself, "Very like I haven't got the smell for 'em." I mean, putting a ghost for a smell, or else contrairiways. And so, I'm for holding with both sides; for, as I say, the truth lies between 'em. And if Dowlas was to go and stand, and say he'd never seen a wink o' Cliff's Holiday all the night through, I'd back him; and if anybody said as Cliff's Holiday was certain sure for all that, I'd back *him* too. For the smell's what I go by.'

The landlord's analogical argument was not well received by the farrier – a man intensely opposed to compromise.

'Tut, tut,' he said, setting down his glass with refreshed irritation; 'what's the smell got to do with it? Did ever a ghost give a man a black eye? That's what I should like to know. If ghos'es want me to believe in 'em, let 'em leave off skulking i' the dark and i' lone places – let 'em come where there's company and candles.'

'As if ghos'es 'ud want to be believed in by anybody so ignirant!' said Mr Macey, in deep disgust at the farrier's crass incompetence to apprehend the conditions of ghostly phenomena.

∽ SEVEN ∾

YET THE NEXT MOMENT THERE SEEMED to be some evidence that ghosts had a more condescending dispositon than Mr Macey attributed to them; for the pale thin figure of Silas Marner was suddenly seen standing in the warm light, uttering no word, but looking round at the company with his strange unearthly eyes. The long pipes gave a simultaneous movement, like the antennae of startled insects, and every man present, not expecting even the sceptical farrier, had an impression that he saw, not Silas Marner in the flesh, but an apparition; for the door by which Silas had entered was hidden by the high-screened seats, and no one had noticed his approach. Mr Macey, sitting a long way off the ghost, might be supposed to have felt an argumentative triumph, which would tend to neutralise his share of the general alarm. Had he not always said that when Silas Marner was in that strange trance of his, his soul went loose from his body? Here was the demonstration: nevertheless, on the whole, he would have been as well contented without it. For a few moments there was a dead silence, Marner's want of breath and agitation not allowing him to speak. The landlord, under the habitual sense that he was bound to keep his house open to all company, and confident in the protection of his unbroken neutrality; at last took on himself the task of adjuring the ghost.

'Master Marner,' he said, in a conciliatory tone, 'what's lacking to you? What's your business here?'

'Robbed!' said Silas, gaspingly. 'I've been robbed! I want the constable – and the Justice – and Squire Cass – and Mr Crackenthorp.'

'Lay hold on him, Jem Rodney,' said the landlord, the idea of a ghost subsiding; 'he's off his head, I doubt. He's wet through.'

Jem Rodney was the outermost man, and sat conveniently near Marner's standing-place; but he declined to give his services.

'Come and lay hold on him yourself, Mr Snell, if you've a mind,' said Jem, rather sullenly. 'He's been robbed, and murdered too, for what I know,' he added, in a muttering tone.

'Jem Rodney!' said Silas, turning and fixing his strange eyes on the suspected man.

'Ay, Master Marner, what do ye want wi' me?' said Jem, trembling a little, and seizing his drinking-can as a defensive weapon.

'If it was you stole my money,' said Silas, clasping his hands entreatingly, and raising his voice to a cry, 'give it me back, - and I won't meddle with you. I won't set the constable on you. Give it me back, and I'll let you have a guinea.'

'Me stole your money!' said Jem, angrily. 'I'll pitch this can at your eye if you talk o' my stealing your money.'

'Come, come, Master Marner,' said the landlord, now rising resolutely, and seizing Marner by the shoulder, 'if you've got any information to lay, speak it out sensible, and show as you're in your right mind, if you expect anybody to listen to you. You're as wet as a drownded rat. Sit down and dry yourself, and speak straight forrard.'

'Ah, to be sure, man,' said the farrier, who began to feel that he had not been quite on a par with himself and the occasion. 'Let's have no more staring and screaming, else we'll have you strapped for a madman. That was why I didn't speak at the first - thinks I, the man's run mad.'

'Ay, ay, make him sit down,' said several voices at once, well pleased that the reality of ghosts remained still an open question.

The landlord forced Marner to take off his coat, and then to sit down on a chair aloof from every one else, in the centre of the circle and in the direct rays of the fire. The weaver, too feeble to have any distinct purpose beyond that of getting help to recover his money, submitted unresistingly. The transient fears of the company were now forgotten in their strong curiosity, and all faces were turned towards Silas, when the landlord, having seated himself again, said –

'Now then, Master Marner, what's this you've got to say – as you've been robbed? Speak out.'

'He'd better not say again as it was me robbed him,' cried Jem Rodney, hastily. 'What could I ha' done with his money? I could as easy steal the parson's surplice, and wear it.'

'Hold your tongue, Jem, and let's hear what he's got to say,' said the landlord. 'Now then, Master Marner.'

Silas now told his story, under frequent questioning as the mysterious character of the robbery became evident.

This strangely novel situation of opening his trouble to his Raveloe neighbours, of sitting in the warmth of a hearth not his own, and feeling the presence of faces and voices which were his nearest promise of help, had doubtless its influence on Marner, in spite of his passionate preoccupation with his loss. Our consciousness rarely registers the beginning of a growth within us any more than without us: there have been many circulations of the sap before we detect the smallest sign of the bud.

The slight suspicion with which his hearers at first listened to him, gradually melted away before the convincing simplicity of his distress: it was impossible for the neighbours to doubt that Marner was telling the truth, not because they were capable of arguing at once from the nature of his statements to the absence of any motive for making them falsely, but because, as Mr Macey observed, 'Folks as had the devil to back 'em were not likely to be so mushed' as poor Silas was. Rather, from the strange fact that the robber had left no traces, and had happened to know the nick of time, utterly incalculable by mortal agents, when Silas would go away from home without locking his door, the more probable conclusion seemed to be, that his disreputable intimacy in that quarter, if it ever existed, had been broken up, and that, in consequence, this ill turn had been done to Marner by somebody it was quite in vain to set the constable after. Why this preternatural felon should be obliged to wait till the door was left unlocked, was a question which did not present itself.

'It isn't Jem Rodney as has done this work, Master Marner,' said the landlord. 'You mustn't be a-casting your eye at poor Jem. There may be a bit of a reckoning against Jem for the matter of a hare or so, if anybody was bound to keep their eyes staring open, and niver to wink; but Jem's been a-sitting here drinking his can, like the decentest man i' the parish, since before you left your house, Master Marner, by your own account.'

'Ay, ay,' said Mr Macey; 'let's have no accusing o' the innicent. That isn't the law. There must be folks to swear again' a man before he can be ta'en up. Let's have no accusing o' the innicent, Master Marner.'

Memory was not so utterly torpid in Silas that it could not be wakened by these words. With a movement of compunction as new and strange to him as everything else within the last hour, he started from his chair and went close up to Jem, looking at him as if he wanted to assure himself of the expression in his face.

'I was wrong,' he said – 'yes, yes – I ought to have thought. There's nothing to witness against you, Jem. Only you'd been into my house oftener than anybody else, and so you came into my head. I don't accuse you – I won't accuse anybody – only,' he added, lifting up his hands to his head, and turning away with bewildered misery, 'I try – I try to think where my guineas can be.'

'Ay, ay, they're gone where it's hot enough to melt 'em, I doubt,' said Mr Macey.

'Tchuh!' said the farrier. And then he asked, with a cross-examining air, 'How much money might there be in the bags, Master Marner?'

'Two hundred and seventy-two pounds, twelve and six-pence, last night when I counted it,' said Silas, seating himself again, with a groan.

'Pooh! why, they'd be none so heavy to carry. Some tramp's been in, that's all; and as for the no footmarks, and the bricks and the sand being all right – why, your eyes are pretty much like a insect's, Master Marner; they're obliged to look so close, you can't see much at a time. It's my opinion as, if I'd been you, or you'd been me – for it comes to the same thing – you wouldn't have thought you'd found everything as you left it. But what I vote is, as two of the sensiblest o' the company should go with you to Master Kench, the constable's – he's ill i' bed, I know that much – and get him to appoint one of us his deppity; for that's the law, and I don't think anybody 'ull take upon him to contradick me there. It isn't much of a walk to Kench's; and then, if it's me as is deppity, I'll go back with you, Master Marner, and examine your premises; and if anybody's got any fault to find with that, I'll thank him to stand up and say it out like a man.'

By this pregnant speech the farrier had re-established his self-complacency, and waited with confidence to hear himself named as one of the superlatively sensible men.

'Let us see how the night is, though,' said the landlord, who also considered himself personally concerned in this proposition. 'Why, it rains heavy still,' he said, returning from the door.

'Well, I'm not the man to be afraid o' the rain,' said the farrier. 'For it 'll look bad when Justice Malam hears as respectable men like us had a information laid before 'em and took no steps.'

The landlord agreed with this view, and after taking the sense of the company, and duly rehearsing a small ceremony known in high ecclesiastical life as the *nolo episcopari*, he consented to take on himself the chill dignity of going to Kench's. But to the farrier's strong disgust, Mr Macey now started an objection to his proposing himself as a deputy-constable; for that oracular old gentleman, claiming to know the law, stated, as a fact delivered to him by his father, that no doctor could be a constable.

'And you're a doctor, I reckon, though you're only a cow-doctor – for a fly's a fly, though it may be a hoss-fly,' concluded Mr Macey, wondering a little at his own "cuteness".

There was a hot debate upon this, the farrier being of course indisposed to renounce the quality of doctor, but contending that a doctor could be a constable if he liked – the law meant, he needn't be one if he didn't like. Mr Macey thought this was nonsense, since the law was not likely to be fonder of doctors than of other folks. Moreover, if it was in the nature of doctors more than of other men not to like being constables, how came Mr Dowlas to be so eager to act in that capacity?

'I don't want to act the constable,' said the farrier, driven into a corner by this merciless reasoning; 'and there's no man can say it of me, if he'd tell the truth. But if there's to be any jealousy and envying about going to Kench's in the rain, let them go as like it – you won't get me to go, I can tell you.'

By the landlord's intervention, however, the dispute was accommodated. Mr Dowlas consented to go as a second person disinclined to act officially; and so poor Silas, furnished with some old coverings, turned out with his two companions into the rain again, thinking of the long night-hours before him, not as those do who long to rest, but as those who expect to 'watch for the morning'.

cઢ EIGHT Ꮟ

WHEN GODFREY CASS RETURNED FROM Mrs Osgood's party at midnight, he was not much surprised to learn that Dunsey had not come home. Perhaps he had not sold Wildfire, and was waiting for another chance – perhaps, on that foggy afternoon, he had preferred housing himself at the Red Lion at Batherley for the night, if the run had kept him in that neighbourhood; for he was not likely to feel much concern about leaving his brother in suspense. Godfrey's mind was too full of Nancy Lammeter's looks and behaviour, too full of the exasperation against himself and his lot, which the sight of her always produced in him, for him to give much thought to Wildfire, or to the probabilities of Dunstan's conduct.

The next morning the whole village was excited by the story of the robbery, and Godfrey, like every one else, was occupied in gathering and discussing news about it, and in visiting the Stone-pits. The rain had washed away all possibility of distinguishing foot-marks, but a close investigation of the spot had disclosed, in the direction opposite to the village, a tinder-box, with a flint and steel, half sunk in the mud. It was not Silas's tinder-box, for the only one he had ever had was still standing on his shelf; and the inference generally accepted was, that the tinder-box in the ditch was somehow connected with the robbery. A small minority shook their heads, and intimated their opinion that it was not a robbery to have much light thrown on it by tinder-boxes, that Master Marner's tale had a queer look with it, and that such things had been known as a man's doing himself a mischief, and then setting the justice to look for the doer. But when questioned closely as to their grounds for this opinion, and what Master Marner had to gain by such false pretences, they only shook their heads as before, and observed that there was no knowing what some folks counted gain; moreover, that everybody had a right to their own opinions, grounds or no grounds, and that the weaver, as everybody knew, was partly crazy. Mr Macey, though he joined in the defence of Marner against all suspicions of deceit, also pooh-poohed the tinder-box; indeed, repudiated it as a rather impious suggestion, tending to imply that everything must be done by human hands, and that there was no power which could make away with the guineas without moving the bricks. Nevertheless, he turned round rather sharply on Mr Tookey, when the zealous deputy, feeling that this was a view of the case peculiarly suited to a parish-clerk, carried it still further, and doubted whether it was right to inquire into a robbery at all when the circumstances were so mysterious.

'As if,' concluded Mr Tookey – 'as if there was nothing but what could be made out by justices and constables.'

'Now, don't you be for overshooting the mark, Tookey,' said Mr Macey, nodding his head aside admonishingly. 'That's what you're allays at; if I throw a stone and hit, you think there's summat better than hitting, and you try to throw a stone beyond. What I said was against the tinderbox: I said nothing against justices and constables, for they're o' King George's making, and it 'ud be ill-becoming a man in a parish office to fly out again' King George.'

While these discussions were going on amongst the group outside the Rainbow, a higher consultation was being carried on within, under the presidency of Mr Crackenthorp, the rector, assisted by Squire Cass and other substantial parishioners. It had just occurred to Mr Snell, the land-lord – he being, as he observed, a man accustomed to put two and two together – to connect with the tinder-box, which, as deputy-constable, he himself had had the honourable distinction of finding, certain recollec-tions of a pedlar who had called to drink at the house about a month before, and had actually stated that he carried a tinder-box about with him to light his pipe. Here, surely, was a clue to be followed out. And as memory, when duly impregnated with ascertained facts is sometimes surprisingly fertile, Mr Snell gradually recovered a vivid impression of the effect produced on him by the pedlar's countenance and conversation. He had a 'look with his eye' which fell unpleasantly on Mr Snell's sensi-tive organism. To be sure, he didn't say anything particular – no, except that about the tinder-box – but it isn't what a man says, it's the way he says it. Moreover, he had a swarthy foreignness of complexion which boded little honesty.

'Did he wear ear-rings?' Mr Crackenthorp wished to know, having some acquaintance with foreign customs.

'Well – stay – let me see,' said Mr Snell, like a docile clairvoyante, who would really not make a mistake if she could help it. After stretching the corners of his mouth and contracting his eyes, as if he were trying to see the ear-rings, he appeared to give up the effort, and said, 'Well, he'd got ear-rings in his box to sell, so it's nat'ral to suppose he might wear 'em. But he called at every house, a'most, in the village: there's somebody else, mayhap, saw 'em in his ears, though I can't take upon me rightly to say.'

Mr Snell was correct in his surmise, that somebody else would remember the pedlar's ear-rings. For on the spread of inquiry among the villagers it was stated with gathering emphasis, that the parson had wanted to know whether the pedlar wore ear-rings in his ears, and an impression was created that a great deal depended on the eliciting of this fact. Of course, every one who heard the question, not having any distinct image of the pedlar as *without* ear-rings, immediately had an image of him *with* ear-rings, larger or smaller, as the case might be; and the image was presently taken for a vivid recollection, so that the glazier's wife, a well-intentioned woman, not given to lying, and whose house was among the cleanest in the village, was ready to declare, as sure as ever she meant to take the sacrament the very next Christmas that was ever coming, that she had seen big ear-rings, in the shape of the young moon, in the pedlar's two ears; while Jinny Oates, the cobbler's daughter, being a more imaginative person, stated not only that she had seen them too, but that they had made her blood creep, as it did at that very moment while there she stood.

Also, by way of throwing further light on this clue of the tinder-box, a collection was made of all the articles purchased from the pedlar at various houses, and carried to the Rainbow to be exhibited there. In fact, there was a general feeling in the village, that for the clearing-up of this robbery there must be a great deal done at the Rainbow, and that no man need offer his wife an excuse for going there while it was the scene of severe public duties.

Some disappointment was felt, and perhaps a little indignation also, when it became known that Silas Marner, on being questioned by the Squire and the parson, had retained no other recollection of the pedlar than that he had called at his door, but had not entered his house, having turned away at once when Silas, holding the door ajar, had said that he wanted nothing. This had been Silas's testimony, though he clutched strongly at the idea of the pedlar's being the culprit, if only because it gave him a definite image of a whereabout for his gold after it had been taken away from its hiding-place: he could see it now in the pedlar's box. But it was observed with some irritation in the village, that anybody but a 'blind creatur' like Marner would have seen the man prowling about, for how came he to leave his tinder-box in the ditch close by, if he hadn't been lingering there? Doubtless, he had made his observations when he saw Marner at the door. Anybody might know – and only look at him – that the weaver was a half-crazy miser. It was a wonder the pedlar hadn't murdered him; men of that sort, with rings in their ears, had been known for murderers often and often; there had been one tried at the 'sizes, not so long ago but what there were people living who remembered it.

Godfrey Cass, indeed, entering the Rainbow during one of Mr Snell's frequently repeated recitals of his testimony, had treated it lightly, stating that he himself had bought a knife of the pedlar, and thought him a merry grinning fellow enough; it was all nonsense, he said, about the man's evil looks. But this was spoken of in the village as the random talk of youth, 'as if it was only Mr Snell who had seen something odd about the pedlar!' On the contrary, there were at least half-a-dozen who were ready to go before Justice Malam, and give in much more striking testimony than any the landlord could furnish. It was to be hoped Mr Godfrey would not go to Tarley and throw cold water on what Mr Snell said there, and so prevent the justice from drawing up a warrant. He was suspected of intending this, when, after mid-day, he was seen setting off on horseback in the direction of Tarley.

But by this time Godfrey's interest in the robbery had faded before his growing anxiety about Dunstan and Wildfire, and he was going, not to Tarley, but to Batherley, unable to rest in uncertainty about them any longer. The possibility that Dunstan had played him the ugly trick of riding away with Wildfire, to return at the end of a month, when he had gambled away or otherwise squandered the price of the horse, was a fear that urged itself upon him more, even, than the thought of an accidental injury; and now that the dance at Mrs Osgood's was past, he was irritated with himself that he had trusted his horse to Dunstan. Instead of trying to still his fears he encouraged them, with that superstitious impression which clings to us all, that if we expect evil very strongly it is the less likely to come; and when he heard a horse approaching at a trot, and saw a hat rising above a hedge beyond an angle of the lane, he felt as if his conjuration had succeeded. But no sooner did the horse come within sight, than his heart sank again. It was not Wildfire: and in a few moments more he discerned that the rider was not Dunstan, but Bryce, who pulled up to speak, with a face that implied something disagreeable.

'Well, Mr Godfrey, that's a lucky brother of yours, that Master Dunsey, isn't he?'

'What do you mean?' said Godfrey, hastily.

'Why, hasn't he been home yet?' said Bryce.

'Home? no. What has happened? Be quick. What has he done with my horse?'

'Ah, I thought it was yours, though he pretended you had parted with it to him.'

'Has he thrown him down and broken his knees?' said Godfrey, flushed with exasperation.

'Worse than that,' said Bryce. 'You see, I'd made a bargain with him to buy the horse for a hundred and twenty – a swinging price, but I always liked the horse. And what does he do but go and stake him – fly at a hedge with stakes in it, atop of a bank with a ditch before it. The horse had been dead a pretty good while when he was found. So he hasn't been home since, has he?'

'Home? no,' said Godfrey, 'and he'd better keep away. Confound me for a fool! I might have known this would be the end of it.'

'Well, to tell you the truth,' said Bryce, 'after I'd bargained for the horse, it did come into my head that he might be riding and selling the horse without your knowledge, for I didn't believe it was his own. I knew Master Dunsey was up to his tricks sometimes. But where can he be gone? He's never been seen at Batherley. He couldn't have been hurt, for he must have walked off.'

'Hurt?' said Godfrey, bitterly. 'He'll never be hurt – he's made to hurt other people.'

'And so you *did* give him leave to sell the horse, eh?' said Bryce.

'Yes; I wanted to part with the horse – he was always a little too hard in the mouth for me,' said Godfrey; his pride making him wince under the idea that Bryce guessed the sale to be a matter of necessity. 'I was going to see after him – I thought some mischief had happened. I'll go back now,' he added, turning the horse's head, and wishing he could get rid of Bryce; for he felt that the long-dreaded crisis in his life was close upon him. 'You're coming on to Raveloe, aren't you?'

'Well, no, not now,' said Bryce. 'I *was* coming round there, for I had to go to Flitton, and I thought I might as well take you in my way, and just let you know all I knew myself about the horse. I suppose Master Dunsey didn't like to show himself till the ill news had blown over a bit. He's perhaps gone to pay a visit at the Three Crowns, by Whitbridge – I know he's fond of the house.'

'Perhaps he is,' said Godfrey, rather absently. Then rousing himself, he said, with an effort at carelessness, 'We shall hear of him soon enough, I'll be bound.'

'Well, here's my turning,' said Bryce, not surprised to perceive that Godfrey was rather 'down'; 'so I'll bid you good-day, and wish I may bring you better news another time.'

Godfrey rode along slowly, representing to himself the scene of confession to his father from which he felt that there was now no longer any escape. The revelation about the money must be made the very next morning; and if he withheld the rest, Dunstan would be sure to come back shortly, and, finding that he must bear the brunt of his father's anger, would tell the whole story out of spite, even though he had nothing to gain by it. There was one step, perhaps, by which he might still win Dunstan's silence and put off the evil day: he might tell his father that he had himself spent the money paid to him by Fowler; and as he had never been guilty of such an offence before, the affair would blow over after a little storming. But Godfrey could not bend himself to this. He felt that in letting Dunstan have the money, he had already been guilty of a breach of trust hardly less culpable than that of spending the money directly for his own behoof; and yet there was a distinction between the two acts which made him feel that the one was so much more blackening than the other as to be intolerable to him.

'I don't pretend to be a good fellow,' he said to himself; 'But I'm not a scoundrel – at least, I'll stop short somewhere. I'll bear the consequences of what I *have* done sooner than make believe I've done what I never would have done. I'd never have spent the money for my own pleasure – I was tortured into it.'

Through the remainder of this day Godfrey, with only occasional fluctuations, kept his will bent in the direction of a complete avowal to his father, and he withheld the story of Wildfire's loss till the next morning, that it might serve him as an introduction to heavier matter. The old Squire was accustomed to his son's frequent absence from home, and thought neither Dunstan's nor Wildfire's non-appearance a matter calling for remark. Godfrey said to himself again and again, that if he let slip this one opportunity of confession, he might never have another; the revelation might be made even in a more odious way than by Dunstan's malignity: *she* might come as she had threatened to do. And then he tried to make the scene easier to himself by rehearsal: he made up his mind how he would pass from the admission of his weakness in letting Dunstan have the money to the fact that Dunstan had a hold on him which he had been unable to shake off, and how he would work up his father to expect something very bad before he told him the fact. The old Squire was an implacable man: he made resolutions in violent anger, and he was not to be moved from them after his anger had subsided – as fiery volcanic matters cool and harden into rock. Like many violent and implacable men, he allowed evils to grow under favour of his own heedlessness, till they pressed upon him with exasperating force, and then he turned round with fierce severity and became unrelentingly hard. This was his system with his tenants: he allowed them to get into arrears, neglect their fences, reduce their stock, sell their straw, and otherwise go the wrong way, – and then, when he became short of money in consequence of this indulgence, he took the hardest measures and would listen to no appeal. Godfrey knew all this, and felt it with the greater force because he had constantly suffered annoyance from witnessing his father's sudden fits of unrelentingness, for which his own habitual irresolution deprived him of all sympathy. (He was not critical on the faulty indulgence which preceded these fits; *that* seemed to him natural enough.) Still there was just the chance, Godfrey thought, that his father's pride might see this marriage in a light that would induce him to hush it up, rather than turn his son out and make the family the talk of the country for ten miles round.

This was the view of the case that Godfrey managed to keep before him pretty closely till midnight, and he went to sleep thinking that he had done with inward debating. But when he awoke in the still morning darkness he found it impossible to reawaken his evening thoughts; it was as if they had been tired out and were not to be roused to further work. Instead of arguments for confession, he could now feel the presence of nothing but its evil consequences: the old dread of disgrace came back – the old shrinking from the thought of raising a hopeless barrier between himself and Nancy – the old disposition to rely on chances which might be favourable to him, and save him from betrayal. Why, after all, should he cut off the hope of them by his own act? He had seen the matter in a wrong light yesterday. He had been in a rage with Dunstan, and had thought of nothing but a thorough break-up of their mutual understanding; but what it would be really wisest for him to do, was to try and soften his father's anger against Dunsey, and keep things as nearly as possible in their old condition. If Dunsey did not come back for a few days (and Godfrey did not know but that the rascal had enough money in his pocket to enable him to keep away still longer), everything might blow over.

◁ NINE ▷

GODFREY ROSE AND TOOK HIS OWN breakfast earlier than usual, but lingered in the wainscoted parlour till his younger brothers had finished their meal and gone out; awaiting his father, who always took a walk with his managing-man before breakfast. Every one breakfasted at a different hour in the Red House, and the Squire was always the latest, giving a long chance to a rather feeble morning appetite before he tried it. The table had been spread with substantial eatables nearly two hours before he presented himself – a tall, stout man of sixty, with a face in which the knit brow and rather hard glance seemed contradicted by the slack and feeble mouth. His person showed marks of habitual neglect, his dress was slovenly; and yet there was something in the presence of the old Squire distinguishable from that of the ordinary farmers in the parish, who were perhaps every whit as refined as he, but, having slouched their way through life with a consciousness of being in the vicinity of their 'betters,' wanted that self-possession and authoritativeness of voice and carriage which belonged to a man who thought of superiors as remote existences with whom he had personally little more to do than with America or the stars. The Squire had been used to parish homage all his life, used to the presupposition that his family, his tankards, and everything that was his, were the oldest and best; and as he never associated with any gentry higher than himself, his opinion was not disturbed by comparison.

He glanced at his son as he entered the room, and said: 'What, sir!

haven't *you* had your breakfast yet?' but there was no pleasant morning greeting between them; not because of any unfriendliness, but because the sweet flower of courtesy is not a growth of such homes as the Red House.

'Yes, sir,' said Godfrey, 'I've had my breakfast, but I was waiting to speak to you.'

'Ah! Well,' said the Squire, throwing himself indifferently into his chair, and speaking in a ponderous coughing fashion, which was felt in Raveloe to be a sort of privilege of his rank, while he cut a piece of beef, and held it up before the deer-hound that had come in with him. 'Ring the bell for my ale, will you? You youngsters' business is your own pleasure, mostly. There's no hurry about it for anybody but yourselves.'

The Squire's life was quite as idle as his sons', but it was a fiction kept up by himself and his contemporaries in Raveloe that youth was exclusively the period of folly, and that their aged wisdom was constantly in a state of endurance mitigated by sarcasm. Godfrey waited, before he spoke again, until the ale had been brought and the door closed – an interval during which Fleet, the deer-hound, had consumed enough bits of beef to make a poor man's holiday dinner.

'There's been a cursed piece of ill-luck with Wildfire,' he began; 'happened the day before yesterday.'

'What! broke his knees?' said the Squire, after taking a draught of ale. 'I thought you knew how to ride better than that, sir. I never threw a horse down in my life. If I had, I might ha' whistled for another, for *my* father wasn't quite so ready to unstring as some other fathers I know of. But they must turn over a new leaf – *they* must. What with mortgages and arrears, I'm as short o' cash as a roadside pauper. And that fool Kimble says the newspaper's talking about peace. Why, the country wouldn't have a leg to stand on. Prices 'ud run down like a jack, and I should never get my arrears, not if I sold all the fellows up. And there's that damned Fowler, I won't put up with him any longer; I've told Winthrop to go to Cox this very day. The lying scoundrel told me he'd be sure to pay me a hundred last month. He takes advantage because he's on that outlying farm, and thinks I shall forget him.'

The Squire had delivered this speech in a coughing and interrupted manner, but with no pause long enough for Godfrey to make it a pretext for taking up the word again. He felt that his father meant to ward off any request for money on the ground of the misfortune with Wildfire, and that the emphasis he had thus been led to lay on his shortness of cash and his arrears was likely to produce an attitude of mind the most unfavourable for his own disclosure. But he must go on, now he had begun.

'It's worse than breaking the horse's knees – he's been staked and killed,' he said, as soon as his father was silent, and had begun to cut his meat. 'But I wasn't thinking of asking you to buy me another horse; I was only thinking I'd lost the means of paying you with the price of Wildfire, as I'd meant to do. Dunsey took him to the hunt to sell him for me the other day, and after he'd made a bargain for a hundred and twenty with Bryce, he went after the hounds, and took some fool's leap or other, that did for the horse at once. If it hadn't been for that, I should have paid you a hundred pounds this morning.'

The Squire had laid down his knife and fork, and was staring at his son in amazement, not being sufficiently quick of brain to form a probable guess as to what could have caused so strange an inversion of the paternal and filial relations as this proposition of his son to pay him a hundred pounds.

'The truth is, sir – I'm very sorry – I was quite to blame,' said Godfrey. 'Fowler did pay that hundred pounds. He paid it to me, when I was over there one day last month. And Dunsey bothered me for the money, and I let him have it, because I hoped I should be able to pay it you before this.'

The Squire was purple with anger before his son had done speaking, and found utterance difficult. 'You let Dunsey have it, sir? And how long have you been so thick with Dunsey that you must *collogue* with him to embezzle my money? Are you turning out a scamp? I tell you I won't have it. I'll turn the whole pack of you out of the house together, and marry again. I'd have you to remember, sir, my property's got no entail on it; – since my grandfather's time the Casses can do as they like with their land. Remember that, sir. Let Dunsey have the money! Why should you let Dunsey have the money? There's some lie at the bottom of it.'

'There's no lie, sir,' said Godfrey. 'I wouldn't have spent the money myself, but Dunsey bothered me, and I was a fool, and let him have it. But I meant to pay it, whether he did or not. That's the whole story. I never meant to embezzle money, and I'm not the man to do it. You never knew me do a dishonest trick, sir.'

'Where's Dunsey, then? What do you stand talking there for? Go and fetch Dunsey, as I tell you, and let him give account of what he wanted the money for, and what he's done with it. He shall repent it. I'll turn him out. I said I would, and I'll do it. He shan't brave me. Go and fetch him.'

'Dunsey isn't come back, sir.'

'What! did he break his own neck, then?' said the Squire, with some disgust at the idea that, in that case, he could not fulfil his threat.

'No, he wasn't hurt, I believe, for the horse was found dead, and Dunsey must have walked off. I daresay we shall see him again by-and-by. I don't know where he is.'

'And what must you be letting him have my money for? Answer me that,' said the Squire, attacking Godfrey again, since Dunsey was not within reach.

'Well, sir, I don't know,' said Godfrey hesitatingly. That was a feeble evasion, but Godfrey was not fond of lying, and, not being sufficiently aware that no sort of duplicity can long flourish without the help of vocal falsehoods, he was quite unprepared with invented motives.

'You don't know? I tell you what it is, sir. You've been up to some trick, and you've been bribing him not to tell,' said the Squire, with a sudden acuteness which startled Godfrey, who felt his heart beat violently at the nearness of his father's guess. The sudden alarm pushed him on to take the next step – a very slight impulse suffices for that on a downward road.

'Why, sir,' he said, trying to speak with careless ease, 'it was a little affair between me and Dunsey; it's no matter to anybody else. It's hardly worth while to pry into young men's fooleries: it wouldn't have made any difference to you, sir, if I'd not had the bad luck to lose Wildfire. I should have paid you the money.'

'Fooleries! Pshaw! It's time you'd done with fooleries. And I'd have you know, sir, you *must* ha' done with 'em,' said the Squire, frowning and casting an angry glance at his son. 'Your goings-on are not what I shall find money for any longer. There's my grandfather had his stables full o' horses, and kept a good house, too, and in worse times, by what I can make out; and so might I, if I hadn't four good-fornothing fellows to hang on me like horse-leeches. I've been too good a father to you all – that's what it is. But I shall pull up, sir.'

Godfrey was silent. He was not likely to be very penetrating in his judgements, but he had always had a sense that his father's indulgence had not been kindness, and had had a vague longing for some discipline that would have checked his own errant weakness and helped his better will. The Squire ate his bread and meat hastily, took a deep draught of ale, then turned his chair from the table, and began to speak again.

'It'll be all the worse for you, you know – you'd need try and help me keep things together.'

'Well, sir, I've often offered to take the management of things, but you know you've taken it ill always, and seemed to think I wanted to push you out of your place.'

'I know nothing o' your offering or o' my taking ill,' said the Squire, whose memory consisted in certain strong impressions unmodified by detail; 'but I know, one while you seemed to be thinking o' marrying, and I didn't offer to put any obstacles in your way, as some fathers would. I'd as lieve you married Lammeter's daughter as anybody. I suppose, if I'd said you nay, you'd ha' kept on with it; but, for want o' contradiction, you've changed your mind. You're a shilly-shally fellow: you take after your poor mother. She never had a will of her own; a woman has no call for one, if she's got a proper man for her husband. But *your* wife had need have one, for you hardly know your own mind enough to make both your legs walk one way. The lass hasn't said downright she won't have you, has she?'

'No,' said Godfrey, feeling very hot and uncomfortable; 'but I don't think she will.'

'Think! why haven't you the courage to ask her? Do you stick to it, you want to have *her* – that's the thing?'

'There's no other woman I want to marry,' said Godfrey, evasively.

'Well, then, let me make the offer for you, that's all, if you haven't the pluck to do it yourself. Lammeter isn't likely to be loth for his daughter to marry into *my* family, I should think. And as for the pretty lass, she wouldn't have her cousin – and there's nobody else, as I see, could ha' stood in your way.'

'I'd rather let it be, please sir, at present,' said Godfrey, in alarm. 'I think she's a little offended with me just now, and I should like to speak for myself. A man must manage these things for himself.'

'Well, speak, then, and manage it, and see if you can't turn over a new leaf. That's what a man must do when he thinks o' marrying.'

'I don't see how I can think of it at present, sir. You wouldn't like to settle me no one of the farms, I suppose, and I don't think she'd come to live in this house with all my brothers. It's a different sort of life to what she's been used to.'

'Not come to live in this house? Don't tell me. You ask her, that's all,' said the Squire, with a short, scornful laugh.

'I'd rather let the thing be, at present, sir,' said Godfrey. 'I hope you won't try to hurry it on by saying anything.'

'I shall do what I choose,' said the Squire, 'and I shall let you know I'm master; else you may turn out, and find an estate to drop into somewhere else. Go out and tell Winthrop not to go to Cox's, but wait for me. And tell 'em to get my horse saddled. And stop: look out and get that hack o' Dunsey's sold, and hand me the money, will you? He'll keep no more hacks at my expense. And if you know where he's sneaking – I daresay you do – you may tell him to spare himself the journey o' coming back home. Let him turn ostler, and keep himself. He shan't hang on me any more.'

'I don't know where he is, sir; and if I did, it isn't my place to tell him to keep away,' said Godfrey, moving towards the door.

'Confound it, sir, don't stay arguing, but go and order my horse,' said the Squire, taking up a pipe.

Godfrey left the room, hardly knowing whether he were more relieved by the sense that the interview was ended without having made any change in his position, or more uneasy that he had entangled himself still further in prevarication and deceit. What had passed about his proposing to Nancy had raised a new alarm, lest by some after-dinner words of his father's to Mr Lammeter he should be thrown into the embarrassment of being obliged absolutely to decline her when she seemed to be within his reach. He fled to his usual refuge, that of hoping for some unforeseen turn of fortune, some favourable chance which would save him from unpleasant consequences – perhaps even justify his insincerity by manifesting its prudence.

In this point of trusting to some throw of fortune's dice, Godfrey can hardly be called old-fashioned. Favourable Chance is the god of all men who follow their own devices instead of obeying a law they believe in. Let even a polished man of these days get into a position he is ashamed to avow, and his mind will be bent on all the possible issues that may deliver him from the calculable results of that position. Let him live outside his income, or shirk the resolute honest work that brings wages, and he will presently find himself dreaming of a possible benefactor, a possible simpleton who may be cajoled into using his interest, a possible state of mind in some possible person not yet forthcoming. Let him neglect the responsibilities of his office, and he will inevitably anchor himself on the chance, that the thing left undone may turn out not to be of the supposed importance. Let him betray his friend's confidence, and he will adore that same cunning complexity called Chance, which gives him the hope that his friend will never know. Let him forsake a decent craft that he may pursue the gentilities of a profession to which nature never called him, and his religion will infallibly be the worship of blessed Chance, which he will believe in as the mighty creator of success. The evil principle deprecated in that religion, is the orderly sequence by which the seed brings forth a crop after its kind.

∽ TEN ∾

JUSTICE MALAM WAS NATURALLY REGARDED in Tarley and Raveloe as a man of capacious mind, seeing that he could draw much wider conclusions without evidence than could be expected of his neighbours who were not on the Commission of the Peace. Such a man was not likely to neglect the clue of the tinder-box, and an inquiry was set on foot concerning a pedlar, name unknown, with curly black hair and a foreign complexion, carrying a box of cutlery and jewellery, and wearing large rings in his ears. But either because inquiry was too slow-footed to overtake him, or because the description applied to so many pedlars that inquiry did not know how to choose among them, weeks passed away, and there was no other result concerning the robbery than a gradual cessation of the excitement it had caused in Raveloe. Dunstan Cass's absence was hardly a subject of remark: he had once before had a quarrel with his father, and had gone off, nobody knew whither, to return at the end of six weeks, take up his old quarters unforbidden and swagger as usual. His own family, who equally expected this issue, with the sole difference that the Squire was determined this time to forbid him the old quarters, never mentioned his absence; and when his uncle Kimble or Mr Osgood noticed it, the story of his having killed Wildfire and committed some offence against his father was enough to prevent surprise. To connect the fact of Dunsey's disappearance with that of the robbery occurring on the same day, lay quite away from the track of every one's thought – even Godfrey's, who had better reason than any one else to know what his brother was capable of. He remembered no mention of the weaver between them since the time, twelve years ago, when it was their boyish sport to deride him; and, besides, his imagination constantly created an *alibi* for Dunstan: he saw him continually in some congenial haunt, to which he had walked off on leaving Wildfire – saw him sponging on chance acquaintances, and meditating a return home to the old amusement of tormenting his elder brother. Even if any brain in Raveloe had put the said two facts together, I doubt whether a combination so injurious to the prescriptive respectability of a family with a mural monument and venerable tankards, would not have been suppressed as of unsound tendency. But Christmas puddings, brawn, and abundance of spirituous liquors, throwing the mental originality into the channel of nightmare, are great preservatives against a dangerous spontaneity of waking thought.

When the robbery was talked of at the Rainbow and elsewhere, in good company, the balance continued to waver between the rational explanation founded on the tinder-box, and the theory of an impenetrable mystery that mocked investigation. The advocates of the tinder-box-and-pedlar view considered the other side a muddle-headed and credulous set, who because they themselves were wall-eyed, supposed everybody else to have the same blank outlook; and the adherents of the inexplicable more than hinted that their antagonists were animals inclined to crow before they had found any corn – mere skimming-dishes in point of depth – whose clear-sightedness consisted in supposing there was nothing behind a barn-door because they couldn't see through it; so that, though their controversy did not serve to elicit the fact concerning the robbery, it elicited some true opinions of collateral importance.

But while poor Silas's loss served thus to brush the slow current of Raveloe conversation, Silas himself was feeling the withering desolation of that bereavement about which his neighbours were arguing at their ease. To any one who had observed him before he lost his gold, it might have seemed that so withered and shrunken a life as his could hardly be susceptible of a bruise, could hardly endure any subtraction but such as would put an end to it altogether. But in reality it had been an eager life, filled with immediate purpose which fenced him in from the wide, cheerless unknown. It had been a clinging life; and though the object round which its fibres had clung was a dead disrupted thing, it satisfied the need for clinging. But now the fence was broken down – the support was snatched away. Marner's thoughts could no longer move in their old round, and were baffled by a blank like that which meets a plodding ant when the earth has broken away on its homeward path. The loom was there, and the weaving, and the growing pattern in the cloth; but the bright treasure in the hole under his feet was gone; the prospect of handling and counting it was gone: the evening had no phantasm of delight to still the poor soul's craving. The thought of the money he would get by his actual work could bring no joy, for its meagre image was only a fresh reminder of his loss; and hope was too heavily crushed by the sudden blow, for his imagination to dwell on the growth of a new hoard from that small beginning.

He filled up the blank with grief. As he sat weaving, he every now and then moaned low, like one in pain: it was the sign that his thoughts had come round again to the sudden chasm – to the empty evening time. And all the evening, as he sat in his loneliness by his dull fire, he leaned his elbows on his knees, and clasped his head with his hands, and moaned very low – not as one who seeks to be heard.

And yet he was not utterly forsaken in his trouble. The repulsion Marner had always created in his neighbours was partly dissipated by the new light in which this misfortune had shown him. Instead of a man who had more cunning than honest folks could come by, and, what was worse, had not the inclination to use that cunning in a neighbourly way, it was now apparent that Silas had not cunning enough to keep his own. He was generally spoken of as a 'poor mushed creatur'; and that avoidance of his neighbours, which had before been referred to his ill-will and to a probable addiction to worse company, was now considered mere craziness.

This change to a kindlier feeling was shown in various ways. The odour of Christmas cooking being on the wind, it was the season when superfluous pork and black puddings are suggestive of charity in well-to-do families; and Silas's misfortune had brought him uppermost in the memory of housekeepers like Mrs Osgood. Mr Crackenthorp, too, while he admonished Silas that his money had probably been taken from him because he thought too much of it and never came to church, enforced the doctrine by a present of pigs' pettitoes, well calculated to dissipate unfounded prejudices against the clerical character. Neighbours who had nothing but verbal consolation to give showed a disposition not only to greet Silas and discuss his misfortune at some length when they encountered him in the village, but also to take the trouble of calling at his cottage and getting him to repeat all the details on the very spot; and then they would try to cheer him by saying, 'Well, Master Marner, you're no worse off nor other poor folks, after all; and if you was to be crippled, the parish 'ud give you a 'lowance.'

I suppose one reason why we are seldom able to comfort our neighbours with our words is that our goodwill gets adulterated, in spite of ourselves, before it can pass our lips. We can send black puddings and pettitoes without giving them a flavour of our own egoism; but language is a stream that is almost sure to smack of a mingled soil. There was a fair proportion of kindness in Raveloe; but it was often of a beery and bungling sort, and took the shape least allied to the complimentary and hypocritical.

Mr Macey, for example, coming one evening expressly to let Silas know that recent events had given him the advantage of standing more favourably in the opinion of a man whose judgement was not formed lightly, opened the conversation by saying, as soon as he had seated himself and adjusted his thumbs –

'Come, Master Marner, why, you've no call to sit a-moaning. You're a deal better off to ha' lost your money, nor to ha' kep it by foul means. I used to think, when you first come into these parts, as you were no better nor you should be; you were a younger a deal than what you are now; but you were allays a staring, white-faced creatur, partly like a bald-faced calf, as I may say. But there's no knowing: it isn't every queer-looksed thing as Old Harry's had the making of – I mean, speaking o' toads and such; for they're often harmless, and useful against varmin. And it's pretty much the same wi' you, as fur as I can see. Though as to the yarbs and stuff to cure the breathing, if you brought that sort o' knowledge from distant parts, you might ha' been a bit freer of it. And if the knowledge wasn't well come by, why, you might ha' made up for it by coming to church reg'lar; for, as for the children as the Wise Woman charmed, I've been at the christening of 'em again and again, and they took the water just as well. And that's reasonable; for if Old Harry's mind to do a bit o' kindness for a holiday, like, who's got anything against it? That's my thinking; and I've been clerk o' this parish forty year, and I know, when the parson and me does the cussing of a Ash Wednesday, there's no cussing o' folks as have a mind to be cured without a doctor, let Kimble say what he will. And so, Master Marner, as I was saying – for there's winding's i' things as they may carry you to the fur end o' the prayer-book afore you get back to 'em – my advice is, as you keep up your sperrits; for as for thinking you're a deep 'un, and ha' got more inside you nor 'ull bear daylight, I'm not o' that opinion at all, and so I tell the neighbours. For, says I, you talk o' Master Marner making out a tale – why, it's nonsense, that is: it 'ud take a 'cute man to make a tale like that; and, says I, he looked as scared as a rabbit.'

During this discursive address Silas had continued motionless in his previous attitude, leaning his elbows on his knees, and pressing his hands against his head. Mr Macey, not doubting that he had been listened to, paused, in the expectation of some appreciatory reply, but Marner remained silent. He had a sense that the old man meant to be good-natured and neighbourly; but the kindness fell on him as sunshine falls on the wretched – he had no heart to taste it, and felt that it was very far off him.

'Come, Master Marner, have you got nothing to say to that?' said Mr Macey at last, with a slight accent of impatience.

'Oh,' said Marner, slowly, shaking his head between his hands, 'I thank you – thank you – kindly.'

'Ay, ay, to be sure: I thought you would,' said Mr Macey; 'and my advice is – have you got a Sunday suit?'

'No,' said Marner.

'I doubted it was so,' said Mr Macey. 'Now, let me advise you to get a Sunday suit: there's Tookey, he's a poor creatur, but he's got my tailoring business, and some o' my money in it, and he shall make a suit at a low price, and give you trust, and then you can come to church, and be a bit neighbourly. Why you've never heared me say "Amen" since you come into these parts, and I recommend you to lose no time, for it'll be poor work when Tookey has it all to himself, for I mayn't be equil to stand i' the desk at all, come another winter.' Here Mr Macey paused, perhaps expecting some sign of emotion in his hearer; but not observing any, he went on. 'And as for the money for the suit o' clothes, why, you get a matter of a pound a-week at your weaving, Master Marner, and you're a young man, eh, for all you look so mushed. Why, you couldn't ha' been five-and-twenty when you come into these parts, eh?'

Silas started a little at the change to a questioning tone, and answered midly, 'I don't know; I can't rightly say – it's a long while since.'

After receiving such an answer as this, it is not surprising that Mr Macey observed, later on in the evening at the Rainbow, that Marner's head was 'all of a muddle', and that it was to be doubted if he ever knew when Sunday came round, which showed him a worse heathen than many a dog.

Another of Silas's comforters, besides Mr Macey, came to him with a mind highly charged on the same topic. This was Mrs Winthrop, the wheelwright's wife. The inhabitants of Raveloe were not severely regular in their church-going, and perhaps there was hardly a person in the parish who would not have held that to go to church every Sunday in the calendar would have shown a greedy desire to stand well with Heaven, and get an undue advantage over their neighbours – a wish to be better than the 'common run', that would have implied a reflection on those who had had godfathers and godmothers as well as themselves, and had an equal right to the burying-service. At the same time, it was understood to be requisite for all who were not household servants, or young men, to take the sacrament at one of the great festivals: Squire Cass himself took it on Christmas day; while those who were held to be 'good livers' went to church with greater, though still with moderate, frequency.

Mrs Winthrop was one of these: she was in all respects a woman of scrupulous conscience, so eager for duties that life seemed to offer them too scantily unless she rose at half-past four, though this threw a scarcity of work over the more advanced hours of the morning, which it was a constant problem with her to remove. Yet she had not the vixenish temper which is sometimes supposed to be a necessary condition of such habits:

she was a very mild, patient woman, whose nature it was to seek out all the sadder and more serious elements of life, and pasture her mind upon them. She was the person always first thought of in Raveloe when there was illness or death in a family, when leeches were to be applied, or there was a sudden disappointment in a monthly nurse. She was a 'comfortable woman' – good-looking, fresh-complexioned, having her lips always slightly screwed, as if she felt herself in a sick-room with the doctor or the clergyman present. But she was never whimpering; no one had seen her shed tears; she was simply grave and inclined to shake her head and sigh, almost imperceptibly, like a funereal mourner who is not a relation. It seemed surprising that Ben Winthrop, who loved his quart-pot and his joke, got along so well with Dolly; but she took her husband's jokes and joviality as patiently as everything else, considering that 'men *would* be so', and viewing the stronger sex in the light of animals whom it had pleased Heaven to make naturally troublesome, like bulls and turkey-cocks.

This good wholesome woman could hardly fail to have her mind drawn strongly towards Silas Marner, now that he appeared in the light of a sufferer; and one Sunday afternoon she took her little boy Aaron with her, and went to call on Silas, carrying in her hand some small lard-cakes, flat paste-like articles much esteemed in Raveloe. Aaron, an apple-cheeked youngster of seven, with a clean starched frill which looked like a plate for the apples, needed all his adventurous curiousity to embolden him against the possibility that the big-eyed weaver might do him some bodily injury; and his dubiety was much increased when, on arriving at the Stone-pits, they heard the mysterious sound of the loom.

'Ah, it is as I thought,' said Mrs Winthrop, sadly.

They had to knock loudly before Silas heard them; but when he did come to the door he showed no impatience, as he would once have done, at a visit that had been unasked for and unexpected. Formerly, his heart had been as a locked casket with its treasure inside; but now the casket was empty, and the lock was broken. Left groping in darkness, with his prop utterly gone, Silas had inevitably a sense, though a dull and half-despairing one, that if any help came to him it must come from without; and there was a slight stirring of expectation at the sight of his fellow-men, a faint consciousness of dependence on their goodwill. He opened the door wide to admit Dolly, but without otherwise returning her greeting than by moving the arm-chair a few inches as a sign that she was to sit down in it. Dolly, as soon as she was seated, removed the white cloth that covered her lard-cakes, and said in her gravest way –

'I'd a baking yesterday, Master Marner, and the lard-cakes turned out better nor common, and I'd ha' asked you to accept some, if you'd thought well. I don't eat such things myself, for a bit o' bread's what I like from one year's end to the other; but men's stomichs are made so comical, they want a change – they do, I know, God help 'em.'

Dolly sighed gently as she held out the cakes to Silas, who thanked her kindly, and looked very close at them, absently, being accustomed to look so at everything he took into his hand – eyed all the while by the wondering bright orbs of the small Aaron, who had made an outwork of his mother's chair, and was peeping round from behind it.

'There's letters pricked on 'em,' said Dolly. 'I can't read 'em myself, and there's nobody, not Mr Macey himself, rightly knows what they mean; but they've a good meaning, for they're the same as is on the pulpit-cloth at church. What are they, Aaron, my dear?'

Aaron retreated completely behind his outwork.

'O go, that's naughty,' said his mother, mildly. 'Well, whativer the letters are, they've a good meaning; and it's a stamp as has been in our house, Ben says, ever since he was a little 'un, and his mother used to put it on the cakes, and I've allays put it on too; for if there's any good, we've need of it i' this world.'

'It's I. H. S.,' said Silas, at which proof of learning Aaron peeped round the chair again.

'Well, to be sure, you can read 'em off,' said Dolly. 'Ben's read 'em to me many and many a time, but they slip out o' my mind again; the more's the pity, for they're good letters, else they wouldn't be in the church; and so, I prick 'em on all the loaves and all the cakes, though sometimes they won't hold, because o' the rising – for, as I said, if there's any good to be got, we've need of it i' this world – that we have; and I hope they'll bring good to you, Master Marner, for it's wi' that will I brought you the cakes; and you see the letters have held better nor common.'

Silas was as unable to interpret the letters as Dolly, but there was no possibility of misunderstanding the desire to give comfort that made itself heard in her quiet tones. He said, with more feeling than before – 'Thank you – thank you kindly.' But he laid down the cakes and seated himself absently – drearily unconscious of any distinct benefit towards which the cakes and the letters, or even Dolly's kindness could tend for him.

'Ah, if there's a good anywhere, we've need of it,' repeated Dolly, who did not lightly forsake a serviceable phrase. She looked at Silas pityingly as she went on. 'But you didn't hear the church-bells this morning, Master Marner? I doubt you didn't know it was Sunday. Living so lone here, you lose your count, I daresay; and then, when your loom makes a noise, you can't hear the bells, more partic'lar now the frost kills the sound.'

'Yes, I did; I heard 'em,' said Silas, to whom Sunday bells were a mere accident of the day, and not part of its sacredness. There had been no bells in Lantern Yard.

'Dear heart!' said Dolly, pausing before she spoke again. 'But what a pity it is you should work of a Sunday, and not clean yourself – if you *didn't* go to church; for if you'd a roasting bit, it might be as you couldn't leave it, being a lone man. But there's the bakehus, if you could make up your mind to spend a twopence on the oven now and then, – not every week, in course – I shouldn't like to do that myself, – you might carry your bit o' dinner there, for it's nothing but right to have a bit o' summat hot of a Sunday, and not to make it as you can't know your dinner from Saturday. But now, upo' Christmas-day, this blessed Christmas as is ever coming, if you was to take your dinner to the bakehus, and go to church, and see the holly and the yew, and hear the anthim, and then take the sacramen', you'd be a deal the better, and you'd know which end you stood on, and you could put your trust i' Them as knows better nor we do, seein' you'd ha' done what it lies on us all to do.'

Dolly's exhortation, which was an unusually long effort of speech for her, was uttered in the soothing persuasive tone with which she would have tried to prevail on a sick man to take his medicine, or a basin of gruel for which he had no appetite. Silas had never before been closely urged on the point of his absence from church, which had only been thought of as a part of his general queerness; and he was too direct and simple to evade Dolly's appeal.

'Nay, nay,' he said, 'I know nothing o' church. I've never been to church.'

'No!' said Dolly, in a low tone of wonderment. Then bethinking herself of Silas's advent from an unknown country, she said, 'Could it ha' been as they'd no church where you was born?'

'O yes,' said Silas, meditatively, sitting in his usual posture of leaning on his knees, and supporting his head. 'There was churches – a many – it was a big town. But I knew nothing of 'em – I went to chapel.'

Dolly was much puzzled at this new word, but she was rather afraid of inquiring further, lest 'chapel' might mean some haunt of wickedness. After a little thought, she said –

'Well, Master Marner, it's niver too late to turn over a new leaf, and if you've niver had no church, there's no telling the good it'll do you. For I feel so set up and comfortable as niver was, when I've been and heard the prayers, and the singing to the praise and glory o' God, as Mr Macey gives out – and Mr Crackenthorp saying good words, and more partic'lar on Sacrament Day; and if a bit o' trouble comes, I feel as I can put up wi' it, for I've looked for help i' the right quarter, and gev myself up to Them as we must all give ourselves up to at the last; and if we'n done our part, it isn't to be believed as Them as are above us 'ull be worse nor we are, and come short o' Their 'n.'

Poor Dolly's exposition of her simple Raveloe theology fell rather unmeaningly on Silas's ears, for there was no word in it that could rouse a memory of what he had known as religion, and his comprehension was quite baffled by the plural pronoun, which was no heresy of Dolly's, but only her way of avoiding a presumptuous familiarity. He remained silent, not feeling inclined to assent to the part of Dolly's speech which he fully understood – her recommendation that he should go to church. Indeed, Silas was so unaccustomed to talk beyond the brief questions and answers necessary for the transaction of his simple business, that words did not easily come to him without the urgency of a distinct purpose.

But now, little Aaron, having become used to the weaver's awful presence, had advanced to his mother's side, and Silas, seeming to notice him for the first time, tried to return Dolly's signs of goodwill by offering the lad a bit of lardcake. Aaron shrank back a little, and rubbed his head against his mother's shoulder, but still thought the piece of cake worth the risk of putting his hand out for it.

'O, for shame, Aaron,' said his mother, taking him on her lap, however; 'why, you don't want cake again yet awhile. He's wonderfully hearty,' she went on, with a little sigh – 'that he is, God knows. He's my youngest, and we spoil him sadly, for either me or the father must allays hev him in our sight – that we must.'

She stroked Aaron's brown head, and thought it must do Master Marner good to see such a 'pictur of a child'. But Marner, on the other side of the hearth, saw the neat-featured rosy face as a mere dim round, with two dark spots in it.

'And he's got a voice like a bird – you wouldn't think,' Dolly went on; 'he can sing a Christmas carril as his father's taught him; and I take it for a token as he'll come to good, as he can learn the good tunes so quick. Come, Aaron, stan' up and sing the carril to Master Marner, come.'

Aaron replied by rubbing his forehead against his mother's shoulder.

'O, that's naughty,' said Dolly, gently. 'Stan' up, when mother tells you, and let me hold the cake till you've done.'

Aaron was not indisposed to display his talents, even to an ogre, under protecting circumstances; and after a few more signs of coyness, consisting chiefly in rubbing the backs of his hands over his eyes, and then peeping between them at Master Marner, to see if he looked anxious for the 'carril', he at length allowed his head to be duly adjusted, and standing behind the table, which let him appear above it only as far as his broad frill, so that he looked like a cherubic head untroubled with a body, he began with a clear chirp, and in a melody that had the rhythm of an industrious hammer, –

> 'God rest you, merry gentlemen,
> Let nothing you dismay,
> For Jesus Christ our Saviour
> Was born on Christmas-day.'

Dolly listened with a devout look, glancing at Marner in some confidence that this strain would help to allure him to church.

'That's Christmas music,' she said, when Aaron had ended, and had secured his piece of cake again. 'There's no other music equil to the Christmas music – 'Hark the erol angils sing.' And you may judge what it is at church, Master Marner, with the bassoon and the voices, as you can't

help thinking you've got to a better place a'ready – for I wouldn't speak ill
o' this world, seeing as Them put us in it as knows best – but what wi' the
drink, and the quarrelling, and the bad illnesses, and the hard dying, as
I've seen times and times, one's thankful to hear of a better. The boy sings
pretty, don't he, Master Marner?'

'Yes,' said Silas, absently, 'very pretty.'

The Christmas carol, with its hammer-like rhythm, had fallen on his
ears as strange music, quite unlike a hymn, and could have none of the
effect Dolly contemplated. But he wanted to show her that he was grateful, and the only mode that occurred to him was to offer Aaron a bit more
cake.

'O, no, thank you, Master Marner,' said Dolly, holding down Aaron's
willing hands. 'We must be going home now. And so I wish you good-
bye, Master Marner; and if you ever feel anyways bad in your inside, as
you can't fend for yourself, I'll come and clean up for you, and get you a
bit o' victual, and willing. But I beg and pray of you to leave off weaving
of a Sunday, for it's bad for soul and body – and the money as comes i'
that way 'ull be a bad bed to lie down on at the last, if it doesn't fly away,
nobody knows where, like the white frost. And you'll excuse me being
that free with you, Master Marner, for I wish you well – I do. Make your
bow, Aaron.'

Silas said 'Good-bye, and thank you kindly,' as he opened the door for
Dolly, but he couldn't help feeling relieved when she was gone – relieved
that he might weave again and moan at his ease. Her simple view of life
and its comforts, by which she had tried to cheer him, was only like a
report of unknown objects, which his imagination could not fashion. The
fountains of human love and of faith in a divine love had not yet been
unlocked, and his soul was still the shrunken rivulet, with only this
difference, that its little groove of sand was blocked up, and it wandered
confusedly against dark obstruction.

And so, notwithstanding the honest persuasions of Mr Macey and
Dolly Winthrop, Silas spent his Christmas-day in loneliness, eating his
meat in sadness of heart, though the meat had come to him as a neighbourly present. In the morning he looked out on the black frost that
seemed to press cruelly on every blade of grass, while the half-icy red pool
shivered under the bitter wind; but towards evening the snow began to
fall, and curtained from him even that dreary outlook, shutting him close
up with his narrow grief. And he sat in his robbed home through the
livelong evening, not caring to close his shutters or lock his door, pressing
his head between his hands and moaning, till the cold grasped him and
told him that his fire was grey.

Nobody in this world but himself knew that he was the same Silas
Marner who had once loved his fellow with tender love, and trusted in an
unseen goodness. Even to himself that past experience had become dim.

But in Raveloe village the bells rang merrily, and the church was fuller than all through the rest of the year, with red faces among the abundant dark-green boughs – faces prepared for a longer service than usual by an odorous breakfast of toast and ale. Those green boughs, the hymn and anthem never heard but at Christmas – even the Athanasian Creed, which was discriminated from the others only as being longer and of exceptional virtue, since it was only read on rare occasions – brought a vague exulting sense, for which the grown men could as little have found words as the children, that something great and mysterious had been done for them in heaven above and in earth below, which they were appropriating by their presence. And then the red faces made their way through the black biting frost to their own homes, feeling themselves free for the rest of the day to eat, drink, and be merry, and using that Christian freedom without diffidence.

At Squire Cass's family party that day nobody mentioned Dunstan – nobody was sorry for his absence, or feared it would be too long. The doctor and his wife, uncle and aunt Kimble, were there, and the annual Christmas talk was carried through without any omissions, rising to the climax of Mr Kimble's experience when he walked the London hospitals thirty years back, together with striking professional anecdotes then gathered. Whereupon cards followed, with aunt Kimble's annual failure to follow suit, and uncle Kimble's irascibility concerning the odd trick which was rarely explicable to him, when it was not on his side, without a general visitation of tricks to see that they were formed on sound principles: the whole being accompanied by a strong steaming odour of spirits-and-water.

But the party on Christmas-day, being a strictly family party, was not the pre-eminently brilliant celebration of the season at the Red House. It was the great dance on New Year's Eve that made the glory of Squire Cass's hospitality, as of his forefathers', time out of mind. This was the occasion when all the society of Raveloe and Tarley, whether old acquaintances separated by long rutty distances, or cooled acquaintances separated by misunderstandings concerning runaway calves, or acquaintances founded on intermittent condescension, counted on meeting and on comporting themselves with mutual appropriateness. This was the occasion on which fair dames who came on pillions sent their bandboxes before them, supplied with more than their evening costume; for the feast was not to end with a single evening, like a paltry town entertainment, where the whole supply of eatables is put on the table at once, and bedding is scanty. The Red House was provisioned as if for a siege; and as for the spare feather-beds ready to be laid on floors, they were as plentiful as might naturally be expected in a family that had killed its own geese for many generations.

Godfrey Cass was looking forward to this New Year's Eve with a foolish reckless longing, that made him half deaf to his importunate companion, Anxiety.

'Dunsey will be coming home soon: there will be a great blow-up, and how will you bribe his spite to silence?' said Anxiety.

'O, he won't come home before New Year's Eve, perhaps?' said Godfrey; 'and I shall sit by Nancy then, and dance with her, and get a kind look from her in spite of herself.'

'But money is wanted in another quarter,' said Anxiety, in a louder voice, 'and how will you get it without selling your mother's diamond pin? And if you don't get it . . .?'

'Well, but something may happen to make things easier. At any rate, there's one pleasure for me close at hand: Nancy is coming.'

'Yes, and suppose your father should bring matters to a pass that will oblige you to decline marrying her – and to give your reasons?'

'Hold your tongue, and don't worry me. I can see Nancy's eyes, just as they will look at me, and feel her hand in mine already.'

But Anxiety went on, though in noisy Christmas company; refusing to be utterly quieted even by much drinking.

ELEVEN

SOME WOMEN, I GRANT, WOULD NOT appear to advantage seated on a pillion, and attired in a drab joseph and a drab beaver-bonnet, with a crown resembling a small stew-pan; for a garment suggesting a coachman's greatcoat, cut out under an exiguity of cloth that would only allow of miniature capes, is not well adapted to conceal deficiencies of contour, nor is drab a colour that will throw sallow cheeks into lively contrast. It was all the greater triumph to Miss Nancy Lammeter's beauty that she looked thoroughly bewitching in that costume, as, seated, on the pillion behind her tall, erect father, she held one arm round him, and looked down, with open-eyed anxiety, at the treacherous snow-covered pools and puddles, which sent up formidable splashings of mud under the stamp of Dobbin's foot. A painter would, perhaps, have preferred her in those moments when she was free from self-consciousness; but certainly the bloom on her cheeks was at its highest point of contrast with the surrounding drab when she arrived at the door of the Red House, and saw Mr Godfrey Cass ready to lift her from the pillion. She wished her sister Priscilla had come up at the same time behind the servant, for then she would have contrived that Mr Godfrey should have lifted off Priscilla first, and, in the mean time, she would have persuaded her father to go round to the horseblock instead of alighting at the door-steps. It was very painful, when you had made it quite clear to a young man that you were determined not to marry him, however much he might wish it, that he would still continue to pay you marked attentions; besides, why didn't he always show the same attentions, if he meant them sincerely, instead of being so strange as Mr Godfrey Cass was, sometimes behaving as if he didn't want to speak to her, and taking no notice of her weeks and weeks, and then, all on a sudden, almost making love again? Moreover, it was quite plain he had no real love for her, else he would not let people have *that* to say of him which they did say. Did he suppose that Miss Nancy Lammeter was to be won by any man, squire or no squire, who led a bad life? That was not what she had been used to see in her own father, who was the soberest and best man in that country-side, only a little hot and - hasty now and then, if things were not done to the minute.

All these thoughts rushed through Miss Nancy's mind, in their habitual succession, in the moments between her first sight of Mr Godfrey Cass standing at the door and her own arrival there. Happily, the Squire came out too and gave a loud greeting to her father, so that, somehow, under cover of this noise she seemed to find concealment for her confusion and neglect of any suitably formal behaviour, while she was being lifted from the pillion by strong arms which seemed to find her ridiculously small and light. And there was the best reason for hastening into the house at once, since the snow was beginning to fall again, threatening an unpleasant journey for such guests as were still on the road. These were a small minority; for already the afternoon was beginning to decline, and there would not be too much time for the ladies who came from a distance to attire themselves in readiness for the early tea which was to inspirit them for the dance.

There was a buzz of voices through the house, as Miss Nancy entered, mingled with the scrape of a fiddle preluding in the kitchen; but the Lammeters were guests whose arrival had evidently been thought of so much that it had been watched for from the windows, for Mrs Kimble, who did the honours at the Red House on these great occasions, came forward to meet Miss Nancy in the hall, and conduct her up-stairs. Mrs Kimble was the Squire's sister, as well as the doctor's wife – a double dignity, with which her diameter was in direct proportion; so that, a journey up-stairs being rather fatiguing to her, she did not oppose Miss Nancy's request to be allowed to find her way alone to the Blue Room, where the Miss Lammeters' bandboxes had been deposited on their arrival in the morning.

There was hardly a bedroom in the house where feminine compliments were not passing and feminine toilettes going forward, in various stages, in space made scanty by extra beds spread upon the floor; and Miss Nancy, as she entered the Blue Room, had to make her little formal curtsy to a group of six. On the one hand, there were ladies no less important than the two Miss Gunns, the wine merchant's daughters from Lytherly, dressed in the height of fashion, with the tightest skirts and the shortest waists, and gazed at by Miss Ladbrook (of the Old Pastures) with a shyness not unsustained by inward criticism. Partly, Miss Ladbrook felt that her own skirt must be regarded as unduly lax by the Miss Gunns, and partly, that it was a pity the Miss Gunns did not show that judgement which she herself would show if she were in their place, by stopping a little on this side of the fashion. On the other hand, Mrs Ladbrook was standing in skullcap and front, with her turban in her hand, curtsying and smiling blandly and saying, 'After you, ma'am,' to another lady in similar circumstances, who had politely offered the precedence at the looking-glass.

But Miss Nancy had no sooner made her curtsy than an elderly lady came forward, whose full white muslin kerchief, and mob-cap round her curls of smooth grey hair, were in daring contrast with the puffed yellow satins and top-knotted caps of her neighbours. She approached Miss Nancy with much primness, and said, with a slow, treble suavity –

'Niece, I hope I see you well in health.' Miss Nancy kissed her aunt's cheek dutifully, and answered, with the same sort of amiable primness, 'Quite well, I thank you, aunt; and I hope I see you the same.'

'Thank you, niece; I keep my health for the present. And how is my brother-in-law?'

These dutiful questions and answers were continued until it was ascertained in detail that the Lammeters were all as well as usual, and the Osgoods likewise, also that niece Priscilla must certainly arrive shortly, and that travelling on pillions in snowy weather was unpleasant, though a joseph was a great protection. Then Nancy was formally introduced to her aunt's visitors, the Miss Gunns, as being the daughters of a mother known to *their* mother, though now for the first time induced to make a journey into these parts; and these ladies were so taken by surprise at finding such a lovely face and figure in an out-of-the-way country place, that they began to feel some curiosity about the dress she would put on when she took off her joseph. Miss Nancy, whose thoughts were always conducted with the propriety and moderation conspicuous in her manners, remarked to herself that the Miss Gunns were rather hard-featured than otherwise, and that such very low dresses as they wore might have been attributed to vanity if their shoulders had been pretty, but that, being as they were, it was not reasonable to suppose that they showed their necks from a love of display, but rather from some obligation not inconsistent with sense and modesty. She felt convinced, as she opened her box, that this must be her aunt Osgood's opinion, for Miss Nancy's mind resembled her aunt's to a degree that everybody said was surprising, considering the kinship was on Mr Osgood's side; and though you might not have supposed it from the formality of their greeting, there was a devoted attachment and mutual admiration between aunt and niece. Even Miss Nancy's refusal of her cousin Gilbert Osgood (on the ground solely that he was her cousin), though it had grieved her aunt greatly, had not in the least cooled the preference which had determined her to leave Nancy several of her hereditary ornaments, let Gilbert's future wife be whom she might.

Three of the ladies quickly retired, but the Miss Gunns were quite content that Mrs Osgood's inclination to remain with her niece gave them also a reason for staying to see the rustic beauty's toilette. And it was really a pleasure – from the first opening of the bandbox, where everything smelt of lavender and rose-leaves, to the clasping of the small coral necklace that fitted closely round her little white neck. Everything belonging to Miss Nancy was of delicate purity and nattiness: not a crease was where it had no business to be, not a bit of her linen professed whiteness without fulfilling its profession; the very pins on her pincushion were stuck in after a pattern from which she was careful to allow no aberration; and as for her own person, it gave the same idea of perfect unvarying neatness as the body of a little bird. It is true that her light-brown hair was cropped behind like a boy's, and was dressed in front in a number of flat rings, that lay quite away from her face; but there was no sort of coiffure that could make Miss Nancy's cheek and neck look otherwise than pretty; and when at last she stood complete in her silvery twilled silk, her lace tucker, her coral necklace, and coral ear-drops, the Miss Gunns could see nothing to criticize except her hands, which bore the traces of butter-making, cheese-crushing, and even still coarser work. But Miss Nancy was not ashamed of that, for while she was dressing she narrated to her aunt how she and Priscilla had packed their boxes yesterday, because this morning was baking morning, and since they were leaving home, it was desirable to make a good supply of meat-pies for the kitchen; and as she concluded this judicious remark, she turned to the Miss Gunns that she might not commit the rudeness of not including them in the conversation. The Miss Gunns smiled stiffly, and thought what a pity it was that these rich country people, who could afford to buy such good clothes (really Miss Nancy's lace and silk were very costly), should be brought up in utter ignorance and vulgarity. She actually said 'mate' for 'meat', "appen' for 'perhaps', and 'oss' for 'horse', which, to young ladies living in good Lytherly society, who habitually said 'orse, even in domestic privacy, and only said 'appen on the right occasions, was necessarily shocking. Miss Nancy, indeed, had never been to any school higher than Dame Tedman's: her acquaintance with profane literature hardly went beyond the rhymes she had worked in her large sampler under the lamb and the shepherdess; and in order to balance an account, she was obliged to effect her subtraction by removing visible metallic shillings and six-pences from a visible metallic total. There is hardly a servant-maid in these days who is not better informed than Miss Nancy; yet she had the essential attributes of a lady – high veracity, delicate honour in her dealings, deference to others, and refined personal habits, – and lest these should not suffice to convince grammatical fair ones that her feelings can at all resemble theirs, I will add that she was slightly proud and exacting, and as constant in her affection towards a baseless opinion as towards an erring lover.

The anxiety about sister Priscilla, which had grown rather active by the time the coral necklace was clasped, was happily ended by the entrance of that cheerful-looking lady herself, with a face made blowsy by cold and damp. After the first questions and greetings, she turned to Nancy, and surveyed her from head to foot – then wheeled her round, to ascertain that the back view was equally faultless.

'What do you think o' *these* gowns, aunt Osgood?' said Priscilla, while Nancy helped her to unrobe.

'Very handsome indeed, niece,' said Mrs Osgood, with a slight increase of formality. She always thought niece Priscilla too rough.

'I'm obliged to have the same as Nancy, you know, for all I'm five years older, and it makes me look yellow; for she never *will* have anything without I have mine just like it, because she wants us to look like sisters. And I tell her, folks 'ull think it's my weakness makes me fancy as I shall look pretty in what she looks pretty in. For I *am* ugly – there's no denying that: I feature my father's family. But, law! I don't mind, do you?' Priscilla here turned to the Miss Gunns, rattling on in too much preoccupation with the delight of talking, to notice that her candour was not appreciated. 'The pretty uns do for fly-catchers – they keep the men off us. I've no opinion o' the men, Miss Gunn – I don't know what *you* have. And as for fretting and stewing about what *they'll* think of you from morning till night, and making your life uneasy about what they're doing when they're out o' your sight – as I tell Nancy, it's a folly no woman need be guilty of, if she's got a good father and a good home: let her leave it to them as have got no fortin, and can't help themselves. As I say, Mr Have-your-own-way is the best husband, and the only one I'd ever promise to obey. I know it isn't pleasant, when you've been used to living in a big way, and managing hogsheads and all that, to go and put your nose in by somebody else's fireside, or to sit down by yourself to a scrag or a knuckle; but, thank God! my father's a sober man and likely to live; and if you've got a man by the chimney-corner, it doesn't matter if he's childish – the business needn't be broke up.'

The delicate process of getting her narrow gown over her head without injury to her smooth curls, obliged Miss Priscilla to pause in this rapid survey of life, and Mrs Osgood seized the opportunity of rising and saying –

'Well, niece, you'll follow us. The Miss Gunns will like to go down.'

'Sister,' said Nancy, when they were alone, 'you've offended the Miss Gunns, I'm sure.'

'What have I done, child?' said Priscilla, in some alarm.

'Why, you asked them if they minded about being ugly – you're so very blunt.'

'Law, did I? Well, it popped out: it's a mercy I said no more, for I'm a bad un to live with folks when they don't like the truth. But as for being ugly, look at me, child, in this silver-coloured silk – I told you how it 'ud be – I look as yellow as a daffodil. Anybody 'ud say you wanted to make a mawkin of me.'

'No, Priscy, don't say so. I begged and prayed of you not to let us have this silk if you'd like another better. I was willing to have *your* choice, you know I was,' said Nancy, in anxious self-vindication.

'Nonsense, child, you know you'd set your heart on this; and reason good, for you're the colour o' cream. It 'ud be fine doings for you to dress yourself to suit *my* skin. What I find fault with, is that notion o' yours as I must dress myself just like you. But you do as you like with me – you always did, from when first you began to walk. If you wanted to go the field's length, the field's length you'd go; and there was no whipping you, for you looked as prim and innicent as a daisy all the while.'

'Priscy,' said Nancy, gently, as she fastened a coral necklace, exactly like her own, round Priscilla's neck, which was very far from being like her own, 'I'm sure I'm willing to give way as far as is right, but who shouldn't dress alike if it isn't sisters? Would you have us go about looking as if we were no kin to one another – us that have got no mother and not another sister in the world? I'd do what was right, if I dressed in a gown dyed with cheese-colouring; and I'd rather you'd choose, and let me wear what pleases you.'

'There you go again! You'd come round to the same thing if one talked to you from Saturday night till Saturday morning. It'll be fine fun to see how you'll master your husband and never raise your voice above the singing o' the kettle all the while. I like to see the men mastered!'

'Don't talk *so*, Priscy,' said Nancy, blushing. 'You know I don't mean ever to be married.'

'O, you never mean a fiddlestick's end!' said Priscilla, as she arranged her discarded dress, and closed her bandbox. 'Who shall *I* have to work for when father's gone, if you are to go and take notions in your head and be an old maid, because some folks are no better than they should be? I haven't a bit o' patience with you – sitting on an addled egg for ever, as if there was never a fresh un in the world. One old maid's enough out o' two sisters; and I shall do credit to a single life, for God A'mighty meant me for it. Come, we can go down now. I'm as ready as a mawkin *can* be – there's nothing awanting to frighten the crows, now I've got my ear-droppers in.'

As the two Miss Lammeters walked into the large parlour together, any one who did not know the character of both, might certainly have supposed that the reason why the square-shouldered, clumsy, high-featured Priscilla wore a dress the facsimile of her pretty sister's, was either the mistaken vanity of the one, or the malicious contrivance of the other in order to set off her own rare beauty. But the good-natured self-forgetful cheeriness and common-sense of Priscilla would soon have dissipated the one suspicion; and the modest calm of Nancy's speech and manners told clearly of a mind free from all disavowed devices.

Places of honour had been kept for the Miss Lammeters near the head of the principal tea-table in the wainscoted parlour, now looking fresh and pleasant with handsome branches of holly, yew, and laurel, from the abundant growths of the old garden; and Nancy felt an inward flutter, that no firmness of purpose could prevent, when she saw Mr Godfrey Cass advancing to lead her to a seat between himself and Mr Crackenthorp, while Priscilla was called to the opposite side between her father and the Squire. It certainly did make some difference to Nancy that the lover she had given up was the young man of quite the highest consequence in the parish – at home in a venerable and unique parlour, which was the extremity of grandeur in her experience, a parlour where *she* might one day have been mistress, with the consciousness that she was spoken of as 'Madam Cass', the Squire's wife. These circumstances exalted her inward drama in her own eyes, and deepened the emphasis with which she declared to herself that not the most dazzling rank should induce her to marry a man whose conduct showed him careless of his character, but that, 'love once, love always', was the motto of a true and pure woman, and no man should ever have any right over her which would be a call on her to destroy the dried flowers that she treasured, and always would treasure, for Godfrey Cass's sake. And Nancy was capable of keeping her word to herself under very trying conditions. Nothing but a becoming blush betrayed the moving thoughts that urged themselves upon her as she accepted the seat next to Mr Crackenthorp; for she was so instinctively neat and adroit in all her actions, and her pretty lips met each other with such quiet firmness, that it would have been difficult for her to appear agitated.

It was not the Rector's practice to let a charming blush pass without an appropriate compliment. He was not in the least lofty or aristocratic, but simply a merry-eyed, small-featured, grey-haired man, with his chin propped by an ample many-creased white neckcloth which seemed to predominate over every other point in his person, and somehow to impress its peculiar character on his remarks; so that to have considered his amenities apart from his cravat would have been a severe, and perhaps a dangerous, effort of abstraction.

'Ha, Miss Nancy,' he said, turning his head within his cravat and smiling down pleasantly upon her, 'when anybody pretends this has been a severe winter, I shall tell them I saw the roses blooming on New Year's Eve – eh, Godfrey, what do *you* say?'

Godfrey made no reply, and avoided looking at Nancy very markedly; for though these complimentary personalities were held to be in excellent taste in old-fashioned Raveloe society, reverent love has a politeness of its own which it teaches to men otherwise of small schooling. But the Squire was rather impatient at Godfrey's showing himself a dull spark in this way. By this advanced hour of the day, the Squire was always in higher spirits than we have seen him in at the breakfast-table, and felt it quite pleasant to fulfil the hereditary duty of being noisily jovial and patronizing: the large silver snuff-box was in active service and was offered without fail to all neighbours from time to time, however often they might have declined the favour. At present, the Squire had only given an express welcome to the heads of families as they appeared; but always as the evening deepened, his hospitality rayed out more widely, till he had tapped the youngest guests on the back and shown a peculiar fondness for their presence, in the full belief that they must feel their lives made happy by their belonging to a parish where there was such a hearty man as Squire Cass to invite them and wish them well. Even in this early stage of the jovial mood, it was natural that he should wish to supply his son's deficiencies by looking and speaking for him.

'Ay, ay,' he began, offering his snuff-box to Mr Lammeter, who for the second time bowed his head and waved his hand in stiff rejection of the offer, 'us old fellows may wish ourselves young tonight, when we see the mistletoe bough in the White Parlour. It's true, most things are gone back'ard in these last thirty years – the country's going down since the old king fell ill. But when I look at Miss Nancy here, I begin to think the lasses keep up their quality; – ding me if I remember a sample to match her, not when I was a fine young fellow, and thought a deal about my pigtail. No offence to you, madam,' he added, bending to Mrs Crackenthorp, who sat by him, 'I didn't know *you* when you were as young as Miss Nancy here.'

Mrs Crackenthorp – a small blinking woman, who fidgeted incessantly with her lace, ribbons, and gold chain, turning her head about and making subdued noises, very much like a guinea-pig that twitches its nose and soliloquises in all company indiscriminately – now blinked and fidgeted towards the Squire, and said, 'O no – no offence.'

This emphatic compliment of the Squire's to Nancy was felt by others besides Godfrey to have a diplomatic significance; and her father gave a slight additional erectness to his back, as he looked across the table at her with complacent gravity. That grave and orderly senior was not going to bate a jot of his dignity by seeming elated at the notion of a match between his family and the Squire's: he was gratified by any honour paid to his daughter; but he must see an alteration in several ways before his consent would be vouchsafed. His spare but healthy person, and high-featured firm face, that looked as if it had never been flushed by excess, was in strong contrast, not only with the Squire's, but with the appearance of the Raveloe farmers generally – in accordance with a favourite saying of his own, that 'breed was stronger than pasture'.

'Miss Nancy's wonderful like what her mother was, though; isn't she, Kimble?' said the stout lady of that name, looking round for her husband.

But Doctor Kimble (country apothecaries in old days enjoyed that title without authority of diploma), being a thin and agile man, was flitting about the room with his hands in his pockets, making himself agreeable to his feminine patients, with medical impartiality, and being welcomed everywhere as a doctor by hereditary right – not one of those miserable apothecaries who canvass for practice in strange neighbourhoods, and spend all their income in starving their one horse, but a man of substance, able to keep an extravagant table like the best of his patients. Time out of mind the Raveloe doctor had been a Kimble; Kimble was inherently a doctor's name; and it was difficult to contemplate firmly the melancholy fact that the actual Kimble had no son, so that his practice might one day be handed over to a successor with the incongruous name of Taylor or Johnson. But in that case the wiser people in Raveloe would employ Dr Blick of Flitton – as less unnatural.

'Did you speak to me, my dear?' said the authentic doctor, coming quickly to his wife's side; but, as if foreseeing that she would be too much out of breath to repeat her remark, he went on immediately – 'Ha, Miss Priscilla, the sight of you revives the taste of that super-excellent pork-pie. I hope the batch isn't near an end.'

'Yes, indeed, it is, doctor,' said Priscilla; 'but I'll answer for it the next shall be as good. My pork-pies don't turn out well by chance.'

'Not as your doctoring does, eh, Kimble? – because folks forget to take your physic, eh?' said the Squire, who regarded physic and doctors as many local churchmen regard the church and the clergy – tasting a joke against them when he was in health, but impatiently eager for their aid when anything was the matter with him. He tapped his box, and looked round with a triumphant laugh.

'Ah, she has a quick wit, my friend Priscilla has,' said the doctor, choosing to attribute the epigram to a lady rather than allow a brother-in-law that advantage over him. 'She saves a little pepper to sprinkle over her talk – that's the reason why she never puts too much in her pies. There's my wife, now, she never has an answer at her tongue's end; but if I offend her, she's sure to scarify my throat with black pepper the next day, or else give me the colic with watery greens. That's an awful tit-for-tat.' Here the vivacious doctor made a pathetic grimace.

'Did you ever hear the like?' said Mrs Kimble, laughing above her double chin with much good-humour, aside to Mrs Crackenthorp, who blinked and nodded, and amiably intended to smile, but the intention lost itself in small twitchings and noises.

'I suppose that's the sort of tit-for-tat adopted in your profession, Kimble, if you've a grudge against a patient,' said the Rector.

'Never do have a grudge against our patients,' said Mr Kimble, 'except when they leave us: and then, you see, we haven't the chance of prescribing for 'em. Ha, Miss Nancy,' he continued, suddenly skipping to Nancy's side, 'you won't forget your promise? You're to save a dance for me, you know.'

'Come, come, Kimble, don't you be too for'ard,' said the Squire. 'Give the young uns fair-play. There's my son Godfrey'll be wanting to have a round with you if you run off with Miss Nancy. He's bespoke her for the first dance, I'll be bound. Eh, sir! what do you say?' he continued, throwing himself backward, and looking at Godfrey. 'Haven't you asked Miss Nancy to open the dance with you?'

Godfrey, sorely uncomfortable under this significant insistence about Nancy, and afraid to think where it would end by the time his father had set his usual hospitable example of drinking before and after supper, saw no course open but to turn to Nancy and say, with as little awkwardness as possible –

'No; I've not asked her yet, but I hope she'll consent – if somebody else hasn't been before me.'

'No, I've not engaged myself,' said Nancy, quietly, though blushingly. (If Mr Godfrey founded any hopes on her consenting to dance with him, he would soon be undeceived; but there was no need for her to be uncivil.)

'Then I hope you've no objections to dancing with me,' said Godfrey, beginning to lose the sense that there was anything uncomfortable in this arrangement.

'No, no objections,' said Nancy, in a cold tone.

'Ah, well, you're a lucky fellow, Godfrey,' said uncle Kimble; 'but you're my godson, so I won't stand in your way. Else I'm not so very old, eh, my dear?' he went on, skipping to his wife's side again. 'You wouldn't mind my having a second after you were gone – not if I cried a good deal first?'

'Come, come, take a cup o' tea and stop your tongue, do,' said good-humoured Mrs Kimble, feeling some pride in a husband who must be regarded as so clever and amusing by the company generally. If he had only not been irritable at cards!

While safe, well-tested personalities were enlivening the tea in this way, the sound of the fiddle approaching within a distance at which it could be heard distinctly, made the young people look at each other with sympathetic impatience for the end of the meal.

'Why, there's Solomon in the hall,' said the Squire, 'and playing my fav'rite tune, I believe – "The flaxen-headed ploughboy" – he's for giving us a hint as we aren't enough in a hurry to hear him play. Bob,' he called out to his third long-legged son, who was at the other end of the room, 'open the door, and tell Solomon to come in. He shall give us a tune here.'

Bob obeyed, and Solomon walked in, fiddling as he walked, for he would on no account break off in the middle of a tune.

'Here, Solomon,' said the Squire, with loud patronage. 'Round here, my man. Ah, I knew it was "The flaxen-headed ploughboy": there's no finer tune.'

Solomon Macey, a small hale old man with an abundant crop of long white hair reaching nearly to his shoulders, advanced to the indicated spot, bowing reverently while he fiddled, as much as to say that he respected the company though he respected the key-note more. As soon as he had repeated the tune and lowered his fiddle, he bowed again to the Squire and the Rector, and said, 'I hope I see your honour and your reverence well, and wishing you health and long life and a happy New Year. And wishing the same to you, Mr Lammeter, sir; and to the other gentlemen, and the madams, and the young lasses.'

As Solomon uttered the last words, he bowed in all directions solicitously, lest he should be wanting in due respect. But thereupon he immediately began to prelude, and fell into the tune which he knew would be taken as a special compliment by Mr Lammeter.

'Thank ye, Solomon, thank ye,' said Mr Lammeter when the fiddle paused again. 'That's "Over the hills and far away", that is. My father used to say to me, whenever we heard that tune, "Ah, lad, I come from over the hills and far away." There's a many tunes I don't make head or tail of; but that speaks to me like the blackbird's whistle. I suppose it's the name: there's a deal in the name of a tune.'

But Solomon was already impatient to prelude again, and presently broke with much spirit into 'Sir Roger de Coverley', at which there was a sound of chairs pushed back, and laughing voices.

'Ay, ay, Solomon, we know what that means,' said the Squire, rising. 'It's time to begin the dance, eh? Lead the way, then, and we'll all follow you.'

So Solomon, holding his white head on one side, and playing vigorously, marched forward at the head of the gay procession into the White Parlour, where the mistletoe-bough was hung, and multitudinous tallow candles made rather a brilliant effect, gleaming from among the berried holly-boughs, and reflected in the old-fashioned oval mirrors fastened in the panels of the white wainscot. A quaint procession! Old Solomon, in his seedy clothes and long white locks, seemed to be luring that decent company by the magic scream of his fiddle – luring discreet matrons in turban-shaped caps, nay, Mrs Crackenthorp herself, the summit of whose perpendicular feather was on a level with the Squire's shoulder – luring fair lasses complacently conscious of very short waists and skirts blameless of front-folds – luring burly fathers in large variegated waistcoats, and ruddy sons, for the most part shy and sheepish, in short nether garments and very long coat-tails.

Already Mr Macey and a few other privileged villagers, who were allowed to be spectators on these great occasions, were seated on benches placed for them near the door; and great was the admiration and satisfaction in that quarter when the couples had formed themselves for the dance, and the Squire led off with Mrs Crackenthorp, joining hands with the Rector and Mrs Osgood. That was as it should be – that was what everybody had been used to – and the charter of Raveloe seemed to be renewed by the ceremony. It was not thought of as an unbecoming levity for the old and middle-aged people to dance a little before sitting down to cards, but rather as part of their social duties. For what were these if not to be merry at appropriate times, interchanging visits and poultry with due frequency, paying each other old-established compliments in sound traditional phrases, passing well-tried personal jokes, urging your guests to eat and drink too much out of hospitality, and eating and drinking too much in your neighbour's house to show that you liked your cheer? And the parson naturally set an example in these social duties. For it would not have been possible for the Raveloe mind, without a peculiar revelation, to know that a clergyman should be a pale-faced memento of solemnities, instead of a reasonably faulty man whose exclusive authority to read prayers and preach, to christen, marry, and bury you, necessarily co-existed with the right to sell you the ground to be buried in and to take tithe in kind; on which last point, of course, there was a little grumbling, but not to the extent of irreligion – not of deeper significance than the grumbling at the rain, which was by no means accompanied with a spirit of impious defiance, but with a desire that the prayer for fine weather might be read forthwith.

There was no reason, then, why the Rector's dancing should not be received as part of the fitness of things quite as much as the Squire's, or why, on the other hand, Mr Macey's official respect should restrain him from subjecting the parson's performance to that criticism with which minds of extraordinary acuteness must necessarily contemplate the doings of their fallible fellow-men.

'The Squire's pretty springe, considering his weight,' said Mr Macey, 'and he stamps uncommon well. But Mr Lammeter beats 'em all for shapes: you see he holds his head like a sodger, and he isn't so cushiony as most o' the oldish gentlefolks – they run fat in general; and he's got a fine leg. The parson's nimble enough, but he hasn't got much of a leg; it's a bit too thick down'ard, and his knees might be a bit nearer wi'out damage; but he might do worse, he might do worse. Though he hasn't that grand way o' waving his hand as the Squire has.'

'Talk o' nimbleness, look at Mrs Osgood,' said Ben Winthrop, who was holding his son Aaron between his knees. 'She trips along with her little steps, so as nobody can see how she goes – it's like as if she had little wheels to her feet. She doesn't look a day older nor last year: she's the finest-made woman as is, let the next be where she will.'

'I don't heed how the women are made,' said Mr Macey, with some contempt. 'They wear nayther coat nor breeches: you can't make much out o' their shapes.'

'Fayder,' said Aaron, whose feet were busy beating out the tune, 'how does that big cock's-feather stick in Mrs Crackenthorp's yead? Is there a little hole for it, like in my shuttlecock?'

'Hush, lad, hush; that's the way the ladies dress theirselves, that is,' said the father, adding, however, in an under-tone to Mr Macey, 'It does make her look funny, though – partly like a short-necked bottle wi' a long quill in it. Hey, by jingo, there's the young Squire leading off now, wi' Miss Nancy for partners. There's a lass for you! – like a pink-and-white posy – there's nobody 'ud think as anybody could be so pritty. I shouldn't wonder if she's Madam Cass some day, arter all – and nobody more rightfuller, for they'd make a fine match. You can find nothing against Master Godfrey's shapes, Macey, I'll bet a penny.'

Mr Macey screwed up his mouth, leaned his head further on one side, and twirled his thumbs with a presto movement as his eyes followed Godfrey up the dance. At last he summed up his opinion.

'Pretty well down'ard, but a bit too round i' the shoulderblades. And as for them coats as he gets from the Flitton tailor, they're a poor cut to pay double money for.'

'Ah, Mr Macey, you and me are two folks,' said Ben, slightly indignant at this carping. 'When I've got a pot o' good ale, I like to swaller it, and do my inside good, i'stead o' smelling and staring at it to see if I can't find faut wi' the brewing. I should like you to pick me out a finer-limbed young fellow nor Master Godfrey – one as 'ud knock you down easier, or's more pleasanter looksed when he's piert and merry.'

'Tchuh!' said Mr Macey, provoked to increased severity, 'he isn't come to his right colour yet: he's partly like a slack-baked pie. And I doubt he's got a soft place in his head, else why should he be turned round the finger by that offal Dunsey as nobody's seen o' late, and let him kill that fine hunting hoss as was the talk o' the country? And one while he was allays after Miss Nancy, and then it all went off again, like a smell o' hot porridge, as I may say. That wasn't my way when I went a-coorting.'

'Ah, but mayhap Miss Nancy hung off, like, and your lass didn't,' said Ben.

'I should say she didn't,' said Mr Macey, significantly. 'Before I said "sniff", I took care to know as she'd say "snaff", and pretty quick too. I wasn't a-going to open *my* mouth, like a dog at a fly, and snap it to again, wi' nothing to swaller.'

'Well, I think Miss Nancy's a-coming round again,' said Ben, 'for Master Godfrey doesn't look so down-hearted tonight. And I see he's for taking her away to sit down, now they're at the end o' the dance: that looks like sweethearting, that does.'

The reason why Godfrey and Nancy had left the dance was not so tender as Ben imagined. In the close press of couples a slight accident had happened to Nancy's dress, which, while it was short enough to show her neat ankle in front, was long enough behind to be caught under the stately stamp of the Squire's foot, so as to rend certain stitches at the waist, and cause much sisterly agitation in Priscilla's mind, as well as serious concern in Nancy's. One's thoughts may be much occupied with love-struggles, but hardly so as to be insensible to a disorder in the general framework of things. Nancy had no sooner completed her duty in the figure they were dancing than she said to Godfrey, with a deep blush, that she must go and sit down till Priscilla could come to her; for the sisters had already exchanged a short whisper and an open-eyed glance full of meaning. No reason less urgent than this could have prevailed on Nancy to give Godfrey this opportunity of sitting apart with her. As for Godfrey, he was feeling so happy and oblivious under the long charm of the country-dance with Nancy, that he got rather bold on the strength of her confusion, and was capable of leading her straight away, without leave asked, into the adjoining small parlour, where the card-tables were set.

'O no, thank you,' said Nancy, coldly, as soon as she perceived where he was going, 'not in there. I'll wait here till Priscilla's ready to come to me. I'm sorry to bring you out of the dance and make myself troublesome.'

'Why, you'll be more comfortable here by yourself,' said the artful Godfrey: 'I'll leave you here till your sister can come.' He spoke in an indifferent tone.

That was an agreeable proposition, and just what Nancy desired; why, then, was she a little hurt that Mr Godfrey should make it? They entered, and she seated herself on a chair against one of the card-tables, as the stiffest and most unapproachable position she could choose.

'Thank you, sir,' she said immediately. 'I needn't give you any more trouble. I'm sorry you've had such an unlucky partner.'

'That's very ill-natured of you,' said Godfrey, standing by her without any sign of intended departure, 'to be sorry you've danced with me.'

'Oh, no, sir, I don't mean to say what's ill-natured at all,' said Nancy, looking distractingly prim and pretty. 'When gentlemen have so many pleasures, one dance can matter but very little.'

'You know that isn't true. You know one dance with you matters more to me than all the other pleasures in the world.'

It was a long, long while since Godfrey had said anything so direct as that, and Nancy was startled. But her instinctive dignity and repugnance to any show of emotion made her sit perfectly still, and only throw a little more decision into her voice as she said –

'No, indeed, Mr Godfrey, that's not known to me, and I have very good reasons for thinking different. But if it's true, I don't wish to hear it.'

'Would you never forgive me, then, Nancy – never think well of me, let what would happen – would you never think the present made amends for the past? Not if I turned a good fellow, and gave up everything you didn't like?'

Godfrey was half conscious that this sudden opportunity of speaking to Nancy alone had driven him beside himself; but blind feeling had got the mastery of his tongue. Nancy really felt much agitated by the possibility Godfrey's words suggested, but this very pressure of emotion that she was in danger of finding too strong for her roused all her power of self-command.

'I should be glad to see a good change in anybody, Mr Godfrey,' she answered, with the slightest discernible difference of tone, 'but it 'ud be better if no change was wanted.'

'You're very hard-hearted, Nancy,' said Godfrey, pettishly. 'You might encourage me to be a better fellow. I'm very miserable – but you've no feeling.'

'I think those have the least feeling that act wrong to begin with,' said Nancy, sending out a flash in spite of herself. Godfrey was delighted with that little flash, and would have liked to go on and make her quarrel with him; Nancy was so exasperatingly quiet and firm. But she was not indifferent to him *yet*.

The entrance of Priscilla, bustling forward and saying, 'Dear heart alive, child, let us look at this gown,' cut off Godfrey's hopes of a quarrel.

'I suppose I must go now,' he said to Priscilla

'It's no matter to me whether you go or stay,' said that frank lady, searching for something in her pocket, with a preoccupied brow.

'Do *you* want me to go?' said Godfrey, looking at Nancy, who was now standing up by Priscilla's order.

'As you like,' said Nancy, trying to recover all her former coldness, and looking carefully at the hem of her gown.

'Then I like to stay,' said Godfrey, with a reckless determination to get as much of this joy as he could tonight, and think nothing of the morrow.

ᘓ TWELVE ᘔ

WHILE GODFREY CASS WAS TAKING DRAUGHTS of forgetfulness from the sweet presence of Nancy, willingly losing all sense of that hidden bond which at other moments galled and fretted him so as to mingle irritation with the very sunshine, Godfrey's wife was walking with slow uncertain steps through the snow-covered Raveloe lanes, carrying her child in her arms.

This journey on New Year's Eve was a premeditated act of vengeance which she had kept in her heart ever since Godfrey, in a fit of passion, had told her he would sooner die than acknowledge her as his wife. There would be a great party at the Red House on New Year's Eve, she knew: her husband would be smiling and smiled upon, hiding *her* existence in the darkest corner of his heart. But she would mar his pleasure: she would go in her dingy rags, with her faded face, once as handsome as the best, with her little child that had its father's hair and eyes, and disclose herself to the Squire as his eldest son's wife. It is seldom that the miserable can help regarding their misery as a wrong inflicted by those who are less miserable. Molly knew that the cause of her dingy rags was not her husband's neglect, but the demon Opium to whom she was enslaved, body and soul, except in the lingering mother's tenderness that refused to give him her hungry child. She knew this well; and yet, in the moments of wretched unbenumbed consciousness, the sense of her want and degradation transformed itself continually into bitterness towards Godfrey. *He* was well off; and if she had her rights she would be well off too. The belief that he repented his marriage, and suffered from it, only aggravated her vindictiveness. Just and self-reproving thoughts do not come to us too thickly, even in the purest air and with the best lessons of heaven and earth; how should those white-winged delicate messengers make their way to Molly's poisoned chamber, inhabited by no higher memories than those of a barmaid's paradise of pink ribbons and gentlemen's jokes?

She had set out at an early hour, but had lingered on the road, inclined by her indolence to believe that if she waited under a warm shed the snow would cease to fall. She had waited longer than she knew, and now that she found herself belated in the snow-hidden ruggedness of the long lanes, even the animation of a vindictive purpose could not keep her spirit from failing. It was seven o'clock, and by this time she was not very far from Raveloe, but she was not familiar enough with those monotonous lanes to know how near she was to her journey's end. She needed comfort, and she knew but one comforter – the familiar demon in her bosom; but she hesitated a moment, after drawing out the black remnant, before she raised it to her lips. In that moment the mother's love pleaded for painful consciousness rather than oblivion – pleaded to be left in aching weariness, rather than to have the encircling arms benumbed so that they could not feel the dear burden. In another moment Molly had flung something away, but it was not the black remnant – it was an empty phial. And she walked on again under the breaking cloud, from which there came now and then the light of a quickly-veiled star, for a freezing wind had sprung up since the snowing had ceased. But she walked always more and more drowsily, and clutched more and more automatically the sleeping child at her bosom.

Slowly the demon was working his will, and cold and weariness were his helpers. Soon she felt nothing but a supreme immediate longing that curtained off all futurity – the longing to lie down and sleep. She had arrived at a spot where her footsteps were no longer checked by a hedgerow, and she had wandered vaguely, unable to distinguish any objects, notwithstanding the wide whiteness around her, and the growing starlight. She sank down against a straggling furze bush, an easy pillow enough; and the bed of snow, too, was soft. She did not feel that the bed was cold, and did not heed whether the child would wake and cry for her. But her arms had not yet relaxed their instinctive clutch; and the little one slumbered on as gently as if it had been rocked in a lace-trimmed cradle.

But the complete torpor came at last: the fingers lost their tension, the arms unbent; then the little head fell away from the bosom, and the blue eyes opened wide on the cold starlight. At first there was a little peevish cry of 'mammy', and an effort to regain the pillowing arm and bosom; but mammy's ear was deaf, and the pillow seemed to be slipping away backward. Suddenly, as the child rolled downward on its mother's knees, all wet with snow, its eyes were caught by a bright glancing light on the white ground, and, with the ready transition of infancy, it was immediately absorbed in watching the bright living thing running towards it, yet never arriving. That bright living thing must be caught; and in an instant the child had slipped on all fours, and held out one little hand to catch the gleam. But the gleam would not be caught in that way, and now the head was held up to see where the cunning gleam came from. It came from a very bright place; and the little one, rising on its legs, toddled through the snow, the old grimy shawl in which it was wrapped trailing behind it, and the queer little bonnet dangling at its back – toddled on to the open door of Silas Marner's cottage, and right up to the warm hearth, where there was a bright fire of logs and sticks, which had thoroughly warmed the old sack (Silas's greatcoat) spread out on the bricks to dry. The little one, accustomed to be left to itself for long hours without notice from its mother, squatted down on the sack, and spread its tiny hands towards the blaze, in perfect contentment, gurgling and making many inarticulate communications to the cheerful fire, like a new-hatched gosling beginning to find itself comfortable. But presently the warmth had a lulling effect, and the little golden head sank down on the old sack, and the blue eyes were veiled by their delicate half-transparent lids.

But where was Silas Marner while this strange visitor had come to his hearth? He was in the cottage, but he did not see the child. During the last few weeks, since he had lost his money, he had contracted the habit of opening his door and looking out from time to time, as if he thought that his money might be somehow coming back to him, or that some trace, some news of it, might be mysteriously on the road, and be caught by the listening ear or the straining eye. It was chiefly at night, when he was not occupied in his loom, that he fell into this repetition of an act for which he could have assigned no definite purpose, and which can hardly be understood except by those who have undergone a bewildering separation from a supremely loved object. In the evening twilight, and later whenever the night was not dark, Silas looked out on that narrow prospect round the Stone-pits, listening and gazing, not with hope, but with mere yearning and unrest.

This morning he had been told by some of his neighbours that it was New Year's Eve, and that he must sit up and hear the old year rung out and the new rung in, because that was good luck, and might bring his money back again. This was only a friendly Raveloe-way of jesting with the half-crazy oddities of a miser, but it had perhaps helped to throw Silas into a more than usually excited state. Since the oncoming of twilight he had opened his door again and again, though only to shut it immediately at seeing all distance veiled by the falling snow. But the last time he opened it the snow had ceased, and the clouds were parting here and there. He stood and listened, and gazed for a long while – there was really something on the road coming towards him then, but he caught no sign of it: and the stillness and the wide trackless snow seemed to narrow his solitude, and touched his yearning with the chill of despair. He went in again, and put his right hand on the latch of the door to close it – but he did not close it: he was arrested, as he had been already since his loss, by the invisible wand of catalepsy, and stood like a graven image, with wide but sightless eyes, holding open his door, powerless to resist either the good or evil that might enter there.

When Marner's sensibility returned, he continued the action which had been arrested, and closed his door, unaware of the chasm in his consciousness, unaware of any intermediate change, except that the light had grown dim, and that he was chilled and faint. He thought he had been too long standing at the door and looking out. Turning towards the hearth, where the two logs had fallen apart, and sent forth only a red uncertain glimmer, he seated himself on his fireside chair, and was stooping to push his logs together, when, to his blurred vision, it seemed as if there were gold on the floor in front of the hearth. Gold! – his own gold – brought back to him as mysteriously as it had been taken away! He felt his heart begin to beat violently, and for a few moments he was unable to stretch out his hand and grasp the restored treasure. The heap of gold seemed to glow and get larger beneath his agitated gaze. He leaned forward at last, and stretched forth his hand; but instead of hard coin with the familiar resisting outline, his fingers encountered soft warm curls. In utter amazement, Silas fell on his knees and bent his head low to examine the marvel: it was a sleeping child – a round, fair thing with soft yellow rings all over its head. Could this be his little sister come back to him in a dream – his little sister whom he had carried about in his arms for a year before she died, when he was a small boy without shoes or stockings? That was the first thought that darted across Silas's blank wonderment. *Was* it a dream? He rose to his feet again, pushed his logs together, and, throwing on some dried leaves and sticks, raised a flame; but the flame did not disperse the vision – it only lit up more distinctly the little round form of the child, and its shabby clothing. It was very much like his little sister. Silas sank into his chair powerless, under the double presence of an inexplicable surprise and a hurrying influx of memories. How and when had the child come in without his knowledge? He had never been beyond the door. But along with that question, and almost thrusting it away, there was a vision of the old home and the old streets leading to Lantern Yard – and within that vision another, of the thoughts which had been present with him in those far-off scenes. The thoughts were strange to him now, like old friendships impossible to revive; and yet he had a dreamy feeling that this child was somehow a message come to him from that far-off life: it stirred fibres that had never been moved in Raveloe – old quiverings of tenderness – old impressions of awe at the presentiment of some Power presiding over his life; for his imagination had not yet extricated itself from the sense of mystery in the child's sudden presence, and had formed no conjectures of ordinary natural means by which the event could have been brought about.

But there was a cry on the hearth: the child had awaked, and Marner stooped to lift it on his knee. It clung round his neck, and burst louder and louder into that mingling of inarticulate cries with 'mammy' by which little children express the bewilderment of waking. Silas pressed it to him, and almost unconsciously uttered sounds of hushing tenderness, while he bethought himself that some of his porridge, which had got cool by the dying fire, would do to feed the child with if it were only warmed up a little.

He had plenty to do through the next hour. The porridge, sweetened with some dry brown sugar from an old store which he had refrained from using for himself, stopped the cries of the little one, and made her lift her blue eyes with a wide quiet gaze at Silas, as he put the spoon into her mouth. Presently she slipped from his knee and began to toddle about, but with a pretty stagger that made Silas jump up and follow her lest she should fall against anything that would hurt her. But she only fell in a sitting posture on the ground, and began to pull at her boots, looking up at him with a crying face as if the boots hurt her. He took her on his knee again, but it was some time before it occurred to Silas's dull bachelor mind that the wet boots were the grievance, pressing on her warm ankles. He got them off with difficulty, and baby was at once happily occupied with the primary mystery of her own toes, inviting Silas, with much chuckling, to consider the mystery too. But the wet boots had at last suggested to Silas that the child had been walking on the snow, and this roused him from his entire oblivion of any ordinary means by which it could have entered or been brought into his house. Under the prompting of this new idea, and without waiting to form conjectures, he raised the child in his arms, and went to the door. As soon as he had opened it, there was the cry of 'mammy' again, which Silas had not heard since the child's first hungry waking. Bending forward, he could just discern the marks made by the little feet on the virgin snow, and he followed their track to the furze bushes. 'Mammy!' the little one cried again and again, stretching itself forward so as almost to escape from Silas's arms, before he himself was aware that there was something more than the bush before him - that there was a human body, with the head sunk low in the furze, and half-covered with the shaken snow.

❧ THIRTEEN ❧

It was after the early supper-time at the Red House, and the entertainment was in that stage when bashfulness itself had passed into easy jollity, when gentlemen, conscious of unusual accomplishments, could at length be prevailed on to dance a hornpipe, and when the Squire preferred talking loudly, scattering snuff, and patting his visitors' backs, to sitting longer at the whist-table - a choice exasperating to uncle Kimble, who, being always volatile in sober business hours, became intense and bitter over cards and brandy, shuffled before his adversary's deal with a glare of suspicion, and turned up a mean trump-card with an air of inexpressible disgust, as if in a world where such things could happen one might as well enter on a course of reckless profligacy. When the evening had advanced to this pitch of freedom and enjoyment, it was usual for the servants, the heavy duties of supper being well over, to get their share of amusement by coming to look on at the dancing; so that the back regions of the house were left in solitude.

There were two doors by which the White Parlour was entered from the hall, and they were both standing open for the sake of air; but the lower one was crowded with the servants and villagers, and only the upper doorway was left free. Bob Cass was figuring in a hornpipe, and his father, very proud of this lithe son, whom he repeatedly declared to be just like himself in his young days in a tone that implied this to be the very highest stamp of juvenile merit, was the centre of a group who had placed themselves opposite the performer, not far from the upper door. Godfrey was standing a little way off, not to admire his brother's dancing, but to keep sight of Nancy, who was seated in the group, near her father. He stood aloof, because he wished to avoid suggesting himself as a subject for the Squire's fatherly jokes in connexion with matrimony and Miss Nancy Lammeter's beauty, which were likely to become more and more explicit. But he had the prospect of dancing with her again when the hornpipe was concluded, and in the meanwhile it was very pleasant to get long glances at her quite unobserved.

But when Godfrey was lifting his eyes from one of those long glances, they encountered an object as startling to him at that moment as if it had been an apparition from the dead. It *was* an apparition from that hidden life which lies, like a dark by-street, behind the goodly ornamented façade that meets the sunlight and the gaze of respectable admirers. It was his own child carried in Silas Marner's arms. That was his instantaneous impression, unaccompanied by doubt, though he had not seen the child for months past; and when the hope was rising that he might possibly be mistaken, Mr Crackenthorp and Mr Lammeter had already advanced to Silas, in astonishment at this strange advent. Godfrey joined them immediately, unable to rest without hearing every word – trying to control himself, but conscious that if any one noticed him, they must see that he was white-lipped and trembling.

But now all eyes at that end of the room were bent on Silas Marner; the Squire himself had risen, and asked angrily, 'How's this? – what's this? – what do you do coming in here in this way?'

'I'm come for the doctor – I want the doctor,' Silas had said, in the first moment, to Mr Crackenthorp.

'Why, what's the matter, Marner?' said the Rector. 'The doctor's here; but say quietly what you want him for.'

'It's a woman,' said Silas, speaking low, and half-breathlessly, just as Godfrey came up. 'She's dead, I think – dead in the snow at the Stone-pits – not far from my door.'

Godfrey felt a great throb: there was one terror in his mind at that moment: it was, that the woman might *not* be dead. That was an evil terror – an ugly inmate to have found a nestling-place in Godfrey's kindly disposition; but no disposition is a security from evil wishes to a man whose happiness hangs on duplicity.

'Hush, hush!' said Mr Crackenthorp. 'Go out into the hall there. I'll fetch the doctor to you. Found a woman in the snow – and thinks she's dead,' he added, speaking low, to the Squire. 'Better say as little about it as possible: it will shock the ladies. Just tell them a poor woman is ill from cold and hunger. I'll go and fetch Kimble.'

By this time, however, the ladies had pressed forward, curious to know what could have brought the solitary linen-weaver there under such strange circumstances, and interested in the pretty child, who, half alarmed and half attracted by the brightness and the numerous company, now frowned and hid her face, now lifted up her head again and looked round placably, until a touch or a coaxing word brought back the frown, and made her bury her face with new determination.

'What child is it?' said several ladies at once, and, among the rest, Nancy Lammeter, addressing Godfrey.

'I don't know – some poor woman's who has been found in the snow, I believe,' was the answer Godfrey wrung from himself with a terrible effort. ('After all, *am* I certain?' he hastened to add, silently, in anticipation of his own conscience.)

'Why, you'd better leave the child here, then, Master Marner,' said good-natured Mrs Kimble, hesitating, however, to take those dingy clothes into contact with her own ornamented satin bodice. 'I'll tell one o' the girls to fetch it.'

'No – no – I can't part with it, I can't let it go,' said Silas, abruptly. 'It's come to me – I've a right to keep it.'

The proposition to take the child from him had come to Silas quite unexpectedly, and his speech, uttered under a strong sudden impulse, was almost like a revelation to himself: a minute before, he had no distinct intention about the child.

'Did you ever hear the like?' said Mrs Kimble, in mild surprise, to her neighbour.

'Now, ladies, I must trouble you to stand aside,' said Mr Kimble, coming from the card-room, in some bitterness at the interruption, but drilled by the long habit of his profession into obedience to unpleasant calls, even when he was hardly sober.

'It's a nasty business turning out now, eh, Kimble?' said the Squire. 'He might ha' gone for your young fellow – the 'prentice, there – what's his name?'

'Might? ay – what's the use of talking about might?' growled uncle Kimble, hastening out with Marner, and followed by Mr Crackenthorp and Godfrey. 'Get me a pair of thick boots, Godfrey, will you? And stay, let somebody run to Winthrop's and fetch Dolly – she's the best woman to get. Ben was here himself before supper; is he gone?'

'Yes, sir, I met him,' said Marner; 'but I couldn't stop to tell him anything, only I said I was going for the doctor, and he said the doctor was at the Squire's. And I made haste and ran, and there was nobody to be seen at the back o' the house, and so I went in to where the company was.'

The child, no longer distracted by the bright light and the smiling women's faces, began to cry and call for 'mammy', though always clinging to Marner, who had apparently won her thorough confidence. Godfrey had come back with the boots, and felt the cry as if some fibre were drawn tight within him.

'I'll go,' he said, hastily, eager for some movement; 'I'll go and fetch the woman – Mrs Winthrop.'

'O, pooh – send somebody else,' said uncle Kimble, hurrying away with Marner.

'You'll let me know if I can be of any use, Kimble,' said Mr Crackenthorp. But the doctor was out of hearing.

Godfrey, too, had disappeared: he was gone to snatch his hat and coat, having just reflection enough to remember that he must not look like a madman; but he rushed out of the house into the snow without heeding his thin shoes.

In a few minutes he was on his rapid way to the Stone-pits by the side of Dolly, who, though feeling that she was entirely in her place encountering cold and snow on an errand of mercy, was much concerned at a young gentleman's getting his feet wet under a like impulse.

'You'd a deal better go back, sir,' said Dolly, with respectful compassion. 'You've no call to catch cold; and I'd ask you if you'd be so good as tell my husband to come, on your way back – he's at the Rainbow, I doubt – if you found him anyway sober enough to be o' use. Or else, there's Mrs Snell 'ud happen send the boy up to fetch and carry, for there may be things wanted from the doctor's.'

'No, I'll stay, now I'm once out – I'll stay outside here,' said Godfrey, when they came opposite Marner's cottage. 'You can come and tell me if I can do anything.'

'Well, sir, you're very good: you've a tender heart,' said Dolly, going to the door.

Godfrey was too painfully preoccupied to feel a twinge of self-reproach at this undeserved praise. He walked up and down, unconscious that he was plunging ankle-deep in snow, unconscious of everything but trembling suspense about what was going on in the cottage, and the effect of each alternative on his future lot. No, not quite unconscious of everything else. Deeper down, and half-smothered by passionate desire and dread, there was the sense that he ought not to be waiting on these alternatives; that he ought to accept the consequences of his deeds, own the miserable wife, and fulfil the claims of the helpless child. But he had not moral courage enough to contemplate that active renunciation of Nancy as possible for him: he had only conscience and heart enough to make him for ever uneasy under the weakness that forbade the renunciation. And at this moment his mind leaped away from all restraint toward the sudden prospect of deliverance from his long bondage.

'Is she dead?' said the voice that predominated over every other within him. 'If she is, I may marry Nancy; and then I shall be a good fellow in future, and have no secrets, and the child – shall be taken care of somehow.' But across that vision came the other possibility – 'She may live, and then it's all up with me.'

Godfrey never knew how long it was before the door of the cottage opened and Mr Kimble came out. He went forward to meet his uncle, prepared to suppress the agitation he must feel, whatever news he was to hear.

'I waited for you, as I'd come so far,' he said, speaking first.

'Pooh, it was nonsense for you to come out: why didn't you send one of the men? There's nothing to be done. She's dead – has been dead for hours, I should say.'

'What sort of woman is she?' said Godfrey, feeling the blood rush to his face.

'A young woman, but emaciated, with long black hair. Some vagrant – quite in rags. She's got a wedding-ring on, however. They must fetch her away to the workhouse tomorrow. Come, come along.'

'I want to look at her,' said Godfrey. 'I think I saw such a woman yesterday. I'll overtake you in a minute or two.'

Mr Kimble went on, and Godfrey turned back to the cottage. He cast only one glance at the dead face on the pillow, which Dolly had smoothed with decent care; but he remembered that last look at his unhappy hated wife so well, that at the end of sixteen years every line in the worn face was present to him when he told the full story of this night.

He turned immediately towards the hearth, where Silas Marner sat lulling the child. She was perfectly quiet now, but not asleep – only soothed by sweet porridge and warmth into that wide-gazing calm which makes us older human beings, with our inward turmoil, feel a certain awe in the presence of a little child, such as we feel before some quiet majesty or beauty in the earth or sky – before a steady glowing planet, or a full-flowered eglantine, or the bending trees over a silent pathway. The wide-open blue eyes looked up at Godfrey's without any uneasiness or sign of recognition: the child could make no visible audible claim on its father; and the father felt a strange mixture of feelings, a conflict of regret and joy, that the pulse of that little heart had no response for the half-jealous yearning in his own, when the blue eyes turned away from him slowly, and fixed themselves on the weaver's queer face, which was bent low down to look at them, while the small hand began to pull Marner's withered cheek with loving disfiguration.

'You'll take the child to the parish tomorrow?' asked Godfrey, speaking as indifferently as he could.

'Who says so?' said Marner, sharply. 'Will they make me take her?'

'Why, you wouldn't like to keep her, should you – an old bachelor like you?'

'Till anybody shows they've a right to take her away from me,' said Marner. 'The mother's dead, and I reckon it's got no father: it's a lone thing – and I'm a lone thing. My money's gone, I don't know where – and this is come from I don't know where. I know nothing – I'm partly mazed.'

'Poor little thing!' said Godfrey. 'Let me give something towards finding it clothes.'

He had put his hand in his pocket and found half-a-guinea, and, thrusting it into Silas's hand, he hurried out of the cottage to overtake Mr Kimble.

'Ah, I see it's not the same woman I saw,' he said, as he came up. 'It's a pretty little child: the old fellow seems to want to keep it; that's strange for a miser like him. But I gave him a trifle to help him out: the parish isn't likely to quarrel with him for the right to keep the child.'

'No; but I've seen the time when I might have quarrelled with him for it myself. It's too late now, though. If the child ran into the fire, your aunt's too fat to overtake it: she could only sit and grunt like an alarmed sow. But what a fool you are, Godfrey, to come out in your dancing shoes and stockings in this way – and you one of the beaux of the evening, and at your own house! What do you mean by such freaks, young fellow? Has Miss Nancy been cruel, and do you want to spite her by spoiling your pumps?'

'O, everything has been disagreeable tonight. I was tired to death of jigging and gallanting, and that bother about the hornpipes. And I'd got to dance with the other Miss Gunn,' said Godfrey, glad of the subterfuge his uncle had suggested to him.

The prevarication and white lies which a mind that keeps itself ambitiously pure is as uneasy under as a great artist under the false touches that no eye detects but his own, are worn as lightly as mere trimmings when once the actions have become a lie.

Godfrey reappeared in the White Parlour with dry feet, and, since the truth must be told, with a sense of relief and gladness that was too strong for painful thoughts to struggle with. For could he not venture now, whenever opportunity offered, to say the tenderest things to Nancy Lammeter – to promise her and himself that he would always be just what she would desire to see him? There was no danger that his dead wife would be recognized: those were not days of active inquiry and wide report; and as for the registry of their marriage, that was a long way off, buried in unturned pages, away from everyone's interest but his own. Dunsey might betray him if he came back; but Dunsey might be won to silence.

And when events turn out so much better for a man than he has had reason to dread, is it not a proof that his conduct has been less foolish and blameworthy than it might otherwise have appeared? When we are treated well, we naturally begin to think that we are not altogether unmeritorious, and that it is only just we should treat ourselves well, and not mar our own good fortune. Where, after all, would be the use of his confessing the past to Nancy Lammeter, and throwing away his happiness? – nay, hers? for he felt some confidence that she loved him. As for the child, he would see that it was cared for: he would never forsake it he; he would do everything but own it. Perhaps it would be just as happy in life without being owned by its father, seeing that nobody could tell how things would turn out, and that – is there any other reason wanted? – well, then, that the father would be much happier without owning the child.

⊂⊃ FOURTEEN ⊂⊃

THERE WAS A PAUPER'S BURIAL THAT week in Raveloe, and up Kench Yard at Batherley it was known that the dark-haired woman with the fair child, who had lately come to lodge there, was gone away again. That was all the express note taken that Molly had disappeared from the eyes of men. But the unwept death which, to the general lot, seemed as trivial as the summer-shed leaf, was charged with the force of destiny to certain human lives that we know of, shaping their joys and sorrows even to the end.

Silas Marner's determination to keep the 'tramp's child' was matter of hardly less surprise and iterated talk in the village than the robbery of his money. That softening of feeling towards him which dated from his misfortune, that merging of suspicion and dislike in a rather contemptuous pity for him as lone and crazy, was now accompanied with a more active sympathy, especially amongst the women. Notable mothers, who knew what it was to keep children 'whole and sweet'; lazy mothers, who knew what it was to be interrupted in folding their arms and scratching their elbows by the mischievous propensities of children just firm on their legs, were equally interested in conjecturing how a lone man would manage with a two-year-old child on his hands, and were equally ready with their suggestions: the notable chiefly telling him what he had better do, and the lazy ones being emphatic in telling him what he would never be able to do.

Among the notable mothers, Dolly Winthrop was the one whose neighbourly offices were the most acceptable to Marner, for they were rendered without any show of bustling instruction. Silas had shown her the half-guinea given to him by Godfrey and had asked her what he should do about getting some clothes for the child.

'Eh, Master Marner,' said Dolly, 'there's no call to buy, no more nor a pair o' shoes; for I've got the little petticoats as Aaron wore five years ago, and it's ill spending the money on them baby-clothes, for the child 'ull grow like grass i' May, bless it – that it will.'

And the same day Dolly brought her bundle, and displayed to Marner, one by one, the tiny garments in their due order of succession, most of them patched and darned, but clean and neat as fresh-sprung herbs. This was the introduction to a great ceremony with soap and water, from which baby came out in new beauty, and sat on Dolly's knee, handling her toes and chuckling and patting her palms together with an air of having made several discoveries about herself, which she communicated by alternate sounds of 'gug-gug-gug', and 'mammy'. The 'mammy' was not a cry of need or uneasiness: Baby had been used to utter it without expecting either tender sound or touch to follow.

'Anybody 'ud think the angils in heaven couldn't be prettier,' said Dolly, rubbing the golden curls and kissing them. 'And to think of its being covered wi' them dirty rags – and the poor mother – froze to death; but there's Them as took care of it, and brought it to your door, Master Marner. The door was open, and it walked in over the snow, like as if it had been a little starved robin. Didn't you say the door was open?'

'Yes,' said Silas, meditatively. 'Yes – the door was open. The money's gone I don't know where, and this is come from I don't know where.'

He had not mentioned to any one his unconsciousness of the child's entrance, shrinking from questions which might lead to the fact he himself suspected – namely, that he had been in one of his trances.

'Ah,' said Dolly, with soothing gravity, 'it's like the night and the morning, and the sleeping and the waking, and the rain and the harvest – one goes and the other comes, and we know nothing how nor where. We may strive and scrat and fend, but it's little we can do arter all – the big things come and go wi' no striving o' our'n – they do, that they do; and I think you're in the right on it to keep the little un, Master Marner, seeing as it's been sent to you, though there's folks as thinks different. You'll happen to be a bit moithered with it while it's so little; but I'll come, and welcome, and see to it for you: I've a bit o' time to spare most days, for when one gets up betimes i' the morning, the clock seems to stan' still tow'rt ten, afore it's time to go about the victual. So, as I say, I'll come and see to the child for you, and welcome.'

'Thank you . . . kindly,' said Silas, hesitating a little. 'I'll be glad if you'll tell me things. But,' he added, uneasily, leaning forward to look at Baby with some jealousy, as she was resting her head backward against Dolly's arm, and eyeing him contentedly from a distance – 'But I want to do things for it myself, else it may get fond o' somebody else, and not fond o' me. I've been used to fending for myself in the house – I can learn, I can learn.'

'Eh, to be sure,' said Dolly, gently. 'I've seen men as are wonderful handy wi' children. The men are awkward and contrairy mostly, God help 'em – but when the drink's out of 'em, they aren't unsensible, though they're bad for leeching and bandaging – so fiery and unpatient. You see this goes first, next the skin,' proceeded Dolly, taking up the little shirt, and putting it on.

'Yes,' said Marner, docilely, bringing his eyes very close, that they might be initiated in the mysteries; whereupon Baby seized his head with both her small arms, and put her lips against his face with purring noises.

'See there,' said Dolly, with a woman's tender tact, 'she's fondest o' you. She wants to go o' your lap, I'll be bound. Go, then: take her, Master Marner; you can put the things on, and then you can say as you've done for her from the first of her coming to you.'

Marner took her on his lap, trembling with an emotion mysterious to himself, at something unknown dawning on his life. Thought and feeling were so confused within him, that if he had tried to give them utterance, he could only have said that the child was come instead of the gold – that the gold had turned into the child. He took the garments from Dolly, and put them on under her teaching; interrupted, of course, by Baby's gymnastics.

'There, then! why, you take to it quite easy, Master Marner,' said Dolly; 'but what shall you do when you're forced to sit in your loom? For she'll get busier and mischievouser every day – she will, bless her. It's lucky as you've got that high hearth i'stead of a grate, for that keeps the fire more out of her reach: but if you've got anything as can be spilt or broke, or as is fit to cut her fingers off, she'll be at it – and it is but right you should know.'

Silas meditated a little while in some perplexity. 'I'll tie her to the leg o' the loom,' he said at last – 'tie her with a good long strip o' something.'

'Well, mayhap that'll do, as it's a little gell, for they're easier persuaded to sit i' one place nor the lads. I know what the lads are; for I've had four – four I've had, God knows – and if you was to take and tie 'em up, they'd make a fighting and a crying as if you was ringing the pigs. But I'll bring you my little chair, and some bits o' red rag and things for her to play wi'; an' she'll sit and chatter to 'em as if they was alive. Eh, if it wasn't a sin to the lads to wish 'em made different, bless 'em, I should ha' been glad for one of 'em to be a little gell; and to think as I could ha' taught her to scour, and mend, and the knitting, and everything. But I can teach 'em this little un, Master Marner, when she gets old enough.'

'But she'll be *my* little un,' said Marner, rather hastily. 'She'll be nobody else's.'

'No, to be sure; you'll have a right to her, if you're a father to her, and bring her up according. But,' added Dolly, coming to a point which she had determined beforehand to touch upon, 'you must bring her up like christened folks's children, and take her to church, and let her learn her catechise, as my little Aaron can say off – the "I believe", and everything, and "hurt nobody by word or deed", – as well as if he was the clerk. That's what you must do, Master Marner, if you'd do the right thing by the orphin child.'

Marner's pale face flushed suddenly under a new anxiety. His mind was too busy trying to give some definite bearing to Dolly's words for him to think of answering her.

'And it's my belief,' she went on, 'as the poor little creature has never been christened, and it's nothing but right as the parson should be spoke to; and if you was no-ways unwilling, I'd talk to Mr Macey about it this very day. For if the child ever went anyways wrong, and you hadn't done your part by it, Master Marner – 'noculation, and everything to save it from harm – it 'ud be a thorn i' your bed for ever o' this side the grave; and I can't think as it 'ud be easy lying down for anybody when they'd got to another world, if they hadn't done their part by the helpless children as come wi'out their own asking.'

Dolly herself was disposed to be silent for some time now, for she had spoken from the depths of her own simple belief, and was much concerned to know whether her words would produce the desired effect on Silas. He was puzzled and anxious, for Dolly's word 'christened' conveyed no distinct meaning to him. He had only heard of baptism, and had only seen the baptism of grown men and women.

'What is it as you mean by "christened"?' he said at last, timidly. 'Won't folks be good to her without it?'

'Dear, dear! Master Marner,' said Dolly, with gentle distress and compassion. 'Had you never no father nor mother as taught you to say your prayers, and as there's good words and good things to keep us from harm?'

'Yes,' said Silas, in a low voice; 'I know a deal about that – used to, used to. But your ways are different: my country was a good way off.' He paused a few moments, and then added, more decidedly, 'But I want to do everything as can be done for the child. And whatever's right for it i' this country, and you think 'ull do it good, I'll act according, if you'll tell me.'

'Well, then, Master Marner,' said Dolly, inwardly rejoiced, 'I'll ask Mr Macey to speak to the parson about it; and you must fix on a name for it, because it must have a name giv' it when it's christened.'

'My mother's name was Hephzibah,' said Silas, 'and my little sister was named after her.'

'Eh, that's a hard name,' said Dolly. 'I partly think it isn't a christened name.'

'It's a Bible name,' said Silas, old ideas recurring.

'Then I've no call to speak again' it,' said Dolly, rather startled by Silas's knowledge on this head: 'but you see I'm no scholard, and I'm slow at catching the words. My husband says I'm allays like as if I was putting the haft for the handle – that's what he says – for he's very sharp, God help him. But it was awk'ard calling your little sister by such a hard name, when you'd got nothing big to say, like wasn't it, Master Marner?'

'We called her Eppie,' said Silas.

'Well, if it was noways wrong to shorten the name, it 'ud be a deal handier. And so I'll go now, Master Marner, and I'll speak about the christening afore dark; and I wish you the best o' luck, and it's my belief as it'll come to you, if you do what's right by the orphin child; – and there's the 'noculation to be seen to; and as to washing its bits o' things, you need look to nobody but me, for I can do 'em wi' one hand when I've got my suds about. Eh, the blessed angil! You'll let me bring my Aaron one o' these days, and he'll show her his little cart as his father's made for him, and the black-and-white pup as he's got a-rearing.'

Baby *was* christened, the rector deciding that a double baptism was the lesser risk to incur; and on this occasion Silas, making himself as clean and tidy as he could, appeared for the first time within the church, and shared in the observances held sacred by his neighbours. He was quite unable, by means of anything he heard or saw, to identify the Raveloe religion with his old faith; if he could at any time in his previous life have done so, it must have been by the aid of a strong feeling ready to vibrate with sympathy, rather than by a comparison of phrases and ideas: and now for long years that feeling had been dormant. He had no distinct idea about the baptism and the church-going, except that Dolly had said it was for the good of the child; and in this way, as the weeks grew to months, the child created fresh and fresh links between his life and the lives from which he had hitherto shrunk continually into narrower isolation. Unlike the gold which needed nothing, and must be worshipped in close-locked solitude – which was hidden away from the daylight, was deaf to the song of birds, and started to no human tones – Eppie was a creature of endless claims and ever-growing desires, seeking and loving sunshine, and living sounds, and living movements; making trial of everything, with trust in new joy, and stirring the human kindness in all eyes that looked on her. The gold had kept his thoughts in an ever-repeated circle, leading to nothing beyond itself; but Eppie was an object compacted of changes and hopes that forced his thoughts onward, and carried them far away from their old eager pacing towards the same blank limit – carried them away to the new things that would come with the coming years, when Eppie would have learned to understand how her father Silas cared for her; and made him look for images of that time in the ties and charities that bound together the families of his neighbours. The gold had asked that he should sit weaving longer and longer, deafened and blinded more and more to all things except the monotony of his loom and the repetition of his web; but Eppie called him away from his weaving, and made him think all its pauses a holiday, re-awakening his senses with her fresh life, even to the old winter-flies that came crawling forth in the early spring sunshine, and warming him into joy because *she* had joy.

And when the sunshine grew strong and lasting, so that the buttercups were thick in the meadows, Silas might be seen in the sunny mid-day, or in the late afternoon when the shadows were lengthening under the hedgerows, strolling out with uncovered head to carry Eppie beyond the Stone-pits to where the flowers grew, till they reached some favourite bank where he could sit down, while Eppie toddled to pluck the flowers, and make remarks to the winged things that murmured happily above the bright petals, calling 'Dad-dad's' attention continually by bringing him the flowers. Then she would turn her ear to some sudden bird-note, and Silas learned to please her by making signs of hushed stillness, that they might listen for the note to come again: so that when it came, she set up her small back and laughed with gurgling triumph. Sitting on the banks in this way, Silas began to look for the once familiar herbs again; and as the leaves, with their unchanged outline and markings, lay on his palm, there was a sense of crowding remembrances from which he turned away timidly, taking refuge in Eppie's little world, that lay lightly on his enfeebled spirit.

As the child's mind was growing into knowledge, his mind was growing into memory: as her life unfolded, his soul, long stupefied in a cold narrow prison, was unfolding too, and trembling gradually into full consciousness.

It was an influence which must gather force with every new year: the tones that stirred Silas's heart grew articulate, and called for more distinct answers; shapes and sounds grew clearer for Eppie's eyes and ears, and there was more that 'Dad-dad' was imperatively required to notice and account for. Also, by the time Eppie was three years old, she developed a fine capacity for mischief, and for devising ingenious ways of being troublesome, which found much exercise, not only for Silas's patience, but for his watchfulness and penetration. Sorely was poor Silas puzzled on such occasions by the incompatible demands of love. Dolly Winthrop told him that punishment was good for Eppie, and that, as for rearing a child without making it tingle a little in soft and safe places now and then, it was not to be done.

'To be sure, there's another thing you might do, Master Marner,' added Dolly, meditatively: 'you might shut her up once i' the coal-hole. That was what I did wi' Aaron; for I was that silly wi' the youngest lad, as I could never bear to smack him. Not as I could find i' my heart to let him stay i' the coal-hole more nor a minute, but it was enough to colly him all over, so as he must be new washed and dressed, and it was as good as a rod to him – that was. But I put it upo' your conscience, Master Marner, as there's one of 'em you must choose – ayther smacking or the coal-hole – else she'll get so masterful, there'll be no holding her.'

Silas was impressed with the melancholy truth of this last remark; but his force of mind failed before the only two penal methods open to him, not only because it was painful to him to hurt Eppie, but because he trembled at a moment's contention with her, lest she should love him the less for it. Let even an affectionate Goliath get himself tied to a small tender thing, dreading to hurt it by pulling, and dreading still more to snap the cord, and which of the two, pray, will be master? It was clear that Eppie, with her short toddling steps, must lead father Silas a pretty dance on any fine morning when circumstances favoured mischief.

For example. He had wisely chosen a broad strip of linen as a means of fastening her to his loom when he was busy: it made a broad belt round her waist, and was long enough to allow of her reaching the truckle-bed and sitting down on it, but not long enough for her to attempt any dangerous climbing. One bright summer's morning Silas had been more engrossed than usual in 'setting up' a new piece of work, an occasion on which his scissors were in requisition. These scissors, owing to an especial warning of Dolly's, had been kept carefully out of Eppie's reach; but the click of them had had a peculiar attraction for her ear, and, watching the results of that click, she had derived the philosophic lesson that the same cause would produce the same effect. Silas had seated himself in his loom, and the noise of weaving had begun; but he had left his scissors on a ledge which Eppie's arm was long enough to reach; and now, like a small mouse, watching her opportunity, she stole quietly from her corner, secured the scissors, and toddled to the bed again, setting up her back as a mode of concealing the fact. She had a distinct intention as to the use of the scissors; and having cut the linen strip in a jagged but effectual manner, in two moments she had run out at the open door where the sunshine was inviting her, while poor Silas believed her to be a better child than usual. It was not until he happened to need his scissors that the terrible fact burst upon him: Eppie had run out by herself – had perhaps fallen into the Stone-pit. Silas, shaken by the worst fear that could have befallen him, rushed out, calling 'Eppie!' and ran eagerly about the unen-closed space, exploring the dry cavities into which she might have fallen, and then gazing with questioning dread at the smooth red surface of the water. The cold drops stood on his brow. How long had she been out? There was one hope – that she had crept through the stile and got into the fields, where he habitually took her to stroll. But the grass was high in the meadow, and there was no descrying her, if she were there, except by a close search that would be a trespass on Mr Osgood's crop. Still, that misdemeanour must be committed; and poor Silas, after peering all round the hedgerows, traversed the grass, beginning with perturbed vision to see Eppie behind every group of red sorrel, and to see her moving always farther off as he approached. The meadow was searched in vain; and he got over the stile into the next field, looking with dying hope towards a small pond which was now reduced to its summer shallowness, so as to leave a wide margin of good adhesive mud. Here, however, sat Eppie, discoursing cheerfully to her own small boot, which she was using as a bucket to convey the water into a deep hoof-mark, while her little naked foot was planted comfortably on a cushion of olive-green mud. A red-headed calf was observing her with alarmed doubt through the opposite hedge.

Here was clearly a case of aberration in a christened child which demanded severe treatment; but Silas, overcome with convulsive joy at finding his treasure again, could do nothing but snatch her up, and cover her with half-sobbing kisses. It was not until he had carried her home, and had begun to think of the necessary washing, that he recollected the need that he should punish Eppie, and 'make her remember'. The idea that she might run away again and come to harm, gave him unusual resolution, and for the first time he determined to try the coal-hole – a small closet near the hearth.

'Naughty, naughty Eppie,' he suddenly began, holding her on his knee, and pointing to her muddy feet and clothes – 'naughty to cut with the scissors and run away. Eppie must go into the coal-hole for being naughty. Daddy must put her in the coal-hole.'

He half-expected that this would be shock enough, and that Eppie would begin to cry. But instead of that, she began to shake herself on his knee, as if the proposition opened a pleasing novelty. Seeing that he must proceed to extremities, he put her into the coal-hole, and held the door closed, with a trembling sense that he was using a strong measure. For a moment there was silence, but then came a little cry, 'Opy, opy!' and Silas let her out again, saying, 'Now Eppie 'ull never be naughty again, else she must go into the coal-hole – a black naughty place.'

The weaving must stand still a long while this morning, for now Eppie must be washed, and have clean clothes on; but it was to be hoped that this punishment would have a lasting effect, and save time in future – though, perhaps, it would have been better if Eppie had cried more.

In half an hour she was clean again, and Silas having turned his back to see what he could do with the linen band, threw it down again, with the reflection that Eppie would be good without fastening for the rest of the morning. He turned round again, and was going to place her in her little chair near the loom, when she peeped out at him with black face and hands again, and said, 'Eppie in de toal-hole!'

This total failure of the coal-hole discipline shook Silas's belief in the efficacy of punishment. 'She'd take it all for fun,' he observed to Dolly, 'if I didn't hurt her, and that I can't do, Mrs Winthrop. If she makes me a bit o' trouble, I can bear it. And she's got no tricks but what she'll grow out of.'

'Well, that's partly true, Master Marner,' said Dolly, sympathetically; 'and if you can't bring your mind to frighten her off touching things, you must do what you can to keep 'em out of her way. That's what I do wi' the pups as the lads are allays a-rearing. They *will* worry and gnaw – worry and gnaw they will, if it was one's Sunday cap as hung anywhere so as they could drag it. They know no difference, God help 'em; it's the pushing o' the teeth as sets 'em on, that's what it is.'

So Eppie was reared without punishment, the burden of her misdeeds being borne vicariously by father Silas. The stone hut was made a soft nest for her, lined with downy patience: and also in the world that lay beyond the stone hut she knew nothing of frowns and denials.

Notwithstanding the difficulty of carrying her and his yarn or linen at the same time, Silas took her with him in most of his journeys to the farm-houses, unwilling to leave her behind at Dolly Winthrop's, who was always ready to take care of her; and little curly-headed Eppie, the weaver's child, became an object of interest at several outlying home-steads, as well as in the village. Hitherto he had been treated very much as if he had been a useful gnome or brownie – a queer and unaccountable creature, who must necessarily be looked at with wondering curiosity and repulsion, and with whom one would be glad to make all greetings and bargains as brief as possible, but who must be dealt with in a pro-pitiatory way, and occasionally have a present of pork or garden-stuff to carry home with him, seeing that without him there was no getting the yarn woven. But now Silas met with open smiling faces and cheerful questioning, as a person whose satisfactions and difficulties could be understood. Everywhere he must sit a little and talk about the child, and words of interest were always ready for him: 'Ah, Master Marner, you'll be lucky if she takes the measles soon and easy!' – or, 'Why, there isn't many lone men 'ud ha' been wishing to take up with a little un like that:

but I reckon the weaving makes you handier than men as do out-door work – you're partly as handy as a woman, for weaving comes next to spinning.' Elderly masters and mistresses, seated observantly in large kitchen arm-chairs, shook their heads over the difficulties attendant on rearing children, felt Eppie's round arms and legs, and pronounced them remarkably firm, and told Silas that, if she turned out well (which, however, there was no telling), it would be a fine thing for him to have a steady lass to do for him when he got helpless. Servant maidens were fond of carrying her out to look at the hens and chickens, or to see if any cherries could be shaken down in the orchard; and the small boys and girls approached her slowly, with cautious movement and steady gaze like little dogs face to face with one of their own kind, till attraction had reached the point at which the soft lips were put out for a kiss. No child was afraid of approaching Silas when Eppie was near him: there was no repulsion around him now, either for young or old; for the little child had come to link him once more with the whole world. There was love between him and the child that blent them into one, and there was love between the child and the world – from men and women with parental looks and tones, to the red lady-birds and the round pebbles.

Silas began now to think of Raveloe life entirely in relation to Eppie: she must have everything that was a good in Raveloe; and he listened docilely, that he might come to understand better what this life was, from which, for fifteen years, he had stood aloof as from a strange thing, where-with he could have no communion: as some man who has a precious plant to which he would give a nurturing home in a new soil, thinks of the rain, and the sunshine, and all influences, in relation to his nursling, and asks industriously for all knowledge that will help him to satisfy the wants of the searching roots, or to guard leaf and bud from invading harm. The disposition to hoard had been utterly crushed at the very first by the loss of his long-stored gold: the coins he earned afterwards seemed as irrelevant as stones brought to complete a house suddenly buried by an earthquake; the sense of bereavement was too heavy upon him for the old thrill of satisfaction to arise again at the touch of the newly-earned coin. And now something had come to replace his hoard which gave a growing purpose to the earnings, drawing his hope and joy continually onward beyond the money.

In old days there were angels who came and took men by the hand and led them away from the city of destruction. We see no white-winged angels now. But yet men are led away from threatening destruction: a hand is put into theirs, which leads them forth gently towards a calm and bright land, so that they look no more backward; and the hand may be a little child's.

◌ぅ FIFTEEN ◌っ

THERE WAS ONE PERSON, AS YOU will believe, who watched with keener though more hidden interest than any other, the prosperous growth of Eppie under the weaver's care. He dared not do anything that would imply a stronger interest in a poor man's adopted child than could be expected from the kindliness of the young Squire, when a chance meeting suggested a little present to a simple old fellow whom others noticed with goodwill; but he told himself that the time would come when he might do something towards furthering the welfare of his daughter without incurring suspicion. Was he very uneasy in the mean time at his inability to give his daughter her birthright? I cannot say that he was. The child was being.taken care of, and would very likely be happy, as people in humble stations often were – happier, perhaps, than those who are brought up in luxury.

That famous ring that pricked its owner when he forgot duty and followed desire – I wonder if it pricked very hard when he set out on the chase, or whether it pricked but lightly then, and only pierced to the quick when the chase had long been ended, and hope, folding her wings, looked backward and became regret?

Godfrey Cass's cheek and eye were brighter than ever now. He was so undivided in his aims, that he seemed like a man of firmness. No Dunsey had come back: people had made up their minds that he was gone for a soldier, or gone 'out of the country', and no one cared to be specific in their inquiries on a subject delicate to a respectable family. Godfrey had ceased to see the shadow of Dunsey across his path; and the path now lay straight forward to the accomplishment of his best, longest-cherished wishes. Everybody said Mr Godfrey had taken the right turn; and it was pretty clear what would be the end of things, for there were not many days in the week that he was not seen riding to the Warrens. Godfrey himself, when he was asked jocosely if the day had been fixed, smiled with the pleasant consciousness of a lover who could say 'yes', if he liked. He felt a reformed man, delivered from temptation; and the vision of his future life seemed to him as a promised land for which he had no cause to fight. He saw himself with all his happiness centred on his own hearth, while Nancy would smile on him as he played with the children.

And that other child, not on the hearth – he would not forget it; he would see that it was well provided for. That was a father's duty.

PART TWO

◌ SIXTEEN ◌

IT WAS A BRIGHT AUTUMN SUNDAY, sixteen years after Silas Marner had found his new treasure on the hearth. The bells of the old Raveloe church were ringing the cheerful peal which told that the morning service was ended; and out of the arched doorway in the tower came slowly, retarded by friendly greetings and questions, the richer parishioners who had chosen this bright Sunday morning as eligible for church-going. It was the rural fashion of that time for the more important members of the congregation to depart first, while their humbler neighbours waited and looked on, stroking their bent heads or dropping their curtsies to any large ratepayer who turned to notice them.

Foremost among these advancing groups of well-clad people, there are some whom we shall recognize, in spite of Time, who has laid his hand on them all. The tall blond man of forty is not much changed in feature from the Godfrey Cass of six-and-twenty: he is only fuller in flesh, and has only lost the indefinable look of youth – a loss which is marked even when the eye is undulled and the wrinkles are not yet come. Perhaps the pretty woman, not much younger than he, who is leaning on his arm, is more changed than her husband: the lovely bloom that used to be always on her cheek now comes but fitfully, with the fresh morning air or with some strong surprise; yet to all who love human faces best for what they tell of human experience, Nancy's beauty has a heightened interest. Often the soul is ripened into fuller goodness while age has spread an ugly film, so that mere glances can never divine the preciousness of the fruit. But the years have not been so cruel to Nancy. The firm yet placid mouth, the clear veracious glance of the brown eyes, speak now of a nature that has been tested and has kept its highest qualities; and even the costume, with its dainty neatness and purity, has more significance now the coquetries of youth can have nothing to do with it.

Mr and Mrs Godfrey Cass (any higher title has died away from Raveloe lips since the old Squire was gathered to his fathers and his inheritance was divided) have turned round to look for the tall aged man and the plainly dressed woman who are a little behind – Nancy having observed that they must wait for 'father and Priscilla' – and now they all turn into a narrower path leading across the churchyard to a small gate opposite the Red House. We will not follow them now; for may there not be some others in this departing congregation whom we should like to see again –

some of those who are not likely to be handsomely clad, and whom we may not recognize so easily as the master and mistress of the Red House?

But it is impossible to mistake Silas Marner. His large brown eyes seem to have gathered a longer vision, as is the way with eyes that have been short-sighted in early life, and they have a less vague, a more answering gaze; but in everything else one sees signs of a frame much enfeebled by the lapse of the sixteen years. The weaver's bent shoulders and white hair give him almost the look of advanced age, though he is not more than five-and-fifty; but there is the freshest blossom of youth close by his side – a blond dimpled girl of eighteen, who has vainly tried to chastise her curly auburn hair into smoothness under her brown bonnet: the hair ripples as obstinately as a brooklet under the March breeze, and the little ringlets burst away from the restraining comb behind and show themselves below the bonnet-crown. Eppie cannot help being rather vexed about her hair, for there is no other girl in Raveloe who has hair at all like it, and she thinks hair ought to be smooth. She does not like to be blameworthy even in small things: you see how neatly her prayer-book is folded in her spotted handkerchief.

That good-looking young fellow, in a new fustian suit, who walks behind her, is not quite sure upon the question of hair in the abstract, when Eppie puts it to him, and thinks that perhaps straight hair is the best in general, but he doesn't want Eppie's hair to be different. She surely divines that there is some one behind her who is thinking about her very particularly, and mustering courage to come to her side as soon as they are out in the lane, else why should she look rather shy, and take care not to turn away her head from her father Silas, to whom she keeps murmuring little sentences as to who was at church, and who was not at church, and how pretty the red mountain-ash is over the Rectory wall?

'I wish *we* had a little garden, father, with double daisies in, like Mrs Winthrop's,' said Eppie, when they were out in the lane; 'only they say it 'ud take a deal of digging and bringing fresh soil – and you couldn't do that, could you, father? Anyhow, I shouldn't like you to do it, for it 'ud be too hard work for you.'

'Yes, I could do it, child, if you want a bit o' garden: these long evenings, I could work at taking in a little bit o' the waste, just enough for a root or two o' flowers for you; and again, i' the morning, I could have a turn wi' the spade before I sat down to the loom. Why didn't you tell me before as you wanted a bit o' garden?'

'*I* can dig it for you, Master Marner,' said the young man in fustian, who was now by Eppie's side, entering into the conversation without the trouble of formalities. 'It'll be play to me after I've done my day's work, or any odd bits o' time when the work's slack. And I'll bring you some soil from Mr Cass's garden – he'll let me, and willing.'

'Eh, Aaron, my lad, are you there?' said Silas; 'I wasn't aware of you; for when Eppie's talking o' things, I see nothing but what she's a-saying.

Well, if you could help me with the digging, we might get her a bit o' garden all the sooner.'

'Then, if you think well and good,' said Aaron, 'I'll come to the Stone-pits this afternoon, and we'll settle what land's to be taken in, and I'll get up an hour earlier i' the morning, and begin on it.'

'But not if you don't promise me not to work at the hard digging, father,' said Eppie. 'For I shouldn't ha' said anything about it,' she added, half-bashfully half-roguishly, 'only Mrs Winthrop said as Aaron 'ud be so good, and – '

'And you might ha' known it without mother telling you,' said Aaron. 'And Master Marner knows too, I hope, as I'm able and willing to do a turn o' work for him, and he won't do me the unkindness to anyways take it out o' my hands.'

'There, now, father, you won't work in it till it's all easy,' said Eppie, 'and you and me can mark out the beds, and make holes and plant the roots. It'll be a deal livelier at the Stone-pits when we've got some flowers, for I always think the flowers can see us and know what we're talking about. And I'll have a bit o' rosemary, and bergamot, and thyme, because they're so sweet-smelling; but there's no lavender; only in the gentlefolks' gardens, I think.'

'That's no reason why you shouldn't have some,' said Aaron, 'for I can bring you slips of anything; I'm forced to cut no end of 'em when I'm gardening, and throw 'em away mostly. There's a big bed o' lavender at the Red House: the missis is very fond of it.'

'Well,' said Silas, gravely, 'so as you don't make free for us, or ask for anything as is worth much at the Red House: for Mr Cass's been so good to us, and built us up the new end o' the cottage, and given us beds and things, as I couldn't abide to be imposin' for garden-stuff or anything else.'

'No, no, there's no imposin',' said Aaron; 'there's never a garden in all the parish but what there's endless waste in it for want o' somebody as could use everything up. It's what I think to myself sometimes, as there need nobody run short o' victuals if the land was made the most on, and there was never a morsel but what could find its way to a mouth. It sets one thinking o' that – gardening does. But I must go back now, else mother 'ull be in trouble as I aren't there.'

'Bring her with you this afternoon, Aaron,' said Eppie; 'I shouldn't like to fix about the garden, and her not know everything from the first – should *you*, father?'

'Ay, bring her if you can, Aaron,' said Silas; 'she's sure to have a word to say as'll help us to set things on their right end.'

Aaron turned back up the village, while Silas and Eppie went on up the lonely sheltered lane.

'O daddy!' she began, when they were in privacy, clasping and squeezing Silas's arm, and skipping round to give him an energetic kiss. 'My little old daddy! I'm so glad. I don't think I shall want anything else when we've got a little garden; and I knew Aaron would dig it for us,' she went on with roguish triumph – 'I knew that very well.'

'You're a deep little puss, you are,' said Silas, with the mild passive happiness of love-crowned age in his face; 'but you'll make yourself fine and beholden to Aaron.'

'O no, I shan't,' said Eppie, laughing and frisking; 'he likes it.'

'Come, come, let me carry your prayer-book, else you'll be dropping it, jumping i' that way.'

Eppie was now aware that her behaviour was under observation, but it was only the observation of a friendly donkey, browsing with a log fastened to his foot – a meek donkey, not scornfully critical of human trivialities, but thankful to share in them, if possible, by getting his nose scratched; and Eppie did not fail to gratify him with her usual notice, though it was attended with the inconvenience of his following them, painfully, up to the very door of their home.

But the sound of a sharp bark inside, as Eppie put the key in the door, modified the donkey's views, and he limped away again without bidding. The sharp bark was the sign of an excited welcome that was awaiting them from a knowing brown terrier, who, after dancing at their legs in a hysterical manner, rushed with a worrying noise at a tortoise-shell kitten under the loom, and then rushed back with a sharp bark again, as much as to say, 'I have done my duty by this feeble creature, you perceive'; while the lady-mother of the kitten sat sunning her white bosom in the window, and looked round with a sleepy air of expecting caresses, though she was not going to take any trouble for them.

The presence of this happy animal life was not the only change which had come over the interior of the stone cottage. There was no bed now in the living-room, and the small space was well filled with decent furniture, all bright and clean enough to satisfy Dolly Winthrop's eye. The oaken table and three-cornered oaken chair were hardly what was likely to be seen in so poor a cottage: they had come, with the beds and other things, from the Red House; for Mr Godfrey Cass, as every one said in the village, did very kindly by the weaver; and it was nothing but right a man should be looked on and helped by those who could afford it, when he had brought up an orphan child, and been father and mother to her – and had lost his money too, so as he had nothing but what he worked for week by week, and when the weaving was going down too – for there was less and less flax spun – and Master Marner was none so young. Nobody was jealous of the weaver, for he was regarded as an exceptional person, whose claims on neighbourly help were not to be matched in Raveloe. Any superstition that remained concerning him had taken an entirely new colour; and Mr Macey, now a very feeble old man of fourscore and six, never seen except in his chimney-corner or sitting in the sunshine at his door-sill, was of opinion that when a man had done what Silas had done by an orphan child, it was a sign that his money would come to light again, or leastwise that the robber would be made to answer for it – for, as Mr Macey observed of himself, his faculties were as strong as ever.

Silas sat down now and watched Eppie with a satisfied gaze as she spread the clean cloth, and set on it the potato-pie, warmed up slowly in a safe Sunday fashion, by being put into a dry pot over a slowly-dying fire, as the best substitute for an oven. For Silas would not consent to have a grate and oven added to his conveniences: he loved the old brick hearth as he had loved his brown pot – and was it not there when he had found Eppie? The gods of the hearth exist for us still; and let all new faith be tolerant of that fetishism, lest it bruise its own roots.

Silas ate his dinner more silently than usual, soon laying down his knife and fork, and watching half-abstractedly Eppie's play with Snap and the cat, by which her own dining was made rather a lengthy business. Yet it was a sight that might well arrest wandering thoughts: Eppie, with the rippling radiance of her hair and the whiteness of her rounded chin and throat set off by the dark-blue cotton gown, laughing merrily as the kitten held on with her four claws to one shoulder, like a design for a jug-handle, while Snap on the right hand and Puss on the other put up their paws towards a morsel which she held out of the reach of both – Snap occasionally desisting in order to remonstrate with the cat by a cogent worrying growl on the greediness and futility of her conduct; till Eppie relented, caressed them both, and divided the morsel between them.

But at last Eppie, glancing at the clock, checked the play, and said, 'O daddy, you're wanting to go into the sunshine to smoke your pipe. But I must clear away first, so as the house may be tidy when godmother comes. I'll make haste – I won't be long.'

Silas had taken to smoking a pipe daily during the last two years, having been strongly urged to it by the sages of Raveloe, as a practice 'good for the fits'; and this advice was sanctioned by Dr Kimble, on the ground that it was as well to try what could do no harm – a principle which was made to answer for a great deal of work in that gentleman's medical practice. Silas did not highly enjoy smoking, and often wondered how his neighbours could be so fond of it; but a humble sort of acquiescence in what was held to be good, had become a strong habit of that new self which had been developed in him since he had found Eppie on his hearth: it had been the only clew his bewildered mind could hold by in cherishing this young life that had been sent to him out of the darkness into which his gold had departed. By seeking what was needful for Eppie, by sharing the effect that everything produced on her, he had himself come to appropriate the forms of custom and belief which were the mould of Raveloe life; and as, with reawakening sensibilities, memory also reawakened, he had begun to ponder over the elements of his old faith, and blend them with his new impressions, till he recovered a consciousness of unity between his past and present. The sense of presiding goodness and the human trust which come with all pure peace and joy had given him a dim impression that there had been some error, some mistake, which had thrown that dark shadow over the days of his best years; and as it grew more and more easy to him to open his mind to Dolly Winthrop, he gradually communicated to her all he could describe of his early life. The communication was necessarily a slow and difficult process, for Silas's meagre power of explanation was not aided by any readiness of interpretation in Dolly, whose narrow outward experience gave her no key to strange customs, and made every novelty a source of wonder that arrested them at every step of the narrative. It was only by fragments, and at intervals which left Dolly time to revolve what she had heard till it acquired some familiarity for her, that Silas at last arrived at the climax of the sad story – the drawing of lots, and its false testimony concerning him; and this had to be repeated in several interviews, under new questions on her part as to the nature of this plan for detecting the guilty and clearing the innocent.

'And yourn's the same Bible, you're sure o' that, Master Marner – the Bible as you brought wi' you from that country – it's the same as what they've got at church, and what Eppie's a-learning to read in?'

'Yes,' said Silas, 'every bit the same; and there's drawing o' lots in the Bible, mind you,' he added in a lower tone.

'O dear, dear,' said Dolly in a grieved voice, as if she were hearing an unfavourable report of a sick man's case. She was silent for some minutes; at last she said –

'There's wise folks, happen, as know how it all is; the parson knows, I'll be bound; but it takes big words to tell them things, and such as poor folks can't make much out on. I can never rightly know the meaning o' what I hear at church, only a bit here and there, but I know it's good words – I do. But what lies upo' your mind – it's this, Master Marner: as, if Them above had done the right thing by you, They'd never ha' let you be turned out for a wicked thief when you was innicent.'

'Ah!' said Silas, who had now come to understand Dolly's phraseology, 'that was what fell on me like as if it had been red-hot iron; because, you see, there was nobody as cared for me or clave to me above nor below. And him as I'd gone out and in wi' for ten year and more, since when we was lads and went halves – mine own famil'ar friend, in whom I trusted, had lifted up his heel again' me, and worked to ruin me.'

'Eh, but he was a bad un – I can't think as there's another such,' said Dolly. 'But I'm o'ercome, Master Marner; I'm like as if I'd waked and didn't know whether it was night or morning. I feel somehow as sure as I do when I've laid something up though I can't justly put my hand on it, as there was a rights in what happened to you, if one could but make it out; and you'd no call to lose heart as you did. But we'll talk on it again; for sometimes things come into my head when I'm leeching or poulticing, or such, as I could never think on when I was sitting still.'

Dolly was too useful a woman not to have many opportunities of illumination of the kind she alluded to, and she was not long before she recurred to the subject.

'Master Marner,' she said, one day that she came to bring home Eppie's washing, 'I've been sore puzzled for a good bit wi' that trouble o' yourn and the drawing o' lots; and it got twisted back'ards and for'ards, as I didn't know which end to lay hold on. But it come to me all clear like, that night when I was sitting up wi' poor Bessy Fawkes, as is dead and left her children behind, God help 'em – it come to me as clear as daylight; but whether I've got hold on it now, or can anyways bring it to my tongue's end, that I don't know. For I've often a deal inside me as 'll niver come out; and for what you talk o' your folks in your old country niver saying prayers by heart nor saying 'em out of a book, they must be wonderful cliver; for if I didn't know "Our Father," and little bits o' good words as I can carry out o' church wi' me, I might down o' my knees every night, but nothing could I say.'

'But you can mostly say something as I can make sense on, Mrs Winthrop,' said Silas.

'Well, then, Master Marner, it come to me summat like this: I can make nothing o' the drawing o' lots and the answer coming wrong; it 'ud mayhap take the parson to tell that, and he could only tell us i' big words. But what come to me as clear as the daylight, it was when I was troubling over poor Bessy Fawkes, and it allays comes into my head when I'm sorry for folks, and feel as I can't do a power to help 'em, not if I was to get up i' the middle o' the night – it comes into my head as Them above has got a deal tenderer heart nor what I've got – for I can't be anyways better nor Them as made me; and if anything looks hard to me, it's because there's things I don't know on; and for the matter o' that, there may be plenty o' things I don't know on, for it's little as I know – that it is. And so, while I was thinking o' that, you come into my mind, Master Marner, and it all come pouring in: – if *I* felt i' my inside what was the right and just thing by you, and them as prayed and drawed the lots, all but that wicked un, if *they*'d ha' done the right thing by you if they could, isn't there Them as was at the making on us, and knows better and has a better will? And that's all as ever I can be sure on, and everything else is a big puzzle to me when I think on it. For there was the fever come and took off them as were full-growed, and left the helpless children; and there's the breaking o' limbs; and them as 'ud do right and be sober have to suffer by them as are contrairy – eh, there's trouble i' this world, and there's things as we can niver make out the rights on. And all as we've got to do is to trusten, Master Marner – to do the right thing as fur as we know, and to trusten. For if us as knows so little can see a bit o' good and rights, we may be sure as there's a good and a rights bigger nor what we can know – I feel it i' my own inside as it must be so. And if you could but ha' gone on trustening, Master Marner, you wouldn't ha' run away from your fellow creaturs and been so lone.'

'Ah, but that 'ud ha' been hard,' said Silas, in an undertone; 'it 'ud ha' been hard to trusten then.'

'And so it would,' said Dolly, almost with compunction; 'them things are easier said nor done; and I'm partly ashamed o' talking.'

'Nay, nay,' said Silas, 'you're i' the right, Mrs Winthrop – you're i' the right. There's good i' this world – I've a feeling o' that now; and it makes a man feel as there's a good more nor he can see, i' spite o' the trouble and the wickedness. That drawing o' the lots is dark; but the child was sent to me: there's dealings with us – there's dealings.'

This dialogue took place in Eppie's earlier years, when Silas had to part with her for two hours every day, that she might learn to read at the dame school, after he had vainly tried himself to guide her in that first step to learning. Now that she was grown up, Silas had often been led, in those moments of quiet outpouring which come to people who live together in perfect love, to talk with *her* too of the past, and how and why he had lived a lonely man until she had been sent to him. For it would have been impossible for him to hide from Eppie that she was not his own child; even if the most delicate reticence on the point could have been expected from Raveloe gossips in her presence, her own questions about her mother could not have been parried, as she grew up, without that complete shrouding of the past which would have made a painful barrier between their minds. So Eppie had long known how her mother had died on the snowy ground, and how she herself had been found on the hearth by father Silas, who had taken her golden curls for his lost guineas brought back to him. The tender and peculiar love with which Silas had reared her in almost inseparable companionship with himself, aided by the seclusion of their dwelling, had preserved her from the lowering influences of the village talk and habits, and had kept her mind in that freshness which is sometimes falsely supposed to be an invariable attribute of rusticity. Perfect love has a breath of poetry which can exalt the relations of the least-instructed human beings; and this breath of poetry had surrounded Eppie from the time when she had followed the bright gleam that beckoned her to Silas's hearth; so that it is not surprising if, in other things besides her delicate prettiness, she was not quite a common village maiden, but had a touch of refinement and fervour which came from no other teaching than that of tenderly-nurtured unvitiated feeling. She was too childish and simple for her imagination to rove into questions about her unknown father; for a long while it did not even occur to her that she must have had a father; and the first time that the idea of her mother having had a husband presented itself to her, was when Silas showed her the wedding-ring which had been taken from the wasted finger, and had been carefully preserved by him in a little lackered box shaped like a shoe. He delivered this box into Eppie's charge when she had grown up, and she often opened it to look at the ring: but still she thought hardly at all about the father of whom it was the symbol. Had she not a father very close to her, who loved her better than any real fathers in the village seemed to love their daughters? On the contrary, who her mother was, and how she came to die in that forlornness, were questions that often pressed on Eppie's mind. Her knowledge of Mrs Winthrop, who was her nearest friend next to Silas, made her feel that a mother must be very precious; and she had again and again asked Silas to tell her how her mother looked, whom she was like, and how he had found her against the furze bush, led towards it by the little footsteps and the outstretched arms. The furze bush was there still; and this afternoon, when Eppie came out with Silas into the sunshine, it was the first object that arrested her eyes and thoughts.

'Father,' she said, in a tone of gentle gravity, which sometimes came like a sadder, slower cadence across her playfulness, 'we shall take the furze bush into the garden; it'll come into the corner, and just against it I'll put snowdrops and crocuses, 'cause Aaron says they won't die out, but'll always get more and more.'

'Ah, child,' said Silas, always ready to talk when he had his pipe in his hand, apparently enjoying the pauses more than the puffs, 'it wouldn't do to leave out the furze bush; and there's nothing prettier to my thinking, when it's yellow with flowers. But it's just come into my head what we're to do for a fence – mayhap Aaron can help us to a thought; but a fence we must have, else the donkeys and things 'ull come and trample everything down. And fencing's hard to be got at, by what I can make out.'

'O, I'll tell you, daddy,' said Eppie, clasping her hands suddenly, after a minute's thought. 'There's lots o' loose stones about, some of 'em not big, and we might lay 'em atop of one another, and make a wall. You and me could carry the smallest, and Aaron 'ud carry the rest – I know he would.'

'Eh, my precious un,' said Silas, 'there isn't enough stones to go all round; and as for you carrying, why wi' your little arms you couldn't carry a stone no bigger than a turnip. You're dillicate made, my dear,' he added, with a tender intonation – 'that's what Mrs Winthrop says.'

'O, I'm stronger than you think, daddy,' said Eppie; 'and if there wasn't stones enough to go all round, why they'll go part o' the way, and then it'll be easier to get sticks and things for the rest. See here, round the big pit, what a many stones!'

She skipped forward to the pit, meaning to lift one of the stones and exhibit her strength, but she started back in surprise.

'O, father, just come and look here,' she exclaimed – 'come and see how the water's gone down since yesterday. Why, yesterday the pit was ever so full!'

'Well, to be sure,' said Silas, coming to her side. 'Why, that's the draining they've begun on, since harvest, i' Mr Osgood's fields, I reckon. The foreman said to me the other day, when I passed by 'em, "Master Marner," he said, "I shouldn't wonder if we lay your bit o' waste as dry as a bone." It was Mr Godfrey Cass, he said, had gone into the draining: he'd been taking these fields o' Mr Osgood.'

'How odd it'll seem to have the old pit dried up!' said Eppie, turning away, and stooping to lift rather a large stone. 'See, daddy, I can carry this quite well,' she said, going along with much energy for a few steps, but presently letting it fall.

'Ah, you're fine and strong, arn't you?' said Silas, while Eppie shook her aching arms and laughed. 'Come, come, let us go and sit down on the bank against the stile there, and have no more lifting. You might hurt yourself, child. You'd need have somebody to work for you – and my arm isn't over strong.'

Silas uttered the last sentence slowly, as if it implied more than met the ear; and Eppie, when they sat down on the bank, nestled close to his side, and, taking hold caressingly of the arm that was not over strong, held it on her lap, while Silas puffed again dutifully at the pipe, which occupied his other arm. An ash in the hedgerow behind made a fretted screen from the sun, and threw happy playful shadows all about them.

'Father,' said Eppie, very gently, after they had been sitting in silence a little while, 'if I was to be married, ought I to be married with my mother's ring?'

Silas gave an almost imperceptible start, though the question fell in with the under-current of thought in his own mind, and then said, in a subdued tone, 'Why, Eppie, have you been-a-thinking on it?'

'Only this last week, father,' said Eppie, ingenuously, 'since Aaron talked to me about it.'

'And what did he say?' said Silas, still in the same subdued way, as if he were anxious lest he should fall into the slightest tone that was not for Eppie's good.

'He said he should like to be married, because he was a-going in four-and-twenty, and had got a deal of gardening work, now Mr Mott's given up; and he goes twice a-week regular to Mr Cass's, and once to Mr Osgood's, and they're going to take him on at the Rectory.'

'And who is it as he's wanting to marry?' said Silas, with rather a sad smile.

'Why, me, to be sure, daddy,' said Eppie, with dimpling laughter, kissing her father's cheek; 'as if he'd want to marry anybody else!'

'And you mean to have him, do you?' said Silas.

'Yes, some time,' said Eppie, 'I don't know when. Everybody's married some time, Aaron says. But I told him that wasn't true: for, I said, look at father – he's never been married.'

'No, child,' said Silas, 'your father was a lone man till you was sent to him.'

'But you'll never be lone again, father,' said Eppie, tenderly. 'That was what Aaron said – "I could never think o' taking you away from Master

Marner, Eppie." And I said "It 'ud be no use if you did, Aaron." And he wants us all to live together, so as you needn't work a bit, father, only what's for your own pleasure; and he'd be as good as a son to you – that was what he said.'

'And should you like that, Eppie?' said Silas, looking at her.

'I shouldn't mind it, father,' said Eppie, quite simply. 'And I should like things to be so as you needn't work much. But if it wasn't for that, I'd sooner things didn't change. I'm very happy: I like Aaron to be fond of me, and come and see us often, and behave pretty to you – he always *does* behave pretty to you, doesn't he, father?'

'Yes, child, nobody could behave better,' said Silas, emphatically. 'He's his mother's lad.'

'But I don't want any change,' said Eppie. 'I should like to go on a long, long while, just as we are. Only Aaron does want a change; and he made me cry a bit – only a bit – because he said I didn't care for him, for if I cared for him I should want us to be married, as he did.'

'Eh, my blessed child,' said Silas, laying down his pipe as if it were useless to pretend to smoke any longer, 'you're o'er young to be married. We'll ask Mrs Winthrop – we'll ask Aaron's mother what *she* thinks: if there's a right thing to do, she'll come at it. But there's this to be thought on, Eppie: things *will* change, whether we like it or no; things won't go on for a long while just as they are and no difference. I shall get older and helplesser, and be a burden on you, belike, if I don't go away from you altogether. Not as I mean you'd think me a burden – I know you wouldn't – but it 'ud be hard upon you; and when I look for'ard to that, I like to think as you'd have somebody else besides me – somebody young and strong, as'll outlast your own life, and take care on you to the end.' Silas paused, and, resting his wrists on his knees, lifted his hands up and down meditatively as he looked on the ground.

'Then, would you like me to be married, father?' said Eppie, with a little trembling in her voice.

'I'll not be the man to say no, Eppie,' said Silas, emphatically; 'but we'll ask your godmother. She'll wish the right thing by you and her son too.'

'There they come, then,' said Eppie. 'Let us go and meet 'em. O the pipe! won't you have it lit again, father?' said Eppie, lifting that medicinal appliance from the ground.

'Nay, child,' said Silas, 'I've done enough for today. I think, mayhap, a little of it does me more good than so much at once.'

❈ SEVENTEEN ❈

WHILE SILAS AND EPPIE WERE SEATED on the bank discoursing in the fleckered shade of the ash tree, Miss Priscilla Lammeter was resisting her sister's arguments, that it would be better to take tea at the Red House, and let her father have a long nap, than drive home to the Warrens so soon after dinner. The family party (of four only) were seated round the table in the dark wainscoted parlour, with the Sunday dessert before them, of fresh filberts, apples, and pears, duly ornamented with leaves by Nancy's own hand before the bells had rung for church.

A great change has come over the dark wainscoted parlour since we saw it in Godfrey's bachelor days, and under the wifeless reign of the old Squire. Now all is polish, on which no yesterday's dust is ever allowed to rest, from the yard's width of oaken boards round the carpet, to the old Squire's gun and whips and walking-sticks, ranged on the stag's antlers above the mantelpiece. All other signs of sporting and out-door occupation Nancy has removed to another room; but she has brought into the Red House the habit of filial reverence, and preserves sacredly in a place of honour these relics of her husband's departed father. The tankards are on the side-table still, but the bossed silver is undimmed by handling, and there are no dregs to send forth unpleasant suggestions: the only prevailing scent is of the lavender and rose-leaves that fill the vases of Derbyshire spar. All is purity and order in this once dreary room, for, fifteen years ago, it was entered by a new presiding spirit.

'Now, father,' said Nancy, 'is there any call for you to go home to tea? Mayn't you just as well stay with us? – such a beautiful evening as it's likely to be.'

The old gentleman had been talking with Godfrey about the increasing poor-rate and the ruinous times, and had not heard the dialogue between his daughters.

'My dear, you must ask Priscilla,' he said, in the once firm voice, now become rather broken. 'She manages me and the farm too.'

'And reason good as I should manage you, father,' said Priscilla, 'else you'd be giving yourself your death with rheumatism. And as for the farm, if anything turns out wrong, as it can't but do in these times, there's nothing kills a man so soon as having nobody to find fault with but himself. It's a deal the best way o' being master, to let somebody else do the ordering, and keep the blaming in your own hands. It 'ud save many a man a stroke, I believe.'

'Well, well, my dear,' said her father, with a quiet laugh, 'I didn't say you don't manage for everybody's good.'

'Then manage so as you may stay tea, Priscilla,' said Nancy, putting her hand on her sister's arm affectionately. 'Come now; and we'll go round the garden while father has his nap.'

'My dear child, he'll have a beautiful nap in the gig, for I shall drive. And as for staying tea, I can't hear of it; for there's this dairymaid, now she knows she's to be married, turned Michaelmas, she'd as lief pour the new milk into the pig-trough as into the pans. That's the way with 'em all: it's as if they thought the world 'ud be new-made because they're to be married. So come and let me put my bonnet on, and there'll be time for us to walk round the garden while the horse is being put in.'

When the sisters were treading the neatly-swept garden-walks, between the bright turf that contrasted pleasantly with the dark cones and arches and wall-like hedges of yew, Priscilla said –

'I'm as glad as anything at your husband's making that exchange o' land with cousin Osgood, and beginning the dairying. It's a thousand pities you didn't do it before; for it'll give you something to fill your mind. There's nothing like a dairy if folks want a bit o' worrit to make the days pass. For as for rubbing furniture, when you can once see your face in a table there's nothing else to look for; but there's always something fresh with the dairy; for even in the depths o' winter there's some pleasure in conquering the butter, and making it come whether or no. My dear,' added Priscilla, pressing her sister's hand affectionately as they walked side by side, 'you'll never be low when you've got a dairy.'

'Ah, Priscilla,' said Nancy, returning the pressure with a grateful glance of her clear eyes, 'but it won't make up to Godfrey: a dairy's not so much to a man. And it's only what he cares for that ever makes me low. I'm contented with the blessings we have, if he could be contented.'

'It drives me past patience,' said Priscilla, impetuously, 'that way o' the men – always wanting and wanting, and never easy with what they've got: they can't sit comfortable in their chairs when they've neither ache nor pain, but either they must stick a pipe in their mouths, to make 'em better than well, or else they must be swallowing something strong, though they're forced to make haste before the next meal comes in. But joyful be it spoken, our father was never that sort o' man. And if it had pleased God to make you ugly, like me, so as the men wouldn't ha' run after you, we might have kept to our own family, and had nothing to do with folks as have got uneasy blood in their veins.'

'O don't say so, Priscilla,' said Nancy, repenting that she had called forth this outburst; 'nobody has any occasion to find fault with Godfrey. It's natural he should be disappointed at not having any children: every man likes to have somebody to work for and lay by for, and he always counted so on making a fuss with 'em when they were little. There's many another man 'ud hanker more than he does. He's the best of husbands.'

'O, I know,' said Priscilla, smiling sarcastically, 'I know the way o' wives; they set one on to abuse their husbands, and then they turn round on one and praise 'em as if they wanted to sell 'em. But father'll be waiting for me; we must turn now.'

The large gig with the steady old grey was at the front door, and Mr Lammeter was already on the stone steps, passing the time in recalling to Godfrey what very fine points Speckle had when his master used to ride him.

'I always *would* have a good horse, you know,' said the old gentleman, not liking that spirited time to be quite effaced from the memory of his juniors.

'Mind you bring Nancy to the Warrens before the week's out, Mr Cass,' was Priscilla's parting injunction, as she took the reins, and shook them gently, by way of friendly incitement to Speckle.

'I shall just take a turn to the fields against the Stone-pits, Nancy, and look at the draining,' said Godfrey.

'You'll be in again by tea-time, dear?'

'O yes, I shall be back in an hour.'

It was Godfrey's custom on a Sunday afternoon to do a little contemplative farming in a leisurely walk. Nancy seldom accompanied him; for the women of her generation – unless, like Priscilla, they took to outdoor management – were not given to much walking beyond their own house and garden, finding sufficient exercise in domestic duties. So, when Priscilla was not with her, she usually sat with Mant's Bible before her, and after following the text with her eyes for a little while, she would gradually permit them to wander as her thoughts had already insisted on wandering.

But Nancy's Sunday thoughts were rarely quite out of keeping with the devout and reverential intention implied by the book spread open before her. She was not theologically instructed enough to discern very clearly the relation between the sacred documents of the past which she opened without method, and her own obscure, simple life; but the spirit of rectitude, and the sense of responsibility for the effect of her conduct on others, which were strong elements in Nancy's character, had made it a habit with her to scrutinize her past feelings and actions with self-questioning solicitude. Her mind not being courted by a great variety of subjects, she filled the vacant moments by living inwardly, again and again, through all her remembered experience, especially through the fifteen years of her married time, in which her life and its significance had been doubled. She recalled the small details, the words, tones, and looks, in the critical scenes which had opened a new epoch for her by giving her a deeper insight into the relations and trials of life, or which had called on her for some little effort of forbearance, or of painful adherence to an imagined or real duty – asking herself continually whether she had been in any respect blamable. This excessive rumination and self-questioning is perhaps a morbid habit inevitable to a mind of much moral sensibility when shut out from its due share of outward activity and of practical claims on its affections – inevitable to a noble-hearted, childless woman, when her lot is narrow. 'I can do so little – have I done it all well?' is the perpetually recurring thought; and there are no voices calling her away from that soliloquy, no peremptory demands to divert energy from vain regret or superfluous scruple.

There was one main thread of painful experience in Nancy's married life, and on it hung certain deeply-felt scenes, which were the oftenest revived in retrospect. The short dialogue with Priscilla in the garden had determined the current of retrospect in that frequent direction this particular Sunday afternoon. The first wandering of her thought from the text, which she still attempted dutifully to follow with her eyes and silent lips, was into an imaginary enlargement of the defence she had set up for her husband against Priscilla's implied blame. The vindication of the loved object is the best balm affection can find for its wounds: – 'A man must have so much on his mind,' is the belief by which a wife often supports a cheerful face under rough answers and unfeeling words. And Nancy's deepest wounds had all come from the perception that the absence of children from their hearth was dwelt on in her husband's mind as a privation to which he could not reconcile himself.

Yet sweet Nancy might have been expected to feel still more keenly the denial of a blessing to which she had looked forward with all the varied expectations and preparations, solemn and prettily trivial, which fill the mind of a loving woman when she expects to become a mother. Was there not a drawer filled with the neat work of her hands, all unworn and untouched, just as she had arranged it there fourteen years ago – just, but for one little dress, which had been made the burial-dress? But under this immediate personal trial Nancy was so firmly unmurmuring, that years ago she had suddenly renounced the habit of visiting this drawer, lest she should in this way be cherishing a longing for what was not given.

Perhaps it was this very severity towards any indulgence of what she held to be sinful regret in herself, that made her shrink from applying her own standard to her husband. 'It is very different – it is much worse for a man to be disappointed in that way: a woman can always be satisfied with devoting herself to her husband, but a man wants something that will make him look forward more – and sitting by the fire is so much duller to him than to a woman.' And always, when Nancy reached this point in her meditations – trying, with predetermined sympathy, to see everything as Godfrey saw it – there came a renewal of self-questioning. *Had* she done everything in her power to lighten Godfrey's privation? Had she really been right in the resistance which had cost her so much pain six years ago, and again four years ago – the resistance to her husband's wish that they should adopt a child? Adoption was more remote from the ideas and habits of that time than of our own; still Nancy had her opinion on it. It was as necessary to her mind to have an opinion on all topics, not exclus-ively masculine, that had come under her notice, as for her to have a precisely marked place for every article of her personal property: and her opinions were always principles to be unwaveringly acted on. They were firm, not because of their basis, but because she held them with a tenacity inseparable from her mental action. On all the duties and proprieties of life, from filial behaviour to the arrangements of the evening toilet, pretty Nancy Lammeter, by the time she was three-and-twenty, had her unalter-able little code, and had formed every one of her habits in strict accord-ance with that code. She carried these decided judgements within her in the most unobtrusive way: they rooted themselves in her mind, and grew there as quietly as grass. Years ago, we know, she insisted on dressing like Priscilla, because 'it was right for sisters to dress alike,' and because 'she would do what was right if she wore a gown dyed with cheese-colouring.' That was a trivial but typical instance of the mode in which Nancy's life was regulated.

It was one of those rigid principles, and no petty egoistic feeling, which had been the ground of Nancy's difficult resistance to her husband's wish. To adopt a child, because children of your own had been denied you, was to try and choose your lot in spite of Providence: the adopted child, she was convinced, would never turn out well, and would be a curse to those who had wilfully and rebelliously sought what it was clear that, for some high reason, they were better without. When you saw a thing was not meant to be, said Nancy, it was a bounden duty to leave off so much as wishing for it. And so far, perhaps, the wisest of men could scarcely make more than a verbal improvement in her principle. But the conditions under which she held it apparent that a thing was not meant to be, depended on a more peculiar mode of thinking. She would have given up making a purchase at a particular place if, on three successive times, rain, or some other cause of Heaven's sending, had formed an obstacle; and she would have anticipated a broken limb or other heavy misfortune to any one who persisted in spite of such indications.

'But why should you think the child would turn out ill?' said Godfrey, in his remonstrances. 'She has thriven as well as child can do with the weaver; and *he* adopted her. There isn't such a pretty little girl anywhere else in the parish, or one fitter for the station we could give her. Where can be the likelihood of her being a curse to anybody?'

'Yes, my dear Godfrey,' said Nancy, who was sitting with her hands tightly clasped together, and with yearning, regretful affection in her eyes. 'The child may not turn out ill with the weaver. But, then, he didn't go to seek her, as we should be doing. It will be wrong: I feel sure it will. Don't you remember what that lady we met at the Royston Baths told us about the child her sister adopted? That was the only adopting I ever heard of: and the child was transported when it was twenty-three. Dear Godfrey, don't ask me to do what I know is wrong: I should never be happy again.

I know it's very hard for *you* – it's easier for me – but it's the will of Providence.'

It might seem singular that Nancy – with her religious theory pieced together out of narrow social traditions, fragments of church doctrine imperfectly understood, and girlish reasonings on her small experience – should have arrived by herself at a way of thinking so nearly akin to that of many devout people whose beliefs are held in the shape of a system quite remote from her knowledge: singular, if we did not know that human beliefs, like all other natural growths, elude the barriers of system.

Godfrey had from the first specified Eppie, then about twelve years old, as a child suitable for them to adopt. It had never occurred to him that Silas would rather part with his life than with Eppie. Surely the weaver would wish the best to the child he had taken so much trouble with, and would be glad that such good fortune should happen to her: she would always be very grateful to him, and he would be well provided for to the end of his life – provided for as the excellent part he had done by the child deserved. Was it not an appropriate thing for people in a higher station to take a charge off the hands of a man in a lower? It seemed an eminently appropriate thing to Godfrey, for reasons that were known only to himself; and by a common fallacy, he imagined the measure would be easy because he had private motives for desiring it. This was rather a coarse mode of estimating Silas's relation to Eppie; but we must remember that many of the impressions which Godfrey was likely to gather concerning the labouring people around him would favour the idea that deep affections can hardly go along with callous palms and scant means; and he had not had the opportunity, even if he had had the power, of entering intimately into all that was exceptional in the weaver's experience. It was only the want of adequate knowledge that could have made it possible for Godfrey deliberately to entertain an unfeeling project: his natural kindness had outlived that blighting time of cruel wishes, and Nancy's praise of him as a husband was not founded entirely on a wilful illusion.

'I was right,' she said to herself, when she had recalled all their scenes of discussion – 'I feel I was right to say him nay, though it hurt me more than anything; but how good Godfrey has been about it! Many men would have been very angry with me for standing out against their wishes; and they might have thrown out that they'd had ill-luck in marrying me; but Godfrey has never been the man to say me an unkind word. It's only what he can't hide: everything seems so blank to him, I know; and the land – what a difference it 'ud make to him, when he goes to see after things, if he'd children growing up that he was doing it all for! But I won't murmur; and perhaps if he'd married a woman who'd have had children, she'd have vexed him in other ways.'

This possibility was Nancy's chief comfort; and to give it greater strength, she laboured to make it impossible that any other wife should have had more perfect tenderness. She had been *forced* to vex him by that one denial. Godfrey was not insensible to her loving effort, and did Nancy no injustice as to the motives of her obstinacy. It was impossible to have lived with her fifteen years and not be aware that an unselfish clinging to the right, and a sincerity clear as the flower-born dew, were her main characteristics; indeed, Godfrey felt this so strongly, that his own more wavering nature, too averse to facing difficulty to be unvaryingly simple and truthful, was kept in a certain awe of this gentle wife who watched his looks with a yearning to obey them. It seemed to him impossible that he should ever confess to her the truth about Eppie: she would never recover from the repulsion the story of his earlier marriage would create, told to her now, after that long concealment. And the child, too, he thought, must become an object of repulsion: the very sight of her would be painful. The shock to Nancy's mingled pride and ignorance of the world's evil might even be too much for her delicate frame. Since he had married her with that secret on his heart, he must keep it there to the last. Whatever else he did, he could not make an irreparable breach between himself and this long-loved wife.

Meanwhile, why could he not make up his mind to the absence of children from a hearth brightened by such a wife? Why did his mind fly uneasily to that void, as if it were the sole reason why life was not thoroughly joyous to him? I suppose it is the way with all men and women who reach middle age without the clear perception that life never *can* be thoroughly joyous: under the vague dullness of the grey hours, dissatisfaction seeks a definite object, and finds it in the privation of an untried good. Dissatisfaction, seated musingly on a childless hearth, thinks with envy of the father whose return is greeted by young voices – seated at the meal where the little heads rise one above another like nursery plants, it sees a black care hovering behind every one of them, and thinks the impulses by which men abandon freedom, and seek for ties, are surely nothing but a brief madness. In Godfrey's case there were further reasons why his thoughts should be continually solicited by this one point in his lot: his conscience, never thoroughly easy about Eppie, now gave his childless home the aspect of a retribution; and as the time passed on, under Nancy's refusal to adopt her, any retrieval of his error became more and more difficult.

On this Sunday afternoon it was already four years since there had been any allusion to the subject between them, and Nancy supposed that it was for ever buried.

'I wonder if he'll mind it less or more as he gets older,' she thought; 'I'm afraid more. Aged people feel the miss of children: what would father do without Priscilla? And if I die, Godfrey will be very lonely – not holding together with his brothers much. But I won't be over-anxious, and trying to make things out beforehand: I must do my best for the present.'

With that last thought Nancy roused herself from her reverie, and turned her eyes again towards the forsaken page. It had been forsaken longer than she imagined, for she was presently surprised by the appearance of the servant with the tea-things. It was, in fact, a little before the usual time for tea; but Jane had her reasons.

'Is your master come into the yard, Jane?'

'No 'm, he isn't,' said Jane, with a slight emphasis, of which, however, her mistress took no notice.

'I don't know whether you've seen 'em, 'm,' continued Jane, after a pause, 'but there's folks making haste all one way, afore the front window. I doubt something's happened. There's niver a man to be seen i' the yard, else I'd send and see. I've been up into the top attic, but there's no seeing anything for trees. I hope nobody's hurt, that's all.'

'O, not, I daresay there's nothing much the matter,' said Nancy. 'It's perhaps Mr Snell's bull got out again, as he did before.'

'I wish he mayn't gore anybody, then, that's all,' said Jane, not altogether despising a hypothesis which covered a few imaginary calamities.

'That girl is always terrifying me,' thought Nancy; 'I wish Godfrey would come in.'

She went to the front window and looked as far as she could see along the road, with an uneasiness which she felt to be childish, for there were now no such signs of excitement as Jane had spoken of, and Godfrey would not be likely to return by the village road, but by the fields. She continued to stand, however, looking at the placid churchyard with the long shadows of the gravestones across the bright green hillocks, and at the glowing autumn colours of the Rectory trees beyond. Before such calm external beauty the presence of a vague fear is more distinctly felt – like a raven flapping its slow wing across the sunny air. Nancy wished more and more that Godfrey would come in.

◁ EIGHTEEN ▷

SOME ONE OPENED THE DOOR AT the other end of the room, and Nancy felt that it was her husband. She turned from the window with gladness in her eyes, for the wife's chief dread was stilled.

'Dear, I'm so thankful you're come,' she said, going towards him. 'I began to get . . .'

She paused abruptly, for Godfrey was laying down his hat with trembling hands, and turned towards her with a pale face and a strange unanswering glance, as if he saw her indeed, but saw her as part of a scene invisible to herself. She laid her hand on his arm, not daring to speak again; but he left the touch unnoticed, and threw himself into his chair.

Jane was already at the door with the hissing urn. 'Tell her to keep away, will you?' said Godfrey; and when the door was closed again he exerted himself to speak more distinctly.

'Sit down, Nancy – there,' he said, pointing to a chair opposite him. 'I came back as soon as I could, to hinder anybody's telling you but me. I've had a great shock – but I care most about the shock it'll be to you.'

'It isn't father and Priscilla?' said Nancy, with quivering lips, clasping her hands together tightly on her lap.

'No, it's nobody living,' said Godfrey, unequal to the considerate skill with which he would have wished to make his revelation. 'It's Dunstan – my brother Dunstan, that we lost sight of sixteen years ago. We've found him – found his body – his skeleton.'

The deep dread Godfrey's look had created in Nancy made her feel these words a relief. She sat in comparative calmness to hear what else he had to tell. He went on:

'The Stone-pit has gone dry suddenly – from the draining, I suppose; and there he lies – has lain for sixteen years, wedged between two great stones. There's his watch and seals, and there's my gold-handled hunting-whip, with my name on: he took it away, without my knowing, the day he went hunting on Wildfire, the last time he was seen.'

Godfrey paused: it was not so easy to say what came next. 'Do you think he drowned himself?' said Nancy, almost wondering that her husband should be so deeply shaken by what had happened all those years ago to an unloved brother, of whom worse things had been augured.

'No, he fell in,' said Godfrey, in a low but distinct voice, as if he felt some deep meaning in the fact. Presently he added: 'Dunstan was the man that robbed Silas Marner.'

The blood rushed to Nancy's face and neck at this surprise and shame, for she had been bred up to regard even a distant kinship with crime as a dishonour.

'O Godfrey!' she said, with compassion in her tone, for she had immediately reflected that the dishonour must be felt still more keenly by her husband.

'There was the money in the pit,' he continued – 'all the weaver's money. Everything's been gathered up, and they're taking the skeleton to the Rainbow. But I came back to tell you: there was no hindering it; you must know.'

He was silent, looking on the ground for two long minutes. Nancy would have said some words of comfort under this disgrace, but she refrained, from an instinctive sense that there was something behind – that Godfrey had something else to tell her. Presently he lifted his eyes to her face, and kept them fixed on her, as he said –

'Everything comes to light, Nancy, sooner or later. When God Almighty wills it, our secrets are found out. I've lived with a secret on my mind, but I'll keep it from you no longer. I wouldn't have you know it by somebody else, and not by me – I wouldn't have you find it out after I'm dead. I'll tell you now. It's been "I will" and "I won't" with me all my life – I'll make sure of myself now.'

Nancy's utmost dread had returned. The eyes of the husband and wife met with awe in them, as at a crisis which suspended affection.

'Nancy,' said Godfrey, slowly, 'when I married you, I hid something from you – something I ought to have told you. That woman Marner found dead in the snow – Eppie's mother – that wretched woman – was my wife: Eppie is my child.'

He paused, dreading the effect of his confession. But Nancy sat quite still, only that her eyes dropped and ceased to meet his. She was pale and quiet as a meditative statue, clasping her hands on her lap.

'You'll never think the same of me again,' said Godfrey, after a little while, with some tremor in his voice.

She was silent.

'I oughtn't to have left the child unowned: I oughtn't to have kept it from you. But I couldn't bear to give you up, Nancy. I was led away into marrying her – I suffered for it.'

Still Nancy was silent, looking down; and he almost expected that she would presently get up and say she would go to her father's. How could she have any mercy for faults that must seem so black to her, with her simple, severe notions?

But at last she lifted up her eyes to his again and spoke. There was no indignation in her voice – only deep regret.

'Godfrey, if you had but told me this six years ago, we could have done some of our duty by the child. Do you think I'd have refused to take her in, if I'd known she was yours?'

At that moment Godfrey felt all the bitterness of an error that was not simply futile, but had defeated its own end. He had not measured this wife with whom he had lived so long. But she spoke again, with more agitation.

'And – O, Godfrey – if we'd had her from the first, if you'd taken to her as you ought, she'd have loved me for her mother – and you'd have been happier with me: I could better have bore my little baby dying and our life might have been more like what we used to think it 'ud be.'

The tears fell, and Nancy ceased to speak.

'But you wouldn't have married me then, Nancy, if I'd told you,' said Godfrey, urged, in the bitterness of his self-reproach, to prove to himself that his conduct had not been utter folly. 'You may think you would now, but you wouldn't then. With your pride and your father's, you'd have hated having anything to do with me after the talk there'd have been.'

'I can't say what I should have done about that, Godfrey. I should never have married anybody else. But I wasn't worth doing wrong for – nothing is in this world. Nothing is so good as it seems beforehand – not even our marrying wasn't, you see.' There was a faint sad smile on Nancy's face as she said the last words.

'I'm a worse man than you thought I was, Nancy,' said Godfrey, rather tremulously. 'Can you forgive me ever?'

'The wrong to me is but little, Godfrey: you've made it up to me – you've been good to me for fifteen years. It's another you did the wrong to; and I doubt it can never be all made up for.'

'But we can take Eppie now,' said Godfrey. 'I won't mind the world knowing at last. I'll be plain and open for the rest o' my life.'

'It'll be different coming to us, now she's grown up,' said Nancy, shaking her head sadly. 'But it's your duty to acknowledge her and provide for her; and I'll do my part by her, and pray to God Almighty to make her love me.'

'Then we'll go together to Silas Marner's this very night, as soon as everything's quiet at the Stone-pits.'

◁ NINETEEN ▷

BETWEEN EIGHT AND NINE O'CLOCK THAT evening, Eppie and Silas were seated alone in the cottage. After the great excitement the weaver had undergone from the events of the afternoon, he had felt a longing for this quietude, and had even begged Mrs Winthrop and Aaron, who had naturally lingered behind every one else, to leave him alone with his child. The excitement had not passed away: it had only reached that stage when the keenness of the susceptibility makes external stimulus intolerable – when there is no sense of weariness, but rather an intensity of inward life, under which sleep is an impossibility. Any one who has watched such moments in other men remembers the brightness of the eyes and the strange definiteness that comes over coarse features from that transient influence. It is as if a new fineness of ear for all spiritual voices had sent wonder-working vibrations through the heavy mortal frame – as if 'beauty born of murmuring sound' had passed into the face of the listener.

Silas's face showed that sort of transfiguration, as he sat in his armchair and looked at Eppie. She had drawn her own chair towards his knees, and leaned forward, holding both his hands, while she looked up at him. On the table near them, lit by a candle, lay the recovered gold – the old long-loved gold, ranged in orderly heaps, as Silas used to range it in the days when it was his only joy. He had been telling her how he used to count it every night, and how his soul was utterly desolate till she was sent to him.

'At first, I'd a sort o' feeling come across me now and then,' he was saying in a subdued tone, 'as if you might be changed into the gold again; for sometimes, turn my head which way I would, I seemed to see the gold; and I thought I should be glad if I could feel it, and find it was come back. But that didn't last long. After a bit, I should have thought it was a curse come again, if it had drove you from me, for I'd got to feel the need o' your looks and your voice and the touch o' your little fingers. You didn't know then, Eppie, when you were such a little un – you didn't know what your old father Silas felt for you.'

'But I know now, father,' said Eppie. 'If it hadn't been for you, they'd have taken me to the workhouse, and there'd have been nobody to love me.'

'Eh, my precious child, the blessing was mine. If you hadn't been sent to save me, I should ha' gone to the grave in my misery. The money was taken away from me in time; and you see it's been kept – kept till it was wanted for you. It's wonderful – our life is wonderful.'

Silas sat in silence a few minutes, looking at the money. 'It takes no hold of me now,' he said, ponderingly – 'the money doesn't. I wonder if it ever could again – I doubt it might, if I lost you, Eppie. I might come to think I was forsaken again, and lose the feeling that God was good to me.'

At that moment there was a knocking at the door; and Eppie was obliged to rise without answering Silas. Beautiful she looked, with the tenderness of gathering tears in her eyes and a slight flush on her cheeks, as she stepped to open the door. The flush deepened when she saw Mr and Mrs Godfrey Cass. She made her little rustic curtsy, and held the door wide for them to enter.

'We're disturbing you very late, my dear,' said Mrs Cass, taking Eppie's hand, and looking in her face with an expression of anxious interest and admiration. Nancy herself was pale and tremulous.

Eppie, after placing chairs for Mr and Mrs Cass, went to stand against Silas, opposite to them.

'Well, Marner,' said Godfrey, trying to speak with perfect firmness, 'it's a great comfort to me to see you with your money again, that you've been deprived of so many years. It was one of my family did you the wrong – the more grief to me – and I feel bound to make up to you for it in every way. Whatever I can do for you will be nothing but paying a debt, even if I looked no farther than the robbery. But there are other things I'm beholden – shall be beholden to you for, Marner.'

Godfrey checked himself. It had been agreed between him and his wife that the subject of his fatherhood should be approached very carefully, and that, if possible, the disclosure should be reserved for the future, so that it might be made to Eppie gradually. Nancy had urged this, because she felt strongly the painful light in which Eppie must inevitably see the relation between her father and mother.

Silas, always ill at ease when he was being spoken to by 'betters', such as Mr Cass – tall, powerful, florid men, seen chiefly on horseback – answered with some constraint, –

'Sir, I've a deal to thank you for a'ready. As for the robbery, I count it no loss to me. And if I did, you couldn't help it: you aren't answerable for it.'

'You may look at it in that way, Marner, but I never can; and I hope you'll let me act according to my own feeling of what's just. I know you're easily contented: you've been a hard-working man all your life.'

'Yes, sir, yes,' said Marner, meditatively. 'I should ha' been bad off without my work: it was what I held by when everything else was gone from me.'

'Ah,' said Godfrey, applying Marner's words simply to his bodily wants, 'it was a good trade for you in this country, because there's been a great deal of linen-weaving to be done. But you're getting rather past such close work, Marner: it's time you laid by and had some rest. You look a good deal pulled down, though you're not an old man, *are* you?'

'Fifty-five, as near as I can say, sir,' said Silas.

'O, why, you may live thirty years longer – look at old Macey! And that money on the table, after all, is but little. It won't go far either way – whether it's put out to interest, or you were to live on it as long as it would last: it wouldn't go far if you'd nobody to keep but yourself, and you've had two to keep for a good many years now.'

'Eh, sir,' said Silas, unaffected by anything Godfrey was saying, 'I'm in no fear o' want. We shall do very well – Eppie and me 'ull do well enough. There's few workingfolks have got so much laid by as that. I don't know what it is to gentlefolks, but I look upon it as a deal – almost too much. And as for us, it's little we want.'

'Only the garden, father,' said Eppie, blushing up to the ears the moment after.

'You love a garden, do you, my dear?' said Nancy, thinking that this turn in the point of view might help her husband. 'We should agree in that: I give a deal of time to the garden.'

'Ah, there's plenty of gardening at the Red House,' said Godfrey, surprised at the difficulty he found in approaching a proposition which had seemed so easy to him in the distance. 'You've done a good part by Eppie, Marner, for sixteen years. It 'ud be a great comfort to you to see her well provided for, wouldn't it? She looks blooming and healthy, but not fit for any hardships: she doesn't look like a strapping girl come of working parents. You'd like to see her taken care of by those who can leave her well off, and make a lady of her; she's more fit for it than for a rough life, such as she might come to have in a few years' time.'

A slight flush came over Marner's face, and disappeared, like a passing gleam. Eppie was simply wondering Mr Cass should talk so about things that seemed to have nothing to do with reality; but Silas was hurt and uneasy.

'I don't take your meaning, sir,' he answered, not having words at command to express the mingled feelings with which he had heard Mr Cass's words.

'Well, my meaning is this, Marner,' said Godfrey, determined to come to the point. 'Mrs Cass and I, you know, have no children – nobody to be the better for our good home and everything else we have – more than enough for ourselves. And we should like to have somebody in the place of a daughter to us – we should like to have Eppie, and treat her in every way as our own child. It 'ud be a great comfort to you in your old age, I hope, to see her fortune made in that way, after you've been at the trouble of bringing her up so well. And it's right you should have every reward for that. And Eppie, I'm sure, will always love you and be grateful to you: she'd come and see you very often, and we should all be on the look-out to do everything we could towards making you comfortable.'

A plain man like Godfrey Cass, speaking under some embarrassment, necessarily blunders on words that are coarser than his intentions, and that are likely to fall gratingly on susceptible feelings. While he had been speaking, Eppie had quietly passed her arm behind Silas's head, and let her hand rest against it caressingly: she felt him trembling violently. He was silent for some moments when Mr Cass had ended – powerless under the conflict of emotions, all alike painful. Eppie's heart was swelling at the sense that her father was in distress; and she was just going to lean down and speak to him, when one struggling dread at last gained the mastery over every other in Silas, and he said, faintly –

'Eppie, my child, speak. I won't stand in your way. Thank Mr and Mrs Cass.'

Eppie took her hand from her father's head, and came forward a step. Her cheeks were flushed, but not with shyness this time: the sense that her father was in doubt and suffering banished that sort of self-consciousness. She dropped a low curtsy, first to Mrs Cass and then to Mr Cass, and said –

'Thank you, ma'am – thank you, sir. But I can't leave my father, nor own anybody nearer than him. And I don't want to be a lady – thank you all the same' (here Eppie dropped another curtsy). 'I couldn't give up the folks I've been used to.'

Eppie's lip began to tremble a little at the last words. She retreated to her father's chair again, and held him round the neck: while Silas, with a subdued sob, put up his hand to grasp hers.

The tears were in Nancy's eyes, but her sympathy with Eppie was, naturally, divided with distress on her husband's account. She dared not speak, wondering what was going on in her husband's mind.

Godfrey felt an irritation inevitable to almost all of us when we encounter an unexpected obstacle. He had been full of his own penitence and resolution to retrieve his error as far as the time was left to him; he was possessed with all-important feelings, that were to lead to a predetermined course of action which he had fixed on as the right, and he was not prepared to enter with lively appreciation into other people's feelings counteracting his virtuous resolves. The agitation with which he spoke again was not quite unmixed with anger.

'But I've a claim on you, Eppie – the strongest of all claims. It's my duty, Marner, to own Eppie as my child, and provide for her. She's my own child: her mother was my wife. I've a natural claim on her that must stand before every other.'

Eppie had given a violent start, and turned quite pale. Silas, on the contrary, who had been relieved, by Eppie's answer, from the dread lest his mind should be in opposition to hers, felt the spirit of resistance in him set free, not without a touch of parental fierceness. 'Then, sir,' he answered, with an accent of bitterness that had been silent in him since the memorable day when his youthful hope had perished – 'then, sir, why didn't you say so sixteen year ago, and claim her before I'd come to love her, i'stead o' coming to take her from me now, when you might as well take the heart out o' my body? God gave her to me because you turned your back upon her, and He looks upon her as mine: you've no right to her! When a man turns a blessing from his door, it falls to them as take it in.'

'I know that, Marner. I was wrong. I've repented of my conduct in that matter,' said Godfrey, who could not help feeling the edge of Silas's words.

'I'm glad to hear it, sir,' said Marner, with gathering excitement; 'but repentance doesn't alter what's been going on for sixteen year. Your coming now and saying "I'm her father" doesn't alter the feelings inside us. It's me she's been calling her father ever since she could say the word.'

'But I think you might look at the thing more reasonably, Marner,' said Godfrey, unexpectedly awed by the weaver's direct truth-speaking. 'It isn't as if she was to be taken quite away from you, so that you'd never see her again. She'll be very near you, and come to see you very often. She'll feel just the same towards you.'

'Just the same?' said Marner, more bitterly than ever. 'How'll she feel just the same for me as she does now, when we eat o' the same bit, and drink o' the same cup, and think o' the same things from one day's end to another? Just the same? that's idle talk. You'd cut us i' two.'

Godfrey, unqualified by experience to discern the pregnancy of Marner's simple words, felt rather angry again. It seemed to him that the weaver was very selfish (a judgement readily passed by those who have never tested their own power of sacrifice) to oppose what was undoubtedly for Eppie's welfare; and he felt himself called upon, for her sake, to assert his authority.

'I should have thought, Marner,' he said, severely – 'I should have thought your affection for Eppie would make you rejoice in what was for her good, even if it did call upon you to give up something. You ought to remember your own life's uncertain, and she's at an age now when her lot may soon be fixed in a way very different from what it would be in her father's home: she may marry some low working-man, and then, whatever I might do for her, I couldn't make her well-off. You're putting yourself in the way of her welfare; and though I'm sorry to hurt you after what you've done, and what I've left undone, I feel now it's my duty to insist on taking care of my own daughter. I want to do my duty.'

It would be difficult to say whether it were Silas or Eppie that was more deeply stirred by this last speech of Godfrey's. Thought had been very busy in Eppie as she listened to the contest between her old long-loved father and this new unfamiliar father who had suddenly come to fill the place of that black featureless shadow which had held the ring and placed it on her mother's finger. Her imagination had darted backward in conjectures, and forward in previsions, of what this revealed fatherhood implied; and there were words in Godfrey's last speech which helped to make the previsions especially definite. Not that these thoughts, either of past or future, determined her resolution – *that* was determined by the feelings which vibrated to every word Silas had uttered; but they raised, even apart from these feelings, a repulsion towards the offered lot and the newly-revealed father.

Silas, on the other hand, was again stricken in conscience, and alarmed lest Godfrey's accusation should be true – lest he should be raising his own will as an obstacle to Eppie's good. For many moments he was mute, struggling for the self-conquest necessary to the uttering of the difficult words. They came out tremulously.

'I'll say no more. Let it be as you will. Speak to the child. I'll hinder nothing.'

Even Nancy, with all the acute sensibility of her own affections, shared her husband's view, that Marner was not justifiable in his wish to retain Eppie, after her real father had avowed himself. She felt that it was a very hard trial for the poor weaver, but her code allowed no question that a father by blood must have a claim above that of any foster-father. Besides, Nancy, used all her life to plenteous circumstances and the privileges of 'respectability,' could not enter into the pleasures which early nurture and habit connect with all the little aims and efforts of the poor who are born poor: to her mind, Eppie, in being restored to her birthright, was entering on a too long withheld but unquestionable good. Hence she heard Silas's last words with relief, and thought, as Godfrey did, that their wish was achieved.

'Eppie, my dear,' said Godfrey, looking at his daughter, not without some embarrassment, under the sense that she was old enough to judge him, 'it'll always be our wish that you should show your love and gratitude to one who's been a father to you so many years, and we shall want to help you to make him comfortable in every way. But we hope you'll come to love us as well; and though I haven't been what a father should ha' been to you all these years, I wish to do the utmost in my power for you for the rest of my life, and provide for you as my only child. And you'll have the best of mothers in my wife – that'll be a blessing you haven't known since you were old enough to know it.'

'My dear, you'll be a treasure to me,' said Nancy, in her gentle voice. 'We shall want for nothing when we have our daughter.'

Eppie did not come forward and curtsy, as she had done before. She held Silas's hand in hers, and grasped it firmly – it was a weaver's hand, with a palm and finger-tips that were sensitive to such pressure – while she spoke with colder decision than before.

'Thank you, ma'am – thank you, sir, for your offers – they're very great, and far above my wish. For I should have no delight i' life any more if I was forced to go away from my father, and knew he was sitting at home, a-thinking of me and feeling lone. We've been used to be happy together every day, and I can't think o' no happiness without him. And he says he'd nobody i' the world till I was sent to him, and he'd have nothing when I was gone. And he's took care of me and loved me from the first, and I'll cleave to him as long as he lives, and nobody shall ever come between him and me.'

'But you must make sure, Eppie,' said Silas, in a low voice – 'you must make sure as you won't ever be sorry, because you've made your choice to stay among poor folks, and with poor clothes and things, when you might ha' had everything o' the best.'

His sensitiveness on this point had increased as he listened to Eppie's words of faithful affection.

'I can never be sorry, father,' said Eppie. 'I shouldn't know what to think on or to wish for with fine things about me, as I haven't been used to. And it 'ud be poor work for me to put on things, and ride in a gig, and sit in a place at church, as 'ud make them as I'm fond of think me unfitting company for 'em. What could *I* care for then?'

Nancy looked at Godfrey with a pained questioning glance. But his eyes were fixed on the floor, where he was moving the end of his stick, as if he were pondering on something absently. She thought there was a word which might perhaps come better from her lips than from his.

'What you say is natural, my dear child – it's natural you should cling to those who've brought you up,' she said, mildly; 'but there's a duty you owe to your lawful father. There's perhaps something to be given up on more sides than one. When your father opens his home to you, I think it's right you shouldn't turn your back on it.'

'I can't feel as I've got any father but one,' said Eppie, impetuously, while the tears gathered. 'I've always thought of a little home where he'd sit i' the corner, and I should fend and do everything for him: I can't think o' no other home. I wasn't brought up to be a lady, and I can't turn my mind to it. I like the working-folks, and their victuals, and their ways. And,' she ended passionately, while the tears fell, 'I'm promised to marry a working-man, as 'll live with father, and help me to take care of him.'

Godfrey looked up at Nancy with a flushed face and smarting dilated eyes. This frustration of a purpose towards which he had set out under the exalted consciousness that he was about to compensate in some degree for the greatest demerit of his life, made him feel the air of the room stifling.

'Let us go,' he said, in an under-tone.

'We won't talk of this any longer now,' said Nancy, rising. 'We're your well-wishers, my dear – and yours too, Marner. We shall come and see you again. It's getting late now.'

In this way she covered her husband's abrupt departure, for Godfrey had gone straight to the door, unable to say more.

◁ TWENTY ▷

NANCY AND GODFREY WALKED HOME UNDER the starlight in silence. When they entered the oaken parlour, Godfrey threw himself into his chair, while Nancy laid down her bonnet and shawl, and stood on the hearth near her husband, unwilling to leave him even for a few minutes, and yet fearing to utter any word lest it might jar on his feeling. At last Godfrey turned his head towards her, and their eyes met, dwelling in that meeting without any movement on either side. That quiet mutual gaze of a trusting husband and wife is like the first moment of rest or refuge from a great weariness or a great danger – not to be interfered with by speech or action which would distract the sensations from the fresh enjoyment of repose.

But presently he put out his hand, and as Nancy placed hers within it, he drew her towards him, and said –

'That's ended!'

She bent to kiss him, and then said, as she stood by his side, 'Yes, I'm afraid we must give up the hope of having her for a daughter. It wouldn't be right to want to force her to come to us against her will. We can't alter her bringing up and what's come of it.'

'No,' said Godfrey, with a keen decisiveness of tone, in contrast with his usually careless and unemphatic speech – 'there's debts we can't pay like money debts, by paying extra for the years that have slipped by. While I've been putting off and putting off, the trees have been growing – it's too late now. Marner was in the right in what he said about a man's turning away a blessing from his door: it falls to somebody else. I wanted to pass for childless once, Nancy – I shall pass for childless now against my wish.'

Nancy did not speak immediately, but after a little while she asked – 'You won't make it known, then, about Eppie's being your daughter?'

'No: where would be the good to anybody? – only harm. I must do what I can for her in the state of life she chooses. I must see who it is she's thinking of marrying.'

'If it won't do any good to make the thing known,' said Nancy, who thought she might now allow herself the relief of entertaining a feeling which she had tried to silence before, 'I should be very thankful for father and Priscilla never to be troubled with knowing what was done in the past, more than about Dunsey: it can't be helped, their knowing that.'

'I shall put it in my will – I think I shall put it in my will. I shouldn't like to leave anything to be found out, like this about Dunsey,' said Godfrey, meditatively. 'But I can't see anything but difficulties that 'ud come from telling it now. I must do what I can to make her happy in her own way. I've a notion,' he added, after a moment's pause, 'it's Aaron Winthrop she meant she was engaged to. I remember seeing him with her and Marner going away from church.'

'Well, he's very sober and industrious,' said Nancy, trying to view the matter as cheerfully as possible.

Godfrey fell into thoughtfulness again. Presently he looked up at Nancy sorrowfully, and said –

'She's a very pretty, nice girl, isn't she, Nancy?'

'Yes, dear; and with just your hair and eyes: I wondered it had never struck me before.'

'I think she took a dislike to me at the thought of my being her father: I could see a change in her manner after that.'

'She couldn't bear to think of not looking on Marner as her father,' said Nancy, not wishing to confirm her husband's painful impression.

'She thinks I did wrong by her mother as well as by her. She thinks me worse than I am. But she *must* think it: she can never know all. It's part of my punishment, Nancy, for my daughter to dislike me. I should never have got into that trouble if I'd been true to you – if I hadn't been a fool. I'd no right to expect anything but evil could come of that marriage – and when I shirked doing a father's part too.'

Nancy was silent: her spirit of rectitude would not let her try to soften the edge of what she felt to be a just compunction. He spoke again after a little while, but the tone was rather changed: there was tenderness mingled with the previous self-reproach.

'And I got *you*, Nancy, in spite of all; and yet I've been grumbling and uneasy because I hadn't something else – as if I deserved it.'

'You've never been wanting to me, Godfrey,' said Nancy, with quiet sincerity. 'My trouble would be gone if you resigned yourself to the lot that's been given us.'

'Well, perhaps it isn't too late to mend a bit there. Though it *is* too late to mend some things, say what they will.'

✑ TWENTY-ONE ✐

THE NEXT MORNING, WHEN SILAS AND Eppie were seated at their breakfast, he said to her, –

'Eppie, there's a thing I've had on my mind to do this two year, and now the money's been brought back to us, we can do it. I've been turning it over and over in the night, and I think we'll set out tomorrow, while the fine days last. We'll leave the house and everything for your godmother to take care on, and we'll make a little bundle o' things and set out.'

'Where to go, daddy?' said Eppie, in much surprise.

'To my old country – to the town where I was born – up Lantern Yard. I want to see Mr Paston, the minister: something may ha' come out to make 'em know I was innicent o' the robbery. And Mr Paston was a man with a deal o' light – I want to speak to him about the drawing o' the lots. And I should like to talk to him about the religion o' this countryside, for I partly think he doesn't know on it.'

Eppie was very joyful, for there was the prospect not only of wonder and delight at seeing a strange country, but also of coming back to tell Aaron all about it. Aaron was so much wiser than she was about most things – it would be rather pleasant to have this little advantage over him. Mrs Winthrop, though possessed with a dim fear of dangers attendant on so long a journey, and requiring many assurances that it would not take them out of the region of carriers' carts and slow waggons, was nevertheless well pleased that Silas should revisit his own country, and find out if he had been cleared from that false accusation.

'You'd be easier in your mind for the rest o' your life, Master Marner,' said Dolly – 'that you would. And if there's any light to be got up the yard as you talk on, we've need of it i' this world, and I'd be glad on it myself, if you could bring it back.'

So on the fourth day from that time, Silas and Eppie, in their Sunday clothes, with a small bundle tied in a blue linen handkerchief, were making their way through the streets of a great manufacturing town. Silas, bewildered by the changes thirty years had brought over his native place, had stopped several persons in succession to ask them the name of this town, that he might be sure he was not under a mistake about it.

'Ask for Lantern Yard, father – ask this gentleman with the tassels on his shoulders a-standing at the shop door; he isn't in a hurry like the rest,' said Eppie, in some distress at her father's bewilderment, and ill at ease, besides, amidst the noise, the movement, and the multitude of strange indifferent faces.

'Eh, my child, he won't know anything about it,' said Silas; 'gentle folks didn't ever go up the Yard. But happen somebody can tell me which is the way to Prison Street, where the jail is. I know the way out o' that as if I'd seen it yesterday.'

With some difficulty, after many turnings and new inquiries, they reached Prison Street; and the grim walls of the jail, the first object that answered to any image in Silas's memory, cheered him with the certitude, which no assurance of the town's name had hitherto given him, that he was in his native place.

'Ah,' he said, drawing a long breath, 'there's the jail, Eppie; that's just the same: I aren't afraid now. It's the third on the left hand from the jail doors – that's the way we must go.'

'O, what a dark ugly place!' said Eppie. 'How it hides the sky! It's worse than the Workhouse. I'm glad you don't live in this town now, father. Is Lantern Yard like this street?'

'My precious child,' said Silas, smiling, 'it isn't a big street like this. I never was easy i' this street myself, but I was fond o' Lantern Yard. The shops here are all altered, I think – I can't make 'em out; but I shall know the turning, because it's the third.'

'Here it is,' he said, in a tone of satisfaction, as they came to a narrow alley. 'And then we must go to the left again, and then straight for'ard for a bit, up Shoe Lane: and then we shall be at the entry next to the o'erhanging window, where there's the nick in the road for the water to run. Eh, I can see it all.'

'O father, I'm like as if I was stifled,' said Eppie. 'I couldn't ha' thought as any folks lived i' this way, so close together. How pretty the Stone-pits 'ull look when we get back!'

'It looks comical to *me*, child, now – and smells bad. I can't think as it usened to smell so.'

Here and there a sallow, begrimed face looked out from a gloomy doorway at the strangers, and increased Eppie's uneasiness, so that it was a longed-for relief when they issued from the alleys into Shoe Lane, where there was a broader strip of sky.

'Dear heart!' said Silas, 'why, there's people coming out o' the Yard as if they'd been to chapel at this time o' day – a weekday noon!'

Suddenly he started and stood still with a look of distressed amazement, that alarmed Eppie. They were before an opening in front of a large factory, from which men and women were streaming for their mid-day meal.

'Father,' said Eppie, clasping his arm, 'what's the matter?'

But she had to speak again and again before Silas could answer her.

'It's gone, child,' he said, at last, in strong agitation – 'Lantern Yard's gone. It must ha' been here, because there's the house with the o'erhanging window – I know that – it's just the same; but they've made this new opening; and see that big factory! It's all gone – chapel and all.'

'Come into that little brush-shop and sit down, father – they'll let you sit down,' said Eppie, always on the watch lest one of her father's strange attacks should come on. 'Perhaps the people can tell you all about it.'

But neither from the brush-maker, who had come to Shoe Lane only ten years ago, when the factory was already built, nor from any other source within his reach, could Silas learn anything of the old Lantern Yard friends, or of Mr Paston, the minister.

'The old place is all swep' away,' Silas said to Dolly Winthrop on the night of his return – 'the little graveyard and everything. The old home's gone; I've no home but this now. I shall never know whether they got at the truth o' the robbery, nor whether Mr Paston could ha' given me any light about the drawing o' the lots. It's dark to me, Mrs Winthrop, that is; I doubt it'll be dark to the last.'

'Well, yes, Master Marner,' said Dolly, who sat with a placid listening face, now bordered by grey hairs; 'I doubt it may. It's the will o' Them above as a many things should be dark to us; but there's some things as I've never felt i' the dark about, and they're mostly what comes i' the day's work. You were hard done by that once, Master Marner, and it seems as you'll never know the rights of it; but that doesn't hinder there *being* a rights, Master Marner, for all it's dark to you and me.'

'No,' said Silas, 'no; that doesn't hinder. Since the time the child was sent to me and I've come to love her as myself, I've had light enough to trusten by; and now she says she'll never leave me, I think I shall trusten till I die.'

❧ CONCLUSION ❧

THERE WAS ONE TIME OF THE YEAR which was held in Raveloe to be especially suitable for a wedding. It was when the great lilacs and laburnums in the old-fashioned gardens showed their golden and purple wealth above the lichen-tinted walls, and when there were calves still young enough to want bucketfuls of fragrant milk. People were not so busy then as they must become when the full cheese-making and the mowing had set in; and besides, it was a time when a light bridal dress could be worn with comfort and seen to advantage.

Happily the sunshine fell more warmly than usual on the lilac tufts the morning that Eppie was married, for her dress was a very light one. She had often thought, though with a feeling of renunciation, that the perfection of a wedding-dress would be a white cotton, with the tiniest pink sprig at wide intervals; so that when Mrs Godfrey Cass begged to provide one, and asked Eppie to choose what it should be, previous meditation had enabled her to give a decided answer at once.

Seen at a little distance as she walked across the church-yard and down the village, she seemed to be attired in pure white, and her hair looked like the dash of gold on a lily. One hand was on her husband's arm, and with the other she clasped the hand of her father Silas.

'You won't be giving me away, father,' she had said before they went to church; 'you'll only be taking Aaron to be a son to you.'

Dolly Winthrop walked behind with her husband; and there ended the little bridal procession.

There were many eyes to look at it, and Miss Priscilla Lammeter was glad that she and her father had happened to drive up to the door of the Red House just in time to see this pretty sight. They had come to keep Nancy company today, because Mr Cass had had to go away to Lytherley, for special reasons. That seemed to be a pity, for otherwise he might have gone, as Mr Crackenthorp and Mr Osgood certainly would, to look on at the wedding-feast which he had ordered at the Rainbow, naturally feeling a great interest in the weaver who had been wronged by one of his own family.

'I could ha' wished Nancy had had the luck to find a child like that and bring her up,' said Priscilla to her father, as they sat in the gig; 'I should ha' had something young to think of then, besides the lambs and the calves.'

'Yes, my dear, yes,' said Mr Lammeter; 'one feels that as one gets older. Things look dim to old folks; they'd need have some young eyes about 'em, to let 'em know the world's the same as it used to be.'

Nancy came out now to welcome her father and sister; and the wedding group had passed on beyond the Red House to the humbler part of the village.

Dolly Winthrop was the first to divine that old Mr Macey, who had been set in his arm-chair outside his own door, would expect some special notice as they passed, since he was too old to be at the wedding-feast.

'Mr Macey's looking for a word from us,'said Dolly; 'he'll be hurt if we pass him and say nothing – and him so racked with rheumatiz.'

So they turned aside to shake hands with the old man. He had looked forward to the occasion, and had his premeditated speech.

'Well, Master Marner,' he said, in a voice that quavered a good deal, 'I've lived to see my words come true. I was the first to say there was no harm in you, though your looks might be again' you; and I was the first to say you'd get your money back. And it's nothing but rightful as you should. And I'd ha' said the "Amens", and willing, at the holy matrimony; but Tookey's done it a good while now, and I hope you'll have none the worse luck.'

In the open yard before the Rainbow the party of guests were already assembled, though it was still nearly an hour before the appointed feast-time. But by this means they could not only enjoy the slow advent of their pleasure; they had also ample leisure to talk of Silas Marner's strange history, and arrive by due degrees at the conclusion that he had brought a blessing on himself by acting like a father to a lone motherless child. Even the farrier did not negative this sentiment: on the contrary, he took it up as peculiarly his own, and invited any hardy person present to contradict him. But he met with no contradiction; and all differences among the company were merged in a general agreement with Mr Snell's sentiment, that when a man had deserved his good luck, it was the part of his neighbours to wish him joy.

As the bridal group approached, a hearty cheer was raised in the Rainbow yard; and Ben Winthrop, whose jokes had retained their acceptable flavour, found it agreeable to turn in there and receive congratulations; not requiring the proposed interval of quiet at the Stone-pits before joining the company.

Eppie had a larger garden than she had ever expected there now; and in other ways there had been alterations at the expense of Mr Cass, the landlord, to suit Silas's larger family. For he and Eppie had declared that they would rather stay at the Stone-pits than go to any new home. The garden was fenced with stones on two sides, but in front there was an open fence, through which the flowers shone with answering gladness, as the four united people came within sight of them.

'O father,' said Eppie, 'what a pretty home ours is! I think nobody could be happier than we are.'

THE SAD FORTUNES OF THE
REV. AMOS BARTON

◦ ONE ◦

SHEPPERTON CHURCH WAS A VERY DIFFERENT-LOOKING building five-and-twenty years ago. To be sure, its substantial stone tower looks at you through its intelligent eye, the clock, with the friendly expression of former days; but in everything else what changes! Now there is a wide span of slated roof flanking the old steeple; the windows are tall and symmetrical; the outer doors are resplendent with oak-graining, the inner doors reverentially noiseless with a garment of red baize; and the walls, you are convinced, no lichen will ever again effect a settlement on – they are smooth and innutrient as the summit of the Rev. Amos Barton's head, after ten years of baldness and supererogatory soap. Pass through the baize doors and you will see the nave filled with well-shaped benches, understood to be free seats; while in certain eligible corners, less directly under the fire of the clergyman's eye, there are pews reserved for the Shepperton gentility. Ample galleries are supported on iron pillars, and in one of them stands the crowning glory, the very clasp or aigrette of Shepperton church-adornment – namely, an organ, not very much out of repair, on which a collector of small rents, differentiated by the force of circumstances into an organist, will accompany the alacrity of your departure after the blessing, by a sacred minuet or an easy 'Gloria'.

Immense improvement! says the well-regulated mind, which unintermittingly rejoices in the New Police, the Tithe Commutation Act, the penny-post, and all guarantees of human advancement, and has no moments when conservative-reforming intellect takes a map, while imagination does a little Toryism by the sly, revelling in regret that dear, old, brown, crumbling, picturesque inefficiency is everywhere giving place to spick-and-span new-painted, new-varnished efficiency, which will yield endless diagrams, plans, elevations, and sections, but alas! no picture. Mine, I fear, is not a well-regulated mind: it has an occasional tenderness for old abuses; it lingers with a certain fondness over the days of nasal clerks and top-booted parsons, and has a sigh for the departed shades of vulgar errors. So it is not surprising that I recall with a fond sadness Shepperton Church as it was in the old days, with its outer coat of rough stucco, its red-tiled roof, its heterogeneous windows patched with desultory bits of painted glass, and its little flight of steps with their wooden rail running up the outer wall, and leading to the school-children's gallery.

Then inside, what dear old quaintnesses! which I began to look at with delight, even when I was so crude a member of the congregation, that my nurse found it necessary to provide for the reinforcement of my devotional patience by smuggling bread-and-butter into the sacred edifice. There was the chancel, guarded by two little cherubims looking uncomfortably squeezed between arch and wall, and adorned with the escutcheons of the Oldinport family, which showed me inexhaustible possibilities of meaning in their blood-red hands, their death's heads and cross-bones, their leopards' paws, and Maltese crosses. There were inscriptions on the panels of the singing-gallery, telling of benefactions to the poor of Shepperton, with an involuted elegance of capitals and final flourishes, which my alphabetic erudition traced with ever-new delight. No benches in those days; but huge roomy pews, round which devout church-goers sat during 'lessons', trying to look anywhere else than into each other's eyes. No low partitions allowing you, with a dreary absence of contrast and mystery, to see everything at all moments; but tall dark panels, under whose shadow I sank with a sense of retirement through the Litany, only to feel with more intensity my burst into the conspicuousness of public life when I was made to stand up on the seat during the psalms or the singing.

And the singing was no mechanical affair of official routine; it had a drama. As the moment of psalmody approached, by some process to me as mysterious and untraceable as the opening of the flowers or the breaking-out of the stars, a slate appeared in front of the gallery, advertising in bold characters the psalm about to be sung, lest the sonorous announcement of the clerk should still leave the bucolic mind in doubt on that head. Then followed the migration of the clerk to the gallery, where, in company with a bassoon, two key-bugles, a carpenter understood to have an amazing power of singing 'counter', and two lesser musical stars, he formed the complement of a choir regarded in Shepperton as one of distinguished attraction, occasionally known to draw hearers from the next parish. The innovation of hymn-books was as yet undreamed of; even the New Version was regarded with a sort of melancholy tolerance, as part of the common degeneracy in a time when prices had dwindled, and a cotton gown was no longer stout enough to last a lifetime; for the lyrical taste of the best heads in Shepperton had been formed on Sternhold and Hopkins. But the greatest triumphs of the Shepperton choir were reserved for the Sundays when the slate announced an ANTHEM, with a dignified abstinence from particularization, both words and music lying far beyond the reach of the most ambitious amateur in the congregation: an anthem in which the key-bugles always ran away at a great pace, while the bassoon every now and then boomed a flying shot after them.

As for the clergyman, Mr Gilfil, an excellent old gentleman, who smoked very long pipes and preached very short sermons, I must not speak of him, or I might be tempted to tell the story of his life, which had its little romance, as most lives have between the ages of teetotum and tobacco. And at present I am concerned with quite another sort of clergy-man – the Rev. Amos Barton, who did not come to Shepperton until long after Mr Gilfil had departed this life – until after an interval in which Evangelicalism and the Catholic Question had begun to agitate the rustic mind with controversial debates. A Popish blacksmith had produced a strong Protestant reaction by declaring that, as soon as the Emancipation Bill was passed, he should do a great stroke of business in gridirons; and the disinclination of the Shepperton parishioners generally to dim the unique glory of St Lawrence, rendered the Church and Constitution an affair of their business and bosoms. A zealous Evangelical preacher had made the old sounding-board vibrate with quite a different sort of elo-cution from Mr Gilfil's; the hymn-book had almost superseded the Old and New Versions; and the great square pews were crowded with new faces from distant corners of the parish – perhaps from Dissenting chapels.

You are not imagining, I hope, that Amos Barton was the incumbent of Shepperton. He was no such thing. Those were days when a man could hold three small livings, starve a curate a-piece on two of them, and live badly himself on the third. It was so with the Vicar of Shepperton; a vicar given to bricks and mortar, and thereby running into debt far away in a northern county – who executed his vicarial functions towards Shepper-ton by pocketing the sum of thirty-five pounds ten per annum, the net surplus remaining to him from the proceeds of that living, after the dis-bursement of eighty pounds as the annual stipend of his curate. And now, pray, can you solve me the following problem? Given a man with a wife and six children: let him be obliged always to exhibit himself when out-side his own door in a suit of black broadcloth, such as will not undermine the foundations of the Establishment by a paltry plebeian glossiness or an unseemly whiteness at the edges; in a snowy cravat, which is a serious investment of labour in the hemming, starching, and ironing departments; and in a hat which shows no symptom of taking to the hideous doctrine of expediency, and shaping itself according to circumstances; let him have a parish large enough to create an external necessity for abundant shoe-leather, and an internal necessity for abundant beef and mutton, as well as poor enough to require frequent priestly consolation in the shape of shil-lings and sixpences; and, lastly, let him be compelled, by his own pride and other people's, to dress his wife and children with gentility from bonnet-strings to shoe-strings. By what process of division can the sum of eighty pounds per annum be made to yield a quotient which will cover that man's weekly expenses? This was the problem presented by the position of the Rev. Amos Barton, as curate of Shepperton, rather more than twenty years ago.

What was thought of this problem, and of the man who had to work it out, by some of the well-to-do inhabitants of Shepperton, two years or more after Mr Barton's arrival among them, you shall hear, if you will accompany me to Cross Farm, and to the fireside of Mrs Patten, a childless old lady, who had got rich chiefly by the negative process of spending nothing. Mrs Patten's passive accumulation of wealth, through all sorts of 'bad times', on the farm of which she had been sole tenant since her husband's death, her epigrammatic neighbour, Mrs Hackit, sarcastically accounted for by supposing that 'sixpences grew on the bents of Cross Farm'; while Mr Hackit, expressing his views more literally, reminded his wife that 'money breeds money'. Mr and Mrs Hackit, from the neighbouring farm, are Mrs Patten's guests this evening; so is Mr Pilgrim, the doctor from the nearest market-town, who, though occasionally affecting aristocratic airs, and giving late dinners with enigmatic side-dishes and poisonous port, is never so comfortable as when he is relaxing his professional legs in one of those excellent farmhouses where the mice are sleek and the mistress sickly. And he is at this moment in clover.

For the flickering of Mrs Patten's bright fire is reflected in her bright copper tea-kettle, the home-made muffins glisten with an inviting succulence, and Mrs Patten's niece, a single lady of fifty, who has refused the most ineligible offers out of devotion to her aged aunt, is pouring the rich cream into the fragrant tea with a discreet liberality.

Reader! *did* you ever taste such a cup of tea as Miss Gibbs is this moment handing to Mr Pilgrim? Do you know the dulcet strength, the animating blandness of tea sufficiently blended with real farmhouse cream? No – most likely you are a miserable town-bred reader, who think of cream as a thinnish white fluid, delivered in infinitesimal pennyworths down area steps; or perhaps, from a presentiment of calves' brains, you refrain from any lacteal addition, and rasp your tongue with unmitigated bohea. You have a vague idea of a milch cow as probably a white-plaster animal standing in a butterman's window, and you know nothing of the sweet history of genuine cream, such as Miss Gibbs's: how it was this morning in the udders of the large sleek beasts, as they stood lowing a patient entreaty under the milking-shed; how it fell with a pleasant rhythm into Betty's pail, sending a delicious incense into the cool air; how it was carried into that temple of moist cleanliness, the dairy, where it quietly separated itself from the meaner elements of milk, and lay in mellowed whiteness, ready for the skimming-dish which transferred it to Miss Gibbs's glass cream-jug. If I am right in my conjecture, you are unacquainted with the highest possibilities of tea: and Mr Pilgrim, who is holding that cup in his hands, has an idea beyond you.

Mrs Hackit declines cream; she has so long abstained from it with an eye to the weekly butter-money, that abstinence, wedded to habit, has begotten aversion. She is a thin woman with a chronic liver-complaint, which would have secured her Mr Pilgrim's entire regard and unreserved good word, even if he had not been in awe of her tongue, which was as sharp as his own lancet. She has brought her knitting – no frivolous fancy knitting, but a substantial woollen stocking; the click-click of her knitting-needles is the running accompaniment to all her conversation, and in her utmost enjoyment of spoiling a friend's self-satisfaction, she was never known to spoil a stocking.

Mrs Patten does not admire this excessive click-clicking activity. Quiescence in an easy-chair, under the sense of compound interest perpetually accumulating, has long seemed an ample function to her, and she does her malevolence gently. She is a pretty little old woman of eighty, with a close cap and tiny flat white curls round her face, as natty and unsoiled and invariable as the waxen image of a little old lady under a glass-case; once a lady's-maid, and married for her beauty. She used to adore her husband, and now she adores her money, cherishing a quiet blood-relation's hatred for her niece, Janet Gibbs, who, she knows, expects a large legacy, and whom she is determined to disappoint. Her money shall all go in a lump to a distant relation of her husband's, and Janet shall be saved the trouble of pretending to cry, by finding that she is left with a miserable pittance.

Mrs Patten has more respect for her neighbour Mr Hackit than for most people. Mr Hackit is a shrewd substantial man, whose advice about crops is always worth listening to, and who is too well off to want to borrow money.

And now that we are snug and warm with this little tea-party, while it is freezing with February bitterness outside, we will listen to what they are talking about.

'So,' said Mr Pilgrim, with his mouth only half empty of muffin, 'you had a row in Shepperton Church last Sunday. I was at Jim Hood's, the bassoon-man's, this morning, attending his wife, and he swears he'll be revenged on the parson – a confounded, methodistical, meddlesome chap, who must be putting his finger in every pie. What was it all about?'

'O, a passill o' nonsense,' said Mr Hackit, sticking one thumb between the buttons of his capacious waistcoat, and retaining a pinch of snuff with the other – for he was but moderately given to 'the cups that cheer but not inebriate', and had already finished his tea; 'they began to sing the wedding psalm for a new-married couple, as pretty a psalm an' as pretty a tune as any in the prayer-book. It's been sung for every new-married couple since I was a boy. And what can be better?' Here Mr Hackit stretched out his left arm, threw back his head, and broke into melody –

> 'O what a happy thing it is,
> And joyful for to see,
> Brethren to dwell together in
> Friendship and unity.

But Mr Barton is all for the hymns, and a sort o' music as I can't join in at all.'

'And so,' said Mr Pilgrim, recalling Mr Hackit from lyrical remi-
niscences to narrative, 'he called out "Silence!" did he? when he got
into the pulpit; and gave a hymn out himself to some meeting-house
tune?'

'Yes,' said Mrs Hackit, stooping towards the candle to pick up a stitch,
'and turned as red as a turkey-cock. I often say, when he preaches about
meekness, he gives himself a slap in the face. He's like me – he's got a
temper of his own.'

'Rather a low-bred fellow, I think, Barton,' said Mr Pilgrim, who hated
the Reverend Amos for two reasons – because he had called in a new
doctor, recently settled in Shepperton; and because, being himself a dab-
bler in drugs, he had the credit of having cured a patient of Mr Pilgrim's.
'They say his father was a Dissenting shoemaker; and he's half a Dissenter
himself. Why, doesn't he preach extempore in that cottage up here, of a
Sunday evening?'

'Tchuh!' – this was Mr Hackit's favourite interjection – 'that preaching
without book's no good, only when a man has a gift, and has the Bible at
his fingers' ends. It was all very well for Parry – he'd a gift; and in my
youth I've heard the Ranters out o' doors in Yorkshire go on for an hour or
two on end, without ever sticking fast a minute. There was one clever
chap, I remember, as used to say, "You're like the wood-pigeon; it says do,
do, do all day, and never sets about any work itself." That's bringing it
home to people. But our parson's no gift at all that way; he can preach as
good a sermon as need be heard when he writes it down. But when he
tries to preach wi'out book, he rambles about, and doesn't stick to his text;
and every now and then he flounders about like a sheep as has cast
itself, and can't get on its legs again. You wouldn't like that, Mrs Patten, if
you was to go to church now?'

'Eh, dear,' said Mrs Patten, falling back in her chair, and lifting up her
little withered hands, 'what 'ud Mr Gilfil say, if he was worthy to know
the changes as have come about i' the Church these last ten years? I don't
understand these new sort o' doctrines. When Mr Barton comes to see me,
he talks about nothing but my sins and my need o' marcy. Now, Mr
Hackit, I've never been a sinner. From the fust beginning, when I went
into service, I al'ys did my duty by my emplyers. I was a good wife as any
in the county – never aggravated my husband. The cheese-factor used to
say my cheese was al'ys to be depended on. I've known women, as their
cheeses swelled a shame to be seen, when their husbands had counted on
the cheese-money to make up their rent; and yet they'd three gowns to my
one. If I'm not to be saved, I know a many as are in a bad way. But it's well
for me as I can't go to church any longer, for if th' old singers are to be
done away with, there'll be nothing left as it was in Mr Patten's time; and
what's more, I hear you've settled to pull the church down and build it up
new?'

Now the fact was that the Rev. Amos Barton, on his last visit to Mrs

Patten, had urged her to enlarge her promised subscription of twenty pounds, representing to her that she was only a steward of her riches, and that she could not spend them more for the glory of God than by giving a heavy subscription towards the rebuilding of Shepperton Church – a practical precept which was not likely to smooth the way to her acceptance of his theological doctrine. Mr Hackit, who had more doctrinal enlightenment than Mrs Patten, had been a little shocked by the heathenism of her speech, and was glad of the new turn given to the subject by this question, addressed to him as church-warden and an authority in all parochial matters.

'Ah,' he answered, 'the parson's bothered us into it at last, and we're to begin pulling down this spring. But we haven't got money enough yet. I was for waiting till we'd made up the sum, and, for my part, I think the congregation's fell off o' late; though Mr Barton says that's because there's been no room for the people when they've come. You see, the congregation got so large in Parry's time, the people stood in the aisles; but there's never any crowd now, as I can see.'

'Well,' said Mrs Hackit, whose good-nature began to act now that it was a little in contradiction with the dominant tone of the conversation, 'I like Mr Barton. I think he's a good sort o' man, for all he's not overburthen'd i' th' upper storey; and his wife's as nice a lady-like woman as I'd wish to see. How nice she keeps her children! and little enough money to do't with; and a delicate creatur' – six children, and another a-coming. I don't know how they make both ends meet, I'm sure, now her aunt has left'em. But I sent 'em a cheese and a sack o'potatoes last week; that's something towards filling the little mouths.'

'Ah!' said Mr Hackit, 'and my wife makes Mr Barton a good stiff glass o'brandy-and-water, when he comes into supper after his cottage preaching. The parson likes it; it puts a bit o' colour into his face, and makes him look a deal handsomer.'

This allusion to brandy-and-water suggested to Miss Gibbs the introduction of the liquor decanters, now that the tea was cleared away; for in bucolic society five-and-twenty years ago, the human animal of the male sex was understood to be perpetually athirst, and 'something to drink' was as necessary a 'condition of thought' as Time and Space.

'Now, that cottage preaching,' said Mr Pilgrim, mixing himself a strong glass of 'cold without', 'I was talking about it to our Parson Ely the other day, and he doesn't approve of it at all. He said it did as much harm as good to give a too familiar aspect to religious teaching. That was what Ely said – it does as much harm as good to give a too familiar aspect to religious teaching.'

Mr Pilgrim generally spoke with an intermittent kind of splutter; indeed, one of his patients had observed that it was a pity such a clever man had a "pediment' in his speech. But when he came to what he conceived the pith of his argument or the point of his joke, he mouthed out his words with slow emphasis; as a hen, when advertising her accouchement, passes at irregular intervals from pianissimo semiquavers to fortissimo crotchets. He thought this speech of Mr Ely's particularly metaphysical and profound, and the more decisive of the question because it was a generality which represented no particulars to his mind.

'Well, I don't know about that,' said Mrs Hackit, who had always the courage of her opinion, 'but I know, some of our labourers and stockingers as used never to come to church, come to the cottage, and that's better than never hearing anything good from week's end to week's end. And there's that Track Society as Mr Barton has begun – I've seen more o' the poor people with going tracking, than all the time I've lived in the parish before. And there'd need be something done among 'em; for the drinking at them Benefit Clubs is shameful. There's hardly a steady man or steady woman either, but what's a dissenter.'

During this speech of Mrs Hackit's, Mr Pilgrim had emitted a succession of little snorts, something like the treble grunts of a guinea-pig, which were always with him the sign of suppressed disapproval. But he never contradicted Mrs Hackit – a woman whose 'pot-luck' was always to be relied on, and who on her side had unlimited reliance on bleeding, blistering, and draughts.

Mrs Patten, however, felt equal disapprobation, and had no reasons for suppressing it.

'Well,' she remarked, 'I've heared of no good from interfering with one's neighbours, poor or rich. And I hate the sight o' women going about trapesing from house to house in all weathers, wet or dry, and coming in with their petticoats dagged and their shoes all over mud. Janet wanted to join in the tracking, but I told her I'd have nobody tracking out o' my house: when I'm gone, she may do as she likes. I never dagged my petticoats in *my* life, and I've no opinion o' that sort o' religion.'

'No,' said Mr Hackit, who was fond of soothing the acerbities of the feminine mind with a jocose compliment, 'you held your petticoats so high, to show your tight ankles: it isn't everybody as likes to show her ankles.'

This joke met with general acceptance, even from the snubbed Janet, whose ankles were only tight in the sense of looking extremely squeezed by her boots. But Janet seemed always to identify herself with her aunt's personality, holding her own under protest.

Under cover of the general laughter the gentlemen replenished their glasses, Mr Pilgrim attempting to give his the character of a stirrup-cup by observing that he 'must be going'. Miss Gibbs seized this opportunity of telling Mrs Hackit that she suspected Betty, the dairymaid, of frying the best bacon for the shepherd, when he sat up with her to 'help brew'; whereupon Mrs Hackit replied that she had always thought Betty false; and Mrs Patten said there was no bacon stolen when *she* was able to manage. Mr Hackit, who often complained that he 'never saw the like to women with their maids – he never had any trouble with his men', avoided listening to this discussion, by raising the question of vetches with Mr Pilgrim. The stream of conversation had thus diverged: and no more was said about the Rev. Amos Barton, who is the main object of interest to us just now. So we may leave Cross Farm without waiting till Mrs Hackit, resolutely donning her clogs and wrappings, renders it incumbent on Mr Pilgrim also to fulfil his frequent threat of going.

❧ TWO ❧

IT WAS HAPPY FOR THR REV. AMOS Barton that he did not, like us, overhear the conversation recorded in the last chapter. Indeed, what mortal is there of us, who would find his satisfaction enhanced by an opportunity of comparing the picture he presents to himself of his own doings, with the picture they make on the mental retina of his neighbours? We are poor plants buoyed up by the air-vessels of our own conceit: alas for us, if we get a few pinches that empty us of that windy self-subsistence! The very capacity for good would go out of us. For, tell the most impassioned orator, suddenly, that his wig is awry, or his shirt-lap hanging out, and that he is tickling people by the oddity of his person, instead of thrilling them by the energy of his periods, and you would infallibly dry up the spring of his eloquence. That is a deep and wide saying, that no miracle can be wrought without faith – without the worker's faith in himself, as well as the recipient's faith in him. And the greater part of the worker's faith in himself is made up of the faith that others believe in him.

Let me be persuaded that my neighbour Jenkins considers me a block-head, and I shall never shine in conversation with him any more. Let me discover that the lovely Phoebe thinks my squint intolerable, and I shall never be able to fix her blandly with my disengaged eye again.

Thank heaven, then, that a little illusion is left to us, to enable us to be useful and agreeable – that we don't know exactly what our friends think of us – that the world is not made of looking-glass, to show us just the figure we are making, and just what is going on behind our backs! By the help of dear friendly illusion, we are able to dream that we are charming – and our faces wear a becoming air of self-possession; we are able to dream that other men admire our talents – and our benignity is undisturbed; we are able to dream that we are doing much good – and we do a little.

Thus it was with Amos Barton on that very Thursday evening, when he was the subject of the conversation at Cross Farm. He had been dining at

Mr Farquhar's, the secondary squire of the parish, and, stimulated by unwonted gravies and port-wine, had been delivering his opinion on affairs parochial and extra-parochial with considerable animation. And he was now returning home in the moonlight – a little chill, it is true, for he had just now no greatcoat compatible with clerical dignity, and a fur boa round one's neck, with a waterproof cape over one's shoulders, doesn't frighten away the cold from one's legs; but entirely unsuspicious, not only of Mr Hackit's estimate of his oratorical powers, but also of the critical remarks passed on him by the Misses Farquhar as soon as the drawing-room door had closed behind him. Miss Julia had observed that she *never* heard any one sniff so frightfully as Mr Barton did – she had a great mind to offer him her pocket-handkerchief; and Miss Arabella wondered why he always said he was going *for* to do a thing. He, excellent man! was meditating fresh pastoral exertions on the morrow; he would set on foot his lending library; in which he had introduced some books that would be a pretty sharp blow to the Dissenters – one especially, purporting to be written by a working man who, out of pure zeal for the welfare of his class, took the trouble to warn them in this way against those hypocritical thieves, the Dissenting preachers. The Rev. Amos Barton profoundly believed in the existence of that working man, and had thoughts of writing to him. Dissent, he considered, would have its head bruised in Shepperton, for did he not attack it in two ways? He preached Low-Church doctrine – as evangelical as anything to be heard in the Independent Chapel; and he made a High-Church assertion of ecclesiastical powers and functions. Clearly, the Dissenters would feel that 'the parson' was too many for them. Nothing like a man who combines shrewdness with energy. The wisdom of the serpent, Mr Barton considered, was one of his strong points.

Look at him as he winds through the little churchyard! The silver light that falls aslant on church and tomb, enables you to see his slim black figure, made all the slimmer by tight pantaloons, as it flits past the pale gravestones. He walks with a quick step, and is now rapping with sharp decision at the vicarage door. It is opened without delay by the nurse, cook, and housemaid, all at once – that is to say, by the robust maid-of-all-work, Nanny; and as Mr Barton hangs up his hat in the passage, you see that a narrow face of no particular complexion – even the small-pox that has attacked it seems to have been of a mongrel, indefinite kind – with features of no particular shape, and an eye of no particular expression, is surmounted by a slope of baldness gently rising from brow to crown. You judge him, rightly, to be about forty. The house is quiet, for it is half-past ten, and the children have long been gone to bed. He opens the sitting-room door, but instead of seeing his wife, as he expected, stitching with the nimblest of fingers by the light of one candle, he finds her dispensing with the light of a candle altogether. She is softly pacing up and down by the red firelight, holding in her arms little Walter, the year-old baby, who looks over her shoulder with large wide-open eyes, while the patient mother pats his back with her soft hand, and glances with a sigh at the heap of large and small stockings lying unmended on the table.

She was a lovely woman – Mrs Amos Barton; a large, fair, gentle Madonna, with thick, close, chestnut curls beside her well-rounded cheeks, and with large, tender, short-sighted eyes. The flowing lines of her tall figure made the limpest dress look graceful, and her old frayed black silk seemed to repose on her bust and limbs with a placid elegance and sense of distinction, in strong contrast with the uneasy sense of being no fit, that seemed to express itself in the rustling of Mrs Farquhar's *gros de Naples*. The caps she wore would have been pronounced, when off her head, utterly heavy and hideous – for in those days even fashionable caps were large and floppy; but surmounting her long arched neck, and mingling their borders of cheap lace and ribbon with her chestnut curls, they seemed miracles of successful millinery. Among strangers she was shy and tremulous as a girl of fifteen; she blushed crimson if any one appealed to her opinion; yet that tall, graceful, substantial presence was so imposing in its mildness, that men spoke to her with an agreeable sensation of timidity.

Soothing, unspeakable charm of gentle womanhood! which supersedes all acquisitions, all accomplishments. You would never have asked, at any period of Mrs Amos Barton's life, if she sketched or played the piano. You would even perhaps have been rather scandalized if she had descended from the serene dignity of *being* to the assiduous unrest of *doing*. Happy the man, you would have thought, whose eye will rest on her in the pauses of his fireside reading – whose hot aching forehead will be soothed by the contact of her cool soft hand – who will recover himself from dejection at his mistakes and failures in the loving light of her unreproaching eyes! You would not, perhaps, have anticipated that this bliss would fall to the share of precisely such a man as Amos Barton, whom you have already surmised not to have the refined sensibilities for which you might have imagined Mrs Barton's qualities to be destined by pre-established harmony. But I, for one, do not grudge Amos Barton his sweet wife. I have all my life had a sympathy for mongrel ungainly dogs, who are nobody's pets; and I would rather surprise one of them by a pat and a pleasant morsel, than meet the condescending advances of the loveliest Skye-terrier who has his cushion by my lady's chair. That, to be sure, is not the way of the world: if it happens to see a fellow of fine proportions and aristocratic mien, who makes no faux *pas*, and wins golden opinions from all sorts of men, it straightway picks out for him the loveliest of unmarried women, and says, *There* would be a proper match! Not at all, say I: let that successful, well-shapen, discreet and able gentleman put up with something less than the best in the matrimonial department; and let the sweet woman go to make sunshine and a soft pillow for the poor devil whose legs are not models, whose efforts are often blunders, and who in general gets more kicks than halfpence. She – the sweet woman – will like it as well; for her sublime capacity of loving will have all the more scope; and I venture to say, Mrs Barton's nature would never have grown half so angelic if she had married the man you would perhaps have had in your eye for her – a man with sufficient income and abundant personal éclat. Besides, Amos was an affectionate husband, and, in his way, valued his wife as his best treasure.

But now he has shut the door behind him, and said, 'Well, Milly!'

'Well, dear!' was the corresponding greeting, made eloquent by a smile.

'So that young rascal won't go to sleep! Can't you give him to Nanny?'

'Why, Nanny has been busy ironing this evening; but I think I'll take him to her now.' And Mrs Barton glided towards the kitchen, while her husband ran up-stairs to put on his maize-coloured dressing-gown, in which costume he was quietly filling his long pipe when his wife returned to the sitting-room. Maize is a colour that decidedly did *not* suit his complexion, and it is one that soon soils; why, then, did Mr Barton select it for domestic wear? Perhaps because he had a knack of hitting on the wrong thing in garb as well as in grammar.

Mrs Barton now lighted her candle, and seated herself before her heap of stockings. She had something disagreeable to tell her husband, but she would not enter on it at once.

'Have you had a nice evening, dear?'

'Yes, pretty well. Ely was there to dinner, but went away rather early. Miss Arabella is setting her cap at him with a vengeance. But I don't think he's much smitten. I've a notion Ely's engaged to some one at a distance, and will astonish all the ladies who are languishing for him here, by bringing home his bride one of these days. Ely's a sly dog; he'll like that.'

'Did the Farquhars say anything about the singing last Sunday?'

'Yes; Farquhar said he thought it was time there was some improvement in the choir. But he was rather scandalized at my setting the tune of "Lydia". He says he's always hearing it as he passes the Independent meeting.' Here Mr Barton laughed – he had a way of laughing at criticisms that other people thought damaging – and thereby showed the remainder of a set of teeth which, like the remnants of the Old Guard, were few in number, and very much the worse for wear. 'But,' he continued, 'Mrs Farquhar talked the most about Mr Bridmain and the Countess. She has taken up all the gossip about them, and wanted to convert me to her opinion, but I told her pretty strongly what I thought.'

'Dear me! why will people take so much pains to find out evil about others? I have had a note from the Countess since you went, asking us to dine with them on Friday.'

Here Mrs Barton reached the note from the mantelpiece, and gave it to her husband. We will look over his shoulder while he reads it: –

'SWEETEST MILLY, Bring your lovely face with your husband to dine with us' on Friday at seven – do. If not, I will be sulky with you till Sunday, when I shall be obliged to see you, and shall long to kiss you that very moment. Yours, according to your answer,

'CAROLINE CZERLASKI'

'Just like her, isn't it?' said Mrs Barton. 'I suppose we can go?'

'Yes; I have no engagement. The Clerical Meeting is tomorrow, you know.'

'And, dear, Woods the butcher called, to say he must have some money next week. He has a payment to make up.'

This announcement made Mr Barton thoughtful. He puffed more rapidly, and looked at the fire.

'I think I must ask Hackit to lend me twenty pounds, for it is nearly two months till Lady-day, and we can't give Woods our last shilling.'

'I hardly like you to ask Mr Hackit, dear – he and Mrs Hackit have been so very kind to us; they have sent us so many things lately.'

'Then I must ask Oldinport. I'm going to write to him tomorrow morning, for to tell him the arrangement I've been thinking of about having service in the workhouse while the church is being enlarged. If he agrees to attend service there once or twice, the other people will come. Net the large fish, and you're sure to have the small fry.'

'I wish we could do without borrowing money, and yet I don't see how we can. Poor Fred must have some new shoes; I couldn't let him go to Mrs Bond's yesterday because his toes were peeping out, dear child! and I can't let him walk anywhere except in the garden. He must have a pair before Sunday. Really, boots and shoes are the greatest trouble of my life. Everything else one can turn and turn about, and make old look like new; but there's no coaxing boots and shoes to look better than they are.'

Mrs Barton was playfully undervaluing her skill in metamorphosing boots and shoes. She had at that moment on her feet a pair of slippers which had long ago lived through the prunella phase of their existence, and were now running a respectable career as black silk slippers, having been neatly covered with that material by Mrs Barton's own neat fingers. Wonderful fingers those! they were never empty; for if she went to spend a few hours with a friendly parishioner, out came her thimble and a piece of calico or muslin, which, before she left, had become a mysterious little garment with all sorts of hemmed ins and outs. She was even trying to persuade her husband to leave off tight pantaloons, because if he would wear the ordinary gun-cases, she knew she could make them so well that no one would suspect the sex of the tailor.

But by this time Mr Barton has finished his pipe, the candle begins to burn low, and Mrs Barton goes to see if Nanny has succeeded in lulling Walter to sleep. Nanny is that moment putting him in the little cot by his mother's bedside; the head, with its thin wavelets of brown hair, indents the little pillow; and a tiny, waxen, dimpled fist hides the rosy lips, for baby is given to the infantile peccadillo of thumb-sucking.

So Nanny could now join in the short evening prayer, and all could go to bed.

Mrs Barton carried up-stairs the remainder of her heap of stockings, and laid them on a table close to her bedside, where also she placed a warm shawl, removing her candle, before she put it out, to a tin socket fixed at the head of her bed. Her body was very weary, but her heart was not heavy, in spite of Mr Woods the butcher, and the transitory nature of shoe-leather; for her heart so overflowed with love, she felt sure she was near a fountain of love that would care for husband and babes better than she could foresee; so she was soon asleep. But about half-past five o'clock in the morning, if there were any angels watching round her bed – and angels might be glad of such an office – they saw Mrs Barton rise up quietly, careful not to disturb the slumbering Amos, who was snoring the snore of the just, light her candle, prop herself upright with the pillows, throw the warm shawl round her shoulders, and renew her attack on the heap of undarned stockings. She darned away until she heard Nanny stirring, and then drowsiness came with the dawn; the candle was put out, and she sank into a doze. But at nine o'clock she was at the breakfast-table, busy cutting bread-and-butter for five hungry mouths, while Nanny, baby on one arm, in rosy cheeks, fat neck, and night-gown, brought in a jug of hot milk-and-water. Nearest her mother sits the nine-year-old Patty, the eldest child, whose sweet fair face is already rather grave sometimes, and who always wants to run up-stairs to save mamma's legs, which get so tired of an evening. Then there are four other blond heads – two boys and two girls, gradually decreasing in size down to Chubby, who is making a round O of her mouth to receive a bit of papa's 'baton'. Papa's attention was divided between petting Chubby, rebuking the noisy Fred, which he did with a somewhat excessive sharpness, and eating his own breakfast. He had not yet looked at Mamma, and did not know that her cheek was paler than usual. But Patty whispered, 'Mamma, have you the headache?'

Happily coal was cheap in the neighbourhood of Shepperton, and Mr Hackit would any time let his horses draw a load for 'the parson' without charge; so there was a blazing fire in the sitting-room, and not without need, for the vicarage garden, as they looked out on it from the bow-window, was hard with black frost, and the sky had the white woolly look that portends snow.

Breakfast over, Mr Barton mounted to his study, and occupied himself in the first place with his letter to Mr Oldinport. It was very much the same sort of letter as most clergymen would have written under the same circumstances, except that instead of *perambulate*, the Rev. Amos wrote *preambulate*, and instead of 'if haply', 'if happily', the contingency indicated being the reverse of happy. Mr Barton had not the gift of perfect accuracy in English orthography and syntax, which was unfortunate, as he was known not to be a Hebrew scholar, and not in the least suspected of being an accomplished Grecian. These lapses, in a man who had gone through the Eleusinian mysteries of a university education, surprised the young ladies of his parish extremely; especially the Misses Farquhar, whom he had once addressed in a letter as Dear Mads., apparently an abbreviation for Madams. The persons least surprised at the Rev. Amos's deficiencies were his clerical brethren, who had gone through the mysteries themselves.

At eleven o'clock, Mr Barton walked forth in cape and boa, with the sleet driving in his face, to read prayers at the workhouse, euphemistically called the 'College'. The College was a huge square stone building, standing on the best apology for an elevation of ground that could be seen for about ten miles around Shepperton. A flat ugly district this; depressing enough to look at even on the brightest days. The roads are black with coal-dust, the brick houses dingy with smoke; and at that time – the time of handloom weavers – every other cottage had a loom at its window, where you might see a pale, sickly-looking man or woman pressing a narrow chest against a board, and doing a sort of treadmill work with legs and arms. A troublesome district for a clergyman; at least to one who, like Amos Barton, understood the 'cure of souls' in something more than an official sense; for over and above the rustic stupidity furnished by the farm-labourers, the miners brought obstreperous animalism, and the weavers in an acrid Radicalism and Dissent. Indeed, Mrs Hackit often observed that the colliers, who many of them earned better wages than Mr Barton, 'passed their time in doing nothing but swilling ale and smoking, like the beasts that perish' (speaking, we may presume, in a remotely analogical sense); and in some of the ale-house corners the drink was flavoured by a dingy kind of infidelity, something like rinsings of Tom Paine in ditch-water. A certain amount of religious excitement created by the popular preaching of Mr Parry, Amos's predecessor, had nearly died out, and the religious life of Shepperton was falling back towards low-water mark. Here, you perceive, was a terrible stronghold of Satan; and you may well pity the Rev. Amos Barton, who had to stand single-handed and summon it to surrender. We read, indeed, that the walls of Jericho fell down before the sound of trumpets; but we nowhere hear that those trumpets were hoarse and feeble. Doubtless they were trumpets that gave forth clear ringing tones, and sent a mighty vibration through brick and mortar. But the oratory of the Rev. Amos resembled rather a Belgian railway-horn, which shows praiseworthy intentions inadequately fulfilled. He often missed the right note both in public and private exhortation, and got a little angry in consequence. For though Amos thought himself strong, he did not *feel* himself strong. Nature had given him the opinion, but not the sensation. Without that opinion he would probably never have worn cambric bands, but would have been an excellent cabinetmaker and deacon of an Independent church, as his father was before him (he was not a shoemaker, as Mr Pilgrim had reported). He might then have sniffed long and loud in the corner of his pew in Gun Street Chapel; he might have indulged in halting rhetoric at prayer-meetings, and have spoken faulty English in private life; and these little infirmities would not have prevented him, honest faithful man that he was, from being a shining light in the Dissenting circle of Bridgeport. A tallow dip, of the long eight description, is an excellent thing in the kitchen candlestick, and Betty's nose and eye are not sensitive to the difference between it and the finest wax; it is only when you stick it in the silver candlestick, and introduce it into the drawing-room, that it seems plebeian, dim, and ineffectual. Alas for the worthy man who, like that candle, gets himself into the wrong place! It is only the very largest souls who will be able to appreciate and pity him – who will discern and love sincerity of purpose amid all the bungling feebleness of achievement.

But now Amos Barton has made his way through the sleet as far as the College, has thrown off his hat, cape, and boa, and is reading, in the dreary stone-floored dining-room, a portion of the morning service to the inmates seated on the benches before him. Remember, the New Poor-law had not yet come into operation, and Mr Barton was not acting as paid chaplain of the Union, but as the pastor who had the cure of all souls in his parish, pauper as well as other. After the prayers he always addressed to them a short discourse on some subject suggested by the lesson for the day, striving if by this means some edifying matter might find its way into the pauper mind and conscience – perhaps a task as trying as you could well imagine to the faith and patience of any honest clergyman. For, on the very first bench, these were the faces on which his eye had to rest, watching whether there was any stirring under the stagnant surface.

Right in front of him – probably because he was stone-deaf, and it was deemed more edifying to hear nothing at a short distance than at a long one – sat 'Old Maxum', as he was familiarly called, his real patronymic remaining a mystery to most persons. A fine philological sense discerns in this cognomen an indication that the pauper patriarch had once been considered pithy and sententious in his speech; but now the weight of ninety-five years lay heavy on his tongue as well as in his ears, and he sat before the clergyman with protruded chin, and munching mouth, and eyes that seemed to look at emptiness.

Next to him sat Poll Fodge – known to the magistracy of her county as Mary Higgins – a one-eyed woman, with a scarred and seamy face, the most notorious rebel in the workhouse, said to have once thrown her broth over the master's coat-tails, and who, in spite of nature's apparent safeguards against that contingency, had contributed to the perpetuation of the Fodge characteristics in the person of a small boy, who was behaving naughtily on one of the back benches. Miss Fodge fixed her one sore eye on Mr Barton with a sort of hardy defiance.

Beyond this member of the softer sex, at the end of the bench, sat 'Silly Jim', a young man afflicted with hydrocephalus, who rolled his head from side to side, and gazed at the point of his nose. These were the supporters of Old Maxum on his right.

On his left sat Mr Fitchett, a tall fellow, who had once been a footman in the Oldinport family, and in that giddy elevation had enunciated a contemptuous opinion of boiled beef, which had been traditionally handed down in Shepperton as the direct cause of his ultimate reduction to pauper commons. His calves were now shrunken, and his hair was grey without the aid of powder; but he still carried his chin as if he were conscious of a stiff cravat; he set his dilapidated hat on with a knowing inclination towards the left ear; and when he was on field-work, he carted and uncarted the manure with a sort of flunkey grace, the ghost of that jaunty demeanour with which he used to usher in my lady's morning visitors. The flunkey nature was nowhere completely subdued but in his stomach, and he still divided society into gentry, gentry's flunkeys, and the people who provided for them. A clergyman without a flunkey was an anomaly, belonging to neither of these classes. Mr Fitchett had an irrepressible tendency to drowsiness under spiritual instruction, and in the recurrent regularity with which he dozed off until he nodded and awaked himself, he looked not unlike a piece of mechanism, ingeniously contrived for measuring the length of Mr Barton's discourse.

Perfectly wide-awake, on the contrary, was his left-hand neighbour, Mrs Brick, one of those hard undying old women, to whom age seems to have given a network of wrinkles, as a coat of magic armour against the attacks of winters, warm or cold. The point on which Mrs Brick was still sensitive – the theme on which you might possibly excite her hope and fear – was snuff. It seemed to be an embalming powder, helping her soul to do the office of salt.

And now, eke out an audience of which this front benchful was a sample, with a certain number of refractory children, over whom Mr Spratt, the master of the workhouse, exercised an irate surveillance, and I think you will admit that the university-taught clergyman, whose office it is to bring home the gospel to a handful of such souls, has a sufficiently hard task. For, to have any chance of success, short of miraculous intervention, he must bring his geographical, chronological, exegetical mind pretty nearly to the pauper point of view, or of no view; he must have some approximate conception of the mode in which the doctrines that have so much vitality in the plenum of his own brain will comport themselves *in vacuo* – that is to say, in a brain that is neither geographical, chronological, nor exegetical. It is a flexible imagination that can take such a leap as that, and an adroit tongue that can adapt its speech to so unfamiliar a position. The Rev. Amos Barton had neither that flexible imagination, nor that adroit tongue. He talked of Israel and its sins, of chosen vessels, of the Paschal lamb, of blood as a medium of reconciliation; and he strove in this way to convey religious truth within reach of the Fodge and Fitchett mind. This very morning, the first lesson was the twelfth chapter of Exodus, and Mr Barton's exposition turned on unleavened bread. Nothing in the world more suited to the simple understanding than instruction through familiar types and symbols! But there is always this danger attending it, that the interest or comprehension of your hearers may stop short precisely at the point where your spiritual interpretation begins. And Mr Barton this morning succeeded in carrying the pauper imagination to the dough-tub, but unfortunately was not able to carry it upwards from that well-known object to the unknown truths which it was intended to shadow forth.

Alas! a natural incapacity for teaching, finished by keeping 'terms' at Cambridge, where there are able mathematicians, and butter is sold by the yard, is not apparently the medium through which Christian doctrine will distil as welcome dew on withered souls.

And so, while the sleet outside was turning to unquestionable snow, and the stony dining-room looked darker and drearier, and Mr Fitchett was nodding his lowest, and Mr Spratt was boxing the boys' ears with a constant *rinforzando*, as he felt more keenly the approach of dinner-time, Mr Barton wound up his exhortation with something of the February chill at his heart as well as his feet. Mr Fitchett, thoroughly roused now the instruction was at an end, obsequiously and gracefully advanced to help Mr Barton in putting on his cape, while Mrs Brick rubbed her withered forefinger round and round her little shoe-shaped snuff-box, vainly seeking for the fraction of a pinch. I can't help thinking that if Mr Barton had shaken into that little box a small portion of Scotch high-dried, he might have produced something more like an amiable emotion in Mrs Brick's mind than anything she had felt under his morning's exposition of the unleavened bread. But our good Amos laboured under a deficiency of small tact as well as of small cash; and when he observed the action of the old woman's forefinger, he said, in his brusque way, 'So your snuff is all gone, eh?'

Mrs Brick's eyes twinkled with the visionary hope that the parson might be intending to replenish her box, at least mediately, through the present of a small copper.

'Ah, well! you'll soon be going where there is no more snuff. You'll be in need of mercy then. You must remember that you may have to seek for mercy and not find it, just as you're seeking for snuff.'

At the first sentence of this admonition, the twinkle subsided from Mrs Brick's eyes. The lid of her box went 'click!' and her heart was shut up at the same moment.

But now Mr Barton's attention was called for by Mr Spratt, who was dragging a small and unwilling boy from the rear. Mr Spratt was a small-featured, small-statured man, with a remarkable power of language, mitigated by hesitation, who piqued himself on expressing unexceptionable sentiments in unexceptional language on all occasions.

'Mr Barton, sir – aw – aw – excuse my trespassing on your time – aw – to beg that you will administer a rebuke to this boy; he is – aw – aw – most inveterate in ill-behaviour during service-time.'

The inveterate culprit was a boy of seven, vainly contending against 'candles' at his nose by feeble sniffing. But no sooner had Mr Spratt uttered his impeachment, than Miss Fodge rushed forward and placed herself between Mr Barton and the accused.

'That's my child, Muster Barton,' she exclaimed, further manifesting her maternal instincts by applying her apron to her offspring's nose. 'He's al'ys a-findin' fault wi' him, and a-poundin' him for nothin'. Let him goo an' eat his roost goose as is a-smellin' up in our noses while we're a-swallering them greasy broth, an' let my boy alooan.'

Mr Spratt's small eyes flashed, and he was in danger of uttering sentiments not unexceptionable before the clergyman; but Mr Barton, foreseeing that a prolongation of this episode would not be to edification, said 'Silence!' in his severest tones.

'Let me hear no abuse. Your boy is not likely to behave well, if you set him the example of being saucy.' Then stooping down to Master Fodge, and taking him by the shoulder, 'Do you like being beaten?'

'No-a.'

'Then what a silly boy you are to be naughty. If you were not naughty, you wouldn't be beaten. But if you are naughty, God will be angry, as well as Mr Spratt; and God can burn you for ever. That will be worse than being beaten.'

Master Fodge's countenance was neither affirmative nor negative of this proposition.

'But,' continued Mr Barton, 'if you will be a good boy, God will love you, and you will grow up to be a good man. Now, let me hear next Thursday that you have been a good boy.'

Master Fodge had no distinct vision of the benefit that would accrue to him from this change of courses. But Mr Barton, being aware that Miss Fodge had touched on a delicate subject in alluding to the roast goose, was determined to witness no more polemics between her and Mr Spratt, so, saying good morning to the latter, he hastily left the College.

The snow was falling in thicker and thicker flakes, and already the vicarage-garden was cloaked in white as he passed through the gate. Mrs Barton heard him open the door, and ran out of the sitting-room to meet him.

'I'm afraid your feet are very wet, dear. What a terrible morning! Let me take your hat. Your slippers are at the fire.'

Mr Barton was feeling a little cold and cross. It is difficult, when you have been doing disagreeable duties, without praise, on a snowy day, to attend to the very minor morals. So he showed no recognition of Milly's attentions, but simply said, 'Fetch me my dressing-gown, will you?'

'It is down, dear. I thought you wouldn't go into the study, because you said you would letter and number the books for the Lending Library. Patty and I have been covering them, and they are all ready in the sitting-room.'

'O, I can't do those this morning,' said Mr Barton, as he took off his boots and put his feet into the slippers Milly had brought him; 'you must put them away into the parlour.'

The sitting-room was also the day nursery and schoolroom; and while Mamma's back was turned, Dickey, the second boy, had insisted on super-seding Chubby in the guidance of a headless horse, of the red-wafered species, which she was drawing round the room, so that when Papa opened the door Chubby was giving tongue energetically.

'Milly, some of these children must go away. I want to be quiet.'

'Yes, dear. Hush, Chubby; go with Patty, and see what Nanny is getting for our dinner. Now, Fred and Sophy and Dickey, help me to carry these books into the parlour. There are three for Dickey. Carry them steadily.'

Papa meanwhile settled himself in his easy-chair, and took up a work on Episcopacy, which he had from the Clerical Book Society; thinking he would finish it and return it this afternoon, as he was going to the Clerical Meeting at Milby Vicarage, where the Book Society had its headquarters.

The Clerical Meetings and Book Society, which had been founded some eight or ten months, had had a noticeable effect on the Rev. Amos Barton. When he first came to Shepperton he was simply an evangelical clergy-man, whose Christian experiences had commenced under the teaching of the Rev. Mr Johns, of Gun Street Chapel, and had been consolidated at Cambridge under the influence of Mr Simeon. John Newton and Thomas Scott were his doctrinal ideals; he would have taken in the *Christian Observer* and the *Record*, if he could have afforded it; his anecdotes were chiefly of the pious-jocose kind, current in Dissenting circles; and he thought an Episcopalian Establishment unobjectionable.

But by this time the effect of the Tractarian agitation was beginning to be felt in backward provincial regions, and the Tractarian satire on the Low-Church party was beginning to tell even on those who disavowed or resisted Tractarian doctrines. The vibration of an intellectual movement was felt from the golden head to the miry toes of the Establishment; and so it came to pass that, in the district round Milby, the market-town close to Shepperton, the clergy had agreed to have a clerical meeting every month, wherein they would exercise their intellects by discussing theo-logical and ecclesiastical questions, and cement their brotherly love by discussing a good dinner. A Book Society naturally suggested itself as an adjunct of this agreeable plan; and thus, you perceive, there was provision made for ample friction of the clerical mind.

Now, the Rev. Amos Barton was one of those men who have a decided will and opinion of their own; he held himself bolt upright, and had no self-distrust. He would march very determinedly along the road he thought best; but then it was wonderfully easy to convince him which *was* the best road. And so a very little unwonted reading and unwonted discussion made him see that an Episcopalian Establishment was much more than unobjectionable, and on many other points he began to feel that he held opinions a little too far-sighted and profound to be crudely and suddenly communicated to ordinary minds. He was like an onion that has been rubbed with spices; the strong original odour was blended with something new and foreign. The Low-Church onion still offended refined High-Church nostrils, and the new spice was unwelcome to the palate of the genuine onion-eater.

We will not accompany him to the Clerical Meeting today, because we shall probably want to go thither some day when he will be absent. And just now I am bent on introducing you to Mr Bridmain and the Countess Czerlaski, with whom Mr and Mrs Barton are invited to dine tomorrow.

◁ THREE ▷

OUTSIDE, THE MOON IS SHEDDING ITS cold light on the cold snow, and the white-bearded fir-trees round Camp Villa are casting a blue shadow across the white ground, while the Rev. Amos Barton and his wife are audibly crushing the crisp snow beneath their feet, as, about seven o'clock on Friday evening, they approach the door of the above-named desirable country residence, containing dining, breakfast, and drawing rooms, etc., situated only half a mile from the market-town of Milby.

Inside, there is a bright fire in the drawing-room, casting a pleasant but uncertain light on the delicate silk dress of a lady who is reclining behind a screen in the corner of the sofa, and allowing you to discern that the hair of the gentleman who is seated in the arm-chair opposite, with a news-paper over his knees, is becoming decidedly grey. A little 'King Charles', with a crimson ribbon round his neck, who has been lying curled up in the very middle of the hearth-rug, has just discovered that that zone is too hot for him, and is jumping on the sofa, evidently with the intention of accommodating his person on the silk gown. On the table there are two wax-candles, which will be lighted as soon as the expected knock is heard at the door.

The knock is heard, the candles are lighted, and presently Mr and Mrs Barton are ushered in – Mr Barton erect and clerical, in a faultless tie and shining cranium; Mrs Barton graceful in a newly-turned black silk.

'Now this is charming of you,' said the Countess Czerlaski, advancing to meet them, and embracing Milly with careful elegance. 'I am really ashamed of my selfishness in asking my friends to come and see me in this frightful weather.' Then, giving her hand to Amos, 'And you, Mr Barton, whose time is so precious! But I am doing a good deed in drawing you away from your labours. I have a plot to prevent you from martyrizing yourself.'

While this greeting was going forward, Mr Bridmain, and Jet the spaniel, looked on with the air of actors who had no idea of by-play. Mr Bridmain, a stiff and rather thick-set man, gave his welcome with a laboured cordiality. It was astonishing how very little he resembled his beautiful sister.

For the Countess Czerlaski was undeniably beautiful. As she seated herself by Mrs Barton on the sofa, Milly's eyes, indeed, rested – must it be confessed? – chiefly on the details of the tasteful dress, the rich silk of a pinkish lilac hue (the Countess always wore delicate colours in an evening), the black lace pelerine, and the black lace veil falling at the back of the small closely-braided head. For Milly had one weakness – don't love her any the less for it, it was a pretty woman's weakness – she was fond of dress; and often, when she was making up her own economical millinery, she had romantic visions how nice it would be to put on really handsome stylish things – to have very stiff balloon sleeves, for example, without which a woman's dress was nought in those days. You and I, too, reader, have our weakness, have we not? which makes us think foolish things now and then. Perhaps it may lie in an excessive admiration for small hands and feet, a tall lithe figure, large dark eyes, and dark silken braided hair. All these the Countess possessed, and she had, moreover, a delicately-formed nose, the least bit curved, and a clear brunette complexion. Her mouth, it must be admitted, receded too much from her nose and chin, and to a prophetic eye threatened 'nut-crackers' in advanced age. But by the light of fire and wax candles that age seemed very far off indeed, and you would have said that the Countess was not more than thirty.

Look at the two women on the sofa together! The large, fair, mild-eyed Milly is timid even in friendship: it is not easy to her to speak of the affection of which her heart is full. The lithe, dark, thin-lipped Countess is racking her small brain for caressing words and charming exaggerations.

'And how are all the cherubs at home?' said the Countess, stooping to pick up Jet, and without waiting for an answer. 'I have been kept in-doors by a cold ever since Sunday, or I should not have rested without seeing you. What have you done with those wretched singers, Mr Barton?'

'O, we have got a new choir together, which will go on very well with a little practice. I was quite determined that the old set of singers should be dismissed. I had given orders that they should not sing the wedding psalm, as they call it, again, to make a new-married couple look ridiculous, and they sang it in defiance of me. I could put them into the Ecclesiastical Court, if I chose for to do so, for lifting up their voices in church in opposition to the clergyman.'

'And a most wholesome discipline that would be,' said the Countess;

'indeed, you are too patient and forbearing, Mr Barton. For my part, *I* lose *my* temper when I see how far you are from being appreciated in that miserable Shepperton.'

If, as is probable, Mr Barton felt at a loss what to say in reply to the insinuated compliment, it was a relief to him that dinner was announced just then, and that he had to offer his arm to the Countess.

As Mr Bridmain was leading Mrs Barton to the dining-room, he observed, 'The weather is very severe.'

'Very, indeed,' said Milly.

Mr Bridmain studied conversation as an art. To ladies he spoke of the weather, and was accustomed to consider it under three points of view: as a question of climate in general, comparing England with other countries in this respect; as a personal question, inquiring how it affected his lady interlocutor in particular; and as a question of probabilities, discussing whether there would be a change or a continuance of the present atmospheric conditions. To gentlemen he talked politics, and he read two daily papers expressly to qualify himself for this function. Mr Barton thought him a man of considerable political information, but not of lively parts.

'And so you are always to hold your Clerical Meetings at Mr Ely's?' said the Countess, between her spoonfuls of soup. (The soup was a little over-spiced. Mrs Short of Camp Villa, who was in the habit of letting her best apartments, gave only moderate wages to her cook.)

'Yes,' said Mr Barton; 'Milby is a central place, and there are many conveniences in having only one point of meeting.'

'Well,' continued the Countess, 'every one seems to agree in giving the precedence to Mr Ely. For my part, I *cannot* admire him. His preaching is too cold for me. It has no fervour – no heart. I often say to my brother, it is a great comfort to me that Shepperton Church is not too far off for us to go to; don't I, Edmund?'

'Yes,' answered Mr Bridmain; 'they show us into such a bad pew at Milby – just where there is a draught from that door. I caught a stiff neck the first time I went there.'

'O, it is the cold in the pulpit that affects me, not the cold in the pew. I was writing to my friend Lady Porter this morning, and telling her all about my feelings. She and I think alike on such matters. She is most anxious that when Sir William has an opportunity of giving away the living at their place, Dippley, they should have a thoroughly zealous clever man there. I have been describing a certain friend of mine to her, who, I think, would be just to her mind. And there is such a pretty rectory, Milly; shouldn't I like to see you the mistress of it?'

Milly smiled and blushed slightly. The Rev. Amos blushed very red, and gave a little embarrassed laugh – he could rarely keep his muscles within the limits of a smile.

At this moment John, the man-servant, approached Mrs Barton with a gravy-tureen, and also with a slight odour of the stable, which usually adhered to him through his in-door functions. John was rather nervous; and the Countess happening to speak to him at this inopportune moment, the tureen slipped and emptied itself on Mrs Barton's newly-turned black silk.

'O, horror! Tell Alice to come directly and rub Mrs Barton's dress,' said the Countess to the trembling John, carefully abstaining from approaching the gravy-sprinkled spot on the floor with her own lilac silk. But Mr Bridmain, who had a strictly private interest in silks, good-naturedly jumped up and applied his napkin at once to Mrs Barton's gown.

Milly felt a little inward anguish, but no ill-temper, and tried to make light of the matter for the sake of John as well as others. The Countess felt inwardly thankful that her own delicate silk had escaped, but threw out lavish interjections of distress and indignation.

'Dear saint that you are,' she said, when Milly laughed, and suggested that, as her silk was not very glossy to begin with, the dim patch would not be much seen; 'you don't mind about these things, I know. Just the same sort of thing happened to me at the Princess Wengstein's one day, on a pink satin. I was in an agony. But you are so indifferent to dress; and well you may be. It is you who make dress pretty, and not dress that makes you pretty.'

Alice, the buxom lady's-maid, wearing a much better dress than Mrs Barton's, now appeared to take Mr Bridmain's place in retrieving the mischief, and after a great amount of supplementary rubbing, composure was restored, and the business of dining was continued.

When John was recounting his accident to the cook in the kitchen, he observed, 'Mrs Barton's a hamable woman; I'd a deal sooner ha' throwed the gravy o'er the Countess's fine gownd. But laws! what tantrums she'd ha' been in arter the visitors was gone.'

'You'd a deal sooner not ha' throwed it down at all, I should think,' responded the unsympathetic cook, to whom John did *not* make love. 'Who d'you think's to mek gravy anuff, if you're to baste people's gownds wi' it?'

'Well,' suggested John, humbly, 'you should wet the bottom of the *duree* a bit, to hold it from slippin'.'

'Wet your granny!' returned the cook; a retort which she probably regarded in the light of a *reductio ad absurdum*, and which in fact reduced John to silence.

Later on in the evening, while John was removing the tea-things from the drawing-room, and brushing the crumbs from the table-cloth with an accompanying hiss, such as he was wont to encourage himself with in rubbing down Mr Bridmain's horse, the Rev. Amos Barton drew from his pocket a thin green-covered pamphlet, and, presenting it to the Countess, said, –

'You were pleased, I think, with my sermon on Christmas Day. It has been printed in *The Pulpit*, and I thought you might like a copy.'

'That indeed I shall. I shall quite value the opportunity of reading that sermon. There was such depth in it! – such argument! It was not a sermon to be heard only once. I am delighted that it should become generally known, as it will be, now it is printed in *The Pulpit*.'

'Yes,' said Milly, innocently, 'I was so pleased with the editor's letter.' And she drew out her little pocket-book, where she carefully treasured the editorial autograph, while Mr Barton laughed and blushed, and said, 'Nonsense, Milly!'

'You see,' she said, giving the letter to the Countess, 'I am very proud of the praise my husband gets.'

The sermon in question, by the by, was an extremely argumentative one on the Incarnation; which, as it was preached to a congregation not one of whom had any doubt of that doctrine, and to whom the Socinians therein confuted were as unknown as the Arimaspians, was exceedingly well adapted to trouble and confuse the Sheppertonian mind.

'Ah,' said the Countess, returning the editor's letter, 'he may well say he will be glad of other sermons from the same source. But I would rather you should publish your sermons in an independent volume, Mr Barton; it would be so desirable to have them in that shape. For instance, I could send a copy to the Dean of Radborough. And there is Lord Blarney, whom I knew before he was chancellor. I was a special favourite of his, and you can't think what sweet things he used to say to me. I shall not resist the temptation to write to him one of these days *sans façon*, and tell him how he ought to dispose of the next vacant living in his gift.'

Whether Jet the spaniel, being a much more knowing dog than was suspected, wished to express his disapproval of the Countess's last speech, as not accordant with his ideas of wisdom and veracity, I cannot say; but at this moment he jumped off her lap, and, turning his back upon her, placed one paw on the fender, and held the other up to warm, as if affecting to abstract himself from the current of conversation.

But now Mr Bridmain brought out the chess-board, and Mr Barton accepted his challenge to play a game, with immense satisfaction. The Rev. Amos was very fond of chess, as most people are who can continue through many years to create interesting vicissitudes in the game, by taking long-meditated moves with their knights, and subsequently discovering that they have thereby exposed their queen.

Chess is a silent game; and the Countess's chat with Milly is in quite an under-tone – probably relating to women's matters that it would be impertinent for us to listen to; so we will leave Camp Villa, and proceed to Milby Vicarage, where Mr Farquhar has sat out two other guests with whom he has been dining at Mr Ely's, and is now rather wearying that reverend gentleman by his protracted small-talk.

Mr Ely was a tall, dark-haired, distinguished-looking man of three-and-thirty. By the laity of Milby and its neighbourhood he was regarded as a man of quite remarkable powers and learning, who must make a considerable sensation in London pulpits and drawing-rooms on his occasional visit to the metropolis; and by his brother clergy he was regarded as a discreet and agreeable fellow. Mr Ely never got into a warm discussion; he suggested what might be thought, but rarely said what he thought himself; he never let either men or women see that he was laughing at them, and he never gave any one an opportunity of laughing at *him*. In one thing only he was injudicious. He parted his dark wavy hair down the middle; and as his head was rather flat than otherwise, that style of coiffure was not advantageous to him.

Mr Farquhar, though not a parishioner of Mr Ely's, was one of his warmest admirers, and thought he would make an unexceptionable son-in-law, in spite of his being of no particular 'family'. Mr Farquhar was susceptible on the point of 'blood' – his own circulating fluid, which animated a short and somewhat flabby person, being, he considered, of very superior quality.

'By the by,' he said, with a certain pomposity counteracted by a lisp, 'what an ath Barton makth of himthelf, about that Bridmain and the Counteth, ath she callth herthelf. After you were gone the other evening, Mithith Farquhar wath telling him the general opinion about them in the neighbourhood, and he got quite red and angry. Bleth your thoul, he believth the whole thtory about her Polish huthband and hith wonderful ethcapeth; and ath for her – why, he thinkth her perfection, a woman of motht refined feelingth, and no end of thtuff.'

Mr Ely smiled. 'Some people would say our friend Barton was not the best judge of refinement. Perhaps the lady flatters him a little, and we men are susceptible. She goes to Shepperton Church every Sunday – drawn there, let us suppose, by Mr Barton's eloquence.'

'Pshaw,' said Mr Farquhar: 'now, to my mind, you have only to look at that woman to thee what she ith – throwing her eyth about when she comth into church, and drething in a way to attract attention. I should thay, she'th tired of her brother Bridmain, and looking out for another brother with a thtronger family likeneth. Mithith Farquhar ith very fond of Mithith Barton, and ith quite dithtrethed that she should athothiate with thuch a woman, tho she attacked him on the thubject purpothly. But I tell her it'th of no uthe, with a pig-headed fellow like him. Barton'th well-meaning enough, but *tho* conteited. I've left off giving him my advithe.'

Mr Ely smiled inwardly and said to himself, 'What a punishment!' But to Mr Farquhar he said, 'Barton might be more judicious, it must be confessed.' He was getting tired, and did not want to develop the subject.

'Why, nobody vithit-th them but the Bartonth,' continued Mr Farquhar, 'and why should thuch people come here, unleth they had particular reathonth for preferring a neighbourhood where they are not known? Pooh! it lookth bad on the very fathe of it. *You* called on them, now; how did you find them?'

'O! – Mr Bridmain strikes me as a common sort of man, who is making an effort to seem wise and well-bred. He comes down on one tremendously with political information, and seems knowing about the King of the French. The Countess is certainly a handsome woman, but she puts on the grand air a little too powerfully. Woodcock was immensely taken with her, and insisted on his wife's calling on her and asking her to dinner; but I think Mrs Woodcock turned restive after the first visit, and wouldn't invite her again.'

'Ha, ha! Woodcock hath alwayth a thoft place in hith heart for a pretty fathe. It'th odd how he came to marry that plain woman, and no fortune either.'

'Mysteries of the tender passion,' said Mr Ely. 'I am not initiated yet, you know.'

Here Mr Farquhar's carriage was announced, and as we have not found his conversation particularly brilliant under the stimulus of Mr Ely's exceptional presence, we will not accompany him home to the less exciting atmosphere of domestic life.

Mr Ely threw himself with a sense of relief into his easiest chair, set his feet on the hobs, and in this attitude of bachelor enjoyment began to read Bishop Jebb's Memoirs.

❧ FOUR ❧

I AM BY NO MEANS SURE THAT IF THE good people of Milby had known the truth about the Countess Czerlaski, they would not have been considerably disappointed to find that it was very far from being as bad as they imagined. Nice distinctions are troublesome. It is so much easier to say that a thing is black, than to discriminate the particular shade of brown, blue, or green, to which it really belongs. It is so much easier to make up your mind that your neighbour is good for nothing, than to enter into all the circumstances that would oblige you to modify that opinion.

Besides, think of all the virtuous declamation, all the penetrating observation, which had been built up entirely on the fundamental position that the Countess was a very objectionable person indeed, and which would be utterly overturned and nullified by the destruction of that premise. Mrs Phipps, the banker's wife, and Mrs Landor, the attorney's wife, had invested part of their reputation for acuteness in the supposition that Mr Bridmain was not the Countess's brother. Moreover, Miss Phipps was conscious that if the Countess was not a disreputable person, she, Miss Phipps, had no compensating superiority in virtue to set against the other lady's manifest superiority in personal charms. Miss Phipps's stumpy figure and unsuccessful attire, instead of looking down from a mount of virtue with an auréole round its head, would then be seen on the same level and in the same light as the Countess Czerlaski's Diana-like form and well-chosen drapery. Miss Phipps, for her part, didn't like dressing for effect – she had always avoided that style of appearance which was calculated to create a sensation.

Then what amusing innuendoes of the Milby gentlemen over their wine would have been entirely frustrated and reduced to nought, if you had told them that the Countess had really been guilty of no misdemeanours which demanded her exclusion from strictly respectable society; that her husband had been the veritable Count Czerlaski, who had had wonderful escapes, as she said, and who, as she did not say, but as was said in certain circulars once folded by her fair hands, had subsequently given dancing lessons in the metropolis; that Mr Bridmain was neither more nor less than her half-brother, who, by unimpeached integrity and industry, had won a partnership in a silk-manufactory, and thereby a moderate fortune, that enabled him to retire, as you see, to study politics, the weather, and the art of conversation at his leisure. Mr Bridmain, in fact, quadragenarian bachelor as he was, felt extremely well pleased to receive his sister in her widowhood, and to shine in the reflected light of her beauty and title. Every man who is not a monster, a mathematician, or a mad philosopher, is the slave of some woman or other. Mr Bridmain had put his neck under the yoke of his handsome sister, and though his soul was a very little one – of the smallest description indeed – he would not have ventured to call it his own. He might be slightly recalcitrant now and then, as is the habit of long-eared pachyderms, under the thong of the fair Countess's tongue; but there seemed little probability that he would ever get his neck loose. Still, a bachelor's heart is an outlying fortress that some fair enemy may any day take either by storm or stratagem; and there was always the possibility that Mr Bridmain's first nuptials might occur before the Countess was quite sure of her second. As it was, however, he submitted to all his sister's caprices, never grumbled because her dress and her maid formed a considerable item beyond her own little income of sixty pounds per annum, and consented to lead with her a migratory life, as personages on the debatable ground between aristocracy and commonalty, instead of settling in some spot where his five hundred a-year might have won him the definite dignity of a parochial magnate.

The Countess had her views in choosing a quiet provincial place like Milby. After three years of widowhood, she had brought her feelings to contemplate giving a successor to her lamented Czerlaski, whose fine whiskers, fine air, and romantic fortunes had won her heart ten years ago, when, as pretty Caroline Bridmain, in the full bloom of five-and-twenty, she was governess to Lady Porter's daughters, whom he initiated into the mysteries of the *pas de basque* and the Lancers' quadrilles. She had had seven years of sufficiently happy matrimony with Czerlaski, who had taken her to Paris and Germany, and introduced her there to many of his old friends with large titles and small fortunes. So that the fair Caroline had had considerable experience of life, and had gathered therefrom, not, indeed, any very ripe and comprehensive wisdom, but much external polish, and certain practical conclusions of a very decided kind. One of these conclusions was, that there were things more solid in life than fine whiskers and a title, and that, in accepting a second husband, she would regard these items as quite subordinate to a carriage and a settlement. Now, she had ascertained, by tentative residences, that the kind of bite she was angling for was difficult to be met with at watering-places, which were already preoccupied with abundance of angling beauties, and were chiefly stocked with men whose whiskers might be dyed, and whose incomes were still more problematic; so she had determined on trying a neighbourhood where people were extremely well acquainted with each other's affairs, and where the women were mostly ill-dressed and ugly. Mr Bridmain's slow brain had adopted his sister's views, and it seemed to him that a woman so handsome and distinguished as the Countess must certainly make a match that might lift himself into the region of county celebrities, and give him at least a sort of cousinship to the quarter-sessions.

All this, which was the simple truth, would have seemed extremely flat to the gossips of Milby, who had made up their minds to something much more exciting. There was nothing here so very detestable. It is true, the Countess was a little vain, a little ambitious, a little selfish, a little shallow and frivolous, a little given to white lies. But who considers such slight blemishes, such moral pimples as these, disqualifications for entering into the most respectable society! Indeed, the severest ladies in Milby would have been perfectly aware that these characteristics would have created no wide distinction between the Countess Czerlaski and themselves; and since it was clear there *was* a wide distinction – why, it must lie in the possession of some vices from which they were undeniably free.

Hence it came to pass that Milby respectability refused to recognize the Countess Czerlaski, in spite of her assiduous church-going, and the deep disgust she was known to have expressed at the extreme paucity of the congregations on Ash-Wednesdays. So she began to feel that she had miscalculated the advantages of a neighbourhood where people are well acquainted with each other's private affairs. Under these circumstances, you will imagine how welcome was the perfect credence and admiration she met with from Mr and Mrs Barton. She had been especially irritated by Mr Ely's behaviour to her; she felt sure that he was not in the least struck with her beauty, that he quizzed her conversation, and that he spoke of her with a sneer. A woman always knows where she is utterly powerless, and shuns a coldly satirical eye as she would shun a Gorgon. And she was especially eager for clerical notice and friendship, not merely because that is quite the most respectable countenance to be obtained in society, but because she really cared about religious matters, and had an uneasy sense that she was not altogether safe in that quarter. She had serious intentions of becoming *quite* pious – without any reserves – when she had once got her carriage and settlement. Let us do this one sly trick, says Ulysses to Neoptolemus, and we will be perfectly honest ever after –

> ἀλλ᾽ ἡδὺ γάρ τοι κτῆμα τῆς νίκης λαβεῖν
> τόλμα· δίκαιοι δ᾽ αὖθις ἐκφανούμεθα.

The Countess did not quote Sophocles, but she said to herself, 'Only this little bit of pretence and vanity, and then I will be *quite* good, and make myself quite safe for another world.'

And as she had by no means such fine taste and insight in theological teaching as in costume, the Rev. Amos Barton seemed to her a man not only of learning – *that* is always understood with a clergyman – but of much power as a spiritual director. As for Milly, the Countess really loved her as well as the preoccupied state of her affections would allow. For you have already perceived that there was one being to whom the Countess was absorbingly devoted, and to whose desires she made everything else subservient – namely, Caroline Czerlaski, *née* Bridmain.

Thus there was really not much affectation in her sweet speeches and attentions to Mr and Mrs Barton. Still their friendship by no means adequately represented the object she had in view when she came to Milby, and it had been for some time clear to her that she must suggest a new change of residence to her brother.

The thing we look forward to often comes to pass, but never precisely in the way we have imagined to ourselves. The Countess did actually leave Camp Villa before many months were past, but under circumstances which had not at all entered into her contemplation.

⊲ FIVE ⊳

THE REV. AMOS BARTON, WHOSE SAD fortunes I have undertaken to relate, was, you perceive, in no respect an ideal or exceptional character; and perhaps I am doing a bold thing to bespeak your sympathy on behalf of a man who was so very far from remarkable, – a man whose virtues were not heroic, and who had no undetected crime within his breast; who had not the slightest mystery hanging about him, but was palpably and unmistakably commonplace; who was not even in love, but had had that complaint favourably many years ago. 'An utterly uninteresting character!' I think I hear a lady reader exclaim – Mrs Farthingale, for example, who prefers the ideal in fiction; to whom tragedy means ermine tippets, adultery, and murder; and comedy, the adventures of some personage who is quite a 'character'.

But, my dear madam, it is so very large a majority of your fellow-countrymen that are of this insignificant stamp. At least eighty out of a hundred of your adult male fellow-Britons returned in the last census are neither extraordinarily silly, nor extraordinarily wicked, nor extraordinarily wise; their eyes are neither deep and liquid with sentiment, nor sparkling with suppressed witticisms; they have probably had no hair-breadth escapes or thrilling adventures; their brains are certainly not pregnant with genius, and their passions have not manifested themselves at all after the fashion of a volcano. They are simply men of complexions more or less muddy, whose conversation is more or less bald and dis-jointed. Yet these commonplace people – many of them – bear a con-science, and have felt the sublime prompting to do the painful right; they have their unspoken sorrows, and their sacred joys; their hearts have perhaps gone out towards their first-born, and they have mourned over the irreclaimable dead. Nay, is there not a pathos in their very insignifi-cance – in our comparison of their dim and narrow existence with the glorious possibilities of that human nature which they share?

Depend upon it, you would gain unspeakably if you would learn with me to see some of the poetry and the pathos, the tragedy and the comedy, lying in the experience of a human soul that looks out through dull grey eyes, and that speaks in a voice of quite ordinary tones. In that case, I should have no fear of your not caring to know what farther befell the Rev. Amos Barton, or of your thinking the homely details I have to tell at all beneath your attention. As it is, you can, if you please, decline to pursue my story farther; and you will easily find reading more to your taste, since I learn from the newspapers that many remarkable novels, full of striking situations, thrilling incidents, and eloquent writing, have appeared only within the last season.

Meanwhile, readers who have begun to feel an interest in the Rev. Amos Barton and his wife, will be glad to learn that Mr Oldinport lent the twenty pounds. But twenty pounds are soon exhausted when twelve are due as back payment to the butcher, and when the possession of eight extra sovereigns in February weather is an irresistible temptation to order a new greatcoat. And though Mr Bridmain so far departed from the necessary economy entailed on him by the Countess's elegant toilette and expensive maid, as to choose a handsome black silk, stiff, as his experi-enced eye discerned, with the genuine strength of its own texture, and not with the factitious strength of gum, and present it to Mrs Barton, in retrieval of the accident that had occurred at his table, yet, dear me – as every husband has heard – what is the present of a gown when you are deficiently furnished with the et-ceteras of apparel, and when, moreover, there are six children whose wear and tear of clothes is something incredible to the non-maternal mind?

Indeed, the equation of income and expenditure was offering new and constantly accumulating difficulties to Mr and Mrs Barton; for shortly after the birth of little Walter, Milly's aunt, who had lived with her ever since her marriage, had withdrawn herself, her furniture, and her yearly income, to the household of another niece; prompted to that step, very probably, by a slight 'tiff' with the Rev. Amos, which occurred while Milly was up-stairs, and proved one too many for the elderly lady's patience and magnanimity. Mr Barton's temper was a little warm, but, on the other hand, elderly maiden ladies are known to be susceptible; so we will not suppose that all the blame lay on his side – the less so, as he had every motive for humouring an inmate whose presence kept the wolf from the door. It was now nearly a year since Miss Jackson's departure, and, to a fine ear, the howl of the wolf was audibly approaching.

It was a sad thing, too, that when the last snow had melted, when the purple and yellow crocuses were coming up in the garden, and the old church was already half pulled down, Milly had an illness which made her lips look pale, and rendered it absolutely necessary that she should not exert herself for some time. Mr Brand, the Shepperton doctor so obnoxious to Mr Pilgrim, ordered her to drink port-wine, and it was quite necessary to have a charwoman very often, to assist Nanny in all the extra work that fell upon her.

Mrs Hackit, who hardly ever paid a visit to any one but her oldest and nearest neighbour, Mrs Patten, now took the unusual step of calling at the vicarage one morning; and the tears came into her unsentimental eyes as she saw Milly seated pale and feeble in the parlour, unable to persevere in sewing the pinafore that lay on the table beside her. Little Dickey, a boisterous boy of five, with large pink cheeks and sturdy legs, was having his turn to sit with Mamma, and was squatting quiet as a mouse at her knee, holding her soft white hand between his little red black-nailed fists. He was a boy whom Mrs Hackit, in a severe mood, had pronounced 'stocky' (a word that etymologically in all probability, conveys some allusion to an instrument of punishment for the refractory); but seeing him thus subdued into goodness, she smiled at him with her kindest smile, and stooping down, suggested a kiss – a favour which Dicky resolutely declined.

'Now do you take nourishing things enough?' was one of Mrs Hackit's first questions, and Milly endeavoured to make it appear that no woman was ever so much in danger of being over-fed and led into self-indulgent habits as herself. But Mrs Hackit gathered one fact from her replies, namely, that Mr Brand had ordered port-wine.

While this conversation was going forward, Dickey had been furtively stroking and kissing the soft white hand; so that at last, when a pause came, his mother said, smilingly, 'Why are you kissing my hand, Dickey?'

'It id to yovely,' answered Dickey, who, you observe, was decidedly backward in his pronunciation.

Mrs Hackit remembered this little scene in after days, and thought with peculiar tenderness and pity of the 'stocky boy'.

The next day there came a hamper with Mrs Hackit's respects; and on being opened it was found to contain half-a-dozen of port-wine and two couples of fowls. Mrs Farquhar, too, was very kind; insisted on Mrs Barton's rejecting all arrowroot but hers, which was genuine Indian, and carried away Sophy and Fred to stay with her a fortnight. These and other good-natured attentions made the trouble of Milly's illness more bearable; but they could not prevent it from swelling expenses, and Mr Barton began to have serious thoughts of representing his case to a certain charity for the relief of needy curates.

Altogether, as matters stood in Shepperton, the parishioners were more likely to have a strong sense that the clergyman needed their material aid, than that they needed his spiritual aid, – not the best state of things in this age and country, where faith in men solely on the ground of their spiritual gifts has considerably diminished, and especially unfavourable to the influence of the Rev. Amos, whose spiritual gifts would not have had a very commanding power even in an age of faith.

But, you ask, did not the Countess Czerlaski pay any attention to her friends all this time? To be sure she did. She was indefatigable in visiting her 'sweet Milly', and sitting with her for hours together. It may seem remarkable to you that she neither thought of taking away any of the children, nor of providing for any of Milly's probable wants; but ladies of rank and of luxurious habits, you know, cannot be expected to surmise the details of poverty. She put a great deal of eau-de-Cologne on Mrs Barton's pocket-handkerchief, rearranged her pillow and footstool, kissed her cheeks, wrapped her in a soft warm shawl from her own shoulders, and amused her with stories of the life she had seen abroad. When Mr Barton joined them she talked of Tractarianism, of her determination not to re-enter the vortex of fashionable life, and of her anxiety to see him in a sphere large enough for his talents. Milly thought her sprightliness and affectionate warmth quite charming, and was very fond of her; while the Rev. Amos had a vague consciousness that he had risen into aristocratic life, and only associated with his middle-class parishioners in a pastoral and parenthetic manner.

However, as the days brightened, Milly's cheeks and lips brightened too; and in a few weeks she was almost as active as ever, though watchful eyes might have seen that activity was not easy to her. Mrs Hackit's eyes were of that kind, and one day, when Mr and Mrs Barton had been dining with her for the first time since Milly's illness, she observed to her husband – 'That poor thing's dreadful weak an' dilicate; she won't stan' havin' many more children.'

Mr Barton, meanwhile, had been indefatigable in his vocation. He had preached two extemporary sermons every Sunday at the workhouse, where a room had been fitted up for divine service, pending the alterations in the church; and had walked the same evening to a cottage at one or other extremity of his parish to deliver another sermon, still more extemporary, in an atmosphere impregnated with spring-flowers and perspiration. After all these labours you will easily conceive that he was considerably exhausted by half-past nine o'clock in the evening, and that a supper at a friendly parishioner's, with a glass, or even two glasses, of brandy-and-water after it, was a welcome reinforcement. Mr Barton was not at all an ascetic; he thought the benefits of fasting were entirely confined to the Old Testament dispensation; he was fond of relaxing himself with a little gossip; indeed, Miss Bond, and other ladies of enthusiastic views, sometimes regretted that Mr Barton did not more uninterruptedly exhibit a superiority to the things of the flesh. Thin ladies, who take little exercise, and whose livers are not strong enough to bear stimulants, are so extremely critical about one's personal habits! And, after all, the Rev. Amos never came near the borders of a vice. His very faults were middling – he was not *very* ungrammatical. It was not in his nature to be superlative in anything; unless, indeed, he was superlatively middling, the quintessential extract of mediocrity. If there was any one point on which he showed an inclination to be excessive, it was confidence in his own shrewdness and ability in practical matters, so that he was very full of plans which were something like his moves in chess – admirably well calculated, supposing the state of the case were otherwise. For example, that notable plan of introducing anti-Dissenting books into his Lending Library did not in the least appear to have bruised the head of Dissent, though it had certainly made Dissent strongly inclined to bite the Rev. Amos's heel. Again, he vexed the souls of his churchwardens and influential parishioners by his fertile suggestiveness as to what it would be well for them to do in the matter of the church repairs, and other ecclesiastical secularities.

'I never saw the like to parsons,' Mr Hackit said one day in conversation with his brother churchwarden, Mr Bond; 'they're al'ys for meddling with business, an they know no more about it than my black filly.'

'Ah,' said Mr Bond, 'they're too high learnt to have much common-sense.'

'Well,' remarked Mr Hackit, in a modest and dubious tone, as if throwing out a hypothesis which might be considered bold, 'I should say that's a bad sort of eddication as makes folks unreasonable.'

So that, you perceive, Mr Barton's popularity was in that precarious condition, in that toppling and contingent state, in which a very slight push from a malignant destiny would utterly upset it. That push was not long in being given, as you shall hear.

One fine May morning, when Amos was out on his parochial visits, and the sunlight was streaming through the bow-window of the sitting-room, where Milly was seated at her sewing, occasionally looking up to glance at the children playing in the garden, there came a loud rap at the door, which she at once recognized as the Countess's, and that well-dressed lady presently entered the sitting-room, with her veil drawn over her face. Milly was not at all surprised or sorry to see her; but when the Countess threw up her veil, and showed that her eyes were red and swollen, she was both surprised and sorry.

'What can be the matter, dear Caroline?'

Caroline threw down Jet, who gave a little yelp; then she threw her arms round Milly's neck, and began to sob; then she threw herself on the sofa, and begged for a glass of water; then she threw off her bonnet and shawl; and by the time Milly's imagination had exhausted itself in conjuring up calamities, she said, –

'Dear, how shall I tell you? I am the most wretched woman. To be deceived by a brother to whom I have been so devoted – to see him degrading himself – giving himself utterly to the dogs!'

'What can it be?' said Milly, who began to picture to herself the sober Mr Bridmain taking to brandy and betting.

'He is going to be married – to marry my own maid, that deceitful Alice, to whom I have been the most indulgent mistress. Did you ever hear of anything so disgraceful? so mortifying? so disreputable?'

'And has he only just told you of it?' said Milly, who, having really heard of worse conduct, even in her innocent life, avoided a direct answer.

'Told me of it! he had not even the grace to do that. I went into the dining-room suddenly and found him kissing her – disgusting at his time of life, is it not? – and when I reproved her for allowing such liberties, she turned round saucily, and said she was engaged to be married to my brother, and she saw no shame in allowing him to kiss her. Edmund is a miserable coward, you know, and looked frightened; but when she asked him to say whether it was not so, he tried to summon up courage and say yes. I left the room in disgust, and this morning I have been questioning Edmund, and find that he is bent on marrying this woman, and that he has been putting off telling me – because he was ashamed of himself, I suppose. I couldn't possibly stay in the house after this, with my own maid turned mistress. And now, Milly, I am come to throw myself on your charity for a week or two. *Will* you take me in?'

'That we will,' said Milly, 'if you will only put up with our poor rooms and way of living. It will be delightful to have you!'

'It will soothe me to be with you and Mr Barton a little while. I feel quite unable to go among my other friends just at present. What those two wretched people will do I don't know – leave the neighbourhood at once, I hope. I entreated my brother to do so, before he disgraced himself.'

When Amos came home, he joined his cordial welcome and sympathy to Milly's. By-and-by the Countess's formidable boxes, which she had carefully packed before her indignation drove her away from Camp Villa, arrived at the vicarage, and were deposited in the spare bedroom, and in two closets, not spare, which Milly emptied for their reception. A week afterwards, the excellent apartments at Camp Villa, comprising dining and drawing rooms, three bedrooms and a dressing-room, were again to let, and Mr Bridmain's sudden departure, together with the Countess Czerlaski's installation as a visitor at Shepperton Vicarage, became a topic of general conversation in the neighbourhood. The keen-sighted virtue of Milby and Shepperton saw in all this a confirmation of its worst suspicions, and pitied the Rev. Amos Barton's gullibility.

But when week after week, and month after month, slipped by without witnessing the Countess's departure – when summer and harvest had fled, and still left her behind them occupying the spare bedroom and the closets, and also a large proportion of Mrs Barton's time and attention, new surmises of a very evil kind were added to the old rumours, and began to take the form of settled convictions in the minds even of Mr Barton's most friendly parishioners.

And now, here is an opportunity for an accomplished writer to apostrophize calumny, to quote Virgil, and to show that he is acquainted with the most ingenious things which have been said on that subject in polite literature.

But what is opportunity to the man who can't use it? An undefecundated egg, which the waves of time wash away into nonentity. So, as my memory is ill-furnished, and my notebook still worse, I am unable to show myself either erudite or eloquent apropos of the calumny whereof the Rev. Amos Barton was the victim. I can only ask my reader, – did you ever upset your ink-bottle, and watch, in helpless agony, the rapid spread of Stygian blackness over your fair manuscript or fairer table-cover? With a like inky swiftness did gossip now blacken the reputation of the Rev. Amos Barton, causing the unfriendly to scorn and even the friendly to stand aloof, at a time when difficulties of another kind were fast thickening around him.

◁ SIX ▷

ONE NOVEMBER MORNING, AT LEAST SIX months after the Countess Czerlaski had taken up her residence at the vicarage, Mrs Hackit heard that her neighbour Mrs Patten had an attack of her old complaint, vaguely called 'the spasms'. Accordingly, about eleven o'clock, she put on her velvet bonnet and cloth cloak, with a long boa and muff large enough to stow a prize baby in; for Mrs Hackit regulated her costume by the calendar, and brought out her furs on the first of November; whatever might be the temperature. She was not a woman weakly to accommodate herself to shilly-shally proceedings. If the season didn't know what it ought to do, Mrs Hackit did. In her best days, it was always sharp weather at 'Gunpowder Plot', and she didn't like new fashions.

And this morning the weather was very rationally in accordance with her costume, for as she made her way through the fields to Cross Farm, the yellow leaves on the hedge-girt elms, which showed bright and golden against the long-hanging purple clouds, were being scattered across the grassy path by the coldest of November winds. 'Ah,' Mrs Hackit thought to herself, 'I daresay we shall have a sharp pinch this winter, and if we do, I shouldn't wonder if it takes the old lady off. They say a green Yule makes a fat churchyard; but so does a white Yule too, for that matter. When the stool's rotten enough, no matter who sits on it.'

However, on her arrival at Cross Farm, the prospect of Mrs Patten's decease was again thrown into the dim distance in her imagination, for Miss Janet Gibbs met her with the news that Mrs Patten was much better, and led her, without any preliminary announcement, to the old lady's bedroom. Janet had scarcely reached the end of her circumstantial narrative how the attack came on and what were her aunt's sensations – a narrative to which Mrs Patten, in her neatly-plaited nightcap, seemed to listen with a contemptuous resignation to her niece's historical inaccuracy, contenting herself with occasionally confounding Janet by a shake of the head – when the clatter of a horse's hoofs on the yard pavement announced the arrival of Mr Pilgrim, whose large, top-booted person presently made its appearance up-stairs. He found Mrs Patten going on so well that there was no need to look solemn. He might glide from condolence into gossip without offence, and the temptation of having Mrs Hackit's ear was irresistible.

'What a disgraceful business this is turning out of your parson's,' was the remark with which he made this agreeable transition, throwing himself back in the chair from which he had been leaning towards the patient.

'Eh, dear me!' said Mrs Hackit, 'disgraceful enough. I stuck to Mr Barton as long as I could, for his wife's sake; but I can't countenance such goings-on. It's hateful to see that woman coming with 'em to service of a Sunday, and if Mr Hackit wasn't churchwarden and I didn't think it wrong to forsake one's own parish, I should go to Knebley Church. There's a many parish'ners as do.'

'I used to think Barton was only a fool,' observed Mr Pilgrim, in a tone which implied that he was conscious of having been weakly charitable. 'I thought he was imposed upon and led away by those people when they first came. But that's impossible now.'

'O, it's as plain as the nose in your face,' said Mrs Hackit, unreflectingly, not perceiving the equivoque in her comparison – 'comin' to Milby, like a sparrow perchin' on a bough, as I may say, with her brother, as she called him; and then all on a sudden the brother goes off with himself, and she throws herself on the Bartons. Though what could make her take up wi' a poor notomise of a parson, as hasn't got enough to keep wife and children, there's one above knows – *I* don't.'

'Mr Barton may have attractions we don't know of,' said Mr Pilgrim, who piqued himself on a talent for sarcasm. 'The Countess has no maid now, and they say Mr Barton is handy in assisting at her toilette – laces her boots, and so forth.'

'Tilette, be fiddled!' said Mrs Hackit, with indignant boldness of metaphor; 'an' there's that poor thing a-sewing her fingers to the bone for them children – an' another comin' on. What she must have to go through! It goes to my heart to turn my back on her. But she's i' the wrong to let herself be put upon i' that manner.'

'Ah! I was talking to Mrs Farquhar about that the other day. She said, "I think Mrs Barton a v-e-r-y w-e-a-k w-o-m-a-n".' (Mr Pilgrim gave this quotation with slow emphasis, as if he thought Mrs Farquhar had uttered a remarkable sentiment.) 'They find it impossible to invite her to their house while she has that equivocal person staying with her.'

'Well!' remarked Miss Gibbs, 'if I was a wife, nothing should induce me to bear what Mrs Barton does.'

'Yes, it's fine talking,' said Mrs Patten, from her pillow; 'old maids' husbands are al'ys well-managed. If you was a wife you'd be as foolish as your betters, belike.'

'All my wonder is,' observed Mrs Hackit, 'how the Bartons make both ends meet. You may depend on it, *she's* got nothing to give 'em; for I understand as he's been having money from some clergy charity. They said at fust as she stuffed Mr Barton wi' notions about her writing to the Chancellor an' her fine friends, to give him a living. Howiver, I don't know what's true an' what's false. Mr Barton keeps away from our house now, for I gave him a bit o' my mind one day. Maybe he's ashamed of himself. He seems to me to look dreadful thin an' harassed of a Sunday.'

'O, he must be aware he's getting into bad odour everywhere. The clergy are quite disgusted with his folly. They say Carpe would be glad to get Barton out of the curacy if he could; but he can't do that without coming to Shepperton himself, as Barton's a licensed curate; and he wouldn't like that, I suppose.'

At this moment Mrs Patten showed signs of uneasiness, which recalled Mr Pilgrim to professional attentions; and Mrs Hackit, observing that it was Thursday, and she must see after the butter, said good-bye, promising to look in again soon, and bring her knitting.

This Thursday, by the by, is the first in the month – the day on which the Clerical Meeting is held at Milby Vicarage; and as the Rev. Amos Barton has reasons for not attending, he will very likely be a subject of conversation amongst his clerical brethren. Suppose we go there, and hear whether Mr Pilgrim has reported their opinion correctly.

There is not a numerous party today, for it is a season of sore throats and catarrhs; so that the exegetical and theological discussions, which are the preliminary of dining, have not been quite so spirited as usual; and although a question relative to the Epistle of Jude has not been quite cleared up, the striking of six by the church clock, and the simultaneous announcement of dinner, are sounds that no one feels to be importunate.

Pleasant (when one is not in the least bilious) to enter a comfortable dining-room, where the closely-drawn red curtains glow with the double light of fire and candle, where glass and silver are glittering on the pure damask, and a soup-tureen gives a hint of the fragrance that will presently rush out to inundate your hungry senses, and prepare them, by the delicate visitation of atoms, for the keen gusto of ampler contact! Especially if you have confidence in the dinner-giving capacity of your host – if you know that he is not a man who entertains grovelling views of eating and drinking as a mere satisfaction of hunger and thirst, and dead to all the finer influences of the palate, expects his guest to be brilliant on ill-flavoured gravies and the cheapest Marsala. Mr Ely was particularly worthy of such confidence, and his virtues as an Amphitryon had probably contributed quite as much as the central situation of Milby to the selection of his house as a clerical rendezvous. He looks particularly graceful at the head of his table, and, indeed, on all occasions where he acts as president or moderator: he is a man who seems to listen well, and is an excellent amalgam of dissimilar ingredients.

At the other end of the table, as 'Vice', sits Mr Fellowes, rector and magistrate, a man of imposing appearance, with a mellifluous voice and the readiest of tongues. Mr Fellowes once obtained a living by the persuasive charms of his conversation, and the fluency with which he interpreted the opinions of an obese and stammering baronet, so as to give that elderly gentleman a very pleasing perception of his own wisdom. Mr Fellowes is a very successful man, and has the highest character everywhere except in his own parish, where, doubtless because his parishioners happen to be quarrelsome people, he is always at fierce feud with a farmer or two, a colliery proprietor, a grocer who was once churchwarden, and a tailor who formerly officiated as clerk.

At Mr Ely's right hand you see a very small man with a sallow and somewhat puffy face, whose hair is brushed straight up, evidently with the intention of giving him a height somewhat less disproportionate to his sense of his own importance than the measure of five feet three accorded him by an oversight of nature. This is Rev. Archibald Duke, a very dyspeptic and evangelical man, who takes the gloomiest view of mankind and their prospects, and thinks the immense sale of the *Pickwick Papers*, recently completed, one of the strongest proofs of original sin. Unfortunately, though Mr Duke was not burdened with a family, his yearly expenditure was apt considerably to exceed his income; and the unpleasant circumstances resulting from this, together with heavy meat-breakfasts, may probably have contributed to his desponding views of the world generally.

Next to him is seated Mr Furness, a tall young man, with blond hair and whiskers, who was plucked at Cambridge entirely owing to his genius; at least I know that he soon afterwards published a volume of poems, which were considered remarkably beautiful by many young ladies of his acquaintance. Mr Furness preached his own sermons, as any one of tolerable critical acumen might have certified by comparing them with his poems: in both, there was an exuberance of metaphor and simile entirely original, and not in the least borrowed from any resemblance in the things compared.

On Mr Furness's left you see Mr Pugh, another young curate, of much less marked characteristics. He had not published any poems; he had not even been plucked; he had neat black whiskers and a pale complexion; read prayers and a sermon twice every Sunday, and might be seen any day sallying forth on his parochial duties in a white tie, a well-brushed hat, a perfect suit of black, and well-polished boots – an equipment which he probably supposed hieroglyphically to represent the spirit of Christianity to the parishioners of Whittlecombe.

Mr Pugh's *vis-à-vis* is the Rev. Martin Cleves, a man about forty – middle-sized, broad-shouldered, with a negligently-tied cravat, large irregular features, and a large head, thickly covered with lanky brown hair. To a superficial glance, Mr Cleves is the plainest and least clerical-looking of the party; yet, strange to say, *there* is the true parish priest, the pastor beloved, consulted, relied on by his flock; a clergyman who is not associated with the undertaker, but thought of as the surest helper under a difficulty, as a monitor who is encouraging rather than severe. Mr Cleves has the wonderful art of preaching sermons which the wheelwright and the blacksmith can understand; not because he talks condescending twaddle, but because he can call a spade a spade, and knows how to disencumber ideas of their wordy frippery. Look at him more attentively, and you will see that his face is a very interesting one – that there is a great deal of humour and feeling playing in his grey eyes, and about the corners of his roughly-cut mouth: a man, you observe, who has most likely sprung from the harder-working section of the middle class, and has hereditary sympathies with the checkered life of the people. He gets together the working men in his parish on a Monday evening, and gives them a sort of conversational lecture on useful practical matters, telling them stories, or reading some select passages from an agreeable book, and commenting on them; and if you were to ask the first labourer or artisan in Tripplegate what sort of man the parson was, he would say, – 'a uncommon knowin', sensable, freespoken gentleman; very kind an' good-natur'd too'. Yet for all this, he is perhaps the best Grecian of the party, if we except Mr Baird, the young man on his left.

Mr Baird has since gained considerable celebrity as an original writer and metropolitan lecturer, but at that time he used to preach in a little church something like a barn, to a congregation consisting of three rich farmers and their servants, about fifteen labourers, and the due proportion of women and children. The rich farmers understood him to be 'very high learnt'; but if you had interrogated them for a more precise description, they would have said that he was 'a thinnish-faced man, with a sort o' cast in his eye, like'.

Seven, altogether: a delightful number for a dinner-party, supposing the units to be delightful, but everything depends on that. During dinner Mr Fellowes took the lead in the conversation, which set strongly in the direction of mangel-wurzel and the rotation of crops; for Mr Fellowes and Mr Cleves cultivated their own glebes. Mr Ely, too, had some agricultural notions, and even the Rev. Archibald Duke was made alive to that class of mundane subjects by the possession of some potato-ground. The two young curates talked a little aside during these discussions, which had imperfect interest for their unbeneficed minds; and the transcendental and near-sighted Mr Baird seemed to listen somewhat abstractedly, knowing little more of potatoes and mangel-wurzel than that they were some form of the 'Conditioned'.

'What a hobby farming is with Lord Watling!' said Mr Fellowes, when the cloth was being drawn. 'I went over his farm at Tetterley with him last summer. It is really a model farm; first-rate dairy, grazing and wheat land, and such splendid farm-buildings! An expensive hobby, though. He sinks a good deal of money there, I fancy. He has a great whim for black cattle, and he sends that drunken old Scotch bailiff of his to Scotland every year, with hundreds in his pocket, to buy these beasts.'

'By the by,' said Mr Ely, 'do you know who is the man to whom Lord Watling has given the Bramhill living?'

'A man named Sargent. I knew him at Oxford. His brother is a lawyer, and was very useful to Lord Watling in that ugly Brounsell affair. That's why Sargent got the living.'

'Sargent,' said Mr Ely. 'I know him. Isn't he a showy, talkative fellow; has written travels in Mesopotamia, or something of that sort?'

'That's the man.'

'He was at Witherington once, as Bagshawe's curate. He got into rather bad odour there, through some scandal about a flirtation, I think.'

'Talking of scandal,' returned Mr Fellowes, 'have you heard the last story about Barton? Nisbett was telling me the other day that he dines alone with the Countess at six, while Mrs Barton is in the kitchen acting as cook.'

'Rather an apocryphal authority, Nisbett,' said Mr Ely.

'Ah,' said Mr Cleves, with good-natured humour twinkling in his eyes, 'depend upon it, that is a corrupt version. The original text is, that they all dined together with *six* – meaning six children – and that Mrs Barton is an excellent cook.'

'I wish dining alone together may be the worst of that sad business,' said the Rev. Archibald Duke, in a tone implying that his wish was a strong figure of speech.

'Well,' said Mr Fellowes, filling his glass and looking jocose, 'Barton is certainly either the greatest gull in existence, or he has some cunning secret, – some philtre or other to make himself charming in the eyes of a fair lady. It isn't all of us that can make conquests when our ugliness is past its bloom.'

'The lady seemed to have made a conquest of him at the very outset,' said Mr Ely. 'I was immensely amused one night at Granby's when he was telling us her story about her husband's adventures. He said, "When she told me the tale, I felt I don't know how, – I felt it from the crown of my head to the sole of my feet".'

Mr Ely gave these words dramatically, imitating the Rev. Amos's fervour and symbolic action, and every one laughed except Mr Duke, whose after-dinner view of things was not apt to be jovial. He said,–

'I think some of us ought to remonstrate with Mr Barton on the scandal he is causing. He is not only imperilling his own soul, but the souls of his flock.'

'Depend upon it,' said Mr Cleves, 'there is some simple explanation of the whole affair, if we only happened to know it. Barton has always impressed me as a right-minded man, who has the knack of doing himself injustice by his manner.'

'Now I never liked Barton,' said Mr Fellowes. 'He's not a gentleman. Why, he used to be on terms of intimacy with that canting Prior, who died a little while ago; – a fellow who soaked himself with spirits, and talked of the Gospel through an inflamed nose.'

'The Countess has given him more refined tastes, I daresay,' said Mr Ely.

'Well,' observed Mr Cleves, 'the poor fellow must have a hard pull to get along, with his small income and large family. Let us hope the Countess does something towards making the pot boil.'

'Not she,' said Mr Duke; 'there are greater signs of poverty about them than ever.'

'Well, come,' returned Mr Cleves, who could be caustic sometimes, and who was not at all fond of his reverend brother, Mr Duke, 'that's something in Barton's favour at all events. He might be poor *without* showing signs of poverty.'

Mr Duke turned rather yellow, which was his way of blushing, and Mr Ely came to his relief by observing, –

'They're making a very good piece of work of Shepperton Church. Dolby, the architect, who has it in hand, is a very clever fellow.'

'It's he who has been doing Coppleton Church,' said Mr Furness. 'They've got it in excellent order for the visitation.'

This mention of the visitation suggested the Bishop, and thus opened a wide duct, which entirely diverted the stream of animadversion from that small pipe – that capillary vessel, the Rev. Amos Barton.

The talk of the clergy about their Bishop belongs to the esoteric part of their profession; so we will at once quit the dining-room at Milby Vicarage, lest we should happen to overhear remarks unsuited to the lay understanding, and perhaps dangerous to our repose of mind.

Ϫ SEVEN ϭ

I DARESAY THE LONG RESIDENCE OF the Countess Czerlaski at Shepperton Vicarage is very puzzling to you also, dear reader, as well as to Mr Barton's clerical brethren; the more so, as I hope you are not in the least inclined to put that very evil interpretation on it which evidently found acceptance with the sallow and dyspeptic Mr Duke, and with the florid and highly peptic Mr Fellowes. You have seen enough, I trust, of the Rev. Amos Barton, to be convinced that he was more apt to fall into a blunder than into a sin – more apt to be deceived than to incur a necessity for being deceitful; and if you have a keen eye for physiognomy, you will have detected that the Countess Czerlaski loved herself far too well to get entangled in an unprofitable vice.

How then, you will say, could this fine lady choose to quarter herself on the establishment of a poor curate, where the carpets were probably falling into holes, where the attendance was limited to a maid-of-all-work, and where six children were running loose from eight o'clock in the morning till eight o'clock in the evening? Surely you must be straining probability.

Heaven forbid! For not having a lofty imagination, as you perceive, and being unable to invent thrilling incidents for your amusement, my only merit must lie in the truth with which I represent to you the humble experience of ordinary fellow-mortals. I wish to stir your sympathy with commonplace troubles – to win your tears for real sorrow: sorrow such as may live next door to you – such as walks neither in rags nor in velvet, but in very ordinary decent apparel.

Therefore, that you may dismiss your suspicions as to the truth of my picture, I will beg you to consider, that at the time the Countess Czerlaski left Camp Villa in dudgeon, she had only twenty pounds in her pocket, being about one-third of the income she possessed independently of her brother. You will then perceive that she was in the extremely inconvenient predicament of having quarrelled, not indeed with her bread and cheese, but certainly with her chicken and tart – a predicament all the more inconvenient to her, because the habit of idleness had quite unfitted her for earning those necessary superfluities, and because, with all her fascinations, she had not secured any enthusiastic friends whose houses were open to her, and who were dying to see her. Thus she had completely checkmated herself, unless she could resolve on one unpleasant move – namely, to humble herself to her brother, and recognize his wife. This seemed quite impossible to her as long as she entertained the hope that he would make the first advances; and in this flattering hope she remained month after month at Shepperton Vicarage, gracefully overlooking the deficiencies of accommodation, and feeling that she was really behaving charmingly. 'Who indeed,' she thought to herself, 'could do otherwise, with a lovely, gentle creature like Milly? I shall really be sorry to leave the poor thing.'

So, though she lay in bed till ten, and came down to a separate breakfast at eleven, she kindly consented to dine as early as five, when a hot joint was prepared, which coldly furnished forth the children's table the next day; she considerately prevented Milly from devoting herself too closely to the children, by insisting on reading, talking, and walking with her; and she even began to embroider a cap for the next baby, which must certainly be a girl, and be named Caroline.

After the first month or two of her residence at the Vicarage, the Rev. Amos Barton became aware – as, indeed, it was unavoidable that he should – of the strong disapprobation it drew upon him, and the change of feeling towards him which it was producing in his kindest parishioners. But, in the first place, he still believed in the Countess as a charming and influential woman, disposed to befriend him, and, in any case, he could hardly hint departure to a lady guest who had been kind to him and his, and who might any day spontaneously announce the termination of her visit; in the second place, he was conscious of his own innocence, and felt some contemptuous indignation towards people who were ready to imagine evil of him; and, lastly, he had, as I have already intimated, a strong will of his own, so that a certain obstinacy and defiance mingled itself with his other feelings on the subject.

The one unpleasant consequence which was not to be evaded or counteracted by any mere mental state, was the increasing drain on his slender purse for household expenses, to meet which the remittance he had received from the clerical charity threatened to be quite inadequate. Slander may be defeated by equanimity; but courageous thoughts will not pay your baker's bill, and fortitude is nowhere considered legal tender for beef. Month after month the financial aspect of the Rev. Amos's affairs became more and more serious to him, and month after month, too, wore away more and more of that armour of indignation and defiance with which he had at first defended himself from the harsh looks of faces that were once the friendliest.

But quite the heaviest pressure of the trouble fell on Milly – on gentle, uncomplaining Milly – whose delicate body was becoming daily less fit for all the many things that had to be done between rising up and lying down. At first, she thought the Countess's visit would not last long, and she was quite glad to incur extra exertion for the sake of making her friend comfortable. I can hardly bear to think of all the rough work she did with those lovely hands – all by the sly, without letting her husband know anything about it, and husbands are not clairvoyant: how she salted bacon, ironed shirts and cravats, put patches on patches, and re-darned darns. Then there was the task of mending and eking out baby-linen in prospect, and the problem perpetually suggesting itself how she and Nanny *should* manage when there was another baby, as there would be before very many months were past.

When time glided on, and the Countess's visit did not end, Milly was not blind to any phase of their position. She knew of the slander; she was aware of the keeping aloof of old friends; but these she felt almost entirely on her husband's account. A loving woman's world lies within the four walls of her own home; and it is only through her husband that she is in any electric communication with the world beyond. Mrs Simpkins may have looked scornfully at her, but baby crows and holds out his little arms none the less blithely; Mrs Tomkins may have left off calling on her, but her husband comes home none the less to receive her care and caresses; it has been wet and gloomy out of doors today, but she has looked well after the shirt buttons, has cut out baby's pinafores, and half finished Willy's blouse.

So it was with Milly. She was only vexed that her husband should be vexed – only wounded because he was misconceived. But the difficulty about ways and means she felt in quite a different manner. Her rectitude was alarmed lest they should have to make tradesmen wait for their money; her motherly love dreaded the diminution of comforts for the children; and the sense of her own failing health gave exaggerated force to these fears.

Milly could no longer shut her eyes to the fact, that the Countess was inconsiderate, if she did not allow herself to entertain severer thoughts; and she began to feel that it would soon be a duty to tell her frankly that they really could not afford to have her visit farther prolonged. But a process was going forward in two other minds, which ultimately saved Milly from having to perform this painful task.

In the first place, the Countess was getting weary of Shepperton – weary of waiting for her brother's overtures which never came; so, one fine morning, she reflected that forgiveness was a Christian duty, that a sister should be placable, that Mr Bridmain must feel the need of her advice, to which he had been accustomed for three years, and that very likely 'that woman' didn't make the poor man happy. In this amiable frame of mind she wrote a very affectionate appeal, and addressed it to Mr Bridmain, through his banker.

Another mind that was being wrought up to a climax was Nanny's, the maid-of-all-work, who had a warm heart and a still warmer temper. Nanny adored her mistress: she had been heard to say, that she was 'ready to kiss the ground as the missis trod on'; and Walter, she considered, was *her* baby, of whom she was as jealous as a lover. But she had, from the first, very slight admiration for the Countess Czerlaski. That lady, from Nanny's point of view, was a personage always 'drawed out i' fine clothes', the chief result of whose existence was to cause additional bed-making, carrying of hot water, laying of table-cloths, and cooking of dinners. It was a perpetually heightening 'aggravation' to Nanny that she and her mistress had to 'slave' more than ever, because there was this fine lady in the house.

'An, she pays nothin' for't neither,' observed Nanny to Mr Jacob Tomms, a young gentleman in the tailoring line, who occasionally – simply out of a taste for dialogue – looked into the vicarage kitchen of an evening. 'I know the master's shorter o' money than iver, an' it meks no end o' difference i' th' housekeepin' – her bein' here, besides bein' obliged to have a charwoman constant.'

'There's fine stories i' the village about her,' said Mr Tomms. 'They say as Muster Barton's great wi' her, or else she'd niver stop here.'

'Then they say a passill o' lies, an' you ought to be ashamed to go an' tell 'em o'er again. Do *you* think as the master, as has got a wife like the missis, 'ud go running arter a stuck-up piece o' goods like that Countess, as isn't fit to black the missis's shoes? I'm none so fond o' the master, but I know better on him nor that.'

'Well, I didn't b'lieve it,' said Mr Tomms, humbly.

'B'lieve it? you'd ha' been a ninny if yer did. An' she's a nasty, stingy thing, that Countess. She's niver giv me a sixpence nor an old rag neither, sin' here's she's been. A-lyin' a bed an a-comin' down to breakfast when other folks wants their dinner!'

If such was the state of Nanny's mind as early as the end of August, when this dialogue with Mr Tomms occurred, you may imagine what it must have been by the beginning of November, and that at that time a very slight spark might any day cause the long-smouldering anger to flame forth in open indignation.

That spark happened to fall the very morning that Mrs Hackit paid the visit to Mrs Patten, recorded in the last chapter. Nanny's dislike of the Countess extended to the innocent dog Jet, whom she 'couldn't a-bear to see made a fuss wi' like a Christian. An' the little ouzel must be washed, too, ivery Saturday, as if there wasn't children enoo to wash, wi'out washin' dogs.'

Now this particular morning it happened that Milly was quite too poorly to get up, and Mr Barton observed to Nanny, on going out, that he would call and tell Mr Brand to come. These circumstances were already enough to make Nanny anxious and susceptible. But the Countess, comfortably ignorant of them, came down as usual about eleven o'clock to her separate breakfast, which stood ready for her at that hour in the parlour; the kettle singing on the hob that she might make her own tea. There was a little jug of cream, taken according to custom from last night's milk, and specially saved for the Countess's breakfast. Jet always awaited his mistress at her bedroom door, and it was her habit to carry him downstairs.

'Now, my little Jet,' she said, putting him down gently on the hearthrug, 'you shall have a nice, nice breakfast.'

Jet indicated that he thought that observation extremely pertinent and well-timed, by immediately raising himself on his hind-legs, and the Countess emptied the cream-jug into the saucer. Now there was usually a small jug of milk standing on the tray by the side of the cream, and destined for Jet's breakfast, but this morning Nanny, being 'moithered', had forgotten that part of the arrangements, so that when the Countess had made her tea, she perceived there was no second jug, and rang the bell. Nanny appeared, looking very red and heated – the fact was, she had been 'doing up' the kitchen fire, and that is a sort of work which by no means conduces to blandness of temper.

'Nanny, you have forgotten Jet's milk; will you bring me some more cream, please?'

This was just a little too much for Nanny's forbearance.

'Yes, I dare say. Here am I wi' my hands full o' the children an' the dinner, and missis ill a-bed, and Mr Brand a-comin'; and I must run o'er the village to get more cream, 'cause you've give it to that nasty little blackamoor.'

'Is Mrs Barton ill?'

'Ill – yes – I should think she *is* ill, an' much you care. She's likely to be ill, moithered as *she* is from mornin' to night, wi' folks as had better be elsewhere.'

'What do you mean by behaving in this way?'

'Mean? Why I mean as the missis is a-slavin' her life out an' a-sittin' up o'nights, for folks as are better able to wait of *her*, i'stid o'lyin' a-bed an' doin' nothin' all the blessed day, but mek work.'

'Leave the room and don't be insolent.'

'Insolent! I'd better be insolent than like what some folks is, – a-livin' on other folks, an' bringin' a bad name on 'em into the bargain.'

Here Nanny flung out of the room, leaving the lady to digest this unexpected breakfast at her leisure.

The Countess was stunned for a few minutes, but when she began to recall Nanny's words, there was no possibility of avoiding very unpleasant conclusions from them, or of failing to see her position at the Vicarage in an entirely new light. The interpretation too of Nanny's allusion to a 'bad name' did not lie out of the reach of the Countess's imagination, and she saw the necessity of quitting Shepperton without delay. Still, she would like to wait for her brother's letter – no – she would ask Milly to forward it to her – still better, she would go at once to London, inquire her brother's address at his banker's, and go to see him without preliminary.

She went up to Milly's room, and, after kisses and inquiries, said – 'I find, on consideration, dear Milly, from the letter I had yesterday, that I must bid you good-bye and go up to London at once. But you must not let me leave you ill, you naughty thing.'

'Oh no,' said Milly, who felt as if a load had been taken off her back, 'I shall be very well in an hour or two. Indeed, I'm much better now. You will want me to help you to pack. But you won't go for two or three days?'

'Yes, I must go to-morrow. But I shall not let you help me to pack, so don't entertain any unreasonable projects, but lie still. Mr Brand is coming, Nanny says.'

The news was not an unpleasant surprise to Mr Barton when he came home, though he was able to express more regret at the idea of parting than Milly could summon to her lips. He retained more of his original feeling for the Countess than Milly did, for women never betray themselves to men as they do to each other; and the Rev. Amos had not a keen instinct for character. But he felt that he was being relieved from a difficulty, and in the way that was easiest for him. Neither he nor Milly suspected that it was Nanny who had cut the knot for them, for the Countess took care to give no sign on that subject. As for Nanny, she was perfectly aware of the relation between cause and effect in the affair, and secretly chuckled over her outburst of 'sauce' as the best morning's work she had ever done.

So, on Friday morning, a fly was seen standing at the Vicarage gate with the Countess's boxes packed upon it; and presently that lady herself was seen getting into the vehicle. After a last shake of the hand to Mr Barton, and last kisses to Milly and the children, the door was closed; and as the fly rolled off, the little party at the Vicarage gate caught a last glimpse of the handsome Countess leaning and waving kisses from the carriage window. Jet's little black phiz was also seen, and doubtless he had his thoughts and feelings on the occasion, but he kept them strictly within his own bosom.

The schoolmistress opposite witnessed this departure, and lost no time in telling it to the schoolmaster, who again communicated the news to the landlord of 'The Jolly Colliers', at the close of the morning school-hours. Nanny poured the joyful tidings into the ear of Mr Farquhar's footman, who happened to call with a letter, and Mr Brand carried them to all the patients he visited that morning, after calling on Mrs Barton. So that, before Sunday, it was very generally known in Shepperton parish that the Countess Czerlaski had left the Vicarage.

The Countess had left, but alas, the bills she had contributed to swell still remained; so did the exiguity of the children's clothing, which also was partly an indirect consequence of her presence; and so, too, did the coolness and alienation in the parishioners, which could not at once vanish before the fact of her departure. The Rev. Amos was not exculpated – the past was not expunged. But what was worse than all, Milly's health gave frequent cause for alarm, and the prospect of baby's birth was over-shadowed by more than the usual fears. The birth came prematurely, about six weeks after the Countess's departure, but Mr Brand gave favourable reports to all inquirers on the following day, which was Satur-day. On Sunday, after morning service, Mrs Hackit called at the Vicarage to inquire how Mrs Barton was, and was invited up-stairs to see her. Milly lay placid and lovely in her feebleness, and held out her hand to Mrs Hackit with a beaming smile. It was very pleasant to her to see her old friend unreserved and cordial once more. The seven months' baby was very tiny and very red, but 'handsome is that handsome does' – he was pronounced to be 'doing well', and Mrs Hackit went home gladdened at heart to think that the perilous hour was over.

∼ EIGHT ∽

THE FOLLOWING WEDNESDAY, WHEN MR and Mrs Hackit were seated comfortably by their bright hearth, enjoying the long afternoon afforded by an early dinner, Rachel, the housemaid, came in and said, –

'If you please 'm, the shepherd says, have you heard as Mrs Barton's wuss, and not expected to live?'

Mrs Hackit turned pale, and hurried out to question the shepherd, who, she found, had heard the sad news at an alehouse in the village. Mr Hackit followed her out and said, 'You'd better have the pony-chaise, and go directly.'

'Yes,' said Mrs Hackit, too much overcome to utter any exclamations. 'Rachel, come an' help me on wi' my things.' When her husband was wrapping her cloak round her feet in the pony-chaise, she said, –

'If I don't come home to-night, I shall send back the pony-chaise, and you'll know I'm wanted there.'

'Yes, yes.'

It was a bright frosty day, and by the time Mrs Hackit arrived at the Vicarage, the sun was near its setting. There was a carriage and pair standing at the gate, which she recognized as Dr Madeley's, the physician from Rotherby. She entered at the kitchen door that she might avoid knocking, and quietly question Nanny. No one was in the kitchen, but, passing on, she saw the sitting-room door open, and Nanny, with Walter in her arms, removing the knives and forks, which had been laid for dinner three hours ago.

'Master says he can't eat no dinner,' was Nanny's first word. 'He's never tasted nothin' sin' yesterday mornin', but a cup o' tea.'

'When was your missis took worse?'

'O' Monday night. They sent for Dr Madeley i' the middle o' the day yesterday, an' he's here again now.'

'Is the baby alive?'

'No, it died last night. The children's all at Mrs Bond's. She come and took 'em away last night, but the master says they must be fetched soon. He's up-stairs now, wi' Dr Madeley and Mr Brand.'

At this moment Mrs Hackit heard the sound of a heavy, slow foot, in the passage; and presently Amos Barton entered, with dry despairing eyes, haggard and unshaven. He expected to find the sitting-room as he left it, with nothing to meet his eyes but Milly's work-basket in the corner of the sofa, and the children's toys overturned in the bow-window. But when he saw Mrs Hackit come towards him with answering sorrow in her face, the pent-up fountain of tears was opened; he threw himself on the sofa, hid his face, and sobbed aloud.

'Bear up, Mr Barton,' Mrs Hackit ventured to say at last; 'bear up, for the sake o' them dear children.'

'The children,' said Amos, starting up. 'They must be sent for. Some one must fetch them. Milly will want to . . .'

He couldn't finish the sentence, but Mrs Hackit understood him, and said, 'I'll send the man with the pony-carriage for 'em.'

She went out to give the order, and encountered Dr Madeley and Mr Brand, who were just going.

Mr Brand said: 'I am very glad to see you are here, Mrs Hackit. No time must be lost in sending for the children. Mrs Barton wants to see them.'

'Do you quite give her up then?'

'She can hardly live through the night. She begged us to tell her how long she had to live; and then asked for the children.'

The pony-carriage was sent; and Mrs Hackit, returning to Mr Barton, said she would like to go up-stairs now. He went up-stairs with her and opened the door. The chamber fronted the west; the sun was just setting, and the red light fell full upon the bed, where Milly lay with the hand of death visibly upon her. The feather-bed had been removed, and she lay low on a mattress, with her head slightly raised by pillows. Her long fair neck seemed to be struggling with a painful effort; her features were pallid and pinched, and her eyes were closed. There was no one in the room but the nurse, and the mistress of the free school, who had come to give her help from the beginning of the change.

Amos and Mrs Hackit stood beside the bed, and Milly opened her eyes.

'My darling, Mrs Hackit is come to see you.'

Milly smiled and looked at her with that strange, far-off look which belongs to ebbing life.

'Are the children coming?' she said, painfully.

'Yes, they will be here directly.'

She closed her eyes again.

Presently the pony-carriage was heard; and Amos, motioning to Mrs Hackit to follow him, left the room. On their way downstairs she suggested that the carriage should remain to take them away again afterwards, and Amos assented.

There they stood in the melancholy sitting-room – the five sweet children, from Patty to Chubby – all, with their mother's eyes – all, except Patty, looking up with a vague fear at their father as he entered. Patty understood the great sorrow that was come upon them, and tried to check her sobs as she heard her papa's footsteps.

'My children,' said Amos, taking Chubby in his arms, 'God is going to take away your dear mamma from us. She wants to see you to say good-bye. You must try to be very good and not cry.'

He could say no more, but turned round to see if Nanny was there with Walter, and then led the way up-stairs, leading Dickey with the other hand. Mrs Hackit followed with Sophy and Patty, and then came Nanny with Walter and Fred.

It seemed as if Milly had heard the little footsteps on the stairs, for when Amos entered her eyes were wide open, eagerly looking towards the door. They all stood by the bedside – Amos nearest to her, holding Chubby and Dickey. But she motioned for Patty to come first, and clasping the poor pale child by the hand, said, –

'Patty, I'm going away from you. Love your papa. Comfort him; and take care of your little brothers and sisters. God will help you.'

Patty stood perfectly quiet, and said, 'Yes, mamma.'

The mother motioned with her pallid lips for the dear child to lean towards her and kiss her; and then Patty's great anguish overcame her, and she burst into sobs. Amos drew her towards him and pressed her head gently to him, while Milly beckoned Fred and Sophy, and said to them more faintly, –

'Patty will try to be your mamma when I am gone, my darlings. You will be good and not vex her.'

They leaned towards her, and she stroked their fair heads, and kissed their tear-stained cheeks. They cried because mamma was ill and papa looked so unhappy; but they thought, perhaps next week things would be as they used to be again.

The little ones were lifted on the bed to kiss her. Little Walter said, 'Mamma, mamma', and stretched out his fat arms and smiled; and Chubby seemed gravely wondering; but Dickey, who had been looking fixedly at her, with lip hanging down, ever since he came into the room, now seemed suddenly pierced with the idea that mamma was going away somewhere; his little heart swelled and he cried aloud.

Then Mrs Hackit and Nanny took them all away. Patty at first begged to stay at home and not go to Mrs Bond's again; but when Nanny reminded her that she had better go to take care of the younger ones, she submitted at once, and they were all packed in the pony-carriage once more.

Milly kept her eyes shut for some time after the children were gone. Amos had sunk on his knees, and was holding her hand while he watched her face. By-and-by she opened her eyes, and, drawing him close to her, whispered slowly, –

'My dear – dear – husband – you have been – very – good to me. You – have – made me – very – happy.'

She spoke no more for many hours. They watched her breathing becoming more and more difficult, until evening deepened into night, and until midnight was past. About half past twelve she seemed to be trying to speak, and they leaned to catch her words.

'Music – music – didn't you hear it?'

Amos knelt by the bed and held her hand in his. He did not believe in his sorrow. It was a bad dream. He did not know when she was gone. But Mr Brand, whom Mrs Hackit had sent for before twelve o'clock, thinking that Mr Barton might probably need his help, now came up to him, and said, –

'She feels no more pain now. Come, my dear sir, come with me.'

'She isn't *dead*?' shrieked the poor desolate man, struggling to shake off Mr Brand, who had taken him by the arm. But his weary weakened frame was not equal to resistance, and he was dragged out of the room.

◁ NINE ▷

THEY LAID HER IN THE GRAVE – the sweet mother with her baby in her arms – while the Christmas snow lay thick upon the graves. It was Mr Cleves who buried her. On the first news of Mr Barton's calamity, he had ridden over from Tripplegate to beg that he might be made of some use, and his silent grasp of Amos's hand had penetrated like the painful thrill of life-recovering warmth to the poor benumbed heart of the stricken man.

The snow lay thick upon the graves, and the day was cold and dreary; but there was many a sad eye watching that black procession as it passed from the vicarage to the church, and from the church to the open grave. There were men and women standing in that churchyard who had band-

ied vulgar jests about their pastor, and who had lightly charged him with
sin; but now, when they saw him following the coffin, pale and haggard,
he was consecrated anew by his great sorrow, and they looked at him with
respectful pity.

All the children were there, for Amos had willed it so, thinking that
some dim memory of that sacred moment might remain even with little
Walter, and link itself with what he would hear of his sweet mother in
after years. He himself led Patty and Dickey; then came Sophy and Fred;
Mr Brand had begged to carry Chubby, and Nanny followed with Walter.
They made a circle round the grave while the coffin was being lowered.
Patty alone of all the children felt that mamma was in that coffin, and that
a new and sadder life had begun for papa and herself. She was pale and
trembling, but she clasped his hand more firmly as the coffin went down,
and gave no sob. Fred and Sophy, though they were only two and three
years younger, and though they had seen mamma in her coffin, seemed to
themselves to be looking at some strange show. They had not learned
to decipher that terrible handwriting of human destiny, illness and death.
Dickey had rebelled against his black clothes, until he was told that it
would be naughty to mamma not to put them on, when he at once
submitted; and now, though he had heard Nanny say that mamma was in
heaven, he had a vague notion that she would come home again tomorrow, and say he had been a good boy and let him empty her work-box. He
stood close to his father, with great rosy cheeks, and wide open blue eyes,
looking first up at Mr Cleves and then down at the coffin, and thinking he
and Chubby would play at that when they got home.

The burial was over, and Amos turned with his children to re-enter the
house – the house where, an hour ago, Milly's dear body lay, where
the windows were half-darkened, and sorrow seemed to have a hallowed
precinct for itself, shut out from the world. But now she was gone; the
broad snow-reflected daylight was in all the rooms; the Vicarage again
seemed part of the common working-day world, and Amos, for the first
time, felt that he was alone – that day after day, month after month, year
after year, would have to be lived through without Milly's love. Spring
would come, and she would not be there; summer, and she would not be
there; and he would never have her again with him by the fireside in the
long evenings. The seasons all seemed irksome to his thoughts; and how
dreary the sunshiny days that would be sure to come! She was gone from
him; and he could never show her his love any more, never make up for
omissions in the past by filling future days with tenderness.

O the anguish of that thought that we can never atone to our dead for
the stinted affection we gave them, for the light answers we returned to
their plaints or their pleadings, for the little reverence we showed to that
sacred human soul that lived so close to us, and was the divinest thing
God had given us to know!

Amos Barton had been an affectionate husband, and while Milly was with him, he was never visited by the thought that perhaps his sympathy with her was not quick and watchful enough; but now he re-lived all their life together, with that terrible keenness of memory and imagination which bereavement gives, and he felt as if his very love needed a pardon for its poverty and selfishness.

No outward solace could counteract the bitterness of this inward woe. But outward solace came. Cold faces looked kind again, and parishioners turned over in their minds what they could best do to help their pastor. Mr Oldinport wrote to express his sympathy, and enclosed another twenty-pound note, begging that he might be permitted to contribute in this way to the relief of Mr Barton's mind from pecuniary anxieties, under the pressure of a grief which all his parishioners must share; and offering his interest towards placing the two eldest girls in a school expressly founded for clergymen's daughters. Mr Cleves succeeded in collecting thirty pounds among his richer clerical brethren, and, adding ten pounds himself, sent the sum to Amos, with the kindest and most delicate words of Christian fellowship and manly friendship. Miss Jackson forgot old grievances, and came to stay some months with Milly's children, bringing such material aid as she could spare from her small income. These were substantial helps, which relieved Amos from the pressure of his money difficulties; and the friendly attentions, the kind pressure of the hand, the cordial looks he met with everywhere in his parish, made him feel that the fatal frost which had settled on his pastoral duties, during the Countess's residence at the Vicarage, was completely thawed, and that the hearts of his parishioners were once more open to him.

No one breathed the Countess's name now; for Milly's memory hallowed her husband, as of old the place was hallowed on which an angel from God had alighted.

When the spring came, Mrs Hackit begged that she might have Dickey to stay with her, and great was the enlargement of Dickey's experience from that visit. Every morning he was allowed – being well wrapt up as to his chest by Mrs Hackit's own hands, but very bare and red as to his legs – to run loose in the cow and poultry yard, to persecute the turkey-cock by satirical imitations of his gobble-gobble, and to put difficult questions to the groom as to the reasons why horses had four legs, and other transcendental matters. Then Mr Hackit would take Dickey up on horseback when he rode round his farm, and Mrs Hackit had a large plumcake in cut, ready to meet incidental attacks of hunger. So that Dickey had considerably modified his views as to the desirability of Mrs Hackit's kisses.

The Miss Farquhars made particular pets of Fred and Sophy, to whom they undertook to give lessons twice a-week in writing and geography; and Mrs Farquhar devised many treats for the little ones. Patty's treat was to stay at home, or walk about with her papa; and when he sat by the fire in an evening, after the other children were gone to bed, she would bring a stool, and, placing it against his feet, would sit down upon it and lean her head against his knee. Then his hand would rest on that fair head, and he would feel that Milly's love was not quite gone out of his life.

So the time wore on till it was May again, and the church was quite finished and reopened in all its new splendour, and Mr Barton was devoting himself with more vigour than ever to his parochial duties. But one morning – it was a very bright morning, and evil tidings sometimes like to fly in the finest weather – there came a letter for Mr Barton, addressed in the Vicar's handwriting. Amos opened it with some anxiety – somehow or other he had a presentiment of evil. The letter contained the announcement that Mr Carpe had resolved on coming to reside at Shepperton, and that, consequently, in six months from that time Mr Barton's duties as curate in that parish would be closed.

O, it was hard! Just when Shepperton had become the place where he most wished to stay – where he had friends who knew his sorrows – where he lived close to Milly's grave. To part from that grave seemed like parting with Milly a second time; for Amos was one who clung to all the material links between his mind and the past. His imagination was not vivid, and required the stimulus of actual perception.

It roused some bitter feeling, too, to think that Mr Carpe's wish to reside at Shepperton was merely a pretext for removing Mr Barton, in order that he might ultimately give the curacy of Shepperton to his own brother-in-law, who was known to be wanting a new position.

Still, it must be borne; and the painful business of seeking another curacy must be set about without loss of time. After the lapse of some months, Amos was obliged to renounce the hope of getting one at all near Shepperton, and he at length resigned himself to accepting one in a distant county. The parish was in a large manufacturing town, where his walks would lie among noisy streets and dingy alleys, and where the children would have no garden to play in, no pleasant farmhouses to visit.

It was another blow inflicted on the bruised man.

◁ TEN ▷

AT LENGTH THE DREADED WEEK WAS come, when Amos and his children must leave Shepperton. There was general regret among the parishioners at his departure: not that any one of them thought his spiritual gifts pre-eminent, or was conscious of great edification from his ministry. But his recent troubles had called out their better sympathies, and that is always a source of love. Amos failed to touch the spring of goodness by his sermons, but he touched it effectually by his sorrows; and there was now a real bond between him and his flock.

'My heart aches for them poor motherless children,' said Mrs Hackit to her husband, 'a-going among strangers, and into a nasty town, where there's no good victuals to be had, and you must pay dear to get bad uns.'

Mrs Hackit had a vague notion of a town life as a combination of dirty backyards, measly pork, and dingy linen.

The same sort of sympathy was strong among the poorer class of parishioners. Old stiff-jointed Mr Tozer, who was still able to earn a little by gardening 'jobs', stopped Mrs Cramp, the charwoman, on her way home from the Vicarage, where she had been helping Nanny to pack up the day before the departure, and inquired very particularly into Mr Barton's prospects.

'Ah, poor mon,' he was heard to say, 'I'm sorry for un. He hedn't much here, but he'll be wuss off theer. Half a loaf's better nor ne'er un.'

The sad good-byes had all been said before that last evening; and after all the packing was done and all the arrangements were made, Amos felt the oppression of that blank interval in which one has nothing left to think of but the dreary future the separation from the loved and familiar, and the chilling entrance on the new and strange. In every parting there is an image of death.

Soon after ten o'clock, when he had sent Nanny to bed, that she might have a good night's rest before the fatigues of the morrow, he stole softly out to pay a last visit to Milly's grave. It was a moonless night, but the sky was thick with stars, and their light was enough to show that the grass had grown long on the grave, and that there was a tombstone telling in bright letters, on a dark ground, that beneath were deposited the remains of Amelia, the beloved wife of Amos Barton, who died in the thirty-fifth year of her age, leaving a husband and six children to lament her loss. The final words of the inscription were, 'Thy will be done.'

The husband was now advancing towards the dear mound from which he was so soon to be parted, perhaps for ever. He stood a few minutes reading over and over again the words on the tombstone, as if to assure himself that all the happy and unhappy past was a reality. For love is frightened at the intervals of insensibility and callousness that encroach by little and little on the dominion of grief, and it makes efforts to recall the keenness of the first anguish.

Gradually, as his eye dwelt on the words, 'Amelia, the beloved wife,' the waves of feeling swelled within his soul, and he threw himself on the grave, clasping it with his arms, and kissing the cold turf.

'Milly, Milly, dost thou hear me? I didn't love thee enough – I wasn't tender enough to thee – but I think of it all now.'

The sobs came and choked his utterance, and the warm tears fell.

❧ CONCLUSION ❧

ONLY ONCE AGAIN IN HIS LIFE HAS Amos Barton visited Milly's grave. It was in the calm and softened light of an autumnal afternoon, and he was not alone. He held on his arm a young woman, with a sweet, grave face, which strongly recalled the expression of Mrs Barton's, but was less lovely in form and colour. She was about thirty, but there were some premature lines round her mouth and eyes, which told of early anxiety.

Amos himself was much changed. His thin circlet of hair was nearly white, and his walk was no longer firm and upright. But his glance was calm, and even cheerful, and his neat linen told of a woman's care. Milly did not take all her love from the earth when she died. She had left some of it in Patty's heart.

All the other children were now grown up, and had gone their several ways. Dickey, you will be glad to hear, had shown remarkable talents as an engineer. His cheeks are still ruddy, in spite of mixed mathematics, and his eyes are still large and blue; but in other respects his person would present no marks of identification for his friend Mrs Hackit, if she were to see him; especially now that her eyes must be grown very dim, with the wear of more than twenty additional years. He is nearly six feet high, and has a proportionately broad chest; he wears spectacles, and rubs his large white hands through a mass of shaggy brown hair. But I am sure you have no doubt that Mr Richard Barton is a thoroughly good fellow, as well as a man of talent, and you will be glad any day to shake hands with him, for his own sake as well as his mother's.

Patty alone remains by her father's side, and makes the evening sunshine of his life.